MULTITUDE

DIMENSION SPACE BOOK TWO

DEAN M. COLE

CANDTOR PRESS

Multitude: Dimension Space Book Two

Published by CANDTOR PRESS

Multitude: Dimension Space Book Two is a work of fiction. Names, characters, places, and incidents are either the products of the author's imagination or are used fictitiously. Any resemblance to actual persons, living or dead, events, or locales is entirely coincidental.

Cover Art © 2018 Raphael Francavilla

Another Great Series by Dean

The Complete *Sector 64* Series
1947 - *First Contact a Sector 64 Prequel Novella*
Today - *Ambush - Book One of the Sector 64 Duology*
Tomorrow - *Retribution - Book Two of the Sector 64 Duology*

(Read the sneak peak of *Ambush* at the end of this book.)

PART I

"Not only is the Universe stranger than we think, it is stranger than we can think."
 —Werner Heisenberg

CHAPTER 1

E verything had gone to shit right in the middle of the best day of
Vaughn's post-apocalyptic life.

That had been two days ago.

Vaughn took a deep breath and then let it out in a long sigh.

My, how time flies…

Shaking his head, he gazed through the forward window of the
yacht's expansive, well-appointed bridge. Blue waves disappeared
beneath the prow of the gently heaving ship. On his left, to the yacht's
port, a long line of limestone cliffs paralleled Vaughn's course.

That fateful "best day" had been a few weeks after he'd rescued
Angela from the International Space Station. Vaughn had introduced
her to this yacht. Having renamed it as the *Angela's Dream*, he'd had
visions of plying the world's oceans with her at his side. They would
winter in places like Aruba or Barbados and spend the rest of the year
exploring the world's far corners.

All of that had been *before* they'd made love, an event that had put
the cherry on top of the icing of that "best day."

Then it had all gone south.

After making love to Vaughn, Angela had dropped the news on
him, had told him of the weird goings-on that she'd seen each time the

space station had flown over Central Europe. In the months after the Disappearance, odd lines had begun to radiate out from Geneva, Switzerland. Those lines had spread across the continent in a pattern that she'd referred to as a Gravity Flower. Gravity because not only had she seen it from orbit, but the flower-shaped pattern had also appeared on the gravity-wave detector that she'd been running aboard the space station.

And one fact tied it all together.

The supercollider sat at the center of that "Gravity Flower," and that damned collider had also been at the center of the Disappearance, the event that had wiped all animal life—including the entire human race—from the surface of the planet.

Just as Angela finished telling him about the Gravity Flower, all of the steel structures around them had suddenly lifted into the air and started streaming toward Europe.

Right on freaking cue!

Movement in his peripheral vision snapped Vaughn out of his thoughts. He looked away from the slowly scrolling line of cliffs and then frowned as a large steel building finished gliding into view overhead. It was just one in a levitating line of thousands of steel structures, the same line that had lured them north and the same one that had painted a petal across her gravity sensors.

Of course, Angela had wanted to follow the line to its final destination at, you guessed it, CERN's supercollider.

Now, instead of heading west into his dream of a sunset, they were sailing straight across the Mediterranean into a nightmare of apocalyptic proportions.

Vaughn shook his head again. "Perfect!"

He flinched as a pair of hands snaked under his arms and then wrapped around him.

Angela pressed the side of her face to his back as she hugged him tightly. "What's perfect?"

"Oh ... Uh, nothing. Just finished reviewing the ship's systems. Everything looks ... perfect."

He felt her head nod against his back. "If you say so."

Vaughn smiled in spite of himself. He'd grown very fond of that sleepy voice.

Forgetting his frustrations for the moment, he hugged her arms to his chest.

With her left cheek still pressed to his back, Angela sighed. "On my way up, I noticed we haven't lost the line."

Vaughn ground his teeth together but managed to keep the frustration from his words. "Yep, still there."

Angela turned her face and pressed her right cheek against his back. She pulled a hand free and pointed east. "By the way, what's that?"

Vaughn tapped a knuckle against the surface of the moving-map display. "According to the charts, that's Sardinia."

She snuggled into him and then sighed. "I know it's not the Caribbean, but at least these cliffs are beautiful."

Vaughn felt his cheeks warm with instant guilt. Inwardly, he shook his head. How long before she saw through him, saw the asshole that everyone else had seen him as?

"What's the matter? You just got all tense."

"N-Nothing."

Vaughn willed his shoulders to relax. Then he nodded toward the coastline. "You're right. They are beautiful."

His eyes swept northward as he continued to study the cliffs. He paused when he spotted an out-of-place, human-made structure. It sat crumpled where the emerald sea met the thin, white beach at the base of the cliff. Waves crashed into the thing, launching geysers of spray.

Angela leaned back as she apparently saw the same object. "Is that an airliner?"

Vaughn nodded. "Yeah."

The structure had resolved as the burned-out and broken hull of a wide-bodied passenger jet.

A colossal shadow crossed over the wreckage, momentarily darkening the airplane's white tail fin and the waves that were crashing against it.

5

Releasing each other, they stepped haltingly to the bridge's side window and stared up into the sky.

Overhead to the left of the ship, the line of levitating structures spanned from horizon to horizon. All of it slowly drifted north barely a thousand feet above the cliffs. The surreal train of steel edifices slowly glided past them, paralleling the rocky shoreline at a speed slightly faster than their yacht.

Angela leaned into him as she continued looking up. "My mind still has a tough time accepting that image."

Vaughn felt a shiver run through her.

He squeezed her tightly. "Yeah, me too."

The ominous specter of that much steel gliding serenely overhead was difficult to process. It looked as if the slightest perturbation would send it all crashing to Earth, converting its stores of potential energy into kinetic in a calamitous collapse.

Not that everything in the line stayed there.

They had seen stuff fall from it, things like concrete and nonmetallic building panels, but as far as he could tell, nothing made of steel ever fell from the line.

"Don't worry. We're safe for now. I'm keeping us out from under it." Still looking up, he pointed forward, ahead of their ship. "Unfortunately, we will have to pass directly beneath it when we cut through the Strait of Bonifacio. Otherwise, we'll have to go all the way around Corsica."

"Wonderful…"

"Yep, that pretty much sums up my thoughts on the subject, but I'll hurry every chance I get."

Angela gestured at the crashed airplane. "Why is that still here?" She looked up. "Why hasn't it been swept up by whatever the hell is doing that?"

Vaughn shrugged. "Was wondering that too. It must be one of the newer airplanes. They're mostly carbon composite. Not as much aluminum as the older ones and even less steel."

Since they'd left the Libyan coast to follow the floating line of structures, Vaughn hadn't seen many variations in its constituent components. As far as he could tell, everything either contained steel or was made of it. They'd even spotted a few boulders floating in the line. He'd guessed they were some kind of metallic ore.

Angela nodded. "Makes sense."

They continued in silence for a while.

Around midday, they reached the end of Sardinia's cliffs, and a channel of water slid into view beyond them.

Vaughn pointed. "There's the Strait of Bonifacio."

To its right was the island of Corsica. The line of steel structures passed directly over the channel and then disappeared behind Sardinia's northern neighbor as they continued on their north-north-east track.

He eyed the line again. "I haven't seen anything fall in a while." Vaughn grabbed the helm and turned the yacht toward the strait. "Looks like about as good a time as any."

Angela chewed her lip for a moment, but then she nodded.

Over the next several minutes, they both watched with nervous anticipation as they passed beneath the line of levitating structures. Now that they were crossing beneath the line, its relative motion appeared faster than it had when they were riding parallel to it. The line's individual components now raced overhead like the fast-moving clouds of a storm front.

It was a storm alright, Vaughn thought wryly.

And now they were sailing right into it.

Another hunk of the metallic ore drew his eye.

Vaughn shook his head and looked down at the large compass that sat in front of the helm's wood and brass wheel. "I don't understand why all of this hasn't affected the compass."

"What do you mean?"

Vaughn pointed overhead again. "All these vessels and that ore, it's all metallic. It must take one hell of a magnetic field to levitate all of it, but it's having no effect on the compass. It still shows magnetic north."

Angela shook her head. "No, it's not magnetism. I already told you that it's focused gravity manipulation."

Vaughn looked at her incredulously. "How can you know that?"

7

Angela raised an eyebrow and then pointed a thumb at herself. "Uh, gravity -wave astronomer here." She looked up and nodded toward the floating structures. "Focused gravity is making all that happen. That's why it showed up on the MONA-LISA's display."

MONA-LISA was the acronym for the name of the gravity-wave detector Angela had been running aboard the space station. It was something about a Modified-Laser-Interferometer-Blah-Blah-Blah. As far as Vaughn was concerned, they may as well have called it the goddamned Dream Shitter.

He shook his head. "What in the hell did your friends at CERN do?"

Angela tensed and pulled back from him. She bristled and thrust an extended finger toward the line of levitating ships. "I've told you, there's nothing they could've done to cause this!"

She pursed her lips as she considered her next words.

Vaughn knew what was coming. They'd already had this discussion several times.

It never ended well.

"It has to be somebody else."

Vaughn shook his head. "What? Please, not the aliens thing again."

Angela crossed her arms. "Well, do you have a better idea?"

"Yeah!" Vaughn said, sounding more confident than he felt. "I think your friends tore a hole in space."

"And what?" Angela scoffed. "They opened some kind of portal?"

Vaughn nodded. "Yeah. Maybe they did open a portal, and maybe there's one of those magneto-stars on the other end of it."

Angela blinked her surprise. "You mean a magnetar?"

Vaughn nodded. He had read an article about magnetar a few months ago before the world had ended. As he recalled, it was a neutron star with an extremely powerful magnetic field.

Doubt suddenly twisted Angela's face, but then she shook her head. "No, it can't be magnetism. You said it yourself. Look at your compass. Normal."

"Well, if it's gravity manipulation, why did water fall from the ships? Why didn't the liquid just hang in globs around the vessels?"

"I told you, it's focused gravity manipulation, as in selective. We're directly beneath it, and we don't feel a thing." She jabbed a finger toward the sky. "Someone or something is shielding those ships from Earth's gravity. There has to be intelligence behind it."

Vaughn rolled his eyes. Then he heard a distant thrumming.

Angela glared at him. "Don't do that! Don't write me off, Vaughn!"

He crossed his arms. "If there's intelligence behind this, why haven't they done anything about us?"

As he spoke, the low-frequency vibration he'd heard grew louder.

They both stepped back and looked at the floor of the yacht.

Was something going wrong with its engines?

Suddenly, the deck heaved beneath their feet, and a roaring crash echoed through the bridge.

Vaughn's eyes widened. "That came from outside!"

Together, they ran through the rear exit and emerged onto the yacht's back deck just as a huge geyser of water jetted into the sky directly behind their ship.

Vaughn looked up and then took an involuntary backward step. "There's something you don't see every day."

Beside him, Angela nodded mutely.

A massive, mile-long suspension bridge was passing overhead. Its cables hummed as it sailed through the atmosphere, generating the low-frequency vibrations they'd heard inside the ship. Their sedate flapping looked like a slow-motion video of vibrating guitar strings, the frequency of the thrumming so low, Vaughn felt it more than he heard it.

Vaughn exchanged a wide-eyed look with Angela and then looked up again.

He swallowed hard. "Well, we can add flying suspension bridges to the list." Extending his fingers, he counted off. "Buildings, trains, tankers, *tanks* ... metallic ore!" He extended a sixth digit. "And now bridges?!"

Suddenly, the entire suspension bridge twisted like a cloth being wrung. As it did, vast sections of its concrete roadbed sloughed off, the twisting motion launching chunks of the stuff in every direction.

"Oh shit!" Vaughn shouted.

They both took several backward steps.

A large section of road was falling directly at them. Before they could react, it plunged into the strait, narrowly missing the back of the yacht.

Vaughn yanked the tablet computer from his leg pocket. Using the bridge remote, he tried to increase the ship's speed.

It wouldn't respond.

The engines were already generating max power.

He looked frantically left and right. Small rocky islands blocked him from turning the yacht. Dead ahead was his only option.

The ship's current course would soon take them out from under the line.

If they survived that long.

They were now on a northwesterly heading, but the steel structures were drifting on a line just left of due north. Considering the length of the suspension bridge and its ability to throw concrete in wide arcs, they were going to be in trouble for some time.

Angela glared at him. "You just had to say it!"

"What?! What did I say?!"

She mimicked his voice and made air quotes. "If there's intelligence behind this, why haven't they done anything about us?" She jabbed a finger at the sky again. "Looks like they—!"

Her eyes widened, and she screamed as another chunk of roadbed arced toward the yacht. It crashed into the ocean mere yards from the ship's port side.

Turning back to Vaughn, she glowered at him. "Looks like they're doing something about us now!"

Vaughn opened his mouth to protest, but then the whistling death song of multiple chunks of plummeting roadbed drowned out his words.

Water geysered up from the ocean in dozens of places as a shotgun pattern of concrete slabs peppered its surface.

Vaughn pointed at the wide distribution of the falling rocks. "Look!" he shouted, again trying to sound more certain than he felt.

"We're not even at the center of the impacts. It's not aimed at us." He looked up. "There's nothing intelligent behind—! Oh shit!"

Another section of pavement was flying directly toward them. This one looked to be a hundred yards long, easily the largest one yet.

Vaughn grabbed Angela's arm, intent on pulling her to safety, but there was nowhere to go.

Frozen in place, they watched the implement of their death as it raced earthward.

Then the massive length of road passed overhead. Vaughn hugged Angela to him as they braced for impact, but somehow it missed the yacht and slammed into the ocean just ahead of it. The ship's bow heaved into the air as the impact launched a wave of water over the boat and rained spray down on Angela and Vaughn.

A moment later, the last of the small islands passed off to their left.

Vaughn tapped the fortunately waterproof tablet computer, commanding the ship to turn toward the open ocean, and it finally pulled entirely out from under the line of levitating structures.

Dripping wet and panting, they stared at the still twisting suspension bridge.

Vaughn pointed. "See? It's still heading northwest. It's not following us. No one is trying to take us out."

Angela's eyes narrowed. The muscles in her jaw worked. "You can be a real asshole, Captain!" Then she turned and stormed away, shouting over her shoulder as she did. "Just tell me when we get to Monte Carlo!"

Vaughn looked down and saw his face reflected in the tablet's screen.

"Well, Captain Asshole, that didn't take long."

CHAPTER 2

The bedroom doors slowly slid open as Angela stormed down the hallway. Impatient, she grabbed the panels and shoved them apart as she walked into the room.

She growled angrily. Who the hell did he think he was?

Exhausted, Angela collapsed into the cozy embrace of the room's expansive circular bed. She could still feel the effects of her extended stay aboard the station. The two weeks that they had spent in Tripoli had helped, but she still tired easily.

During her months trapped aboard the station, Angela had tried to stay in shape, exercising regularly. However, as her food supplies had dwindled, she had abandoned those efforts. No sense in being physically fit if it would only lead to starving to death, leaving behind an emaciated but nicely toned cadaver.

By the time Vaughn had discovered her existence and then made his way to the space station, she had been near death.

The descent back to Earth had nearly killed them both.

After bailing out of the ship moments before it exploded, each of them had narrowly survived their separate parachute crash-landings on North Africa's Mediterranean coastline.

Angela's anger withered as she recalled the series of events that nearly killed them again when they had reunited in Tripoli's port. Vaughn had spent the next two weeks nursing her back to health.

Over that time, she had grown fond of her rescuer, had even made love to him once she'd recovered enough to do so.

Angela felt the rest of her anger melt away as she remembered the tentative, almost frightened way he had held her as if worried he might break her.

Her spreading smile faltered as she thought about the look that periodically crossed Vaughn's face. It wasn't creepy or anything like that. It was as if she could see doubts marching across his face. About what, she didn't know. When it happened, Vaughn would suddenly withdraw from her, become distant.

Doubts?

About what?

Me?

Angela's brow furrowed. Could it be that? They had only known each other for a couple of weeks. Maybe he—

A knock interrupted her thoughts.

Raising her head, Angela stared at the door. "Hello?"

The two panels slid apart to reveal Vaughn. He stood silently, a sheepish grin on his face. Then he produced something from behind his back, and Angela burst into laughter.

He shook the yellow bag of Funyuns. "Are you hangry?" A look of mock horror crossed his face. "Sorry, sorry! I meant, are you hungry?" He sat on the edge of the bed.

Angela smirked, giving Vaughn the stink eye as she snatched the Funyuns.

He shook his head, eyebrows raised with exaggerated innocence. "No, not *hangry*," he scoffed. "I have *no* idea where that even came from."

Angela rolled over to Vaughn's side of the bed. Smiling devilishly, she tore the bag open with her teeth and then dug out a ring and crunched it theatrically. Crumbs fell, tumbling off her lap and onto his portion of the sheets.

"Oops."

Vaughn stared at her silently for a moment. Then he laughed and lunged across the bed. Throwing his arms around her, he rolled over, pulling her on top of him.

He kissed Angela and then looked into her eyes. "Sorry for—"

She pressed a finger to his lips. "You had me at Funyuns. Now, less talking, more kissing."

CHAPTER 3

Vaughn hoisted heavy lids. Trying to blink the sleep from his eyes, he stared up at the mahogany ceiling of the yacht's spacious quarters. Angela was lying on his left shoulder. She murmured and then fell back into sleep, resuming the cadence of her soft breathing.

Running a finger along the curve of her chin, Vaughn shook his head. Angela was starting to see him for the jackass that he was. He might be the last man on Earth, but considering his history, it wasn't like he was going to let a little thing like that stop him from screwing it up.

Angela flinched as an alarm next to the bed began to blare.

Vaughn had set the yacht's autopilot for Monte Carlo. Before falling asleep, he'd also set the alarm to wake him before they got too close to the coastal city. Because he was still in no rush to get to Geneva and he figured they needed a good night's rest, he'd set the yacht's speed at just above idle, making an overnight affair out of the relatively short trip from the strait to Monte Carlo.

He mashed a button on its top, and the blaring ceased.

Still lying on his shoulder, Angela began to stir. Her eyes flickered and then opened.

He smiled self-consciously. "It's time."

After a moment, her eyes focused and then she nodded. "Okay."

They climbed from the bed and dressed in silence. Then Angela grabbed the remains of the Funyuns bag and held it up. "I know who will love the rest of this."

She walked into the closet that he had converted into a habitat for her little white mice.

Seeing Angela approach, Nate Junior and his family scampered to the yellow habitat's near side. She lifted the lid, and the little guys stood on their hind legs, squeaking in anticipation. She gave each a golden ring. With their ridiculously large snacks clutched firmly in their tiny mouths, they ran off in different directions, bouncing clumsily off corners and tubes as they sought a place to eat in privacy.

After exchanging amused glances, Vaughn and Angela left the bedroom and headed to the bridge.

Earlier, they had plotted the levitating line of steel on the map and determined that it would cross Europe's Mediterranean coast a few miles east of Monte Carlo. Intent on using the city-state's harbor, they had set it as their destination.

"We should be in sight of the city now," Vaughn said.

Angela nodded as she entered the control room ahead of him, but then stopped mid-step. "Oh no…"

Vaughn nearly ran into her back. "What?"

When she didn't respond, he gently placed his hands on her shoulders and guided her the rest of the way onto the bridge.

Then he too froze. "Oh shit!"

They were in sight of it alright, but what he saw didn't look very welcoming.

The port and the entire hillside city beyond it was nothing but a charred remnant of its former glory. In the bay's royal blue water, a few metal-hulled yachts stood tall above row upon row of ruined ship remnants. Most of the boats in the harbor had burned to the waterline, leaving nothing but the jagged outlines where their hulls barely protruded from the surreally tranquil water.

Vaughn tore his eyes from the catastrophic scene and looked right.

Overhead to the east, the line of steel structures that they'd followed across the Mediterranean crossed the beach right where they had estimated. From there, it continued north by northwest, its far end blocked from sight by the mountains that it crossed.

Vaughn looked left and then pointed. "Look!"

In the distance to their west, barely discernible through the midday haze, a second line of levitating structures was now visible as it slowly scrolled over the coastline.

It was the adjacent petal of the Gravity Flower.

Judging by its angle, Vaughn estimated that it would indeed converge with their line over Geneva.

Vaughn stepped up to the helm. He had programmed the autopilot to bring the ship to a stop at this location. Now he guided the yacht closer to the harbor so they could get a closer look.

Several minutes later, he stopped the ship again.

It looked as if the fire had started in the port area and then climbed up Monte Carlo's steep, rocky slopes.

Giving the entire image a surreal highlight, a cascading waterfall had cut through the city, turning the remnants of its many switchback roads into a multi-tiered waterfall. Where the torrent splashed down into the bay, the late morning sun cast a wide, arcing rainbow over the tragic scene.

Vaughn closed his eyes and gnashed his teeth.

Why had he ever agreed to this fool's errand?

Against all reason, he had hoped that they could at least have a mini-vacation here in Monte Carlo, that they could relax and recuperate for a few more days before continuing inland, but this version of the city-state left them with only two real choices. Either they continued via helicopter, using the one stored in the yacht's hangar, or they turned this bus around and headed toward some tropical paradise.

Vaughn knew what would ensue if he suggested that second option.

However, Angela only needed one look at his face to know that it was on his mind again.

"Vaughn, whoever …" She paused and then shook her head. "Sorry, *whatever* caused this …" She gestured toward the shoreline with the broad sweep of her arm. "This and everything else, it may not be finished."

Vaughn nodded. "Exactly! *That* is why we need to get as far away as we can, get to safety before something reaches out and snatches us as well."

Angela continued shaking her head. "I know you don't think there is an external force at work, but whatever caused this, it didn't stop until it swept across the entire planet. I saw it with my own eyes. If something like that happens again, it won't matter if we're in the Caribbean or even Tahiti. We won't be able to get far enough away."

He shook his head, but before he could speak, she continued.

"If it is a rift, as you say, maybe we can do something about it. Maybe we can shut it down. Then we can live in peace wherever you want."

Vaughn's mouth fell open as he realized that she had used his own argument to back him into a corner.

He sighed and cursed under his breath. "Shit."

Finally, he nodded. "Alright, I'll get the helicopter ready."

Angela smiled. "Thank you, Vaughn. I'll pack a bag for us." Then she kissed him on the cheek and darted from the room.

Vaughn turned and glared through the bridge's window. She just couldn't accept that her friends at CERN had caused this.

He looked up, warily eyeing the converging lines of steel structures. He worried that the closer they got to Geneva, the more likely it was that they would get sucked into whatever force was dragging in all of that steel.

And Angela was willing to risk it.

"Of course she is," Vaughn said, shaking his head. "Why would she want to live happily ever after with Captain Asshole?"

CHAPTER 4

Angela watched as another mountain peak glided past the helicopter. An hour ago, they had left the burned-out husk of Monte Carlo. Now a beautiful landscape scrolled beneath their aircraft. Over that hour, she'd seen many Alpine villages that would have looked entirely at home on a postcard. The months-long absence of humanity hadn't appreciably tainted their beauty. Houses with steep-pitched roofs dotted lush, green fields. Only sporadic patches of overgrown vegetation along with the periodic burned-out structure or washed-out bridge hinted at the land's dark and lonely desolation.

Angela glimpsed an incredible sight as Vaughn guided the helicopter through another mountain pass. She leaned forward and peered across him. Her eyes widened. She pointed, extending an arm so quickly it slammed into Vaughn's chest. "Look at that!"

He cast an annoyed glance at her. Then he turned in the indicated direction and did a double take.

Angela and Vaughn watched in silent amazement as they flew past a large, levitating ferryboat. Even though the ship was upside down, the automobiles on its deck stuck to it like a formation of inverted geckos clinging to a ceiling. The ferry had a full complement of vehicular passengers. It appeared that not a single car or truck had fallen away from its upside-down deck.

The ship and its impossible cargo disappeared behind them as the helicopter's significantly faster pace carried it farther down the seemingly unending line of steel.

Vaughn had held the aircraft at a respectable distance from the parade of levitating structures. Unfortunately, the helicopter didn't have sufficient power to cross the top of the mountains. They had only moved this close to the line because it intersected with the same mountain pass that they'd been forced through.

Angela saw Vaughn glance down at the instrument panel, a worried look on his face.

"What's wrong?"

"We need fuel." He tapped one of the panel's computer screens, pointing at two vertical ribbons. They were empty but for slivers of yellow at their bottoms.

Angela realized the ribbons must be fuel level indicators.

"If we don't find some in the next ten minutes, I'm going to have to land this thing."

"Why is the fuel so low?"

Vaughn gave her an embarrassed look. "I wanted to get more in Tripoli, had planned to top off the helicopter's fuel there." He smiled self-consciously. "But after all those hundred-foot-wide steel fuel tanks started ripping out of their mounts and flying into the sky, it no longer seemed like such a good idea."

The helicopter flew out of the mouth of the pass and emerged over another valley.

Vaughn peeled the chopper away from the steel structures.

Ahead, the line of them tilted downhill and began to descend toward a point where it passed just above the lower ridgeline ahead of them on the far side of the valley.

As Angela peered through a cut in that lower line of hills, she saw a flicker of light.

Squinting her eyes, she pointed ahead at the reflective surface. "Do you see that?"

Vaughn continued to scan the valley floor beneath them. "See what?"

"I see something through that cut in the next ridge." She tapped his shoulder and then jabbed her finger ahead. "Is that Lake Geneva?"

Vaughn looked up and suddenly tensed. After a long moment, he gave her a sideward glance but didn't comment.

"What?" Angela looked from him and furrowed her brow as she tried to resolve the distant fuzzy reflection. "What's wrong?"

Still Vaughn didn't respond, but the uneasy look on his face had Angela concerned.

Through slitted eyes he continued to silently stare ahead.

Angela couldn't stand it any longer. "What?!"

Vaughn glanced at her again and then shook his head. He shifted his gaze to the valley floor. "We better land. I've been looking for a place to get fuel, but every airport has either been burned up or is missing its fuel tanks."

As Vaughn spoke, Angela squinted as she tried to resolve the distant glint of light.

Vaughn released one of the helicopter's control levers and pointed to their front left. "Check out that airfield. I'd settle for siphoning fuel from other aircraft, but now, even they are gone."

Reluctantly, Angela pulled her gaze from the mysterious reflection and looked down. She scanned the field's ramps and taxiways but didn't see anything, no structures or equipment. If not for the recognizable pattern of grass and concrete, it would have been difficult to tell it had ever been an airport.

She looked at the fuel gauge. "How much longer till—?"

Suddenly, the noise coming from the helicopter changed.

Angela gripped the sides of her seat, her nails digging into the fabric.

"What happened?! Did we run out of fuel?"

"No!" Vaughn shouted. He grunted with exertion as he fought with the aircraft's controls. The veins of his arms pulsed with the effort.

The engines screamed, their high-pitched squeals oscillating insanely.

21

Both of their upper bodies lunged to the left as the helicopter lurched right.

"What are you doing?!"

Vaughn shook his head. "That wasn't me!"

Angela screamed and slammed a hand into the ceiling as her body floated up out of the seat.

The helicopter began to fall out of the sky.

Her shoulders pressed painfully into the harnesses as the straps became the only thing that kept Angela in her seat.

Vaughn reached over and slammed down the lever that extended the retractable landing gear. "I'm getting us on the ground, now!"

The helicopter rocked again.

Vaughn grunted as he yanked the controls and righted the chopper. "That wasn't me either! Must be mountain turbulence." He shook his head. "But I've never felt it this bad!"

The aircraft continued its emergency descent.

The valley floor rushed up toward them.

At the last possible moment, Vaughn flared the helicopter. He pulled the center stick back, and the aircraft's nose heaved upward. Their speed and rate of descent slowed precipitously, but the helicopter's gyrations and oscillations continued throughout the maneuver.

By the look on Vaughn's face and the veins still popping out on his arms, he was having a hard time keeping the craft under control.

They hit the ground hard, but the aircraft still had significant speed.

Rolling forward on its tires, the helicopter hopped and lurched as it careened across mounds in the grass field.

Finally, it skidded to a stop.

Vaughn rapidly flipped switches and yanked levers. One of them must've been a brake made for the rotors because they quickly stopped turning.

The aircraft lurched again, throwing Angela against her harnesses.

Somehow, the helicopter continued to bounce around ... even *without* the blades turning.

Vaughn cast off his seat belts and motioned for Angela to do the same. "Get out!"

She unbuckled her harness and kicked the door open.

Suddenly, the aircraft leaped up from the ground and started to levitate.

Angela jumped through the open door and landed in the field, collapsing into a ball in its deep grass.

Vaughn yelled something from behind her.

She rolled onto her back and looked up to see him standing inside the helicopter, throwing their bags out.

The helicopter lurched higher.

Angela jumped to her feet. She tried to grab the aircraft, but it was already out of reach.

"Get the hell out of there!"

Vaughn nodded and then jumped. Landing next to Angela, he too collapsed into a heap.

The aircraft shot skyward.

Lying on their backs and breathing heavily, Angela and Vaughn watched as the helicopter, its previously stationary blades now wind-milling slowly, joined the line of metallic structures flowing toward Geneva.

Angela rolled over and threw her arms around Vaughn, burying her face in the crook of his neck. "You crazy man. You could've been taken up there with it."

She felt him swallow and then nod.

He sat up and pulled one of the bulkier bags to them. He unzipped it. Holding it open, he showed Angela the bag's contents.

"I couldn't let these guys get pulled up there."

She stared down into the opening, and tears suddenly welled in her eyes.

Nate Junior and family—all twitchy, pink noses and jittery, white whiskers—looked up at her from inside the yellow box that Vaughn must have pulled from the habitat.

She threw her arms around him again. "Oh, thank you, thank you, thank you!" She pulled his face to hers and kissed him deeply.

She pulled back and stared into his eyes. "I thought you said we should leave them since we'd be back in a few days. I even left out a bunch of food and water."

"I know. Brought that, too."

"But ... why?"

He shrugged. "The look on your face ... Guess I started feeling guilty."

Angela looked at him for a long moment. "Thank you. You're a good man, Captain. Crazy, but good."

An odd look crossed his face, but after a moment he smiled self-consciously.

They looked up at the line of objects.

Angela could no longer see the helicopter.

Vaughn shielded his eyes. "Guess we know what happened to all of the aircraft around here."

"About that, I thought you said the helicopter didn't have any steel."

"No. I said it was mostly aluminum and carbon composite. There's plenty of steel hardware. The transmission is full of it." He nodded toward the flying structures. "But I had hoped it wouldn't be enough to get sucked into that."

He shifted his gaze and looked north, toward the next ridge. As it passed over that geologic feature, the far end of the parading structures scrolled out of sight, fading into the haze as they continued toward their unknown purpose in Geneva.

Vaughn pointed. "I think we'll be able to see the city from those hills." Lowering his arm, he turned and looked at her. "But we're on foot now, so we better get going if we're going to make it before dark."

"Yeah." Angela nodded. "But we'll have to leave some of this stuff. There's too much to carry."

She scanned the field. Around them, waist-high grass undulated lazily, swaying with the gentle push of the valley's late spring breeze. The babble of a nearby creek was the only sound that rose above the soft rustling of the grass.

Angela sighed. "I guess this will do."

Vaughn screwed up his face. "This'll do for what?"

Ignoring him, she bent down and kneeled next to the bag he had opened. She pulled out the yellow box and walked toward the gurgling sound.

Realizing her intention, Vaughn stood and followed her.

A moment later, the grass parted, revealing a small creek.

Dropping to a knee, Angela gently placed the box on the ground. She fished out the mice and set them next to the stream, Nate Junior last. Then she laid out their food and water.

For a moment, they went back and forth, from her to the water and then back. Peering through their whiskers, the mice looked at Angela. Then one of them started to chew on a long blade of the tall, green grass. The mouse squeaked, and the others scurried over for a taste of their own.

Only Nate lingered.

He looked at Angela. Then the squeaks of his family proved too great a lure, and he also ventured into the vegetation.

Stepping carefully, Vaughn joined her.

"Are you sure about this?"

Angela wiped away a tear and then nodded. She looked around the valley. "It's beautiful here." She smiled weakly. "And they'll have the whole place to themselves."

Vaughn studied her face for a moment. Then he nodded as well. He handed her a backpack. "These have everything we'll need for a few days." He pointed to a village a couple of miles to their west. "Once we've had a peek over the hill, we can head over there for more provisions."

Taking the heavy bag, Angela slung it over her shoulders.

Vaughn donned his and then gazed into her eyes. "Are you sure you're okay?"

Angela looked back toward the mice and chewed her lip. Finally, she nodded. "Yeah. I'm fine."

She started to walk but then pulled up short.

"Wait a minute!" She eyed Vaughn curiously. "You've been itching for a reason to turn around." Angela pointed at the line in the sky. "I think you even mentioned something about us getting sucked into that ... like ten times, and now that it's almost happened to us, you're suddenly anxious to continue? Why?"

Vaughn's eyes dropped from hers. He looked toward the ground and started picking at it with the toe of his boot. Finally, he stopped fidgeting. He looked up and locked eyes with her. "I'm starting to think I was wrong."

"What?! Why? What's changed?"

Vaughn turned and pointed toward the next pass. "That was no lake you saw. Didn't you notice something odd about it?"

Angela shook her head. "No. Just saw a flicker of light, a shimmer really. Figured it was sunlight reflecting off the lake."

"You didn't see it, then." It was a statement, not a question.

"See what?"

"All the angles?"

Angela continued shaking her head. "Angles? No, I didn't see anything but the lake. It was a little fuzzy. My eyes haven't quite recovered from all that time spent in zero-G. Distance vision has been a little sketchy ever since." She gave a short, ironic laugh. "Probably should see an optometrist."

Vaughn didn't laugh. Instead, he cast another nervous glance toward the low ridgeline.

Her smile faltered. "What did you see? Did you get a glimpse of the city, of Geneva?"

Vaughn shook his head. "I'm not sure what I saw, but it definitely wasn't Geneva. It was too big ... too organized." He appeared to consider his words for a moment. Then he frowned. "I think you were right. Your friends didn't cause this. It was someone else, and we need to find out who."

Angela tilted her head quizzically. "I thought that's what we were doing."

Vaughn's head lowered, and he stared at the ground.

She felt her face flush. "You never intended to go through with it, did you?"

He shrugged. "I don't know. Didn't really have a plan. Guess I was

26

just hoping that you'd change your mind once we got close enough to see whatever the hell was drawing all of this toward the collider. Then we'd head back to the yacht." He gestured to the airfield around them and its absence of aircraft. "Unfortunately, I never anticipated this." Then he pointed toward the pass. "Nor what I saw through there."

Angela gnashed her teeth and shook her head angrily. She pointed at Vaughn. "Don't patronize me! I know what I'm talking about, Captain. And I don't need you second-guessing me just because … because you think I'm too young!"

Confusion twisted his face.

Angela was reminded of how little they actually knew about each other.

Vaughn shook his head. "It wasn't that. I just …" He sighed. "Never mind."

The look on his face drained the anger from her.

Angela stepped to Vaughn and touched his cheek.

When he looked up, she gazed into his eyes. "Just talk to me, Vaughn. We have all the time in the world."

He nodded. "Okay, I will." He raised an eyebrow as he looked overhead at the parading structures. "Although I'm afraid that all the time in the world ain't what it used to be."

CHAPTER 5

A ngela kicked at a hardened puddle of melted plastic. It skittered across the intersection's scorched pavement. "This trip would've been much easier if we could've at least found a bicycle."

Vaughn nodded.

They had passed through a small village and were now walking up its last road. It led in the general direction of the pass. Looking ahead, he could see that they'd soon have to leave the paved surface and finish the trip walking cross-country, most of it up steep hillsides and across rocky ledges.

When they had entered the village, the two of them had searched several houses. They hadn't expected to find any cars. However, they couldn't even find a bicycle. Many of the Swiss-styled dwellings had been damaged. You could see where metal items had punched through walls as they broke their way out of the structures that had tried to contain them.

Most of the buildings in the village were made of wood and concrete. However, in a few places, empty foundations sat where steel structures had once resided. It looked as if a tornado had swept those buildings completely from the planet. Vaughn gazed into the sky. Yeah, like a tornado alright, sucked right up into the air. Only those structures wouldn't come crashing down here or even in Toto's Kansas.

The next blob of melted plastic that Angela kicked didn't budge. It had fused with the scorched pavement.

She regarded Vaughn with a hoisted eyebrow and pointed at the burn mark. "What do you think caused all this?"

Vaughn shrugged. "Probably a carbeque."

"A what?"

He gestured at the intersection. "Barbecued cars. After the Disappearance, they clogged a lot of intersections. Don't you remember seeing them in Tripoli?"

Angela smiled self-consciously. "I only drove through the town twice. The first time is kind of a blur. I barely remember it. And the second time, someone had a blindfold on me."

"Sorry." He gave her a crooked grin. "Wouldn't have done that if I'd known it was going to be our last trip."

He gestured at the intersection again. "Anyway, burned-out cars still clogged a lot of the intersections back home." He pointed at the line of levitating ships. "But then there wasn't someone sucking up all the steel." He tilted his head. "At least ... there wasn't when I left."

Angela gestured ahead. "What do you think they're doing with all of it, all that metal?"

Vaughn followed her gaze. As they had done several times, the pair stopped walking and stared at the surreal sight of so many structures slowly gliding through the air.

Now three lines of levitating steel filled the sky. Judging by their angles, Vaughn guessed that the lines converged at an unseen point less than twenty miles beyond the ridge.

A shiver tried to snake its way down his spine as he considered what might await them there.

Angela began to speak again, snapping Vaughn from his thoughts.

"Is that what you saw through the pass? Do you think it's just all the metal stacking up on top of CERN?"

Vaughn blinked and then shook his head. "Sorry. I zoned out for a moment."

"You said you saw angled structures through the pass." She gestured at the sky. "Could it be all these metal objects stacking up on top of the collider?"

He pulled up the mental image of what he'd glimpsed through the haze. It had seemed more organized than that, but considering the distance and amount of haze that still clung to the region, he really couldn't be sure.

"I don't know." He rocked his head equivocally. "Maybe, but even for me it was a little blurry. Seems to be more haze here than what we've been seeing."

Ahead of them, the road started to bend, veering off to the left. Beyond it, the land began to rise in earnest.

Fortunately, this ridge was significantly smaller than the Alpine peaks they'd flown over to get this far. The ridge was more foothill than mountain, but the hike up it was going to be strenuous nonetheless.

Suddenly, Angela grabbed his arm and yanked him sideways. "Watch out!"

Vaughn looked at her and then down. "Oh shit!"

Side-by-side, they stared into the shadowed depths of a jagged hole in the middle of the street.

"You almost stepped right in that thing."

He arched his brows. "That would've messed up my whole weekend. Thanks for stopping me."

Angela laughed and then shook her head. "Anyway, what do you think made the hole?"

Vaughn bent over. Shielding his eyes, he peered deeper into the opening. "Looks like a sewer access." Then he realized what had happened. He pointed down. "There used to be a manhole cover there." Glancing overhead, he added, "You can guess where it went."

Angela looked up and then frowned.

Vaughn knew how she felt. The sight of the lines converging overhead sent his pulse rate into overdrive every time he looked up. Those lines served as a stark reminder of the scale and weirdness of the mystery that lay ahead of them, and each step took them ever closer to a revelation of apocalyptic magnitude. It was too big, too extreme to wrap his mind around, so he kept himself occupied with the journey. He tried to focus on the ground ahead and the steps required to traverse it, but invariably the lines of levitating structures drew his eyes and his thoughts. Then his steps would falter while his heart raced.

Finally, he forced his gaze back to the ground and waved. "Come on, Angela. Burning daylight."

After a moment, she nodded and fixed her gaze on the pavement ahead of them.

Giving the jagged edge of the deep hole a wide berth, they walked to the outer side of the road's curve. Stepping onto the overgrown grass, they left the last of the town and its streets behind.

An hour later, with the mid-afternoon sun beginning to cast long shadows, they were halfway up the slope.

Vaughn reached back and helped Angela over a rocky ledge. "So when did you get into theoretical physics?"

Clearing the rock, she released his hand and then shrugged. "Guess I've been fascinated by the subject since I was a kid."

"Oh." Vaughn smiled wryly. "So for a whole year now?" He winced inwardly as a hurt feeling briefly crossed Angela's face.

She smiled and slugged him hard in the shoulder. "Watch it, Captain."

Vaughn raised hands in surrender. "Yes, ma'am."

They continued up the remnants of the old trail they'd been following. The vegetation had grown over much of it, but enough remained for them to discern its path.

Angela negotiated one of its cutbacks. Then she continued speaking. "When I was twelve, I told my mom I wanted to go to MIT." Her eyes took on a far-off look. She smiled. "My mom jumped online and started searching for preparatory schools, schools that had a high conversion rate for funneling their students into MIT. She found a really good one. I was so excited when she told me about it."

She paused. Her face darkened, and she looked at the ground.

"Go ahead," Vaughn prompted. "I'm listening."

She gave a quick, curt nod. When she began speaking again, her words were choked. "What she didn't tell me was how expensive it was. She started working two jobs. Said it was because the landlord had raised the rent." Angela shook her head. "I was clueless."

Unsure of what to say, Vaughn simply nodded.

Angela stepped over another rock and then continued speaking. "Anyway, a few months later, I received a letter from the preparatory school. I had been accepted!"

"Wow! That's awesome."

Angela nodded and smiled weakly.

"How did it go? I'm guessing pretty well." Vaughn gave her a crooked smile. "I mean, you did go to MIT, after all. I bet your mom was very proud of you."

Angela's smile faltered. One corner of her mouth quivered. Then she gave a barely perceptible nod. "She would have been."

Vaughn stopped walking and turned toward her. "Oh, Angela. I'm so sorry." He stepped toward her, but Angela pushed him away.

"I'm okay. That was a long time ago."

After an awkward silence, they started walking again.

Finally, Angela raised her eyes to Vaughn. "You've never spoken of your parents. Were they still ... You know, when it happened?"

It was Vaughn's turn to look down. "My mom was."

"I'm sorry, Vaughn. I shouldn't have asked."

He waved a hand. "No, it's okay. I've come to terms with it. Guess there's no easy way to go through that." He gave her an understanding look. "Regardless of how it happens."

Teetering on the verge of another awkward silence, Vaughn gave Angela a self-deprecating smile. "How 'bout them Yankees?"

She guffawed. "I know, right? Those guys ...!"

For the next several minutes, the steep, traversing climb provided a welcome diversion, occupying their otherwise wandering thoughts.

Another turn of the trail brought them to a section of jagged rocks that protruded at multiple odd angles. Some of them looked precariously balanced. Vaughn gave the entire setup a quick once-over. Spotting his route, he held up a hand to Angela. "Wait here, let me check it out."

Without pausing for a response, he hopped onto the first ledge and then onto one of the large boulders. It rocked beneath his feet, so Vaughn let his inertia carry him onto the next rock. Two additional loping jumps brought him to the top of the ledge. He looked down at Angela and held his arms out to his side. "Ta-da!"

To his surprise, Angela was shaking her head, her face ash-white. "God protects drunks and idiots."

"What do you mean? That was pure skill."

"No, that was pure idiocy." She pointed down over the ledge. "If you had tripped or if that boulder had toppled, you'd have fallen a thousand feet."

Vaughn followed the line of her finger. Looking down, he felt his stomach turn. He'd been so intent on analyzing the best route across the obstacle, he hadn't noticed that it stuck out over a cliff ... a damned high one!

When that rock had shifted under his feet, he'd been teetering above a drop of over a thousand feet.

Suddenly, Angela burst into snorting laughter. "Oh my God! You should see ... the look on your face!"

Vaughn looked at her and shook his head. "Laugh it up." He crossed his arms. "I'm here. You're there. How are you going to get up?"

After a few more snorts, she stopped laughing, finally. A serious look took over her face.

He watched as she studied the hillside. As she'd done innumerable times during that long climb, she overanalyzed every option, a trait that was starting to drive him crazy.

"Any day now."

Angela nodded. "I'll be right there."

She turned and walked away from him, disappearing into the tree line.

Vaughn stared into the woods for a while. He smirked and then cupped his hands around his mouth. "I don't think capitulation or surrender is a viable …"

He faltered as Angela emerged from the forest a few feet to his side, now standing on his upper ledge.

"Close your mouth, Captain. You'll attract flies."

She smiled whimsically and shook her head. "I can't believe you survived long enough to actually rescue me." She arched her eyebrows and grinned. "Although in the end, I guess it was me that rescued you, wasn't it?"

She walked past Vaughn, not waiting for him.

Left in her wake, he could only shake his head. "Guess I had that coming," he said under his breath.

Speaking over her shoulder, Angela continued up the steep slope. "Yep, you sure did."

Vaughn thought they must be nearing the top. The levitating line of steel looked closer than ever. However, when he reached the next rise, it proved to be just another false pass. They had encountered several of them. Each time they crested one ledge, they found another waiting above them.

Angela reached the top of the next one and then froze mid-step.

"What is it?!"

She didn't respond.

Having lagged a few dozen feet behind her, Vaughn sprinted the rest of the way up the hill. As he reached Angela, he grabbed her elbow. "What's the ma—?"

His hand fell, as did his jaw.

Staring in shocked silence, Vaughn and Angela stood fixed in place for a long moment.

He felt his mind lock up as he tried and failed to process the image. This was no false pass.

Angela and Vaughn had indeed reached the top of the hill.

Now they stood at the southern end of the long, V-shaped ravine that cut a notch across the small ridge. It was the same narrow cut that they'd seen from the helicopter.

Vaughn could only see a sliver of Geneva through the far end of the ravine.

But a sliver was all he needed.

The image painted across the triangular canvas of horizon visible through the ravine's opposite end said significantly more than a thousand words. It spoke of a fallen society, a lost people, and now, Vaughn realized, a lost war as well.

The narrow sliver of city visible through the distant end of the pass revealed an entirely new city where Geneva had once stood. There was no doubting this assertion. The structures eclipsed anything man had ever built.

Enormous silver edifices now towered above the floor of the valley that once housed Geneva. Where the city used to sit, now countless structures of varying sizes and shapes blotted out the land. Instead of façades of stone and wood, everything in this surreal metropolis sported a skin of shiny, polished metal.

On his left, Angela was slowly shaking her head. "It was a war."

Through a suddenly dry throat, Vaughn said, "Yeah ... Yeah, it was." He shook his head. "A war that ended before we even knew it had started."

CHAPTER 6

Angela breathed heavily as she crawled along on her belly. Tall grass cocooned her. The late afternoon sun beat down on her back. A trickle of sweat ran down the line of her nose.

They had dropped off their backpacks at the mouth of the ravine. Not wanting to be silhouetted in the V-shaped pass, they were crawling on their bellies, or low-crawling, as Vaughn had called it.

Angela looked up, warily studying the bottom of another ship as it floated silently past them, gliding only a hundred feet above their heads. This was the closest they'd been to the line of levitating structures.

Her gaze returned to front. Not that she could see anything in that direction—at least not yet. The tall grass obscured all but the sky and its steel cargo.

Her knees churned, one after the other, as she slowly inched toward the Geneva side of the cut.

"You're too high," Vaughn whispered harshly. "Get your butt down. Pretend like you're crawling under barbed wire … just like in the movies."

Angela nodded and dropped flat.

Crawling through the tall grass at the bottom of the draw

reminded her of her childhood and playing in the parks. It even smelled the same. The sweet aroma of the pines and grasses seemed crazily disjointed when taken in with the scenery that waited ahead.

That and the sky full of floating ships and buildings.

There was another aspect that she hadn't noticed during their climb. It was the utter silence. Aside from the periodic rustle of the breeze, there were no other sounds, no chirping crickets or birds.

Angela stopped moving and held her breath.

Beside her, Vaughn also stopped.

Tilting her head, Angela listened. The world suddenly felt like a movie minus its soundtrack. The sound of her racing heart rose to fill the void.

"What are you doing?"

Angela looked at Vaughn and released the held breath. Panting again, she shook her head. "Nothing."

He gave her an odd look but then nodded.

They started crawling again.

"Not like that!" Vaughn whispered urgently. "Keep your knees off to the side, like this."

Angela looked over to him and then dropped her belly, displacing her knees to the side like Vaughn.

Whispering seemed ridiculous. They were still miles from the city, but she couldn't help it. She supposed it was for the same reason that they were crawling up for a better view.

As they neared the far end of the ravine, Angela began to glimpse silvery glints through the tall grass. The nervous feeling in her stomach grew as each subsequent shuffling crawl brought more and more of the alien city into view.

She still couldn't see the ground, just the huge structures rising from it.

Obviously, Vaughn had more experience with this whole low-crawly thing. As they neared the edge, his faster pace had him half a body length ahead of her. Angela could barely see his arms through the grass.

Suddenly, his whole body flinched and then froze. She heard Vaughn swearing under his breath as he began to breathe harder.

Angela stopped crawling. "What is it?!"

He motioned for her to move up. "Come on up … but be careful. There's a drop-off."

Angela verged on hyperventilating as she nosed her way through the weeds. A foot later, the vegetation disappeared altogether.

As did the land.

"Oh, my …!" Angela's panting breath hitched in her throat.

Vaughn swallowed and then nodded. "I know."

The scale of the panorama painted across what had been Geneva Valley shocked Angela's system.

It was … too much … too big.

Her mind balked at the unreal reality.

She suddenly felt light-headed and dizzy.

They had emerged from the edge of the grass, their heads now peering out over a thousand-foot-high cliff. Usually, the sight of that much empty air between her and the fallow farmland below the rocky precipice would have been enough to make her blood run cold, but that incredible sight paled in comparison to the disjointed alien vista that spanned the horizon.

A metropolis populated by colossal silver buildings stretched out as far as she could see left and right.

"It's huge! I mean …" She swallowed hard, fighting to rein in her breathing. "Those buildings …!" She paused, struggling for the right words. "They're as tall as mountains."

Vaughn nodded. "I can't wrap my head around it, the scale of it all."

Angela's mind reeled. Questions bounced through her thoughts like careening pinballs.

What did it all mean?

Why would someone wipe out a world only to build a city of steel?

Who were they?

And why here? How did it all tie into Geneva's supercollider?

In the hazy distance, the three lines of structures that were passing overhead and to Angela's left and right appeared to terminate just before reaching the outer limit of the alien metropolis. After crossing over the ridgeline, the ships, buildings, and bridges that made up the levitating rows of steel soared a thousand or more feet above the land, but even their lofty altitude paled in comparison to the massive buildings that towered over their far ends.

Through the smog, Angela could just make out an enormous cruise-ship near the front of the levitating line. Even though several hundred feet lay beneath its hull and the ground beneath, the top of the huge ship reached less than a quarter way up the nearest building.

Vaughn's voice broke through her trance. "I don't see anything moving." He pointed up. "Other than this stuff."

Angela nodded. Then her eyes narrowed as a flicker of orange drew her gaze to a place on the ground near the outer edge of the city.

Sudden recognition slammed home.

She scanned left and right and saw two additional vermillion spots sitting exactly where she remembered.

She pointed. "Look! I saw those from space."

"What?"

"Those orange spots."

At her extreme distance, Angela could barely discern them. From above, they had looked round, but her current oblique viewing angle gave them a squat, oval shape. As she'd seen from the space station, each line appeared to terminate at its own spot of orange.

Still pointing, she swept her arm left and right. "It looks like there's one for each line. Can you tell what they are?"

Vaughn shook his head. "No, still too far away. But damn! They're huge, a lot bigger than anything in these lines. Looks like they're even bigger than a stadium!"

For long moments, they stared at the scene silently.

Miles of undeveloped countryside sat between them and the closest edge of the alien city.

Fallow farm fields dotted by small communities filled the land below their vantage point. Beyond it, Angela could see the wrecked and burned remnants of Geneva's outskirts. The periphery of the original city protruded from beneath the outer edge of the massive alien metropolis like the ejected entrails of squashed roadkill.

The analogy turned her stomach, but Angela realized it was all too accurate. Humanity had become roadkill, crushed under the invading wheel of uncaring aliens.

Flickering light drew her gaze east toward Lake Geneva. Then she saw why the body of water had appeared to have spilled out of its banks. When Angela had first seen the area's changes from space, she'd thought that Lake Geneva had spread out and covered the surrounding land, but now she saw that the lake still sat in its original banks. It hadn't grown at all, but currently she was having a hard time discerning its surface against the ocean of silvery buildings that now surrounded and reflected off it. Everything blended, appearing as one just as it had when she'd seen it from the space station's 200-mile altitude.

Her eyes returned to front. Ahead of them, a line of shadows drifted across the bizarre milieu. Cast by the slowly drifting rows of steel structures, the dark silhouettes dotted the land between their vantage point and the city.

Angela shook her head. "There's no way we will ever find a way into the collider. We can't get to CERN. It's impossible."

Vaughn looked at her. His eyes narrowed. "You don't know that."

She pointed to the city. "We don't stand a chance against someone that can build something this big and complicated. None of this was there a few months ago. We'll be like cavemen trying to pick a fight with gods."

"We're not going to fight them," Vaughn said. "I thought you wanted to find out what happened in the collider ... how it all links to CERN!"

Angela's eyes widened. "How in the hell are we gonna get in there?!" She thrust a finger toward the distant skyline. "It's buried under all that!"

Vaughn pursed his lips as he turned and stared at the surreal metropolis. After a moment he shrugged. "I don't know, but I'm not ready to give up. Not yet."

"Then what?" Angela looked at him. "What in the hell can we do?"

He turned from her and studied the land ahead of them. Then he glanced up at a truck that was gliding overhead.

Incredulous, Angela thought she could see him formulating a plan.

Finally, Vaughn looked around their hiding position and then nodded. "Let's backtrack out of this cut. Then we can move farther down the ridge and set up camp. We'll watch things for a while, see what they're doing, and maybe, just maybe, we'll figure out a way into the city."

"I thought you were ready to head for the Caribbean." She extended an arm toward the mountainous pillars of steel. "Now you want to take on this?"

He pointed up at the sky. "We haven't seen any spaceships, no invading hordes. Where did all of this come from? Who is doing it?" His head lowered, and he stared out at the ruined land. "And why here? Why us? Why in the hell did they erase humanity?"

Angela stared at the thin sliver of Geneva's ruined remnants and chewed her lip as Vaughn listed the same questions that were racing through her own thoughts.

"Come on," he said softly.

Rolling onto her side, Angela looked at Vaughn.

He smiled self-consciously. "Let's scout it out for a day or two." He winked. "Then we can decide whether or not to retreat to that island paradise."

Angela chewed her lip for a moment longer. Finally, she nodded. "Okay, you're right." She scanned their surroundings and then looked back to Vaughn. "Let's go see if we can find a spot under the trees, somewhere that's not this exposed."

Vaughn's head bobbed slowly. "Okay."

Angela rolled onto her belly and looked out over the city.

She heard a rustling sound and turned to see Vaughn backing away from the precipice. The tall grass soon hid him from sight.

She glanced at the city again and swallowed. Then she too began to back away from the ledge, crawling backward on her belly.

Suddenly, the ground shook beneath her as a thunderous noise split the air.

Angela froze.

Had something fallen from the levitating line? The image of concrete roadbed falling from that suspension bridge flooded into her mind's eye.

Was it happening again?

She rolled onto her back and stared up into the sky.

Nothing.

Then the ground began to roll beneath her. The screech of renting metal split the air. It seemed to come from everywhere, but then Angela heard the sound of falling rocks.

She sat up, looking back toward the far end of the cut, where they had first entered the ravine.

"Oh no!"

A giant ship, a supertanker by the looks of it, was grinding its way through the pass. The front of its bulbous prow was plowing up the ground, throwing rocks and boulders into the air as it careened through the narrow cut. In spite of the incredible drag generated by its ground contact, the ship continued inextricably, grinding its way toward them.

Vaughn jumped to his feet. He scooped up their packs in one hand. With his other, he grabbed Angela.

"Run!"

CHAPTER 7

Angela took Vaughn's hand and jumped to her feet.

They ran to the nearest side of the ravine. It looked too steep to scale. Out of options, Angela threw herself at it, but only managed to climb a few feet before the steep slope sent her sliding back to the bottom.

She glanced at the slowly approaching ship and then at the opposite end of the ravine. The thousand-foot drop and its alien overlook sat a mere ten feet away.

She turned to see Vaughn trying to climb the opposite side of the cut, but he had the same result, sliding back into the ravine in a cloud of dust.

Angela ran over and joined him.

Together, they tried twice more, but still couldn't scale the side of the ravine.

Vaughn even got behind Angela and tried to push her up.

It was no good. The sides were too steep and the soil too loose.

As she slid back to the bottom, Angela turned and saw Vaughn frantically scanning the ravine.

The quaking of the ground amplified as the inexorable ship closed on their dwindling wedge of space.

Painfully loud, high-pitched squeals of scraping metal punctuated the low, rumbling roar of the supertanker's grinding passage.

Angela looked from the approaching wall of steel and desperately scanned every surface of the ravine, seeking some avenue out of the ever-shrinking pass.

Suddenly, Vaughn ran past her, straight at the ship.

"What are you doing?!"

He pointed to the front left. "We can hide there!"

Close on Vaughn's heels, Angela looked around his bobbing shoulder and then nodded.

He was heading for a hollow in the ravine's wall. The notch was small, not much bigger than a phone booth, but it should be large enough to hold the two of them until the ship passed.

A moment later they skidded to a stop in the concavity.

Breathing heavily, Angela and Vaughn pressed themselves into the depression and watched with wide eyes as the narrow, bulbous prow of the ship crossed in front of them.

The ground heaved beneath them.

After the narrow nose of the ship slid past, the hull began to widen as its wedge-shaped bottom pushed into their end of the ravine.

Angela clawed her fingers into the earthen wall at her back as she watched the near surface of the ever-widening hull draw closer.

As the gap narrowed, the heaving ground threatened to knock her from her feet.

Something moved to their side.

Angela leaned forward and glanced across Vaughn on her left.

"Oh no!"

Vaughn looked at her. "What?!" He started to lean out too, but Angela yanked him back just as another boulder tumbled down and slammed into the ground at his feet.

The widening side of the colossal ship was launching an avalanche of dirt and boulders from the ravine's walls.

Looking at the coming landslide, Angela realized that the rock that had almost crushed Vaughn had been the first salvo of what would soon be a deadly cascade.

She grabbed his arm. "Come on!"

They burst from cover just as the slope began to collapse above them.

Angela didn't look back, but the dirt that kicked at their heels and the dust that flew up from behind them told her that they'd narrowly missed being crushed by the landslide.

Side-by-side, Vaughn and Angela ran alongside the bulbous nose of the advancing ship's hull. Fortunately, a slow jog was enough to match its laggardly pace.

But even at that speed, the two of them were quickly running out of options.

They were trapped in a narrow strip of land that was shrinking in both length and width.

The slowly advancing hull formed a wall of steel on their left. The ravine's steep slope towered over their right. The surreal alien skyline waited ahead at the strip's far end.

At the base of a thousand-foot cliff!

Capping off the whole thing was the running avalanche of rocks that was chasing them toward the drop like lemmings to the fall.

They searched everywhere, scanning every surface, desperately seeking a way out of their shrinking universe.

Angela screamed in frustration.

There was nothing! Not one goddamned way out.

They were either going to be crushed between the ship and the side of the ravine or knocked over the cliff.

She hazarded a glance over her shoulder and saw the unending rockfall nipping at their heels.

Great! Add being crushed by falling rocks to the list of screwed-up ways the afternoon could end.

Suddenly, a gently undulating length of an enormous levitating chain drew up alongside Angela.

Still jogging, she blinked and then stared at the horizontal span of thick, floating links.

Its untethered end flapped as if in slow motion. Each link was the size of her torso. Seeing where it protruded from the side of the supertanker, she realized that it was the ship's anchor chain, sans the anchor.

Angela batted at Vaughn's shoulder. "Look!"

He turned wide, terrified eyes toward Angela and then looked past her.

With only fifteen yards left between them and the rapidly approaching cliff, Angela had no time to describe her plan.

She threw her body onto the gently writhing chain and wrapped her arms around it.

The massive links didn't budge. They held fast beneath her, continuing to leisurely float alongside the relentlessly advancing supertanker.

A wave of vertigo washed over Angela as gravity's direction seemed to shift.

She shook off the sensation and extended a hand toward Vaughn. "Jump on!"

A large chunk of ravine wall sloughed off behind him. As it fell toward Vaughn, he yelled and jumped ahead a few feet, narrowly avoiding the crushing collapse, but now even closer to the cliff's precipice.

Angela thrust her hand toward him again. "Jump now, dammit!"

They were out of time.

Vaughn reached the end of the ravine. Still running, he planted his foot on the last piece of solid ground and launched himself over the cliff.

At the top of his leap, he grabbed her extended arm with one hand and jabbed his other into the loop of one of the massive links.

His lower body swung out into space, nothing but a thousand feet of air between the bottom of his hiking boots and the French countryside.

The veins in both of their arms throbbed as they struggled to rein in the inertia of his swing.

Vaughn threw a leg over one of the links. A moment later he climbed all the way onto the chain, straddling it just ahead of Angela.

"Thank you!" he managed between pants.

They both looked down on the fallow farmland that now hung several hundred feet beneath them.

Clutching the chain with renewed desperation, Angela dragged her eyes from the horrifying sight. She looked fixedly at Vaughn ahead of her.

Eyes round, he stared at the distant ground.

"Vaughn!"

No response.

"Vaughn!"

He flinched and then looked at her.

Not wanting to release her grip on the chain, Angela tilted her head, nodding toward the point ahead of Vaughn where the chain entered the side of the ship. "We need to climb through there!"

Vaughn suddenly looked nauseous. "Do you feel that?!"

Angela nodded. "Yes, gravity is all wrong here. Up doesn't quite feel like up anymore." She pointed toward the hole in the ship. "Up down, whatever! Just go! Hurry!"

Vaughn swallowed and then nodded. He began to shimmy up the chain.

Angela tried not to look down. Instead, she hazarded a backward glance.

The bulk of the ship was still in the ravine. They needed to get up onto the deck and then run back toward the land. They might be able to jump off the side and onto the ridgeline before the whole ship was hanging in space and taking them God knows where.

She followed Vaughn into the hole.

It turned out to be a long pipe.

As Angela traversed its length, she felt gravity fluctuate radically. For several feet, it even felt as if she were crawling across a horizontal surface, even though the pipe was vertical. However, by the time Angela reached the end of the tube, it again felt as if she were climbing upward, the normal sense of up and down reasserted itself.

Using the links like a ladder, Angela and Vaughn crawled out of the pipe and stepped onto the tanker's main deck near the forward point of its bow.

The ship trembled beneath their feet. Judging by the changing pitch of the noise and the lowering frequency of the vibrations, Angela thought the tanker might be slowing as it continued to grind roughly against the ravine's walls.

She shouted, waving for Vaughn to follow. "Come on!"

Angela started running toward the back of the ship.

A moment later, she felt the deck begin to tilt beneath her feet.

Not looking up, Angela continued running aft.

She kept her eyes glued to the deck and shouted to Vaughn. "Hurry! It's tilting!"

"Right behind you!"

Still concentrating on the surface immediately in front of her boots, Angela sprinted rearward, leaning toward the left railing to stay on her feet.

Suddenly Vaughn's panic-filled voice rang out from behind her. "Angela!"

"What—?!" She looked up. "Oh shit!"

Angela stopped running and clutched desperately at the nearest handrail.

Not wanting to trip or fall, she had been focusing on the deck immediately in front of her feet, completely unaware that the world had somehow fallen onto its side. When she had looked up, the sight of an insanely tilted horizon had filled her vision.

Slamming into her backpack, Vaughn wrapped an arm around her and grabbed the railing with his free hand.

Panting in raspy breaths, he looked over her shoulder. "How is this happening?"

Staring at an impossibly skewed horizon, Angela shook her head. "I don't know."

Not only was the ship listing, but it also looked as if the entire Earth had tilted.

The previously horizontal ridgeline now looked as if it ran uphill from right to left.

The supertanker still appeared to be running straight through the ravine, its deck square to the top of the ridge.

Gravity-wise, it looked and felt as if straight down no longer pointed anywhere close to the center of the Earth.

Understanding washed over Angela. The ship hadn't tilted. It wasn't listing.

It was gravity that had shifted! This was another manifestation of what they had felt while crawling through the anchor chain's guide pipe.

Somehow, Angela's reference for straight down on this portion of the supertanker was about forty degrees off from what it would be on the ground. It was as if the planet's gravitational center had suddenly shifted to the middle of the ship.

From where they stood, clutching the railing, it felt as if they were going to start sliding toward the center of the tanker's deck.

Another fact screamed for her attention: they had gained ground. She and Vaughn had run backward faster than the ship was moving through the cut in the ridgeline.

Angela grabbed Vaughn's hand and squeezed it. "It's gravity manipulation, but we can talk about that later!" She pointed toward the near side of the ridge and pulled out of his grasp. "We're almost there! Go, go, go!"

Leaning insanely, they started running again.

Waves of vertigo washed across Angela. She kept a hand on the railing to stabilize herself and to prevent the disorienting image of the skewed horizon from sending her sprawling across the deck.

However, in spite of it all, they continued to make progress, each lurching step drawing them closer to the waiting ridge.

The friction of its contact with the ground had slowed the ship precipitously. Running backward as the tanker inched forward, they were catching up with the land again.

Tall trees topped the adjacent hill. Some of their larger branches hung over the railing ahead.

That was their out!

They could jump onto one of the ridge's trees and then climb down to safety after the ship cleared the ravine.

A tremendous metallic renting noise came from beneath them. It sounded as if a chunk of the ship's hull had broken away.

Suddenly, the tanker lurched ahead.

The trees at the top of the hill trembled and rocked as the ship ground against them. Leaves littered the deck.

"Grab it!" Vaughn urged from behind her.

Angela thrust out an arm. Her hand latched onto a large limb.

"Got it—"

Vaughn shouted over her. "Oh shit! Watch out!"

Something slammed painfully into Angela's torso.

The branch yanked out of her grasp.

Air burst from her lungs as she bounced backward.

She had run straight into the ship's back rail.

Wrapping his arms around her, Vaughn caught Angela, pinning her and her backpack between himself and the railing. He looked over her shoulder as he had earlier. Clutching the barricade and struggling to draw breath, they watched the ridgeline retreat.

Still behind her, Vaughn hugged Angela to him with his free arm. "Are you alright?!"

Finally catching her breath, she swallowed hard and then gave a short nod. "Yeah, I'll live." With mounting dread, she watched the receding land. "But I'm not sure how long that'll last."

They continued to grip the back rail tightly. Because of its perceived list, the top bar appeared to stand taller on their left. Looking at its tilt, Angela realized that she would have tumbled over the railing if she hadn't been leaning to compensate for the shifted gravity.

Still breathing heavily, Angela began to move to her right, waving for Vaughn to follow.

A moment later, they reached the middle of the back deck, and the world appeared to have righted itself. It no longer felt as if the ship were listing, and the ridge behind it now etched a normal horizon across the sky.

Looking around, Vaughn shook his head. "What the hell?"

Angela pointed down. "We're feeling the local changes in gravity. I told you they must be manipulating it. That's why it showed up on my gravity-wave detector."

Vaughn nodded. Experimentally, he walked a few paces toward the opposite side of the tanker. With each step his upper body leaned farther out.

From Angela's perspective, it looked as if he was leaning away from her and should be falling over.

He walked back to her.

Together, they peered over the handrail and looked down.

Angela's hands clenched it tightly. Her heart raced, its pulse pounding in her ears as she looked down and watched the French countryside scroll past a thousand feet beneath them.

Vaughn looked at her. "We're stuck on this thing."

Unable to speak, Angela nodded.

He was right. They wouldn't be getting off this ship until it reached its final destination.

A shiver ran down her spine as she remembered the enormous orange discs that sat at the end of the line.

Angela had no idea what those spots might be, but she did know one thing.

They would soon gain an up close and personal familiarity with all of it.

PART II

"Valor is stability, not of legs and arms, but of courage and the soul."
    —Michel de Montaigne

CHAPTER 8

Holding onto the railing and peering down at the distant countryside, Vaughn experienced an unwelcome sense of déjà vu. His stomach churned as he recalled the last time he'd clung to a handrail this high above the ground. Stacking the memory of his suicidal Royal Gorge visit on top of this wonderful little cruise fashioned the perfect shit sandwich.

Vaughn shook his head, and then he and Angela exchanged frightened glances. She looked like he felt: scared shitless—save the aforementioned sandwich.

What the hell were they going to do now?!

He looked back down at the sphincter-tightening sight of the too distant ground. Even as a helicopter pilot, Vaughn had no affinity for high places, and nearly falling from that suspension bridge had done little to assuage that sentiment.

His hair started waving in the breeze as the ship, no longer dragging across the ground, returned to its original pace.

One thing was certain: they were along for the whole ride now, all the way to the goddamned destination.

Standing behind the tanker's four-story-tall bridge section, he could no longer see the ginormous steel skyscrapers.

Vaughn stepped away from the back rail and waved for Angela to follow. "Come on. We're about to have a bird's-eye view of the city. May as well take advantage of it."

She hesitated.

Vaughn stopped and gently took her shaky hand in his own unsteady one.

Angela yanked hers free. "I'm fine!"

A flush crept up her face. Her gaze fell to the decking. After a moment, her eyes lifted back to meet his. She frowned. "Sorry, you didn't deserve that."

Vaughn shrugged and smiled crookedly. He pointed over his shoulder. "Water. Duck's back. No problem."

Grinning self-consciously, Angela closed her eyes and took a deep breath. Then she nodded and gestured toward the front of the ship. She stepped closer and slipped her tremulous hand back into his.

Vaughn squeezed it. Puckering his forehead, he looked into her eyes. "I'm scared, too."

A mixture of emotions scrolled across her face, but then she nodded and gestured ahead toward the front of the tanker. "Lead the way, Captain."

Vaughn squeezed her hand again and then started walking toward the right edge of the ship's office building-sized bridge.

As they moved laterally away from the middle of the deck, Vaughn began to feel as if he were walking uphill.

Ever since they had boarded the tanker, the sense of down always seemed to point toward the middle of the ship's hull, as if the thing had somehow gained its own planetary-strength gravity field. The gravity shift … or manipulation—whatever the hell Angela had called it—made it feel like the longitudinal axis of the ship was the center of the Earth, as if someone had taken a black hole and stretched it into a long rod and then skewered the supertanker with it.

As they walked down the length of the ship, they didn't have to lean forward or backward. However, when Vaughn moved left or right, he had to keep his feet between him and the center of the ship like an ant walking along a length of horizontal pipe.

Now leaning right, Vaughn reached the starboard edge of the building and peered around the corner, expecting to spot a sky full of polished steel monstrosities.

Angela whispered over his shoulder. "What do you see?"

"Nothing. The prow is too tall."

She leaned out, peeking around him. "The what?"

"The front of the ship. It's too tall. Sides too. Can't see a damned thing."

"Good!" Angela released his hand. She stepped from behind Vaughn and walked out into the open. "If we can't see them, they can't see us."

"Someone is feeling better."

Angela shrugged. "We've come this far, and it's not like we have a choice. So you're right, we might as well go see what's coming."

"You sure about this?"

She cocked an eyebrow and gestured forward. "Move it, Captain. Don't make me pull this bus over."

"Yes, ma'am!"

Leaning against the shifting gravity, they walked along the side of the bridge structure and then traversed back to the central catwalk where the sense of down returned to its normal angle, making the deck feel level again.

A few minutes later, they approached the front of the ship. Vaughn climbed a short ladder that led to the prow. As he reached the elevated deck, his eyes widened and he ducked down.

From the higher vantage point, he could now see the tops of the city's tallest buildings.

Crouching, Vaughn scurried up to the black steel wall at the front of the V-shaped foredeck.

Now that they'd reached the front of the long ship, Vaughn could hear a deep rumble drifting over the shielding wall of the prow's black bulkhead.

He looked back just as Angela's head rose into view.

As she saw the building tops, her eyes went round, and she froze.

Vaughn waved urgently. "Move it, Commander Brown!"

She blinked and then looked at him.

He waved Angela over, motioning for her to stay low.

She chewed her lip for a moment and then nodded.

Moving lithely, she crested the ladder and crawled up next to him and sat.

With their backs pressed to the four-foot-tall bulkhead, they exchanged nervous glances.

Angela leaned in, placing her mouth next to Vaughn's ear. "Now what?"

"We're far enough away. I think we can hazard a peek." Vaughn pointed at the collection of pipes and small structures that crowded the prow's upper deck. "We won't stand out with all of that stuff behind us."

Angela chewed her lip for a moment.

Vaughn watched her struggle to rein in her emotions.

He knew exactly how she felt.

Finally, Angela nodded.

He returned the gesture and then rolled onto his knees. Now facing the wall, he placed his hands on the rounded top of the black bulkhead.

Angela did the same.

Vaughn winked at her. "Ready?"

She gave him a curt nod. "Yep."

Moving slowly, they raised their heads.

As Vaughn emerged from behind the prow's shield, the low rumble they'd been hearing crescendoed into an unending tumult of rolling thunder.

His breath caught in his throat as an incredible panorama slid into view.

A short cry escaped Angela. "Oh my God ...!"

She turned pleading eyes toward Vaughn as if asking him to make it all go away.

If only he could.

It was all too much.

His mind reeled as he tried to grasp the scale of the scene and the dark horrors it portended.

Everything was huge, every component of the surreal tapestry a colossal feature on its own.

Angela said something, but her words were lost to the din. Then her hand was in his again.

Vaughn clutched it tightly as he stared ahead.

He'd known that the city's towers were huge. They'd seen as much from the ridge before being scooped up by the damned ship. However, that previous view, hazed by the combined effects of distance and smog, couldn't have prepared him for the overwhelming scale of what he now saw. No longer encumbered by those deficits, Vaughn now looked upon a scene that had him bordering on shock.

The bow of the tanker was only a few miles from the outskirts of the city. The clarity of their 'front-row seats' revealed its true scale. The insane skyline towered well above the ship's thousand-foot altitude. The tallest buildings appeared miles high, many times the height of humanity's greatest structures. They varied dramatically in size and shape. Some looked almost organic. One had an odd egg shape. Strange, wavy ridges protruded from the sides of many of the buildings, extending earthward like the exposed roots of a giant ficus tree.

Vaughn could see elevated roadways snaking through the metropolis. However, no vehicles traversed their lanes.

Narrow towers dotted the cityscape, tall, pointed structures with a light at the top of each.

The surreal panorama would have bordered on beautiful if not for the framing perimeter of horror.

Concentric bands of destruction and construction ringed the outskirts of the alien city.

Therein lay the mechanisms of Angela and Vaughn's terror.

A sweeping tide of black specks swarmed around the area. Vaughn blinked, trying to resolve the scene. Swarming like ants, lines of black dots streamed inward from the city's perimeter and flowed up the sides of the outermost structures. There they congregated atop each building. The upper extremities of those incomplete structures looked as if cleaved by a giant blade. Below the line delineated by the swarming dots, the exterior of the buildings had the same polished metal finish as those in the rest of the city.

Vaughn dropped his gaze back to the source, the point of origin for all those lines of black specks and for the dread that was consuming what remained of his sanity.

His breathing rate increased as he watched the ant-like black points spill out of a massive industrial complex.

An intricate network of pipes and machinery sat ahead of their levitating supertanker, resting beneath a recognizable feature: one of the glowing orange discs that Angela had seen from orbit.

Only, it wasn't anything as benign as a disc.

From farther away, the circle had been more of a burnt orange. However, now it shined bright, glowing in a vibrant amber hue.

Shimmering, brilliant material filled the top of a bowl-shaped structure. A part of his mind already accepted what that giant, stadium-sized container represented, but Vaughn shook his head. It couldn't be that.

Shifting his gaze from the disturbing image, he studied the ground beneath the basin's near side. The industrial complex that appeared to be birthing the black dots surrounded three sides of the giant bowl, but mounded earth had piled up against the portion that faced Angela and Vaughn.

Staring at the mass, he realized it wasn't dirt. The pulverized remains of the old city had piled up in front of the stadium-sized structure. Even from this distance, Vaughn could see the jagged lines of broken buildings protruding from the heap.

As he watched, a cloud of dust kicked up as a large chunk of masonry wall toppled from the mound and tumbled down its face.

Eyes widening, Vaughn looked back at the orange-topped structure.

"The damned thing is moving!"

He looked over at Angela.

She'd seen it too. Beneath her undulating mane of auburn hair, her face had a ghostly pallor. He began to worry that she might be more than on the verge of shock, but then she returned his gaze and nodded soberly. "It is moving, but look." She pointed. "Is there something sticking out of that orange stuff?"

Vaughn reluctantly returned his gaze to the top of the stadium-sized bowl.

Angela was right. Something was protruding from it.

The now amber surface had grown so bright that it was becoming painful to look directly at it, and as they drew ever closer, he could now see that the air above it shimmered with heat waves.

As Vaughn knew it would, the protruding item gradually sank beneath the luminous surface.

"Shit. Shit. *Shit!*"

Angela's head snapped toward him. "What?!"

Vaughn pointed ahead at a large, steel crane that was floating at the front of the parade of steel. It was one of the mega structures that you'd typically see at a shipping port. The massive derrick looked large enough to pluck an office building from its foundation.

As Vaughn knew it would, the giant steel edifice began to sink toward the luminous amber surface.

"What's it doing?!"

He looked at Angela and then nodded meaningfully, tilting his head toward the descending crane. "It's heading to the same place we are." He pointed at the orange-topped bowl. "Into that cauldron of molten metal."

Dawning comprehension spread across her face followed quickly by abject horror. She pointed ahead. "That big-assed thing is a vat … of liquified steel?!"

He nodded. "Ah-yep."

"Oh no! No, no, no …" She looked around, searching the sky around them. "We have to get off this thing!"

Vaughn grabbed the shoulder strap of his backpack. "Unfortunately, I left my parachute at the cleaners."

Angela glared at him. "Now's not the time for your inner asshole to show up, Captain! Think! Help me find a way out of here!"

Vaughn frowned but then nodded. He pointed ahead. "There's still another ship and all those boulders of ore ahead of us. It'll take a while for them to process all of it. That'll buy us some time."

As he spoke, his gaze returned to the cauldron. The lowest portion of the crane penetrated the surface of the lake of molten steel. Black smoke erupted from the point of contact as its coat of paint burst into flames.

Vaughn looked at the next item in the line: the leading boulder of metallic ore.

Suddenly, it dropped toward the luminous surface, falling much faster than had the crane. The giant boulder plunged into the vat, slamming into the viscous surface next to the still sinking crane. The impact launched long ribbons of glowing material. The liquefied metal shot into the air like lava blasted from a volcano. It splashed down on the ruined bits of city that surrounded the cauldron's advancing side.

Vaughn flinched. "Son of a bitch!" Then he blinked and looked up as all the hunks of ore ahead of them split off from their line and headed toward the adjacent cauldrons.

"Aw, crap …!" He closed his eyes and shook his head.

"What? Where are they going?"

He looked at Angela. "It's nickel. They're converting the metal into stainless steel."

"What do you mean?"

"Those boulders, they must be nickel ore. They probably dragged it up here from the mines in South Africa. Mix that with steel in the right ratio, and you get stainless steel." He pointed at the silver city. "Polished, it looks like that."

Angela looked at the skyline.

Vaughn shook his head again. "But now we have another problem."

As he spoke, the supertanker began to drift forward, moving up to occupy the portion of the line vacated by the reassigned nickel ore.

He nodded at the ship ahead of them. "When they're done with that one, we're next."

The last of the crane sank out of sight, its massive boom and swinging hook slipping beneath the coruscant surface.

Movement ahead drew Vaughn's eyes. The back of the next ship was lifting into the air. A few moments later, the entire vessel had pivoted to the vertical, its front or bow now pointing straight down.

Frozen in place, Vaughn watched as the ship began to lower into the vat.

Considerably smaller than their supertanker, it sank quickly. Within moments, half of its length had already disappeared into the stadium-sized cauldron.

The tanker beneath their feet began to move forward again.

The motion snapped Vaughn out of his horrified trance.

He grabbed Angela's arm and turned toward the back of the ship. "Run! Go now!"

A minute later, they had covered half the distance between the bow and the tanker's tall, building-sized bridge structure. Vaughn had been watching his feet, making sure he didn't trip over anything. When he looked up to check on their progress, something looked very wrong.

It appeared as if the entire world had rolled on its side.

But this wasn't like last time. The elevated catwalk that they were running on spanned the length of the deck's center. They hadn't veered from it. Straight down still felt as if it passed through the middle of the ship beneath his feet, but while his brain and his inner ear told him that the vessel was still perfectly upright, his eyes said that the tanker and its bridge had fallen on its side.

Their supertanker had rolled over, but because of the artificial gravity, he hadn't felt it.

Vaughn grabbed the railing to stabilize himself as the visual disconnect between what he was seeing and feeling sent another wave of vertigo washing over him.

Angela ran into his back, nearly knocking him to his knees. Panting, she shouted, "Why did you—?" Then seeing the vertical line of the horizon, she grabbed the railing, too. "Oh shit! It's rolling over!"

She was right. It hadn't fallen over. It was rolling. The ship no longer looked as if it were lying on its side. Its bridge section was starting to point toward the ground.

Then it flipped completely inverted, finishing its slow-motion capsize.

Now gripping both rails with white-knuckled death grips, Vaughn looked straight up. The ruined remnants of Geneva hung a thousand feet above his head. He stood there for a long moment, frozen in place, unable to move as he stared at the surreal sight.

"Come on!" Angela screamed from somewhere below ... above him. "Get under here!"

Vaughn looked down toward his feet. Angela was climbing into the three-foot-tall crawl space beneath the elevated catwalk and the deck.

"We need to get under here." She pointed up, toward the ground. "In case normal gravity—"

Vaughn's head spun, and the traditional sense of up-and-down suddenly reasserted itself ... with a vengeance.

The tanker lost its gravitational pull and, instantaneously, Earth reasserted its dominance.

His feet fell from the catwalk, and then Vaughn was hanging from the handrail, nothing but his death grip preventing him from plummeting into old Geneva.

Angela screamed. "Vaughn!"

He couldn't pull his eyes away from the ground. He tried to speak, but his suddenly dry throat only managed a weak croak.

All he could do was stare down past his swinging hiking boots at the distant, crumbled remains of the old city.

He kept expecting the ground to rush up and squash the two of them like bugs, but somehow the ship held its lofty elevation despite the return of normal gravity.

"Vaughn!"

He flinched, Angela's words yanking him out of his shocked trance.

Finally able to wrench his gaze from the ground, he looked up and saw her now lying prone on the backside of the catwalk.

From Vaughn's radically revised perspective, the catwalk's metal grating now looked like a shelf suspended from a steel ceiling.

Angela extended her arm, reaching for Vaughn.

She growled in frustration. "I can't reach you!"

Vaughn glanced at his white knuckles. Again they reminded him of his aborted suicide at the Royal.

His hands had almost failed him then.

He sure as hell hoped they held this time!

"Hold on, Vaughn!"

Angela climbed out from her perch. She placed a foot on the middle bar of the inverted handrail.

The flipped perspective made it appear that she had moved from her suspended shelf to a split-level pull-up bar.

Hanging onto one of the vertical members, she laced her leg around the bar and hooked her calf over one of the midspan pipes.

Vaughn looked down and then looked back up at her with wide eyes. "No, Angela! You'll fall!"

"Just give me your hand!"

Vaughn shook his head. "No! I'll end up pulling you down."

"Dammit, Captain! Give me your goddamned hand!"

He shook his head. Then he started swinging back and forth, intent on throwing a leg over the handrail-turned-monkey bar.

"What are you doing?! You'll fall!"

He heard tears in Angela's voice.

"Vaughn! Please!"

The muscles in his hands and forearms burned as if on fire.

Gnashing his teeth, he thrust his right leg upward, trying to hook his heel over the bar. However, it bounced off ineffectually and accelerated his backswing.

The inertia threatened to rip the railing out of his hands.

He could feel ... his fingers ... prying apart!

Suddenly, Angela's hands were on both of his wrists. She was now standing on the railing with her back pressed to the deck-turned-ceiling. She wasn't holding his entire weight, but her assistance allowed his hands to win their battle. He reestablished his grip, and then they both screamed with exertion as he swung his legs up and finally hooked a calf over the rail.

A moment later and breathing heavily, they both crawled onto the backside of the inverted catwalk.

Vaughn rolled onto his back and massaged the blood back into his hands. He looked at Angela. "Thank you … You saved my life."

She shook her head. "You stubborn man."

She peered down. "Now what?"

Vaughn scoffed. "No clue."

"Me neither." She glanced at the deck over their heads. "I don't understand why the gravity failed, why we almost fell even though the ship is still in the air."

Vaughn frowned. "I think it's kind of obvious. They must have seen us and decided to drop us off in the old city."

Shaking her head, Angela looked into his eyes. "I don't think that's it." She pointed toward the front of the ship. "Why bother? We're already heading toward—"

They both flinched as the entire ship shuddered.

A tremendous, metallic screech pierced the atmosphere.

With wide eyes, Angela and Vaughn watched as large portions of the deck to either side of them suddenly wrenched open as if cut with a giant can-opener. Thick torrents of black liquid burst through the openings and plunged earthward.

An acrid stench filled the air, burning Vaughn's eyes and sinuses.

The two of them began to cough.

Angela held a sleeve over her lower face. "What is that?!"

Vaughn coughed again and then spat. "Crude oil!"

Beneath them, the supertanker's entire cache of the thick, black substance, some two million barrels of crude, began to splash down across the ruined remnants of Geneva.

Angela looked at him. "Alien or not, who would do that?"

Vaughn pointed at the metallic metropolis. "Someone willing to wipe life from an entire planet just so they could pave it over with steel."

CHAPTER 9

On hands and knees and trying not to look down, Vaughn followed Angela. They crawled frantically rearward through the three-foot gap between the catwalk and the inverted deck over their heads.

A moment later, they rounded a bend and came to a steel plate.

A dead end. It blocked their passage completely.

Angela slammed her clenched fist into the grating. "Dammit!"

Hazarding a downward glance, Vaughn saw a hatchway just beneath the inverted walkway. He recognized it as the door into the bridge structure. A latched, long-handled lever held it closed.

During their two previous treks down the length of the ship, they had gone around the bridge.

That wasn't an option now.

Angela and Vaughn had to find a way through it to get to the back of the ship.

Vaughn knew that either way, they were likely dead, but he'd just as soon put that off as long as physically possible.

He was funny that way.

The ground below them appeared to have slipped farther away. Looking right, he identified the problem.

His fingers clutched anxiously at the steel grating. "Oh shit!"

Ahead of him, Angela nodded. "I see it too!"

The back of the ship had already begun to rise as the whole thing tilted earthward in preparation for its death dive.

Vaughn resisted the urge to look back. He really didn't need a closer look at that giant cauldron of molten metal.

Ahead of him, Angela began to shimmy sideways. "I'm going to open the hatch!"

Before he could stop her, she had swung her legs out over the edge of the catwalk and then scooted off it.

Vaughn felt his bowels loosen as he watched her hang suspended, nothing but hundreds of feet of empty air between her and the ground.

On hands and knees, he lunged forward and grabbed Angela's wrists. He held her hands to the edge of the grating. "I got you!"

Angela looked up at him and nodded.

Vaughn glanced sideways and spotted the handrail that Angela had used when she'd helped him earlier. Inexplicably, it stopped several feet short of the building's entrance. It sat too far away to help them this time.

Hanging from her hands, Angela batted at the latched lever with the toes of her hiking boots.

Vaughn felt the tendons and muscles in her arms strain and flex under his grasp.

On her third try, Angela hooked a toe under the handle and pried it toward the deck. The door unlatched and slowly swung open.

Watching it, Vaughn realized that the change in the gravity field hadn't affected the steel. With the ship's increasing tilt, the door should have slammed open.

Whoever was controlling all of this had changed the gravity manipulation, focusing it solely on the steel. In a sudden insight, Vaughn realized they must have changed it to allow the crude oil to drain while leaving the ship up in the air.

The gravity shift that had nearly launched them from the ship hadn't necessarily been aimed at them. The powers that be might not know about the two of them, yet.

With a little urging from Angela's boots, the door finally swung out of the way.

"Great job!"

She looked up and then nodded to his hands. "Let go of my wrists."

Vaughn hesitated.

She winked at him. "I'll be okay."

He nodded and reluctantly released her, leaving imprints of his fingers pressed into her skin.

Angela began to swing her body back and forth, hanging from the edge of the catwalk like a trapeze artist on a monkey bar.

Her feet swung out and then back into the open door. Timing it perfectly, she released the grating and landed on the ceiling of the room beyond the door.

Vaughn released the breath he'd been holding. He crawled to the edge of the catwalk. Not wanting to look at the ground, he focused on the hatchway.

Squatting inside the upside-down building, Angela glanced down and then looked up at him with anxious eyes. She waved urgently. "Hurry!"

He took a deep breath and then started to slide his body over the ledge. A heart-pounding moment later and now hanging from the catwalk, he began to swing his legs like she had, kicking his boots toward the hatchway. On the second arc, he released his grip and dropped through the open hatch, landing next to Angela.

Unfortunately, he didn't have her perfect timing.

The energy of Vaughn's swing didn't carry him all the way into the room beyond.

He started to fall backward.

His flailing hands bounced ineffectually off the jamb, the traitorous bastards again failing to save him.

"Shit!"

Angela grabbed the front of Vaughn's shirt. She couldn't hold him up, but her efforts arrested enough of his slow-motion fall that his hands finally managed to find purchase.

With a final heave, Angela yanked him forward.

Tumbling into the inverted room, he landed hard on his hands and knees on its sloping ceiling.

Still clutching his shirt, Angela pulled him insistently toward the back of the ship. "We have to hurry!"

Breathless, Vaughn nodded and pointed for her to lead the way.

They ran aft, scuttling up the increasingly tilted ceiling as the tanker continued to angle down toward its ultimate demise.

Angela scurried upward, now on all fours. "It's getting steep!"

Still trying to catch his breath, Vaughn could only manage another nod.

Legs churning and soles squeaking, they scurried up the painted surface of the tilted steel plates. Negotiating the maze-like interstices of the building's interior, they hurried rearward, hopping over exit signs and sprinkler heads along the way. All the while, the upward tilt of the ceiling kept getting steeper.

Vaughn knew that if he and Angela didn't reach the back of the ship soon, they never would.

After an agonizingly long detour down a dead-end side corridor, they finally found one that led to a hatch at the back of the bridge. The rubber soles of their boots now slipped with every step, squealing their protest with increasing volume as the two tried to run up the ever-steepening slope.

Angela reached the door a step ahead of Vaughn. She wrenched the handle open, grunting with exertion. It unlatched, squealing as she turned it ninety degrees.

As he watched her, Vaughn feared that the now considerable tilt of the ship would pin the door closed. If so, they would have to lift the door's significant weight. However, the hatch swung outward with surreal slowness, as if the ship were still level.

Vaughn's boots began to slip.

Angela lunged for the edge of the doorway. "Grab the lip!"

Vaughn wedged his boots into the angle where ceiling met wall.

Using that leverage, he jumped for the side of the open hatch and caught it with one hand.

For a precarious moment, he hung there, his already fatigued fingers threatening to drop him back into the bridge.

Finally, he managed to grab the jamb with his other hand.

Vaughn pedaled his feet like a madman. Next to him, Angela did the same.

Fortunately, the ceiling panel beneath their shoes had just enough tilt remaining to afford them a measure of traction.

They clambered onto the now horizontal back wall of the super-tanker's bridge just as the ship rolled completely vertical.

Panting, they stood and hugged each other tightly.

Vaughn released Angela and cocked his head. "Do you hear that?"

A distant, unending roar filled the air. It was the same endless rolling thunder that they'd heard when the two of them had stood at the front of the ship. However, now that the tanker was directly over the cauldron, Vaughn could feel his insides shaking to the beat of the colossal machine's heart.

He grabbed her hand. "Come on. Let's go see."

Angela's lips pressed white, thin as potato chips, but then she nodded.

Crouching and stepping cautiously with hands held out for balance, they eased toward the nearest end of the toppled bridge's back wall.

Vaughn's heart raced as they neared the ledge where it dropped to unknown depths.

With no handrail between him and the ledge, Vaughn became keenly aware of the fact that the slightest jostle of the building under-foot could send the two of them over the edge. Plummeting a thou-sand feet into a vat of molten metal didn't seem like the best way to end the day, so he dropped to hands and knees and crawled the last few feet.

Beside him, Angela did the same.

As they drew closer, intense heat blasted their faces, and the noise level seemed to double.

They winced and dropped to their bellies.

Squinting and covering their ears, Vaughn and Angela exchanged nervous glances. Then they inched up to the edge and peered down.

In the moments before the intense heat and bone-rattling sound chased him back, Vaughn stared in pained, horrified amazement at the incredible scene.

Huge machines, each as big as a city block, worked feverishly on three sides of the cauldron.

Rivers of glowing, molten steel poured from multiple ports in the bottom of the vat and streamed into one end of each of the three mechanical monstrosities. Vaughn could see multitudinous arms and manipulators moving about the exposed innards of the giant mechanisms. Glowing embers arced into the air as thousands of skittering appendages shaped and processed the steel with insectile dexterity.

At their far ends, the giant robots spat out steady streams of formed and polished stainless-steel parts in myriad sizes and shapes. It appeared that the entire process was draining the cauldron as quickly as the incoming parade of steel structures filled it.

The black dots they'd seen streaming from the area now resolved as an army of black-bodied worker bots. Multiple lines of them coursed past the ends of the giant robots. As they crossed the area, each one of them received a unique, freshly minted stainless-steel part. Without so much as a hiccup in their step, they then streamed out of the facility and coursed up the sides of the nearest of the buildings.

Vaughn couldn't see the tops of those mountainous structures, but he could envision what was happening at the far end of those lines. The bots would install their assigned part and then return to the base to get their next allotment.

His attention returned to the industrial complex, and he saw that giant metal links formed tracks that lined the left and right side of the cauldron and its collection of machinery. They looked like the tracks you would see on a military tank or a bulldozer, but these were each as wide as an interstate highway.

Seeing the twinned lines of colossal links, Vaughn realized that they'd been right.

The whole thing was moving.

The damned cauldron was the centerpiece of a self-propelled, city-sized construction robot, an industrial facility that wouldn't stop moving. It would continue across the land, depositing buildings in its wake until it ran out of planetary surface or raw materials.

Vaughn gave a final, forlorn glance at the all-too-close cauldron of molten steel and then slid back from the edge. The sound dropped precipitously. Pulling his hands from his ears, he shook his head. "Son of a bitch!" He looked at Angela. "Out of the freaking frying pan and into the damned fire!"

Angela had pulled back as well. She rolled onto her side and looked at him. Now splotched with red, her face had reacquired its ghostly pallor. She shouted above the din. "What are we going to do, Vaughn?"

He almost scoffed. What the hell could they do? But then Vaughn realized Captain Asshole was the last person Angela needed to hear from right now.

He placed a hand on her arm and lied. "We'll figure out something."

They both flinched as suddenly it felt like they were in a descending elevator.

They exchanged frightened glances and then peered over the edge again.

The ship had started to descend in earnest. The prow where they'd gotten their first close look of the alien city was drawing near to the glowing surface. Smokey fumes were already beginning to rise from its thick coat of black paint.

Vaughn glimpsed an item descending in formation with the super-tanker. Looking around, he realized that the ship was not the only vessel heading toward that luminous pool. Hundreds of smaller steel structures were descending with them.

Again, the scorched air chased him back from the edge. As soon as he passed out of the cauldron's direct line of sight, the heat again dropped as did the noise level.

Beside him, Angela did the same. She rolled toward him and nodded. Then she began to shout, her words now barely audible over the growing cacophony. "We're going to have to jump!"

Vaughn's eyes widened. "Jump?! Are you in a hurry to end it all?" He glanced back over the edge and then hoisted an eyebrow as he regarded her. "I'm pretty sure that would do the job, although being barbecued on the way down might not be the quick, painless death you're envisioning."

Angela shook her head and then pointed over his shoulder. "We can jump onto that!"

Turning to follow her gesture, he spotted an old, subcompact automobile of uncertain origin flying in formation with the supertanker. He hadn't seen it earlier because it was a couple of dozen feet to his left. Descending at the same speed as the ship, the car hung in the air about ten feet from that portion of the bridge's back wall.

Vaughn did a double take and then stared at Angela, eyebrow now flying at full skepticism. "Are you crazy?" He pointed at the car. "As soon as we land on that thing, it'll start falling faster!"

Angela shook her head. "I don't think so. Whatever or whoever is doing all of this is adding material at a controlled rate. Didn't you say something about needing to keep the ratios at a specific level to create stainless steel?"

Vaughn nodded. "Yeah, but that's one hell of an assumption. If you're wrong, we'll look like toasted marshmallows by the time we reach the bottom."

Angela's face twisted with disgust. "Thanks! Could have done without that mental image."

They both flinched again as the deck began to vibrate roughly.

Still lying prone, they crept side-by-side back to the ledge and looked down again. A thousand feet beneath them, the bow of the tanker had disappeared in the pool of molten metal. Huge flames licked up from the point of contact as paint and other materials combusted in the incredible, all-consuming heat.

The flames lazily worked their way up the exterior of the tanker. Then they found the residual crude oil and exploded into a frenzied conflagration. Renewed heat blasted their faces as a roiling orange and black mushroom cloud raced toward them.

Vaughn and Angela scrambled back from the edge. Standing, they raced to the center of the bridge section's rear wall. A moment later, the expanding, superheated gases shot past and soared heavenward. The roiling cloud scorched the place where they'd just been lying.

The black pall swelled overhead, darkening the sky.

Smoke began to engulf the entire ship and started obscuring their view of the outside world.

Angela turned to Vaughn and shouted, screaming above the sound of shredding air. "We have to jump, now!"

Vaughn pursed his lips and then nodded.

Angela pulled away from him.

He turned and studied the gap, estimating the speed and distance of the jump he'd need to make. His heart raced at the thought.

He walked backward, stepping out the needed distance. Then he swallowed hard and shouted over his shoulder. "I'll go fir—"

Suddenly, Angela zipped past him and then, reaching the scorched edge of the back wall, leaped into the air.

"Angela!"

She flew through the smoke and then disappeared.

"Oh shit!"

Vaughn stumbled forward as he tried to spot her through the churning black wall. Through a gap he saw her straddling the roof of the floating car.

It didn't fall. Its descent hadn't even accelerated.

Angela glanced down from her perch. Her eyes widened, and she looked back to Vaughn and waved urgently, motioning for him to jump.

She yelled something, but a loud explosion drowned out her words.

Vaughn took a couple of quick backward steps and then shook his head. "And she calls me reactionary!"

He stared at the ledge, again trying to estimate the required speed and trajectory, but then he saw Angela waving frantically.

"Shit! Screw it!"

He ran straight at the precipice.

His heart raced, threatening to burst from his chest.

Then he was flying through the air.

Incredible heat wrapped around him.

Looking down, Vaughn saw a rapidly rising cloud of roiling black smoke. It appeared that the entire lower half of the supertanker's deck was now fully engulfed in fire.

The heat dropped precipitously as his feet hit the hood of the car, but then the hot gases of the rising smoke assaulted his back.

Vaughn tumbled into Angela, but somehow they managed to stay on the car.

The temperature dropped, the metal bulk of the automobile shielding them from the worst of the massive fire's radiant heat.

Fortunately, even the addition of his weight did not accelerate the vehicle's descent. However, the inertia of their bodies had transferred some lateral movement to the car.

It was now drifting sideways, away from the supertanker.

Wincing from the heat assaulting their faces, the two of them peered down. Half the tanker had disappeared into the churning cauldron of molten metal. Less than five hundred feet now separated them and its searing surface.

Vaughn pointed over Angela's shoulder. "Keep going!" He jabbed his finger toward a nearby hunk of floating steel.

Angela nodded. A moment later, she leaped onto the item—the ship's no longer missing anchor. It was too small to support both of them at the same time, so she continued and jumped onto the next piece, a floating, slowly rotating I-beam. Fortunately, it was horizontally oriented and didn't cant when Angela landed on it.

From the hood of the car, Vaughn ran across the roof of the small vehicle.

He planted his foot on its trunk and lunged for the anchor.

The sheet metal buckled underfoot.

Robbed of its full force, the jump came up short.

Vaughn watched his intended landing spot slide out of reach.

"Ah, sh—!"

Air exploded through his lips as his upper body slammed into the side of the anchor.

The impact knocked the wind out of him, but somehow Vaughn managed to latch his arms around it. His feet swung, almost wrenching him from the anchor.

A moment later, he finally managed to pull himself onto the floating hunk of metal. As he fought to draw breath from the too hot atmosphere, he searched frantically for Angela.

Then he spotted her.

Still on hands and knees, she had shimmied halfway down the length of the I-beam.

Vaughn struggled to his feet. Mentally calculating the timing, he watched as the end of the slowly rotating beam swung toward him.

"Three … Two … *One!*"

He jumped!

The full heat of the rising air accosted him as he passed out of the anchor's shadow.

He landed unsteadily, hopping on one foot, his arms windmilling as he struggled to keep his weight centered over the beam.

Finally, Vaughn won his battle. He dropped to hands and knees and clutched the beam desperately.

Angela looked over her shoulder and waved impatiently. Somehow, her voice broke through the cacophony. "Hurry up!"

Vaughn rolled his eyes. "Nag, nag, nag!"

He looked down, and his momentary smile faltered as he stared into the pool of molten metal. It now sat less than five hundred feet beneath him. Its caustic fumes and tremendous heat assaulted his senses. Fortunately, the thick metal of the I-beam shielded him from the worst of it, and it still retained some coolness.

Angela's voice again pierced the din. "Vaughn!"

His head snapped up, and he nodded to her. "I'm coming!"

Vaughn crawled feverishly, following Angela as she dashed down the length of the I-beam. Scrambling on all fours, they looked like a pair of caffeinated toddlers.

Despite its thickness, the steel was beginning to warm beneath Vaughn's hands.

Ahead of him, the wild torrents of heated air rising from the pool of liquid steel blew Angela's hair straight up.

As their path down the I-beam carried them closer to the outer edge of the cauldron, Vaughn felt welcome torrents of cooler air mixed with the hot gases.

The steel beam was a good sixty feet long, and as it descended beneath a hundred feet, both the heat of the air and the heat of metal beneath Vaughn's hands began to rise dramatically. Ahead of him, Angela was struggling with the same problem. She was hopping from hand-to-hand and shaking them with evident pain.

The rim of the cauldron looked very close now. The distant end of the I-beam appeared to hover just above its lip, which was a good thirty feet above the pool. Fortunately, the mounded debris of old Geneva waited beyond the rim.

The heat became too much.

Vaughn jumped to his feet. "Go, go, go!"

Angela needed no prodding. She had leaped to her feet at the same time as he had.

Arms out to keep their balance, they ran toward the far end of the I-beam.

Angela jumped into the air and disappeared over the rim of the cauldron. A cloud of dust rose up, marking the spot where she'd landed on the debris field.

Then Vaughn was flying through the air as well.

He only had a moment to enjoy the sudden drop in temperature before he landed painfully on the mounded detritus that ringed that portion of the cauldron.

A couple of tumbles later, he came to a halt lying next to Angela.

They looked at each other for a shocked moment. Then they threw arms around each other, laughing and crying at the same time.

Angela squeezed him tightly as she rained kisses onto the side of his head. She laughed manically. "I can't believe we made it!"

Vaughn returned the hug and nodded. A moment later, he released Angela and rolled onto his back. Staring up at the machine city, he raised both hands and extended his middle fingers. "We're still here, assholes!"

CHAPTER 10

Angela mentally inventoried her body as she watched Vaughn flip off the alien city. No single part of her hurt any worse than the others, although the rolling impact had left her feeling as if electrical jolts were coursing through her. Pulverized bits of brick and concrete had partially cushioned her landing, leaving her with nothing worse than a few small cuts and scrapes.

Thankfully, she hadn't been impaled on anything and, judging by his reaction, neither had Vaughn. Angela didn't see metal protruding from any of the debris. She guessed the aliens or whoever had already stripped out all of the steel.

In spite of the pain caused by the tumbling impact, she was relieved that it had carried her into a depression in the piled debris. The only thing she could see in the direction of the city was its nearest incomplete buildings. The massive towers appeared to have no windows, and so far, nothing here had seemed to take notice of her and Vaughn, despite his current tirade.

Angela rolled toward him. Her breath launched a cloud of dust from the shattered masonry between them. "Are you hurt?"

He ran hands along his body and then shook his head. "No. A little singed, but nothing's broken. What about you?"

"Same."

"Good."

Vaughn looked up at the towering buildings. "I've had about enough of this goddamned city. We need to get the hell out of here." Still breathing heavily, he glanced at the low spot they'd landed in. "But I think we should lie low, stay out of sight until dark."

Angela cocked an eyebrow and held up her hands. "I'm not the one screaming and flipping off our alien overlords."

Vaughn smiled sheepishly. "Yeah, kinda got caught up in the moment there."

A sudden realization slammed home. Angela's eyes widened, and she stared up into the sky as she remembered how the big rocks had dropped into the molten metal. The impacts had launched ribbons of the glowing stuff into the air. Afterward, it had rained down onto the debris pile, landing not far from where they were now lying.

Dragging her gaze from the sky, Angela turned her rounded eyes to Vaughn. "We have to go now!"

He glanced at the sky and then knitted his brows.

"Now, Vaughn! Before we get burned up!"

Comprehension dawned on his face. "No, I think they only drop the boulders of ore like that. Probably to break it up, make it mix better."

She cast a doubtful glance at the cauldron.

Vaughn smiled reassuringly. "It only takes a little nickel to make stainless, and I don't see any ore in the line right now. We're okay for the moment." Smirking, he gestured at the tanker that was still sinking behind them. "Well, as safe as we can be after that superduper shitbus dropped us off in the middle of freaking alien Grand Central Station."

Angela nodded and then tilted her head. "We still don't know that no one saw us. If someone is coming to investigate, I'd feel a lot better if we could see them before they were right on top of us."

After chewing on her words for a moment, Vaughn nodded. "You're right. Let's crawl up to the edge of this hole. Might be able to see down the slope without exposing ourselves too much."

Angela smiled. She leaned over and kissed him. Then she rolled onto her belly, launching more dust into the late afternoon air. Low-crawling like Vaughn had taught her, she headed for the downhill-facing side of the depression.

She regarded Vaughn over her shoulder. He hadn't moved. He was just lying there with a silly, puppy-dog grin.

Angela smiled inwardly, would have laughed if their situation weren't so dire. Even in the middle of the apocalypse, a simple kiss was enough to jam a stick into Vaughn's mental spokes.

She cocked an eyebrow. "Any day now, Captain."

Vaughn coughed, and the goofy look fell from his face. He rolled onto his stomach and crawled up to Angela.

Side-by-side again, they continued up to the edge. A few dusty moments later, they eased up to it and peeked through gaps in the piled material.

Black smoke from the tanker's still burning oil residue had filled the sky, blocking much of the setting sun's light. Beneath those dark clouds, the fire's orange luminescence and the glow emitted by the cauldron of molten metal was casting everything in dark, earthen shades.

From their new position, Angela could see a portion of the slope that faced the stainless-steel towers, but ridges blocked their views to left and right. She couldn't see the industrial complex or the remnants of the original city that she'd spotted earlier. Ahead, a hillock several hundred yards beneath their perch obscured the bases of the enormous skyscrapers.

In the wan light, Angela didn't see anything moving on the visible portion of the hill.

It appeared that nothing was coming for them.

Not yet, anyway.

She looked up and watched the columns of black assembly bots march up and down the side of the nearest building. A shudder ran through her as she remembered the lines of them that snaked around the perimeter of the alien city.

She pointed up. "The last thing I want is a run-in with an army of those things."

Vaughn gazed up at them and then nodded. "About the only thing we've got going for us is our size."

"What do you mean?"

The corner of his mouth curled. "We're gnats compared to the scale of this place. I think that's why they haven't noticed us."

Angela glanced up uncomfortably. "Maybe, but I'd rather not test that assumption any longer than absolutely necessary." She scanned their surroundings. "We need to find cover."

After a short chuckle, Vaughn nodded toward the alien city ahead. "Not going that way. I already told you my thoughts on that matter. I'm done with this place."

Craning her neck, Angela looked right and pointed. "I can't see it from here, but what's left of the old city should be that way."

Vaughn looked around and then nodded. "Yeah, it is, but I can't see shit from here." He started to crawl in that direction. "Come on."

Angela followed. Her eyes watered from the combination of gritty dust and acrid fumes. The mixture seemed to permeate everything, filling her sinuses and burning her eyes. The dust worsened as they crawled toward higher ground.

A moment later, they topped a rise and finally had an unobscured view of the no-man's-land that lay between the two industrial complexes.

Ahead of Angela, a mile of ruined city lay between this cauldron's piled detritus and that of the next giant vat. The landscape between the two looked like an image straight out of a World War II photograph of postwar Berlin. A grid of rubble-strewn streets filled the land, most of it no more than a few feet tall. However, blackened husks of burned-out buildings dotted the terrain, jutting from the panorama like dark sentinels of the apocalypse.

All of it looked similar to what they'd seen in Monte Carlo but somehow worse.

To Angela's left, closer to the alien city, lines of machines were flattening the rubble. From here, she couldn't even see a cab on the bulldozers. They appeared to be fully autonomous. Behind them, other machines with less apparent purposes worked piles of debris, leaving the ground behind them smooth.

Her eyebrows furrowed. "Have you seen anybody?"

Slowly shaking his head, Vaughn continued to stare at the machines. "No, I haven't, not a single living thing. It looks like the whole damned lot is running on autopilot." He pointed at the dozers working the leading edge of rubble. "I don't even see supervisor bots. Everything is just happening en masse as if choreographed."

"Yeah, that's what I was thinking, but then what is it all for? *Who* is it for?"

"No clue."

Angela nodded toward the incomplete end of an elevated highway. It protruded from between the bases of two of the unfinished towers. "I don't think those roads were made for the bots. It must be for someone else."

"Maybe, but where are they, then?"

"It's already a big city. There could be millions of … of whatever they are … hiding in the middle of it."

Vaughn rocked his head equivocally.

Suddenly, the ground shook beneath them! The shock wave of a tremendous crash started Angela's ears ringing.

At the same time, debris geysered into the sky to her right.

Angela pressed her face into the gravelly surface and threw arms over her head.

Had the aliens seen them?

Gravel rained down, pelting her back.

Angela tilted her head toward Vaughn. "What the hell was that?!" She paused, coughing dust. "Are they shooting at us?"

"I don't know!" Having covered his head as well, Vaughn lifted an elbow and glanced upward. Then his eyes went round. "Oh shit!"

He reached over and grabbed Angela.

"What are you do—?"

Vaughn yanked her sideways. Dragging her bodily, he pulled her across himself and then dropped her onto the ground on his far side. Then he rolled over on top of her.

Something slammed into the hillside right next to them with a tremendous crash. The ground lurched, tossing Angela and Vaughn across the slope.

They scrambled to their feet.

Angela looked around, frantically searching for their attacker.

Vaughn shook his head and pointed overhead at a large truck that was levitating near the front of the line of advancing steel structures. "It's shit falling from that thing!"

Proving his assertion, something suddenly burst through the skin of the floating eighteen-wheeler's trailer.

Angela stared, frozen in place as it fell straight toward her.

Vaughn yanked her backward as cases of cargo slammed into the ground at their feet. Dust and debris sprayed her painfully as it shot out from the point of impact.

Now gazing heavenward, Angela squeezed Vaughn's hand. "Thank you!"

"Oh, that?" he said with a scoff. "I was trying to use you as a shield, but your big ass pulled me right over." He gave her a quick sideways glance and winked. "Anyway, we need to get out from under this shit storm." Watching the sky again, he pointed down the hill. "You find us a place to hide. I'll keep an eye out."

Angela nodded and then reluctantly tore her gaze from the levitating truck. She scanned Geneva's ruined cityscape but didn't see any structures that might work. What little still stood looked like Swiss cheese. They wouldn't provide much in the way of cover and even less as protection.

How was anything in that desolate remnant of old Geneva going to help them?

Next to her, Vaughn rolled his index finger impatiently. "Anytime now!"

"I'm looking!"

Several desperate moments later, she spotted a small, recognizable structure.

Suddenly, Angela knew what they needed to do.

"I have an idea." She paused, pulling her eyes from the small building and looking overhead. "I think we can—Oh shit!"

Angela screamed as another box of cargo launched from the slowly tumbling eighteen-wheeler.

"Run!" Vaughn shouted.

This time, Angela needed neither prompting nor assistance. She was already two loping strides down the slope of broken debris.

The hillside shook beneath her as the cargo slammed into the ground behind her.

Angela's eyes went wide.

"Vaughn!"

She spun around and stared at the dust cloud. Then he came barreling out of the flying debris, still on his feet and running.

Coughing, he pointed down the hill. "Go, go, go!"

She turned and ran, hopping from a mound of gravel to a protruding chunk of concrete and then onto a pile of bricks.

To her right, Vaughn jumped and leaped as they worked their way down the hill toward old Geneva.

Angela hazarded a look over her shoulder. Behind them, black smoke billowed from the top of the conical mountain of broken masonry. The whole thing could've been mistaken for a volcano if not for the back of the supertanker protruding from its center.

Smoke had blotted out much of the sky, casting a pall over everything, but an eerie glow radiated from the fires and the underlying lake of molten steel. It illuminated the sides of the still protruding portion of the ship's vertical hull and its enigmatically rotating prop.

Staring at the incredible, surreal sight, Angela tripped and nearly sprawled headlong down the debris field. She returned her attention to front. A few precarious minutes later, they finally reached street level and slowed to a walk.

Under the mantle of black smoke, flickering light cast by the burning residue of the supertanker's oily cargo painted the dead city in shades of umber.

As they worked their way down the rubble-strewn streets, the tremendous roar of the cauldron and its rushing air subsided behind them. However, the din of giant machinery still echoed from the ruined buildings.

Reaching a corner, Angela looked left and right, trying to spot her quarry. She pointed right and then turned and walked in that direction.

"What are you looking for?"

Angela spoke over her shoulder as she continued scanning the sides of the road. "A street I saw from the hill." She shook her head. "But now that we're down here, they all look the same."

They emerged into a wide intersection, and Angela smiled as she stared down the long, straight thoroughfare she'd spotted from the hill.

Blackened, limbless tree trunks backed by ruined storefronts lined each side of the once majestic street.

Angela spotted her quarry a block down on the right and started running toward it.

As she neared the spot, Vaughn ran up behind her. "Where the hell are you going?"

A ten-foot-tall concrete archway stood on the walkway ahead. Angela could already see a dark patch behind it. She pointed at the arch. "Right there. The metal signs and handrails are gone, but I think that's it."

"That's what?"

As she stepped up to the opening, Angela nodded toward the embossed words that lined the top of the masonry arch.

"Marché Station."

"The subway?" Vaughn said doubtfully. He glanced toward the alien city. "Why in the hell would we go down there? We made it. We're out!" He pointed toward the distant ridgeline. "We need to keep heading south, get the hell out of here before the machines overrun us."

"I thought we came here to find out what happened."

Vaughn's eyes widened. He turned and held his arms out toward the alien skyline. "This happened, Angela! And thank you very much,

I've already had as close of a gander as I intend to get. What more do you need to see to know that we are in *way* above our heads?!"

Angela placed a hand on his dusty sleeve and stared into his eyes. "We need to get to the collider." She glanced at the sky. "Something here doesn't add up."

Seeing the look on Vaughn's face, Angela held up a hand. "Something other than the obvious. Why haven't we seen anybody, any spaceships?" She pointed toward the alien city. "Where are all the people for that?"

"You think we'll find answers at CERN," Vaughn said. It wasn't a question.

Angela nodded. "Yes, I do." She released his arm and pointed into the dark recess beyond the stone archway. "And I think we may be able to reach it through there. The subways are new. There are only a few lines, and I know one of them leads to the collider."

Vaughn looked doubtful.

"I thought you wanted to find out what happened?"

He nodded. "I did, and I've seen enough to know we can't do anything about it. We need to get the hell out of here while we still can."

She shook her head vigorously. "What would we be running to, Vaughn? The planet is dead." She jabbed a finger toward the alien city. "Those bastards killed everybody! Every human! Every animal! We owe it to them to find out why and maybe do something about it."

"Do something about it?" Vaughn scoffed. "Like what?"

Angela dropped her arm and lowered her voice. "I don't know for sure, but if this is somehow connected to the collider, then we might be able to break it. I know CERN's computer systems. I think my account access was still active when ... you know. Anyway, I'll crash the whole damned thing if I have to."

Vaughn gazed into the subway entrance and then turned back to Angela, a mixture of emotions clouding his face.

Angela thought she saw doubt.

About what? Her?

She bristled and was about to dig in her heels, but then his eyes cleared, and he nodded.

"Okay. But I'm leading the way."

Momentarily taken aback by his sudden reversal, Angela blinked. Finally, she nodded and pointed toward the subway entrance. "Be my guest."

He stepped past her and descended the steps, disappearing into the darkness.

Angela looked toward the mounded debris in time to see the tanker's rudder and stern disappear into the volcano-like cauldron.

She swallowed hard and then tilted her head and spoke under her breath. "Careful what you wish for, Angela."

CHAPTER 11

A ngela bumped into something, and a stifled scream escaped her lips. Then she heard Vaughn stumble forward.

In the dark, she frowned and shook her head. "Sorry."

Only a few steps into the tunnel and its now complete darkness had her spooked. She felt silly. It's not like there would be people or animals down here, although she knew that much worse likely lay ahead.

Suddenly, a light blossomed, illuminating Vaughn's dust- and soot-covered face. He had pulled off his backpack and fished a headlamp from it. He slipped it over his forehead and then threw the pack over his shoulder. Then he handed her a water bottle and an energy bar.

Angela took a sip of the water and then guzzled the entire bottle. She hadn't realized how thirsty she was until the water touched her lips.

She peeled open the protein bar. The chocolate inside had melted due to the heat given off by the cauldron. However, Angela devoured this as well. Then she pulled the headlamp out of her backpack and slipped it on.

The circle of light cast by Vaughn's lamp scrolled across dusty wall tiles. Then it fell on Angela. He leaned in and spoke softly, his words barely audible above the noise still pouring in through the subway entrance. "Where do we go from here?"

"CERN."

"Yeah, got that. How?"

"The subway connects all the way through to it." Doubt twisted her face. "Or at least it used to."

In the light of Angela's headlamp, Vaughn considered her words. He shrugged. "Only one way to find out." Then he turned and continued walking down the dark passageway.

Angela started after him but then stopped as her light fell across a dust-covered briefcase. Panning her lamp farther down the corridor, she bit back a sob as she spotted a taller item standing amongst the articles.

Vaughn's light turned toward Angela. "What's wrong?"

Swallowing against the lump that was trying to form in her throat, she raised a hand and pointed.

Turning toward the item, Vaughn added his light to it. He stopped walking. "Oh, man ..."

A poignant reminder of the massive tragedy that had unfolded here stood near the center of the corridor.

As if in silent vigil, the two of them stared at the lonely and long-emptied stroller.

After a long moment, she felt Vaughn's hand on her elbow. He spoke softly. "I'm sorry, Angela. Wish I could tell you it gets easier, but ..." He paused and then nodded ahead. "Anyway, we need to keep going."

Angela pursed her lips and gave a short nod. She squeezed the hand he'd placed on her elbow. "Let's go."

A few steps later, they stopped at the top of a steep flight of stairs. Their lamps only revealed the first few steps. Beyond that the descending treads disappeared into the darkness. Huge, gaping holes lined both sides of the steps. Angela couldn't see where they ended. Then she realized what they represented.

She pointed at the ragged edge of the twinned openings. "That must be where the escalators had been."

"Yeah. Looks like they ripped all of it right out of the concrete." He started down the central stairway and gestured off to the side. "Handrails are gone, too. Be careful."

As Angela moved to follow him, a chill ran down her spine. Fear of the unknown began to sink into her soul. Up to this point, everything had happened so fast that she hadn't had time to worry. It had been a race to survive, but now her stomach began to churn as she contemplated what might lie ahead.

The cacophonous outside world faded with each step deeper into the dark abyss. Then it was gone altogether, as was the odor of the surface. Dank, stale air had replaced the acrid stench of burned metal and tortured masonry.

Their raspy breaths and periodic coughs echoed loudly in the tunnel's claustrophobic, catacomb-like depths. The sound of her pulse raced in Angela's ears.

She flinched as Vaughn's voice broke her trance.

"I hope we brought enough batteries."

"Uh … what?" She blinked and then nodded. "Oh, yeah. Me too."

"How far is this station from the collider?"

Angela turned toward Vaughn as she considered his question. "Crap. You're right." She paused and tried to remember the layout of the original city. "From what I remember on the map, we have a few miles to go."

Vaughn squinted as the spot from her headlamp fell on his face.

Angela chuckled nervously and glanced around. "I hope batteries are the worst of our problems." She turned off her lamp. "Guess we don't need them both right now. I'll save mine for later."

Suddenly, a breeze cooled her sweat-dampened face.

"Did you feel that?"

Vaughn's headlight bobbed up and down. "Yeah, just a little breeze. No big deal. Feels good, actually."

Angela nodded hesitantly. "I guess so."

He started down the stairs again. His head tilted down, and the lamp's yellow circle of light traced the edges of the jagged hole where the escalator had been. "Stay right behind me."

She nodded and placed a hand on his backpack. "Don't worry. I'm staying right here."

Fortunately, the stairs were relatively clear of dropped possessions. Angela thought they had likely been dragged out with the missing escalators.

A few moments later, her lamp's beam fell on a dusty landing at the bottom of the long stairwell.

Angela sighed and smiled. "Finally." Then she tilted her head as she saw something else. "Do you see that?"

"What?"

Suddenly alarmed, she lowered her voice and grabbed his arm. "Turn off your headlamp."

"What? Why?"

"Shh!" Angela tugged urgently at Vaughn's sleeve as she continued to stare past him. "Just do it!"

He glanced over his shoulder, regarding her with raised eyebrows.

She squinted and held up a hand to shield her eyes from his light.

Finally, he turned it off. "I don't see what..."

Vaughn paused and then turned to look forward. "What the hell?"

An opening at the far end of the new tunnel glowed softly. The light was extraordinarily faint but bright enough to reveal the checkerboard pattern of the intervening floor tiles as well as the arcing white walls and ceiling of the passageway. Dropped belongings dotted the corridor, cutting long shadows across its floor.

Angela stepped up and stood next to Vaughn. They exchanged confused glances. The wan light imparted no color, painting his face in pale gray.

She started forward, trying to step lightly but then winced as dusty gravel crunched underfoot.

A few moments later, they reached the opening.

The hallway beyond bent sharply right. She leaned tentatively into it and peered in that direction. Its far end glowed brightly under two illuminated fluorescent light fixtures.

Leaning back, Angela turned to look at Vaughn and spoke softly. "There's power down there. The lights are on."

He peeked around the corner and then looked at her with raised eyebrows. "How in the hell can the electricity be on?" he said, whispering as well. He pointed up, toward the city over their heads. "They leveled everything. There's no infrastructure left."

Angela furrowed her brow. "I don't know."

Leaning in again, she stared down the hall for a long moment, unsure of what to do.

Vaughn touched her arm. "Let's get closer."

Angela nodded and stepped forward.

Her heart raced as she considered what may lie ahead. Visions of subterranean aliens haunted her thoughts. She swallowed hard, and continued down the hallway silently, keeping the fears to herself.

Some things were better left unspoken.

As she walked down the hall, Angela weaved between dust-covered briefcases and suitcases. Resting a hand on the strap of her pack, she wondered why there weren't any backpacks among the dropped belongings. From her previous visits, Angela knew that people regularly traveled these corridors with knapsacks and book bags slung over their shoulders, but she hadn't seen a single one among the fallen articles.

She mentioned the fact to Vaughn.

"Yeah, I noticed that back in Boulder. There wasn't any clothing left behind either. The light took everyone and anything they were wearing." His voice was suddenly heavy with emotions. "It left behind everything else."

A pang of sorrow washed over Angela as she remembered Vaughn's description of finding his mother's dropped, lipstick-lined coffee mug.

Lost in thought, he now appeared to be staring through the floor.

Angela looked away. Her gaze fell upon the posters that lined the corridor's walls. Dulled by the long shadows cast by the still distant lights, the colorful advertisements written in French and Italian announced shows and exhibitions. Beautiful models smiled toothily, pedaling products that promised everything from eternal youth to whiter teeth and even a better sex life. One of the latter advertised underarm deodorant. It depicted a man surrounded by a virtual harem. Powerful stuff, Angela mused, but then the smile fell from her lips as she thought of the fate that had consumed them all.

A few moments later, they reached another right turn at the end of the hallway.

Angela squinted against the bright light as she crept up and peeked around the bend. It opened up on another stairwell, this one much shorter than the last and significantly brighter. LED light strips illuminated it as well as the landing beneath.

After exchanging nervous glances, she and Vaughn eased around the corner and walked tentatively down the steps.

In the subterranean silence, even the floor's light coating of dust seemed to crunch beneath their boots. Nearing the bottom and feeling exposed, they crouched and hugged the wall. As they continued to creep forward, a platform began to inch into sight. Each downward step revealed more of the subway station. If not for the smattering of dropped goods, it would have looked like a normal platform.

Reaching the landing, they stood glued to the right wall for a long moment listening for anything out of place.

No sounds rose above those of their rhythmic breaths and the buzz of multitudinous lights.

Angela leaned toward Vaughn. "Maybe the subway is on its own grid."

She turned to see him shaking his head. "I think they left it powered up on purpose."

"They? Who?"

Vaughn pointed upward. "The aliens."

"What makes you think that?"

He gestured into the station. "Look at the tracks."

Angela leaned out and studied the near end of the ledge where the platform dropped off.

She shrugged. "They look normal to me."

"Exactly!"

"So?"

He gave her a meaningful look. "Angela, they're made of steel."

Her eyes slowly widened as the implication of the fact registered. Then she shook her head. "Maybe this is too deep to reach with their gravity manipulation."

Vaughn started to reply, but then a blast of air suddenly washed across them.

They both flinched as a warbling metallic squeal shattered the station's silence.

Angela instantly recognized it as the unmistakable screech of a moving subway train.

She turned and pushed Vaughn back up the stairs. "Hide!"

They retreated up the treads.

Angela heard the train pull into the station behind them and then stop. A moment later, there was a whoosh that she thought must be the sound of all its doors opening simultaneously.

Still walking upward, she cocked her head, listening for other sounds, but heard none.

Grabbing Vaughn's backpack, she pulled him to a stop.

Angela pointed to her ear and then mouthed, "Listen."

For long seconds, there was no other sound. Then they both twitched as a burst of compressed air shattered the silence. She heard the doors sliding closed again. Then the train rushed back out of the station, leaving nothing but the faint buzz of humming electricity in its wake.

Air rushed past them to fill the void left by the departing train, drawn into the subway's wake like fluid pulled into a syringe by a plunger.

Again, the two of them tilted their heads as they listened for the slightest sound.

After long moments of silence, they exchanged a look and then began to creep back down the stairs. When they reached the bottom, everything was as they had left it. Nothing had disturbed any of the lost articles nor the dust that covered it all. No foot had treaded upon the tiled floor, alien or otherwise.

Angela stood straight and walked into the station.

Vaughn whispered urgently after her, "What are you doing?!"

"The automated system must still be running." She sounded more confident than she felt. "We can ride it all the way to the collider."

A quick check of the station's signage told her that they had emerged on the inbound deck. For a welcome change, things had finally gone their way. They were on the side of Marché Station that serviced trains headed toward the collider.

Was she really considering riding the subway? Then she started thinking about Vaughn's assertion and stopped walking.

He moved to stand next to her on the station's platform. "What is it?"

"I don't know about this." Angela shook her head, suddenly unsure. "What if you were right?" She pointed upward as Vaughn had earlier. "What if *they* did keep this running for their own purposes?" Pausing, she turned and looked at the tunnel that led toward CERN. "Maybe we should walk. It's only a few miles."

Vaughn shook his head. "The tunnel is just wide enough for both of us and the train *here*, but we don't know how wide it is farther down. If it gets much narrower, we'll be crushed by the next train that comes our way."

Then they felt the rush of wind and heard the sound of another approaching subway.

Vaughn and Angela exchanged concerned glances and then retreated to the stairwell.

This time, Angela paused just inside it. When the train came to a stop, she peered into the station.

A perfectly ordinary subway sat silently. The glow of its internal lights spilled from the open doors of the cars and pooled onto the platform, casting rectangles of yellow light onto its white tile floor and its collection of dropped belongings.

A moment later, the doors slid shut, and the train departed as the last one had.

Walking tentatively, Angela and Vaughn emerged from the stairwell.

Arching his brows, he turned to her. "What do you think? Should we take the next one?"

After a pause, Angela nodded. "Yeah …" She gave a nervous chuckle. "As long as it's empty, too."

Smirking, Vaughn nodded. "Agreed."

A few minutes later, rushing wind and a building roar announced the arrival of the next train. After hiding … just in case … they heard the whoosh of opening doors.

Vaughn glanced around the corner. "All clear."

Crouching and moving purposefully, they stepped out of the stairwell and dashed through the nearest of the train's open doors, entering the lead car of the subway.

Dropping to their hands and knees, they hid inside as the doors slid shut and the train departed the station.

The world outside of their car darkened as it passed into the waiting tunnel.

Both of them jumped as a French-speaking human voice suddenly blared from hidden speakers.

Angela laughed nervously. "It just announced the next station."

The whole thing seemed surreally normal, but as Angela looked around, she had a nagging sensation that something was wrong.

No, not wrong.

Something was out of place.

She looked at Vaughn. Confusion was twisting his features.

Her pulse ratcheted up from its already insane pace. "What is it?"

"Where's all the stuff?"

Angela frowned. "What stuff?"

Vaughn gestured at the seats and the floor. "The briefcases … The strollers."

That was it! That's what had been bothering her. The railcar was too clean. There wasn't anything left behind, and it appeared to be free of the ubiquitous dust as well. It even smelled sterile.

As Angela glanced around the car, Vaughn stood and peered aft, looking toward the back of the subway. His forehead puckered. "The train is completely empty."

Angela slowly shook her head.

The tunnel walls began to glow, signaling the approach of the next station.

She grabbed Vaughn's backpack and pulled him to the floor just as the train rushed into the brightly lit space.

Afraid to raise her head, Angela watched the speed-blurred passage of the new station's white ceiling tiles. Then the train ground to a stop. A moment later, its doors opened with a burp of compressed air.

From their crouched position, Angela listened for any sound. Hearing none, she hazarded a peek through the nearest open door. Vaughn did the same.

It looked like the last one. Dropped belongings littered the deck. A thick coat of dust covered it all.

They turned and looked at the opposite half of the station.

Angela's sense of foreboding deepened at the sight of a platform utterly devoid of humanity's remnants. Not a single briefcase or stroller sat on the shiny tiles of its dust-free floor.

They exchanged glances, and then both flinched as the doors suddenly rolled closed.

A moment later, the subway passed out of the pool of light as it plunged into the darkness of the waiting tunnel.

Uncomfortable on the hard floor, Angela climbed up and dropped into one of the train's seats.

Vaughn sat next to her.

She looked at him. "The other half of the station is empty now."

"Yeah, it even smells cleaner, less musty."

Nodding, Angela turned and studied her reflection in the dark window. "I noticed that, too." Then she looked at Vaughn. "What does it all mean?"

He scoffed. "Hell if I know. I'm just glad—"

Suddenly, light streamed into the car as the subway emerged into the next station. It had been a much shorter passage than the previous ones.

Vaughn looked forward. "That was quick."

They both froze as another train pulled into its far end.

Angela's eyes went wide. "Oh shit!"

Something was moving inside the other subway.

They both slid out of their seats and ducked out of sight, dropping to their hands and knees on the floor.

She looked at Vaughn. "What was that?!"

Breathing heavily and cursing, he shook his head. "Shit if I know. Didn't get a good look."

Squeals echoed through the station as both trains slowed and then stopped.

The doors of their subway opened, and Angela heard those of the opposite train do the same.

Then her heart threatened to leap through the wall of her chest as a riotous din suddenly filled the tiled chamber.

She and Vaughn exchanged frightened glances.

It sounded as if an army of excited soldiers had entered the station.

Angela slowly raised her head. The roof of the other subway slid into sight.

"What are you doing?!"

She stared at the top of the other train, her pulse pounding in her ears. "I have to see them."

"Dammit, woman, you're gonna be the death of me." In spite of his protestations, Vaughn started raising his head as well. "What do you see?"

"Nothing yet. Just the roof of the next train."

"What are you waiting for?" He continued to rise slowly but then froze. "Oh, shit ..."

Angela glanced at Vaughn. His eyes looked like saucers on a whitening cloth.

She touched his arm. "What do you see?"

His Adam's apple bobbed. Then he reached over and pulled her up.

Angela slowly rose. The bottom of the train and the platform beyond it slid into view. She gasped. "Oh my God."

She tried to swallow, but her suddenly dry throat refused to work.

Staring in frozen horror, she watched a swarm of multi-armed, headless beings pour out of the other subway.

Her heart now pounded so hard she was sure the things on the opposite platform could hear it. She closed her eyes for a moment, struggling to rein in her emotions.

Vaughn pulled her back down. "We're too exposed here."

She opened her eyes and looked at him. "Did you get a good look at them?"

"Not really. Just what I could see through the other train's windows." She saw him shake off a shudder. "Looked like a bunch of flailing white arms."

Chewing her lip, Angela glanced in the direction of the beings. The wall of the train blocked them from view. "We need a better look."

Vaughn's head shook. "I don't know. I'd rather not jump out and say, 'Here we are. Come eat us.'"

Angela glared at him. "Not helping."

Vaughn shrugged.

She turned and looked through the open doors of their own subway. Dust and lost belongings covered the floor of this side of the station just as it had on the last one.

She tapped Vaughn's arm and then pointed. "Nobody's been over here yet."

They both flinched as the public address system activated again, announcing the next destination. Then the doors slid shut.

Vaughn started to peek above the bottom of the window.

Angela saw his hair shining under the train's overhead lights. She pulled him down. "You're right. They'll see us. We're too lit up, too exposed."

As the train entered the tunnel, Vaughn looked at her with raised eyebrows. "We came here to see who did this, didn't we?"

Angela shook her head. "No ... I mean, yes, but the primary reason was CERN. I want to know why here." She pointed at the ground to emphasize her words. "I want to know why the collider is at the geometric center of this entire mess. But if we get captured or killed before we get there, we'll never know."

The subway train rocked and squeaked as it rounded a bend in the tracks.

Feeling the turn, Angela pointed up. "We are under the city now."

Vaughn nodded. "Yeah, we have been since shortly after we left the second station. Maybe that's why we're starting to see activity now."

They both looked forward as the tunnel ahead of them brightened, signaling the coming of the next station.

Angela scanned the train behind them and noticed that the lights were out at the far end of the next train car.

She began to crawl toward it and motioned for Vaughn to follow.

"Where are you going?"

"Just come on, Captain!"

Angela heard him curse under his breath as he shuffled across the floor, rushing to catch up.

As she crawled, her backpack shifted left and right. She stayed low to make sure it wasn't visible above the bottom of the subway's windows.

They entered the next car. The door slid shut behind them just as the train slid into the next station.

Angela reached the back door and pulled Vaughn up next to her and whispered into his ear. "We can look from here. Our heads won't be lit up or silhouetted."

Vaughn nodded. He raised his head slowly and then stopped, eyes widening.

Angela sat frozen in place. Had they seen him?

Vaughn didn't say anything. He just kept staring, unmoving. Finally, he reached out, motioning for her to look.

Heart racing, Angela slowly raised her head. As the opposite platform slid into sight, she too seized, motionlessly staring over the window's lower frame.

Her throat hitched.

What she saw was like something out of a science fiction movie.

No train occupied the far side of the station this time. She now had an unobscured view of the beings. Hundreds of them were milling about on the far platform.

The things stood in groups, appearing to chat amongst one

another. If not for their body form, it would've looked like an ordinary gathering of humans.

But these things were far from human.

They had hips that angled rearward to a point where they attached to the tops of long, white legs. Legs with knees that bent in the wrong direction.

To Angela, their hips and legs looked like those on the two-legged, walking tanks from the Star Wars movies.

However, that was where the similarities ended.

Their upper bodies sported two pairs of arms for a total of four, each tipped with three-fingered hands. They had no visible head. It was impossible to tell from here for sure, but Angela thought she saw a low-profile disc sitting atop the torso. Beneath their chest, a narrow black abdomen tapered to only a few inches wide where it attached to the rearward angled hips. Seen from the side, the line of their body, hips, and legs formed an elongated S shape.

Angela watched them mix and mingle. The way they stood in small groups made it appear as if they were chatting. She could even hear them.

Vaughn tilted his head. "Are they talking?"

She nodded. "I think so."

Heard from her remote observation point, their mid-range, monotone voices blended together, the individual words of their conversations indistinguishable above the riotous din.

Their actions looked almost human, but something about the way they moved screamed 'machine.' However, instead of hard, angular lines, their limbs appeared sleek, almost organic.

Angela finally found her voice. "Are they robots?"

Beside her, Vaughn shook his head. "I don't know. Maybe."

They heard the rush of another arriving train.

Then the doors of their subway closed, and it started to exit the station.

Just before their car slid into the tunnel, Angela glimpsed the next train and its cargo.

It brimmed with robotic aliens.

CHAPTER 12

The dark tunnel whizzed by unseen as Angela gazed through the black windows. In their reflections, she saw Vaughn staring at her, an odd look on his face.

"Uh, you do know ..." He paused. His forehead furrowed and he sighed. "You do know this is a one-way trip, right?"

Angela shook her head and spoke sharply. "No, I don't know that, and neither should you."

Vaughn blinked. He pointed toward the front of the train. "We're stuck. We were trapped the minute we passed a station full of robots. There's no way back out, and the deeper we go, the worse it gets."

Angela considered his words for a moment and then shook her head again. "I refuse to accept that." She thrust an arm toward the opposite window and pointed outside. "There are side tunnels, other subways that lead to different parts of the city. Maybe the robots aren't in them."

She turned to face him and saw doubt clouding his face. "Vaughn." She palmed his cheek, turning him to face her. "We'll get into CERN, find out what the hell happened there, change anything that we can ... I'll break it if I can, and then we'll get the hell out of there."

"How are we going to do any of that?"

"I don't know." She grinned devilishly. "But I think the man that flew a rocket with a nose cone made from Home Depot garage sale signs can figure it out."

Vaughn guffawed and then shook his head, a crooked smile on his face.

Angela kissed him and then leaned back.

Staring at his reflection again, she winked. "Afterward, we'll make our way back to the yacht and head for those islands you've been talking about."

He stared at her. After a moment he gave her a forlorn smile and then nodded. "Yes, ma'am."

Angela knew Vaughn wasn't entirely onboard with her optimistic outlook. To be honest, neither was she. However, all those months stranded alone on the space station had taught her the value of hope. They needed it right now. They needed to believe that if they tried hard enough, they could find a way through or around any obstacle. Otherwise, they might give up, packing it in before they exhaust all possibilities. Lord knows she'd been tempted to do just that on numerous occasions while stranded aboard the ISS, but the idea of Vaughn, of potential rescue, had seen her through the darkest of those times.

She squeezed his hand and then stared through the dark window again.

"I think they are robots," Vaughn said.

Angela nodded. She had come to the same conclusion five stations earlier. "Yeah, I think so, too." She twisted her face. "But are they the masters or the servants?"

"Huh?"

Turning toward Vaughn, she held out her hands, palms up. "Did they invade on their own, or are they just here to pave the way for someone else?"

Vaughn shook his head. "No way to know."

Shrugging, she continued. "And if there is someone else, are they here yet?"

"Not that I've seen." Vaughn pointed outside. "So far, all these things look identical to one another. If anything, I think the bots that are building the city are working for these robots."

Tilting her head, Angela considered his suggestion. Then she looked at Vaughn. "Maybe these are the manager bots you were looking for outside."

Vaughn scrunched up his face. "I don't think so. There are too many of them. You typically have more workers than managers. Not the other way around, especially in a system as automated as this one."

Flinching, Angela looked up as the recorded French voice ruptured the silence again. This time she was relieved to hear the male voice announce: "Conseil Européen pour la Recherche Nucléaire, CERN."

"Did he just say what I think he did?"

Angela nodded.

Vaughn tilted his head back and closed his eyes. "Oh, thank you!"

The announcement had elicited the same response from Angela. The stress of waiting for discovery or capture over these last several stops had been grueling. At each station, she had expected the doors to open on a platform full of the alien beings. However, several stations later, they still hadn't seen any of them on their side of the rail system. The robots appeared to be heading in only one direction: away from CERN.

Angela looked at Vaughn and shook her head. "It's like they're spreading out to fill in the city that the bots built for them, but I don't understand where they can be coming from. It's been an unending, outbound migration. We've seen thousands of them. Where in the hell are they coming from?"

"I don't know." Vaughn pointed ahead. "Maybe they have a landing site somewhere on the far side of Geneva and are working their way across the city from there."

"Then where are the transports?" Angela gestured overhead. "We never saw anything in the sky, other than the line of floating steel anyway."

"Maybe they landed a large ship before we got here."

Angela nodded thoughtfully, chewing her lip while she considered the idea. "Maybe." Then she shook her head. "But I don't know. From what I saw in orbit, the collider is right at the center of the city. There has to be a connection."

Vaughn cocked an eyebrow. He gestured to the outbound side of the tracks. "You think they're coming from inside CERN?"

Angela shrugged. "No idea." Strictly speaking, that was not one hundred percent true. She was beginning to form a hypothesis, but she was reluctant to utter the words, lest they speak the possibility into existence.

The tunnel ahead began to glow as they neared CERN Station. Then their train emerged fully into the light.

From their shadowed corner, Angela and Vaughn gazed across the station. Another subway sat on its opposite side. A zigzagging line of the beings, hundreds long, stood waiting to enter the railcars. They looked like amusement park visitors waiting their turn to ride the roller coaster.

Angela agreed with Vaughn. These were almost certainly robots, but they didn't act like machines. She could see them fidgeting and turning their bodies as if looking around. In places, groups of them conversed, their arms flailing about, gesticulating as a human would. However, their bodyparts looked too mechanical. Metallic, softball-sized joints connected their two legs to the outside of their reverse-angled hips. The same mechanisms formed shoulders where they attached all four of their arms to the rearward-sloping upper torso.

Angela turned and searched her side of the platform, desperately seeking a place to hide. Fortunately, the train would block them from being observed by the robots, but the last thing they needed was to be standing in the open when it departed.

Staying onboard wasn't an option either. According to the signage, this was the line's last stop. Beyond this station, there must be a turn-around facility that would guide the train onto the opposite tracks and feed them right into the waiting line of robots. Angela winced at the unfortunate pun as she remembered Vaughn's comment about shouting for them to 'come eat us.'

The train ground to a stop, and she spotted a potential path. About twenty yards to their left, farther up the platform, a dark passageway led away from the station.

The doors of their train opened with a whoosh, and the echoing noise of multitudinous robotic conversations flooded the railcar.

Angela dropped to the floor and waved for Vaughn to follow.

She had to stay low. If they didn't, the beings on the other platform would see them through the windows that lined both sides of the trains.

On hands and knees, she crawled through the car's closest door and onto the station's tiled floor.

Angela had only covered half the distance to the dark opening when the subway's doors slid closed behind them.

Her eyes widened, and she whispered urgently. "Oh shit! Faster!"

Vaughn had already pulled up alongside her. Now the two of them skittered across the platform like toddlers amped up on double-shot caffè mochas.

As they closed to within five yards, the train began to roll.

"No, no, no!" Vaughn said under his breath.

They passed into the shadowed hallway just as the last car rolled out from between them and the hordes of robots.

Vaughn seized up. "Stop!"

Angela froze mid-crawl.

She looked straight ahead, afraid to move. "Why are we stopping? We're in the shadows."

"It might not be dark to their eyes. They might be able to see us in here."

Vaughn started to slowly lower his body, flattening himself against the floor.

Angela did the same, lying flat next to him.

A few feet ahead, the corridor made a sharp right turn.

Now moving like tranquilized sloths, they began to *slowly* inch their way down the hall.

A couple of minutes later, they finally rounded the bend and passed out of the line of sight of the boisterous robots.

Angela and Vaughn stood and started knocking dust off their

clothing. Behind them, the robotic beings continued their loud discussions.

During their trek down the dark passageway, Angela had listened to them, but she still couldn't make out individual words. The first time she had heard the robots, their voices had sounded monotone, but occasionally, one raised, the speaker becoming more animated, as if in argument. It almost seemed as if they were yelling and shouting.

Tilting her head in the direction of the din, Angela looked at Vaughn and raised her eyebrows. "Kind of odd behavior for robots."

"I know. If you close your eyes, they almost sound like a crowd of people heading into a football game."

Angela nodded. She finished knocking off the dust and then stood upright and gestured ahead. "We have to get into CERN." She hitched a thumb toward the unseen robots behind them. "But the entrance is over there."

"How in the hell are we gonna get through all of them?"

"We're not. I know a way around." She pointed overhead. "A tunnel connects the two sides. It's off the beaten path. Hopefully, these alien robot thingies haven't found it. On the far side of the footpath, there's an employee access point." She left out the part about the lock on the access door requiring a code that may no longer work.

Vaughn stepped back and extended an arm. "Lead the way, Commander."

They spent the next several minutes inching down long hallways, constantly worried that someone or something would suddenly poke its head out—not that these things appeared to have heads.

Angela finally found the stairs and guided Vaughn up two flights. They led to the long corridor that crossed over the subway station.

When she got to the stairs at the far end, she grabbed Vaughn's arm and pulled him close. "This leads to the employee entrance."

He looked around nervously. There were no other exits, no way to go but down. They could already hear the tumultuous voices of the gathered robots. The noise of their cacophonous conversations had risen with each step down the long hallway.

Vaughn turned back to her and inclined his head toward the stairs. "Sounds like it also leads down to that robot-infested platform."

Angela shrugged. "We'll just have to make sure they don't see or hear us."

Vaughn gave her his eyebrow-o-skepticism. "How in the *hell* are we going to do that?"

"I'm pretty sure that the employee entrance is only one flight down from here."

"Pretty sure?!"

"Yep. We should find it before we stumble into our friends." She looked down the stairs. "Any-who, I just hope they haven't changed the security code since last time I was here."

Vaughn did a double take. "Wait ... What?!"

Looking up and to the left, Angela smiled self-consciously. "Well, the lock requires a code, and I'm pretty sure mine was still active when ... you know, when it happened."

"And you're just now telling me this?"

Angela turned her smile to Vaughn and shrugged. "Ready, Captain?"

He frowned and the eyebrow hoisted another notch, but then he sighed and pointed ahead. "Come on, princess. Let's do this."

They descended the stairs.

The volume of robotic conversations rose with each downward tread.

Soon they reached a landing where the stairs cut back in the opposite direction.

It sounded as if the main body of the robots might be just around the corner.

Perched on the landing, Angela slowly peered around the smooth, white wall. None of the quad-armed machines waited.

She leaned farther out, and the door for the employee entrance slid into view on the next landing.

Angela said a silent thank you.

She gave Vaughn the all-clear sign and headed down the stairs.

Reaching the next landing, she stepped up to the small panel adjacent to the door and punched in her code.

They both flinched as a short beep accompanied each keystroke. Even against the cacophony generated by the crowd of robots below them, the beeps seemed horribly loud. After she punched the final key, a series of four additional beeps rang out, and the word error streamed across the keyboard's screen.

The sound of metal scraping across concrete issued from the lower portion of the stairwell.

Tilting her head to listen, Angela realized it was one of the robots coming up the stairs!

With shaking fingers, she tried the code again.

And again received the same results.

"Shit!"

The footsteps grew louder.

Angela was about to try the code another time when Vaughn reached around her and grabbed the handle.

He twisted the lever.

The door opened.

Immediately, he and Angela rushed into the dark room beyond, careful not to make any additional noises.

Vaughn drew the door closed behind them. It latched with a light snick.

Angela stood, frozen in place and holding her breath as a shadow passed across the light that streamed under the door. For long moments, the robot on the other side stood motionlessly, just outside their door, but then it finally moved on.

Angela sighed, releasing her held breath as she turned to head deeper into the facility. She glanced at Vaughn. "Good thinking."

Turning to follow her, he nodded. "I thought it might be open. I'll bet all the doors in this place have been unlocked. Probably wouldn't be much of a challenge to these machines to hack every security code in the place."

Now inside CERN, they spent the next several minutes negotiating hallways and stairways, each taking them deeper underground. The sounds of the robotic horde quickly faded in their wake. Soon only the faint buzzing of the facility's ubiquitous fluorescent lights followed them through the corridors and stairwells.

After what seemed like a thousand cutbacks, they finally reached the bottom landing where another door blocked their passage.

Breathing hard, Angela tried its latch. It too was unlocked. She released the handle without opening the door.

Vaughn leaned over and whispered into her ear. "What are you waiting for?"

"Th-This is the main floor. We're only two rooms away from the Atlas control room."

"So?"

"It's … It's where we used to focus and collect data from our most powerful experiments."

Vaughn raised his eyebrows and looked at the door appraisingly. "So this is where the rubber meets the road."

"Yeah, I guess that's one way to put it."

"Then this is what we came to see." He pointed at the latch. "Let's go."

Nodding, Angela chewed her lip. She extended a trembling hand toward the lever.

Her heart raced as she grasped the handle and slowly twisted it.

It released with a barely audible click.

She swallowed and then eased the door open, revealing an ever-widening wedge of the dark, unlit room beyond. She scanned left and right.

It appeared vacant.

Breathing again, Angela relaxed her bunched-up shoulders. "Oh, thank goodness."

Vaughn peeked around her and then pushed the door fully open. "Come on."

Crouching, they slid through the opening and then started across the office. Desks and computer consoles crowded the right side of the room.

Passing out from behind the door, Angela heard noise. Seeking the source, she glanced left.

Suddenly a momentary flash of blindingly bright light washed out the scene and then vanished.

Blinking in the dark, Angela tried to clear the blue spots from her vision. "Where did that light come from?"

Vaughn shook his head.

Angela heard the noise again. She looked left and then seized up as she saw motion.

A large window lined the office's full length, affording the room a view of the brightly lit, long hallway that paralleled it.

Beside her, Vaughn had seized up as well.

Side-by-side, the two of them stared wordlessly at the tightly packed, single-file row of robots that was shuffling down the hallway. As with the others, these appeared to be chatting amongst themselves, their arms gesticulating in rhythm to their animated conversations. They were moving from right to left at a slow walk.

Fortunately, none of the robots had seen them in the dark room, even when the light had flashed.

A sudden realization struck Angela. She grabbed Vaughn's hand and pulled him down.

Moving slowly, they dropped out of sight and slipped behind a filing cabinet. Then they weaved their way between desks and retreated to the room's far side, placing the maximum distance between themselves and the robots.

Angela pulled Vaughn close. "They *are* coming from the Atlas detector facility!" She gestured toward the far end of the corridor. "That's one of its exits."

Vaughn peered in the indicated direction and then leaned toward her. "Why here? What makes Atlas so special?"

"It's one of the collider's primary collision points. Remember how I was saying that we were hoping to create some micro black holes?" She pointed toward the Atlas Facility. "That is where we expected to see them."

Ethereal, sourceless light suddenly flooded the room again.

Angela flinched and blinked several times.

Blinking as well, Vaughn looked at her. "Where does that light keep coming from?"

"I don't know." She pointed over Vaughn's shoulder. "Let's move to the next room over. We might be able to tell from there. It's the Atlas Facility's control room. It overlooks the detector."

She began to creep toward the control room door.

Crawling beside her, Vaughn leaned in close to her. "What if they are in there."

Angela shook her head. "This is it. This is what we came all this way to see." Giving him a meaningful look, she pointed at the door. "And there's a collider control interface in that room."

Vaughn closed his eyes for a moment. Then he nodded ahead. "Go."

Angela reached the door and then slowly twisted the lever. Fortunately, as Vaughn had theorized, it was unlocked. It opened easily.

Bright light washed out the scene again. As it did, Angela squinted. In the afterglow, she glimpsed two beings at the far end of the control room. They appeared to be looking right at her. Barely containing a scream, she quickly shut the door. Fortunately, it closed silently.

They both peered over their shoulders. Apparently not seeing or hearing them, the Chatty Cathy robots continued to shuffle down the hallway.

Beside her, Vaughn whispered urgently. "What was it? Did you see where the light came from?"

Angela turned to look at Vaughn. "I saw two people on the far side of the room."

He looked at her for a long moment and then released a short laugh.

"What?"

Vaughn shook his head. "Thought you'd seen something else." He reached up and slid the door back open. Then he grinned as he pointed at a glass door that sat on the room's opposite wall. "You're jumping at your own reflection."

Angela felt her face flush as she spoke defensively. "It looked like more than a reflection."

"It's alright. I'm spooked too."

She extended a palm toward him. "Whatever. Come on."

Still on hands and knees, she pushed through the open door.

Angela glanced around and then waved Vaughn in. "It's clear."

Fortunately, this room was dark as well. She knew that a metallic film coated the detector side of the control room's wide windows. It presented a mirrored finish to anyone on the other side and stopped errant radiation from entering the room.

From her position on the floor, Angela couldn't see the center of the detector yet, although the top third of its eighty-foot-tall, ringed complex of radiating pipes and conduits filled the massive panorama visible through the wide window.

The scale of the supercollider had always amazed her, and this was its largest single feature. Atlas was so big that, by itself, it weighed as much as the Eiffel Tower.

Angela craned her neck but still couldn't quite see the central point of the giant, starburst-shaped complex of pipes and conduits. Its midsection sat just below her line of sight.

Vaughn nodded toward Atlas. "What's causing that noise?"

"It's the collider. It's still running." Angela had noticed the sound as soon as they'd opened the door at the bottom of the stairwell. The low-frequency hum had grown in volume as they'd approached this room. Now she could feel it pulsing through her very bones.

Staring through the large window, she continued to study Atlas, looking for and finding no changes in its architecture. She couldn't see any of the robots either, but the floor of the facility lay some forty feet beneath the control room's window.

Angela motioned for Vaughn to raise himself up. "The other side of the glass is mirrored. They won't be able to see us."

He looked at her dubiously. "Willing to bet our lives on that?"

Regarding him with a cocked eyebrow, she pulled a desk chair from one of the consoles and sat in it. "We are way past tha—"

Angela stopped mid-word as she turned to look through the window.

The focal point of the Atlas facility was now visible. Everything looked as she remembered, save one incredible detail.

A metallic sphere now floated at the geometric center of the detector complex.

Slowly shaking her head, Angela felt her gut wrench as she stared at the horrifying confirmation of her worst fear. "It happened."

Next to her, Vaughn slowly raised himself to her eye level. "What happened?" Then he froze.

Surreally levitating at the center of the facility, the perfectly smooth surface of the floating metallic sphere reflected a fish-eyed view of Atlas. At its center, Angela saw the elongated mirrored surface of the control room window. The repeated reflections within it painted a shrinking, mirror-house effect across the center of the metal ball.

Vaughn slowly shook his head.

Before Angela could answer, brilliant white light suddenly washed out everything.

They winced and threw their hands up to shield their eyes.

In the receding afterglow, Angela saw that the flash had come from the sphere. In an instant, it had flared phosphorescent white. Then it ramped down through less painful levels of luminosity until the light was gone.

Blinking the blue spots from her vision, Angela stared at the no longer glowing ball.

Then a series of concentric rings rippled across the sphere's suddenly liquid surface.

The whole thing quivered like a rung bell.

Angela and Vaughn exchanged confused glances. Then new movement drew their eyes back to front.

The mercurial sphere's near side began to bulge outward.

Vaughn stood from the desk and walked closer to the glass wall.

Unable to stop herself, Angela did the same. She moved up to stand next to him in front of the large window.

Side-by-side, they stared at the growing protuberance with rapt awe.

With an audible crack, the silvery surface split like a popping bubble.

Angela and Vaughn lurched, each taking an involuntary backward step as the upper torso of one of the robots suddenly popped out of the three-foot-wide orb.

Its arms slid from the mass. All four of them extended forward as if reaching for her.

Vaughn stepped back again. "Son of a bitch!"

Angela placed a hand on his arm. "It's okay. It can't see us."

She saw him nod in her peripheral vision.

In a couple of seconds, the robot's entire body slid from the metallic ball. Getting her first close look, Angela saw that the thing did have a head after all, but the way the neckless thing blended with the torso had made them appear to be headless. Now completely clear of the sphere, it levitated in the air in front of the control room. Then it rotated ninety degrees and began to descend toward the floor. A moment later, it disappeared out of sight.

Vaughn stepped closer again, gazing intently at the undulating metallic surface of the sphere. "Is it some kind of 3D printer? Are they making the robots from that material?"

Angela shook her head. "I don't think so."

No, she didn't believe that for a second. She felt ill, her stomach twisting as she grew ever more certain that this was the manifestation of her worst fear, the one she'd refused to verbalize lest doing so breathed life into the nightmare.

Over the next couple of minutes, they watched as three more flashes announced the upcoming arrival. Each time, a robot emerged in the same manner.

As the sphere flashed a fourth time, Angela looked at Vaughn, shaking her head again. "No way there's enough material in that ball to create these robots." She pointed toward the orb. "That's a doorway."

"A doorway?" Vaughn looked at her dubiously. "A doorway to where?"

"I think it's the end of a wormhole."

His eyes widened, and he looked from her to the sphere and then back. Then he pointed at it. "How in the hell is that a hole?"

Angela blinked. "What?" Then she nodded. "We don't think they're actually holes. A hole is a two-dimensional construct. They're great for drawing a picture on paper, but the real world exists in all three dimensions. So instead of a hole," she pointed through the window, "you end up with a sphere."

Vaughn stared at it and shook his head. "I thought wormholes were science fiction."

Angela pointed at the next robot coming through the gateway. "Not anymore."

"How did it get here?"

"We must have finally created a micro black hole." She pointed to the window. "And somehow they latched onto it. It should have evaporated in a flash of Hawking radiation, but they must have stabilized it somehow."

"They? Who? The engineers here at CERN?"

Angela shook her head. "No, we don't have anything close to that level of technology. We weren't even sure we could create an MBH." She gestured at the now floating robot. "They did it. Whoever the hell *they* are. They latched onto the black hole and then somehow opened up a wormhole from their home system."

He regarded her through knitted eyebrows. "You mean from a different solar system?"

Angela shrugged. "Yeah, maybe. I doubt it's from a nearby ship. If you could fly one all the way here, why open a wormhole for the last portion?"

"But how would they detect a black hole from that far away?"

"I don't know." Angela shook her head again. "The energy signature of a black hole's creation would radiate out from that point at the speed of light. Even its gravity would be restricted to that speed. So I don't know how they could remotely detect it."

Vaughn looked as if he was about to ask another question. Angela held up a hand.

"Listen. Right now, I feel like a pig staring at a wristwatch. I might not know how to make it work, but just like that pig, I can break it."

"How?"

Angela tilted her head. "Without CERN, I don't think they could have reached Earth. And if we can take the collider away, these robots will be marooned. We can close down this end of the wormhole. I'll pump in a bunch of power—not so much to overload the coils, that would cause an explosion and kill us. I'll add just enough to distort and disrupt this end of the wormhole. Then I'll crash the system so that they can't reopen it."

"What good will that do? They're machines. They can probably fix other machines and computers."

Angela nodded thoughtfully. "We'll sneak back out of the city and then come back with something big enough to kill them before they do."

"How are we going to do that?"

"I don't know. You're the military man."

Vaughn shook his head. "No. I mean how in the hell can we sneak out of here?"

Angela pursed her lips and stared at him for a moment. That was a good question. She looked at the computer screen. The displayed power reading drew her eye again. It was an incredibly high number. She wouldn't have thought the system could handle that much power. It sure as hell wasn't coming from this side. The electricity's frequency and phase were shifted, not quite the normal values. They weren't off enough to cause system failures, but enough that Angela thought it wasn't the native electrical state normally produced by whatever was generating it.

She pulled up the electrical phase and frequency for the facility's grid and compared it to that of the Atlas grid.

Angela looked up with raised eyebrows.

"What?"

She pointed at the screen. "The power they're pumping through the wormhole ... I think it's powering ... everything."

"What do you mean everything?"

"I mean *everything* on this side. The facility for sure and probably a lot of the subway system, maybe all of it."

Vaughn began to nod slowly. "Okay, so what does that mean for us?"

Angela canted her head. "Well, when I crash the system, the wormhole should collapse."

Understanding blossomed on Vaughn's face. Nodding, he finished the thought for her. "And cut the electricity."

"Yeah, like you said before, they've wrecked the old city's infrastructure. As soon as the wormhole closes, this side should go dark."

"What if it doesn't?"

Angela stared at the display and chewed on her lip. Finally, she shrugged. "We'll cross that bridge when we come to it. Just have that flashlight of yours ready. Hopefully, we're going to need it." She glanced toward the unseen line of machines. "Although, unless you want to be chased by a horde of pissed-off alien robots, I wouldn't turn it on until we're back in the stairwell."

CHAPTER 13

Vaughn watched as Angela punched commands into the computer interface.

She looked at him and tilted her head toward Atlas. "Going to time the surge to happen between robot arrivals, when there's not one coming through the wormhole. Can't chance their mass changing the variables."

Multiple prompts popped up on the screen. Angela looked at them and cursed under her breath. This had happened several times.

"What's wrong?"

She finished clearing the messages and then shook her head. "Nothing. Actually, it's going easier than I expected. Thought I'd have to override a lot more safeties than this." She gave Vaughn a sideward glance and then tilted her head toward the Atlas Detector again. "It looks like our friends out there already bypassed most of them."

A brilliant flash announced the arrival of the next robot.

A moment later, Angela's fingers stopped their keyboard dance. Her index finger hovered over the enter key. As she watched the next bot begin to slip through the wormhole, she spoke over her shoulder. "Are you ready?"

Vaughn glanced at the exit door and again memorized its distance and angle from their current position. He had already done this several times. If Angela's surge worked, the whole place could be plunged into absolute darkness. The emergency lights should work, but considering how long it had been since any of them had been inspected by a human, Vaughn didn't want to count on them. He needed to be able to make the crossing in the dark.

Finger still hovering, Angela turned a raised brow to Vaughn.

He nodded. "Let's do this."

Returning her gaze to front, she watched the alien robot slide out of the mercurial sphere.

It popped free, and Angela pressed the enter key, toggling the command to start the surge. "That should do it!"

Angela and Vaughn stared expectantly through the control room's window.

A barely perceptible humming whine suddenly ramped up in intensity, setting his teeth on edge.

The floating mercurial sphere quivered and then quaked.

Vaughn pointed. "Something's happening!"

Angela shook her head. "Yeah, but not enough. I'm going to boost the power."

He turned widening eyes toward her. "I thought that would blow us up!"

She smiled, still shaking her head. "Not going to add that much power."

Another keystroke sent the whine up another notch.

The sphere's quaking redoubled.

Vaughn took an involuntary backward step as the quivering ball suddenly swelled in size, rapidly expanding to fill the visible portion of the facility. The sphere now spanned the full height of the control room's observation window, and its equator appeared to be touching the glass.

Then the window seemed to bow inward, flexing toward Angela at the console.

"Oh shit!" Vaughn lunged forward and grabbed her chair.

It wasn't the window.

The sphere itself had expanded into the control room, passing through the glass like smoke through a sunbeam.

Vaughn released the seat back and jammed his hands under Angela's arms. He yanked her backward, dragging her out of the chair. The seat tilted and then fell, clanging loudly as he pulled her away from the convulsing, mercurial ball.

Another violent quake sent shock waves racing across the wormhole's surface.

Then it exploded outward and swallowed Vaughn and Angela.

CHAPTER 14

B lindingly bright light flooded into Vaughn's eyes.

This wasn't like the previous flashes. Unrelenting, the rays burned through his eyes and stabbed into his brain like white-hot daggers.

Still holding Angela with his left arm, he threw his right one over his eyes. The light and the pain it had wrought subsided.

Then the floor fell away.

Angela screamed.

Just as Vaughn registered that they were falling, they slammed into a hard surface and tumbled backward. He landed hard on his ass.

His arm fell away from his face and light flooded into his eyes again. However, the radiance that now streamed through his lids no longer elicited the same level of pain.

Angela had landed on top of him. Recovering from the impact, they both raised their arms defensively, ready to fend off fire, brimstone, or the wrath of their robotic overlords.

But nothing came.

The whine of ramping electrical fields had vaporized, leaving them in disjointed silence.

Wait!

There was sound.

A deep rumble and a … a sloshing noise?

With his eyelids squeezed shut, Vaughn frantically probed the air around them.

His arms swung freely. They didn't contact anything but the ground.

The control consoles that had surrounded them were gone.

He ran his fingers across the floor. Instead of smooth tiles, he found a grooved surface that felt as if it might be made of plastic.

Pressing against the floor, Vaughn pushed himself up to a seated position.

He held Angela tightly and whispered into her ear. "Are you okay?"

"Yeah. I think so."

With his free hand, Vaughn continued to probe around them blindly. "What happened? I can't see."

"Me neither …" Angela paused. "Wait! I feel movement."

Vaughn felt it too. The ground was heaving beneath them.

His eyes began to adjust to the intense light that was pouring through his closed lids.

The sloshing sound returned, and this time Vaughn recognized it.

He stopped moving and listened intently.

There it was again.

He leaned back and turned his head left and right. "That … That can't be."

Angela started to squirm against him. "Let me go!"

Vaughn complied.

She pushed off him and stumbled away.

He clambered to his feet and stood unsteadily on a surface that gently undulated beneath him.

Vaughn finally managed to crack open one eyelid. Tears blurred his vision, but he glimpsed churning water.

Blinking, he gazed around. Angela was standing next to him. They were both hunkered over, staying low to keep their balance.

"Angela! Are you seeing this?"

Her head bobbed. "Yeah, I think so. Is that water?"

Vaughn finally managed to open both eyes. Tilting his head, he screwed up his face as he watched a two-foot-tall wave roll past. Then he winced as its peak sloughed off and collapsed into a bright cap of churning foam.

The two of them swayed as the floor heaved again.

Vaughn tried to look down. He winced and raised a hand to shield his eyes.

Light reflected off the brilliant white surface beneath his feet, drilling fresh daggers of pain into his brain.

Blinking, he slowly resolved it and then glanced around with shocked amazement.

Standing beside him, Angela did the same. Squinting, she looked at him. "We're on a boat?"

Vaughn looked to his right and did a double take. He shook his head. "No, not *a* boat, *the* boat. We're back on *Angela's Dream*!"

They were standing on the ship's aft deck. Its rear-facing windows and doors filled a portion of the bright sky.

The deck lurched again, and water sprayed off to the sides. The thing was underway. The rumbling he'd heard was its engines.

They exchanged confused glances.

Looking around, Angela began to shake her head slowly. "This doesn't make any sense."

"I'll say." Vaughn looked at his wrist. Both hands of the simple watch he wore still pointed straight up. He raised his arm and gestured at the timepiece. "It was almost midnight a minute ago." Squinting, he glanced at the sky. "Now it looks like high noon! How can that be?"

"I don't know." Angela shielded her eyes with visored hands and began to turn slowly. "Can you tell where we are?"

Vaughn slowly pivoted, scanning the horizon. He spotted a finger of land. It appeared to be an island, but he couldn't be certain.

As he turned further, another piece of land came into view.

Vaughn stopped as his eyes fell on a recognizable formation of rocks.

"Son of a ..." His words fell away. His hands slowly lowered as if forgotten. Then he reached out and tapped Angela's shoulder. He pointed toward the rocks. "Look."

"What?" She followed the line of his finger. "What is it?"

"We're back in the strait."

"The strait by Corsica?"

Vaughn nodded. "Yeah …" He dug for the name. Then it came to him. "The Strait of Bonifacio." His still watering eyes widened. "Oh crap!"

This was where falling concrete had almost crushed them.

Full of trepidation, Vaughn looked up and stared into the sky. Beside him, Angela did the same.

Blocking the sun with their hands, they scanned the azure atmosphere for the line of levitating buildings and ships.

Angela shook her head. "They're gone! Are you sure we're in the same strait?"

Vaughn tore his gaze from the empty sky and scanned the islands. "Yeah, positive!"

He looked up again. Nothing hung in the sky, not even the faintest wisp of a cloud adulterated the dome of blue sky above the *Angela's Dream*.

Vaughn looked at Angela. "What does it mean?"

She shook her head and looked down, studying the deck. Then she turned her attention to the surrounding island. Finally, she nodded, a smile spreading across her face.

"What is it?" Vaughn looked at the land, trying to see what had made her smile.

"I think …" She paused and turned her widening smile to Vaughn. "I think we reset the timeline."

He blinked and dragged his gaze from the island. "Wh-What?"

Angela turned and stared across the water, and she suddenly looked lost in thought.

She started to nod slowly. "That was a wormhole, right?"

Vaughn raised his eyebrows. "You're asking me?"

Angela looked at him as if she'd forgotten he was there. "Shut it, mister." She hitched a thumb at herself. "Scientist trying to think, here."

Vaughn held up his hands. "Don't let us idiots slow you down."

She turned her gaze out to sea again. "Yes, it was a wormhole, and a wormhole is a rift in spacetime." She paused and then nodded slowly. "So when my energy surge closed the hole, it must have also reset the wormhole's effect."

Vaughn shook his head. "You lost me."

Angela looked at him, her eyes now focused. The smile returned to her face. "Don't you see? It's causality."

"You mean like cause and effect?"

Angela nodded. "Yeah. A wormhole connects two unique points in both space *and* time. When we collapsed this end of the hole, the far end must have shut down as well."

Her eyes lost focus as she continued to mull it over.

Angela held her hands out. "That must have reversed some of the events created by its existence."

Vaughn frowned. "How in the hell does that tie in with cause and effect?"

"Because without the reversal of those events, an outside observer could have seen the effect before the cause." She paused, doubt clouding her face. "Unless …" She shook her head. "No, that has to be it, right?"

Vaughn grabbed her arm and laughed. "Angela! None of that makes any sense to me, but at this point, I couldn't give two shits less." He pointed at the empty sky and laughed again. "You did it! They're gone!"

He swept Angela up in his arms and spun her across the deck of the yacht. "You did it!"

He stopped spinning and set her down.

Angela blinked and her eyes focused on him. Then she looked into the sky. Her smile returned, and she laughed. She wrapped her arms around Vaughn's neck and kissed him deeply.

She pulled back. "Wait!" Fresh hope blossomed in her eyes. "How big of a reset was it? Did we bring everybody back?"

Vaughn's eyes widened. "Holy shit!" He glanced at the sky and then looked at Corsica. "Is that even possible?"

Angela shook her head. "I don't know." She scanned the horizon. Doubt returned to her face. "I don't see anyone on the islands, and I don't see any planes or boats."

"Yeah, but we don't know how much of that was visible from here before."

Angela pointed to the nearest big island. "Corsica still looks the same."

Turning, Vaughn studied the island, but then light glinted off something in the distance. Their ship was about to pass out of the strait. The flash had come from a distant feature that was just visible above a low spot on the island's nearing edge. He realized that it must be one of the Alps' peaks.

Sunlight continued to reflect off the remote feature. Vaughn narrowed his eyes. Something about it looked weird. Then it struck him. It was too bright. Last time they'd passed through this area, he had glimpsed their white-capped peaks. They had looked dull, barely brighter than the hazy background. Now the snowcap looked vibrant, standing out starkly against the haze.

Seeing his reaction, Angela tensed and squinted as she too gazed north. After a moment, she shook her head. "What do you see?"

"I don't know," Vaughn said distractedly as he continued to stare at the mountains. Then he had an idea. "Follow me."

He turned from the sight and jogged into the ship. He didn't stop until they reached the bridge. He grabbed a pair of binoculars from a shelf.

After taking a moment to catch his breath, Vaughn raised the field glasses to his eyes.

His breath hitched. "Aw shit!"

He tried to swallow, but his suddenly dry throat refused to budge. "What?!"

The binos drooped. Vaughn shook his head. "Fuck me!"

"What is it?!"

He held out the binoculars.

Angela snatched them from his hands and raised them to her eyes. Then she flinched. Her breathing rate accelerated. "No! No! No!"

The ship pulled clear of the strait's narrow confines. No longer blocked from view, a thin strip of silver stood above the distant northern horizon. Last time they had plied these waters, they hadn't been able to see the European mainland from here, but now it glistened under a bright sky.

Vaughn retrieved the binoculars from Angela. He had to pry them from her suddenly paralyzed hands. Hesitantly, he raised them to his eyes. Already knowing what he would see, he slowly scanned the horizon, panning from west to east.

Distorted by the atmosphere, silvery buildings shimmered and wavered in the distance, covering the land from horizon to horizon and from shoreline to mountain peak.

Finally, his too dry throat relented. "What did we do?"

CHAPTER 15

Lying on his back, Vaughn stared at the ornate ceiling of their master suite. Night had fallen. Darkness filled the cabin's port windows. Soft amber light streamed from the Habitrail-filled closet, casting its yellow pallor across the room.

What the hell were they going to do now?

Angela had been right the first time she had seen the machine city: they had already lost.

When they had made it into CERN, the two of them had hoped to stop the robots. Then, for an elated moment, they thought they'd reversed the robotic invasion, but instead, it now appeared that the bastards had already paved over the rest of Europe, if not the world.

Now what were they going to do? How do you undo something this big? Undo it? Shit, how in the hell were they going to survive? They'd be lucky to last another day.

After seeing that the machine city now appeared to cover the entire European continent, they had decided to take refuge in a Corsican port. Vaughn had worried that a dash across the Mediterranean would leave them too exposed. Fortunately, it looked like the robots had elected not to occupy Corsica. It was free of the mainland's steel structures, so they'd headed toward one of its harbors, looking for a place to hide and regroup.

He had tried to use the GPS, but now the unit couldn't find any satellites, so Vaughn had plotted their position and navigated to the harbor using the unit's built-in map. He had a difficult time of it. The island's shoreline looked subtly different from that depicted on the GPS's detailed map.

Then the mystery had deepened.

As they'd neared the land, Vaughn and Angela hadn't seen any evidence of humanity's previous existence. All of the buildings were gone. Even their foundations had vanished. The land looked raw as if it had never been developed.

Vaughn had no idea how far into the future Angela's reset had thrown them, but for things to have changed this much, it must have been pretty damned far.

They had agreed that it had to be time travel. That's the only thing that made sense.

Could they have jumped millennia into the future? And if they had traveled ahead in time, why had the boat still been here?

Vaughn closed his eyes and massaged his temples. The unending circle of questions was giving him a headache, eroding the little bit of rest he'd managed.

After guiding the yacht into the protection of the cove, they had dropped anchor.

Exhausted mentally and physically, out of energy and ideas, Vaughn and Angela had stumbled into their quarters. The events in Geneva followed by the subsequent emotional roller coaster had left them spent, exhausted to the point of collapse.

For Vaughn, a hot shower and a few hours of sleep hadn't helped him find the answer to their most pressing question: where should they go from here?

Angela stirred in his arms. Her eyes fluttered and then opened. She gave him a sad smile. Her gaze shifted to the ceiling. Her brow furrowed. "How did that get here?"

"What?" Vaughn looked up again. "I don't see … Wait … Where did that come from?"

With arched eyebrows, he stared at the slowly twisting figurine, a ballerina that now hung suspended from the room's ornate chandelier. Over the past week, he had lain here staring at that ceiling enough to know that the figurine hadn't been there before.

Angela shivered. Then she turned perplexed eyes on him. "Did you do that?"

Vaughn shook his head. "Never seen it before."

"I have." Angela shivered again. "I left it on the station. My daddy gave that ballerina to me when I was a little girl. I meant to bring it down with me, but between being sick and in a hurry to get the hell out of there, I forgot. I've been regretting it ever since." She shook her head. A tear rolled down her cheek. She looked at him and smiled. "How did you know to grab it?"

"Angela …" Vaughn stared at the slowly pirouetting figurine and shook his head. "I didn't. I mean, I would have if I'd known, but I didn't, and I didn't see it." He paused and looked back at the slowly spinning ballerina. "I've *never* seen it before now."

For a long moment, Angela looked at him incredulously. Finally, she nodded. "Okay, sure."

Vaughn blinked in surprise. She didn't believe him.

Angela pointed to one of the room's expansive closets. "I suppose next you'll tell me you had nothing to do with the changes in there either."

"What changes?"

"You rearranged the Habitrail."

"What?"

She rolled her eyes. "I saw it just before I crashed in here. Went in there to check on Nate Junior and the gang, to make sure that they'd been reset too. Was worried that they might still be in that field. Anyway, they were sleeping way in the back, so I didn't disturb them."

She paused and looked toward their closet. "I bet they're awake now."

She pulled the covers off and rose from the bed. "I'm gonna go say hello. Check their food and water."

Vaughn shook his head again and climbed out of bed. "I don't know what you're talking about."

Ahead of him, Angela stopped and extended a hand, gesturing toward the inside of the closet. "How long did that take you?"

"I didn't change any ..."

The words died in his mouth as the closet's interior slid into view. Dumbfounded, he stared at the completely rearranged complex of yellow Habitrail tubes.

He frowned and cast a concerned look at Angela. Had she snapped? The figurine? And now this? All things considered, it seemed like an odd time for her to start pulling practical jokes.

Had all of this been too much for her?

Vaughn supposed he could relate.

He moved to stand between her and the complex of plastic pipes. Arching his brows, he took her hands in his. "What's going on, Angela? Are you okay?"

Confusion twisted her features. Then her eyes flared angrily. "Dammit, Vaughn! I'm not the one ..." Her head tilted, and she peered over his shoulder. "There they are!"

Her face morphed into a mask of horror.

"What?!" Vaughn spun around, raising his arms defensively. Then he relaxed. It was just the mice coming to greet them.

He smiled. "Nate! How's it ...? What the hell?"

It wasn't Nate or any of his family members.

Shit, they weren't even mice!

Four small reptiles scurried excitedly toward them. The pudgy animals looked wrong.

Wrong? Hell, they looked alien!

The things walked on six legs, each tipped by two finger-like claws and one smaller, opposable appendage, like a clawed thumb. The small reptiles moved like tiny monkeys, but their scaly tails wagged like those of excited dogs.

Speechless, Vaughn and Angela exchanged confused glances and then gaped at the chubby, reptilian monkeys. Having reached the nearest portion of their habitat, each one of the three-inch-tall animals looked up at them and smiled toothily.

Vaughn swallowed. His throat clicked.

He pointed at the closest reptilian monkey and its wagging tail.

"That ain't Toto ... and we sure the hell aren't in Kansas anymore."

PART III

"Nonsense is that which does not fit into the prearranged patterns which we have superimposed on reality...Nonsense is nonsense only when we have not yet found that point of view from which it makes sense."
—Gary Zukav

CHAPTER 16

Hanging her arm over the edge of the small boat, Angela watched her fingers slice through the smooth water as the dinghy's silent motor pushed it across the bay's glassy surface. Goose bumps raised on her arm as the boat passed into a pocket of cool, early morning air.

She shook off the chill and looked at Vaughn. "I don't understand any of this. The mice! How could that happen?!" She gestured north. "And the robots? ... I mean, it looks like we've jumped years into the future." She shook her head. "But that makes no sense."

Standing at the skiff's helm and still appearing perplexed, Vaughn looked from the map to the shoreline. "I don't know, Angela." He gave her a sideways glance and then shrugged. "Earlier, you thought the power surge had sent us back in time. Couldn't it have sent us forward just as easily?"

Angela screwed up her face. "That's the thing. I don't think it could have, not like this anyway."

As the boat slid into a small inlet, Angela gazed at the rugged land that surrounded them. The scent of the salt-laden air mixed with that of the island's trees, generating an aroma that engendered a sense of nostalgia entirely at odds with their situation.

Angela wrapped arms around herself and shook her head.

She couldn't make sense of any of it.

Her original theory had fallen apart in the face of what they had seen on the northern horizon.

She and Vaughn hadn't traveled back in time.

They hadn't created a paradox that had wiped the robots from the planet.

Quite the opposite.

If the buildings of the machine city now covered even the Alps, they had likely spread across the entire European continent. At the very least, the structures had covered every square inch of land from Geneva to the Mediterranean coast, including those craggy mountain peaks.

Angela looked at Vaughn. "If we went forward in time, then how did we end up back in the yacht?"

"Yeah, that's been bothering me too."

She turned and gazed across the water, slowly shaking her head. "And why are so many things different?"

Beyond the radical change in the mice, they had discovered several subtle differences. All of their clothing had gone missing, replaced by oddly cut garments that didn't fit either of them. As they'd motored away from the yacht, she had discovered that Vaughn's handiwork no longer adorned its rear bulkhead. Instead of *Angela's Dream*, unknown script now scrolled out an illegible name across the ship's transom.

Vaughn pointed ahead of their small boat, gesturing to the nearing shoreline. "None of it makes sense to me, but maybe we'll find some answers up there."

Angela nodded absent-mindedly, her thoughts returning to the metamorphosed mice. In this already messed up and strange day, the site of those reptilian critters crawling around in Nate Junior's habitat had shocked her the deepest.

How could they have changed?

Had the robots released a virus that had altered their DNA?

Were she and Vaughn going to change into reptiles?

Angela knew that didn't fit the evidence, but that didn't stop her from checking the back of her hand.

No scales had sprouted from her skin ... yet.

There was another possibility, but after the complete collapse of her previous theory, she wasn't about to volunteer a new one, not until she'd had a chance to work through every angle.

"Angela!" Vaughn said, his tone indicating it wasn't the first time.

Blinking and wringing her hands, she looked at him. "Huh?"

"I asked if you noticed our clothes and backpacks?"

She looked down at her light jacket. "What about them?"

"They didn't change. They're exactly the same." He knocked masonry dust from his pant leg. "Albeit a little worse for wear."

Studying her soiled and singed clothing, Angela nodded. The effects of their close encounter with the vat of molten metal and rolling through the rubble of Geneva had stayed with them. In spite of the time reset or time travel—or whatever the hell had happened—those parts of their experience remained unchanged.

"What do you think it means?"

Angela shook her head. "Wish I knew. I had a theory." She hitched a thumb over her shoulder, pointing north, toward the distant mainland and its carpet of alien structures. "But that sight blew it out of the water."

Vaughn pursed his lips and nodded.

They fell into an uncomfortable silence.

In the wan light of early morning, the skiff glided silently across the calm surface of the cove. The glowing eastern sky was already painting the surrounding hills in shades of pink. Angela guessed they had half an hour before sunrise.

Vaughn looked down at the GPS clutched in his hand and shook his head. He had retrieved it from his backpack. Somehow the thing had survived their trip through Geneva. He looked up from it and stared at the island. Then he pointed at the shoreline to the right of the boat. "This is wrong. Not all of it, not the big stuff." He shifted the gesture. "That hill is where it should be." Then he pointed off to the right. "And that one there, too." Then he indicated two other features.

"But those smaller hills don't exist on this map." He swept his arm in a broad left to right arc. "And this entire shoreline is off. It doesn't quite match the map."

"I thought you said there were no GPS satellites."

Vaughn nodded. "None. They're either all dead or ... gone."

"Then how do you know you're in the right bay?"

He cocked an eyebrow. "Angela, I've been an Army aviator for most of my adult life. I know how to navigate. I don't need satellites to tell me where I am."

Angela raised an eyebrow and then nodded toward the shoreline. "Then how do you explain these differences?"

Vaughn gave her a meaningful look. "You tell me how we ended up with a set of plump, six-legged dog-lizards, and I'll tell you why this land doesn't match the map."

Angela frowned and looked away.

They continued the next mile up the V-shaped cove in renewed silence.

Vaughn slowed the boat as it neared the water's end. He gestured right, pointing at the land along the south bank of the inlet. "That's the town of Propriano."

Angela shook her head. "I don't see a town."

"Exactly!" He smacked the steering wheel. "This doesn't make any goddamned sense."

A long, white beach slid into view. Vaughn turned the boat toward it.

"According to the map, there should be a point of land and a light-house right here, not a beach."

Angela stood and looked over his shoulder. She studied the map and then shoreline. "You're right. It doesn't match." She looked up from the GPS and scanned the coastline. "You sure this is the right cove?"

Vaughn gave her the stink-eye again, so she let it go.

A moment later, he cut the power to the dinghy's electric motor, and it ground to a soft stop on the beach's white sand.

Angela peered over the boat's edge, studying the clear, shallow water. No minnows scurried beneath its small waves. Colorful shells of long-dead mollusks littered the beach, but no bubbling clam holes dotted the point where the water lapped at the sand.

She and Vaughn jumped down onto the beach just as the morning sun rose above the island's central hills. The light revealed disjointed splendor.

Blue-green water lapped at the cove's white sand, painting a beautiful contrast in colors so vibrant they almost hurt her eyes. Squat, fragrant trees and scrub vegetation carpeted the hills that surrounded them. The land looked like a misplaced piece of Southern California.

Vaughn walked past her. "Come on, the center of the old town should be just behind these trees."

As Angela followed him up the beach, she scanned ahead. She saw no evidence that anyone had ever touched this land. It appeared to be utterly undeveloped. It looked as if she and Vaughn had walked into the remote end of a national park.

A few minutes later and a hundred feet higher in elevation, they emerged from the trees to find themselves on a rocky bluff that overlooked the bay's turquoise water.

Angela turned slowly, scanning the panorama for any manner of development. She found none. Not so much as a building foundation nor an ancient roadbed marked the land where the city should have been. "It's not here. Looks like it never was."

Beside her, Vaughn nodded. "I know. So how far into the future would we have to go for things to change this much?"

Angela froze, stopping mid-turn as a rustling noise suddenly came from the trees on her left.

Vaughn seized up as well, his hand clamping down on hers like a vice.

A moment later, two robots stepped onto the bluff. They looked identical to the ones she'd seen in the subway stations.

For a long, unreal moment, the two couples—one biological, one synthetic, both pairs holding hands—simply gaped at one another.

Pinned by fear, Angela stared at the apparent robotic lovers. Her eyes fell to their clutched, four-fingered graspers. They were holding hands, just like her and Vaughn, but instead of one hand, the quad-armed machines held two.

The robots broke the stalemate. All eight of their combined arms raised as if in slow motion. A mechanical digit extended from each of their hands, and they pointed at her and Vaughn in an all too human gesture.

Then Angela flinched as a high-pitched siren shattered the silence.

CHAPTER 17

Vaughn darted between two trees, dragging Angela behind him. The screech of the robotic screams filled the air, the sound chasing them down the tree-covered hillside.

Angela tried and failed to pull free of his grasp. "Let go of my hand!"

A branch swung back and slapped her in the face before she could block it.

"Dammit!" She yanked her hand back again and finally freed it.

Vaughn looked over his shoulder.

She pointed ahead. "Go! I'll keep up."

He nodded and pushed deeper into the trees.

Angela followed close on his heels, all the while dodging swinging branches.

They emerged into a small clearing and ran across it. As they reached the trees on its far side, Vaughn shouted over his shoulder. "Are they following us?"

Angela glanced back. The slope behind them looked clear. "No! Not yet, but I can still hear them."

She turned forward just in time to catch another branch to the face. "Shit!"

"What?"

"Nothing!" She pointed down the hill. "Just keep going!"

A moment later, they burst out of the tree line and ran onto the beach. Not slowing, they sprinted for the waiting skiff.

Vaughn began to pull ahead of Angela. Reaching the small boat, he dropped a shoulder and plowed into its inflated rubber hull like a football lineman hitting a practice sled.

The skiff lurched backward and slid into the water. Vaughn jumped onto its bow just as Angela caught up to him.

This time, she accepted his offered hand. He pulled her onboard and then jumped behind the controls.

A moment later, the boat surged backward as it pulled free of the sandy bottom.

Looking across the beach, Angela saw the two robots emerge from the trees.

She pointed. "We've got company!"

Wildly waving all eight of their arms, the robotic pair continued to scream at them. At first they had sounded like sirens, but now they seemed almost organic.

Having finished backing the skiff away from the shoreline, Vaughn placed the boat in drive and hammered its throttle. The electric motors thrummed, the bow surged into the air, and then the dinghy sped them away from the beach.

Angela looked back.

The robots had stayed close to the trees. They seemed reluctant to venture onto the beach. She had a moment to wonder if they feared damage from the sand or the salt water, but then she saw more movement. Several additional robots had emerged, some in pairs, others in trios, and a few appeared to be solo.

"Vaughn!"

He glanced over his shoulder and then did a double take.

"Oh shit!"

Dragging his eyes from the sight, he looked ahead and turned the boat, aiming it straight for the waiting yacht. It floated idly in the middle of the bay, about a mile ahead of them.

Glancing back at the gathering bots, Angela shook her head. "What the hell are we going to do?"

"Let's just get in the yacht and head out to sea. Maybe we can get clear of the area before they call for help."

Angela pursed her lips. She imagined these machines didn't need things like telephones or walkie-talkies to call for help. They probably had built-in communication devices.

She glanced back at the beach and then shook her head. "We need to run for cover. The yacht is too big. We'll stick out like a sore thumb!"

Vaughn pointed at the robots that now crowded the tree line. "The entire island might be crawling with those things." He shifted his gesture to point at the yacht. "We need to get on that and head out to sea."

Angela shook her head vigorously. "They'll see us."

"They already do, but not for long. We'll get out of here, head southwest. We'll be out of sight over the horizon before someone comes looking."

Angela glanced back at the still gesticulating robots and then nodded reluctantly. "Okay."

She flinched and then stooped, as a tremendous thunderclap cracked the clear morning air. It sounded as if it had come from directly above their speeding skiff.

Angela threw up her hands defensively. She looked overhead and saw a stubby, wingless ship rocketing straight toward them.

"Vaughn! Watch out!"

He looked up and flinched, causing the boat to rock.

The white vessel slowed rapidly. It matched the speed of the boat, flying a few feet above their heads. Perfectly pacing the rushing dinghy, the egg-shaped craft hung silently above them, blotting out most of the sky.

"Hold on!" Vaughn shouted.

He yanked the skiff's wheel left and then right, trying to throw off the vessel, but it perfectly matched each jink of the boat.

A brilliant fan of white light shot down from the center of the strange ship's belly. It looked like the flat beam of a laser show. The bright wedge of white light held steadfastly, blocking their forward view.

Squinting and shielding his eyes with a raised hand, Vaughn jerked the wheel back and forth in another futile attempt to throw off their pursuer, but the egg-shaped ship held fast above them. The fan of light that was streaming from its belly remained in place as if anchored to the front of the boat.

Angela reached out and grabbed the skiff's throttle and yanked it back, hoping that the sudden drop in speed would cause the craft to lose lock.

It didn't work.

The vessel matched the boat's deceleration, and the beam held fast.

Angela released the throttle and turned sideward. "Jump!"

She launched herself overboard, diving headlong for the water. In her peripheral vision, she saw Vaughn jumping from the boat's opposite side.

Then, in a flash, the light washed over her falling body.

Darkness swallowed Angela.

All noise vanished.

She cried out in pain as her extended arms and upper body slammed into a hard surface.

Angela rolled painfully and then came to rest facedown. Gritty dust filled her mouth.

What the hell? Had she landed on a sandbar?

Her stomach lurched as a godawful smell nearly overwhelmed her.

Coughing and wheezing, she rolled onto her back and looked up.

The ship and its beam of white light were gone. The egg-shaped vessel had disappeared. It no longer hung overhead.

Still coughing, Angela stared into the suddenly empty sky. Confusion twisted her features.

The sky was ... wrong, still cloudless, but now brown, as if filled with dust.

Hearing Vaughn coughing and hacking, she turned to see him

sitting up. He had landed a few feet away. Rust-colored dust covered him from head to toe.

Sitting up, Angela saw that grime also covered her.

They looked around and then exchanged confused glances.

The water was gone, too.

This wasn't a sandbar.

Angela's head was spinning.

Her heart raced. She scanned the air and then the horizon, frantically looking for the water, the skiff, their yacht.

All of it was gone.

In an instant, the indigo atmosphere and its underlying ocean of blue water had morphed into brown land under a dust-choked, ochre sky.

A series of low hills surrounded them. Beyond those, the craggy peaks of tall mountains scratched at the soiled sky. The range stared down on them from above the thick, dusty haze that obscured the base of the mountain chain.

Somehow, those distant peaks looked familiar.

Vaughn stood. Covered in dust, he walked over to her, his eyes darting left and right beneath knitted brows.

Angela accepted Vaughn's offered hand and stood.

"Where ...?" He paused and looked around. His voice had a panicked edge that unnerved her further. Finally, he locked eyes with her. "Where the hell are we?"

Angela wrinkled her forehead. "I-I don't know!" After a quick sideways glance at their surroundings, she looked at him. "I'm scared."

Vaughn released a short laugh that hitched. "Don't feel like the Lone Ranger."

Another wave of nausea washed over Angela. "That smell ... It's horrible."

Nodding, Vaughn leaned over and spat. "Smells like death." He pointed over her shoulder. "Let's head to the top of this hill. Maybe we'll see more from there."

Angela spat as well, then she nodded. "Okay."

As she began to walk, something crunched under her foot. She

149

stopped and glanced down. Splinters of broken white twigs protruded from under her hiking boot. Scanning the ground, she saw several more of the small, desiccated branches sticking out of the dust around them. They appeared to cover the entire hillside. The brittle twigs only protruded a couple of inches above the sandy soil, but their coat of dust made them difficult to discern.

"Are you okay?"

Angela looked up and nodded. "Yeah."

Vaughn was standing farther up the hill. He waved her on. "Let's see what we can see."

She caught up with him, and they continued up the hill. With each step, more of the weathered branches crunched underfoot.

Her eyes returned to the distant mountain peaks. They still looked naggingly familiar.

Could those be …

Angela shook her head, refusing to complete the thought. It was too crazy.

Halfway up the hill, she began breathing heavily. She felt short of breath.

Panting beside her, Vaughn appeared to be having the same problem.

A few moments later, they finally crested the rise. Its far slope had significantly more of the brown scrub brushes. The short scraggly branches of the withered plants protruded everywhere. Softball-sized rocks dotted the ground on this side of the hill.

In her peripheral vision, Angela saw Vaughn scanning the horizon. Then his body tensed. "Oh shit. We're back!"

Angela looked up from the field of dead plants, and then her breath hitched. "Oh no …" She shook her head. "No, no, no. This can't be."

Wide-eyed and now panting, she stared at the all-too-familiar range of mountains.

"I'm afraid it is." Vaughn pointed. "Those are definitely the Alps."

Angela slowly nodded.

Somehow, they had teleported back to the Geneva area or at least some hellish version of the Franco-Swiss border town. However, unlike that verdant, forested region, the land here offered nothing green. It appeared dead in every sense of the word.

Considering the smell and their respiratory difficulties, Angela was also starting to think that the air was dead as well, its oxygen level too low.

A tan disc slowly rose from behind the easternmost mountains.

She watched it rise for a moment. Then recognition struck. "Is that the sun?"

Vaughn nodded. "Yep."

Angela stared at the dim orb. The atmospheric dust was so thick she could look directly at the sun.

The loose soil shifted beneath Angela. Something cracked loudly under her hiking boots. She looked down and her whole body tensed.

Wide-eyed, Angela pulled her gaze from the exposed item and slowly scanned the slope beyond it.

A soft cry escaped her lips. Finally, she managed to speak. "V-Vaughn ..."

"What?" he said, still staring at the dirty skyline.

She pulled weakly at his sleeve.

Finally, Vaughn looked at her. Fresh concern took over his features. "What is it?"

Choking back tears, Angela pointed at the ground.

Vaughn followed her gesture. His eyes went round, and he stepped back. "Oh shit!"

When the soil had shifted beneath them, it had exposed a skeletal human arm and a grinning skull. As Angela and Vaughn stood transfixed, the skull's hollow eye sockets seemed to glare back at them accusingly.

"How did that get here?" Vaughn said, his voice now reedy.

"That's not the only one." Angela gestured ahead, and her voice cracked. "They're covering the whole hillside!"

Vaughn looked down the slope. His jaw quivered, and his throat bobbed. Then he spoke, his words barely audible. "Stone the fucking crows ..."

A field of dust-covered bones blanketed the slope, and what she had initially mistaken as small rocks now proved to be hundreds of skulls.

Angela took a couple of trembling backward steps. Then her legs buckled, and she collapsed to her knees.

Vaughn stood beside her, confusion twisting his face. "Who are they?"

"It's them ..." A short sob escaped her. "All of them."

Vaughn shook his head. "Who?"

"Every—" The word caught in her throat. She swallowed and then swept an arm across the scene. "Everybody!"

The rise and fall of the ones that surrounded it weren't hills at all.

Angela and Vaughn were standing on the piled bones of millions, no, billions of dead, Earth's entire human population.

She swallowed again and then looked up at Vaughn. "It's humanity ... All of it. The entire human race."

Vaughn turned and stared at the surrounding mounds. Then he too fell to his knees.

Angela stared across the scene. "This is where everyone went." She shook her head. "And now we've joined them."

CHAPTER 18

Vaughn tried to rein in the effects of the adrenaline that had dumped into his system. He was already short of breath. Now his heart hammered in his chest, and his respiratory rate had redoubled.

The scope of Angela's revelation threatened to end him. He'd known they had lost billions, but that had been a number without weight. Of course, he had grasped the fact that they had lost the whole of humanity. That truth had driven him to the edge of suicide, but beyond his personal losses—those of friends and relationships—he'd had a hard time wrapping his mind around the true scale of the tragedy. Above a particular value, numbers became meaningless ... weightless. However, as he stood atop the mounded heaps of uncountable millions, Vaughn felt something in his mind threatening to snap, the irrefutable truth trying to undo him, to steal his sanity.

This was real, tangible ... and undeniable.

Part of his tortured mind latched onto the realization that millions of the dead must have survived the transition only to perish under an ever-increasing pile of new arrivals.

Vaughn shook his head.

It was all too much!

Had his mother ended that way, buried under a growing mound of humanity and the rest of Earth's discarded life?

He grasped his head with both hands.

He had to stop!

Vaughn found himself kneeling next to Angela with no recollection of how he'd gotten there.

Wrapped in each other's arms, they hugged tightly.

Angela sobbed inconsolably, her face buried in his chest.

Vaughn resisted the urge to tell her everything would be alright.

How in the hell would anything ever be okay?

All along, he'd secretly held out hope that maybe everyone had been transported elsewhere, to some higher plain or something like that.

This was no *higher plain*.

This was Hell.

Stop it! he shouted inwardly.

But he couldn't hold back the avalanche of thoughts that plowed through his mind.

He and Angela had been banished to the same place as had the whole of humanity, dropped from a churning blue ocean of water onto a brown sea of the dead.

And judging by the landscape, they'd soon be going the same way as had the billions before them.

Vaughn shook his head. Screw that!

They had come this far. He'd be damned if he would give up now. He wasn't about to just lie here and wait for the end.

Grabbing Angela by the shoulder, Vaughn held her at arm's length. The pain manifest in her green eyes almost broke his resolve.

He shook his head again.

"Angela!"

She blinked, and then her bloodshot eyes focused on his.

Holding her gaze, Vaughn tilted his head toward the distant mountains. "When is this, Angela?"

"What?"

"If this is the Geneva area, then what version of it?" He shook his head. "No. I mean what point in time? Did the robots send us into the ancient past?" He looked around again and then added, "Or is this the distant future?"

He watched her struggle with the same emotions, the soul-crushing thoughts that had threatened to quit him only moments before. The knot in his gut eased a notch as he saw her also starting to gain the upper hand.

Angela closed her eyes for a moment. She took a deep, hitching breath and then let it out with a sigh. She rubbed the tears from her face with the back of her hands, smearing mud across her cheeks.

Finally, Angela looked at Vaughn. "No." She sniffled and then pointed at the surrounding mountains. "The geography lines up too closely with our Geneva."

"Okay." Vaughn was glad to see her focus on something other than their immediate surroundings. He prodded her to continue. "What's that have to do with the timeline?"

She took a hitching breath and then drove on. "We'd have to go back a billion years to find Earth this lifeless. If you went even a few million years back, the mountains here would have a different shape if they existed at all."

Vaughn nodded slowly. He held her gaze, afraid that not doing so would open a door for one or both of them to slip back into the abyss. "That's because of plate tectonics?"

Angela nodded. "Yes. Even a change of a few million years would alter the shape and location of the mountains." She paused and looked around. "We'd have to go back a hell of a lot farther to see Earth this … lifeless."

She sighed again and then turned back to Vaughn. The barely contained desperation hovering behind her eyes threatened to push him back over the edge.

He focused on her words, pushing out the doubts before they could take root. "What about the distant future? Could they have … I don't know … beamed us a million years forward?"

Angela shook her head again. "Same problem." She pointed at the mountains. "Things would've moved. Besides, why would they do that to us? Their city looked pretty permanent to me. Why would they send us into their own future? And if they did send us forward, where are all the buildings? Those stainless-steel monstrosities would take eons to revert to rock and dust."

Vaughn chewed on that for a minute. As he thought, he looked up at the sky. He could stare directly at the sun. The filtering effect of the atmospheric dust rendered it as nothing more than a bright, sharply defined disc. The murky atmosphere reminded him of photos of the Martian sky taken by NASA's Opportunity rover.

Angela's voice snapped him out of his reverie.

She was pointing at a nearby line of hills. "That's the ridge that the supertanker swept us off of." She looked to their left. "So the city center should be over there. Let's head that way. Maybe we'll find some answers."

Vaughn nodded. It was good to see Angela participating, evaluating their options. Even if it was all busywork, doing something, anything, was better than waiting here to die.

They stood. Vaughn took a step, and then they both flinched as a bone cracked under his boot.

Angela shook her head and then muttered under her breath, saying something about it being nothing but scrub plants. Looking up and seeing him watching her, she pointed down the hill. "Just go." Echoing his internal thoughts, she added, "We can't sit here waiting for the end."

An hour later and a mile farther down the slope, they still hadn't seen evidence of previous structures, nor had they reached the ground. They were still traversing the mountain of dead. Along the way, they had spotted the bones of thousands of animals protruding from the dust. Large and small, beasts of all sorts had died alongside and on top of the billions of discarded humans.

Vaughn began to envision what it must have been like. Then a chill ran down his spine, and he suddenly felt nauseous. The mental images threatened to toss him back into the black abyss. He shook the thoughts from his head.

Beside him, Angela jumped with a start as an unusually large bone snapped beneath her feet. Its report sounded like a shotgun blast. Stepping back, she closed her eyes and released a long sigh.

Vaughn moved to stand in front of her. "Angela?"

She nodded. "Don't worry. I'm okay ... for now."

Angela opened her eyes and gave him a wan smile. Then she canted her head and looked over his shoulder. "What is that?"

Vaughn turned and looked down the hill. "I don't see any ..." He paused as a glint of muted light pierced the haze. It appeared to be sunlight reflecting off a distant shiny surface.

Up until now, the only metallic objects they had seen had been belt buckles and capped teeth, and most of those items had been so dust covered as to be all but unrecognizable. However, this reflection was too big to be a tooth or a buckle.

Angela turned raised brows toward Vaughn. "Could that be one of their buildings?"

"You mean from the machine city?"

She nodded.

Vaughn shrugged. "Only one way to find out."

"What if someone is down there waiting for us?"

Shaking his head, he gestured to their surroundings. "Don't think we're going to find anyone lying in wait, not in these dead lands." He gave her a crooked grin. "But if we do, I'm going to give them a piece of my mind."

Angela snorted and started down the hill again. "Careful, Captain. You don't have a lot of that to give away."

Vaughn followed her. "I'm serious. I have complaints to lodge. This place stinks."

Angela guffawed. Then she flinched as another bone crunched underfoot.

Short-lived, the levity died, withering as had everything else in that desiccated land.

A torturous half hour later, they finally approached the edge of the piled remnants of Earth's lost life.

Near the bottom of the macabre mountain of bones and tattered clothing, windblown dust covered all but the highest protrusions.

As Vaughn approached the foot of the hill, he stepped onto a stone outcropping that appeared to be native rock. The steep-sided protuberance extended from the massed dead like a dark monument.

Breathing heavily, he rubbed his temples. The atmosphere's low oxygen content already had his head throbbing. Looking up, he searched the land ahead for the glint that had lured them in this direction.

Gazing across the small dunes that dotted the lifeless, rocky surface around the mounded dead, Vaughn could now see that the reflected light was coming from multiple points.

Angela walked past him quickly. Several crunchy steps later, she finally reached solid ground and stopped. Panting, bent at the waist with hands on her knees, she whispered 'Thank you' over and over.

After a moment, she stood and began rubbing her temples as Vaughn had. She glanced down at a small dust dune. Then her shoulders slumped. A small cry escaped her lips. She slowly looked up and scanned the surrounding dunes.

"No ... Oh, no ..." Dread filled her voice. "This is too much!"

"What?" Vaughn leaped down from the rocky ledge and ran toward Angela. Each footfall launched a small dust cloud, but the dry breeze quickly carried them past Angela's frozen form.

Vaughn slid to a stop next to her. "What is it ...?"

He looked down. "Ah, shit!"

The upper half of the skeletal remnants of a human couple protruded from the small sand dune at Angela's feet. Lying on their sides, the pair still held each other, their foreheads touching in a permanent embrace.

Vaughn saw that some of their bones were badly broken. He didn't think those had happened post-mortem. In his mind's eye, he could see the couple extracting themselves from the pile after being partially crushed by the unending arrival of new victims.

Had they known each other or had they huddled together, two lost souls tossed onto the shores of a writhing sea of the dead and dying?

He shuddered and then forced the image from his mind. Instead, he focused on Angela's face. She was looking at the surrounding dunes. Vaughn didn't need to look. He already knew that each hummock would tell its own story of loss, of pain and suffering.

"Angela."

She didn't respond.

"Angela!"

A shudder rocked her body. Then she blinked several times and looked at Vaughn as if waking from a dream.

It was a dream alright, a goddamned nightmare.

He held her gaze. "Focus, Angela. There's nothing we can do for them." He pointed toward their goal and tried to sound more confident than he felt. "We have to get over there, see what it is."

Angela stared back at him for a long moment. Finally, she swallowed hard and then nodded. "Okay, but you lead the way. I don't want to look ... look down."

Vaughn nodded and took her hand. For the next half hour, he led Angela through a minefield of heartbreak.

He'd been hardened by witnessing the ravages of war, but even for him, this was too much. At times, it was all he could do to continue, not to break down and collapse as they weaved around entire families, parents wrapped protectively around their children, all of them partially buried in the dunes. Vaughn's imagination all too easily added expressions of pain and agony to their grinning visages.

Along the way, he had seen all manner of animal carcasses, many of their bones scattered in a way that made it evident that they'd become food for someone or something.

On more than one occasion, he heard a choked sob escape Angela's lips.

Gradually, the field of ravaged bodies thinned. The reflective objects still stood several hundred yards away, but no skeleton-filled dunes cluttered the land ahead.

A full-blown migraine now chewed its way through Vaughn's head. He'd also began to feel nauseous. Angela's look and periodic winces told him that she was experiencing the same sensations.

He squeezed her hand. "We're out of it. No more bodies here."

She nodded curtly and pointed ahead. "I'm sure there are plenty more out there somewhere." Hitching a thumb over her shoulder, she gestured behind them. "Anyone who wasn't too injured to walk would've gotten as far away from that as they could."

"Do you think there might be some still alive?"

Breathing heavily, Angela released his hand and started rubbing her temples. She shook her head. "No, I don't think anyone can live long here." She gave him a sad, resigned look. "And we won't either. The oxygen level is too low."

Suddenly, she bent over and wretched. The food she'd eaten that morning splashed across the ground.

Vaughn moved up to help, but Angela waved him off.

She stood and wiped a sleeve across her mouth. "We're already presenting symptoms of high-altitude sickness." She pointed at him and then herself. "The headaches, the nausea, all signs of oxygen deprivation."

Vaughn nodded and started walking again. He'd felt on the verge of throwing up for the last twenty minutes. "I was wondering why we haven't seen any evidence of long-term survival. It doesn't even look like anybody made fires for cooking."

Angela shook her head and took another deep breath. "Not enough oxygen. Wouldn't be able to keep a fire going." She looked ahead. "There might be someone out there, people from higher elevations. If they survived their initial arrival, they might have made it a little farther than most, but I think even they would have succumbed eventually."

She kicked at the ground with the toe of her boot. "Back home this was a lush valley. There should be lakes, ponds, and rivers all over the place. Those mountains should be snowcapped. They're not, and we haven't seen so much as a stream. If it's this dead and dry here, I doubt anyone found an oasis elsewhere. Even if they could survive the low oxygen level, the lack of water and vegetation would have killed off them and any animals that they might have gathered for food stock."

Angela dragged her boot, plowing a furrow through the layer of dead bugs that covered everything. She released a long sigh. It was a sad, mournful thing. Then she nodded at the ground. "Even the flies ran out of food and water."

Vaughn nodded slowly. Then he looked up and was surprised to see that they had reached their goal.

He stopped and touched her arm. "Angela!"

She stutter-stepped, almost losing her balance. "What?" She looked up. "Oh my …"

They stood in the middle of a cluster of toppled, four-foot-long metallic cones. The things littered the ground around them. It looked as if some giant kid had left his toys strewn about.

Seeing characters stenciled across the side of one, Vaughn dropped to a knee next to it. Then he blinked in surprise as he recognized not only the writing but also its true meaning.

He stood and quickly backed away from the object.

Angela looked at him, her eyes widening. "What?!"

Vaughn waved for her to follow as he quickly placed some distance between them and the field of cones, although he knew it was a futile effort.

"What did it say?"

"L-G-M One-One-Eight-Alpha!" He dragged his eyes away from the devices. "Those are Peacekeepers!"

Vaughn saw a question forming on Angela's lips. He held up a hand and gave her a meaningful look. "We just found your missing nukes."

Angela stared at Vaughn, apparently not comprehending his meaning. Then her eyes widened. "Oh shit!" She looked ready to bolt, to try and put more distance between herself and the nuclear weapons.

Vaughn held up a hand again. "We can't get far enough away from these bad boys, but if they were going to go off, I think they already would have by now."

"What about radiation?"

Vaughn pursed his lips. "I don't know." Then he shook his head. "They're intact. Probably got here the same way we did. Doesn't even look like they were scratched by the trip."

A confused look crossed Angela's face. "I thought ICBMs were a few feet wide."

"The missile is, but the Peacekeeper carries ten smaller, independently guided reentry vehicles under its nose cone."

Angela nodded. She pointed beyond the field of nukes. "Then what the hell is that?"

Again, Vaughn did a double take. A larger device lay in the dirt a few hundred yards beyond the cones. He shook his head. "I ... I don't know."

They spent the next several minutes circumnavigating the field of nuclear devices, still reluctant to get too close.

Finally, they came to a stop in front of the new device. It had been designed for flight, but it looked like no aircraft Vaughn had ever seen. It appeared to be a cross between a cruise missile and a futuristic concept car, like an oversized Lamborghini designed for flight.

Suddenly, Angela took a couple of backward steps. "What the hell is that?!"

Vaughn looked at her and then shifted his eyes to the ground, and he too stepped back. "Son of a bitch!"

What he'd mistaken for a boulder was the exoskeleton of a long-dead alien beast.

"It's huge!"

"Yes, it is," Vaughn said as he stared at the monstrosity.

The being looked like a six-legged minotaur. Looking around, Vaughn saw that it was just one of many. Unlike this one, most of the others appeared to be incomplete. Their scarabs had shattered and crumbled. They looked like the product of lobsters mating with crabs, but instead of pincers, they had articulated fingers on the end of the long, skinny arms. It also had matching digits on each of its six legs.

Moving hesitantly, Angela stepped in for a closer look. "Who were they?"

"I don't know. Maybe they made the robots."

She turned widening eyes toward him. "You think the robots work for them? Could this be one of their masters?"

Vaughn mulled it over and then shook his head. "On second

thought, I doubt it. They look aquatic. Probably not native to this shit hole. Besides, why would the robot's creators be here?"

Angela looked from Vaughn to the dead alien and then nodded. "I think you're right."

She suddenly swayed. Her hand went to her stomach.

Vaughn reached out to stabilize her. "Are you okay?"

"Just another wave of nausea."

He looked at the sun. It now hung low in the western sky. In their weakened state, it had taken them the better part of a day to traverse the mountain of dead and the land beyond.

"It's going to be dark soon. We should find somewhere to hole up for the night."

Discomfort blossomed anew on Angela's face, but then she nodded. She pointed to the backside of the alien device. "That's higher than anything within a few miles. Maybe we can shelter behind it. If the winds get any stronger, it should protect us."

Vaughn nodded. They walked to the leeward side of the alien ship and set up camp.

A few hours later, the moon rose. Aside from the muted lunar disc, only the light from the brightest stars and a couple of planets penetrated the hazy atmosphere.

Angela had pointed out that the moon was in the same phase here as it had been when they'd left Tripoli.

Vaughn could tell that Angela was working on a new theory, but when he pushed her on the subject, Angela would only shake her head. Either she didn't think it was worth discussing, or there was something else going on.

At this point, Vaughn was too tired to think about it.

The temperature had fallen precipitously when the sun had set. They had joined their sleeping bags so that they could share body heat.

Lying next to Angela in the warm confines of their combined bags, Vaughn rolled onto his side and looked at her. She was staring into the sky. In the wan light cast by the dust-filtered moon, he saw a muddy track left in the wake of a slowly rolling tear.

Vaughn pulled Angela close and gently kissed her cheek. Then he cupped her chin and turned her to face him. He stared into her eyes. "Angela, I don't know how, but we'll get through this."

She sighed. After turning to gaze into the sky again, she shook her head. "Don't make promises you can't keep, flyboy."

Deep sorrow washed over Vaughn. He didn't know what to do next. The only thing they'd accomplished was to find out what was reflecting the light. They were still no closer to understanding when or where the robots had sent them.

Where would they go from here?

How much time did they have left?

Angela was right. He couldn't know anything right now except that they were just as screwed as the billions who had come before them.

Vaughn flinched as something touched his cheek.

He blinked. His eyes cleared, and he saw Angela staring at him.

Cradling his face in her hands, she smiled weakly. "Thank you for all you've done, Vaughn." She kissed him. "I needed a hero, and you showed up larger than life." She nuzzled into his neck and began to sing, her breath warm on his neck. Her voice rose and fell as she breathily rendered the lyrics of the eighties tune she'd sung to him over the radio back when she was still stranded aboard the space station.

Vaughn swallowed and hugged her tightly. "You still make that old song sound so beautiful."

Angela started another stanza, but her words soon faltered.

A moment later, her rhythmic breathing told Vaughn she'd fallen asleep.

Exhausted beyond words and lying in the darkness with Angela held in his arms, Vaughn felt himself drifting toward slumber as well. A moment later, he too surrendered to the cold, dark sanctuary of sleep.

Vaughn flinched as a blindingly bright light jolted him awake.

Then the ground fell away.

Before Vaughn could process this information, he and Angela plunged into warm water.

Angela screamed.

Her shriek devolved into a gurgling wail as they dropped below the surface.

They started sinking.

Vaughn tried to extend his arms to paddle, but he couldn't free them from the enveloping sleeping bag.

Craning his neck, he stretched for the water's too bright surface. Its churning waves may as well have been a hundred feet away. He couldn't reach them, couldn't draw the breath he so badly needed.

Angela flailed against him as she too tried to free herself from the sinking bag.

Then she was out.

Her boot grazed his cheek as she shot upward.

Now that Vaughn had more space, he wormed his arms out of the sleeping bag and pulled it down. Then he too swam for the surface.

A moment later, Vaughn broke through the waves. Throwing his head back, he tried to inhale but only gasped and coughed. Painful moments later, he finally managed to draw in dry air.

Treading water next to Angela, he raised a hand to shield his eyes from the bright blue sky, but the loss of that hand's paddling threatened to send him back beneath the waves.

Spitting and coughing, he tried to look around, but couldn't resolve much through his slitted eyes.

"What the—?" He coughed again. "What happened?!"

Water sprayed his face as Angela shook her head. "You're asking me? Weren't you awake?!"

Vaughn tried to shield his eyes again, but with his boots on, he couldn't keep his head above water without using both hands to paddle. He spit out salt water. "Think I was out too."

Still squinting, he tried to look around. Luckily, the choppy waves were less than a foot high. His eyes were starting to adjust to the light. Vaughn could just make out a blue sky above the water. Part of it was blue anyway. It appeared that a white cloud was obscuring half of the sky, but everything was too bright. He couldn't see any of it clearly.

Angela bumped into him. Dark rivulets of brown mud streamed from her hair and ran down her face. She rubbed her eyes and tried to look around. "Can you see anything?"

Vaughn nodded. "Yeah. A little bit. Looks like it's midday." He paused to spit out another mouthful of salt water. "There's a blue sky." He pointed behind her. "But it looks like clouds are blocking half of it." He winced as he tried to resolve the white mass. It was too bright.

Angela turned to look. Then she screamed and started backpedaling. "Oh no! No, no, no, no!"

She scrambled backward. The back of her head slammed painfully into Vaughn's nose. In panicked flight, Angela ran over him, her boot kicking him one final time as she swam away, her flailing arms churning the water into a white froth.

Staring after her, Vaughn shook his head. "Where are you going?!"

Clumsily, he tried to rub his sore nose and head but quickly sank. Another mouthful of water was the only reward for his efforts.

Spitting it out, he turned toward the cloud.

Finally, his eyes adjusted enough that he could stand to look at it for more than a second.

The white mass started to resolve.

He tilted his head. "What is that?"

Vaughn's entire body tensed as recognition slammed home.

Open-mouthed, he stared at the curtain of white energy. It looked like an all too straight aurora borealis. The wall of light stretched skyward from the surface of the water. It extended left and right to the limit of Vaughn's field of view, blocking out half of the sky.

Vaughn shook his head. "Ah, son of a bitch! Really?!"

CHAPTER 19

V aughn turned from the light. "Angela! Come back!" As he swam after her, he kept glancing backward, watching the towering wave of energy.

Looking at the thing, Vaughn realized that they must have returned to the beginning of it all, back to when the invaders had first cast their life-stealing ray of light across the planet.

Apparently, the robots hadn't been satisfied with tossing Angela and Vaughn into the desiccated and lifeless version of Earth all by themselves. The bastards had brought them back to the beginning just so they could send them back again. Now the two of them were going to be deported to that hellish rendition of Earth at the same time as the rest of humanity. When that light swept across him and Angela, it would deposit them into the middle of the ever-expanding pile of discarded life at its other end.

Even as he watched his coming death, Vaughn couldn't help but be awed by the sheer scale of the energy wave. In horrified amazement, he scanned its full height. Bisecting the midday sun, the wall of light blocked out half the sky, looking as if another planetary body had merged with Earth's surface at a ninety-degree angle.

This was Vaughn's first time to see it in person. The descriptions he'd found on his mother's computer had done the damned thing no justice. The immensity of it took his breath away—that and the gallon of salt water that tried to flow into his mouth with every breath.

The wave of light had better hurry, or the watery ones were going to beat it to the finish line.

Something splashed behind Vaughn. He turned to see Angela swimming back to him.

"I'm sorry." She looked at the approaching wall of energy. "I ... I just ..."

He swam toward Angela. "Stop it. Come here." He wrapped his arms around her, hugging her tightly, but then they both began to sink.

Something bumped into Vaughn. At first he thought it had been Angela's leg, but then one of their backpacks bobbed up between them. A moment later, the other one surfaced a few feet away.

They released each other and grabbed their packs. Using the buoyancy of the bags, they floated hand-in-hand and turned to watch the coming wall of light.

Squinting, Angela took a hitching breath. Her lower lip quivered as she spoke. "You know ... we'll be inside the pile this time."

Vaughn gave Angela a sideways glance and then nodded.

What could he say? That they wouldn't be crushed? Maybe they would end up on top of the pile or on its edge?

Were those possibilities any better than the faster end Angela was envisioning?

Likely not. Those were probably just slower means to the same end.

The outcome wouldn't change either way.

Angela looked at him expectantly.

He squeezed her hand. "Whatever comes, we'll face it together."

She pursed her lips and gave a curt nod.

They turned and watched the wall of light, continuing their silent vigil.

No longer in a frenetic battle to keep his head above water, Vaughn got his first clear look at the base of the thing.

The curtain of energy still obscured half the sky, but he couldn't see where it touched the water.

Vaughn released Angela's hand.

"What is it?"

"Hang on a second."

Trying to get a higher vantage point, he propped himself up on the backpack. Kicking his feet and craning his neck, he could finally see more than a few feet.

Vaughn tilted his head. There was still a lot of ocean surface between them and the base of the light wave.

Miles and miles of it.

He couldn't see the point where the two met. It was too far away.

Based on Angela's description of the light wave's speed, he thought it should have already swept over them, but it didn't look any closer.

In fact … it was starting to shrink!

Vaughn's eyes widened. "It's moving away!"

"What?" Angela scrambled onto her bag and craned her neck. "You're right!" She closed her eyes and released a long sigh. "Oh, thank you!"

Vaughn watched the light as it continued to retreat. Then a black outline emerged from the energetic, white curtain. It was a long island to their front left. Blinking, Vaughn studied its craggy peaks.

"I recognize those mountains …" Pausing, he kicked his booted feet and turned. Another island sat right where he thought it would. The island wasn't very far away. He would've seen it earlier if he hadn't been struggling to stay afloat.

Vaughn tilted his head. "We're back?"

Angela turned to face him. "Back where?"

He pointed at the land that had been revealed by the receding light wave. "That's Sardinia."

"How can you know that?"

Vaughn grabbed her shoulders and gently turned her toward the new island he'd spotted. "Because that's Corsica. We're back in the Strait of Bonifacio."

He watched Angela process the information. Then her eyes flew open. "Oh shit!" She looked up at the sky. "We have to warn them!"

Following her gaze, Vaughn stared up into the sky. "Warn who?"

"Me! ... You!"

"What? That doesn't make ..." Then it struck Vaughn. His eyes went round. "Oh, crap!"

He looked at the now visibly retreating curtain of light. Angela was right.

If they had jumped all the way back to the beginning, back to a point in time when the light wave was still crossing the planet, then at this very moment, there were still billions of people alive!

Including the earlier versions of themselves!

Angela desperately clutched at his sleeves. "We have to warn Bill and Teddy! They can't leave the station!"

Not waiting for his reply, Angela turned and started swimming toward Corsica, still clutching her backpack.

Vaughn looked after her for a moment and then followed. As he churned through the water, he tried to process the new paradigm. If the light wave was crossing the Med, it had just left Europe. There were still billions of people left.

People like his mother.

He caught up with Angela. They swam side-by-side.

Thoughts for his mom rushed through Vaughn's mind.

Was there a way he could save her?

A soul-crushing realization slammed home: he couldn't save his mother.

He couldn't save anyone.

The only reason he and Mark had survived was because of the unique way they were disconnected from the planet. Given the time available, there was no way for him to get anyone to safety.

Except ...

Another realization slammed home.

He could save Matt!

Just like Angela, Vaughn needed to get a message to himself.

Then it hit him. There was one person with whom they had both spoken.

"Angela! We need to call—"

"McCree!" Angela said, cutting him off. "I know! He's the link. The Director spoke with both of us. Randy can save Bill and Teddy." She glanced at him. "And he can warn you and Mark to stay away from the airport."

Vaughn nodded again and continued swimming.

If they could speak with Director Randall McCree, they could tell him to warn their opposites not to make the same mistakes. They could save Mark from his appointment with that tumbling jet engine, and they could stop Angela's crew-mates from boarding the Soyuz descent module.

Unbearably long minutes later, they finally made landfall. The two of them scrambled up the beach, heading toward a huge rock. Then Vaughn realized it was actually a villa with a door and several windows cut into its smooth, gray surface. It looked like no home he had ever seen. Its seamless, curving lines made the dwelling look as if it had been carved from a single, building-sized boulder.

Not slowing to study the villa further, Vaughn sprinted toward its front door.

Angela shouted breathlessly from behind him. "Find a phone, and I'll call Randy directly! I still remember his number."

"On it!" Vaughn slowed as he neared the entry. He didn't see a handle, so he reached out and lunged at the front door, intending to push it open, but then his hand passed through empty air as the panel suddenly slid aside.

He tumbled forward. "Oh shit!"

Vaughn stumbled through the opening and sprawled face first across the floor of the dwelling.

He scrambled back to his feet and then continued into the home, Angela close on his heels.

The villa's interior was even odder than its outside. The walls of the room beyond the doorway had the same organic, flowing lines as had the building's exterior, but inside the home, the light fixtures appeared to have grown right out of the ceiling and walls. The furniture and the floor all looked as if sculpted from one block of stone. Even the paintings and family photos had been installed in recesses cut into the dark, rock walls.

As he ran past one of the larger family portraits, Vaughn did a double take and then slid to a stop. "What in the world?!"

Angela ran into the back of him. "Why are you stopping?!"

Still staring at the portrait, Vaughn raised a hand and pointed at the large photograph.

Angela turned and then started to shake her head slowly. "I ... I don't understand."

Vaughn swallowed. His mind reeled as he tried to comprehend what they were seeing.

He looked around, scanning the room's other pictures. They were all the same.

Angela's voice dropped to a whisper. "Those aren't people."

Scanning the room, Vaughn nodded. "You got that right."

He turned back to the large portrait and stared at the family of clothed, fish-headed beings—amphibians, he guessed. These weren't doctored photos either. There were too many details, stuff in the background that looked all too real. Then there was the shape of the room's furnishings, both in the photo and in the house around Angela and Vaughn. None of it looked like anything a human would use. It was all tailored to the shape of those beings.

Impersonating the amphibian rebel commander from Star Wars, Vaughn said, "It's a trap."

Neither of them laughed.

CHAPTER 20

Vaughn looked around the room. He couldn't process the information streaming through his eyes. It made no sense.

Beside him, Angela stared at the surreal family portrait and slowly shook her head. "I don't understand this." She looked at him. "What's going on?"

"I'm just as confused as you."

Vaughn turned and walked around the room. A vaguely fishy smell permeated the space, and the air was oppressively humid. The outside atmosphere had been dry. Inside the house, it felt artificially elevated, as if someone had left a humidifier on high.

Angela spoke up from behind him. "This can't be real, can it?"

"Looks pretty genuine to me."

"Maybe we stumbled into an amusement park."

Vaughn raised an eyebrow. "You see any roller coasters when we swam up to the beach?"

"No ... but maybe it's more of a theme park."

He looked around the room. Nothing in the place appeared contrived. Details like those he'd seen in the photo lay strewn about the dwelling. It had the look of everyday use, not that of a display or a sideshow attraction.

Glancing at Angela, Vaughn puckered his forehead. He didn't want to shit on her hopes, but she was grasping at straws.

Turning from her, he rocked his head equivocally and then stepped up to an elevated portion of the floor. It looked like a chaise lounge made for a hot tub. A fist-sized clump of something sat in a small puddle of water at the center of the concave seat bottom.

Vaughn bent over to inspect the item.

Angela stepped up next to him. "What is it?"

"Looks like a hunk of fish."

"How can that be? I thought the light wiped away all life."

"It does if it's alive." He grabbed the piece and held it up. "This has a bite taken out of it. It's food."

Angela nodded. "See, it must be a theme park." She pointed at a nearby portrait. "If these were really fish people, they wouldn't eat fish. That would be cannibalism."

"Why wouldn't they eat fish?" Vaughn shrugged. "We eat mammals."

She regarded him through knitted brows and then shook her head. "Whatever. We still need to call Director McCree."

Vaughn's eyes went round. No longer able to contain his skepticism, he swept an arm in a horizontal arc. "After seeing all this, you think you can still reach someone, anyone who'll even speak our language?"

Doubt clouded Angela's face. "I don't know! But we have to try."

After a moment, Vaughn nodded. "Okay, sure. Let's go see what we can find."

Finding nothing in the family room, they continued deeper into the villa. They passed through an apparent kitchen and several bedrooms.

They found a touch-screen device lying in the middle of a hallway. It looked like it might be a smartphone. Angela picked it up, and the screen came alive. A series of unreadable characters marched across its display.

She pressed a couple of the virtual buttons that were floating across the screen. Nothing happened at first. Then she tapped a third one and flinched as a low-pitched voice rang out.

Angela held the phone up to her lips. "Hello?"

The voice continued to drone on.

Vaughn suppressed a grin. The deep voice had a gravelly, wet quality … just like that of Admiral Ackbar in Star Wars.

Angela shook her head. "It's a recorded voice."

Pointing at the device, Vaughn gave her a meaningful look. "I've been all over the world, and I've never heard a language that sounded like that."

Angela glowered at him. "You don't know everything, Vaughn."

Vaughn bit his tongue. There was quite a lot he didn't know, but he figured that if it walked and talked like a fish-headed alien and if it smelled like a fish … it was probably a goddamned fish-headed alien.

Angela turned her sneer toward the communication device. The recorded voice was still streaming through its speakers. She started jabbing virtual buttons. Finally, one of them worked, and the odd voice cut out mid-word.

She cycled through another set of inscrutable menu items, proceeding blindly as the illegible text that filled each option was still written in characters that Vaughn had never seen.

A moment later, something approximating a ringtone blared from the device.

Angela looked at Vaughn triumphantly. Then she turned back to the screen. Her jaw went slack as a head suddenly filled the display. The dark-skinned amphibian appeared as surprised as did Angela. Its broad, fishy mouth fell open, and its impossibly wide eyes somehow expanded.

The fish-head was standing in a domicile much like the one Angela and Vaughn currently occupied. The walls behind it had the same curved stone surfaces.

The being spoke. It sounded indignant as if thinking someone was playing a practical joke. Its voice had the same raspy, wet sound as the recorded voice.

The looks on both of their faces were hilarious.

Vaughn tried and failed to stifle a laugh.

The screen flashed white.

When the light faded, the talking amphibian had vanished. The feed hadn't died. The stony dwelling in the background looked unchanged, but the indignant fish-head no longer filled the center of the display.

Vaughn's laugh died in his suddenly tight throat. "Oh shit!" he said in a dry croak. "The light got him."

Angela looked at Vaughn, her face ash white. "They're wiping out another race?"

"Yes they are, but why is there another race in the first place? Why have things changed again? First, lizard dog-monkeys replaced the mice." Vaughn pointed at the device in her hand. "And now fish-heads have replaced us? What the hell?!"

Angela shook her head. "I don't understand. None of this makes sense." She looked down at the live image of the now empty home on the other end of the connection. Then her forehead furrowed. "Unless …"

"Unless what?"

Angela chewed her lip. "Could it be?" Then a soft cry escaped her lips. "Oh God. Bill and Teddy …" Her gaze dropped to the floor. "We can't save them. We never could, not from here."

Thrown by the sudden change, Vaughn blinked and screwed up his face. "Wait … What?"

She wiped a tear from her cheek and looked at him. "There's something that might explain some of this, but first, I need to figure out a few things."

"Like what?"

"Like, why would the robots send us here—wherever this is? They already had us where they wanted us."

Vaughn had wondered the same thing. He started pacing back and forth as he tried to work it through. Finally, he shrugged. "I don't know. I was pretty sure they meant to send us to that dead version of Geneva. That flying egg hit us with that light, and suddenly we're in Hell. Seemed pretty intentional to me."

"That's a good name for it?"

Vaughn stopped pacing and looked up. "Huh?"

"That place, it was like being in Hell."

"Hell?" Mental images of their trek through the place paraded through his mind. He nodded. "Yeah, it was."

Through force of will, Vaughn pushed out the memories and started walking back and forth again. "Anyway, I think the robots sent us to Hell, as you say, on purpose. It makes sense. They saw us where they didn't want us, so they sent us to the same place or time where they had sent the rest of Earth's animal life."

Vaughn started counting off fingers. "They sent all of Earth's animal life to Hell, and they deposited the missiles there that we shot at them." He extended his thumb. "And lastly, they dump off anything else that happens to poke its head up." He waved his index finger fore and aft, gesturing theatrically at the two of them. "Like you and me."

"I agree."

Vaughn held up a hand. "But now we have bigger fish to fry." He winced and extended a palm toward the amphibian in the photo. "Sorry, bad choice of words." He turned back to Angela and gestured at their surroundings. "So how does your idea reconcile all this?"

Angela frowned. "Something still doesn't add up."

Vaughn scoffed. "Other than pretty much everything, what doesn't add up?"

"You said that it made sense that they would send us to Hell, and I think you're right. Did they also send us back here, freeing us from a prison of their making?"

Vaughn wagged his head. "Maybe they have other plans for us."

Angela pursed her lips. "Maybe, but I don't think so. How long were we in Hell?"

Vaughn checked his watch. Angela had been giving him unending shit about his need to wear a timepiece, often asking if he had post-apocalyptic appointments to keep, so now he made a show of studying its face.

Angela rolled her eyes.

"It's showing one o'clock now."

"PM or AM? Did the watch's time change when we jumped back here?"

Vaughn raised his eyebrows. "Oh. Now you want to know something about time?"

"Shut up and answer the question, Captain."

He shrugged. "Don't know. This is a simple watch. No AM or PM, no date either."

Angela frowned. "So, either it didn't change, and it's showing one AM, or it did, and it's showing the current time of one PM?"

Vaughn gave her an odd look. "What makes you think it would have changed time, and why would the time be one PM?"

Angela shrugged. "Maybe I'm wrong." She held up air quotes. "You're the Army 'aviator.' You saw the position of the sun. What time do you think it is?"

Vaughn thought about it for a moment. The sun had been directly overhead when they'd landed in the water. That had been about an hour ago. He smiled self-consciously. "Guess it's about one."

Angela nodded. "So how long were we in Hell?"

"It was about eight AM when we ran into the robots in Corsica."

"Okay, so how long were we in Hell?"

"Well, I think it was about the same time of day there as it had been in Corsica. The sun rose over Hell's taller mountains right after we arrived. It had crested Corsica's hills before the bastards beamed us out of there, but considering the different elevations of the two features, I think the sun was probably at the same height at both places. I doubt that means anything, but it gives us a starting point."

Angela looked at him impatiently. "How. Long. Were. We. In. Hell?!"

"I wasn't checking my watch. Kinda seemed like a moot point at the time."

Angela stared at him with her eyebrows raised expectantly.

Vaughn glanced at the ceiling and did some quick math. "Assuming we beamed back here at midnight, I think it was about sixteen hours."

She shook her head. "Like pulling freakin' teeth. Would it have been so hard to say that in the first place?"

Vaughn ignored her. "Now that we've settled that, what are you getting at?"

"I'm not done." Angela crossed her arms. "First, tell me how much time passed between the wormhole power surge and our arrival in Hell."

Vaughn opened his mouth, but Angela held up a hand.

"The short answer, please."

He closed his mouth and then checked his watch. They had beamed to the alternate version of the yacht at high noon and had arrived in Hell around eight the next morning. After some quick mental math, he said, "Twenty hours, give or take."

Angela nodded. "So about thirty-six hours between them."

"Between what?"

"Our two arrivals in the strait. Thirty-six hours after we were dropped onto the deck of the yacht that wasn't ours, we splashed down into the same geographic location, sans the boat." Angela paused. Then her eyes widened. "Wait! How long did it take us to get to CERN?"

"From where?"

Angela rolled her eyes. "From the first time we passed through the strait, of course."

"What?"

She sighed and spoke slowly. "How long from the first time we passed through this strait until we overpowered the wormhole?"

Vaughn thought back to that first time through the area. It seemed like an eternity ago. It had been around noon when they crossed the strait, but they hadn't flown out of Monte Carlo until the next day. By the time they'd gone down into the tunnels, the sun had been setting. Considering how long it took them to find and catch a train, it must have been close to midnight when they tried to overload the wormhole.

Vaughn looked at Angela. "Thirty-six hours again. It was a day and a half both times."

She nodded. "Yep. Thirty-six hours from our first pass through the strait until I overloaded the wormhole, and then another thirty-six hours after that, we get sucked out of Hell and end up in the same place!"

"I don't see how that's relevant. It must be a coincidence. We certainly didn't go back a day and a half. All three trips through this damned strait had to have been at different points in time."

Angela gave him an unreadable expression. "I'm not so sure about that."

"Pfft!" Vaughn nodded toward a picture of what looked to be amphibian toddlers playing in a park. "I never visited Corsica before the Disappearance, but I'm pretty sure I would have heard about a settlement of Admiral Ackbar wannabes walking its streets. There's no way we only jumped thirty-six hours this time."

Tilting her head, Angela shrugged. "Actually, there might be a way." She set the communication device on a shelf and walked toward the front room.

Vaughn narrowed his eyes. "How?"

Angela disappeared through the opening at the far end of the hallway.

Shaking his head, Vaughn walked after her. He stepped into the apparent living room.

Angela was standing in front of the largest of the amphibian family portraits. She looked lost in thought.

Vaughn held out his hands. "Come on already. What's you're theory? Do you think your little trick back in CERN had something to do with these changes?"

Angela looked at him appraisingly. Then she nodded. "Yeah, but calling it a trick might be giving me too much credit. I was only trying to break the thing. This was the first time I or any other human ever messed with a wormhole. It's uncharted territory." She paused and then nodded. "But yes, what we're seeing fits my theory."

"Let's hear it, then."

Angela chewed her lower lip and then gave a short nod. "Thirty-six hours, right?"

"Yeah, thirty-six hours ... twice."

Angela shook her head. "No, I think it was four times."

"Four? How in the hell do you get that many?"

"The first thirty-six-hour period began here and ended when we overloaded the wormhole."

Nodding, Vaughn held up two fingers. "Yeah, and the second one was the thirty-six hours it took us to travel through Corsica and Hell."

Angela shook her head. "That wasn't the second; it was the third."

Vaughn screwed up his face. "What? Uh, I don't think so. Pretty sure I'd remember an extra day and a half."

"We didn't experience it. We traveled through it ... twice."

"What are you talking about?"

"We've been dropped into the strait twice, once onto the back of a boat and once into the water. It was noon both times." Angela extended two fingers. "Same place, same time of day." Giving Vaughn a meaningful look, she extended a third finger. "And the same exact day."

"I was with you right up until that last part." Vaughn shook his head. "What on Earth would make you think it's the same day?"

"You're thinking that the timeline is the variable in this equation, but it's not. I think *Earth* is the variable."

"Come again?"

"The land is the same, and the location is too, but ..." Angela paused. She tilted her head. "The location is the same ...?" Then her eyes widened, and she grabbed his arm. "Oh no, Vaughn!"

"What?!"

She released him and started looking around frantically as if searching for something.

Then she ran out of the villa.

Confused, Vaughn stared after her for a moment. Then he ran after her.

Standing in the yard, Angela turned, visually searching the shoreline. "No, no, no! I can't believe this is happening. I've wasted so much time!" Apparently not finding what she sought, she looked back toward the house. Finally, she looked at him, her eyes still wide.

Vaughn held his hands out. "What is it? What's wrong?"

"We need to get to the mainland!"

He frowned. "Why? What's that got to do with your theory?"

"This isn't about my theory ... Well, actually, it is, but that's not the problem. It's the robots! They're doing it again!"

Vaughn felt his short hairs trying to stand on end. He looked up, expecting to see another egg-shaped ship bearing down on them, but all he saw was an empty sky.

Angela shook her head. "No, not here."

"Where, then? What are they doing?"

"Wiping out another race."

Vaughn looked at her. Then his shoulders relaxed as he realized they weren't in imminent danger. "Geez, Angela. You scared the shit out of me."

He looked at her as a new worry set in. Was she having a psychotic break? Had all of this been too much for her?

"Listen, Angela." He said softly. "We already knew that, right?" He pointed at the villa. "We saw what the bastards did to the people in the house. We even saw it happen to the guy on the phone, saw it in real time."

Angela stopped scanning the area around the villa and turned a confused look toward him. Then her eyes cleared and she shook her head. "No, Vaughn. It's not past tense. They're still doing it!"

He thought about their close call with the light wave and then shook his head. "No, we thought we were back home, in our own time, so we thought that light wave had come from Geneva." He gestured toward the alien villa. "Now we have no idea where the light came from. As far as we know, we saw the last bit of the wave's action."

Her eyes flared with anger. "Dammit, Vaughn! Don't you see?"

"See what?"

Angela growled and shook her head. "It's coming from Geneva again. We have to get there!"

Vaughn stared at her for a moment. Finally, he said, "How can you know that? I mean, we don't even know *when* this is." He shook his head and pointed at the villa. "But judging by what we saw in there, it must be one hell of a long way into the future. Besides, why on Earth would you want to go back to that machine city?"

She shook her head impatiently. "I don't think it's there anymore." Seeing Vaughn open his mouth, she held up a hand. "Every moment we stand here, there could be millions more dying." She turned away from him and started across the yard, walking quickly toward the left side of the villa. She yelled over her shoulder, "I'll explain it later! Just help me find a way out of here!"

Vaughn ran after her. "Angela! What about the robot city?" He gestured north, toward the mainland. "It's covering everything up there!"

"I told you, I don't think it is." Angela shook her head. "Not here, anyway."

"Can you at least tell me what you meant about Earth being the variable?"

"Not now!" She continued to scan their surroundings. "We're wasting time! You have to help me find a way to Geneva."

"Fine." Vaughn threw his hands up. He looked around. "Maybe we can find a car. There has to be a port on this island. We'll drive there and see if we can find a boat."

Angela gave him a pained look. "I hope we can find something faster than a boat!"

Vaughn looked past her and then shrugged. "Not sure how we're going to do any of that, though." He pointed at the rising terrain behind the rock-shaped villa. "There's no road here."

Angela walked up to a smaller structure that sat adjacent to the house. It too looked like a giant boulder, but its fixtures and wide doors gave it a familiar look. She pointed at it. "Then what's in this garage?"

"Not sure," Vaughn said with a shrug. He walked up to the building's largest door. As he neared it, the entire panel began to slide downward, slowly disappearing into a slot in the ground. At the same time, a portion of the roof immediately above the door retracted into itself.

Vaughn stared at the large, organic-looking sphere that sat in the center of the garage's floor. Finally, he found his voice. "That's not a car."

Angela stepped up next to him. "No, it's not."

Vaughn finally broke his paralysis and walked up to the ten-foot-wide orb. It appeared to be a mix of stone and large, curved sections of glass. It had four short, frog-footed legs, each tipped with three toes. The feet looked similar to those he'd seen on the amphibians in the villa's portraits.

A large window spanned the portion of the sphere that faced the garage doors. The glass panel wrapped around the forward third of the orb. To Vaughn, it looked like an aircraft's windscreen. Two oval panels bracketed the windshield, one on each side of the craft. The four-foot-wide convex ovals looked like hatches.

Vaughn reached out to touch one. Then he yanked his hand back as the transparent panel popped out of its frame an inch. The opposite one had moved at the same time.

They flinched and stepped back as both doors silently shot open, revealing person-sized portals on each side of the sphere.

After exchanging glances, he and Angela cautiously stepped up and peered through the nearest hatch. At the center of the forwardmost section of the craft, a pair of apparent joysticks protruded from a console beneath the main window.

Angela looked at Vaughn. "Do you think it flies?"

"I don't know." He knocked on the exterior skin. "This looks and feels like stone." Then he pointed at the joysticks. "But those look like controls. Maybe it walks, or it could be a boat. We are by the water."

Angela gave the ship's undercarriage a skeptical glance. "The legs look too short and rigid for that."

Vaughn shrugged. "Must be a boat then, but I don't see a trailer or any way to get it to the water."

"We don't have time to fart around." Angela gestured impatiently toward the interior of the sphere. "Let's go already. Give it a shot."

He did a double take. "Are you sure?"

Angela waved him forward. "Move it, Captain!"

Vaughn held his hands up. "Yes, ma'am." He stepped through the hatch and then stood in front of the controls.

Holding his breath, Vaughn reached tentatively for the joysticks. He paused as he remembered his previous failure in the Aurora.

"What are you doing?!"

"Are you sure about this? We don't even know what this thing does."

Angela held out her hands and shook them. "Come on, Vaughn. What happened to, 'I'm a pilot, it's what I do'?"

Vaughn didn't reply. He just continued to look at her, unsure of what to think or say. Finally, he found his voice. "You call *me* impetuous? ... Who are you, and what have you done with Angela?"

A look of desperation broke through her impatient visage. "Vaughn, every moment we delay means thousands more might die. We have to hurry!"

Shaking his head, Vaughn pointed north, toward the mainland. "What is it you think we'll find up there, and how does it all tie into this theory of yours?"

"If this thing can get us moving, I promise I'll tell you once we're on our way." She raised an eyebrow and then jabbed a finger toward the controls. "Now hurry it up, mister. You can do this."

Vaughn looked at her for a long moment. Then he nodded. Stepping forward again, he tentatively touched the controls and then clutched one stick in each hand. Feeling them give a bit, he slowly applied pressure in various directions, trying to get a feel for how the sticks moved.

Angela stepped up next to him. "What the hell are you doing?!"

"I need to see what these do."

They both turned with a start as the doors suddenly slid shut.

Before Vaughn could consider whether they were locked in, a loud hum came up from the floor. Even as he registered the sound, he saw the outside world shift as the vehicle lifted to a one-foot hover.

Angela grasped his upper arm. "You're doing it!"

Vaughn held his hands up. "I'm not doing anything ..." He smiled wryly. "Well, not yet, anyway."

Testing its reaction and purpose, Vaughn moved the left control, incrementally displacing the joystick fore and aft. The spherical ship responded by moving in the indicated directions while holding its one-foot altitude.

Angela's grip on his arm tightened.

Vaughn nodded. Then he experimented with the right stick. As he'd already discovered, it didn't move laterally. It only moved up and down like the handle of a butter churn. He applied slight upward pressure on the control. The craft responded by moving up a foot. He released the stick, and the sphere stopped. Then he pressed it down, and the thing lowered to its original altitude.

He regarded Angela with a cocked eyebrow. "I got this. The controls are backward, but that won't be a problem."

"What do you mean?"

"Their positions are reversed from what you'd find in a helicopter."

"You think you can fly it?"

He looked at Angela and smirked. "You asked for it."

"Would you just hurry—?"

A shocked scream burst through Angela's lips, cutting off her words as the sphere rocketed straight up with incredible acceleration.

Vaughn had yanked up on the right stick. The resulting vertical G-forces had almost buckled his knees.

Angela clutched him desperately. "What the hell are you doing?!"

Glancing over his shoulder, Vaughn grinned again. "I'm a pilot." He shrugged. "It's what I do."

He relaxed the upward pressure on the stick, and the craft slowed, making them both nearly weightless for a moment.

A short chuckle escaped Angela's lips, but when Vaughn looked, she only glared at him.

He released the controls, and the sphere came to a stationary hover a few hundred feet above the shoreline. Vaughn looked down through the glass floor. The garage was still directly below them.

Angela's fingers were two-knuckles deep into Vaughn's upper arm, but she nodded. "Okay, although I thought you'd settle for a few feet above the surface. Why did you have to go all the way up here?"

"When this thing popped up to a one-foot hover, I realized two things." Vaughn held up his thumb. "First: these people have either perfected something like our Q-Drive, or they've figured out how to manipulate gravity." He extended his index finger. "Anybody who can do either of those things would make this thing idiot-proof."

He held up a hand. "And before you ask, yes, that means it's even Vaughn-proof."

"Uh, your Q-Drive ship wasn't Vaughn-proof."

"Hey! That wasn't my fault. That thing was a one-off." He pointed ahead, at the land beyond the seaside villa. From their higher vantage point, they could now see more of the mountainous island. "Look. They don't have any roads. That means pretty much everyone on this island has one of these things or something like it. They're likely mass-produced and standardized."

Angela gestured at the instrument panel. The spartan display didn't have much on it, but what was there was written in alien lettering. "Can you read any of that?"

"Nope," Vaughn said curtly.

His matter-of-fact tone appeared to annoy Angela. "What if it runs out of power?!"

He shrugged. "I already told you it's Vaughn-proof. Any device this advanced will have multiple redundancies and fail-safes. If it loses power, the ship will auto-land or deploy an alternate means of descent like a parachute."

Angela pursed her lips but then nodded. "We're up here now. Just go, already, but be careful."

Vaughn started to tell her that was up to the machine but thought better of it.

He grabbed the two joysticks. The sphere accelerated northward. It tilted forward like a helicopter. The vehicle's angle perfectly matched its acceleration, keeping them from being thrown backward in the seatless craft.

The land beneath them looked utterly undeveloped. Aside from several boulders that might have been of the same construction as the villa, Vaughn saw nothing that looked like a town or even a small village.

He guided the sphere higher. It climbed above the island's small, craggy mountains. Then the mainland's highest peaks slid into view above the watery northern horizon.

Vaughn narrowed his eyes. He didn't have binoculars this time, but he could already see a difference in the tops of the mountains. They no longer sported a stainless-steel glint.

He glanced at Angela. She was squinting as she stared ahead.

Vaughn remembered the lingering problems with her vision. "You were right. The buildings are gone."

Angela only nodded.

As the sphere accelerated toward the mainland, the full height of the snow-capped Alps and the land beneath them slid into view above the Mediterranean's blue waters.

Vaughn still didn't see any sign of the buildings.

Beside him, Angela continued her mute survey of the scene.

He pointed at the land and repeated himself. "They're gone. How did you know?"

"I'll tell you my theory soon, but I need a closer look at the mainland first. Can this thing go any faster?"

Vaughn pushed harder on the stick in his left hand, but the portion of the craft's display that appeared to indicate speed remained unchanged. "That's all I can get out of it, but it won't be long. We're hauling ass."

Again Angela didn't respond. She merely stared ahead, studying the land through slitted eyes.

Several minutes later, they approached the rocky shoreline of what should have been Monte Carlo. The lay of the land looked similar. It had many of the same twists and curves, but this time, it looked undeveloped. Only scrub trees and large boulders covered the ground.

Vaughn started to slow the sphere.

Angela looked at him. "What are you doing?"

"Thought you wanted a closer look."

"I told you, we need to get to Geneva. Fly lower, but keep your speed up."

Vaughn shook his head but did as she asked.

As he watched the land rush toward them, he half-worried that this was all an illusion. He kept expecting the image of the undeveloped land to waver and then vanish like a massive mirage, revealing the hidden machine city in all its horror.

Angela pointed down. "Is that another villa?"

Vaughn blinked and followed her gesture. "I think so." He guided the craft lower. The structure appeared to be made from the same material as the villa. Its smooth, rocky features looked as if grown into its purposeful shape. As they zipped past it, Vaughn glimpsed the same type of windows cut into the villa's curved surface.

Angela tapped his arm and pointed to another rocky structure that featured the same design.

Vaughn looked around and realized that thousands of them covered the terrain. Many of the structures were tucked under trees. They blended perfectly with their surroundings. An entire city sat hidden in plain sight. It looked like a version of Monte Carlo created in near perfect harmony with its environment.

Beside him, Angela suddenly tensed.

Following her gaze, Vaughn saw light reflecting off debris in the center of a patch of damaged vegetation. It took him a moment to realize what he was seeing. Then he blinked in recognition. A shattered ship, similar to the one in which they now flew, had spread itself across the ground in an incredibly violent impact.

A moment later, the scene passed out of sight as the blazing speed of the flying sphere carried the two of them farther inland.

Looking around, Vaughn spotted several additional ships dotting the area. Most were still intact. It appeared that the few shattered ones had flown into the area's cliffs. They must have been flying directly at the rocky inclines when their occupants had vanished, too close for their automated systems to intervene and prevent a collision.

He cast a wary glance at the interior of their ship. He sincerely hoped that was what had caused the crashes anyway.

The scene reminded Vaughn of the piled cars that had littered many intersections after the robots had stripped them of their drivers. However, in this case, it appeared that the fail-safe features of the ships had saved all but a few, not that it had mattered to their missing occupants.

He shook his head. "This still doesn't make sense. What's going on, Angela?"

She didn't respond, but a look of consternation took over her features. Angela looked as perplexed as he felt.

"What's up?"

She shook her head slowly. "You're right." Her eyes cleared and looked into his. "It doesn't make sense. Maybe it will in Geneva."

"Why Geneva?" He pointed at the alien structures. "Why would anything there be different from this? I doubt these people even developed the area? This isn't anywhere close to our timeline."

"I think it is, but I need to see the Geneva area to know for sure."

Vaughn ground his teeth. This was going nowhere. Angela was talking in circles. He jabbed a finger toward the surrounding city. "Why in hell would Geneva matter?" He held his hands out. "This doesn't even look like our version of Earth!"

Angela gave him a double take. Then she shook her head. "Just humor me, please."

Vaughn glared at her for a long moment. Finally, he looked forward and turned the sphere toward the Alps. "I sure as hell hope they have beer up there."

CHAPTER 21

Angela watched Vaughn fly the craft across the Alpine foothills north of Monte Carlo. He looked frustrated. She knew he wasn't happy with her putting off the sharing of her theory, but she wasn't sure about it herself. Angela needed to work her way through her thesis before she could defend it, had to think through all of its potential holes.

Turning from Vaughn, she looked down and scanned the craft's instruments. Its numbers and characters were completely alien. However, all of the digits glowed green. In spite of his assurances about the aircraft being 'Vaughn-proof,' Angela couldn't help but worry that green-for-good might not be universal.

"You sure everything is okay with this thing? We're not going to run out of gas or electricity?"

Vaughn shrugged. "Everything is green."

Angela frowned and cocked an eyebrow. After a moment, she sighed and gave him a curt nod.

The vessel began to climb in earnest as they flew up the tree-lined slopes of the Alps. Angela spotted a few more of the rocky domiciles. There weren't as many here, but the tragedy represented by all those empty homes threatened to undo her. However, there was one thing that kept her going. She knew that it was still happening at this very moment, that millions of these amphibians along with the rest of this world's animal life were even now falling to that damned light.

The sphere banked left as Vaughn steered it through a cut in the mountains.

Studying the lay of the land, Angela realized that it was the same pass they'd gone through in the helicopter when they had trailed the line of levitating ships en route to Geneva.

During that previous trip, they had flown over uncountable expanses of farm fields, but now Angela gazed down on a valley covered by wide swaths of shallow water. The multi-tiered terraces covered the land. She pointed at one of them. "Looks like rice paddies. Maybe they cultivate aquatic plants."

Vaughn shrugged. "Maybe not just plants. Those look like the crawfish paddies we had in Southeast Texas and Louisiana."

Multiple mountain ridges crossed the land ahead of the ship. Layered one over the other, each subsequent ridgeline painted a lighter shade across the sphere's windshield. The farthest peaks were barely perceptible in the hazy distance. Angela wondered what they would find beyond it.

She felt Vaughn staring at her.

"Stop changing the subject, Angela."

"Huh?"

Vaughn pointed ahead. "Uh, Geneva. You know, the city you wanted to see. It's time you share this theory of yours."

Angela looked down and then back at Vaughn. "I think we might find the collider."

"What makes you think there's a collider anywhere in this timeline?"

"Because of the light wave we saw here. I think that's how the robots linked to our world. They used our collider against us. They might have done the same thing to these people."

Nodding slowly, Vaughn looked at her with brightening eyes. "Okay, that makes sense. The fish-heads must have found our old one and somehow reactivated it."

Angela shook her head. "No, not the same collider. It wasn't ours. It was one made by these people."

"Why wouldn't it be our old collider?" Vaughn gestured at the surrounding land. "To me, it's starting to look like we've fallen into a misguided re-envisioning of the goddamned Planet of the Apes. You know, the one where giant, fish-headed salamanders learned to talk. Then they kicked Woody Harrelson's ass and eventually went on to knock us off the top of the food chain."

Angela opened her mouth, but Vaughn held up a hand.

"Bald Woody aside, who's to say these fish-heads didn't find our now ancient collider and bring it back online?"

As he spoke, Vaughn guided the sphere through a broad, arcing circle around a particularly tall mountain. The path took them over a small lake. A sparse collection of stone huts dotted its shoreline, blending perfectly with their surroundings in a manner that had its own beauty.

The thought made Angela all the more angry at what had happened to these people.

She shook her head and then looked at Vaughn. "I don't think we jumped in time." She gestured outside. "That doesn't fit with what we see here, nor with what we saw in Hell."

Raising his eyebrows, Vaughn tilted his head. "Come again?"

"You're assuming we were sent to another point in time, but I've already told you why that doesn't work."

Vaughn's confused look persisted.

Angela sighed. "Tectonic plates? Mountains still in exactly the same place? Any of that ring a bell?"

He nodded quickly. "Oh, yeah. But we know the robots' technology can transport us through time. We've already seen it at least twice! You even said that it was four times. If those events aren't separate points in Earth's timeline," he shrugged, "then what?"

"I have an idea about that. I've been holding off because I haven't worked my way through the whole thing yet." She pointed down. "But before I go into that, let's talk about how we ended up here."

Vaughn glanced ahead. Having cleared the mountain, he steered the craft back onto their original course-line. "Go ahead." He nodded at the instrument panel. "We're going pretty fast, but this thing ain't setting any speed records."

Nodding, Angela continued. "When I saw Hell's sun in the same position as it had been over Corsica, I started wondering if the two places might be linked." She shook her head. "However, that hypothesis fell apart when we dropped out of there in the middle of the night only to plunge into the ocean in the middle of the day here. How could they be linked if the time of day was different from one place to the next?"

Another ridge slid beneath the craft.

Vaughn glanced at her and shrugged. "That doesn't mean we couldn't have jumped farther into the past or the future."

Watching two mountain peaks slip past the flyer, Angela held up a hand. "Bear with me. I'm going somewhere with this."

Vaughn looked at her and then nodded. "Go ahead."

"When you realized that we had jumped back to the Strait of Bonafatchio."

"Strait of Bonifacio," he corrected.

"Whatever. When we realized that we had ended up back at the same place as we had after I tried to break the wormhole, I realized that there might be another explanation, a single fact that would resolve almost all of these mysteries."

Vaughn had been watching the terrain around them, but then he looked at her with expectant eyes. "Go on."

Angela nodded. "Each time we've ... jumped, or whatever you want to call it, some things have been different, but the location and time of day weren't."

He shook his head. "No. The time of day was different when we jumped here."

"No," Angela said. "They were exactly the same as the first time it happened."

Vaughn tilted his head. "Okay, you've lost me."

In imitation of Vaughn's finger counting exercise, she extended her thumb. "First, thirty-six hours after we passed through the strait of whatever, we jumped back thirty-six hours and ended up back in the strait." She extended her index finger. "Then thirty-six hours later, we're back there again."

He shook his head. "I think *you* caused the first one, not the robots. The ones we ran into in Corsica weren't looking for us. Hell, they had no idea we were there. We practically stumbled into them. But when they did see us, they intentionally sent us to Hell."

"Exactly!"

"Exactly, what?"

"We caused the first one, and they didn't know we were there. And you're right. They did send us to Hell." She paused and tapped the floor of the flyer. "But I don't think they know we're here this time, any more than they did last time." She gestured behind them. "If the robots had sent us here intentionally, they would have dropped us on the other side of that energy wave."

Vaughn nodded slowly. "So what does that mean?"

"We already figured out that we jumped back thirty-six hours when I overloaded the wormhole."

"Yeah, and we ended up back in the strait after another thirty-six hours passed." Vaughn shook his head. "But that's where the cycle ended." He nodded toward a passing alien village. "We jumped a lot farther than thirty-six hours this time."

Angela grinned. "I don't think we did."

"What the hell are you talking about?" Vaughn shook his head. "That makes no sense." He waved his hands in front of him, palms out. "Not that any of this shit does. But there's no way this is the same timeline!"

"Actually, there is one way, and if you'd shut the hell up for more than a second or two, I'll tell you what it is."

He opened his mouth but appeared to reconsider. Then he nodded and held his hands out. "Please."

"Dimensions."

"Dimensions?" Confused, he looked around. "What's the size of this place have to do with anything?"

"Vaughn! Listen with your ears, not your mouth."

"Sorry." He looked outside and guided the craft toward another pass. "Go ahead."

Angela sighed and then nodded. "I'm not talking about dimensions of size or scale. This is about dimensions of space."

He stopped scanning outside and slowly turned to look at her again.

Angela gave him a wan smile and continued. "You touched on it earlier when you said this doesn't look like our version of Earth. It's not. We're not traveling between different *time periods* of the planet, Vaughn. We're traveling between different *versions* of Earth."

Vaughn raised a hand like a student requesting permission to speak.

Angela rolled her eyes. "Go ahead."

"Dimensions of space? I thought we only had four dimensions: three spatial and one time."

Angela nodded appreciatively, glad that Vaughn wasn't completely clueless on the subject. "Yes. Those are the dimensions that we can directly observe, but scientists have long theorized about the possibility that there may be additional dimensions that exist outside of our perceptions."

Vaughn looked skeptical. "Couldn't these machines ... these robots just be a bunch of asshole time-travelers?"

Glancing outside, Angela nodded. "They're definitely assholes, but like I said, if the robots sent us forward in time—if Hell was just a place in Earth's future—the amount of time change required to explain the disappearance of their very permanent structures would've changed the lay of the land."

Doubt continued to cloud Vaughn's face. "So you're saying we're hopping to other versions of Earth? To other dimensions?"

"Yep."

"How?"

Angela held her hands out. "You've heard of dark matter, right?"

Vaughn blinked at the apparent non sequitur, but then he nodded. "Yeah, it's supposed to make up the majority of the universe. You scientists use it to explain why galaxies don't fly apart."

Angela smiled and nodded again. "I'm glad you paid attention in your physics classes. Yes, galaxies rotate too fast to be held together by the combined gravity of their visible components. At the rates that galaxies rotate, all of the stars, planets, and dust that we can detect can only provide a small fraction of the gravity required to hold it all together. So we deduced that there must be a lot of matter that we can't see or perceive."

"Yeah," Vaughn said. "Dark matter." He pointed outside. "But what's that got to do with all of this?"

Angela raised her eyebrows. "I'm starting to think we were wrong."

"Why?"

"Because there was an alternate theory that fits perfectly with what we're seeing."

Vaughn looked at her expectantly.

"The proponents of the theory postulated that the additional gravitational forces bled through from heavenly bodies that existed in multiple parallel dimensions. They hypothesized that all these layered versions of Earth and the Sun, along with every heavenly body in the universe, traveled through space gravitationally locked in a perpetual dance that held each version in the same spatial position, regardless of which dimension it occupied."

"Wait!" Vaughn paused as he guided the sphere around another peak. "These scientists thought that there were multiple versions of Earth sitting on top of one another?"

Angela rocked her head from side to side. "Not stacked, more like overlaid, but you have the idea. The theory says there are a bunch of Earths that each occupy the exact same point in space, but not just our planet. Every star, planet, and moon in the universe would exist in multiple dimensions. We mainly feel the gravity produced by our dimension, but they theorized that enough gravity leaked from each dimension to explain effects we've observed at the galactic level. I used to laugh at their idea." She glanced forlornly outside. "But I'm not laughing anymore."

They stared out silently for a moment. Then Vaughn nodded. "I think you're right." He pointed to their surroundings. "Kind of hard to call bullshit with all of this happening. Inter-dimensional travel starts sounding pretty plausible when you're magically hopping from one reality to another." He paused and then looked at her. "How many of them?"

"How many dimensions?"

He nodded.

Angela shrugged. "Depends on how much gravity leaks from each dimension. If the shared portion is minuscule, there could be thousands of worlds layered over one another."

"Son of a bitch," Vaughn said under his breath. Then he looked at her, comprehension dawning on his face. "The robots didn't come from another star system, did they?"

Angela shook her head. "No, they didn't. If I'm right, they didn't cross space at all, not regular space, anyway."

Vaughn's eyes narrowed. "The bastards attacked us from another dimension." He looked outside. "And this isn't our Earth at all." He began to nod slowly. "That explains a lot."

Angela nodded as well. "Yeah, it does. It's why the land looks roughly the same, but the situation and even the people are different."

"So Hell is just another layer, too."

Angela blinked. "What?"

"The land we've been calling Hell. It's just another dimension of Earth."

"Yeah, it is."

Vaughn shook his head angrily. "The goddamned robots are using it like a trash can, dumping off anything that gets in their way."

"Yep. All of Earth's life." Angela paused and looked at Vaughn. "And probably all of the life from the dimension that was home to those dead lobster-crab aliens that we saw in Hell."

Pointing outside, Vaughn said, "And now you can add these poor bastards to the list."

Angela shuddered as she recalled their trek down that dimension's pile of dead humanity. She didn't even want to think about what that place must be like now.

"Wait," Vaughn said, suddenly looking confused. "If they're all different, unique worlds, why did things look almost exactly the same when the wormhole knocked us back to the strait? The yacht looked so similar that we didn't notice the differences until the next morning. Hell, for that matter, why was a boat there at all?"

Nodding, Angela held out her hands. "That was one of the things that got me thinking about the Dimension Space theory. Its proponents believed that neighboring versions of the planet might be almost identical, but the farther you got from your own dimension, the more things would change."

Vaughn frowned and raised his eyebrows. "Considering that we're now on a planet populated by huge, fish-headed salamanders, I'd say we've gone pretty damned far afield." Then he looked at her. "But despite that, you thought there was a collider here?"

Angela nodded. "I still do. The robots linked to our dimension by latching onto a micro black hole created by CERN, and they probably got here by connecting to one made by these people. I was thinking the ability to latch onto that singularity depended on geographic proximity." She looked at the scattered rocky homes around them. "But now I'm starting to think you're right. We've traveled so far from our home dimension, the collider might be anywhere on this planet."

The sphere passed between two mountain peaks, and Lake Geneva slid into view. Angela's eyes widened, and she placed a hand on Vaughn's arm. "But there's a chance I was right about the proximity thing." She pointed toward the west end of the city. "If so, their collider should be in that area. So head that way, and hurry, please."

Vaughn turned the ship. "Okay, but this is as fast as it'll go."

Angela felt her body tensing as she scanned the valley. There was one aspect of their approach to the city that she had kept to herself. The nuclear weapons they'd seen in Hell had gotten there because the robots had zapped them out just before they had impacted. She could only hope the same didn't happen to her and Vaughn. She reasoned that since the two of them had gotten all the way into the machine city without being detected, the robots must only look for threats that rise above a certain threshold.

Hopefully, the approach of the two of them didn't rise to that level.

Casting a wary glance at their flight pod, Angela resisted the urge to cross her fingers.

Agonizingly long minutes later—and still inhabiting the same dimension—they finally approached the outskirts of the city of Geneva, or at least where it would've started in their homeworld.

Over the next minute, Angela felt some of the tension leaving her body. If they were going to be zapped to Hell, it should've happened by now. The missiles had disappeared the moment they had arrived.

The surrounding mountains still sat in the same places. Even the nearer hills and the lake looked unchanged. However, as with everything else they'd seen since arriving, this land looked wild and untamed. No roads cut across the terrain. Aside from the ubiquitous stone habitats, no bridges or visible structures stood out either. The area contained significantly more homes than any place that they'd yet seen, but still, it looked undeveloped.

Angela shook her head. "I expected to see … more than this. Where are all their roads?" She pointed at yet another wrecked flight pod. "Surely, these things aren't the only way they get around."

"I don't know," Vaughn said, scanning the area. "There are a lot of them, but I think you're right, not enough to supply everything this many people would need."

Vaughn looked around and then pointed ahead to their left. "The supercollider's main entrance was in that area, right?"

She looked in the indicated direction and then nodded sharply. "Yes! Hurry!"

Vaughn adjusted the controls. A few moments later, he dropped the craft to a lower altitude and began to slow.

Angela pointed at a small rise. "Over there!"

Nodding, he shifted the ship.

From their elevated vantage point, Angela scanned the ground and the scattered stone structures, desperately looking for any sign of an entrance to an underground facility.

She growled and shook her head. "Dammit! Nothing but villas!"

Vaughn turned the ship to the north and pointed ahead. "Let's do a wider search."

Pursing her lips, Angela gave a short nod, but based on what she had seen so far, she doubted they would find anything. Outwardly, it appeared these people had shunned industry and science, but the technology of this ship and that of the communicator they'd found in that first stone hut indicated otherwise.

As he flew the sphere across the ground, Vaughn started shaking his head.

Angela gave him a sidelong glance. "What?"

"You know. I'm sure you're thinking the same thing I am."

"I am, but we have to try. There's so much on the line."

Pressing his lips into a thin line, Vaughn nodded. He started flying the craft in a zigzagging pattern, doing a systematic search of the land around the rising terrain.

A fruitless hour later, the setting sun began to cut long shadows across their path, painting the stony villas in amber hues. In the darkening day, an ethereal blue-green light began to radiate from many of the area's homes.

Vaughn started shaking his head again.

Angela ignored him. She shifted her gaze to the west. The sun was slipping below the horizon. Amber sky faded to umber. Around them, aqua light streamed from thousands of windows. The entire scene looked otherworldly.

With every passing second, Angela could feel the lives of thousands passing through her fingers like grains of sand. On the verge of tears, she began to shake her head as well. "I don't think we're going to find it, not here anyway, and not in time to save anyone."

"Me neither. There's nothing that looks like an entrance." Vaughn paused and looked at her soberly. "You did your best, Angela. It was a good idea. I'm sorry we didn't find anything."

Unable to speak, she merely nodded.

Vaughn brought the craft to a stationary hover and released the controls. He pointed at a shortened and now amber strip on the craft's instrument panel. "I think that indicates our remaining power." He gestured at a nearby house. It had a huge yard. Light streaming from it illuminated its wide, flat yard. "I'm going to land there."

Angela felt the weight of the day's events pushing down on her. Looking at Vaughn, she could see her exhaustion, both physical and mental, reflected in his face. "Okay. Thank you for trying. I know this has been hard on you too."

Vaughn ran the back of his hand across his cheek, batting away a tear. Then he wrapped his arms around her.

This time, Angela let him.

They held each other tightly. Angela buried her face in Vaughn's chest. The stress flowed from her in hot tears. It was too much. No one should ever have to take on this responsibility. In that realization, she finally found a measure of solace.

They had done their best, had done everything they could in the face of an incomprehensible chain of events. They hadn't created this. It wasn't their fault.

After a moment, Vaughn kissed the top of her head. Then he released her and stepped back to the controls. He guided the sphere toward the illuminated yard. Apparently sensing Vaughn's intentions, the ship deployed a ring of lights to illuminate the landing zone further. As soon as the craft touched down, its doors slid open. Then the sphere's lights shifted to light up their path to the villa.

Exhausted beyond words, Angela and Vaughn walked on wobbly legs. A moment later, they stepped into the stone hut. Wordlessly, they walked into its kitchen. They found food similar to what they'd seen in the first one and began to eat.

Angela found a bread analog and another type of meat. They seemed to fit a craving that she hadn't realized she had. Deep in thought, she made a makeshift sandwich and was halfway through another before she noticed the way Vaughn was looking at her.

"What?"

He smiled. "I was just thinking that it's a good thing my hand wasn't anywhere near that maw."

Angela blinked and then looked down. Half the loaf was gone along with a sizable portion of the fishy meat.

She felt a blush reddening her cheeks. Guess I was hungry.

Vaughn smiled and held out a hand. "Enjoy. I have to go, uh ... Take care of some business. I'll be right back."

Angela took another bite and then nodded.

A few minutes later, while she was chewing on a taffy-like candy, Vaughn returned. Angela turned to see him smiling.

"Got something I'd like to show you."

She wiped a hand across her mouth. "What?"

He gestured for her to follow and then walked out of the kitchen.

Angela set the food down and went after him. As they entered a long hallway, she saw smoke issuing from an opening ahead. She also heard the sound of falling water coming through the apparent door.

Vaughn stepped through the opening. Seeing how the vapors wrapped around him, she realized it was actually steam.

She followed him into the room. It had a huge mirror. Angela glimpsed her reflected image beneath the line of condensation that fogged the mirror's upper reaches. Weary eyes peered from her dirt-streaked face. Apparently, their oceanic swim hadn't purged all of the grime that their trek through Hell had deposited in her hair.

Angela turned and saw the source of the noise. A huge bathtub that would've passed for a large hot tub back home sat at the room's center. Rising steam churned above its roiling surface.

Vaughn walked ahead of her and stuck his hand in it. "Perfect!"

Angela had her backpack and half her clothes off before she realized she had started to disrobe. A moment later her aching, filthy body slid into the churning water.

A long sigh escaped her lips. "Thank you, thank you, thank you."

Looking up, she realized she was alone. Vaughn had left the room silently.

Angela laid her head back. The last of the day's tears mixed with the warm water as it washed away the dirt and stress of the day.

Slipping deeper into her watery refuge, Angela lost herself in the small universe of steam.

∼

Angela woke with a start. She spent a panicked moment trying to remember where she was. It all seemed too unreal. Her sleep-addled mind balked, refusing to accept the reality of her fuzzy memories. Then the sensation that had woken her returned. Nausea passed through Angela like a rogue wave, doubling her over. She scrambled out of her and Vaughn's makeshift bed and ran back to the bathroom.

After finishing her business, she found a cloth and wiped her face. The piece of fabric had been covering a recessed button on the countertop. The tub's jets still churned its deep, steaming water. Tentatively, she reached for the switch. After a moment, she pressed it, and the jets fell silent.

Angela stepped into the hallway and then pulled up short. It wasn't a perfect silence. Another noise had risen to fill the void left by the quietened water. Tilting her head, she listened for a moment and then started to walk down the long hallway, following the sound toward its source.

A moment later, she stepped up to a closed door. The low, whistling sound seemed to be coming from the entire perimeter of the gray panel. A dark pad sat on the wall next to it.

Angela touched the small, black rectangle.

A muffled gasp escaped her as the door lurched, popping backward an inch out of its frame. The whistle turned into a howl as air rushed around the partially open panel and blew past her. Then the door slid sideways and disappeared into the adjacent wall, and the torrent of rushing wind subsided.

Aqua light from the hallway spilled into the gloomy corridor beyond the open door. Her shadow cut a long void across its floor.

Angela leaned through the opening. Craning her neck, she peered into the darkness.

A gust whipped her auburn hair around her face as the suddenly reversed wind rushed in from behind Angela. Then brilliant overhead lights flared to life, illuminating the hallway beyond the open door.

The gust subsided. Squinting, she stared into the corridor. The light had the same blue-green hue as had everything else in the strange city.

Then she realized that it wasn't a hallway but a long ramp that led downward.

Wait! They were at ground level. Did the ramp lead underground?

Turning to look toward the front of the villa, Angela tried to envision the exterior of the home. The land here had been relatively flat.

Nodding, Angela looked down the descending corridor. It had to be going below ground level. They hadn't gone up any stairs since entering the house.

Stepping cautiously through the opening, she started walking down the ramp. It looked like the passageway continued its downhill trek for at least a hundred feet. Beyond that, it appeared to level off.

Angela looked over her shoulder. She really should go and get Vaughn, but curiosity was driving her now.

Initially, she stepped cautiously. The floor looked shiny, almost wet. If it proved to be as slippery as it appeared, she would probably slide to the bottom and then never be able to make her way back up. Worsening the situation, the passageway had no handrails. Fortunately, the floor proved very sticky. Beneath her bare feet, it felt almost rubbery.

Walking faster, Angela soon emerged onto the lower level. It opened up on a small room, perhaps ten feet wide by twenty feet long. The ceiling of the rectangular space glowed softly. The long wall on her right appeared to be made from the same gray stone as had everything else. However, the one on her left bowed out along its entire length. It looked like the convex surface of a massive, ten-foot-thick pipe running horizontally down the whole stretch of the room.

A door-sized panel sat near the center third of the long tube. To either side of it, Angela saw odd symbols, each annotated with arrows that pointed either left or right.

One of the icons drew her attention.

"Could that be ...?"

She leaned in for a closer look.

Angela's eyes went wide. She stood bolt upright.

"I can't believe it!"

CHAPTER 22

Vaughn pulled on his pants and stood. He rubbed the sleep from his eyes and then looked at Angela. "What are we doing?"

"I'll tell you in a moment." She threw her backpack over her shoulder and then grabbed his and tossed it onto the bed next to Vaughn. "Bring everything. We won't be coming back."

He looked at the bag and then back at Angela, but she was already heading toward the door. On her way out, she glanced over her shoulder. "Hurry!"

Vaughn scrambled to stuff the last of his belongings into the bag and then ran after her. Emerging into the dim hallway, he turned left and started to head toward the front of the villa. Then Angela's voice came from behind him.

"No, this way!"

He turned to see her standing at the opposite end of the hall, backlit by a rectangle of soft, aqua light. It took him a moment to realize she was standing in an open doorway, one he hadn't seen earlier.

He reversed course and stepped up to Angela.

"What's that?"

Angela turned and walked through the door. She waved for him to follow. "Come on. You're not going to believe this."

Vaughn stared at her for a moment. Then he did a double take as he realized she was descending. "Oh shit. It's a ramp?"

"Yeah, now move it, Captain!"

Vaughn followed her down the sloping corridor. When they reached the bottom, he pulled up short. "That looks like a pipe."

Angela shook her head. "It's a tunnel. I think it's a Hyperloop, kinda like the one SpaceX is ... was building between Los Angeles and San Francisco."

Vaughn cocked an eyebrow. He pointed at the curved black surface of the large horizontal tube. "You get all that from this big sewer pipe?"

Angela frowned at him and shook her head. "I don't think they would put an underground room next to a sewer. This has to be for transportation." She pointed at the ceiling. "That's why there are no roads on the surface, no way to get around other than through the air. They have this underground system. I bet it's a network that links every home in the area."

Angela had moved to stand in front of the center of the convex wall. Next to her, Vaughn saw the outline of a potential hatch etched across the middle of the long pipe. Directly opposite the possible door, a two-foot-tall logo sat at the center of the long wall.

Vaughn studied the large starburst symbol. Then he turned back toward Angela and saw several additional icons adorning the curved surface to the left and right of the outlined hatch. Stepping closer, he studied the seam. "I don't know. That's one hell of a leap in logic."

"Not really." Angela pointed at a rectangular pad adjacent to the hatch. "That looks just like the ones that activate all the other doors in this place."

She was right. The pad and door configuration was the same as those they had seen in both the Corsican villa and in the house above them. But still ...

Vaughn shook his head. "I don't know. It could just as easily be a complex sewer system or trash disposal network."

Angela frowned and then gestured to the icons that adorned the curving wall to either side of the apparent door. "Look at these. I think they're symbols for stations that the Hyperloop services." Then she stepped to the right and gave Vaughn a meaningful look. She pointed at an icon in the middle of the group. "And check out that circular one."

Vaughn looked at it quizzically. It was a ring with a few short lines crossing it at right angles. He shook his head. "I don't think that's what you think it is. Sometimes a circle is just a circle."

Angela frowned. "No. See these segments? I think they represent the collider's detectors. The spacing is right." She leaned in and then pressed two fingers to the icon. It began to glow aqua green.

Vaughn's eyes widened, and he held out a hand. "What are you doing?! We don't know what that does!"

"I'm proving you wrong."

Vaughn cocked an eyebrow. "I sure hope you're right. If that hatch pops open and I drown in a sea of alien fish shit, I'll be really pissed."

Angela laughed and then shook her head. "It's a personal transportation system. Has to be. Like I said, it probably links all of the homes."

A low whistling sound began to fill the room. Vaughn leaned in close and realized it was coming from the paper-thin gap around the hatch. He reached out to touch the pad next to it.

Angela threw out her hand. "Wait!"

Vaughn yanked back his arm, but it was too late. His finger had already grazed the pad.

Nothing happened. He looked at Angela and held up his hands. "What?"

A loud clank rang out.

Both of them twitched and then stepped back.

The hatch popped an inch out of its jam. A howling blast of mist-filled air ringed the door.

The wind shoved Vaughn and Angela around as it raced past them, but then it died as the panel slid aside and the curved surface of a shiny beige cylinder scrolled across the now open hatch.

Vaughn stared at the apparent pod for a moment. "Son of a bitch. You were right."

Face flushed with anger, Angela spun toward him. "Dammit, Vaughn!" She took a deep breath and then shook her head. "If this thing *is* like the Hyperloop, there could have been vacuum on the other side of that door! We could have been sucked right the hell in!"

He shrugged. "Vaughn-proof. Besides, I thought you wanted to go to the collider." He pointed through the now open inner door. "Your coach awaits."

Angela glared at him for another moment and then finally relented. She turned to look in the pod.

Vaughn stepped closer and then poked his head into the vehicle. It looked like a short, stubby subway car with forward-facing seats lining both of its sides. Fortunately, the amphibians had been about the same size as a human. The two of them would have no problem fitting into the seats.

Brushing past him, Angela entered the pod and walked up to its front.

Stepping up next to her, Vaughn studied the console. "Those look similar to the controls in the flight pod."

Angela pointed excitedly at the panel's display. "Look! There's the symbol again. It has to be their collider."

Vaughn stared at it and twisted his face. "Maybe." He reached out to touch it but then hesitated.

"What are you waiting for?" Angela waved her hands impatiently. "You're the pilot. Push the damned button already."

He regarded her with his eyebrows raised. "Now who's the reactionary?" He took off his backpack and sat down.

"Come on, Vaughn. We need to hurry!"

He gave her a crooked grin and then nodded toward the seat beside him. "Unless you want to go keister over teakettle and get real familiar with that back wall, you may want to sit down first. If this is like the Hyperloop, it'll probably accelerate pretty quickly."

"Oh … yeah." Angela's face flushed. She peeled off her pack and dropped into the seat.

Vaughn toggled the control.

The outer hatch slid silently shut, followed shortly by the inner one.

Both of them lurched in their seats as a pair of white straps slid out from between Angela and Vaughn and then wrapped around them.

To Vaughn, the soft, wide harnesses felt like reinforced neoprene as they snugged down, sucking the two of them into the seats.

He heard a rush of air. His ears popped as the cabin pressurized. Then he was pressed back into his seat as the pod raced down the chute.

Suddenly, the G-forces let off and then reversed, pressing Vaughn into his harness as the pod slowed just as quickly as it had accelerated.

Everything fell silent.

Angela looked at Vaughn. "Did we break it?!"

He tried to shrug, but the straps made it impossible. "I don't know."

The harnesses released them and snaked out of sight, disappearing into the seats.

Vaughn and Angela exchanged confused glances.

Then the pod's door slid open.

Leaning back to see past Angela, Vaughn saw a room similar to the one they had left.

They both stood and stepped tentatively toward the hatch. Stopping at the door, they eased their heads through the opening and scanned left and right. The room looked similar to the last one except for the main symbol. Like the previous station, this one also had a large icon directly across from the pod exit.

Angela pointed at the three-foot-wide, segmented circle. "There it is!"

"Yeah!" Vaughn said, scoffing. "Congratulations, you're the first human to successfully navigate an alien subway." He shrugged. "We still don't know that there's a collider here. Maybe you just found the merry-go-round."

Angela frowned and then stepped past him onto the platform. She looked left and right, studying the opposing ends of the narrow station. Smiling triumphantly, she turned back to Vaughn. "Well then, Captain," she pointed left and then right, "why does this station have two exits, one going up and one going down?"

Vaughn joined her on the platform and looked in the indicated directions. To their right, a ramp led upward, just as it had at the first station. However, unlike that one, this platform had an additional down-sloping passageway at its far left end. It led deeper underground.

Angela had been right. This dimension's version of the supercollider likely lay somewhere beneath them. He recalled the points of her argument: the direction of the movement of the light wave that the two of them had seen when they'd arrived in this dimension, the segmented, circular icon, and now a ramp leading farther underground at the station marked with that symbol.

It all added up.

The wave had started here.

The epiphany left Vaughn feeling exposed and vulnerable. He looked at Angela and held a finger to his lips.

She shook her head, but when Angela spoke, she whispered. "Don't you think it's a little late to start worrying about stealth? They would've noticed us by now if they were going to."

"Well, Commander Brown, *I* noticed that *I'm* not the only one whispering." Vaughn paused and looked down the descending hallway. Then he extended a hand toward it, palm out. "But if it blows your skirt up, feel free to prance down there in your skivvies shouting dilly dilly!"

Grinning and shaking her head, Angela turned and walked toward the ramp. "I doubt those xenophobic robots would deign so low as to share a planet with even one living soul. In this dimension, I think the only thing that's come through the wormhole so far is the light wave."

Following after her, Vaughn frowned. "I don't know. They took out our missiles. There must have been someone around to do that."

Angela stopped. She turned and stared at Vaughn with a perplexed look. Then her eyes cleared. "No. They'd have to shut down the energy curtain before they could send physical items through the wormhole. As far as I know, the light never so much as flickered after it started to sweep across our dimension. Did you see any reports of it blinking or wavering?"

"No, but then how did they take out our missiles?"

Angela held out her hands. "I don't know for sure. Remote sensing, I guess. You should be able to send and receive multiple forms of energy through a wormhole simultaneously, but the passage of any kind of matter through it would distort or collapse the wave and alter any signals."

"So you're saying we're alone in here?"

She screwed up her face. "Probably, but no, I'm not about to go running down there in my skivvies." She turned from him and continued walking toward the left ramp. Angela glanced over her shoulder and gave Vaughn a knowing look. "And quit trying to picture it, Captain."

He held his hands up. "Don't know what you're talking about."

Angela scoffed and turned away from him. "Just try not to look like an incoming missile, and we should be—"

She stopped abruptly.

Vaughn narrowly avoided running over her.

"Why are you ...?" Looking over her shoulder, he saw an all too familiar sight. "Aw, crap."

Beyond Angela, bags and personal belongings cluttered the floor. Judging by the dispersal patterns of the dropped items, it appeared that several of the amphibians had been running up the ramp in a mad dash to escape the facility.

"Oh shit." Vaughn shook his head. "They must have known something was happening."

Angela nodded. "Looks like a few of them did, anyway."

Vaughn started to place an arm around her, but she shrugged it off. "I'm fine!"

They both winced as Angela's words echoed loudly.

They stood transfixed for a long moment, looking around expectantly.

Vaughn tilted his head, listening for any sign that someone had heard Angela.

No robots pounced.

A wedge of white light didn't sweep them from the planet.

Having not been beamed back to the trash can dimension or Hell, Vaughn gestured for Angela to continue. "Come on. Let's go see where this leads."

Several minutes later and multiple ramps deeper underground, they rounded yet another corner and then stopped, frozen in place, their conversation forgotten.

Ahead of them, a rather stout looking white panel blocked the entire passageway.

To Vaughn, it looked like a blast door. A window at its center flared and strobed brilliantly as radiant white light from an unseen source flooded the space beyond it.

Squinting, they both stared at the foot-wide window.

The harsh white light that streamed through it had the same hue as that of the energy curtain.

Angela started walking down the ramp.

"Where are you going?"

She didn't stop or look back. "This is it. This is what we came to find."

Vaughn took a deep breath and then sighed. He swallowed hard and then followed after her. "Penny ... pound, in for the whole ball of nine yards, or whatever."

They arrived at the small window and leaned in to peer through it.

The floor immediately beyond the blast door looked normal, having the same seamless matt-white finish they'd seen throughout the facility. However, a slanted curtain of white light obscured every-thing beyond twenty feet. It looked like a giant teepee formed by a fan of laser beams. The bright, inverted cone appeared to originate from a single point that sat above the window's line of sight.

Stooping, Vaughn craned his neck, looking upward, but still couldn't see the light's origination point.

Suddenly animated, Angela started pointing at something beyond the window. "I think that's a control panel."

Vaughn looked down, following the line of her finger. A pedestal with multiple icons and touch pads stood just a few feet to the right of the inverted light-cone's base.

He nodded. "Yeah, it is."

Backing up from the large door, Vaughn searched the walls to its left and right. He couldn't believe what he was contemplating. He spotted a touch pad. It looked just like the ones they had been using to open doors ever since they'd entered the first villa. He walked over to it and then looked back to Angela.

She nodded and then whispered urgently. "Push it!"

"Are you sure?"

Angela nodded again. "Hurry!"

In for a penny, my ass. This was the whole goddamned pension plan. Pressing his lips together, he placed two fingers and a thumb on the pad and pressed.

Nothing happened.

Then the floor started to vibrate.

An earsplitting squall pierced the silence as the massive blast door began to rise ponderously. The loud wail was coming from the room beyond.

The door had only risen a couple of feet when Angela dashed under it.

"Shit! Really?" Vaughn did a quick scan of their six. After verifying that no one was approaching from behind them, he too dove under the slowly rising door.

As he slid to a stop, Vaughn jumped to his feet. The noise rose to painful levels. The scent of ozone mixed unpleasantly with the fishy odor left by the room's previous occupants.

Vaughn looked around the cavernous room. It was as big as a concert hall. Massive pipes radiated out from a central point. It looked almost identical to the configuration of the Atlas Detector back in CERN.

Looking up, Vaughn could now see the source of the inverted cone of light.

Unfortunately, this facility shared another similarity with CERN's collider: a mercurial sphere hung in midair, suspended at the geometric center of the arrangement of pipes and conduits. Anchored to the silvery globe, the fan of white light angled down from it, making the whole thing look like an ethereal, forty-foot-tall Christmas tree topped by a three-foot-wide ball of liquid metal.

Vaughn looked down and saw that Angela had already crossed to the control pedestal. He jogged over and stood next to her. "What are they doing? Why's the light shooting down at the floor?"

Desperately scanning the panel, Angela didn't look up. "I told you! They're still sweeping them from this dimension!" She jabbed a finger at the fan of light. "That cone is going all the way through the planet. Somewhere on the far side of the world, probably around this dimension's version of Australia and New Zealand, there are still people inside that circle. The light hasn't swept across them yet."

Vaughn looked down at the base of the cone. Studying the area where it touched the floor, he realized that it was slowly shrinking. The movement was barely perceptible, but Angela was right. The circumference of the circle was constricting. Vaughn envisioned its opposite end sweeping across the far side of the planet, drawing an ever-tightening noose around the countless millions of people trapped within it.

He clutched at the side of the console. "We have to save them! What can I do to help?"

Angela shook her head. "I can't make heads or tails of this damned thing."

"Screw it!" Vaughn said as he pointed at the screen. "Start pushing buttons. We can't just stand here!"

Angela chewed her lip. Then she nodded and pressed a small red portion of the control panel's screen.

It had no effect. Nothing happened.

She started tapping other parts of the display.

Still, nothing changed.

A frustrated growl shot from Angela. She looked around frantically. Then she dashed away from the pedestal, looking in every direction.

Vaughn hurried after her. "What are you looking for?"

Angela shouted over her shoulder, her words barely perceptible above the light wave's eerie wail. "Find something we can use to hammer that thing!" She jabbed a finger toward the control pedestal. "Get an ax. Hell, anything to stop these bastards before they finish wiping out these people!"

Vaughn nodded and changed direction, heading toward a different part of the facility. Scanning the ground, he nodded. Impact engineering. He was completely onboard with that.

Vaughn spotted a massive tool propped against the far wall. It looked like a pipe wrench.

"I found something!"

He ran over to it. Grabbing the heavy steel tool, Vaughn slung it over his shoulder and then turned and ran back toward the pedestal.

Angela's voice rang out from the far side of the facility. "Me too!"

He saw her running with a stout length of metal pipe. Clutching it with both hands, Angela held the heavy, three-foot-long tube across her body like a warrior carrying a maul into battle.

Approaching the pedestal from opposite sides, they were each about twenty feet from the control panel and running toward it at top speed when two sections of the cone of light peeled away and swept toward them. The closest one engulfed Vaughn in an instant.

The light vanished, plunging him into total darkness. At the same time, the ground lurched under his feet, sending Vaughn sprawling headfirst through the air.

CHAPTER 23

In the sudden darkness, Vaughn smacked into the floor. The large wrench in his hands lurched, twisting his wrist painfully. The impact with the ground yanked the thing from his grasp.

He heard a muffled ring, and Angela cried out. Then her metal pipe rang again as it, too, clattered from her hands.

Vaughn slid to a stop facedown. Dust filled his mouth and sinuses. He rolled onto his back, coughing and spitting.

Something crunched beneath him.

It sounded like snapping twigs.

No, not twigs, bones.

"Ah, shit! Not again!"

Blinking the dust from his eyes, Vaughn stared up into Hell's muted star field. Like dark sentinels of the apocalypse, the region's surrounding mountain peaks peered down on him, their bases lost in the hazy atmosphere.

"Vaughn?!"

"Over—!" Vaughn coughed and spat out more dust. He sat up. "Over here! Are you okay?!" Looking west, he glimpsed the moon just as the last part of it dropped below the horizon.

He saw Angela scramble to her feet, her silhouette barely

discernible. He watched her profile as she looked around frantically. "We're back?"

Vaughn spat again. "Yeah, guess we forgot not to look too much like a goddamned missile."

"Oh no! No, no, no! I can't do this again, Vaughn!"

Standing, he walked to her side. Vaughn placed a hand on Angela's shoulder. "Come on, let's head for lower ground."

Her silhouette nodded sharply.

She took a step, and another bone crackled beneath her feet. A short cry escaped her lips.

Vaughn urged her forward with his hand. "Keep going."

Angela began to walk again, but a few steps later another bone snapped underfoot. This time a sharp keening burst from her. She bolted, running down the mountain of the dead. Angela cried out each time another bone snapped under her boots.

An indeterminate amount of time later, they found themselves standing amongst the cadaver-seeded dunes that ringed the perimeter of the macabre mountain.

Panting and coughing, Vaughn struggled to catch his breath, but Hell's low oxygen level made it difficult. He looked over and studied Angela's face. Now that his eyes had adjusted to the lower light level, he could see more than just her profile. In the wan light, he saw that her eyes were glistening with tears. She shook her head. "We couldn't save them."

Vaughn stepped over to Angela and wrapped his arms around her. "We did all we could." He left unsaid that they'd now pay the ultimate price for that effort.

She nodded and leaned into him.

In Hell's timeless night, they stood transfixed, holding each other. At some point, they pulled apart and stared into the sky.

Angela slowly shook her head. "Where are they?"

Vaughn pulled a rag from his backpack and used it to wipe the dust from Angela's face. "What do you mean? Who?"

"The amphibians."

Vaughn stopped wiping and tilted his head. "You're right. They ought to be here."

"Yeah, they should, but this place looks exactly the same." Angela looked at the hillside and hugged herself tightly. Turning from the image, she looked at Vaughn. "Even now, they're still being wiped from their world. Why aren't they here?"

Vaughn shook his head. "I don't know. They're probably being sent to some other part of Hell or maybe to a whole other dimension. Either way, I'm glad they're not here."

Angela gave him a confused look. "What do you mean?"

"To them, we'd be the aliens. If we weren't buried under the pile, if we survived our arrival, the Fish-Heads that had survived their own arrival would likely think we did this to them."

Nodding, Angela stared across the land. Vaughn thought he saw something change in her. Her eyes cleared. Then she gave a short nod. She took the cloth and wiped the muddy tears from her cheeks.

Vaughn looked away from Angela and pursed his lips. The threat of alien retaliation hadn't been his only reason for being thankful for the absence of the amphibs. His forehead furrowed as he gazed across the necrotic dunes. He thought the place smelled bad enough without adding a few million dead and dying Fish-Heads, but he kept that part to himself.

"Now what?"

Canting his head, Vaughn shrugged. "Good question."

They were back in Hell, permanently this time. They'd be here for the rest of their lives. Not that that was saying much.

No, he couldn't think that way. They had to stay busy, had to have a goal.

Vaughn pointed across the dusty plain. "Want to see if we can find that alien ship? It's getting cold. We can shelter there again."

Angela nodded and took his arm. "Lead the way, Captain."

Vaughn did a double take. Why was she suddenly so calm? Aside from freaking out about being back on top of the mounded dead, Angela seemed almost tranquil now, especially in comparison to their

219

last visit to the place. That time she'd been despondent. Hell, then as now, it had been all he could do to keep his shit too.

"What is it?"

Blinking, Vaughn shook his head and looked away. "N-Nothing." Stepping over the protruding finger of an elongated dune, he pointed ahead. "I think the alien ship is this way."

CHAPTER 24

Nearly a day later and now lying within the confines of their conjoined sleeping bags, Vaughn held a slumbering Angela. Staring at the eastern horizon, he watched the moon's dust-muted disc reappear as it rose above this dimension's denuded Alps. It looked exactly the same as it had the first time they'd ended up in this desiccated, dead land.

His migraine was back with a vengeance. The planet's dead atmosphere and its low oxygen level had resumed its assault on their minds and bodies early on during the cross-country trek of the previous night.

They had found the nukes and the derelict alien ship in the exact same location as last time, even without the glints of reflected sunlight to guide them. However, upon arriving, they'd found no evidence of their previous visit to the site. The area was free of their boot marks and discarded food wrappers.

Presently, Angela stirred in his embrace. She murmured something about her head hurting. Then her light snoring told him she'd fallen back into the safe harbor of sleep.

That was for the best. Her apathetic disposition had continued throughout the day and into their second night.

Vaughn didn't know if it was just a coping mechanism or if Angela had snapped. He'd opted not to dissuade her of this outlook. It wasn't exactly sunny, but it was decidedly more optimistic than had been her previous disposition. It almost seemed as if she were biding her time. In expectation of what, he didn't know.

As far as Vaughn could tell, they were well and truly screwed this time. They had been here going on twenty hours now. He'd quickly run out of busy work, and now he could feel his body dying.

Vaughn envied Angela. If only he could face their impending demise with her level of blissful ignorance.

Sometime later, he too began to drift off. Part of him wondered if they'd ever wake. Another part of him was starting not to care.

Maybe Angela was onto something.

Suddenly, bright light burned through Vaughn's closed lids.

The ground heaved. Then it liquified.

"What the—?!" He spasmed with a body-racking cough as salt water flooded into his open mouth.

Instantly waterlogged, the conjoined sleeping bags dragged Vaughn and Angela beneath the surface.

The brilliance of the light burning through his squeezed-shut lids began to subside.

Opening his eyes, Vaughn looked up to see a blurry image of receding, brightly lit waves.

As one, he and Angela fought to free themselves from the confines of their bags.

Vaughn's lungs burned as the urge to release another cough became almost irresistible. Remembering how this had gone last time, he grabbed Angela and pushed her through the bag's opening.

Again, she kicked his head on her way out.

No longer fighting with her for the exit, Vaughn quickly extricated himself from the cloth cocoon.

Reaching up, he kicked frantically for the surface.

Impossibly long seconds later, his head burst through the waves, emerging under a cloudy sky. The long-held cough exploded from his lips.

Treading water and spitting, he scanned the area.

"Angela!"

No reply.

"Angela!"

Then he glimpsed her between a set of waves. She was treading water several feet to his right, mutely staring into the sky and shaking her head.

"Hang on! I'm coming!"

A few moments later, Vaughn pulled up next to Angela. "What happened?"

"We're back, that's what."

"What?" Knitting his brows, Vaughn looked at the clouds and then back to Angela. "Back where?"

"We're back in the strait."

He looked around and glimpsed a familiar land mass. "Oh shit. You're right. It's the Strait of Bonifacio."

Angela nodded and then looked up again. Her choked words came out in a hoarse whisper as if she were talking to herself. "It *is* a loop. We're stuck in a goddamned loop."

CHAPTER 25

Waterlogged and coughing, Angela crawled onto the sandy beach. Beside her, Vaughn did the same.

They'd spent the better part of an hour working their way toward the shoreline. After retrieving their sleeping bags, they had alternated between swimming and resting while hanging onto their buoyant backpacks.

So far, they hadn't seen any activity, robotic or native. However, they'd picked this particular beach due to its hidden nature. Its short, arcing span sat at the base of a tall cliff. On this rock-strewn radius of sand, they'd be hidden from all but someone standing on the very precipice of the hundred-foot-tall cliff that overlooked it.

Finally climbing above the waves, she collapsed and rolled onto her back. As Angela fought to catch her breath, Vaughn crawled up and plopped down next to her, his chest rising and falling. "I don't understand ... What happened?" His head lolled toward her. "And what did you mean about it being a loop?"

"I think ... I think we're trapped in a loop, a time loop. And I caused it."

"Trapped like how?"

"It's a recurring cycle, and we're stuck in it."

Starting to catch his breath, Vaughn sat up partially and wedged an elbow under him. He ran fingers through his wet hair and then looked at her from under a cocked eyebrow. "Couldn't it just be the robots screwing with us?"

Spitting out the last of the salt water, Angela turned to Vaughn and shook her head. "I don't think so. When it comes to us, they seem pretty disinterested. They didn't even react to our presence until we were about to cut their connection. I can't see them expending that much energy just to screw with us." She shrugged. "I think it comes down to the same question as last time. Why would they free us from the prison that they'd already sent us to?"

Vaughn considered her logic for a moment. Finally, he nodded. "Okay, then. What makes you think you caused it?"

She pointed to his watch. "What time is it?"

He waved dismissively. "I don't need to look. It's been thirty-six hours again. We spent a little more than half a day in Fish-Head Land and a little less than a whole day in Hell, but that still doesn't tell me why you think you caused it."

Angela stood and looked around the small beach. She turned back to Vaughn. "I think that when we tried to overload the wormhole in our Geneva, it somehow created a … I don't know … not just a time loop …" She paused and then nodded. "Not just a time loop but an inter-dimensional or trans-dimensional loop. Whatever you want to call it, that's what is resetting us to other dimensions." She began to pace as she worked through the logic. Thinking out loud, she continued. "It makes sense. I mean, we definitely created a loop. I don't think it's the robots doing this. I think that every time it resets, they no longer know we exist."

Vaughn nodded. "Makes sense. Guess that's why the robots don't know we're there. We're jumping thirty-six hours back in time, showing up in another dimension a day and a half before they ever knew we existed."

"Exactly!"

Vaughn glanced at his arm and then looked at her. "It's not a full reset, though." He showed her a scratch on his forearm. "I got this during our first trip through Hell." He pointed to a green stain on his pant leg. "And I got that from a plant outside of that first villa on Corsica."

"Yeah, so?"

"That means we're not in a true time loop, at least not like the one Bill Murray's character experienced in Groundhog Day. His injuries didn't follow him. Hell, he even died a few times, but when the day reset, so did he." He pointed at her and then at himself. "We're not."

Studying a cut on her arm, Angela nodded. She'd gotten it during one of their trips through Corsica. "Shit, you're right. If we break a leg or die, it's all over. No reset, no get-out-of-jail-free card." Lowering her arm, she looked out over the waves. "We have to find a way out of this, or eventually it *will* kill us."

Through her peripheral vision, Angela saw Vaughn nod as he too shifted his gaze to stare across the water. He sat up and pointed toward the strait. "Why do we keep coming back here?"

"I've been working on a theory. I think it's tied to the amount of power we fed into the wormhole."

Vaughn screwed up his face. "How would that have anything to do with it?"

"Wormholes connect two points in space, right?"

"If you say so. You're the physicist."

Angela waved a hand. "Yes, I say so. They connect two points in space, but what a lot of people don't realize is that they also connect two points in time. Even when wormholes were just a theoretical construct, we believed they also bridged time itself."

"Why?"

"It's really complex. The problem ties into relativity and how time is a variable portion of the universe's fabric."

"Break it down for me Barney-style, then."

Angela blinked. "Huh?"

Vaughn's eye gleamed and he smiled. "Nothing. Just give me the simple explanation."

She looked up at the sky and tried to think of an example. Then she nodded. "Say you were standing outside of a wormhole that connects to a point a couple of hundred thousand miles away. On the far side of that hole, you have a telescope. You step through the wormhole, and instantly you move to its far end. If you then used the telescope to look back toward the start point, you'd see yourself stepping into the opposite end of the wormhole a little more than a second later because that's how long it takes light to travel the distance."

"Isn't that just a speed of light restriction?"

"Actually, it's a space-time thing. Bottom line: information in the form of you traveled faster than light, so effect preceded cause."

Vaughn's eyes were glazing over.

Angela shook her head. "You're the one that wanted it Barnet-style."

"Barney."

"Whatever. Anyway, in a greatly oversimplified way, effect preceding cause ties into the time travel aspect of wormholes."

"Okay, so what does all that have to do with how much power you pumped into the damned thing?"

"I think that the wormhole somehow links to every point in time touched by its existence just like it links to various dimensions."

Angela's eyes widened as an incredible epiphany slammed home. "That's it!"

Vaughn sat bolt upright and looked around. "What's it?"

"That's our out!" She threw her hands up. "That's how we fix this!"

Vaughn stopped searching the horizon and looked at her. "How in the hell do we fix any of this, Angela?"

She started pacing up and down the rocky beach again. "If I'm right about this, we might be able to reset … *everything*!" Her heart raced as if trying to keep pace with the possibilities that were running through her mind.

She stopped walking and turned toward Vaughn. "We could reset the entire timeline!"

He shook his head. "Wait, what? We can reset it? We can break the loop?!"

Angela began to shake her head but then nodded. "Yes, but much more than that. If I'm right, then the same mechanism that sent us back this far could be used to send us to any point in the lifespan of the wormhole!"

"What mechanism?"

Angela sighed. "Don't you see? It was the power! I didn't pump enough of it into the wormhole last time, so it just sent us back here." She gestured excitedly toward the strait. "To this point in the wormhole's lifespan."

Vaughn stared at the sky for maddeningly long moments as he mulled over her words. Then he looked at her and tilted his head. "Let me see if I got this right."

Angela tried and failed to resist the urge to roll her eyes.

Seeing her reaction, Vaughn held up a hand. "Sorry, but I'm just a helicopter pilot, and you made some pretty big jumps there, so bear with me."

Angela pressed her lips together, but she waved her hand in a go-ahead gesture.

Vaughn nodded. "So you're saying that the power you dumped into the wormhole back in CERN created a ... a time loop that pushes us back thirty-six hours every day and a half and that the distance the loop pushes us back is tied to the amount of power that you put into the wormhole?"

Angela nodded. "Yes, yes! We landed at a point in the wormhole's lifespan because I didn't use enough power to reach its far end."

Vaughn's face twisted. "Why does the power level matter?"

Sighing impatiently, Angela threw her hands up. "Don't you see? If I had pumped in more power, we might have been sent all the way back to the beginning of the singularity's life, but since we fell short, we don't have an anchor, so we keep dropping into parallel dimensions, not our own. Eventually, we will return to our version of Earth, and when we do, I can pump all of the power that was coming through the wormhole back into it." She paused and gave him a meaningful look. "Listen to me, Vaughn! This is the important part, the part that changes everything. When I do that, we'll be sent back to the point in time when the robots created the wormhole, maybe farther, and because that is the anchoring end of the connection, we should stay in our own dimension."

She watched as realization dawned on Vaughn's face. Then a look of fragile hope took root there. "And that ...?" He swallowed. "That would bring ... everybody back?"

Angela smiled and nodded. "Yes! We would return to the beginning, to a point in time when they were all still alive. Every person, every animal ... every living being will return, all of them back, all of them alive!"

CHAPTER 26

"Holy crap!" Vaughn jumped to his feet. He grabbed his backpack and slung it over a shoulder.

His mind raced with the possibilities of Angela's proclamation.

Thoughts of what this could mean for his mother and Mark shot to the front.

Then he realized it was so much bigger than that.

A whole world bigger.

"Where are you going?"

"Huh?"

"I asked where you're going."

Vaughn stopped walking and looked up from his feet.

Glancing around, he saw that he'd walked halfway up the beach. Looking back to Angela, he smiled self-consciously. "Not a clue."

Still holding his backpack, Vaughn turned. Facing the ocean, he stared across the waves. "I can't believe it." He looked at Angela. "Are you sure we can do it? Go back in time ... reset everything?"

"I think so. It fits with what's been happening and with what science has speculated about the nature of both singularities and wormholes."

As Angela spoke, Vaughn started walking in a wide circle around her. His arcing path took him from the water's edge below Angela to the dry sand up the beach from her.

"This is ...!" He searched for the right words and failed. Unable to stop his manic circling, he began to walk across his previous steps, cutting a circular groove in the sand with Angela at its center. "We can save the whole world!" Even as he said the words, Vaughn couldn't accept the weight of the statement. It seemed unreal, but still, his heart pounded in his ears, and he started breathing heavily.

He dropped the bag and then stopped his circuitous pacing as he reached the water's edge again. Standing with his fingers laced across the top of his head, Vaughn stared out to sea. Inch-high waves lapped at his toes.

Everything they'd lost—all that *the world* had lost—could be returned? He had never permitted himself that hope, hadn't even considered it, but now ...

The horizon wavered as tears clouded his vision.

Vaughn took a deep breath and then blinked his eyes clear.

Not wanting Angela to see his face, he continued to look across the water as he spoke. "Is there anything we can do to expedite things?"

"No. Unfortunately, we'll have to wait until the loop takes us back to our home dimension."

Vaughn's face darkened. Then he slowly shook his head. He should've known that her theory was too good to be true. Blinking the last of the moisture from his eyes, he dropped his arms and turned to face Angela. As he looked at her, he could feel a muscle twitching in his clenched jaw.

"Come on, Angela! What makes you think we will ever get back to our Earth? Didn't you say there could be thousands of dimensions?" His frustration boiled over. "We could be stuck in this loop for years! Shit! We probably won't live long enough to see home!"

Angela's eyes flared. "No, Vaughn! I told you, I think we will return. We'll—"

"Sure we will!" he said acidly, cutting her off. "After what, a couple of years stuck in this loop? Lot of good it'll do us!"

Angela started to say something, but Vaughn held up a hand.

"You've seen what these loops are doing to us. Our bodies aren't resetting, not physically anyway. Even if we somehow manage to survive long enough to reach our Earth, we'll be too malnourished and weak to make our way back into the collider."

"Damn you, Vaughn!" Angela squared on him, nostrils flaring. "If you'd shut up and listen for a moment, I'll tell you why that's not going to happen!"

Vaughn's head rocked back as if slapped. His teeth clicked as his mouth shut. Feeling his cheeks warm, he looked around, suddenly too ashamed to look her in the eye.

Blinking, Vaughn stepped back from Angela and held up his hands. He took a deep breath and then sighed. "Sorry. I ..."

She shook her head. "Just listen."

Finally managing to look her in the eyes, he nodded.

Angela sighed and then continued. "Remember how I said the robots are crossing into dimensions by latching onto the micro black holes created by powerful colliders?"

"Yeah. You said that as soon as they detect one, they lock onto it and then open up the wormhole. We've seen what happens after that."

"Exactly, and because of that, I think these robots are limited to invading versions of Earth where the native inhabitants have advanced enough to create supercollider technology."

Vaughn frowned. "We've been over that."

"Yes, but now we're trapped in a loop that's hopping between dimensions, and you were right. There probably are thousands of dimensions." Seeing his reaction, she held up a hand. "But the vast majority of them won't be accessible to our loop."

Vaughn tilted his head. "Why not?"

"We now know of two worlds that the robots have invaded in the span of a few months, ours and the amphibians. The first world, the one with the robot-infested Corsican nature park, must have been invaded long ago, but both our world and the amphibians' were hit in the same year."

"Yeah, it sucks, but what's your point?"

"Vaughn, don't you see? That's two worlds that reached the same level of collider technology within a few months of each other."

Then Vaughn did see. His heart sank as he finally understood Angela's point. Considering the length of Earth's geologic timeline, the fact that two societies reached that level of technological advancement at virtually the same time pointed to thousands of dimensions, probably a lot more than that.

"That's why I said you were right about the number of dimensions."

He felt the muscle twitching in his jaw again. "Angela, that's worse, not better."

She nodded. "Yes, that part is, but I still think we'll come full circle sooner rather than later."

Vaughn looked up. In spite of the nagging doubts, he felt hope trying to take root again. He raised his eyebrows. "How? ... Why?"

Angela pointed down. "The loop is depositing us here because it's along the path we traveled and this is as far back as the overload I generated could send us."

"Right." Vaughn nodded. "Because the wormhole connects to all dimensions. But isn't that the problem? That's why we'll have to go through thousands of them to get back home."

Angela shook her head. "No. The wormhole doesn't connect to *all* dimensions, only to the ones that have been affected by it, and more importantly, only to versions where the collider is in roughly the same geographic area."

Vaughn looked up from the sand, his eyes widening. "You're saying we'll only cycle through dimensions they've already invaded?"

Angela nodded. "And only the ones where the collider is close enough geographically for cross-dimensional interaction. That's why the collider has been in roughly the same position in each version."

"Oh." Vaughn nodded appreciably. "And that's why you were so sure there had to be a collider in Fish-Head Geneva."

"Actually, I wasn't sure. I was just beginning to think we were stuck in a loop. My biggest fear was that I was wrong about the proximity thing. If so, we could have had many more dimensions standing between us and home."

Vaughn smiled. "Yeah, like a few thousand, but I think you're right. It all makes sense."

Angela held a finger to the back of her ear. "I'm sorry. What was that?"

"You're right. I'm wrong. And yes, I've learned my lesson."

She smiled back at him. "Good. Just remember that next time."

Vaughn smirked. "Sorry I was such an ass."

"It's okay, Captain." She sighed and looked around. "We've been through one hell of an emotional roller coaster."

Vaughn glanced at the cliff and then tilted his head. "Any idea how many dimensions we'll have to pass through to find ours?"

Angela blew a curly strand of damp hair from her eyes and then frowned. "No, just that it'll be a lot less than it might have been."

Vaughn felt the worry trying to return, but this time he managed to push out the thoughts.

He nodded. "Okay, what's the plan when we get back to our home dimension?"

Angela pointed toward the strait. "We'll probably end up back here, so we'll have to get to the collider before the thirty-six hours end. Otherwise ..."

"Otherwise, we'll start it all over again," Vaughn finished for her.

"Yeah, pretty much. Then there's the whole thing about sneaking back into a city of killer robots, all while dodging flying supertankers and not getting dumped into a stadium-sized vat of molten metal."

Vaughn scoffed and then grinned. "Can of corn! Easy-peasy!"

They both laughed at that.

As he started to mull over the possibilities, Vaughn resumed his circular pacing. He glanced at Angela and waved dismissively. "When we've done all that easy stuff, and you supercharge the wormhole, we'll be sent back to the beginning?"

Angela nodded.

Vaughn gave her a meaningful look. "Where do *we* end up? Will we still be together?"

He widened his arc, leaving the circular groove he'd cut into the sand. Then he heard a hollow echo reverberate from beneath him.

Vaughn stopped and looked down. "What the—?"

Suddenly, the ground fell out from under him.

It hadn't been thirty-six hours yet!

Why was he falling?!

The thoughts had barely formed when Vaughn plunged into water. Waist-deep water.

About a half-yard of loose sand dumped on top of his head, nearly pushing him below the shallow water.

The onslaught of earth subsided, and Vaughn rose to a crouched position, an arm held overhead to ward off further sandy barrages.

Blinking, he tried to scan the area around him. Instead of being assaulted by blindingly bright light, his eyes had a hard time making out his now dark surroundings.

A contrast of dusty light and glistening shadows cut through the middle of his suddenly shrunken universe.

One of the shadows reached out for him.

Vaughn screamed and jumped about a foot off the ground.

Sending up a frenetic spray, he backpedaled and then fell, landing hard on his ass in the shallow water.

"Vaughn?!"

He looked up to see Angela peering down from an opening, her head cutting a notch into the mote-filled shaft of light that streamed through it.

Angela shifted position, causing her shadow to move again. She peered down at him with wide eyes. "Oh my goodness! Are you okay?!"

From the floor of his watery cell, Vaughn squinted and blinked against the combined assault of trickling sand and contrasting light.

"I think—" A cough cut off his words, launching a spray of salty sand into the bright beam. He waved it away and then looked up again. "I think so."

"Are you sure?"

Vaughn glanced down and then back up at Angela. He shrugged.

"Guess that depends on your definition of okay. I mean, none of my limbs are pointing in the wrong direction." Raising a hand, he shielded his eyes against the glare. His forehead furrowed and he glanced heavenward. "But then again, it looks like I've dropped into a large animal's lair."

Placing the hand against his forehead, Vaughn craned his neck and peered nervously into the murky shadows of his subterranean prison. He lowered his voice. "And it suddenly occurs to me ... we don't know for sure that we're alone in this world."

CHAPTER 27

V aughn inched his way across the watery room, wincing as the noise of his movement echoed off the rock walls of the enclosure.

As he passed out of the column of light streaming through the hole he'd fallen through, Vaughn found he could see much better. Reflected light glistened from every surface. Shiny, floor-to-ceiling tubes filled much of the space. Then he noticed gaps where the upper and lower halves didn't quite meet in the middle.

Vaughn leaned in close to inspect the oddly shaped columns and then nearly shit himself as Angela's voice cracked the silence.

"Where are you going?!"

"Geez, woman!" he whispered harshly. "Why don't you just ring the goddamned dinner bell?"

"Oh shit ... sorry."

"Now she whispers," Vaughn grumbled as he shook his head.

"What do you see?"

He looked around. The space was an odd mix. Six smooth walls surrounded him. Through the glistening stony columns, he could just make out the outline of a hatch on one wall of the hexagon.

"It's a room, but I don't think anybody's been here in a long time."

"Why?"

"There are stalactites and stalagmites all over the place."

Vaughn's eyes narrowed as he studied an angular construct that was protruding from one of the stone columns. "There's something that looks like it might have been a shelf or a desk, but it's partially encased in limestone."

Seeing the shiny surface of the rock formation flowing over the remnants of an apparent computer display, Vaughn shook his head. He stood upright from his crouched position and raised his voice. "No, nobody's been in here for a long, long time."

"Well, then, come on out of there."

Glancing up at Angela, Vaughn frowned and hoisted an eyebrow. "Sure! Just lower that rope down to me."

"Oh …! Well, shit."

"Exactly. Next time we're in Home Depot, remind me to pick up a spool of it."

"You don't have to be such a smart ass about it."

The light level in the room increased.

Vaughn looked up again. Angela's head no longer hung over the opening.

"Where'd you go?!" His words echoed loudly in the small room.

Angela's voice came to him weak and fading. "I'm going to see if I can find a vine in the local *Home Depot.*"

"What?!"

"In the jungle. I'll be right back."

Vaughn barely heard the last part.

"Wait!"

It was no good. She was gone, the only remaining sound the constant drip, drip, drip of water falling from the few stalactites that had yet to join their stalagmite mates.

Vaughn looked around and then closed his eyes. "Wonderful …" He sure as hell hoped there weren't any robots waiting for her up there. He took a deep breath and then released it in an echoing whistle.

Looking around, Vaughn spotted the outline of the room's

apparent door. "Hmm. Where do you lead?"

He splashed through the thigh-deep water. As he neared the door, he tried to step between a couple of the limestone columns.

In spite of all the weight he'd lost since the Disappearance, Vaughn couldn't squeeze through. He turned, looking for another route but found none.

He waded back toward the center of the room and then tripped over something. It sent him sprawling headlong into the water. Fortunately, he managed to arrest his forward momentum before injuring more than his pride.

His hand brushed against something on the floor as he righted himself.

Vaughn probed around until he found it again. It was a thin slab of rock, probably from the hole he'd punched in the room's ceiling.

His probing fingers landed on a hard, smooth surface.

Something was pinned beneath the rock slab.

His tongue protruded from the corner of his mouth, and a distant look took over his features as he ran his fingers down the length of the pinned item. The portions that protruded from beneath the slab felt like segmented metal. It had multiple four-inch spans interrupted by apparent knobby joints.

Vaughn finally managed to wedge two fingers beneath one of the segments. He pulled, and it reluctantly slid out from under the rock. Clutched in his hand, the articulated metal structure emerged from the water. Oxidation had dulled the finish of the six-foot-long device, giving it a greenish hue. Apart from a series of shallow, parallel gouges, the construct appeared intact.

The thing looked like a high-tech mechanical toy snake. If he held it in one orientation, it would slump, but if he turned it ninety degrees, it became rigid and undulated just like the multi-hinged toy snakes of his youth.

Holding the piece at eye level, Vaughn studied its full length. Turning it around, he inspected its opposite end. The thing was tapered, fat at one end, narrow at the other. The entire span was hollow as if made to fit over something.

He studied its narrow end. It had a socket that appeared to accommodate attachments. Pulling it closer, Vaughn spotted a small button set into the inner edge of the device's tapered end. He wormed his index finger through a gap in the side of its final segment and pushed the button. There was a metallic click, and then the whole thing went rigid.

Vaughn tried rolling it ninety degrees as he'd done earlier. However, unlike last time, the six-foot-long device didn't slump. Instead, it remained unyielding. To Vaughn, it now looked like a long, cone-shaped baseball bat.

Feeling its newly acquired strength, he eyed the columns that were blocking him from the exit.

Vaughn shrugged. "Worth a try."

He trudged through the water and then levered the narrow end of the device between two of the limestone pillars. The thinner of the two quickly surrendered to the leverage afforded by the mechanical snake's six-foot length.

A crack formed in its middle. Then the center third of the column's floor-to-ceiling span fell away, dropping into the water with a tremendous splash and striking the floor beneath with a loud thunk.

Now Vaughn found he could squeeze between the remnants. He stepped up to the door, searching for a knob or a latch. He found none. The panel was recessed about an inch into the wall. Unlike those in the last world, this door had no touch pad next to it. Not that he expected any of the ancient electronics of this place to work still.

Vaughn glanced back toward the opening in the ceiling.

"Angela!"

No reply.

What was taking her so long?

Setting his jaw, Vaughn shook his head and turned back to the door. "Need to get the hell out of here."

He knocked on the panel with the fat end of his makeshift club. A metallic ping rang out. The door sounded thin. He gave the long construct in his hands an appraising glance and then shrugged.

"Screw it."

He stepped back. Holding the narrow end of the device, Vaughn swung the thing like a six-foot-long baseball bat. In the middle of the swing, the end of the club clipped a stalagmite. The device struck the door ineffectually.

"Shit!"

Vaughn repositioned himself. After verifying his clearance, he took another swing. This time, he landed a blow that would have jacked a baseball out of the park.

The end of the makeshift club struck the door with significantly more force. A satisfying bark rang out from the point of impact.

Suddenly, a vertical crack zipped down the entire length of the panel, but before Vaughn could celebrate his success, water began to spew from the full span of the fissure. Then the door started to bow inward as it began to yield to the pressure of the water on its far side.

Vaughn's eyes went round. "Oh crap!"

He lunged forward and jammed his hands against the door, one on each side of the vertical crack. He grunted as he leaned into it with all his weight.

A loud groan issued from the door.

Then it blew open.

A massive wave of water blasted through the opening and washed Vaughn across the room, barreling him right through one of the limestone pillars. The stone column snapped and vanished beneath the rising torrent.

The water washed over Vaughn's head, the torrential currents pulling him down. He flipped end over end like a rag doll caught in a clothes dryer.

Light and shadow swirled around him.

His lungs burned with the need for air.

The swirling currents began to ebb.

Unable to tell up from down, Vaughn frantically searched the now murky water, trying to find the light of the opening in the ceiling.

Vaughn squeezed his lips together as the fire in his chest threatened to override his self-control.

One portion of his universe appeared brighter than the rest.

He swam toward it, arms and legs flailing.

His face broke the surface, and he drew in a lungful of blessed air.

The water was still swirling, carrying him around in a slow arc. Its level had risen significantly. The hole in the ceiling was now only a foot above him.

The twisting current carried him under the opening just as a long, fat tree branch slid down from above.

Vaughn reached for it, but his hand bounced off the branch before he could grab the thing.

"Shit!"

As the circling water took him around the room, Vaughn spotted Angela through the opening.

Holding the far end of the long limb, she shoved it toward him.

Kicking his feet, he thrust his arms forward and finally managed to grab the branch.

"Got it!"

The current tried to pull him away from the opening.

Tendons showed in Angela's skinny arms as she tried to pull him toward it.

As he neared the opening, Vaughn released one hand and grabbed at the stone ledge. Finally catching a break, he managed to snag it on the first attempt. Fortunately, it felt sturdy, solid.

He released the branch and threw his arm up through the opening. Kicking as hard as he could, Vaughn levered his elbow onto the top of the sandy ledge.

He began to slip backward.

Then Angela was there. She grabbed the back of his shirt and pulled, grunting with exertion.

With her support, Vaughn extended his other arm through the opening and planted that elbow onto the rock as well.

Finally, he rose high enough to get a knee over the edge.

Then he was out.

They collapsed onto the sand, rolling onto their backs and breathing heavily.

A few moments later, Angela's head lolled toward him. "What the hell did you do?"

"I was trying to open the door. Guess the next room was flooded."

Angela shook her head. "You did a whole lot more than open a door."

Finally starting to catch his breath, Vaughn rolled his head toward Angela. "What are you talking about?"

Her forehead creased. "You don't know." It was a statement, not a question.

She sat up and pointed toward the water. "Look."

Vaughn raised himself to a seated position and then froze.

Ten feet from them, the beach just ... ended. They had been a good fifty feet from the water's edge. Now undulating waves of deep water lapped at a zigzagging rocky ledge. The bottom forty feet of the beach had fallen into the ocean.

Breaking his trance, Vaughn shook his head. "Where did the beach go?"

"You tell me. I was running back here with this tree branch when the entire beach collapsed." Sweeping her arm from left to right, Angela gestured at the full width of the short span of arcing waterfront. "It all collapsed at the same time! Water and sand shot into the air like a two hundred-foot-wide geyser."

Angela shook her head. She looked at him, her eyes glistening with tears. Then she threw her arms around Vaughn and hugged him tightly.

"I thought I'd lost you!"

The breath of her muffled words warmed the chilled skin of his neck.

Vaughn felt a lump form in his throat as he realized the terror and loneliness, however short-lived, that the sight must have engendered within Angela.

After a moment, she released him and dabbed her eyes.

Vaughn was glad for the dripping water that prevented him from having to do the same.

Angela gestured at the dark opening by their feet. "I couldn't believe it when I saw you swirling around in there. I've never been so relieved in my life."

"Th-That—" Vaughn coughed and then smiled self-consciously as he glanced sidelong at her. "That makes two of us."

Angela kissed him passionately.

Vaughn returned it, lacing his fingers through her hair and pressing his lips to hers. When it ended, they sat in comfortable silence, their foreheads pressed together.

Sometime later, they stood and then cautiously walked toward the newly formed ledge, checking the stability of the ground with each step. Finally, they reached the lip and stood side-by-side looking out over the water.

As Vaughn had seen earlier, the drop-off etched a jagged line across the beach. However, now he saw that the small precipice followed a precise pattern. Beyond the drop-off, rising and falling waters revealed broken walls that followed the same, six-sided form as had Vaughn's temporary prison. He looked left and right and saw that the pattern continued to the end of the short stretch of beach. It looked as if a parking lot-sized honeycomb had broken off the edge of the island.

Partially submerged, tilting slabs littered the scene. Vaughn pointed at them. "Those panels must have been the ceilings."

"Why did it all collapse?"

He shrugged. "I think the whole thing had been on the brink of it for a long time. All I did was open a door. Guess the sudden pressure change tripped a cascading collapse." He shook his head slowly. "But what were these? The whole thing looks like a giant beehive."

Angela shook her head as well. "No idea. Living quarters maybe."

"I guess, but why would someone build something like that below the waterline?"

"You said it looked like they'd been empty for a long time." She pursed her lips. "Might not have been below it when they were built. These could've been oceanside villas."

Scoffing, Vaughn gestured at the tightly packed rooms. "Who would want to live like that? Looks more like a prison than a resort."

"Could be that too. Kind of hard to tell now."

Angela paused and then kneeled on the top of the ledge and gazed down into the water. After a moment she frowned.

"What do you see?"

"Nothing. That's the problem. I don't see any fish, not even a minnow."

"You think they wiped this world, too?"

Angela looked up and nodded. "Yeah, we already knew the robots had to have visited this dimension. Otherwise, the wormhole wouldn't have dropped us here." She nodded toward the complex. "I already thought that they'd wiped this world before all this. When we were swimming up to the beach, I didn't see barnacles or coral on any of the rocks in the surf."

"Yeah, I noticed the same thing, but if the robots did wipe out this world, it must've been a long time ago." He pointed at a broken piece of limestone. Still attached to a now inverted section of ceiling, the pillar jutted into the sky. "Those stalactites take thousands and thousands of years to get that long."

Angela nodded. "Yeah, I doubt those columns were part of the original design of the place."

"Exactly! So where *are* the robots? Why aren't they crawling all over this island?"

"Maybe they've set this area aside. Could be a park like the one we were in the first time they sent us to Hell."

Vaughn cast a wary overhead glance. Angela did the same. Thankfully, there was still no sign of the egg-shaped craft that had chased them across the water and beamed them to that trash world.

After a moment, he nodded and pointed at the large branch. "Where did you get that?"

She pointed toward the trees at the top of the nearby cliff. "I found it up there."

"See any evidence of the robots?"

"No, but I didn't exactly have time to look around. Besides, it's pretty dense up there."

Nodding, Vaughn stared up the cliff. The foliage of this dimension of Corsica appeared to be much lusher than the ones they had already visited. Instead of the squat scrub trees that had dotted the arid landscape of those previous iterations, a verdant jungle covered this apparently tropical version of the island.

"Let's go check it out now. Maybe we'll find something up there."

Angela affixed Vaughn with a sober stare. "Okay, but let's make sure nothing finds us. I can't handle another trip across that mountain of the dead."

Vaughn nodded. "Noted. Should we run into any more no-necks, we'll try not to look like incoming missiles."

Angela rolled her eyes. "How about we just try not to be seen at all."

Smirking, Vaughn extended a hand toward the base of the cliff. "Lead the way, Commander Brown."

He spent the next couple of minutes following Angela up the steep slope. Fortunately, a network of ledges cut diagonal paths across the face of the escarpment. They followed a zigzagging path that made easy work of the climb.

As they neared the top, Vaughn smelled a familiar aroma. A light, offshore breeze carried the sweet scent of vegetation across them as it headed out to sea.

After reaching the top and verifying that no robots lay in wait—at least not in the immediate area—they turned and looked toward the big island to their south.

Across the strait's indigo waters, Sardinia shimmered in lush greens. Scattered clouds hung in the afternoon's azure sky, dotting the ocean and land with their inky shadows.

Angela suddenly latched onto his arm.

Vaughn turned, half expecting to see a troop of robots or the flying egg.

He released the breath he'd held and relaxed as he saw that nothing around them had changed, but his relief was short-lived. Angela's face had suddenly gone ash white.

"What?! What's wrong?"

Wordlessly, she pointed at the water.

Looking down, Vaughn followed the line of her gesture and then understood as he felt his own body respond to the horrible truth revealed by this new, higher vantage point. If he hadn't been focused on Sardinia, he would have seen it as well.

Visible through the crystal-clear water that surrounded Corsica, Vaughn could now see that the structures they'd discovered along the shoreline were just the outskirts of what appeared to be a vast undersea metropolis.

Through the turquoise water, he saw the outlines of multiple structures. Many of them had the same hexagonal shape as the much smaller habitats along the shore. He also glimpsed long, underwater tubes. Sections of them appeared to have broken away, but enough of the tubes remained that he could still see the winding path they took through the city.

Angela found her voice first. Emotion choked her words. "They killed them … all of them. Another whole world wiped out by those bastard robots or whoever controls them."

Vaughn had been nodding, but then something occurred to him. "I don't think there is anyone else controlling them."

"Why not?"

He pointed at the city. "Whatever these people were, I doubt they ever smelted iron."

"If the robots found them, they must have created a collider."

Vaughn rocked his head. "Maybe, but they could've gone about it in a different way than we did, might have found another way to mash atoms or whatever. My point is, there wasn't a ready supply of steel lying here for the robots to use. They didn't come here for that." He cast a hand toward the scene. "I think there's another reason that the Necks did this."

"If not for someone else, then why?"

"For the same reason the Cylons wanted to wipe out humanity."

"Cylons?"

Vaughn shook his head. "Battlestar Galactica?"

"Never heard of it."

Vaughn tried to think of another example. Then he nodded. "Skynet!"

Angela gave him a blank stare.

"You know, the computer intelligence that tried to wipe out humanity in the Terminator movies."

"Never saw Terminator. Wait, movies? There was more than one?"

Vaughn's shoulders slumped. He stared at her, resisting the urge to roll his eyes. "You really led a sheltered life."

Angela crossed her arms and then pointed a thumb at her chest. "Multiple PhDs. What's your excuse?"

He took a deep breath and then sighed. "It comes down to one thing."

"What's that?"

"Do unto others before they can do unto you."

"What does that even mean?"

"I think it means that the effing no-neck-having robots see all animal life as potential competition."

"Competition for what? Steel?"

Vaughn shook his head. "No. For space, dimension space."

"That doesn't make sense. We were no threat to them." She pointed at the aquatic alien city. "And I doubt these people were either."

Vaughn nodded. "You're right. We weren't a threat to them, yet."

Angela shook her head. "We were never going to be a threat to them."

Vaughn wagged his head equivocally. "I'm not so sure about that." He held up a hand. "Hear me out."

She nodded.

"This ability to cross dimensions by latching onto micro black holes, do you think we would've discovered it eventually?"

Angela's mouth skewed as she considered the question. Then she nodded. "Yeah, I suppose so."

He returned the gesture. "I think you're right. I'll take it a step further. Once we mastered the technology, jumping between dimensions could conceivably become easier than flying across a continent."

"Maybe."

"Okay, so what do you think we would do when we eventually ran across a land-hungry race, robotic or not, that was spreading across every dimension like a virus, even if they weren't preemptively wiping out all animal life?"

"We would just avoid them."

He tilted his head and knitted his eyebrows. "Really? We discover an all-consuming race of robots that can cross into our world easier than catching a flight across the pond, and you think we would settle with just avoiding them?"

Her eyes flared, but Vaughn also saw doubt clouding her face. "Why do you always have to be such a condescending asshole?"

It wasn't the first time he'd heard that. Remembering his last conversation with Mark, Vaughn felt his face flush. "Sorry."

Angela nodded and held out a hand. "I guess you're right, but why all animal life? Why do they wipe out everything that isn't plant-based?"

"I've wondered about that too. Could be a limitation of their tech." He shrugged. "Or maybe they just don't give a shit, but I think it goes deeper than that." He pointed at the aquatic city. "If they did this to proactively wipe out a potential competitor, I think their xenophobia extends to all animal life."

"I don't understand. Why would they fear all of it? They even wiped out the insects."

"Taking the long view with an eye toward evolution, maybe they see all animal life as a potential future threat. We are their scourge. To them, life is the virus, something that simply needs to be cleaned from each version of Earth."

As Angela considered his words, she wrapped arms around herself. She looked out at the underwater structures and then shuddered. "I think you're right." She turned suddenly hardened eyes toward Vaughn. "And we'd have been right to do it."

"To do what?"

"To wipe the bastards out." She jabbed a finger at the alien city. "Anyone that would do this to world upon world doesn't deserve to exist."

PART IV

"*Physics is often stranger than science fiction, and I think science fiction takes its cues from physics: higher dimensions, wormholes, the warping of space and time, stuff like that.*"
—Michio Kaku

"*For the wise man looks into space and he knows there is no limited dimensions.*"
—Lao Tzu

CHAPTER 28

Vaughn glanced at his empty wrist, the force of habit driving the action. By now, even the missing watch's tan-line had faded. He frowned and wiped an arm across his sweaty forehead. It came away caked with grimy mud.

He looked up at the stars appraisingly. Seeing the now familiar position of the few visible celestial bodies, Vaughn glanced down at Angela. "Only a few minutes to go."

She nodded wearily and continued to massage her left temple. With her other hand, she aimed a silvery device at a nearby rock. The mechanism looked like a blaster right out of Star Wars. Angela pulled the trigger. This time the thing didn't even give the high-pitched squeal generated by earlier attempts to fire it.

Angela had spotted the apparent gun earlier that morning, almost a full day after their arrival. To preserve their withering sanity, they'd gotten in the habit of leaving the mounded dead as soon as they arrived in Hell. Unfortunately, they had been discovered shortly after the beginning of the latest loop cycle, so they'd had nearly the full thirty-six hours to burn in Hell.

Vaughn smirked inwardly at the unintentional pun.

Anyway, they had traveled farther than any of their previous visits to the trash world. The two of them had ventured well past the field of nukes when Angela had seen light from the dusty sun glinting off an exposed corner of the partially buried device. She had pulled it from the soil and wiped it down. It was plainly alien. All efforts to get it to fire had failed. The first couple of trigger pulls had generated nothing more than a short pop followed by a high-pitched whine that lasted a second or two before it fell silent.

Angela pulled the trigger again. Nothing happened.

Vaughn shrugged. "Guess it's all the way dead now."

She frowned and then stuffed the device into her tattered backpack.

As he watched her, Vaughn massaged his temples. The low oxygen content of this dimension's atmosphere had generated throbbing headaches and gut-wrenching nausea for both of them.

He studied Angela's features. Her ghostly pallor concerned him. She now looked nearly as drawn and gaunt as she had when they'd first met aboard the space station.

But then again, now he looked almost as thin.

They had burned through the last of their food stores several loops back—about the time when his watch had died. Since then, they'd been reduced to scavenging for sustenance in the versions of Earth that held most closely to their own. Unfortunately, Angela was still having a hard time adapting to alien foods.

Not that Vaughn was immune to it.

He had vomited his fair share of native grub along the way.

Angela only had a narrow lead in the race to starvation.

Making matters worse, many of the worlds through which they had traveled were more like the one they'd dropped into mid-yesterday: already entirely covered by the robots and their global machine cities.

Each loop iteration still took them back to the strait between Sardinia and Corsica, but in many of the dimensions, those islands had been either covered with buildings or swarming with robots.

When they arrived in those worlds, Vaughn and Angela would seek shelter, trying to stay out of sight of the no-neck bots, but somehow the xenophobic bastards invariably detected them. A couple of times, they hadn't even made landfall before a Tater, the windowless, egg-shaped craft, had shown up and beamed them to the trash world for the first time … again.

Vaughn thought the ships looked like a giant egg, but Angela said they looked more like a skinned, boiled potato. So now they just called them Taters.

Anyway, this trip to Hell had been particularly … hellish. The fact that a Tater had found them so early after their arrival yesterday meant that this time they'd spent nearly the full thirty-six hours in the place.

During their multiple visits to Hell, they had never found any evidence that this world of refuse had ever had a collider. However, it may have just been covered up by all of the layers of shit deposited by the Necks. Hell's history and how the robots had latched onto it remained a mystery.

On the bright side, or on the not-quite-as-dark side, the fact that they were always looping back thirty-six hours meant that when they inevitably ended up back on this hellish version of Earth, it was always the same day.

Vaughn stared up at the dust-hazed stars. Returning to the same place and time over and over again was like being Bill Murray in the movie Groundhog Day. However, he and Angela didn't have the comedic relief of waking every morning to the same Sonny and Cher song blaring from a clock radio.

Realizing that he was still staring at the sky, Vaughn shook his head. He'd found his mind going off on these tangents more and more over the last several weeks.

Where had he been?

Oh yeah. The not-quite-as-dark side.

Vaughn had come to see the loop's time resets as a blessing of sorts.

Originally, he had worried about what would happen if they dropped into Hell only to be greeted by millions of angry Fish-Heads, but during their weeks and now months of time-loop travels, they still hadn't seen any sign of the amphibians or any of the peoples from the multiple other eradicated cultures through which they had drifted. Survivors from those events likely would have seen Angela and Vaughn's alien features and thought them to be the progenitors of their demise.

Pretty sad for a bright side, but it was all he had.

Angela sighed, pulling Vaughn from his ruminations. Looking down, he saw that she had tried to wipe sweat from her brow. As it had with him earlier, the effort had only smeared gritty mud across her face.

Stooping beside her, Vaughn used a slightly less dirty section of his shirt to wipe some of the grime from her face. "I think this is our longest stay at Motel Hell." He paused and inspected her face. Then he grinned wryly. "I'm actually looking forward to the big plunge this time."

Angela reflected his wry smile. "Yeah, anything will be better than this." Tired hope blossomed in her eyes. "Maybe this'll be the one."

Vaughn tried to look optimistic, although he was anything but.

During the first several loop iterations after they'd inferred the true nature and intentions of the robots, they had looked forward to each new jump, confident that their home dimension, their Earth, lay at the end of that next loop. However, after weeks and now months of passing through multiple iterations of the same soul-crushing scenery, Vaughn had long ago lost his optimism.

Stifling his doubts, he nodded dutifully and raised his eyebrows. "I hope so, too."

Unable to hold her eyes, Vaughn scanned the distant horizon, studying the fuzzy line where land met star field. Then he looked at the sky again. "Should be any second n—"

Brilliant light suddenly burned into his dark-adapted eyes. He squeezed them shut and braced for impact with the water. But then his knees buckled painfully as his feet struck a hard surface. Unprepared for the contact, he crumpled into a pile. Squinting and blinking, he looked over to see Angela just as she collapsed into the same surface. He barely had time to register the event before a thought blasted into his mind.

Vaughn scrambled to his feet and tried to look around, but his burning eyes had a hard time differentiating anything through the tears flooding into them. From what little he could see, they were standing on a gently rolling boat deck surrounded by blue water.

Could this be their Earth?!

Still squinting, Vaughn looked at Angela and pointed at the blurred horizon. "Are we back?"

Blinking and holding up a hand to shield her eyes, Angela turned to scan their surroundings. Then her eyebrows rose hopefully. "Could it be?"

Squinting and peering from beneath his own raised hand, Vaughn fought to resolve the horizon fully. Finally, his watering eyes adjusted enough for him to look up. The day wasn't as bright as he'd first thought.

Vaughn stared at a cloud-filled, leaden sky. Then he flinched and took an involuntary step back.

Dark shadows stitched a straight line across the bellies of the low-hanging, tumescent clouds.

He pointed up. "Oh shit … Look!"

Angela turned and gazed at the gloomy, overhead mantel. Then a short cry escaped her lips.

Vaughn didn't know if it had been a cry of horror or elation.

Probably it had been both.

The two of them stared wordlessly at the incredible sight. Parts of structures glided in and out of the low clouds. The pointed crest of a toppled radio tower poked out of a vaporous gray cotton ball.

"Could it be?" Angela whispered. "Is this home?"

Vaughn canted his head. "I don't know. Wasn't the sky blue that day?"

"I think you're right, but …" Angela paused as she turned to follow the line northward visually. "Maybe it's a different day."

Vaughn shook his head. "How could that …?" His words trailed off as a large, dark cloud directly overhead suddenly birthed a structure like none he'd ever seen. It would be several times larger than Earth's biggest skyscraper. The evident building had soft, flowing angles and probably had stood a mile tall before being uprooted. To Vaughn, it looked like something humanity might have built a hundred years from now ... if they hadn't already been swept from the damned planet.

In his peripheral vision, he saw Angela shaking her head as she continued to look in the wrong direction. He reached out and tapped her arm and then pointed up.

Angela turned and then flinched. "What in the world is that?"

Vaughn pulled his eyes from the image and looked down at the boat deck underfoot. Again, the lines of the ship were all wrong and so were its colors. He shook his head and sighed. He pointed at the giant skyscraper. "We didn't build that." He shifted the gesture toward the deck beneath their feet. "And this ain't the *Angela's Dream*. We're not home."

With mounting dread, Vaughn turned and looked at Corsica. A machine city didn't yet cover this world's version of the island. Judging by the levitating line of steel structures, the Necks hadn't progressed that far here.

As Vaughn studied the land, he saw that this iteration of Corsica sported architecture that would've almost looked at home in their version of Earth.

Suddenly, a sorrowful wail came from next to him. He looked over to see Angela staring at the island, shaking her head, tears welling in her eyes. "I can't take this anymore!" Collapsing to the deck, she sat down and hugged her knees to her chest. "It's too much."

Vaughn squatted next to her. He pointed toward the island. "At least the Necks aren't here already. We should be safe for a while."

Angela shook her head. "It's not that, Vaughn."

The gentle heaving of the boat and sway of her head conspired to push a tear from its reservoir. It rolled down her cheek, cutting a path in the grime and soot deposited by their passage through Hell.

Angela pointed toward the land. "It's this. It's what happened to these people." She turned shimmering red eyes toward him. "Another entire race wiped from *another* planet. Just when I think it can't get any worse, that we must have seen the last of these tragedies, we run into yet another world where the damned Necks have wiped out an entire culture." Angela batted muddy tears from her cheek. Anger hardened her tone. "It's just too goddamned much!"

Finally understanding, Vaughn sat next to her and swallowed hard. Looking down at the deck, he nodded absently. Angela was right. He had gotten so involved in their struggles, their fight to stay alive, to find their way home, that he had grown numb. He'd stopped giving more than passing consideration to the weight of the loss suffered by the former inhabitants of each new world through which the time loop had dragged them.

Vaughn tried to pull Angela to him, but she shrugged him away.

"I'm fine!"

She sounded anything but.

A moment later, Angela shuddered and then turned back to him. She buried her face in his chest.

Vaughn held her as she sobbed.

It was all he could do not to join her.

Sometime later, he placed two fingers under her chin.

Angela's still muddy face tilted up, her red eyes staring into his. She smiled weakly and then kissed him. Afterward, they held each other tightly.

As his adrenaline waned, Vaughn's utter exhaustion reasserted itself.

Angela took a deep breath. Apparently feeling her own fatigue, she pulled away from him and leaned back. Practically collapsing onto the deck, she stared into the sky and released a long sigh.

Surrendering to gravity, Vaughn dropped onto his back as well.

Lying side-by-side, they stared at fat, steel-gray clouds that bulged with apocalyptic booty.

Vaughn's head lolled to the side. His gaze shifted to Angela's prone body. Her emaciated form tore at his heart.

Like memories, scrapes, and bruises, even weight loss carried forward from one loop to the next. Over the weeks and now months since this loop had begun, each day had chipped away at Angela and Vaughn, grinding down the two of them.

Soon there'd be nothing left to strip away.

Angela saw him looking at her. Worry clouded her eyes. "What are we going to do if we can't break the loop before … before we—?"

"That's not going to happen," Vaughn said, cutting her off.

"What if it does? All of this will have been for nothing."

He gently caressed her cheek. Then he stood and offered Angela his hands. "Come on. We need to find you some edible food."

Angela accepted his assistance and stood. Vaughn's legs almost buckled in spite of her light weight.

She cocked an eyebrow at him. "We need to find *both* of us some food. You can't keep giving all the good stuff to me. You need your strength."

Ignoring her words, Vaughn walked unsteadily to the edge of the boat. His head felt as if it were spinning. He couldn't remember the last time he'd eaten.

Angela placed a steadying hand on his upper arm. She gazed across the water, staring at Corsica. "This place looks more like home than anything we've seen in a while." She hitched a thumb toward the yacht's quarters. "Maybe we can find some food aboard this thing."

Still clutching the railing, Vaughn nodded.

About an hour later and still famished, they motored up to the beach in a dinghy. They had found it aboard the yacht after they'd each washed off the worst of Hell's grime. This version of the ship had been oddly bereft of food, so they had decided to try their luck in Corsica.

From the pictures and the evidence they'd seen aboard the yacht, these people had been bipedal, almost human. Not the hybridized fish nor any of the other variants they'd indirectly encountered thus far. In a poorly lit room, one of them could have likely passed for a normal person. Unfortunately, the articles of clothing they'd found aboard the ship had proven too small. Vaughn and Angela had washed their clothes as they'd showered, leaving the drain clogged with necrotic detritus.

Leaning over the side of the small boat, Vaughn spat. Despite ridding himself of Hell's residue, he felt he could still smell and taste it with every breath. Each passage through that dead land left a long-lingering imprint on his soul and his sinuses.

The dinghy slid up onto the shore. Vaughn stepped over the edge of the boat and shakily lowered himself onto the sand. His knees buckled and threatened to toss him to the ground.

Angela caught him. "Why don't you let me go on the scavenging run. You wait here."

"No, I'm coming with you."

He shook off her hands and stood unsteadily. "Come on."

Angela gave him a worried look but then nodded. "Okay, just lean on me."

Vaughn started to shake his head but then thought better of it.

Arm in arm, they stumbled up the beach, carrying each other.

Breathing heavily, Vaughn looked around. The lay of the land followed roughly the same zigzagging lines as had all the previous iterations. It looked like they were pretty close to where the light-house had been on their version of the island. However, instead of a lighthouse, this place featured a rocky prominence.

A few minutes later, the pair stumbled into the coastal town. Again the place struck Vaughn as a futuristic version of their world. Many of the structures would look at home on an Italian postcard, but the flowing lines of the cars that dotted the road made it all appear as if it were something out of a science fiction movie.

They walked hesitantly into an unmistakable restaurant. Vaughn guessed there were certain aspects of that type of business that wouldn't change even a hundred years into the future.

Angela deposited him into a cozy booth and then disappeared through a pair of doors at the back of the room.

Vaughn soon found he was having a difficult time keeping his eyes open. They seemed to weigh a thousand pounds, but he didn't want to fall …

The most wonderful smell he'd ever encountered flooded into him. Vaughn opened his eyes to see a steaming plate of spaghetti and meatballs on the table. Angela was standing off to the side struggling to uncork a wine bottle.

The sun now hung low in the sky. Its umber rays streamed through the restaurant's expansive, western-facing windows. The light of the setting sun cast the tranquil bay waters in fiery golds and brilliant oranges.

Vaughn inhaled, pulling more of the beautiful smells into himself. Then the soft pop of a liberated wine cork accented the moment, lending a melancholy tilt to an image that was both sanguinely beautiful and heart-achingly tragic.

He turned to see Angela looking at him. A wan smile curled one corner of her mouth. The trail of a solitary tear glistened on her cheek.

She turned and gazed through the window. "Beautiful, isn't it?"

Vaughn sighed. He nodded. "Yes, it is." Then his eyes locked onto the spaghetti. His mouth had started to water. He licked his lips. "That smells incredible." He returned Angela's smile. "Have I died and gone to Heaven?"

She looked out the window again and then chuckled wistfully. "No, but at least it ain't Hell."

She filled their wine glasses and pushed one to Vaughn.

He grabbed the vessel and held it up to Angela. "I'll drink to that."

They clinked glasses and then drank.

Angela pointed at his steaming plate of spaghetti. "Dig in."

Vaughn didn't need to be told twice. He nodded and grabbed his fork. Pausing, he pointed the silvery utensil at Angela. "What about you?"

She smiled sheepishly. Extending her pinky, she delicately dabbed the corner of her lips with a napkin. "Sorry, couldn't wait." Then she dropped the cloth onto the table and took another swig of wine. As Angela lowered the glass, her eyes rolled back and then closed. She released a long, contented sigh. Then she saw him gawking at her. "Eat, already."

Vaughn smiled. Guess he did need to be told twice.

Sometime later, they finished and made their way to a local hostel.

The place didn't have electricity, but somehow it still had hot and cold running water.

Still feeling Hell's residue, they bathed.

Not a shower. A steaming hot bath.

What a sensation!

Vaughn hadn't felt anything that good since ... Well, suffice it to say that at the moment, the sensation was a close runner-up to sex.

Speaking of sex ...

Nope.

Didn't happen.

Exhausted beyond all words and suffering from a severe case of calorie coma, the two of them found a bed and did nothing but collapse into it, passing out the moment their heads hit the pillow.

The next morning, Vaughn woke to find Angela lying next to him, awake and staring at the ceiling.

He rolled toward her. "Penny for your thoughts."

She slowly shook her head. "We can't keep doing this, Vaughn. We have to stop them."

He nodded. "We will, just as soon as we get back to our dimension."

Her head continued to rock side to side. "No. I mean, we need to do it now." She looked at him. "We have to stop them here. Now."

"Stop them?" Vaughn scoffed. "How in the hell are we going to do that here?"

"The same way I planned to do it in our dimension. We'll work our way into this world's collider and overload it."

Vaughn stared at Angela, unable to believe the words that were coming out of her mouth. He shook his head. "Even if we manage to get inside this dimension's collider and overload it," he gestured at a nearby group photo, "we'll just end up in their past."

She looked at the ceiling again, an intense sadness clouding her eyes. "We have to—"

Vaughn sat up. "No, Angela! We have to get back to our home first."

She raised herself to a seated position as well and shook her head.

263

"I think we should stop trying to get back to our world. We've been so worried about the destination that we've overlooked what the Necks are doing to all of these other dimensions."

Vaughn spread his arms. "You don't know how many people were lost on each of these worlds, but we *know* that a few billion were eradicated from ours." He clutched her hands. "We need to get back there. Reset our *own* timeline. That comes with a known quality, a *known* quantity."

She stared at him for a long moment, then her brow furrowed. "How many billions have died while we've been idly waiting for our turn to be home?"

Vaughn blinked at the question. "That's not fair, Angela. We didn't do this. We didn't cause it!"

She raised her eyebrows. "And we haven't done anything to stop it, either."

"What *can* we do?" He gestured toward their surroundings. "Look around you, Angela. These aren't our people. Even if we could reset the time loop here, what would we do?" He placed a hand on her shoulder. "If we did manage to reset it here, how would we warn them? We show up and tell the locals ... what? That there's a race of robots about to eradicate them? As far as they'd be concerned, we would be the aliens."

Angela shrugged his hand from her shoulder. "What, then?! We just wait for the next loop reset and hope that it takes us home? What if it's just another freshly eradicated society?" She shook her head. "I can't keep doing this, Vaughn."

He gestured to the empty hostel and the city beyond its walls. "In the long run, how is anything we do going to change this outcome?"

Angela shook her head. "I don't know, but we don't know that it won't change something."

"We don't know that it won't change things for the worse," Vaughn said. "We could make our way to this planet's collider, and if you could figure it out and overload it, you could reset the timeline and completely wipe ourselves out of existence." He shook his head. "Then these people would likely be no better off, and any chance our version of Earth had of being reset disappears."

Angela seemed to ponder that for a moment. While she did, Vaughn continued. "We landed on a boat this time. Maybe that means we're getting closer to our home dimension." He pointed at their surroundings. "This culture even looks like it could be related to ours."

Finally, Angela nodded. "That boat's existence tells me that two people in this dimension paralleled our path, and you're right, it does look a lot like our world. A world where someone just like you, the sole male survivor, spent the last several months living an existence much like yours, another man that had to find the place where his mother had fallen."

Angela's words hit Vaughn like a slap to the face.

Apparently seeing the effect, she drove on. "We can go on through more cycles, sitting idly by as more people fall to these damned robots, or we can save that guy. We can go to this world's collider and blow it. Damn the consequences."

Vaughn looked at Angela for a long moment. "Damn the consequences, huh?" He nodded and raised his eyebrows. "That sounds more like me than you."

She shrugged. "Maybe, but I just can't live with sitting idly by as another cycle of the loop renders us witnesses to the demise of yet another wiped-out civilization."

He turned and stared at the scenic countryside visible through the room's wide window for a long moment.

Finally, Vaughn swallowed and then nodded. He looked at Angela. "Better get started, then. We're burning daylight."

CHAPTER 29

A ngela craned her neck as she visually inspected the structure.
Then she pointed at it. "Let's look in this one."

Not waiting for Vaughn, she walked up and pushed one of the
building's doors. It opened easily, as had every door they'd encountered. The people of this dimension seemed to have no use for locks.

As she stepped through the house, Angela paid no heed to the
home's interior beauty and its seamless integration of technology.
She'd already seen it in all of the previous buildings. Instead, she made
a beeline for the area where most of the homes they'd searched had
sported garages. Those attached structures had a retractable roof, but
all of them had been empty. They had deduced that some type of
aircraft might lie beneath them normally, but so far they hadn't
found one.

Angela pushed open an interior door and was finally greeted by
something other than an empty garage. However, the natural, curving
lines of the futuristic vehicle that lay within the small structure made
it difficult to discern the device's use, but she thought the closed yet
obviously retractable roof belied its purpose.

This had to be an aircraft.

Frowning, Angela studied its sleek surface. She had always thought of humanity as being technologically advanced. However, she and Vaughn had encountered multiple societies from other dimensions with highly advanced technologies. Much of it had baffled both of them. Personal flying crafts were an everyday staple of at least two of them, probably more. It was starting to make their version of Earth feel like a backwater world.

Was humanity's home the dimension-space equivalent of Amish country?

She pointed at the craft and then looked at Vaughn. "What do you think? Does it fly?"

He shrugged. "Looks like it. The thing definitely has aerodynamic lines. I don't see wings or any other way of creating lift, but we already know that's not always required."

Nodding, Angela stepped up to the machine's hatch. It slid open soundlessly. She entered the vehicle and studied its instrument panel. A domed, three-inch-wide switch sat in the center of the console. It looked like a big, green easy-button. After a furtive sideward glance, Angela reached out and pressed it. A whirring sound filled the cabin. She looked up to see the retractable roof opening.

Angela raised her eyebrows and nodded appreciably. No keys required. No locks. Further signs that these people had lived in a seeming utopia ... until the bastard robots had wiped them out anyway. She was feeling better and better about her decision to attempt the reset here. These people deserved a second chance. If she could overload their wormhole and reset their timeline to a point sometime before the Necks had invaded, then maybe they'd figure out a way to stop the event altogether.

Of course, the big question was just how far back in time the reset would send them. If Angela and Vaughn only went back to the opening of the wormhole, they'd have little chance of stopping anything. Then they'd end up sharing the same fate as this dimension's people.

Was she dooming herself and Vaughn to be dropped into Hell with the inhabitants of this world?

Angela shook her head. Regardless of the outcome, they had to do something while they still could. In spite of her original optimism, she now believed that the two of them would perish long before they could reach home if they continued on their previous path. Their deaths would be meaningless, and all that they had learned would be lost with them.

Vaughn chuckled. "That's a damned big garage door button."

Nodding, Angela glanced up. The hole in the roof wasn't much bigger than their aircraft. Scanning the instrument panel, she recalled how Vaughn had activated the flight pod they'd used in the Fish-Heads' world or as he had taken to calling it: Mon Calamari. Something to do with the homeworld of a Star Wars character named Admiral Ackbar. Anyway, this vehicle's console appeared to have many of the same functions as had the Calamarian one.

As she reached out to toggle a command, Angela could feel Vaughn's insistent gaze. She waved for him to join her.

As he stepped hesitantly to her side, Angela toggled another command. Four white masts suddenly extended, one rising from each corner of the vehicle. They didn't stop until they protruded through the corners of the overhead opening.

A high-pitched whine suddenly emitted from the craft. It took Angela a moment to realize that the noise was coming from the shafts. They had begun to rotate about their long axis. The smooth, white surface of the masts made it difficult to discern the motion, but as the shafts spun ever faster, white propeller blades began to grow outward from the top of each one.

Angela turned toward Vaughn.

He was staring at her in wide-eyed amazement.

She shrugged. "What?"

Vaughn held up both hands in surrender. "Nothing. Glass houses … stones. I've got no room to speak." He chuckled and shook his head. "Guess I'm just a little bit shocked by the sudden role reversal."

Angela regarded him with a cocked eyebrow. "Considering all we've been through, this seems like the safest thing we've done in quite a while."

Nodding, Vaughn held out a hand. "Your controls, Commander."

Casting a wary glance upward, Angela placed her hands on the two cue ball-sized controls that sat in the center of the console. She applied gentle upward pressure on the left one.

Nothing happened.

She pulled up on the other control.

Again, nothing.

A new icon started flashing. Vaughn pointed at it. "I think it wants us to sit down."

The symbol did look like the profile of a person sitting in a seat.

Angela turned and stared at the chairs behind them. The vehicle had four of them, two bucket seats up front as well as another pair behind them. She shook her head. "I won't be able to reach the controls."

"Yeah, neither would I." He shrugged and sat down. "Let's give it a shot. See what happens."

"Okay."

Angela sat in the front left chair. Then she flinched as something snaked out of the corners of the seat. Before she realized what it was, the apparent harness had wrapped itself around her and sucked Angela into the chair.

The instrument panel that had been two feet in front of her split in half and moved to the seat's left and right armrests, a cue ball-shaped control on each.

Vaughn patted his harness. Then he smiled and pointed at the now extinguished chair icon. "Problem solved."

Angela gave a short nod. She'd just have to trust that the belt would let her go once it was no longer required.

Chewing her lip, she glanced up again. With her elbows on the armrests, Angela grasped a control ball in each hand. She pulled up on the left one. It didn't move, but the craft lifted from the garage floor, rising steadily through the opening in spite of her shaky movements. As she had anticipated, it was stabilized.

Vaughn grinned and winked at her. "Guess they're Angela-proof, too."

She scoffed and then blew a strand of auburn hair out of her eyes.

"Whatever."

He was right, though. Just as he'd pointed out when they'd been on Mon Calamari, they wouldn't have had one of these things in every garage if they required highly specialized training to fly.

Angela relaxed the pressure on the control. The craft came to a stop, hovering over the house.

Vaughn leaned in as if to tell her what to do.

Angela pressed him back with her elbow. "I've got this."

She cast a wary glance at the levitating steel structures parading overhead. As the day had warmed, the clouds had lifted to expose the entire line.

After a calming breath, Angela moved the simple controls and guided the quadcopter to follow the line.

The craft quickly accelerated and climbed. Soon they left this planet's version of Corsica behind. As they neared the mainland, she saw Vaughn shifting nervously.

Angela looked at him askance. "What?"

Vaughn shook his head. "Something doesn't look right."

Looking forward again, Angela scanned the horizon. "What do you mean? I don't see anything."

He pointed overhead. "The angle, it's all wrong. This line is moving more northwest than north."

Angela studied the line and slowly nodded. "You're right."

Then she saw another problem, and her heart sank. "Shit!" She raised an arm and pointed left and right. "We're missing the other lines, too."

If their collider was in this dimension's version of Geneva, then the converging lines of levitating steel structures should already be visible to the left and right of the line they were following.

Vaughn scanned the horizon, slowly shaking his head. "Crap. You're right. Their collider must be in a different place."

Angela eyed the craft's instrument panel. The gauge that she assumed to be battery power showed all green. She nodded toward it. "I hope that means we have enough power to get to the point where the lines *do* converge."

CHAPTER 30

Angela began to worry that this society might have installed their collider farther north, like above the Arctic Circle north. She and Vaughn were not exactly dressed for that locale. As it was, she could already feel the vehicle's glass chilling in response to the falling outside air temperature.

Thanks to their waterless landing aboard the yacht, the two of them had been able to dawn the light, and thankfully dry, jackets that they kept in their tattered backpacks.

During the hours since they'd crossed over the local version of Monte Carlo, they had flown over the aftermath of a few uncontrolled fires, but nothing like what they'd seen during their first trek to Geneva.

On their way to this point, they had watched in silent vigil as emptied, futuristic-looking cities and surrealistically mundane farm-land scrolled beneath their craft.

Now a couple of hours into their flight and with the last of the Alps well behind them, Angela had to fight the nagging doubts that were haunting her thoughts.

Was she doing the right thing?

Were they squandering their only chance, dooming both their society and this one, as well as all the others?

But what else could they do?

A light snore came from beside her. Vaughn had fallen asleep. He looked so drawn and weak.

Angela shook her head. No, they couldn't keep going like this.

She was doing the right thing.

Turning her attention back outside, Angela saw that storm clouds now lined the western horizon. She started to look away, but then snapped her head back to the left.

Those weren't storm clouds!

She looked right and saw a matching line converging from the east.

Angela took a deep breath and then sighed. "Oh, thank you!"

It appeared that the lines would converge somewhere over Northern Europe, probably where Amsterdam would be in their home dimension.

She glanced down at the now half-diminished power icon.

They were going to make it.

The tension that had been building in her shoulders loosened a notch.

She sighed and nodded again. "Thank you!"

Sitting beside her, Vaughn flinched. "Huh?" He blinked and then looked around. "Where'd the mountains go?"

"Left them behind about a half hour ago."

As she spoke, Vaughn looked forward. His eyes narrowed. Then terror overtook his face.

"Oh shit!"

Angela followed his gaze. On the horizon, light glinted off this planet's now visible steel city.

Vaughn sat up and jabbed a finger at the ground. "Get down! We're too high. We need to be lower!"

Pointing down at the flat, featureless terrain beneath them, Angela shook her head. "That's no good. We'll still stand out like a sore thumb."

They both looked up.

The floating line of steel structures hung several hundred feet above them on their right side. Angela had kept the aircraft offset to the left so that a chunk of falling debris wouldn't knock them from the sky.

"Okay," Vaughn said and then gestured upward. "Let's merge with the traffic."

Shaking her head, Angela didn't adjust the controls. "I was trying to keep my distance. Didn't want to get too close and get sucked into the stream."

"We should be okay. I doubt there's any steel in this thing. Must be made of composites. Otherwise, we wouldn't have found the thing still sitting in its garage."

"A lot of the garages around it were empty."

"They just hadn't been home when it happened. If the Necks had snatched these to get at the steel, there would've been holes in those garage roofs." Vaughn looked nervously from the line of structures overhead to the robotic city and then pointed to her controls. "Sooner would be better."

Angela chewed her lip for a second.

Vaughn moved as if to take the aircraft from her.

She brushed him back. "I got it!"

Grabbing the controls, Angela guided the craft upward. "I'll just travel above the line. That should keep us out of sight, at least until we get closer to the city."

She swung the copter up the left side. A tangled ball of tractor trailers fell past on their right. Then she had the quadcopter racing along just above the line of steel.

Multiple structures slid beneath them as they flew toward the city at a significantly higher speed than that of the line. Angela watched as a slowly undulating steel bridge passed below them followed shortly by a massive ship. As with many of the vessels, this one's curving, organic lines made it look like a cruise ship right out of a science fiction movie.

Ahead of their craft, the line tapered into the hazed distance, coming to a fine point where it dead-ended into the towering steel city that dwarfed all else.

Vaughn pointed at it. "Have you given any thought as to how in the hell we are going to get in there? It didn't exactly go smoothly last time."

Angela's hands tightened on the controls. "Yeah, I have." She gave Vaughn a sideward glance. "These robots don't seem too keen on security. Based on how easily we got in last time, I think that, once they finish wiping a planet, they stop actively searching for life." She pointed ahead. "If this steel city is anything like ours was, we should be able to fly right into the heart of it."

"That doesn't seem like much of a plan, more like a hope and a prayer."

Angela shrugged. "Do you have a better idea?"

He turned to look at the city, his pressed together lips forming a straight line. Finally, Vaughn shook his head. "No ... No, I don't. Just try not to look too much like an incoming missile."

Angela smiled weakly. She placed her withered hand on his too skinny arm. "This is it, Vaughn. We *will* make it ... Whatever it takes, we'll make it."

He smiled weakly and then squeezed her hand. He nodded. "Yes, we will."

After a tense silence, Angela gestured ahead. "When we get closer and these structures begin their death dives into the cauldron, we'll make a dash for the city center."

Beside her, Vaughn shifted uncomfortably.

Angela turned a raised eyebrow toward him. "What?"

His forehead creased. "Don't you think I should be flying now?"

She was about to chastise him but then thought better of it. He was a combat helicopter pilot, after all. They might get into a situation that demanded more from this thing than she could manage.

Stepping out of the chair, Angela extended a hand. "Your controls, Captain."

Vaughn gave a short nod and then swapped seats.

He spent the next few minutes acquainting himself with the craft's flight characteristics by doing a few sharp turns and quick altitude changes.

During one particularly abrupt maneuver, Angela grunted and gripped her armrest tightly. "Is that really necessary?"

"Hopefully, I won't need to do any wifferdills." He shrugged. "But I don't want to bet our lives on it." He adjusted the controls, and the craft leveled off. "No worries, though. This thing responds just like a helicopter, albeit a very stabilized one."

Frowning, Angela nodded. She gazed out the large side window. Looking down through the floating cloud of metallic detritus, she watched the alien world scroll past. European style farmhouses dotted a landscape striped by tracts of alternating green and yellow crops.

The familiar look of the land triggered a deep sense of melancholy within Angela. Except for the feral appearance of the unkempt fields, it looked perfectly normal, as if she were flying across the countryside back in their home dimension.

These people had suffered the same fate as had hers. How many other worlds had gone the way of theirs?

Watery waves blurred the image as she stared down at the incredible loss represented by all those emptied homes, fields, and structures.

Pulling her eyes from the disturbing image, she stared ahead.

That only made matters worse.

The city looked closer now.

Angela wished she hadn't relinquished the controls. Flying duty had distracted her from the more poignant aspects of this world's loss, but now that she was no longer preoccupied, she could find no quarter for her mind and no way to escape the fact that they were rapidly approaching a resolution, one that was likely to be final ... one way or the other.

Vaughn brought the craft closer to the floating steel assemblages. He glanced at her. "Looks like we're okay. I don't feel anything trying to pull at this thing. Must be no steel in it."

Angela nodded and chewed her lip nonetheless. She watched the nearest of the mountainous stainless-steel structures of the alien metropolis slowly rise in apparent height as every second drew them closer to the city.

She felt incredibly exposed.

Apparently, Vaughn was feeling it too. He slowed the craft and then merged with the levitating line, slipping the quadcopter into the clear air between a twisted building and a large structure that looked like a modernized version of the Eiffel Tower.

Vaughn's eyes kept darting upward. He gestured at the area around the rotor blades. "Keep an eye out for smaller pieces. If we fly into something, we'll throw a blade."

"What would we do if that happened?"

"Likely, this thing has an automatic parachute." Pointing at the distant ground and all of the sharp-edged debris below them, he shook his head. "But it probably wouldn't end well."

Angela nodded and swallowed.

Her suddenly dry throat clicked loudly in her ears.

The enormous buildings now towered over them.

As she scanned the sky for any threats, Angela tried to slide lower in the seat, but the harness held her firmly in place. "Almost there."

Vaughn nodded. "Yep," he said lightly. Then he looked at her, grinning sheepishly. "Why are we whispering?"

Angela giggled nervously but stopped short, afraid doing more might lead to crying or, even worse, to one of her snort storms.

Her breath hitched as she looked down, staring into the shimmering heat waves rising from this column's dedicated vat of boiling, molten metal. Her blood ran cold as she remembered how close they had come to falling into the last one.

The floating building ahead of them began to twist and undulate. Nonmetallic panels and pieces fell from it. Watching this, Angela realized that it was the same thing that had happened to the oil tanker. The robots were discarding nonferrous material from the structures before introducing them into the vat.

Suddenly, the near side of the wracked, cube-shaped structure heaved into the sky. The building's now-naked frame began to lower into the vat. The rapid pitching moment had launched several pieces of dislodged material. The debris flew toward the base of the city on a ballistic arc.

Vaughn grabbed the controls. "That's our chance!" He glanced at her. "Tighten your seat belt!"

Angela gave her harness a confused glance.

Vaughn wrenched the controls, and the copter rocketed forward, rising on a path that followed the flying debris.

She grabbed the sides of her seat and tightened her abs against the coming weightlessness as the quad reached the apex of the ballistic arc.

Vaughn adjusted the controls to follow the flying debris as it began to fall toward the outskirts of the robot city.

Both of their backpacks floated up off the floor. Ahead, the building's thrown off panels and broken concrete began to rain down, launching dust and rocks into the air.

Angela screamed as the ground rushed up to greet them.

At the last moment, Vaughn pulled back on the controls. The ship skimmed over the piles and then began a rapid climb.

They were heading toward a narrow gap between the nearest buildings. The quadcopter was climbing fast, but the structures were too high to clear.

Angela glanced at the wide path cut by the rotor blades that extended from each corner of the copter and then back at the rapidly approaching alleyway.

Her eyes went wide. "It's too narrow! We won't fit!"

Vaughn glanced at her and grinned. "Hang onto something."

"Wh-What—?!"

He yanked one control to the right and twisted the other.

Angela screamed again as the quadcopter snap-rolled ninety degrees onto its right side and then passed between the buildings.

Wide-eyed, she looked up through the quad's glass roof. For a surreal moment, she stared at the reflection of her horrified face in the polished side of the building. The image wavered under the spinning rotor blades as they whirled mere inches from the shiny surface.

The upward momentum that had carried the craft deep into the crevice began to wane. Without the lift usually generated by the now sideways rotor blades, the quad reached the zenith of its trajectory and then began to fall earthward.

Angela dragged her eyes from her reflection and watched the ground start to rush up at them.

"Vaughn!"

"I know." His voice was maddeningly calm.

Angela felt something in the seat's armrest break under her death grip. "Oh God—!"

Suddenly, the buildings that were hemming in the copter passed out of sight.

Vaughn shoved the controls to the left.

The craft snapped level. Its landing gear kissed the ground. Then the quadcopter bounced back into the air. Flying a couple of feet above the ground, the craft now screamed down a blessedly wide expanse of roadway.

Vaughn gave Angela a crooked grin and raised an eyebrow. "I think they don't even know we're here—"

Both of them flinched as something slammed into the front of the quadcopter with a tremendous report. The noise left Angela's ears ringing. The force of the blow rocked the craft, throwing them forward into their seat belts.

Angela saw a plastic-covered white arm fly through the air.

As they continued to rocket down the street, she and Vaughn watched the disembodied arm arc toward the building on their right. It flew through the air as if in slow motion. Then the robotic appendage ricocheted off the wall's gleaming surface and burst into pieces.

Another impact followed by several additional ones knocked the vessel from side to side.

Angela's head snapped to front. She gasped at the site of dozens of the no-neck robots bouncing off the nose of the quadcopter.

Beside her, Vaughn struggled to rein in the violently bucking aircraft. A moment later, he managed to coax it higher. They began to gain altitude, but not before plowing through three more robots.

As the copter raced upward, Angela gave Vaughn a sidelong glance and raised an eyebrow. "They know now!"

Vaughn scoffed. "Screw 'em. That felt good."

Angela guffawed. "Yeah, it did!"

She leaned forward and looked up through the top of the windscreen. The aircraft was rocketing straight up, but the buildings around it stretched high overhead. Angela couldn't even see their tops. "What now?"

Beside her, Vaughn craned his neck as well. "I *was* planning to land in the street and see if we could sneak into one of these buildings. Figured we could work our way down into whatever passes for this city's underground." He shook his head. "Not sure what to do now, but we need to find cover quick, fast and in a goddamned hurry!"

As the quad continued to rocket into the sky, the upper extremity of a relatively shorter building slid into view at the top of the windshield. Then Angela saw its broad, flat roof and pointed. "Land there!"

Vaughn looked and then shook his head. "On that roof? Where would we go after that? How in the hell will we get down?"

"One bridge at a time. Let's just land and find cover before a Tater shows up. This quad is pretty fast, but we'll never outrun one of those things."

He turned a wary eye toward the sky and then nodded. "I guess so. I just hope we can find a hatch."

Vaughn began to maneuver the craft for landing.

Angela's heart raced. She had already been more frightened than at any other point in their travels, but now her adrenaline level ratcheted up another notch at the mere prospect of landing the craft in this city. She felt her hand tightening on the already broken armrest. Through force of will, she loosened her grip as she watched Vaughn guide the vessel toward the rooftop.

As they drew closer, she scanned its smooth, metallic surface, desperately seeking any sign of a door or a hatch.

Vaughn shook his head. "I don't see a way in."

"Just land it. There must be something." She searched the surrounding sky, looking for one of the potato-shaped craft. The things were fast, significantly more so than this quad. "If a Tater shows up before we can get in, we'll be sent back to Hell." She shook her head. "I don't think we'll survive another trip, Vaughn. It's now or never."

"Dammit, Angela, I know that! But if there's no way in from up here, we'll just be sitting d—!"

"Right there!" Angela pointed excitedly. "I think that's a hatch."

Vaughn followed her gesture and then, with his lips pressed into a thin line, gave a curt nod. Adjusting the trajectory, he guided the vessel to a soft landing on the roof. A moment later, the scene quietened as the quad shut down and retracted its rotors.

Now standing breathlessly inside the vehicle, they exchanged nervous glances.

Angela half-expected a cannon to pop up from a hidden port and hammer bullets into them.

Several tense seconds later and still bullet-free, they stepped out onto the roof. It felt solid underfoot.

Angela shied away from the edge. No handrail or cornice adorned the precipice. At its periphery, the reflective metal simply curved away and dropped toward the city below.

Looking up at the surrounding structures, Angela felt utterly exposed. On three sides, the taller buildings towered above them. The metallic canyon cut by the road that they'd flown down provided the only gap.

Tearing her eyes from the scene, she scanned the deck and then spotted the rectangular outline of the hatch.

Vaughn had exited the far side of the aircraft.

Looking at him, Angela waved and pointed. "Over here!"

Suddenly, a mechanical, high-pitched whirring noise emitted from in front of her. She turned and stared as the three-foot-wide panel suddenly dropped down a couple of inches. Then the sound changed, and the door slid sideways, disappearing under the roof.

Vaughn ran past her. As he approached the opening, he looked back and held up a hand for her to hold fast.

Angela nodded.

Stepping cautiously, Vaughn eased up to the opening.

Then a robot rose through it.

"Vaughn!" Angela screamed, but it was too late.

Each of the machine's four hands reached out, snatching Vaughn and pulling him from his feet.

For an eternal second, Angela stood frozen in place. Then she found the alien gun in her hand. She couldn't recall pulling it from her pack and wasn't sure why she had bothered. When they tried to fire the damned thing in Hell, it had only whistled and whined.

Out of options, Angela pointed the device at the robot and squeezed the trigger. As with the previous attempts, the gun only emitted a pop followed by a high-pitched whine and then fell silent.

She was about to throw the useless piece of crap at the robot, but then she stopped.

The machine had seized.

The robot no longer moved.

Angela blinked and then turned the gun sideways, looking at it with open-mouthed amazement. Then she saw Vaughn struggling to get out of the now inanimate Neck's hands.

Sliding the gun under her belt, she sprinted across the roof and then skidded to a stop next to the opening.

Vaughn freed himself, falling hard onto the roof deck.

Angela dropped to a knee next to him. "Are you okay?"

He waved her off and quickly scrambled to his hands and knees. "Yeah, I'm fine." He looked down through the opening and then nodded.

Vaughn began struggling to pull the robot out of the way. "Help me move this jackass before the rest of his buddies show up."

Angela nodded and then grabbed hold of one of the dead Neck's arms. The thing felt as if it weighed a ton. Peering through the opening, she saw that one of its clawed feet still rested on the top rung of a ladder that disappeared into the depths below. Complicating the situation, its backward bending knee was hanging up on the inside of the opening.

She pulled the machine toward her, trying to free up its lower leg.

The robot lunged.

It pushed Angela across the roof and then pinned her to the deck.

She screamed and kicked at the Neck's white torso, but the worn soles of her old hiking boots found no purchase.

Vaughn shouted something at her, but Angela screamed over him. "Get it off me!"

"Angela! It's okay!" Vaughn's urgent words finally penetrated her panic. "It's still dead."

She stopped struggling. Breathing heavily, she looked at Vaughn.

He nodded and started tugging on the machine. "It just fell on you. Help me move it!"

Finally reining in her panic, Angela gave a short nod and then pushed against the robot with hands spread wide, gripping it as if she were bench-pressing a heavy Olympic bar.

The thing barely budged.

Gnashing her teeth, Angela kicked at it again. "It weighs a ton!"

She saw veins popping out on Vaughn's starvation-withered and now shaking arms.

Angela took a deep breath and held it. Then she pushed with all the strength she could muster.

Finally, the machine drifted a few inches upward. Together, they guided it sideways. As the white and silver monstrosity passed off to the side, Angela gave it a final push, allowing the movement to roll her in the opposite direction, out from under the machine.

Just as she tried to roll onto her left shoulder, she felt the metallic surface of the roof curve away from her.

"Watch out!" Vaughn yelled.

Angela had landed closer to the edge than she'd realized.

Too close!

Her momentum started to carry her over the side of the building.

"Oh shit!" She swung her arms, batting at the surface ineffectually as she continued to slide. "No, no, no!"

Vaughn's hands latched onto her lower legs.

The rolling motion had carried Angela onto her stomach. Her hands clawed at the curved precipice, desperately seeking purchase.

"I got you," Vaughn said, his voice straining under the effort. "Now, please, stop struggling so I can pull you back."

Angela swallowed hard and then forced herself to stop flailing.

Vaughn grunted with the effort as he slowly pulled her back from the ledge an inch at a time.

Safely back on the roof, Angela rolled onto her back, her head tilting as it rested on the edge's sloping transition.

A new sound rose above her raspy breaths.

"Where's that noise coming from?"

Vaughn plopped down next to her, panting heavily and staring at the sky. "It's your toy gun. That's the same noise it made after we test-fired it back in Hell."

She drew the weapon out from under her and held it up in front of the two of them.

The thing looked like a ray gun out of a science fiction movie. She had pulled the trigger more out of desperation than a belief that it would work. "Guess it's not a toy after all."

Beside her, Vaughn shook his head. "Nope."

The high-pitched squeal continued ramping up. She knew that soon it would fall silent as it had before. The thing's matching vibrations made her fingers tingle.

Angela wrinkled her nose. "Do you smell that?"

"Yeah. Smells like ozone." He pointed at the dead robot. "It's coming from that. I think your gun fried its electronics."

Angela nodded. She opened her mouth to respond, but then a new, all too familiar noise rose from behind them.

"Oh shit!" they both shouted as they rolled over.

Peering down over the edge of the building, they saw a white craft rising toward them. It was a goddamned Tater!

Angela extended her arms over the precipice and aimed the gun down, pointing it at the rapidly rising machine.

Not wanting to pull the trigger until assured of hitting her target, she waited excruciatingly long moments while the egg-shaped craft drew closer—not that Angela had an inkling of the weapon's range. Even now, she could hear and feel the gun's rising whine.

Finally, the Tater filled the weapon's small sights.

Angela squeezed the trigger.

Click.

No snap or crackle, no squeal.

Eyes widening, she glanced at the uncooperative gun and then beyond it at the onrushing Tater.

Angela squeezed the trigger again and again with no effect.

"Shit!"

Suddenly, Vaughn was yanking on Angela's backpack and dragging her away from the edge.

"Come on! The gun hasn't finished charging. We gotta go!"

She nodded and scrambled to her feet.

Vaughn had released her and was already halfway to the still open roof hatch. Reaching the opening, he dropped through the hole and fell out of sight.

Angela slid to a stop beside the open hatch. Just then, the Tater climbed above the lip of the roof and started moving toward her. As it did, it rose overhead, positioning itself to banish them to Hell.

Still staring at the white craft, Angela shouted down into the hole. "Vaughn?!"

His voice rose from it. "Jump! Hurry!"

Having raced up the side of the building, the craft now approached with menacingly slow speed.

Angela tore her eyes away from it and looked down into the hole.

Vaughn stood on a deck about ten feet below her, his arms outstretched. "Jump!"

Needing no further motivation, Angela dropped through the opening and into Vaughn's arms. The two of them collapsed into a heap on the metal floor.

Untangling from each other, they scrambled back to their feet just as the machine moved to hover above the still open hatchway.

Angela saw the probe mounted to its belly start glowing. "No, no, no!"

Vaughn grabbed her arm and pulled. "Run!"

Illuminated by glowing overhead panels, the checkerboard pattern of the wide corridor's floor blurred as the two of them ran down it.

Angela glanced back over her shoulder just as a sphere of white light blossomed through the opening and started to chase them down the hallway.

She pushed on Vaughn's back, urging him forward. "Hurry! The light's coming!"

They had made it so far! She couldn't let the bastards knock them back now.

It occurred to Angela that, considering she and Vaughn had killed one of the Necks, the light might do worse than banish them this time.

With this new thought in mind, Angela looked back with widening eyes.

The rapidly growing sphere had swallowed the entire hallway. Like a miniature version of the curtain of energy that had swept life from Earth, the light now formed a white wall that looked bent on enveloping them.

It was moving too fast.

They couldn't outrun it.

The gap narrowed.

The wave nipped at their heels.

Angela lunged forward, bowling Vaughn over as she did.

They crashed to the floor.

Scrambling backward, they watched as the light chewed up the gained footage.

"Dammit!" Vaughn growled.

The gun still clutched in Angela's hand suddenly stopped vibrating.

She glanced at it and then raised the weapon.

Pointing through the wall of light, Angela aimed at the unseen Tater.

She pulled the trigger just as the surface of ethereal light enveloped their feet.

Then the wave faltered, slowing to a crawl halfway up their legs.

Angela tried to scamper away from the energetic curtain, but suddenly her legs felt as if they were anchored in concrete.

Vaughn's arms flailed, and his upper body heaved as he too tried to pull himself free of the light's iron grip.

Suddenly, the wave shattered, dissolving into a million shimmering pieces.

Angela felt a sideways wrenching sensation in her gut as the twinkling fragments flew apart and vanished.

CHAPTER 31

Blinking furiously, Vaughn tried to clear the light's afterimage from his vision. He and Angela exchanged confused glances in the sudden silence.

She held up the gun. "I think it worked."

Vaughn nodded hesitantly. Still blinking, he stood and then reached down, helping Angela to her feet.

As the spots faded from his vision, he looked around and then tilted his head. "What the …?"

Turning, Angela slowly shook her head. "I don't understand."

They had been in a hallway, a long, skinny one, about the size of what you'd see in a typical office building, but now they were in a large, open room. The floor had a similar pattern to the one they'd run across in the corridor. However, the walls of this chamber were a good twenty or thirty feet away, and the ceiling stood significantly higher than had the hall's.

Vaughn saw something else new and pointed at it. "Angela, look."

An open door sat at the far side of the cavernous room.

He started walking toward it. Speaking softly, he waved for her to follow. "Let's check it out."

As they neared the door, Vaughn heard a distant rumble coming through the opening. With each step, the sound ramped up another notch. Soon it had risen to a dull roar. He could feel the metal floor vibrating in time with the din.

Angela caught up with him and placed a hand on his arm. "What's making that noise?"

Before Vaughn could respond, a new sound joined the cacophony.

Rhythmic metallic pinging stabbed the air, and the gut-shaking rattle of massive machinery shook his bones.

Vaughn reached the opening. He took up a position along the wall to the right of the doorway and motioned for Angela to get behind him. She raised an eyebrow in protest but finally pressed herself to the wall next to him.

After a moment, he peered outside and then flinched, quickly pulling back out of sight.

Standing with his back to the wall, breathing heavily, Vaughn tried to comprehend the scene that he had glimpsed.

Angela gave him a questioning look.

Not wanting to shout above the din coming through the opening, he pointed two fingers at his eyes and then gestured for her to look outside. He stepped aside, letting her move to the door.

Angela gazed through it and then looked back at Vaughn.

He saw his confusion reflected on her face.

The scene outside made no sense.

They had entered the building through a panel in the roof, and the structure had been in the center of a sprawling alien metropolis. Now they were on the ground floor and had somehow moved to the edge of the city.

When Vaughn had peeked through the door, he'd expected to see a sky choked with building tops.

Instead, he'd seen the ground and an open swath of cloud-covered sky. The bases of the tall, stainless-steel structures flanked the left and right sides of their building, but nothing but construction materials and broken concrete lined the ground opposite the open door.

Well, there was one other thing. The source of the tremendous noise that even now threatened to dislodge Vaughn's teeth.

The near side of a massive, automated, all-in-one city constructor sat only a few hundred feet away, blotting out the lower portion of the leaden sky. Black smoke billowed frantically above its stadium-sized cauldron of molten metal.

Vaughn looked over Angela's head and peered through the opening again.

He stared awestruck at the roiling black cloud that billowed above the vat. Then a dark structure appeared through a gap in the smoke.

Vaughn's breath hitched.

He shook his head.

It couldn't be...

Could it?

Forgetting their exposed position, he stepped from cover and stood in the center of the door. Vaughn stared at the vertically oriented supertanker. Half of its bow was already immersed in the cauldron.

Suddenly, Angela was at his side, tugging at his arm, trying to drag him back into the building. She was screaming something, probably for him to get back in, but it was impossible to hear her over the storm of sound emanating from the city builder and its burning cache.

Angela was focusing on him. She hadn't noticed the ship.

Vaughn grabbed her hand and pulled her back to him. Then he pointed up, toward the highest portion of the ship, the back of the nose-diving tanker.

Angela tore nearly panicked eyes from Vaughn and looked in the indicated direction.

She stopped pulling on him. Her now limp hand fell to her side.

Sporadically visible through gaps in the smoke, two people were leaping from one floating structure to the next. Each frenzied vault landed them on a descending hunk of metal closer to the molten surface of the cauldron but also closer to its outer edge.

As Vaughn had known they would, the very familiar-looking couple jumped onto a slowly rotating I-beam. Then they used it to propel themselves out of the clutches of the massive machine's ever-thirsty maw.

Then the months-younger versions of Angela and Vaughn landed on the pulverized remnants of Geneva's destroyed buildings and rolled out of sight.

CHAPTER 32

B reathing hard, Angela struggled to keep up with Vaughn.
They were back in their home dimension, back in their version of Earth. No doubt about it, but as Angela continued to run, one question kept cycling through her mind:

How?

How had they returned?.

Vaughn glanced back at her and shouted over his shoulder. "We have to stop them!"

Angela nodded. Too winded to speak, she merely waved for him to continue.

How in the hell had they returned to their home dimension?

And it certainly was home.

The timing of the jumps made by the earlier version of herself had removed all doubt. Seeing herself leaping from floating hunks of steel in the exact same manner as she had on that fateful day, Angela had known this was home.

She glanced at the sky. Even the shape and spacing of the clouds of smoke matched her memories.

But how had they returned?

Ahead of her, Vaughn rounded a corner. Angela's legs burned, but she stayed on his heels.

She shook her head. Had the EMP gun killed the Tater?

It must have. That's why the light had collapsed.

It had been in the process of beaming them back to Hell, but when the light had died, it must have spit them out.

Her eyes went round. That's what had caused the gut-wrenching sensation.

But it hadn't left the two of them where they'd been. Somehow, the partial application of the light's power had dropped them back into their home dimension.

Was it another anchor point? Was their version of Earth a hard stop?

It would make sense. She already theorized that a hard stop existed at the beginning of the wormhole's life, at the point in time when it was formed.

Angela filed away the knowledge for later.

Vaughn looked back at her, his eyebrows raised. Red blotches dotted his too pale face. He looked like she felt.

Angela paused for a breath and then waved him on. "Keep going!"

Unlike the city that they had entered today, the streets of this one were fortunately just as empty as the first time they'd visited it. So far, there was no sign that they'd been spotted during their run through the periphery of the metropolis.

Another question had occurred to Angela the moment she'd realized they were back:

Had they broken the loop?

Angela and Vaughn had intuited the answer to that one immediately.

The fact that there were currently two versions of themselves running through the streets of post-apocalyptic Geneva pointed to the loop's continued existence.

There was another fact that supported the idea. The egg-shaped vessel that always banished them to hell never sent them to a different time of day. Even this aborted dimensional shove hadn't changed it. The thing had simply pushed them back to their homeworld.

No. Killing the Tater might have sent them back to their Earth, but it hadn't broken the loop.

That was why she and Vaughn were running.

They had to intercept their earlier versions and stop themselves from creating the loop in the first place.

Vaughn halted behind the ruined corner of an old building. Panting, he leaned out and scanned the area. Apparently not seeing any robots, he pointed ahead. "Just a few more blocks ... Keep an eye out. We should be ... coming from that direction," he said between breaths.

He stepped out from behind the corner and waved for her to follow. "Come on."

Trotting to catch up, Angela peered around Vaughn. Then she saw movement followed by a bright, bluish-white flash.

Seeing the light as well, Vaughn dove for cover behind a jagged edge of a burned-out building.

Before they had entered the wrecked streets of Geneva, Angela and Vaughn had seen—and kept well clear of—the automated bulldozers and the insectoid cargo bots that were working the periphery of the metropolis. However, since they'd left the city behind, they had observed no movement, no sign of robots.

Until now.

Peering around the husk of the ruined structure, Angela and Vaughn stared at a pair of machines rummaging through the rubble. They were shorter than the no-neck bots and stood on four, stubby legs instead of the two sported by the main robots, although they were similarly equipped with four hands or graspers.

One of them pulled a large chunk of masonry or concrete from a debris pile. A mangled span of rusted steel reinforcement stuck out from it. The robot grasped the ends of the metal. Then the machine stopped moving, becoming suddenly inanimate. The protruding metal began to glow. Initially, it took on a dark orange hue, but then the light emanating from the rod ramped up to a bright yellow.

A loud crack shot out, and the shattered masonry fell to the ground. The bot tossed the now naked piece of glowing metal into the air. Just when it reached the top of its arc and began to fall earthward, the steel rod lurched and then shot sideways, flying toward the vat of molten metal.

Vaughn looked at Angela and then whispered harshly. "They must be scavenger bots."

She nodded.

He began to look around, scanning the area. "Shit! They're blocking our path to the subway entrance."

Angela nodded and then whispered urgently. "I know! Let's go around."

After a quick scan of her own, she checked the bots one more time. They appeared to be looking the other way.

Still crouching, Angela stepped out from behind the cover and darted between piles of debris. She could hear Vaughn following just behind her.

A few minutes later, they rounded another corner. Having circumnavigated the bots, they were now heading straight for the part of town where the subway entrance should be. Unfortunately, their circuitous path had taken them uncomfortably close to the outskirts of the steel city and its tenant dozers and insect bots.

Angela finally spotted their destination. "This way!"

She turned away from the alien metropolis and began to trot down the length of an old, rubble-strewn Geneva street.

Reaching a wide, circular roundabout, Angela stopped and took cover in the shadow of a toppled statue that sat in its center. Her eyes narrowed as she visually scanned the area a few blocks ahead, looking for the subway entrance.

She spotted movement.

Angela pointed. "I see them ... I mean us!"

Vaughn squatted next to her and craned his neck. "Where?"

She opened her mouth to respond but then saw them drop out of sight, disappearing into the tunnel.

"They just went under—"

A tremendous, siren-like alarm shattered the air.

Both their heads snapped left as they sought the source of the noise.

A couple of hundred feet away, in the center of an intersecting road, a scavenger bot stood waist-deep in a pile of debris. As it continued to blare its alarm, both of the robot's large, camera-lens eyes remained locked on Angela and Vaughn.

Suddenly, it dropped the chunk of debris that it had been working on and began to scurry toward the two of them, its four short legs kicking up dust in its wake. Three of its claw-like graspers reached out menacingly. A blowtorch grasped in its other appendage flared to life.

Angela's eyes widened. "Run!"

She jumped from their hiding position and started in the direction of the subway entrance, but then movement above the opening stopped both of them in their tracks.

"Oh shit," Vaughn said hoarsely.

It was a goddamned Tater! The thing must have spotted the original version of themselves descending into the subway and gone to investigate.

Angela glanced over her shoulder. The scavenger bot was rapidly closing on them.

She scanned their surroundings, frantically looking for cover or a way out of this poop sandwich. Caught out in the open, they were too exposed. They'd never outrun the bot. The Tater was probably too far away to hear the robot's alarm, but even if it hadn't already been notified by radio, the flying potato would soon see them for itself if they didn't find cover.

Angela grabbed Vaughn's arm and pulled him toward the steel city. Running as fast as her tired legs could muster, she headed back in the direction from which they'd come.

Passing through an area clear of the dozers and cargo bots, Angela reentered the machine city, seeking cover in its narrow alleyways.

Both of them were breathing heavily.

Looking back, Angela peered around Vaughn.

The scavenger bot was hot on their heels. Fortunately, they'd seen no sign of the Tater. It hadn't appeared to have followed them.

Angela pulled the gun out from her belt and aimed it over

Vaughn's shoulder, but he knocked it aside before she could pull the trigger.

"Don't waste the shot," he said breathlessly. "There's just one of them."

Angela nodded curtly and tucked the gun back into the waistline of her pants. Then she darted into a skinny alleyway, one that she hoped was too narrow for the bot.

As she passed between the mirror finishes of the two buildings, she saw multiple hazy reflections of both herself and Vaughn to her left and right.

A loud clunk told her that the alleyway had prevented the bot's entrance. It screamed in frustration.

Unsure of what other routes the machine might find to give chase and how many friends it may have called in, Angela continued to run deeper into the city. Several twists and turns later, she decided they must have gone far enough to lose the bot.

She turned and was surprised to see that Vaughn was no longer right behind her. A moment later, he exited from the last alleyway, his face flushed and covered with a thin layer of sweat. His breathing was labored.

Angela felt her stomach sink. This was her fault. Vaughn wouldn't be this drawn and weak if not for his giving her extra rations to make up for what she had lost to illness.

Panting and bent over, Vaughn rested his hands on his knees. Then he pointed off to the side. "We need to head back ... back toward the subway entrance."

Still twenty feet away, he hitched a thumb over his shoulder, pointing behind them. "I think we lost—"

Suddenly, the robot darted out from between two buildings.

Vaughn flinched and tried to jump away.

The scavenger reached out and snatched him by the wrist.

A scream of pain burst from Vaughn's lips.

Angela broke through her shock and ran toward him. "Vaughn!"

Digging under the tail of her flapping shirt, she groped for the gun.

Before Angela could produce the weapon, the bot reversed itself, backing into the crossing passage and yanking Vaughn out of sight.

She sprinted toward the alley.

Finally freeing the weapon from her waistband, Angela raised it to eye level just as she slid to a stop in front of the entrance to the narrow lane.

It was empty.

Vaughn and the bot had already disappeared.

Then another scream echoed through the city.

Running as fast as she could, Angela followed the sound of Vaughn's shouts. A moment later, she rounded a bend and saw them.

Vaughn kicked and screamed as the scavenger dragged him backward down the street. Blood trickled down his arm. It was coming from the point where the machine's grappler was digging into his wrist.

"Angela!"

The bot stopped with a lurch.

Vaughn's face contorted with pain. He tried again to pull his arm free, but it wouldn't budge.

The narrow passageway had slowed the machine. She could see scratch marks left by the bot's hips where they had rubbed the walls that framed the alley.

Angela ran toward it, gun outstretched.

"Leave him alone, you damned toaster."

Suddenly, a six-foot-long flame shot from the torch grasped in one of the machine's other appendages.

Angela screamed and jumped back, falling on her butt. Her teeth clicked together, and the coppery taste of blood filled her mouth. She batted down the small flames that clung to the tattered legs of her worn pants.

Heat waves from the still-blasting flamethrower rippled the air between her and Vaughn.

Then Angela saw that the bot no longer moved. Its legs continued to churn, but it had ground to a stop. The thing had jammed itself between the buildings.

Vaughn was still struggling to free himself from the grasp of the robot, his face twisting with pain.

Frozen, Angela stood with the gun aimed at the bot.

Vaughn again tried and failed to free himself.

The scavenger shifted the torch's flame toward Vaughn.

He looked at Angela. "Feel free to shoot the damned thing anytime now!"

"I don't want to hit you!"

Vaughn shook his head. "The gun won't hurt me."

The robot inched the torch closer to its hostage.

Vaughn looked at the open flame. His face glowed beneath its amber light. "Now that, on the other hand ...!"

Angela nodded. She spat out a bloody wad, and then aimed at the machine's body. She screwed up her face, worried that the gun might hurt Vaughn in spite of his reassurances. An electromagnetic pulse shouldn't harm living tissue, but she didn't know for sure that the weapon only fired an EMP.

Cringing, Angela squeezed the trigger.

It popped and squealed.

The robot stopped moving.

The flame withered and died.

On his back and with his arm pinned overhead, Vaughn struggled to get his feet under him. The now inanimate robot's mechanical claw still clasped his wrist. Bloody streaks trailed down his arm. With his free hand, he tried to pry open the machine's claw.

Angela ran to his side. She grabbed the bot's grasper and also tried to pry its halves apart. She pulled as hard as she could, screaming with the effort. "It. Won't. Budge!"

Beneath her, Vaughn continued to struggle with the mechanism.

Angela searched frantically, looking for something with which she could pry it open. Then she saw several rods protruding from a slot in the robot's back. She didn't know what they were, maybe giant welding rods, but they looked strong enough. She grabbed one and pulled it out.

Vaughn stopped struggling and eyed the rod warily. Then he nodded. "That should do it."

Angela wedged its end into a gap between the grasper's two halves. With raised eyebrows, she looked at Vaughn. "Ready?"

He nodded. His face now looked even whiter than it had earlier.

Angela swallowed and then began to count down. "Three, two, one!"

She hefted her weight into the rod.

Creaking loudly, the metal jaws slowly opened.

Vaughn yanked his arm free just before the end of the rod broke off and the claws snapped shut.

Vaughn clamped a hand over the injured wrist. "Holy crap!" Face glistening with sweat, he stared at the blood-covered claws. "That was close!"

Breathing heavily, Angela plopped down next to him. She reached for his arm. "Let me see."

Looking as if afraid of what he might see, Vaughn continued to clasp his injured wrist. Still wide-eyed, he regarded her with his too white face.

Angela hoped he wasn't going into shock.

Haltingly, Vaughn extended the arm toward her and slowly opened his other hand.

Chewing her lip, Angela inspected his injuries. Fresh blood oozed from the abrasions on either side of his wrist. Fortunately, no arterial blood spurted, although some of the cuts were deep enough to need stitches.

She nodded. "It's pretty swollen, but I think you'll be alright. I'll wrap it up."

Vaughn nodded.

Angela began to dig through her backpack, soon producing a strip of cloth she had set aside for this very purpose. She wrapped it around his wound. The bleeding had already begun to slow. It stained the bandage but didn't look like it would get any worse.

"That should do for now."

Vaughn studied her handiwork and then nodded again.

Standing, she helped him to his feet.

They looked up at the narrow sliver of sky visible overhead.

Breathing heavily, Vaughn said, "It's already getting dark. We're falling behind. We have to catch up to them ... to us!"

Angela grabbed her backpack and stuffed everything into it. "Okay." She looked around. "Which way?"

"I don't know, but we can't just wait here." Vaughn looked left and right. "Screw it." He pointed right and then started jogging unsteadily in that direction. "Let's try this way."

Angela glanced down at the gun clasped in her right hand. The grimy, thrumming device still emitted a high-pitched whine. She sure as hell hoped the thing finished charging before they ran into any more robots. It was their only weapon. As she had the thought, Angela saw the metal rod. She bent over and picked it up and then followed Vaughn.

The two of them ran down the zigzagging network of alleys and roads. They didn't run into any other robots. Unfortunately, they didn't find a way out of the steel city either.

As they worked their way through the metropolis, Angela noticed that the surface of the ground alternated between new metal surfaces and periodic stretches of Geneva's original streets. It appeared that the robots had no affinity for dirt, but they didn't mind leaving the existing road surface where it suited them.

They rounded another turn only to find another long expanse of steel-lined corridor, but still no sign of the city's perimeter.

Vaughn stopped and looked at the sky.

"Shit! Shit! Shit! I don't know where in the hell we are!"

Angela shook her head. "Me neither."

With so much of the sky blocked by buildings and with no sunlight left, it was impossible to tell which way they were going.

Exhausted, she lowered the end of the heavy rod to the ground. It hit with a hollow, metallic report.

Vaughn suddenly became very animated. "What the heck?!" He dropped to a knee at her feet.

In the dark, Angela saw his hands sweeping across the ground.

"That sounded like a ..." He stopped moving and then looked up at her, his smile glowing in the darkness. "It is!"

She crouched next to him. "What is it?"

"It's a utility access!"

Kneeling beside Vaughn in the gloomy alley, Angela slid her hands across the surface and soon found the recognizable ridged pattern of concentric rings. He was right. This was another section where the robots had opted to leave the original street surface in place.

Angela looked at Vaughn. "It is, but so what?" She wrinkled her nose. "We need to get to the subway, not the sewer."

He looked around and then back at her. "You know which way to go?" he whispered. "Because I sure as hell don't." Pointing down for emphasis, he added, "This leads down and probably connects to the subway. If you have a better idea, I'm all ears."

A soft breeze shuffled Angela's matted hair. At the same time, she heard a low, hollow-sounding whistle, like air blowing across the top of a soda bottle. She probed the surface of the access cover with her fingers and soon found the source of the sound. Air was blowing out of an inch-wide hole near the edge of the steel disc.

She looked up. In the alley's darkness, she could just make out a smile on Vaughn's nodding face.

"That's wind from subway movement."

Angela shook her head. "We don't have a light. How are we going to find our way into the subway?"

"Just follow the air," Vaughn said, his voice straining with fresh exertion. "If we can get the damned thing open." He grunted again. "Shit! It won't budge."

Angela glanced at the dark silhouette of the metal bar in her hand. Reluctantly, she held it in front of her. "This should help."

"Perfect!" Vaughn said too loudly. The word echoed off the surrounding walls, returning to them multiple times, each more twisted and distorted than the previous.

Angela winced at the noise. "Shh!" She looked down and then back at Vaughn. "Are you sure about this?"

Suddenly, the high-pitched screech of an approaching Tater split the night. Then it appeared in the narrow gap visible between the buildings.

"Shit!" Angela shoved the bar into Vaughn's hands and whispered urgently. "Here, take it!"

Fortunately, the potato-shaped ship was several blocks from their location. With any luck, it still didn't know exactly where they were.

Vaughn took the bar.

The grating squall of steel on steel rang out as he slid the unbroken end of the rod into a hole in the cover. Then he grunted as he tried to pry up the cast-iron disc. His ghostly white arms trembled visibly in the dark.

"Here, let me help."

Vaughn shifted, opening a space on the bar for her. She grabbed the end and added her weight to his.

The heavy plate refused to budge.

Angela feared that it might snap off like it had when she'd pried open the bot's claws, but fortunately it held. Then with a loud, echoing squawk the opposite side of the cover lifted.

Angela and Vaughn fell to the pavement, pinning the rod to the surface. Thankfully, the heavy steel disc didn't fall off the end of the bar.

She glanced toward the distant Tater and then nodded. "I don't think it heard us."

Kneeling now, she placed a hand on top of Vaughn's. "Keep holding it down."

"I got it."

In the darkness, she crawled to the far side of the cover.

Vaughn's silhouetted head nodded.

Knowing that a slip of the bar would cost her dearly, Angela slid fingers under the propped-up lid. After a hard swallow, she grasped the steel disc and pulled with all of the strength she could muster.

Sounding like the screech of a steel-throated eagle, the manhole cover slid from the opening. The metallic rasp echoed harshly.

Then a terrifying sound rose to replace it.

Wide-eyed, Angela and Vaughn looked down the alley.

The Tater was rushing toward them. It had already closed to within a few blocks.

Vaughn pointed into the inky void.

"Go!"

Angela swung her legs into the opening's black maw. Groping with her feet, she found a step. Then she reached down and found the top metal rung and descended into the black as fast as she dared.

She froze for a horrified moment as a roar rose from beneath her.

She felt the rush of air that signaled the distant passage of another subway.

She looked up. The onrushing Tater now illuminated Vaughn's face.

He looked back down as he swung his legs into the hole. "Go faster!"

Angela nodded and began to shimmy down the steps. Her foot bounced off one of them, and she started to fall.

She swiped desperately at the rungs and just managed to grab one with her left hand.

The Tater's brilliant searchlight flooded the vertical tunnel as it moved over the access hole.

Angela glanced down.

"Oh no!"

Her breath caught in her throat at the sight of rungs disappearing into the darkness beneath them. The hole continued straight down as far as she could see.

Unless they just dropped, there was no way they'd get far enough down the ladder to outrun the light wave that was only moments away.

Still hanging from her left hand, Angela quit trying to find footing and dug out the gun with her free hand.

She pointed it upward, but Vaughn was blocking her shot.

"Move left!"

Vaughn shifted sideways, and the belly of the Tater slid into view.

Its light-wave emitter was already starting to glow.

Angela pointed the gun at it and pulled the trigger.

The weapon snapped and squealed.

Then impenetrable blackness swallowed Angela.

CHAPTER 33

The entire vertical tunnel rocked, shaking the rungs in Vaughn's hands as the now dead Tater fell ten feet to the surface and landed on top of the manhole.

Coughing, he squinted and blinked against the acrid dust that suddenly filled his lungs.

Then he heard grunts and coughs coming from beneath him.

"Angela! Are you okay?!"

"Yeah ..." She grunted again. "Lost my footing for a moment there. Got some grit in my eyes too, but I'm fine. What about you?"

Vaughn glimpsed up, but the Tater was invisible in the darkness. However, the knowledge it sat mere inches from his face sent a shiver down his spine.

"We need to hurry—!"

A rustling sound cut off his words. It was Angela descending the steps.

"Already ahead of you. Try to keep up, Captain. We have to catch ourselves before it's too late."

He nodded and began to lower himself down the ladder.

Several times, his weary hands threatened to drop Vaughn down on Angela, but somehow he managed to hang on in spite of the sweat that was wetting his hands.

After a seeming eternity, he heard a change in Angela's footfalls.

"I found the bottom."

Another roar filled the void.

A stiff breeze swept across Vaughn's sweat-covered brow. He swept a sleeve across it. The feeling of grit smearing across his skin momentarily reminded him of Hell.

The wind changed direction.

Vaughn realized that the subway must have passed the opening that they were seeking. It had gone from pushing air into their passage to pulling it out as it had continued down the line.

Blinking, he realized he could just make out her silhouette. There was light down here, although he couldn't see the source.

Then both the wind and the sound died, taking the momentary illumination with it.

Angela tugged his arm in the renewed darkness. "This way, I think."

Vaughn followed her, feeling in the dark with outstretched hands. Periodically, water splashed underfoot, and he felt damp stone walls to their sides.

Gradually, Vaughn started seeing details as light from another unseen source began to fill the narrow tunnel. This time it was brighter. He could see the tubing of several electrical conduits running overhead.

A few yards later, they came to a Y-shaped intersection where their small tunnel merged with a much broader and taller passageway. It took a moment for Vaughn to realize that it was a subway tunnel.

They'd found it!

They had also found the source of the light.

A subway station sat less than a hundred yards away.

In front of their feet, the station's light reflected from the triple rails that guided and powered the trains.

Vaughn grabbed Angela's arm. "Careful," he whispered and then pointed at the farthest length of steel. "Don't touch the third rail."

DEAN M. COLE

Looking back at him, she nodded. Then her eyes widened as a new light source shone on her face.

He looked left and squinted against the blindingly bright light that suddenly filled the tunnel. A subway had rounded a corner and was heading straight for them, its headlight slicing the darkness ahead of it.

Vaughn reached out and snatched Angela. He pulled her back into the service corridor just as the train zipped past.

Brightly illuminated railcars careened past them.

Then he heard the squeal of brakes, and the subway slowed.

Angela clutched him. "Did they see us?"

Vaughn shook his head. "I don't think so."

The train's last car scrolled past the service tunnel's exit. Then the subway came to a stop, its back only a few yards down the tracks.

He pointed at it. "Let's go. We need to get on."

Angela's eyes widened. She pulled him down until her lips brushed his ear. "Are you crazy?" she whispered harshly.

Vaughn leaned in. "I didn't see any robots on it. I think it's one of the returning subways. It should take us back to the source." He paused and gave Angela a meaningful look. "Back to CERN."

She glanced from him to the train and then back.

"How can you know that?"

"Last time we saw the robots riding the subway, they were standing in the cars, not sitting." He pointed at the train again. "Even from down here, I would've seen them if they were onboard. This one is empty. It's going back for another load, just like the one we rode the first time."

Finally, Angela nodded. "Okay."

Crouching, they emerged from their hiding spot and crept up to the rear car.

Angela stepped onto the short, three-rung ladder that led to its rear deck.

The subway began to roll forward.

Vaughn cursed under his breath and shook his head. "Really?!"

306

Fortunately, Angela managed to scramble onto the small platform quickly. She turned and waved him up.

"Hurry!"

Vaughn gnawed his teeth. He was trying to hurry, but his spent legs were having a hard time getting him up to speed. He could barely manage the jog currently required just to keep up with the steadily accelerating train. He didn't need Angela to remind him that if he didn't get on that deck soon, he'd be running through a brightly lit subway station, possibly with an audience of freshly deposited robots.

Grimacing, Vaughn shook his head. "Freaking wonderful!"

The white, tiled walls visible around the periphery of the rear car began to glow from the light of the nearing station.

"Shit! Shit! Shit! Shit!" Vaughn chanted under his breath, the words coming in rhythm with each footfall. And of course, each of those steps was taking him closer and closer to the station.

Vaughn achieved his maximum speed just as he caught up to the train. He reached for the top rung of the short ladder, but his hand bounced off it.

"Come on!"

The accelerating train began to pull away from him.

Like a baseball center fielder diving for a hard hit line drive, Vaughn lunged for the back of the subway.

And caught it!

The train continued to accelerate, dragging Vaughn into the station.

He pulled his feet toward the bottom rung. Looking down, he saw his right foot drifting toward the electrified third rail.

"Oh, hell no!"

Tapping the last of his reserves, Vaughn drew his knees up and finally climbed onto the three-foot-wide platform.

Angela pulled him to her. Clutching each other desperately, they huddled on the worn steel deck, hiding behind the sheet-metal side skirting that ran from the handrails to the floor. The solid panel blocked the pair from view as they passed through the subway station.

When they passed into the tunnel at the far side of the station,

Vaughn caught a momentary glimpse of a group of robots chatting on the opposite deck. Fortunately, none of them seemed to have noticed the two stowaways on the back of the departing train. They just continued their oddly human-like animated discussions.

As the subway bore deeper into the tunnel, Vaughn reached over Angela's head and pressed a button next to the car's back door. It slid aside with a burp of compressed air.

After a quick scan of the thankfully empty railcar, they crawled into its well-lit interior and collapsed onto the floor, lying next to each other.

Breathing heavily, Vaughn rolled his head toward Angela. "That ... was ... damned close!"

She gave him a quick nod.

Angela looked around again and then regarded Vaughn with raised eyebrows. "This might be *the* train."

"What do you mean?"

"This might be the same subway we rode to CERN!"

Vaughn paused. Then he shook his head. "Can't be. We lost too much time running from that damned scavenger bot."

"No. Remember? It took us a while to get on the train."

He considered her words. How long had they wandered around down there that day? It had been evening the first time they had entered the subway station, but once they'd descended below ground level, he had lost all track of time.

Vaughn raised his empty wrist. Looking at the faded tan-line left by the discarded watch, he had no better grasp on the time of day now than he'd had back then.

Vaughn looked at Angela. "Maybe." He gestured forward. "Let's go find ourselves."

She smiled weakly and nodded.

They climbed to their feet. Staying crouched, the pair searched from cabin to cabin, peering over the lower lip of each car's back window before opening its door.

Twice they dropped to the floor, hiding as a brightening of the tunnel announced their arrival at the next station.

As they passed into the second station, they sat on the floor again to stay out of sight. Then Angela tapped Vaughn's shoulder. She pointed excitedly at the name placarded on the station's white, tiled wall. "We passed through here last time! We *are* on the right train!"

Vaughn nodded. "Let's keep working our way forward. Maybe we can catch up to ourselves and end this now."

The subway started moving. A moment later darkness engulfed the train again as it passed back out of the station.

They exchanged nervous glances and then rose to their feet. Still crouching, they advanced to the next car.

Several nerve-racking searches later, they reached the forward-most railcar.

Angela looked dejected. "It's empty!" She plopped onto her butt.

Vaughn dropped to the floor next to her. "Crap!" He leaned back against the door they'd just come through. He resisted the urge to look at his wrist. "They ... *We* are probably already in CERN."

She nodded but didn't say anything.

Pointing to his empty wrist, Vaughn looked at Angela. "We have to get there before *we* start this whole loop ... again."

Nodding, Angela stared through the car's windows. Outside, the tunnel walls began to brighten. Then she flinched as the disembodied French voice announced: "Conseil Européen pour la Recherche Nucléaire."

Unlike his first trip down this subway line, Vaughn knew the announcement signaled their arrival at CERN.

Angela confirmed the fact. "This is it!"

"Let's not end up low-crawling the last twenty feet this time."

She nodded again. "As soon as the door opens, we head for the exit."

The train rolled to a stop. Vaughn spotted the station's name: CERN.

Bent at the waist, the two of them scrambled through the parting doors. They ran across the platform and darted into the waiting hallway beyond.

Behind them, the subway's doors closed with a burp of

compressed air. Then a breeze ruffled Vaughn's hair as the train rushed out of the station, pulling a shaft of atmosphere with it.

Unlike their previous exit, they had already passed out of the opposite platform's line of sight before the subway departed.

Angela hesitated.

Vaughn still remembered the path they had taken. He placed a hand on her elbow, urging her forward.

She relented, although her eyes still had a far-off look to them. Angela appeared distracted.

"What is it?" Vaughn said as they jogged down the long corridor.

She shook her head. "Not sure."

"About ... what?" he said, already winded. "We have to stop ourselves ... before ..." He pointed to the tattered remnants of their weathered and worn clothing. "Before this shit happens again."

Angela didn't respond, but she allowed Vaughn to guide them down the same steps and corridors that they had navigated on their first trip to CERN.

This time, they didn't have to peek around each corner. Vaughn knew where they had encountered the line of robots, knew that all of the other passageways were clear.

He urged Angela down another corridor. When they were halfway down its long expanse, Vaughn pulled up short.

"Oh shit." He looked around, slowly scanning the walls. Unfamiliar signs and portraits covered both sides. "I think I took a wrong turn."

Angela's eyes cleared, focus chasing away her distant gaze. She looked around and then nodded. "I know where we are." Turning slowly, she pointed to a door about twenty feet farther down the hall. "Go in there."

Needing no further prodding, Vaughn ran toward the glass door. He threw it open and started to step through, Angela at his side.

Suddenly, she froze.

Vaughn stopped mid-step.

"What?"

A door across from them flew open. Just as Vaughn saw the earlier version of himself step into the opening, Angela suddenly yanked him backward. Crouching again, she pulled him back down the hallway.

Angela whispered urgently in his ear. "Get down! They can't see us again."

Vaughn looked at her incredulously. "Again?" He shook his head and tried to pry her fingers from his arm. "What are you doing?! We have to stop them!"

Angela's head shot left and right. "No!" She pointed back down the hallway. "We have to run!"

Vaughn stopped trying to peel off her hands. Squatting, he grabbed her shoulders and turned her to face him. "You're not making sense, Angela! We have to stop ourselves from creating the loop. Otherwise, we'll just end up going through all of this again."

With infectious dread, Angela looked over his shoulder and then stared hard into Vaughn's eyes. She pointed toward the adjacent room. "Right now, we're in there discovering the truth about where the robots are coming from. And in a couple of minutes, I'm going to try to overload the wormhole."

Vaughn nodded. "Exactly! We have to stop that from happening."

Angela shook her head again. "No." She pointed at the floor. "We wouldn't be here, wouldn't know about what these bastards have been doing to all of these worlds if we hadn't started this loop."

She looked over her shoulder and started trying to tug Vaughn back in the direction from which they'd come.

He stopped her and placed a finger on the side of her chin.

She turned to look at him.

"Okay, Angela," Vaughn said, speaking softly. "I guess you might be right."

Looking more frightened than ever, she pulled desperately at his elbow.

Vaughn gave her a reassuring look. "I believe you, Angela. I won't try to stop them."

"Vaughn!" Angela said in a barely contained shout. She pulled at him. "If we're caught in the light when I ..." She shook her head. "When the earlier me overloads the wormhole, we'll be sucked in too."

Vaughn's blood ran cold. He froze for a horrifyingly wasted moment.

Misreading his hesitation, Angela continued. "We'll be wiped from existence!"

Finally, Vaughn broke his paralysis and jumped to his feet. He pointed past Angela. "Run!"

CHAPTER 34

As they jumped to their feet and started running down the hallway, Vaughn could already hear the ramping up, high-pitched whine of Angela's previous manipulations.

Placing a hand on her back, he urged her forward. "Hurry, you've already started!"

Angela nodded. Her tangled mat of hair bobbed up and down with the motion.

Reaching the end of the empty corridor, she jammed both hands against the latching bar and shoved.

It didn't give.

The door stayed shut.

Angela simply bounced off it, ricocheting backward into Vaughn.

Recovering quickly, she bent over the keypad and punched in her code, but just as she was about to press the last key, the lights flickered, and the pad's display blinked out as it lost power.

"No!" Angela fruitlessly pressed several additional keys, but they no longer beeped, and when she finished entering her code, nothing happened.

Vaughn pulled her aside. Then he kicked at the bar as hard as he could.

Still, the door didn't budge.

Behind them, the crescendoing squeal of the collider's increasing power output rose to painful levels.

Vaughn exchanged a frightened glance with Angela. Then they turned to look back down the hall.

Shaking his head, Vaughn grabbed Angela's hand and started to run down the passageway, intent on backtracking to another exit.

Suddenly, the leading edge of the quivering, mercurial mass of the expanding wormhole appeared. In an instant, it swallowed the far end of the corridor and rushed toward the two of them as they skidded to a stop.

Reversing directions, Angela and Vaughn ran back toward the locked door. As they neared it, Vaughn leaped into the air, leading with the sole of his right hiking boot. It slammed painfully into the lock bar.

Still it refused to yield.

Vaughn kicked two more times in rapid succession.

Nothing. The damned thing wouldn't open!

Angela tugged at his sleeve. "Vaughn!"

He turned and then pressed his back to the door as he watched the mercurial wall's oddly rippling surface. Its now slowing advance swallowed the corridor foot by foot.

For a brief, surreal moment, Vaughn stared at their growing reflection in its undulating surface.

"No, not like this," Angela said weakly. She leaned into Vaughn, pressing the side of her face into his chest. "Please, don't let it end like this."

Vaughn wrapped his arms around her. Together they watched as the silvery wall continued to advance, steadily swallowing the corridor.

Then it began to slow.

At first Vaughn thought it wishful thinking, but then he saw that its advance was indeed slowing.

The squealing, grating whine of the collider's power source plateaued, and its painful, tooth-rattling frequency held unchanged.

At the same moment, the mercurial wall ground to a stop mere inches from Angela and Vaughn's faces.

Staring at their wavering reflections, Vaughn had to resist the urge to reach out and touch the undulating, silvery surface.

The shape of the slowly traversing waves shifted. Then a pattern began to emerge. The surface directly across from Vaughn, the portion reflecting his and Angela's faces, began to protrude, bulging outward as if something inside it were reaching out for them.

Angela pressed harder into Vaughn as she started to scream.

They both flinched as the head and shoulders of one of the no-neck-having bastards suddenly emerged from the mass with a wet pop.

The thing stared across the narrow void, first at Angela. Then it turned its glass eyes on Vaughn. It was impossible to see emotion in that mechanical face, but Vaughn thought he could feel malevolent intent pouring from its lifeless eyes.

Four hands suddenly emerged from the surface. Flexing and grasping, they reached for Vaughn and Angela.

Yep, malevolent alright. The bastard certainly didn't have rainbows and kittens on its mind.

Suddenly, Angela pulled away from Vaughn. With incredible speed, she produced the EMP gun and jammed it onto the robot's small forehead. "Go to Hell, Fucker!"

The Neck's hands grasped her forearms.

Angela pulled the trigger.

A snap and pop rang out.

The robot froze.

Then the screaming power source suddenly quietened.

At the same moment, the wormhole contracted. Its mirrored surface retreated down the corridor and then disappeared at its far end.

Angela and Vaughn flinched as a loud, metallic clank echoed down the now empty hallway.

Vaughn looked down to see the severed remnants of the robot's upper body and hands rocking on the floor at their feet.

Angela pointed the now whining EMP gun at it. She balled her other hand into a fist and then stomped the robot's head, crunching its glass eyes under the sole of her boot. "Die, you son of a bitch!"

Vaughn touched her arm lightly. "Angela?"

She didn't respond, just continued stomping on the bot's head and hands.

Angela growled. It was a primal sound that ended with a scream. It carried months of pent-up frustration.

"Angela!"

"What?!"

"It's dead!" He released her arm and pointed toward the exit. "We need to get out of here!"

Panting, Angela looked around as if remembering where she was. She raised her hands and stared at them and the gun. "We're still here …"

"Angela!" Vaughn looked around nervously. "We *need* to get moving!"

She looked at him and smiled. "Don't you understand? We're out!"

Vaughn shook his head. "Uh, no. We are still very much in!" He looked around again. "And if we don't get the hell out of here, we won't be alone much longer!"

"No, Vaughn. Not out of here. We're out of the loop. We broke it!"

Vaughn had been looking back at the door that had blocked their exit. Eyes widening, he turned back to Angela. He started to glance at his empty wrist. The watch was long gone, but he didn't need it to know that the time was past midnight.

Thirty-six hours had passed, and they were still here!

He grinned. "Holy crap! You're right! We're out!"

Angela's smile grew. "We are!"

Both of their grins faltered as a rustling noise broke the relative silence left in the wake of the power source's collapse.

Vaughn tilted his head. "What the hell is that sound?"

Then something crashed into the door at the far end of the hallway.

After exchanging horrified glances, they turned to the locked door at their backs, the one that had blocked their egress.

Angela glanced at the now steady overhead lights. "I hope that keypad works now!"

Behind them, the opposite exit rattled in its frame again.

The rustling had grown into a steady rumble as if an avalanche of boulders were heading their way.

Vaughn shuddered. "I don't like that sound."

Angela shook her head. "Me neither!"

She punched in her code. A click rang out when she pressed the pound key.

Angela shoved the lock bar.

The door opened.

She stepped forward. "Come on!"

A Neck on the door's far side yanked it fully open.

Angela stumbled backward, running into Vaughn's chest.

She dug behind her and produced the gun. Pointing it at the advancing robot, she pulled the trigger.

Click.

Nothing happened! The Neck just kept coming.

Vaughn grabbed Angela and shoved her behind him. He felt her jump as another loud crash rocked the door at the opposite end of the corridor. It sounded as if an entire army of the Necks were trying to get in from that direction.

He glanced around the advancing robot. Through the sliver of hallway visible beyond the machine's narrow waist, Vaughn could see tens of additional robots, all headed for their location.

"Ah, shit."

"Vaughn!"

He looked over his shoulder and saw Angela standing in the side door that led back to the Atlas Detector's control room.

Holding it open, she waved frantically. "Hurry!"

Vaughn spun away from the robot just as it reached out for him.

One of its hands clutched his jacket.

The material started to tear, but to his horror, the tattered garment held, stopping him dead in his tracks.

Then the powerful machine yanked Vaughn backward.

He threw his arms behind him. Wriggling, Vaughn freed himself from the jacket and the robot's grasp and then ran toward Angela.

Beyond her, the far door suddenly flew open as another group of robots burst into the hallway's opposite end.

Vaughn ran into the control room.

Angela slammed the door closed just as the two groups of robots converged on it! She punched nine-one-one into a keypad next to the latch, and the light above the door cycled red.

"That should keep them out!"

The door rattled in its frame.

One of the Necks glared at them through its foot-wide window.

The robot shifted sideways, and then one of its arms reared back.

Its three-fingered hand curled into a fist.

The arm blurred as it pistoned forward and punched the glass.

The entire door shook in its frame, but the glass didn't yield.

Angela leaned in and glared at the Neck. Then she held up her middle finger. "It's bulletproof, asshole!"

The robot leaned in and inspected the glass. Seeing it unaffected, it stepped sideways again.

Angela and Vaughn jerked as the Neck's arm pistoned rapidly, its fist pounding the glass like a jackhammer.

Then a tremendous crash erupted from behind the two of them.

They turned.

Vaughn's shoulders slumped. "Crap ... Really?!"

Several additional reports rang out as he and Angela stared through the Atlas control room's wide window. Robots were crashing through every visible door and hatch. A sea of the Necks was flooding into the Atlas Detector's cavernous facility.

Converging from multiple points, all of them were sprinting straight at Angela and Vaughn.

The wormhole still hung suspended at the center of the Atlas facility. In spite of Angela's earlier efforts, the mercurial sphere had returned to its original size and state, although no robots were coming through it at the moment.

Small favors, Vaughn thought.

He pointed at the advancing bots. "I thought you said they couldn't see through the glass."

Angela shrugged and sat down at the console. It was the same one she'd used last time. "I think our secret's out." She looked up at Vaughn and pointed at the approaching horde. "We should be okay for a moment. This window is thirty or forty feet above the floor."

Nodding, Vaughn glanced over his shoulder. The Neck-turned-jackhammer had pulverized the door's 'bulletproof' window. The glass was still in its frame, but it was beginning to bow inward. He looked at Angela. "Whatever you're planning to do, you'd better do it fast."

Ahead, the first wave of charging robots had disappeared beneath the frame of the observation window, but dozens more still streamed into the facility, coming in from every direction.

Suddenly, a dozen or more robots leaped into view.

It was the first wave.

"Uh ... Angela!"

Not looking up, she continued to punch commands into the computer terminal. "Kinda busy here."

The Necks flew through the air on ballistic arcs aimed at the control room window.

"Angela!"

"What?!" She looked up, and her eyes went round. "Oh shit!"

Having jumped forty feet into the air, the clutch of robots crashed into the control room's glass wall.

The floor shook with the force of the impact.

In the window, Angela and Vaughn's reflections quaked crazily, but the glass held.

The Necks fell out of sight, but then another wave of the bastards flew into view.

They slammed into the glass.

Cracks radiated out from the point of impact, and then those robots fell out of sight as well.

Angela bent over the console again. Her fingers were a blur of activity. "I'm almost done! There's still a massive amount of power flowing into the system."

Another group of robots slammed into the glass.

The window held, but more cracks radiated out from its center.

Angela nodded toward the wormhole. "The energy has to be coming through that."

Vaughn gave her a nervous look. "You sure about this, sure we won't just get sucked back into the loop?"

Angela shook her head. "I'm not sure of anything." As she continued to type, she gave him a sideways glance. "Except that, if we don't try, nothing will change."

Vaughn eyed the mechanical horde and then nodded. "Okay, what do we do?"

"*We* don't do anything. I'm going to do what I should have the first time. I'll divert the power they're pumping through the wormhole. If I feed all of it into the collider's magnetic coils, it should blow the whole thing."

"Uh ..." Vaughn dragged his gaze from the ant-like swarm of robots and looked at Angela. "Didn't you say something about that causing an explosion ... one that would kill us?"

Angela turned glistening eyes toward him.

"It will."

Vaughn stared at her, unable to speak for a moment. Then he shook his head. "I thought this was supposed to reset the entire time-line, send us back to the beginning."

"I'm hoping it will." She pointed at the computer terminal. "But I don't think we'll survive this reset."

"What?!"

Another wave of Necks slammed into the glass.

It bowed inward.

Angela held up her emaciated arm. "We've carried every scratch and condition with us from loop to loop. Like I said before, I think it's over if we die."

"What, then?" Vaughn said, shaking his head. "What happens to our previous selves? We just ... disappear from the timeline?"

"Yes, no, maybe ... I don't know, Vaughn! I don't have all the answers."

Standing on the piled masses beneath them, dozens of Necks were now pounding their clenched fists into the glass wall.

Something clattered behind Vaughn.

He turned to see the Jackhammer-Neck sticking one of its arms through the door's now destroyed window.

Angela looked from it to Vaughn. "All I know is that if we don't do something now, we won't be able to do anything soon."

Looking from the computer and then at the swarming robots, Vaughn swallowed and then nodded. He pulled a chair over and sat next to Angela. "Is there anything I can do to help?"

Angela leaned in and then kissed him with salty, tear-dampened lips.

Vaughn returned the kiss.

After a moment, she pulled back and placed a hand on his cheek. "I got this."

She turned back to the computer terminal. Her fingers blurred as they whizzed across its keyboard.

As if detecting Angela's intent, the robots suddenly redoubled their efforts. The ground itself began to tremble as the walls and glass panels shook violently.

"All the safeties are still bypassed. That's how I was able to ramp up the power as much as I did last time."

"Is there enough electricity ... to ... to do what you need?"

Angela glanced at him and then nodded grimly.

Vaughn thought of the amount of energy that it would take to power the massive cauldrons of boiling, molten metal that ringed the machine city. Yeah, that should be more than enough to blow the place three times over.

He returned her nod.

Angela spoke as she continued entering commands. "There's still a chance that this changes something. If the loop completely resets the timeline. Maybe it'll break the robot's connection to our dimension."

Pressing a final key, Angela looked at the wall of pounding robots. She lifted her too skinny arm toward them and then extended her middle finger. She grinned menacingly. "Either way, you bastards are toast."

Vaughn heard the wine of ramping electrical power rising above the cacophony of the invading robots. He glanced at the computer and swallowed again. "Is that it?"

Angela pointed at the keyboard. "Just have to hit the enter key when the power peaks." She looked at him. A tear rolled down her right cheek.

Vaughn hugged her tightly. "We've done the best we can."

Angela flinched as the robotic assault reached thunderous heights. Then she reached hesitantly for the computer's enter key.

Her hand hovered shakily above its plastic surface.

She looked at Vaughn again and nodded toward the robots that were still streaming into the facility. "With all of the extra power they're pumping in, every one of the collider's superconducting magnets should blow, all seventeen miles of them, but the worst of it will be right here."

"What will happen to us?"

Angela shivered in his arms. Her hand still hovered above the keyboard. "It should be quick."

This was it, Vaughn realized. This is where it was all going to end.

Glaring, he gestured at the mass of machines fighting to enter the control room.

"At least we'll take these assholes with us."

Angela smiled wryly. "Yes ... Yes, we will."

He rested his hand on the one she had hovering over the keyboard. "Angela, I ... I."

The very earth shuddered under the escalating robotic onslaught.

Angela leaned into him. She kissed his cheek and then rested her head on his shoulder. "I know, Vaughn. Me too."

The control room glass collapsed inward.

Dozens of robots streamed through the opening.

The incredible roar of ramping electrical energy peaked with bone-grinding intensity.

Vaughn closed his eyes. "Now?"

Angela's head bobbed. "Yes."

They pressed the key.

Instantly, all noise seemed to die.

Vaughn opened his eyes.

Every robot he could see stood frozen in place, seized up. The Necks had stopped right in the middle of their attack. Several were still standing with their arms raised like statues of protesters.

The floor heaved, nearly throwing both Vaughn and Angela to the ground.

Several of the inanimate bots toppled.

Looking above the piled Necks, Vaughn stared through the open frame of the control room window. He watched in horrified amazement as a jet of white-hot plasma exploded into the far side of the Atlas facility.

The blossoming flames shot out of the central point where the collider's massive ring deposited its seventeen-mile-long run of pipes and conduits into the Atlas experiment.

Expanding rapidly, the exploding gases raced out of the center of the detector and flew toward the back of the still hovering, spherical wormhole.

As it burned through the facility, the fireball obliterated the paralyzed swarm of invading robots.

In Vaughn's suddenly dilated perception of time, he watched as pieces of the no-neck bots flew ahead of the blast wave as if in slow motion.

At the same moment, hundreds of brilliant bolts of electricity arced through the air.

Coming from the massive formation of radiating steel conduits, all of the lightning bolts burned into the mercurial sphere.

The wormhole distorted.

Sharp-edged waves raced across its face as it ballooned outward.

In the blink of an eye, the sphere swelled to fill the visible portion of the Atlas facility.

Jagged metallic spikes rose and fell from its spasming surface.

Then it swallowed the front half of the control room.

Horrified, entranced, expecting to die at any moment, Vaughn stared at the wormhole's violently quaking surface.

He and Angela exchanged confused glances.

Another volley of lightning bolts burned into the quaking sphere.

Suddenly, the wormhole's size halved and then redoubled in a spasm that engulfed the two of them.

Vaughn plunged into a lightless, silent void of impenetrable darkness.

CHAPTER 35

Vaughn floated in an ocean of nothing.

He couldn't feel his body. Neither light nor sound penetrated his perceptions.

It was as if he'd become a disembodied intellect stuck in a perfect sensory deprivation tank.

Was this death?

Heaven?

Or was it Hell?! Not the smelly and dusty one but the one with pitchforks and fires?

Light suddenly banished the all-consuming black.

Then he was falling.

Shit! It was the loop all over again.

Vaughn didn't know whether to laugh or—

Air burst from his lungs as he slammed face first into a hard surface.

He gasped, fighting to draw a breath. "Son of a bitch ... that hurt."

Blinking, still lying prone, he stared at the surface that hung in the air a couple of inches from his nose.

Was that concrete?

"That was graceful, Captain."

Vaughn blinked.

That hadn't been Angela.

The speaker was male!

"Are you going to lie there all day?"

He knew that voice!

Vaughn froze. He didn't even breathe for fear that anything he did or said might shatter the illusion.

"Vaughn?! Are you okay?"

He released the held breath.

His view of the pavement hazed.

No, not hazed, fogged ... fog on the inside of a visor.

"M-Matt?" Vaughn said hesitantly. "Is that you?"

"No, it's the tooth fairy." Mark chuckled. "Of course it's me. Were you expecting someone else?"

Tears began to cloud Vaughn's vision.

In the corner of his eye, he saw Matt's booted foot step up next to him. Then the man dropped to a knee and placed a hand on Vaughn's shoulder.

"Don't worry about the fall. Happens all the time, especially to people new to these things. As long as you didn't break anything, we'll be okay."

Mark started to bend down.

Vaughn reached for the top of his own helmet. He had more than tears to hide from Mark. Looking down, he could see his beard on his cheeks.

Finding the lever for the helmet's mirrored visor, Vaughn slid it down, obscuring his too thin face and its furry surface.

Myriad thoughts raced through his mind.

Had he died? Was this a flashback?

No. Everything was too real, too solid.

Then what?

Had they created another loop?

No. Well, maybe, but now Vaughn understood.

This was Angela's full reset.

He remembered how the ramping up power had rattled his teeth.

He shuddered at the image, still fresh in his mind's eye, of the wall of fire racing at them, blowing apart the suddenly inanimate Necks.

Then he recalled the wormhole swallowing it all, including him and Angela, just as it had the first time they'd screwed with the thing. However, he now knew that Angela's first attempt had been a fart in a hurricane compared to the ferocity of this reset.

Another realization pounded home: if Mark was alive again, so was the rest of the world!

Or were they?

Had they stopped the damned robots altogether, broken their link to this dimension, to this Earth?

Maybe.

What if they hadn't stopped anything?

Could he save more people? Could Vaughn get more of them into the vacuum chamber?

How? No one would believe him.

In the two or three seconds that all of these epiphanies blazed through his mind, one realization reigned roughshod over all else: If Vaughn didn't get his ass up right freaking now, he risked changing something about this morning's test of the Q-Drive.

If he changed anything, the timing of that test might change.

That would doom them all!

If Angela's efforts hadn't broken the link permanently, and the robots had already opened the wormhole, he and Mark would only survive if they were hovering inside the vacuum chamber at the moment the light reached them.

Where was Angela?

Had she returned to the space station?

He shook his head. *You can figure that out later. Move it, Captain!*

He scrambled back to his feet. Turning to Mark, he pointed at his helmet's now mirrored visor. "It's too bright out here. Couldn't see my feet."

Mark smiled. "The sun isn't the problem, friend." He pointed to Vaughn's abdomen. "It's your belly …"

As Mark glanced down at Vaughn's midsection, his words faltered, and he did a double take. "What the hell?"

Vaughn looked down and saw his feet—something he couldn't have done that day, not with all of the extra weight he'd been carrying around. The space suits they had used for the vacuum chamber didn't have the hard-shelled torso of Angela's EVA suit, so the change in his body was perceptible.

Vaughn bent at his waist and made a show of inspecting himself. At the same time, he adjusted his suit's internal pressure, hoping Mark didn't see him doing it. His friend hadn't shown him this trick. Vaughn had learned how to change the pressure while preparing for his flight to the space station.

As he felt the suit begin to expand, he pooched out his belly and stood upright.

He patted his stomach. "Told you not to be illin' on the toolshed."

Mark stared at him wordlessly. Then he grinned wryly and shook his head.

Vaughn placed a gloved hand on Matt's arm and steered him toward the vacuum chamber.

"Come on, Colonel."

With his free hand, Vaughn gestured ahead.

"We have a date with destiny."

CHAPTER 36

Angela pushed back from the console, trying to get away from the undulating spikes that were extending and retracting from the wormhole's insanely manic surface.

Suddenly, it spasmed again.

The mercurial surface swallowed Angela, plunging her into inky blackness.

It seemed to go on forever.

Angela lost herself in it.

Blinding light flooded into her eyes. She squeezed them shut against the painful assault.

She was falling!

Had they triggered another loop?

Were she and Vaughn being sent back yet again?

Still falling?

Too long!

She windmilled her arms.

"Oh, no! Please, no ...!"

She was going to slam into the ocean, the boat, or whatever the hell was beneath them this time.

"No, no—!"

A male voice cut her off. "Angela! What's wrong?"

"Vaughn?"

Silence greeted her question.

No, not Vaughn. Who had that been? She knew that voice.

Her body went rigid as she tensed with the realization that she was still falling.

Angela tried to open her eyes, but each attempt drove a spike of pain into her brain. All she could see was a spot of brilliant light hovering in front of her.

"We passed out of the shadow," the disembodied voice said. The man's voice sounded reedy, as if coming through a ... speaker?

Angela stopped spasming.

She canted her head.

"Bill? ... Is that you?"

"Uh, yeah. Unless someone else joined us out here," Major Bill Peterson said with a light laugh. "You'll be alright. Just lower your visor. Then you'll be able to see again."

Angela brought up her hands, but before they could touch her face, they ran into a hard surface. She heard a click like two pieces of hard plastic colliding.

Something bumped into the back of her.

"Here, let me help. I'm right behind you."

An arm wrapped around her right side, coming over her shoulder.

A click.

The sound of sliding plastic.

The pain in her eyes halved. A moment later, it faded completely.

Angela lids fluttered open. A blurry mess of white shapes back-dropped by a field of black filled her vision.

Finally, Angela blinked the image into focus.

The space station!

She was back in space?!

"Better?"

Angela flinched. Then she found Bill's arm and spun herself around to look at him.

The astronaut's visor blocked his face from view, but Angela saw his name tag.

"Bill!"

She threw her arms around him.

Major Peterson grunted as her sudden movement dislodged him from his perch.

They started a slow tumble.

"Oops," Angela said with a giggle. Then something yanked her feet.

She pulled back from Bill and looked toward her boots.

They were latched into the station's manipulator arm.

Angela looked up with widening eyes. She scanned their immediate surroundings. The pair of astronauts were floating across from each other.

Major Peterson waved for her attention. "What? What's wrong?"

A new voice joined them.

"Yo, Command-Oh. What's going on out there? You okay?"

Angela looked over to the Cupola. "You're alive! You're both alive!" Angela managed between sobs.

"Uh," Major Peterson paused and then cleared his throat. He reached over and cycled a switch on the sleeve of her space suit. "Sorry, just wanted to make sure you weren't transmitting. What the hell is wrong with you, Commander?" he asked sharply.

His tone snapped Angela out of her reverie.

"Is your mixture screwed up?"

Angela shook her head, but of course he couldn't see her face. Then something else drew her eye.

Between Bill and Angela lay the same stubborn electrical connector that had given them so much trouble that day.

This day!

"Oh no, no, no ..." Angela whispered.

They were floating beneath the port end of the space station's 300-foot-long solar array truss structure.

Exactly as they had been when—

"Oh shit!"

Angela toggled her radio. "Control! This is Commander Brown! Come in!"

"Go ahead, Commander. This is Control. Is everything alright?"

"No ... Definitely not?"

Angela's head was spinning.

It had worked.

The reset had sent them all the way back to the beginning.

"Commander Brown?"

Everyone was back!

The whole world!

But would the robots find them again?

Angela's eyes widened.

"Control!" she said in a shout. "Call CERN. Tell them to shut it down! Shut it down, now!"

The radio remained deathly quiet for a long moment. Angela was about to key the mic again, but then a new, very familiar voice came over the speakers in her helmet. "Uh, Angela? Are you okay?"

"Director McCree! This is extremely urgent. I need you to call Doctor Hans Garfield at CERN. Tell him—"

"Sorry to interrupt you, Angela," McCree said. "I have to admit, I'm sorely confused as to why you'd need me to contact someone in Europe, especially considering the request I was about to make."

"Oh God ..." Angela said in a hoarse whisper. "I'm too late!"

"Sorry, Commander, I didn't catch that. Your radio was weak and unreadable, but hold that thought. I have something I need you to take a look at."

Angela shook her head vigorously. "No, Director McCree. I have something I need to show you."

She pointed to the Quest module. It sat a hundred fifty feet away. "Bill, start making your way to the airlock."

After turning to follow her gesture, Bill's suit turned back toward Angela. "Commander?"

"Now, goddammit!"

After a short hesitation. He turned and started to work his way toward the center of the station.

"Commander Brown?!" Director McCree said, raising his voice. "What are you doing?"

"Sir, I need you to head to your office and stand by for a video conference. I'll call you back from inside the station."

"Dammit, Commander, I have something of the utmost importance, something I need you to take a look at."

Angela guided the manipulator arm so that she followed close behind Major Peterson. "I already know what it is, Randall. And I can tell you that it is not an aurora. There's more that I need to tell you, but it'll have to wait until we're inside."

A long silence greeted her proclamation. When the director's voice returned, he sounded thoroughly confused. "Uh, okay ... I-I'll be standing by. Make it fast, please."

Angela nodded. "Will do, sir."

She hated losing any time, but without proof there was no way the director or anyone else was going to believe what she was about to tell them.

A few minutes later, Angela and Bill completed the airlock cycle. They floated into the spacious lower half of the Quest module. Major Peterson had already doffed his suit, but Angela still had hers on. She'd also left her mirrored visor down.

"Teddy! Where are you?" She had to yell to be heard through the suit's still closed helmet.

The cosmonaut floated into the module. "Right here, Command-Oh!"

Angela pointed her gloved finger at the device in his hand.

"Is that thing on?"

Teddy screwed up his face. "Why are you still in your suit?"

"She refuses to take it off," Bill said. "Won't even raise the mirrored visor."

Angela ignored them. She jabbed a gloved finger at the camera in Teddy's hand. "Is it on? Are we connected to the Director?!"

A hurt look crossed Teddy's face, but he nodded. "Y-Yes, it is."

The director's voice suddenly blared from a speaker mounted to the module's wall. "I'm here, Angela. And I can see you just fine ...

well, I see your suit, anyway. Now would be a really good time to tell me just what in the hell is going on!"

Angela held up a gloved finger. "I have many things to tell you, things you'll never believe, not without strong evidence."

She pointed to Major Peterson. "Bill, do you remember what I was wearing when we donned our space suits?"

"What?"

"Humor me."

Thoroughly confused, he looked at her for a moment and then shrugged. "Yeah, the same thing as me: the thermal suit-liner we all wear during spacewalks."

Angela nodded and then reminded herself that they still couldn't see her head. "Yes, exactly." She turned and pointed. "And Teddy, what did you say about my hair this morning?"

Teddy smiled. "Da, Command-Oh." He pulled off his Roscosmos hat. No longer held in check, his curly blond mane swelled to fill a good portion of the module. "I said, if you had not cut your hair so short, it could have been as pretty as mine. Yours used to be so beautiful. Why did you cut it like that? I mean, it's only a few inches long now. That's ridiculous."

Director McCree's voice rang from the speaker. "Commander Brown, where are you going with this? I have the president waiting for a report!"

Angela began to unlatch her suit. "He'll wait."

McCree said something else, but she couldn't hear him over the rustling of her suit. Angela had disconnected its waistline coupler and was currently struggling to pull the top half of the suit over her head.

A moment later, she finally shrugged out of the upper shell and shoved it aside.

Angela shook her head, and her hair floated free.

Suddenly, all conversation ceased.

Angela's too skinny face stared into the camera lens. Then she looked at the two men that floated to either side of it.

Her now foot-long and matted auburn hair filled an appreciable portion of the module's interior space.

She untucked the dirty, tattered shirt from her worn and equally filthy jeans, neither of which bore any resemblance to the thermal suit-liner they'd seen her wearing earlier.

Bill and Teddy exchanged confused glances.

The speaker crackled back to life.

"Commander Brown, uh, I don't know—"

"No, you don't," Angela interrupted. "But I do. I know a lot."

She stared into the camera. "Randall, I have a plan, but for my plan to work, you have to do exactly what I say and exactly *when* I say."

"Angela …" Director McCree said, his voice suddenly shaky. "Who … or what did this to you? Is it tied to that … that thing in Europe?"

Angela nodded. "Yes, sir, it is."

Her eyes narrowed.

"But don't worry. I have a plan for those bastards, too."

Find out what happens next!
Continue to the next page for information about
Amplitude: Dimension Space Book Three

Amplitude: Dimension Space Book Three
Coming 2019

Get Notified When Amplitude is Available.
Visit deanmcole.com/notify

Following the incredible events of Solitude and Multitude, Vaughn and Angela must find a way to save their friends. Then it's time to take the battle to the enemy.

Thank you for reading Multitude: Dimension Space Book Two!

Dear Reader,

I hope you enjoyed *Multitude*. Thanks for riding along with me on this journey.

I appreciate your feedback. Actually, you are the reason I develop these apocalyptic tales. While I work on my next novel, I'd love to hear from you. Tell me what you liked, what you loved, even what you hated. You can email me at dean@deanmcole.com and visit me on the web at www.deanmcole.com.

Finally, I need to ask a favor. If you're so inclined, I'd truly appreciate a review of *Multitude*. In this day of e-marketing, you have the power to make or break a book. Please post a review for *Multitude* to its page on your favorite book retailer's website.

Thank you so much for reading *Multitude: Dimension Space Book Two* and for being my copilot on this adventure. Don't forget to follow me on your favorite site by clicking the appropriate links on the About the Author page.

Fly safe!

Dean M. Cole

Sector 64: Sneak Peek

The *Sector 64* Timeline
1947 - *First Contact* a *Sector 64* Prequel Novella
Today - *Ambush* - Book One of the Sector 64 Duology
Tomorrow - *Retribution* - Book Two of the Sector 64 Duology

Seventy years after the events of *First Contact*, most of humanity is completely unaware of the coming changes. We live and die believing we are alone. In 2017, Air Force fighter pilots Jake Giard and Sandra Fitzpatrick discover the decades-old secret project to integrate Earth into a galactic government, but then the plot renders our world a disposable pawn. An interstellar war spills onto our shores, plunging the planet into an otherworldly post-apocalyptic hell. Can Jake and Sandy save humanity from extinction? If you like action-packed, page-turning novels, then you'll love the electrifying action in this apocalyptic thriller.

SECTOR 64: AMBUSH SNEAK PEEK

Captain Sandra Fitzpatrick's steady rhythmic breathing, a technique born through years of cardio training, belied the horror gripping her soul. The teddy bear, oh God, the teddy bear. An image she couldn't shake, the vision would haunt her for the rest of her days.

Earlier, while jogging toward the distant terminal building, Sandy came across a still idling airport transfer bus. Hoping to use it to expedite the crossing, she peered into its closed glass doors. In spite of the eastern glow of the coming sunrise, she couldn't discern details through its dirty windows. However, the bus looked empty.

Jamming her fingers into the rubber gap between the panels, Sandy tried to pry the split glass doors apart. After a fruitless, half-minute struggle, she finally noticed a backlit, recessed emergency-release button left of the door. Activating it, Sandy heard a short blast of compressed air. She jumped as the doors popped two inches out of their opening and then parted, each sliding in opposite directions.

"Hello?"

No reply rose above the bus's droning diesel engine.

She took a tentative step into the opening. "Is anybody in here?"

Standing half in the doorway, Sandy screamed as two strong hands, squeezing from both sides, grasped her shoulders. Another blast of compressed air burped from under the bus, and the door trying to close on her retracted.

"Shit!" Sandy kicked the right panel of the retreating glass door and shook her head. Keep it together, Captain Fitzpatrick. She stepped all the way into the bus, and its doors slid closed. Air-conditioner blower noise replaced the engine's. Getting over her skittishness, she stepped into the driver's compartment. In the dawn's wan light, the seat looked empty. Groping in the darkness, Sandy worked her way closer. A few awkward seconds later, she finally dropped into it.

Something was wrong with the seat. It felt like someone had left a towel or cloth on it. Running her fingers across the material's loose, rippled surface, Sandy froze, remembering what she saw while peering down into the empty F-18's cockpit. An uncomfortable hard object dug into her right thigh. Wide-eyed in the dark, she leaned left and pulled it out from under her leg. Breathlessly holding the object up, she studied its angular silhouette against the deep turquoise hue of the early morning sky. A round ball on one end and a long rod on the other, it felt metallic. With her opposite hand, she blindly searched the instrument panel for a light switch. A huge windshield wiper arm sparked to life, its dry, rubber blade chattering against the dirty glass. Another switch later, the bus's cabin lit up like an exam room. Sandy blinked and squinted as the sudden blast of light burned her dark adapted eyes.

Finally able to see, she squinted at the device in her hand. Struggling not to scream, Sandy dropped the artificial hip. Jumping to her feet, she looked down to see a bus driver's uniform strewn across the compartment. While the driver's shirt was on the floor, the pants, belt still buckled, lay in the seat. She saw several shiny objects littering the interior of the pants. Bending, she looked closer. In a sudden epiphany, she recognized the parts as titanium screws.

What the hell could do that? She looked from the strewn articles, to the screws, and finally to the artificial hip where it had landed next to her right foot. Why isn't there any blood?

Backing away in shocked dismay, Sandy stumbled. Regaining her footing in the bus's central corridor, she looked aft and froze. Visible in the cabin's stark, white light, emptied articles of clothing littered the entire bus.

A glint of light drew her attention to one of the front left seats. A teddy bear's half-open, glass-bead eyes peered from under a vacated toddler's outfit. On the narrow bench, a little girl's tiny white and yellow dress sat between piled clothes of an apparent mother and father. Worn in anticipation of an early morning departure to some exciting destination, the tiny girl's yellow ribbons and pink bows now lay strewn about her emptied clothes.

Sandy had a mental image of the parents casting horrified glances at the monstrosity hovering overhead while they tried to calm their frightened little girl. But in Sandy's vision, she and Jake were the anxious couple. The child between them was the little girl with golden locks that she'd often imagined would grace their future. Unconsciously, her hand drifted to the point where the baby bump would soon show.

As a tear threatened to breach the levee of her lower eyelid, Sandy extended a trembling hand toward the stuffed animal. After a short hesitation, she caressed its furry belly.

The teddy bear's lifeless, doll-like eyes snapped wide open. "Are you my mommy?"

Find out why this happened and what happens next!
Get the Sector 64 Series Today!

ABOUT THE AUTHOR

Author Dean M. Cole, a combat helicopter pilot turned airline first officer, has written multiple award-winning, apocalyptic tales. The audiobook for *Solitude*, book one of his newest series, *Dimension Space*, won the ABR Listeners Choice Award for Best Sci-Fi of 2018, and it was a finalist for the 2017 Voice Arts Awards. Previously, IndieReader named Dean's first full-length novel, *Sector 64: Ambush*, to their Best of 2014 list.

Follow Dean on BookBub!
bookbub.com/authors/dean-m-cole

For More Information:
www.deanmcole.com
dean@deanmcole.com

facebook.com/authordeanmcole

twitter.com/deanmcole

instagram.com/deanmcole

Made in the USA
Coppell, TX
22 December 2020

THE GREEN GUIDE
Switzerland

St. Bernard Dog and Matterhorn, Photo: Christof Sonderegger/Switzerland Tourism

General Manager   Cynthia Clayton Ochterbeck

THEGREENGUIDE SWITZERLAND

Editorial Manager	Jonathan Gilbert
Editors	Rachel Mills, Clive Hebard
Principal Writers	Laurent Gontier, John Malathronas, Paul Shawcross
Production Manager	Natasha G. George
Cartography	Alain Baldet, Michèle Cana, John Dear, Peter Wrenn
Photo Editor	Yoshimi Kanazawa
Proofreader	Hannah Witchell
Interior Design	Chris Bell
Cover Design	Chris Bell, Christelle Le Déan
Layout	Michelin Apa Publications Ltd., John Higginbottom
Cover Layout	Michelin Apa Publications Ltd.

Contact Us

The Green Guide
Michelin Maps and Guides
One Parkway South
Greenville, SC 29615, USA
www.michelintravel.com
Michelin Maps and Guides
Hannay House
39 Clarendon Road
Watford, Herts WD17 1JA, UK
✆01923 205240
www.ViaMichelin.com
travelpubsales@uk.michelin.com

Special Sales

For information regarding bulk sales, customized editions and premium sales, please contact our Customer Service Departments:
USA   1-800-432-6277
UK   01923 205240
Canada 1-800-361-8236

HOW TO USE THIS GUIDE

PLANNING YOUR TRIP

The blue-tabbed PLANNING YOUR TRIP section gives you **ideas for your trip** and **practical information** to help you organize it. You'll find tours, practical information, a host of outdoor activities, a calendar of events, information on shopping, sightseeing, kids' activities and more.

INTRODUCTION

The orange-tabbed INTRODUCTION section explores **Switzerland Today**, including food and wine, while the **History** section spans from Roman rule to Swiss-EU relations in the early 21C. **Architecture** and **Art** are covered, as well as Switzerland's **Nature,** geology and climate.

DISCOVERING

The green-tabbed DISCOVERING section features Principal Sights by region, featuring the most interesting local **Sights**, **Walking Tours**, nearby **Excursions**, and detailed **Driving Tours**. Admission prices shown are normally for a single adult.

ADDRESSES

We've selected the best hotels, restaurants, cafes, shops, nightlife and entertainment to fit all budgets. See the Legend on the cover flap for an explanation of the price categories. See the back of the guide for an index of hotels and restaurants.

Sidebars

Throughout the guide you will find blue, orange and green-colored text boxes with lively anecdotes, detailed history and background information.

😊 A Bit of Advice 😊

Green advice boxes found in this guide contain practical tips and handy information relevant to the sight in the Discovering section.

STAR RATINGS★★★

Michelin has given star ratings for more than 100 years. If you're pressed for time, we recommend you visit the ★★★ or ★★ sights first:

★★★   **Highly recommended**
★★   **Recommended**
★   **Interesting**

MAPS

😊 Regional Driving Tours map, Places to Stay map and Sights map.
😊 Region maps.
😊 Maps for major cities and villages.
😊 Local tour maps.

All maps in this guide are oriented north, unless otherwise indicated by a directional arrow. The term "Local Map" refers to a map within the chapter or Tourism Region. A complete list of the maps found in the guide appears at the back of this book.

© Brian Lawrence Images/Pictures Colour Library

PLANNING YOUR TRIP

INTRODUCTION TO SWITZERLAND

CONTENTS

Peter Mathis/Bettmeralp Tourismus/Switzerland Tourism

DISCOVERING
SWITZERLAND

Welcome to Switzerland

Switzerland, perhaps the most culturally, linguistically and geographically diverse country in western Europe, is located right at its centre, bordered by Germany in the north, Austria in the east, Italy in the south and France in the west. The country is divided into 26 cantons that have been organised into seven regions for the purposes of this Guide and which comprise French-speaking Suisse Romande, bilingual Valais, the mostly German-speaking Bern and Jura, Graubünden, North and Centre, and Italian-speaking Ticino.

SUISSE ROMANDE (p84–183)

This, the most French of the Swiss regions, is often referred to by French speakers as Romandie. It shares a border with France, and the cosmopolitan city of Geneva – home to the monumental Jet d'Eau and the headquarters of many of the world's international organisations – is almost totally surrounded by France. With two of Switzerland's largest lakes, Lakes Geneva (Lac Léman) and Neuchâtel, the region offers much for the visitor to explore, from the mountainous cheese-producing Gruyères region to the medieval city of Fribourg, and Lausanne, world capital of the Olympic Movement.

BERN AND JURA CANTONS
(p184–239)

Until 1979 the Jura was part of the ancient canton of Bern but opted to leave mainly for linguistic and religious reasons. With no large towns, the Jura is characterised by mountains and valleys and is a major winter sports destination. The Swiss capital, Bern, has a beautiful old town with street after street of arcades and shops to keep even the most enthusiastic shopper happy. The crowning glory of the region is the Bernese Oberland where the iconic mountains of the Eiger, Monch and Jungfrau stand above Brienzer See and Thuner See lakes, and the resort of Interlaken.

THE VALAIS (p240–287)

The French- and German-speaking Valais covers southwest Switzerland and boasts three world-famous ski resorts – Verbier, Crans-Montana and Zermatt – where a full range of winter sports for any ability is available.

Skiiing in Zermatt, Valais

Simon Stark/Valais Tourism/Switzerland Tourism

Martigny has a fine Roman heritage with a 2C amphitheatre still used for events such as the quirky "Queen of Queens" cow contest. Named after the valley along which the River Rhône flows, the Valais is Switzerland's third largest canton and has 14 mountains over 4 000m/13 123ft, including the iconic Matterhorn.

TICINO (p288–317)

Italian-speaking Ticino, the southernmost canton of the Confederation, combines Latin flair with legendary Swiss orderliness. A mountainous area with the Lepontine Alps in the north, the canton is divided by three river systems. The barrier

Gandria by the Lake Lugano, Ticino

Bruno Meier/Switzerland Tourism

formed by the massif shelters the shores of Lake Maggiore and Lake Lugano, gracing their resorts with a pleasant Mediterranean climate. Bellinzona with its three castles and well deserved UNESCO World Heritage status is an essential city to visit, while for sheer excitement try the *Goldeneye* bungee jump from the Verzasca Dam near Locarno. This southernmost part of the Alps can be fully appreciated when taking the St Gotthard or Lukmanier Pass roads on one of our driving tours.

CENTRAL SWITZERLAND
(p318–353)

Central Switzerland comprises the cantons of Lucerne, Zug, Schwyz, Uri, Unter-walden and Nidwalden. Apart from Zug, these cantons are all adjacent to scenic Lake Lucerne or, as it is known to most Swiss, the Vierwaldstätter See. The bustling university town of Lucerne, with its fascinating covered wooden bridges, is also the place to embark on the many wonderful boat trips offered on historic vessels such as the *Schwyz* and the *William Tell*. Nearby Mounts Pilatus and Rigi can be accessed by cogwheel railway from Alpnachstad or Vitznau respectively.

GRAUBÜNDEN *(p354–385)*

This canton is bordered by Austria, Italy and the tiny state of Liechtenstein. Though the majority of the population speak German or Italian, Graubünden is the only canton where the ancient Romansh language continues to be spoken. Several unforgettable train journeys can be taken here, including the amazing Glacier Express. The capital is the fascinating city of Chur, located close to the mighty river Rhine which has its source in the high Alps in the west of the region. Graubünden also boasts the world-renowned and ritzy resorts of St Moritz, Davos and Klosters.

THE NORTH *(p386–447)*

The North consists of the Cantons of Basle-Land and Basel-Stadt, Aargau, Zürich, Schaffhausen, Thurgau, St Gallen and Appenzell, most of which share a border with Germany or Austria and are therefore German-speaking. Zürich, the financial centre of Switzerland and of the Reformation in German-speaking Switzerland has a fantastic arts scene, world-class museums and great nightlife. The surrounding lush grasslands are epitomised by the green hills of the Emmenthal, traditional dairy-farming country.

Typical houses of Appenzell, the North

Renato Bagattini/Switzerland Tourism

Village of Grindelwald, Wetterhorn In the background, Canton Bern

Michelin Driving Tours

GRAND TOURS

🐚*These tours are highlighted on the map on the inside front cover.*

SUISSE JURA AND LAKE GENEVA

(650km/400mi)

This tour takes in four splendid lakes (including two of the three largest in Switzerland), the undulating central Swiss Plateau and, for good measure, a few magnificent mountains.

Starting from Geneva and heading north along the shores of Lake Geneva with mountain ranges on either side, you come to the walled town of Nyon. Continuing around the Lake leads to Lausanne and the beautifully situated Montreux. From here the route heads north onto the plateau of the Mittelland past Murten See and on up to the old town of Solothurn. The drive then goes north over the last ridge of the Jura, the Weissenstein, and onto Basel and the River Rhine. The return trip goes into the Jura Mountains before dropping down into Neuchâtel and its vineyard-fringed lake. After leaving the Lake the tour proceeds through the Vallée de Joux, the jewel of the Vaud Jura, and back down to Geneva via Nyon and the tranquil waters of Lac Geneva.

VALAIS AND BERNER OBERLAND

(950km - 590 miles)

The Valais and Berner Oberland drive includes offers a taste of Swiss scenery at its best. It includes some of the most well-known mountains, two or possibly three spectacular mountain passes, a couple of small lakes and a 188km/117.5mi journey along the banks of one of Europe's major rivers, the Rhône.

Beginning at the Swiss capital city of Bern the drive heads south to Thun where there is the option of heading up to the resort of Kandersberg via the beautiful lakeside town of Spiez. Return to the main route and onto Interlaken where again a spur leads to Grindelwald and Murren which both have to views of the magnificent Jungfrau, Monch and Eiger, not to mention most of the Bernese Oberland. Retuning to Interlaken, the route heads to the Susten Pass and the resort of Andermatt which lies at the junction of the St Gotthard and Furka Passes. Here the tour joins the course of the Rhône and follows it along the Furkastrasse all the way to Brig at the foot of the road to the breathtaking Simplon Pass. As the drive continues through the Valais there are various other side routes to barrages and resorts until eventually the wine town of Aigle is reached. The drive turns east here passing over the Alpes

Postal bus at the Furka Pass with a view to Grimsel Pass and Finsteraarhorn, Valais

Christof Sonderegger/Switzerland Tourism

Vaudoises to the resort of Gstaad and then travels through the renowned Gruyères region up to the medieval city of Fribourg before returning to Bern.

GRAUBÜNDEN
(700km/435mi)

The Alpine canton of Graubünden is the country's largest. This driving tour is the best way to enjoy its dramatic and varied landscapes, as well as to reach the little-known Italian-speaking canton of Ticino to its south. Departing from dynamic Davos, head east along the lateral valleys of the Flüela in to the Engandin and stop off at the pretty village of Guarda, before following the Inn river to the spa town of Schuls, set dramatically amid rocky slopes and scattered forests. The route along the lower plateau of the Upper Engandin takes you to the high-altitude resort of Zuoz before you reach sunny St Moritz, "Top of the World" and beloved by winter sports enthusiasts. There's a stunning panorama in almost every direction, especially at the Bernina Massif, right at the edge of Graubünden. Next, head south and west on the historic transalpine San Bernardino Pass to Bellinzona in the sunny Lower Ticino Valley. Lugano, Morcote and Locarno look and feel entirely different from their northern neighbours, and it's easy to linger in any of Ticino's warm and welcoming lakeside resorts. Head north along the St Gotthard Pass road to Andermatt and then east along the thickly wooded Valley of the Vorderrhein, popular with biking, hiking and swimming enthusiasts. Finish at Chur, historical, administrative and religious capital of Graubünden for more than 500 years.

LAKES AND APPENZELLERLAND
(600km/375mi)

Gently rolling hills, flowery meadows and rugged mountains typify Appenzellerland, in the northeast corner of the country, while the lovers of classic lake views will enjoy driving along the shores of some Switzerland's most pristine bodies of water.

Head north from Zürich to Roman Winterthur and then Renaissance Schaffhausen, stopping off at Europe's most powerful waterfalls, Rheinfall. Follow the Sitter Valley next to tranquil Lake Constance to the UNESCO World Heritage Site of St Gallen and then drive south in to the heart of Appenzellerland, before reaching the tiny principality of Liechtenstein. The route skirts the south of Walensee and then takes in Glarus at the foot of the Vorder Glärnisch and numerous lakeshore towns, such as exclusive Seelisberg, pretty Zug and up the Ibergeregg Road to the pilgrimage site of Einsiedeln, in pine-clad, rugged hills. Return to Zürich by driving along the south side of Lake Zürich, the chain of Albis hills stretching up to your left.

LOCAL DRIVES

Use the Discovering section to explore Switzerland's hidden routes in:

- **LES ALPES VAUDOISES**
- **ALTO TICINO**
- **VAL D'ANNIVIERS**
- **LA CHASSERAL**
- **ENGELBERG**
- **ROUTE DE LA FORCLAZ**
- **FURKASTRASSE**
- **INTERLAKEN**
- **VALLÉE DE JOUX**
- **KANDERSTEG**
- **LAKE GENEVA**
- **LOCARNO**
- **LUGANO**
- **MONTREUX**
- **VAL DE MORGINS**
- **SACHSELNER STRASSE**
- **SAN BERNARDINO-STRASSE**
- **ST GALLEN**
- **ST MORITZ**
- **LE VALAIS**
- **LAKE LUCERNE**
- **ZÜRICH**

When and Where to Go

WHEN TO GO

Switzerland's dramatic Alpine peaks, rolling meadows and sparkling lakes change with each season, adding new facets to this natural playground with every visit. This sense of movement is reflected in Switzerland's cosmopolitan cities, which buzz with culture and nightlife, while the rural villages still prefer a timeless, traditional lifestyle.

Europeans have sought Switzerland's snow-covered Alps in **winter** ever since skiing was first invented. Today, skiers and snowboarders alike delight in the country's world-famous resorts (*see WHAT TO SEE AND DO)*; Zermatt is the iconic destination, lounging at the foot of the iconic Matterhorn; exclusive St Moritz is considered to be the oldest ski resort in the world and has hosted the winter Olympics twice (1928 and 1948); while celebrity-studded Gstaad is known for luxurious hotels, shopping and high-society nightlife. The skiing hard core tend to seek out the quieter, but more challenging slopes of Titlis and the glacier plateau of Les Diablerets. Winter is also a magical time to visit Ticino, where a downhill piste can end with palm trees and flowering bushes in this surprisingly temperate Alpine micro-climate. Here on the Italian border, the warmth of Italian *brio* (vigor) tempers legendary Swiss efficiency.

Switzerland's network of hiking and biking trails is open throughout **spring**, **summer** and **autumn**. The routes take in monumental glaciers, churning rivers swelled by glacial meltwater (excellent for white-water rafting) and serene boating and fishing lakes that polka-dot the countryside. Let us not forget golf; one of the highest courses in the world is in Arosa, where golfers often share the 18-hole course with grazing cows. Warmer weather is ideal, too, for a relaxing lake cruise, especially

at sunset; or take a cable car or cog railway to the top of a mountain such as Rigi or Pilatus, and marvel at the unfurling panorama of Alpine peaks.

Festivals abound year-round (*see WHAT TO SEE AND DO)*, celebrating the culture and history of Switzerland and the world at large. The Montreaux Jazz Festival each July attracts the world's top musicians; while Christmas markets in numerous cities and villages focus on traditional crafts.

Switzerland's turbulent history has created a chain of **historic castles**, while the historic districts of many major cities, such as Basel, Zürich, Lucerne and Bern, have survived the test of time unscathed. Today, the sandstone city centre arcades house modern shops and boutiques, while the lofty turrets of castles such as Chillon, immortalized by Lord Byron's poem, can be explored for a small fee.

CLIMATE

The climate is temperate, with temperatures rarely higher than 86F/30C in summer, and rarely colder than 41F/-5C in winter, except high in the mountains. The warmest regions are Ticino (Lucarno and Lugano claim 298 sunny days a year), and Valais, south of Lake Geneva. Even so, capricious wind patterns can turn a bright, sunny day into a rainy or snowy one in minutes.

There is no excessive heat or humidity, so the air is always crisp. Southern Switzerland has subtropical vegetation and enjoys year-round mild temperatures.
Weather Reports - *162.*

IDEAS FOR YOUR VISIT
SHORT BREAKS (2 DAYS)
Bern

Begin your visit to Bern (*see BERN)* at the **Bear Park** with a 20-minute multimedia tour of the city and a stop at the **Tourist Center** for the audio tour package (2hr) or tickets to the **Old Town Tour** (1hr30min). Follow this with a relaxing river tour of the

View over the Old Town, Bern

Terence du Fresne/Bern Tourismus/Switzerland Tourism

city by **dinghy**, and then make your way to the **Clock Tower** for a narrated show (1hr). Don't miss the **Botanical Gardens** (1–2hr), as well as the city tours by **horse-drawn carriage** and **tram** (to the summit of the Brienz Rothorn, 1-3hr). The **Postbus** system offers a full day ride through four passes (Grimsel, Nufenen, Gotthard, and Susten) departing from and returning to Bern. Information and tickets are available through the Tourist Office (℘(0)31 328 12 12; www.berninfo.com).

Geneva

Don't miss out on Geneva's (*see GENEVA)* **boat tours**, with your choice of paddle wheeler or steamer, and durations of 1hr to one day, many including meals (℘0848 811 848; www.cgn.ch). **Minitrains** offer short (35-55min) trips past the lakefront and rose gardens and parks with the option to stop off at various sites and rejoin the tour at your own pace (**Pâquis Express & Vielle Ville** departing from Rotonde du Mont-Blanc; ℘(0)22 781 04 04; **Trans Eaux-Viviens** deparing from Jardin Anglais ℘(0)22 310 53 00). Geneva also offers a multitude of **cable-car rides** (leave at least 1 hour for round trip with sightseeing) to surrounding peaks and spectacular views (www.geneve-tourisme.ch).

Lucerne

A visit to Lucerne (*see LUCERNE)* should begin at the **Chapel Bridge** (30min), followed by a leisurely walk along the stunning shores of **Lake Lucerne**, or a guided tour of the city either by foot (2hr) or by **horse drawn carriage** (1hr; www.Lucerne.org). A trip on the world's steepest cogwheel train to the peak of **Pilatus** (4-5hr) may be combined with boat and cable car rides for the ultimate tour of the region (℘(0)41 227 17 17; www.pilatus. ch). Visit the summit of **Mount Titlis** by train and cable car (5hr total) to explore its glacial caves (www.titlis.ch).

Neuchâtel

A visit to Neuchâtel (*see NEUCHÂTEL)* is well begun with the **city tour by train** (45min). A guided walking tour provided by the Tourist Office includes a visit to the Old Town's stunning **castle**, which houses the Cantonal Government (1-2hr) and a panoramic view of the town from the **Prison Tower**. The **Laténium Museum** covers 50 000 years of the region (1-2hr), while the **Papilliorama-Nocturama** in nearby Kerzers is home to exotic butterflies and animals. No visit is complete without a cruise on **Lake Neuchâtel**, with options to explore two other lakes in the same trip (2-4hr). For more information: www.neuchateltourisme.ch.

ONE WEEK

While Switzerland is not a large country it is probably best to concentrate on one region or even one city and its immediate locality if you only have a week at your disposal. With such cultural and linguistic diversity things differ considerably from region to region and there is much to see in each. Most regions are relatively compact and most cities have plenty of interesting sights and attractions either in the centre or nearby. There is also a good selection of local drives at the beginning of the Planning Your Trip chapter (&see p13) which are described in detail in the relevant part of the Discovering Section. By selecting one of the cities which is also beside a lake the possibilities are almost endless! Not only that, but Swiss train and bus services are legendary in terms of their service and reliability so it's possible to explore without your own vehicle. Some suggestions are given below:

The Suisse Romande

Geneva is the obvious choice of destination here. Right at the southern end of the Romandie, the city, canton and nearby Vaud have it all. Lake Geneva comes right to the edge of the City centre where it turns into the River Rhône. The magnificent Jet d'Eau can be viewed at fairly close quarters by joining one of the organised walking tours of the harbour and lake shores. There is much of interest in the old city which clusters around the cathedral and will be forever associated with the Reformation.

Ticino

The Ticino in the far southeastern corner of Switzerland provides a little Italian flair combined with legendary Swiss organisation. Both Lugano and Locarno combine beautiful lakeside settings with interesting sights and attractions while the stronghold of Bellinzona offers three amazing castles as well as being a good base for touring the canton.

TWO WEEKS

In two weeks it should be possible to explore parts of at least two regions especially if you have access to a car. A Swiss Rail Pass (&see p35) which allows unlimited access to trains, boats and buses throughout the country should enable you to see quite a lot of Switzerland if you wish in this time. it is also possible to include any, or even two or three, of the four driving tours suggested at the beginning of Planning Your Trip (&see p12). Further suggestions are:

Jura and Berne

The Jura is one of the more relaxed parts of Switzerland and its green mountain scenery combined with

View of the Bernese Alps from Weissenstein, Jura

Christof Sonderegger/Switzerland Tourism

the absence of large towns make it the ideal place for relaxing walks in summer and skiing in the winter. The Berne canton further south offers the fascinating Swiss capital city of Bern with the UNESCO World Heritage Site of its medieval old town together with first-class shopping. To the south east, however, is what most people associate the Canton with: the Bernese Oberland above Interlaken, which makes a fine base from which to access the legendary mountains of the Jungfrau, Monch and Eiger.

Central Switzerland
The city of Lucerne and the Lake of the same name are at the centre of arguably the most typically Swiss region of all. The old city with its amazing flower decked covered wooden bridges and medieval buildings and squares provides a good base from which to tour the surrounding region. Boat trips around the lake should not be missed.

Valais
The appropriately named Valais in the southeast is an unspoiled region with the fascinating cities of Sion and Martigny to explore as well having the world famous mountain resorts of Zermatt and Crans-Montana to enjoy.

What to See and Do

WINTER SPORTS
Thanks to its mountainous landscape, Switzerland has always been *the* ideal place for a winter holiday. It is, in fact, the first country where winter sports were developed on a large scale. Villages such as St Moritz started to welcome British tourists for the winter season from the early 19C.
In most Swiss resorts, the winter season is from just before Christmas through to early April with the best conditions usually between mid-January and mid-March, depending on the altitude. The latter part of the season offers the advantages of longer days, mild temperatures and far fewer people. In the higher resorts (Zermatt, Saas Fee, St Moritz), snow coverage is generally satisfactory until Easter, even early May in locations above 2 500m/8 202ft. Spring snow is ideal for off-piste skiing.
Most Swiss ski resorts are above the tree line, giving even inexperienced skiers access to summits reaching some 4 000m/13 123ft, and frequently commanding panoramic views. Many resorts have winter hiking trails for long treks along gentle slopes.
If you would rather just bask in the winter sun, you can pull up a chair as a spectator at any of the numerous competitions and events that take place throughout the winter season.

ALPINE SKIING
Switzerland simply has some of the world's best skiing and the world's best known resorts. The largest are the duo of **Davos** (248km/154mi of prepared pistes) and **Klosters** (170km/105.6mi), followed by the ensemble of the Four Valleys (**Verbier** as the main resort with 400km/248.5mi of pistes and the Jungfrau region of **Interlaken, Wengen, Murren**, with 220km/136.7mi of pistes). Some individual resorts are equally as expansive, such as **St Moritz** (230km/143mi of pistes in the Engadin Valley) and **Zermatt** (313km/194.5mi of pistes, including on the Klein Matterhorn glacier).
Each resort has impressive modern networks of mountain railways, funiculars, cable cars and drag lifts (t-bars on the glaciers), while the terrain suits all levels of skiers and

Snowshoe excursion in the Chablais region, Valais, Dents-du-Midi in the background

Christian Perret/Valais Tourism/Switzerland Tourism

snowboarders. Even resorts that are smaller by comparison, such as **Engelberg-Titlis** (82km/51mi of pistes) and **Aletsch** glacier (99km/61.5mi of pistes) have enough terrain to satisfy a ski holiday. Because of their proximity, it is possible to stay in one resort and visit another by train or bus for a day.

Some border resorts have teamed up with their French, Italian or Austrian counterparts, such as the Franco-Swiss resort of **Les Portes du Soleil**, offering 600km/372.8mi of pistes lying mainly in the French resorts of Avoriaz and Morzine Châtel. **Zermatt**'s partnership with Breuil-Cervinia In Italy requires purchase of a separate ski pass for each country. Lastly, there is **Samnaun**, linked to the Austrian resort of Ischgl.

Many Swiss resorts are sought for their charming **architecture**, inspired by local tradition. Some developed from existing villages (Klosters, Arosa, Saas Fee, Zermatt, Adelboden). The chalet style has been preserved in larger resorts like Verbier, which can provide accommodation for up to 25 000 visitors. However, a boom in the popularity of winter holidays spurred the construction of vast, impersonal developments lacking traditional Swiss charm. This is the case with Davos, St Moritz-Bad, Thyon and even Crans-Montana.

SNOWBOARDING

All Swiss resorts welcome snowboarders and many have snowparks with facilities such as half-pipes, boardercross and high jumps, as well as competitive events. The best equipped are Les Diablerets, Saas Fee and Laax, where World Cup events are held every year. Snowboarding was introduced as an official skiing event at the 1998 Winter Olympic Games held in Nagano, Japan.

CROSS-COUNTRY SKIING

Cross-country skiing is one of the most popular sports after downhill skiing. The prettiest sites are in Graubünden (150km/94mi of pistes near St Moritz, 75km/47mi in Davos), at Laax-Flims and in the Gstaad region.

OTHER SNOWSPORTS

Ski touring is a combination of cross-country and alpine skiing. The boots are fastened to the heel for downhill skiing but left free for upward walking. The Swiss Alps offer countless opportunities for this sport, especially between Chamonix and Zermatt and at Engadin. Always use the trails in the company of an experienced mountain guide.

Skijoring, in which one is towed behind a galloping horse, requires the skier to be of moderate skill or better.

St Moritz is one of the resorts which regularly organizes skijoring races.

Walking: All resorts feature signposted packed snow trails near the villages and much higher up *(access by chairlifts)*. Some of these trails are more suitable to walking with **snowshoes**. If you are going off the beaten track, it is advisable to go with a guide, especially to avoid areas prone to avalanches.

Many resorts set aside gentle slopes for **snow-tubing**, in which you sit in an inflated donut-like tube. Also, many villages offer **dogsledding**.

Ice-rink sports are a popular feature of Swiss resorts, with many natural or artificial **skating rinks**, both indoors and outdoors. The Swiss are also fond of **ice hockey** and **curling**.

Switzerland is a great place for **sledding**. Many resorts offer kilometres of signposted trails where the snow has been carefully packed. Grindelwald and Saas Fee boast outstanding facilities, with reserved hillsides. Bobsled runs are available for those in search of high-speed excitement , such as the descent (with a pilot) at St Moritz.

OUTDOOR FUN
HIKING AND WALKING

Switzerland's network of public footpaths is one of the world's longest with 68 000km/42 500mi of marked paths. Signs give the length and duration to various stops on the walk. Some footpaths are suitable for children and for wheelchairs. The most attractive of these include the walk around the Tomlishorn on Mount Pilatus, the "cheese circuit" (Käserstatt) on the Halisberg, and the panoramic walk around Aletsch Glacier.

Trail Markings
Signposts with **black on a yellow background** and a yellow lozenge indicate footpaths suitable for children and inexperienced walkers. Mountain hikes for experienced walkers in good physical condition are marked by **yellow signs with a white arrow and red line** and a red lozenge. Difficult footpaths across glaciers, scree or snowfields, which require experience in rock-climbing, are indicated by **blue signs with a white arrow and a thin blue line**; tricky sections are specifically marked and have safety rails and ropes. Signs with **white text on a brown background** highlight cultural sights of interest.

The Swiss Path
Built to celebrate the 700th anniversary of the Swiss Confederation in 1991, this 35km/21.7mi trail edges the fjord-like Lake Uri, the southernmost end of Lake Lucern. Marble markers bearing the

Nordic walking in the Engelberg valley, Central Switzerland

Christian Perret/Engelberg-Titlis Tourismus/Switzerland Tourism

19

coats of arms of each canton and other information mark different sections of the route, with boat, bus or train connections at each destination. Visit www.weg-der-schweiz.ch for more information.

Information
The **Swiss National Hiking Association** publishes maps and guides, many of which can be bought at bookshops in the country.
A selection of walks is listed at **www.myswitzerland.com**, as well as information on hiking safety and links to organisations such as the Swiss Alpine Club and Wandersite.
If you are interested in a serious hiking holiday, it would be worth contacting the **Swiss National Hiking Association** (ASTP) (Im Hirshalm 49, 4125 Riehen, ✆(0)61 606 93 40).

HIKES AND WALKS

Bassins Du Doubs
The hikes in this region explore the River Doubs, Lake Brenets, and Chatelot Dam, which form a section of the border with France. A wooded path (2hr15min) leads from the small town of Les Brenets to Brenets Lake's overflow at Doubs Fall (27m/88.6ft). The hike from Les Brenets to Les Roches de Mauron has pleasant views and is quite short (45min). *See p182.*

Val d'Hérens
Alpe Bricola is easily ascended for spectacular views of glaciers and the valleys below (5hr); allow at least 5hr to explore the Cabane des Aiguilles Rouges. *See p263.*

Zermatt
Allow a half day to explore Schwarzsee to Zermatt (*see ZERMATT*) on foot, while experiencing views of the Matterhorn as well as the Zmutt and Arben Glaciers; alternate views are on the hike to Grünsee, Grindjisee and Leisee (beginning with a rack railway ride). Allow at least half a day.

BOAT TOURS
Explore the main Swiss lakes and parts of some major rivers on the large white boats that can be seen cruising up and down. A few of these boats still feature the original paddle wheels.

Cycling along the Lake Champfer, Graubünden

CYCLING

Swiss Federal Railways (SBB/CFF) and most private railway companies accept bicycles as **accompanied baggage**. Bicycles can be rented in over 100 railway stations and returned to a different station.
The **train + bike** formula includes transport, bicycle hire, and civil liability insurance in case of an accident. Contact the Rail Service ℘0900 300 300; www.rail.ch.

Cycle Routes and Paths

There are nine national cycle routes (3 300km/2 050mi), each starts near a railway station and follows a clearly marked route with signs indicating distances, destinations and altitude differentials. One of the most challenging is the "Alpine Panorama" (480km/298mi); it crosses a dozen mountain passes and finishes at the Klausenpass (alt 1 948m/6 391ft). Switzerland also has over 3 000km/1 864mi of cycle paths. **La Suisse à vélo** publishes detailed guides and a list of hotels specifically recommended for cyclists, with covered bike shelters and repair kits. (P.O. Box 8275, CH 3001 Berne; ℘(0)31 307 47 40. www.suisse-a-velo.ch).

MOUNTAINEERING

Climbing routes pop up throughout Switzerland. The largest is the **Via Ferrata Tälli** in the Bernese Oberland, open to all experience levels, including beginners: the route has 78m/256ft of ladders and 550 steel pitons embedded into the wall of the imposing Gadmerflue, at the Susten Pass. In Liechtenstein, the steep walls of the Eggstöcke, above Braunwald, are also suitable for serious climbing enthusiasts.
The www.myswitzerland.com website lists suggested climbs. Most major resorts have their own **climbing school** plus expeditions with trained guides and instructors.

BEACHES

Some of the country's most attractive lakeside beaches are at Lenzerheide on the Heidsee, on Lake Cauma (whose waters are heated by underground streams), and Estavayer-le-Lac, the country's largest natural sandy beach.

Sailing, Windsurfing and Water-skiing

Most larger lakes have their own sailing school. Visit www.myswitzerland.com for further information.

WATER SPORTS

Switzerland's wild Alpine rivers provide some of the best white-water **rafting** in Europe.
For more information contact **Swissraft** ℘081 911 5250; www.swissraft.ch.
The Rotsee near Lucerne is a particular favorite for **rowing**. **Canoeing and kayaking** are available on many lakes and rivers. **Water parks** are extremely popular and often feature wave machines, huge water slides and swimming pools. Two of the largest are the Säntispark at Abwill, near St Gallen, and the Alpamare at Pfäffikon, near Zürich.

FISHING

Switzerland's 32 000km/19 883mi of rivers and 135 000ha/333 592 acres of lakes are a paradise for anglers. For further information on seasons, regulations and licences, apply to local Tourist Information Centers or **Schweizerischer Fischerei-Verband** (Swiss Fishing Federation), Seilerstrasse 27, Postfach 8218, CH-3001 Bern, ℘(0)31 386 17 10, www.sfv-fsp.ch.

HANG-GLIDING AND PARAGLIDING

Hang-gliding and paragliding competitions are frequently held in Villeneuve in the Lake Geneva region. For information, contact:

Paragliding over Lake Thun

Office de Tourisme, 15 Grand-Rue, 1844 Villeneuve; ℘(0)21 960 22 86; www.redbull-vertigo.com.

ACTIVITIES FOR KIDS

In this guide, sights of particular interest to children are indicated with a ♣♣symbol. Some attractions may offer discount fees for children. In Switzerland, children can enjoy;

Aigle Adventure Park Vaud *⚓see p142*

Appenzell Museum Inner Rhoden *⚓see p442*

Basel Zoo *⚓see p411*

Adventure Playground Parco Civico Lugano Ticino *⚓see p292*

Verkehrshaus Transport Museum Lucerne *⚓see p328*

St Bernard Dog Museum Martigny *⚓see p248*

Tierpark Peter und Paul St Gallen *⚓see p439*

Naturhistorisches Museum Bern *⚓see p193*

SPAS

Switzerland has a wealth of thermal spas fed by natural hot springs, often accompanied by luxurious man-made swimming pools, Jacuzzis and saunas. Spas are open to visitors of all ages and are particularly suitable for families. The baths at Saillon and Leukerbad, in the Valais mountains, are popular in summer. **Schweizer Heilbäder**, Avenue des Bains 22, 1400 Yverdon-les-Bains; ℘(0)24 420 15 21; www.heilbad.org.

SHOPPING
OPENING TIMES

Most shops open from 9am–noon and 2–6.30pm (Sat 4pm or 5pm) although in large towns they may not close for lunch. Most towns have a late opening evening often until 9pm. All shops close on Sunday. Some cafés open early and close when the shops close. Others open at lunchtime or later and become bars in the evening, often closing at midnight or even 1am in some cities. Restaurants serve meals only at normal mealtimes and close in between.

TIMEPIECES & JEWELLERY

Bucherer produces timepieces and jewellery, famous for their exceptional craftsmanship (*www.bucherer.com*). Smaller shops operated by fine goldsmiths and watchmakers can be found throughout Switzerland.

SWISS ARMY KNIVES

Victorinox is the country's leading producer of pocket knives and multi-tools, whose line also inlcudes apparel, luggage and other products celebrating the highest quality of the Swiss-made tradition. (Schmiedgasse 57, CH-6438 Ibach-Schwyz; ℘(0)41 818 12 11; www.victorinox.com).

The Swiss Army Knife

The Swiss penknife, an essential part of any Boy Scout's kit, is recognizable by its red handle, white cross logo and rounded corners (accept no imitations). This gem of the miniature cutlery industry was originally created over a century ago as a Swiss army field knife. Within a short time, the **"Schweizer Militärmesser"**, or Swiss Army Knife, became world famous and was adopted by outdoor and do-it-yourself enthusiasts worldwide. Today there are over 400 different models, ranging from the most basic to extremely sophisticated, including models specifically for left-handed users. Designs can include an altimeter, a barometer, a computer USB memory card, and a range of fashionable colours. It deserves its nickname as the world's smallest toolbox, one which can cut, slice, file, carve, sharpen, remove bottle tops, tighten, loosen, measure, download and more.

The Swiss Army Knife is made by Victorinox, whose factory is in Schwyz (♻ *See Shopping*).

GOURMET FOODS

Swiss Chocolate

Switzerland is home to some of the world's finest chocolatiers. Internationally recognised brands, such as Lindt and Frey, can be found in most grocery and speciality shops.

Cheese

Over 450 cheese makers produce local varieties as well as the popular Emmental (Swiss Cheese), Appenzeller, Gruyère, Sbrinz, and Tête de Moine. For traditional national recipes and information on specific dairies (often open for visits and tours) contact **Switzerland Cheese Marketing AG**, Brunnmattstrasse 21 Postfach, 3001 Bern; ℘(0)31 385 26 26; www.switzerland-cheese.ch.

VAT REFUND

With the **Global Refund** system, any non-resident can get back the 7.6% VAT on any purchase of CHF400 or more as long as it is exported within the thirty days. Vouchers received at the time of the purchase are stamped by customs officials, and then turned in with several payment options. **Global Refund** *AG, Zürichstrasse 38, 8306 Brüttisellen; ℘01 805 60 70. www.gobalrefund.com.*

Cheese for sale, Ticino

Markets

Adelboden – Adelboden traditional autumn market; early Oct. Culinary specialities and arts and crafts produced locally and nationally are offered for sale in the bustling main street.

Les Mosses – The country's highest grocer's market and flea market Jun–Sept, Sun; www.lesmosses.ch.

Vevey – Vevey Folk Market, 2nd week July until end August. Known locally as *Marchés Folkloriques*, these markets attract at least 2 000 visitors who come to buy and listen to brass bands and folk music.

DUTY-FREE

The **Zürich Airport** offers one of the largest duty-free malls available. ℘(0)43 816 22 11; www.flughafen-zuerich.ch/info/visitorservices.

SIGHTSEEING
ALPINE TRAINS

Swiss Pre-Alps

The **Voralpen-Express** running between Romanshorn and Lucerne provides a link between Lake Constance and Lake Lucerne. This 2hr30min trip affords delightful views of the pre-Alpine ranges and lakeside country; www.voralpen-express.ch.

The **Train du Chocolat** runs between Montreux, on the Swiss Riviera, and Gruyères, home of the famous cheese and milk chocolate.

The trip includes coffee and croissants, entrance to the château and cheese factory at Gruyères, and a visit to the **Cailler-Nestlé** chocolate factory, including a tasting (🕐open Jun–Oct, Wed, Jul–Aug Mon and Wed; www.mob.ch).

The **GoldenPass Line** offers panoramic views between Lucerne and Montreux via the Brünig Pass, Lake Brienz to Interlaken (6hr). You can stop at Interlaken for the excursion to Jungfraujoch (3 454m/11 332ft), on the highest railway in Europe; www.goldenpass.ch.

The **Train du Vignoble** (13km/8mi) operates between Vevey, Chexbres and Puidoux in the Lavaux, along the shores of Lake Geneva, passing through wine-growing countryside with several vineyard, wine cellar and museum stops.

Graubünden (Grisons)

The **Bernina-Express** links Chur to St Moritz and the Bernina Pass (2 253m/7 392ft) in 4hr, with an onward bus connection to Tirano (Italy) and Lugano.

The **Heidi-Express** travels between Landquart and Tirano (Italy) via Davos and the Bernina Pass (4hr).

The famous **Glacier-Express** links Zermatt and Chur to St Moritz or Davos (7hr 30min), passing through the majestic Alps, crossing 291 bridges, and negotiating 91 tunnels. The route crosses the Oberalp Pass (2 033m/6 670ft) by rack railway from Andermatt; www.glacierexpress.ch.

The **Engadin Star** links Landquart to St Moritz (9hr), passing through the new Vereinatunnel and crossing the Engadin; www.rhb.ch.

Valais

The **Saint Bernard Express** runs from Martigny to Orsières (30min) through the Vallée de la Dranse. In summer (Jun–late Sept), there is a bus connection to Champex-Lac, La Fouly and the Great Saint Bernard hospice (55min); www.momc.ch

The **Mont Blanc Express** runs through the Trient and Vallorcine valleys, linking France and Switzerland between Martigny and Le Fayet, stopping at Argentière, Chamonix and Les Houches.

The **Allalin-Express** leaves from Bern or Interlaken to Brig; continue by bus to Saas Fee, a charming village closed to road traffic. You then have the option of taking the **Alpin-Express** (45min) to a huge glacial cave

Heidi-Express on Alp Grüm, Graubünden

Peter Donatsch/Rhaetische Bahn/Switzerland Tourism

hollowed out of the landscape at an altitude of 3 500m/11 483ft.

Ticino

The **William Tell Express** links central Switzerland to the Ticino area, taking passengers by paddle boat from Lucerne to Lugano or Locarno on Lake Maggiore. The journey (6hr) then continues by train. The trip only runs from north to south from May–Oct. The **Centovalli Railway** connects Berne to Locarno through the Simplon Tunnel to Domodossola in Italy (4hr); www.centovalli.ch.

STEAM TRAINS

Steam trains operate during the summer, especially weekends.

Vaud canton:
- Blonay-Chamby ℘(0)21 943 21 21
- Le Pont-Le Brassus ℘(0)21 845 17 77
- Lausanne-Échallens-Bercher nicknamed "La Brouette" (The Wheelbarrow) ℘(0)21 886 20 00
- Montreux-Caux-Naye Rocks ℘(0)21 963 65 31.

Neuchâtel canton:
- St Sulplice-Travers ℘(0)32 863 24 07. www.vvf.ch

Bernese Mittelland:
- Bern Weissenbühl-Interlaken Ost-Brienz ℘(0)33 952 22 22,
- Flamatt-Laupen-Gümmenen ℘(0)31 740 62 62

Steam train of Dampfbahn Furka-Bergstrecke AG at the Rhone glacier, Valais

Christof Sonдеregger/Switzerland Tourism

Boat cruise on the Lake Geneva

- Huttwil-Ramsei-Huttwil
  ℘(0)34 422 31 51,
- Worblaufen-Worb Dorf/Solothurn
  ℘(0)31 925 55 55.

Solothurn canton:
- Solothurn-Burgdorf-Thun-
  Solothurn ℘(0)34 422 31 51.

Ticino canton:
- Capolago-Generoso Velta
  ℘(0)91 648 11 05.

BUS TOURS

The **Palm-Express** links St Moritz
with Lugano by post bus, crossing the
Upper Engadin region before heading
to Val Bregaglia and Lake Como.
The **Romantic Route Express**
leaves Andermatt by the Furka Pass
(2 431m/7 973ft) and follows the
Rhône Glacier as far as Gletsch.
The tour passes over the Grimsel Pass
(2 165m/7 101ft), through the Hasli
Valley, to Meiringen and Grindelwald,
at the foot of the north face of the
Eiger; www.post.ch.

LAKE BOATS

The steamer is another familiar site.
Many serve meals. On Greifensee, Lake
Brienz, Lake Constance, Lake Geneva,
Lake Lucerne, Lake Maggiore, Lake
Thun, and Lake Zürich, traditional
steamboats also provide regular ferry
services. The **Swiss Boat Pass** gives
unlimited 50% discount travel for one

or two weeks; sold at harbor ticket and
Tourist Offices. www.vssu.ch or
www.myswitzerland.com.

MUSEUM PASS

The **Swiss Museums Passport**
provides entry to 400 museums,
including temporary exhibitions. The
pass can be purchased at major Tourist
Offices or participating museums.
(Hornbachstrasse 50, Zürich ℘(0)44
389 84 56; www.museumspass.ch).

BOOKS
SWITZERLAND / REFERENCE

The Early Mountaineers by Francis
Gribble (1899). Accounts of pre-
19C Alpine exploration and
engineering.
Winter in the Alps: Food by the Fireside
by Manuela Darling-Gansser (2008).
Exploration of Swiss culture
through its cuisine; includes
cookbook section.
Turner in the Alps by David Hill (1992).
Accounts of travels in France &
Switzerland in 1802.
Historical Dictionary of Switzerland by
Leo Schelbert (2007). Swiss history, part
of the Historical Dictionaries of
Europe series.
*Target Switzerland: Swiss Armed
Neutrality in World War II* by Edward
Whymper (1998). Discusses the
controversy around WWII and
Swiss neutrality during and after
the Nazi threat.

BIOGRAPHY

François de Bonivard and his Captivity —The Prisoner of Chillon by Lord Byron (2004).

FICTION

Swiss Family Robinson by Johann David Wyss, edited by Johan Rudolf Wyss (1812, 1996). Chidren's story about a family stranded on an island.

Heidi by Johanna Spyri (2005). Enchanting story of a girl's youth in the Swiss Alps.

The Cow by Beat Sterchi (2000). A first novel about a Spanish guest worker in Switzerland who works on a dairy farm and later an abattoir, experiences which finally destroy him.

Dr Fischer of Geneva or The Bomb Party by Graham Greene (1980). A satire on capitalism and how greed can corrupt, Set in Geneva and around Lake Geneva.

FILMS
FILMED IN SWITZERLAND

Star Wars III: Revenge of the Sith (2005). Continuation of the Star Wars saga. Grindelwald Mountains appear as a backdrop.

Syriana (2005). A political thriller starring George Clooney, Matt Damon (as an analyst based in Geneva), and Jeffrey Wright.

GoldenEye (1995). Modern adventures of the classic James Bond tales, starring Pierce Brosnan. Verzasca Dam base jump.

Frankenstein (1994). Oscar-nominated performance by Robert DeNiro of Mary Shelley's classic horror tale. Scenes shot in the Swiss Alps.

A View to a Kill (1985). More action from Ian Fleming's James Bond series, starring Roger Moore and Christopher Walken. Various Swiss Alps locations.

On Her Majesty's Secret Service (1969). Starring George Lazenby, this James Bond thriller was nominated for a Golden Globe. Scenes shot on Piz Gloria and in Bern.

Goldfinger (1964). The adventures of Ian Fleming's James Bond, starring Sean Connery who won an Oscar for his role in this film. Located outside Geneva.

Heidi (1954). The classic book brought to life, starring Elsbeth Sigmund. Various Swiss locations.

The Bourne identity (2002). A spy film based on a novel of the same name by Robert Ludlum starring Matt Damon and set partially in Zürich.

Five Days One Summer (1982). A romance directed by Fred Ziinemann starring Sean Connery who plays a middle-aged Scottish doctor on holiday in the Alps.

Heidi (1954)

© UPPA/Photoshot

Calendar of Events

The Swiss find something to celebrate all year round and many regional Tourist Offices publish brochures listing local festivals, fairs, carnivals and other events. Forthcoming events can also be found on their websites. The National Day on 1 Aug (⚲*see p29*) is celebrated around the country. From regionally celebrated Swiss home-cooking to Switzerland's popular haute cuisine, there are myriad festivals that make the best of the country's ingredients and rich culinary heritage.

JANUARY
Solothurn — Swiss Film Festival
Davos— World Economic Forum
Château D'Oex — International Hot Air Balloon Week
Basel—Vogel Gryff - Festival of the Griffin (in Kleinbasel)

FIRST MONDAY IN LENT
Basel — Carnival (3 days)

Carnival, Basel
Philipp Giegel / Switzerland Tourism

FEBRUARY
Dorf Lenk, Gadmen — International Sled Dog Races
Engadin — International Free-Ride Competition

late Feb:
Ticino — Traveling carnival with risotto served outdoors

MARCH
early Mar:
Fribourg — International Film Festival
Bellinzona —Rabadan Carnival
Geneva — International Motor Show
Caprices — Caprices Festival (Music)
Basel — European Watch, Clock and Jewellery Fair

APRIL
Geneva — Chocolate Festival
Zürich — Sechseläuten: a spring festival to mark the end of winter; including burning of "Böögg" (Old Man Winter)
late Apr:
Aarberg — Second-hand market
Appenzell — Landsgemeinde: open-air assembly
mid Apr–mid-May:
Morges — Tulip Festival
late Apr–early May:
Montreux — International "Golden Rose" Television Festival
late Apr–early May:
Zürich — 2nd International Bach Days

MAY
first Sun in May:
Glarus — Landsgemeinde
Berne — International Jazz Festival
late May–early Jun:
Sierre — International Comic Book Festival
Beromünster — Ascension Day
May or Jun:
Appenzell, Fribourg, Saas-Fee Lötschental: Kippel, Ferden, Wiler, Blatten — Corpus Christi Thursday processions

JUNE
Basel — International Art Fair (modern and contemporary art)
Boverasse—Absinthe Festival (mid-June)
late Jun–early Jul:
Ascona — New Orleans Jazz Festival

Jazz Festival on the Piazza della Riforma, Lugano

Lugano Turismo

late Jun–Sept:
Interlaken — Open-air performances of Schiller's *William Tell* in German

JULY
Fribourg (even years) — International Jazz Festival
Lausanne — Athlétissima: International Athletics Meeting
Lugano — Jazz Festival
Montreux — International Jazz Festival
Nyon — Paléo Festival: International Open-Air Rock and Folk Music

LATE JULY/EARLY AUGUST
Montreux, Vevey, La Tour-de-Peilz — Léman Tradition Festival

LATE JULY/EARLY SEPTEMBER
Gstaad/Saanen — Classical Music Festival

AUGUST
Geneva — Genevese festivities; floral floats and fireworks
Locarno — International Film Festival
Saignelégier — National horse show, fair and horse racing (second weekend in August)
Montreux — Comedy Festival
mid Aug–early Sep:
Lucerne — International Music Weeks
late Aug:
Fribourg — International Folk Festival

Vevey — Street Theatre Festival
Aarberg — Second-hand Antique Market
late Aug–early Oct:
Ascona — International Classical Music Festival
Brunnen—More than 25 private providers turn the village into a huge restaurant (late Aug). www.brunnentourismus.ch.

SEPTEMBER
Saas-Fee — Pilgrimage to the Hohen Stiege Chapel — Early Sept
Zürich (Albisgütli) — Knabenschiessen (Shooting

The National Festival

Throughout Switzerland the anniversary of the alliance sworn on 1 August 1291 by the representatives of Uri, Schwyz and Unterwalden, is commemorated with patriotic demonstrations, fireworks displays and spectacular mountaintop bonfires. It has been held every year since and is thought to be the first national day to be celebrated anywhere in the world. The historic sites of Lake Uri, especially the Rütli Field where a vow of brotherhood was taken, and the Axenstrasse, are floodlit for the occasion.

Christmas Markets and Fairs

Christmas Market at Klosterplatz Square, Einsiedeln

Christof Sonderegger/Switzerland Tourism

Brunnen – The city's former wine cellars are turned into the venue for over 50 Christmas stalls.

Einsiedeln – Held in the Klosterplatz Square; over 140 themed wooden huts.

Lucerne – Christkindlimarkts at both the railway station and Löwenplatz

Ticino – Local townships and villages celebrate with markets and fairs. Markets at Airolo and Bellinzona mid Dec; Biasca and Locarno just before Christmas.

Pilatus – At 2 132m/6 995ft and held in the restaurant during mid-November, this is probably the highest Christmas Market of all.

Zürich – Zürich Christkindlimarkt, the largest indoor Christmas Market in Europe claiming to have over 15,000 visitors per day. Late Nov–Christmas Eve.

Contest): a competition for Zürich schoolchildren

mid Sept:

Locarno—Festival of Grapes (mid-Sept)

Lausanne — Swiss Trade Fair (Late Sept)

Neuchâtel — Grape Harvest Festival

Charmey — Fête de la Désalpe

Martigny — Valais Fair

Vevey — Festival Images (photography, cinema, multimedia)

Pratz—Wine Festival (late Sept)

OCTOBER

St Gallen — National Show for the Dairy and Farming Industry

Lugano — Autumn Festival

Châtel-St-Denis — Bénichon (Benediction or harvest) festival

Bulle— Gruyère gastronomic fair (late Oct–early Nov

Basle —Basel Wine Fair (late Oct-Nov)

NOVEMBER

Bern — Zibelemärit (4th Monday)

DECEMBER

Geneva — Feast of the Escalade

Fribourg — St Nicholas parade and fair

Feast of the Escalade, Geneva

Know Before You Go

USEFUL WEBSITES

www.myswitzerland.com

The Swiss National Tourist Office (SNTO) website is full of practical information on destinations, accommodations, weather, events and festivals. Another section provides suggestions for specific types of holiday experiences, including family, golf, wellness spas and, of course, skiing. There are links to each region, within which there are links to individual destinations.

www.alpseurope.com

The Alpine Tourist Commission is a marketing organization for the five Alpine countries of Austria, France, Germany, Italy and Switzerland, with links to tour operators, airlines and special travel package offers.

www.visiteurope.com

The European Travel Commission provides useful travel information for 27 countries, plus links to rail schedules, car rental agencies, weather reports and more.

www.swissinfo.org

This website has comprehensive information about Swiss business, industry, education and politics. There also are links to developments in the arts, science and technology that involve Switzerland.

www.switzerland.tv

A guide to Swiss products and services, including chocolate, watches, cheese, private medical clinics and spas, plus banks and business centres. There also are links to shopping by city or category of product.

www.swisstravelsystem.ch

Comprehensive information about the various Swiss Pass options for train, bus, boat, cable car and other public transport.

TOURIST OFFICES
SWISS NATIONAL TOURIST OFFICES (SNTO)

For information, brochures, maps and assistance in planning your trip, contact the relevant national office. (www.myswitzerland.com)

♦ **Headquarters**
Schweizerische Verkehrszentrale Bellariastrasse 38, Postfach 695, CH-8027 Zürich; ℘01 288 11 11; Fax 01 288 12 05.

♦ **United Kingdom**
Swiss Center, 1st Floor Bedford St, London WC2E9ED, ℘0800 100 200 30 (toll free)

♦ **United States**
Swiss Center, 608 Fifth Avenue, New York City, NY 10020-2303, ℘00800 100 200 30 (international toll free); or 212 757 5944 or 1877 794 8037 (USA only).

150 North Michigan Avenue, Chicago, IL 60601, ℘312 630 5840.

222 Sepulveda Boulevard, El Segundo, Los Angeles, CA 90245; ℘310 335 5980.

Other Locations

There are also SNTO locations in the following cities: Amsterdam, Brussels, Frankfurt, Madrid, Milan, Paris, Rome, Stockholm, Tokyo and Vienna.

TOURIST INFORMATION

Information Centres

Look for the 🛈 on town maps.
Tourist Information Centres (Verkehrsbüro; office de tourisme; ente turistico) can be found in most large towns and tourist resorts. Their contact details are shown after the introduction to each principal sight, where applicable.

Information Association

A total of 23 towns from several different cantons have joined to form an organisation providing information to visitors. The towns involved are Appenzell, Baden, Basel, Bellinzona, Bern, Biel/Bienne, Chur, Fribourg, La Chaux-de-Fonds, Geneva, Lausanne, Lugano, Montreux, Neuchâtel, St Gallen, Schaffhausen, Sierre, Sion, Solothurn, Winterthur, Thun, Zug and Zürich.

For further information, contact:
Information and Reservation Center, Chur Tourismus, Grabenstrasse 5, CH-7002 Chur; ☏(0)81 252 18 18;

Hotel Association
Swiss Hotel Association
(Schweizer Hotelier-Verein) –
Monbijoustrasse 130, CH 3007 Bern;
☏(0)31 370 41 11; Fax (0)31 370 44 44;
www.swisshotels.ch.

INTERNATIONAL VISITORS
SWISS EMBASSIES AND CONSULATES ABROAD

United Kingdom
Swiss Embassy, 16-18 Montagu Place, London W1H 2BQ; ☏020 7616 6000; www.eda.admin.ch.

Republic of Ireland
Swiss Embassy, 6 Ailesbury Road, Ballsbridge, Dublin 4; ☏353 1 269 25 15; www.eda.admin.ch/dublin.

United States
Swiss Embassy, 2900 Cathedral Avenue NW, Washington DC 20008, ☏202 745 7900; www.eda.admin.ch/washington (with consulates in 26 major cities and Puerto Rico).

Canada
Swiss Embassy, 5 Marlborough Avenue, Ottawa ON K1N 8E6, ☏613 235 1837; www.eda.admin.ch/canada (plus seven provincial consulates).

FOREIGN EMBASSIES AND CONSULATES IN SWITZERLAND

United Kingdom
♦ **Embassy**, Thunstrasse 50, CH-3000 Bern 15; ☏(0)31 359 77 00; www.ukinswitzerland.fco.gov.uk.

♦ **Consulate General**, rue de Vermont 37-39, Geneva; ☏(0)22 918 2400.
♦ **Vice-Consulate**, Hegibachstrasse 47, CH-8032 Zürich; ☏(0)44 383 65 60.

Republic of Ireland
♦ **Embassy**, Kirchenfeldstrasse 68, CH-3005 Bern; ☏(0)31 352 14 42.
♦ **Consulate General**, Claridenstrasse 25, Postfach 562, 8027 Zürich; ☏01 289 25 15.

United States
♦ **Embassy**, Jubiläumstrasse 93, 3001 Bern; ☏(0)31 357 70 11; http://bern.usembassy.gov.
♦ **Consulate General**, Route de Pregny 111292 Chambésy; ☏(0)22 840 51 60.
♦ **Consulate**, Dufourstrasse 101, c/o Zürich America Center, 8008 Zürich; ☏(0)43 499 29 60.

Canada
♦ **Embassy**, Kirchenfeldstrasse 88, 3000 Bern 6, ☏(0)31 357 32 00; www.canada-ambassade.ch.
♦ **Consulate** , 5 avenue de l'Ariana, 1202 Geneva; ☏(0)22 919 92 00.

ENTRY REQUIREMENTS

Visitors travelling to Switzerland must have a valid national passport, including citizens of European Union countries (in case of loss or theft, report to the embassy or consulate and the local police). Entry visas are required for Australian, European, New Zealand, Canadian, and US citizens if the intended stay exceeds 90 days. The nearest Swiss consulate or embassy will help if there is any doubt. US citizens may find the booklet **Safe Trip Abroad** useful for information on visa requirements, customs regulations, medical care, etc when travelling in Europe.

Contact the Superintendent of Documents, *PO Box* 371954, Pittsburgh, PA 15250-7954; ☏(202) 512 1800; www.access.gpo.gov; www.bfm.admin.ch.

CUSTOMS REGULATIONS

There are no restrictions concerning the import, export and exchange of Swiss francs. Switzerland is not a member of the EU and has stricter conditions for the import and export of goods; contact the Swiss Tourist Office (&see Tourist Offices) for more information. Tourists under the age of 17 are not allowed to import or export alcohol or tobacco.

Pets brought into Switzerland require a veterinary certificate stating that the animal has been vaccinated against rabies in your home country, except for puppies and kittens aged under-3 months, which simply require a health certificate issued by a veterinary surgeon. For further information, contact: **Swiss Federal Veterinary Office (FVO)**, Schwarzenburgstr. 155 CH-3003 Berne; &(0)31 323 30 33.

HEALTH

Visitors are strongly advised to have medical or travel insurance to cover personal accident and sickness. There is no state health service in Switzerland and patients are required to pay for all medical treatment (keep any receipts). Special winter sports policies should be arranged where required.

For more information contact the **International Association for Medical Assistance to Travellers** (www.iamat.org).

ACCESSIBILITY

Many of the sights described in this guide are accessible to those with special needs. Sights marked with the & symbol offer wheelchair access. However, it is always advisable to check beforehand by telephone. More than 170 Swiss railway stations have wheelchair ramps. Trains that do not have lifts may be accessed by notifying the **SBB Call Center** (&0800 00 71 02) at least one hour prior to boarding. Those travelling from abroad should call for assistance 3 days ahead of arriving &41 51 225 71 50. Some cog

railways and mountain cable cars also are wheelchair accessible, but the volunteer system **Compagna** will respond to any request for help accessing sites not already equipped &41 71 220 16 09. Local Tourist Offices can also give information on accessibility options.

Larger lake steamers are wheelchair-accessible, but it is best to avoid purchasing a first-class ticket, which requires climbing steep stairs.

An **International Wheelchair Badge** on the dashboard of your vehicle is required to park in designated spots. Large modern and renovated hotels and holiday apartments usually have special disabled facilities such as wide-door bathrooms and roll-in showers; inns and *pensions* may have only cramped elevators. Larger cities and towns have wheelchair-accessible public toilets, most often unisex facilities, marked with the & wheelchair symbol.

Mobility International Switzerland (MIS) publishes a guide for wheelchair users. Froburgstrasse 4, CH-4600 Olten, &62 206 88 35 or www.mis-ch.ch.

Access-Able (http://access-able.com) provides a multitude of resources for the disabled and elderly.

SwissTrac wheelchair power unit attaches to your existing or rented chair, and enables ease of movement over all terrains including curbs, grass, and nature paths &(0)41 854 80 20, www.swisstrac.ch.

Mobility assistance at Zürich Airport
Careport AG

Getting There and Getting Around

BY PLANE

The world's top airlines, including the Swiss National Airline, Swiss Air, operate scheduled flights to Basel, Geneva and Zürich, plus budget airlines such as easyJet (www.easyjet.com). There is also a domestic service to Lugano.

CONNECTIONS WITH AIRPORTS

Geneva and Zürich airports both have rail stations with regular services to all major cities and to their own city centres; shuttle buses also operate from Basel, Bern and Lugano airports (between 15min and 20min). Taxis are available at each airport.

Fly-Rail

This service allows visitors flying into Zürich or Geneva to have their luggage transported directly to the railway station nearest to their destination. It also operates for out-going flights from 50 railway stations in Switzerland to the passenger's final destination. **Swiss Federal Railways** ℘0900 300 300; www.rail.ch.

BY TRAIN
INTERNATIONAL RAIL

For travellers coming from the UK, **Eurostar** (℘08705 186 186; www.eurostar.com) operates high-speed passenger trains (**TGV**) to Paris from London St Pancras International. From Paris, the high-speed trains run to a number of cities in Switzerland, including Geneva, Lausanne (with some trains calling at Montreux, Aigle, Bex, Martigny, Sion, Sierre, Visp and Brigue) and Zürich (with stops at Neuchâtel and Berne). All trains leave from the Gare de Lyon, with the exception of the train to Basel, which operates from the Gare de l'Est. Direct TGV trains also run to Neuchâtel and Bern from Dijon.

Switzerland's Main Railway Bridges
Sitterviadukt (St Gallen): 97m/319ft
Wiesenviadukt (Graubünden): 92m/302ft
Solisbrücke (Graubünden): 85m/278ft
Viaduc de Grandfey (Fribourg): 82m/269ft
Reussbrücke (Uri): 77m/252ft
Meienreussbrücke (Uri): 71m/232ft
Langwiesviadukt (Graubünden): 66m/216ft
Landwasserviadukt (Graubünden): 65m/214ft

NATIONAL RAIL

Within Switzerland, the extensive Swiss railway system operates a frequent and efficient service. For tickets, prices and discounts apply to:

- **Rail Europe**, 178 Piccadilly, London W1; ℘08448 484 064; www.raileurope.co.uk.
- **Swiss Federal Railways** (SBB/CFF); ℘0900 300 300 (within Switzerland); www.rail.ch.
- **Railaway** Zentralstrasse 7, Lucerne ℘(0)51 227 36 40; www.railaway.ch.

The Swiss rail network covers about 4 989km/3 100mi. Swiss trains are famous worldwide for running on time. All major cities and large towns have excellent connections and regular services. Trains include fast intercity trains (IC); regular direct trains; regional trains serving destinations normally considered to be off the beaten track; rack railways

Switzerland's Longest Railway Tunnels
Lötschber base Tunnel (Bern, Zermatt): 34.6km/21.5mi (2007)
Simplon (Valais): 19.8km/12mi (1906)
Furka (Valais, Uri): 15.4km/9.5mi (1982)
St Gotthard (Uri, Ticino): 15km/9.3mi (1882)
Ricken (St Gallen): 8.6km/5.4mi
Grenchenberg (Solothurn, Berne): 8.6km/5.4mi
Hauenstein (Solothurn, Basel): 8.1km/5mi

in the mountains; scenic railways and steam railways; not forgetting funicular railways, cable-cars, chairlifts and underground trains. Motorail services also operate between Kandersteg and Goppenstein (Lötschberg), Brig and Iselle di Trasquera in Italy (Simplon), Thusis and Samedan (Albula), Oberwald and Realp (Furka) and Andermatt and Sedrun (Oberalp).

SWITZERLAND'S LONGEST ROAD TUNNELS

St Gotthard (Uri, Ticino):
16.3km/10.2mi (1980)

Seelisberg (Nidwalden, Uri):
9.3km/5.8mi (1981)

San Bernardino: 6.6km/4mi (1967)

Gr St Bernhard (Graubünden):
5.9km/3.6mi (1964)

Belchen (Solothurn, Bern): 3.2km/1.9mi

Landwasser (Graubünden): 2.8km/1.7mi

Isla Bella (Ticino): 2.4km/1.4mi

Binn (Valais): 1.9km/1.1mi

SWISS TRAVEL SYSTEM

The Swiss public transport system is second to none, especially in large cities where buses, trams and trolleycars operate a highly efficient service. Automatic **ticket machines** are available at each stop (exact change often required). **Swiss Pass** holders are entitled to free, unlimited travel.

TRAVEL PASSES

The **Swiss Travel System** (STS) offers several different 1st and 2nd class passes. These can be purchased from Swiss National Tourist Offices, local travel agents or railway stations upon presenting a passport or identity card. The **Swiss Pass** allows visitors unlimited travel on a network of 16 000km/12 000mi of trains, boats, postal buses, tramways and urban bus services in 35 Swiss cities and towns. Discounts are also offered on many mountain and panoramic railways and

a 15% reduction is available for two people or more. The Swiss pass is valid for 4, 8, 15, 22 days or one month, and also serves as a discount card for many museums and sightseeing tours.

The **Swiss Flexipass** allows 3, 4, 5, or 6 days unlimited travel in a one month period, with a 15% discount for two people or more, also serving as a discount card.

The **Swiss Youth Pass** is a discounted version of the Flexipass for those under 26 years of age; children up to the age of 16 traveling with at least one parent with a valid STS ticket travel free of charge on the entire network.

The **Swiss Card** entitles visitors to a 50% discount on trains, postal buses and mountain railways in one area. For groups of 2 to 5 , the **SaverPass** provides unlimited travel on the Swiss Travel System including trains, buses and boats . Passes are available for 4, 8, 15, or 22 days and one month and include the discount benefits on local attractions and tours as well.

The **Swiss Transfer Ticket** includes two transfers by rail between any Swiss airport or border town plus any one destination in Switzerland plus a 50% discount on all further train, bus or boat travel in between. Each transfer must be completed in one day.

The **Swiss Museum Passport** provides free entry to more than 420 museums and exhibits. Family and plus passes available for those traveling with children ℘(0)44 389 84 56, www.museumspass.ch.

POSTAL BUSES

The famous **postal buses** (postauto) usually leave from train stations or post offices and for many visitors provide a leisurely, inexpensive and scenic way to visit remote villages. **Swiss PostBus Lt. Tours & Travel**. Aareckstrasse 6, CH-3800 Interlaken, ℘(0)33 828 88 28, www.postauto.ch.

BY CAR

MAIN ROUTES

Visitors traveling by road from one of the Channel ports can choose one of two main routes: via **Calais** and the French motorway system through **France** (A 26 to Troyes, A 5 to Langres, A 31 to Beaune, A 6 to Mâcon and A 40 to Geneva—about 800km/500mi); or via **Ostende** and then through **Belgium, Luxembourg, France** and **Germany** (along E 40 to Liège, E 25 to Luxembourg, A 31 to just north of Metz, and the A 4 to Strasbourg, where you cross the Rhine and the German border to pick up the E 35 (A 5) to Basel—about 700km/450mi).

PLANNING YOUR ROUTE

Michelin's national Swiss map 729 covers all of Switzerland, including a list of towns and enlarged maps of the main cities. More detailed orange maps covering the North (551), South-West (552) and South-East (553) indicate very narrow roads (single track, where overtaking is difficult or impossible), gradients, difficult or dangerous roads, tunnels and the altitudes of passes.

The itineraries described in this guide often follow local roads that may intimidate drivers unfamiliar with mountain driving. All of these roads are accessible, at least in summer. The Michelin maps mentioned above highlight **snowbound roads** (with their opening and closing dates) as well as the location of emergency telephones.

Michelin offers a computerised route-finding system integrating information about roads, tourist sights, hotels and restaurants available on the **internet** at www. ViaMichelin.com. For route planning, specify your point of departure and destination, stipulate your preference for motorways or local roads and it will do the rest. The website also gives information on campsites and interesting sights en route.

DOCUMENTS

A valid driving licence or international driving permit, car registration papers (log-book) and a nationality licence plate are required. An International Insurance Certificate (Green Card) is available from your insurance company and is the most effective proof of insurance coverage, recognised by all Swiss police and other officials.

ROAD TAX

Instead of tolls, an annual road tax called a **vignette** is levied on cars and motorbikes using Swiss motorways. The *vignette* is valid from 1 December until 31 January of the following year; it must be displayed on the windscreen. The *vignette* costs 40CHF (trailers an additional 40CHF) and is available at border posts, post offices, petrol stations, garages and cantonal car registration offices. To avoid delays at the border, purchase the *vignette* in advance from the Swiss National Tourist Office (*see Tourist Offices*).

ROAD REGULATIONS

Laws are strictly enforced and police are authorised to collect on-the-spot fines. Drivers must be at least 18 years old. **Seat belts** are compulsory; children under-12 are required to sit in the back. **Dipped headlights** are compulsory in tunnels. A red **warning triangle** or **hazard warning lights** are obligatory in case of a breakdown. Use of the **horn** is discouraged except on mountain roads with blind turns. **Studded tires** are forbidden on motorways; on other roads, they are permitted only between 1 November and 30 April. **STOP signs** at crossings should be strictly obeyed. **Tram and light railway systems** are modern and run at high speed; take great care at unguarded crossings, where the warning is generally three red blinking lights, arranged in a triangle and connected with a bell. **Pedestrians** getting on or off buses and trams have priority over motorists.

It is strictly prohibited to overtake on the right, even on motorways. On **mountain roads**, if you want to pass another vehicle and meet an on-coming vehicle, it is the responsibility of the car coming down to pull over and if necessary reverse back to a suitable stopping place. **Post buses**—easy to recognise by their yellow colour and distinctive three-note horn (the first notes of Rossini's overture to *William Tell*)—always have priority.

Trailers are restricted to 2.5m/8.2ft in width and 12m/39.37ft in length. Owners of larger trailers registered outside the country can apply to the Customs Office for authorisation to drive them in the country (20CHF tax). The Klausen, Nufenen, Schelten and Weissenstein Passes are closed to these cars; access is permitted to Bürgenstock and Diemtigtal.

SPEED LIMITS

Maximum speed on motorways is 120kph/75mph; on other roads 80kph/50mph and in towns and villages 50kph/31mph. Police radar speed trap detectors are forbidden. The speed limit for cars towing trailers is 80kph/50mph (up to 1t) or 60kph/37mph (over 1t) on all roads, including motorways.

PARKING

There is a charge for most city-centre parking; areas (marked by a blue sign) permit parking up to 90min. Visitors should buy a **parking disc** from the local police station or Tourist Office.

ROAD SIGNS

Motorways are indicated by signs in white on a green background. There are priority roads, numbered and marked by arrows in white on a blue ground. Secondary roads are marked and numbered in black on a white ground. These green signs are not to be mistaken for those used for indicating diversions, known as *itinéraires bis*.

CAR RENTAL

There are car rental agencies at airports, railway stations and downtown locations in most larger cities. Except at airports, rental agencies are closed Sundays; most non-airport locations close before 6pm weekdays and Saturdays. Smaller vehicles have manual transmissions; automatics require advance reservations. Drivers must be over 21 years of age (**SIXT-Eurorent** will rent mini-cars to drivers 18 to 21); drivers must be at least 25 for some luxury vehicles and large SUVs. Avis does not charge for an additional driver. Fly-drive packages are generally less expensive than renting separately. For longer stays, 17 days to six months, **Renault EuroDrive** offers a short-term lease that can be less costly than renting. ℘1-888-532-1221 (in USA); www.renaultusa.com.

Car rental companies
Avis: www.avis.ch
Kemwel: www.kemwel.com
AutoEurope: www.autoeurope.com
SIXT-Eurorent: www.esixt.com

PETROL (GASOLINE)

Most petrol stations are closed at night, even on motorways; self-service petrol pumps remain open (10CHF or 20CHF notes). Four-star and unleaded petrol are cheaper than the European average, whereas diesel is more expensive. Unleaded petrol is widely available.

EMERGENCIES

Emergency telephones are available on motorways, larger roads and in the mountains; motorist help calls can also be made from any telephone 24hr a day by dialling ℘140. Automobile associations include the **Touring Club of Switzerland** (TCS) (4 chemin de Blandonnet, 1214 Vernier, ℘(0)22 417 22 20; www.tcs.ch) and the **Swiss Automobile Club** (ACS) (Wasserwerkgasse 39, CH-3000 Bern 13, ℘(0)31 328 31 11; www.acs.ch).

Where to Stay and Eat

🎧 Hotel and Restaurant recommendations are located in the Address Books throughout the Discovering Switzerland section of this guide. For coin ranges and for a description of the symbols used in the Address Books see the legend on the cover flap.

WHERE TO STAY
USEFUL WEBSITES

www.switzerlanddirect.ch
The Switzerland direct site (also www.suissedirect.ch) allows internet searching and booking of hotels by region. Also special offers.

www.switzerlandhotels.ch
Direct links to many hotels and apartments in the large cities and some resorts. Also links to descriptions by the Switzerland Hotel Association.

www.rooms.ch
Direct links to 200 Swiss budget hotels in all regions. Budget holidays are also available where your entire stay can be organised for you.

www.myswitzerland.com
The Swiss National Tourist Office offers a list of child-friendly accommodations on its website, arranged by region with complete contact details.

FINDING A HOTEL

For an exhaustive list of hotels consult the *Michelin Red Guide Switzerland*. The **Swiss Guide to Hotels** (Guide Suisse des Hôtels), published by the Swiss National Board of Hotel Owners, classifies hotels by region or canton and is available from **Schweizer Hotelier-Verein Hotel-Boutique**, Monbijoustrasse 130 Postfach CH-3001 Bern; ℘(0)31 370 41 11. www.swisshotels.ch.

VELOTELS, APARTMENTS, BED AND BREAKFAST

Velohotlels, distinguishable by their sign, cater specifically to cyclists. (℘01 680 22 23) (🎧see Outdoor Fun). The publication **Vacances à la Campagne** lists furnished flats, bed and breakfasts, lodgings with full- or half-board, communal accommodation, mainly for German-speaking Switzerland; it is available from **Caisse Suisse de Voyage Reka** (Neuengasse 15, 3001 Bern, ℘(0)31 329 66 33; www.reka.ch). Charming bed and breakfast accommodations throughout Switzerland can be recognised by signs along the road. **Bed and Breakfast Switzerland** has over 100 members (www.bnb.ch). Highly recommended B & B accommodation all checked regularly can be selected by canton or by a simple alphabetical search. A 504 page book, Guide to Swiss B & Bs, is available and also vouchers valid for 2 years to give to friends and family.

STAYING ON A FARM

Bauernhof Ferien (Holiday Farms) provides information on stays at over 250 farms. Participating farms must

Hospitality Industry Terms

Bündnerstube – Traditional sitting room from Graubünden, furnished and decorated in accordance with the local custom.
Café – Tea room (in German-speaking Switzerland).
Carnotzet – In hotels of the Vaud and the Valais, a room where local cheese and wines are served.
Gasthaus – Inn.
Kurhaus – Spa. There are also thermal and mountain *Kurhäuser*.
Restaurant – Establishment serving lunch and dinner. In some German-Swiss towns, "restaurants" may provide only drinks, as in cafés, unless there is a notice saying *Speise-Restaurant*.
Wirtschaft – Very modest inn or pub, used mainly by local people.

meet criteria, including quality of rooms and a range of animals; some offer extra facilities such as horse riding. **Swiss Holiday Farms**, Reka, Neuengasse 15, 3000 Bern, ℰ(0)31 329 66 99; www.agrotourismus.ch.

YOUTH HOSTELS

Switzerland has 67 youth hostels, open to visitors of all ages who belong to a youth hostel association. Hostels are popular with families, especially during school holidays. To join in the UK, contact the **Youth Hostels Association**, Trevelyan House, Dimple Road, Matlock, Derbyshire DE4 3YH, UK. ℰ0870 770 8868 or 01629 592 700; www.yha.org.uk; or **Hostelling International-American Youth Hostels**, 8401 Colesville Road, Suite 600, Silver Spring, MD, ℰ(301) 495-1240; www.hiayh.org.
A full list of Swiss youth hostels is available at www.youthhostel.ch.

CAMPING AND CARAVANNING

Camping is only permitted on authorised sites. Maps and lists of sites with prices and facilities are published by the **Swiss Camping and Caravanning Federation** (www.swisscamps.ch) and the **Swiss Touring Club** (CP 820, CH-1214-Vernier, ℰ(0)22 417 22 20). A full list of Swiss camping associations and information is available from the Swiss National Tourist Office (*see Tourist Offices*).

MOUNTAIN HUTS

The **Swiss Alpine Club** (Club Alpin Suisse) manages numerous mountain huts. Contact SNTO or the Swiss Alpine Club (Schweizer Alpenclub – SAC), Monbijoustrasse 61, CH-3000 Bern 23, ℰ(0)31 370 18 18; www.sac-cas.ch. SAC members have priority over other applicants.
The **Swiss Backpackers Association** offers mountain and family-friendly accommodations (Alpenstrasse 16, CH-3800 Interlaken; ℰ(0)33 823 46 46; www.swissbackpackers.ch).

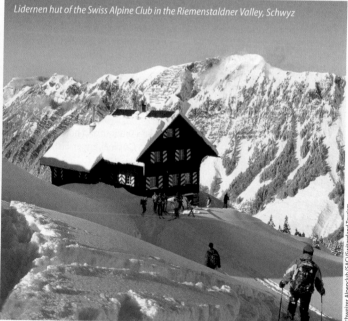

Lidernen hut of the Swiss Alpine Club in the Riemenstaldner Valley, Schwyz

Schweizer Alpenclub (SAC)/Switzerland Tourism

WHERE TO EAT

Address Books in the sight descriptions have dining suggestions and their prices (see the Legend on the cover flap for coin ranges). An exhaustive list can be found in the Michelin Red Guide Switzerland.

USEFUL WEBSITES

www.viamichelin.co.uk
Click on 'Restaurants' and enter the location you require in order to find a selection of eating places some of which are also in the Michelin Red Guide.

www.foodeu.com
By selecting Switzerland on the drop down menu you can browse and select restaurants, bistros, brasseries, cafés and bar in all cities and regions.

EATING OUT

Some **restaurants** levy a cover charge, which may include bread *(pain et couvert)*. At lunch, the *plat du jour*, or dish of the day, usually represents good value.

REGIONAL SPECIALTIES

Be sure to try **perch fillet**, caught in Lake Geneva, with a glass of Fendant or Perlan; a cheese **fondue** with Gruyère or Vacherin with a dry white wine; a tasty **raclette**, cheese melted in a wood oven or grill and served with potatoes; or **tripe à la neuchâteloise** with an Oeil de Perdrix rosé. Meat specialties include **game** from the Valais with a Cornalin wine, dried and smoked **beef** from Graubünden enhanced by a velvety Pinot Noir, or Zürich-style **veal slices** *(geschnetzeltes Kalbfleisch)*. Other specialities include the Bernese dish of **assorted cold meats**, spicy meat balls *(polpettone)* from the Ticino region, **papet vaudois**, a winter dish of sausages with cabbage, leeks and potatoes, **Rösti** (delicious diced potatoes, fried then baked); and traditional **veal sausage**, a nationwide specialty. Desserts favour cream pastries, and the mouth-watering chocolates for which the country is world famous.

DRINKS

Wine – Switzerland produces some 200 million bottles of wine a year.

Whites: Fendant (Valais), Perlan (Geneva), Chasselas (Neuchâtel, Vaud) and Johannisberg (Valais).
Reds: Gamay (Geneva), Pinot Noir (Graubünden, Neuchâtel), Dôle (Pinot Noir and Gamay; blend, Valais).
Rosé: Oeil de Perdrix (Neuchâtel), Merlot Rosato (Ticino).

Wines are served in two- to five-decilitre carafes or may be sampled by the glass in a **weinstub** (wine bar).

Beer – Draught and bottled beer (Adler, Cardinal, Egger, Eichhof, Feldschlösschen, etc) are popular. In German-speaking areas, the **bierstub** is similar in atmosphere to a *weinstub*.

Mineral water – Most Swiss order bottled water in restaurants, either still or sparkling mineral water. Swiss brands are Henniez and Passuger.

Coffee – This is often served with a small pot of cream *(Kaffeesahne)*.

Raclette

Valais Tourism/Switzerland Tourism

Useful Words and Phrases

GERMAN	ENGLISH	FRENCH
Bahnhof	Railway station	Gare
Brücke	Bridge	Pont
Burg	Feudal castle	Château
Denkmal	Monument or memorial	Monument
Fähre	Ferry	Ferry
Fall	Waterfall	Cascade
Garten	Garden	Jardin
Gasse	Street, alley	Ruelle
Gletscher	Glacier	Glacier
Hafen	Port, harbor	Port
Haupt...	As a prefix: main, chief, head	Principal...
Kirche	Church	Église
Kleintaxi	Small taxi	Minicab
Kloster	Monastery, convent, abbey	Monastère
Kursaal	Casino	Casino
Markt	Market	Marché
Münster	Important church (cathedral)	Cathédrale
Ober...	High, upper	Haut...
Rathaus	Town hall	Mairie
Schloss	Castle, château	Château
Schlucht	Gorge	Gorge
Schwimmbad	Swimming pool	Piscine
See	Lake	Lac
Spielplatz	Sports ground	Aire de jeu
Strandbad	Bathing beach	Plage
Strasse	Street	Rue
Tal	Valley	Vallée
Talsperre	Dam	Barage
Tobel	Ravine	Ravine
Tor	Gate (of a town)	Porte
Unter...	Under, lower	Bas...
Verboten	Forbidden, prohibited	Interdit
Wald	Forest, wood	Forêt
Zeughaus	Arsenal	Arsenal

VOCABULARY FOR SKIERS

GERMAN	ENGLISH	FRENCH
Skischule	Ski school	École de ski
Abfahrt	Ski run	Départ, piste
Schi, Ski (Bergski, Talski)	Top ski, bottom ski	Ski (amont, aval)
Kanten	Ski edges	Carres
Bindung	Ski bindings	Fixation
Skistock	Ski stick	Bâton
Skiwachs	Ski wax	Fart
Schussfahrt	Straight run	Descente directe
Schneepflug, Stemmen	Snow-plough position	Position de chasse-neige

GERMAN	ENGLISH	FRENCH
Abrutschen	Side slipping	Dérapage
Kurvenschwung,	Curve, swing, turn	Bogen Virage
Wedeln	Wedling	"Godille"
Riesenslalom	Giant slalom	Slalom géant
Abfahrtslauf	Clear run	Descente libre
Kombination	All-round test	Combiné
Langstreckenlauf	Long-distance race	Course de fond
Sprungschanze	Ski jumping	Tremplin de saut
Skilift	Ski lift	Téléski, remonte-pente
Sessellift	Chairlift	Télésiège
Kabinenbahn	Cable car	Télécabine
Schwebebahn	Cable car	Téléphérique
Drahtseilbahn	Funicular	Funiculaire
Lawine	Avalanche	Avalanche
Schutzhütte	Refuge	Refuge
Skiwerkstatt	Ski-repair shop	Atelier de réparation de skis
Rodelbahn	Sledge run	Piste de luge
Eisbahn	Skating rink	Patinoire

Basic Information

BUSINESS HOURS

Shops are usually open Mon–Fri 8am–6.30pm; Sat 8am–4pm or 5pm. Banks are open Mon–Fri 8.30am–4.30pm. Shops generally close at 4pm on Saturday afternoons. In large towns, department stores are closed on Monday mornings, but have late-night shopping until 9pm once a week.

LAST ADMISSION TIMES

In the Discovering section of the guide the times we generally give are opening hours: 10am–6pm means the site *closes* at 6pm. In practise many places have a last admission time of 30mins to an hour before closing time. If the last admission time is more than an hour before closing time (normally only larger attractions stipulate this) or the attraction specifically states last admission time (as opposed to closing time) we also state this. In general however it is always best to arrive at least 90min before an attraction closes.

COMMUNICATIONS

Credit cards are accepted in many phone boxes. Telephone cards, called **Taxcards**, are available from post offices, railway kiosks and hotel reception desks for 10 or 20 CHF. The minimum cost of a call is 0.60 CHF. Calls are cheaper after 7pm and on weekends.

For calls within Switzerland, the number is formed by a three-figure code starting with 0, given in brackets, followed by another group of five, six or seven figures. When calling within the same telephone district, do not dial the area code.

For **international calls** dial 00 plus the following country codes:
Australia: ℰ61
Canada: ℰ1
New Zealand: ℰ64
UK: ℰ44
USA: ℰ1

If calling from outside the country, the international code for **Switzerland** is 41. Dial the international access code,

USEFUL TELEPHONE NUMBERS

1181: Directory enquiries for Switzerland

117: Police in case of an emergency

118: Fire brigade

187: In winter, snow reports and avalanche bulletins; in summer, tourist information provided by the Swiss National Tourist Office

140: Car breakdown service (open 24 hours)

144: Emergency doctor; ambulance

161: Talking clock

162: Weather forecast

163: Information on snow-bound roads, traffic conditions

187: Avalanche bulletin

1141: International numbers and information on calling abroad

followed by 41, then the area code without the first 0, followed by the correspondent's number; for example, when calling Bern from the UK, dial 00 41 31, followed by the correspondent's number.

The international dialling code for the **Principality of Liechtenstein** is 423. There is a 24hr **English-speaking** information and help line called Anglo-Phone: ℘157-5014, which costs 2.13 CHF per minute. The operators speak French, German and Italian depending on the region; English in main cities and major resorts.

The Swisscom Mobile network covers 99% of Switzerland; for additional information contact www.swisscom-mobile.ch.

EMERGENCIES
Police: ℘17
Fire Brigade: ℘118
Ambulances: ℘144

ELECTRICITY
220 volts (AC) is the usual voltage; most power sockets are designed for three-pin round plugs. Adaptors for two pin plugs are available in most hotels.

MAIL/POST
All letters to Switzerland should have the international abbreviation CH and the post code number before the name of the town, e.g. CH-3000 Bern. In the cities, post offices often have a café serving sandwiches and pastries, and a stationery store selling anything from paper clips to DVDs. Offices are closed on Saturdays from noon onwards. Stamps are sold at two rates: priority mailing and standard (usually arriving within three days).

- Airmail postcards and letters to the USA and Canada: 1.90CHF.
- Airmail postcards and letters to the UK (up to 20g): 1.40CHF.
- Postcards and letters within Switzerland: 1CHF.

Additional information is available online at www.post.ch.

MONEY
CURRENCY
The currency is the Swiss Franc. The abbreviation, CHF is the official financial ISO code, which stands for Confederation Helvetica France, Switzerland's formal Latin name. Advertisers and stores tend to prefer Fr. Denominations in circulation are: 5, 10, 20 and 50 *centimes* (*rappen* in German-speaking areas) and 1, 2 and 5 francs (coins), 10, 20, 50, 100, 200, 500 and 1 000 francs (notes).

BANKS
Traveller's cheques and foreign currency can be exchanged in banks and official exchange offices. Your passport is necessary as identification when cashing checks. Commission charges vary, with hotels charging more than banks. Generally, banks are open from 8am–4.30pm (Mon–Fri). Money can also be withdrawn from cash dispensers by using your credit or debit card. Always check with your bank whether your debit or credit card will be accepted. You may have more difficulty when trying to use your debit card to pay for items at a till.

CREDIT CARDS

Major **credit cards** (American Express, Diners Club, Eurocard/MasterCard, Visa, EC-Maestro, EC-Cirrus, Japan Card Bank, etc) are accepted in shops, hotels, restaurants and ATMs, although perhaps not in the smallest villages where cash is preferred. The **euro** is accepted by some establishments on the borders of Germany, France, Italy and Austria. Geneva and Basel in particular have been keen to accommodate the European single currency.

PUBLIC HOLIDAYS

Various general holidays are observed throughout the country. Public offices, banks, and major companies will be closed on public holidays.

January 1 and 2—New Year
March—Good Friday
March—Easter Sunday and Monday
May—Ascension Day
May—Whitsunday and Monday
August 1—Swiss National Day
December 25—Christmas Day
December 26—Boxing Day

Other holidays tend to vary from canton to canton. Thanksgiving (*Jeûne Fédéral* in French; *Buß- und Bettag* in German), not to be confused with the American holiday, is observed in all the cantons, except Geneva, on the third Sunday in September. The *Jeûne Fédéral* is a period of fasting and penitence, accompanied by processions and pilgrimages. The Geneva canton observes Thanksgiving on the second Thursday in September. Many areas observe local and regional holidays as well, including Labor Day (May 1) and Corpus Christi (June 7).

REDUCED RATES

Discounts on admissions and fares are available for children and groups traveling together at most major sites, including all-inclusive passes such as the Museum Pass and Swiss Pass. *See GETTING THERE AND GETTING AROUND for travel discounts.*

TAXES & TIPPING
TAXES

7.6% VAT is included in the retail price of most goods. Foreign tourists who shop in stores with the sign "Tax Free" and whose purchases equal or exceed 400CHF can claim back the VAT on their purchase when they leave the country. Ask the store for the form.

TIPPING

Tips are included on all restaurant, hotel, hairdresser, and taxi bills, so you are not usually expected to leave anything extra.

SMOKING

Switzerland has very few restrictions regarding smoking, most of which are town-wide bans during times of heightened forest fire risk. Those sensitive to smoke should remember that it is still allowed in most public buildings, including banks, restaurants, and even trains.

TIME

Switzerland is 1hr ahead of GMT, 6hr ahead of EST (USA/Canada) and 9hr ahead of PST.
In summer, the country operates a daylight-saving scheme when clocks are advanced by an hour. The actual dates are announced annually but always occur over weekends in March and October.

Christmas time in St Moritz

Christof Sonderegger/Switzerland Tourism

CONVERSION TABLES

Weights and Measures

1 kilogram (kg)	**2.2 pounds (lb)**	**2.2 pounds**	*To convert*
6.35 kilograms	14 pounds	1 stone (st)	*kilograms*
0.45 kilograms	16 ounces (oz)	16 ounces	*to pounds,*
1 metric ton (tn)	**1.1 tons**	**1.1 tons**	*multiply by 2.2*
1 litre (l)	**2.11 pints (pt)**	**1.76 pints**	*To convert litres*
3.79 litres	1 gallon (gal)	0.83 gallon	*to gallons, multiply*
4.55 litres	1.20 gallon	1 gallon	*by 0.26 (US)*
			or 0.22 (UK)
1 hectare (ha)	**2.47 acres**	**2.47 acres**	*To convert*
1 sq kilometre (km²)	**0.38 sq. miles (sq mi)**	**0.38 sq. miles**	*hectares to acres, multiply by 2.4*
1 centimetre (cm)	**0.39 inches (in)**	**0.39 inches**	*To convert metres*
1 metre (m)	**3.28 feet (ft) or 39.37 inches**		*to feet, multiply*
	or 1.09 yards (yd)		*by 3.28; for*
1 kilometre (km)	**0.62 miles (mi)**	**0.62 miles**	*kilometres to miles, multiply by 0.6*

Clothing

Women					Men			
	35	4	2½			40	7½	7
	36	5	3½			41	8½	8
	37	6	4½			42	9½	9
Shoes	38	7	5½		Shoes	43	10½	10
	39	8	6½			44	11½	11
	40	9	7½			45	12½	12
	41	10	8½			46	13½	13
	36	6	8			46	36	36
	38	8	10			48	38	38
Dresses	40	10	12		Suits	50	40	40
& suits	42	12	14			52	42	42
	44	14	16			54	44	44
	46	16	18			56	46	48
	36	6	30			37	14½	14½
	38	8	32			38	15	15
Blouses &	40	10	34		Shirts	39	15½	15½
sweaters	42	12	36			40	15¾	15¾
	44	14	38			41	16	16
	46	16	40			42	16½	16½

Sizes often vary depending on the designer. These equivalents are given for guidance only.

Speed

KPH	10	30	50	70	80	90	100	110	120	130
MPH	6	19	31	43	50	56	62	68	75	81

Temperature

Celsius (°C)	0°	5°	10°	15°	20°	25°	30°	40°	60°	80°	100°
Fahrenheit (°F)	32°	41°	50°	59°	68°	77°	86°	104°	140°	176°	212°

To convert Celsius into Fahrenheit, multiply °C by 9, divide by 5, and add 32.
To convert Fahrenheit into Celsius, subtract 32 from °F, multiply by 5, and divide by 9.
NB: Conversion factors on this page are approximate.

Hiking trails in the vineyards between Lausanne
and Montreux by the Lake Geneva, Vaud
© Urs Achermann/Lausanne Tourisme Switzerland Tourism

The Country Today

Switzerland remains a fascinating mix of traditional and modern, pastoral and cosmopolitan. No other nation has a greater density of museums, a more efficient transport network, or as well-educated a population more skilled in welcoming tourists. The Swiss enjoy one of the best standards of living in the world, with a strong currency, driven in part by the country's political stability and international neutrality. Beyond Alpine panoramas, cheese, chocolate and trains that run on time, the country is a scenic, gastronomic and cultural delight.

21ST CENTURY SWITZERLAND

POPULATION

Switzerland's population stands at 7 701 856 with a large foreign contingent (21.7%). Of the latter, about 37% originate from the big surrounding countries of Germany, Italy and France and about two-thirds from all EU states. Although it is relatively easy for EU citizens to live and work in Switzerland, naturalisation is extremely difficult and costly. This explains why 40% of those still claissified as foreign have lived in Switzerland for more than 10 years and 20% have actually been born in the country. The population is not spread out evenly, as most people tend to live in the central plateau stretching from Lake Geneva to Lake Constance and in the Rhône Valley, while the mountains in the south are almost empty.

LIFESTYLE

As one might expect from their history of banding together against their neighbours, the Swiss are a conservative and reserved people whose primary commitment is to their family and their local community. Despite this, they are remarkably liberal in social matters: same-sex registered partnerships were adopted through a referendum in 2005, and two euthanasia charities operate lawfully. Although espousing neutrality, they are also well prepared for war, via nuclear shelters for the whole population (prescribed in building regulations) and a citizen's militia: every able male between 18 and 34 does three weeks of military service per year and keeps his personal weapons at home.

LANGUAGE AND RELIGION

One of the successes of the Swiss Confederation is the coexistence of four languages and several religions in a single community.

Languages

German-speaking Swiss represent 64% of the Helvetian people. **Schwyzerdütsch** (Swiss German) is a dialect of the Alemannic group, with many local variations. It can be difficult to follow at first, even for native Germans and Austrians. It is used in daily conversation, while classical German (*Hochdeutsch*)

Landsgemeinde in Appenzell

Stephan Engler/Switzerland Tourism

Traditions and Folklore

Swiss folklore can always point to a rich collection of local costumes, and it is in the mountains that visitors have the best chance of seeing people who wear their traditional costumes every day, especially in Gruyères and the Valais.

The *armailli* (herdsman) of Gruyères still wears the *bredzon*, a short cloth or canvas jacket with puffed sleeves which dates back to the Empire period, embroidered with thorn-points and with edelweiss on the lapels. The straw toque edged with velvet is called a *capette*. Similar costumes are found in the pastoral districts of the Bernese Oberland, although less often, but the man's jacket from this area is often made of velvet.

Stone throwing in Unspunnen, Bernese Oberland

Christof Sonderegger/Switzerland Tourism

At Evolène the women's working dress includes a simple frock, with a red and white neckerchief, and a straw hat with a brim edged with velvet and turned down over the ears; the crown is encircled by crochet-work ribbons arranged in bands. On high feast days the women of Evolène put on a rustling silk apron and the *mandzon* (a sort of jacket with long sleeves), and a very flat, round felt hat on top of a white lace bonnet.

Pastoral traditions are still very much alive in mountain districts like the Val d'Anniviers, where life is governed by the movements of cattle from the villages to the *mayens* and the high Alpine pastures (*alpe*). The trek to summer pastures creates joyful and picturesque parades *(late May, early June)*. Scores of beasts with beribboned and flower-decked horns move along the roads with cowbells tolling, escorted by herdsmen carrying necessities for living in the chalets, including a huge cheese-boiler on a yoke. In the Valais the end of the journey is marked by **cow competitions**, after which the "queen" of the herd may wear the giant bell reserved for her.

Midsummer festivals lessen the loneliness of the *armaillis* by bringing a crowd of friends and relatives up from the valleys. The return from the alp, referred to as the *désalpe*, is equally spectacular and lively. The open-air performances of *William Tell* at Interlaken begin with a procession of this kind.

Urban traditions – These are generally patriotic and civic, like the commemoration of the Escalade in Geneva or the *Knabenschiessen* in Zürich (see Calendar of Events). In quite a different spirit, more like the Rhenish customs, Basel Carnival, in which there are masked dances and processions preceding Lent, brings a touch of frivolity to the city of Erasmus. From behind the mask of some grotesque figure the merrymaker is free to taunt and tease friends and acquaintances.

Traditional rustic sports survive only at certain village fêtes in German Switzerland, where you might see games like wrestling on the grass, stone throwing, flag throwing and, most inscrutable of all, *Hornussen*, a team sport in which defenders with paddles try to deflect a puck which is hit, like a golf tee shot, as far as possible up the field. A summer festival in the Emmental is also the place to hear the cavernous tones of the great trumpet, the Alpenhorn.

Sport in Switzerland

The Swiss take full advantage of the outdoor opportunities their country offers, with one in four being a member of a sports club. Summers are spent **sailing** in the lakes or **hiking** on the mountains, with several prestigious alpine marathons on offer. The most spectacular is the **Zermatt Run** on the lower slopes of the Matterhorn, starting at an altitude of 1 600m/5 249 ft and ending in 2 585m/8 481ft. However, winter sports predominate with everyone capable of **skiing**, **ice skating** and **tobogganing** from a young age, a fact reflected in recurring Swiss successes in the Winter Olympics (nine medals in 2010). **Ice hockey** is extremely popular and teams from smaller towns compete in the professional league alongside metropolitan giants. This is not possible in **football** where money plays an important role and where, unsurprisingly, teams from Zürich and Basel predominate. The national team has been improving recently and made the headlines in the **2010 World Cup** with a memorable win over Spain.

is reserved for official business and the written word. On the other hand, the French-speaking group (18%) have seen their dialect fall more and more into disuse. Italian (11%) is spoken almost entirely throughout the Ticino and in part of Graubünden.

Romansh was recognised as a fourth national language in 1938. The Romansh League has done all it can to preserve and even spread its use in schools and in the press. Of Latin origin, Romansch is used by 7% of the Swiss in Graubünden canton, especially in the Engadin and Graubünden Oberland.

German, French and Italian are the official languages of the Confederation and are used by the authorities and the federal civil service. At least two languages are taught compulsorily in schools.

Religion

Until the middle of the 19C, the religious question seemed an obstacle to unity in the Confederation. This was proved by the Sonderbund War of 1847, but since 1848 complete tolerance is the rule. Today Protestants represent only 35% of the population, the Roman Catholics 42%, while 11% claim no religious affiliation.

The Swiss Protestant temperament, in its fundamentally democratic and patriotic aspects, owes more to the forceful personality of a man like Zwingli than to the strict doctrine of Calvin, whose influence was felt chiefly in Geneva. The flexible organization of Protestant churches reflects the federalist structure of the country and allows subsidised state churches to exist alongside free churches supported by donations.

Roman Catholics are attached to their dioceses: Basel (& see SOLOTHURN), Lausanne-Geneva-Fribourg (& see FRIBOURG), Sion, Chur, St Gallen and Lugano. Clergy are distributed among some large abbeys like those of St Maurice, Einsiedeln and Engelberg.

The small Jewish population lives mostly in large cities such as Basel and Zürich.

THE SWISS CANTONS

Under the shield: The name of the canton and its official abbreviation (used for car registration).

On the map: The boundaries of the cantons and their capitals. Cantons are listed alphabetically by their local names with their English version and/or alternative name. Area, population, language, and religious majorities follow.

ABBREVIATIONS:

F: *French*, **G**: *German*, **I**: *Italian*, **P**: *Protestant*, **RC**: *Roman Catholic*.

AARGAU (Argovia)

- 1 404sq km/542sq mi
- population 591 632 (**G-P**).

The name means "the country of the Aare" and the river is represented by wavy lines. The three stars represent the three districts which together form the canton.

APPENZELL

Innerrhoden (AI):
- 172sq km/66sq mi
- population 15 549 (**G-RC**).

Ausserrhoden (AR):
- 243sq km/94sq mi
- population 53 504 (**G-P**).

The bear, which represents the Abbey of St Gallen, adorns the shield of the canton. (AR includes the letters VR.)

BASEL (Bâle)

Basel District (BL):
- 482sq km/165sq mi
- population 271 214 (**G-P**).

Basel Town (BS):
- 52sq km/20sq mi
- population 186 672 (**G-P**).

Coat of arms include a bishop's crosier (red for Basel District, black for Basel Town).

BERN (Berne)

- 6 050sq km/2 659sq mi
- population 969 299 (**G-P**).

For the origin of the coat of arms see BERN.

FRIBOURG

- 1 670sq km/645sq mi
- population 268 537 (**F-RC**).

The shield of Fribourg is black and white, the colours of the dukes of Zähringen.

GENEVA (Genève, Genf)

- 282sq km/109sq mi
- population 446 106(**F-P**).

For the origin of the coat of arms see GENEVA.

GLARUS

- 684sq km/2 654sq mi
- population 38 370 (**G-P**).

Its coat of arms represents St Fridolin, the patron saint of the district.

GRAUBÜNDEN (Grisons)

- 7 106sq km/2 744sq mi
- population 190 459 (**G-P**).

The modern history of Graubünden, also referred to as Les Grisons (French), Grigioni (Italian), Grischun (Romansh) and *Rhaetia* in ancient times, begins with the alliance of the three Leagues in the 14C and 15C. The Gray League (shield half sable, half argent, black and white), which means Graubünden, ruled the upper Rhine Basin. The banner of the Ten Jurisdictions League (a cross of gold and blue quartering) flew in the Prättigau, the district of Davos and Arosa.

JURA

- 837sq km/323sq mi
- population 69 822 (**F-RC**).

The canton was formed 24 September 1978 by popular vote ratifying a Federal decree of 9 March 1978. Its three districts, Delémont (the capital), Porrentruy and Les Franches Montagnes were formerly part of the canton of Berne.

LUCERNE (Lucerne, Luzern)

- 1 492sq km/576sq mi
- population 368 742(**G-RC**).

NEUCHÂTEL

- 797sq km/308sq mi
- population 170 924 (**F-P**).

The present coat of arms dates from the proclamation (1848) of the Republic of Neuchâtel. The white cross on a red background commemorates its adhesion to the Confederation.

ST GALLEN

- 2 014sq km/778sq mi
- population 471 152 (**G-RC**).

The fascine on the shield recalls the union of the various districts which were joined in 1803, when the canton was formed.

SCHAFFHAUSEN

- 298sq km/115sq mi
- population 75 303 (**G-P**).

SCHWYZ

- 908sq km/350sq mi
- population 143 719 (**G-RC**).

The shield of Schwyz used to be plain red. Later, it was charged with a white

APPENZELL (AR/AI)

AARGAU (AG)

BASEL-LAND (BL)

BASEL-STADT (BS)

BERN (BE)

FRIBOURG (FR) GENÈVE (GE) GLARUS (GL) GRAUBÜNDEN (GR) JURA (JU) LUZERN (LU) NEUCHÂTEL (NE)

cross and became the emblem of the entire Swiss Confederation.

SOLOTHURN
- 791sq km/305sq mi
- population 251 830 (**G-RC**).

TICINO (Tessin)
- 2 811sq km/1 085sq mi
- population 332 736 (**I-RC**).

THURGAU
- 1 013sq km/391sq mi
- population 241 811 (**GP**).

The two lions pictured on the coat of arms were borrowed from the arms of the counts of Kyburg.

UNTERWALDEN

Nidwalden (NW):
- 276sq km/107sq mi
- population 40 737 (**G-RC**).

Obwalden (OW):
- 491sq km/190sq mi
- population 34 429 (**G-RC**).

The arms bear the keys of St Peter: Those of Nidwalden are on a red background; those of Obwalden on a red and white background.

URI
- 1 076sq km/415sq mi
- population 35 162 (**G-RC**).

SH	SCHAFFHAUSEN (SCHAFFHOUSE)
	Schaffhausen
	DEUTSCHLAND
	Bodensee
TG	THURGAU (THURGOVIE)
	Frauenfeld
ZH	ZÜRICH
	Zürich
	Sankt Gallen
AR	APPENZELL
	Herisau
AI	Appenzell
SG	SANKT GALLEN (SAINT GALL)
	ÖSTERREICH
	LIECHTENSTEIN
ZG	ZUG (ZOUG)
	Zug
SCHWYZ	
SZ	
	Glarus
GL	GLARUS (GLARIS)
	Schwyz
NW	
	Stans
UNTERWALD	
	Altdorf
UR	URI
	Chur
	Inn
	Rhein
GR	GRAUBÜNDEN GRIGIONI (GRISONS)
	ITALIA
TI	TICINO (TESSIN)
	Ticino
	Bellinzona
	Toce
	Lago Maggiore

Demi-cantons / Semi-cantoni
Halbkantone / Half-cantons
Semi-cantones

Appenzell	AI	Innerrhoden (Rhodes intérieures)
	AR	Ausserrhoden (Rhodes extérieures)
Basel Bâle	BS	Basel-Stadt (Bâle-ville)
	BL	Basel-Landschaft (Bâle-campagne)
Unterwalden Unterwald	NW	Nidwalden (Nidwald)
	OW	Obwalden (Obwald)

ZÜRICH (ZH)

ZUG (ZG)

LIBERTÉ PATRIE — VAUD (VD)

VALAIS (VS)

URI (UR)

OBWALDEN (OW)

ST. GALLEN (SG) · SCHAFFHAUSEN (SH) · SCHWYZ (SZ) · SOLOTHURN (SO) · TICINO (TI) · THURGAU (TG) · NIDWALDEN (NW)

VALAIS (Wallis)

- 5 226sq km/2 018sq mi
- population 303 241 (**F-RC**).

The shield is red and white to commemorate the episcopal banner of Sion. It bears 13 stars representing the 13 *dizains* (districts) of the canton.

VAUD (Waadt)

- 3 219sq km/1 243sq mi
- population 688 245 (**F-P**).

The green flag was adopted when the Lemanic Republic was founded in 1798. The white flag with the motto "Liberté et Patrie", or "Freedom and Homeland", was adopted when Vaud joined the Confederation in 1803.

ZUG

- 239sq km/92sq mi
- population 110 384 (**G-RC**).

ZÜRICH

- 1 729sq km/667sq mi
- population 1 332 727 (**G-P**).

GOVERNMENT

The Constitution of 1848, revised in 1874 and more recently in 1999, set up a modern federal state in place of the former Confederation of Cantons. Each canton had its own coinage, postal services, and customs.

THE COMMUNITIES

Liberty of the individual, liberty of faith and conscience, liberty of the press and of association are recognised by the Constitution, which gives every Swiss citizen over the age of 18 the right to vote and to be elected. Women, at last, obtained the vote in federal elections in 1971 but still do not always have a say in cantonal and community affairs. The whole regime, however, rests upon the principle of the sovereignty of citizens living in 2 905 free communities and forming the basis of the national will.

In all matters the community is competent to decide in the first instance. The canton intervenes only on appeal. So powerful is the citizenry that foreigners must first be admitted to the "corps of citizens" of a given community in order to acquire Swiss nationality.

CANTONAL AUTHORITY

Each canton has political sovereignty, with its own constitution and legislative body. In each of the 23 cantons (26 including the half-cantons—⏱see Welcome to Switzerland) executive power belongs to the State Council and legislative power to the Grand Council.

The practice of direct democracy survives in a few mountain cantons like Appenzell, Glarus and Unterwalden. Here, each spring, citizens vote by a show of hands on questions affecting the community. These highly ceremonial meetings are called the **Landsgemeinden** (⏱see Calendar of Events).

THE FEDERAL AUTHORITIES

Legislative power is exercised by two assemblies, the National Council and the Council of States; executive power by a collegial of seven members called the Federal Council. The two assemblies, when sitting jointly, form the Federal Assembly. The National Council represents the people, with one deputy being elected for more than 30 000 inhabitants (200 members); each canton or half-canton is represented by at least one seat. The Council of States, which represents the cantons, has 46 members: two per canton and one per half-canton, regardless of the size of the population.

This bicameral system, similar to American and parliamentary institutions, protects the interests of the small communities.

Executive power resides with the Federal Council. Its seven members are elected for a four-year term by the Federal Assembly, and each administers a department, or ministry. The annual election of the President—whose official title is President of the Confederation—and of the Vice-President, appears to be a mere formality: The Vice-President invariably succeeds the President and his successor is chosen from a roster drawn up by agreement.

THE SOVEREIGN PEOPLE

Decisions by the Federal Assembly can be taken only after a favourable vote by both chambers. Here again, however, popular sovereignty has a role to play. If, within 90 days after a decision by the Assembly, signatures can be obtained from 50 000 citizens, the entire population is then called upon to decide whether a law should finally be accepted or rejected. This is the **right of referendum**, which in practice has a conservative influence. Citizens of Vaud, according to tradition, are fond of saying: "The referendum is our right to say No when Bern has said Yes." During a referendum in December 1992, the Swiss nation answered no to joining the EEE (*Espace Économique Européen*).

The Swiss also have the right to **initiate legislation**. Thus, 100 000 citizens may demand an amendment of the articles of the Constitution or the adoption of new articles. Therefore, the popular will finds expression at every level of political activity and exercises permanent control over the country's institutions.

NATIONAL SERVICE

Although Switzerland is known to be a neutral country, military service plays a prominent part in the life of its citizens, though there is a provision for performing civilian service instead of military service since 1996. The **Swiss Army** is a militia without "regular" units. "Active" service begins only at general mobilisation. The Army has a general only in time of war or general mobilisation, the last being General Guisan, in 1939–1945. In 2003, voters approved a major military reform, *Army XXI*, reducing the size of the army by half to 220 000 conscripts and reducing mandatory service to 260 days. Service is required for able-bodied men; for women, it is voluntary.

The Swiss soldier keeps all his equipment at home: Uniform, rifle, ammunition, and gas mask against nuclear, biological, or chemical weapons. While landlocked Switzerland does not have a navy, **military boats** patrol Swiss border lakes Lake Geneva, Lake Maggiore and Lake Constance. There is also a Swiss **Air Force**, which defended national air space from Allied and Axis incursion in the Second World War.

Electoral Duty

Communal, cantonal and federal elections occur with a frequency that may seem surprising to outsiders. In cantons like Bern and Zürich, which are very much attached to strict control of their budgets, it is a common joke that voting is as frequent as *Jass*, the Swiss game of poker. As a result, many elections, which are usually scheduled on a Sunday, have low turn-outs (35–50% participation); with cantonal voting, attendance can be as low as 30%.

ECONOMY

Switzerland enjoys one of the highest standards of living in the world. Its economic success relies on a thriving services sector, a highly skilled and motivated workforce, strong currency and stable political situation. Swiss industry, known to be both traditional and innovative, is efficient, but depends heavily on exporting its goods. A mountainous country where only 10% of the land is arable, it is also highly dependent on the import of raw materials to meet the needs of its population. Even so, the overall mentality remains protectionist and immigration is subject to strict regulation.

Swiss voters decided in 1992 not to join the European Community (now the European Union), but in 1995, Switzerland became a member of the International Trade Organization (ITO). In the 21C, bilateral treaties with EU countries and entry into the Schengen area in December 2008 have made it an EU member in all but name. The country remains a **"haven of peace"** and a refuge for many foreigners. Geneva is the seat of many international organizations, including GATT and specialised agencies of the United Nations, including the High Commission for Refugees.

WORLD FINANCE

Zürich is the country's economic capital, where most banks have their headquarters. Swiss neutrality has done much to attract foreign capital, thanks to a strong, steady currency and its famous bank confidentiality: 40% of the world's personal savings are concentrated in Switzerland. However, in 2009, banking spats with Germany and most notoriously with the US forced Switzerland to co-operate in lifting elements of the banking secrecy to help in cases of suspected tax evasion.

The banking system also supports important insurance and shipping industries; vasts amounts of international financial trade passes through Switzerland. Life insurance is a prosperous sector, and it is said that Swiss citizens enjoy the best and most comprehensive insurance in the world. Rentenanstalt/Swiss Life, Winterthur and Zürich dominate.

AGRICULTURE

Agriculture enjoys a privileged status. Strongly protected, heavily subsidized by the state, and closely integrated into rural life and the Swiss landscape, it is simultaneously an integral part of Swiss culture and a major tourist attraction. Livestock farming accounts for 75% of the agricultural production.

Since the Swiss farming industry can grow only enough to satisfy 60% of the country's needs, everything grown is consumed in the home country; the remainder is imported.

LINGUISTIC SWITZERLAND	German	Romansh	Ethnic boundary between Alamans and Burgundians in the 9 C.
	French	Italian	Zürich — University town

Cereals, heavily subsidised by the government, remain expensive, although the use of chemical fertilisers has increased yield. Such farming methods, thought to damage the environment, are not well accepted by the population. Organic farming is very much en vogue, but is still too costly to be applied on a large scale.

Half the cheese made in Switzerland (25% of dairy production) is exported. The country is famous worldwide for its Gruyère (from the Gruyères region) and Emmental (from the Emmen valley). **Forestry** has been carefully regulated since 1993. Forests cover about one-third of the land and contribute to the prevention of natural disasters such as avalanches and landslides. For these reasons, deforestation is strictly forbidden.

INDUSTRY AND TRADE

Swiss industry is characterised by extremely high standards of quality—an attitude which has earned it a worldwide reputation of excellence. The most prosperous sectors are those of machinery (machine tools, farming and printing equipment) and electro-mechanics, representing 45% of Swiss exports. Zürich, Baden, and Winterthur are the major industrial centres.

The chemical and pharmaceutical industries, largely concentrated in the Basel area, are flourishing; research and development are extremely active. Swiss pharmaceutical groups are among the world's most powerful: Roche and Novartis (resulting from the merger of Ciba and Sandoz), two of the world's largest, are headquartered here; others have major offices here.

Watchmaking has also come to symbolise Switzerland. Renowned as the "international custodian of time," Switzerland boasts artisans that specialise in luxury timepieces, producing high-quality products that utilise classic hand-crafting and modern techniques. Swiss clocks and watches are universally appreciated and the "Made in Switzerland" label enjoys worldwide esteem; indeed 95% of the national production is exported.

The **food-processing industry** is booming. Swiss **chocolate** enjoys an excellent reputation abroad; just over half the annual production is exported. The rest is consumed by the Swiss, whose sweet teeth consume an esti-

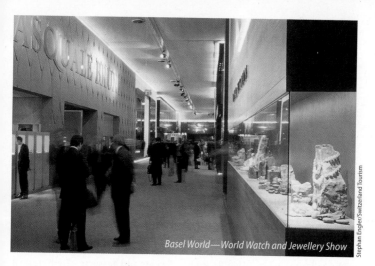

Basel World—World Watch and Jewellery Show

Stephan Engler/Switzerland Tourism

mated 11.7 kg per person per year. The designation "Swiss chocolate" is carefully controlled; it must be made entirely in Switzerland out of cocoa beans, cocoa paste, cocoa butter, sugar, and sometimes milk. Swiss chocolate pioneers include François-Louis Cailler, Philippe Suchard, Rodolphe Sprungli, Rudolf Lindt and Henri Nestlé.

The Swiss **textile industry** has had the same problems as other nations with comparably high labour costs against the onslaught of low-cost Asian products. However, its embroidery still has a niche in haut-couture, and was recently given a strong impetus by Michelle Obama's presidential inauguration yellow dress made by textiles from St Gallen.

Protecting the Environment

Preserving nature is equally important to private firms, public authorities and the population. The Swiss show great awareness of ecological issues and are careful to recycle their rubbish individually, with 78% of currently recyclable items being recycled.

FINANCIAL

Services are the backbone of the Swiss economy: They employ 70% of the working population and account for 70% of the GDP. The national currency attracts many foreign investments.

TOURISM

Picturesque chalets, beautiful landscapes, and a tradition of hospitality have made Switzerland an ideal holiday destination for generations. Switzerland also benefits from its reputation as one of the safest destinations in Europe.

After metalworking and pharmaceuticals, tourism is the country's main industry, attracting an international clientele. German tourists account for the highest number of visitors, followed by the British and the Dutch. Destinations such as Zermatt and Grindelwald also attract Japanese and American tourists. More recently, the use of the Alps in Bollywood films (instead of the Himalayas) and high-tech immigration has led to a slew of Indian visitors. Where winter and summer seasons were once distinct, increasing tourism has created a year-round season as visitors take advantage of discounts and offers in non-peak times, especially for wellness retreats at Swiss spas and resorts. Switzerland is renowned for the excellence of its hotel industry, with some establishments over 100 years old.

Many multinational companies are headquartered or have subsidiaries here, boosting business-related tourism. International organizations, such as the United Nations in Geneva, and the International Olympic Committee in Lausanne, also perform this role.

FOOD AND WINE
SWISS SPECIALTIES

Swiss cuisine combines the culinary traditions of France, Germany, and Italy.

Cheese dishes – The great hard cheeses, Gruyère and Emmental, which carry the fame of the Swiss dairy industry abroad, are the basis of **fondue**, which is a national institution among the French Swiss. Every canton, especially Vaud, Neuchâtel and Fribourg, claims the perfect mix of Gruyère, Emmental, Vacherin, and other ingredients.

Raclette, a Valais specialty, is prepared by toasting one side of a slice of Valais cheese (the soft cheese of Bagnes or Conches – Goms) at a fire. The melted cheese is scraped directly onto the plate with a knife or a wooden blade. *Raclette* is eaten with gherkins and bread or potatoes cooked in their jackets.

Beef, Pork and Fish – The most original Swiss specialty is the dried meat of Graubünden, **Bündnerfleisch**. This is raw beef smoked and air-dried, served in thin slices. The most frequent meat dishes are fillet of veal *(Schnitzel)* and pork chop. A popular Zürich dish is minced veal or calf's liver with cream *(geschnetzeltes Kalbsfleisch)* and *Leberspiessli* (calf's liver cooked on a spit, with bacon). There is an extraordinary variety of *Wurst* (sausage). *Gnagi* (knuckle of pork, much enjoyed in Berne for an afternoon snack), *Klöpfer* (saveloy) in Basel, *Schüblig* (long pork sausage) in St Gallen, *Kalbsbratwurst* (veal sausage) in Zürich and *Salsiz* (small salamis) in the Engadin. The national dish of German Switzerland is **Rösti**: Potatoes boiled, diced, fried and finally baked with fried onion rings and bacon bits).

The French Swiss prefer smoked sausages with a stronger taste (*boutefas* in Payerne, *longeole* in Geneva). The monumental **Berner Platte** (Bernese platter) combines bacon, sausages, ham, sometimes boiled beef, pickled cabbage (*Sauerkraut*) and potatoes.

Swiss rivers and lakes produce a wide variety of fish such as trout, pike, tench, carp, and perch (a specialty from Lake Geneva). All are seasoned according to local tradition.

Sweets and desserts – Fresh cream is used in many sweets and desserts, such as meringues and *Schaffhauserzunger* (baked biscuits with fresh cream). The *kirschtorte* of Zug and the *Leckerli* of Basel—spiced bread with honey and almonds—are also enjoyed. Swiss chocolate, of time-honored reputation, is used to make delicious cakes and sweets.

SWISS WINES

Switzerland's vineyards produce only 36% of the wine consumed nationally. Vaud's best-known white-wine vintages are Lavaux, Dézaley, Aigle, and Yvorne. Fendant is the best known of the Valais white wines. Dôle, the most popular Valais red is a fragrant, fruity blend of Pinot and Gamay grapes.

The Geneva canton produces whites for fish dishes: Perlan; Aligoté; Pinot Gris. Oeil de Perdrix, the rosé version of Pinot Noir, is best served chilled. Although Cortaillod is a heavy red wine, most wines from Neuchâtel, such as Auvernier, Boudry, and Colombier are lighter whites drawn from a noble vine, the Chasselas, grown in chalky soil. Ticino vines yield highly alcoholic wines, such as Mezzana and Nostrano, which are pleasant with dessert. The red, white and rosé wines (*Süssdruck*) from the eastern region and the Alpine Valley of the Rhine are most appreciated for their light and subtle quality.

Fondue

Andy Mettler/Switzerland Tourism

History

Unlike the popular perception, Switzerland's history is full of bloody wars and internecine strife, as one might expect for a country right in the middle of Europe. Its famed neutrality has been mostly a product of the late 19C and early 20C.

TIME LINE
EARLY HELVETIA

3C — Cro-Magnon man is believed to have lived about 12000 BC, an estimate reinforced by a Cro-Magnon skull discovered in the Jura.

200 BC — The **Helvetii** cross the Rhine. This powerful Celtic, semi-nomadic tribe settles on a territory stretching from Lake Constance to Geneva, from the Alps to the Jura.

100 BC — The Helvetii are driven out by the Germanic Alemanni. Their exodus into Gaul is hindered by the Romans, led by Julius Caesar; the battle of Bibracte (Autun) takes place in 58 BC. This leads to the foundation of several settlements extending into the heart of the Alps, including those of Nyon and Augusta Raurica.

AD 1C — Helvetia becomes a province of the Roman Empire, with Vindonissa as its capital.

2C — Helvetia's geographical location compels the Romans into large-scale construction of roads and fortifications. The golden age of Aventicum (Avenches), founded by Augustus.

3C–5C — The **Burgundians**, originally a northern tribe, settle in the western part of Helvetia which becomes part of the Kingdom of Burgundy. The **Alamans** occupy Aventicum and colonise central and eastern Helvetia.

6C–9C — In 530 Franks invade the country. Their supremacy over the Merovingians and Carolingians extends to western Helvetia until 888. Irish monks, led by Columba, arrive in Helvetia to preach to the population and help build several monasteries. St Gallen, founded by Gallus, becomes a major seat of learning in Europe.

THE MIDDLE AGES

1032 — Death of Rudolph III of Burgundy. The country passes to the rulers of Germany.

11C–13C — Feudal lords and their free cities are given the power to rule over Helvetia, although they are officially accountable to the kings and subsequently the emperors of Germany.

1191 — The city of Bern is founded.

1291 — **Rudolph of Habsburg** bequeaths Helvetia to his sons, the dukes of Austria.

1 Aug 1291 — The three original forest cantons (Waldstätten) of Uri, Schwyz and Unterwalden, refuse to submit to the Habsburgs and the bailiffs and conclude a pact of mutual assistance and take the **Oath of the Everlasting League** at Rütli. This pact is the founding document of the **Helvetic Confederation** (named Switzerland in 1350). The legend of archer **William Tell**, stems from this time and he eventually becomes a national hero.

1315 — The Confederates defeat Duke Leopold of Hapsburg at **Morgarten**.

1386 — The cantons (eight by now) are again victorious at **Sempach**.

15C — The **St Gotthard issue**: in order to gain possession of this strategic route, the Swiss occupy part of the Ticino, Aargau, Thurgau, St Gallen and Graubünden regions. Encouraged by the King of France, Louis XI, they invade the Pays de Vaud.

BURGUNDIAN WARS AND ITALIAN WARS

1476 — Charles the Bold, **Duke of Burgundy**, is defeated by the Swiss at **Grandson (VD)**, then at **Murten (FR)**. Burgundy ceases to exist as a state.

1513 — The number of cantons is extended from eight to 13.

1515 — Allied with the Pope and the Milanese, the Swiss are defeated at Marignano by the King of France, **Francis I**, with whom they then sign a treaty of alliance.

1525 — The crushing Franco-Swiss defeat at Pavia, where the Swiss are wiped out by Emperor Charles V, marks the end of Switzerland's political and military history outside its own borders.

REFORMATION TO THE 18C

16C — The **Reformation** preached by Zwingli and Calvin is spread throughout Romansh Switzerland and heavily influences the 13 cantons.

1536 — Bern regains possession of the Pays de Vaud from the Duke of Savoy.

1648 — Swiss independence and neutrality is officially acknowledged with the **Peace of Westphalia** after the Thirty Years War which Switzerland escaped unscathed.

18C — A united country where several languages and religions coexist, Switzerland is influenced by theories of the **Age of Enlightenment**, supported by such philosophers as **Jean-Jacques Rousseau**; revolutionary ideas spread.

1798 — The French Republican army marches into Bern and occupies the city. A centralised Helvetic Republic is founded.

19TH CENTURY

1803 — Disputes between conservative and progressive forces lead Bonaparte to introduce a new Federal constitution and annex Geneva and the Valais to Switzerland.

1804–15 Switzerland becomes a battlefield of Napoleon's troops.

1815 — The **Congress of Vienna** reaffirms Switzerland's neutrality. The number of cantons is extended to 22. Part of the French Jura is annexed to the Bern canton.

1846 — Deep religious divisions lead to a separatist League of Roman Catholic cantons, known as the **Sonderbund**. It is soon disbanded by the Diet, reunited in Bern. General Dufour, Commander of the Confederate Army, ends hostilities and paves the way for a general reconciliation.

1848 — A new constitution introduces centralised, secular rule.

1863 — **Henri Dunant** from Geneva founds the Red Cross.

THE 20TH CENTURY

1914–18 — Switzerland guards its frontiers and extends hospitality to those exiled by war.

1919 — Tribute is paid to Swiss neutrality by making Geneva the seat of the **League of Nations**.

1939–45 — During the Second World War, Swiss troops are sent to their frontiers under the command of **General Guisan**. In the post-war years, Geneva, site of European UN headquarters, undertakes diplomatic conferences.

Famous Swiss

Despite its small size, Switzerland boasts many world-famous citizens, and many more have decided to make their homes there during their careers. The greatest problem the Swiss seem to have is that of recognition since their famous offspring is often mistaken as French (Le Corbusier), German (Max Frisch) or Italian (Alberto Giacommetti).

14C – The mythical William **Tell**; Arnold von **Winkelried**.

15C to 17C – St Nicholas of **Flüe**, Cardinal Matthew **Schiner**; Ulrich **Zwingli**; Joachim von Watt, known as **Vadian**; Theophrastus Bombastus von Hohenheim, known as **Paracelsus**, natural scientist and alchemist; François de **Bonivard**; Domenico **Fontana**, architect, and his student Carlo **Maderno**; Kaspar Jodok von **Stockalper**.

18C – Mathematicians Jakob, Johann and Daniel **Bernoulli**, Leonhard **Euler**; painters Jean-Étienne **Liotard** and Salomon **Gessner**; philosopher Jean-Jacques **Rousseau**; Albrecht von **Haller** anatomist; and physicist Horace Bénédict de **Saussure**.

19C – Jacques **Necker**, financier and statesman; Johann Kaspar **Lavater**, poet and physiognomist; Johann David **Wyss**, writer; Johann Heinrich **Pestalozzi**, educator; General Frédéric de **Laharpe**, politician; Guillaume-Henri **Dufour**, Swiss army general; Léopold **Robert**, painter; Albert Bitzius, known as Jeremias **Gotthelf**, writer; artist Rodolphe **Toepffer**; Louis **Agassiz**, geologist; Nikolaus **Riggenbach**, engineer; Jacob **Burckhardt**, philosopher; Gottfried **Keller**, poet; Henri Frédéric **Amiel**, writer; Conrad Ferdinand **Meyer**, author and poet.

20C – Arnold **Böcklin**, painter; Henri **Dunant**, founder of the Red Cross; César **Ritz**, hotelier; Carl **Spitteler**, poet; Ferdinand **Hodler**, painter; Ferdinand **de Saussure**, linguist; Félix **Vallotton**, painter; Carl Gustav **Jung**, psychoanalyst; Charles Ferdinand **Ramuz**, writer; Ernest **Ansermet**, orchestra conductor; Frédéric Sauser, known as Blaise **Cendrars**, writer; Édouard Jeanneret-Gris, known as **Le Corbusier**, architect; Frank Martin and Arthur **Honegger**, musicians; Michel **Simon**, actor; Alberto **Giacometti**, painter and sculptor; Mario **Botta**, architect; Hans **Erni**, painter; Jean **Tinguely**, sculptor; Max **Frisch**, writer; Friedrich **Dürrenmatt**, writer; Ursula **Andress**, actress and sex symbol; Clay **Regazzoni**, racing driver; **H.R.Giger**, sculptor, painter and most famously set designer for the **Alien** films.

21C – Roger **Federer**, tennis player; Martina **Hingis** tennis player (naturalised).

Famous Swiss Residents

Other famous residents are foreigners, including painters **Konrad Witz** and **Holbein** the Younger; **Richard Wagner** who lived in Triebschen near Lucerne for six creative years; Visual artists **Paul Klee** and **Daniel Spoerri**; author **Hermann Hesse**; film director/actor **Charlie Chaplin**; **Vladimir Ilyich Lenin** who spent 18 months in Zürich, where in 1916 he wrote **Imperialism, the Highest Stage of Capitalism**; writer **Georges Simenon**; father of artist Commissaire Maigret; writer **James Joyce** who visited and lived in Zürich several times and who is buried there; singer/composer Charles **Aznavour**; actress Audrey **Hepburn**; fashion designer Coco **Chanel**; author Frédéric **Dard**; writer **Graham Greene** who is also buried in Vevey; and Albert **Einstein**, who did much of his work on the Theory of Relativity while living in Bern. Currently, many famous people, such as singers **Tina Turner** and **Céline Dion**, director **Roman Polanski** and British actor **Roger Moore** have made their homes in Switzerland.

The National Flag

Franziska Pfenniger/Switzerland Tourism

All the boats gliding along Swiss lakes and rivers can be seen proudly sporting their national banner—a white cross on a red background. It was on 21 July 1840 that the Diet officially adopted this national emblem. Formerly, each contingent serving in the federal army fought under the colours of their own canton. As early as 1815, General Dufour, who was colonel at the time, had advocated the creation of a single flag in order to reinforce national unity and foster feelings of patriotism and comradeship. The flag is inspired from the white cross featured on the banner belonging to the mercenaries of the canton of Schwyz, which had been bestowed by Emperor Frederick II as a token of his appreciation.

1954 — The first disarmament talks bring together Eisenhower, Dulles, Eden and Faure from the West and Bulganin and Molotov from Russia.

1971 — The **World Economic Forum** is held for the first time in Davos, where it will become an annual summit of the world's political and economic leaders.

1978 — The Jura canton is created. Cantons now number 23.

1986 — 76% of the electorate votes not to become a member of the United Nations. However, the country continues to be active in UN-specialised agencies and programmes.

1989 — The Swiss vote to maintain their federal army.

1991 — The voting age drops from 20 to 18.

1992 — Switzerland decides not to join the European Community but becomes a member of the International Monetary Fund and the World Bank.

1995 — The International Trade Organiation (ITO), replaces the GATT (General Agreement on Tariffs and Trade). Headquarters are in Geneva.

1999 — Ruth Dreifuss becomes the first woman elected President of the Swiss Confederation.

1999 — Swiss scientist Bertrand Piccard and British co-pilot Brian Jones befome the first balloonists to circumnavigate the globe with a non-stop, non-refuelled flight. It takes 19 days, 21 hours.

THE NEW MILLENNIUM

2000 — 67% of the electorate votes for bilateral agreements to strengthen economic ties with the European Union.

2002 — 54.6% of the electorate votes to join the United Nations. Switzerland becomes the UN's 190th member state.

2003 — Roger Federer, the tennis star, becomes Swiss of the Year.

2007 — Lavaux Vineyard Region was named a UNESCO World Heritage Site.

2008 — European Championships in Bern, Basel, Geneva and Zürich. Switzerland joins the Schengen area.

2009 — After pressure from the G20, Switzerland abandons its banking secrecy and agrees to co-operate in matters of tax evasion.

2010 — A drilling machine completes the world's longest tunnel beneath the Alps.

Art and Architecture

ts position at the crossroads of three important civilizations—French, Italian and German—has made Switzerland a melting pot combining the cultural characteristics of its neighbours, drawing on their cultural and artistic heritage, and adapting them to suit its own traditions. Swiss art did not acquire its own identity until the late 19C, but it soon influenced the Continent's cultural history rapidly, carving a niche in the international avant-garde art scene.

UNDER ROMAN RULE

Roman customs and traditions exerted a strong influence over early Swiss cultural heritage: Vestiges of the Roman period bear the signs of Imperial art, but with strong regional and popular characteristics. Some sites contain many remains dating back to this period. One of the most famous, the site of **Augusta Raurica** (Augst) near Basel, provides a fascinating insight into daily life under the Romans and some of their remarkable technological achievements, such as villas fitted with sewers and central heating.

Mosaics and frescoes also reflect the high degree of sophistication and taste for refinement of this civilization. The **Roman Villa** at **Orbe** features magnificent mosaics depicting mythological scenes; the **Villa Commugny** near **Nyon** boasts vivid murals with gold leaf, still brightly coloured when excavated in 1904.

EARLY MIDDLE AGES

The collapse of the Roman Empire in the 5C led to a slackening of artistic activity. Eventually, a new aesthetic—inspired by Christianity—revived artistic life as the Church played a key role in art throughout Europe. The early Middle Ages were characterised by the development of religious mural paintings.

The only remaining example, the **ceiling of Zillis church**, has scenes illustrating the Life of Christ, featuring angels, allegorical figures and mythological beasts. Evangelisation spread throughout the country from the 7C, evidenced by the construction of many convents, which became bastions of artistic activity and were seen as temples of cultural life.

The **Abbey of St Gallen** exerted considerable influence within Europe between the 8C and 10C. This flourishing of the arts was reflected in the superb illuminations and manuscripts from the 9C that have been carefully preserved in the library.

ROMANESQUE AND CLUNY

Switzerland underwent a variety of influences, illustrated by its churches, which imbibed the artistic movements

Ceiling of Saint Martin Church in Zillis, Graubünden

Roland Gerth/Switzerland Tourism

of surrounding countries and then moulded them to suit the Swiss national character. The stamp of Lombard art can be observed in most churches in the Ticino area, such as the **Chiesa di San Nicolao** in **Giornico**, with its doorway columns resting on crouching beasts. Likewise, in the **Chiesa dei Santi Pietro e Paolo** in **Biasca**, the basilica, displaying three naves and a single apse closing off the chancel, is typical of Lombard architecture. Lastly, in Zürich, the north doorway of the Grossmünster cathedral is shaped like a triumphal arch, a common occurence in Italy.

Burgundian influence is best observed in **Basel Cathedral**, whose original late Romanesque figure was destroyed by an earthquake in 1356 and rebuilt in part-Gothic style, with a three-tier elevation, lancet arches, and the polygonal chancel. The carved tympanum on the famous "**St-Gallen Doorway**," on the east side, is the best example of Romanesque carving in the whole of Switzerland. Inside the cathedral, the **Apostle panel** and the **St Vincent panel** are masterpieces of late Romanesque sculpture that sit side to side with the remarkable late Gothic **pulpit**. Lastly, Germanic Romanesque art is very well illustrated by the **Münster zu Allerheiligen in Schaffhausen**, distinguished by stark geometry surrounding a square and pure architectural lines.

The influence of Provence is especially evident in the sculpture of Romandie. The four statue-columns depicting the Apostles in **Chur Cathedral** bear a strong resemblance to earlier sculptures in Saint-Trophime at Arles with the tight folds of their robes falling stiffly over their legs. However, the capitals in **Geneva Cathedral** are more reminiscent of those found in Lyon or Vienne.

The foundation of **Cluny Abbey Church** in 910 led to the creation of several hundred convents over the next two centuries. Cluny left its mark on many of these buildings, which featured the same tall, slender proportions. The abbey churches in Romainmôtiers and Payerne in the Vaud canton were early examples of Romanesque architecture influenced by Cluny Abbey. Romainmôtiers' abbey is a replica of the Cluny Abbey Church. The abbey in **Payerne**, with its double elevation, chapels, apsidioles, and its narthex at the entrance, represents pure Cluniac tradition.

The 12C saw the golden age of Romanesque art in Romandie with the emergence of a new Christian community the Cistercian Order. Simplicity, austerity and formal perfection were its dominant traits. **Bonmont Abbey** near Nyon is a fine example of Cistercian architecture with its plan designed in the shape of a Roman cross.

Bonmont Abbey, Vaud

SCULPTURE

The various figures and motifs represented in sculpture tended to reflect their architectural environment; they did not seek to depict reality but to express the supernatural. Imagery was extremely rich and punctuated by references to the Old and New Testaments. The capitals of the **Église St-Jean-Baptiste de Grandson** are among the most minutely executed in Switzerland, including the "Eagle with Spread Wings" and "St Michael Slaying the Dragon."

GOTHIC PERIOD

Gothic art and the ribbed arch were introduced to Switzerland in the 13C by Cistercian monks. In architecture, the Gothic style was conveyed by systematic use of lancet arches and flying buttresses to support the imposing nave and high clerestory windows enhanced by stained glass. In sculpture, it led to the creation of statues carved out of the same block of stone as the column. This new movement paved the way for many great construction projects, including **Geneva Cathedral**. In the 13C and the 14C, the Franciscan and Dominican religious orders developed an unadorned style of their own.

The **abbey** at **Königsfelden**, founded in 1308 by the Franciscans, reflects such austerity, with its flat, wooden ceiling crowning the bare nave.

PAINTING

Economic recovery was instrumental in allowing art to expand throughout Europe. From the 14C onward, foreign artists were often called upon for projects in Switzerland, bringing with them many styles and techniques. Byzantine influence was evident in paintings such as the frescoes adorning the narthex of the 13C **Payerne Abbey Church**, devoted to the theme of the Apocalypse. Paintings often associated religious and secular elements: In Romainmôtiers, episodes from Genesis were depicted alongside scenes of musicians. In Gothic art, paintings were often replaced by stained glass.

Gothic painting flourished under such artists as **Konrad Witz** (1400–1446), who worked in Basel and Geneva. His most famous canvas, *The Miraculous Draught of Fishes* (1444), represents Lake Geneva and its shores and displays both astounding realism and minute attention to detail. The religious subject is presented, perhaps for the first time, in a recognisable, rather than an idealised, landscape. However, in this he appears to have been an exception, since most of his contemporaries remained closer to the symbolic, more iconic representation associated with the Gothic tradition. Up to 1536, painting prospered with a fair amount of creativity. On the eve of the Reformation, fewer works were commissioned as reformers turned against visual imagery, and ended the last remaining vestiges of medieval art.

SCULPTURE

Gothic sculpture displays a far freer approach, shedding Romanesque aesthetics for a more humane, graceful representation. Burgundian, Germanic and Lombard influences were still felt in projects involving artists working elsewhere, such as the German sculptor **Johann Parler**, member of the famous Parler family, who executed the chancels in the cathedrals of Fribourg and Basel around 1350. In the late 14C, an international style spread to all of Europe. Works of art became smaller so they could be transported more easily and foster cultural exchanges among countries. The Marian cult and the worshipping of saints became widespread and many sumptuous altarpieces were commissioned; the one designed for **Chur Cathedral** is an outstanding example. Sculpted doorways also drew inspiration from Gothic art; the celebrated **painted doorway in Lausanne Cathedral** is a telling example. Remarkably well-preserved, the polychrome panel illustrates the *Dormition of the Blessed Virgin* and is clearly based on the one in Senlis Cathedral. This religious imagery was exceptional for the Gothic period. Such works were seen as decorative as well as intended to enlighten the faithful.

Peter Maurer/Switzerland Tourism

Last Judgement on the doorway of Bern Cathedral

The ultimate expression of Flamboyant Gothic is the doorway of **Bern Cathedral**, portraying the *Last Judgement*. The graphics are said to be the most detailed in Europe and every episode is conveyed by a sculpture.

Sculpted furniture also was key to the development of Gothic art and exemplified the artistic changes occurring between the 13C and the Reformation.

THE RENAISSANCE

The late 15C and the early 16C were characterised by flourishing arts and political upheavals. Large altarpieces were replaced by painted panels and canvases. The Renaissance also added a touch of humanism.

ARCHITECTURE

Arcades, considered to be typically Renaissance, were becoming more widespread in Switzerland; the **Hôtel de Ville de Palud** in Lausanne is the most representative building of this period. Architects from Bern, including Abraham **Düntz** and Samuel **Jenner**, displayed a novel approach to their art from 1667, advocating a plain, sober style devoid of Baroque embellishments. It was in this spirit that the oval became a popular feature of many buildings. This simple geometrical figure allowed the faithful to be reunited in an area that was both simple and aesthetically pleasing, as is evidenced by the **Temple de Chêne-Paquer** (1667) in the Vaud canton.

Although the Reformation gave a new lease of life to civil architecture, the building of religious sanctuaries slowed down during the 16C, with reformers appropriating those Catholic churches which already existed.

In German-speaking Switzerland, Late Gothic architecture, influenced by Germanic art, coexisted with Renaissance tradition in good harmony. The city of **Schaffhausen** is a perfect example of this trend with its richly sculpted "olliers." These Gothic towers, originally placed at the corners of houses, were subsequently moved to the centre of the façade above the main entrance. Italian influence gradually spread to the Ticino canton. This was reflected in the frescoes adorning **Santa Maria degli Angeli** in Lugano or those displayed in the former town hall of Lucerne. These two different manifestations of Renaissance art, associated with the north and the south respectively, are indicative of distinct cultural traditions.

PAINTING AND ENGRAVING

Artists such as the Bern painter **Niklaus Manuel Deutsch** (1484-1530) successfully negotiated the transition between Gothic and the more modern approach of the Renaissance. **Hans Holbein the Younger**, a German who settled in Basel, not only produced the portrait of his patron Erasmus (displayed in the city's Museum of Fine Arts), but undertook many influential façades and frescoes. The Reformation seriously jeopardised his career and painting at large. Although reformers objected to religious images, they tolerated decoration with foliated scrolls, such as those in the **Temple of Lutry** (1577).

This period was marked by the invention of printing, which spread the views advocated by the Reformation. Printing was first introduced into Basel in 1468, and from then onwards, books replaced manuscripts. The new medium made it possible to popularise ideas more quickly and effectively. **Urs Graf** (1485-

1527), a famous engraver, depicted macabre, erotic and military scenes, which carried strong dramatic impact.

SCULPTURE

The stiffness that characterised this period was to replace the ornamental profusion of Late Gothic. The decline in commissions from the clergy led to the construction of fountains to enhance urban landscapes, a feature typical of Renaissance art in Switzerland. The centre of the basin was taken up by a tall sculpted and gilded column, frequently surmounted by an allegorical figure such as Justice. A monument of this type can be found in Lausanne: it portrays a woman with her eyes blindfolded holding a pair of scales and a sword.

18C

Society became more refined, elegant and sophisticated. Literary salons and musical societies flourished. Geneva and Lausanne dazzled the rest of Europe and attracted foreign artists and intellectuals. The period was symbolised by a taste for the extravagant and a strong spirit of imagination, fantasy, and freedom.

ARCHITECTURE

Up to 1770, Switzerland was mainly dominated by Baroque architecture, sculpture, painting, and applied arts.

To serve the views of the Counter-Reformation, Baroque was applied to religious buildings, becoming Rococo. The **abbey church** in **Einsiedeln** built by **Kasper Moosbrugger** (1656–1723) between 1674 and 1745 is a perfect example, as is the **abbey church** and **library of St-Gallen** designed by **Peter Thumb** (1681–1766) and **Johann Michael Beer**. Jesuits and Franciscans encouraged construction of Baroque chuches in **Lucerne**, **Fribourg** and **Solothurn**.

This grand era produced sumptuous creations featuring scrolls, painted ceilings, and lavish ornamentation. The **abbey church** in **Disentis/Mustér** (1695–1712) shows the influence of Austrian Baroque.

The association of painting and sculpture with architecture is a typical feature of Baroque art. *Trompe-l'œil* motifs extended architectural plans, as do the paintings in St Gallen by **Johann Christian Wentzinger** (1710–1797).

In the 18C, French architects such as Saussure came to work in Switzerland, strongly influencing local artists. In Bern, the Swiss adapted Mansard's principles to their own country's traditions. The most outstanding architectural achievements derived from the French model are to be found in Geneva—**Hôtel Buisson**, **Hôtel de Saussure**—and in Solothurn—**Hôtel de la Couronne**.

Abbey church in Einsiedeln, Schwyz

Heinz Schwab/Switzerland Tourism

PAINTING

The art of the portrait, much en vogue during the 18C, marked the revival of painting with the Geneva-born artist **Jean-Étienne Liotard** (1702–1789), with realistic style, and a light, confident hand featuring bold colour contrasts and finely observed details. At the end of the 18C, it became fashionable to give free rein to one's feelings; in his portraits **Anton Graff** (1736–1813) depicts his subjects with a modish Romantic sensibility.

After 1750, historical painting returned to fashion with the emergence of Neoclassical style. Events of national importance were commemorated and the country began to develop a patriotic consciousness and sense of national identity; the Geneva artist **Jean-Pierre Saint-Ours** (1752–1809) worked on the Allegory of the Republic of Geneva in 1794. These portrayals of Swiss history remained popular until the mid-20C.

At the end of the 18C, a new genre appeared: Landscape painting.

Celebrating Mother Nature in lush landscapes became a feature of Swiss painting and, for the rest of Europe, defined Switzerland in the popular imagination. The two forerunners of this movement were **Wolf** (1735–1783) and **Johann Heinrich Wüest** (1741–1821), The most famous English exponent was **JMW Turner**, whose views of Lake Geneva, Lucerne and Montreux fired a growing British enthusiasm for the Alps and helped launch the Swiss tourism industry.

Around this period, many Swiss artists travelled abroad (Rome, Paris, or Munich) to complete their training, and some settled in those countries. **Heinrich Füssli** (1741–1825), anglicised as Henry Fuseli, became well known in London. His tortured, obsessive visions often draw on literary works and are thought, in turn, to have been one source of inspiration for Mary Shelley's *Frankenstein*.

Dismissed as a sensationalist by some critics, his weird, nightmarish canvases exerted considerable influence on his peers and on following generations.

19C

Republican ideals and nationalistic values found natural expression in the Neoclassicism that permeated official art and academic works. With this return to themes taken from Antiquity, new genres emerged, characterised by strong emphasis on emotion and feelings.

ARCHITECTURE

The gradual fading of Baroque led to sober Neoclassicism, which embodied the republican ideal. In Lausanne, the edifice housing the Great Council, is a perfect example. Designed by the architect **Alexandre Perregaux** in 1803–1806, it became a symbol for the Vaud canton. In Avenches, the Casino, a private club, was conceived as a small temple of antiquity. The masterpiece of Palladian architecture remains the **Gordanne** in Féchy; with its cupola and its portico flanked by Ionic columns it seems to date back to Antiquity.

After 1840, the trend turned toward classical landscaped gardens and mock ruins. The **Château de l'Aile** in Vevey, conceived by **Philippe Framel** and **Jean-Louis Brocher** in 1840–1842, is an excellent representation of this lighter, neo-Gothic current.

PAINTING

Alongside academic Neoclassicism, new genres caused a revival of the pictorial art form, namely Romanticism, Symbolism, poster art and satire.

Nostalgia and sentimentality reflected the romantic spirit of the century, aptly conveyed by the works of **Charles Gleyre**, whose tender, graceful characters are bathed in a soft light. **Landscape painting** also took on a sentimental dimension, with light playing an essential part of the composition.

Alexandre Calame (1810–1864) paid tribute to Alpine landscapes by revealing their grandiose, mysterious nature. **Arnold Böcklin** (1827–1901) adopted a similar approach; his *Isle of the Dead* (1880–1886) is an eerie landscape shrouded in silence and mystery, said to have inspired the famous symphonic poem by Rachmaninoff.

Detail of Verdun, tableau de guerre interprete *(1917) by Félix Vallotton*

© akg-images/Alamy

At the end of the 19C, painting explored a new form of expression under the influence of Symbolism, which offered a spiritual or even mystical explanation for reality. **Ferdinand Hodler** (1853–1918) is seen as a Symbolist for his symmetry that reveals a sense of unity inherent in the world (*Truth*, 1903). **Félix Vallotton** (1865–1925), a member of the Nabis movement, contributed to Symbolism by describing the social mores of his time in accordance with the theoretical principles of a pure and symbolic art form.

Lastly, **poster art** and **satire** developed considerably throughout the 19C thanks to Vallotton, **Théophile-Alexandre Steinlen** (1859–1923) and **Eugène Grasset** (1845–1917).

Their role was to expose injustice, to defend the oppressed, and to describe daily life in a simple manner, making art accessible to a wide cross-section of the population.

SCULPTURE

Sculpture saw a tremendous revival during the 19C. Salons in particular were instrumental in popularising small sculptures among private collectors, especially those belonging to the bourgeoisie. In the public sector, this art form was expressed through the decoration of theatres, casinos, banks and rail stations. It accompanied the other changes affecting Swiss urban landscapes and fostered deep feelings of patriotism and national identity.

The exuberance of Rococo was replaced by the grandiose dignity of Neo classicism. The early 19C was also marked by a return to the styles and qualities of the Middle Ages, particularly in painting and architecture. Nostalgia for the past and for bygone feudal traditions can be felt in the creations dating from this period, resulting in a neo-Gothic trend.

To counter this Neoclassical movement, **Vincenzo Vela** (1820–1891) produced naturalistic sculptures and developed the concept of *Vérisme*. He was much appreciated in France, where, in 1866, he painted *The Last Days of Napoleon I*, which portrays the emperor as an ageing, disillusioned man. Vela was known for speaking out in favour of the oppressed and his political commitment took shape in *Memorial to the Victims of Work* in 1883. In the latter part of the 19C, sculpture flourished with a new freedom of expression. The Symbolist movement and Art Nouveau both gave a new lease of life to sculpture. **Auguste de Niederhäusern**, known as Rodo, drew on Rodin's Symbolist theories and produced sculptures from which matter projected, like his *Jet of Water* from 1910–11. The different arts were skillfully combined under the influence of **Art Nouveau**. This approach was successfully explored by **Hermann Obrist**, who strove to achieve the merging of art, spirit and nature through his utopian reflection on the spiral—the ultimate expression of vital energy.

69

Rural Architecture

Valais house
(Évolène)

Central Switzerland house
(Lucerne area)

Appenzell house
(Trogen area)

Bernese Country house
(Évolène)

Bernese Oberland house
(Jungfrau region)

R. Corbel/Michelin

Rural Architecture

Carefully adorned with flowers, the Swiss peasant house shows, especially in German Switzerland, a remarkable care for comfort and propriety as well as a highly developed practical sense.

The Bernese Oberland House
The Swiss chalet style features a low-pitched roof, with wide eaves on all sides; in the high valleys, it is still covered with shingles weighted down by large stones. The ornamentation is profuse: The beams are carved with facets and the props of the roof are elaborately finished.

The Central Switzerland House
A highly distinctive style of building, recognisable by its steep roof and separate weatherboards sheltering the row of windows on each storey. The ground floor is high above the ground.

The Appenzell House
In this rainy district, farm buildings are grouped together to form a single block and wooden shingles cover the roof and sometimes part of the façade. The gable invariably faces the valley, and the windows of the cellar are located at "ground level" to aid in an even temperature.

The Bernese Country House
A huge roof extending down to the first floor at the sides also covers a large barn. The wealthier country dwellers, imitating townspeople, often choose to remove the triangular roof surmounting the gable and replace it with an imposing timber arch with wood paneling.

The Ticino House
A stone building of a somewhat primitive design with outdoor stairs and wooden galleries. Because of the uneven shape and size of the stones used in its construction, the Ticino house has very thick walls (up to 0.9m/3ft) and is roofed with stone slabs.

The Valais House
Living quarters (wooden section) are joined by open-side galleries to the kitchen area (masonry section). Nearby stands a **raccard** (🕙 *for illustration see The VALAIS*), a small wooden barn perched on piles and used as a granary or storehouse. These are known as a *torba* in the Ticino area.

The Engadin House
The typical Engadin house, a massive grey structure, has plenty of room under a broad gable crowning a façade. Floral, geometrical or heraldic designs frequently adorn the white walls. These may be decorated by a technique known as **sgraffito**, obtained by applying a layer of rough gray plaster, covering with a coat of limewash, and scraping the surface into designs such as rosettes and foliated scrolls.

Wonderful examples of local furnishings are at the Engadin Museum at St Moritz. The most typical room is the **sulèr**, a covered court common to the barn and living quarters, which serves both as a study and a meeting room. This cool, dark room, featuring carefully kept stone flags, a low, whitewashed vault and coffered ceiling, is lit only by an opening in the carriage gate.

20C AND EARLY 21C

Switzerland was part of the cultural wave that swept through Europe, most notably after 1930. The country was the recipient of artistic trends from abroad and began playing an active role in the international art scene.

ARCHITECTURE

During the 1920s, Swiss architecture was heavily influenced by the Bauhaus movement of Walter Gropius. Artistic creation was seen as a means of associating all art forms to create a new architectural identity. The notion of "order" was abandoned and buildings were stripped of their ornamentation. **Robert Maillard** (1872–1940) specialised in designing bridges with "aesthetic perfection." **Charles Édouard Jeanneret** (1887–1965), alias **Le Corbusier**, opted for functional architecture and became known as the "builder of radiant cities." Most of his work was carried out abroad, as his unusual views on architecture were not always well received at home. **Karl Moser** developed a new art form using modern materials such as reinforced concrete to design huge areas where light played an essential role. **St Antonius Kirche** in Basel is his most typical work.

In Lucerne, his work was continued by his pupils Fritz Metzger (St Charles' Church) and Otto Dreyer (St Joseph's Church).

Post-war architecture developed mainly in the Ticino area, Basel, Baden and French-speaking Switzerland, as economic growth required building up areas which, hitherto, had remained unexploited. Switzerland's national road network was the main achievement of this period.

In this utilitarian atmosphere, **Christian Menn** and **Rino Tami** produced outstanding creations, such as the south entrance to the St Gotthard tunnel at Airolo (Ticino), designed by Tami.

With the decline of industry, disused warehouses and factories were converted into arts centres, a trend which became a distinguishing feature of the period. Contemporary architecture became linked to the prestigious image of firms which offered their patronage and for which it acted as a showcase.

Since the mid-1970s, environmental concern has spurred an ecological approach to architecture.

In the 1960s, **Aldo Rossi** reacted against the "radiant cities" of Le Corbusier and advocated a universal vision of townscapes. Each building is designed for a particular purpose but nonetheless remains open to change if the situation requires it. His example was followed by architects **Luigi Snozzi**, **Aurelio Galfetti**, and **Mario Botta**, known for his pure, geometrical proportions. Botta conceived the **Tinguely Museum** in Basel, the **Cappella di Santa Maria**

Chiesa di Santa Maria degli Angeli on Monte Tamaro

Jean Tinguely

Born in Freiburg on 22 May 1925 but raised in Basel where he went to school, worked as a youth and finally studied in the town's Fine Arts Academy (1941–45), Jean Tinguely is the most interesting plastic artist to emerge from Switzerland—some would say, Europe—in the 20C. His assemblages already appear strange to the eye, looking like three-dimensional versions of Dali canvases, but what makes them even weirder is that most of them have been designed for movement, having parts that interlock, turn and shift in the most unexpected manner. Her made his name with self destroying sculptures (**Homage to New York, End of the World Part 2**) although his most popular works are the gigantic **Meta-Harmonie** a crazy hotchpotch of musical instruments welded together making a mighty noise when switched on, and his playful, public fountains in Basel and by the Pompidou Center in Paris. He died in Bern on 20 August 1991.

degli **Angeli** on Monte Tamaro and what is considered his masterpiece, the Church of **San Giovanni Battista** in the village of **Mogno**, Ticino. Post-Modernism explored the history of architecture, focusing on its structure, materials and motifs. **Bruno Reichlin** and **Fabio Reinhart** drew inspiration from past masters such as Andrea Palladio in the 16C and Francesco Borromini in the 17C. **Jacques Herzog** and **Pierre de Meuron** developed an aesthetic based on surprising and unexpected juxtapositions of materials.

In the second half of the 20C, modern architecture returned to fashion as buildings originally designed in the 1920s and 1930s needed restoration and the designs of **Karl Moser**, **Rudolf Gaberel**, and **Maurice Braillard** were updated. The talent of Swiss architects did not pass unnoticed abroad: **Bernard Tschumi** took part in the Parc de la Villette project in Paris, and **Mario Botta**, as Switzerland's most celebrated architect, was commissioned to design buildings in Tokyo, San Francisco and Paris.

PAINTING AND SCULPTURE

The Modernist movements which spread to Europe at the end of the First World War were represented in Switzerland only through temporary exhibitions. Swiss painting became isolated as ideas from abroad were perceived as a threat. Themes of isolation and escape became common in the work of Alberto Giacometti and **Meret Oppenheim**. However, from 1915–20, Zürich and Geneva became the center of opposition to conventional art.

This was Dadaism, which abolished logic, concentrating on absurd and irrational aspects of everyday life. In this period of World War I, the barbaric products of civilisation were denounced through collages, photomontages and poetry. It was abroad that avant-garde Swiss sculpture truly blossomed, with **Hans Arp**, **Sophie Taeuber-Arp**, and **Alberto Giacometti**. In the 1920s, **Hermann Scherer** and his highly Expressionist wooden sculptures introduced a touch of novelty.

The inter-war period saw a revival of Swiss sculpture. **Alberto Giacometti** (1901–1966) renewed the representation of human figures with his symbolic creations, inspired by tribal art. His spindly, elongated sculptures present a rough texture bearing the imprint of his thumbs and the blade of a knife, and convey the fleeting, elusive nature of man. **Max Bill** was a staunch defender of Concrete Art, which advocated order and rationality. Both his paintings and smooth, aesthetic sculptures (*Endless Ribbon*, 1935) are governed by rigorous mathematical considerations.

Simultaneously, a form of national art emerged, with many public buildings commissioned by the State. The government wanted to maintain calm and order and encouraged art aimed

Beautifully painted Haus zum Ritter, Schaffhausen

Schaffhausen Tourismus/Switzerland Tourism

Urban Architecture

Swiss villages and cities generally have an old quarter still unchanged from medieval times. The best examples are in **Stein-am-Rhein**, **Schaffhausen**, **St Gallen** and **Chur**.

Fountains – Always charmingly decked with flowers, fountains are a welcoming note to the lively squares and streets of Swiss cities.

Arcades – Originating beyond the Alps, arcades (*Laufen* in German) became popular from the 14C onwards, when they were adopted by Bern.

Painted Façades –Such painting (not to be confused with *sgraffito*, *"The Engadin house"*) has been popular since the Renaissance, especially in German Switzerland. Throughout Switzerland, the shutters of historic monuments and public buildings are painted with chevrons in the colours of the canton's coat of arms.

Covered Bridges – These are especially popular in German Switzerland. In addition to providing towns like Lucerne with pleasant sheltered walks, the roof protects the walkway, reducing maintenance on a structure made wholly of timber. The latest covered bridge built in Switzerland was in 1943 (Hohe Brücke, on the road from Flüeli to Kerns – *See p333*).

Oriel Windows – These corbelled loggias (*Erker* in German), sometimes built over two storeys, are to be seen in northeastern towns and the Engadin region where they are often elaborate works of art decorated with carving and painting.

Official Buildings – Public buildings testify to the quality of civil architecture in the Gothic, Renaissance and Classical periods. Their rooms are richly ornamented and furnished with stucco, woodwork, glazed cabinets, and magnificent porcelain stoves. Important buildings, like the great Gothic cathedrals, are Swiss specimens of foreign styles.

Covered bridge of Baden

at achieving a state of well-being. Any doctrine straying from this vision of happiness and seeking to combine different art forms was deemed degenerate and was systematically rejected (Meret Oppenheim, Sophie Taeuber-Arp).

During the Second World War, Switzerland became a refuge for many European artists, for example **Germaine Richier**, who expressed the war's traumas through highly imaginative sculptures, with strange mutilated surfaces featuring human, vegetable and animal motifs. Some Swiss artists returned to their home country, such as **Paul Klee** (1879–1940), who explored the inner world of dreams and imagination, creating a new style halfway between Abstract and Figurative art, based on colour and perspective.

Sculpture returned to vogue after the Second World War, and Zürich artist **Hans Äschbacher** (1906–1980) created precariously superimposed blocks of marble or granite that seem to defy the laws of gravity. **Walter M Förderer** (b. 1928), designed St Nicholas Church in Hérémence as a huge concrete sculpture. **Walter Bodmer**, a forerunner with his experimental wire paintings, undertook research in monumental iron works, focusing on lightness and transparency. The iron sculptures of **Bernard Luginbühl** (b. 1929) and **Jean Tinguely** (1925–1991) were far more imposing, overpowering, and excessive: The former showed nostalgia for the bygone era of the Industrial Revolution, while the latter expressed his contempt for history and the art trade through ephemeral, self-destructive machines. His sculpture, *Eureka*, exhibited at the 1988 World Fair in Brisbane (Australia) was crafted with the precision that has earned the Swiss their worldwide reputation.

During the 1960s, **André Thomkins**, **Daniel Spoerri**, **Dieter Roth**, and **Karl Gerstner** spearheaded the Fluxus movement. Thomkins worked on the notion of changing identity and function while Spoerri paid tribute to objects with his ironical booby-trapped paintings.

Since the 1980s, **Samuel Buri** and **Markus Raetz** have worked on the concept of metamorphosis. **Buri** is perhaps best known for his life-size polyester cows which he exhibits at shows and fairs, while **Raetz** studies the changes occurring in the human body and head, the effect of shade and movement.

Stephan Engler/Switzerland Tourism

Sculptures by Alberto Giacometti, Fondation Beyeler, Basel

Art Lovers

Art lovers will enjoy admiring works typifying the following famous painters and artistic movements:

Paul Klee in the Zentrum Paul Klee in Bern

Jean Tinguely in the Musée Jean-Tinguely in Basel

Arnold Böcklin and Konrad Witz in the Musée des Beaux-Arts in Basel

Félix Vallotton in the Musée des Beaux-Arts in Lausanne

Impressionism in the Fondation Collection EG Bührie in Zürich and the Stiftung "Langmatt" Sidney und Jenny Brown in Baden

Post-Impressionism in the Villa Flora in Winterthur and the Fondation Beyeler in Riehen

Contemporary art in the Kunsthaus in Zürich and the Kunstmuseum in Basel.

Nature

Switzerland consists of a lowland area (the Mittelland or Middle Country) between two mountain barriers: the Alps and the Jura. Both of these highlands arose in the Tertiary Era, 65 million years ago.

THE SWISS ALPS

The Alps cover three-fifths of Swiss territory, making Switzerland the second most Alpine country in Europe after Austria. Apart from the part of Graubünden to the east of the Hinterrhein Valley—a high valley like the Engadin, which, with its extra continental climate, is more typical of central Europe—the Swiss Alps, like the French ones, belong to the western Alpine group: the steepest and most contorted chain, and therefore, the most affected by erosion.

The pinnacle of this world of lakes and glaciers is the Dufour Peak at Mount Rosa 4 634m/15 203ft), although the St Gotthard Massif (highest point: Pizzo Rotondo: 3 192m/10 473ft), which represents the cornerstone of the whole structure. Any motorist crossing a pass like the St Gotthard is made aware of the sharp contrast between the relatively gentle slopes of the north face and the sudden descent which occurs on the south. In the longitudinal direction, the remarkable depression which slashes through the mountains from Martigny to Chur and is drained in opposite directions by the Rhône and the Vorderrhein, forms a great strategic and tourist thoroughfare.

GLACIERS

The Swiss Alps comprise about 2 000sq km/772sq mi of glaciers. Most typical are the valley glaciers, of which the Aletsch Glacier (see GOMS) is the most extensive in Europe (169sq km/65sq mi). Moving downstream, a **névé** (Firn in German), or snowfield, in which snow accumulates and is compacted into ice, is succeeded by a slowly moving **glacier** (Gletscher in German) traversed by a close network of crevasses. Breaks or 'steps' in the downward slope, which in the case of a torrent would form cascades or rapids, are marked by unstable masses of ice (séracs).

Moraines are accumulations of rocky debris brought down by the glacier. They often soil the whiteness of its tongue of ice and sometimes mask it completely, as at the Steingletscher. Once they halt they form characteristic embankments, known as lateral moraines.

About 1 000 years ago, the predecessors of present glaciers completely filled in the depression between the Jura and the Alps, reaching gigantic proportions. The Rhône Glacier, in what is now the Valais, was at least 1 500m/5 000ft thick. As glaciers withdrew, they created the rocky bars or **bolts** obstructing certain valley floors, as well as tributary **hanging valleys**, described as **scoops** because of their U-shaped cross-sections. When the ice disappeared, the new river flow began to soften these contrasts. **Connecting gorges** then made deeper cuts through the bolts, as in the Aareschlucht, or connected valleys, as in the Trient Gorges.

Alpine torrents were not only destructive, they also built up obstacles in the form of **cones of rubble**. The largest example in Switzerland is the cone of Illgraben as seen from Leuk.

ALPINE VEGETATION

Vegetation is closely bound to climatic and soil conditions as well as altitude and the degree of exposure to prevailing winds and sun. Above the agricultural land, which extends to about 1 500m/4 921ft, is the zone dominated by coniferous forest.

At 2 200m/7 218ft this makes way for mountain pasture (alpe) where sturdy, short-stemmed species, bilberry and Alpine flowers grow. At 3 000m/9 842ft, the mineral zone, moss and lichen cling to the rock faces of an otherwise desolate landscape.

Forests

These are the most familiar types of conifers in the Swiss Alps.

Alpine flax

©Alberto Nardi/Tips Images

Purple Columbine

Giorgio Perbellini/iStockphoto

Alpine Clover

Arco Images/Tips Images

Alpine Squill

Arco Images/Tips Images

Edelweiss

Chromorange/Tips Images

Norway spruce

In French: *épicéa*; in German: *Fichte*; in Italian: *abete rosso*. Found on north-facing slopes, it has a slim, pointed crest and a generally "hairy" appearance, with branches curled like a spaniel's tail. The reddish bark becomes very wrinkled as it grows old, and it bears prickly needles.

Spruce or fir

In French: *sapin*; in German: *Tanne*; in Italian: *abete bianco*. The tree has a broad head, flat on the top, like a stork's

nest in older specimens. The bark covers various shades of gray. Cones stand up like candles and, when ripe, disintegrate on the branch, dropping their scales.

Larch

In French: *mélèze*; in German: *Lärche*; in Italian: *larice*. This is the only conifer in the Swiss Alps that sheds its needles in winter.

The tree is found on sunny slopes in the high mountains, especially in the Valais and Graubünden. Cones are very small.

Arolla pine

In French: *pin arolle*; in German: *Arve*; in Italian: *pino cembro*. A characteristic feature of the many species of pine is the arrangement of their needles in tufts of two to five, held together by a scaly sheath. Their cones have hard, tough scales.

The arolla pine can be recognised by the shape of its branches, which are deeply curved, like those of a candelabrum. The tree is often damaged by the wind.

Flora

The term "Alpine plants" is reserved for those which grow above the upper limits of the forests. The early flowering of these species, which are usually small and strong, reflects the brevity of the growing season (June to August). Disproportionately large blossoms, compared with the plants as a whole, and bright colouring, are directly related to the high ultraviolet content of the light at high altitude.

Protection of Alpine flora

The picking of certain Alpine flowers that are particularly threatened, including cyclamen, Alpine aster, primrose, and edelweiss, is strictly prohibited.

ALPINE CLIMATE

Differences in altitude, mountain formation, and exposure create many variables. During the warm season, daily temperature variations produce winds called *brises*, similar to sea and land breezes elsewhere. Toward noon, the warm, expanding air rises and causes clouds to form around the mountain tops—a sign of steady, fine weather. Walkers should head for viewpoints early, since the valley breeze dies away at about 5pm, and the air suddenly turns cold, especially in the shade.

The Föhn – This relatively warm wind, most keenly felt on the north side of the Alps in the upper Aare and Reuss valleys, unleashes torrential rainstorms and causes thundering avalanches. The arrival of the *Föhn* first sheds its moisture on the Italian side of the Alps, then pours violently over the crest-line, finally growing warmer and becoming dry. Increased risk of disastrous forest fires prompts some communities to apply strict rules, often posted in cafés.

The Majestic Peaks

Swiss mountains over 4 000m/
13 123ft include:

- **Monte Rosa** (Valais):
  4 634m/15 203ft
- **Dom** (Mischabel; Valais):
  4 545m/14 911ft
- **Weisshorn** (Valais):
  4 505m/14 780ft
- **Matterhorn** (Valais):
  4 478m/14 692ft
- **Dent Blanche** (Valais):
  4 357m/14 295ft
- **Grand Combin** (Valais):
  4 314m/14 153.5ft
- **Finsteraarhorn** (Valais):
  4 274m/14 022ft

Some go so far as to forbid smoking completely. But the Föhn also melts the snow, enabling earlier crops and extended grazing time for animals.

THE SWISS JURA

The Jura massif in Switzerland curves for 200km/125mi between the Dôle (alt 1 677m/5 502ft) and the Lägern (alt 859m/2 819ft above Baden) and ends at the Crête de la Neige (alt 1 723m/5 653ft) in France. The last ridges of the Jura mountains rise above the Mittelland to more than 1 000m/3 280ft to face the Bernese Alps and the Mont Blanc Massif. This mountain chain was created in the Tertiary Era (65 million years ago). Beside this "fixed swell" of valleys and hills there are high, almost level plateaus such as the Franches Montagnes (*see Les FRANCHES MONTAGNES*).

Erosion has developed lush valleys and laid bare dramatic rock escarpments. The slashes made by erosion on the hills form the **ruz**.

The **cross-valley** cuts across the hill, connecting two valleys. The **coomb** runs longitudinally along the top of a hill; its escarped edges are called **crests**.

MITTELLAND OR MIDDLE COUNTRY

From Lake Geneva to the Bodensee, between the Alps and the Jura, stretches a gently sloping plateau. All the drainage from here feeds the Rhine through a furrow running along the foot of the last ridge of the Jura. Before the Ice Age, the Rhône itself flowed through this depression, in which a string of lakes (those of Biel and Neuchâtel) and marshy areas now lie.

WILDLIFE

The Alpine slopes are naturally rich in wildlife. Like the flora, fauna has adapted to a hostile environment: protection against cold (dark colour for better heat retention, hibernation), or against predators (white colour to blend with the snow). Of these, man has been the worst. **Chamois** has been greatly hunted and the species, which now numbers 90 000 individuals, has only

Conquest of the Heights

The victories of the 19C over the supposedly inaccessible peaks gradually destroyed the superstitious dread with which they were regarded (𝒞 see PILATUS). Switzerland, with many of its summits exceeding 4 000m/13 123ft (𝒞 see left), is a paradise for climbers. One of the first mountains to be climbed here was glacier-covered Titlis in 1744, by four friars from Engelberg. In 1792, Spescha, a monk from Disentis, conquered Oberalpstock. In 1811, the **Meyer brothers**, rich merchants from Aarau, reached the Valais via Grimsel and, starting from Lötschental, climbed the **Jungfrau** (4 158m/13 642ft).

At the same time, Frenchmen and Austrians were attacking the highest alpine peaks. In 1786 French guide **Jacques Balmat** reached the **Mont Blanc** summit and repeated his expedition in 1787 with the Swiss physicist De Saussure (𝒞 see Michelin Green Guide French Alps). Austrians summited **Grossglockner** (3 797m/12 457ft) in 1800. Breithorn (4 165m/13 665ft) was conquered in 1813, Tödi in 1824, and Piz Bernina (4 049m/13 284ft) in 1850.

The British also recorded some famous first ascents, including **Stockhorn** in 1842 and **Wasenhorn** in 1844, by JD Forbes; **Pic Dufour** (4 634m/15 204ft) in 1855 by the three **Smyth brothers**; **Eiger** in 1858 by **Charles Barrington**; and, above all, in 1865, **Matterhorn** (Mont Cervin 4 478m/14 692ft) by **Edward Whymper**. These achievements, with those of the French and Italians, make the 19C the golden age of mountaineering.

---

survived thanks to draconian regulations. The **Ibex** was not so lucky and was exterminated in the mid 19C. They were reintroduced in 1920 and their current number is 15 000 individuals in Graubünden, Valais and Oberland. **Lynx** spontaneously colonised the central and southern Alps since its reintroduction in the 1960s. **Gray Wolves**—extinct for 100 years—are also slowly returning to Switzerland from Italy, where strong protection measures led to an increase in their population. The **Marmot**, which hibernates for nearly six months, is common in the Alps and in some parts of the Jura. The **Golden Eagle**, a protected species since 1953, spends its life in an altitude of 1 500–3 000m, which covers around 100sq km in the Alps. The **Bearded Vulture** disappeared from the Alps in the late 19C, but was successfully reintroduced in 1986 and gradually resumed possession of its original habitats. The Swiss Biodiversity Monitoring (BDM), established in 2001 by the Federal Office of Environment, monitors biodiversity. Although such diversity is surprisingly well-developed on the alpine slopes thanks to the variety of climate, elevation and relief, it is much reduced on the overpopulated Central Plateau. Of the 2 729 species recorded in the country, 132 have disappeared and 969 are threatened; of the 195 recorded species of birds, 77 are endangered or extinct.

Marmot in Valais

Max Schmid/Switzerland Tourism

Village of Bettmeralp, Goms, Valais
Peter Mathis/Bettmeralp Tourismus/Switzerland Tourism

SUISSE ROMANDE

The Suisse Romande (Romandie) is the most westerly region of Switzerland, sharing its border with France in the northwest and the west, and with the canton of Bern to the east. It boasts a wide variety of landscapes ranging from two of the country's largest lakes, Lake Geneva (Léman) and Neuchâtel, to world-renowned mountain summits such as the Matterhorn and the Dent Blanche. The central Swiss Plateau (Mittelland) between the Jura mountains and the Swiss Alps covers a third of the country and is the most densely populated region. While the countryside offers a wide range of activities—from hiking arond La Chaux-de-Fonds to lazing on the beach beside Lake Geneva—the cities of Suisse Romande could keep you busy for weeks.

Highlights

1 Vineyard tour of **Lake Geneva** (p108)
2 **Lausanne**'s Olympic Museum (p128)
3 Attending a festival in chic **Montreux** (p137)
4 Cable car to **Scex Rouge** (p142)
5 Musée International d'Horlogerie at **La Chaux de Fonds** (p180)

A Bit of History

The Suisse Romande actually refers to French Switzerland and is synonymous with the French-speaking area of the country adjacent to France. It consists of six cantons: Jura, Neuchâtel, Vaud, Fribourg, Geneva and Valais, although for the purposes of this Guide, Jura and Valais are treated separately. The cantons of Romandie came relatively recently into the Swiss Confederation as their histori-

cal and linguistic connections tended to be with the Latin world, rather than with their Germanic neighbours, despite being part of the German Holy Roman Empire for a time. Fribourg was the first to join in 1481 but the others came later: Vaud in 1803; Valais, Neuchâtel and Geneva in 1815; and Jura in 1979.

The Canton of Geneva

Geneva is the westernmost canton and as such is almost surrounded by France, with the cosmopolitan city of Geneva at its centre and isolated from all the other cantons except Vaud. Before 1798 Geneva was actually an independent republic although it had been allied to the Swiss Confederation since the late 16C. During the Napoleonic Wars it was annexed to France until liberation in 1813, before finally joining the Swiss Confederation two years later.

Geneva is a very important financial and trading centre with many Swiss banks and international corporations having their headquarters in the city. It is one of

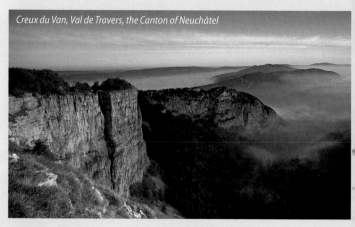

Creux du Van, Val de Travers, the Canton of Neuchâtel

the centres of the renowned Swiss watch industry with several famous manufacturers based in the canton. There are also numerous international organisations based here, from the Red Cross to the World Trade Organisation, not to mention the European headquarters of the United Nations.

The Canton of Vaud

Vaud, pronounced "*Voh*" in English, is situated in the southwest of Switzerland and shares its borders with Geneva in the south, Neuchâtel in the north and Valais, Bern and Fribourg in the east. In the west lie the Ain, Jura and Doubs *départements* of France.

The Romans, under Julius Caesar, defeated the Celtic Hevetia tribe and founded Lausanne, the modern capital of the Vaud. They were followed by Alemans, Burgundians, Franks, Germans and the Counts of Savoy before the neighbouring Bernese took control. Invading French troops were welcomed by the population in 1798 and by 1803 the Vaud had joined the Swiss Confederation as a canton.

Today Vaud has a flourishing service sector based around finance, tourism and telecommunications, plus a strong manufacturing sector mostly concentrated around Lausanne producing watches and pharmaceuticals. Agricululture remains important too and white wine is produced, mostly in the vineyards above Lake Geneva. Lausanne houses the headquarters of the International Olympic Committee.

The Canton of Fribourg

Fribourg, the first canton in the Suisse Romande to join the Swiss Confederation in 1481, lies at the eastern edge of the Suisse Romande surrounded by Bern in the north and east and by Vaud in the south and west. The Lac de Neuchâtel forms the northwestern frontier and the city of Fribourg is the capital. Although undoubtedly French, there are many German speakers in the east and both Fribourg and Murten are bilingual towns. The west of the canton is part of the Mittelland Plateau, but towards the

southeast the land rises to the Pre-Alps with peaks over 2 000m/6 560ft—these pastures make up the Gruyère region renowned for its cheese.

The Romans were here but left few traces, most of which can be found around Fribourg which became a city state in 1157 under the Zähringrens from Germany. It passed to the Habsburgs at the end of the 13C and began to expand before being passed to the Dukes of Savoy. As the power of the Dukes waned, Fribourg became a Free Imperial City in 1478, paving the way for entry to the Swiss Confederation.

The economy of the canton relies heavily on its agricultural sector with cattle breeding, dairy farming, cereal, fruit and tobacco production all being significant. Manufacturing mostly takes place around Fribourg while tourism is becoming very important, especially around the lakes and in the mountains.

The Canton of Neuchâtel

Neuchâtel is sandwiched between France in the west and the lake of the same name in the east. It stretches from Bern canton in the north to Vaud in the south and occupies the eastern slopes of the Jura mountains. There are three regions: the Vignoble on the lake shores, Les Vallées (Val de Travers and Val de Ruz) and the Neuchâtelais mountains above the Val de Travers.

The name of the canton goes back to the Roman designation Novum Castellum (new castle). Following their withdrawal, the area was subjected to alternating claims of Franks, Burgundians and Germans. In 1707 the lands eventually came under the control of the Hohenzollerns who ruled until 1848. Despite not being a Republic, Neuchâtel became part of the Swiss Confederation in 1815 and in 1848 a revolution removed the Hohenzollerns for good.

Neuchâtel is one of the main centres of Swiss watch-making and it is famous for the wines produced on the shore of the lake. Also important are dairy farming, horse and cattle breeding and, of course, the notorious beverage of Absinthe is concocted in the Val de Travers.

SUISSE ROMANDE

GENÈVE	★★★	Highly recommended
Lausanne	★★	Recommended
Gsteig	★	Interesting
Avenches		Other sight described in this guide
		Driving tour
LES BELVÉDÈRES DU DOUBS		See detailed driving tour map

0 ___ 8 km
0 ___ 4 miles

BESANÇON

N 57

Morteau

Doubs

La Brévine

Môtiers

Tra

D 437

10

Pontarlier

Lac de
Saint-Point

N 57

LE CHASSERON

1607

Sainte-Croix

Les Rasses

Grandson

Mont de
Baulmes

1285

Yverdon-
les-Bains

DÔLE

N 5

FRANCE

Doubs

D 437

Orbe

Dent de
Vaulion

Vallorbe

Romainmôtier

1482

La Sarraz

Écha

Lac de
Joux

Le Sentier

A 1

Saint-Laurent-
en-Grandvaux

Orbe

Vallée de Joux

VAUD

9

Lac des
Rousses

D 419

Vufflens-le-Château

Lausanne

La Garenne

A 1

Saint-Sulpice

Les Rousses

Saint-Cergue

Morges

Lu

Saint-
Claude

LA DÔLE

1677

Rolle

Corn
de Lo

LAKE GENEVA

D 496

Abbaye de
Bonmont

Prangins

Évian-
les-Bains

Nyon

Thonon-
les-Bains

Gex

Crans

D 1005

Dranse

D 902

Coppet

RHÔNE

GENEVA

D 1206

Dranse de Morzine

D 884

A 1

GENÈVE

FRANCE

D 1005

LYON ◆ BOURG-EN-BRESSE

Carouge

Annemasse

Abonda

Arve

D 902

Mo

Mont Salève

A 40

Bonneville

D 1508

A 41

A 410

A 40

Cluses

Geneva★★★

An exceptional location makes Geneva one of Switzerland's most privileged cities; it is blessed with a mild climate and its natural environment is carefully protected to guarantee the best possible living conditions. The result is that despite its cosmopolitan and international atmosphere and sprawling residential suburbs, Geneva retains the feel of a small and pleasant town. Geneva is the second seat of the United Nations (after New York) and houses the headquarters of several specialised UN agencies devoted to economic issues and social and humanitarian causes (disarmament, etc.), and international bodies such as the European Centre for Nuclear Research, the International Committee of the Red Cross, and the International Labour Organization. Clustering around its cathedral remains the town of Calvin and the stronghold of the Reformation. The metropolis of French-speaking Switzerland, it is an intellectual city which has welcomed many naturalists and teachers. It is also known for its busy streets and shopping centers. A very Helvetian atmosphere of order and discipline binds these three Genevas into one. Visitors will be charmed by the opulent mansions, the harbour and its fountain, and the shimmering shores of the lake, set against a backdrop of lush vegetation and wooded mountains.

A BIT OF HISTORY

2000 Years of History – The first settlement here dates from around 3000 BC. It became a Roman city when Julius Caesar drove off an attack by the Helveti and its strategic location on the banks of the Rhône caused the city to be conquered and reconquered repeatedly, by Burgundians, Francs, Merovingians, Carolingians, and in 1032, Germanic emperors; all this time the city was

▶ **Population:** Geneva 183 287.

Michelin Map: National 729: C7. Includes Town Plan.

Info: Rue du Mont-Blanc 18 – 1211. ℰ(0)22 909 70 00. www.geneva-tourism.ch.

Location: The city sits around the southwest corner of Lake Geneva, much of which is bordered by pedestrian walkways. Alt. 375m/1 227ft.

Parking: There is a handy park-and-ride system as well as metered parking.

Don't Miss: The *Jet d'Eau* (Water Fountain), a man-made geyser that sends up a 122m/400ft fountain over the lake, the city's symbol.

Timing: At least 3 days for the city and its museums. To explore more, go on excursions to nearby vineyards and summits, and take a lake cruise.

Kids: The Science and History Museum, with dinosaurs, reptiles, and minerals.

ruled by its bishops. Geneva developed into an important commercial center in the Middle Ages, but its independence was threatened by Savoy, whose princes tried unsuccessfully from the 13C–15C to control it. The city's autonomy was saved in the early 16C by the intervention of the Swiss cantons of Fribourg and Bern, and Geneva became a republic in 1535. Geneva's coat of arms reflects its status until then as an Imperial town (half-eagle) and a bishopric (symbolised by a golden key).

The Town of Calvin – From 1532 onward reform was preached successfully in Geneva by French humanists. Shortly after Calvin settled in the town (1536), he dictated laws, decreed laws, built new ramparts, welcomed Marot, Theo-

Geneva and the Jet d'Eau

Lucia Degonda / Switzerland Tourism

dore Beza and others, and sentenced the Spanish doctor Miguel Serveto to be burnt at the stake for his religious opinions. Meanwhile, the dukes of Savoy could not resign themselves to the loss of their state's leading city, and in 1602, Charles-Emmanuel delivered an unexpected night attack on Geneva. This was the famous unsuccessful attempt at scaling the rampart walls (*L'Escalade*), which the Genevese still commemorate annually (*see Calendar of Events*). The first flood of Protestant refugees to Geneva in the mid-16C followed by second wave at the end of the 17C fleeing Louis XIV's persecution of Protestants in France turned the city into a beacon of faith and learning.

GETTING THERE
PUBLIC TRANSPORT

The public transport company Transports Publics Genevois (TPG) operates the city's tram, bus, and trolleybus network. The city is divided into zones (zone 10 is the city center; zones 21, 31 and 41 cover the suburbs; while zones 51, 61 and 71 are in France). The lines serving zone 10 are numbered (1, 2, 3, etc.), those serving zones 21, 31, 41, 61 and 71 are identified by letters (A, B, C, etc.), and line 51 is operated by Transports Annemassiens Collectifs (TAC). Information and tickets are available from TPG agents at Cornavin Railway Station, Rond-Point de Rive and Bachet de Pesay. The main ticket office can be contacted at *(0)22 308 34 34* (Mon–Fri). Tickets and day passes can also be purchased from automatic ticket machines at bus stops in zone 10, as well as from licensed vendors. Geneva Transport Cards are provided at no extra cost when you check in at your hotel or hostel. The card provides free access to public transportation for the duration of your stay. *www. unireso.com*.

BOATS – The two banks of the lake are connected by boat, with departures every 10min from 9am–7pm. Line M1 operates between Pâquis and Molard, and M2 from Pâquis to Eaux-Vives. (**CGN** – *(0)84 881 18 48; www.cgn.ch*). Boat trips are available to visitors, from a trip round the harbour to a grand tour of the lake.
See Lake Geneva.

WHERE TO STAY		WHERE TO EAT	
Auteuil (Hôtel)	①	Bourse (La)	③
City Hostel Geneva	⑦	Dix Vins (Le)	⑤
Mon-Repos	⑩	Negociants (Café les)	⑨
Montbrillant (Le)	⑬	Vallon (Le)	⑮

Geneva, Capital of the Mind – Intellectual life flourished in the 18C: Jean-Jacques Rousseau, Mme d'Epinay, the banker Necker and his daughter Germaine (the future Mme de Staël), Dr Tronchin, the mountaineer and scientist, De Saussure, the painter Liotard, and Voltaire were citizens of Geneva by birth or by adoption. Diderot and D'Alembert had several volumes of their controversial 18C French encyclopaedia, *L'Encyclopédie*, printed here from 1777 to 1779. The city was annexed by France in 1798 and for 16 years the town was the capital of the French *département* of Léman. It joined the Swiss Confederation, after the collapse of the Napoleonic Empire, in 1815, when the unification treaty was signed. In 1846, a revolution led by James Fazy overthrew the government of the Reforation and established the constitution that is still in force today. Geneva's tradition of intellectual and religious freedom set the stage for its becoming an international city: Henri Dunant (1828–1910) had governments sign the Geneva Convention in 1863, limiting the effects of war, which led to the creation of the International Red Cross and cemented the city's reputation of a centre of peace and humanism and commerce, including watchmaking.

WALKING TOURS

1 OLD TOWN★★
1hr 30min.

With its narrow cobbled streets, the old town is a labyrinth of architectural gems spanning the 12C–18C, and is dotted with fine restaurants and vibrant bistros and cafés.

Place Neuve

This large square is surrounded by several majestic buildings dating from the 19C: the Music Conservatory, the work of Jean-François Bartholoni, and the Grand Theatre and the Rath museum, housed in a Greek architecture-inspired building which acts as a exhibition venue, are the focal point for culture in Geneva. In the middle of the square there is a bronze statue of the 19C Swiss hero General Dufour, on horseback.

Musée Rath (Rath Museum)

Place Neuve. 🕐*Open 10am–6pm, Wed 1pm–9pm.* 🕐*Closed Mon.* 🎟*10CHF* ✆ *(0)22 418 33 40. www.ville-ge.ch/mah.*

This museum, fronted by a portico, was built in the 19C in Greek classic style. It features temporary exhibits organised by the Art and History Museum. Special emphasis is placed on archeology and ancient art and on contemporary and modern art.

Promenade des Bastions

These public gardens, located at the foot of the city's ramparts, date from the eighteenth century. In the middle of the gardens, on the left hand side, you will find the vast mural (100m/109yds long) the **Monument de la Réformation**★ (Protestant Reformation), built against a 16C rampart and kept deliberately plain. The great statues of the four Genevese reformers Farel, Calvin, Beza, and Knox stand in the centre underneath the motto *Post Tenebras Lux*. The memorial (erected 1917) and its other statues and low reliefs with explanatory texts recall the origins of the Reformed Church and its repercussions in Europe. In front of it the arms of Geneva—bishop's key and imperial eagle—appear on the pavement between the Bear of Bern and the Lion of Scotland

On the other side, the boundary of the park is the University and the university library (🕐 *open Tue–Fri 10.00am– noon;* 🕐*closed for one week over Easter, Dec 25– Jan 1 and on Geneva's public holidays;* 🎟*free entry;* ✆ *(0)22 418 28 00;).* The Ami-Lullin section has a permanenet exhibition of manuscripts, books and archive documents on the subject of the Reform movement and Geneva's literary pedigree, plus the JJ Rousseau museum which has momentoes of the writer as well as a bust by Houdon.

▶ *Leave the promenade des Bastions, opposite the Place Neuve, by rue St-Léger, then turn to the left passing under the bridge.*

Place du Bourg-de-Four

Fairs used to take place during the Middle Ages on this quaint square in the heart of old Geneva. It is flanked by old houses, some of which have kept their former inn signs. Antiques shops, art

---

General Dufour, a National Hero

Guillaume-Henri Dufour was born in 1787 in Germany to Swiss parents in exile. He attended military studies in Paris and became an officer in Napoleon's Grand Army, resigning his commission in 1817 to return to Switzerland, where he was appointed captain in the federal forces and *chef du génie genevois*. He helped to found the **Military Academy** at Thun in 1819 and was a military instructor until 1830; soldiers he trained included Prince Louis **Napoleon Bonaparte**, the future Emperor Napoleon III. Dufour reorganised the armed forces and was appointed Chief of Staff, commanding the Swiss Army against the rebels of separatist Catholic cantons in the Sonderbund War (1847). Between 1832-64 he surveyed Switzerland, publishing a series of topographical maps on a scale of 1:100 000, known as the **Dufour Map**. Perhaps his most enduring legacy was **the national flag**, officially recognised by the Diet on 21 July 1840. When he died on his estate at Contamines in 1875, he was honored with a hero's funeral. The highest point of Mount Rosa, Pointe Dufour (alt. 4 634m/15 202ft), was named in his honour.

GENEVA
map II

0 ———— 300 m
0 ———— 300 yds

N

LAKE GENEVA

FOUNTAIN

Pierre du Niton

2

Ador

Gustave

Quai

R. du Décembre

Vives

Rue des Eaux

R. de la Scie

R. Versonnex

hône

R.-P. Fation

P

Pl. des
Eaux-Vives

Av. Pictet de Rochemont

Av. du Frontenex

ld -Pt
Rive

Bd Helvétique

R. de la Terrassière

■ La Clarté

Rue F. Hodler

POL

Villereusse

P

**Natural
History
Museum**

R. de

M

Holy Cross
Orthodox
Church

Rte de Malagnou

**Baur
ollection**

Tranchées

Contamines

des

Rte de Florissant

Rue

E

WHERE TO STAY

Armures (Les).........................①

Bel'Espérance.........................③

Best Western
Strasbourg & Univers.............⑤

Cigogne (La)...........................⑦

Cornavin.................................⑨

Du Midi...................................⑩

Suisse.....................................⑬

Tourelles (Les)........................⑮

WHERE TO EAT

Centre (Café du)....................①

Chez ma cousine....................③

Favola (La)..............................⑤

Halles de l'Île.........................⑦

Opéra Bouffe.........................⑨

Papon (Café)..........................⑪

Romantica (La).......................⑬

galleries and cafés surround the flower bedecked fountain.

 Walk along rue des Chaudronniers and then down rue Charles-Galland.

Musée d'Art et d'Histoire★★ (Art and History Museum)

Open Tue–Sun, 10am–6pm. Closed 1 Jan and 25 Dec. 5CHF (no charge for the permanent collection). (0)22 418 26 00. www.ville-ge.ch/mah.

The Art and History Museum collections present an outline of the history of civilisation, from prehistoric times up to the 21C. The largest sections are devoted to archaeology and painting. Several rooms of a castle have been reconstructed, complete with raised panelling and 17C furniture.

Archeology – Several rooms in succession are devoted to prehistory (objects of local origin), Egypt, Mesopotamia, the Near East, Greece, Rome and the Etruscans. The Numismatic Room contains a wide range of ancient monetary weights and coins.

Painting – The celebrated altarpiece by **Konrad Witz** (1444), one of whose panels shows the New Testament story of the miraculous draught of fishes, is generally held to be the first exact representation of landscape in European painting: Geneva and Le Môle can be glimpsed in the background. Other

rooms pay tribute to the Italian and Dutch Schools. These are succeeded by pictures of the 17C and especially the 18C. There are a number of masterpieces by Quentin de la Tour, including *Abbot*. Tribute is paid to the Impressionist movement, with works by Pissarro (*The Harbor in Rouen*), Monet (*Peonies*), Cézanne (*The House in Bellevue*), Renoir (*Summertime*) and Sisley (*The Lock at Moret-sur-Loing*).

 Continue along rue Charles-Galland.

Cathédrale Orthodoxe Russe de l'Exaltation de la Sainte-Croix (Holy Cross Orthodox Church)

Open Tue–Sun, 9.30am–noon, 2.30pm–5pm in summer; 2.30pm–5pm only in winter. (0)22 346 47 09.

This beautiful Russian Orthodox church dates from the late 19C. The golden domes of its cupolas are in the style of old Moscow churches, reproducing the plan of a Greek cross. Inside, walls, vaulting and pillars are ornamented with paintings inspired by Byzantine art. The nave is separated from the chancel by the iconostasis, forming five arches in Carrara marble, finely carved and adorned with icons.

In the center stands the sacred doorway, carved in cypress pine, gilded with intricate relief work.

Courtyard, Musée d'Art et d'Histoire

The Geneva Escalade

This traditional festival commemorates the successful defence of the town against the Savoyards who attemped to scale *(escalader)* the walls. Celebrations include a torchlit procession with the Genevese in period costume through the narrow streets of the town and along the banks of the Rhône. The procession stops along the way when a herald on horseback reads out the official proclamation claiming victory over Savoy. Local confectioners make chocolate cauldrons, symbolising the heroic deed of one semi-mythical Genevese housewife who put the enemy to flight by pouring the boiling contents of a cauldron over their heads. Fireworks and a religious service in the Cathédrale St-Pierre complete the day's festivities.

🏛️Musée d'Histoire Naturelle★★ (Natural History Museum)

1 Rte Malagnou. ◑*Open Tue–Sun, 10am–5pm.* ◑*Closed 1 Jan and 25 Dec.* 🎫*No charge.* ♿ ✆*(0)22 418 63 00. www.ville-ge.ch/mhng.*

The Natural History Museum was originally founded in 1820. It is the largest such museum in the country. The first floor, set aside for tropical birds and mammals, takes visitors from the African savannah to the South and North Poles, as well as Asia and Latin America. You can see several species of tiger, some of which have become extinct, as well as the dodo, a bird which used to inhabit the Mauritius and Réunion Islands. The second floor shows reptiles and amphibians from around the world.

The third floor focuses on paleontology, geology and mineralogy, giving a chronological account of the history of the earth, other planets, and meteorites. Note the dinosaur display with its huge triptych in the background, explaining three prehistoric ages. Another fascinating exhibit is the fossil of a *Xiphactinus audax*, a predatory fish from the Cretaceous period (96 to 75 million years ago). The section devoted to the *Hominidae* is illustrated by Lucy, who was discovered in Ethiopia in 1974 and whose origins are thought to go back some 3.5 million years.

The fourth floor focuses on the geology of Switzerland.

▷ *Retrace your steps along rte. de Malagnou and go left up blvd. des Tranchées. Take the second road on the right (rue Charles Sturm) and then turn immediately left on to rue du Mont de Sion.*

Collections Baur★

8 rue Munier-Romilly. ◑*Open Tue–Sun, 2pm–6pm (8pm Wed).* 🔎*Guided tour first Wed of the month.* ◑*Closed 1 Jan and 25 Dec.* 🎫*5CHF.* ✆*(0)22 704 32 82. www.fondation-baur.ch.*

This museum, housed in a 19C mansion, is devoted to art from the Far East amassed over a half-century by Swiss collector Alfred Baur (1865–1951) plus temporary exhibitions. The permanent collection features porcelain, stoneware, celadon jade, and other items from China and Japan.

▷ *Walk down rue Munier-Romilly, left on to rue François-le-Fort and right down rue St Victor. Return to Place duBourg-de-Fer, then take promenade de Pin and then rue Étienne-Dumont. Pass the Mortimer café, at number 2, to access the stairs which lead to the cathedral.*

Cathédrale St-Pierre★★ (St Peter's Cathedral)

◑*Open Jun–Sept, Mon–Sat 9.30am–6.30pm, Sun noon–6.30pm; Oct–May, Mon–Sat, 10am–5.30pm, Sun and public holidays, noon–5.30pm.* ✆*(0)22 311 75 75. www.saintpierre-geneve.ch.*

This vast cathedral, erected 12C-13C, partly rebuilt during the 15C, has been a Protestant church since 1536. It was given a surprising neo-Grecian façade in the 18C. The interior is plain but impressive. It was here that John Calvin preached his fierce, protesting sermons; you may see Calvin's seat, 15C stalls and the tomb of the Duke de Rohan, who was the head of the Reformed Church in France during the reigns of Henri IV of Navarre and Louis XIII.

The Chapelle St-Pierre or Chapelle des Macchabées opens out of the first bay in the south aisle. It is an elegant structure in the Flamboyant Gothic style, built by Cardinal de Brogny at the beginning of the 15C and heavily restored in the 19C in the neo-Gothic tradition after designs by the famous architect Viollet-le-Duc.

North Tower

🕐 *Same opening times as the cathedral (last admission 30min before closing time).* 🎫*2CHF.*

The top of the tower commands a superb **panorama**★★ of Geneva, the lake, the Jura, and the Alps.

▶ *Once out of the cathedral you come to the Cour St-Pierre.*

Site Archéologique★

🕐*Open Tue–Sun 10am–6pm. Last admission 30min before closing time.* 🕐*Closed Mon except Easter, Whitsun and Jeûne federal holiday.* 🎫*8CHF.* 📞*(0)22 311 75 74. www.site-archeologique.ch.*

In front of the west face of the Chapelle des Macchabées a staircase leads down to the archeological site found under the present cathedral. A chronological itinerary leads the visitor through the excavations, some of which date back over 2 000 years.

Cross Cour St-Pierre and turn right into rue du Soleil-Levant.

On the corner of the street stands a bronze statue of the Prophet Jeremiah, executed by Rodo.

▶ *Turn right as you leave the crypt.*

Musée International de la Réforme★

4 rue du Cloître. 🕐*Daily Tue–Fri 10am–5pm.* 🕐*Closed Mon, except Pentecost and Jeune Fédéral.* 🎫*10 CHF (-16 years,*

5 CHF). ♿ 📞*(0)22 310 24 31. www.musee-reforme.ch.*

This museum which was opened in 2005, presents the history of the Reformation in an attractive and engaging style. The movement turned Geneva life on its head in the 16C with thousands of refugees escaping to the city from France, Italy, the Netherlands and Scotland. Pictures, drawings, Calvin's manuscripts, unusual works of art and other rare objects are displayed in 12 rooms, each having a different theme (Calvin and Geneva, the religious wars, the 19C Reformation and so forth). In the fine central room, decorated in 18C style, a 15min informative audiovisual film is shown every hour (at quarter past). In another room, a virtual banquet has been laid out, and there you can listen to Rousseau and Calvin exchanging views on the issue of predestination.

▶ *Turn left along the Rue du Cloître, bear right and head along the Rue de l'Evêche to the Rue du Puits.*

Maison Tavel★ (Tavel House)

6 Rue du Puits-St-Pierre. 📞*(0)22 310 29 00.* 🕐*Open Tue–Sun 10am–6pm.* 🕐*Closed 25 Dec and 1 Jan.* 🎫*Temporary exhibition 3CHF.* ♿ 👥*For guided tours, contact* 📞*(0)22 418 37 00. www. ville-ge-ch/mah.*

This house is the oldest in Geneva. After the great fire of 1334—which ravaged more than half the town—it was rebuilt and gradually acquired its present appearance. Its elegant stone façade features amusing stone effigies representing heads of animals and human beings. A niche above one of the windows on the first floor carries the sculpted coat of arms of the Tavel family. Displays focus on the history of Geneva between the 14C and 19C. The town's ramparts, architecture, religious and political activities, and day-to-day life are vividly evoked through a collections of coins, early photographs, locks, door panels, and roof ornaments.

▶ *Turn left from the Maison Tavel and left again at Rue Jean Calvin.*

Musée Barbier-Mueller★ (Barbier-Mueller Museum)

10 r. Jean-Calvin. ⏲*Open daily 11am–5pm.* ♿*(ground floor only).* 👁*8 CHF (-12 years free of charge).* ☎*(0)22 312 02 70. www.barbier-mueller.ch.*

Drawing its riches from a family collection, amounting to more than 7000 items, this museum has a rotating exhibition of ancient works of art, plus sculptures, masks, ceramic pieces, jewellery and material from "primitive" civilisations throughout the world. Creative use of lighting adds to the appreciation of the works.

▷ *Follow rue Calvin, turn left to join the Grand'Rue.*

Grand'Rue

This picturesque street, one of the best preserved in the old city, offers visitors a remarkable choice of bookstores, art galleries, and antique shops. Several buildings are associated with famous people: number 40 is where **Jean-Jacques Rousseau** was born; the great actor **Michel Simon** (1895–1975) was born at number 27.

▷ *When you reach the place du Grand-Mézel, ornamented with a flower-decked fountain, turn left.*

Rue des Granges

Lined with large, comfortable residences in the style of French 18C architecture. The Hôtel de Sellon at number 2 houses the **Musée-Fondation Zoubov** (👣*guided tours (50min) mid-Jun–late Sept, Mon–Fri 3.45pm; Oct–mid-Jun, Thu at 5pm, Sat at 2.30pm and 3.30pm;* 👁*5CHF; unguided visits Mon–Fri 2.30pm–5pm;* 👁*no charge;* ⏲*closed two weeks at Easter and three weeks at Christmas;* ☎*(0)22 311 92 55. www.ge-ch/zoubof)* made up of Countess Zoubov's personal mementoes and brought back from her many trips abroad, including *cloisonné* enamels from Peking and painted enamels from Russia (imperial palaces of St Petersburg).

Furniture pieces signed by the greatest 18C French cabinetmakers, portraits executed by court painters such as Vigée-Lebrun, the Baron Gérard, Lampi the Elder and Lampi the Younger, as well as sumptuous carpets and tapestries decorate the various rooms of the Hôtel: the private entrance, the dining hall, the vast lounge, the bedrooms, and the boudoir of Catherine II. At number 7 stands the house where **Albert Gallatin** (1761–1849) was born, who emigrated to America and became an American statesman, including as peace commissioner to Ghent in 1814.

Église St-Germain – *Call ahead on* ☎*(0)22 311 41 30 to organise a visit to this church.* Rebuilt in the 15C, this church as a bell tower which dates from the 13C. Christian relics, dating back to the 5C, including the remains of a primitive altar are also evident.

Modern stained glass allows light to illuminate the interior of the church. One of the most interesting features is a fountain and sundial work.

▷ *At the end of rue des Granges, you come out on rue Henri-Fazy and the Hôtel de Ville.*

Hôtel de ville (City Hall)

This building dates mainly from the 16C and 17C with an older (1455) tower, the Baudet. Go into the courtyard to see an unusual spiral ramp, paved with pebbles, which allowed visitors to gain access to higher floors without having to get off their horses or climb out of their sedan chairs.

On the ground floor, visit the Alabama room where the first Red Cross agreement (named the Geneva agreement) was signed on 22 August 1864.

In the summer (July and August) the Hôtel de Ville acts as a stage for a variety of concerts from jazz to classical. Entry to the **Summer Musical Festival** (☎*(0)22 418 36 18; www.ville-ge.ch/culture/mus_ete/infos.html)* is by ticket only.

▷ *At the bottom of rue Henri-Fazy, head down towards the Place Neuve via the promenade and the Treille ramp.*

A Monumental Jet of Water

Most big cities boast a recognisable landmark which identify it: The Eiffel Tower in Paris, London's Big Ben, New York's Statue of Liberty, Rome's Colosseum, Athens has the Acropolis and Geneva has its monumental jet of water. It gushes not from the earth but from the lake at a speed of around 200kph/125mph to a height of 140m/460ft. This gigantic white column, on which the Genevese pride themselves and which tourists flock to admire, is operated by a powerful pumping system driven by electrical engines which draw in lake water and shoot it into the air at a rate of 500l a second. The water falls in a fine spray which, if a strong wind is blowing, can take tourists by surprise! To avoid any problems, particularly with boats crossing the lake, the jet is subject to strict wind and weather regulations. A meteorological center inside the machine room and a team of technicians are on duty to monitor the city's symbol. The *Jet d'Eau* is traditionally turned on on the first day of the Salon de l'automobile in March, and operates until 31 October.

2 THE LEFT BANK

3hrs. Start from Pont du Mont-Blanc.
The quays along the south of the lake are flanked by lawns planted with trees and flower beds.

Jardin Anglais

A floral clock dominates the part of the English garden which looks out onto Quai Général-Guisan. The clock consists of 6 500 different flowers and symbolises the expertise of Geneva's clock-making industry. The terrace affords an interesting panorama of the harbour and, farther back, the Jura mountain range. One of the most famous landmarks of Geneva is the harbour and its magnificent **Jet d'Eau,** whose great white plume marks the city from afar. It is now the emblem of Geneva and for a good, close-up view of the fountain, situated at the end of the Jetée des Eaux-Vives, take a walk along Quai Gustave-Ador. There, an impressive collection of sailing boats are moored to an artificial marina, confirming Geneva's reputation as an important yachting harbour.
The lake itself, teeming with many boats, including paddle steamers and the famous mouettes, is a memorable sight.

Parc de la Grange★

It features the finest rose garden in Switzerland (flowering season mid-June) and, in the centre of the grounds,

an elegant 18C residence. Next to it lies the charming **Parc des Eaux-Vives★**.

3 THE RIGHT BANK

Take a walk along **Quai du Mont-Blanc** which runs parallel to the north bank of the lake and which features stately mansions decked with flags. The route offers distant **views★★★** of the surrounding mountains (Voirons, Môle, Salève, Mont Blanc on a clear day).

▷ *Start from the junction formed by the bridge, the street and Quai du Mont-Blanc.*

The prow of the **Île Jean-Jacques Rousseau** juts out downstream from the bridge. On it stands a statue of the famous writer.
The Quai du Mont-Blanc is a bustling centre of activity, frequented by both local residents and tourists, who enjoy strolling along the lake shores and visiting the cafés and souvenir shops.

Mausolée du Duc de Brunswick (Mausoleum)

The mausoleum of Charles II of Brunswick (b. 1804, d. in Geneva 1873), a distinguished benefactor of the town, was built in 1879 in the style of the Scaliger tombs in Verona.

▷ *Proceed along Quai Wilson, the continuation of Quai du Mont-Blanc, or go to the Débarcadère des Pâquis and use the "Mouettes Genevoises", a regular shuttle service linking several points of the harbour.*

Parc Villa Barton, La Perle du Lac, and Parc Mon Repos★★

These three connected parks form the finest landscaped area in Geneva. There are elegant mansions within the gardens and around its perimeter.

Farther on there is a good view of the **Little Lake** towards Lausanne.

👥 Musée d'Histoire des Sciences (Museum of the History of Science)

◷Open Wed–Mon, 10am–5pm. ◷Closed 1 Jan and 25 Dec. ✏No charge. ✆(0)22 418 50 60.

In La Perle du Lac stands the stately Bartholoni Villa (1825), lavishly decorated with mural paintings, now a museum devoted to scientific equipment from the 18C and 19C. One room pays tribute to the Genevese physicist De Saussure (inventions, personal instruments, and mementoes); others display exhibits relating to astronomy (sundials, planetaries), navigation (sextants, compasses) and surveying (theodolites).

Other historical medical artifacts include stethoscopes, portable first-aid kits), electricity and electromagnetism, meteorology (thermometers, barometers), and physics (models of steam engines, various measuring devices, including an acoustic spoon used for calculating the speed of sound crossing water).

THE INTERNATIONAL DISTRICT
Musée Ariana★★

Avenue de la Paix 10 ◷Open Wed–Mon 10am–5pm. ◷Closed 1 Jan and 25 Dec. ✏5CHF. ♿ ✆(0)22 418 54 50. www.ville-ge.ch/mah.

The museum, founded by Gustave Revilliod (1817–1890), was built by Émile Grobety between 1879 and 1884 in the style of an Italian palace. The collections provide a riveting illustration of 1 000 years of ceramics in Europe, Asia and the Middle East, from the first earthenware pieces (a 9C bowl from Mesopotamia) to Italian Renaissance maljolica and Delft earthenware up to early Meissen pottery at the beginning of the 18C. The building also houses the headquarters of the International Academy of Ceramics.

Palais des Nations★★ (Palace of Nations)

Entrance at 14 avenue de la Paix, Portail de Pregny. 🎧Guided tours (1hr) daily in Jul and Aug, 10am–5pm; Sept–Mar Mon–Fri, 10am–noon, 2–4pm; Apr–May daily 10am–noon, 2–4pm. ◷Closed Nov to Mar, Sat–Sun and two weeks before Christmas. ✏10CHF. ♿ ✆(0)22 917 48 96. www.unog.ch.

The palace in Ariana Park was built between 1929 and 1936 as the headquarters of the League of Nations. Since 1946 it has been the second centre of the United Nations, the seat of which is located in New York City. A new wing added in 1973 is said to be one of the most active conference centres in the world. The **Salle des Pas-Perdus**, adorned with various kinds of marble donated by UN member countries, leads into the great **Salle des Assemblées** (capacity 2 000 people) where plenary meetings are held. Pass along a gallery onto which several meeting rooms

The Last Days of Sissi

Elisabeth, Empress of Austria and Queen of Hungary, wife to Emperor Franz-Joseph, died in Geneva in 1898. Just as she was stepping onto a boat, Sissi, as she was affectionately known by the population, was stabbed in the heart by Italian anarchist Luigi Lucheni. She staggered on board and collapsed. Rushed to the private suite which she occupied at the Hôtel Beau-Rivage, on Quai du Mont-Blanc, she died of her wounds soon afterwards. To mark the centenary of her death, the Hôtel Beau-Rivage organised an exhibition devoted to the sovereign including her poems, which she had bequeathed to Switzerland. A bust in her memory stands on the lake opposite the hotel.

Palais des Nations

open, to reach the **Salle du Conseil** where the most important conferences take place. It is also known as the Spanish Room in honour of Francisco de Vitoria, who is considered by many to be the founder of international law. The Spanish artist José Maria Sert decorated this room with huge frescoes depicting the technical, social and scientific achievements of mankind. The visit ends with a film explaining the role of the UN and its famous peacekeeping forces.

Musée International de la Croix-Rouge et du Croissant-Rouge★ (Red Cross Museum)

Access to the museum is through the Avenue de la Paix. ◑*Wed–Mon 10am–5pm.* ◑*Closed 1 Jan, 24, 25 and 31 Dec.* ◉*10CHF.* ♿ ✆*(0)22 748 95 25. www.micr.org.*

In the entrance hall, a bronze by US sculptor George Segal entitled *The Petrified* symbolises the violation of human rights.

Genevese businessman **Henri Dunant** witnessed the Battle of Solférino, during which 40 000 men were killed or wounded in one day. He decided to launch a movement to aid the wounded. Four years later, he founded the Red Cross. Eleven exhibition areas describe the activities of the Red Cross and the

Red Crescent throughout the world. Also on display is the uniform worn by Napoleon III during the battle. The museum provides a moving insight into the history of mankind, inviting both respect and contemplation.

Conservatoire et Jardin Botanique★ (Botanical Gardens and Conservatory)

◑*Open Apr–Oct, daily 8am–7.30pm; Oct–Mar, daily, 9.30am–5pm. Greenhouses open all year 9.30– 4.30pm.* ◈*Guided tour Nov–Apr, Tue at 12.30pm; May–Oct, by appointment.* ◉*No charge.* ✆*(0)22 418 51 00. www.ville-ge.ch.*

This 17ha/42-acre garden is both a pleasant recreational spot and a living museum of the plant kingdom.

It features a **rock garden★★**, where the different plants are divided into geographical groups, a deer pen and aviary, and a series of hothouses with a superb winter garden, containing many luxuriant species from both equatorial and tropical countries. Noticeboards direct visitors to the most interesting flower varieties. There are more than 16 000 plant species from around the world and the herbarium of 5.5 million samples makes it one of the five largest in the world.

PLAINPALAIS DISTRICT

From Cornavin station take number 13 or 15 tram to Cirque station on boulevard Georges-Favon.

The three museums below are located on the other side of the Plainpalais plain. This enormous piece of land seems to be nondescript at first site, but has markets on several days of the week (*see p107*) and on the north side an area is dedicated to enthusiasts of skateboards and rollerskates.

Patek Philippe Museum★★

Open Tue–Fri, 2pm–6pm; Sat, 10am–6pm. Guided tours by appointment. Closed public holidays. 10CHF (0)22 807 09 10. www.patekmuseum.com.

The history of Patek Philippe began in 1839, when Antoine Norbert de Patek founded a watch and clock manufacturers with his compatriot, François Czapek. Czapek retired in 1845 and the French watchmaker Adrien Philippe, inventor of the keyless watch, joined the company, which soon built an international reputation for unparalleled technical expertise and aesthetic style. A beautifully restored factory now houses the Patek Philippe Museum, which exhibits a collection of magnificent timepieces collected over a period of 30 years. Each floor focuses on a particular aspect of watchmaking and history.

Musée d'Ethnographie (Museum of Ethnography)

Open Tue–Sun, 10am–5pm. 5CHF for temporary exhibitions, no charge for permanent collections and 1st Sun of month. (0)22 418 45 50. www.ville-ge.ch/meg.

The Museum of Ethnography presents miscellaneous collections from all over the world, featuring both works of art and simple objects for everyday use. It also hosts temporary exhibitions, each focusing on a specific theme or ethnic group.

MAMCO

Open Tue–Fri, noon–6pm; Sat-Sun, 11am–6pm. Closed 1 and 2 Jan, Good Fri, 1 May, 1 Aug, first Thu of Sept (Jeûne Genevois), 25 and 26 Dec. 8CHF. (0)22 320 61 22. www.mamco.ch.

This Museum of Modern and Contemporary Art, housed in an old factory, displays recent avant garde works (post-1960), taken from over 40 private and public collections, both in Switzerland and abroad. Relying for the most part on unusual or relatively unknown artists, the museum's aim is to surprise and provoke visitors, whether they be seasoned critics or simply amateur art lovers.

ADDITIONAL SIGHTS

Bibliothèque Universitaire (University Library)

1 Promenade des Bastions. Open Mon –Sat 9am–noon, 2pm–6pm, Sat 9am– noon only. Closed Easter, 1 May, Ascension, Whitsun, 2nd Thu in Sept and school holidays. (0)22 418 28 00. www.ville-ge.ch/bge.

The Ami-Lullin library room is reserved for a permanent display of manuscripts, books and archives relating to the history of the Reformation and literary life in Geneva. The room named after **Jean-Jacques Rousseau** contains personal mementos belonging to the writer (manuscripts, prints, and a bust by Houdon).

Fondation Bodmer★★ (Bodmer Foundation)

19-21 rte du Guignard (from Rive, take bus A, to Cologny-Temple stop or bus 33, Croisée de Cologny stop). Every day except Mondays and Hols. 2pm–6pm. 15 CHF. (0)22 707 44 36. www.fondationbodmer.org.

The Bodmer foundation has drawn together the most notable of the documents written by scholar, collector and bibliophile Martin Bodmer (1899-1971). In 2003 a new underground museum, designed by Swiss architect Mario Botta was opened. This has a lovely above ground terrace with a lake view. The foundation has an enviable collection of works from the dawn of time up to modern day, including ancient tablets, Greek and Coptic papyrus documents, among which figure manuscripts written by John the Baptist. Under muted lights there are also works from leading philosophers, writers and well known people over the centuries—among the Dante, Napoleon I, Zola, Kierkegaard and Tolstoy.

Microcosm

CERN, route de Meyrin. From Geneva, follow the signs for the airport, Lyons or Meyrin. From Meyrin, continue to St-Genis. The CERN is on the left, just after the French border. ○*Tours Wed and Sat 9am and 2pm. Reception open Mon–Fri 8.45am–5.45pm and Sat 8.30am–5.15pm.* ✆ *(0)22 767 84 84. http://public.web.cern.ch/public.*
The European Organisation for Nuclear Research explains wider issues of the universe as well as the work of scientists in this field. A combination of audiovisual and multimedia presentations, games and hands-on exhibits allow visitors to get to grips with complex issues such as the forces of nature and how a particle accelerator functions.

Domaine de Penthes

18 chemin de l'Impératrice, Pregny-Chambésy. Access via Avenue de la Paix to the N and then the road to Pregny.
Located within grounds of 12 hectares/ 29.6 acres of beech groves, the Penthes château is rich with history, having been built during the 14C and then often remodelled until the 1800s. Among notable visits was that, in the 1850s, of the Duchess of Orléans and her sons, the Count of Paris and the Duke of Chartres.

Musée des Suisses dans le Monde★

○*Open Tue–Sun, 10am–noon, 1–5pm.* ○*Closed over Mon, Christmas and New Year.* ⊛*5CHF.* ✆ *(0)22 734 90 21. www.chateau-de-penthes.ch.*
This museum devoted to Switzerland's relations with the rest of the world from the Middle Ages to today, focuses on economic, military, diplomatic, scientific, cultural and literary aspects of Swiss society. Emphasis is on the Franco-Swiss alliances from 1444 to 1830, and on the armed forces or famous Swiss personalities who served the European powers. In the Le Fort Room, enhanced by delicate wainscoting, are several portraits worth noting and an oval embossed silver platter depicting the oath of alliance taken by Louis XIV and the Swiss cantons after a tapestry by Le Brun.
The first floor captures the French Revolution and its tragic result for Louis XVI's Swiss Guards, the French Occupation, and the role of the Swiss regiments during the Empire, as well as traditions followed by the Papal Guard, founded during the 16C). Mementoes of Beatus von Fischer, Switzerland's first postmaster, and of the national postal system, are presented in the Salon des Dieux, decorated with lovely **woodwork★**, seven gilded and painted panels representing the Gods of Olympus, taken from Reichenbach Château near Bern. The exhibition rooms on the second floor are devoted to Swiss celebrities who acquired a worldwide reputation: archeologists (Burckhardt), leading figures in industry and aeronautics (Breguet), forerunners of the modern banking system (Necker), diplomats (Gallatin) and statesmen (Haldimand), writers (Blaise Cendrars), scientists and physicians (De Haller), artists (JH Füssli), and famous women (Sybille Merian).

Musée Militaire Genevois

○*Open Tue–Sat 2pm–5pm, Sun 10am–noon, 2pm–5pm.* ○*Closed Mon and Christmas.* ⊛*No charge.* ✆*(0)22 734 48 75.*
The former stables of Penthes Château presently house a small museum which explains the history of the Genevese troops from 1814 to 1815, when Geneva joined the Confederation, up to the present day. The landmarks in Geneva's military history are illustrated through collections of arms, equipment, documents, and around 30 figures in uniform.

Musée International de l'Automobile★

Palexpo, halle 7, along the bypass on the road to Ferney. P *Leave your car in car park P26.* ◐ *Open Wed–Fri 1.30pm–6.30pm, Sat–Sun 10am–6pm.* ➿*12CHF.* ♿ & ♟*(0)22 788 84 84. www.cilma.ch.*

Laid out over two 7 000sq m/8 300sq yd exhibition areas, the Automobile Museum presents around 400 vehicles in chronological order, grouped together by make and country of manufacture. All the cars are in perfect condition. General Patton's Jeep, Mussolini's Fiat, General Guisan's Buick, Stalin's Zis, as well as a Cadillac and a Ferrari which belonged respectively to Elvis Presley and Sophia Loren, are the star attractions. Of particular note are the Swiss models (Ajax, Felber, Monteverdi, etc.) and the superb Italian machines, such as Ferrari, Lamborghini and Maserati, to name but a few.

Finally, a number of exceptional automobiles will not fail to seduce even the most hardened professionals: three Bugatti T35 models (1926, 1927 and 1929), Voisin C14 (1930), Auburn Speedster (1932), Hispano-Suiza (1934), Alfa-Romeo 2500 (1939), Allard 81M (1945), Facel-Vega HK500 (1959) Austin Healy MKIII (1967), and a gull-wing Mercedes-Benz SLR McClaren (2005).

Les Schtroumpfs

North bank, rue Louis-Favre and rue I.-Eberhardt.

These modern housing blocks (1982–89) in the Grottes district near Cornavin Station bring to mind the work of the Spanish architect Gaudí.

Institut et Musée Voltaire★

25 rue des Délices, 1203 Geneva. ◐*Open Mon–Sat, 2pm–5pm; Ascension, Whit Mon and Jeûne Genevois, 2pm–6pm.* ◐*Closed 2 Jan, Good Fri, Easter Mon, 24, 26 and 31 Dec.* ➿*No charge.* ♟*(0)22 418 95 60. www.ville-ge.ch/bge/imv.*

"Les Délices"—Voltaire's residence in Geneva (1755-65) has become a centre for research into his life and the period in which he lived. The Institute, which published the very first edition of the author's vast correspondence and which houses an impressive library, presents a series of exhibits retracing the career of **François-Marie Arouet**, the famous author better known as Voltaire. Displays contain an original edition of *Candide*, and handwritten documents, mainly letters signed by or addressed to Voltaire. Another curiosity is the collection of 199 wax seals bearing his heraldic insignia he used in his correspondence. Among the portraits of the author, note the painting by Largillière, representing him at the age of 24 (*ground floor*) and a terracotta replica of Houdon's famous statue *Voltaire Seated* (*first floor*). An audio-visual presentation (*45min*) enlightens visitors on Voltaire's stay in Geneva.

EXCURSIONS
Carouge★

◐ *2km/1.25mi S of Geneva City Centre.* Founded in the late 18C by Victor-Amadeus III, Duke of Savoy and King of Sardinia, the town has often been in conflict with its neighbour, Geneva. Many left puritan Geneva to enjoy themselves in the cabarets and inns of Carouge. The town was annexed to the Geneva canton in 1816 by the Treaty of Turin. The old district still has streets which were laid out in the 17C.

Mont Salève

Alt. 1 380m/4 525ft. 7km/4.4mi from Geneva. A lift is located at the frontier at Veyrier (accessible by the number 8 bus. Get off at the Veyrier terminus, cross the border in to France, from where the lift is 500m/1 640ft away). From Switzerland ♟ *00 33 450 39 86 86.* ◐*Open Apr and Oct daily except Mon 9.30am–6pm, May–Sept daily 9.30am–6pm(weekends).* ➿*16.80 CHF (children 8.40 CHF).*

Known as the "Mountain of Genevese" le Salève in France is the playground for walkers, as well as mountain bikers, rock climbers, paragliders and handgliders.

ADDRESSES

🛏️STAY

🛏️ **City Hostel Geneva** – *2 rue Ferrier. ℰ(0)22 901 15 00. www.cityhostel.ch. 54 rooms (dormitory style and private).* This hostel is in a good location, just a 5min walk from Cornavin railway station. Each room has a washbasin; toilets and showers are on the landing. Kitchen available for guest use. Good place for those on a tight budget.

🛏️🛏️ **Bel'Espérance** – *1 rue de la Vallée. ℰ(0)22 818 37 37. www.hotel-bel-esperance.ch. 40 rooms.* Traditional establishment with an interesting location halfway between the old city and the shores of Lake Geneva.

🛏️🛏️ **Best Western Strasbourg & Univers** – *10 rue Pradier. ℰ(0)22 906 58 00. www.hotel-strasbourg-geneva.ch. 51 rooms.* Comfortable hotel at the top of rue du Mont-Blanc near the railway station but away from the bustling Place Cornavin and rue des Alpes, a one-way street which channels traffic from the lake shores towards the station.

🛏️🛏️ **Les Tourelles** – *2 boulevard James-Fazy. ℰ(0)22 732 44 23. www.destourelles.ch. 22 rooms.* Excellent value given its location on the banks of the Rhône. Simple rooms which are refurbished regularly.

🛏️🛏️🛏️ **Hôtel Auteuil** – *33 r. de Lausanne. ℰ (0)22 544 22 22. www.manotel.com. 104 rooms. ⚏26 CHF.* One of the six hotels in the Manotel Froup in Geneva, which each have their own particular design—Swiss, Feng Shui, Colonial etc.). The rooms are designer inspired and comfortable, with quality furnishings in dark wood.

🛏️🛏️🛏️ **Mon Repos** – *131 rue de Lausanne. ℰ(0)22 909 39 09. www.hmrge.ch. 80 rooms.* Cosy, traditional hotel near Lake Geneva, opposite the Mon Repos park. Convenient location near UN headquarters and other international organisations.

🛏️🛏️🛏️ **The Neu Midi** – *4 place Chevelu. ℰ(0)22 544 15 00. www.hotel-du-midi.ch. 78 rooms. ⚏24CHF.* Just off Quai des Bergues, surrounded by lively narrow streets, this is an ideal starting-point for visiting the old quarter and the right bank of the city.

🛏️🛏️🛏️ **Suisse** – *10 place Cornavin. ℰ(0)22 732 66 30. www.hotel-suisse.ch. 62 rooms.* Facing the station, on the corner of rue du Mont-Blanc and its pedestrian zone. At the end of this main street lie the harbour, the landing-stages and, on the left bank, the old city. Restaurant with flower-decked terrace.

🛏️🛏️🛏️🛏️ **Les Armures** – *1 rue du Puits-Saint-Pierre. ℰ(0)22 310 91 72. www.hotel-les-armures.ch. 32 rooms.* Sophisticated 17C hotel with great charm close to the Cathédrale Saint-Pierre. An unforgettable experience.

🛏️🛏️🛏️🛏️ **La Cigogne** – *17 place Longemalle. ℰ(0)22 818 40 40. www.relaischateau.com/cignone. Restaurant 🛏️🛏️. 52 apartment-style rooms.* Luxury hotel at the heart of the old city offering excellent service with a personal touch. Quality furnishings and quiet, peaceful atmosphere.

🛏️🛏️🛏️🛏️ **Le Montbrillant** – *2 rue de Montbrillant. ℰ(0)22 733 77 84. www.montbrillant.ch. 82 rooms.* A comfortable hotel in a 19C building directly behind Cornavin station. The rooms are soundproofed; those on the top floor decorated with wood paneling. No parking facilities.

🛏️🛏️🛏️🛏️ **Cornavin** – *23 boulevard James-Fazy. ℰ(0)22 716 12 12. www.fassbindhotels.com. 169 rooms.* A modernised establishment, the upper floors have beautiful views of the lake. Rooms are spacious and soundproofed, with cherry-wood furniture and light, airy bathrooms. Note the unusual 30m/98ft-high clock, whose clockface is on the 8th floor. The panoramic breakfast room is on the same floor.

🍽️EAT

At lunchtime, many restaurants offer reasonably priced menus or plats du jour (dishes of the day), which include a main dish and a salad, for around 20CHF. À la carte dinner with good wine can easily cost around 70-80CHF.

🍽️ **Chez ma Cousine** – *6 pl. du Bourg-de-Four. ℰ(0)22 310 96 96. Open daily.* Near the cathedral, this colourful restaurant (yellow walls, green tables) serves chicken in all its forms.

🍽️ **La Romantica** – *3 place des Trois-Perdrix* 📞*(0)22 311 41 10. Closed Sun lunchtime.* A pizzeria located at the bottom of the Old Town. Simple fare but well prepared. Friendly welcome.

🍽️🍷 **Café du Centre** – *5 place du Molard* 📞*(0)22 311 85 86. www.cafeducentre.ch. Mon–Fri 6am–1am (midnight on Mondays), Sat 9am–1am, Sun 9am–midnight.* Well located restaurant in an area populated with smart shops, coffee houses and good restaurants. Excellent fish.

🍽️🍷 **Aux Halles de l'Île** – *1 place de l'Île.* 📞*(0)22 311 52 21. www.brasseriedes hallesdelile.ch.* Situated on an island in the middle of the River Rhône. Very popular at lunchtime, with its magnificent panoramic dining room overlooking the river. The restaurant serves simple, traditional cuisine and offers a number of different menus. Jazz some nights of the week.

🍽️🍷 **Café Papon** – *Old town. 1 rue Henry-Fazy.* 📞*(0)22 311 54 28. www.cafe-papon.com. Closed Sat lunchtime in winter, and Sun.* In part of the historical building housing the town hall and gives onto a pretty, shaded square. Rustic dining hall with bare stone walls and undeniable charm. The clientele includes local politicians.

🍽️🍷 **La Favola** – *Old town. 15 rue Jean-Calvin.* 📞*(0)22 311 74 37. www.lafavola.com. Closed 1–15 Aug, Sat lunchtime and Sun. Booking recommended.* This attractive restaurant is in a 17C building with a wooden façade. One dining room is on on the ground floor and one on the first floor, linked by a narrow spiral staircase. The restaurant serves well-presented, inventive cuisine from Ticino.

🍽️🍷🍷 **Opéra Bouffe** – *5 avenue de Frontenex* 📞*(0)22 736 63 00. www.opera bouffe.ch. Tue–Fri noon–3pm, 7pm–12.30am, Sat 7pm–12.30am, closed Sun and Mon.* Romantic atmosphere in the evenings with candle-lit tables and interior design along the opera theme. The menu changes frequently and there are often special offers at lunchtime.

🍽️🍷🍷 **Le Vallon** – *182 route de Florissant.* 📞*(0)22 347 11 04. www.chateauvieux.ch.* A small restaurant with informal décor situated in Conches 5km/3mi southeast of Geneva. Excellent wine selecion.

CAROUGE

🍽️🍷 **Café Les Négociants** – *29 rue de la Filature.* 📞*(0)22 300 31 30. www.negociants.ch. Closed Tue.* Good food at reasonable prices. Customers can select wine directly from the wine cellar, or order by the glass.

🍽️🍷🍷 **L'Ange du Dix Vins** – *31 rue Jacques-Dalphin.* 📞*(0)22 342 03 18. Closed 29 Jul–20 Aug, Christmas and New Year.* Two dining rooms, one of which is bistro-style. Good service and fine cuisine, including some delicious desserts.

🍽️🍷🍷 **La Bourse** – *7 place du Marché.* 📞*(0)22 342 04 66. www.resto.ch/labourse.* A brasserie in the Parisian style. The menu is broad and inviting with seafood, sausage and a variety of meat, including a tartare of seabass and a horse steak. Traditional cuisine is served on the ground floor, and pizzas and meat pierrades in the more informal vaulted basement.

🎭 NIGHTLIFE

At night, the neighbourhood between Cornavin station and Les Pâquis is always bustling with people on account of the many cinemas, bars, pubs and restaurants, mainly serving exotic food.

The **Les Brasseurs** (*20 Place Cornavin;* 📞*(0)22 731 02 06; www.les-brasseurs.ch*) micro-brewery produces its own beer on the premises, and has a brewing room and fermentation vats. If there are several of you and you get a seat, it's worth ordering a *colonne* of beer, which comes in either 3l/0.8gal or 5l/1.3gal measures. Three types of beer are on offer: *blonde, blanche* and *ambrée.*

The **Casino de Paris** on Quai du Mont-Blanc attracts a lively crowd. If you prefer the tango, cha-cha, or the waltz, visit to the **Palais Mascotte** (*rue de Bern*) after 10pm.

In the old district, centred around Place du Bourg-de-Four, the **Mortimer** is an unusual place with its collection of advertising posters, early gadgets and splendid zinc counter. In summer, enjoy a drink on the terrace of the **Clémence** (fountain and huge chessboard).

For Irish beer and ambience, try the busy **Flanagan's Irish Pub** (*4 rue du Cheval Blanc*), which often hosts live music. The fashionable **Demi-Lune** café (*3 rue Étienne-Dumont*) attracts an international clientele, especially late in the evening. Décor is traditional, in keeping with its location in the old town, and the atmosphere jazz-inspired. A range of snacks, including tapas, salads, and hamburgers, are served until 11.30pm.

There are also several smart cinemas and establishments around place du Molard, popular at aperitif time or later in the evening. These include the **Brasserie Lipp** (*8 rue de la Confédération; ℘(0)22 318 80 30; www.brasserie-lipp.com*) the antechamber of world finance and trade.

Many of the stylish cafés in the Eaux-Vives quarter are patronised by foreign dignitaries or executives. **La Coupole** (*116 rue du Rhône*) features two types of atmosphere, depending on your mood. For an aperitif or after-dinner drink, the comfortable **Café or American Bar** has a large choice of alcoholic and non-alcoholic cocktails, and a wide selection of fine whiskies. If you feel like dancing, climb the stairs to the café's nightclub, **Le Dancing**. **L'Opéra Bouffe**, in avenue de Frontenex, is a favorite haunt among artists, journalists and intellectuals, with opera music playing in the background.

OUTSIDE GENEVA
Head out on the Thonon road to Vésenaz, where you can't miss **Le Trois-Huit** café on the side of the road. With their leather armchairs and sofas, the **Night Café** and **Bibliothèque** (*open 7pm–5am*) have a cosy, almost British ambience. From 10pm, the Night Café alternates as a piano-bar and disco-bar with a live DJ; on Sunday afternoons it holds tea dances. The **Bibliothèque** (lined with bookshelves, as the name suggests), is quieter and more suited

to a drink and a chat. The café has a good choice of drinks, with over 70 different types of blended and pure malt whiskies.

In France, in **St-Julien-en-Genevois** (going southbound along the A 40 motorway then the N 201 towards Annecy), the **Macumba** is the largest nightclub complex in Europe, with 17 themed club rooms and 7 restaurants (*℘33 4 5049 2350; www.macumba. net*). The nightclub is very popular on Saturdays, with people coming here from miles around. **Le Gk** is for lovers of electronic music, while **La Villa** attracts Latin aficionados with its classic Spanish theme and a full Tapas bar. Each of the city's diverse clubs has its own unique niche. For a romantic night out, try **Les Mille et Une Nuits** with its Arabian Nights gossamer, or **la Mere** for a more traditional night out.

⬭SHOPPING

The main shopping areas, with a huge range of stores to suit all tastes and budgets, are in the following streets:

North bank – Quai des Bergues, quai du Mont-Blanc and rue du Mont-Blanc. **Manor** department store (*6 rue Cornavin*).

South bank – Rue du Rhône, rue de la Confédération, rue du Marché, galerie Jean-Malbuisson, rue Neuve du Molard, rue de la Croix-d'Or (which includes the Confédération Centre shopping mall),

Rues des Basses - main thoroughfare of the South Bank

rue de Rive, cours de Rive and rue de la Corraterie.

Globus department store (48 rue du Rhône and rue de la Confédération).

MARKETS

Geneva has several colourful local markets, offering visitors the chance to soak up the atmosphere of the city.

NORTH BANK

Place de la Navigation – Tue and Fri, 8am–1pm: fruit and vegetables.

Place de Grenus – Sat, 8am–1.30pm: fruit and vegetables.

SOUTH BANK

Plaine de Plainpalais – Geneva's largest markets are held in this square. Tue and Fri, 8am–1pm; Sun, 8am–6pm: fruit and vegetables. Wed and Sat, 8am–5pm: flea market; wide selection of antique and second-hand goods.

Boulevard Helvétique – Wed and Sat, 8am–1pm. Fruit and vegetables.

Place de la Fusterie – Wed and Sat, 8am–6pm: fruit and vegetables. Thu, 8am–6.45pm: handicrafts. Fri, 8am–6.45pm: second-hand books.

Place du Molard – A flower market is held in this square every day.

THEATRE AND MUSIC

Grand Théâtre – *5 place Neuve.* *(0)22 418 30 00. Reservations* *(0)22 418 31 30. www.genevaopera.ch.* Modeled after the Paris Opera, this well-known theatre hosts performances of opera, ballet and music.

Bâtiment des Forces Motrices – *2 place des Volontaires.* *(0)22 322 12 20. www.bfm.ch.* An annex of the Grand Théâtre, this is a venue for plays, opera, and conferences. Excellent acoustics.

Comédie de Genève – *6 boulevard des Philosophes.* *(0)22 320 50 01. www.comedie.ch.* Contemporary and classical drama.

Les Salons – *6 rue Bartholoni. Reservations* *(0)22 807 06 30. www. les-salons.ch.* Musical performances and plays by modern authors.

Théâtre le Poche – *7 rue du Cheval-Blanc.* *(0)22 310 37 59. www.lepoche.ch.* This small theatre in the old town has developed a reputation for its contemporary works, with a focus on experimental drama.

Casino-Théâtre – *42 rue de Carouge.* *(0)22 418 44 00. www.ville-ge.ch/ culture/casinotheatre.* Satirical reviews, operetta, and variety shows.

Forum Meyrin – *1 place des Cinq-Continents, Meyrin.* *(0)22 989 34 34. www.forum-meyrin.ch.* The theatre's varied program includes drama, dance, and classical and modern music.

Théâtre de Carouge – *57 rue Ancienne, Carouge.* *(0)22 343 43 43. www.theatre decarouge-geneve.ch.* This renowned theatre offers a varied international programme of drama, with works by classical and modern playwrights, including Racine, Molière, André Roussin, Chekhov and Pirandello.

Victoria Hall – *14 rue du Général-Dufour.* *(0)22 418 35 00. www.ville-ge.ch/vh.* For over a century this impressive auditorium with its superb acoustics has hosted classical concerts by the Orchestre de la Suisse Romande and visiting orchestras.

Conservatoire de Musique – *Rue de l'Arquebuse* *(0)22 319 60 60. www.cmusge.ch.* Classical music concerts performed by renowned soloists.

FOR KIDS

Les Marionnettes de Genève – *3 rue Rodo.* *022 418 47 77. www.marionnettes.ch.* This puppet-theatre group presents works by the Grimm Brothers, Russian fairy tales and contemporary stories written by the group. For children of any age.

Am Stram Gram – *56 route de Frontenex.* *(0)22 735 79 24. www.amstramgram.ch.* Traditional favourites for children and parents alike. The repertoire includes Beauty and the Beast, Peter Pan and Robinson Crusoe.

Lake Geneva ★★★

Known to the French as Lac Léman, the area spreads its great arc fringed with vineyards successively along the last slopes of the Jura, the ridges of the Swiss Plateau, and the foothills of the Vaud Alps. This shore, especially in the Vevey-Montreux section, became, after Jean-Jacques Rousseau had stayed there, the refuge of the Romantics. The pilgrimages which became more and more frequent among nature lovers started a great tourist industry.

- **Michelin Map:**
  National 729: C7.
- **Info:** Rue du Mont-Blanc 18.
  ℘(0)22 909 70 00,
  www.geneve-tourisme.ch.
- **Location:** The Swiss shore of Lake Geneva.
- **Parking:**
  Public transportation is most sensible for most parts of this region.
- **Don't Miss:**
  The vineyard tour.
- **Timing:** Allow one day to complete both tours.

🚗 DRIVING TOURS

In addition to the following itineraries, the corniche section of the main road connecting Vevey and Rennaz affords wonderful views of the Upper Lake.

1 VINEYARD TOUR★

70km/43mi – about 3hr.

▷ Leave Geneva by the shore road to Lausanne (which does not leave Geneva's built-up area until after Versoix).

Coppet

This little town 9.7km/6mi southwest of Nyon is crossed from end to end by a main street lined with arcaded houses built after the invasion by Bernese troops in the 16C.

Château★

🔎 Guided tours (35min) Easter–Oct 2pm–6pm (last admission 5.30pm). 8CHF. ℘(0)22 776 10 28.
Rebuilt in the 18C, the château overlooks Lake Geneva. It once belonged to Jacques Necker, a banker from Geneva who was Minister of Finance to Louis XVI. His dismissal by the king in 1789 was one of the decisive moments which drove France to revolution. His daughter, Mme de Staël, spoke out against Napoleon's regime and was sent into exile; she fled to Coppet, where she remained until the Restoration. Here she wrote Corinne, Ten

Years in Exile, Literature Seen in Relation to Social Institutions and her often cultural critique, On Germany. Coppet soon became a sort of literary principality, frequented by celebrities such as Benjamin Constant, Lord Byron, Schlegel, Chateaubriand and Mme Récamier.
The château has remained in the same family ever since. The interior is lavishly decorated. The rooms remain unchanged since the Revolution.
Visitors are shown round the library, Mme de Staël's bedroom, Mme Récamier's suite and, on the first floor, the Great Salon embellished with Aubusson tapestries and a Portrait Gallery displaying works by Duplessis, Gérard, Carmontelle and Mazot. In the park, in a grove near a shaded path, lie the remains of Mme de Staël and other members of her family.

▷ Continue along the Route de Suisse (shore road) for 6km/3.75mi until Crans and turn left into the Route du Port.

Crans

The château, which boasts good lines and proportions, is a fine example of the Louis XV period. The small church nearby offers a nice view of the vineyard, the lake, and in the far distance, the French Mountain range.

▷ Return to the Route de Suisse and turn left towards Nyon.

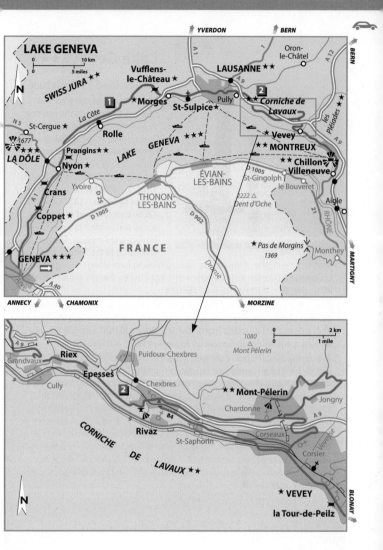

Nyon★ – *See NYON.*

▷ *Leave Nyon by the Route de Lausanne and in 2km/1.25mi turn left to Prangins.*

Château de Prangins★★

2km/1mi NE by the road to Lausanne. ○*Open Tue–Sun 11am–5pm.* ○*Closed 1 and 2 Jan and 25 Dec.* ◎*7CHF.* ゟ *(0)22 994 88 90. www.landesmuseen.ch.*

In a landscaped garden dominating Lake Geneva, the Château de Prangins, which successively fulfilled the role of seigneu-

rial manor, prince's residence, school and private house, currently houses a branch of the **Swiss National Museum** of Zürich. It presents the history of 18C and 19C Switzerland, focusing on its political, economic and cultural background.

Ceremonial rooms on the **ground floor** explore the theme of *The Dream of the Enlightenment.*

Note the beautiful music box in the shape of a bird's cage in the living room. In room 7 farther along, the optical instrument in the shape of a house (1781), known as "the television of the

109

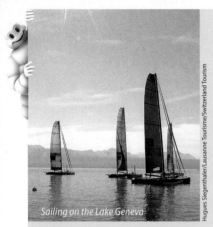

Sailing on the Lake Geneva

Hugues Siegenthaler/Lausanne Tourisme/Switzerland Tourism

Lake Geneva★★★

Switzerland in Miniature

Characterised by geographical diversity that reflects the country as a whole, the region around Lake Geneva encompasses the peaceful shoreline, gentle wooded slopes, lush green fields and snow-capped mountain peaks. It is 310m/1 018ft deep with a surface area of 58 000ha/143 323 acres, 72km/45mi long and 13km/7.5mi across at its widest point, between Morges and Amphion. The folding of the Alps in the Tertiary Era reversed the incline of the valleys, causing lakes to form along the edge (Lake Lucerne and Lake Geneva). Exchange of heat between the lake waters and the atmosphere produces a very mild **climate**.

Crescent-shaped Lake Geneva is Switzerland's largest lake (the southern shore belongs to neighbouring France). It is the body of water into which the River Rhône flows from its source high in the St Gotthard Massiff, entering the near Montreux and exiting at Geneva on its journey to the Mediterranean.

The narrow western end of the lake, known as the Little Lake, between Geneva and Yvoire is often considered separately from the Great Lake. The latter is the widest section, within which the so-called Upper Lake can be seen off Vevey-Montreux. Since the line of Swiss altimetry was fixed at the Niton Rock (alt. 374m/1 227ft above the level of the Mediterranean), the level of the lake may be regarded as the general standard of altitude in Switzerland. Lake Geneva has been a study centre for naturalists since the Reformation and during the 1960s it was found that the it had become very polluted. A massive clean-up operation restored Lake Geneva to its former condition and a full range of activities including swimming, sailing, wind surfing and scuba diving can safely take place again.

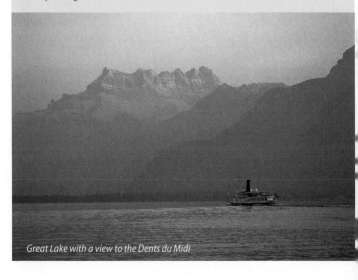

Great Lake with a view to the Dents du Midi

Ancien Régime", was an object of entertainment.

The **first floor** is dedicated to the period from the Revolution to the Federal State (1750–1920), a period of great upheaval. Note the **hat of liberty**, which symbolised the Swiss Republic in 1798 and took the form of William Tell's hat in the 17C. Switzerland became an urban society in the 19C; middle-class life in this period is depicted by the reconstruction of a living room (1850) and the development of transport portrayed through a collection of old bicycles and motorcycles, including several dandy-horses for children. An unusual circular shower is one of the exhibits devoted to health and hygiene. In the first-floor corridor, a striking painting by the pastor Jean-Élie Dautan entitled *Famous Swiss* appeals for unity and tolerance. Note also the small carriage known as a *char de côté*, very popular at the time, where passengers sat on the side of the carriage.

On the **top floor**, Switzerland's immigration, emigration, import and export, is explored, as is development of the country's tourist industry. The reconstruction of a storehouse for colonial foodstuffs near Seewen station (1883) is particularly worthy of note. The **cellars** are devoted to the history of the château, wine and cereals, energy, heating and light. Note the hail-cannon, much in vogue around 1900; blank shots were fired to disperse hail. The **vegetable garden** laid out in an old moat was planted in accordance with designs of the period; fruit and vegetables are grown here as they would have been in the 18C. From the garden, there are splendid views of Mont Dôle, with the Jura Mountains in the distance.

▷ *Take the Route de l'Étraz, direction Lausanne, via Luins and Bursins to Rolle.*

After Luins and the church standing in a clump of cypresses, it is a fast trip to Bursins and then on to Mont-sur-Rolle. Besides the Savoy shore of the lake— with Thonon—and the summits of the Haut-Chablais, you see the Vaud shore from Rolle Bay to the Naye Rocks with Lausanne in between. The south-facing hills which slope down to the lake are one of the great wine-growing areas of Switzerland.

Rolle

This town lies on the north shore of Lake Geneva halfway between Geneva and Lausanne. The triangular 13C **castle** was built by a Prince of Savoy. On a small artificial island is an obelisk erected to the memory of **General Frédéric de Laharpe** (1754–1838).

The road from Mont-sur-Rolle to Aubonne reveals typical villages surrounded by vineyards such as Féchy. The **views**★★ open out toward the Little Lake as far as Geneva and the Salève. Immediately after leaving Aubonne, toward Lavigny, the crossing of the Aubonne Ravine offers an attractive general view of the town.

▷ *Drive to the A1 autoroute and head towards Lausanne. After 14km/8.75mi take exit 15 towards Vufflens.*

Vufflens-le-Château★

Vufflens Castle stands on a plateau overlooking the ravine of the Morges, with a view of the Jura, Lake Geneva and the Alps. The castle was entirely rebuilt with brick in the 15C in the Italian tradition and extensively restored in the 19C.

▷ *Drive S along the Route du Village and Route de Morge for 4km/2.5mi.*

Morges★

Alt. 378m/1 240ft. Rue du Château 1110. ℘ (0)21 801 32 33. www.morges.ch.

The little town of Morges is an important wine-growing centre on the Vaud hillside. It has a pleasant site on the shore of Lake Geneva, facing the Savoy Alps. The port, built from 1691 to 1696, was busy with trade between the Vaud district and Geneva until the development of the railway system. Now, it is a **pleasure-boat harbor**. From the quay, near the castle (a former residence of the Bernese bailiffs) is an excellent **view**★ of Lake Geneva at its widest point and beyond it of the Alps, from Mount Salève to the Fribourg Alps, including the Savoy Alps, among which the Dent d'Oche and the Mont Blanc are prominent.

Musée Alexis-Forel★★

54 Grand'Rue. ⏱*Open mid-Mar–Nov, Wed–Sun 2pm–6pm.* ⏱*Closed Dec–mid-Mar.* ⌨*8CHF.* ☎*(0)21 801 26 47. www.museeforel.ch.*

Founded by the engraver **Alexis Forel** and his wife, the museum is housed in part of the Blanchenay Mansion, a handsome residence from the 15C, 17C and 18C. Note the panelled ceilings (15C and 16C), the 17C carved Burgundian doors and the two monumental fireplaces. Each exhibition room pays tribute to a particular period in history: 15C–19C French and Swiss furniture, most of which Forel collected himself; mementoes (17C and 18C salons), porcelain from Nyon and the East India Company; 16C–19C glasswork, 18C and 19C silverware. An exhibition of dolls occupies two floors, displaying numerous 18C–20C pieces together with their accessories.

Castle

⏱*Open Jul and Aug, Tue–Sun 10am–5pm, Sept–Jun, Tue–Sun 10am–noon, 1.30pm–5pm, Sat–Sun and public holidays 1.30pm–5pm.* ⏱*Closed Easter Mon, Whit Mon and mid-Dec–31 Jan.* ⌨*10CHF.* ☎*(0)21 316 09 90. www.chateau-morges.ch.*

Built on a strategic location west of the town, this massive 13C fortress, flanked by four circular corner towers defining four bulwarks arranged around a central courtyard, houses the collections belonging to three museums.

The **Swiss Figurine Museum** (*ground floor*) presents a series of dioramas with lead or tin soldiers which illustrate major historical events from Antiquity to the 19C, including Babylon, the Aztec rebellion against Spanish settlers, the Field of the Cloth of Gold and the Berezina Crossing on Napoleons's retreat from Russia. Each figurine has been painstakingly reconstructed with minute attention to detail.

The **Vaud Military Museum** (*ground floor and first floor*) presents an exhaustive collection of the weapons, uniforms and types of headdress associated with the Swiss Army from Napoleonic times to the present day, including the Pope's famous Swiss guard. A succession of rooms recreate particular periods of history: the Tower of Justice or the Tower of Torture, the Davel Room, devoted to Major Jean-Daniel Abraham Davel, a Vaud patriot executed in 1723 for having fought against the Bernese authorities, or the room paying tribute to General Guisan, Commander-in-Chief of the Swiss army between 1939 and 1945 (military record, personal belongings). The **Artillery Museum**, set up in a series of fine cellars enhanced by barrel vaulting, displays around 40 real exhibits along with miniature models which explain the development of this weapon: early artillery pieces from the 16C, mountain artillery carried by beasts of burden, 75mm/3in field canon and carriage; an unusual boule-shaped 12mm/0.5in mortar able to revolve around its axis, adjustable on slopes, with a range of 3km/1.8mi.

▷ *Between Morges and Lausanne leave road no. 1 to make a detour through St Sulpice.*

St Sulpice★

The little **St-Sulpice Church**★ is a pure specimen of Romanesque within sight of Lake Geneva and the Savoy Alps. The interior is austere and simple but tempered by multicoloured decoration.

▷ *Return to road no. 1 for the drive to Lausanne.*

2 LAVAUX CORNICHE★★ FROM LAUSANNE TO VILLENEUVE

39km/24mi – about 1hr 30min.

The road described here, which crosses the motorway after the La Croix crossroads, is the same road that is sandwiched between the motorway and the coastal road (no. 9) as far as the outskirts of Vevey. If traffic is too heavy, take the small road from Chexbres to the Puidoux railway station (5km/3mi), which then links up to the road described. It, too, borders and overlooks the motorway. You can catch splendid views from this road, though they are often interrupted by the many tunnels.

▷ *Leaving from Ouchy, you can join up with the tour at Grandvaux by taking coastal road no. 9. After leaving Lutry, turn left into the "Route de la Petite Corniche", then follow directions to Riex.*

Lausanne★★
See LAUSANNE.

▷ *Leave Lausanne by avenue de Béthusy going toward La Rosiaz.*

After this the road runs through a residential suburb and wooded ravines and emerges on a slope planted with fruit trees within view of the Upper Lake and its Savoy shore. This is marked from left to right by the Meillerie Cliffs, the green undulations of the Gavot Plateau (behind Évian) and the Drance Delta.
After the crossroads at La Croix, the whole of the Great Lake (Grand Lac) can be seen: the curves of the Vaud shore make a bend at the foot of the Jura, beyond the houses of Lausanne.

The Yvoire Point juts out from the far shore.

▷ *After a steep descent you will cross the motorway and railway.*

The road then enters the **Lavaux vineyard**, where its slopes plunge down into the Upper Lake opposite the shores of Savoy. Then come the wine-growing villages of Riex and Epesses enclosed by terraces of vines. The slope steepens and you enter the Le Dézaley district. Where the road skirts a sharp little spur, a **viewpoint★★** offers the Valais Rhône Valley through a gap in which the snowy Grand Combin summit appears in the distance. Beyond are the towns of Vevey and Montreux. They cover every bend in the shore at the foot of the characteristic Dent de Jaman and the cliffs of the Naye Rocks.
The Vinorama at Rivaz *(2 rte. du Lac;* ◷ *open Wed–Sun 10.30am–9.30pm;* ◌*free;* ℘*(0)21 946 31 31; www.lavauxvinorama.ch)* has an informative film and an opportunity to buy local wines.
From this area, you can visit **Vevey★**, **Mont-Pélerin★★** (*see VEVEY*) and **Montreux★★** (*see MONTREUX*).

▷ *Drive S along the Avenue de Chillon for 2.5km/1.6mi.*

Terraced vineyards of Lavaux

Stephan Engler/Switzerland Tourism

The Prisoner of Chillon

The castle and its dungeons have been used as a state prison more than once, but **François de Bonivard** remains its most famous prisoner. Bonivard attempted to introduce the Reformation when he was Prior of St Victor at Geneva. His theories displeased the Duke of Savoy, a staunch supporter of Catholicism. Bonivard was arrested and cast into the castle dungeons which have borne his name ever since. He lived chained to one of the pillars and it is said that his footprints can still be traced in the rock. He remained there for four years until he was freed by the Bernese in 1536. When **Lord Byron** visited Chillon in 1816, he commemorated the captivity of Bonivard in a poem, *The Prisoner of Chillon*, which contributed to making the castle Switzerland's most popular monument.

Château de Chillon★★

⏱*Open Sept–Jun, Sun 11.30am–3.45pm; Jul–Aug, daily 11.30am–3.45pm.* 🎫*12CHF.* ✆*(0)21 966 89 10. www.chillon.ch.*

Vaud/Chillon Castle is built on a rocky islet; its towers are reflected in the waters of Lake Geneva. The picturesque **site**★★ lies at the centre of the lake, within sight of Montreux, the French shore and the Alps: the Dents du Midi are clearly visible. The first fortress was built in the 9C to guard the road from Avenches to Italy, which crossed the Great St Bernard after skirting Lake Geneva. The castle became the property of the bishops of Sion, who enlarged it, and then of the counts of Savoy from 1150. It took on its present appearance in the middle of the 13C.

The drawbridge which once spanned the moat has been replaced by an 18C bridge. The dungeons, used as magazines for the Bernese fleet in the 17C and 18C, have fine ogive vaulting and are hewn from the rock. While he was visiting the prison, Byron carved his name on the third pillar in Bonivard's cell.

The Great Hall of the Bailiffs, which bears the coat of arms of Savoy, has an imposing 15C fireplace. The former

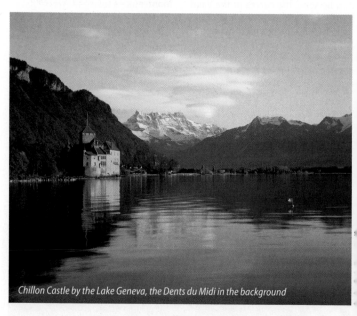

Chillon Castle by the Lake Geneva, the Dents du Midi in the background

Banqueting Hall (Aula Nova) houses the **museum**; the collections comprise pewter, armour, furniture and weapons. The visit ends with a section of the wall-walk and two fortified towers, converted into a prison during the 17C.

▶ *Continue S along the Avenue de Chillon for 2km/1.25mi.*

Villeneuve
Located at the east end of the lake, this small town has a pleasant lake front. The Grand'Rue has kept its old narrow houses fronted by wooden gates.

Several shops have façades decorated with quaint wrought-iron signs. Near the Place du Temple and its pretty fountain stands **St Paul's Church** (12C), noted for its stained-glass windows. Not far from the station, an unusual town hall has been set up in the former chapel of the hospital. Many world celebrities fell in love with the town and decided to make it their home. Among those whose name will forever remain associated with Villeneuve were writers like **Byron** (one hotel is named after him), Victor Hugo, and Romain Rolland.

ADDRESSES

STAY

⊝⊜ **Auberge du Chasseur** – *10 rte. d'Yverdon, 1028 Préverenges.* ℘*(0)21 811 50 80. 12 rooms.* �½. This charming hotel is only a 5-minute drive away from Morges and a 10-minute drive from Lausanne and offers comfortable rooms including free Wi-Fi. The restaurant serves local and international cuisine. Buffet breakfast is included in the room rate. The beach on Lake Geneva is only 600m away; free car park.

⊝⊜🍽 **Pré Fleuri** – *1 rue du Centre – St. Sulpice.* ℘*(0)21 691 20 21. Fax (0)21 697 40 40. http://pfen.hotelprefleuri.ch/. 17 rooms.* Rooms overlook a charming garden with pool. Meals (arrange beforehand) can be served in a pretty dining room or on the terrace.

⊝⊜🍽 **Romantik Hotel Mont Blanc au Lac** – *Quai du Mont-Blanc, 1110 Morges.* ℘*(0)21 804 87 87. www. hotel-mont-blanc.ch.* �½. *45 rooms.* Built in 1857 on the lakeside of Morges opposite the majestic Mont Blanc, this legendary hotel offers elegant rooms, most with superb lake views. During the summer season you can enjoy the beautiful shaded terrace. The proximity of the water and the serenity of the place provide ideal conditions for relaxing after a long day.

EAT

⊝⊜ **Rive-Bleue** – *La Lagune, route de la Plage, La Bouveret.* ℘*(0)24 482 42 82.* A welcoming dining hall extended by a terrace facing Lake Geneva. Traditional cuisine with by a wide choice of dishes.

⊝⊜ **La Plage** – *5 ave de la Plage, Préverenges.* ℘*(0)21 803 07 93. www. hotel-laplage.ch. Closed Nov–Feb and Sun–Mon Mar–Apr.* On a walk around the lake, discover this café, fine restaurant and terrace serving modern cuisine. Neat, clean, tidy rooms also available. Pretty garden for relaxation at the rear.

⊝⊜🍽 **L'Ermitage** – *26 route du Vilage, Vufflens-le-Château.* ℘*(0)21 804 68 68. www.ravet.ch. Closed 23 Dec–15 Jan, 1–19 Aug, Sun and Mon.* An entire family looks after diners in this charming old residence featuring a garden with lakes. Classical yet creative delicacies and spit-roasted specialities from the father and son. Personalised rooms and junior suites for extending your stay.

SIGHTSEEING
THE LAKE BY BOAT

The steamers of the Compagnie Générale de Navigation *(www.cgn.ch)* offer many trips including the Tour of the **Little Lake** (Petit Lac—starting from Geneva) and the more interesting Tour of the **Upper Lake** (Haut Lac—starting from Ouchy-Lausanne).
A round trip of the lake takes 11hr-12hr.

Nyon★

A pleasant town above Lake Geneva, Nyon was founded by Caesar under the name Colonia Julia Equestris (succeeding the Helvetian burg of Noviodunum). In the 16C Nyon was occupied by the Bernese. Examples of their style of architecture can be seen in the castle and the arcaded houses on Place du Marché. Today Nyon is at the centre of the vineyards on the southeast facing hillsides above the Lake and the wine cellar at the château is well known to wine lovers.

▶ **Population:** Vaud 18 269.
◔ **Michelin Map:** National 729: C6.
▯ **Info:** Av. Viollier 8. ℘(0)22 365 66 00. www.geneva-tourism.ch.
▷ **Location:** On the north-western shore of Lake Geneva. Alt. 410m/1 345ft.
▣ **Parking:** Park in designated areas; many streets restricted.
◈ **Don't Miss:** A walk around the city walls.
◔ **Timing:** Allow the better part of a day to visit the sights and go on an excursion to the summit of La Dôle.

OLD TOWN
Walk around the Town Walls★
The walk skirts the ivy-covered walls (19C) and widens onto the Esplanade des Marronniers from where there is a pretty view of the town, the Little Lake as far as Geneva, the Salève and Mont Blanc. Roman columns add a romantic touch to the scene.

Castle★
◔*Open daily exc Mon and public hols Apr–Oct, 10am–5pm; Nov–Mar 2pm–5pm.* ♿ ☜*free of charge.* ℘*(0)22 363 83 51. www.chateaudenyon.ch.*
Heavily altered in the 16C, the feudal castle has five different towers, all crowned with pepper-pot roofs. From the terrace there is a nice **view** of the Rive quarter and the Little Lake (*viewing table*). This château, which was re-opened in 2006 after six years of restoration, houses the History and Porcelain Museum. It was much altered during the fifteenth century during the Bern Period, is of fuedal origin and was owned by the town of Nyon from 1804. It has five towers of differing design but all finished with a "pepper pot" cap. From the terrace, which has an orientaton table, there is a fine view over the Rive district and the Petit Lac.
The entrance to the museum is from the basement. The ground floor is dedicated to temporary exhibitions. On every floor there are pictures of the people of Nyon over the centuries, some of which are very moving.

First floor – divided into several rooms which house the finest collection of Nyon porcelain from between 1781 and 1813. The original use of the rooms is indicated, including the "Coat of Arms Room". You can also see a large outside gallery, decorated with murals which date from 1690.

Second floor – a floor used for ceremonial purposes in the sixteenth century, until 1836 when it was used as a town court and the local council. It has been redecorated using wallpaper based on original styles. The rooms contains ceramics from the 19C and furniture ordered for the château before it was repurchased by the town of Nyon.

Third floor – the top floor served as storage space and a torture chamber in the 17C, and was converted in 1832 to provide a prison, plus a flat for the gaoler and his family. The cells were still used until 1979 and have been preserved in their original state. Graffiti scrawled on the walls by prisoners can be seen.

Musée Romain
◔*Open Apr–Oct, Tue–Sun 10am–noon, 2pm–6pm; Nov–Mar, 2pm–6pm.*
◔*Closed Mon (except Jul, Aug, and*

Paléo Festival

For more than 20 years, Nyon has hosted a lively international music festival. Concerts are held in a large meadow near the shores of Lake Geneva, where several stages are set up for performances. All styles of music are represented: Rock, jazz, blues, reggae, salsa, rap, country, techno, and even classical music. Performers have included Johnny Clegg, Joe Cocker, Eddy Mitchell, Noa, Al Jarreau, Placebo, Patricia Kaas, Mc Solaar and Alan Stivell. The event attracts large crowds of locals and visitors from abroad and the atmosphere is noisy and convivial. The Prix de la Scène is a prize awarded to a young singer or group from Switzerland by an international panel made up of professional performers. During the Paléo Festival, the town of Nyon becomes a living stage, with improvised shows taking place in the streets: theatre, dance, mime, circus and magic (www.paleo.ch).

Philippe Dutoit/Switzerland Tourism

public holidays), 1 Jan and 25 Dec. 6CHF (ticket gives admission to the other museums). Guided tours available for a hefty charge). ₰ (0)22 361 75 91. www.mrn.ch.

This underground museum is marked above ground by a statue of Caesar. On the façade of the neighbouring house there is a drawing of how the Forum must have looked during the Roman era. The excavated part of this vast 1C public building (more than a third of its foundations) is the centrepiece of the museum.

Around it are artefacts excavated from digs at Nyon and its environs: fragments of mosaics with simple geometric patterns or foliage motifs (including the famous Artemis mural), stone debris (capitals, military milestones), domestic objects (lamps, ceramics, crockery, coins) and a host of **amphorae** of different origins.

Quartier de Rive

A park and quays with attractive flower beds border the small sheltered yachting harbour and provide views of Lake Geneva and France on the far side. Farther along on Quai des Alpes stands the 11C Tour César (Caesar's Tower). Note, high up, the Roman masque of the god Attis, consort of the Great Mother of the gods (Cybele).

Musée du Léman

Same opening times as the Musée Romain. 6CHF (ticket gives admission to the other museums). ₰ (0)22 361 09 49.

The museum is housed in an 18C hospital overlooking the harbour. The origins of Switzerland's largest lake and its flora and fauna (aquariums are home to several species of fish) are the themes of the first exhibition.

The next section illustrates the various activities associated with the lake: fishing (boats, nets, and tools), forestry and timber-working (barges used to transport the logs prior to the advent of the railway) as well as the history of shipping (from the early lateen-sail fishing boats, so typical of the lake, to machinery from the steamer Helvétie II).

The first floor is dedicated to artists, both Swiss and non-Swiss, who have been drawn to Lake Geneva in the past; an area devoted to the Swiss General Navigation Company contains a collection of models, including one of the first steamboats ever used on the lake (1823).

EXCURSIONS
Abbaye de Bonmont

▶ *10km/6.2mi W by the road to Divonne. Then take the narrow road on the right.* ⏱*Open Jul–Aug, daily 1pm–5pm; Sept–Oct, Mon, Sat–Sun 1pm–5pm.* ⏱*Closed most public holidays and during concerts and other events.* ⚲*6CHF.* ☏*(0)22 369 23 68.*

At the foot of the Vaud Jura, a few buildings remain from the former Bonmont Abbey, which became Cistercian during its construction (1131). Over the centuries, it was used as a cheese dairy and even as a garage, and consequently has not suffered too much damage. Built in the same Burgundian style as the Abbaye de Clairvaux—designed like a Latin cross, with a tripartite nave and a flat east end flanked by oblong chapels—and recently restored, the austere church nonetheless has elegant lines and boasts a fine porch enhanced by capitals with floral motifs.

La Dôle★★★
Alt. 1 677m/5 500ft.

La Dôle can be reached by car via two routes. From Nyon go to the La Barrillette parking ground (about 20km/12.5mi). From St-Cergue go to the St-Cergue parking ground (about 21km/13.1mi) The travelling time is 1h10mins from La Barillette and 1h35mins from St-Cergue. Walking boots required.

Leave the car at the foot of La Dôle and continue on foot. Follow the path on the left, marked out in yellow. It leads to the summit, where a navigation beacon and radar station have been constructed.

A vast **panorama**★★★ extends over the Alps right up to the peaks of the Valais (Matterhorn) and the Oisans (Meije). Mont Blanc looms between the two towers, with Lake Geneva in the foreground. Looking right round, you can see the Jura including Mount Tendre and the Chasseron on one side and the Valserine as far as the Reculet, on the other.

Saint-Cergue★
Alt. 1 044m/3 480ft. 15km/9.4mi. Leave Nyon and drive NE by Route Signy and Route Blanche. Place Sy-Vieuxville.
☏*(0)22 360 13 14. www.st-cergue.ch.*

The high-altitude resort of Saint-Cergue has long been known to the Genevese and the French for its bracing mountain climate. St-Cergue stands at the point where the corridor of the Girvine Pass opens out within sight of the Mont-Blanc Massif and Lake Geneva. There are many belvederes near the resort, from which there are good views of the forest-clad foreground and the giant of the Alps.

Borsattaz Meadow

Those interested in botanical phenomena should go to the Borsattaz meadow, where giant pine trees, known locally as *gogants*, prosper; they are to be found only in the Jura. You reach the meadow from the Lausanne road; after 1.5km/1mi turn left into a tarred road (Route de la Prangine et du Plumet); 1.5km/1mi farther on bear right at the Carrefour des Fruitières. St-Cergue offers more than 50km/31mi of trails for **cross-country skiing** and a variety of training grounds and fairly difficult ski runs for **downhill skiing.**

Belvédère du Vieux Château★★
30min on foot there and back by a path signposted Le Vieux Château. Splendid view of Lake Geneva and Mont Blanc.

Parc Jurassien Vaudois★★★
Rte du Marchuairuz 2. ☏*(0)22 366 51 70 www.parc-jurassien.ch.*

In 1973, 13 communities and a number of private landowners combined to create this regional natural park to preserve the mountain sides of the Jura for future generations, Now comprising more than 100sq km/38.6mi in 23 towns on the Jura highlands above the northern shores of Lake Geneva, the park includes not only woodlands but pasture lands lined with dry masonry stone walls as well. The pastures are home to the cattle that provide the milk for the region's

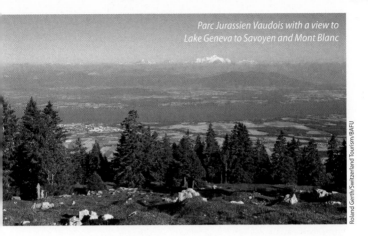

Parc Jurassien Vaudois with a view to Lake Geneva to Savoyen and Mont Blanc

Roland Gerth/Switzerland Tourism/BAFU

famed Gruyère cheese. Throughout the year the lands are available for public uses and the park administration has a number of programmes available to the public explaining the natural and human history of the region. Saint Cergue is at the southwest end of the park.

🚗 DRIVING TOUR

1 VALLÉE DE JOUX★★

From Nyon to Vallorbe. 90km/56mi – allow approx 2hrs. ⚠The Marchairuz road (Le Brassus to St-George) is usually blocked by snow from November to April.

The jewel of the Vaud Jura, the Joux Valley and its lake, presents an agreeable stop on an otherwise hilly road linking Lake Geneva to the French border. Thanks to its lake, pastures, pine forests and the mountains which surround it, the Joux valley is the jewel in the crown of the Jura in the Vaud area.

Zoo de la Garenne

ⓘ*Open daily, 9am–6pm (5.30pm Dec–Feb). ⚫10CHF. www.lagarenne.ch.*
This small zoo presents mostly European species (wolf, lynx, eagle etc). The hairpin section between Burtigny and Begnins offers particularly open **views**★★ of the Savoy shore of Lake Geneva.

▷ *Return to Marchissy and continue to St-George.*

From St-George, the panorama from Sapin to Siméon provides a lovely view over the Mont Blanc massif, the Aravis chain of mountians, plus the plateau and ranges of the Glières and the Grand Salève.

▷ *Continue to Brassus.*

The road crosses the Amburneux valley at the heart of the Vaud's Jurassic Park, one of Switzerland's largest parks. The countryside is distinctive due to its dry stone walls which were built between the end of the 19C and the beginning of the 20C. They were built to divide the pastures and to fence in animals.

▷ *At Brassus, turn right to return to the village.*

Vallée de Joux★★

Rue de l'Orbe. ☏(0)21 845 17 770. www.myvalleedejoux.ch.
The road then leads into the Joux Valley, gently hollowed out between the minor ranges around Mont Risoux and Mont Tendre. After the small Lake Brenets and the villas and hotels of Le Pont (facilities) scattered around it, Lake Joux, the largest of the Jura lakes, appears. Its calm waters are frozen during the long harsh winter. Until a few years after the World War I this ice, cut into regular blocks, was stored at Le Pont in underground ice-houses before being sent to Paris by rail.

View of Lake Joux from the Dent de Vaulion

Follow the south shore, bordered by wooded hills, wide pastures and hospitable villages, which are both pleasant country resorts and small industrial centres employed in watch and clock-making. The **Espace Horloger de la Vallée de Joux** (○*open Tue–Sun, 2pm–6pm;* ◉*8CHF;* ℘*(0)21 845 75 45*) at **Le Sentier** introduces visitors to a display of splendid clocks and watches dating from the 16C–19C and a reconstruction of a typical watchmaker's workshop. The climb from Le Brassus (facilities) to the Marchairuz Pass affords pleasant views of Lake Joux and its valley, closed by the bold spur of the Dent de Vaulion.

▷ *Take the south bank from Joux lake (l'Orient, les Bioux). After Abbaye village, take the road to Lausanne-Cossonnay. At Petra Felix, turn left towards Vaulion. Several kilometres further on turn left again towards the Dent de Vaulion chalet.*

Dent De Vaulion★★
Alt. 1 482m/4 865ft.
Dent de Vaulion, one of the steepest summits in the Swiss Jura, offers a sweeping panorama of the Alps, from the Jungfrau to the Meije and the Joux Valley.

Climb to the Dent
From the road from Romainmôtier to L'Abbaye, 5km/3mi – allow 45min.
The access road, tarred as far as the chalet on Dent de Vaulion, branches off from the main road on the ridge between the Vaulion Valley and the Joux Valley. It soon becomes very narrow (*passing only possible at certain points*). From the chalet you can see your way to a signpost marking the summit (*viewing table*).

Panorama★★★
The great glory of this view is the Mont-Blanc Massif beyond the mists of Lake Geneva; the first ridges of the Jura towards the Joux Valley and its lakes are also a majestic sight. Beware the alarming precipice: a sheer drop of over 200m/600ft.

Vallorbe
Alt. 769m/2 523ft. Grandes-Forges 11.
℘*(0)21 43 25 83.*
www.vallorbe-tourisme.ch.
The town of Vallorbe owes its activity to its varied industries (light engineering, plastic products) and especially to its frontier station, well-known to users of the Simplon line.

Musée du Fer et du Chemin de Fer
The Carte Trèfle (◉*30CHF) is a ticket valid from Palm Sunday to All Saints giving access to the caves, the Iron and Railway Museum, the Parc du Mont-d'Orzaires, and the Vallorbe fort. Contact the sights for further information. ○Open Apr–Oct, daily 9.30am–noon, 1.30pm–6pm; Nov–Mar, Tue–Fri at the same times. ◉10CHF.*

(0)21 843 25 83. Access to the Iron and Railway Museum is through the Tourist Information Centre.

On the former site of the Grandes Forges, the **Iron Museum** celebrates the history of the region's iron industry. In addition to early forges, displays include anvils, grinding-stones, and other tools manufactured on site, as well as modern products made through precision engineering.

Vallorbe's golden age as one of the stops on the Simplon line is vividly evoked at the **Railway Museum**. There is a maquette of the station in 1908: plus historic railway tools and equipment, tickets, old posters, and an inspector's uniform. On the second floor, visitors can follow the adventures of their favorite train on a miniature toy circuit: *micheline*, high-speed *TGV*, regional Swiss trains.

Grottes de Vallorbe★

Open Mar–Nov, 9.30am–4.30pm (5.30pm Jun, Jul and Aug). 15CHF, 7CHF children). *(0)21 843 25 83.

The Orbe rivier has created underground chambers which are among the most spectacular in Switzerland. The grottos hadn't been explored much before the 1960s. Having passed through a large artificial gallery, there is a succession of lakes and grottos rich with stalactites, stalagmites and concretions (masses formed of solid particles). Just before the exit, it is worth visiting the Trésor des Fées (Fairies' Treasure) where 250 examples of minerals from around the world, are displayed.

Fort de Vallorbe

Guided tours (1hr30min) Jul and Aug, daily 10.30am–4pm; May–Nov, Sat–Sun 11am–3.45pm. 12CHF. *(0)32 843 25 83.

This stronghold, carved out of rock and facing the French border, was built shortly before the Second World War. It consists of three small forts and six heavily guarded blockhouses and watchtowers, connected by a maze

of underground galleries. 30m/98.4ft below ground level sits a machine room, ammunition dump, telephone exchange, barracks, dormitory, kitchen, mess, canteen, infirmary, dental surgery, and operating theatre. Figurines, weapons, documents, and sound effects complete this evocation of military life in the Fort de Pré-Giroud, which could house around 100 men.

Source of the Orbe

3km/1.8mi—plus 30min on foot there and back. Leave Vallorbe by the road to the Joux Valley, and then take the road to the left marked Source-Grottes, sloping gently downhill. Leave your car near the power station.

Walk along a shady path and you will reach the end of the little rocky hollow where the Orbe rises: a reappearance of the waters of the Joux and Brenet lakes.

ADDRESSES

STAY

Hostellerie du 16e siècle – *Pl. du Marché.* *(0)22 994 88 00. www.16eme.com. 19 rooms.* . In the centre of Nyon next to the château, this hotel housed in a lovely old building offers light and pleasant rooms together with a restaurant which offers very good value for money considering the quality of the cuisine.

Hôtel Ambassador – *26 r. St-Jean.* *(0)22 994 48 48 - www.hotel-ambassador-nyon.ch. 20 rooms.* . Comfortable spacious rooms with traditional muted decor. Several of the rooms have a large terrace overlooking the lake.

EAT

Le Rive – *15 r. de Rive.* *(0)22 362 34 46. www.lerive.ch. Non-stop meals available every day.* Simple but good fare in this brasserie on the lake. The menu includes crêpes. Friendly welcome and terrace.

Lausanne★★

Lausanne is a welcoming, cosmopolitan city, much loved by its university students and its high society, who enjoy the scenic views of the lake and the surrounding Alps. The city is built on uneven ground. After being confined to the promontory of the present city for several centuries, Lausanne spread southward to the delightful shores of Ouchy, a former fisherman's hamlet. Its new quarters contrast sharply with the old, steep, narrow streets that lead to the cathedral.

A BIT OF HISTORY

The life of the city is concentrated within Place de la Riponne, rue du Bourg, Place Saint-François, rue du Grand-Chêne and Place Bel-Air. These are joined by the Grand Pont, spanning the valley where the Flon torrent once flowed.

An important centre for both art and entertainment, Lausanne has acquired a worldwide reputation for the famous ballet troupe directed by Maurice Béjart and the classical concerts performed by the French Swiss Orchestra and the Chamber Orchestra of Lausanne. The Palais de Beaulieu and the Théâtre Municipal are frequently used to host dance performances and musical shows.

The municipality of **Vidy**, part of Lausanne, enjoys Olympic status since it houses the International Olympic Committee (IOC), which was founded in 1894 by Baron Pierre de Coubertin. The Olympic Museum, opened in Ouchy in 1993, has made Lausanne the world capital of the **Olympic movement**.

Early days – Recent excavations show Lausanne was originally built on the site of the present city, perched on the promontory where Neolithic skeletons have been uncovered. Southwest (at **Vidy**), part of the former Roman Lousonna has been excavated. Of particular interest is a section of Roman road, located exactly where the Geneva-Lausanne road is today.

▶ **Population:** Vaud 114 518.

◔ **Michelin Map:** National Map 729: D6. Includes Town Plan.

▯ **Info:** 4 place de la Gare – 1000. ✆(0)21 613 73 73. www.lausanne-tourisme.ch.

◖ **Location:** 62km/36mi northeast of Geneva, on the lakeshore. Alt. 455m/1 493ft.

▯ **Parking:** Leave the car; use the rapid subway between lakefront and city centre.

◉ **Don't Miss:** The Olympic Museum in a beautiful park on the lake, where the Olympic flame has burnt uninterrupted since opening.

◔ **Timing:** Allow at least two days for the museums and a lake excursion.

Cathedral City – At the end of the 6C Bishop St Marius came to live in Lausanne; the first cathedral was built two centuries later. In the Middle Ages, religious leadership combined with economic and political expansion: the quarters of Place de la Palud, the Bourg, St Pierre, St Laurent and St François were added to the town. In the 13C many religious orders settled here and the Prince-Bishop Guillaume de Champvent consecrated the new cathedral; later Pope Gregory X dedicated it in the presence of Emperor Rudolf I of Habsburg. The city or upper town was the religious and intellectual centre; commercial activities flourished in adjoining districts.

From the Reformation to Bernese domination – The Reformation scored a sweeping success at Lausanne; it was preached there by Guillaume Farel. In 1536 the town and all of the Vaud Country were occupied by the Bernese. All of Lausanne's churches except for the cathedral and the Church of St Francis disappeared. In 1723 the Bernese

View of Old Town

Regis Colombo/Lausanne Tourisme/Switzerland Tourism

harshly suppressed an attempt by the Vaud people to regain their independence; Davel, the instigator of the revolt, was beheaded at Vidy. It was not until 1803 that the Vaud region attained political autonomy, with Lausanne as its capital. In 1874 it became the seat of the Federal Court of Justice.

The Age of Enlightenment – The 18C was an era of prosperity. Lausanne came under French influence; Voltaire stayed in the city, where his play *Zadig* was performed. Byron and Shelley visited Lausanne in 1816, as did Wordsworth in 1790 and 1820; Dickens resided here twice: in 1846, where he was visited by, among others, Thackeray and Tennyson; and again in 1853. It was during his stay in Lausanne (1921–22) that **TS Eliot** wrote *The Waste Land*, which secured his international reputation. Literary salons flourished. The best known local figures, however, were Dr Tissot, who lived in the 18C and was known as the "Healer of the Sick of Europe", Dr Jules Gonin, an eye surgeon who specialised in operating on detached retinas, and Maurice Lugeon (d. 1953), an outstanding geologist and an authority on the Alps.

Today, the city hosts festivals throughout the year, including cultural Festival de la Cité, Athlestissima at Olympic stadium, and a marathon in the autumn.

☙ WALKING TOUR

OLD TOWN

1hr. ☙ Longer guided tours from May–Oct every Tue and Fri at 3pm; ⊜40CHF. For further information, contact Lausanne Tourist Office. Depart from place St François.

Place de la Palud

Lined by old houses and by the Renaissance façade of the town hall, which proudly bears the arms of the city of Lausanne, this square is adorned with the Fountain of Justice (16C–18C). Nearby, an animated clock strikes the hours of the day, exhibiting a gallery of historical figures. The curious covered **staircase** beyond the fountain leads through to the cathedral.

Cathedral★★

ⓘ *Open 7am–7pm, Sat–Sun 8am–7pm (5.30 pm in winter). ℘(0)21 316 71 61.*
This is the finest Gothic building in Switzerland. Its construction began during the episcopate of St Amadeus (1145–59) and was completed in the mid-13C; it was consecrated in 1275 and entirely restored in the late 19C. The east end abuts two picturesque square towers, dominated by the lantern-tower at the transept crossing. Both it and the bell tower are reminiscent of Anglo-Norman

architecture, clearly marking the transition from Romanesque to Gothic.

The **south door**, known as the Painted Doorway, is adorned with a fine group of 13C sculptures. The pillars supporting the roof bear figures of the Prophets. The lintel is carved with low reliefs. The Montfalcon Doorway is named for the bishops Aymon and Sébastien de Montfalcon (1517, restored in the early 20C). In a chapel on the right, murals (1505) portray the life of the Virgin Mary.

Other features are influenced by the English Gothic style: note the original arrangement of sturdy columns, alternating with pairs of slender pillars. The rare and unusual 13C **stalls** feature exceptionally fine figures on the cheek pieces. Other stalls, in the Flamboyant style (16C), are in the St-Maurice chapel. In the south arm of the transept a 13C rose window, *Imago Mundi* (elements, seasons, months, and signs of the Zodiac), is remarkably harmonious. In the chancel rests the tomb of Othon I of Grandson. In the ambulatory note the tomb of the 13C bishop-builder Roger de Vico-Pisano.

Lausanne is one of the last towns to maintain a nightwatch. From the top of the cathedral tower the nightwatchman cries the hour between 10pm and 2am.

Tower

Access to the stairway (224 steps) at the end of the south aisle. ⓞ*Ascent 8.30am–11.30am, 1.30pm–5.30pm (4.30pm in winter), Sun 2pm–5.30pm (4.30pm in winter).* ⓞ*Closed 1 and 2 Jan and 25 Dec.* ⊜*4CHF.* ℘*(0)21 316 71 61.* From the top of the tower there is a fine **view**★ of the town, Lake Geneva, and the Alps. The parvis of the cathedral affords bird's-eye views of the town and the lake.

Go round the cathedral to the left of the east end, rue Cité-Derrière, a small medieval street decorated with wrought-iron signs.

▸ *Two museums are located just to the right of the cathedral.*

Musée de Design et d'Arts Appliqués Contemporains (Museum of Contemporary Design and Applied Arts)

🕐*Open 11am–6pm.* 🕐*Closed Mon (except Jul and Aug), 1 Jan, and 25 Dec.* ✆*10CHF (combined ticket with Musée Historique* ✆*15CHF). Free entry 1st Sat of month.* ♿ 🖉*(0)21 315 25 30.*

This museum devoted to design and contemporary art includes early exhibits coming from Egypt and China along with glass sculptures made by contemporary artists.

Musée Historique de Lausanne

🕐*Open Tue, Wed, Thu 11am–6pm; Fri, Sat–Sun 11am–5pm.* 🕐*Closed Mon (except in Jul and Aug, open 11am– 6pm) and religious holidays.* ✆*8CHF.* 🖉*(0)21 315 41 01. www.lausanne. ch/mhl.*

Rooms of the former bishop's palace have been restored to house these collections, which recall the town's history from prehistoric times to today. The first section features a vast miniature model of the city as it was in 1638. Several 19C displays include a general store, grocery shop, printing house and photographer's studio. Note the safe which once belonged to the Kohler House (1828) with its original and elaborate ironwork.

Château St-Marie

This 15C brick and stone castle was originally the residence of the bishops of Lausanne and then the Bernese bailiffs. The cantonal government sits there today. The terrace affords a sweeping **view** of Lausanne and Lake Geneva.

▷ *Continue along rue Cité-Derrière. Then turn left into avenue de l'Université, which leads to Place de la Riponne, situated at the foot of the promontory.*

PALAIS DE RUMINE

Built in the early 20C it houses the library and these five museums:

Musée des Beaux-Arts★

🕐*Open Tue, Wed and Thu 10am–6pm, Fri, Sat–Sun and public holidays, 11am– 5pm.* 🕐*Closed Mon, 1 Jan and 25 Dec.* ✆*8CHF.* ♿ 🖉*(0)21 316 34 45.*

Most of the paintings in this Museum of Fine Arts in the first three rooms are the work of Swiss nationals, many of whom were born in the region. There are many works by Lausanne artist Félix Vallotton, of whom the museum possesses the largest **state collection★**.

This section ends with French painters, namely Largillière, Géricault, Courbet, Cézanne, Bonnard, Renoir, Degas, Matisse, Marquet, Vlaminck, Vuillard, and Utrillo. Also, sculptures of Rodin and Giacometti are exhibited alongside

Palais de Rumine

Christof Schuerpf/Switzerland Tourism

more recent works by Nauman and Boltanski.

Musée de Géologie
First floor, on the left. ⏱*Open Tue–Thu 11am–6pm (5pm Fri and Sat–Sun).* ⏱*Closed 1 Jan and 25 Dec.* ⊜*6CHF, no charge first Sat in the month.* ✆*(0)21 316 33 90. www.unil.ch/meg.*
The Geological Museum contains rock specimens from the country plus relief models and a skeleton of a mammoth.

Musée de Paléontologie
On the right, opposite the Geological Museum.
A collection of plant and animal fossils and skeletons.

Musée de Zoologie
Second floor. Same hours as the Musée de Géologie.
The Zoology Museum houses specimens of flora from countries all over the world. Displays include a comparative anatomy between Man and the animal race, a living Mexican ant colony, and a gallery of mineralogy.

Salle d'Archéologie et d'Histoire
Sixth floor. Same hours as the Musée de Géologie.
The History and Archaeology Museum displays artefacts discovered during excavations of local sites.

PROMENADE DE SAUVABELIN
1h30mins. Take the number 16 bus from Place St-François or Lausanne-Flon and get off at the Lac de Sauvabelin stop.
A pleasant walk for the family, this pretty rural route heads to the Sauvabelin Lake, to the north of the town, to Château St-Maire, near to the cathedral. From time to time the paths crosses the route of St-Jacques-de-Compostelle.
On Sundays, families from Lausanne come here to relax in the countryside, just a stone's throw from the town.
It is possible to cross the lake in a boat or to take a walk around the perimeter. There's also a restaurant, childrens' playgrounds and animals (sheep, pigs and goats. Take the path beside the Pinte à Fromage restaurant.

Sauvabelin Tower
⏱*Summer 9am–9pm, winter 9am–5pm.* ⊜*No charge.* ✆*(0)21 315 42 74. www.tour-de-sauvabelin-lausanne.ch.*
This 35m wooden tower was erected in 2003 and has ever since been the major attraction of the park. After the climb of 151 steps visitors can enjoy a 360 degree view over Lausanne, Lake Geneva, the Alps, the back country and the Jura.
At the base of the tower, take the gently inclining path and then turn left.
At the crossroads, go straight ahead (following the yellow tourist markers) until reaching a road bordered with a stand of trees. Go past the Chalet Suisse restaurant.

Vue du Signal★★
Alt. 643m/2 109ft.
This belvedere *(viewing table, telescope)* affords a pleasant **view** of Lake Geneva, the Savoy, Fribourg and the Vaud Alps and, in the foreground, the historic centre of Lausanne.

Fondation de l'Hermitage (Hermitage Foundation)
2 route du Signal. ⏱*Exhibitions from 25 Jan–28 May and 21 Jun–28 Oct. Every day except Mon, 10am–6pm (Thu 9pm).* ⏱*Closed between the exhibitions.* ☜*Guided visits (1hr) Thu 6.30pm and Sun 3pm.* ⊜*5 CHF in addition to the 15 CHF entry ticket (children free).* ✆*(0)21 320 50 01 or (0)21 312 50 13 to find out more about the exhibitions. www.fondation-hermitage.ch.*
This former abode of the Vaud Family, the Bugnion was built in 1841 and is surrounded by gardens with rare plants. It hosts temporary art and history exhibitions. From the lawns there is a good view of Château St-Maire, the cathedral and the lake.
Follow the yellow markers to return to the town. The path which goes through woodland, leads to the Place de la Barre which has a pretty fountain, close to Château St-Maire.

Collection de l'Art Brut

Christof Schuepf/Switzerland Tourism

ADDITIONAL SIGHTS
Collection de l'Art Brut★

🕐 *Open Tue–Sun 11am–6pm.*
Also open Mon Jul-Aug, pub hols.
8CHF. ℘(0)21 315 25 70.
www.artbrut.ch.

The four floors of this unique museum—housed in the former stables of Beaulieu Château (18C)—present 1 000 objects (out of some 5 000) collected by the painter Jean Dubuffet since 1945 and donated to the city.

The paintings, drawings, sculptures, modeling, and embroidery are the work of schizophrenics, inmates confined to prison cells or psychiatric hospitals, spiritualist mediums, and others.

Montriond Park

On this spot where, in 1037, the first Truce of God was proclaimed in the district, there is a great esplanade reached by a ramp and a staircase.

The **view**★★ extends southward over Ouchy, the shores of Lake Geneva and to the Alps. One section of the park is by a **botanical garden** (🕐 *open May–Sept, daily 10am–6.30pm; Mar–Apr and Oct, daily 10am–5.30pm; no charge; museum open by appointment; ℘(0)21 316 99 88*).

It consists of an arboretum, an alpine garden with mountain flora, flowers, succulents, and a variety of medicinal, carnivorous, and aquatic species.

Parc Mon Repos

This pleasant garden is also the site of the Empire style villa where Voltaire used to live. To the north of the park the Federal Court of Switzerland is housed in a huge building.

Musée Romain de Lausanne-Vidy

24 chemin du Bois-de-Vaux (from Lausanne, follow signs to Geneva)
🕐 *Open every day except Mon, 11am–6pm (8pm on Thu). Closed 24, 25, 31 Dec and 1 Jan. 8 CHF, No charge 1st Sat of month. ℘(0)21 315 41 85. www.lausanne.ch/mrv.*

This museum was built in 1993 on the remains of Gallo-Roman site called Lousonna which lasted until the fourth century. The settlement which lies on the banks of the lake had a population of between 1 500 and 2 000 people. From the house a well and a room decorated with frescoes has been preserved. The room also displays items of furniture from the time and relics from everyday life, as well as temporary exhibitions.

Pully

The old village of Pully has become a residential suburb of Lausanne.
From the terrace of the Church of St Germain a charming **view**★ opens out onto the eastern part of Lake Geneva to the French side of the lake from Évian to Meillerie.

In the church precincts stand a museum and the remains of a Roman villa.

Musée de Pully

⊙*Open Wed–Sun 2pm–6pm.* ⊙*Closed Easter, Christmas and according to temporary exhibitions.* ☞*7CHF.* ♿ ♪*(0)21 729 55 81.*

The museum is located near the house where **Charles-Ferdinand Ramuz** (1878–1947) lived until his death. The museum displays souvenirs of Ramuz together with paintings by contemporary artists from Pully. Visitors may also admire clay sculptures by Derain and precious objects (writing desk, model of royal barge) that belonged to the King of Siam, a resident of Pully between 1925 and 1945.

OUCHY★★

Ouchy is linked to Lausanne by its *métro*, an electrically-driven funicular once known as the "rope" (cable-driven) and later as the "tire" (mounted on wheels). Ouchy—a famous hotel resort and popular spot for Sunday strollers—is also one of the liveliest navigation centres on the lake, now that its time as a fishing port has passed. The large sailing port adjoining Place de la Navigation has been refurbished and is now reserved for pedestrians, who can enjoy its charming fountains and four giant chess games. Many leisure boats are also available for cruises. The shaded quays, adorned with tropical plants and flowers, stretch for over 1km/0.6mi and are prolonged eastward by the lakeside path. This charming route offers lovely **views**★★ of the harbour, Lake Geneva and the Chablais mountains.

Musée Olympique★★ (Olympic Museum)

⊙*Open 9am–6pm.* ⊙*Closed Mon (except Easter Mon), 1 Jan, and 25 Dec.* ☞*14CHF.* ♿ ♪*(0)21 621 65 11.*

This museum sits on the shores of Lake Geneva, with a public garden enhanced by statues, fountains, and pavilions. The **park** extends across terraced slopes, offering nice views. All along the path to the museum entrance (420m/1 378ft, the length of an Olympic stadium), a series of statues symbolises the marriage of sport and culture.

The modern ensemble, inspired by a Greek temple, is the work of architects Pedro Ramirez Vázquez and Lausanne native Jean-Pierre Cahen. In front of the white marble façade (the stone is from the Greek island of Thassos), two rows of four columns carry the names of the towns which have hosted the Olympic Games and the names of the Olympic Committee presidents. In a granite bowl, decorated with allegorical motifs illustrating the myth of Prometheus, the Olympic flame burns forever.

Musée Olympique

see map II

LAUSANNE
map I

| 0 | 200 m |
| 0 | 200 yds |

LAKE GENEVA

WHERE TO STAY		WHERE TO EAT	
Agora	1	Lacustre (Le)	2
Angleterre & Résidence. de	3	Olympique (Restaurant du musée)	4
Aulac	5	Pêcherie (La)	6
Mirabeau	7	Port de Pully	8
Pierrettes (Les)	9		
Pré Fleuri	10		

Ground Floor – Largely devoted to the history of the Games, with particular emphasis on ancient Greece. Terracotta figures, marble and bronze sculptures, vases decorated with figures of athletes, gold laurel wreaths, and *strigils* are exhibited.

Also on display: all the torches that have carried the Olympic flame, from the Berlin Games of 1936 to the present.

Note two fine bronze statues—*The American Athlete* by Rodin and *The Archer* by Bourdelle.

Level 1 – One side is devoted to the Summer Games, the other to the Winter Games. Videos enable visitors to relive great moments of Olympic history and share the physical effort and strong emotions experienced by top-level

129

athletes. Opening and closing ceremonies are re-enacted on huge screens and interactive terminals provide answers to thousands of questions about the Games, the different events, the athletes, the records, etc.

EXCURSIONS
Lutry
▶ 4 km/2.5mi E of the town, via Avenue de l'Élysée, then road number 9.

This village with narrow streets is worthy of a short stop. It sits on Lake Geneva with its own small marina and the plus of a fine view of the Alps. The central square has an attractive fountain and a white painted church with an ornate Roman porch. As you leave the village, an imposing château (now a medical centre) can be seen among the vines.

Échallens
▶ 15km/9mi by avenue d'Échallens then take road number 5.

Located in a fertile cereal-growing agricultural area, this small town boasts a fascinating **Maison du Blé et du Pain** (◐open 8.30am–6pm; ◐closed Mon and two weeks at the end of the year; ⌾8CHF; ℘(0)21 881 50 71), set up in a restored 18C farmhouse.

The daily lives of peasants, millers, and bakers throughout the ages are illustrated by a diorama, a collection of farming tools, granaries, and a display of different types of baking ovens and mills. At the end of the visit, rolls, loaves, and croissants are prepared and baked before your eyes.

▲▲ Zoo de Servion
▶ 18km/11mi by the road to Bern.
◐Open 9am–7pm (6pm in winter). Last admission 1hr before closing.
⌾10CHF. ♿ ℘(0)21 903 16 71.

This estate is home to a wide range of animal species. After the Monkey Pavilion, visitors enter the tropical hothouse with exotic birds. Alongside the Ostrich Pavilion you will find Chilean flamingoes, as well as crowned cranes and pink-backed pelicans from Africa. Next come the red deer, American buffaloes, brown bears, and wolves.

Romainmôtier★
Alt. 676m/2 163ft. 44km/27.5mi N on the Pontarlier road. 323 Romainmôtier.
℘(0)24 453 14 79.
www.romainmotier.ch.

It is impossible to miss the charm of this old village encircling a plain but graceful Romanesque church. The church belongs to the abbey founded in the 5C by St Romanus and handed over to the monks of Cluny in the 10C.

The **church**★ (◐open daily 9am–noon, 1.30pm–6pm, Sun 1.30pm–5pm; exhibition and slide show (30min) 9am–noon, 1.30pm–6pm; ⌾4CHF; ℘(0)24 453 14 65) was built with Jura stone in the 11C and later modified, inspired by the church St-Pierre-le-Vieux. The transept and nave date from the 11C. A large, early-

St-Pierre-le-Viex, Romainmôtier

12C narthex is preceded by a 13C Gothic porch. Inside are 13C murals; pointed arches (13C) have replaced the original timbering; aisles have semicircular vaulting. The chancel contains priors' tombs of the 7C. The church has been Protestant since 1536. To the right of the façade, stands the former prior's house (now a tea room) dated 1605—but going back to the 13C—with a pepper-pot roofed turret and an embossed doorway.

Château de la Sarraz

▶ *27km/16.9mi N via road number 9. Guided visits available Jun–Aug.* ◷*Jun–Aug open every day except Mon 1pm–5pm; Apr–May, Sept and Oct, weekends 1pm–5pm.* ⊜*9 CHF.* ✆*(0)21 866 66 64.* This château is just outside the village. Built in the 11C and re-built in the 15C and 16C. The château sits in its own grounds and is an unusually shaped building, dominated in the centre by two square towers. A guided visit really

allows the visitor the chance to appreciate the wealth of fine furniture in its rooms, plus silverware, china items and chandeliers dating from between the 17C and 19C, paintings and precious antiques. In an old chapel close to the château there is an amazing 14C carved cenotaph of François de la Sarra.

Mosaïques d'Urba

▶ *2km/1m N of Orbe on the road to Yverdon.* ◷*Open Easter–Oct, 9am–noon, 1.30pm–5pm, Sat–Sun and public holidays 1.30pm–5.30pm.* ◷*Closed 1 Nov and Easter.* ⊜*5CHF.* ✆*079 745 98 47.*
Alongside the road, four separate pavilions house **Roman mosaics** dating back to the early 3C. Starting from the farm nearby, the themes are: Calendar of Divinities, the loveliest, consisting of polychrome medallions; pastoral scene with chariots, the most evocative; maze with lion and birds; geometric mosaic in black and white.

ADDRESSES

🛏STAY

⊜ **Les Pierrettes** – *In Saint-Sulpice, on the route Cantonale 19. 22 rooms.* ✆*(0)21 691 25 25.* Conveniently situated at the western entrance to Lausanne. Each room has a private terrace with a table and garden chairs. Relax on the lawn or by the outdoor pool in summer.

⊜ **Les Voyageurs** –*19 rue Grand-St-Jean.* ✆*(0)21 319 91 11. www.voyageurs.ch. 33 rooms.* This hotel, nestling in the old part of Lausanne, is an ideal starting-point to discover the city on foot.

⊜⊜ **Agora** – *9 avenue du Rond-Point.* ✆*(0)21 555 59 55. www.fhotels.ch. 82 rooms.* Modern hotel decorated in bold colours: blue, pink and silver. Large rooms. The lobby features a sculpture of white marble.

⊜⊜ **Aulac** – *In Ouchy, 4 place de la Navigation.* ✆*(0)21 612 15 00. www.aulac.ch. 84 rooms.* Hotel situated just opposite the lake, near the landing stage for excursions to Évian (trip there and back overnight).

⊜⊜ **City** – *5 rue Caroline.* ✆*(0)21 320 21 41. www.fhotels.ch. 51 rooms.* Located near the Pont Bessière (no restaurant).

⊜⊜ **Pré Fleuri** – *1 r. du Centre, St-Sulpice* ✆*(0)21 697 40 40. www.hotelprefleuri.ch. 21 rooms.* ⊠. A pleasant hotel with rooms overlooking a garden and swimming pool.

⊜⊜⊜ **Angleterre et Résidence** – *In Ouchy, 11 place du Port.* ✆*(0)21 613 34 34. www.laresidence.ch. 75 rooms.* Three imposing pavilions exuding great charm, including an 18C hôtel particulier, located just off the lakeshore. Outdoor pool and ornamental garden. Complete the experience with delicious meal at the gourmet restaurant.

⊜⊜⊜ **Mirabeau** – *31 Avenue de la gare* ✆*(0)21 341 42 43. www.mirabeau.ch. 72 rooms.* An attractive hotel close to the station and the centre of town. The style is art deco, with every comfort offered in its rooms. Half of the rooms have a balcony, a third of them a lake view.

♥/EAT

Restaurant du musée Olympique – *1 quai d'Ouchy, Ouchy. ℘(0)21 621 67 08. www.olympic.org. Open daily 9am–6pm. Closed Sun and Nov–end Apr.* Worth dining here especially if you are visiting the museum on a fine day as there is a good view of Ouchy, the lake and the museum's gardens. Good value traditional style cooking.

Brasserie Bavaria – *10 rue du Petit-Chêne. ℘(0)21 323 39 13. www.la bavaria.ch. Closed Sun & Mon.* On the boundaries of the old city, an old-fashioned restaurant with a nostalgic décor serves sauerkraut and cold meats made from pork. Remarkable choice of beers.

Le Lacustre – *In Ouchy, on the landing stage, quai Dapples. ℘(0)21 617 42 00. Closed mid-Dec–mid-Feb.* The Brasserie offers nice views of the lake, while the Café Français offers views of the park.

Port de Pully – *rue du Port 7, In the port of Pully, skirting the lake to the E. ℘(0)21 728 78 78. www.pullyport.ch. Closed Sun night & Mon.* Charming establishment facing the marina. Dining choices are brasserie, traditional restaurant or rotisserie.

Café Romand – *2 place St-François. ℘(0)21 312 63 75. www.caferomand.com. Closed Sun and public holidays.* Typical old Lausanne brasserie gathers a local crowd. Specialties such as cheese fondue and *tête de veau* (head of veal).

Mövenpick – *In Ouchy, 4 avenue de Rhodanie. ℘(0)21 612 76 12. La Pêcherie restaurant closed in Jul and Sat lunch.* Pleasant location facing the lake and its marina. **La Pêcherie** is one of several restaurants where meals are served in a pleasant setting. Large choice of dishes. In the restaurant Le Général, where prices are more affordable, the life of General Guisan is illustrated with paintings and panels displayed on the walls.

À la Pomme de Pin – *11 rue Cité-Derrière. ℘(0)21 323 46 56. Closed Sat at lunchtime, Sun, public holidays.* A friendly establishment in a narrow street lying behind the cathedral.

Clients can choose between two dining rooms: simple fare in the café or a more elaborate and more expensive meal in the restaurant.

⚇NIGHTLIFE

Nestling in its superb setting on the shores of the lake, the **Ouchy** district is extremely lively, both during the day and at night. On a fine day, you can enjoy the many pavement cafés and their sunny terraces. Those yearning for an English atmosphere can go to **Sherlock's Pub** in Avenue de Rhodanie, where a disc jockey will liven up the evening. For beer drinkers, the **Bavaria** (rue du Petit-Chêne), one of the oldest cafés in town (1872), offers a selection of 22 different beers.

Finally, for those who appreciate jazz, the **Pianissimo** (rue des Deux-Marchés) with its outstanding pianist is definitely the place to go; live concerts of jazz-soul and occasionally rock are held at the **V.O.** (Place du Tunnel). The old vaults of a 14C cellar are the hallmark of the unusual **Disco Zille** (Rue Cité-Devant 10).

🛒 SHOPPING

Most main shopping streets are located in the old district and include: place St-François, rue des Terreaux, rue de l'Ale, rue Mauborget, rue Chaucrau, rue St-Laurent, rue de Bourg, rue St-Jean and rue St-François. **Department store:** Innovation (rue Centrale).

⚇THEATRE AND MUSIC

The high season is September to June.

Théâtre Arsenic – *57 rue de Genève. ℘(0)21 625 11 36. www.theatre-arsenic.ch.* Centre of Contemporary Drama.

Théâtre Vidy-Lausanne – *5 avenue E.-Jacques-Dalcroze. ℘(0)21 619 45 45. www.vidy.ch.* Stage performances.

L'Octogone – *41 avenue de Lavaux-Pully. ℘(0)21 721 36 20. www.theatre-octogon.ch.* Theatre, concerts, dance.

Le Petit Théâtre –*12 place de la Cathédrale. ℘(0)21 323 62 13. www.lepetittheatre.ch.* Theatre, plays for children.

Vevey★

Vevey occupies a beautiful site★★ facing the Savoy Alps at the mouth of the Veveyse Valley and the foot of Mount Pèlerin, with the blue sheet of Lake Geneva and the Alps making a splendid backdrop.

A BIT OF HISTORY

Already capital of the Lavaux vineyards, in the 19C Vevey became the cradle of the Swiss industry of milk and dietetic products, and also chocolate. The powerful Nestlé group has its headquarters here, together with its central laboratory and an experimental factory. Picturesque traditional markets (*Saturday mornings*) are held on place du Marché in July and August.

Nestlé

This world food-processing giant was founded by **Heinrich Nestlé**, who was born in Frankfurt am Main in 1814 and settled in Vevey in 1843, having first worked as a pharmacist. He had inherited a small business that manufactured fertiliser and mustard, and later developed an interest in baby food. Nestlé's baby cereal, introduced in 1867 and made from milk, wheat flour and sugar, became a great success. In the previous year, the Americans George and Charles Page had turned Cham into the leading European manufacturer of condensed

▶ **Population:** Vaud 17 676.
◔ **Michelin Map:**
   National 728: E6.
▧ **Info:** rue de Théatre
   ✆(0) 848 86 84 84.
   www.montreux-vevey.com.
▶ **Location:** Between
   Lausanne and Montreux.
   Alt. 400m/1 312ft.
☺ **Don't Miss:**
   The Alimentarium
   at Nestlé's former
   headquarters.
◔ **Timing:** Allow two days
   for museums and a
   lake excursion.
👪 **Kids:** The antique carousel
   along the lake front.

milk. In 1905, Nestlé and Cham merged under the name of Nestlé and Anglo-Swiss Condensed Milk Company. Other companies were later purchased by the group turning Nestlé into one of the world's leading companies.

A Distinguished Resident

Charles Spencer Chaplin was born in London in 1889 to a family of impoverished music-hall artistes. Charles and brother Sydney began performing at an early age in pantomime shows, which enabled them to travel abroad. During a tour of the United States in 1913,

Vevey

Stephan Engler/Switzerland Tourism

133

young Charles made the acquaintance of Mack Sennett, who directed and produced burlesque movies in Hollywood. Sennett immediately offered the young man a job, which led to the birth of the **The Little Tramp** character and his legendary silhouette. With his moustache, derby hat, baggy trousers falling onto out-sized shoes, tight frock coat and cane, distinctive shuffling gait and pale features, Chaplin became highly popular and gained international acclaim.

During the 1920s, his tumultuous private life was strongly criticised by the American press; after his second divorce, authorities requested that he be expelled from the country. In 1952, during McCarthy's anti-Communist campaigns, Chaplin left America with his family and settled in Corsier-sur-Vevey. In 1975, he was knighted by Queen Elizabeth II, and on 25 December 1977, he passed away in his Swiss home.

A statue of Chaplin has been erected by the city of Vevey on the shores of Lake Geneva, in front of the Alimentarium; his former home is to become the Chaplin Museum in 2012.

SIGHTS
Église St-Martin
The present church (1530) stands on a site originally occupied by an 11C sanctuary whose walls were discovered during excavation work.

The church is dominated by a large, square tower and four corner turrets. The terrace (viewing table) affords a sweeping **view**★ of the town, the Alps and Lake Geneva.

Musée Jenisch
◷Open Tue–Sun 11am–5.30pm. Closed 25 Dec and 1 Jan. ⌕12CHF. ♿ ℘(0)21 921 29 50. www.museejenisch.ch.
Inside this 19C neoclassical building are two museums. The ground floor houses the **Cantonal Prints Gallery**, presenting engravings by great masters of the past (Dürer, Rembrandt, Lorrain, Belletto, Corot) and by modern Swiss artists, which are shown in rotation. The **Fine Arts Museum** on the first floor displays temporary exhibitions of

works by Swiss and foreign artists from the 19C and 20C.

Musée Historique du Vieux-Vevey
◷Open Apr–Oct, Tue–Sun 11am–5pm; Nov–Mar 2pm–5pm only. ◷Closed 1 Jan and 25 Dec. ⌕6CHF. ℘(0)21 921 07 22. www.museehistoriquevevey.ch.
This museum is housed in the castle which was once the residence of the Bernese bailiffs. It relates the history of the area and contains a fine collection of furniture from the Gothic period to the 17C, small wrought-iron objects and caskets, costumes and local mementoes. On the first floor, visit the **Museum of the Wine-Growers Fraternity** (Confrérie des Vignerons), where models of the costumes worn at wine-growers' festivals (since 1791) are kept, together with prints, records and banners used during these festivities.

Musée Suisse de l'Appareil Photographique★
99 Grande-Place. ◷Open Tue–Sun, 11am–5.30pm. ◷Closed 25 Dec. ⌕8CHF. ♿ ℘(0)21 925 34 80. www.cameramuseum.ch.
The five floors of this **Swiss Camera Museum** present the history of photography, its famous inventors, and its techniques through a remarkable collection of cameras dating from early models to the most recent and sophisticated devices including digital imaging. One floor is devoted to photographic equipment made in Switzerland.

The camera obscura in the entrance hall provides an insight into the birth of photography. Magic lanterns illustrate the theory of projection; the importance of photography in the army is explained via spy cameras that can be hidden in everyday objects.

Another section includes the first small cameras, first flashes, early Swiss cameras (Alpa, Escopette de Darier), famous names such as Kodak and Leica (1930–40), multi-image cameras, miniature cameras, image transmission and projection, and tracing the development of photography and film industries.

Alimentarium

Andy Mettler/Switzerland Tourism

The "**clic-clac**" studio introduces children to the art of photography.

Alimentarium★★

Quai Perdonnet. ⏰*Open Tue–Sun 10am–6pm.* ⏰*Closed Mon exc Easter Mon and Pentecost, 1 Jan, 24, 25 and 31 Dec.* 💳*10CHF.* ☎*(0)21 924 41 11. www.alimentarium.ch.*
Since 1985 this neoclassical mansion, formerly headquarters of Nestlé, has housed a food museum. Exhibits are arranged by themes. *Cuisiner* (Cooking) illustrates cooking methods found around the world at different periods in history and in various ethnic and social environments, as well as various utensils. *Manger* (Eating) illustrates the importance of pleasure and communication in eating, as does the art of laying a table. This section highlights plants and animals eaten by humans, celebratory and everyday meals, and how the act of eating differs by culture. The New York push-cart and snack trolley men can be considered to be the precursors of the fast-food industry, also explored here. *Acheter* (Buying) resembles a supermarket and explores agricultural and production methods, food safety, and our eating habits. *Digérer* (Digestion) is portrayed through biology, including the importance of sports. The Nestlé Room traces the history and importance of the now-global company, including advertisements and packaging dating back to

1867. There is also, of course, chocolate! There are cooking classes for adults and children (*in French only*) and a garden planted with herbs and vegetables, interspersed with picnic areas.

EXCURSIONS
Mont-Pèlerin Resort★★

Alt. 810m/2 657ft. ▷ *Round trip of 25km/15.5mi about 30min.*
♿*Consult the local maps under LAKE GENEVA. Leave Vevey by the Châtel-St-Denis-Fribourg road 2.5km/1.5mi after having passed the road to Chardonne on your left, turn left toward Attalens, then sharp left again toward the Pèlerin or Pilgrim Mountain.*
Several of these roads run corniche fashion among the vines. From a point near the arrival station of the funicular, there is a fabulous wide open **view**★★ of Lake Geneva and the crest of the Vaud Alps (Dent de Jaman, Rochers de Naye, Aï Tower). The drive back through Chardonne and Chexbres is along roads with magnificent views of the Dents du Midi and the summits of the Haut-Chablais in Savoy.

La Tour-de-Peilz

▷ *2km/1.2mi by road number 9 heading towards Montreux.*
The castle was commissioned by the Comtes de Savoie (13C, altered in the 18C). The ramparts, moats, and two corner turrets still stand. Inside the

former keep is the **Musée Suisse du Jeu** (○*open Tue–Sun 11am–5.30pm and Mon during public holidays;* ○*closed 1 Jan and 25 Dec;* ☞*9CHF;* ℘*(0)21 977 23 00. www.museesuisse.ch*), a collection of games from all countries and all epochs. These are split into five groups: educational games, strategic games, simulation games, games of skill, and games of chance. Each section stresses the qualities required for playing and is illustrated by a series of examples. Visitors may test their own natural ability by playing, learning, and even creating new games. If you bypass the castle on the left, you will come to the yachting harbour; from there you can take a pleasant walk along the shores of the lake. Opposite stands the Grammont, dominating the landscape from a height of 2 172m/6 800ft.

Oron-Le-Châtel

Alt. 720m/2 362ft. 25km/15.6mi.
▶ *Take the motorway from Vevey (direction Lausanne) and exit at J15 following Bern and then Oron.*
This little medieval village is dominated by the imposing mass of its fortified castle (℘*(0)21 907 88 14; http://oron-le-chatel.ch*).

Castle

☞*Guided tours (45min) Apr–Sept, Sat–Sun, 10am–noon, 2pm–6pm.* ☞*10CHF.* ℘*(0)21 907 90 51.*
This forbidding citadel on a rocky promontory was built in the late 12C and early 13C. An impressive display of various families' coats of arms is in the main hall. For 241 years the castle was the official residence of the Bernese bailiffs. The rooms on the first floor give a good idea of French middle-class life The dining hall houses some superb collections of Sèvres and Limoges porcelain, as well as pieces of Wedgwood. The library is believed to contain around 18 000 books dating from the 16C to the 19C.
The visit ends with a series of tastefully decorated rooms: music room, smoking salon decorated with wallpaper printed with hunting scenes, playroom and study for the children, tea parlor

(Louis XV commode in rosewood), prior's bedroom, etc.

ADDRESSES

▨STAY

◌◌ **Hôtel des Négociants** – *27 r. du Conseil.* ℘*(0)21 922 70 11. www.hotel negociants.ch. 23 rooms.* ⬚. A hotel located in the pedestrian zone, conveniently located near to the lake, the station and the town's cinemas. Airy plain rooms decorated with jolly colours.

◌◌ **Hostellerie de Genève** – *Pl. du Marché 11.* ℘*(0)21 921 45 77. www.hotelgeneve.ch. 23 rooms.* ⬚.
A small but well located hotel on the liveliest of the squares in Vevey, next to the markets. Comfortable rooms with a shaded terrace; ideal for the summer months

◌◌◌◌ **Hôtel du Lac** – *1 rue d'Italie.* ℘*(0)21 921 06 06. 50 rooms.* A stone's throw from the harbour and the lake, this venerable hotel features comfortable rooms and a lovely terrace with a private pool giving onto the lake.

♟/EAT

◌◌ **La Terrasse** – *Corseaux, 8 chemin du Basset.* ℘*(0)21 921 31 88. Closed Mon and 23 Dec–22 Jan.* Good food and reasonable prices, whether you choose the set menu or go à la carte. In summer, meals are served on the terrace.

◌◌◌ **Hostellerie chez Chibrac** – *Mont-Pèlerin.* ℘*(0)21 922 61 61. www. chezchibrac.ch. Closed Sun eve, Mon and mid-Oct–1 Mar.* A simple establishment with a congenial atmosphere.

◌◌◌ **Á la Montagne** – *Chardonne, 21 rue du Village* ℘*(0)21 921 29 30. Closed Mon, Sun, 23 Dec–7 Jan and 30 Jun–15 Jul.* A small, unassuming family inn offering tasty dishes, and affordable prices.

◌◌◌◌ **Restaurant Denis Martin "Le Château"** – *2 Rue du Château.* ℘*(0)21 921 12 10. Open eve only. Closed Sun, Mon and 23 Dec–15 Jan.* Located in a baronial villa with creative cuisine to match. Fixed price menus include one with 15 mini courses.

Montreux★★

Thanks to its beautiful **site**★★ and pleasant surroundings—which have won literary fame since **Jean-Jacques Rousseau** chose the village of Clarens, now a suburb, as the setting for *La Nouvelle Héloïse*—Montreux is the most frequented resort on Lake Geneva and has acquired an international reputation. It stretches along the shores of a large bay facing south and rises in tiers to heights covered with woods and vineyards which shelter it from winds. Its sumptuous palaces and Edwardian hotels are reminiscent of the French Riviera. It is an important cultural city, hosting many festivals and major world events such as the International Choral Festival (the week following Easter), the Golden Rose Television Festival (spring), a jazz festival (July) and the September Musical Concert (*see Calendar of Events*).

▶ **Population:** Vaud 24 520.
◔ **Michelin Map:** National Map 729: E6.
🚩 **Info:** 5 rue du Théâtre. ✆(0)848 86 84 84. www.montreux-vevey.com.
◐ **Location:** Montreux is on the eastern edge of Lake Geneva. Alt. 398m/1 305ft.
⊕ **Don't Miss:** The panorama from Les Pléiades on the Avants-Sonloup driving tour.
◔ **Timing:** Allow two or three days for the city and nearby excursions; longer if you are attending the world-famous Montreux Jazz Festival (July).
♟ **Kids:** The Museum of Food at former Nestlé headquaraters in nearby Vevey, easily reached by public transport.

SIGHTS

Many local trains leave Montreux station for the nearby summits, offering panoramic views of Geneva, the Mont Blanc, the Matterhorn: the two most famous are the Montreux-Oberland Bernois (MOB) and the Montreux Crystal Panoramic Express (*reservations necessary*).

Steamboat cruises are available for tours of the Upper Lake.

Walk up through old Montreux to the terrace of the church for a lovely **view**★★ of Clarens-Montreux-Territet and the lake with the Château de Chillon, the mountains of the Savoy Chablais and the sparkling Dents du Midi.

Montreux

© Adam Gilinski/Montreux-Vevey Tourisme

CHÂTEL-ST-DENIS

★★**les Pléiades**
1360

le Molard
△ 1752

Bains de l'Alliaz

Lally

St-Légier-
la-Chiésaz

Cape au Moine
1941 △

Blonay

LAUSANNE

Baye de Clarens

Saumont

A 9

Brent

Sonloup Pass
1149

Chailly

Chaulin

1188
△

les Avants ★

le Châtelard

Chamby

LAUSANNE

Chernex

Baye de Montreux

Dent de Jaman
△ 1874

9

Sonzier

Clarens

Glion

Caux

★★**MONTREUX**

2042 ★★
★★★**ROCHERS DE NAYE**

la Veraye

LAKE GENEVA

Territet

MONTREUX

★★Chillon

N

0   1500 m
0   1500 yds

MARTIGNY

The Vaud Riviera

The mild climate (average annual temperature 10°C/50°F) and lake shore earns it the name of Vaud Riviera. This exceptional climate produces varied and luxuriant vegetation: vines grow at an altitude of nearly 600m/1 968.5ft, walnut trees up to 700m/2 296.5ft and fruit trees up to 1 000m/3 281ft.

Fig, bay, almond and mulberry trees and even cypresses, magnolias and palm trees flourish on the lake shores at truly Mediterranean temperatures. In spring, the fields overlooking the town are covered with narcissi.

Musée du Vieux-Montreux

40 rue de la Gare. ○*Open Mar–7 Nov, daily 10am–noon, 2pm–5pm.* ◎*6CHF.* ℘*(0)21 963 13 53.*

In the heart of the old quarter, the museum presents a lively account of

the region's eventful history. Prehistoric times, Roman era, Middle Ages, reconstruction of interiors from different centuries, the expansion of tourism, technology, coins, architecture and town planning are some of the themes presented on three levels, explaining the development of the city of Montreux throughout the ages.

Audiorama

At Montreux-Territet, route de Chillon, Villeneuve. ○*Open Tue–Sun 1pm–6pm.* ◎*10CHF.* ℘ *℘(0)21 963 22 33.*

The **Swiss National Audio-visual Museum** presents major events in the history of radio and television through equipment used at the time.

The Champ-de-Mars to Lausanne transmitter (1922), created to ensure aircraft security can be seen on the ground floor.

View from Rochers de Naye

Stephan Engler/Switzerland Tourism

EXCURSIONS
Rochers de Naye★★★

2 042m/6 699ft. About 3hr there and back, including 2hr by rack railway.
In summer, an old-fashioned steam train departs every hour, except at noon, from 9.05am–5.05pm. In winter, last departure at 3.05pm. ⊛*Fare there and back 59CHF. Other tourist train— Montreux, Bernese Oberland—MOB: 12 panoramic-express trains per day in summer, Sat–Sun all year round.*
From the summit of Rochers de Naye you will enjoy a bird's-eye view east of Lake Geneva and a splendid panorama of the Bernese, Valais and Savoy Alps and the Jura.

🚗 DRIVING TOUR

AVANTS-SONLOUP TOUR★★
27km/16mi - allow approx 1hr.

🖐*See map p138. Leave Montreux by the route signed "Les Avants".*

On the left, the Château du Châtelard, with its large rectangular 15C crenellated tower stands out.

◗ *4km/2.5mi from Montreux turn left towards Chernex-Les-Avants, then left 200m/220yd farther on before Chamby (two bends) and cross the railway line, and another right turn for Les Avants.*

Blonay
4km/2.5mi E. 29 Grande-Place, Vevey – 1800. ☎(0)21 922 20 20.
The **Chemin de Fer-Musée Blonay-Chamby** (*Musée Blonay-Chamby;* 🕐*operates May–Oct, Sat–Sun 10am– 6pm; Jul–Aug, Thu and Fri 2pm–6pm;* ⊛*14CHF;* ♿ *☎(0)21) 943 21 21*) has given new life to a railway section which opened in 1902 and closed down in 1966. Electric trams and early steam-driven trains take travellers along a steep, winding route covering a distance of 2.95km/1.8mi. Halfway up the hill stands the former shed. It has been converted into a museum displaying early vehicles, including a 1914 postal van, a 1904 tram from the Fribourg area, and a steam engine which once linked Le Locle to Les Brenets.

Les Pléiades★★
From Lally 30min on foot there and back.
From the Les Pléiades summit (alt. 1 360m/4 462ft) there is a **panorama**★★ of Lake Geneva, the Molard, the Dent de Jaman, the Rochers de Naye, the Savoy Alps, and the Mont Blanc Range.
Return by the Blonay road which and reveals, to the right, **Château de Blonay**, dating back to the 11C.

Les Avants★
Alt. 968m/3 176ft.
This is a small resort overlooked on the southeast by the Dent de Jaman and the Naye Rocks.

Col de Sonloup
Alt. 1 149m/3 769.5ft.
A fine **view**★ of the Rochers de Naye, the Dents du Midi and the Savoy Alps.

◗ *The return to Montreux is via the villages of Saumont, Chamby and Chernex. Narrow at first, this road reveals new glimpses of the lake and of the Vevey-Blonay region.*

ADDRESSES

🛏 STAY

🍴🛏 **Auberge des Planches** – *2 rue du Temple.* ℘*(0)21 963 49 73.* **36 rooms. Closed Jan.** Located on a steep street on the outskirts of town. Rooms tend to be large and decorated in rustic style. The Don Chico Restaurant has Mexican-style décor and serves typical Mexican dishes.

🍴🛏 **Hôtel du Pont** – *12 rue du Pont.* ℘*(0)21 963 22 49.* **10 rooms.** Congenial establishment in the old district, at the foot of the funicular. Restaurant offers traditional cuisine, and Italian specialties.

🍴🛏 **Eden Palace au Lac** – *11 rue du Théâtre.* ℘*(0)21 966 08 00. www.eden montreux.ch.* **100 rooms. Closed Jan.** Who hasn't dreamed of spending the night in a sumptuous, turn-of-the-century palace? The rates may seem outrageously high but they are definitely worth it. The Victorian architecture, period furniture, lofty rooms, gastronomic cuisine, and romantic atmosphere will transport you back in time, while offering all the advantages of modern sophistication!

🍴🛏 **Eurotel Riviera** – *81 Grand-Rue.* ℘*(0)21 966 22 22.* **152 rooms.** Centrally located hotel with a pontoon for mooring boats and the choice between two restaurants: the Bel-Horizon and the Matara.

🍴🛏 **Golf-Hôtel René Capt** – *35 rue de Bon-Port.* ℘*(0)21 966 25 25. www.golf-hotel-montreux.ch. Closed 22 Dec–mid-Jan.* **75 rooms.** Away from the bustling town centre, this hotel has a pretty garden overlooking the lake shores.

🍴🛏 **Masson** – *In Veytaux, 5 rue Bonivard.* ℘*(0)21 966 00 44. www.hotel masson.ch. Closed 18 Oct–25 Mar.* **31 rooms.** The oldest hotel in Montreux (1829) has undeniable charm, evoking the splendor of bygone times. The small garden is perfect for long, relaxing afternoons in the shade.

🍽/EAT

🍴🛏 **Restaurant du Montagnard** – *In Villard-sur-Chamby, 7km/4.3mi N.* ℘*(0)21 964 36 84. Closed Mon, Tue.* A genuine 17C mountain farmhouse serving traditional fare. Lively evenings with folk music.

🍴🛏 **Auberge de la Cergniaulaz** – *In Les Avants, 8km/5mi N by the Col de Sonloup and the road to Orgevaux.* ℘*(0)21 964 42 76. Closed Mon, Tue, and Jan–Mar.* Traditional Swiss specialties served on a lovely terrace.

🍴🛏 **Caveau des Vignerons** – *30 bis rue Industrielle.* ℘*(0)21 963 25 70. www.caveaudesvignons.ch.* Décor focuses on grapes and the art of oenology (display of tools used during grape harvesting). The restaurant serves fondue, raclette, and meat on hot slates, and local wines.

🍴🛏 **Le Museum** – *40 rue de la Gare.* ℘*(0)21 963 16 62. www.museum-montreux.ch. Closed Sun and Mon.* This former convent house dating back to the 13C features three fine dining halls with vaulted ceilings. Fondue, raclette, and grilled meat are served in a rustic décor with an open fireplace.

🎭 NIGHTLIFE

The Grand-Rue has live music: the **Sunset Bar and Piano Bar,** located in the Hôtel Royal Plaza (97) and **Harry's New York** Bar (Raffles Le Montreaux Palace Hotel, 100) offers hundreds of cocktail varieties.

At night, a lively, bustling crowd can be found in rue du Théâtre, where the **Casino de Montreux** complex (9 rue du Théâtre) caters for all tastes. **Le Piano Bar** (*in the hotel Mirador Kempinski, Mont-Pelerin*) is a stylish bar with fireplace, breaktaking view of Lake Geneva, and more than 70 varieties of champagne.

🛍 SHOPPING

Many shops and boutiques are on avenue des Alpes, Grande-Rue, avenue du Casino, and rue de la Paix. **Department store:** Innovation (*avenue du Casino*).

🎼 THEATRE AND MUSIC

Théâtre Montreux-Riviera –*36 Rue du Pont.* ℘*(0)21 961 11 31. www.theatre-montreux-riviera.ch.*
Auditorium Stravinski – *95 Grand-Rue.* ℘*(0)21 962 21 19.*

The Alps★★

The Vaud Alps owe their strong individuality to their landscape of wide green valleys and limestone escarpments, forming majestic snowy summits. Their mountain people speak French, are Protestant, and build houses like those of the Bernese Oberland. A striking feature of the local landscape is the extraordinary scattering of these chalets over the slopes above the Grande Eau and the Sarine.

GEOGRAPHY

The Ormonts and Enhaut district valleys around Lake Geneva and the Bernese Oberland are dotted with holiday resorts such as Château-d'Oex or Les Diablerets. Higher up, on terraced sites 1 000m/3 280ft above the Rhône Valley and facing the Dents du Midi, Leysin and Villars-Chesières draw the world of sport and fashion.

This is ideal walking country with well signposted trails and beautiful panoramas with high peaks, green valleys and mountain lakes.

- **Michelin Map:** 729 F6-F7.
- **Info:** Les Diablerets rue de la Gare. ℰ(0)24 492 00 10. www.diablerets.ch. **Leysin** Place Large ℰ(0)24 493 33 00. www.leysin.ch. **Gstaad** Haus des Gastes ℰ(0)33 748 81 81. www.gstaad.ch.
- **Location:** The Vaud Alps are divided between the Rhône and Aare basins (Upper Sarine Valley).
- **Don't Miss:** A cable car ride to Scex Rouge.
- **Time:** Leave at least a full day for tour itineraries and visiting sites.

🚗 DRIVING TOURS

1 VALLÉE DES ORMONTS★★

From Aigle to Saanen 45km/28mi – allow approx 1hr30min. ⊗The Col du Pillon is usually blocked by snow from November to April.

141

Aigle

Alt. 417m/1 369ft. 5 Rue Colomb, 1860.
℘ (0)24 466 30 00. www.aigle.ch.
A wine and industrial centre as well as a military depot, Aigle is a small, pleasant town surrounded by famous vineyards. Stroll along the shaded Gustave-Doré Avenue (beside the torrent of the Grande Eau) and into the town centre by the unusual Jerusalem Alley (Ruelle de Jérusalem), with its covered wooden galleries decked with flowers.

Castle

This 13C feudal fortress originally belonged to the House of Savoy but was captured and rebuilt by the Bernese in the 15C. It now houses a local museum.

Musée de la Vigne et du Vin

⊙*Open 25 Apr–31 Oct, Tue–Sun 11am–6pm.* ⊙*Closed Nov–24 Apr* ⊜*11CHF.*
℘ (0)24 466 21 30. www.chateauaigle.ch.
The Wine Museum displays wine making items from the 17C up to the present day.

♣♣Aigle Adventure Park

⊙*Open 27 Mar–Oct. Jul–29 Aug daily 9am–6pm. Other times see website.* ⊜*36CHF; discounts for a family group.*
℘ (0)24 466 30 30. www.parc-aventure.ch.
Offers over 100 outdoor adventures including five skill levels, welcoming ages 4 and up.

Leysin★

From the touring route, 4km/2.5mi by a road on the left before reaching Le Sépey.
The splendid terraced **site**★★ of Leysin, overlooking the Rhône Valley and facing the Dents du Midi, enjoys a mild climate and strong sun: An ideal location for either summer holidays or winter skiing.

Les Diablerets✳

Chief town of the Ormonts Valley. The resort is spread over a widening basin of meadows dotted with ash trees and maples. The **site**★★ is both delightful and impressive, with very fine chalets, built and decorated in the traditional style of the Bernese Oberland. Here the wall of the Les Diablerets Mountain curves deeply to form a cirque (Creux de Champ) between the Scex Rouge spur and the Culan.

Between Les Diablerets and the Pillon Pass, a bend in the ravine crossed by the Bourquin Bridge affords glimpses, between the trees, of white monoliths, formed by the dissolution of gypsum. On the opposite slope the Dard Torrent escapes in thin cascades from two overlapping rock **cirques**★.

The Ski Area

The Diablerets resort is renowned for its snowfields, spread out over three massifs: Le Meilleret (1 949m/6394ft), which can be reached by skiing from **Villars-sur-Ollon**★ (&see VILLARS-SUR-OLLON), Isenau (2 120m/6 955ft at Le Floriettaz) and the **Scex Rouge Glacier** (2 979m/9 774ft). In spite of its small size (50km/31mi of slopes) and somewhat impractical equipment, the resort offers several splendid slopes. Intermediate skiers will appreciate the Isenau area, the long forested pistes around Le Meilleret and especially the red trail between Cabane and Oldenegg. Seasoned skiers can swoop along the **Combe d'Audon**★★, starting from Scex Rouge, which features high-quality snow and breathtaking vistas. Snowboarders will find snowparks laid out along the Isenau in winter and Scex Rouge in summer. The **Forfait Intégral des Alpes Vaudoises** ski pass grants visitors unlimited access to 220km/137mi of slopes and 77 cable cars covering Villars, Leysin and Les Mosses. Cross-country skiers have at their disposal 31km/20mi of pistes at high altitude as well as lower down in the valleys.

Scex Rouge★★★

⛷*Access: 35min by cable car from the Pillon Pass (Col du Pillon) or by cable car leaving from Reusch.*
During the ascent, marmots and chamois goats take a backseat to the dramatic view of the Les Diablerets Basin and the splendid escarpment immediately before you reach the upper station.

"*Breitling Orbiter 3 over the Alps following its launch from Château d'Oex 1 March 1999*

© EPA/Photoshot

Round the World in a Hot-Air Balloon

On 28 January 1998, French navigator Olivier de Kersauzon lit the burners of *Breitling Orbiter 2* with the Olympic flame, which had been specially brought from Lausanne for the occasion. At precisely 9.56am, the Swiss hang-gliding specialist Bertrand Piccard (whose grandfather Auguste Piccard invented the bathyscaph), Belgian Wim Verstraeten and Andy Elson from Great Britain slowly rose into the air in a pear-shaped Rozier balloon made of aluminium and filled with helium. This non-stop flight around the world, which seemed to spring from the pages of a Jules Verne novel, would last three weeks and follow a specific flight path—Italy, Greece, Cyprus, Israel, Saudi Arabia, India, China, the Pacific Ocean, California, Florida, Bermuda Islands, Canary Islands and North Africa—achieving an unprecedented feat in the history of aviation.

The mission suffered a serious setback when Chinese authorities denied them access for national security, despite strong diplomatic pressure from the International Olympic Committee, and the *Breitling Orbiter 2* team was forced to abandon the operation. Then, China changed its mind and gave permission for the balloon to fly over the country, but it was too late. The delays incurred by China's indecision slowed the flight so the balloon could no longer reach the jet stream, a narrow belt of high-altitude, fast-moving winds which would have propelled *Breitling Orbiter 2* over the Pacific Ocean at around 200kph/124.3mph. The team nonetheless continued their flight and eventually landed in Burma after 9 days, 17 hours and 51 minutes, having covered a distance of 8 473km/5 265mi. Although they failed to complete their full orbit, the team did succeed in establishing a new world record for living in a hot-air balloon.

A little over a year later on 21 March 1999, Swiss balloonist Bertrand Piccard and British pilot Brian Jones finally achieved their world record round-the-world flight in *Breitling Orbiter 3*. Sponsored by the renowned Swiss watchmaker, they took off from the Swiss resort of Château d'Oex at 8.05am on 1 March and eventually landed in the Eygyptian dessert 19 days, 21 hours and 55 minutes later. The distance they travelled was 40 814km/25 361mi (the circumference of the Earth is 40 075km/24 901mi at the equator) climbing to altitudes of 11 735m/38 500ft, a world record for this type of balloon. Amongst the first people to congratulate Picard and Jones were rival balloonist and entrepreneur Richard Branson who had made earlier unsuccessful attempts with Per Lindstrand and the late Steve Fossett.

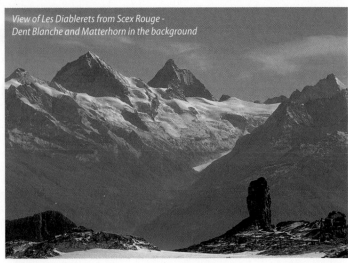

View of Les Diablerets from Scex Rouge - Dent Blanche and Matterhorn in the background

From here, a staircase (○*open only in summer*) leads to the Scex Rouge Peak (alt. 2 971m/9 747ft) where there is a magnificent **panorama**★★★: Southward from the Swiss Alps (Matterhorn) and French Alps (Mont Blanc) to the nearby peaks of Les Diablerets and the superb **Les Diablerets Glacier**★★ (an extension to the north of the Tsafleuron Glacier). Northward the view extends to the Tornette and Palette peaks, which rise behind the Ormonts Valley.

Lac Retaud★

1.5km/1mi by a narrow mountain road from the Pillon Pass (Col du Pillon).
This pretty sheet of green water fills a hollow opposite the double cirque of the Dard, dominated on the left by the Oldenhorn and on the right by the Scex Rouge. A third cirque lies between the spurs of the Oldenhorn (in the Oldenbach Valley) from Col du Pillon to Gsteig, ending in sight of the solidly buttressed Spitzhorn pyramid.

Gsteig★

The rocky hanging valley farther upstream between the escarpments of the Spitzhorn and the Mittaghorn, and from which a powerful cascade flows, leads to the Sanetsch Pass, which used to be a well-traveled link between the Oberland and the Valais.

Gstaad★★

Alt. 1 080m/3 543ft. Haus des Gastes.
℘(0)33 748 81 81. www.gstaad.ch.
Gstaad lies on the boundary between the Bernese and Vaud Alps at the junction of four gently sloping valleys: The Upper Sarine Valley, the Lauenen Valley, the Turbach Valley and the Saanenmöser Depression.
The resort at Gstaad, with its carefully restored old chalets and many luxury boutiques, is pleasing for its restful setting and the variety of its sporting and social facilities. Popular with celebrities in winter, Gstaad offers a number of pleasant walks in summer: explore the **Eggli** (alt. 1 557m/5 108ft) and the nearby plateau, accessible by cable car. Helicopter rides of the area are available from Gstaad-Grund heliport.

The Skiing Area

Thanks to the blue trains of the local railways, the resort shares with Saanenmöser (alt. 1 272m/4 173ft—facilities) and even with Zweisimmen (equipped with a large cable car for ascents to the Rinderberg) a magnificent ski area served by about 60 ski lifts. There are more than 85km/53mi of groomed local runs and more than 250km/155mi in the region, which encompasses six ski resorts with inteconnected lifts. The Eggli (alt. 1 671m/5 483ft) has good, long intermediate runs and connects with nearby Rougemont. Wassergrat (alt. 1 942m/6 372ft) is for intermediates and experts, offering both open snowfields and piste routes through the trees. Cross-country skiers can enjoy 100km/62mi of classic tracks and 40km/25mi of skating tracks.

Saanen

The road from Lausanne to Interlaken (via Bulle or the Mosses col) leaves the Sarine Valley (Saane in German) en route to the Saanenmöser by the Simme valley. Saanen is a charming and peaceful place in contrast to its neighbour Gstaad. Even in winter the area preserves its individual style, and has an extensive network of chair lifts - Kalberhöni-Vorder Eggli.

The sun kissed wooden chalets of the area often have large overhanging traditional roofs bedecked with hanging baskets. Some of the chalets date from the sixteenth century (note the dates). Visitors can see the fine bell tower from afar. Inside the church, the chancel is decorated with wall paintings dating from the fifteenth century. The paintings portray biblical scenes, events during the life of the Virgin Mary and the martyr St Maurice, the patron of the sanctuary. Information is provided by the pulpit.

2 PAYS D'ENHAUT★★

From Saanen to Aigle. 45km/28mi – allow 1hr (excluding visits).

Lying between Saanen and Château-d'Oex, the short **Défilé des Allamans** marks the boundary between the cantons of Bern and Vaud as well as the switch from French to German. The slim, rocky point aptly named Rubli (carrot), continually catches the eye.

Rougemont

This charming village was the site of a Cluniac priory between the 11C and the Reformation. The church is typical of early Swiss Romanesque structures. Note the crane mascot in the stained-glass windows.

La Videmanette★

Alt. 2 140m/7 021ft. Access by cable car in 18min leaving from Rougemont.
The upper station is on top of the Videmanette Mountain, situated between the Rubli and Rocher Plat summits. From the restaurant's roof terrace, the **vista**★ encompasses (*right to left*): The three summits of La Tornette, Les Diablerets, Lake Arnensee, and Lake Retaud; behind, the Gummfluh, the Oldenhorn Range, the Jungfrau Mountain range in the distance; to the far left, the Eiger.

Réserve de la Pierreuse★

On foot: allow half a day.
At Les Granges bear left (hairpin bend) onto the downhill road from Gérignoz, which goes through a tunnel and crosses a bridge over the Sarine. Before a large sawmill bear right and take the road up the opposite side of the valley.

Leave the car before the Les Leyssalets Bridge and proceed on foot.

This nature reserve, at the foot of the rocky north face of the Gummfluh, lies at an altitude of between 1 300m/4 264ft and 2 460m/8 068ft, a hilly **site**★ covering approximately 880ha/2 174 acres. The flora and fauna (spruce trees, ibexes, marmots) are protected. The twin Gummfluh peaks can be glimpsed through a gap formed by the tributary valley of Gérignoz.

Château-D'Oex

Alt. 1 000m/3 281ft. La Place – 1837. (0)26 924 25 25. www.chateau-doex.ch.
Château-d'Oex (pronounced Château Day) is a little pre-Alpine mountain centre which has long lived apart, spreading its chalets and hotels at the foot of the last wooded slopes of the Gummfluh and the Vanils. This is a typical Vaud Alps family resort, highly popular because of the many water sports facilities it offers.

The Balloon Festival

Château d'Oex is the self-styled "world capital of ballooning" and it organises an international hot-air ballooning event each year in late January. More than 80 balloons from 20 different countries take part over ten days. Look out for the special event for unconventionally shaped balloons (bagpipes, roosters, tortoises etc). The venue is at the junction of the Saanen road and the one to Col des Mosses. Staying elsewhere in the valley will help you to avoid paying higher accommodation costs. An entry fee of 10CHF is payable if you wish to enter the venue. *www.festivaldeballons.ch.*

Musée d'Art Populaire du Vieux Pays d'Enhaut★

Open Tue–Sun, 2pm–5pm. Closed 1 Jan, Easter and 25 Dec. 7CHF. *(0)26 924 65 20.*

Located in a three-storey building, the museum illustrates the region's rich historical past (12C–19C). Exhibits include parchment, engravings, drawings, photographs, popular or religious works of art, weapons, beautifully carved tools, old-fashioned utensils and other objects, painted or inlaid furniture, and reconstructed interiors: blacksmith's forge, peasant's kitchen, bourgeois kitchen, and bedrooms belonging to a herdsman and a weaver. Stained glass, a fine collection of 19C paper cuttings, and black bobbin pillow lace are also worth noting. Reconstituted in two separate pavilions are a chalet which housed herders up in the mountain pastures: note the cheese room with its gigantic copper cauldron (800l/211gal), and the carpenter's workshop. Also part of the museum, but located at the end of the town, is the **Étambeau Chalet**, which houses artifacts of regional architecture. Visitors are also shown the cheese cellar and the barn, which houses an exhibition on Alpine transport.

Winter sports in Château d'Oex

Downhill and cross-country skiing and winter hiking are also available in Château d'Oex. For more information, see *www.ess-chax.ch.* 70CHF. *Open 14 Dec–3 Jan/31 Jan–28 Feb 9am–1.30pm and 3.30pm-6pm. Low Season: 9am-10.30 and 3.30-6pm.* *(0)26 924 68 48.*

Gorges du Pissot

A **viewpoint**★ on a curve allows you to appreciate the steepness of this rocky cleft, through which the Torneresse flows. After passing through the Pissot Gorges, the road curves to the Etivaz Valley, you will then come to the extensive lowland of Mosses with its woods and fields.

At La Lécherette you reach the upper valley of the Hongrin. On the Ormonts slope the view extends along the Comballaz to Les Diablerets; on the left, the Scex Rouge and the Oldenhorn.

Looking down the Grande Eau Valley, you can pick out the spa and large hotels of Leysin and, on the horizon, the Dents du Midi.

Between Le Sépey and Aigle the road runs along a ledge above the wooded **Grande Eau Gorges**★, and after a few hairpin bends, goes down to the floor of the Rhône Valley. The town of Aigle, dominated by its castle, nestles in a vineyard setting.

③ CROIX PASS ROAD★★

From Aigle to Les Diablerets via Villars. 29km/18mi – allow 1hr. The Croix Pass is only open in summer.

Aigle – See p142.

Ollon

This is a charming wine-growers' village. The road climbs, tortuous but excellent, along a *corniche.* 3km/1.8mi after Ollon a superb **view**★★ opens onto the Grand Muveran and Les Diablerets, the Pas de Cheville Valley between.

Villars-Sur-Ollon✳, Chesières and Arveyes

Alt. 1 253m/4 111ft. Rue Centrale,
℘(0)24 495 32 32. www.villars.ch.
Together Villars, Chesières, and Arveyes form a resort perched 800m/2 625ft above the Lower Valais. It is the most highly developed mountain resort in French Switzerland and offers a panorama of the French Alps, the Dents du Midi, and the Muverans Range with Mont Blanc, the Trient Glacier, and the peaks of Les Diablerets in the distance. These resorts are recommended to residents who are looking for peace and quiet rather than fashionable society. The panorama from Chesières includes the Mont-Blanc Massif, between the Trient Glacier and the Aiguille Verte.

Villars

The town lies along an esplanade of parkland in an attractive rural setting dotted with low mountains. Villar's summer facilities include a golf course, swimming pool, 300km/186.4mi of hiking trails, and 150km/93mi of mountain-bike tracks. In winter, the skating rink and sledge piste attract large crowds. Villars hosts many cultural events, including classical music concerts.

Skiing Area

The Villars-sur-Ollon skiing area is smaller than some neighboring resorts (220km/136.7mi of ski slopes), a definite plus for families and others looking for a leisurely resort pace and a variety of novice and intermediate terrain on sunny slopes. The two main peaks (Grand Chamossaire and Croix des Chaux) are perfect for intermediates. Try the Combe d'Orsay, with its **views**★ of Leysin, and one of the many forest trails. Seasoned skiers can tackle slopes running from Croix des Chaux to La Rasse or Les Fracherets. A skiing pass now enables you to go skiing all over the Vaud Alps including Les Diablerets and its glacier (50km/31mi of challenging slopes, accessible by the Conches chairlift) as well as Leysin (60km/37mi of pistes) and Les Mosses (40km/25mi), which can only be reached by car. There

are also 44km/27mi of cross-country trails around the resort.

Bretaye

Alt. 1 806m/5 925ft. ▤Rack railway.
Pretty route crossing the forest. After reaching Col de Soud, there are stunning views of Croix des Chaux and the impressive Diablerets peaks.

Grand Chamossaire

Alt. 2 120m/6 955ft. ⌇ Access to skiers
by chairlift starting from Bretaye.
Sweeping panorama of the Vaud Alps mountain range (Leysin, Gryon, Les Diablerets) with the Valais, Mont Blanc and Dents du Midi nestling in the background.

AROUND VILLARS
Gryon

Alt. 1 114m/3 655ft.
Old terraced village overlooking the Avançon Valley. The road dips rapidly, winding between fir and larch. Bear left toward Les Plans 2km/1mi before Bex. At Frenières note on the left the perched village of Gryon. After Les Plans the road climbs through woodland, running parallel to a stream.

Bex Salt Mines (Mines de Sel de Bex)★

Route des Mines de Sel, Les Dévens.
⊙Guided tours daily Apr–Oct, every
90mins 9.45am–3.45pm, advance
booking suggested, English tours
available. ▤19CHF. ℘(0)24 463 03 30.
www.mines.ch. Refer to website for
times of visits.
The two-hour tour begins with an audio-visual show and a long underground narrow-gauge train ride, continuing on foot through passageways carved deep into the mountain. Wear sturdy shoes and a warm jacket.
This 300-year-old **salt mine** is still fully operational (the only one in Switzerland) producing 150 tons of salt daily and has been worked since the 15C. The salt is obtained through traditional means: A stream of fresh water is injected into the salt rock, flooding every crevice, until

147

the brine shows a salt content of 30%. This technique is known as leaching. Water is then evaporated through boiling, leaving a salt deposit at the bottom of the container. The mine consists of 40km/25mi of shafts, passageways and steps, originally hollowed out by chisels and sledgehammers.

Part of the mine has been made into a **museum** which can be visited on foot and in a small train. Exhibits include tools and machinery which have served the mining industry over the past centuries.

La Barboleusaz
Alt. 1 211m/3 973ft.

This winter sports resort is located in a lovely site overlooked by Les Diablerets. From here you can get to the ski fields of **Les Chaux**★ (5km/3mi by a narrow, winding road; in winter access by cable car) or to the **Solalex Refuge**★ (alt. 1 466m/4 809ft)—via a small picturesque road (6km/3.5mi) following the Avançon torrent—in a cirque of Alpine pastures at the foot of Les Diablerets.

Pont de Nant★
A lovely cirque at the base of the Grand Muveran Glaciers. An Alpine rock garden can be visited (water lily pond; more than 2 000 kinds of Alpine or medicinal plants from all over the world).

ADDRESSES

🏠STAY
LES DIABLERETS
⊜⊜ **Hôtel des Diablerets** – *Chemin des Ormonts. ℰ(0)24 492 09 09. www.diablerets.com. Closed May and Oct–Nov. 59 rooms.* Treat yourself to one of the higher-priced rooms with sumptuous views of the glacier. Covered pool.

⊜⊜ **L'Ours** – *Towards l'Église (hamlet 2km/1.25mi from Diablerets) ℰ(0)24 492 44 00. www.aubergedelours.ch. 6 rooms. Closed Nov and Apr.* Plain wood lined rooms, but pleasant and airy.

⊜⊜⊜ **Du Golf** – *r. Centrale, Villars-sur-Ollon. ℰ(0)24 496 38 38. www.hotel-golf.ch. 70 rms.* A hotel just 100m/109yds from the chairlifts. Spacious rooms.

⊜⊜⊜ **La Renardière** – *rte des Layeux, Villars-sur-Ollon. ℰ(0)24 495 25 92. www.larenardiere.ch. 20 rooms. Open mid-Dec–mid-Apr and mid-Jun–mid-Nov.* Attractive rooms in a peaceful setting. Three large chalets linked by walkways, near to a forest. Prices for each of the chalets vary considerably. The rooms in the annexe are less expensive.

⊜⊜⊜ **Hostellerie Les Sources** – *Chemin du Vernex. ℰ(0)24 492 01 00. www.hotel-les-sources.ch. Closed May and mid-Oct–Nov. 48 rooms.* A family friendly hotel with the finest of modern amenities. Pleasantly situated near the village centre, overlooking the Diablerets Massif.

🍴EAT
LES DIABLERETS
⊜ **Café de la Couronne** – *ℰ(0)24 492 31 75. Closed Wed in low season.* Delicious homemade charcuterie.

⊜⊜ **Les Lilas** – *ℰ(0)24 492 31 34. www.hotellelilas.ch. Closed 22 May–8 Jun, Sun evenings and Mon in low season.* This charming chalet converted into a guesthouse serves regional cuisine.

⊜⊜ **Miroir d'Argentine** – *Solalex. 9km/5.6mi E of Villars-sur-Ollon. ℰ(0)24 498 14 46. www.solalex.ch. Open early May–end Oct, daily exc Mon and Tue.* A restaurant, beautifully positioned, surrounded by mountains. Friendly welcome with excellent traditional cuisine. Well recommended.

⊜⊜⊜ **Restaurant de Plambuit** – *Plambuit. 6km/3.75mi N of Villars-sur-Ollon. ℰ(0)24 499 33 44. www.plambuit.com. Open 1 May–31 Oct, Wed lunchtime–Sun lunchtime.* A rustic dining room offering food which is created from local market produce. As places are limited, it is best to reserve in advance. Terrace with a wide ranging view.

Gruyères★

This little fortified town is perched on a hill in a harmonious landscape. It charms visitors to Romansh Switzerland by its friendly atmosphere, derived from the time when the whole Sarine Valley lay under the benevolent rule of the counts of Gruyères (12C–16C).

SIGHTS

Visitors will immediately be charmed by the locality of Gruyères, which they approach by its main street. It is lined with old houses with twin windows and wide eaves, and slopes down to the town fountain before rising again toward the castle.

Go up to the castle on foot, noticing on the right the old grain measures hollowed out of a stone block, and then, on the left, the house with delicately carved 16C window frames of the jester Chalamala, who became famous at the court of the counts of Gruyères.

Castle★

Guided tour (1hr) Apr–Oct, 9am–6pm; Nov–Mar, 10am–4.30pm. Last admission 30min before closing time. Closed 1 Jan and at Christmas. 6CHF. (0)26 921 21 02. www.chateau-gruyeres.ch.

Most of the former castle of the counts of Gruyères dates from the late 15C

▶ **Population:** Fribourg 1 753.
Michelin Map: National Map 729: F6.
Info: 1663 Gruyères. (0)24 424 424. www.gruyeres.ch.
Location: In the Fribourg region of western Switzerland. Alt. 830m/2 657ft.
Parking: Cars should be parked outside the town (car park).
Don't Miss: The HR Giger Museum, as well as Historial Suisse, a wax museum located in the La Locanda restaurant in Moléson village.
Timing: Allow at least a full day.

(façades on the courtyard of the main dwelling). The internal arrangement recalls both the feudal period (kitchen and guardroom) and 18C refinements. Their decoration, more or less tasteful, is largely the work of the Bovy family, a dynasty of artists who saved the castle from destruction in the 20C and welcomed many foreign artists (namely Corot). The heraldic crane of the counts of Gruyères can be seen in many places, over doors, in stained-glass windows

Château de Gruyères

Roland Gerth/Switzerland Tourism

and on firebacks. The most valuable pieces assembled here are the three mourning **copes**★ of the Order of the Golden Fleece, used by almoners of Charles the Bold to celebrate masses for the repose of knights who died in the campaign of 1476. These sumptuous vestments became, for the people of Fribourg, their most glorious trophy of the Battle of Murten. Four 16C Flanders tapestries depicting scenes from the Old Testament are displayed in the count's bedroom, whose ceiling is typical of the Savoyard period. In the Baroque Salle des Baillis, note the impressive sculpted wood furniture. The Salle des Chevaliers, notable for its size and decoration, has a coffered ceiling with hanging keystones and walls painted with scenes illustrating the history of the counts' lands.

The 15C **Chapelle St-Jean** stands on a pleasant terrace within view of the Lower Gruyères (Bulle-Broc district), partly drowned by the reservoir of the Rossens Dam, and of the two graceful Dent de Broc peaks. Near the chapel, on the ramparts, is a splendid view of the surrounding area, including the Moléson and the Jura chain (viewing table).

Musée HR Giger

🕐Apr–Oct, 10am–6pm; Nov–Mar, Tue–Fri 1pm–5pm, Sat–Sun 10am–6pm. ⊛12.50CHF. ℘(0)26 921 22 00. www.hrgiger.info.

This museum is a must-see destination for art and science-fiction film fans. Housed in Château St-Germain, the museum is dedicated to Swiss sculptor HR Giger, who created the *Alien* life forms. The *Birth Machine* sculpture at the entrance sets the tone for a visit, which includes a room dedicated to the movie, with various sketches used for the film, paintings, sculptures, and unique pieces of furniture made from glass, plexiglass, polyester, metal and rubber and artifacts from the artist's other major works, *Species, The SpellI-IV* and *Harkonnen*.

Tibet Museum

4 Rue du Château. 🕐Open daily Apr–Oct 11am–6pm (Nov–Mar Fri 1am–5pm, Sat–Sun 1am–6pm). ⊛12CHF

(5CHF) ℘(0)26 921 30 10. www.tibetmuseum.ch.

Adjacent to the Musée HR Giger is this recently opened collection of Buddhist and Himalyan art.

▷ *Follow the main street, which offers a view of the Moléson (see below), the most typical Gruyères peak. Turn right in front of the fountain.*

Maison du Gruyère

1km/0.6mi away, at the entrance to Pringy. 🕐Open 9am–7pm (6pm Oct–Mar). ⊛6CHF ♿ ℘(0)26 921 84 00. www.lamaisondugruyere.ch.

This former industrial cheesemaking factory houses a demonstration cheese dairy. The ground floor contains the cellars where the cheeses are stored. The first floor features the ripening area, an exhibition on local customs, a videotape explaining cheesemaking techniques and galleries overlooking the demonstration area where Gruyère is made in wheels of 35kg/77lb.

EXCURSIONS
Moléson-sur-Gruyères

▷6km/3.7mi to the SW. 6 Place de l'Aigle, 1663. ℘(0)26 921 85 00.

This pretty village features a **Fromagerie d'Alpage** (🕐open mid-May–26 Sept, 10am–6pm; ⊛2.50CHF; by prior appointment to Madame Sylvia Magnin on ℘(0)26 921 10 44; www.fromagerie-alpage.ch), an Alpine cheese dairy set up in a 17C chalet, with a roof made up of 90 000 shingles. After an audio-visual presentation (in French) of regional specialities, visitors are shown the humble sleeping quarters of a local cowherd (*armailli*). Then they can watch a cowherd prepare Gruyère cheese according to traditional methods, baking it in an old-fashioned stove fuelled by firewood. Fresh products are kept in the milk room and the more mature cheeses are stored in the salting house, a small square building located near the farm.

A cable car will take you up to the **Observatoire de Moléson** (alt. 2 002m/6 568ft) (🚡cable car leaving from Moléson-Village; does not operate from Easter to mid-May and mid-Oct to mid-Dec; ⊙the observatory is open mid-Dec–mid-Apr, 9am–4.30pm; mid-May–mid-Oct, 9am–6pm, and until 11pm Fri and Sat in Jul and Aug; evening introductory sessions to astronomy, by appointment 5pm–9am; ⊶25-33CHF; ℘(0)26 921 29 96) which commands a panoramic view of the Gruyères area and the Swiss plateau. The observatory organizes evening classes on the subject of astronomy (telescopes). During the winter season 35km/20mi of carefully marked-out ski runs are available to tourists.

Bulle

Alt. 769m/2 523ft. 4 Avenue de la Gare, 1630. ℘(0)26 912 80 22.
Bulle is the capital of the "green Gruyères", one of the most attractive districts in Switzerland with its peaceful scenery and quaint folklore. The market town deals in timber and cheese, and the black-and-white Fribourg cattle.

Musée Gruérien★★

⊙Open Tue–Sun, 10am–noon, 2pm–5pm; Sun and public holidays, 2pm–5pm. ⊙Closed 1 Jan and 25 Dec. ⊶8CHF. ℘(0)26 916 10 10. www.musee-gruerien.ch.
Founded by the writer **Victor Tissot**, the Museum of the Gruyères Region is in the basement of a modern building at the foot of the castle. Exhibits are superbly arranged and include some 10 000 pieces of rural furniture, craft objects and documents illustrating the cycle of the seasons. The first section contains several reconstructed peasant interiors, including a cheese room and a typical Fribourg house. Note the pyramid-shaped fireplace in one of the kitchens and painted scenes of the life of the prophet Elijah in one of the bedrooms.
Myriad objects highlight the **folklore of the Gruyère region**. Large paintings (19C) known as "poyas" (from the verb poyî," to move up the mountain") show the herds being led up to mountain pastures. One of these is by a master of the genre, Sylvestre Pidoux. The armaillis (cowherds) are depicted in their bred-

Cream spoons, Musée Gruérien

Stephan Engler/Switzerland Tourism

zon (short jacket with puffed sleeves), with their loyi (bag of salt) slung over their shoulder. Also admire the large variety of fine **old furniture**: Tables, beds, chests, wardrobes, sideboards, decorated cribs, and chairs, such as the 16C bench from Fribourg. The 18C Gruyères **regional costumes** are also worth noting as well as the wax crèches from the same period. Also on display are 18C–19C medallions on cut-out paper, religious statues, church plate (gold monstrance dated 1752), cowbells and horns from the Alps, and a diorama of the local fauna.
The second section contains 16C–17C engravings and paintings from the Italian School. Also represented are the French School, with works by Corot and Courbet, including a lovely portrait of a young Bulle girl, and the Swiss School (Vallotton, Alexis Grimou), and the painted cupboard by Netton Bosson.

Castle

⊶Not open to the public.
The castle is an imposing 13C building, built for Bishop Boniface of Lausanne in the style of Burgundy and Savoy.

Jaunpassstrasse

Jaun Pass Road. 381 Hauptstrasse. ℘26 929 81 81. www.jaun.ch.
The **Jaun Pass Road** is the most mountainous in the Fribourg Alps. For the

Cailler, Suchard, Kohler, Nestlé, Lindt, Tobler...

Attractive presentations and mouth-watering contents characterize the high-quality confectionery of Swiss chocolate-makers, many of whom have been making chocolate since the 19C. As in the case of a good wine, one should savor the aroma and taste. Dark, white or milk chocolate comes in many forms—cakes, mini-slabs, figurines, sweets, and in a variety of shapes—and is often combined with various other ingredients such as nuts, raisins, or ginger.

sightseer it combines lakes, rocky crests and stretches of pasture.

Broc

From the garden in front of the town hall, you will enjoy a lovely **view**★ of the Gruyères area with Vanil Blanc, Vudalla and Moléson summits as a backdrop. The **Nestlé-Callier chocolate factory** (🕙 open Apr–Oct Mon–Fri 10am–6pm; 🎟10CHF; 𝒫(0)26 921 51 51; www.cailler. ch) is open to the public (short film and tasting).

Electrobroc (🕙 open Mar–Dec, Mon–Sat 9am–noon, 1.30pm–5pm, except public holidays; audio-guides; 🎟 no charge; 𝒫(0)26 921 15 37), next to the factory, is run by the Fribourg electricity company and introduces visitors to the world of electricity, with information on consumption, distribution and production, as well as explaining how a hydroelectric plant works. The tour finishes with an impressive audio-visual display of the effects of lightning.

Charmey

The **Musée du Pays et Val de Charmey** in the Tourist Office (𝒫(0)26 927 55 80; www.charmey.ch) houses a collection of objects relating to life in the region.

Jaun

This little town, quite close to the dividing line between Romansh and German Switzerland, still features several fine old chalets and a church with a traditional shingle roof.

ADDRESSES

🏨 STAY

Those wishing to sample local specialities should taste these dishes: The traditional fondue and raclette, jambon (ham) and meringue à la crème de la Gruyère (sweet topped with cream).

😑😑 **Fleur de Lys** – 𝒫(0)26 921 82 82. ww.hotelfleurdelys.ch. Closed Feb and Nov–Easter. 10 rooms. Rooms decorated with pretty wainscoting. Large, rustic dining hall where traditional meals are served.

😑😑 **Hostellerie de St-Georges** – 𝒫(0)26 921 83 00. www.st-georges-gruyeres.ch. 14 rooms. Old inn dating back to the 16C. Peace and quiet guaranteed. Lovely views of the ramparts and surrounding mountains.

🍴 EAT

😑😑 **Le Chalet** – 𝒫(0)26 921 21 54. Closed 25 Dec. A country chalet serving local cuisine in the heart of the town centre.

😑😑 **Auberge de la Halle** – 𝒫(0)26 921 21 78. www.la-halle.ch. Restaurant with a rustic setting offering regional dishes and a charming atmosphere.

😑😑 **Hôtel de Ville** – 𝒫(0)26 921 24 24. www.hoteldeville.ch. Closed Wed low season, 1–20 Dec and 3–17 Jan. 8 rooms. Located in the main street, this old-fashioned, rustic hotel has a restaurant which serves regional cuisine.

Fribourg★★

Fribourg is a remarkable **site**★★ on a rocky spur circled by a bend of the Sarine. The old quarters extend from the river to the upper town; bristling with church towers and monasteries, they still bear the appearance of a medieval city. Fribourg boasts many **sculpted fountains** gracing the squares and along the streets, built during the Middle Ages as outlets for the many springs which supplied the town with water. Later, in the 15C, they were adorned with elegantly chiselled basins and stone columns, the work of renowned artists such as Hans Geiler, Hans Gieng and Stephan Ammann.

A BIT OF HISTORY

From its foundations to the Reformation – In 1157 **Berchtold IV of Zähringen** founded Fribourg at a ford on the Sarine and made it a stronghold to command this important thoroughfare. After the Zähringen family died out, the town changed hands several times. It passed to the Kyburgs and then to the Habsburgs, but finally to the rule of Savoy. Fribourg joined the Confederation in 1481 after having acquired extensive lands in the Vaud Country. Here the Reformation had no decisive influence and the Catholic Restoration inspired by Father Canisius reaffirmed the Catholic

- ▶ **Population:** Fribourg 34 084.
- **Michelin Map:** Map: F5.
- **Info:** 1 avenue de la Gare – 1700. ℘(0)26 350 11 11. www.fribourgtourisme.ch.
- **Location:** Fribourg is located 29km/18.2mi east of Estavayer-Le-Lac. Alt. 640m/2 100ft.
- **Parking:** Use public parking areas and explore by foot or public transport
- **Don't Miss:** A tour of the Old Town on foot.
- **Timing:** Allow at least half a day to explore the city and its sights; a full day to include an excursion.

feelings of the town, which became the seat of the Bishopric of Lausanne, Geneva, and Fribourg.

A bastion of Catholicism – In the 17C many religious orders were added to those already settled in Fribourg during the 13C: Franciscans, Jesuits, and other communities made it the Catholic capital of Switzerland. Among the most famous and brilliant establishments were the College of St Michael, founded by the Jesuits, the Capuchin Church and Monastery, the Franciscan Monastery, and

View of Fribourg

the Monastery of Maigrauge, built by the Cistercians in the 13C.

The university – In 1889 the foundation of a Catholic state university gave a new impulse to the crucial role played by religious instruction in modern times. Fribourg University, one of the most prestigious seats of learning, still enjoys an excellent reputation in Switzerland and abroad. Its five faculties (theology, law, social and economic sciences, languages, and natural sciences) and 15 independent institutes (computer technology, journalism, and more) welcome students from all over the world.

⏴⏴WALKING TOUR

This route explores the history of Fribourg. Visitors can appreciate the modern areas of the town and then immerse themselves into the medieval streets, having taken in the town's museums and the cathedral. Allow 1h30 for the walk, not including a museum visit. Start from the Place de la Gare and then follow the Rue de Romont, pass place Georges-Python and go down rue Lausanne to place Nova-Friburgo. Go down rue Pierre Aeby and the Murtengasse.

Art and History Museum★

◷ Open Tue–Sun 11am–6pm (8pm Thu).
◷ Closed 24, 26, 31 Dec, 1 Jan. ⊗8CHF.
♿ ☏(0)26 305 51 40. www.mahf.ch
The collections displayed in the Hôtel Ratzé, an elegant Renaissance building (16C), and in a former slaughterhouse converted in 1981, illustrate the art and history of Fribourg from its origins to the present day. Many exhibits date back to the Middle Ages, a period rich in artistic events.
Note the Late Gothic collections of remarkable works of art executed by local artists such as Martin Gramp, Hans Fries, Hans Gieng and Hans Geiler. Fries—the city's official poet from 1501 through 1510—exerted a strong influence over his contemporaries and several of his works are on display. The 17C is present with works by Pierre Wuilleret and Jean-François Reyff, the 18C with paintings attributed to Gottfried Locher.

In the room devoted to regional guilds and associations, a series of engravings and watercolours present the city of Fribourg and its canton. The artifacts displayed in the archeological section can be traced back to prehistoric times, ancient Rome and the early Middle Ages.
The stone museum, set up in the former slaughterhouse, features a fascinating collection of fourteen **15C stone statues**★ taken from the Cathedral of St Nicholas, depicting the Annunciation and the Apostles. Visitors may also admire a splendid 11C Crucifixion scene from Villars-les-Moines and a group of 16C sculptures attributed to Hans Gieng, contrasting sharply with the monumental compositions of Jean Tinguely. The rest of the exhibition consists of a rare collection of objects in silver and gold (14C–18C), some stunning pieces of Burgundian jewellery (7C–8C) and works by Marcello (the pseudonym of the native artist the Duchess Castiglione Colonna, née Adèle d'Affry), extremely popular during the 20C. A number of 19C and 20C works, including several by Eugène Delacroix, Félix Vallotton and Ferdinand Hodler, are in the attic room above the former slaughterhouse.

▷ Continue down Murtengasse.

Franciscan Church

A Franciscan community settled in Fribourg in 1256. The monastery buildings were completed about the end of the 13C and remodelled in the 18C. The monastery, which then had a superb bookbinding workshop and the richest library in town, received the most influential people passing through Fribourg.
The first chapel on the right contains a gilded and carved wood **triptych**★ made in about 1513 for Jean de Furno, which shows Alsatian influence. The central panel depicts the Crucifixion, with Mary Magdalene at the foot of the Cross; the panel on the left shows the Adoration of the Shepherds, and that on the right, the Adoration of the Magi. The folding shutters on the left illustrate the

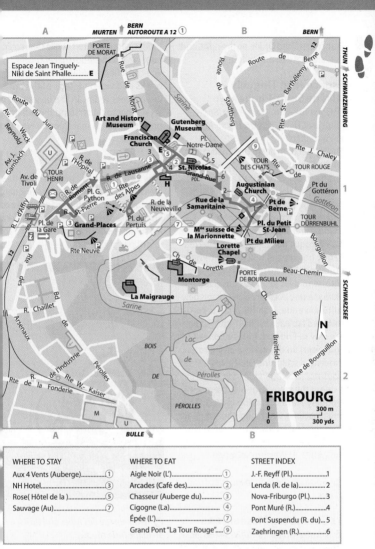

FRIBOURG

0   300 m

0   300 yds

Annunciation; those on the right present
a pretty Coronation of the Virgin.

The **chancel** is a good example of
13C Franciscan architecture, with four
keystones in the vaulting bearing the
symbols of the Evangelists. It contains
oak **stalls**★ dating from c.1280. On the
left of the chancel is the altarpiece of
St Anthony, known as *The Death of the
Usurer*, painted in 1506 by the Fribourg
artist Hans Fries. The picture illustrates
the words of the Gospel: "Where a man's
treasure is, there will his heart be too."
Over the high altar stands the magnificent **altarpiece**★★ by the Masters of

the Carnation, painted at Solothurn and
Basel in 1480. The picture is very large
(8 x 2.7m/26 x 8.5ft) and was installed
during the restoration of 1936, replac-
ing a 1692 Baroque altarpiece. The central scene represents a Crucifixion; it is
flanked by four Franciscan saints: St Ber-
nardine of Siena, St Anthony of Padua,
St Francis of Assisi, and St Louis, Bishop
of Toulouse. The Adoration of the Shepherds is on the left shutter, that of the
Magi on the right; the background suggests the Fribourg Alps. Folding shutters
feature an Annunciation in their centre,
St Elizabeth of Hungary, patroness of the

Franciscan Third Order, on the right, and St Clara of Assisi on the left.

Espace Jean Tinguely – Niki de Saint-Phalle★

⊙*Open Tue–Sun, 11am–6pm (8pm Thu).* ⊛*8CHF.* ♿ ℘*(0)26 305 51 40. www.mahf.ch .*

The former tram depot designed in 1900 by the Fribourg architect Léon Hertling, has been converted into a gallery displaying the works of the famous artists Jean Tinguely and Niki de Saint-Phalle; and temporary exhibitions. Fronted by an imposing façade and decorated with neo-Baroque gables, the gallery permanently houses the Niki de Saint-Phalle donation. The artist (Jean Tinguely's wife, who died in 2002) conceived her *Monumental Relief* especially for this new cultural venue: A series of 22 brightly coloured tableaux evoking Jean Tinguely's stay in Fribourg (left-hand wall as you enter). In the middle of the room, the central sculpture, *Retable to Western Opulence and Totalitarian Mercantilism*, is one of the many large altarpieces that Tinguely started making in 1981. This huge machine, which grinds into motion at regular intervals, is decorated with toys and various objects symbolizing the wealth of Western society.

▷ *Go along the road to the left of the square.*

♟♟ Gutenberg Museum★★

16 pl. Notre-Dame. ℘ *(0)26 347 38 28. www.gutenbergmuseum.ch.* ♿ ⊙*Open daily except Mon and Tue 11am–6pm (8pm Thu, 5pm Sun),* ⊛*5 CHF. Audio-guide.*

Just behind the Espace Jean Tinguely, the Swiss museum of Graphic Art and Communication is located in a building which was built in 1527, and served its purpose as a customs office, among other roles. The museum explores the history of the written word and the printing process across the centuries, from Gutenberg to the technology driven world today. The exhibitions are educational and appeal to children as well as adults. The first floor concen-trates on former times, while the second floor covers the industrial era.

The third floor contains both very old books and video footage of the printing process today. In the basement it is possible to understand the different processes which make up the creation of a book

Grand-Place

This square which includes lawned areas, is graced with the Jean-Tinguely fountain, dedicated by the Swiss artist to his deceased friend, the driver Jo Siffert. On summer days the open areas attract lots of people.

La fontaine de Jo Siffert' by Jean Tinguely at Grand-Places

▷ *Walk up rue des Alpes and turn left on to the little square.*

Hôtel de Ville★ (H)

The town hall stands near a square famed for its lime tree, planted, it is said, on 22 June 1476 to celebrate the victory of the Confederates over **Charles the Bold** (⟲*see INTRODUCTION: History)* in Murten. This fine, early-16C building, with its canopy and double staircase (17C) is dominated by a large roof of brown tiles. The belfry and its Jack-o'-the-clock figure are crowned with pinnacle turrets. On the square stands the Fountain of St George (1525), featuring a group of sculptures by Hans Geiler.

▷ *Go along the Grand Rue and take the first pedestrianised street on the right.*

Cathédrale St-Nicolas★

⊙*Open Mon–Fri 9.30am–6pm, Sat 9am–4pm and Sun 2am–5pm.*

The cathedral rears its fine Gothic tower above the roofs of the old town. The first stone was laid in 1283; the cathedral was intended to take the place of the church built a century earlier by the founder of the town, Berchtold IV of Zähringen. The far end of the church was altered in the 17C by the rebuilding of an apse with three walls and five bays to replace the flat east end. The tower, 76m/250ft high, was built in the 14C, on the octagon completed c.1490 with a crown of pinnacles in the style of the period.

The **tympanum**★★ of the main porch, surmounted by a rose window, is devoted to the Last Judgement: Heaven and Hell are shown on either side of the Weighing of Souls; the archivolts portray the Angels, Prophets and Patriarchs; the doorway, the Apostles. The sculptures in the south porch date back to the 14C. Inside, a square vestibule is formed by the lower part of the tower, with side walls adorned with fine arcades, precedes the ogive-vaulted nave. Pictures from the 17C adorn the corner-pieces of the great arcades, which is surmounted by clerestory windows (the work of Alfred Manessier in 1983). The aisles, which also feature ogive vaulting, are lit by windows designed by the Polish painter Mehoffer.

The side chapels (16C and 17C) received Baroque altars in the mid-18C. The chancel, with a Gothic wrought-iron screen, is adorned with 15C **stalls**★ representing the Prophets and Apostles. A beam supports a large Calvary carved in the first half of the 15C. To the right, the Chapel of the Holy Sepulchre contains a fine **Entombment** (433) and more stained glass by Alfred Manessier.

The late-15C font on the south side of the chancel is made of finely carved stone. Its wooden cover is 17C. The organ, one of the glories of 19C Fribourg, was built in 1834.

Tower of Cathédrale St-Nicolas and the belfry of Hôtel de Ville

Stephan Engler/Switzerland Tourism

▷ *Descend towards the Vieille Ville by rue du Pont-Suspendu, turn right into rue de Zaehringen, follow by Stalden, then turn left along rue de la Lenda.*

Augustinian Church

The interior of the church, commissioned by the mendicant orders, presents a large nave divided into four bays, separated by Gothic arches resting on spherical pillars. The furnishings are characteristic of the Baroque period. The wooden retable surmounting the high altar—gilded and painted to resemble marble—is the work of Peter and Jacob Spring: Three levels, two of which feature niches flanked by columns, portray religious scenes, mostly taken from the Life of the Virgin. The two retables placed at the entrance to the chancel were made at the Ryeff workshops. The one on the right features an elegant polychrome composition, *Virgin and Child*. On the square is an annex to the church: A gallery with six arcades, supporting a first floor reinforced by half-timbering.

▷ *Go down rue des Agustins and then turn left on to rue d'Or.*

Pont de Berne

A charming wooden bridge with oak supports spans the River Sarine.

▷ *Take the road opposite the bridge.*

Place du Petit-St-Jean

This square, located south of the Auge district, extends up to the Pont de Berne and owes its name to St-Jean-de-Jérusalem, a former Knights' Chapel built in the 13C and demolished in the 19C.

The Fontaine de Ste-Anne (1560), a tribute to the city's patron saint of tanners, is the work of Hans Gieng; note the lovely façade at number 29.

▷ *Take the road uphill.*

Rue de la Samaritaine

This steep, paved street will return you to **place du Petit St-Jean**. The Samaritans' Fountain (1551), yet another token of Hans Gieng's talent, represents Jesus and the Samaritan at Jacob's well. Level with the fountain, note the impressive Late Gothic façade, punctuated by eight picture windows embellished with Flamboyant tracery.

At number 34 the **Musée Suisse de la Marionnette** (*open daily, 10am–5pm, guided visits only Mon–Tues; closed Jan, during Carnival, Easter and 25 Dec; 5CHF; (0)26 322 85 13; www.marionette.ch*) will whisk you away to the magical world of dolls, puppets, paper or chiffon figurines, shadow pantomimes, masks, and similar games from countries all over the world. Performances can be arranged on a regular basis.

▷ *By going back up route des Alpes and on to rue St-Pierre you can reach the Grand Place, which has a Tinguely fountain dedicated to his late racing driver friend, Jo Siffert. Rejoin avenue de la Gare.*

SIGHTS
Musée d'Histoire Naturelle

In the Faculty of Science on the route de Marly (not on the map) via the boulevard de Pérolles. Open daily 2pm–6pm. Closed 1 Jan, Good Fri and 25 Dec. The museum closes at 4pm on 24 and 31 Dec. No charge. (0)26 305 89 00.

The Natural Science Museum occupies seven rooms on the first floor. The first rooms display fossils (geological and paleontological sections), a relief model of the Aletsch Glacier and its region, and a splendid collection of minerals, along with a reconstruction of a crystal cave. The other rooms are devoted to zoology. Stuffed specimens of local fauna are presented in their natural setting and a diorama shows a variety of bird species complete with their recorded songs. Other displays include animals from the five continents. The fascinating world of insects is given special attention. Morphology, reproduction, evolution of the species, recorded stridulations of the grasshopper and cricket, and studies conducted under a microscope.

Schwarzsee

EXCURSIONS

Schwarzsee★

⟫ 27km/17mi – about 1hr. Leave Fribourg across the Zaehringen Bridge on the road to Bourguillon and then road N 74.

When you reach Tafers, turn right on to a picturesque road offering charming views towards the Berra on the right and towards the Guggershorn on the left.

After Plaffeien, a pretty village of varnished wooden chalets, the road climbs through the Sence Valley to end at the **Black Lake** (Schwarzee—*angling*) in a pretty mountain **setting**★. A pleasant resort has grown up beside the lake.

Barrage de Rossens★

⟫ Round tour of 55km/34mi. Leave Fribourg by road number 12. After 13km/8mi take the Rossens road on the left.

A large dam was built across the Sarine in 1948, upstream from the village of Rossens. The dam is arched, 320m/1 049ft long and 83m/272ft high. The 14km/8.5mi-long reservoir, forming a magnificent pool in a pretty, steep-sided setting, is known as **Lake Gruyères**. To enjoy a good view, follow the road on the right towards Pont-la-Ville. At La Roche take road 77 on the right and cross the lake at Corbières. At Riaz you rejoin road number 12 to Fribourg.

Abbaye de Hauterive

⟫ 7km/4.3mi SW of Fribourg by the road to Bulle. After 4.5km/3mi take the Marly-le-Grand exit and turn right.

⟫ Guided tour (1hr), Mon–Sat 9.45–11.30am, 2pm–5pm, Sun and public holidays, 11.00–11.30am, 3pm–4pm. ✆(0)26 409 71 02.

After Chesalles, a road on the left leads to the abbey, which stands in a loop of the Sarine. The Cistercian abbey, founded in 1138 by 12 French monks, was secularised in 1848 but resumed the life of prayer and work in 1939. It is the oldest remaining Cistercian abbey in Switzerland. Situated on the route to St-Jacques-de-Compostela, it extends hospitality to pilgrims or other travellers wishing to go into retreat.

The church, built in 1160, has undergone many alterations, especially in the 14C and 18C. It was furnished with stained-glass windows (14C and 15C) in the chancel with fine stalls with panels carved with human figures and crowned with open-work canopies, a 16C mural painting and in the north side aisle the recumbent figure of a knight whose feet rest on a lion. The monastery buildings were rebuilt in the 18C, with a Baroque façade. Inside, the main staircase is adorned with elegant wrought-iron balustrades. The Gothic **cloisters**, entirely remodeled in the 14C, are roofed with painted groined vaulting featuring finely carved keystones.

🚗 DRIVING TOUR

LE PLATEAU VAUDOIS

Avenches

4km/2mi S of Lake Murten – Alt. 473m/ 1 574ft. 3 place de l'Église – 1580. ✆(0)26 676 99 22. www.avenches.ch.

Avenches is built on the site of the former capital of the Helvetii. The Roman city of Aventicum, founded by the Emperor Augustus and expanded into a colony by Vespasian, had some 20 000 inhabitants and flourished throughout the 2C AD and destroyed in AD 259. The château, with the Renaissance façade which stands in the centre of the town, dates from the late 13C. It was commissioned by the bishops of Lausanne. In the 16C, the château was enlarged by the authorities in Bern into a residence for their bailiffs.

Roman legions – The town was defended by a ring of fortifications about 6km/3.7mi round, with walls over 7m/23ft high, crowned with battlements; semicircular towers were used as observation posts; one of them, the Tornallaz, is still standing but it has been badly restored. Visitors are allowed to visit the remains of the amphitheatre, the Roman arena (on the Fribourg road) and a large sanctuary known as the "storkery", of which only one pilaster has survived. Recent excavations have revealed the ruins of a portico and temple podium.

Amphitheatre – The amphitheater is thought to date from the end of the 1C AD. Duels between gladiators and fights against wild animals were staged in this elliptical arena, which, in its heyday, was able to seat up to 16 000.

Today – The modern town is much smaller than the Ancient city, whose size can be judged from the excavated ruins. These became the property of the town in 1804. General Guisan, commander-inchief of the Swiss army from 1939–45, was born here; his bust stands in the plaza in front of the post office.

Musée Romain d'Avenches★

Open Apr–Sept, Tue–Sun, 10am–noon, 1pm–5pm; Oct–Mar, 2pm–5pm. Closed 1 and 2 Jan, 25, 26 and 31 Dec. 2CHF. (0)26 671 17 27. www.aventicum.org.

The museum is housed in a square tower, built in the Middle Ages over the main entrance to the amphitheatre. It contains objects discovered during the excavations. On the ground floor are displayed a very fine statue of a wolf suckling Romulus and Remus, several inscriptions, mural paintings, and mosaics; an audio-visual presentation explains the history of Avenches.

On the first floor, admire the copy of a golden bust of the Emperor Marcus Aurelius (the original is in the Musée des Beaux-Arts in Lausanne), along with some bronze pieces (Bacchus, Silenus, votive hand, Gaul divinity), marble sculptures (Minerva, Mercury, funerary art) and a collection of coins minted at Aventicum.

The second floor displays old tools and pottery pieces recreating Roman daily life in Switzerland in a lively and evocative manner.

▶ 6km/3.75mi W . Take the road in the direction of Estavayer-le-Lac.

Musée Romain de Vallon

Open Jun–Sept Wed–Sun, 2–6pm, 1 Oct–31 May, Wed–Sun 2–5pm. Closed Mon, Sun, 1 & 2 Jan, 24–26 & 31 Dec.

6 CHF. (0)26 667 97 97. www.museevallon.ch.

A Gallo-Roman villa has been uncovered at the base of Caringan's rocky outcrop, where a water course had been planned. A museum has subsequently been created. The findings confirm that several large domaines existed in the countryside around Aventicum. Here there is evidence of three large buildings with a total of some 40 rooms. The rooms of note boast a superb mosaic depicting Bacchus and Ariadne, as well as hunting scenes—the latter of 97sq m/116sq yd being the largest in the Northern Alps area. Among the exhibits in the museum are a collection of small bronze statues of Lares—deities believed to protect the household.

▶ Continue in the direction of Estavayer-le-Lac and after 1km/0.6mi turn left to Payerne.

Payerne★

Alt. 450m/1 476ft 1 place Général Guisan – 1530. (0)26 660 61 61.

Payerne boasts a remarkable abbey church, once attached to a Benedictine abbey. This abbey is believed to have been founded in the 10C by Empress Adelaide, wife of Otto the Great, first of the Holy Roman Emperors and daughter of the legendary Queen Bertha, nicknamed Bertha the Spinner, the widow of Rudolph II, King of Trans-Jura Burgundy.

Abbey Church★★

Open Tue–Sun 10am–noon, 2pm–6pm (5pm Nov–Apr). Closed Good Fri. 3CHF. (0)26 662 67 04.

The 11C church is virtually all that remains of this once large Cluniac abbey. The church fell into disuse when the Bernese introduced the Reformation into the Vaud district. It was converted into a storehouse and barracks and suffered considerable damage. Large-scale renovation has restored this Romanesque church to its former glory.

Interior – The plain nave is lit by tall windows and crowned with barrel vaulting; harmony of proportion con veys an impression of grandeur but also of severity, emphasised by sparse decoration. Remarkable capitals adorn tall windows of the chancel and transept pillars. Their crude but expressive design dates them back to the abbey's founding. Beautiful 13C frescoes can be seen in the choir, transept and narthex, including Christ at the Last Judgement, with the 24 Elders of the Apocalypse seated before him.

Adjoining the church, the elegant **chapterhouse** with groined vaulting houses an exhibition on the history of the church. Note the two original bronze knockers (10C).

Museum – The museum is reached through the right arm of the transept. Permanent collections are devoted to two famous natives of the area.

Aimée Rapin (1868–1956) was an artist born without arms who painted with her toes. Her work was presented at the Paris World Fair in 1888, when she gained widespread recognition. Her wide-ranging talent is clearly expressed in her still life works (*Fruit, The Hunt*), portraits (*Young Girl at the Lake, Man with Pipe*), and drawings in charcoal and crayon (*Portrait of Monsieur Pierre Libaud, Woman Sitting*).

General **Antoine-Henri Jomini** (1779–1869) served under Napoleon I, becoming aide-de-camp to Marshall Ney and subsequently his Chief of Staff. After a misunderstanding with the marshall, Jomini left the French army and served under the Tsar of Russia, Alexander II. He died in Passy, near Paris, in 1869.

Lucens

This small town is associated with Sherlock Holmes, since the famous detective's author, Sir Arthur Conan Doyle, once owned a château here and founded a museum. The **Musée Sherlock Holmes** (👥🔓🕐*open Wed, Sat–Sun 2pm–5pm;* ◉*4CHF;* ✆*(0)21 906 73 33*) is dedicated to Sir Conan Doyle and his well-known, fictitious hero, and is worth a visit.

Moudon

Alt. 522m/1 713ft. Place de la Douane – 1510. ✆*(0)21 905 88 66.*
www.moudon.ch.

Moudon enjoyed great prosperity under the counts of Savoy (14C): most of the buildings which give the town its medieval air date from that time. From the bridge over which the N 1 secondary road crosses the Broye, there is a pleasing view of the old quarter with its 15C-17C houses.

Église St-Étienne

This church, built in the 13C and early 14C, has an imposing fortified belfry, once part of the town walls. The Gothic nave, roofed with vaulting, bearing coats of arms, has lovely stained-glass windows and an organ (1764). The chancel contains fine stalls (early 16C and early 17C). Original 16C frescoes, which have undergone extensive restoration, are noteworthy.

Rue du Château

Start from Place de la Grenette.

This is the main street of the old quarter, beginning with a fountain depicting Justice. Farther along, the 12C Broye Tower (in ruins) stands on the right of the street, which is lined on either side by houses dating from the 15C, 16C and 17C; note the Bernese-style house at number 34. Midway to the left the view overlooks the river, spanned by a covered bridge; at the end of the street are the museums (on the right) and a second fountain (1557) called Moses.

Musée du Vieux-Moudon

🕐*Open Apr–late-Nov, Wed, Sat–Sun 2pm–6pm.* ◉*5CHF, 8CHF (combined ticket with Musée Eugène-Burnand).* ✆*(0)21 905 27 05.*

Housed in the 13C Maison de Rochefort in the upper town, this museum is dedicated to local and regional history, including documents, weapons, and a period kitchen. Additional sections are dedicated to the town (old wrought-iron signs that once hung outside cafés in Moudon, finials and paintings) and rural areas (tools, ploughing instruments and

View of Romont

Stephan Engler/Switzerland Tourism

cow bells). A spiral staircase leads to the first floor, where a model of the town as it was in 1415 is displayed.

Musée Eugène-Burnand

Ⓛ*Open Apr–Nov, Wed, Sat–Sun 2pm–6.30pm. ⊜5CHF, 8CHF (combined ticket with Musée du Vieux-Moudon), (-16 years, no charge). Visit by appointment 10 days in advance to the Tourist Office on ℘(0)21 905 88 66.*
The Bâtiment du Grand'Air houses works by Eugène Burnand, who was born in Moudon in 1850 and died in Paris in 1921.

Romont

*Alt. 760m/2 736ft. 112Rue du Château.
℘(0)26 651 90 55. www.romont.ch.*
The little town of Romont was built by Peter II of Savoy in the 13C, and is still encircled by some of its ramparts. Its occupies a picturesque **site**★ on a crest overlooking the valleys of the Glâne and the Glâney.

Collégiale Notre-Dame-de-l'Assomption

Ⓛ*Open Apr–Oct, 9am–7.30pm; Nov–Mar, 9am–6.30pm. ⸰⸰Guided tour, contact the Tourist Office for further information ℘(0)26 651 90 55.*
This collegiate church is one of the finest Gothic churches in Romansh country. Don't miss the 15C **chancel**★ (adorned with carved stalls) and 14C and 15C stained-glass windows.

Castle

The castle dates from the 13C, as can be seen from the keep of Peter II of Savoy, but has been remodelled several times. The main gateway (16C) is surmounted by several coats of arms of Fribourg and Romont.
Since 1981, the castle has housed the **Musée Suisse du Vitrail** (Ⓛ*open daily 23 Mar–31 Oct, Tue–Sun 10am–1pm, 2pm–6pm; 4 Nov–22 Mar Thu and Sun, 10am–1pm, 2–5. ⊜10CHF. ℘(0)26) 652 10 95. www.vitromusee.ch*). The museum collections include medieval stained glass and Swiss heraldic glass as well as works by non-Swiss glass-makers.

ADDRESSES

⌂STAY

⊜⊜ **Auberge Aux 4 Vents** – *2km/ 1.25mi N of Fribourg, exit N. 124 route de Grandfey. ℘(0)26 347 36 00. www.auberge.aux4vents.ch. Closed 3 weeks Jan. 8 rooms.* A well renowned hotel, worth a detour. Easy to find despite its rural location, the hotel's rooms are a real experience. In the Blue Room, which is the best known, the bath is half suspended outside the window which gives the impression of being in the water and above the garden. The Angel room is truely romantic and the luxury of the Babylon room is exceptional. Anyone on a lesser budget can opt for the Dormitory room which has four beds. Outdoor swimming pool and good restaurant.

⌣⌣ **Hôtel de la Rose** – *1 rue de Morat.*
℘(0)26 351 01 01. www.hoteldelarose.ch.
40 rooms. Located a stone's throw from
the Cathédrale Notre-Dame and the
Église des Cordeliers.

⌣⌣⌣ **NH Hotel** – *14 Grand-Places.*
℘(0)26 351 91 91. www.nh-hotels.com.
122 rooms. Just 300m/328yds from
the station, a modern hotel with
comfortable rooms.

⌣⌣⌣ **Hôtel du Sauvage** –
12 Planche-Supérieure. ℘(0)26 347 30 60.
www.hotel-sauvage.ch. 16 rooms. This
hotel in the heart of the old city is easy
to spot because of its sign. It offers a
choice of different rooms, each with its
own personality and charm.

⌣/EAT

⌣ **Café des Arcades** – *1 place des
Ormeaux. ℘(0)26 321 48 40. www.cafe
desarcades.ch. Closed Mon.* A good
choice for lunch, located just next to
the cathedral. Service can be slow at
busy times.

⌣ **L'Épée** – *39 Planche-Supérieure.
℘(0)26 322 34 07. Closed mid-Jul–mid
Aug, Mon evenings and Sun.* Carefully
prepared dishes at reasonable prices.

⌣⌣ **L'Aigle Noir** – *10 rue des Alpes.
℘(0)26 322 49 88. www.aiglenoir.ch.
Closed 25 Dec–12 Jan, Sun and Mon.*
Choose to dine in a traditional room,
one opulently furnished with antiques
to evoke old-fashioned Switzerland, or
on the terrace with a lovely view of the
old city and the mountains.

⌣⌣ **Auberge du Chasseur** – *10 rue de
Lausanne. ℘(0)26 322 56 98. Open daily
exc Mon. Closed 1–15 Jun.* In the town
centre. Fondues and raclettes are the
speciality of the house.

⌣⌣ **Grand Pont "La Tour Rouge"** –
*2 route de Bourguillon. ℘(0)26 481 32 48.
Closed Tue, Wed and Sun evenings.*
Traditional restaurant and brasserie (La
Galerie). Terrace commanding pretty
views of the Sarine River and the old city.

⌣⌣ **La Cigogne** – *24 rue d'Or.
℘(0)26 322 68 34. www.la-cigogne.ch.
Closed Sun and Mon, and last two weeks
Feb.* Bistro near Pont de Berne in the
old district providing good, affordable
cuisine.

⛒ SHOPPING

The main shopping streets are
boulevard de Pérolles, from the train
station to the Jardin des Pérolles, **rue
de Romont**, **rue St-Pierre**, and **rue
de Lausanne.** There is a **vegetable
and flower market** on place Georges-
Python every Wednesday morning and
on place de l'Hôtel-de-Ville on Saturdays.
Regional produce can be bought from
La Clef du Pays, 4 route des Alpes.

⛉ THEATRE AND MUSIC

Aula Magna, avenue Louis Weck-
Reynold.
Église St-Michel, rue St-Pierre Canisius:
Classical music.
Centre Frison, route de la Fonderie:
Modern music.
Le Nouveau Monde, Arsenaux 12A:
Jazz, rock, salsa, reggae etc.

⛎ NIGHTLIFE

The **Rock Café** features rock 'n' roll
music and décor: Gold and platinum
records and instruments which
belonged to famous performers
(Johnny Hallyday, Elton John, etc.).

Near pont de Zaehringen, in the street
bearing the same name, the **Golden
Gate** (enter through the Auberge
de Zaehringen) offers a pleasant 13C
setting (rough walls with pebble
masonry, sturdy wooden beams
and pillars).

In the vicinity of place de Notre-Dame:
The **Gothard** (typical fondue from the
Fribourg area) with its young, trendy
crowd; **Les Arcades**, a more relaxed
restaurant and bar; **La Cave** (basement
dance hall situated below the Hôtel de
la Rose) has a fine vaulted cellar with
thick stone walls and opens its doors at
10pm, although the place livens up later
in the night. **Banshee's**, a Celtic pub
offering a remarkable choice of beers
and live folk music on weekends, is the
place to go, especially on St Patrick's
Day, when the atmosphere is at its
wildest. The **Baccara** nightclub in the
Hôtel au Parc has a DJ.

Murten★★

Murten has a yachting marina which attracts visitors. This former fortified city, which has kept most of its ramparts and towers, exudes picturesque charm.

👣WALKING TOUR

Hauptgasse

The main street runs through the heart of the **old town** with arcaded houses, fountains and the Bern Gateway, surmounted by a graceful pinnacle.

▶ *Take Deutschekirchgasse which starts just before the Berntor, go around the German Protestant church, behind which a wooden stairway leads to the walls.*

Stadtmauer★

Take the wall-walk, covered with an attractive timber roof, to the right. It affords pretty views over the old town, the castle and the lake. Mount Vully and the Jura foothills rise on the horizon. At the end of the wall-walk, climb the tower for views of the castle and the lake in the distance.

▶ *Retrace your steps and leave the wall-walk by the square tower.*

Schloss

Built in the 13C by Duke Peter of Savoy, this is a grim, imposing castle.

Historisches Museum

🕑*Open Mar–Dec, Tue–Sun 2pm–5pm; Jan and Feb, Sat–Sun 2pm–5pm.* 📷*8CHF.* 📞*026 670 31 00. www.museummurten.ch.*

The historical museum is located in the town's restored 18C watermill. Exhibits include prehistoric and Gallo-Roman relics, local historical objects from the Middle Ages to the 18C, Burgundian treasures, and exhibits on the crucial Battle of Murten.

▶ **Population:** Fribourg 6 024.
🕭 **Michelin Map:**
National Map 729: F5
🗎 **Info:** Französische Kirchgasse 6 – 3280. 📞026 670 51 12. www.murten tourismus.ch.
▶ **Location:** On the eastern shore of Lake Murten. Alt. 458m/1 503ft.
👁 **Don't Miss:** The wall-walk on Stadtmauer.
🕐 **Timing:** Allow at least two hours to visit the sights.
👫 **Kids:** Papiliorama—tropical forest environment.

Rathausgasse

This street leads to the small **French church**, with its single nave and ogival-vaulted choir.The balcony has views of the lakes and the foothills of the Jura mountains in the distance.

▶ *Französischegasse leads to the Berntor and back to the main street.*

NEARBY

Murtensee (Morat Lake)

The Murtensee runs parallel to the northern part of Lake Neuchâtel and is linked to it by the Broye Canal. Lake Murten has a bird sanctuary on its north shore and a beach on its south shore.

👫 Papiliorama-Nocturama

At Kerzers(Chiètres), 13km/7.5mi NE of Morat. 🕑*Open summer, 9am–6pm; winter, 10am–5pm.* 📷*17CHF.* 📞*(0)31 756 04 61.*

The **Papiliorama** and **Nocturama,** housed in two enormous bubbles, give visitors a chance to experience tropical forests. The Papiliorama exhibits very humid tropical heat, and the cooler Nocturama introduces animals from South America in a moonlit atmosphere. Unusual creatures here include the spectacled owl, the paca, the nine-striped armadillo, the night monkey and the ocelot.

Neuchâtel★★

Neuchâtel enjoys a charming site between its lake, with 4km/2.5mi of quays, and Chaumont Hill. The pleasant, attractive town stands in the middle of vineyards; its pale ochre houses prompted Alexandre Dumas to say it was carved out of a pat of butter. The silhouettes of the collegiate church and the castle dominate the scene.

OLD TOWN
Lake Neuchâtel
This is the largest wholly Swiss lake, being nearly 38km/23.6mi long and 8km/5mi wide. Canals used by pleasure boats join it with Lake Biel and Lake Murten. Its iridescent waters and hilly, vine-clad shores are favorite subjects for painters and writers; André Gide is one of many to have been inspired in the past.

A BIT OF HISTORY
Middle Ages – The name Neuchâtel is derived from a structure built as a stronghold during Burgundian rule (1011). Later, the town became the property of the French Orléans-Longueville family. It is said that in order to celebrate his entry into the town during a 1657 visit, Henri II of Orléans had 6 000l/1 585 gal of the local red wine poured into the Griffin Fountain, which still stands in rue du Château. Neuchâtel became the personal property of the King of Prussia after 1707.

Struggle for independence – After being placed under the rule of Marshal Berthier (Chief of Staff of Napoleon I) as a principality (1806-14), Neuchâtel joined the Swiss Confederation in 1815 and was then in a peculiar political position as a Swiss canton bound to the King of Prussia.
An independence effort in 1831 failed, but succeeded in 1848, and the Republic was proclaimed. The King of Prussia finally recognised the canton's independence in 1857 but kept the courtesy title of Prince of Neuchâtel. The French

▶ **Population:** Neuchâtel 32 592.
Michelin Map: National Map 729: E5.
Info: Hôtel des Postes. ℘(0)32 889 68 90. www.neuchateltourisme.ch.
Location: At the feet of the Jura hills in western Switzerland. Alt. 440m/1 444ft.
Parking: It is easiest to use public or hotel car parks.
Don't Miss: The old town or an excursion to the observation tower at Chaumont.
Timing: A stay of at least two days is recommended in order to enjoy the most important sights.

spoken at Neuchâtel is considered by many to be the purest in Switzerland. Neuchâtel today is an important watch and clock research centre, whose observatory gives the official time to all of Switzerland. It is also a wine market— a great wine harvest procession takes place here in September.

SIGHTS
Old Town★
Guided tours (1hr) mid-May– Oct, at 9am and 11am. 7CHF. Contact the Tourist Office ℘(0)32 889 68 90.
A picturesque quarter (rue du Château, rue du Trésor, rue du Seyon, rue du Pommier, rue des Moulins) with old houses, 16C and 17C fountains (Fontaine de la Justice, Grand-Rue; Fontaine du Banneret, on the corner of rue du Château and rue du Trésor; Fontaine du Lion, on the corner of rue du Temple-Neuf and rue du Bassin) and defensive towers, extends between the town hall (1788), a classical building by the architect and painter Paris (1747–1819), from Besançon, and the group formed by the collegiate church and the castle. On the oblong Place des Halles (Market Square) are 17C

houses, and, at the far end, the Renaissance house Maison des Halles.

Collegiate Church and Château★

Guided tour (45min) Apr–Sept, Mon–Sat hourly 10am–noon, 2pm–4pm, Sun and public holidays at 2pm, 3pm, 4pm. No charge. (0)32 889 60 00.

The **collegiate church** is a fine 12C and 13C construction with multicoloured glazed tiles, and was heavily restored during the 19C. A statue of the protestant reformer **Guillaume Farel** (1489–1565) faces the main church entrance. Under an arcade in the chancel, the cenotaph of the counts of Neuchâtel (14C) is a striking example of medieval sculpture: This superb stone composition comprises 14 stiff, impressive polychrome statues depicting knights and noblewomen at prayer. The south portal, Romanesque, decorated with archivolts and carved capitals, is flanked by the statues of St Peter and St Paul.

The **Castle** (15C and 16C, restored) is the seat of the cantonal government. The main entrance gate is flanked by two crowned towers and embellished with broken arches. Under the passageway, the arms of Philippe de Hochberg, Lord of Neuchâtel, can be seen. In the northern wing, you may visit the former kitchen area, the antechamber, the semicircular Great Council Hall, seat of the cantonal government (note the stained-glass windows by Georges Froidevaux, representing municipal coats of arms), and the Knights' Hall, the largest room in the castle, used for receptions.

In the south wing, visitors are shown the room named after Mary of Savoy, niece of Louis XI and wife to Count Philippe de Hochberg (the count's arms hang above the stone fireplace), the Philippe de Hochberg Gallery, and the States' Room or Tribunal Room, whose walls recount the history of the Neuchâtel district. The wall-walk offers lovely views of the town.

Prisons Tower

Open Apr–30 Sept, 8am–6pm. 2CHF. (0)32 717 75 00.

The Prison Tower sits at the foot of the hill on which the castle stands, in rue Jehanne-de-Hochberg. The interior contains two wooden dungeons used until 1848 and two maquettes of Neuchâtel from the late 15C and late 18C. The viewpoint affords a fine **panorama** of the town and the lake.

Art and History Museum★★

Start from the Fine Arts section. Open Tue–Sun 11am–6pm. Closed 26 Sept, 1 Jan, 24, 25 and 31 Dec. 5CHF. No charge Wed. (0)32 717 79 20. www.mahn.ch.

Fine Arts (*Upper floor*) – A staircase decorated with frescoes by Paul Robert and stained glass by Clement Heaton leads to

Collegiate Church and Castle of Neuchâtel

this part of the museum, which houses a retrospective of Swiss painting occupies five halls, presenting works by Léopold Robert (*Weeping Woman at the Water's Edge*), Ferdinand Hodler (*Autumn Evening*) and Albert Anker (*Bernese Peasant Reading his Newspaper*). Another room is largely devoted to French Impressionism (*The Boat-Workshop* by Monet).

History and Decorative Arts (*Ground floor and mezzanine*) – A series of large and small galleries display regional crafts and the history and lifestyle of the canton via collections of gold and silver plate, coins and porcelain. Gallery 4 includes timepieces from Neuchâtel and three delightful **automata**★★, made in the 18C by Jaquet-Droz and Sons as well as by Jean-Frédéric Leschot: they are the Musician, the Writer and the Draughtsman. Do not miss the admirable **Strübin Collection**★, presenting weapons, armour, and uniforms from the French Revolution, the First Napoleonic Empire, the Restoration and the Second Empire.

Museum of Ethnography★

◷*Open Tue–Sun 10am–5pm.* ◷*Closed Mon, 1 Jan, 24, 25 and 31 Dec.* ⊜*8CHF. No charge Wed.* ℘*(0)32 718 19 60. www.men.ch.*

The **Museum of Ethnography**'s modern annex is used exclusively for themed temporary exhibits. The northern façade has a huge mural, *The Conquests of Man,* by the Swiss painter **Hans Erni**.

Ground floor rooms are dedicated to Ancient Egypt, with collections of *shabti* statuettes and funerary boats, wooden sculptures dating from the 6th and 10th Dynasties, and exhibits explaining the ritual of mummification. Another room displays artifacts from the Himalayas, including Tibetan statues and a collection from Bhutan. On the first floor is the private study of the traveller and collector Charles-Daniel de Meuron (1738–1806), containing his collections. This floor also houses traditional ethnographical collections, with exhibits that include a Tuareg tent, spears, Angolan musical instruments, masks from New Caledonia, Nigeria and Angola, a reliquary head from Gabon and an androgynous "Uli" statue from New Ireland, near Papua New Guinea.

Quai Osterwald

Viewing table. Superb **view**★★ of the lake and the Alpine range.

♟♟ Natural History Museum

◷*Open Tue–Sun, 10am–6pm.* ◷*Closed 25 Dec and 1 Jan.* ⊜*8CHF.* ♿ ℘*(0)32 717 79 60. www.museum-neuchatel.ch.*

The Natural History Museum houses exhibitions of mammals, as well as several species of aquatic and sylvan birds, displayed in dioramas which reproduce their natural setting.

Hôtel Du Peyrou

An elegant building in the style of Louis 16th which was built in the eighteenth century by the financier DuPeyrou; a friend of Jean-Jacques Rousseau. The entrance allows visitors to appreciate the clean lines of the outside of the building and leads to a French style garden. The centre piece within a water feature is a statue, the Bather, by A. Ramseyer.

Red Church★

The Église Notre-Dame de Neuchâtel is a neo-gothic structure, built between 1897 and 1906, which was classified as a national monument in 1986. Fourteen years of restoration then took place. The style of the church is certainly original, from its artificial stone walls and vaulted ceilings, to which coloured cement (reminiscent of Alsatian work) was added, to its British Victorian Gothic and even Portuguese influences.

There is also an unusual gallery as well as a ceiling adorned with 10 000 stars. Above the main altar is a splendid depiction of Christ created by the Swiss sculptor Marcel Feuillat in the early twentieth century. The stained glass windows, installed in 1903 are also notable.

Dürrenmatt Centre

74 Chemin du Pertuis-du-Sault.
The centre is located a little farther out of town than the Jardin Botanique. Bus

number 9, alighting at the Chapelle de l'Ermitage. ○Open Wed–Sun 11am–5pm. ☞8CHF. ℘(0)32 720 20 60. www.cdn.ch. Although Swiss author Friedrich Dürrenmatt is best known as a novelist and playwright, he was also an avid artist who wanted his paintings and drawings to be accessible to the public after his death. His widow donated the villa and garden he had purchased in 1952 to the Swiss Confederation and commissioned the Ticino architect Mario Botta to design an exhibition and research centre, which involved adding an unusual slate-covered building.

The Sistine Chapel on the same floor as the cafeteria is one of the museum's outstanding works.

EXCURSIONS
Laténium★★ (at Hauterive)

▶4km/2.5mi E along the Bern road. ○Museum open Tue–Sun 10am–5pm. ○Closed 1 Jan, 31 Dec. ☞9CHF. First Sun of month no charge. Free access to the gardens. &. ℘(0)32 889 69 17. www.latenium.ch.

The Laténium retraces 50 000 years of regional history via artifacts found during archaeological digs in the canton of Neuchâtel and on the site.

Visitors may wander through the lakeside **Parc de la Découverte** before or after the museum visit; exhibits include a lake house, piles symbolising a 6 000-year-old village, a Gallo-Roman barge, a Celtic bridge, and a

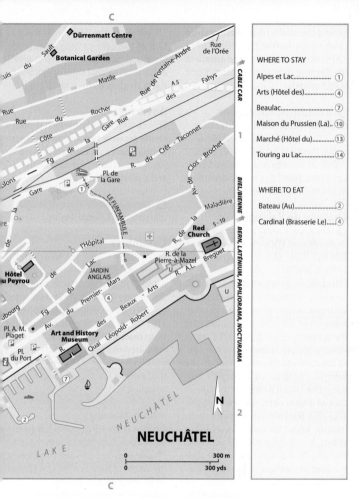

NEUCHÂTEL

pool showing the level of the lake in the distant past. The modern **Musée d'Archéologie** features a permanent exhibition entitled *Yesterday… between the Mediterranean and the North Sea*. The Gallo-Roman barge from Bevaix (copy) is the showpiece in the navigation section (*Room 4*); dating back to AD 182. Other exhibits cover the environment, daily life of the Celts, and the weapons, tools and jewellery from the site of **La Tène** (*Room 5*), which gave its name to the second phase of the Iron Age. Room 6, dedicated to lake dwellings, has a fine exhibition of everyday objects and a statue-menhir from Bevaix-Treytel, discovered in 1997.

Le Landeron
▶ *16km/10mi E of Neuchâtel, heading for the Bel/Bienne motorway.*

Not far from the Bel/Bienne lake, this well preserved medieval town is an ideal spot to wander between antique shops, art galleries and restaurants. The Town Hall, dating from the fifteenth century, is split between its civil duties and the Dix-Mille Martyrs Chapel. Of note is a museum of local history.

Chaumont★★
▶ *8km/5mi. Take the road to Chaumont on the right.*

🅿 Leave your car at the upper Neuchâtel-Chaumont funicular station (alt. 1 087m/3 576ft). To the left of and behind the station is an **observation tower** (⊙*turnstile: 2.20CHF; ☎(0)32 720 06 00*). An immense **panorama** of the Bernese Alps and the Mont Blanc Massif unfolds.

▷ *It can also be reached by the* ***funicular*** *(departures from La Coudre about once an hour, 9.30am–7.30pm;* ⊙*fare there and back: 9.20CHF; ☎032 720 06 00; www.tn-neuchatel.ch) from La Coudre, 3km/1.8mi from the centre of Neuchâtel, allow 12min.*

Château de Valangin

▷*4km/2.5mi N along the La Chaux-de-Fonds road.* ⊙*Open Mar–mid-Dec, Tue–Sun 11am–5pm. (morning only Fri).* ⊙*7CHF. ☎(0)32 857 23 83.*

This castle dates to the 12C and was considerably extended under the Lords of Valangin in the 14C and 15C. Used as a prison in the 17C, it then became the property of the Neuchâtel Canton History Society at the end of the 19C. Rooms open to the public include the Salle Louis XVI (Louis XVI-style furniture); the Salle d'Armes (a fine collection of swords and sabres from the 17C–19C); the Salle des Chevalier (sideboards, beautiful sculpted wedding chests, Neuchâtel clocks and watches); the Salle René de Challant, named after the Lord of Valangin; the Salle de Guillemette de Vergy (lace cushions and *abigans*, globe-shaped objects used by lacemakers); and the oratory (Neuchâtel lace, an important industry in the 18C, along with exhibits of clock- and watchmaking and painted canvases, also known as Indian canvases).

Visitors may also tour the guardroom and the prison cell known as Farel's cell, where the French reformer is said to have been imprisoned.

🚗 DRIVING TOURS

1 LAKE NEUCHÂTEL

From Neuchâtel to Estavayer. 65km/40.6mi. 45mins without visits.

This drive, as the name indicates, is a tour of the Lake passing through villages and pleasant small towns giving a choice of regional roads or motorways if you are pressed for time.

Auvernier

This charming village which is both a centre for wine production and a residential haven, is centred around its fountains, a church dating from the 15C and a pretty château from the 16C.

▷ *Leave Auvernier by rue de la Bâla and continue 1.5km/0.9mi.*

Colombier

This village near Lake Neuchâtel is renowned for its white wines. It is dominated by its imposing castle, built in the 15C in Late Gothic style and enlarged during the two following centuries. In 1762 the philosopher **Jean-Jacques Rousseau** stayed at the castle, which remained the property of the counts of Neuchâtel for many years. Today the building is a barracks and military museum.

Military Museum

⊙*Open 11 Apr–19 Dec, Tue–Sun 10am–noon, 2pm–5pm; otherwise by request.* ⊙*Guided tours (1hr15min) first Sun in the month at 3pm.* ⊙*9CHF. ☎(0)32 889 54 99. www.military.ch/EIM.*

Patriotic frescoes adorn the walls of the Knights' Hall on the first floor and, on the second floor, important historical events in medieval Switzerland are highlighted. Also displayed are hundreds of arms (14C–20C), either cutting and thrusting weapons or firearms, armour, flags and regimental memorabilia (portraits, uniforms, etc). A large gallery on the third floor exhibits cannons. There is also a display of textiles made in the area in the 18C and 19C.

▷ *Drive SW on the same road for 3km/1.9mi.*

Boudry

10km/6.2mi S along the Yverdon road or by tramway, starting from Esplanade du Mont-Blanc.

This small medieval-looking town was the birthplace of the French revolutionary leader **Jean-Paul Marat**, editor of *L'Ami du Peuple*, murdered in his bath by Charlotte Corday in 1793. A sculpture called *Marat-L'œil* has been erected in his honor near the house where he was born. This 14m/46ft-high structure in painted steel slowly revolves, creating dazzling effects of light. The renowned chocolate manufacturer **Philippe Suchard** was born at 7 rue Louis-Favre in 1797 and spent many childhood years in the house at number 37, which is now the town hall.

The 13C–16C castle, which served alternately as a counts' residence and a prison, houses the **Musée de la Vigne et du Vin** (◷*open Wed–Sun 2pm–6pm;* ◷*closed for 3 weeks after Christmas;* ◉*7CHF;* ℘*(0)32 842 10 98*), founded by the Compagnie des Vignolants. The wines of Neuchâtel are made with grapes grown on a vineyard extending between Neuchâtel Lake and the Jura. The visit begins with a history of the wine bottle, ranging from the amphora to the wine box, and provides a review of regional wine-making from the 18C through today. The exhibition explains the work of the wine-grower, defined by the seasons and the equipment used, diseases of the vine, harvesting techniques, and the process right up to bottling.

▷ *Follow the A5 towards Lausanne and take exit 3.*

Grandson★

Alt. 440m/1 442ft.
Genève Tourisme, 18 Rue du Mont-Blanc.
℘*(0)22 909 70 00. www.geneve-tourisme.ch.*
Situated near the southern end of peaceful Lake Neuchâtel, not far from the foothills of the Jura, the little town of Grandson was the backdrop to a major historical event: the humiliating defeat suffered by Charles the Bold, Duke of Burgundy, in 1476.

Castle★★

◷*Open Apr–Oct, 8.30am–6pm; Nov–Mar, 8.30am–5pm.* ◷*Closed 1 Jan and 25 Dec.* ◉*12CHF.* ℘*(0)24 445 29 26.*
www.chateau-grandson.ch.

The first stronghold was built at the beginning of the 11C by the lords of Grandson, but the castle as we know it today dates from the 13C. After 1476 Grandson became the property of the town of Bern and Fribourg; the castle became the bailiffs' residence and was rearranged inside. Its high walls, large round towers and a covered watch-path, occupy a remarkable **site**★★ on the shore of the lake. There are rooms of historic interest and collections of ancient arms. The wall-walk particularly should be seen, also the Knights' Hall (fine Renaissance stalls), a museum devoted to the Burgundian wars (dioramas) and to Charles the Bold, the great armoury, the fortresses' museum, the dungeons and the chapel as well as a

The Battle of Grandson

Charles the Bold, Duke of Burgundy and rival of the King of France Louis XI, longed to recreate former Lotharingia, which extended from the Alps to the North Sea including the Swiss Confederation. In 1476, the duke's troops besieged the city of Grandson and its castle and the garrison was forced to surrender. Charles the Bold ordered his enemies hanged. The Confederates raised an army of around 18 000 men and marched on Grandson. It was a cruel, bloody battle. The Confederates defeated the Burgundians, who only survived by fleeing. Charles abandoned the whole of his camp: horses, artillery, and his precious treasure, which accompanied him on all his campaigns. This bitter Battle of Grandson is a famous landmark in Swiss history and has inspired many authors, novelists, and playwrights.

museum devoted to the Grandson District. An **Automobile Museum** occupies the basement. The collection includes an 1898 Delahaye as well as the 1927 white Rolls-Royce Phantom which once belonged to Greta Garbo.

Église St-Jean-Baptiste

The church is half-Romanesque, half-Gothic, with a striking contrast between the very simple nave and the chancel, which is lit by many stained-glass windows. A fine fresco depicting the Entombment is in the chapel on the south side of the chancel. The acoustic drums are also noteworthy. Leave the church, go around to the east end and the fountain (1637); then, to the right of the church, note the former Bailiff's House, which has a sun with a human face supported by savages, wearing loincloths and brandishing clubs, carved on its pediment.

Follow the road along the Lake shore for 4.5km/2.8mi.

Yverdon-les-Bains

Alt. 439m/1 440ft.
2, avenue de la Gare. ℰ(0)24 423 61 01.
www.yverdonlesbains-tourisme.ch.
Yverdon-les-Bains is a well-known spa because of the healing properties of its waters, which feature a high content of sulphur and magnesium, and which for many centuries have sprung from

a depth of 500m/1 640ft. A pleasant lake side beach also adds to the town's attractions. A group of menhirs, known as the Promenade des Anglais are the remains of a Celtic settlement. The only Roman remains are a *castrum* (fortified citadel), located near the graveyard. The town hall (Louis XV façade) is worthy of attention.

Castle

This castle dates from the 13C, built by Peter II of Savoy, who captured the town in 1259 and erected this imposing fortress with its four round towers. After extensive restoration, the castle has become an important arts centre, housing the Museé d'Yverdon-les-Bains et de sa région (⚲open Jun–Sept, Tue–Sun 11am–5pm; Oct–May, Tue–Sun 2pm–5pm; ⚲closed 1 Jan and 25 Dec. ⚲8CHF; ℰ(0)24 425 93 10). The collections recall the history of the area since prehistoric times. Regional fauna is also represented. One room in the northeast tower presents an exhibition on the famous teacher Pestalozzi (⚲see TROGEN).

Maison d'Ailleurs

⚲Open Wed–Fri, 2pm–6pm, Sat–Sun, noon–6pm. Open Jeune Féderal. ⚲9CHF. ℰ(0)24 425 64 38. www.ailleurs.ch.
This unique museum dedicated to science fiction, utopia, and extraordinary

A Brilliant Educator

Born in Zürich in 1746, **Johann Heinrich Pestalozzi**, the son of an Italian-born surgeon and the grandson of a priest, was influenced from an early age by the educational principles of Jean-Jacques Rousseau's *Émile*, to such an extent that he devoted most of his life to educating poor children, mainly in rural areas. His theories about education are clearly presented in *Léonard et Gertrud* (1781-87). In 1804, he accepted the invitation extended by the city of Yverdon to teach deprived children. The following year, he founded an institution on the castle premises, which gained a Europe-wide reputation. In 1806, he opened an institute for girls next to the town hall, in which the teaching standards were the same as those for boys. After twenty years in Yverdon, Pestalozzi returned to the Maison de Neuhof. He died in Brugg in 1827.

His philosophy and his achievements are neatly summed up in the words which he had inscribed on the pedestal of his statue: "I myself chose to live like a beggar, so that beggars might learn to live like men."

journeys hosts temporary exhibitions of sculpture, art, and design. The amusing and often disturbing exhibits are displayed on three floors.

▷ *Follow the road along the Lake shore for 19km/11.9mi or the A1.*

Estavayer-Le-Lac
Alt. 454m/1 489ft.
Place du Midi. ℘*(026) 663 12 37.*
www.estavayer-le-lac.ch.
The little town of Estavayer is built on a hill overlooking the south shore of Lake Neuchâtel. It has preserved its medieval city look (ramparts, towers, old houses). Its pleasure-boat harbor makes it a popular resort among water sports enthusiasts.

Église St-Laurent
A Late Gothic church crowned with a large square tower. Inside, the **chancel** is embellished with fine 16C stalls and a painted and gilded high altar in the Baroque style, enclosed by an elaborate wrought-iron screen.

Museum
⊙*Open daily Mar–Oct, 10am–noon, 2pm–5pm; Nov–Feb 2pm–5pm.*
⊙*Closed Mon Mar–Jun, Sept and public holidays.* ⊛*5CHF.* ℘*(0)26 664 80 85.*
www.museedesgrenouilles.ch.
This yellow sandstone mansion (1435) features tiered bay windows. It houses a Regional History Museum with a remarkable collection of stuffed frogs parodying human scenes (a card game, a political gathering), impressive collections of weapons and early engravings, a reconstruction of an old kitchen and utensils, and an exhibition room devoted to railway transport (Swiss trains, lanterns).

② LE VAL DE TRAVERS★
From Neuchâtel to Sainte Croix. 52km/ 32.5mi. Allow 1hr20mins without visits.

15 Clos-Pury. ℘(0)32 889 68 96. www.neuchateltourisme.ch.

The River Areuse winds through this wide lush valley where fields of crops are interspersed with attractive towns, and slopes are blanketed with firs. This valley, one of the main crossover points between France and Switzerland (the road from Pontarlier to Neuchâtel passes through) offers two pleasant walks: the Areuse Gorges and the Creux du Van Nature Reserve.

Gorges de l'Areuse★★
Tourisme Neuchâtelois – Val-de-Travers. ℘(0)32 889 68 96. www.neuchatel tourisme.ch.
Located in the Val de Travers, which stretches from Lake Neuenburg across the Jura.

Hiking
🚶 *About 1hr on foot from Noiraigue railway station, where there is a car park.* Beyond the Plan-de-l'Eau hydroelectric power station the path descends to follow the Areuse. Steep limestone sides of this gorge rise to jagged crests. A viewpoint halfway offers a plunging view of the narrowest part of the gorge where the torrent gushes over cascades. An old humpbacked bridge adds a romantic touch to this attractive **beauty spot**★.

Champ-du-Moulin
A surfaced path leads through the woods to this hamlet.
Champ-du-Moulin stands at the southern end of the gorge, don't miss the house where the famous French philosopher **Jean-Jacques Rousseau** lived in exile in 1764. Climb back up to Champ-du-Moulin railway station *(30min on foot)* for another good view of the southern end of the gorge. Take one of the many trains back to Noiraigue, or walk back.

Creux du Van★★
From the Ferme Robert allow 2hr30min there and back to walk up to the Soliat by a path to Dos d'Ane, 1km/0.6mi E of the Soliat.
This nature reserve (flora and fauna, protected chamois, ibexes) covering 11sq km/4sq mi, includes a typical example of a Jura blind valley crowned by a superb cirque of cliffs which open

in a U-shape toward the Areuse Gorges and look down on rocks blanketed by fir trees. From its highest point, the Soliat (alt. 1 463m/4 800ft), there is a **view**★★ to the south onto Neuchâtel Lake and the of the Alps beyond. From paths along the cliffs are views onto the hills of the nature reserve and onto the Jura heights.

▶ *From Noiraigues drive SW along the Valley towards Couvet 8.5km/5.9mi. The Mines are on the left before Couvet.*

Mines d'Asphalte

Guided tours (1hr30min) Apr–Oct at 10.30am and 2.30pm (Jul and Aug, additional tours 12.30pm and 4.30pm); Nov–Mar, Sun only at 12.30pm and 2.30pm. 14CHF. Temperature around 8°C and 1 km/0.6mi walk; wear warm clothes and good shoes. ℘(0)32 964 90 64.

The first deposit of asphalt here was discovered in 1711 by Eirini d'Eyrinys. Two million tons were exported between 1830 and 1986. Visitors are first shown the **Mining Museum** (geological cross-sections, diagrams explaining asphalt extraction and exploitation, photographs of miners, of early mining equipment, lumps of asphalt etc), from where you continue on foot through several galleries (*helmets and electric torches are provided*) with stops for commentary on the various aspects of mining, bringing to life an important chapter in the industrial and social history of the Val de Travers.

▶ *From Couvet follow the signs for Môtiers 2.5km/1.6mi.*

Môtiers★

This village has well preserved 17C and 18C houses and a church, a former Gothic abbey rebuilt in 1679.

Its two small **museums** (*Guided tours (1hr) May to mid-Oct, Tue, Thu, Sat-Sun 2.30pm–5.30pm; 5CHF; ℘(0)32 725 84 74*) are worthy of attention: the Jean-Jacques Rousseau Museum (memorabilia) located in the house Rousseau lived in from 1762 to 1765, and the local museum set up in an 18C home, known locally as the Maison des Mascarons.

Sainte-Croix/Les Rasses★

Alt. 1 069m/3 507ft.
Balcon du Jura Vaudois Tourisme.
Rue Neuve 10. ℘(0)24 455 41 42.
www.sainte-croix.ch.

The twin townships of Sainte-Croix and Les Rasses lie on a sunny shoulder of the Chasseron, facing the Alps, approximately 9.5km/6mi west of lake Geneva. They deserve a special place among Swiss Jura resorts for their commanding situation and their excellent tourist organization. In winter, Sainte-Croix-les-Rasses is recommended for beginners or intermediate skiers who want to enjoy themselves rather than break records. Where cross-country skiing—the specialty of the Jura—is concerned, the resort offers more than 80km/50mi of marked trails.

The Village of Sound

The history of Sainte Croix since the mid-19C is a good example of the adaptability of Swiss industry to international economic changes. Around 1850, like most small towns in the Jura, the village was making watches. The establishment in the United States of great watch and clock making factories with sophisticated machine tools caused a grave crisis at Sainte Croix, which turned to the musical-box industry. But when Edison developed the phonograph, the public lost interest in little musical boxes with their tinkling notes, considered childish. Sainte Croix moved with the times and switched to making gramophones. Since then the popularity of radio has required more changes in the workshops, but today musical boxes again play an important part in local industry and Sainte Croix is still "the village of sound".

Resorts

Sainte-Croix lies in a pastoral basin well protected from the winds at the mouth of the wooded pass of the Covatannaz Gorges, through which a wide section of the Bernese Alps can be seen. **Les Rasses**★ is an annexe of Sainte-Croix with several hotels and scattered chalets enjoying a magnificent terraced **site**★★ within view of the Alps.

For those interested in hiking, there are more than 200km/124mi of paths.

♣♣ Centre International de la Mécanique d'Art

Guided tours (1hr15min) Apr–Sept 10.30am, 2pm, 3.30pm and 5pm; reduced times Oct–Mar. ◯*Closed Mon.* *13CHF.* *(0)24 454 44 77.* *www.musees.ch.*

Step into this old music-box factory (display of disused machinery) and be transported into a wonderful, magical world where you discover the vibrant melodies coming from beautiful handmade instruments, masterpieces of acoustics and cabinetmaking. This **music box museum** gives a new lease on life to musical boxes operated by discs or cylinders (the first model dates from 1796), radio sets, phonographs, pianos, street organs, automata (clowns, acrobats, Pierrot writing to Colombine), barrel organs and bird-organs.

The **Salle Guido Reuge**, named after the famous industrialist from the Jura, contains a remarkable collection of exhibits donated by his widow, presented in a superb setting portraying a magic forest.

Musée Baud

Guided tours (1hr) all year round on Sun and public holidays, 10am–noon, 2pm–6pm; Jul–Sept, daily 2pm–5pm. ◯*Closed at Christmas.* *8CHF.* ♿ *(0)24 454 24 84. www.museebaud.ch.* This small museum displays and keeps in working order an exceptional **collection of old musical instruments**★ (Utrecht organ, barrel organ, player organ) and phonographs (note especially the ones dating from 1900, 1912 and 1920). Also exhibited and functioning are automata and animated scenes. In display cases, music boxes, mechanisms, bonbonnières, etc. can be admired.

▷ *Follow the same road to Sainte Croix and turn left to Les Rasses.*

Le Chasseron★★★

Alt. 1 607m/5 272ft. From Les Rasses, 3km/1.8mi – 1hr15min by a small, winding, tarred road (there is also a chairlift ending at Les Avattes, about 1hr walk from the summit).

Follow the road from Sainte-Croix to Les Rasses, 0.5km/0.3mi beyond the Grand Hôtel des Rasses. Turn left on the Chasseron road. At the Avattes crossroads, bear right toward the Hôtel du Chasseron. On emerging from the woods, leave the car at the hotel car park.

Walk to the Hôtel du Chasseron and the summit *(signpost)* where you will see a sweeping panorama of the Alps, the Jura and Lake Neuchâtel.

▷ *Take the Route du Château from Bullet and return to the main road. Turn left to Vuiteboeuf and right to Baulmes.*

Mont de Baulmes

Alt. 1 285m/4 216ft. From Sainte-Croix 4.5km/2.8mi – about 30min by a narrow mountain road, steep toward the end but wholly paved, plus 15min on foot there and back.

Leave Sainte-Croix by the level-crossing at the railway station and continue through the hamlets of La Sagne and Culliairy. Leave the car at the Chalet-Restaurant of Mount Baulmes, and go along an avenue to the viewing table, on the edge of the precipice, for a **bird's-eye view** of the Swiss plateau, its lakes (in particular Lake Neuchâtel), and the Alps.

③ VUE DES ALPES ROAD★★

From Valangin near Neuchâtel to the Vue des Alps. 10km/6mi. Allow 45min to 1 hour excluding the walk up to the Tête de Ran.

Valangin

Between Neuchâtel and Valangin the road follows the wooded Seyon Gorges.

This picturesque little town nestles at the foot of an attractive 12C and 15C castle protected by an imposing curtain wall with towers (levelled).

The 16C Gothic collegiate church (inside, interesting tombs and funerary plaques), the town gate with a clock tower and 16C to 17C houses make a nice, old-fashioned picture.

▶ *Drive N on the road to La Chaux de Fonds for 10km/6mi to the Vue des Alpes.*

Vue des Alpes★
Alt. 1 283m/4 209ft.

The viewing table will enable the visitor to fit names to the peaks in this tremendous **panorama**★: Finsteraarhorn, Jungfrau, Weisshorn, Dent Blanche, and Mont Blanc. The best light is in the late afternoon.

Tête de Ran★★
Alt. 1 422m/4 655ft. From the Vue des Alpes, 2.5km/1.5mi to the Tête de Ran Hotel, plus 30min on foot there and back to reach the summit, climbing straight up the steep ridge overlooking this hotel on the right.

Lovers of panoramic views may prefer this view (*steep stony path*) to that of the Vue des Alpes: Tête de Ran is better placed for a wide view of the Jura ridges in the foreground (Val de Ruz, Chasseral and Chaumont Chains), even though fir trees hide the view to the northwest; most of Lake Neuchâtel can be seen. On the way down through the fir trees of the southern slope are interesting views of the **Ruz Valley** depression. This immense "ship's hold" has struck geographers with the regularity of its features: *ruz* has, therefore, become a scientific term to describe the first stages of erosion on the side of a mountain (*see INTRODUCTION*).

▶ *Take route number 20 to La Chaux-de-Fonds.*

La Chaux-de-Fonds –
See La Chaux-de-Fonds.

ADDRESSES

STAY

⊖ **Hôtel du Marché** – *4 place du Marché. ℰ(0)32 723 23 30. www.hotel-dumarche.com. Closed Sun. 10 rooms.* Very pleasant hotel in the heart of the village. Rooms with toilets and showers on first floor.

⊖⊖ **Hôtel des Arts** – *3 rue Pourtalès. ℰ(0)32 727 61 61. www.hotel-des-arts.ch. 46 rooms.* This friendly, recently renovated, modern hotel enjoys a good location near the lake and the town centre; suites & apartments available.

⊖⊖ **Alpes et Lac** – *2 place de la Gare. ℰ(0)32 723 19 19. www.alpesetlac.ch. 30 rooms.* This hotel is located away from the centre but is conveniently close to the station. Views of town and lake.

⊖⊖ **Touring au Lac** – *1 place Numa-Droz. ℰ(0)32 725 55 01. www.touring-au-lac.ch. 30 rooms.* ⊂*10CHF.* Conveniently located next to the harbour, a stone's throw from the bustling town centre with its pedestrian streets. Try to book a room with views of the lake.

⊖⊖⊖ **Beaulac** – *2 esplanade Léopold-Robert. ℰ(0)32 723 11 11. www.beaulac.ch. 94 rooms. Restaurant and Sushi Bar* ⊖⊖⊖⊖. Splendid location on the lake shore, near the marina. Forget about price and reserve a room overlooking the lake.

⊖⊖⊖⊖ **La Maison du Prussien** – *Gor du Vauseyon by rue de St-Nicolas. ℰ(0)32 730 54 54. www.hotel-prussien.ch. 10 rooms. Restaurant* ⊖⊖⊖⊖. For a change of scene, take a room at this 18C former brewery nestled among trees, offering large, rustic-style bedrooms named after local people. The Chambre Jean Chambrier is most unusual.

EAT

One of the region's specialities is a cheese fondue known as "moitié-moitié", literally meaning half Gruyère, half Vacherin. Leave Neuchâtel and drive a few miles towards the Jura. Stop at one of the many inns dotting the countryside around Valangin, Dombresson or Vallon de St-Imier, settle down on the terrace and sample the fondue with a glass of white wine.

Brasserie Le Cardinal – *9 rue du Seyon.* *(0)32 725 12 86. www.lecardinal-brasserie.ch. Closed Sun and last week Jul and first week of Aug.* The interior of this traditional brasserie is decorated with a mixture of brightly coloured tiles. The food is non-pretentious, delicious and not too expensive. Fish is a speciality and the menu is changed regularly. A "must".

Au Bateau – *Neuchâtel Harbour.* *(0)32 724 88 00. www.aubateau.ch. Closed Mon.* If you dream of gliding along the water, then step aboard this old steamboat moored along the quays. Reasonable prices, delicious meat and fish dishes and an original setting.

🛒 SHOPPING

The main shopping area is concentrated in the largely pedestrianised old town, bordered by rue du Coq-d'Inde, rue de la Place-d'Armes, rue de l'Hôtel-de-ville and rue de l'Écluse.

The two main department stores, **Migros** (*12 rue de l'Hôpital*) and **Globus** (*14 rue du Temple-Neuf*) are also located here. On Saturdays, the **Place de Halles** market brims with regional produce, cheese, and olives.

BOAT TRIPS

Boat trips on the lake run through the year, although visitors will have a greater choice of excursions between May and October. For further information, contact the Société de Navigation sur les Lacs de Neuchâtel et Morat at the port. *(0)32 729 96 00.*

🎭 THEATRE AND MUSIC

Théâtre du Passage – *Passage Max-Meuron.* *(0)32 717 79 07. www.theatre dupassage.ch.* This theatre hosts comedies and dramas by both Swiss and non-Swiss playwrights.

Maison du Concert – *Rue de l'Hôtel-de-Ville.* *(0)32 724 21 22. www.maison-du-concert.ch.*

Temple du Bas – *Rue du Temple-Neuf.* *(0)32 717 79 08.* Classical and choral music.

🎭 NIGHTLIFE

The **Amiral Bar** of the Hôtel Beaulac features a lovely terrace looking out onto the sailing harbor. Themed evenings can be arranged and a wine exhibition is open to customers. The bar of the **Hôtel Beau-Rivage** attracts a friendly crowd and commands lovely views of the lake; there is a nightclub in the basement.

Train enthusiasts or those looking for an elegant but unique experience will love the **Orient Express**, located at the main station; cocktails, light food.

Visitors looking for good beer and a pub-like atmosphere should try the Highlander (*rue de l'Hôpital*) or **Sherlock's** (*rue du Faubourg-de-l'Hôpital*). The **Bleu Café** (*faubourg du Lac 27*), popular with students, is next to the Bio cinema and offers an all-inclusive café-cinema option, which includes a snack. The **King** café (**rue du Seyon 38**) has live jazz several nights a week.

Night-owls should make for the **B Fly** nightclub (*ruelle du Port, in the basement*), which has a dynamic DJ and is particularly lively on a Thursday night.

Port of Neuchâtel

Stephan Engler/Switzerland Tourism

La Chaux-de-Fonds

La Chaux-de-Fonds is the biggest watch and clockmaking centre in Switzerland as well as being one of the most important towns for the Swiss farming industry. The town was almost entirely destroyed by fire in 1794 and afterwards rebuilt to a geometrical plan. The cradle of the clockmaking industry since the early 18C, this city also plays an important part in the production of microtechnology, electronics and mechanics, as well as in the tertiary sector.

- ▶ **Population:** Neuchâtel 37 240.
- **Michelin Map:** National Map 729: E4.
- **Info:** Tour Espacité, Place Le Corbusier. ℘(03)2 919 68 95. www.neuchatel tourisme.ch or www.chaux-de-fonds. ch (in French only).
- **Location:** The main town of the Neuchâtel mountains, La Chaux-de-Fonds lies in an upper valley of the Jura. Alt. 992m/3 254ft.
- **Don't Miss:** The Musée International d'Horlogerie.
- **Timing:** The watchmaking, history, and art museums are grouped together conveniently (allow at least half a day).

A BIT OF HISTORY
Local Celebrities
La Chaux-de-Fonds is the native town of the automaton maker **Pierre Jaquet-Droz** (1721–1790), the painter Léopold Robert (1794–1835), automobile designer **Louis Chevrolet** (1870–1941) ,and writer Frédéric Sauser, better known as **Blaise Cendrars** (1887–1961), who, with Guillaume Apollinaire, heralded the age of Surrealism. Like his literary work, his personal life was governed by his overriding passion for travel, both across land and in his own mind.

The Cradle of Clockmaking
From Geneva to the Jura – In the 16C, the reformer Calvin compelled the goldsmiths to turn their attention to making watches, forbidding them to make "crosses, chalices and other instruments of popery and idolatry." The development of this industry was spurred on by the arrival of French Huguenots driven from their country. Clockmaking soon spread from Geneva to the Neuchâtel Jura.

Daniel Jean Richard and the Horse Dealer – In 1679 a horse dealer returning to the Neuchâtel mountains from London brought back a watch which was admired by everyone until, one day, it stopped. The people of Sagne, a village near La Chaux-de-Fonds, advised him to have his watch exam-ined by Daniel Jean Richard, who was said to be highly skilled. He managed to repair the watch, studied its mechanism and decided to make watches himself. This he did, using tools of his own design, and subsequently settled at Le Locle, where he trained many others. The watch industry gradually spread throughout the Jura.

A World-Famous Industry – Most of the watchmaking industry today is concentrated in French-speaking Switzerland, and especially in the Jura. Many firms are located in La Chaux-de-Fonds, Le Locle, Biel, Neuchâtel, Solothurn, and Granges. They employ about 32 000 white-collar employees and manual workers. Workshops have sophisticated technical equipment which enables them to produce a quantity of high-quality watches. However, perfection has always been very important to Swiss watchmakers. At present the precision tolerance for the industry's working parts is of the order of 1/400th of a millimetre—1/10 000th of an inch. In certain workshops, the daily production of 1 000 workers could be carried

Maison Blanche

Christof Schuerpf/Switzerland Tourism

Le Corbusier Villas

Charles-Édouard Jeanneret was born on 6 October 1887. After studying painting and architecture at the local art school, he embarked upon a European tour. In 1918 he gained recognition as a painter and published the *Purist Manifesto* with Amédée Ozenfant. "After Cubism" advocated formal simplicity, economy of means and mathematical precision without denying emotion. The same principles were to guide his work as an architect. In 1920 he changed his name and became known as Le Corbusier. The same year, together with Ozenfant and the poet Paul Dermé, he founded the literary magazine *L'Art Nouveau*, which remained in circulation until 1925.

Le Corbusier was an inventive man who believed in structuring man's habitat along vertical lines. He invented the "living machine," which illustrated his views on the relationship between society and technology. His accomplishments in the field of community housing stand out on account of their revolutionary conception; he established an artful balance between the different elements, combining a variety of building materials and using light to enhance the cement blocks and exploit their full potential. His work was by no means limited to Europe and many examples of his creative genius can be seen in Russia, Brazil, Japan and India. Strongly criticised or highly praised, Le Corbusier remains one of the undisputed masters of 20C architecture and his impact on modern urbanism was considerable. He died in 1965.

There are three Le Corbusier house which can be visited at La Chaux de Fonds.

Villa Turque – *167 r. du Doubs.* ℘*(0)32 912 31 23. 1st and 3rd Sat of each month, 11am–4pm. Visit 1 hour of which 20 min for film. No charge.* Built in 1916–17 for a clockmaker, Anatole Schwob, this house is the best known Le Corbusier creation in the town. The name of the house is thanks to its neo-Greek style, flat roof and terra cotta brick cladding. However, the project finally drove Le Corbusier to move to Paris and later it was bought by Ebel.

Maison Blanche – *12, ch. de Pouillerel.* ℘*(0)32 910 90 30. www.maisonblanche. ch. Fri–Sun, 10am–5pm. Visit 30min–1 hour.* ⊜*10 CHF.* Le Corbusier built this home for his parents in 1912, after a trip to the Orient. It was his first private project, built in a neo-Classic style, at odds from the Art Nouveau influences of the time.

Villa Fallet – *1 ch. de Pouillerel.* A young Le Corbusier was involved with the creation of this villa in 1906, thanks to Charles L'Eplattenier. The result is an Art Nouveau style with local influence.

away in a jacket pocket. Precision has improved with the introduction of computer technology. Together with chemical products and machinery, clockmaking is one of the country's largest export industries. It plays a major role in the economy, and in spite of fierce competition from Japan and Southeast Asia, it remains a key factor in the stability of Switzerland's balance of trade.

SIGHTS
Musée International d'Horlogerie★★

🕐Open Tue–Sun, 10am–5pm and Dec 24, 25, 31, Jan 1. ⊚15CHF. ♿ ℘(0)32 967 68 61. www.mih.ch.

Founded in 1902, this fascinating **International Watchmaking Museum** has been housed since 1974 in basement rooms with the entrance on the north side of the park.

The museum illustrates the ways time has been measured throughout history, with more than 3 000 items from all over the world. The museum also has a centre for the restoration of antique clocks and watches; be sure to stop at the glassed-in workshops to watch craftsmen working. The main gallery displays instruments for measuring time and Renaissance, 17C (exquisite enamel watches) and 18C instruments. Marine chronometers, watches from the Neuchâtel region and other countries, as well as unusual astronomical instruments, musical clocks, and amusing 19C automata are also displayed.

UNESCO Recognition

La Chaux-de-Fonds and neighbouring Le Locale were recognised in 2009 by UNESCO for their exceptional universal value as examples of mono-industrial manufacturing towns. Successful urban planning has accommodated the transition from a cottage industry to 21C factory production, evident on a walk through the town centres, which reveal how residential housing and workshops stand side by side.

Continue on to the centre of scientific clocks and watches (astronomical, atomic and quartz-crystal clocks). The belfry offers a pleasant view of the museum's park; proceed into a raised gallery which introduces modern clockmaking techniques. Outside is the imposing **Carillon**, a 15t tubular steel structure made by the sculptor Onelio Vignando erected in 1980. Every quarter hour it chimes (the tune varies according to the season) and at night it offers a captivating light show.

Musée des Beaux-Arts★ (Fine Arts Museum)

🕐Open Tue–Sun, 10am–5pm. 🕐Closed 1 Jan and 25 Dec. ⊚10CHF. ♿ ℘(0)32 967 60 77. http://cdf-mba.ne.ch.

Built in the 1920s in the Neoclassical style, the Fine Arts Museum is devoted to regional art in Switzerland and abroad. Beyond the entrance hall with mosaic tiling, rooms display works by artists Charles L'Eplattenier (Springtime, The Doubs River), François Barraud (Self-Portrait), Charles Humbert (Friends) and Charles-Édouard Jeanneret, later known as Le Corbusier (Woman in Bathrobe, The Musicians). Elsewhere, daily lives and working conditions of the local population are vividly illustrated by such artists as Édouard Kaiser (Engraver's Workshop, Box Maker's Workshop), Albert Anker (The Grandparents), and Édouard Jeanmaire (Leaving the Stables). Swiss painting is represented by the work of Félix Vallotton (Nude with Green Scarf) and Ferdinand Hodler (Marignan Warriors).

The prestigious **René and Madeleine Junod Collection** features masterpieces of Modern Art, in particular from France: Delacroix (St Sebastian Released by the Saintly Women), Renoir (The Colettes), Derain (L'Estaque), Matisse (Young Girls in a Garden). It also includes pictures by Liotard (Marie Favart), Constable (Dedham from Langham) and Van Gogh (Young Girl with Tousled Hair). Abstract art is present with painters belonging to various movements that blossomed after 1950: Manessier (The Passion of Our Lord Jesus Christ), Bissière (The Angel in the Cathedral) and Graeser, Christen and Glattfelder for Concrete Art in Switzerland.

Musée d'Histoire Naturelle

On the 2nd floor (lift) of the main post office. ⏱ *Open Tue–Sat, 2pm–5pm, Sun and public holidays 10am–noon, 2pm–5pm.* ⏱ *Closed 1 Jan and 25 Dec.* ⊛ *6CHF.* ☏ *(0)32 967 60 71. www.mhnc.ch.*

The **Museum of Natural History** houses a wonderful collection of stuffed animals. Various Swiss and exotic species (of African origin, particularly from Angola) of mammals, birds, and reptiles are exhibited in dioramas of their natural setting. A room devoted to marine fauna displays several hundred types of seashells.

Musée d'Histoire

⏱ *Open Tue–Fri 2pm–5pm, Sat, Sun and public holidays 10am–5pm.* ⏱ *Closed 1 Jan and 25 Dec.* ⊛ *6CHF.* ☏ *(0)32 967 60 88. www.cdf-mh.ne.ch.*

The **Local History Museum** is housed in a former mansion used for the meetings of the town council. A collection of 17C to 19C Neuchâtel interiors are on show on the first floor: Bedrooms with sculpted ceilings, kitchens complete with cooking utensils, etc. The Medal Room presents collections of local and foreign coins, along with medals bearing the effigy of famous personalities from Switzerland (Calvin, General Dufour, Le Corbusier) and abroad (Abraham Lincoln, Louis XVI, Queen Victoria).

Musée Paysan

SW of the town, at 148 Rue des Crêtets. ⏱ *Open Apr–Oct, Tue–Sun, 2pm–5pm; Nov–Mar, Wed, Sat-Sun, 2pm–5pm.* ⏱ *Closed 1 Jan, Mar and 25 Dec.* ⊛ *6CHF.* ♿ *summer only.* ☏ *(0)32 926 71 89.*

The **Peasant Museum** is located in an old Jura farmhouse (1612). Although restored, the farmhouse has preserved some Gothic elements (mullioned windows on the ground floor) of the original 1507 building. It is an imposing shingled structure with its triangular gable and discreet, carved decoration. The interior has a pine framework with a large

central fireplace. The life of a wealthy 17C farmer is re-created. There is a clockmaker's workshop, a cheese room, a still, as well as furniture, utensils, tools, and porcelain stoves. Local lacemakers can be seen at work on the first Sunday of every month. The life of peasants is illustrated by temporary exhibitions held every year.

EXCURSIONS
La Sagne

▶ *10km/6.2mi S and after 4km/2.5mi by a road on the right which runs along the railway line.*

Fine 16C–18C Jurassian farms are interspersed along the road. Daniel Jean Richard was born in this village in the 17C. The church (15C and 16C) was partially restored in 1891 and more thoroughly in 1952 and 1983. The nave features ogive vaulting. Modern windows are glazed in plain glass in pale shades of green, yellow, gray, and violet.

Le Locle

▶ *9km/5.6mi from La Chaux de Fonds via Rue de Locle and Rue Girardet. 31 rue Daniel-Jean Richard – 2400.* ☏ *(0)32) 931 43 30.*

Le Locle is in the Jura Valley, linked to Franche-Comté by the Rock Pass (Col-des-Roches). This small town owes its prosperity to **Daniel Jean-Richard**, a young goldsmith who introduced the art of clockmaking into the area during the 18C.

Musée d'Horlogerie★

⏱ *Open May–Oct, 10am–5pm; Nov–Apr, 2pm–5pm only.* ⏱ *Closed Mon (except on public holidays), 1 Jan and 24 Dec.* ⊛ *8CHF.* ☏ *(0)32 931 16 80. www.mhl-monts.ch.*

The **Château des Monts** is an elegant 18C mansion on the heights of Le Locle, surrounded by a lovely park. The site houses a museum containing many superb artifacts from many countries and is seen as the indispensable complement to the Horology Museum of La-Chaux-de-Fonds. The ground floor is a showcase for 18C interior decoration: a large drawing room, an antechamber, a panelled dining hall, a library—all tastefully furnished and decorated—provide the charming setting for a splendid collection of clocks delicately worked in silver and gold. The AL Perrelet Room illustrates the history of clockmaking from the very first timepiece with automatic rewinding to the tiniest digital watch. The Maurice-Yves Sandoz Room presents clocks with miniature automatons, like the Carabosse fairy, a gilt copper figure portraying an old woman walking with great difficulty. The second floor explains the science of horology (old instruments, clocks, watches, chronometers, precision tools etc). Look around the workshop of a local clockmaker, faithfully reconstructed.

Musée des Beaux-Arts

🕑Open Tue–Sun 2pm–5pm. 🕑Closed 24 Dec–1 Jan. ༄8CHF. 𝒫(0)32 931 13 33 www.mbal.ch.

In addition to rooms devoted to Swiss painting and sculpture in the 19C and 20C (Girardet, Koller, Kaiser, Mathey) the Fine Arts Museum features an interesting display of work by foreign artists including *Richard Wagner* by Félix Vallotton, *The Studio* by Alberto Giacometti, *First Snowfall* by Lermite, *The Dancing Stars* by Dufy, *Portrait of Claude* by Renoir.

Moulins Souterrains du Col-des-Roches

༄Guided tours (1hr) May–Oct, daily 10am–5pm; Nov–Apr, weekdays 2pm–5pm & Sat–Sun (guided visits only) 2.30pm & 4pm. ༄14CHF. 𝒫(0)32 931 89 89. www.lesmoulins.ch. 🏠Temperature is 7°C, so wear warm clothes.

Built in the 16C to use the waters of the Le Locle Valley as a new energy source, these underground mills expanded rapidly from the mid-17C to the late 19C: the gushing waters of the river activated huge wheels, which in turn operated beaters, baking ovens, and sawmills. In the early 20C the mills were turned into slaughterhouses, subsequently abandoned, and then restored to their former glory. Exhibitions explain different types of mills, their roles and

mechanisms. The downstairs grotto is certainly worth a visit, featuring numerous wells and galleries that the men had to dig with their bare hands. The grotto also contains several remarkable pieces of machinery (gear mechanisms, flour mills, saws, superimposed wheels).

La Brévine

▶ 24km/15mi SW of La Chaux de Fonds. This small plateau has received the nickname "Swiss Siberia" because of its bitter winters: it registers the lowest temperatures in Switzerland. The plateau is sprinkled with chalets and has as its centre La Brévine (alt. 1 043m/3 422ft) at the edge of an immense combe of high pastures.

🏃 HIKING
LE SAUT DU DOUBS

🏃 16km/10mi to the S, in the direction of Le Locle by car, then on foot (by a forest path bordering the E bank) 2hr15min there and back or 1hr plus return trip by boat. By boat: 1hr there and back plus 20min there and back on foot. 🕑Summer service May–Sept, departures every 45min starting at 10am. ༄Fare there and back 12.50CHF. 𝒫(0)32 932 14 14. www.nlb.ch.

Les Brenets

A small border town pleasantly terraced on the slopes which plunge into **Lac des Brenets**★. This lake was a bend in the Doubs transformed into a reservoir following a series of landslides. It is 3.5km/2mi long and averages a width of 200m/656ft. At one point its sides become extremely narrow, forming two basins: the first (average depth 10m/32.8ft) spreads over an area between gentle slopes; the second (average depth 30m/98ft) flows between abrupt limestone cliffs—crowned with fir, Norway spruce and beech trees—the crests of which, here and there, are said to resemble famous people in profile (Louis-Philippe, Calvin and others). The federal cross painted onto the rock face in 1853 and the so-called Grotto of the King of Prussia can be seen on the Swiss side.

Saut du Doubs★★★

The waterfall can be reached by the landing stage which marks the end of the lake, via a forest path.

This famous waterfall, the overfall of Brenets Lake, 27m/89ft high, is far more spectacular when it is seen from the French side. The site is heavily wooded.

LES BELVÉDÈRES DU DOUBS

14km/8.75mi by car, towards Biaufond, then les Planchettes, leads to the hamlet of Recrettes. A further 2hrs (the circuit) on foot following a signposted route and you reach the three look out areas mentioned below.

After leaving Les Brenets in the direction of Le Locle, bear left at the crossroads onto the road towards Les Planchettes. The road passes through woods, climbs to the plateau, and arrives near the hamlet of Les Recrettes.

Les Recrettes viewpoint★

Alt. 1 074m/3 524ft. 30min on foot there and back.

From the belvedere there is a good **view**★ onto the loop of the Doubs made by Châtelard Mountain on the French

side and the hinterland covered with fir trees and pastures.

Just before the farm *(Ferme Modèle)* bear left onto a path *(private: close the gates after you)* and continue along it for about 700m/765yds until you are right by the cliff.

Point de vue de l'Escarpineau

Alt. 1 198m/3930ft.

From this wonderfully located view point it is possible to see the dam, the area around Chatelot, as well as the peaks over in France.

▷ *Turn left in front of the model farm. Before the village of Plancettes, take a tree lined road to the left.*

Les Roches de Moron

Alt. 1 076m/3 530ft.

Walk to the viewpoint near the restaurant, from where there is a plunging view onto the Doubs, hemmed in by the Châtelard Promontory and the Chatelot Dam.

BERN AND JURA CANTONS

For many visitors, the time spent in Bern and its hinterland has provided the highlight of their visit to Switzerland. No wonder, since it offers the unbeatable combination of superbly well preserved old town centres such as Bern and Solothurn, the glacial lakes of Thun, Biel and Brienz, the high-adrenaline sports playground of Interlaken and the superb mountain vistas at Schynige Platte, in Lauterbrunnen and from the Jungfraujoch rack railway.

Highlights

1 The **famous view** of Old Bern from the Rosengarten (p191)

2 A stroll in the **Baroque town** of Solothurn (p210)

3 The driving tour along the shore of photogenic **Lake Thun** (p214)

4 The **Alpine panorama** from Schynige Platte (p222)

5 The magnificent **railway trip** to Jungfrau (p224)

A Bit of History

The transformation of the belligerent, patrician society that used to charac-terise Bern to a tourist paradise could form a parable for the whole of Switzer-land. It's difficult to conceive today the power of the city during the late Middle Ages up until the Napoleonic Wars, yet a glimpse of the grand throne of the town's mayor in the Historical Museum of Bern is enough to convince any doubt-ers, for this was a seat fit for a king or an emperor. Unlike other city and cantonal democracies in Switzerland, Bern was an oligarchy with power restricted to a handful of patrician families: you can see their arms in the window recesses of the Münster that used to be Catholic chapels pre-Reformation. Napoleon's invasion ended abruptly the rule of the *ancien régime* along with much of its territory, and with typical diplomatic skill Bern succeeded in presenting and re-inventing itself as the capital of the Swiss Confederation. In the early 20C when the English-led new craze of Alpi-nism took hold, the Bernese had the foresight to build a network of tunnels, cable cars and railways to reach villages and mountain tops that transformed the landscape and catapulted the canton into the forefront of the tourism indus-try. Finally, in the 1960s and 1970s when the political cracks threatened Swiss unity with the troubles in the Jura, Bern defused the explosive situation via peaceful and constitutional means, as if final proof was needed of its politi-cal maturity.

Solothurn on the bank of the Aare

La Neuveville— a town in the canton of Jura

Stefan Boegli/Jura bernois Tourism/Switzerland Tourism

Jura: Switzerland's Newest Canton

In 1815 the Congress of Vienna, granted the Jura (largely French-speaking and Catholic) to Bern (largely German-speaking and Protestant) in compensation for the loss of the territory of Vaud. In 1947 a Jura independence initiative was born and by the 1960s a secession struggle had began involving riots, arson attacks and embassy occupations by the separatist *Béliers* (Battering Rams) movement. There was a whiff of Northern Irish politics in the air for a while, as the southern part of the Jura (French-speaking but Protestant) wanted to remain under Bern and formed its own anti-independence group the *Sangliers* (wild boars). A series of constitutional referendums defused the situation and northern Jura achieved canton status in 1979. Still, the question never really went away: a *Béliers* member, Christophe Bader, died in Bern in 1993 when his explosive device detonated early; in 1994 the German-speaking district of Laufental seceded from Jura and joined Basel-Land; and in 2004 a Federal Commission proposed the unification of the two Francophone Jura sections as two half-cantons.

BERN AND JURA CANTONS

| 0 | 10 km |
| 0 | 5 miles |

BERN ★★★ Highly recommended

Thoune ★★ Recommended

Bienne ★ Interesting

Hünegg Other sights described in this guide

Driving tour

ROSENLAUITAL See detailed driving tour map

Bern★★★

The seat of the Swiss federal authorities, 70 embassies and the headquarters of several international organisations, Bern is situated on a spur overlooking a verdant loop of the river Aare, facing the Alps. The old town, a UNESCO World Heritage Site, is characterised by its medieval grid, although the buildings date from the 19C. Its 6km/3.7mi of arcaded streets make it one of the longest shopping centres in Europe. The town, with its attractive towers and flower-decked fountains, is best explored on foot: access by car to the city centre is restricted, giving the old town a rather provincial air, despite its lively atmosphere.

▶ **Population:** Bern 122 925.
Info: Bahnhof – 3000.
℘ (0)31 328 12 12.
www.berninfo.com.
◑ **Location:** Bern is built on a U-turn of the river Aare, within 1hr30min by train from all major swiss towns and is best explored on foot.
☺ **Don't Miss:** The Zentrum Paul Klee, with some 4 000 works by this native son; the Zytgloggeturm at noon.
▲ **Kids:** The Bear Park in the centre of town.
◔ **Timing:** Allow at least two days for museums and attractions in Old town.

A BIT OF HISTORY

Foundation of Bern – A 15C chronicle describes the foundation of the town by **Duke Berchtold V of Zähringen** in 1191 as follows: Wishing to create a city, the duke asked for the advice of his huntsmen and his chief master of hounds. One of them answered, "Master, there is a good site in the river bend where your Castle of Nydegg stands." The duke visited the spot, which was then thickly wooded, and ordered that a moat be dug on the present site of the Kreuzgasse (a street running up to the cathedral). However, it was thought better to draw the line of the moat farther west, where the clock tower stands today. As game was very abundant the duke agreed with his advisers to give the new town the name of the first animal caught at the hunt. It so happened that this was a bear (*Bär*). The duke, therefore, named the town Bärn (Bern) and gave it a bear as its coat of arms. At the end of the 15C, the bear appeared in engravings of the town.

View of Bern from Rosengarten

GETTING AROUND

As much of the city centre is closed to cars, visitors are advised to explore Bern on foot, by **tram** or by **bus**. Special passes (for 1, 2 or 3 days) can be bought at the Tourist Office or at hotels. A night bus service operates from the railway station until 3.15am on Fri, Sat, and Sun. **Bicycles** can be rented from the rail station; *0512 20 23 74*. Cycle lanes are marked by yellow lines.

VISITOR'S CARD

This card, available from the town's Tourist Office (Bern Tourismus), grants you free and unlimited access to all forms of local transport.

GUIDED TOURS

Tour of the town by bus (2hr) Apr–Oct, 2pm daily; Nov–Mar, Sat only. 24CHF. Tour of the old town on foot (1hr30min) Jun–Sept, 11am daily. 16CHF. Contact the Tourist Office for further information. *(0)31 328 12 12*.

Expansion – From the 14C to the 16C, Bern followed a clever policy of expansion and played a dominant part in the Confederation. Many annexations, such as those of Burgdorf and Thun after the struggle with the Kyburgs, secured its hegemony on both banks of the River Aare. In the 15C, the conquest of Aargau enabled it to extend to the Lower Reuss, and its resolute attitude in the Burgundian wars placed it in the front rank of Swiss cantons. In the 16C, by annexing the Gruyères and Vaud districts, Bern ruled over all the country between the Lower Reuss and Lake Geneva.

Bern in the Confederation – When the Constitution of 1848 was drafted after the defeat of the Sonderbund, Bern was chosen by common consent as the seat for the federal authority. The choice was amply justified on account of the leading political part the city had played for several centuries and its privileged position at the heart of the Confederation and at the dividing line between the Latin and Germanic cultures. Though the city became the seat of the Federal Chambers, the civil service and the federal postal and railway services, this did not make it the administrative centre of its country in the manner of London and Washington. The federal system prevented any one town from enjoying political supremacy.

Ferdinand Hodler

One of the most important Swiss painters of the 20C, Hodler was born in Bern in 1853 (d 1918 in Geneva). Orphaned at the age of 12, he was apprenticed to Ferdinand Sommer, a painter of Swiss landscapes for tourists in Thun. At 19 he went to Geneva to copy the romantic landscapes by Calame. With the help of his professor Barthélemy Menn (1815–1893), a student of Ingres and friend of Corot, Hodler broke with conventional painting. A trip to Spain (1878–79) enabled Hodler to admire the technique of Velázquez. During this period Hodler painted many landscapes: The Alps and Thun Lake were his preferred subjects.

Although the major artistic currents (Realism, Symbolism, Art Nouveau) of the time are echoed in his works, from 1885 Hodler branched off to adopt Parallelism. This style can be found in his allegorical works (*Night*, 1889–90; *Day*, 1899–1900), as well as his historical canvases (*The Defeat at Marignano*), which earned Hodler first prize in an 1897 competition organised by the Swiss National Museum in Zürich. At the end of his life, Hodler was painting what he called "planetary landscapes," curious compositions consisting only of lines and space, with no trace of life or death.

⚜️WALKING TOUR

OLD BERN★★

Allow 2hr30min.

The old town, rebuilt in yellow-green sandstone after the terrible fire of 1405, is full of winding streets and terraced gardens overlooking the river. From Easter to the end of October the main monuments are floodlit until midnight. In the summer, the sound of horse-drawn carriages echoes through the streets.

Holy Spirit Church

The Baroque Heiliggeistkirche was built between 1726 and 1729. Spitalgasse is a bustling street lined with arcades which boasts many shops. A Piper's Fountain (16C and 19C) stands in the centre.

Bärenplatz

In former days, this square was occupied by a large bear pit. Today it is a vast esplanade, a lively meeting place surrounded by pavement cafés.

Marktgasse★

The smart and lively Marktgasse, with luxury shops and many florists' windows, is the main street of the old town. Fine mid 19C houses present a series of arcades, lending remarkable unity to the whole. The 16C–17C fountain (Seilerbrunnen) is dedicated to Anna Seiler, who in 1354 provided the town with its first hospital. Farther on, the Marksman's Fountain (Schützenbrunnen, 1543) depicts a standard-bearer with, between his knees, a small bear wearing armour and firing a gun.

On **Kornhausplatz**, to the left, the Ogre Fountain (Kindlifresserbrunnen) represents an ogre devouring a small boy and holding other children in reserve under his left arm.

Zytgloggeturm★ (Clock Tower)

⚜️*Guided tour May–Oct, daily 2.30pm. ⊛12CHF. ☎(0)31 328 12 12.*

This famous Bern landmark acts as the reference point from which all distances from the city are measured. Built between 1191 and 1250, the clock

Zytgloggeturm

Terence du Fresne/Bern Tourismus/Switzerland Tourism

tower once marked the western limits of the city. Note the 15C Jack (on the Kramgasse side of the gate) and the two ducal crowns above the gilded clock-face. Chimes strike at four minutes to the hour, and the many painted **figurines** (15C–17C) then start to move: the cockerel crows, flapping his wings, a procession of bear cubs march to the sound of pealing bells, followed by a second cock crow. The god Chronos turns his apron upside down and the large bell sounds the hour, struck by Hans von Thann, a knight made of lime wood and dressed in gilded armor. At the same time, Chronos counts the strikes and waves his sceptre, while the lion turns his head. The show ends with a third cock crow. A tour inside the **clock** enables visitors to admire its elaborate, sophisticated mechanism.

Kramgasse★

Kramgasse is a more crowded extension of Marktgasse. Along Kramgasse notice the Zähringen Fountain (16C) with its bear wearing armour and holding the Zähringen coat of arms in its paw, and the Samson Fountain (16C), surmounted by a statue of the giant prising apart the jaws of a lion.

At nnumber 49 stands **Einsteinhaus** (🕐*open Apr–Nov, daily 10am–5pm; Oct–Dec, Tue–Fri 10am–4pm;* 🕐*closed public holidays, Jan;* ⊛*10CHF;* ☎*(0)31 312 00 91; www.einstein-bern.ch*). It was here, on the second floor, that the great scientist Albert Einstein wrote his Theory of Relativity in 1905. Einstein spent seven years in Bern (1902–09). Visitors are able to view his study and bedroom, as well as a collection of portraits and photos. In 1909 Einstein was appointed Professor of Physics at Zürich University.

▷ *At the end of Kramgasse, turn left into Kreuzgasse leading to Rathausplatz.*

Rathausplatz is decorated with a fountain bearing a banneret (Vennerbrunnen) by Hans Gieng (1542).

City Hall
The Rathaus is the seat of the Bern Municipal Council (legislative assembly of the city of Bern) and the Grand Council (legislative assembly of the canton). It was erected between 1406 and 1417 and has been heavily restored, although its double staircase and covered porch make it one of the most typical buildings in the city.
Return to Kreuzgasse which leads to Gerechtigkeitsgasse, where the **Justice Fountain** stands. Its shaft is crowned by a Corinthian capital (1543).
Nydeggasse, which is a continuation of Gerechtigkeitsgasse, contains the Church of the Nydegg (*Nydeggkirche*) built in the 14C on the foundations of a 13C fortress.

Nydeggbrücke
The bridge spans the Aare and affords an attractive **view**★ of the quarters huddled in the meanderings of the river and the wooded slopes which overlook it.

▲▲ Bear Park★
◷*Open 9.30am–5pm (4.30pm in winter).* ◉*No charge.* ℘*(0)31 357 15 15.*
The old bear pit has closed and a new larger and more animal-friendly bärenpark opened in October 2009. The bears of Bern have been local celebrities. They receive many visits, not only from tourists but also from the Bernese, who are particularly fond of them. Near the bear park, the **Bern Show** uses video and an

animated model to recount the history of the town.

▷ *At the number 12 bus stop take the steepest path up signed Rosengarten.*

Rosengarten (Rose Garden)
From here, you have the best view of the **old city**★★★. The garden contains 200 varieties of roses, all kinds of irises and many rhododendrons.

▷ *Turn round. At the entrance to Gerechtigkeitsgasse turn left into Junkerngasse.*

Junkerngasse★
This street is lined with old houses. Note the **Erlacher Hof** at number 47, a fine Baroque dwelling influenced by French architectural style, now home to the city hall.
Approaching the cathedral from the east, there is a general view of the tall tower, the nave and flying buttresses, and the pinnacles surmounting the buttresses. Skirt the building to the left until you come to a fine terrace planted with trees and flowers. From the terrace there is a bird's-eye **view**★ of the Aare locks and, to the right, the Kirchenfeldbrücke, which spans the river over a distance of 40m/135ft.

St Vincent's Cathedral★
◷*Hours vary significantly; 10am–5pm in summer.* ◉*Closed Mon.* ◉*No charge.* ℘*(0)31 312 04 62.*
www.bernermuenster.ch.
One of the last great Gothic churches in Switzerland, the Münster St Vinzenz dates from 1421. Construction continued until 1573, and the bell tower, over 100m/328ft high, the highest in Switzerland, was only completed in 1893.
The splendid **tympanum**★★ of the main portal, by the Master Erhard Küng, was spared the destruction of the Reformation. It illustrates the Last Judgement (1495) with 234 figures, some of which are still painted. *The Damned* and the *Elect* are very realistically treated. There are statues of Prophets on the recessed arches, *Wise and Foolish Virgins* in the

embrasures (*left and right respectively*) and *grisaille* frescoes dating from the early 16C on either side of the portal. The nave is a vast structure with reticulated vaulting and 87 painted keystones adorned with coats of arms. Note the Bern Bear Keystone over the choir. The chancel has great 15C stained-glass windows by Hans Acker, depicting the *Passion* and the *Crucifixion*; other windows depict the Victory of the 10 000 Knights, and the Magi. Stalls, which date from the Renaissance (1523), are richly sculpted with scenes from everyday life. Visitors who do not mind a climb can take the spiral staircase of 254 steps to the tower platform (*open summer Tue–Sun, 10am–4.30pm (11.30am Sun); winter Tue–Sat, 10am–11.30am, 2pm–3.30pm (4.30pm Sat), Sun 11.30am–1.30pm; closes 30min before the cathedral; 4CHF; (0)31 312 04 63*) for a **panorama★★** encompassing, in the foreground, the various quarters of the town, with their fine reddish-brown tiled roofs, many turrets and belfries, the bridges over the Aare and, in the background, the majestically spreading chain of the Bernese Alps.

▷ *On leaving the cathedral, cross Münsterplatz and turn left into Münstergasse (several narrow covered passages leading to Kramgasse) to Casinoplatz. Just before reaching the bridge (Kirchenfeldbrücke) take Bundesterrasse on the right.*

Federal Palace
Guided tours (45min) daily except Sat–Sun, at 9am, 10am, 11am, 2pm, 3pm and 4pm, preferably at 11am, 4pm for individual visitors. Book a day in advance. Closed public holidays and during parliamentary sessions (access to the public galleries only during this period). No charge. (0)31 322 85 22. www.bundeshaus.ch.

The Swiss Government (Federal Council) and **Swiss Parliament** (National Council and Council of the States) are housed in the Bundeshaus, a heavy, domed building (1902), whose design was inspired by the Florentine Renais-

sance. A guided tour describes the workings of Swiss democracy (*see INTRODUCTION*). The view from the terrace encompasses the Aare, the town and in the background, the Bernese Alps.

▷ *After the Bundesplatz, rejoin Bärenplatz and cross Kirchenfeldbrücke to Helvetiaplatz where you can find many museums.*

Note the Kunsthalle on your left—this is where Paul Klee's first exhibition was panned and where Christo's first wrapping installation in 1968 made him a household name. It is worth checking what is on show when you are around.

MUSEUMS
The following three museums are all on or around Helvetiaplatz.

Bern Historical Museum/ Einstein Museum★★
Open Tue–Fri 10am–5pm. 18CHF (additional charge for special exhibits). (0)31 350 77 11. www.bhm.ch.
This French château-like building, constructed in 1881, contains a vast, historic, prehistoric, ethnographic and numismatic collection on the ground floor and basement and on the top floors it is devoted to the life and times of Albert Einstein who spent so much of his life in Switzerland.

The bottom two floors are divided in five sections: **Medieval concept of the world**: here are bronzes and gilded ornaments and sarcophagi from the Alemanni and Burgundian period as well as the originals from the Münster's Last Judgement Portal; **City of Bern**: the focus here is on the painting cycle from the Rathaus depicting the city's legendary foundation by Humbert Mareschet, a Huguenot refugee and the Dance of Death from the Dominical Convent in Bern painted by Niklaus Manuel; **War and Public Life**: here you will find mediaeval armour and weapons from chainmail to cannon balls; **Private Life**: domestic exhibits from the old patrician families of Bern; and **Glory and Decline of Ancien Regime**: here there is almost a complete reconstruction of the old Council Hall in Bern (check out the Mayor's throne, fit for a King) as well as paintings and furniture that shows the power of the city's patriciate.

The first floor led through a sci-fi glass construction is an excellent multi-media exhibition of **Einstein's life**, from his birth in Ulm and his Jewish roots to his childhood in Munich, schooldays in Aarau, study in Zürich and life in Bern where he published the first relativity paper (the originals are all displayed) that changed science forever. It continues to his life in Berlin and escape to America up to his death in 1955. All this plus "special relativity in four easy lessons". Unbeatable.

Swiss Alpine Museum★★

🕐 *Open 10am–5.30pm (from 2pm Mon).* 🕐 *Closed 1 Jan, 1 Aug, 24, 25 and 31 Dec.* 🚷 *12CHF.* 📞 *(0)31 350 0440. www.alpinesmuseum.ch.*

Soon to be renovated and expanded, the Schweizerisches Alpines Museum is dedicated to the Alps, which cover 60% of the country's total area. Visitors view an audio-visual presentation called "A Mountainous Country." Several relief maps—the early ones date back to 1750—connect the famous summits and their valleys: Bietschhorn, the Matterhorn, Dents-du-Midi, Jungfrau, Säntis, Bernina, etc.

A series of interactive booths focus on specific aspects of the exhibition (history, geology, transportation and industry, tourism, climate, flora and fauna); all the commentaries are in German, French, English, and Italian. On the first floor "Mountains seen through Maps" covers the 16C–18C and is followed by presentations on art, popular traditions and regional lore, as well as habitat.

The last room is the raison d'être for any visit: it is decorated with seven huge canvases by Ferdinand Hodler, *The Climb and the Fall*, inspired by the conquest of the Matterhorn. It also presents the evolution of climbing gear and life-saving equipment in the Alps. In the centre there is a huge raised map of the Bernese Oberland. The top floor

has been earmarked for exhibitions on Alpine photography since the 19C.

👥👤 Natural History Museum★★

🕐 *Open Mon 2pm–5pm, Tue–Fri 9am–5pm (6pm Wed), Sat–Sun 10am–5pm.* 🕐 *Closed most public holidays.* 🚷 *8CHF.* 📞 *(0)31 350 71 11. www.nmbe.ch.*

The museum is surprisingly child-friendly: no wonder when the first thing you see when you enter is Barry, the stuffed St Bernard dog (1800–1814) who saved 40 lost souls in his brief life. On the ground floor there is a fossil of an ichthyosaurus to be admired in the hall. In the basement, dioramas display Asian fauna as well as minerals (reconstructions of all famous diamonds among them). The ground floor contains Alpine and African fauna while the first floor contains, amphibians, fish and snakes as well as the skeletons of several whales. The second floor has the must-see skeleton of a Plateosaurus found in Frick (1983) while the top floor is devoted to insects and includes a completely closed anthill ecosystem.

👥👤 Communication Museum★

🕐 *Open Tue–Sun, 10am–5pm.* 🕐 *Closed 1 Jan, 24, 25 and 31 Dec.* 🚷 *12CHF.* ♿ 📞 *(0)31 357 55 55. www.mfk.ch.*

This museum explains the history of communications from early smoke signals through the transmission of highly sophisticated digital systems. Special coverage is given to the history of postal institutions (founded in 1849) and philately (more than 500 000 stamps displayed).

Art Museum★★

Hodlerstrasse 8-12 🕐 *Open Tue–Sun, 10am–5pm (9pm Tue).* 🕐 *Closed most public holidays.* 🚷 *9CHF (price varies for temporary exhibitions).* ♿ 📞 *(0)31 328 09 44. www.kunstmuseumbern.ch.*

This Fine Arts Museum contains a splendid collection of 13C–20C paintings. Its renowned collection of works by **Paul Klee** has been moved to the new Zentrum Paul Klee (👉 *see Zentrum Paul Klee, p196*) although some are still exhibited.

BERN

0 _____ 200 m
0 _____ 200 yds

WHERE TO STAY

WHERE TO EAT

B

C

AUTOBAHN, ZÜRICH, BASEL

AUTOBAHN, INTERLAKEN

PAUL KLEE CENTRE, ABEGG FOUNDATION

ST. NICOLAS CHURCH

INTERLAKEN, AUTOBAHN

ZÜRICH, BASEL

1

2

Breitenrainstr.

Greyerzstr.

Mosersstr.

Waldhöheweg

Beundenfeldstr.

Viktoriapl.

Viktoria-

Blumenberg-

strasse

Spitalackerstr.

Kasernenstrasse

strasse

Papiermühle

Laubeggstr.

KURSAAL
SCHÄNZLI

Schänzli-

Str.

Schänzlistr.

Aargauer Stalden

Rose Garden

Altenbergstr.

Brunngasse

Untertorbrücke

13

Brunngasshalde

Postgasshalde

NYDEGGKIRCHE

Pont de
la Nydegg

Kornhausbrücke

Brunngasse

City Hall

Postgasse

Kornhauspl.

Rathausgasse

Rathausplatz

Nydeggasse

22

Clock
Tower

7   13

Münster-
gasse

Kramgasse

Gerechtigkeitsgasse

22

Junkerngasse

Bear

aterplatz

4

Albert
Einstein's
House

St. Vincent's
Cathedral

Kreuzgasse

Gerberngasse

Park

Casinopl.

Münster-
platz

Erlacherhof

MATTE

Muristalden

CASINO

Plattform

Mühlenpl.

Aarstr.

Schifflaube

Gr.

Schlosshaldenstrasse

16

AARE

Muristrasse

wiss Alpine
Museum

Helvetiaplatz

Marienstr.

KIRCHENFELD

Thunstr.

Luisenstrasse

Str.

Jungfraustr.

strasse

Ensingerstr.

Bern Historical
Museum

Museum of
Communication

Natural
History
Museum

Helvetia

Dufour

Thunstr.

Seminar-

Thunstr.

10

Aegertenstr.

Str.

Kirchenfeldstr.

Helvetia

Jubiläumsstrasse

Kirchenfeldstr.

Elfenstr.

B

DÄHLHÖLZLI ZOO

C

Paul Klee

Paul Klee was born in 1879 at Münchenbuchsee and spent his youth in Bern, where he painted scenes of the city and surrounding landscape: the meanders of the Aare, the Niesen mountains and the quarries at Ostermundigen. He was an ironic observer of social conventions and also drew caricatures. In 1906, he travelled to Munich, where he made contact with members of the Blauer Reiter movement, including Franz Marc, Wassily Kandinsky and Alexej von Jawlensky. A violinist and a poet, he taught in the Bauhaus (1921–33). Considered to be a "degenerate artist" by the Nazis, Klee saw his teaching contract at the Dusseldorf Academy terminated in 1933. He spent the latter part of his life in Bern, where he died in 1940. The Zentrum Paul Klee opened in Bern in 2005.

The focus has recently changed from permanent to special exhibitions which occupy around 50% of the museum space.

Basement – This is the most interesting part of the permanent exhibition, being devoted to Italian early artists of the 13C to 15C, including Fra Angelico (*Madonna and Child*) and Duccio, whose *Maestà* (c.1290) reflects the Byzantine style characteristic of the Siennese School and works by the Swiss Primitives (15C–16C), especially *Master with Carnation from Berne*. The 16C school also is represented by Bernese painter Niklaus Manuel Deutsch (c.1484–1530), whose style and composition were akin to the art of the Renaissance: *Triptych of St John the Baptist, St Luke Painting the Virgin, Temptation of St Anthony*. Also note the two excellent portraits of Luther and his wife from the workshop of German painter Lucas Cranach. Adjoining rooms exhibit works by 17C artists from Bern.

Ground floor – The French School is fully represented here by leading Impressionists such as Monet, Manet, Cézanne (*Self-portrait in a Felt Hat*), Sisley, Pissarro, Renoir, Matisse (*The Blue Blouse*), and Bonnard (*In a Garden*).

First floor – A special exhibition is devoted to native-born artist **Ferdinand Hodler**. Along with large allegorical frescoes that reflect his concern for death (*Day, Night, The chosen*),there are his portraits (*Young Girl with a Poppy*) and self-portraits (he depicts himself with wild, menacing features in *The Madman*). There are also many works by Anker and Cuno Amiet who favoured a palette of bright, vivid colours. Other galleries display Expressionist painters Chagall, Soutine and Modigliani, and a large collection of Cubist paintings by Braque, Picasso, Juan Gris and Fernand Léger (*Contrasts of Form*), Kandinsky, Masson and Miró. Contemporary art is represented by Swiss artists Meret Oppenheim, Franz Gertsch and Markus Raetz, and the Americans Jackson Pollock and Mark Rothko.

Zentrum Paul Klee ★★★

Take bus 12 or 5 to the final stop.
⏱ *Open Tues–Sun 10am–5pm.* 🚫*16CHF.*
♿ ✆ *(0)31 359 01 01. www.zpk.ch.*

The Paul Klee Museum opened in 2005 to house more than 4 000 paintings (*Steinbruch, Monument in Fruchtland*), gouaches, watercolours and drawings, plus archives and biographical material of one of the most significant and prolific artists of the 20C (1879–1940). It is impossible to exhibit them all, so special exhibitions try to group them together (*Klee in Morocco, Klee and Picasso* and so on).

Klee's striving for colour effects gave rise to square paintings (*Pictorial Architecture in Red, Yellow and Blue*), to Divisionist works (1930–32, *Ad Parnassum*) and paintings with figures and signs against a coloured background (*Flowers with Stone,* 1940). The collection is believed to be the largest single collection of a major artist in the world. The artwork is housed in a dramatic building designed by award-winning Italian architect Renzo Piano; three soaring hills of steel and glass offer natural light to showcase

Zentrum Paul Klee

Terence du Fresne/Bern Tourismus/Bern Tourismus/Switzerland Tourism

Klee's colourful creations, which seem to blend primitive art, surrealism and cubism with gentle humor and allusion to dreams. The main exhibits are in the centre section; the other sections contain restaurants, shops, galleries, and a performance theatre. There is also a separate children's museum within the complex. Temporary exhibits focus on the connection between Klee and other artists, such as Kandinsky and Max Beckmann. The site includes a sculpture park. **Wege zu Klee** (Theme Path) from the city centre to the museum is punctuated by additional information about the artist and his works.

During the excavation, boulders buried by the retreating Aare Glacier more than 10 000 years ago were unearthed; these now form a natural landscape around ponds on the park-like site, which includes the 19C Villa Schöngrün, summer home of one of Bern's patrician families.

ADDITIONAL SIGHTS
Botanical Garden★

This vast botanical garden, with its fountains and pools, descends to the banks of the Aare in terraces. Some 6 000 plants, including a wide variety of Alpine species, grow in the garden, which covers an area of 2ha/5 acres. The seven greenhouses contain a collection of tropical plants, such as ferns, grasses, and orchids.

Dählhölzli Zoo★

Entrance in Jubiläumstrasse.
⊙*Vivarium open summer 8am–6.30pm; winter 9am–5pm.* 8CHF. &
℘*(0)31 357 15 15. www.tierpark-bern.ch.*
The 13ha/32-acre Tierpark Dählhölzli, overlooking the Aare, is home to a number of European and Nordic animal species, including otters, musk ox, lynx, wolves, bison, elk, reindeer, and black grouse. The aviary contains hundreds of tropical birds, butterflies, rare specimens of local fauna, a termites' nest, and an ant hill. There is also a children's playground and a picnic area.

EXCURSIONS
Gurten★★

Alt. 858m/2 815ft – 2.5km/1.5mi – about 30min including 10min by funicular.
Take tram 9 direction Wabern until stop Gurtenbahn. *Operates all year round.* 5CHF one-way; 9CHF there and back.
℘*(0)31 961 23 23. www.gurtenpark.ch.*
The Gurten, a magnificent belvedere with a **panorama**★★ of Bern and the Bernese Oberland, is a pleasant place in which to stroll; it also has a good sit-down and self-service restaurant and a fun-filled children's playground.

Abegg-Stiftung★★

Closed until 2011. Check information at www.abegg-stiftung.ch.
As you enter **Riggisberg** town from the north (Bern road), bear right onto the

road to the Abegg Foundation; the modern buildings of this prestigious cultural venue are located on the mountainside in a verdant and peaceful setting.

The Foundation was established in 1961 by **Werner and Margaret Abegg** for conducting scientific research in applied arts, especially textiles, and their preservation. Collections include exhibits from Europe and the Middle East dating from Antiquity to the Renaissance. In addition to its vast library boasting around 160 000 titles, there are displays of Neolithic pottery, marble pieces from the Cyclades, Iranian ceramics and gold, bronzes from Luristan, Pharoic Egyptian pieces, ivory plaquettes from the pre-Achaemenid Era, and Byzantine ceramics.

The foundation runs a university-level degree course on the conservation and restoration of textiles, and maintains a related research library (open to the public), and an online catalogue. It also issues regular publications on subjects such as applied arts, textile art, and other applicable subjects.

Jegenstorf

16km/10mi N of Bern via route 12.

The houses in this cheerful, flowered town cluster around a Late Gothic church, with a saddleback roof and a shingled bell tower. The interior is decorated with woodwork; the stained-glass windows are 16C–18C. The town's **château** (*open mid-May–mid-Oct, Tue–Sun 10am–noon, 2pm–5pm; 7CHF; (0)31 761 01 59*), an 18C town house added to a feudal tower, stands in a small wooded park and presents temporary exhibitions in lovely 18C period rooms.

DRIVING TOUR

EMMENTAL★

100km/62mi – Leave aside one whole day.

Leave Bern from the N/NE via the route to Bolligen Burgdorf.

The Emmental (The Emmen Dale) whose name immediately brings to mind the well-known Swiss cheese, is cut across by the River Emme, a tributary of the Aare, into which it flows east of Solothurn. Originating in the Hohgant Massif north of Lake Brienz, the River Emme crosses first a mountainous area, and then runs through an area of forest and fields dotted with flower-decked chalets. The area's wealth comes from forestry, crop farming, and cattle raising.

Burgdorf

Poststrasse 10 – 3400. (0)34 422 24 45 www.burgdorf.ch.

At the entrance to the Emmental, Burgdorf is a busy little town in the canton of Bern. The modern district, with its large textile works, is overlooked by the old quarter, crowned by its **castle**, built by the dukes of Zähringen at the end of the 12C.

Museum

Open Apr–Oct, daily 2pm–5pm (11am Sun); Nov–Mar, Sun only 11am–5pm. 6CHF. (0)34 423 02 14.

The museum occupies three floors in the tower. Visit the Knights' Hall, with fine furniture, Emmental costumes, porcelain, an instrument collection, and mementoes of **Johann Heinrich Pestalozzi**, who worked here (1799–1804). From the top floor there is a **view** of Burgdorf and the Bernese Alps.

Leave Burgdorf by the road to Wynigen.

On leaving town you will cross two ferro-concrete bridges over the Emme. After 1.5km/1mi take a narrow, winding road to the right which passes through Gutisberg. Leave a byroad to Wynigen on your left and park the car after the Lueg restaurant.

Belvedere Lookout★

Alt. 887m/2 910ft. 8.5km/5.3mi – about 30min.

You reach the top of the bluff along a very steep path among fir trees. A monument commemorating the Bernese cavalry (1914–18) has been erected on the open space; from here the semicircular **panorama**★ includes the Jura and the Bernese Alps on the horizon.

👥 Affoltern Show Dairy

🕐 *Open Apr–Oct 9am–6.30pm, Nov–Mar, 9am–5pm.* 🎫 *Free.* 📞 *(0)34 435 16 11. www.showdairy.ch.*
A trip to the Emmen valley is not complete without a visit to this modern cheese dairy, the only one in the region open to the public. Equipped with an audio guide, visitors can attend several times a day and watch behind windows the famous regional cheese being made. Butter-making takes place every Tuesday and Friday morning. Demonstration of the old-fashioned cheese production is made in the small cottage dated from 1741 and located next to the modern cheese factory. A shop and restaurant offering fondue and raclette bring the gastronomic visit to the end.

🚗 *Head E and join the B 23, driving S to Sumiswald.*

Sumiswald

This pretty Bernese village has fine wooden houses characteristic of the region: A large façade carries one or two tiers of windows close together; the overhanging roof is immense; the gable is often painted and decorated with designs in bright colours. The **Kramerhaus** and the **Zum Kreuz Inn** are quite remarkable.

Lützelflüh

This lovely village on the Emme has a church that was built in 1494 (modernised). Inside the church are six old stained-glass windows and an organ loft (1785). Outside the door is the tomb of Albert Bitzius (pseudonym of Jeremias Gotthelf), pastor and writer during the 19C, whose unsentimental depictions of Emmenthal village life were based on his time as a curate here.

Hasle

On the west bank of the River Emme, this village is linked to the Rüegsauschachen (east bank) by a remarkable **covered**

bridge (1838). Built entirely of wood, the bridge crosses the river in one span. The Protestant church, a former chapel rebuilt in the 17C, is worth noting. Inside are small 17C stained-glass windows, heraldic bearings and 15C frescoes showing the *Last Judgment* and the *Crucifixion*.

🚗 *Retrace your steps and take the direction to Langnau-im-Emmental.*

Langnau-im-Emmental★
Schlossstrasse 3 – 3550.
📞 *(0)34 402 42 52.*
The picturesque town of Langnau lies on the banks of the Ilfis (spanned by a covered bridge), a tributary of the River Emme. Its commerce is based on forestry and Emmental cheese (main exporting centre for the latter).

ADDRESSES

🛏 STAY

🛏 **Hotel Glocke** – *Rathausgasse 75.* 📞 *(0)31 311 37 71. www.bernback packers.com. 12 rooms.* Those on a limited budget will like this hotel, located in the heart of old Bern. Shared rooms are simple and clean. Those on the top floor overlook the rooftops and cathedral.

⊖ **Zum Goldener Schlüssel** – *Rathausgasse 72.* ✆*(0)31 311 02 16. www.goldener-schluessel.ch. 48 rooms.* This reasonably priced and friendly hotel is situated in a picturesque street in the old town. A good restaurant on the ground floor, under the arcades, serves a range of meat (especially game) and vegetarian dishes.

⊖⊖ **Landhaus** – *Altenbergstrasse 4/6.* ✆*(0)31 331 41 66. www.landhausbern.ch.* 🅿 *32 beds (dormitory or room).* A short walk from the bear enclosure, this old house has been brilliantly converted into a hotel for backpackers. Hygienic conditions in the dorms *(from 30CHF)*, and beautiful views of the Gurten in the attic rooms. Affordable restaurant on the ground floor.

⊖⊖ **Kreuz** – *Zeughausgasse 41 -* ✆*(0)31 329 95 95. www.kreuzbern.ch. 100 rooms.* Almost all the rooms in this three star hotel have been tastefully renovated. Its central location, set back from the street, makes it a good base for exploring the city on foot. Avoid the rooms at the front, which can be rather noisy, especially on weekends. Nice view of the city and the Bernese Alps from the rooftop terrace.

⊖⊖ **La Pergola** – *Belpstrasse 43.* ✆*(0)31 343 43 43. www.hotel-lapergola.ch.* 🅿 *55 rooms.* Three stops away from the train station on bus number 3, this hotel scores in that it provides parking space. But rooms are small, there are no cupboards (just shelves) and the Internet reception is unreliable.

⊖⊖ **Bern** – *Zeughausgasse 9.* ✆*(0)31 329 22 22. www.hotelbern.ch. 95 rooms.* Cosy hotel a stone's throw from the lively shopping district and its picturesque arcades. Piano bar in a sophisticated setting.

⊖⊖⊖ **Belle Époque** – *Gerechtigkeit 18.* ✆*(0)31 311 43 36. www.belle-epoque.ch. 17 rooms.* As soon as you cross the threshold, you are transported back to the turn of the last century. "Toulouse Lautrec" bar and Art Nouveau furniture, decoration, vases and paintings. This elegant establishment could almost qualify as an art museum.

🍴/**EAT**

On menus in Bern, Gschnätzeltes are thin slices of veal (or émincé), Suurchabis is Sauerkraut and Gschwellti are potatoes boiled in their skins.

⊖ **Klötzlikeller** – *Gerechtigkeitsgasse 62.* ✆*(0)31 311 74 56. www.kloetzlikeller.ch. Closed Sun in winter, Sun and Mon in summer.* A typical Bernese wine bar which has traditionally been run by women for over 100 years: in 1635, there were more than 230 of these establishments in the city. The Klötzlikeller also serves light meals.

⊖ **Vatter** – *Bärenplatz 2.* ✆*(0)31 313 11 21. Closed Sun. www.vatter.ch.* Above the shop of organic products of the same name, this is an organic restaurant for those on tight budgets. Use the extensive buffet (salads, pasta), then pay by weight. For an exotic touch, taste Indian and vegetarian specialties. Pleasant terrace balcony on Bärenplatz.

⊖ **Verdi** – *Gerechtigkeitsgasse 5.* ✆*(0)31 312 63 68. Closed 24 & 25 Dec.* The famous composer himself would not turn up his nose at gnocchi with truffles or spaghetti alla scapara in this fine Italian diner in old Bern. The decor pays tribute to the maestro: old scores, red velvet curtains, candles at night—romantico!

⊖ **Zum Äusseren Stand** – *Zeughausgasse 17.* ✆*(0)31 311 32 05. www.aeussererstand.ch. Closed Sun.* This restaurant is housed in the former town hall where the Constitution of the Bern canton was first drawn up in 1831. In this building, representatives of 22 countries gathered in 1874 to found the Universal Postal Union. The huge dining hall upstairs, decorated in the Empire style, is reserved for formal banquets.

⊖⊖ **Punkt** – *Rathausgasse 73.* ✆*(0)31 318 18 88. www.restaurant-punkt.ch. Closed Sun.* For a change from Bern staples sausages and fried potato, try this excellent Asian place. The Thai, Chinese, Japanese and Indian flavours and convivial décor make for a charming atmosphere. Those of a suspicious demeanour can monitor the chefs at work via a camera placed in the kitchen.

Kornhauskeller – *Kornhausplatz 8*. *(0)31 327 72 72. www.bindella.ch. Closed Mon lunchtime in summer.* In the early 18C, a warehouse used for storing wheat and wine was dug out beneath the old covered market. Converted into a village hall in 1896, it currently houses this restaurant. The paintings dating from that period are the work of the Bernese artist Rudolf Mänger. The huge barrel set up in the main dining hall can contain up to 41 055 litres. An unusual yet welcoming place where diners can sample traditional Bernese cuisine.

Harmonie – *Hotelgasse 3.* *(0)31 313 11 41. www.harmonie.ch. Closed Sat evenings, Sun and Mon lunchtime.* Old-fashioned café, whose décor has remained exactly the same since 1915. Famous for its fondues.

Brasserie Bärengraben – *Muristalden 1.* *(0)31 331 42 18.* Situated at the end of Nydeggbrücke, towards Bärengraben. Small, congenial restaurant with mouthwatering homemade desserts.

Schwellenmaetteli – *Dalmaziquai II.* *(0)31 350 50 01.* www.schwellenmaetteli.ch. Closed Mon. Salmon and perch are popular with the Bernese in this restaurant-bar conveniently located down by the main Aare lock. The old city spreads out on the other side of the river. There is also a snack bar on stilts over the water and a romantic cocktail bar. Reached via a staircase on the side of the Helvetiaplatz or, better by car, as the way up afterwards is steep.

NIGHTLIFE

It is true that Bern lags behind Zürich and Lausanne in nightlife, but it is by no means a cemetery town. Try walking the streets behind the railway station, in particular Neuengasse, Aarbergergase and Speichergasse, and you will find that there are many busy clubs and bars under the arcades.

At number 35, there is a gay bar, **Samurai** (*www.samurai-bar.ch*). Outside this area you can find **Club Viente Sur** (*Lerchenweg 33*) for dancehall and reggae, the **ISC**

(*Neuenbrueckestrasse 10, isc-club.ch*) which offers nights for every taste (rock to hiphop and goth), and next door the Reitschule Bern (*Neubrückstrasse 8, www.reitschule.ch*), an alternative cultural centre with live music.

You can enjoy some good jazz at **Marian's Jazzroom** in the basement of the Hotel Innere Enge (*Engerstrasse 54 www.mariansjazzroom.ch*). Very popular among connoisseurs.

SHOPPING

The main **shopping streets** are Spitalgasse, Marktgasse, Kramgasse and Gerechtigkeitsgasse. Note the late shopping on Thursdays until 9pm. The new pride of Bern is the recently opened **Westside** shopping centre designed by **Daniel Libeskind**. Containing hundreds of shops, it is just eight minutes from Bern main railway station by S-bahn nos. S5, S51 and S52. www.westside.ch.

There are **markets** selling fruit, flowers, vegetables and, various other articles every Tuesday and Saturday morning on the Bundesplatz. The traditional **onion market (Zwiebelmarkt)** is the fourth Monday in November at various locations around the city. The **Christmas market** takes place on Münsterplatz.

THEATRE AND MUSIC

Stadttheater – *Kornhausplatz 20.* *(0)31 329 51 11. www.stadttheaterbern.ch.*

Puppentheater (*Puppet Theater*) – *Gerechtigkeitsgasse 31.* *(0)31 311 95 85. www.berner-puppentheater.ch.*

Kursaal – *Kornhausstrasse 3.* *(0)31 339 55 00.* A complex featuring restaurants, a casino, a hotel, a piano bar, a nightclub and a cabaret (international variety shows).

Biel/Bienne★

Biel is a good excursion centre and its beach, not far from Nidau, is much appreciated. The city marks the linguistic frontier between French and German: one third of the inhabitants speak French. The ugly modern town contrasts with the quaint old quarters of the upper city.

A BIT OF HISTORY

The population of Biel (Bienne in French) has increased ten-fold within a century, thanks to the watch and clock industry, which still employs about 6 000 people. The first Omega watch factory was set up here in 1879. Other industries have been established to ward off possible economic crises (precision machine-tool works, wire-mills and graphic art workshops).

Biel is also a shining example of successful bilingualism, even by Swiss standards: German and French are official languages on an equal footing, with street signs in both languages. It is not unusual to come across two locals conversing without difficulty, each in his own language. In summer, the place to see and be seen is **Strandboden**, the park on the lake.

OLD TOWN★

This area of town is very picturesque, with many fountains and façades decorated with remarkable wrought-iron

Watch Mecca

Since the mid 19C, Biel/Bienne has seen itself as the capital of the watch industry: the first factory—Omega—was founded here in 1879; it is the home of Swatch, the biggest company in the watch industry; and is an important site for Rolex, too. Thanks to the watch industry, the city has seen its population increase tenfold in a century.

▶ **Population:** Biel/Bienne 50 455.

Info: Zentralstrasse 60. ℘(0)32 329 84 84. www.biel-seeland.net.

◐ **Location:** Biel/Bienne lies at the foot of the last spurs of the Jura and on the shore of the lake that bears its name; approx 30 min form Bern. Alt. 438m/1 437ft.

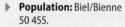

signs, often painted in bright colours. O the main street, **Burggasse**, stand th town hall, notable for its stepped gabl and façade adorned by windows wit red sandstone mullions, and a Fountai of Justice dating from 1744. **Obergass** is lined with houses influenced by bot Bernese and French architectural style To the right, the houses are arcaded an accessible directly from street level; t the left, short flights of steps lead to th entrances.

Ring

This charming square was the centre c old Biel when the town was governe by the prince-bishops of Basel, from th 11C to the Revolution.

Justice was rendered here; the accuse appeared before members of the Coun cil seated in a semicircle, and it was from this arrangement that the Ring drew it name. In the middle of the Ring is th curious **Banneret Fountain** (1546) symbolizing the militia and war. Th houses, with their arcades and turret form a fine architectural group.

Note the massive tower of the Goth Church of St Benedict and the frescoe to the left as you enter. The highl decorated corner house with a turre is particularly attractive. Now home t the local registry office, it was once th forest workers' house.

Obergasse leads to **Juraplatz**, anothe picturesque square surrounded b arcaded houses. Note the beautifu Angel's Fountain (1480), decorate with an angel holding a lamb in its arm which it is protecting from the devil.

Center PasquArt★★

71-75 Faubourg du Lac. ⏰*Mon–Fri 2pm –6pm, Sat–Sun and holidays 11am– 5pm* ⏰ *11 CHF.* ✆*(0)32 322 55 86. www.pasquart.ch.*

A place to visit as much for its works on display as for its architecture. This centre of contemporary art with a programme of innovative exhibitions is distributed in two buildings: a former hospital, and since 2000, an absolutely modern vast cube by the firm of Diener & Diener. The artists exhibit large volumes of works and the brightness of rooms provides a dream space for expression. The first floor houses the Foto Forum, dedicated to photography. Temporary exhibitions occupy the 2nd and 3rd floors.

Neuhaus Museum

26 Promenade de la Suze . ⏰*Tue–Sun 11am–5pm (11am–7pm Wed.)* ⏰ *7CHF (children free).* Guided tours on Wed (free). ✆*(0)32 328 70 30/31. www.mn-biel.ch.*

Located in one of the city's oldest fabric-printing factories to contribute to Biel's prosperity, this museum brings together several regional exhibitions devoted to the industrial history of Biel: local bourgeois life in the 19C, animal and plant watercolours from the Robert family, collection, artefacts from brothers Robert (a writer) and Karl (a painter) Walser, and numerous pieces of equipment, such as old and new projectors to illustrate the history of cinema.

Museum Schwab★

⏰*Open Tue–Sun 2pm–6pm, Sun and public holidays, 11am–6pm.* ⏰*Closed 1 Jan, 24 and 31 Dec.* ⏰*5CHF.* ✆*(0)32 322 76 03. www.muschwab.ch.*

Housed here are collections made from discoveries by Colonel Schwab (1803–1869), a pioneer in the research of the prehistoric epoch in Romansh Switzerland. The museum contains the best-known examples of the lake-dwellers' era. Artefacts uncovered in the lakes of Biel, Neuchâtel and Murten are displayed alongside those from the Gallo-Roman settlement at Petinesca and La Tène (excavated by Schwab in 1857).

EXCURSIONS
Magglingen★

8km/5mi – about 30min.

▶ *Leave Biel by the road to Delémont and 200m/220yd after going under a bridge between two bends, turn left onto the byroad to Evilard.*

At Magglingen, also known as Macolin, you will find an extensive **panorama**★ of the Swiss plateau, the lakes at the foot of the Jura and the Alps. Magglingen is known for its Federal School of Gymnastics. *Accessible by funicular from Biel (W on the town plan).*

Aarberg

▶ *11km/6.8mi S (road number 22).*

A canal links this small yet prosperous town to Biel Lake. The upper town, joined to the lower town by a covered bridge (16C) spanning the River Aare, is well worth a visit. Its main square, **Stadtplatz**★, oblong in shape and paved, is embellished with two flower-decked fountains and lined with classical façades and a small 15C church (restored). A picturesque second-hand fair is held annually on the last weekend in April.

Le Chasseral ★★★

▶ *Drive 30km/18.5mi to the W by Highway 5 to La Neuveville, then towards Nods (signposted). After the toll, go to the hotel Chasseral where you can park your car.* Caution: the road is narrow and is usually blocked by snow *from December to April. Jura Bernois Tourisme, 4 Rue du Marché. 𝒫(0)32 751 49 49. www.jurabernois.ch.*

The highest point of the northern Jura (alt. 1 607m/5 272ft), Le Chasseral has a famous panorama of the Swiss Alps.

Panorama★★★

The Hotel Chasseral, situated just below the route's highest point, marks the end of the public thoroughfare. The nearby viewing table allows visitors to take their bearings on the main peaks of the Bernese and Valais Alps and the Mont Blanc Massif. This wonderful backcloth extends for some 250km/156mi.

Walk to the Chasseral beacon *(1hr there and back by a wide, gently sloping path)* near a Swiss postal service's telecommunications relay station. From the beacon you get a **circular view★★★** of the horizon, extending from the Swiss Alps to the northern Jura, the Vosges and the Black Forest.

Motorists can return to Biel via **St-Imier**. This bustling watch and clock-making centre is located on the south face of Mount Soleil. St-Imier's past is recalled by the Tower of St Martin (or Queen Bertha), all that remains of an 11C church, and its 12C former **Collegiate Church** (now a Reformed Church). The interior features a narthex with archaic capitals (heads on the right), an apse with oven vaulting and a chancel with ogive vaulting and mural paintings.

🚗 DRIVING TOURS

BIELER SEE★

55km/34mi – Allow 1hr15min. www.bielersee.ch.

▶ *Leave Biel/Bienne via Route 5, W.*

Lake Biel (Lac de Bienne) is of glacial origin. It was once larger; when the water level dropped about 2m/6.5ft in 1878, it uncovered a score of lake-dwellings on the south shore. At the same time some of the waters of the Aare were deflected from the lake. "The shores of Lake Biel are wilder and more romantic than those

of Lake Geneva... but they are not less smiling," wrote French philosopher Jean-Jacques Rousseau.

The north shore, with charming French-speaking villages such as La Neuveville nestling amid vineyards, is more picturesque.

La Neuveville

4 rue du Marché – 2520. 𝒫(0)32 751 49 49. www.jurabernois.ch.

The town's economic activity includes wine-producing, precision engineering, and tourism. An old-world feeling lingers about the town with its paved streets, lanterns and five towers (remains of the fortifications), and it is an excellent base for excursions to Île St-Pierre, the three lakes (Biel, Neuchâtel, and Murten) and Le Chasseral.

Two hours is ample for exploring this pleasant area, including Tour de Rive (1312–18), the entrance to the town, whose heavy oak door is adorned with the arms of the town. From the place de la Liberté, take a look at the houses on the left on **Rue de l'Hôpital**, whose top floor, protected by a roof overhang, is equipped with a winch that was used to bring goods up the attic.

Rue du Marché★, a long street, with two old gates at either end (Tour de Rive and Tour Rouge), pretty Renaissance fountains in-between and flower-decked houses (two of which dated from 1647 and 1697) in between.

The Old Town Hall houses the **Museum of History of Neuveville**, which contains the trophies of the Burgundy wars, antiques and paintings. It also hosts temporary art exhibitions (*Apr–Oct, Sun afternoon; ⚹admission free*).

Blanche Église

E of town towards Biel/Bienne, on the left. To visit, contact the Tourist Office, 4 rue du Marché in La Neuveville. 𝒫(0)32 751 49 49.

This Carolingian building remodelled in the Gothic period and restored in 1915 is surrounded by 17C and 18C tombstones. Inside are a painted wooden pulpit (1536) and remains of 14C frescoes on the right of the chancel: Temptation of

Christ, Christ Reviled, Entrance to Jerusalem, Adam and Eve.

St Petersinsel★★

By boat from Biel or la Neuveville.
Allow half a day for the whole excursion.
⏱Departure from Biel Apr–mid-Oct,
9.45am–4.45pm (times vary according
to the season). ⛟Fare there and back
30.40CHF. ℘(0)32 329 88 11. Departure
from La Neuveville Apr–mid-Oct,
10.30am–5.15pm (times vary according
to the season: Weekends only in winter).
⛟Fare there and back 18.40CHF from
La Neuveville. ℘(0)32 329 88 11.

St Peter's Island, at the extreme southwest end of the lake, effectively became a peninsula when the lake's water level was lowered, but it has retained its former name of island. In the autumn of 1765 it was visited by **Jean-Jacques Rousseau**, who recalls his idyllic stay there in *The Confessions* and in *Musings of the Solitary Walker*.

The visitor can walk round the north side of the island easily and enjoy pretty glimpses of the lake, especially toward the village of Ligerz (Gléresse). After seeing the small landing stage used by Rousseau, you will come to the house in which he lived. St Peter's Island and its neighbour, the small **Rabbits Island** (joined to the shore by a strip of marshy land since the waters of the lake were lowered), are nature reserves, providing a delightful haven of peace for migratory birds, as well as hare, and deer.

Cressier

Set back from the lake, this wine-growing village has preserved some of its old buildings; on Rue des St-Martin there is a house (1576) with an oriel window and the Vallier Château (1610) with its pointed turrets lies nearby.

Le Landeron

Nearer to the lake, this small hamlet is hemmed in by vegetable gardens and orchards. The charm of this village lies in its unique, long shaded square adorned with two fountains with bannerets. It is defended at each end by a fortified gate (1659 north side, 1596 south side)

and lined with old houses. The town hall (15C) is built onto the Martyrs Chapel. At 36 note a house dating from 1550.

GORGES DU PICHOUX★

From Biel to Porrentruy 61km/38mi –
Allow 2hr30mins (not including visits).
From Lake Biel to the Ajoie region (area around Porrentruy), deep gorges, pastures, fir or deciduous forests follow the road which, in the Sorne Valley, runs between the Franches Montagnes and the Delémont region.

▷ *Leave Biel by Madretschstasse and the road to Solothurn and Zürich, and at Bözingen take a path just before the Suze Bridge, near a wire-mill.*

From Biel to Sonceboz the road climbs quickly above the suburbs of Biel and halfway up the slope threads its way through the Taubenloch Gorges.

Taubenlochschlucht★

🚶 *Allow about 1hr30min.*
These gorges, often wild and mysterious, are served by an excellent tourist path.
The road goes up the industrialised Suze Valley. Between Sonceboz and Tavannes, the **Pierre-Pertuis** section resembles a small Alpine pass. This corridor has been used since the beginning of the 3C by the Roman road from Aventicum (Avenches) to Augusta Raurica (Augst) and takes its name from the arch under which the former road passed on the Tavannes slope.

Tavannes

This town, situated in the Upper Birse Valley, at the foot of the rock of Pierre-Pertuis, is known for its clock-making industry. The modern Roman Catholic church was decorated by artists of its **Société St-Luc**, a school of sacred art well known in Romansh Switzerland. The mosaic on the façade, representing the Ascension is by Gino Severini.

▷ *Turn left after the church in the direction of Delémont.*

Abbaye de Bellelay

⏱ *Open early Jan–mid-Jun & Sept–Dec, 8am–6pm; otherwise, 10am–noon, 2pm–6pm.* ⏱ *Closed for a week in Jun.* 🚌 *4CHF.* 📞 *(0)32 484 72 37.*

The **abbey church** (built 1710–14) features an imposing array of Baroque architecture in the interior, which art lovers may compare to that of St Urban and Rheinau. The **interior**★ is remarkably impressive. The Fathers of Bellelay hold the secret of making Tête-de-Moine, a semi-hard cheese.

After winding through wooded pastureland, the road glides into the depths of the gorges cut by the Sorne.

Gorges du Pichoux★

This cutting is the deepest of the *cluses*, or transverse valleys, hollowed out by the Sorne between Le Pichoux and Berlincourt. The gorges have limestone cliffs to which cling forests of fir trees. The **climb**★ from Boécourt to the Les Rangiers Pass at first crosses the flank of an open slope planted with birch and oak. The Doubs slope is reached when the road joins the itinerary called the Jura Corniche.

▶ *Finish at Porrentruy.*

Porrentruy★

Porrentruy, a small town in the northeast of the Bernese Jura and the 16C residence of the prince-bishops of Basel, has many tourist attractions. Its pedestrianised old town is full of colourful façades and wrought-iron signs. Many museums tell the history and geology of this region that was annexed by revolutionary France in 1793. The city of Porrentruy became the capital of the Mont-Terrible *département*, which included the present Jura canton and Bernese Jura as far as Biel/Bienne.

ADDRESSES

🛏 STAY

🛏 **Villa Lindenegg** – *Lindenegg 5.* 📞 *(0)32 322 94 66. www.lindenegg.ch.* 🅿. *8 rooms.* Restaurant in the evening (except Sat) and weekend lunchtimes. Closed Tues . A taste of la dolce vita in this elegant 19C building, carefully restored and surrounded by a beautiful garden. Enough to want to stay on after a drink on the terrace and dine in the excellent Bistro.

🍴 EAT

🍽 **Restaurant Pfauen** – *Ring 7, Altstadt. Closed Wed.* 📞 *(0)32 322 49 13.* Spectacular views of the beautiful fountain and watchtowers of the Ring from the tables on the terrace of this restaurant. In the cosy room, with its parquet floor and light walls, let yourself be tempted by the seasonal dishes on offer.

🍽🍽 **Elite** – *Bahnhofstr. 14. Closed Sat lunch, Sun and mid Jun–mid Aug.* 📞 *(0)32 328 77 77. www.hotelelite.ch.* In a 1930s Art Deco atmosphere, this brasserie serves traditional, quality fare.

▶ **Population:** 6 637.
ℹ **Info:** 5 Grand-Rue – 2900. 📞 *(032) 466 59 59.*
▶ **Location:** In the centre of the Ajoie region in the Jura. Alt. 445m/1 460ft.
🅿 **Parking:** There is no parking in the old town; use car parks and walk in.
⊘ **Don't Miss:** The château, or the Grottes de Réclère.
👥 **Kids:** Exploring the Grottes de Réclère.
⏱ **Timing:** This town is not on many tourists' radar, making weekend visits easier for the casual visitor.

OLD TOWN

The **Porte de France**, marks the entrance to the old town. The town centre features many wealthy residential mansions with inner courtyards and turrets worthy of note *(22 Grand-Rue)* magnificent 16C fountains that are the work of Laurent Perroud: The Banneret Fountain *(rue des Malvoisins)*, the Samaritan Fountain *(Grand-Rue, in front of a corner house with oriel windows)* and the Gilded Sphere Fountain *(rue des Annonciades)*.

Musée de l'Hôtel-Dieu

Open May–mid-Nov, Tue–Sun, 2pm –5pm. Closed 1 Nov and mid-Nov– Apr. 5CHF. (0)32 466 72 72. www.museehoteldieu.ch.

Devoted to local history, this museum features an exhibit about the hospital's **pharmacy**, a fine example of 19C cabinet-making and presents an interesting display of pots and phials made of glass and porcelain.

The other exhibit is the treasury of St Peter's Church, which contains precious objects, some dating back to the Gothic period: A 1487 crucifix used in processions and a large monstrance known as Ostensoir de Morat (1488).

Château

Perched on a rocky spur, the castle's silhouette rises above the Allaine Valley. Only the Tour Réfous (45m/148ft, pretty views from the top) remains of this medieval stronghold, a round tower standing near a group of buildings now housing administrative offices. One corridor inside the Law Courts displays portraits representing prince-bishops (1575–1737) including Jacques-Christophe Blarer from Wartensee, a charismatic figure whose strong personality was to mark the history of the town.

Botanical Garden

Garden 10am–5pm, greenhouses 2pm–5pm. Free. (0)32 466 30 15. www.mhdp.ch.

The gardens border the former bishop's residence whose front yard is home to an impressive Foucault pendulum, which demonstrates the rotation of the

---

Jurassic Era

In 1795 the German naturalist Alexander von Humboldt was on a scientific expedition in the Swiss Jura mountains when he realised that the limestone deposits which make up these mountains were a new, unknown strata which he called "Calcaire de Jura". Although he originally dated the deposits wrongly, he had discovered a complete geologic era in the Earth's history (between c.200 and 145 million years ago), which was characterised by the prevalence of dinosaurs on land (and sea) and wide conifer forest cover.

Earth. The tropical greenhouses hold a fine collection of tropical plants including carnivorous plants and orchids.

Jurassic Museum of Natural Sciences

Within the botanical garden.
Tue–Sun 2pm–5pm. Closed Dec 25 & 1–3 Jan. 3 CHF (-16 years free). (0)32 467 37 10. www.mhdp.ch.
While this museum traces the history of the universe, two rooms are devoted to the natural heritage of Jura such as fauna and fossils (this is where the word Jurassic and the corresponding era originate).

EXCURSIONS
Grottes de Réclère

15km/9.5mi by the road to Besançon. Guided tour of the caves (1hr) Apr– Nov, 10am–noon, 1pm–5pm (9am– 6pm Jul–Aug). Closed Dec–Mar. 9CHF (14CHF caves and park).
These caves, located 100m/328ft underground, were discovered in 1886. Admire the fine array of stalactites and stalagmites; the latter feature "the great dome", said to be the largest in the country (13m/43ft high for 250 000 years of age). The tour may be combined with that of **Préhisto-Parc** *(opening times same as above; closed Dec–mid-Apr; 8CHF (14CHF caves and park); (032) 467 61 55),*

an area of the forest filled with life-size replicas of prehistoric creatures.

Delémont

◐ *30km/18mi E via the A 16, exit Delémont. 12 place de la Gare – 2800.* ℘ *(0)32 422 97 78.*

Until 1792 Delémont was the summer residence of the prince-bishops of Basel, whose crosier appears in the arms of the town. Today it owes its importance to its watch and precision-instrument factories. Since 1978 it has been the capital of the new canton of Jura.

The **old town** or high town, on either side of rue du 23 Juin, has kept its monumental gates, 16C Renaissance fountains and noble 18C classical buildings.

Musée Jurassien d'Art et d'Histoire

◐ *Open Tue–Sun, 2pm–5pm.* ◐ *Closed 1 week between Christmas and New Year.* ◐ *6CHF.* ℘ *(0)32 422 80 77. www.mjah.ch.*

The regional Art and History Museum contains archeological finds from the prehistoric to the Merovingian Era discovered in the area, ancient religious objects, mementoes of Napoleon, and examples of local crafts and furniture. Also included are works by artists from the Jura.

Chapelle du Vorbourg

◐ *2km/1.2mi NE of Delémont.*

This pilgrimage shrine is reached by a shady road offering beautiful views of Delémont. The chapel with its Baroque altars and walls adorned with votive offerings of the 18C and 19C, stands in a wild and woody site over a deep valley.

🚗 DRIVING TOURS

LES FRANCHES MONTAGNES★

41km/25.5mi from Porrentruy to Saignelégnier – Allow 2hrs (not including visits).

◐ *Exit Porrentruy SE by Highway 6 in the direction of Delémont. At Courgenay, just after the church toward Courtemautruy, take a right and then the panoramic de la Croix pass. After a steep incline (18%) is Saint Ursanne.*

Saint-Ursanne★

Alt. 494m/1 621ft. 18, rue du Quartier ℘ *(0)32 461 37 16. www.juratourisme.ch* Lying away from the main roads deep in the Doubs Valley, Saint Ursanne, a quaint old town that has remained unchanged since the beginning of the 19C, makes a charming place to stop when cross

Saint-Ursanne

ing the Swiss Jura. It originated with the hermitage that Ursicinus, a disciple of Columba set up in the 7C.

You enter this medieval town through fortified gates surmounted by a bear carrying the symbolic crosier of the prince-bishops of Basel. The town is littered with medieval architecture, including collégiales, a church, a cloister, ruins of a 14C castle, and a hermitage. There is a good **view**★ from the bridge over the Doubs River. The town roofs are dominated by the church tower and the castle.

Collegiate Church

🕓 Open daily except Sun am, 7.30am–7pm (8pm Jun–Oct). 𝒫(0)32 461 31 74.

The east end and apse are Romanesque and comprise a single-arched **doorway**★ adorned with statues. The Romanesque chancel has a Baroque canopied altar; the nave is early Gothic (13C).

⬤ From Saint Ursanne, rejoin road 18A at the place called Les Manettesheading towards Delémont.

The high plateau of the Franches Montagnes (average altitude 1 000m/3 281ft) between the Doubs Valley and Mount Soleil Chain is known as the "Watch Valley." Its low houses, pastures dotted with fir trees and natural parks where bay horses and milk cows graze, are most attractive.

Tourism flourishes in winter because of the popularity of cross-country skiing, and in summer thanks to the temperate climate and abundance of natural sites.

Saignelégier

The chief town of the district, it is well-known throughout the Jura for its **August Horse Fair** (🕓see Calendar of Events).

While visiting, you may also want to take a tour through **Gruère pond**, where signs along the log path explain the fascinating 20 000-year history of this 40ha/98.8-acre peat bog.

ADDRESSES

🏠 STAY

⊖⊜ **Hôtel Bellevue** – 46 route de Belfort. 𝒫(0)32 466 55 44. www.bellevue-porrentruy.ch. 10 rooms. Restaurant. At the gates of the town, a low building where the rooms offer the usual level of comfort. The Brasserie offers simple but good meals of pizza, pasta, fish and meat (⊖⊜⊜menus, ⊖dish of the day).

⊖⊜ **De la Gare** – 2, rue de la Petite-Gilberte, Courgenay (3km/1.8mi to the SE). 𝒫(0)32 471 22 22. Closed 4–8 Jan. 6 rooms. Opposite the station, an establishment with individually designed and named rooms, some with antique furniture. Reserve the one called Gilberte, which is also the name of the hotel brasserie (⊖⊜⊜; closed Sun & Mon). Beautiful quiet patio at the back.

🍴 EAT

⊖⊜ **Les Grottes** – 2912 Réclère. 𝒫(0)32 476 61 55. Restaurant near the Réclère caves and the Prehistoric Park. It allows for a nice break between visiting the two. There is a possibility of accommodation in small cabins and Mongolian yurts which can take a families up to 5 persons.

⊖⊜ **Hôtel du Bœuf** – 7 rue de l'Eglise, Courgenay (3km/1.8mi to the SE). 𝒫(0)32 471 11 21. www.boeuf-courgenay.ch. Closed 3–24 Feb, 5–13 Oct plus Tue & Wed. This restaurant offers "effet bœuf", the signature dish of this family business whose pink facade stands in the middle of the village. Meals for every taste, carefully chosen menus.

Market in Porrentruy

Jura Tourisme/Switzerland Tourism

Solothurn★★

Solothurn lies at the foot of the last ridge of the Jura (Weissenstein) and today extends to both banks of the Aare. On the north bank of the river the old nucleus of the town, still encircled by its 17C walls, has justifiably acquired the reputation of being the most beautiful Baroque town in Switzerland.
The Krummturm (Crooked Tower) is the most striking feature of this fortified group.

▶ **Population:** 15 623.
ℹ **Info:** Hauptgasse 69 – 4500. ℘(0)32 626 46 46. www.solothurn-city.ch.
▶ **Location:** The town of Solothurn is in Solothurn canton, and lies at the foot of the Jura (Weissenstein). Alt. 436m/1 430ft.
⊚ **Don't Miss:** St Ursenkathedrale.
⊙ **Timing:** Allow at least a day to enjoy the sights properly.

A BIT OF HISTORY

Solothurn remained Catholic until 1792 and was chosen as a residence by the French ambassadors to the Swiss Diet. Intellectual and artistic exchanges flourished between the two countries; Bourbon court fashions were adopted and the town's fortifications were built (1667) according to principles of the French military engineer Vauban.

OLD TOWN★

The Basel Gate (**Baseltor**) and the Biel Gate (**Bieltor**) access the old quarter, with picturesque streets lined with houses featuring brightly painted shutters, wrought-iron signs, half-timbered facades with window boxes overflowing in colourful flowers, and overhanging roofs. **Hauptgasse**, **St-Urbangasse**, and **Schmiedengasse** are noteworthy. **Marktplatz**, the heart of the old town, is adorned with a fountain with 16C painted figures (St Ursen Brunnen). This is one of eleven painted wooden fountains for which the town is famous. It is dominated by the 12C clock tower (Zeitglockenturm) whose astronomical clock face is surmounted by three figures (the King between Death and Saint Ursus, patron saint of the town).

St Urs Cathedral★

This imposing Baroque building was designed in the Italian style (18C) by two Ticino architects, dedicated to St Ursus and St Victor, martyrs from the Theban Legion who, having escaped the massacre of Aguane (℮ see ST MAURICE),

were beheaded at Solothurn. The vast nave is supported by piers with engaged pilasters and capitals embellished with floral motifs. This decoration continues along the false gallery under the clerestory. The carved pink marble pulpit and the paintings in the chancel and at the transept crossing are the main ornamental features. Pleasant gardens are laid out behind the east end of the St Ursenkathedrale.

Jesuits Church

The Jesuitenkirche (end of the 17C) features a **nave**★ consisting of three bays decorated with frescoes and stucco work. A gallery runs along the first two bays, so that the third one appears to form a transept. The gigantic high altar is adorned with a great painting representing the Assumption, framed between two large green marble pillars. The organ-loft is delicately decorated.

Old Arsenal Museum

⊙Open 1pm–5pm; Sat–Sun 10am–5pm. ⊙Closed Easter, Christmas and 1 Jan. ∞6CHF. ℘(0)32 624 35 28. www.museum-alteszeughaus.ch.
The **Museum Altes Zeughaus** contains a large collection of weapons and uniforms dating from the Middle Ages up to the 20C. The second floor boasts 400 breastplates and suits of armor; the ground floor displays a German tank used in the World War II and a collection of cannons, both old-fashioned and modern.

SOLOTHURN

0   200 m
0   200 yds

BLUMENSTEIN CASTLE

KLOSTER ST-JOSEF

RÖTIHOF

Art Museum

Old Arsenal Museum

Porte de Bâle

St. Urs Cathedral

Nictumgässlein

Market Pl.

Clock Tower

Jesuits Church

Klosterplatz

Natural History Museum

Porte de Bienne

CROOKED TOWER

AARE

LYSS

WHERE TO STAY		WHERE TO EAT	
Roter Turm	①	Stadtbeiz	③

Kunstmuseum Solothurn★

🕐 Open Tue–Sun, 11am–5pm, Sat-Sun 10am–5pm. 🕐 Closed 1 Jan, Good Fri, Easter, Whitsun and Christmas. 💰 Donation. 📞 (0)32 622 23 07. www.kunstmuseum-so.ch.

This is maybe the best small Fine Arts museum in Switzerland with an excellent collection mostly of Swiss art from 1850 onwards—and it's free! The most interesting collections are on the first floor. Alongside some of the best works by Ferdinand Hodler (his *William Tell* is here 👆 p318) and many known works by Félix Vallotton and Cuno Amiet, both contemporary painters of his. Take note of two stunning portraits executed by bygone masters: **Virgin with Strawberries**★ is a painting on wood from

the Rhenish School (c.1425), remarkable for its strong, vivid colours (blue, green, gold, crimson, ruby) and the graceful attitude of the two characters. As for the **Madonna of Solothurn**★—the work of Holbein the Younger—it is full of majesty and shows strict composition in which gold, red and blue predominate. Visitors may also admire works by Klimt, Van Gogh, Renoir, Matisse, Leger and Degas.

Natural History Museum

🕐 Open Tue–Sun, 2pm–5pm, Sun 10am –5pm. 🕐 Closed 1 Jan, Easter, Whitsun and Christmas. 👆 📞 (0)32 622 70 21. www.naturmuseum-so.ch.

The Naturmuseum enlightens the visitor on the human race and regional fauna

211

(alive and fossilised). The second floor contains displays on Swiss geology and mineralogy. Of interest are the fossilised tortoises, starfish and dinosaur footprints. The basement houses temporary exhibitions.

Museum Schloss Blumenstein

Access NW of the town centre (follow directions for Schloss Blumenstein) ○*Open Tue–Sat 2pm–5pm, Sun 10am –5pm.* ∞*Free.* ℘*(032) 622 54 70. www.museumblumenstein.ch.*
This large 18C building, surrounded by a small park, exhibits furniture, tapestries, sculpture (religious and cult objects), costumes, ceramics and musical instruments. On the ground floor veranda, note the lovely 16C stained-glass windows.

EXCURSIONS
Weissenstein★★★

▷ *10km/6.2mi from Solothurn. The most difficult section of mountain road can be avoided by taking the chairlift from Oberdorf station (4km/2.5mi N of Solothurn) to Kurhaus Weissenstein (16min). Allow 2hrs.*
The crests of Weissenstein, standing like a rampart above the Solothurn lowland, offer one of the most impressive panoramas in the Jura. There is a chairlift from Oberdorf to the spa hotel at the summit.

Panorama★★★

⛰○*Operates Apr–Oct, 8.30am–6pm (8am Sun), Nov–Mar, 9am–5pm (8am Sun).* ○*Closed three weeks in spring and autumn.* ∞*Return fare 19CHF.* ℘*(0)84 884 15 25. www.seilbahnweissenstein.ch.*
When driving from Solothurn or Gänsbrunnen, the summit is marked by a pastoral coomb. Turn into the road to the Kurhaus, which stands on the crest. Walk down the path (7km/4.3mi) on the road to Gänsbrunnen.
Park at the restaurant; here views of the great barrier of the Alps can be seen, from the Säntis on the left to the Mont Blanc on the right.

Utzenstorf
This lovely shaded and flowered village has a small church with 16C stained-glass windows.
North of Utzenstorf stands the 17C and 18C white turreted **Schloss Landshut★**, the residence of the bailiffs of Bern until 1798 (○*open May–Oct, Tues–Sat 2pm–5pm, Sun 10–5;* ○*closed public holidays;* ∞*7CHF;* ℘*(0)32 665 40 27; www.schloss-landshut.ch).* Interior decor includes heavy period furnishings and huge porcelain stoves. It houses the **Swiss Hunting Museum** with trophies, decoys, and a remarkable collection of seignorial hunting arms from the 16C–20C.

ADDRESSES

STAY

⊜⊜⊟ **Roter Turm** – *Hauptgasse 42.* ℘*(0)32 622 96 21. www.roterturm.ch. 36 rooms.* Next to the clock tower, this family hotel is located in the historic district of the city. All rooms with modern conveniences. Great view of the tower from the fifth floor.

EAT

⊜⊜ **Stadtbeiz** – *Friedhofplatz 10.* ℘*(0)32 622 11 09. www.alterstephan.ch. Closed 1–5 Apr, 1–9 Aug, 17–31 Oct, 24 Dec–4 Jan.* On the ground floor of the chic restaurant **Zum Alten Stephan, Stadtbeiz** has nothing to envy in terms of the quality of the food it serves—and at better prices. Excellent traditional and regional dishes.

BOAT TRIPS

From Biel/Bienne, four daily boats travel eastward on a 2hr30min trip along the River Aare to Solothurn. ℘*(0)32 622 33 22. www.bielersee.ch*
The scenery is pastoral with reedy banks, farmhouses and birds along the glacial blue-green river. Half-timbered towns along the shore add interest, especially in **Büren**, where a covered bridge crosses the river. **Altreu** is a popular stop for its stork colony where the nests can be seen from the river.

Thun★★

Thun is one of the most typical Swiss towns, occupying an admirable site★★ within view of the Bernese Alps. The city, which has been populated since the Stone Age, was first established on an islet in the Aare where the river flows out of Lake Thun (Thunersee), and it gradually spread over the neighbouring shores at the foot of the Schlossberg, while passing from the hands of the Zähringens (☞see BERN) to those of the Kyburgs (1218). The second dynasty having become extinct in its turn, Thun came under the control of the Patriciate of Bern in 1384. The old quarters lie on the right bank of the Aare but the modern town with its ironworks has spread westward over the left bank.

- ▶ **Population:** 42 129.
- ◔ **Michelin Map:** Town plan in Michelin Red Guide Switzerland.
- ▤ **Info:** Seestrasse 2/Bahnhof. ℘(0)33 225 90 00. www.thun.ch.
- ▷ **Location:** Thun is located where the river Aar flows out of Lake Thun. Alt. 560m/1 837ft.
- ◈ **Don't Miss:** A cruise on Lake Thun, past castles and palaces and sun-blackened wooden chalets; excursion boats stop directly at the train station.
- ◔ **Timing:** This town can be very busy on weekends and holidays so plan accordingly.

THE OLD TOWN

The bustling **Obere Hauptgasse★** has an amusing feature: the flower-decked terraces of the houses serve as foot-paths, so that one walks on the roofs of the shops installed in the arcades at ground level. From the upper part of this street with its broad overhanging roofs a curious covered staircase (Kirchtreppe) to the church and the Zähringen Castle. Look for the city's narrowest house, only 2m/6.6ft wide, at No 61.

The **Rathausplatz★** is surrounded by arcaded houses and adorned with a flower-decked fountain. Dominated by its castle, the Rathausplatz makes a fine picture. A covered wooden bridge (Obere Schleuse), crosses the Aare.

Schloss

Reached by the covered staircase (Kirchtreppe) mentioned above.

The castle is is a massive Romanesque construction—flanked by four towers—which now houses the Schlossmuseum, at the north end of the Schlossberg.

Schlossmuseum★

◔*Open Jun–Sept 10am–5pm, Feb and Mar, 1pm–4pm, Nov–Jan, Sun 1pm–4pm. ◛8CHF; guided tours available.*

℘(0)33 225 90 00. www.schlossthun.ch. The magnificent Knights' Hall contains beautiful tapestries—one from the tent of Charles the Bold, seized by the Confederates after the Battle of Grandson in 1476—together with standards, breast-plates, chests, ceramics (a fine collection of old "Heimberg" pieces), archeological artefacts, items relating to local folklore, instruments, furniture and popular art-work evoking Thun in the 18C.

Above the Knights' Hall are special exhibits, such as Swiss Army firearms and uniforms. From the top floor of the tower you can reach the four corner turrets for a **panorama★★** of the town, the Aare, Lake Thun and the Bernese Alps from the Stockhorn in the west to the Niesen in the south, embracing the Jungfrau, the Eiger and the Mönch.

Stadtkirche

At the opposite end of the Schlossberg stands the parish church, its large octagonal tower and the steeple covered with small round tiles, dominating a porch decorated with frescoes.

From the terrace of the church, there is a beautiful **view★★** of the city, the lake and the Alps.

THE LAKE SHORE
Jakobshübeli★★
From this hill equipped as a belvedere (*viewing table*), there is a semicircular **panorama**★★ toward the Stockhorn and the Jungfrau.

Schadau Park and Castle★
Access by bus number 1 from the station. www.schloss-schadau.ch.
Set on the lake shore, this pleasant garden surrounding **Schadau Castle** offers a fine **view**★★ (*viewing table*) of the summits of the Bernese Alps, particularly the Finsteraarhorn (alt. 4 274m/14 022ft), which is the highest point of this mountain group. The Castle houses the Arts Restaurant and the **Swiss Gastronomy Museum** (◷*Tue–Thu 2pm–5pm; ∞5 CHF; www. gastronomiemuseum-thun.ch*) which displays books, menus and old utensils. The library is unique in its kind, bringing together more than 5 000 cookbooks in several languages, including some rare copies of 16C first editions. Just at the left of the entrance to the park, do not miss the Scherzligen church with its 9C Romanesque nave where modern furniture (altar, benches) rubs shoulders with ancient frescoes painted in the nave, the apse and the porch (13C–16C).

Wocher Panorama★
◷*Open May–Oct, Tue–Sun, 10am–5pm (9pm Wed). ∞5CHF. ✆(0)33 225 84 20.*
Schadau park is also the setting for the rotunda housing Marquard Wocher's panorama portraying Thun and its environs from 1814. It is the oldest circular painting in existence.

EXCURSION
Einigen
▶ *11km/6.5mi S by Frutigenstrasse.*
Halfway between Thun and Spiez, the charming village of Einigen is located on the south bank of Lake Thun, across from a lovely mountain landscape. The small Romanesque church, with a brilliant roughcast façade and 15C and 16C stained-glass windows, is topped by a pinnacle turret. With the tiny cemetery surrounding it, and sloping down in terraces to the lake, the church forms a picturesque **scene**★.

🚗 DRIVING TOUR

Thunersee★★ (Lake Thun)
From Thun to Interlaken 23km/14.3mi. Allow about 1hr. www.bls.ch.

Lake Thun 18km/11mi long, almost 4km/2.5mi wide and 217m/712ft deep, is one of the loveliest and largest sheets of water in Switzerland. Countless tourists have been captivated by its location amid green mountains and the snow-capped summit of the Jungfrau.

▶ *After the pretty residential suburbs of Thun, the road to Oberhofen remains within view of the summits of the Bernese Alps (Eiger-Mönch-Jungfrau and, more to the right, the three characteristic snowy ridges of the Blümlisalp). In the foreground, on the opposite shore, the Niesen pyramid and the rocky Stockhorn are prominent.*

Schloss Hünegg★★
◷*Open daily mid–May to mid–Oct, 2pm–5pm, Sun 11am–5pm. ∞9CHF. ✆(0)33 243 19 82. www.schlosshuenegg.ch.*
Located in a wooded park that slopes down to the lake, this large edifice (1863), in spite of its size, cannot be seen from the road. The apartments (1900) have been arranged into a museum of *Jugendstil (Art Nouveau)*. One room evokes the life of the Swiss student at the time (uniforms, duelling weapons etc.); works by the Bernese painter Martin Lauterburg (d. 1960) are exhibited on the second floor.

Oberhofen
This 12C **castle**★★ (◷*open mid–May–mid-Oct, Tue–Sun 11am–5pm, Mon 2pm–5pm; ∞8CHF; ✆(0)33 243 12 35*) jutting into the waters of the lake, forms an enchanting fairytale picture (*illuminated at night*), opposite the summits of the Bernese Alps. Enlarged and restored (17C to 19C), is now a branch of the Ber-

Oberhofen Castle by Thunersee

Max Schmid/Switzerland

nisches Historisches Museum displaying period furniture (Louis XIV, Louis XV, Empire) and collections of popular art illustrating life in the Bernese Oberland. The landscape park on the shores of the lake is one of the most pleasant features of the visit.

Before leaving Oberhofen, visit the **Museum of Timepieces and Mechanical Music Instruments** (⏱*open mid-May–mid-Oct, daily 2pm–5pm;* 🎟*10 CHF;* 📞*(0)33 243 43 77; www.uhrenmusem. ch*), housed in a 16C building in a large park by the lake. The museum displays a splendid collection of watches and musical instruments spanning seven centuries.

Between Oberhofen and Merligen, there is a superb **run along the quays★★**, facing Spiez and the mouth of the Kander Valley, the best side of the lake for sun and flowers. The Blümlisalp Massif, clearly visible through this gap, now draws near.

Merligen

At the end of a deeply cut valley, the village lies between green hillsides and the lake. It is known for its music, with frequent concerts, and for its 250-year cheese-making tradition, celebrated each September in a fair.

After Merligen, the road becomes a corniche along the steep slopes of the Nase (Nose) promontory over the eastern basin of the lake, whose lonely shores form a contrast with the little Riviera you have just come through.

Niederhorn★★

Alt. 1 950m/6 397ft 🚡*1–2hrs round trip, including the funicular ride from Beatenbucht to Beatenberg. Operates Jun–early Nov, daily 8am–5pm.* 🎟*48CHF.* 📞*(0)33 841 08 41.*

A gondola lift carries hikers and sightseers to the top of the Niederhorn, where views stretch across the Bernese Alps, including the three summits of the Eiger, Mönch, and Jungfrau and down across Thuner See. A short trail leads to a viewing platform with a telescope and map. During the descent through several tunnels, beginning 1km/0.6mi after Beatenbucht (the starting-point of the Beatenberg funicular), the view opens over the Bödeli Plain, between the wooded chains of the Harder (on the left) and the Rugen (on the right, dominated in the background by the rocky points of the Schynige Platte). Before Unterseen, the road passes at the foot of the St Beatus Caves with a cascade tumbling down.

Beatenberg ★ (St Beatus Caves)

Allow 1hr15min, including 1hr for the guided tour. Remember to dress warmly since the temperature is between 8°C/45°F and 12°C/55°F. 🚶*Guided tour (50min) every half hour Apr–Oct,*

10.30am–5pm. 16CHF. (0)33 841
16 43. www.beatushoehlen.ch.

It is in these caves, according to legend, that the 6C Hermit St Beatus spent his life in prayer (and slew a dragon while he was at it). In the 18C the only access was along the picturesque pilgrims' path which can also be traversed today starting from **Beatenbucht** (60–70 mins) or from Interlaken itself (2hr30min). This was an important pilgrimage centre and the ruins of an old Pilgrim's inn can be seen after the entrance on the right.

Of the 14km/8.8mi of galleries which have been excavated, only 900m/985yd are open to the public. They are reached by a steep path (10min) running alongside a pretty **waterfall**★.

First you will come across a series of caves evoking man's life in prehistoric times. Then you enter the actual grottoes, of which the most notable features are the Domed Grotto (11m/36ft high), the Mirror Grotto (note the stalactites' reflection in the sheet of water), the Witches' Cauldron and the Snake's Grotto. You can also visit a small **Cave Museum** (Tue–Sun 11.30am–5.30pm) devoted to geology and speleology, which displays several panels explaining the history of Swiss Caving.

Unterseen

This peaceful village, contiguous to Interlaken has a church, whose rustic steeple with a steep sloping gabled roof provides a very photogenic composition with the Mönch (left) and Jungfrau (right) in the background.

Just steps away, the small **Jungfrau Region Touristikmuseum**★ (Jungfrau tourist region museum, Obere Gasse 28; open mid May to mid–Oct, Tue–Sun 2pm–5pm; 5CHF, children 2CHF; 033 822 98 39; www.touristikmuseum. ch) traces the increase in tourism in the region since the early 19C. Exhibits illustrate a century of road transport in the Oberland: the Habkern postal carriage, models of other postal vehicles and the first bicycle to have been used in Inter-

laken. The milestone (studenstein) indicated the distance and length of time required for those on foot to reach Bern. Other displays illustrate the expansion of the hotel industry (accommodation in private homes, inns and hotels) and development of the railway network (model of a locomotive from the Brünig Pass's rack railway). Nautical instruments and furnishings are grouped together in the boat section. The most interesting exhibit is undoubtedly a miniature model of the Bellevue, the very first boat to sail on Lake Thun. There are additional displays on winter sports, with a section on development of skis and sledges, the growth of mountain railways such as those on the Giessbach, Wetterhorn and Jungfrau, and the sport of mountaineering. The top floor is reserved for temporary exhibitions.

Interlaken★★★
See INTERLAKEN.

ADDRESSES

STAY

Pension-Restaurant zum Lärch – 3988 Obergesteln. (0)27 973 10 01. www.laerch.ch. Cosy guesthouse with restaurant.

Krone – Rathausplatz 2. (0)33 227 88 88. www.krone-thun.ch. 27 rooms. Located in the heart of the old town, with recently renovated and refurbished, elegant rooms.

EAT

Arts Schloss Schadau – Seestrasse 45. (0)33 222 25 00. www. schloss-schandau.ch. Closed Mon in Feb and Tue Nov–Apr. This 19C chateau in the sumptuous setting of a leafy park on a lake, has a restaurant and a bistro for different budgets.

NIGHTLIFE

Dancing and socializing on five levels at **Musikpark** (Scheibenstrasse 49-51).

Spiez★

This charming little town at the foot of the Niesen enjoys a beautiful site★, best seen from a terrace at the exit from the town beside the road to Interlaken. Spiez is a pleasant summer resort and a good excursion centre.

SIGHTS
Schloss

The medieval **castle**, crowned with several massive towers, stands on a spur of the Spiezberg overlooking the lake and the bay. It was built in the 12C and 13C and has since been enlarged and restored several times.

From the public garden on the esplanade in front of the castle entrance, you overlook the harbour containing sailing and pleasure boats. Many chalets nestle among the greenery on the far shore. The Castle Museum (☉open mid-Apr–mid-Oct, Mon 2pm–5pm (6pm Jul–mid-Sept), Tue–Sun 10am–5pm (6pm Jul–mid-Sept); ☞5CHF; ℘(0)33 654 15 06) contains mementoes of the former owners of the castle, the Erlachs and Bubenbergs, and some fine Gothic, Renaissance and Baroque inlaid furniture. The rooms are adorned with ornate woodwork and stained-glass windows.

From the top of the great tower you can admire a fine **panoramic view**★★ of the lovely sites of Spiez, Lake Thun, the Niesen in the south and the Beatenberg in the east.

Schlosskirche

This Romanesque church (late 10C, now disused) near the castle was designed as a basilica with three aisles and semicircular apses (fine frescoes). Especially remarkable are, to the left of the chancel, the Baroque tomb of Sigismond of Erlach (1700) and the grave of Jeanne de la Sararz , second wife of Adrian von Budenberg (15C)

▶ **Population:** 12 453.
🛈 **Info:** Info-Centre – 3700 Spiez. ℘(0)33 654 20 20. www.spiez.ch. Hauptstrasse, Kanderthal. ℘(0)33 675 80 80. www.kandersteg.ch.
◉ **Location:** On the south shore of Lake Thun. Alt. 628m/2 060ft.
◉ **Don't Miss:** The castle museum.

🚗 DRIVING TOURS

KANDERTAL★

From Spiez to Kandersteg 26km/16mi – about 2hr30min. ⓐThis excursion ends in a cul-de-sac at Kandersteg, but the railway is fitted out to take cars through the Lötschberg Tunnel to the Valais.

This valley is divided into two sections orientated differently: firstly the Frutigtal which goes southwest as far as Frutigen; then the Kandertal which goes south to Kandersteg.

▶ *Leave Spiez SW by the Kandersteg road and stop in Mülenen.*

Crossing the spur which separates Spiez from the Kander, the road drops towards the valley floor and begins to encircle the huge Niesen Pyramid.

Climb to the Niesen★★★

Alt. 2 362m/7 749ft. ⌇ From Mülenen station, about 2hr round trip, including 1hr by funicular. ☉Operates Jun–Nov. Departure every 30min (15min if busy), 8am–5pm (enquire in advance). ☞Return fare 55CHF. ℘(0)33 676 11 12. The funicular rides above the Frutigtal and stops at Schwandegg (alt. 1 669m/5 474ft), before continuing to Niesen Kulm, from where there is a magnificent **panorama**★★★ of the Berner Oberland. A footpath leads to the summit *(allow half a day)*, where visitors will find a hotel-restaurant.

Frutigen

15min on foot there and back to go up to the church (following the Adelboden road for a moment and then turning up the first ramp to the right).

This large village at the confluence of the Kander and the Engstligen, is the best-equipped medium altitude resort in the Lötschberg district. The church is built high up within view of the Balmhorn and the Altels.

Crossing the Kander at the foot of the Tellenburg ruins your approach to the Bühlstutz ridge. This separates the Kandergrund shelf from the Kandersteg Basin and compels the Lötschberg railway to make a hairpin loop around the Felsenburg ruins, which stand out clearly on their rocky spur.

Blausee★

About 45min walk and trip by boat.
🕘 *Nature reserve open from Apr–Oct, 9am–5pm; Nov–Mar 10am–5pm.*
🎫 *Admission 4.50CHF, including boat trip.* 🕿 *(0)33 672 33 33.*

This site comprises not only a little lake with incredibly clear, blue water, lying deep in the forest within view of the snowy Doldenhorn summit, but also a mass of rocks among the woods, a trout farm, and a restaurant. The road now takes on the Bühlstutz ridge in a more austere landscape of fields and woods dotted with rocks. At last you emerge into the Kandersteg Basin with steep slopes laced with waterfalls.

Kandersteg★

Alt. 1 176m/3 858ft. Hauptstrasse.
🕿 *(0)33 675 80 80. www.kandersteg.ch.*

Lying at the foot of rugged escarpments, which frame the snow-peaks of the Blümlisalp to the east and dip into a green Alpine basin, Kandersteg is best known today for its position at the north end of the **Lötschberg Tunnel**.

This railway tunnel, 14.6km/9mi long (Kandersteg–Goppenstein), has created, since 1913, a direct link between Bern and the Rhône Valley and can also convey cars.

As a mark of the close co-operation between Eurotunnel and the Swiss

railway system, one locomotive of the Bern-Lötschberg-Simplon train has been given the name *Eurotunnel*. Likewise, one of the engines which carries passengers across the Channel is called *Lötschberg*. *(For information on how to transport your car through the tunnel, ask at Tourist Information Centres or railway stations.)* The life of the locality is kept going in summer by the proximity of natural wonders like Lake Oeschinen and, in winter, by facilities for skiers.

▷ *Follow the main road towards the floor of the valley and leave your car at the lower cable-car station at Stock.*

Klus★★

1hr on foot there and back.
Climb, on foot, a little road that goes into a tunnel over the Klus. Go on to the bridge over the Kander after a second tunnel. Sure-footed tourists will prefer to descend by the steep path, sometimes wet with spray, which leaves the road between the two tunnels.

ENGSTLIGENGRAT VALLEY

30km/18.5mi from Spiez to Adelboden – Allow 2hrs. www.engstligenalp.ch.
This tour follows the same route as above, then branches off to turn right to Frutigen to Adelboden.

Adelboden

Alt. 1 356m/4 446ft. Dorfstrasse 23, 3715.
🕿 *(0)33 673 80 80. www.adelboden.ch.*
Adelboden lies in the wide, sunny **basin**★ at the upper end of the Engstligen Valley. It is one of the highest of the fashionable resorts in the Bernese Oberland both in summer and in winter, and is known for its healthy and agreeable climate. The village clusters halfway up the slope, facing a majestic skyline of limestone mountains. The most striking feature is the snow-covered, flat top of the Wildstrubel (alt. 3 243m/10 640ft), completing the great mountain circle of the Engstligenalp, from which the powerful Engstligenfälle bursts forth, leaping from a rocky shelf to form an impressive spectacle.

⚡ The Skiing Area

Adelboden skiing area, linked to that of Lenk, comprises 160km/99.5mi of pistes and some 50 lifts. Its highest point is Luegli (alt. 2 138m/7 014ft); it is particularly suitable for intermediate skiers.

Engstligenfälle★★★

4km/2.5mi along the Adelboden road, ⚡ then access by cable car (ascent 5min). ⚠ Bring warm, waterproof clothes and sturdy shoes.

From the top, the **view**★ of Adelboden is dominated by Gsür (2 708m/8 884ft), the Gross Lohner Massif, and the upper part of the Engstligen Falls. To the south extend the Engstligenalp pastures.

🚶 Hikers can choose several **itineraries**, including those leading to Ammerten Pass (*2hr climb*, 2 443m/8 015ft) and the **Ammertenspitz** summit (*2hr30min climb*, 2 613m/8 573ft), for a splendid **panorama** of Steghorn, Tierhorn, Les Diablerets and the Walliser Alpen. The most spectacular excursion leads down past the falls, featuring a vertical drop of 476m/1 562m (*1hr30min on foot*). From Engstligenalp, follow directions for "Unter dem Berg" and continue towards "Wasserfall."

After 30min, you will discover a breathtaking **view**★★★ as you approach the bridge spanning the falls. Follow directions for "Engstligenfall," within sight of the cable-car terminal. A steep, narrow path leads to Alpine columbine, a rare mountain species. Finally you reach the **belvedere**★★ overlooking the lower falls, which are equally spectacular. Return to the car park by following directions for "Unter dem Berg" (*10min*).

🚶 HIKES DEPARTING FROM KANDERSTEG

Oeschinensee★★★

⚡ About 1hr30min there and back, including 7min by chairlift, plus a 20min walk. ⏱ Operates Dec–Oct; times vary according to the season. Departure every 30min. ⚡ Fare there and back 20CHF. ☎(0)33 675 11 18. www.oeschinensee.ch.

The road leading to the lower chairlift station branches off the main road from Kandersteg directly after the bridge over the Oeschinenbach, on the left. From the upper station a road leads down to the lake shore (*bear to the right at a fork after a 5min walk*) encircled by a vast amphitheatre of cliffs, crowned by the snowy Blümlisalp Peaks. After reaching Lake Oeschinen, good walkers can continue to Kandersteg by the direct road, others can return to the upper chairlift station.

Oberbergli★★★

Allow at least 3hr15min or even a whole day if you plan to climb up towards the Blüemlisalp refuge. ⚠ Not to be attempted in wet weather. Sturdy mountain shoes are necessary.

A path (*good condition*) skirts Lake Oeschinen and reveals splendid **views**★★★ of the steep surrounding summits: Doldenhorn, Fründenhorn, Oeschinenhorn, and Blüemlisalphorn. At the far end of the lake, a steep path leads to Oberbergli. To enjoy a sweeping panorama of the glacier, continue climbing for 1hr (⚠ *very steep slope*) toward the Blüemlisalp refuge until you reach a small lake.

ADDRESSES

🏨 STAY

⚓⚓ **Seerose** – *Interlakenstrasse 87 Faulensee. 2km/1.2mi SE of Spiez. ☎(0)33 654 10 25. www.seerose-faulensee.ch. 🅿 ⚡. 13 rooms. Closed Jan & Feb. ⚓⚓ Restaurant open daily for lunch and dinner, closed Mon & Tue Mar–Apr, Oct–Dec.* This house overlooks Lake Thun in a small village.

🍴 EAT

⚓⚓⚓ **Restaurant Im Schloss** – *Schlossstrasse 16. ☎(0)33 654 94 74. 🅿 www.im-schloss.ch. Open May–Oct Thu–Sat evenings and by appointment.* A gastronomic stop to enjoy the atmosphere of Spiez castle. Original local cuisine from chef Bruno Wüthrich.

Interlaken★★★

Interlaken is the tourist centre of the Berner Oberland. It is renowned for its superb view of the Jungfrau Massif, which is home to the highest railway station in Europe. Framed between the small wooded ranges of the Rügen and the Harder, the town extends over the low plain of the Bödeli, formed by deposits from the Lombach in the north and the Lütschine in the south. These finally divided the single lake (into which the Aare used to flow between Meiringen and Thun) into two distinct sheets of water, Lake Thun and Lake Brienz (Thunersee and Brienzersee).

A BIT OF HISTORY

The Latin sound of the name Interlaken recalls the clerical origin of the town; it grew up between the lakes from the 12C onwards, around an Augustinian monastery of which traces, such as the cloister gallery, can still be found in the block of buildings formed by the castle and the Protestant church. The resort is extremely popular in the summer months, when its many souvenir shops are busy with tourists.

▶ **Population:** 5 319.
⚅ **Michelin Map:** Town plan in The Michelin Red Guide Switzerland.
🗎 **Info:** Höheweg 37 – 3800. ☎(0)33 826 53 00. www.interlakentourism.ch.
◐ **Location:** Interlaken has two train stations, West and Ost. West station goes to the city centre; take Ost station for excursions to nearby villages and peaks such as Grindelwald and Jungfraujoch.
⊙ **Don't Miss:** An excursion to one, if not all, of the majestic summits: Schilthorn, Jungfrau, Eiger.

SIGHTS
Höheweg★★
This famous avenue is bordered on one side by the lawns and flower beds of the Höhematte, on the other by a row of grand hotels and behind them, the casino (Kursaal). The promenade links the urban centre of Interlaken West with the much more scattered township of Interlaken East. It offers dazzling

Interlaken in winter with a view to Eiger, Mönch and Jungfrau

Interlaken Tourismus/Switzerland Tourism

SUSTEN, GRIMSEL, FURKA

★★ Niederhorn 1950
★ Beatenberg
Harderkulm ★★ 1323
Unterseen
INTERLAKEN ★★★
Lake Brienz
A 8
N

Lake Thoune
670 Heimwehfluh ★
★★★ FAULHORN 2681
★★ Bachalpsee
2101 SCHYNIGE PLATTE ★★
★★ First 2168

A 8
Lütschine
Schwarze Lütschine
★★ Grindelwald

2249 Morgenberghorn
MÄNNLICHEN ★★★ 2343
Wengwald
Wengen
Alpiglen

Lauterbrunnen Valley
Lauterbrunnen
★★ Cascade du Staubbach
Kleine Scheidegg ★★
Wengernalp
Eigerwand ★★
3970 Eiger
Eismeer

★★★ SCHILTHORN 2970
★★ Mürren
Eigergletscher
TRÜMMELBACH FALLS ★★★
Mönch 4099
4049 Fiescherhorn

★★★ JUNGFRAUJOCH 3475
Mönchsjochhütte

★ Sefinen Falls
Stechelberg
Weisse Lütschine
4158 Jungfrau

INTERLAKEN
0   4 km
0   2 mile

views★★★ of the Jungfrau, through the opening of the lower Lütschine Valley. It is pleasant to stroll beneath the trees, glancing at the pavilion of meteorological instruments or the well-known floral clock in the casino gardens. A second attraction on the opposite bank of the River Aare is the open-air swimming pool and miniature golf course. These are both popular weekend activities during the summer season.

EXCURSIONS
Harderkulm★★
Alt. 1 323m/4 341ft. ⛰ *About 1hr there and back, including 10min by funicular from Interlaken East.* ⏱*Operates daily, Apr–Oct, 8.10am–5.45pm. Departures every 20 or 30min.* ⚙*Fare there and back 25CHF.* ☎*(0)33 828 73 39.*
A small park near the lower funicular station is home to a variety of animals typically found in the Alps. From the panoramic restaurant at the summit, there is a clear view of the two Interlaken lakes and the Jungfrau Massif.

Heimwehfluh★
Alt. 670m/2 218ft. 1–2hr round trip, including 5min by funicular.
⏱*Operates mid-Apr–Nov 8.30am–5.30pm. Departures every 15min.*
⚙*Return fare 11CHF.* ☎*(0)33 822 34 53.*
A cool, shady hill overlooking Lake Thun and Lake Brienz. Don't miss the unique toboggan run for both children and adults, as well as a model railway display and playground.
There are many shaded walks, especially on the slopes of the Rügen or the Harder.

Beatenberg★
Alt. 1 150m/3 773ft.
The winding but excellent road (connecting to Scheidgasse in Unterseen), climbs amid fir trees, offering good glimpses of Interlaken, the Jungfrau and Lake Thun. Beatenberg, a terraced resort, extending along more than 7km/4.5mi, consists mainly of hotels and holiday chalets nestling in the trees. It overlooks Lake Thun and, farther to the right, the Niesen; on the

left you can admire the sweeping ranges of the Jungfrau and the Mönch. For an all-encompassing view, go up to the Niederhorn *(10km/6.2mi from Interlaken; access also by funicular from the Thun road).*

Niederhorn★★

Alt. 1950m/6397ft. Access by chairlift. Chairlift operates (generally) 8am–5pm in summer and 8am–6pm in winter. Fare there and back 34CHF. (0)33 841 0841.

From the summit *(viewing tables)* of this mountain covered with Alpine pastures is a spectacular **panorama★★**: south beyond Thun Lake onto the glaciers of the Jungfrau Massif; southwest onto the Niesen and far in the distance Mont Blanc, barely visible; west onto the summit of the Stockhorn; northwest as far as the Neuchâtel and Murten lakes; north onto the mountains preceding the Emmental; and east beyond Lake Brienz, onto the cliffs of the Brienzer Rothorn.

🚗 DRIVING TOUR

LAUTERBRUNNENTAL★★★

23km/14mi from Interlaken to Stechelberg – about 3hr including 2hr 45min cable-car and sightseeing.

▷ *Leave Interlaken from the S on the Lauterbrunnen road and stop at Wilderswil.*

Schynige Platte★★

Alt. 2 101m/6 891ft. About 4hr there and back, including 2hr by rack railway starting from Wilderswil station. Operates Jun–Oct. Departure every 50min, 8am–6.30pm. Fare there and back 55CHF. (0)33 828 72 33. www.jungfraubahn.ch.

This climb is especially suited to tourists who have no time to venture farther into the Jungfrau Massif. Schynige Platte is one of the most popular destinations for vacationers staying in Grindelwald (see GRINDELWALD.)

Near the upper station, an Alpine garden and a botanical section have been laid out over an area of 8 000sq m/9 570sq yds, presenting some 500 varieties of flowers (edelweiss, gentian), plants and ferns. The panoramic terrace of the hotel affords easy access to the nearest summit (alt. 2 076m/6 812ft—viewpoint overlooking the Jungfrau, Interlaken and its lakes). Note the Alpine dairy on the Iseltenalp, where fresh dairy produce is made daily (milk, butter, cheese and the ricotta-like serac).

The road runs into the wooded Lütschine defile, losing sight of the Jungfrau for the time being.

▷ *Continue on the same road.*

The valley soon widens, framed, as you go upstream, by the huge rock walls which make the Lauterbrunnen Gorge a classic example of the glacial feature: a U-shaped valley (*illustration, see INTRODUCTION: Alpine relief*). Ahead, on either side of the slopes of the Schwarzmönch, appear the snowy summits of the Jungfrau (on the left) and those of the Mittaghorn-Grosshorn group (straight ahead).

Lauterbrunnen

This village has heavy through traffic. **P** *Motorists who wish to go to Wengen must leave their cars in the car park.* Here the **Staubbachfall★**, which Byron compared with the "tail of the pale horse ridden by Death in the Apocalypse," plunges 300m/1 000ft from the terrace at Mürren, dissolving almost entirely into fine spray. In line with the valley you will see the Breithorn summit, clearly detached to the right of the Grosshorn.

Wengen★★

Alt. 1 275m/4 183ft.

Wengen is situated on a sunny and wind-sheltered mountain terrace at the foot of the Jungfrau massif, dominated by the Jungfrau and the Eiger. One of the most fashionable and best equipped mountain resorts in the Bernese Oberland, it is popular year-round for its picturesque old-fashioned charm and car-free streets.

The **site★★★** is a perfect starting point for walks, which follow well-

Wengen at the foot of Eiger, Mönch and Jungfrau

Wengen-Muerren-Lauterbrunnental Tourismus AG/Switzerland Tourism

maintained paths, even in winter with 500km/310.6mi of posted hiking trails. The **ski resort** has 44 lifts leading to more than 200km/124mi of pistes; beginner areas are ideal for families. Kleine Scheidegg (alt. 2 061m/6 762ft) is reached by the mountain railway from the centre of town. From here, you can ski the famous Lauberhorn, site of the men's downhill World Cup **Lauberhorn race**, which takes place in early January; the railway also accesses the Eigergletscher. There are 50km/32mi of groomed toboggan runs, some are illuminated at night.

▷ *At the exit from Lauterbrunnen, turn to the direction of Stechelberg.*

Trümmelbachfälle★★★

3hr to 4hr on foot there and back.
🕐*Open Jul and Aug, 8am–6pm; Apr, May, Sept and Oct, 9am–5pm.*
💶*11CHF.* 🅿*Leave your car in the Trümmelbachfälle car park. Take waterproof clothes.* 📞*(0)33 855 32 32.*
A lift passing through the rock leads to the beginning of the galleries. These are well sited over the winding fissure where the Trümmelbach leaps and boils, forcing its way through a series of great eroded potholes. On returning to the lower entrance of the funicular, be sure to walk up the path to the left (to the right when facing the mountain) to see

the incredible gush of water coming from the second last falls of the Trümmelbachfälle.

Return to your car and drive up the valley to Stechelberg, the Mürren-Schilthorn cable-car station and the place from where you can see, to the south *(1km/0.6mi)* the lovely, almost vertical **Sefinenfall**★.

Mürren★

Alt. 1 650m/5 413ft. 🚡*Access: 10min by cable car. Mürren Tourismus.* 📞*(0)33 856 86 86. www.muerren.ch.*
Perched on a shelf of Alpine pasture forming a balcony overlooking the steep

Trümmelbachfälle

Marcus Gyger/Switzerland Tourism

cleft of the Lauterbrunnen Valley, Mürren faces a series of giant peaks carved out of rock or ice: from left to right, the view encompasses the Eiger, the Mönch, the Jungfrau, the Breithorn, and the Gspaltenhorn range (far right).

The **site**★★ of this village, completely free of car traffic, and its surrounding ski slopes, which bristle with every conceivable obstacle, account for the resort's popularity. The development of tourism in the area was largely due to the British, who came here at the turn of the last century to indulge in their favourite winter sports and succeeded in recreating a cosy, congenial atmosphere. It was here that the Kandahar Ski Club was founded in 1924 named after its founder, Earl Roberts of Kandahar. 1928 saw the start of the **Arlberg-Kandahar competition**, now regarded as the unofficial world championship of winter sports for the Alpine countries Mürren has only 350 inhabitants and is the highest-lying settlement in the canton of Bern, belonging politically to the municipality of Lauterbrunnen. .

Schilthorn★★★

Alt. 2 970m/9 744ft. About 1hr15min including 17min by cable car, leaving from Mürren. There is also a cable car leaving from Stechelberg down in the valley. www.schilthorn.ch. ⛷ Round trip about 2hr including 1hr cable car via Stechelberg. ⏱Operates every 30 mins from 7.05am–6.03pm high season

Summit of Schilthorn

Interlaken Tourismus/Switzerland Tourism

to 5:03pm low season ⚌Fare there and back 92CHF. For information on periods of closure, call ✆(0)33 856 21 41.

From the top, in a desolate landscape of torrents and scree, is a **panoramic view**★★★ of the Jungfrau Massif with only the Lauterbrunnen cleft between that and the observer. Part of Lake Thun and a total of 200 mountain peaks and 40 glaciers are visible. The panoramic restaurant features a popular revolving plateau; it makes a complete turn in 55min. This aluminum establishment with a futuristic look and exceptional location is famous and familiar for its role in the James Bond film *On Her Majesty's Secret Service*; several scenes were shot on the premises (1967–68). Every year in January the locality hosts **Inferno**, an Alpine skiing competition in which contestants race from the Schilthorn summit down to Lauterbrunnen, a 16km/10mi circuit and a vertical drop of 2 134m/7 001ft in barely 20min. Seasoned skiers can follow the route on other days without racing.

ROUND TOUR OF THE JUNGFRAU BY RAILWAY★★★

This panoramic tour is magnificent. Reductions are available on the first train of the morning: ask for a Good Morning Ticket. Allow a whole day and choose one when the atmospheric conditions are the best possible in order to enjoy spectacular scenery; a veil of cloud on the summits is enough to spoil the excursion. Wear warm clothes, and if you want to go out into the open, take sunglasses and wear sturdy shoes.

The first part of the journey is to Kleine Scheidegg, where passengers change trains. The train then makes its way through tunnels cut into the Eiger, stopping occasionally to allow passengers to admire the glaciers, to reach the **Top of Europe** station (alt. 3 454m/11 329ft). Some of the slopes along this unforgettable route have gradients of 25%.

Wengernalp

Alt. 1 873m/6 145ft.

A wild site at the foot of the rock and glacier slopes of the Jungfrau. The deep

Conquest of the Eigerwand

One of the most dramatic climbs after the conquest of the Matterhorn was that of the north face of the Eiger (see INTERLAKEN). In 1858 the summit (3 970m/13 025ft) was reached by the Irishman Charles Barrington and Swiss guides Christian Almer and Peter Bohren. The south and southwest spurs were conquered in 1874 and 1876. From 1935 onwards there were many deadly attempts to climb the north face: that year, two Germans were killed; the next year, three roped teams of Germans and Austrians fell to their deaths.

These tragedies raised such a storm of protest that cantonal authorities in Bern forbade any further attempt. The ban was lifted in 1937, marked by the failure of the Austrian Rebitsch and the German Wiggerl Vörg. However, the follvowing year, Vörg and his companion, Anderl Heckmair, made secret preparations for an attempt. Though two Austrians, Kasparek and Harrer, started before them, they overtook them on the second day and decided to join forces with the rival team. Their slow and difficult progress, threatened at every step by the danger of storms and avalanches, was watched anxiously from the valley. Thanks to international press and radio, the whole world eagerly awaited details of their progress. When they surmounted the final crest, blinded by fatigue and storm, they were not even immediately aware of their victory. Their difficult descent by the west face, in the midst of a blizzard, sealed the success of their expedition.

Trümmelbach Gorge in the foreground makes the height of this wall of rock even more impressive, and it is not unknown to witness an avalanche. To the left of the Jungfrau you will recognize the snowy cleft of the Jungfraujoch—the terminus of the excursion (the Sphinx observatory is visible)—and then the Mönch, the Eigergletscher Glacier and the Eiger.

Kleine Scheidegg★★
Alt. 2 061m/6 762ft.
This mountain resort, isolated on the ledge linking the Lauterbrunnen Valley to the Grindelwald Valley, is a favourite with skiers, who find abundant snow here even late in the season. In summer it is frequented by tourists seeking tranquillity. Tourists who do not go up the Jungfraujoch may admire the Grindelwald Basin and pick out the Eiger-Mönch-Jungfrau group in excellent conditions by going up to the **belvedere**★★ on the north side of the pass (*1hr to 2hr on foot there and back.*)

Eigergletscher
Alt. 2 320m/7 612ft.
This stop near the snout of the Eiger Glacier, much broken and stained with morainic deposits, marks the beginning of the underground section, 7km/4mi long, which leads to the Jungfraujoch. In spring, great numbers of skiers come here.

Eigerwand★★
Alt. 2 865m/9 400ft.
The station is cut out of the rock. Ventilating bays giving on to the north face of the Eiger afford a bird's-eye view of the Grindelwald Basin and the Interlaken district. The situation is all the more impressive when you remember the dramatic efforts of mountaineers to conquer this rock wall, which was only climbed for the first time in 1938.

Jungfraujoch★★★
Alt. 3 475m/11 401ft.
This mountain resort, now marketing itself as Top of Europe, is the highest in Europe to be served by a **rack railway**. It presents a memorable and grandiose setting hemmed in by high mountains, with spectacular views of the surrounding mountain glaciers.
The site includes the famous summits of Mönch, the Eiger and the Jungfrau, as well as the Aletsch Glacier, and has been a UNESCO World Heritage Site since

Jungfrau Railway with a view of Jungfrau summit

Jungfrau Railways/Switzerland Tourism

The Highest Railway Line in Europe

In 1893 the industrialist Adolf Guyer-Zeller, a member of the Alpine Club, had the idea of an "altitude metro". Extending the railway from the Wengernalp, a train would enter a tunnel and then climb the Eiger through to the heart of the Jungfrau. From there, a lift would lead tourists on the summit. The construction lasted sixteen years because the conditions were difficult, with the wind and snow, avalanches and fog complicating the assault against the rock by teams of "mole workers" digging in three shifts a day. The summer pastures between the neck of the Kleine Scheidegg and the Eiger Glacier were invaded by hundreds of workers, with carts and mules. Provisions were transported and stored for the winter. Adolf Guyer-Zeller designed everything, even the panoramic windows carved into the rock for the tourists. The line was inaugurated on 1 August 1912, Swiss National Day, in dense fog.

2001. This was the first natural region in Switzerland—539sq km/208sq mi in the Bern and Valais cantons—to be declared a World Heritage Site.

Sphinx-Panoramaterrasse ★★★
Alt. 3 571m/8 435ft.
Access by the fastest lift in Switzerland (108m/355ft gained in 25 seconds with a maximum speed of 6.3m/20ft a second halfway up), then by 19 steps.
Breathtaking **panorama** of the Aletsch Glacier as it flows majestically like a wide river, sparkling among the rocky peaks. It is framed by the Mönch (4 099m/13 447ft), the Fiescherhorn (4 049m/13 282ft), the Aletschhorn (4 193m/13 755ft) and the Jungfrau (4 158m/13 641ft).
To the north, the steep Guggigletscher Glacier can be seen. The view includes

the Schilthorn, the Niesen, Interlaken and the Faulhorn.
A restaurant serving drinks and light meals is located at the summit of the Jungfraujoch. The Sphinx houses a research laboratory and an astronomical cupola. The pure quality of the air and easy access by railway are undeniable assets to carry out scientific experiments—you can actually observe some.

Aletschgletscher★★★
Go back down by lift and follow directions for Aletschgletscher. You will reach the glacier itself, used as a piste for summer skiing (gentle slope, 100m/330ft).

Eispalast★
10min access on foot and 15min visit.
The Ice Palace is a grotto carved out of the blue-tinged ice up to 8m/25ft in

depth, containing sculptures, particularly of animals.

Walk to the Mönchsjochhütte★★★
Alt. 3 629m/11 905ft.
This walk can be undertaken by any hiker wearing good mountain boots (🖐*do not stray from the beaten track—crampons are not necessary).*
A 1hr energetic walk up a steep slope will take you to a stunning **setting**★★★ and then to the small refuge at the foot of the Mönch. The pass (Obere Mönchsjoch) commands a pretty **view**★★ of the Schreckhorn.

▷ *Walk back along the same path.*

Wengwald
Alt. 1 182m/3 878ft.
Between this stopping-place and Wengen the route offers a splendid **view**★★★ of the Lauterbrunnen rift; the **Jungfrau** emerges in the distance. This is flanked on the right by the Silberhorn, a dazzling white, conical snow peak.

ADDRESSES

🏠 STAY

INTERLAKEN

🛏🍽🍽 **Seehotel La Terasse** – *Seestrasse 22.* 📞*(0)33 822 07 70. Fax (0)33 822 07 40. www.seehotelterrasse.ch. 40 rooms.* Hotel with terrace situated on the shore of Brienz lake. Peace and quiet guaranteed.

🛏🍽🍽🍽 **Beau Site** – *Seestrasse 16.* 📞*(0)33 826 75 75. www.beausite.ch. 50 rooms.* Superb views of the Jungfrau. Enjoy the pleasant garden after a hard day's trekking in the snow.

🛏🍽🍽🍽 **Goldey** – *Obere Goldey 85.* 📞*(0)33 826 44 45. www.goldey.ch. 41 rooms.* Lovely hotel at the water's edge. The starting-point for many excursions, it will provide a warm, cosy welcome when you return at the end of the day.

🛏🍽🍽🍽 **Hirschen** – *In Matten, Hauptstrasse 11.* 📞*(0)33 822 15 45. www.hirschen-interlaken.ch. 25 rooms.* Attractive wooden chalet typical of the region, dating from the 16C. Breathtaking panorama of the Jungfrau range from the terrace. Traditional cuisine and restful atmosphere.

THE JUNGFRAU

🛏🍽🍽🍽 **Belvedere** – *3818 Grindelwald.* 📞*(0)33 854 57 57. www. belvedere-grindelwald.ch. 54 rooms.* Stunning setting and panoramic views.

🛏🍽🍽🍽 **Bodmi** – *3818 Grindelwald.* 📞*(0)33 853 12 20. www.bodmi.ch. 23 rooms.* Idyllic setting with personal service.

🍴 EAT

INTERLAKEN

🍽🍽🍽 **Restaurant Luegibrüggli** – *Kienbergstrasse 1, Unterseen-Interlaken* 📞*(0)33 822 27 53. www.interlakentourism.ch* Located halfway between Interlaken and Beatenburg, serving traditional Bernese cuisine with excellent views.

🍽🍽 **Restaurant Aarburg** – *Beatenbergstrasse 1, Unterseen.* 📞*(0)33 822 26 15.Closed Sun.* Small, 30-seat dining room on a terrace overlooking the town, serving local fare.

🍽🍽🍽 **Chalet Oberland** – *Postgasse 1, Interlaken.* 📞*(0)33 827 87 87. www.chalet-oberland.ch.* Offers vegetarian meals, and a folklore night every Tuesday.

🍽🍽 **Gastro-Galerie** – *Schifffstation Interlaken Ost, Ländte Nr. 2, Interlaken.* 📞*(0)33 823 02 22.* Provides light fare and snacks.

THE JUNGFRAU

🍽🍽🍽 **Hotel Alpenhof** – *3818 Grindelwald.* 📞*(0)33 853 52 70. www.alpenhof.ch.* This restaurant prides itself in using products from its own farm in most of its dishes.

🍽🍽 **Berghaus Bort** – *3818 Grindelwald.* 📞*(0)33 853 17 62. www.berghaus-bort.ch.* Located beside the first intermediate station of the Jungfraujoch cableway.

Grindelwald★★

On an unforgettable site, Grindelwald, the Eiger village, is the only great mountain resort in the Jungfrau area which can be reached by car. It therefore attracts not only holidaymakers—mountaineers or skiers depending on the season— but also crowds of day trippers from the Interlaken area. The bustling crowds which, on fine winter or summer days, surge exuberantly along the little town's main street, plunge the newcomer straight into the atmosphere of an Alpine capital. Events throughout the year include the famous **World Snow Festival**, held each January on the natural skating rink at the heart of the village: Several teams from different countries make ice and snow sculptures.

SIGHTS

The Skiing Area

The Grindelwald skiing area, linked to those of **Wengen** and **Mürren**, consists of about 200km/125mi of slopes suitable for downhill skiing, served by 49 ski lifts, and dominated by the hulking grandeur of the Eiger. Surprisingly, many of the pistes in this staggeringly steep terrain are mild enough for intermediate level skiers and snowboarders. The Bodmi area is for novices, where lifts rise to

▶ **Population:** 3 826.
Info: Postfach 124.
  ℰ(0)33 854 12 12.
  www.grindelwald.ch.
▶ **Location:** Grindelwald is in the Bernese Oberland, central Switzerland.
  Alt. 1 034m/3 392ft.
Don't Miss:
  The Jungfraujoch—Top of Europe, from where you can see the longest glacier in the Alps. On the way to the top you pass Kleine Scheidegg with a spectacular view of the famous Eiger-Monch-Jungfrau triptych.
Kids: Children will love the ride up Jungfraujoch, as well as the cable car journey up the Männlichen.
Timing: Visitors should allow a minimum of two days to explore the top sights, but plan on at least three days to fully tour the area's numerous mountains.

First and Oberjoch (alt. 2 468m/8 097ft) before opening onto vast, sunny snow-fields. The descent between Oberjoch and Grindelwald via piste 22 offers

Grindelwald at night

superb **views**★★ of the surrounding landscape and quaint villages. A carving piste and a snowpark have been laid out at the top. Kleine Scheidegg offers opportunities for splendid walks towards Grindelwald, especially at sunset. Seasoned skiers should choose the "Lauberhorn Rennstrecke" slope above Wengen, often used in official competitions for Alpine skiing. Steep and challenging slopes can be found on the Schilthorn Massif (including the Eiger Glacier), which is somewhat difficult to reach (train ride followed by a bus and four separate funiculars) but boasts the best pistes. For cross-country skiers, 35km/22mi of loops are available between Grindelwald and Burglauenen. Despite the low altitude, the snow coverage is usually satisfactory at the bottom of the valleys because there is little sunlight during the winter season.

The area also offers many opportunities for hikers, with 80km/50mi of marked out trails and 20km/12.4mi of pistes for sledges. One recommended route is to walk up to Faulhorn from First (2hr30min) and then to go back down to Grindelwald by sledge via Bussalp; this 12.5km/8mi itinerary is the longest sledge piste in Europe.

The area boasts an important Sports Centre (Centre Sportif) with facilities for a number of sports, a skating rink, indoor swimming pool, curling rink, gymnasium, etc.

The Town★★★

The site of Grindelwald combines a foreground full of country charm—fields planted with fruit trees or maples and containing pretty dwellings—with a grand rocky barrier stretching from the shoulder of the Wetterhorn to the pyramid of the Eiger. On one hand are the high mountains, a playground for mountaineers or skilled skiers; on the other, between the Grosse and Kleine Scheidegg Ridges, with the Faulhorn in between, is an immense amphitheatre-like shape of Alpine pastures and woods perfectly suited to cross-country skiing. Access is provided by the Wengernalp railway—much appreciated by skiers in early spring—which serves the high altitude annex of the Kleine Scheidegg, and by the chain of chairlifts at First.

CABLE-CAR VIEWPOINTS

🚠🚶 Jungfraujoch★★★

Allow at least one day for this exceptional excursion. We recommend that you choose the round tour of the Jungfrau by railway (🕐 see p224). ✆Circular ticket Interlaken-Jungfraujoch-Interlaken: 172CHF; when taking one of the two first morning trains (Nov–Apr) and the trains with direct interconnection: 126CHF. Ticket for departure from Lauterbrunnen: 148CHF; when taking the two first trains: 154CHF. Ticket for departure from Grindelwald Grund: 149CHF; when taking the first train and return before noon (May–Oct): 103CHF. Circular ticket Interlaken-Kleine Scheidegg-Interlaken (not going up to Jungfraujoch): 68CHF.

🚠🚶 Männlichen★★★

🚡 *Access by the longest cable car ride in Europe (6.2km/4mi), 15min on foot from the centre of the resort. Allow 2hr there and back including 1hr by cable car.*
🏃 *The main attractions of this summit are the walks and hikes that it offers (🕐see below).*

The final platform (alt. 2 227m/7 306ft) commands a splendid view of Grindelwald, at the foot of the Wetterhorn and

Walking in Männlichen—Mönch in the background

Grindelwald Tourismus/Switzerland Tourism

the Schreckhorn. Go to the nearby viewpoint dominating the Lauterbrunnen Valley for a **panorama**★★★ of the legendary Eiger-Mönch-Jungfrau triptych, the sparkling Silberhorn, Breithorn and, down below, the village of Wengen, with Lake Thun lying to the north.

To enjoy a complete circular view of your surroundings, climb up to the top of the Männlichen (alt. 2 343m/7 687ft). The view is quite clear to the north.

First★★

🚠 *Access by cable car. Allow 1hr30min including 1hr by cable car. The excursion can be combined with a walk.*
🕐*Operates from 8am or 8.30am, times vary according to the season.* 🕐*Closed in Nov and Apr.* 🚠*Fare there and back 50CHF.* 📞*(0)33 828 77 11.*

When you reach the third section (alt. 2 168m/7 113ft), go to the restaurant's panoramic terrace (*viewing table*). Magnificent **view**★★ of the Grindelwald Basin in its wooded setting and the summits of the Wetterhorn, Grosser Fiescherhorn, Eiger, Jungfrau, Morgenhorn and Schreckhorn, hemmed in by the Upper and Lower Grindelwald Glaciers. The Titlis and the Sustenhörner can be glimpsed in the far distance. Lush pastures extend to the northwest, at the foot of the Faulhorn (note the hotel right on top).

🚶 HIKING TRAILS

Grindelwald is a great rambling and climbing centre, offering all types of excursions of varying degrees of difficulty (300km/187mi of paths at an altitude of 1 000–3 600m/3 280–11 810ft). Some of the more interesting circuits are listed below. There are also 100km/62mi of marked trails for mountain bikes.

Faulhorn★★★

🚠 *Access to First by cable car. 2hr20min climb (500m/1 640ft difference in altitude). Inexperienced hikers can stop at Bachalpsee (50min easy walking).*

Bachalpsee★★ is one of Switzerland's most beautiful lakes. It affords a spectacular **view**★★, enhanced by the twinkling reflections of the mountain cirque. From the verdant shores of the lake, you can admire the jagged crest of the Finsteraarhorn, framed between the Schreckhorn and the Fiescherhorn. The climb to Faulhorn is along a steep but even path. At the top (alt. 2 681m/8 796ft), you reach one of the highest mountain hotels in Europe, and certainly the oldest (opened in 1832) from where there is a sweeping **panorama**★★★ of the Bernese Oberland. To the south, you can see First, the Mönch, and the Breithorn. To the north, you overlook Lake Brienz and Lake Thun, lying at the foot of the Brienzerrothorn and the Niederhorn respectively. In the far distance, farther east, note the Pilatus and Rigi peaks.

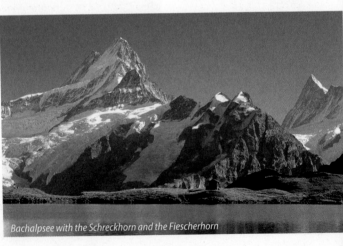
Bachalpsee with the Schreckhorn and the Fiescherhorn

From Faulhorn to Schynige Platte★★★

3hr15min walk with a 600m/1 968.5ft difference in altitude. 🔺 *This excursion is for experienced hikers only (sturdy mountain boots necessary) and can be undertaken after the walk to Grindelwald.* 🚫 *Do not attempt to go in wet weather. The return to Grindelwald is by train (enquire beforehand about times).*

The fascinating **path along the crest** offers a wonderful panorama at all times. After 1hr walking, heading towards the Mädlenen Restaurant, the rocky track becomes more tiring and more difficult to negotiate. It commands nearby **views**★ of Lake Sägistal and the formidable slopes of the Faulhorn. It then wends its way through mountain pastures before revealing a fantastic **panorama**★★★ of the Jungfrau Massif, extending from the Schreckhorn to the Morgenhorn. On reaching the Schynige Platte, those climbers who still have some energy left will discover an Alpine garden.

▶ *The climb down to Wilderswil is by rack railway. Then take the train back to Grindelwald.*

Mönchsjochhütte★★★

Alt. 3 629m/11 906ft. 1hr climb. Access from Jungfraujoch (⚙ see p225).

Stieregg and Bänisegg★★

🚠 *Access to Pfingstegg (alt. 1 391m/ 4 563.6ft) in 4min by cable car. Allow 1hr climb to reach the Baregg Restaurant (260m/853ft difference in altitude) and an extra 1hr to get to Bänisegg (160m/525ft difference in altitude).*

From Pfingstegg, look for an overall **view**★ of Grindelwald and the First area and an even path following the mountain slope. After 30min, you will admire a fantastic **view**★★ of the Lower Grindelwald Glacier and especially Fiescher-gletscher. Note the waterfalls gushing down the slopes of the Eiger. The path now becomes steeper and leads past local flora (orchids, rhododendrons, and forget-me-nots) and the occasional sheep. Allow 1hr30min to reach the Bar-

Hikers on Stieregg

Walter Storto/Switzerland Tourism

egg Restaurant (alt. 1 650m/5 413ft) commands an even more impressive **view**★★ of the majestic glacial cirque dominated by the Grossfiescherhorn (alt. 4 048m/13 280ft).

Experienced hikers who do not suffer from vertigo and who are equipped with proper mountain boots can continue toward Schreckhornhütte. Although it is still wild, the setting now features more and more species of regional flora and fauna. After a series of short ups and downs, the path follows a very steep course to reach Bänisegg (alt. 1 807m/5 927ft). From a bend to the left, you can discover the long ice tongue of the Ischmeer. It is a truly breathtaking **site**★★, with the Finsteraarhorn looming at a height of 4 274m/14 021ft.

▶ *Go back down along the same path (1hr30min).*

From Pfingstegg, you can reach the **Milchbach Chalet** by a gently sloping track (*allow 1hr*). This route will take you past the mineral paradise of Breitlouwina (Gesteinparadies Breitlouwina), characterised by a remarkably wide range of sediments dating from several million years ago. View of the Upper Grindelwald Glacier, in which an **ice cave** has been set up. Visitors will be impressed by the blue ice walls of the cave, which is almost 30m/98.4ft deep.

Allow an extra 20min to climb down to the Hôtel Wetterhorn, where a bus will take you back to Grindelwald.

From Männlichen to Kleine Scheidegg★★

🚡 *Take the Männlichen cable car. 1hr 15min walk along an easy, pleasant path (170m/558ft difference in altitude).* All along the way, there are superb **views★★** of the Eiger, Mönch, Jungfrau and Grindewald Basin.

▶ *From Kleine Scheidegg, continue with the walk to Eigerwand or return to Grindelwald by train.*

Eigerwand★★

Access to the Eigergletscher resort (alt. 2 320m/7 611ft) by train. Allow 2hr for the climb down to Alpiglen (700m/ 2 297ft difference in altitude). 👢*Good mountain boots essential. Do not stray from the beaten track, which cuts across a protected area for local fauna.*
Follow the railway tracks for 100m/328ft going downwards, then cross them and take the "Eiger-Trail" itinerary on the right. Walk a short distance up to the foot of the Eiger. The path goes through steep Alpine pastures and mounds of fallen rocks, following the imposing mountain face, offering pretty views of Grindelwald and the Wetterhorn. Reaching a steep slope, it leads to the Alpiglen pastures (alt. 1 615m/5 297ft). The climb down can be undertaken on foot or by train.

Gletscherschlucht★

2.5km/1.5mi on a very narrow road beginning at the far end of the village, on the right, after a church. Allow 30min sightseeing. 🕐*Access May–mid-Oct, 10am–5pm; mid-Jul–late Aug, 9am–6pm (9pm Tue and Thu); Sept–Oct, 10am–5pm.* 🕐*Closed in winter.* 👛*6CHF.* *(033) 853 60 50.*
A rocky fissure, at the bottom of which the tail of the Lower Grindelwald Glacier (Unterer Grindelwaldgletscher) appears as a narrow strip of ice. This

impressive geological formation was once described by Byron as a "frozen hurricane".

ADDRESSES

🛏STAY

Lehmann's Herberge – *3818 Grindelwald.* *(0)33 853 31 41. www. lehmanns-herberge.ch.* 🅿 *12 rooms.*
A nice young couple owns this B&B in the centre of Grindelwald, which will delight the budget-conscious. In the dormitory rooms, comfort is limited (toilets on the landing upstairs) but the view of the Eiger and Männlichen is beautiful from rooms 5 and 10.

Alpenhof – *3818 Grindelwald.* *(0)33 853 52 70. www.alpenhof.ch. Closed November and several weeks after Easter.* 🅿 *12 rooms.* Guests will enjoy the view over the Alps and the quiet location at the foot of the ski slopes. Simple and comfortable modern rooms soberly arranged. The restaurant offers gourmet products from their own farm.

Gletschergarten – *(0)33 853 17 21. www.hotel-gletschergarten.ch. Closed Apr–May and Oct–Christmas.* 🅿*. 26 rooms.* If you are looking for an intimate or romantic atmosphere or if you dream of a warm fireside return after your hike or skiing, you will love this charming wooden cottage which will sooth and relax you.

🍽EAT

Hilty-Stübli – *Marktgasse 57.* *(0)33 854 40 80. www.kirchbuehl.ch. Closed Apr– mid May, end Oct–beginning Dec.* The restaurant of hotel Kirchbühl offers good rustic fare.

Chalet Hotel alte Post – *Dorfstrasse.* *(0)338 534 242. www.altepost- grindelwald.ch. Closed Wed and end Oct–end Dec.* In a cottage whose entry appears to be guarded by an old stagecoach, this restaurant serves delicious mountain cuisine. The tasty cheeses on the platter are produced in-house.

Brienz★

Brienz is one of the best preserved, old-fashioned summer resorts in the Bernese Oberland. The town is a great woodcarving centre and a technical school was founded here to keep up the tradition, as well as a music academy for stringed instruments. Most of the carvings of bears in all sizes and positions sold as souvenirs come from local workshops.

▶ **Population:** 2 996.
ℹ **Info:** Hauptstrasse 143, Brienz 3855. ℘(0)33 952 80 80. www.alpenregion.ch.
◖ **Location:** Brienz lies along the shore of its lake, facing the Giessbach Falls. Alt. 570m/7 871ft.
◈ **Don't Miss:** The panoramic views from the Brienzer Rothhorn.

SIGHTS
Jobin Living Museum★
Hauptstrasse 111. ◷*Open Apr–May and Sept–Oct, Mon–Fri 8.30am–noon, 1.30pm–6.30pm, Sat–Sun 9am–5pm; Jun–Aug Mon–Fri 8am–6.30pm, Sat–Sun 9am–6.30pm, Nov–Dec Tue, Thu, Fri, Sat 1.30pm–5pm.* ◷ *Closed Christmas.* ◉*5CHF (15CHF guided tour in English on request).* ♿ *℘(0)33 952 13 00. www.jobin.ch.*
Founded in 1835, the workshop continues the tradition of local Jobin woodcarving. Visitors can freely attend to the work of craftsmen who work by hand or machine, in a bright and modern environment. Upstairs, a small museum features music boxes, wooden animals carved miniature cottages and utensils which have made the reputation of the workshop and the city. The boutique store sells some of the production line, also including some antiques.

EXCURSIONS
Brienzer See★
Shorter, narrower, perhaps less picturesque but nonetheless wilder than Lake Thun (◔*see p214*), Lake Brienz is linked to its "twin" by the River Aare. The main drive is along the **North shore**★—from Interlaken to Meiringen 30km/19mi—while the southern part of the lake can be visited more easily with a boat from Interlaken. The North shore is a beautiful 45-minute drive which can take longer depending on where you choose to spend your time.

From Interlaken the road runs through woods, climbing to the last slopes of the Harder and when you reach Ringgenberg, there are attractive views of the lake and the mountains from the lake shore, immediately overlooking Interlaken. A **church** was erected in 1670 on the ruins of a castle (Burg) whose keep was used again in the building of the belfry. Between Ringgenberg and Brienz, especially on the Oberried-Brienz section, the view opens out over **Brienzer See** and the south shore, enclosed by the Brienzer Rothorn Chain and the foothills of the Faulhorn. The best place to stop is 600m/656yds northeast of **Oberried-am-Brienzer-See**: Return to the lake shore, where, upstream, you begin to see the Sustenhörner Range, which reaches its highest point of 3 503m/11 493ft in the dome-shaped Sustenhorn, and Brienz in the distance.

Brienzer Rothorn★★★
Alt. 2 350m/7 710ft. Allow 3hr there and back (2hr 20min by rack railway). ◷*Open Jun–Oct, 7.30am–5.20pm.* ◉*Fare there and back 74CHF. ℘(0)33 952 22 22. www.brienz-rothorn-bahn.ch.* Panoramic view of the Bernese Alps, Lake Brienz *(Brienzersee)* and Hasli. For an unforgettable experience, take the steam-powered Brienz Rothorn Bahn that takes you up the steep, 25% gradient to the top. The ride starts at the restored valley station, close to the Brienz railway terminal and the lake steamer landing.

Brienzer Rothorn overlooking Brienzersee and the Alps of Berner Oberland

Robert Boesch/Switzerland Tourism

Ballenberg Freilichtmuseum (Swiss Open-Air Museum)★★

2.5km/1.5mi. Leave Brienz E on the Hofstetten road which branches left off the main street (follow directions for Freilichtmuseum). ⊙*Open mid-Apr– end Oct, daily 10am–5pm.* ⊜*20CHF, concessions apply* ⚿ *&* ℰ*(0)33 952 10 30. www.ballenberg.ch.*

In a vast and superb wooded setting designed for pedestrians, this open-air museum, opened in 1978, is spread out over 80ha/200 acres. There is a free shuttle service bus between the west (nearest Brienz) and east entrances. Genuine examples of regional architecture from practically all the country's cantons were transported here and re-assembled piece by piece, along with ancient furniture. Within each building are daily demonstrations of crafts, from needlework to wood sculpture, and an Alpine cheese dairy, bakery, and blacksmith. Divided into 13 groups by geographical origin, the traditional rural houses are connected by paths complete with picnic spots, play areas and small enclosures with 250 domestic animals.

The most noteworthy buildings are: The Chaux-de-Fonds multi-purpose dwelling, typical of the Haut-Jura district; the Oberentfelden (Aargau) chalet (1609) crowned by a huge thatched roof; the half-timbered Old Bear Inn moved from Rapperswil; the chalet from Ostermun-

digen, with its *trompe-l'œil* windows beneath the gable; the imposing farmhouse from Lancy, originally a small outbuilding containing a winepress; the Richterswil house with pretty half-timbering, built in the Zürich area around 1780; the 17C dwelling from Erstfeld, a masterpiece of Late Renaissance "St Gotthard" style; and the Adelboden chalet (17C), notable for its lovely beams. Three inns serve traditional cuisine and shops sell local craftwork, usually made on the premises.

There's an impressive group of foaming waterfalls in a wooded setting at **Giessbachfälle★★**.

Starting from Brienz

Allow 2hr there and back, including 45min by boat and funicular. ⊙*Daily service during summer season.* ⊜*From Brienz, return fare 12CHF by boat in 2nd class, 6CHF by funicular. There is a regular bus from the railway station at Brienz to Ballenberg West or Ballenberg East.*

Starting from Interlaken

About 3hr there and back, including 2hr by boat and funicular. ⊜*From Interlaken, return fare 23CHF by boat in 2nd class; 5CHF by funicular. Contact the Tourist Office,* ℰ*(0)33 952 80 80.* Separate Interlaken-Brienzersee or Bönigen embarkation stages.

ADDRESSES

🏨 STAY

🍴🛏 **Lindenhof** – *Lindenhofweg 15.*
*📞(0)33 952 20 30. www.hotel-lindenhof.
ch. Closed Jan–mid March. 71 rooms.
🍽 Restaurant (🍴🛏) closed Mon & Tue
March–April and Nov–Dec.* Lovely
quiet hotel, consisting of six buildings
overlooking the village. The rooms
are individually decorated in various
themes, and partly look at the lake. The
restaurant has a mountain restaurant,
conservatory and terrace are also with a
view of the lake.

🍴 EAT

🍴🛏 **The Red-Carpet** – *📞033 952 25 25.
www.giessbach.ch. Closed mid Oct–mid
Apr.* Cuisine in a classic and elegant
atmosphere. On the terrace, you take
your meals with superb views of the
lake and waterfalls.

Meiringen★

Meiringen is an important tourist
centre as the starting-point for
excursions to the Aare Gorges and
the Reichenbach Falls and also a
convenient stop on the Grimsel and
Susten roads. The generally accepted
birthplace of meringue which are
sold by weight in every shop, it has
been overshadowed by its Sherlock
Holmes connections: The great
fictional detective supposedly fell
to his death from the ledge of the
Reichenbach Falls; today an "X"
marks the spot and you can have a
photo with a Holmes cut-out by the
waterfall. This has led, unsurprisingly
to a big Sherlock Holmes tourist
market.

THE TOWN
Sherlock Holmes Museum
🕐*Open May–Sept, Tue–Sun 1.30pm–
6pm; Oct, Wed–Sun 3pm–6pm.* 🎫*5CHF.
📞(0)33 971 42 21.*
This museum, based in an old church,
has a collection of Holmes memorabilia
and a reconstruction of the famous, fictitious London drawing room at number
221B Baker Street.

Kirche
The church (1684) is in a part of the village where wooden houses recall old
Meiringen, ravaged by fire in 1879 and
1891. This is the fifth church built on this
spot, succeeding others swept away by
the flooding of the Alpbach, a waterfall
located behind the building. For this rea-

- ▶ **Population:** 4 723.
- 🛈 **Info:** Bahnhofstrasse 22 –
  3860. 📞(0)33 972 50 55.
  www.haslital.ch.
- ◐ **Location:** Meiringen is
  the chief town in the Hasli
  Valley, 13.5km/8.4mi east of
  Brienz. Alt. 595m/1 952ft.
- 🅿 **Parking:** Use the public
  car park and stroll to
  the sights, all nearby.
- 👁 **Don't Miss:** Walk to
  Hochstollen via Planplatten.
  Also visit Reichenbachfälle
  (Reichenbach Waterfall),
  the site of the fictional
  disappearance of Sherlock
  Holmes and Moriarty.
- 🕐 **Timing:** Allow two hours
  for town sights; a day-and-
  a-half for all excursions.

son, its detached Romanesque tower has
foundations over 7m/23ft deep. During
restoration the remains of the original
11C structure, now the crypt, and a series
of Romanesque frescoes in the upper
church, representing scenes from the
Old Testament, were discovered.

EXCURSIONS
Planplatten★★
*Alt. 2 245m/7 365ft. 1hr by ski lift, then
cable car (3 sections).*
Stunning **route**★★ overlooking pretty
pastures and forests. When you reach
the top, bear right toward the viewing
table. Superb **panorama**★★ present-

Arthur Conan Doyle

On the square named after the Scottish novelist **Arthur Conan Doyle** (1859–1930), the creator of Sherlock Holmes, stands a bronze statue of the celebrated fictitious detective by the English sculptor John Doubleday. Conan Doyle, who loved Switzerland, was made an honorary citizen of Meiringen.

ing many different landscapes: To the east the summits and glaciers of Rhonestock, Sustenhorn, and Wendenstöcke; to the south the sparkling, snow-capped peaks of the Bernese Alps (Wetterhorn, Schreckhorn, Finsteraarhorn); to the west Lake Brienz; and to the north the Glogghüs dominating the Alpine gorges around Meiringen.

Planplatten is a popular departure point for microlite flying and hang-gliding and as a starting-point for hikes and walks 🚶. Less experienced hikers can stop after reaching the two lakes Tannensee and Melchsee (*allow 5hr*); those in excellent physical condition can continue on the route described below.

Walk to the Lakes and Hochstollen★★★

Leave Planplatten early in the morning to allow enough time to catch the last cable car back at the end of the day. Allow 5–6hr depending on your choice of route, not including stops.

It is essential to wear shoes with non-slip soles.

Walk to **Balmeregg** (alt. 2 255m/7 397ft) in 1hr by a track following the mountain slope. **View**★★ of the three lakes (Engstien, Tannen and Melch), the Titlis and Wendenstöcke. Pretty **mountain path**★★ heading towards **Tannensee**★, then a flat track until **Melchsee**★ (*allow 1hr30min;* to save 1hr, go directly from *Balmeregg to Melchsee*).

Bear left and walk round Melchsee: the lovely postcard view from the tip of the lake is enhanced by shimmering **reflections**★★ on the Titlis. Climb up to small **Blausee**★. The route becomes very steep and after 1hr you will reach **Abgschütz Pass** (2 263m/7 424.5ft), which commands a sublime **view**★★. However, you will be able to get an even broader **panorama**★★★ of the surrounding landscape if you go up to **Hochstollen** (2 481m/8 140ft, marked out by a cross) along a strong, impres-

Melchsee at Melchsee-Frutt

sive incline. There are splendid views of the lakes and the Bernese Oberland, from the Eiger to Finsteraarhorn. Panoramic descent toward Käserstatt until you get to the track running down the slope before joining up with a path leading to **Mägisalp** (1 689m/5 541ft, allow 45min). Take the two cable cars to go back to the car park.

🚗 DRIVING TOURS

SUSTENPASS★★★
50km/31mi from Meiringen to Sustenpass – Allow 1hr30min.
Built from 1938 to 1945 from Wassen to Innertkirchen, the Susten road (from the French "Souste" meaning "goods warehouse"), this was the first of the major Swiss Alpine roads which has been subsequently studied extensively for its motor traffic. It is a masterpiece of civil engineering, which can be best appreciated in good weather.

▷ *From Meiringen, follow the road to Grimsel Innetkirchen, then head in the direction of the Sustenpass. The Gadmen valley begins 4km/2.5mi after Innetkirchen.*

A few kilometres before Nessental, at a bridge, turn left onto a small toll road. This detour is justified especially for hikers; Engstlenalp occupies a cul-de-sac at the bottom of the Gental valley. The road rises above the forest and runs through beautiful pastures with grazing cows. You then discover little by little, as you look behind, some remarkable **perspectives**★★ of the Bernese Oberland (Finsteraarhorn and Wetterhorn).

Engstlenalp★
A 13km/8mi detour intended mainly for seasoned ramblers.
A short distance below Nessental, level with a bridge, turn right into a narrow toll road *(at 4km)* that climbs up into the forest, passing through lovely pastures where cows are put out to graze. Behind you extend splendid **views**★★ of the Bernese Oberland (Finsteraarhorn,

Wetterhorn). Several walks leave from the final car park: the stunning lake, the **Engstlensee**★★ *(10min)*, then proceed to **Joch Pass**★★ by chair-lift, to **Trübsee**★★ *(second chair-lift going down)* and finally **Titlis**★★★ (🚗 *see ENGELBERG, allow a whole day)*. Alternatively, you may choose to visit lakes **Tannensee**★, **Melchsee**★ and **Blausee**★ *(2hr to get there, 1hr 45min to get back)*.

▷ *Between Innertkirchen and Meiringen you follow the road to the Grimsel.*

Gschletter Hairpin Bend★
🅿 *Park inside the bend.*
This loop forms a **belvedere**★ overlooking the lower Gadmental and the Gadmerflue and Wendenstöcke. Very high up, the massive walls of the Gadmerflue and the Wendenstöcke stand out. Between Gadmen and Innertkirchen is the Nessental shelf. At the last rise before arriving in the Innertkirchen Basin, the view opens out to the summits which enclose the Urbachtal, on the left of the crests of the Engelhörner.

Steingletscher★
1km/0.6mi before Himmelrank.
The enormous Steingletscher glacier seems almost overcome by a mass of reddish earth in places; a portion of the glacier reappears form the ground on the banks of a small nearby lake, in to which miniature floating icebergs often break off.
Ever since the hotel Steingletscher was built, the footpath to the glacier joins that of Steinalp and can be reached in 2hrs there and back. Motorists can also access it through a small toll road *(15 min walk from the car park upon arrival)*.

Himmelrank★★
🅿 *Park inside the bend.*
The road-builders named this Paradise Bend; it winds across a rocky slope formerly called Hell Upstairs by the people of Gadmental. Note the **view**★★ of the Gadmen and the Sustenhörner Summits (Sustenhorn, Gwächtenhorn).

Sustenpass★★

🅿 *Large car park at the west end of the tunnel (Bernese slope).*

The road reaches its highest point (2 224m/7 296ft) in the 325m/1 067ft long tunnel under the pass (alt. 2 259m/7 411ft—*which can be reached on foot*). From this point on, the finest **scenery**★★★ is the 4km/2.5mi between the western entrance and the Himmelrank. In the foreground the flow of the **Steingletscher** dies away under a mass of reddish morainic deposits; the foot of the glacier reappears on the shores of a lake, where miniature icebergs float. View the Sustenhörner group summits at the Swiss Touring Club viewing table 2km/1.2mi below the pass.

GRIMSELSTRASSE★

33km/20.5mi from Meiringen to Grimselpass – Allow 1hr30min.

The Grimsel road, rising from the upper valley of the Aare (Haslital), runs through a setting of rounded rocks, polished by ancient glaciers. But at each level of the valley, dams and power plants are reminders of modern civilization.

Outside Meiringen, the valley is obstructed by the rocky mound of the Kirchet which cuts the Aare gorge (the Aareschlucht), invisible from the road. The basin is perfectly level at Innertkirchen, dominated by great escarpments of Burg and the pyramid of Bänzlauistock.

Aareschlucht★★

2km/1.2mi, plus 30min sightseeing.
🅿 *The road to the gorges' car park branches off from the Grimsel road (number 6) on leaving Meiringen for Innertkirchen, 200m/219yds upstream from the bridge over the Aare.*

The gorge cut by the Aare through the Kirchet bolt between Meiringen and Innertkirchen, are among the most popular curiosities in the Bernese Oberland. The viewing galleries lead into the narrowest part of the gorge, the walls of which, sometimes sheer, sometimes polished and hollowed by erosion (traces of potholes and glaciated rocks), are very impressive. Stranger still is the dim light in the depths of the cleft where the jade-green stream of the Aare flows.

▷ *After about 1.5km/1mi within view of a tributary waterfall you arrive at the far end of the gorge (the last hairpin bend before Innertkirchen).*

Guttannen

This is the only community in the Oberhasli which can be called a village. Its **Kristallmuseum** (🕙 *open Jun–Sept, daily except Sat-Sun, 8am–5pm; Oct–May, Sat–Sun, open by appointment;* 👛*3CHF;* 📞*(0)33 973 12 47*) displays a wide variety of minerals and crystals.

The climb continues from level to level in a **setting**★★ of rounded greenish rocks, snowfields and waterfalls. In some places the road cuts through huge blocks of extraordinarily polished, light-coloured granite.

Handeggfall★

The River Arlenbach and River Aare mingle their waters in a Y-shaped cascade which falls into a narrow gorge.

After the turquoise sheet of the reservoir-lake of **Räterichsboden** comes the great artificial lake of Grimsel, whose muddy waters are held back by two dams anchored to the Nollen Rock—the site of a hotel which took the place of the Grimsel hostel, now submerged. In line with the drowned valley, the **view**★ reaches the crests of the Finsteraarhorn (alt. 4 274m/14 022ft, highest point of the Bernese Alps) in the distance.

Gelmerbahn★★

Leaving from Handegg. 🕙*Open mid Jun–Oct 9am–4pm, 8am–5pm in Jul–Aug if the weather permits.* 👛 *25CHF return (children 15CHF return, 2nd child free).*

Inaugurated in 1926 but open to the public only since 2001, the steepest funicular in the world (106%) climbs a 10min path to Lake Gelmer (Gelmersee), set in the mountains through untouched Nature. At the top, visitors have the choice between doing a tour of the lake (1h45mins) and continue to the Gelmer refuge (Gelmerhütte, 2hrs).

Grimselpass★★

Alt. 2 165m/7 103ft.

A "Lake of the Dead" recalls the fighting between the Austrians and the French in 1799. From the mound behind Hotel Grimselblick, the **view**★★ includes the desert region where the Rhône rises near the Rhône Glacier and, from left to right, the snowy Galenstock summit, the foot of the Rhône Glacier, the Furka Gap and its long, bare, monotonous crests stretching between the Upper Valais and the Piedmontese Toce Valley. Facing northwest you will see in the far distance the walls of the Lauteraarhorn (alt. 4 042m/13 261ft). The road then drops towards the **Gletschboden**, a desolate valley floor. The country loses its Arctic character and becomes more typically Alpine. The road develops hairpin bends on the Meienwand slopes and the terminal cataract of the Rhône Glacier, comes into sight, overlooked by the snowy dome of the Galenstock. You will also see Gletsch in the distance.

Rosenlauital★★

14km/8.7mi – about 1hr – by a narrow mountain path.

> ▶ *Leave Meiringen by the Grimsel road. After the bridge over the Aare at a crossroads, turn right and leave the car by the station of the Reichenbach funicular.*

Reichenbachfälle★

1km/0.6mi, 30min there and back, including 10min by funicular. Leave Meiringen by the road to Grimsel. After the bridge over the Aare, turn right and leave your car at the Reichenbach funicular station. ⊙*Operates mid-May–mid-Oct, every 15min, 8.15am–11.45am, 1.15pm–5.45pm.* ⊛*Fare there and back 7CHF.* ℘*(0)33 972 50 50.*

Crossing the lower falls on a viaduct, the funicular ends at a terrace from where you can view them from below, and there is a 10min steep walking path to a viewing platform at the top. At Willi-

gen, turn right toward Rosenlaui which, after a series of sharp hairpin bends, enters the lonely Reichenbach Valley, dominated by the extraordinary rock formations of the Engelhörner. Soon you will see ahead, from left to right, the Rosenlaui Glacier, the Wellhorn and the Wetterhorn. A bridge over the bed of the Reichenbach leads to the fields of Gschwandtenmad and a striking **view**★★★: The rocky shoulder of the Welhorn behind fir woods to the right of the Rosenlaui Glacier. This flanks the icy cone of the Wetterhorn, which stands above the Grosse Scheidegg Depression—a broad shelf over which you can walk from Rosenlaui to Grindelwald.

The mountaineering resort of **Rosenlaui** has given its name to a climbing school which has trained several guides for the conquest of the Himalayas. Here tourists may visit the **Gletscherschlucht**★ (⊙ *open May–Oct, 9am–5pm (6pm Jun, Jul and Aug);* ⊛*6CHF;* ℘*(0)33 971 24 88)*, the glacier gorges hollowed out by the waters from the melting ice of the Rosenlaui Glacier *(⊕45min of rather difficult walking)*. The scenery now becomes quite rocky. On arriving at Schwarzwaldalp, at the end of the road suitable for cars, you will find a slope wholly planted with maple trees.

ADDRESSES

🛏 STAY

⊜ **Schweizerhof** – *Gotthardstrasse 85, Andermatt.* ℘*(0)41 887 11 89. www. schweizerhof-andermatt.ch. 28 rooms. Restaurant*⊜⊜*.* Centrally located chalet-style lodgings.

⊜⊜⊜ **Hotel Sonne** – *Gotthardstrasse 76, Andermatt.* ℘*(0)41 887 12 26. www. hotelsonneandermatt.ch. 40 rooms. Restaurant*⊜ ⊜⊜*.* Located two minutes from Gemmstock cable car.

🍴 EAT

⊜⊜⊜ **Gasthaus Ochsen** – *Gotthardstrasse 72, Andermatt.* ℘*(0)41 887 14 20. ochsen-andermatt.ch.*

THE VALAIS

The Valais is one of the most isolated cantons of Switzerland, an area of the highest Alpine peaks and numerous glaciers. Almost completely cut off from the economic centres of German Switzerland, it has been kept busy for 2 000 years by intense international traffic through the Great St Bernard and Simplon Passes. It owes its distinctive regional character to the Mediterranean clarity of its sky, the deep Catholic beliefs of its people, and its impressive industrial development, which nevertheless does not prevent the survival in the high valleys of the most ancient ways of life.

Highlights

1. The **Roman Amphitheatre** at Martigny (p248)
2. The international panorama from **Mont Fort** (p258)
3. The **fortified hills** of Valère and Tourbillon at Sion (p262)
4. Visiting the **Barrage de la Grande Dixence** (p263)
5. View of the **Matterhorn** from Zermatt (p276)

Valaisans and Walser

All along the Rhône Valley, travellers might think they were in a purely Latin civilisation. Beyond Sierre, and especially near Brig, however, they will start to hear a Germanic dialect and the name Valais yields to Wallis. The Upper Valais was invaded from the 6C onward by Germanic peoples who probably came down from the Grimsel and pushed on as far as Sierre. Later, these restless "Walser" infiltrated other southern Alpine valleys, forming centres of German culture in otherwise French-speaking districts, as at Davos. These hardy mountaineers, especially those of the Conches Valley, represented the most fiercely democratic element (Raron, Saillon), reducing the temporal rights of the prince-bishops of Sion and claims of local feudal lords by force.

Geography

Here you must not expect gentle pastoral scenes, but dramatic, high mountain landscapes like those of the **lateral valleys**★★★, dotted with chalets and *raccards* or *mazots* (small barns perched on piles and used as granaries or storehouses). In these wild, uninviting regions, it is common to find wayside wooden crosses, set up to protect trav-

Raccards—old-fashioned Valais barns in Val d'Anniviers

ellers and local residents from the dark dangers of the mountain.

The Canton is so named because it is effectively one big L-shaped valley, with several smaller valleys connected to it, through which the river Rhône flows on its journey from the Lepontine Alps in the east to Switzerland's largest body of water, Lake Geneva in the west. Flanked on both sides of the valley by massive mountain ranges, in the north lies the insurmountable (by road at least) Bernese Oberland which includes the Jungfrau, the Eiger and Mönch, while in the south lies the Valais or Pennine Alps, with the Matterhorn and Monte Rosa traversed only by the renowned Great St Bernard and Simplon Passes and Tunnels.

One fifth of the Canton is covered by glaciers but despite this the Valais is drier and sunnier than the rest of Switzerland. There are no large cities, the largest towns being the old roman town of Martigny and the capital of the canton, Sion, a bishopric founded in the 4C, both in the west. Sierre is the last French-speaking town before German-speaking Brig in the east. High up in the valleys the terrain is wild and desolate and resorts such as Zermatt and Crans-Montana are some of the only signs of human habitation.

History

Being surrounded by mountains, the Valais has always been difficult to access. But the indomitable Roman Army led by Julius Caesar invaded during the 1C BC by crossing the Alps via the Great St Bernard Pass. As he advanced east, the general was confronted by the fierce Aleman tribe and was effectively halted at Sierre, which helps to explain why even today this is the point where the French language, derived from Latin, stops and German, which derived from the language spoken by the Alemans, begins.

The Romans withdrew from the western Valais in the 5C, but Christianity, which was brought over Great St Bernard Pass by merchants and priests, had already established itself. Disputed by Franks and Burgundians, the latter eventually took control during the late 9C and their King Rudolph III appointed the Bishop of Sion as Count of the Valais. Soon after, however, the Bishop was unable to prevent the Lower Valais being taken over by the Dukes of Savoy but by 1475 he managed to retake the territory with the help of the communes of the Upper Valais.

Due to its relative isolation, the Reformation passed the Valais by and it became a republic controlled by the Bishop until he was eventually removed by Napoleon in 1798. The Valais remained a semi-independent republic until 1810 when it was absorbed into France before finally becoming a canton of the Swiss Confederation in 1815. By the mid 19C many people in Switzerland were concerned about increasing centralisation of power and the Valais joined with six other Roman Catholic cantons to form the Sonderbund. The so-called Sonderbund War broke out in early November 1847 but by the end of the month it was all over with the Valaisians surrendering to the Confederate Army.

Today

The Valais is today heavily dependent on agriculture with dairy farming, cattle breeding and wine production the most important sectors. The climate is ideal for growing fruit and there are many orchards especially in lower Valais. Year-round tourism is also very important, with winter sports fans flocking to world-famous resorts such as Crans-Montana above Sion and Sierre, while during the summer months tourists are attracted by the excellent sunshine record of the canton.

The Chablais region, just south of Lake Geneva, is not only known for its fine wines it is also the home of much of the canton's industry, which consists of pharmaceuticals, agribusiness, oil-refining and other light industry. The region can also boast the world's highest gravity dam at Grande Dixence (285m/935ft), in the mountains south of Sion near Zermatt which collects the melt water of 35 glaciers.

THE VALAIS

0   12 km
0   7 miles

BULLE

THUN, INTERLAKEN

A   B

LAUSANNE

GENEVA

SALLANCHES

Château-d'Oex

Montreux

LAKE GENEVA

Le Bouveret

Leysin

Aigle

Valais Alps

Scex Rouge 2971

Sanetsch Pass 2243

PLAINE MORTE
2927

Leukerk

Bella Lui 2543

Pt Mt Bovin 2412

Alb

Vermala

Villars-s-Ollon

Les Diablerets 3210

Derborence Nature Reserve

Lac souterrain de St-Léonard

Crans Montana

Sierre

Châtel

Pas de Morgins 1369

Morgins

St-Maurice

St-Séverin

Chand

V^ée d'Anniviers

St

Croix de Culet 1963

Val d'Illiez

RHÔNE

St-Pierre-de-Clages

Sion

Vex

Grimentz

V^ée Zina

Champéry

G^ges du Trient

Saillon

Pyramides d'Euseigne

Val d'Hérens

V^ée de Moiry

Zin

Salvan

A 9

Verbier

Mt Gelé

Evolène

Les Marécottes

Martigny

Le Levron

3023

3329

Aiguilles Rouges

Me 28

Ferpècle

Barrage Emosson

1526

Col de la Forclaz

Drance

MONT FORT

2810

Les Haudères

Lac Bleu

Champex

Orsières

GRANDE DIXENCE

Arolla

3540

La Breya

Aig^le du Tour

2374

Entremont Valley

2365

Praz Gra

MAUVOISIN 1961

PETIT CER

FRANCE

D 1506

CHAMONIX

3820 Mt Dolent

Col du Gd St-Bernard 2469

Bourg-St-Bernard

447

MONT BLANC 4807

Mont Blanc Tunnel

Tunnel du Grand St-Bernard

AOSTA

AOSTA

A   B

SPIEZ · INTERLAKEN · C · GRINDELWALD · D · LUCERNE

ANDERMATT · AIROLO

SCHILTHORN 2970
LAKE ÖESCHINEN
Kandersteg
Mürren
JUNGFRAUJOCH 3475

RHÔNE GLACIER 2431
Realp
Gletsch
Furka Pass
Oberwald

BERNESE OBERLAND
Gletscherstafel
Lonza
...schbergtunnel
Kippel
Raron
Brigerbad
Brig
9
19
Rhône

ALETSCH GLACIER
Moosfluh 2335
Riederalp
EGGISHORN 2927
Bellwald
Ernen
Münster
Reckingen

Toce

9

Simplonpass 2005

S 33

HOHSAAS 3098
Hannig
Saas-Fee
ALLALIN 2570
Plattjen
LÄNGFLUH 2870
Britannia
Gondoschlucht

Weisshorn 605
Täsch

I T A L Y

...rmatt
Rothorn 3103
...ner ...ges
...ac Noir 3135
Allalinhorn 4027 3030
Lac de Barrage Stausee Mattmark
STOCKHORN 3532
2868
Monte Moropass

Breithorn 4164
GORNERGRAT

EGGISHORN	★★★	Highly recommended
Emosson	★★	Recommended
Grimentz	★	Interesting
Kippel		Other sight described in this guide
		Driving tour

N

C · D

243

St Maurice★

The little town of St Maurice occupies a picturesque site★. Agaune (from the Celtic name *acauno*, meaning a rock) was the chief village of the Nantuates tribe. After the Roman conquest it became the capital of the present Valais under the Emperor Augustus. Today St Maurice is a picturesque small town attracting tourists and pilgrims as it has done for hundreds years and it is an ideal base from which to explore the nearby towns of Montreux and Martigny.

▶ **Population:** 4 013.
◔ **Michelin Map:** Michelin National Map 729: F7.
🛈 **Info:** 1 avenue des Terreaux. ℘(0)24 485 40 40. www.saint-maurice.ch.
◖ **Location:** Saint-Maurice is dominated to the west by the Dents du Midi and to the east by the Dent de Morcles. Alt. 422m/1 384ft.
◈ **Don't Miss:** The Abbey Treasury.
◔ **Timing:** Allow a minimum of 2hrs.

A BIT OF HISTORY
The Field of Martyrs
In the 3C an African legion commanded by **Maurice** was massacred for refusing to worship Roman gods. The community took charge of the martyrs' tombs, and the foundation of the Abbey of St Maurice was prompted by King Sigismund of Burgundy and in the 9C the town took the name of its illustrious patron saint. St Maurice became one of the holy places of Christianity.

SIGHTS
Église Abbatiale
The fine **belfry**★ is 11C and the stone spire 13C, although the **abbey church** itself dates only from the beginning of the 17C and has been restored. On the altar there is a fine mosaic by Maurice Denis.

Treasury★★
🔊*Guided tours (1hr)* ◔*Jul and Aug 10.30am, 2pm and 3.15pm; Sept–Oct and May–Jun 2.45pm; Jan–Apr, (Tue and Wed) 2.45pm. Open Easter Mon and Pentecost.* ◔*Closed Mon, Sun mornings and public holidays.* ⊛*10CHF.* ℘*(0)24 486 04 04. www.abbaye-stmaurice.ch.*
This is one of the richest ecclesiastical treasuries in the Christian world. Pay special attention to a sardonyx vase, the Merovingian casket of Theodoric made of gold encrusted with pearls and cameos, the golden 9C ewer, said to be Charlemagne's, and the reliquary of St Mau-

rice. Two other reliquaries of the 12C and 13C, the reliquary-bust of St Candid (on the plinth, his martyrdom by beheading) and the reliquary-monstrance given by St Louis, complete the priceless collection.

Fouilles de Martolet
◔*Same admission times and charges as for the abbey treasury.*
Near the belfry, at the foot of the rock overlooking the abbey, excavations have uncovered foundations of the buildings that preceded the present church from the 4C onward; their plan stands out clearly. You may see traces of a baptistery and graceful modern cloisters in the Romanesque style. Visit the catacombs, narrow underground galleries leading to the crypt and tomb of St Maurice.

Castle
Overlooking the Rhône and sheltered by the eastern slopes of the Dents du Midi, this castle dates from the early 16C. The square keep and bastions were added in the 18C and now house the **Musée Cantonal d'Histoire Militaire** (🔊*guided tours, Jun–Sept, 1p,m–6pm;* ⊛*12CHF, no charge the first Sun in the month;* ℘*(0)24 485 24 58*). On display are banners, medals, arms, and uniforms; another section includes models of the fortifications built along the Swiss borders during both World Wars. The dungeons house heavy artillery from the Second World

Valais Rhône

From the Glacier to the Vines

Issuing from the famous cataract of the Rhône Glacier, the river is born at an altitude of 2 200m/7 218ft, crosses the Gletschboden Basin and enters the Conches Valley (also known as Goms). Its volume doubles at Brig where it receives waters of the Massa flowing from the Aletsch Glacier. It then ceases to be a mountain torrent and flows onto the floor of the alluvial plain between steep rocky banks at Visp (Viège) and Gampel.

Rhône Glacier

Max Schmid/Switzerland Tourism

The double obstacle created by the cone of debris of the Illgraben, cloaked in the Finges Forest (Pfynwald), and by the Sierre landslide, results in a wide break in the valley. This is where the boundary between German-speaking Upper Valais and French-speaking Valais developed (👁see INTRODUCTION: Language and Religion).

The Central Valais between Sierre and Martigny is sheltered from winds by mountain barriers and is the driest area in Switzerland. Favoured by this Mediterranean climate, the local vines (👁see INTRODUCTION: Food and Wine) flourish on rugged, sun-baked ridges of south-facing slope, opposite the wooded and pastoral slopes of the **mayens** (pastures where the herds wait in May for the snow to melt on the higher Alps).

At Martigny, the Rhône receives the Dranse and turns sharply north. Deflected toward the last foothills of the Bernese Alps by the cone of debris from the St Barthélemy Torrent, the river passes through St Maurice and opens out into the Lower Valais. This marshy plain, which spreads as it extends toward the shores of Lake Geneva, belongs politically to the Valais on the left shore of the lake.

The tumultuous natural phenomenon of the waters' meeting (👁see Lake Geneva) is the last sign of this 170km/106mi long mountainous Rhône.

The Rhône running through the Finges Forest

Roland Gerth/Switzerland Tourism/BAFU

War and anti-aircraft guns occupy the courtyards. On the ground floor the elegantly furnished reception room is typical of the 18C.

Grotte aux Fées

Reached by path starting from the level of the castle and a bridge at the north entrance to the town. ⏱*Open mid-Mar –mid-Nov, daily 10am–5pm (until 6pm Jul & Aug); winter by reservation.* ◉*8CHF.* ✆*(0)24 485 10 45. www.grotteauxfees.ch.* This grotto is formed by a natural gallery about 900m/990yds long leading to an underground lake and waterfall. From the terrace of the nearby restaurant there is a fine **view**★ of St Maurice and the Dent de Morcles.

🚗 DRIVING TOUR

VAL DE MORGINS★

34km/21mi – from Monthey to Châtel. Allow approx 2hrs. Swiss customs control near the pass, French customs at Vonne.

The Morgins Pass is the only international route in the pre-Alpine Chablais Massif joining the pastoral valleys of Dranse d'Abondance and Morgins, with their many large chalets. On the Valais side it is a modern road offering views of the Dents du Midi.

On leaving Monthey the road climbs quickly in hairpin bends above the Rhône Valley, overlooked (going upstream) by the summits of the Les Diablerets, Grand Muveran and Dent de Morcles. Ahead, in line with the Illiez Valley, are the snowy Dents Blanches and Dents du Midi. Fields planted with walnut trees succeed vineyards.

Champéry✷✷

Champéry lies on the mountainside at the beginning of the **Val d'Illiez**★★, in the shadow of the Dents du Midi Range. The resort clusters around its single narrow street and exudes a family atmosphere despite its international clientele. It is a favourite place for rock-climbers. A

local feature is the church **belfry** roofed with a curious pierced stone crown. In winter the Panachaux Basin, served by several ski lifts, offers fine, sunny slopes to skiers.

Croix de Culet★★

From Champéry, about 45min, including 15min by cable-car and 1hr on foot. Jul–Aug, departure approximately every 30min, 9am–5.30pm; Jun, Sept and Oct, departures approximately every hr, 9am–5pm; Dec–mid-Apr, 9am–5pm. ⏱*Closed late-Oct–beginning of the skiing season.* ◉*15CHF there and back.* ✆*(0)24 479 20 20.* From the upper station of the Planachaux cable-car, climb on foot, along the crest, to the cross (alt. 1 963m/6 440ft). There is an open view of the various peaks of the Dents du Midi, Mount Ruan, Dents Blanches and the Vaud Alps. The road continues to make hairpin bends, offering a widening **view**★ of the Rhône Valley, to the south of the Illiez Valley, the Dents du Midi Cliffs and, to the right of these, Mount Ruan. The road then becomes a corniche above the wooded ravine of the Vièze; it then reaches the floor of the softly shaped Alpine combe of the Morgins Valley. Here, chalets nestle under wide-eaved roofs covered with shingles; their two-storey balconies have a double overhang, forming a gallery.

▶ *Return towards Monthey and turn left at Troistorrents taking the Pass road.*

Pas de Morgins★

Alt. 1 369m/4 491ft. The road, falling slightly, slips into this forest dell containing a small lake in which fir trees are reflected. South-eastward, in the middle distance, the Dents du Midi summits can be seen. The steeper descent into the Dranse d'Abondance Valley reveals the majestic **site**★ of Châtel. Ahead, the horizon is now barred by the slopes of Mount Chauffé (left) and the Cornettes de Bise (right).

Martigny

The town of Martigny, dominated by the Tour de la Bâtiaz and surrounded by vineyards, is an international road junction and a choice stopping-place for tourists. In this elbow of the Valais Rhône, where the Drance joins it, the flow of traffic from the Simplon and the Great St Bernard routes, and that from the Forclaz Pass all converge.

A BIT OF HISTORY

Martigny boasts several stone ruins dating to Roman times. Forum Claudii Augusti was a small town situated in the Forclaz Pass, linking Italy directly to France. Originally founded between AD41 and 47 under the Emperor Claudius, it was renamed Forum Claudii Vallensium (*guided tours: the tourist office organises archeological tours*).

WALKING TOURS
AROUND THE FONDATION PIERRE GIANADDA

Allow 3hrs to include visiting the museums at the cultural centre.

▷ *Begin at the Fondation Pierre Gianadda, S of the town centre.*

Fondation Pierre Gianadda★★

Open Jul–Oct, 9am–7pm; Nov–Jun, 10am–6pm. 18CHF. (0)27 722 39 78. www.gianadda.ch.
Léonard Gianadda opened this cultural centre named after his brother, who died in a tragic accident. It is built around the site of an ancient Celtic temple, the oldest of its kind in Switzerland. In addition to permanent collections, there are temporary exhibitions of works by such renowned artists as Goya, Renoir, Picasso, Klee, Braque, Degas, Manet, Dufy, Kandinsky, Van Gogh, Miró, and Modigliani.
The **Gallo-Roman Museum** displays statuettes, coins, jewellery, domestic utensils, and fragments of sculpted stones dating back to the 1C–4C. Do not miss the bronzes of Octodurum, including the tricorn head of a bull.

▶ **Population:** 15 635.
Michelin Map: Michelin National Map 729: F7.
Info: Ave de la Gare – 1920. (0)27 720 49 49. www.martigny.com.
Location: On the Rhône in the lower Valais. Alt. 476m/1 562ft.
Don't Miss: Fondation Pierre Gianadda or the Amphithéâtre Romain (Roman Amphitheatre).
Kids: The St Bernard Dog Museum.
Timing: Allow a minimum of one day for the highlights.

The **Automobile Museum** presents unique early vehicles, still in perfect working order, dating from 1897 to 1939. The oldest is an 1897 Benz with a maximum speed of 25kph/15.5mph. All the great names of the car industry are represented: Rolls-Royce, Bugatti, De Dion-Bouton, Delaunay-Belleville. The museum also displays cars made in Switzerland: Pic-Pic (1906 double-phaeton), Sigma (1910–11), Martini (1912 torpedo), Fischer (1913 six-seater torpedo), and Stella (1911).

The **Louis and Evelyn Franck Collection**, features Impressionists, including prominent works by Cézanne, Van Gogh, Ensor, Van Dongen, and Picasso. The **Garden** is an open-air sculpture museum, dotted with archeological ruins and more modern works by Henry Moore (*Reclining Figure*), Joán Miró (*Head*), Brancusi (*The Big Rooster*), Dubuffet (*Contortionist Element of Architecture V*), Segal (*Woman with Sunglasses on Park Bench*) and Rodin (*Meditation Scene with Arm*). Every year, from April to October, an exhibition dedicated to Leonardo da Vinci is held in the old arsenal of the foundation.

▷ *Turn left into chemin de Surfrête, then left again into route du Levant.*

Cow fights, Amphithéâtre Romain

Cow Fights

Popular cow fights take place in the Valais during spring and autumn when at least 100 contestants, usually of the Hérens breed, a sturdy, muscular race of cattle with curved horns and a lively, belligerent character bred primarily for their beef but also used for dairy production. They are grouped into categories according to age and weight and the fights take place before the cows are put out to grass or when they combine with another herd, these springtime contests deciding the Queen Cow who leads the herd to the summer pastures. Heads are lowered for the clash, horns are locked and the struggle begins with the weaker animal retreating, often chased by the winner. Organised fights determine regional and cantonal queens and a jury awards prizes to the first six in each category. The grand final is held in Martigny, where an overall champion emerges and is given the title "Queen of Queens".

Amphithéâtre Romain

The **Roman Amphitheatre** dates back to the 2C and bears witness to the prosperity of the Roman community that was here. Excavation work exposed ruins of residences, temples and public baths. The amphitheatre has been restored and is the site of open-air shows, concerts, and re-enactments of Roman gladiator fights and races.

St Bernard Dog Museum

Route du Levant 34 in the old Arsenal building adjacent to the Roman Ampitheater; take the CFF bus to Pierre Gianadda Foundation. Open daily 10am–6pm. 10CHF. (0)27 720 49 20. www.musee-saint-bernard.ch.

This museum is dedicated to the history of the Great St Bernard hospice and pass and the history and role of the legendary St Bernard dogs. There are special programs and exhibits for children, and a picnic area nearby.

Turn around; route du Levant leads back to Place du Bourg.

Place and rue du Bourg

Pleasant small square with its turreted house (1609 heavily restored) and picturesque street. On the left note the old town hall (Maison de Commune du Quartier du Bourg—1645) with arcades supported by seven marble columns.

TOWN CENTRE
Tour de la Bâtiaz

20min on foot there and back by Chemin du Château.

Set in a strategic site, high on a rocky promontory, the circular keep and its defensive wall are all that remain of a 13C fortress. From the tower there is a lovely **view**★ of the Martigny Basin and surrounding vineyards.

◐ *Just before the bridge, turn right along the west bank of the river.*

Chapelle Notre-Dame-de-Compassion

This 17C sanctuary contains an elegant Baroque gilt altarpiece and an unusual collection of ex-votos in the form of small paintings.

◐ *Cross the 19C wooden covered bridge (pont couvert) to avenue Marc-Morand.*

The 16C **Grand'Maison**, recognisable by its elegant spire-like shingle roof, was a hostel where a number of 18C and 19C European notables stayed.

On the right, at the beginning of Avenue du Grand-St-Bernard, is a powerful bronze bust by Courbet symbolising Liberty.

Return to Place Centrale and enter the 19C town hall to see the brilliant **stained-glass window**★ (55sq m/ 592sq ft) which illustrates the Rhône contemplating the Drance. There are also other fine stained-glass windows by **Edmond Bille** of Valais.

◐ *Continue to the Église Notre-Dame-des-Champs on Place du Midi.*

Église Notre-Dame-des-Champs

Rebuilt in the 17C in the Tuscan style and flanked in the 18C by a neo-Gothic bell tower (50m/164ft high), outstanding features are a monumental doorway with finely carved panels, a 17C baptismal font, a pulpit carved by local artisans, 18C statues of the Apostle, and a large Crucifix dating to 1495.

Go as far as rue des Alpes to see the restored **Maison Supersaxo**, an interesting example of 15C architecture. Take rue de la Délèze, rue Octodure, and rue du Forum, which passes in front of the Forum Claudii Vallensium, a Gallo-Roman site.

EXCURSIONS
Saillon

Alt. 522m/1 713ft. ◐*19km/12mi NE. Route du centre thermal.* ✆*(0)27 743 11 88. www.saillon.ch.*

The village of Saillon, a wine-making centre since Roman times, sits on the banks of the River Rhône surrounded by vineyards (200ha/494 acres) and market gardens. This wide, sunny valley has an ideal climate for the cultivation of grapes, strawberries, pears, apricots and asparagus.

Old Town

The old town, with its gray rooftops clustered around the ramparts, enjoyed a strategic position of vital importance before the Rhône changed its course in

The Bisses

In the middle section of the Valais (from Martigny to Brig) cultivation of tablelands overlooking the Rhône Valley caused irrigation problems. The lack of water in the gorges inspired the Valaisans to invent the *bisses,* narrow canals (207 at the turn of the last century; total length of 2 000km/1 243mi) that draw the glacier waters from the Rhône tributaries. They carry water along the mountainsides through wooden troughs, the upkeep of which requires dangerous acrobatics. The maintenance of the irrigating *bisse* and the distribution of its water among those who are entitled to it, hold an important place in the lives of these communities. The filling of the canals in early spring is still accompanied in some places by a religious ceremony. Technical progress in water supply has led to the abandonment of many of these rustic aqueducts, but some wooded sections offer tourists charming scenes for walks on level ground.

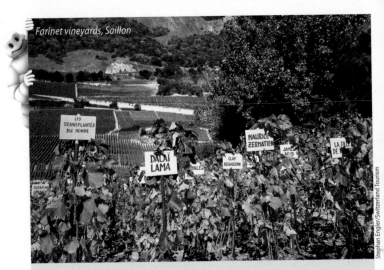

Farinet vineyards, Saillon

Stephan Engler/Switzerland Tourism

Joseph-Samuel Farinet

A Kind-hearted Crook

Born near the Grand-St-Bernard in 1845, Joseph-Samuel Farinet was a lively character who led an eventful life. A dedicated, self-proclaimed adventurer and forger, this Swiss Robin Hood would hand out the money he had forged to the poor and needy. Rebelling against the Establishment and forever on the run from the Swiss *gendarmes*, this kind-hearted, unorthodox figure was widely admired by the local population, who condoned his sense of justice and soon hailed him as a national hero. Hounded by the police, he was hit by a bullet and died in the Salentze Gorges, near Saillon, aged 35. He is buried in Saillon cemetery, at the foot of the church tower.

This outlaw is still seen by many as a benefactor who devoted his life to the poor. He remains a symbol embodying the values of freedom and mountain hospitality. His life story has inspired a ballad by the Vaud writer Charles-Ferdinand Ramuz and a film starring Jean-Louis Barrault, *Farinet et la Fausse Monnaie*. Barrault went on to create the Friends of Farinet Association which turned Saillon into a place of pilgrimage.

The Smallest Vineyard in the World

Planted by a group of admirers to mark the 100th anniversary of Farinet's death, this vineyard in the Colline Ardente consists of just three vines, covering an area of 1.67sq m/1.8sq yds. In 1999 the Dalaï Lama, appointed by the "Amis de Farinet" took possession of these vines, following in the footsteps of the renowned Abbé Pierre, champion of the poor, and Jean-Louis Barrault. Other celebrities who have symbolically tended the vine include Gerard Depardieu, Maurice Béjart, Peter Ustinov, Danielle Mitterand, Roger Moore, Princess Caroline of Monaco, the Lord Mayor of London, Gina Lollobrigida, Paul-Émile Victor, Auxerre football coach Guy Roux, Zinedine Zidane and Michael Schumacher. Rocks carried from countries all round the world signifying that true friendship has no boundaries lie beneath the vines. Every year, wine produced by the three stocks is blended with the best Valais vintage. One thousand bottles are made, specially labelled and sold at an auction to benefit a charity fund in memory of Farinet.

this part of central Valais. The impressive ruins of the castle and the church, with its Romanesque belfry, are quite picturesque.

View★

From the village, a steep path soon leads to the foot of the great tower of the castle (a former keep), from where there is a lovely view of the terraced vineyards carpeting the slopes plain with its orchards. The Pennines can be seen like a massive wall in the distance.

Farinet's Path

↞↞*45min walk.*

Leaving from the foot of Saillon hill, this path is dotted with 21 stained-glass works depicting human experiences, such as childhood, love, suffering, and death. It wends its way through wine-growing fields to end up at the smallest registered vineyard in the world. **Farinet's Footbridge** was opened in 2001.

Spa

The spa complex (*Route de Centre Thermal, 1913, Saillon; check website for opening times and charges; ℘(0)27 743 11 70; www.bainsdesaillon.ch*) opened in 1983 carries on a tradition that dates back to Roman times. The hot springs of the Salentze provide four thermal baths ranging in temperature from 28°C/82°F to 34°C/93°F; the complex also has three steam baths, two saunas, swimming pools and foot baths.

🚗 DRIVING TOURS

ROUTE DE LA FORCLAZ★★

36km/22.5mi – about 55min – tour of the Emosson Dam and trek to the Trient Glacier not included. The road leading from the Le Châtelard to the Dam is narrow and winding with some steep climbs/descents.

The convenience of a direct link between the resort of Chamonix and the great Valais road junction of Martigny makes the Forclaz Pass Road one of the great international routes of the Alps.

▷ *24km/15m SW of Martigny. Take the Chamonix road from Martigny.*

▷ Col de la Forclaz

Alt. 1 527m/5 010ft.

To the south the view is cut off by the detached crests of the Aiguille du Tour (visible on the extreme left, above the Grands Glacier). To the north the snowy peaks of the Bernese Alps seldom emerge from the bluish mist which rises from the great Valais Depression on fine summer days; the rocky Pierre-Avoi Peak, between the valleys of the Rhône and the Drance, is easier to distinguish. From the Forclaz Pass, many long signposted walks in the midst of the Valais mountains (*Information on trails: Marécottes, ℘(0)27 761 31 01*) are available to visitors keen on wild nature. One of these walks, leading to the **Trient Glacier★** (*allow 3hr there and back, ⊖inaccessible in winter because of snow*) follows an outflow channel (natural duct draining glacier waters toward the valley) along the mountainside and through a forest of larch, spruce and arolla pines. The path offers an open view of the Grands Glaciers and Dzornevattaz Valley, and the Pétoudes d'En Haut and Herbagères pastures below the Balme Pass. The ascent toward the Trient Glacier is breathtaking. The tongue of snow—a massive powdery stretch which appears to have frozen in mid-air like a lava flow—sparkles with bluish tints as one draws gradually nearer.

Halfway up the mountain, enjoy a well-deserved break at the Trient refreshments stall: This former refuge, rebuilt after an avalanche in 1978, was used in the late 19C as accommodation for workers farming the ice for commercial use. From the pass to Martigny the view of the Martigny Basin and the gap formed by the Valais Rhône really opens out only 2.5km/1.5mi below the ridge. The rocky snag-like Pierre-Avoi is still prominent in the foreground; soon you will pick out the narrow furrow of the Drance forming a way through to the Great St Bernard. The site of Martigny and La Bâtiaz Tower become visible where the road runs between vineyards.

Glacier du Trient★

Access: from Col de la Forclaz.
Park in the car park and take the
waymarked footpath from the pass (alt.
1 526m/5 006ft). Follow signs to the
"Glacier du Trient et Fenêtre d'Arpette".

An easy walk (1hr) leads to a **snack bar** with views of the glacier, which is 5km/3mi long and 500m/547yds to 900m/984yds wide. The path continues to the tongue of the glacier along a more difficult route that follows the right bank of the river (1hr). From here, a **glacial hike** leads up the gentle slopes of the Trient, then up the steeper strips overlooking the river. Experience of glacial hiking is essential for this section of the walk, as are crampons and ice picks; beginners wishing to tackle the walk should contact a mountain guide.

▷ *Turn sharp right at Le Châtelard.*

A winding road (8km/5mi, closed in winter) leads from Le Châtelard, on the border between Switzerland and France, via Finhaut to the Emosson Dam. As the flower-and pine-tree lined road nears the dam, there are extensive views towards Mont Blanc in the distance.

Barrage d'Emosson★

Alt. 1 850m/6 068ft. ⏱*Open May–Oct (exterior). For further information, contact the Parc d'attractions on* ℰ*(0)27 769 11 11.*

The dam of Emosson—the second largest in Switzerland after the Barrage de la Grande Dixence—was a joint Franco-Swiss project (1967–72). It rises to 180m/590ft, just below the Gueulaz Pass (alt. 1 970m/6 463ft) and harmonizes perfectly with its rocky, mountainous setting.

The reservoir has a capacity of 225 million cu m/7 946 million cu ft and a surface area of 327ha/808 acres. It replaced the old Barberine dam, which now lies 42m/138ft below the surface of the water when it was at its highest level. The water in the lake comes mostly from the Mont-Blanc Massif, on the other side of the valley. The sub-glacial water is

collected at a higher altitude than the dam and is then transported here via underground tunnels and siphoned up to the lake.

The hydroelectric power station on the upper stage at Châtelard-Vallorcine is in French territory; the Swiss power station on the lower stage (la Bâtaz) lies on the floor of the Rhône Valley. Annual production of some 850 million kWh is shared between the two national electricity companies EDF (France) and ATEL (Switzerland).

Access by funicular★★

From **Le Châtelard-Giétroz** take the funicular (one of the steepest in the world, with a gradient of 78%) which goes from the C.F.F. (Swiss Railway) power station to the water tower, and which offers lovely **views** of the Rhône Valley to one side and Mont Blanc to the other (⚞*Access by funicular from Châtelard-Château d'Eau, Emosson train and Emosson mini-funicular;* ⏱*operates Jun–mid-Oct, 9.30am–12.30pm, 1.30pm–5.30pm;* ⚞*Fare there and back 44CHF;* ℰ*(0)27 769 11 11; www.chatelard.net).*

A little train runs from here to the base of the dam. A second funicular, known as "Le Minifunic", then leads to the Gueulaz Pass (alt. 1 970m/6 461ft). Inaugurated on the occasion of the 700th anniversary of the Swiss Confederation in 1991, this ingenious piece of engineering can rise to a height of 260m/854ft in two minutes.

View★★

From the dam, there is a magnificent view of the Mont Blanc Massif (right to left) from Aiguilles Rouges to Mont Blanc, including Mont Maudit, Mont Blanc du Tacul, Aiguille du Midi, Aiguille du Dru, Aiguille Verte, the Aiguilles du Chardonnet and Argentière, Aiguille du Tour and Le Tour Glacier, and Grands Glaciers.

Above the café-restaurant stands the modern Chapelle Notre Dame des Neiges (Chapel of Our Lady of Snow), whose interior features pretty stained-glass windows depicting Alpine flowers and animals.

Climbing the Dam

In 1996, a climbing route was opened on the smooth side of the dam by climbers Marc Volorio, Paul Victor Amaudruz, Samuel Lugon Maulin, and Thierry Amaudruz from the Valais region. This is the highest artificial climbing wall in the world, with two sloping sections, a vertical section, and two final sections which curve back at 13m/42ft over a height of 60m/197ft. Around 600 synthetic resin footholds have been screwed into and stuck on to the concrete wall. This spectacular 150m/492ft route is very popular with experienced climbers.

Emosson Lakes★
3-4hr walk, there and back.

A wide paved path crosses the dam, leading to a route which follows the left bank of the **Lac d'Emosson**. The tranquil lake is almost Scandinavian in feel. The **Lac du Vieux Emosson** stands at the western end of the lake. The path climbs up to the Vieux Emosson Dam, where there is a snack bar. From here, there are fine views of the Cirque du Cheval Blanc (alt. 2 831m/9 285ft) and the Pointe de Finive (2 625m/8 610ft).

In the footsteps of the dinosaurs★★
5-6hr walk, there and back.
It is strictly forbidden to remove rocks or stones.

Follow the left bank of the Lac d'Emosson. At the end of the lake, a footpath signposted to Col de la Terrasse climbs up to this protected site (alt. 2 400m/7 872ft) discovered on 23 August 1976 by the French geologist, Georges Bronner. The site contains more than 800 fossilised dinosaur footprints, left over 250 million years ago, before the Alps even existed. The dinosaurs stood at a height of 3–4m/10–13ft and weighed several tons. They have left prints 10–20cm/4–7.8in long and 5cm/2in deep. The space between the prints shows that these animals had a stride of up to 2m/6.6ft.

VALLÉE DU TRIENT★

12km/7.2mi (excl Vallon de Van).
Allow 20-25 minutes driving time.

Beyond the covered bridge or the new bridge over the Drance in Martigny, a winding road heads toward Salvan (8km/5mi). The road, occasionally cut into the rock, then climbs above the Rhône Valley and enters the wild scenery of the Trient Valley, a perfect destination for mountain walkers. The valley is particularly popular with cross-country and downhill skiers during the winter season.

Trient Gorge

Thomas Andenmatten/Valais Tourism/Switzerland Tourism

Gorges du Trient★★
At Vernayaz.

Beginning in the Trient glacier, this stream gushes through a rocky fissure 200m/656ft high followed by a **way-marked footpath** and bridge across the gorge. Nearby, the old **Pont du Gueu-roz** (1934) is now a listed monument. Cross the bridge on foot for a bird's-eye view of the gorge.

Vallon de Van

The narrow road overhanging the Rhône Valley at a height of 800m/2 625ft provides an exciting route to Van d'en Haut.

253

The drive back to Salvan offers views of the Vallon de Van and Martigny.

▷ *Return to Salvan, then follow the Trient Valley as far as Les Marécottes.*

Les Marécottes

Les Marécottes 1923. ℘(0)27 761 31 01. www.marecottes.ch.
A mountain village with wooden chalets. A cable-car heads up to **La Creusaz** (alt. 1 777m/5 800ft), from where you can enjoy a panorama of Mont Blanc and the Valais Alps. Near the village, on the right as you come down the road, the **♣⚲Zoo des Marécottes** (◷*open mid-May–mid-Sept, daily, 9am–nightfall;* ◷*closed Mon & Tue in Sept and Oct;* ⊚*10CHF;* ℘(0)27 761 15 62; www.zoo-alpin.ch) is home to a wide variety of Alpine animals including chamois, reindeer, ibex, Valais goats and mouflons, llamas and bears.

GRAND-ST-BERNARD PASS★

From Martigny to the Great St Bernard Pass. 55km/34mi – allow approx 3hr30min. Bourg-St-Pierre 1946. ℘(0)27 783 32 48. www.saint-bernard.ch. ⊛Once beyond the fork in Bourg-St-Bernard the road demands careful driving because of its numerous bends. When the road is blocked by snow, tourists should travel via the tunnel. Swiss and Italian customs control are at the top of the pass in summer. Those using the tunnel will find the customs control all the year round at Gare Nord in Switzerland and Gare Sud in Italy.
The Great St Bernard Pass, connecting the valleys of the Drance and Dora Baltea, carries the most famous, historic transalpine route. The great tradition of hospitality has continued here since the 11C and such popular memories as that of Napoleon's crossing of the Alps in 1800 have drawn crowds. The opening of the tunnel beneath the pass has helped to separate the mass of hurried tourists crossing the frontier from the genuine pilgrims.
A short distance after Martigny, the road follows the deeply sunken Drance Valley as far as Les Valettes. The smallest valleys are still planted with vines and fruit trees (*ℂsee "VALAIS RHÔNE" box, p245*). The small road from Les Valettes to Champex is difficult. There are 22 hairpin bends, mostly sharp and awkward above the Durnant which flows through 1km/0.6mi of the impressive gorges (⊛*sightseeing facilities; inexperienced mountain drivers are advised to take the route via Orsières*).

Champex★★

Alt. 1 465m/4 806ft.
Champex stands high above the Orsières Basin at the mouth of a deep wooded valley containing a delightful lake. It is an elegant resort with views of a series of snowy summits; the Combin (Combin de Corbassière on the left, Grand Combin on the right). Those in search of views can see the range at their leisure while strolling along the Signal road connecting the hotel-belvederes of the resort. An alpine garden is open to visitors in summer.

La Breya★★

Alt. 2 374m/7 789ft. ⚡1hr30min there and back, including 15min by chairlift. ◷Operates mid-Jun–late Sept, 8.30am–12.30pm, 1.30pm–4.30pm; winter 9.15am–4.30pm. ⊚Fare there and back 12CHF; 151CHF for a 6-day pass. ℘(0)27 783 13 44.
A pleasant ascent by chairlift above Lake Champex; panorama of the Valais Alps.From Champex to Orsières, the winding, surfaced road (well laid out) within sight of the Combin Massif and the Valais foothills of the Mont Blanc sloping down to the Ferret Valley, lies between broad fields of strawberries. The scenery is wonderful.
The road passes **Bourg-St-Pierre** on its right, with its rust-coloured roofs nestling at the mouth of the Valsorey Valley and its waterfall. After crossing the Valsorey and its gorges, the road overlooks the Les Toules Dam of which there is a magnificent view (*a small section of the old pass road from Bourg-St-Pierre before you reach the dam is not surfaced*). Afterwards glaciated and striated rocks and rifts filled with landslides make the landscape more harsh.

Tunnel du Grand-St-Bernard

Entrance at Bourg-St-Bernard. Cars: 29.80CHF one-way, 47.40CHF there and back; motorbikes: 17.50CHF one-way, 23.60CHF there and back.

In view of the ever-increasing road traffic between the Rhône Valley and the Aosta Valley and to overcome the problem of snow blocking the road through the pass for over six months of the year, the Swiss and Italian governments combined to build a road tunnel, from 1959 to 1964, which would be open all year round and shorten the distance from Basel to Turin to 450km/279.6mi. Some sections of the road on the Italian side are not protected. Throughout the length of the road you can admire the daring construction of this freeway, with its viaducts high above the Artanavaz Gorges. Access roads on either side of the tunnel are generally covered and have a maximum gradient of 6%; they lead from below Bourg-St-Pierre on the Swiss side and above St Oyen on the Italian side.

After the Combe des Morts, it is a fast run to the Great St Bernard Pass (Col du Grand-St-Bernard).

Col du Grand-St-Bernard★

Alt. 2 469m/8 100ft.

The Great St Bernard hospice stands right at the top of the pass in a rocky gully, almost continually swept by an icy wind, on the edge of a lake which is frozen, on average, 265 days of the year and where the winter season lasts for more than eight months. It is open throughout the year to all travellers seeking a quiet haven.

The hospice was founded in 1050 as a refuge for those who had suffered at the hands of bandits or been victims of the mountain. Before the road, all supplies had to be carried by mules. The hospice continues to offer accommodation and meals to skiers, hikers, climbers, and all visitors.

The refuge exemplifies the survival of an admirable Christian tradition of assistance and hospitality. For nine centuries, the monks established here by St Bernard from Aosta—regular canons

belonging to the Augustinian Order—have taken in, comforted and rescued travellers in winter. A statue in honour of this "Hero of the Alps" has been erected at the summit of the pass, on Italian soil.

Church

This 17C Baroque church, fully incorporated into the hospice, was built on top of an early 13C sanctuary, presently serving as the crypt. The high altar is graced with statues of St Bernard and St Augustine. The carved walnut stalls and the painted vaulting in the chancel, wildly ornate with strong, bold colours, are characteristic of the Baroque period. The Holy Trinity is pictured surrounded by scenes taken from the New Testament: the Adoration of the Three Wise Men, the Annunciation and a Nativity scene. To the left, is the altar of St Bernard, bearing the gilt walnut casket containing the remains of the illustrious saint.

The **treasury** features a fine collection of sacred objects: a 13C polychrome bust-reliquary of St Bernard, sculpted in wood and ornamented with embossed gold and precious stones; a silver pilgrim's cross gilded and studded with gems (13–14C); a *Virgin and Child* dating from the 15C; and an illuminated 15C breviary.

ADDRESSES

STAY

MARTIGNY

Alpes et Rhône – *11 avenue du Grand-Saint-Bernard.* ℘*(0)27 722 17 17. www.alpes-rhone.ch. 50 rooms.* This hotel has a great restaurant serving international cuisine, using local and seasonal ingredients. There is also a bistro and a lovely terrace. Modern hotel conveniently located in the town centre.

Forclaz-Touring – *15 rue de Leman.* ℘*(0)27 722 2 7 01. www.hotelforclaz touring.ch. 100 rooms.* Family-run hotel in the heart of Martigny. From the La Coupole restaurant on the 7th floor you can enjoy panoramic views over the Rhône Valley. During various themed months Mexican, Indian, seafood or game dishes are served.

🍴🛏 **Mercure Hotel du Parc** – *19 rue Marconi. ℰ(0)27 720 13 13. 90 rooms.* Modern hotel with distinctly contemporary architecture. 5 mins from the town centre museums of the world renowned Gianadda Foundation. Sophisticated cuisine and wine bar.

GREAT ST BERNARD PASS

🍴🛏 **Glacier** – *Endweg. ℰ(0)33 853 10 04 www.glacierhotel.ch. 19 rooms.* This restored chalet, situated below the ski resort, is the starting-point for many excursions. The quiet, peaceful terrace commands magnificent views of the Eiger. Fine restaurant on-site.

🛏 **Fiescherblick** – *Hauptstrasse. ℰ(0)33 854 53 53. www.fiescherblick.ch. 25 rooms.* This grand old restored chalet serves generous helpings of tasty regional cuisine. Quiet, restful atmosphere, superb views and warm welcome guaranteed.

LES MARÉCOTTES

🍴🍴🛏 **Aux Mille Étoiles** – *ℰ(0)27 761 16 66. www.mille-etoiles.ch. 24 rooms.* A cosy chalet near the skiing pistes will welcome you during the winter season. Splendid views. Covered pool. Peace and quiet guaranteed.

♟/EAT

BARRAGE D'EMOSSON

🍴 **Restaurant du Barrage d'Emosson** – *Rossens. ℰ(0)27 768 12 74. www.emossonresto.com. Closed mid-Nov–Apr.* This secluded restaurant overlooking the dam is an ideal stop for a meal. Its exceptional location and breathtaking views of the surrounding mountains will strongly impress any visitor.

🍴🍴🛏 **Brasserie des Alpes** – *1937 Orsières. ℰ(0)27 783 11 01. Closed 13–27 Dec, 15–30 May, Tues & Weds.* Traditional brasserie run for the past 30 years by the Joris family, who make the most of local Valais produce, and also specialise in excellent risotto.

Restaurant on Place Centrale, Martigny

Stephan Engler/Switzerland Tourism

MARTIGNY

🍴 **Au Chapiteau Romain** – *51 rue du Bourg ℰ(0)27 722 00 57. Closed Sun and 1–20 Aug.* À la carte menu only. Raclette and fondue served in the cellar.

🍴🍴 **Les Trois Couronnes** – *8 place du Bourg 1.3km/0.8mi from Martigny. ℰ(0)27 723 21 14. ad3c@net.plus. Closed 1–13 Feb, 9–14 Aug, Sun–Mon.* Located in a historic building dating from 1609 in a small square with a fountain. Serves traditional cuisine in a modern rustic atmosphere.

🍴🍴 **Le Virage** – *3km/1.8mi on the road leading to the Col de la Forclaz. ℰ(0)27 722 11 53. www.surlescex.ch. Closed Wed.* This panoramic chalet-restaurant enjoys pretty views of Martigny and the Rhône Valley. Wide choice of traditional specialities.

🍴🍴 **Les Touristes** – *2 rue de l'Hôpital. ℰ(0)27 722 95 98. Closed 24 Dec–12 Jan, 27 Jun–20 Jul, Sun & Mon.* Two brothers run this in the centre of town. There's a separate bar, recently refurbished dining room and sunny terrace. Fresh, tasty food with a Mediterranean twist.

🍴🍴🛏 **Le Belvédère** – *Chemin Dessous 1927 Chemin. 4.5km/2.8m S via Route de Chemin. ℰ (0)27 723 14 00. www. le belvedere.ch. Closed Sun eve, Mon–Tue.* This pretty pink chalet-gazebo above Martigny has a bright veranda in pale wood where you can admire the Rhône valley. Meticulous cuisine whichi s good value for money. Pleasant café.

Verbier✳✳

Preceded by **Verbier-Village with its two churches,** the resort of Verbier is scattered over the sunny slope of the Bagnes Valley within view of the Grand Combin, the Dents du Midi and Mont-Blanc massifs, with luxurious hotels and traditional chalets in a glorious site✶. Its proximity to Geneva and good access to the Swiss motorway system makes it a popular weekend retreat year-round.

▶ **Population:** 2 163.
◔ **Michelin Map:** Michelin National Map 729: F7.
▤ **Info:** Place Centrale – 1936. ℘(0)27 775 38 88. www.verbier.ch.
◖ **Location:** Southwestern corner of the Valais region. Alt. 1 500m/4 921ft (resort).
⊛ **Don't Miss:** Mont Fort (international panorama), or Mont Gelé.
◷ **Timing:** The resort is very crowded during holidays.

VISIT

The cirque of regular slopes converging here offers ideal topographical and climatic conditions for the great majority of present-day skiers, who find spacious and restful surroundings and considerable mechanical equipment suitable for downhill skiing. Verbier is also known to long-distance skiers as the starting-point of the High Road run, of which Zermatt or Saas-Fee is the terminus.

SKIING AREA

Verbier is the main attraction of **Les Quatre Vallées** (the Four Valleys), a huge skiing complex boasting a total of 410km/254.7mi of pistes and 100 chair-lifts, one of the most interesting and varied Alpine ski resorts in Switzerland. A 150-person cable-car and an unusual lift combining a gondola and a six-passenger chair have enhanced uphill capacity significantly. The pistes around Verbier are fairly easy (Ruinettes and Savoleyres sector) but those on Mont Fort (highest summit of the complex), the Col des Gentianes, Mont Gelé, and the Plan-du-Fou Massif are recommended for experienced skiers (many steep slopes and bumpy sections). Some high-mountain itineraries are very impressive because of the austere landscape and the gradient of the slopes (Vallon d'Arbi from the Col des Mines, Mont Gelé, and Mont Fort toward Tortin and its legendary bumps). The long cruiser piste from Col des Gen-

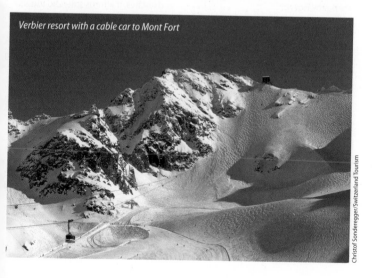

Verbier resort with a cable car to Mont Fort

Christof Sonderegger/Switzerland Tourism

tianes to La Chaux has fantastic views; this red piste and those from Savoleyres to La Tzoumaz and from Greppon Blanc to Siviez are ideal for intermediates. The resorts connected to Verbier (La Tzoumaz, Nendaz, Siviez, Veysonnaz, Mayens-de-l'Ours, Thyon, and Les Collons) offer gentle slopes more attuned to beginners. The adventurous should take the opportunity to go paragliding in tandem with an experienced pilot-guide.

EXCURSIONS
Mont Fort★★★
Alt. 3 329m/10 922ft. ⛷ *Access: by cable-car (allow 45min) from Verbier to Les Ruinettes; by shuttle (5min), or on foot (30min) up to La Chaux; by jumbo cable-car to Les Gentianes, then take another cable-car up to the top.* ⏰*Open daily 3 Jul–22 Aug, weekends late Aug & Sept, 8.45am–3.45pm; Dec–Apr, 9.15am–3.30pm.* ⛷*Fare there and back 34CHF, 49CHF for sunrise breakfast lift.* ☎*(0)27 775 25 11.*

A favourite with skiers and snowboarders for long-lasting snow and ice, including in summer, Mont Fort on a clear day offers a sweeping **international panorama★★★** (*viewing tables*) of the Alps, covering Italy (Matterhorn), France (Mont Blanc), the Valais (Mont Fort, Grand Combin) and the Bernese Oberland (Eiger).

Mont Gelé★★
Alt. 3 023m/9 918ft. *Access (about 45min) via cable-car from Verbier to Les Ruinettes, then change and take another cable-car to Attelas I and change again for Attelas II (near the top).* ⏰*Operates from mid-Dec–mid-Apr only, 9.40am–12.15pm, 1pm–3.30pm or 4pm.* ☎*(0)27 775 25 11.* From the cross, which indicates that you are at the rocky summit of the Mont Gelé, admire the **circular view★★**: to the south Grand Combin Massif and its glaciers; to the east Mont Fort and its glaciers; to the north the peaks of Les Diablerets; to the west the Pierre d'Avoi Mountain and below, Verbier and the Entremont Valley.

Round tour of the passes★
Starting from Sembrancher, 14km/ 8.7mi from Verbier.
When the weather is fair this excursion is very pleasant. The road continues through Vollèges (elegant bell tower), **Le Levron** (terraced mountain village), the passes of Le Lein (a rocky larch-filled hollow), Le Tronc and Les Planches (restaurant) and the tiny village of Vens (*join the road to Mauvoisin*). It is a forest road at the beginning (*unsurfaced for 5km/3mi between Le Levron and Les Planches Pass*), becomes a corniche and then passes through woods of fir trees and larches. It affords splendid **views★** of the neighbouring valleys, the Pierre

Summit of Mont Fort

Avoi Mountain (northeast), the snowy summits of the French Alps (Mont Blanc) to the southwest and the Pennine Alps (Grand Combin) to the southeast.

Barrage de Mauvoisin★★★
Alt. 1 961m/6 433ft. 30km/18.5mi Se of Verbier.

The Mauvoisin Dam, which blocks a wild ravine in the Upper Bagnes Valley, is one of the highest arched-type dams in the world (237m/778ft). This huge wall has created a reservoir of 180 million cu m/ 40 000 milliongal of water to feed the turbines of the Fionnay and Riddes power stations.

▶ *At Mauvoisin, make for the visitors' car park* P *halfway between the hotel and the dam. After parking the car, take the path to the crown of the dam.*

☜☝Walk to the Chanrion refuge★★
This strenuous walk (*6hr*) affords good views of the lake but requires hikers to be in excellent physical condition. It is possible to spend the night at the refuge to spread the outing over two days. Bear right and proceed down the long covered passageway (30min) then continue around the lake by a smooth path, walking for more than an hour. At the tip of the lake, you discover the Bec de Chardoney and the Bec de l'Épicourne. Go up to the refuge (1hr30min) by following the words "piétons" on rocks, then the "red and white" signposting. On reaching the top (alt. 2 462m/8 077ft), enjoy the **view**★★ of the Épicourne Glacier and, to the west, Mont Avril, Tour de Boussine, Combin de Tsessette (4 141m/13 586ft) and Tournelon Blanc, forming an imposing rocky barrier. The setting is enhanced by Lake Chanrion, where many plant and flower species thrive in this ideal location. Follow a charming path until the Col de Tsofeiret; the first part is relatively easy and offers **views**★ of the Brenay Glacier.

The pass (alt. 2 635m/8 645ft) affords a lovely **view**★ of Lake Tsofeiret. The expedition finishes by going down the gentle slope (2hr or more), glimpsing

Milk on Tap
In difficult hilly terrain such as the Swiss Alps, there can be a problem transporting large quantities of milk from the milking stations to the dairies. The resourceful Swiss farmers above Verbier have come up with an ingenious way of transporting milk by pipelines. These milk ducts, which run between the Alpine pastures and the dairies, have a total length of about 220km/138mi. Problem solved!

plunging **views**★★ of Lake Mauvoisin along the way.

ADDRESSES

🏃🏔SPORTS AND RECREATION
SUMMER ACTIVITIES
Summer is very popular for many sports and leisure activities. On Switzerland's largest state territory (296sq km/114sq mi), you can choose between **walks** covering altogether 400km/248.5mi: the most famous hike is the 🔲 **Sentier des Chamois**★★ between the Mont Fort refuge and Termin Pass. Moreover, 200km/124mi of lanes have been laid out for mountain bikes. Verbier also boasts facilities for hang-gliding and an 18-hole golf course. The **sports centre** (*rue de la Piscine;* ⏱*open daily 10am–9pm;* 🎫*8CHF;* ✆*(0)27 771 66 01*) features an indoor and an outdoor pool and a huge skating rink.

SIGHTSEEING
Tourists interested in traditional Swiss architecture can visit the picturesque villages of Bruson, Fionnay, and Sarreyer.

🎭EVENTS AND FESTIVALS
Verbier hosts one of the world's most prestigious classical music festivals to be held in a mountain setting (*last two weeks Jul, see www.verbierfestival.com for all times and charges. Some concerts free of charge*).

Sion★★

The attractive **site**★★ of the town of Sion has been inhabited for over 2 000 years: It can be fully appreciated when coming from Martigny or again when climbing to Savièze. The appearance of the two rocky Valère (Rhône side) and Tourbillon (mountainside) peaks, each crowned with episcopal fortresses, gives an immediate sense of history.

A BIT OF HISTORY
The Bishopric of Sion
The bishopric of Sion was founded in the 4C AD and played a key role in the religion and politics of the Middle Ages. In the early 11C the last King of Trans-Juran Burgundy, Rudolf III, made the bishop a temporal lord and a sovereign prince, enjoying full royal prerogatives: Dispensing justice, levying fines, minting coins. When the Communes were emancipated, these privileges disappeared one by one. However, until 1848 the Bishop of Sion was elected jointly by the canons and the Valais Diet, and subsequently by the Grand Council until 1918. Since then, the appointment has been the responsibility of the Vatican.

👣 WALKING TOUR
Allow half a day.

▷ *From Place de la Planta go along rue de Conthey before turning left onto rue St Théodule.*

Église St Théodule
Named after the first bishop of the Valais, the church was built under the episcopate of Matthäus Schiner at the beginning of the 16C. The vaults of the choir were decorated by the painter Hans Rinicher.

▷ *The Cathedral is adjacent.*

Notre-Dame du Glarier Cathedral
The 11C and 13C Romanesque **belfry**★ is adorned with Lombard arcades and

▶ **Population:** 29 304.
🚗 **Michelin Map:** Michelin National Map 729: G7.
ℹ️ **Info:** Place de la Planta 1950. ℘(0)27 327 77 27. www.siontourism.ch.
▷ **Location:** In the inner Valais plain. Alt. 512m/ 1 680ft.
🔭 **Don't Miss:** The church-fortress of Tourbillon surrounded by vineyards.
🕐 **Timing:** Allow a minimum of a day to take in the best of the sights; two days to fully enjoy the town.

ends in a graceful octagonal steeple. The ogive-vaulted nave was completed at the beginning of the 16C. The chancel contains 17C stalls and is decorated behind the high altar with a gilded wood **triptych**★ depicting the Tree of Jesse. To the northwest stands the Sorcerers' Tower (Tour des Sorciers), originally part of the medieval fortifications.

▷ *Walk along rue de l' Église and cross the rue du Grand Pont.*

Town Hall
👣*Guided tours of the town hall included in tour of the town.* 🕐*Open Mon–Fri 8am–noon, 2pm–5.30pm.* 🕐*Closed public holidays. For further information, contact the Tourist Office on ℘(0)27 327 77 27.*
The entrance of the 17C Hôtel de Ville is an elaborately carved wooden **door**. Roman inscriptions are exhibited in the entrance hall, one of which is Christian (377). The **Burgesses' Council Chamber**★ on the first floor has splendid woodwork and gorgeous furnishings.

▷*Ascend the rue des Châteaux.*

Art Museum
🕐*Open Tue–Sun, 1pm–6pm (5pm Oct–May).* 🕐*Closed 1 Jan, 25 Dec and following certain exhibitions.*

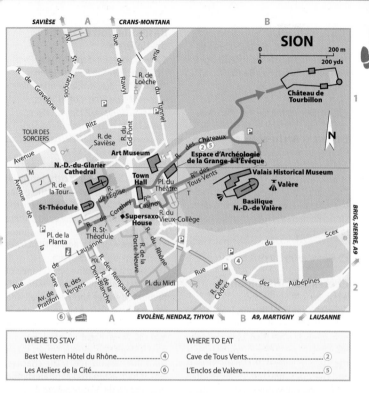

SAVIÈSE · A · CRANS-MONTANA · B

Av. St-François
R. de Gravelone
Rue du Ravyl
R. de Loèche
Rue du Tunnel
Ritz
R. de Savièse
R. du Gd-Pont
TOUR DES SORCIERS
Avenue
N.-D.-du-Glarier Cathedral
Art Museum
R. des Châteaux
Espace d'Archéologie de la Grange-à-l'Évêque
Château de Tourbillon
SION
0   200 m
0   200 yds
N
Town Hall
Pl. du Théâtre
R. des Tous-Vents
Valais Historical Museum
Valère
Basilique N.-D. de Valère
St-Théodule
R. de la Tour
R. de l'Église
R. de Conthey
Casino
R. du Vieux-Collège
Supersaxo House
R. St-Théodule
R. de la Porte-Neuve
R. du Rhône
Pl. de la Planta
Lausanne
R. des Remparts
R. de la Dent-Blanche
Rue
R. du Scex
R. des Cèdres
R. des
Aubépines
Av. de Pratifori
R. des Vergers
Pl. du Midi
BRIG, SIERRE, A9

EVOLÈNE, NENDAZ, THYON · A9, MARTIGNY · LAUSANNE

WHERE TO STAY	WHERE TO EAT
Best Western Hôtel du Rhône..................④	Cave de Tous Vents.................②
Les Ateliers de la Cité..................⑥	L'Enclos de Valère..................⑤

Vineyards of Sion with a view to the twin hills of Tourbillon and Valère

Roland Gerth/Switzerland Tourism

Guided tour first Thu in the month at 6.30pm. 5CHF. (0)27 606 46 99.
The Majorie and the Vidomat house the **Musée Cantonal des Beaux-Arts** (old prints, paintings by local artists).

▶ *Continue up the rue des Châteaux.*

Espace d'Archéologie

Same admission times as the Musée Cantonal d'Histoire. 4CHF. (0)27 606 47 00.
This small but interesting Museum of Archaeology exhibits carved prehistoric, Roman, and Greek artefacts from local digs.

▶*Ascend to the car park at the top.*

Château de Tourbillon★

Allow 1hr
From the car park, a path leads up to the imposing ruins of a former stronghold whose crenellated walls circle the hill. During the ascent (*rather steep*), the **view** of Valère, its church-fortress and the surrounding hillsides planted with vines, is breathtaking. The building and the chapel were erected in the late 13C by Bishop Boniface de Challant. Although originally defensive structure, the castle became a summer residence for bishops in times of peace. Repeatedly besieged and rebuilt in the 15C, it was razed to the ground by a terrible fire in 1788. After walking through a first doorway, pierced in a ring of ramparts, one enters the enclosure of the castle, dominated by its keep.

▶*Return to the car park.*

Valais Historical Museum★

Open Tue–Sun, 1pm–5pm. Closed 1 Jan and 25 Dec. 3CHF. (0)27 606 47 30.
Originally the canon's residence, this 12C castle, the interior of which was recently renovated, houses alternate exhibitions presenting the history of the Valais area.

▶ *The church is adjacent to the museum.*

Basilique Notre-Dame-de-Valère★

Open daily Jun–Sept, 8.30am–7pm; Oct–May, Tue–Sun 8.30am–6pm.
Guided tours available from mid-Mar–mid-Nov, Mon–Sat 10.15am, 11.15am, 12,.15pm, 2.15pm, 3.15pm, and 4.15pm, afternoons only on Sun. Closed 1 Jan and 25 Dec. 3CHF. (0)27 606 46 70/47 15.
The church, the former residence of the Chapter of Sion, is built on the top of the hill of Valère and overlooks the valley from a height of 120m/394ft. Inside the fortified area at the end of a ramp there is a terrace (*viewing table*) which affords a fine **view**★ of Sion and of the Lower Valais, looking downstream.
The church has all the appearance of a fortress, with its curtain wall, battlemented tower and north wall and internal wall-walk. Building began in the early 12C and continued until the mid-13C. Magnificent 17C **stalls**★★ with panels depicting various scenes taken from the Passion adorn the chancel, which has historiated capitals dating from the Romanesque period and 16C frescoes. Note the organ-loft and organ, this is the world's oldest still-functioning organ (1390), and is played every year at the International Festival of the Old Organ.

▶ *Descend to the lower town via the roulles des Tout Vents and Casino, cross rue du Grand Pont to rue de Conthey.*

Supersaxo House

Open Mon–Fri 8am–noon, 1.30–6pm. Closed public holidays. (0)27 327 77 27.
This sumptuous dwelling was built in 1505 by Georges Supersaxo, who wished to dazzle his rival, Cardinal Matthäus Schiner, with its luxury.
The house has a very large, high **room**★ with a radially patterned woodwork ceiling with a huge rose-shaped pendant in the centre showing the Nativity of Christ. Around the room are 12 alcoves containing busts of the Magi and the Prophets.

EXCURSIONS

Barrage de la Grande Dixence ★★★

400m/437.4yds downstream from the original work, at an altitude of 2 365m/7 759ft (crest of the dam). ℘(0)27 328 43 11. www.grande-dixence.ch.

The new Grande Dixence Dam, the greatest feat of civil engineering the Swiss have ever undertaken, is of the dead-weight type and 284m/932ft tall. The first Dixence Dam, 87m/285ft, completed in 1935, had a storage capacity of 50 million cu m/1 765 million cu ft feeding the Chandoline power station on the floor of the Rhône Valley opposite Sion with an average fall over 1 750m/5 700ft. This was already the most powerful hydroelectric installation in Switzerland and the biggest head of water in the world.

The dam has been built up in stages is now more than two and a half times the height of St Paul's Cathedral in London. About 6 million cu m/208 million cu ft of concrete were required—enough to build two Great Pyramids. A further part of the project involved drilling about 100km/62mi of underground tunnels to bring water from the foot of the Matterhorn Glacier. The water was then distributed not only to the new power station at Fionnay in the nearby Bagnes Valley, but also to the Riddes-Nendaz and Chandoline power stations in the Rhône Valley. The hydroelectric output of Switzerland has been increased by an annual 1 600 million kWh.

Lac Souterrain de St-Léonard

6km/3.5mi by on the road to Brig and then left; from the car park. Allow 10min on foot there and back. ◷Open 15 Mar–May 9am–5pm, Jun–Sept 9am–5.30pm, Oct–1 Nov 9am–5pm. ∞10CHF. ℘(0)27 203 22 66. www.lac-souterrain.com.

The lake and cave were formed by water infiltrating the gypsum bed and dissolving it little by little. The level of the lake is maintained by pumping (its dimensions are 300m/984ft long, 20m/65.5ft wide and 15m/49ft). The electric lighting enhances the site: The tormented relief and contrasting shades of colour (whitish gypsum, coal schist and gray marble) of the vaulting and rocky surfaces reflect onto the lake surface.

🥾 Alpe Bricola★★

Alt. 2 415m/7 923ft. 🅿 Park the car at Salay/Ferplècle. 2hr15min up, 1hr30min down. A comparatively easy ascent.

This outing offers lovely **views**★★ over the glaciers of Ferplècle, Mont-Mine and La Dent Blanche. For a sweeping panorama of the landscape, continue to climb a little higher toward the Dent Blanche Hütte refuge.

Barrage de la Grande Dixence

© Dawn Cranie/fotolibra

🏃 Cabane des Aiguilles Rouges★★

Alt. 2 810m/9 219ft. 3hr up, 2hr down. Check timetables in advance to get back to Arolla from La Gouille hamlet in the evening. 🅿 *Park the car at the foot of the Guitza ski lift. This lovely route requires considerable stamina over a variety of landscapes.*

Leaving behind the ski lift, proceed up a steep forest path commanding magnificent **views**★★ of Pointe de Tsa, Mont Collon and Pigne d'Arolla to a lovely path crossing an Alpine lawn (*avoid the winding lane*). After about 1hr, you reach the pretty perched village of **Remointse de Pra Gra** (2 479m/8 133ft), Start climbing towards the refuge, at the foot of the Aiguilles Rouges of Arolla (follow red signs when crossing the chasms).

The refuge affords a **sweeping panorama**★★ of the whole valley: the Aiguille de la Tsa, Pointe des Genevois, Dent de Perroc and La Grande Dent de Veisivi form a huge stone barrier.

The descent is steep leading down to the shores of **Lac Bleu**★★ (2 090m/6 857ft). Walk down to La Gouille hamlet and catch a bus back. 🚫*Avoid the path going from Lac Bleu to Arolla; it is both tiring and dangerous.*

🏃 Pas de Chèvres★★

Alt. 2 855m/9 367ft. 2hr up, 1h30min down, difference in height 850m/2 789ft. 🅿 *Park the car on leaving Arolla, just before you get to the highest chalet.*

Follow the lane for 50m/55yds, then take the steep path on the right, facing the slope, until you reach the broken-down hillocks (*40min*). Take the path opposite that winds its way through an open **landscape**, skirting the impressive Tsijiore Nouve Glacier and Pigne d'Arolla (3 796m/12 454ft). Around 30 min later, after crossing a track, the path becomes steeper. At the next fork, turn left. The pass offers beautiful **views**★★ of Mont Collon and the Aiguille de la Tsa. Go back down along the path on the right in the middle section, near the ski lift.

🚗 DRIVING TOURS

DERBORENCE ROAD★

24km/15mi. Leave Sion by S and follow road number 9 as far as Pont-de-la-Morge.

The road climbs through vineyards and crosses the villages of Conthey, Sensine and **St-Séverin** (church with stone bell tower) where you go left. After Erde, vineyards are replaced by shrubbery; in the bend before the Aven chalets is a good view of the Rhône Valley. After St Bernard's Church (last nice view of the valley), the road goes northward along the wild Triquent Valley, where the Lizerne runs.

After the first tunnel, there is a view of the Les Diablerets blocking the combe to the north, The landscape is picturesque with snowfields here and there, pine trees, a torrent (the Lizerne, which the road crosses three times) surrounded by erratics, cascades.

The valley then opens into a **cirque**★★ of rocks, pine and larch. Bear left onto the rocky path, which ends in the Derborence Nature Reserve in a rock **corrie**★ created in the 18C, after an avalanche of the Les Diablerets.

SANETSCH PASS ROAD★★

33km/20.5mi. Leave Sion by S and follow road 9 to Pont-de-la-Morge.

After crossing the Morge, the narrow road through the vineyards climbs to Chandolin, offering views of neighbouring slopes covered with vineyards and the Rhône Plain. At the Pont du Diable the corniche descends, meets up with the torrent and then enters a landscape with fir trees and a lovely cascade.

At the junction of the road to Conthey (on the left), the rocky Crêta Besse summit stands straight ahead. A steep climb (15%—1 in 6.5) through woods ends at the chalets of Plan-Cernay.

2km/1mi farther, in front of the Zenfleuron Inn, the road crosses the Morge and in a corniche stretch passes the east slope, and after a tunnel, a **view** of the valley and at the opposite end

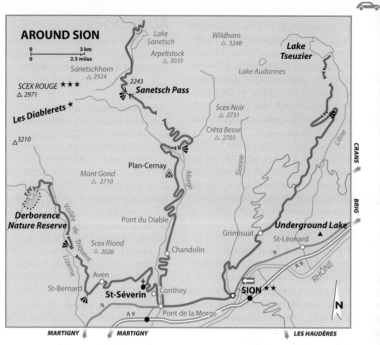

AROUND SION

0   3 km
0   2.5 miles

Lake Sanetsch
Wildhorn △ 3248
Lake Tseuzier
Arpelistock △ 3035
Lake Audannes
Sanetschhorn △ 2924
SCEX ROUGE ★★★ △ 2971
2243 **Sanetsch Pass**
Scex Noir △ 2731
Les Diablerets ★
Crêta Besse △ 2703
△3210
Plan-Cernay
Morge
Sionne
Liène

CRANS
BRIG

Mont Gond △ 2710
Derborence Nature Reserve
Pont du Diable
Underground Lake
Grimisuat   St-Léonard
Scex Riond △ 2026
Chandolin
9
RHÔNE
A 9
Vallée de Triquent
Lizerne
Aven
St-Bernard   St-Séverin   Conthey   SION ★★
9   Pont de la Morge
A 9

N

MARTIGNY   MARTIGNY   LES HAUDÈRES

onto the mountaintops (where three torrents tumble from melting glaciers). This is followed by a climb which opens, before the second tunnel, at the foot of the rocky face of the Sex Noir facing the snowy barrier of Les Diablerets.
After the last tunnel, the route continues its spectacular climb to the **Sanetsch Pass** (2 243m/7 359ft; lovely **view**★★ of Les Diablerets preceded by the Tsanfleuron Glacier), then descends to and halts at the dam's reservoir (Sanetsch Lake).

TSEUZIER ROAD★

23km/14mi. Leave Sion on the road to Crans-Montana to the N.

3km/1.8mi after Grimisuat bear left onto the road to Ayent and at St-Romain follow the narrow but easy road signposted Barrage de Tseuzier, which climbs amid fir trees above the Liène Valley and soon offers some lovely glimpses of the valley and the terraced resort of Crans-Montana beyond (a wide **view**★, especially at the entrance to the first tunnel).
At the end of the road *(restaurant)* is the small lake of Tseuzier Dam in its rocky basin.

VAL D'HÉRENS★★

29km/18mi – about 2hr
(see THE VALAIS map).

The Hérens Valley is one of the most accessible of the lateral valleys in French-speaking Valais. The Évolène district, located in a very fine setting of high mountains, overlooked by the Dent Blanche (alt. 4 357m/14 290ft), has retained many traditional local customs. Sights like that of haymaking between Évolène and Les Haudères are among the most attractive in picturesque Switzerland. When you see the women working in the fields or driving herds of cows, you are often tempted to forget the rigours of their mountain life. The men seldom feature in these pastoral scenes. Most of them find work in local timber yards or factories.

Skiing Area

In winter, skiers can tackle 100km/62mi of downhill runs, two cross-country skiing tracks (33km/20.5mi) and two open-air ice rinks.
From Sion, crossing the Rhône and leaving on the right the Chandoline

power station, fed by the Grande Dixence Dam, the road climbs in hairpin bends, affording good views of the site of Sion, marked by the fortified heights of Valère and Tourbillon. On arriving at **Vex**, the first village in the Hérens Valley, the superb rock pyramid of the Dent Blanche begins to emerge from the Ferpècle Corrie.

The road, which runs almost horizontally along a ledge, approaches the ravines overlooking the confluence of the Borgne and the Dixence. The eye will be caught by the astonishing ridge of broken country from which the Pyramids of Euseigne spring.

Pyramides d'Euseigne★

The road passes through a tunnel under the crowned columns cut out by erosion from masses of soft morainic debris and saved from destruction by their unstable, rocky crowns. The valley shrinks and the gradient grows steeper. Arrival in the Evolène Basin is marked by the reappearance of the Dent Blanche. To the right of the Dent Blanche, in the foreground, stand the twin sharp-edged pyramids of the Dents de Veisivi.

Évolène★

Alt. 1 400m/4 593ft.

The tall, flower-decked **wooden houses**★★ of this resort are among the finest in the Valais. Évolène is a popular mountaineering centre (Mount Collon and the Dent Blanche Massifs) with a climbing school in the village.

Les Haudères

The chalets stand in picturesque disorder. From here roads lead to **Ferpècle** (alt. 1 770m/5 807ft; 9km/5.6mi from Les Haudères), at the foot of the Dent Blanche, and Arolla (12km/7.4mi) at the foot of Mont Collon. The road passes through the hamlets of La Sage, Villa and La Forclaz, with their beautiful slate-roofed chalets, and offers clear views of the Upper Hérens Valley.

ADDRESSES

Despite the growth in tourism in Sion over the past few years, the choice of hotels in the town remains limited.

STAY

Les Ateliers de la Cité – *6 avenue de la Gare, Sion.* ℘*(0)27 324 41 41. 13 rooms.* This accommodation offers a new type of hotel service which is primarily targeted at businessmen. However, its tasteful and well equipped studios are also convenient for holiday makers, plus the prices for two people are very competitive.

Best Western Hôtel du Rhône - *10 rue du Scex, Sion.* ℘*(0)27 322 82 91. www.bestwestern.ch/durhonesion. 44 rooms.* 🚗. A hotel in the middle of Sion with modern rooms. A comfortable option even if not the most charming.

Hôtel des Vignes – *9 rue du Pont, Uvrier 1958 (5km/3mi E of Sion). ℘(0)27 203 16 71. www.hoteldesvignes.ch. 39 rooms.* 🚗. *Closed Sun even and Mon.* A really charming hotel just a stone's throw from Sion, in its own grounds with vineyards closeby. Good size airy rooms.

EAT

SION

Cave de Tous Vents – *16 rue des Châteaux* ℘*(0)27 322 46 84. www.cave-tous-vents.ch. Closed in Aug, Mon in May–Jun.* Dining in the lovely cellar which dates from the 13C, you can enjoy dishes from the Valais region.

L'Enclos de Valère – *18 rue des Châteaux.* ℘*(0)27 323 32 30. www.enclosdevalere.ch. Open May–Sept, closed Sun eve and Mon, Oct–Apr, closed Sun and Mon.* Good quality French restaurant with one of the best terraces in Sion. During the summer guests will appreciate its calm and shade.

NEARBY

Relais du Mont d'Orge – *La Muraz (NW by route de Savièse). ℘(0)27 395 33 46. www.ricou.ch. Closed hols, one wk end of Jun, Sun eve and Mon.* Modern cuisine with a good choice of Valais wines.

Sierre

Sierre is one of the sunniest cities in Switzerland. It lies in the Valais Rhône, below the vineyards of the Noble Country (Noble Contrée) and at the mouth of the Val d'Anniviers. A huge landslide in prehistoric times explains the unique site★ of the town, in a landscape like "a gravel pit dug and turned over with a spade." Sierre (Siders) marks the language boundary between French and German Switzerland (&see INTRODUCTION: Language and Religion).

▶ **Population:** 15 574.
& **Michelin Map:** Michelin National Map 729: G7.
▌ **Info:** Place de la Gare 10. &(0)27 455 85 35. www.sierre-salgesch.ch.
▶ **Location:** Valais region, southwestern Switzerland. Alt. 534m/1 752ft.
& **Don't Miss:** Château de Villa.
◷ **Timing:** The city is crowded during the international festival in May and early June.

A BIT OF HISTORY

Several strongholds such as the Castle of the Vidômes and the Goubin Tower, perched on its rock, recall the part played by Sierre at the time of episcopal and feudal Valais. Shortly before his death in 1926, the Austrian poet **Rainer Maria Rilke** stayed in the former Château de La Cour, which now houses the town hall.

SIGHTS
Hôtel de Ville

Formerly a manor house and a hotel, the town hall dates from the 17C and 19C. The **interior**★ is sumptuous in its decoration (elegant painted ceilings, frescoes, paintings and stained-glass windows) and yet it retains a certain intimacy. It houses a small museum: The **Musée des étains** (◷open Mon–Fri, 9am–11am, 3pm–5pm; ◷ closed on public holidays in the Valais canton; ◌no charge; &(0)27 452 01 11) Set up in the cellar, it displays approximately 180 pewter objects (tableware, utensils) from the 17C–19C.

Rue du Bourg

A small picturesque street with old houses. Note the unusual building with bartizans, known as the Château des Vidômes and the Catholic Church of St Catherine (17C–19C). Inside the church are a Baroque chancel, a carved pulpit and a lovely organ loft. At number 30, on the ground floor, the Maison Pancrace

de Courten houses the **Fondation Rainer Maria Rilke** (◷open Mar–Oct, Tue–Sun 2pm–6pm; ◌6CHF; &(0)27 456 26 46; www.fondationrilke.ch), a tribute to the Austrian poet, who is buried nearby (&see RARON, p283).

Château de Villa

The **Musée Valaisan de la Vigne et du Vin** (◷open 27 May–Nov, Tue–Sun 2pm–5pm; ◷closed in winter; ◌5CHF; &(0)27 456 45 25; www.museevalaisan-duvin.ch) has been set up in one of the château outbuildings. The visit to the

The International Comics and Graphic Art Festival

Every year, in late May and early June, the city of Sierre celebrates the joy of reading by staging a world festival devoted to comics and strip cartoons. Writers, illustrators, publishers and second-hand booksellers all gather in Sierre to attend Sismics. This popular festival also involves many exhibitions, street performances and concerts combining originality and humour. Children will be delighted since they, too, are included in the festivities, with a wide choice of games, quizzes, make-up workshops and drawing competitions.

Wine Museum begins with a video film about traditional techniques for pressing grapes. The two following rooms are devoted to wine presses. The second one explains the work of people employed in the cellars. The visit ends with a display of the different types of containers (bottles and labels, pewter pots, barrels) associated with the business of wine and the role it has played in society throughout the ages.

EXCURSIONS
Salgesch
▶ *From Sierre head E, take Gemmistrasse and then Unterdorfstrasse towards Salgesh.*

A 6km/3.8mi-long **Wine Route** linking Sierre to Salgesch (**Salquenen** in French) enables you to discover part of the vineyard. The route is dotted with signposts which describe the different grape varieties (Chasselas, Pinot, Sylvaner, Malvoisie), the quality of the soil, the various pruning methods and the long-standing tradition of *vignolage* (a day's work in the vineyard in springtime, accompanied by fife and drum music). In this quiet village, the 16C **Maison Zumofen** (🕐*open Apr–Nov, Tue–Sun, 2pm–5pm;* 🕐*closed Dec to Mar;* 🎫*5CHF;* 📞*(0)27 456 45 25)*, easily recognisable by its double-gabled wooden roof, presents an exhibition which complements those of the **Musée Valaisan de la Vigne et du Vin** in Sierre. Several rooms enlighten visitors on the art of winemaking: Soil, grape varieties, techniques and tools used in wine making, and finally grape harvesting, conducted with the blessing of St Théodule, the patron saint of this noble profession.

Kippel★
▶ *Leaving Sierre take the E62 E and after 18km/11.2mi turn off to Gempeland head N to Kippel.*
6 Rue Pré-Fleuri, Sion. 📞*(0)27 327 35 70. www.valaistourism.ch.*

This is the most typical village in the the remote Alpine valley of Lötschentala and visitors not pressed for time may want to spend the whole day here. In the area around the church are numerous blackened **wooden houses**★★ with delicate friezes of dog-tooth and rosette patterns. The crowds which gather for High Mass make Sundays and feast days most spectacular events for lovers of folklore, but the Corpus Christi Procession (🔖*see Calendar of Events*), with its procession of God's Grenadiers, is the most colourful spectacle. For this occasion flags are flown and the local men bring out their old-fashioned outifts, including plumes, bearskin caps and belts.

The valley remained cut off from the outside world until the Lötschberg railway tunnel was built between Kandersteg in the north and Goppenstein, in 1913. The River Lonza flows southwards through the valley to join the Rhône. In the past, when it was extremely difficult to maintain an open road in the lower sections of the valley, because of the frequent avalanches, the main access was by passes at an altitude of 2 500m/8 200ft. The people of this remote valley remain very attached to their traditional way of life.

Crans-Montana★★
Alt. 1 500m/4 921ft. 13km/8mi NW of Sierre. Avenue de la Gare, Montana – 3962. 📞*(0)27 485 04 04 and Crans-sur-Sierre – 3963.* 📞*(027) 485 08 00. www.crans-montana.ch.*

This resort, formed by the neighbouring towns of Crans and Montana, extends for 2km/1.2mi along a wooded plateau dotted with small lakes, facing the impressive backdrop of the Valais Alps. Seen from Montana, the Valais Alps give the impression of rising from the near background, whereas in fact the Rhône Valley lies between them and the observer. The road to Crans-Montana from Sierre is a succession of hairpin bends, climbing through vineyards and then pastures. On reaching Montana, motorists wishing to return to the floor of the Rhône Valley by a different road can find their way down along the by-road from Crans to road number 9—an interesting route which offers fine views of the Pennine Alps. Its splendid location, facing due south at an altitude of

1 500–1 700m/ 4 921–5 577ft, was initially responsible for the development of luxury hotels and sanatoria between the two wars. It was here that **Katherine Mansfield** stayed in 1921 and wrote some of her charming stories (*The Garden Party, The Doll's House*). Renowned for its skiing, Crans-Montana attracts visitors, who can spend their time away from the slopes playing golf or squash, or window-shopping in the many luxury boutiques. Despite its cosmopolitan attractions, the resort lacks the charm of a traditional Alpine village. However, in summer waymarked footpaths allow visitors to escape the modern buildings and busy roads in search of more typically Alpine scenes. *A map of footpaths (a total of 280km/174mi) is available from the Tourist Office.*

The skiing area – The skiing area of Crans-Montana, consisting of 160km/ 99.4mi of slopes served by 41 lifts, including four gondolas, is one of the most important in Switzerland. It is especially popular among beginners and intermediate skiers for its wide, groomed trails. Experts will find many off-piste opportunities, tree-skiing through the forest and some mogul sections around Bella Lui and La Toula. However, the most superb skiing slopes are on the Plaine Morte, which offers opportunities for skiing both in winter and summer, and where the vertical drop is considerable (1 500m/4 921ft to the resort). There are also opportunities for **cross-country skiing**, with 50km/31mi of loops extending over the lovely wooded plateau of Crans at Aminona and the Plaine Morte Glacier. A funicular (12min) connects Crans-Montana with Sierre.

Excursions and walks from Crans-Montana

Bella Lui★★
Alt. 2 543m/8 340ft. ⏏*Access by cable-car. 1hr30min there and back. Cable-car leaving from Crans and Montana.*
🕐*Service to Cry d'Er 8.30am–4.30pm, Jul–mid-Sept. Departure every 20min.*
🚟*Fare there and back 22CHF.*
📞*(0)27 485 89 10.*

Stop at Croix (or Cry) d'Er (alt. 2 263m/ 7 422ft with TCS viewing table) for a magnificent ascent by cable-car over the Rhône Valley, with a great panorama of the Valais Alps. To reach Bella Lui by foot, take the path from Vermala to Cry d'Er (2hr45min) around Mont Lachaux, then carry on to Bella Lui (45min).

Aminona
Alt. 1 515m/4 969ft.
This small modern resort, to the east of Montana, is the departure point for the **centenary walk**, designed in 1993 to commemorate the resort's centenary. This easy walk (*4hr30min there and back*) winds its way through parks and forest and crosses Crans-Montana by La Comba (1 428m/4 684ft) and Les Mélèzes (1 450m/4 756ft). Three orientation boards give information on the surrounding peaks of Brig and Martigny. *A bus service operates back to the resort.*

Petit Bonvin★★
Alt. 2 400m/7 873ft. Access by cable-car from Aminona. **View★★** of the Crans-Montana surrounded by spruce, the Bella Lui, the Grand Combin and the Dent Blanche.

Vermala★★
Alt. 1 670m/5 479ft. 1.5km/1mi.
🅿*Leave your car below the Café-Restaurant du Cervin and go to the viewpoint on the right, at the edge of a small escarpment.*
Enjoy a bird's-eye view of the Rhône Valley with a sweeping panorama of the high summits enclosing the Val d'Anniviers (especially the Weisshorn and the Zinalrothorn and, in the far distance, the Matterhorn).

Housed in an old Alpine chalet, the small **Colombire Museum** recalls life in the mountains in the 1930s, with information on cheesemaking and other rural activities. *Snacks available, guided walks at dawn, plus a typical mountain breakfast.* This chalet is the departure point for the **Bisse du Tsittoret**, an easy walk suitable for children across fields and through woodland (*4hr30min there and back*). Take the path toward the Marolires, Courtavey, Colombire caves and the Tièche (alt. 1 969m/6 460ft).

Plaine Morte★★★

9min by the Violettes Express cable-car reaching an altitude of 2 267m/7 437ft (Barzettes Station). Then take the Funitel to reach Plaine Morte. 5min on foot up a short but steep slope.

The summit (alt. 3 000m/9 843ft) affords an exceptional **panorama**★★★ of the Valais Alps. To the southwest loom the Grand Combin, Mont Blanc and, on the distant horizon, the Meije (on the frontier with the southern French Alps). To the north extends the gently sloping Plaine Morte Glacier, dominated by the Wildstrubel (3 243m/10 639ft).

Plans Mayens★★

Alt. 1 622m/5 322ft. 1.5km/1mi.
It's possible to stop at the edge of the road, beside the terrace of the Restaurant du Mont-Blanc.

A wide panorama of the Valais Alps extends to the Mont-Blanc Massif in the distance. A picturesque walk (3hr 30min) can be followed from here along the old **Bisse du Ro** up to Er de Chermignon (1 733m/5 684ft). ✋*The path is steep in parts and not suitable for children or those who suffer from vertigo.* Follow the path near the Hôtel de la Dent-Blanche. Return to Crans-Montana via Pra du Taillour and the Pas de l'Ours.

🚗 DRIVING TOURS

DALA VALLEY

28km/17mi. Allow 1 hour. Leave Sierre on road number 9, heading E.

Leuk

Alt. 750m/2 461ft. Bahnhof 5.
𝒞(0)27 473 10 94. www.leuk.ch.

Leuk sits above the Rhône Valley at the mouth of the Dala Gorges. The first stronghold encountered on entering the town is the Château des Vidommes: vidames were secular deputies appointed to command armies or to represent the interests of French abbots or bishops under the Ancien Régime.

This building has become the town hall. From the castle's esplanade there is an astonishing view★ of the valley floor. The great fluvial cone of rubble from the Illgraben, covered with a mixture of heath and forest vegetation (Forest of Finges or Pfynwald), stands below. This obstruction still forms the natural boundary between the French-speaking Central Valais and the Upper Valais with its German-Swiss culture.

Farther on, the 15C Château des Majors still features its square crenellated tower.

 Continue towards Leukerbad and turn left in to a narrow road to reach Albinen.

Albinen

This picturesque village is one of the most beautiful in the Valais. It contains a number of wooden houses that cling to the steep, sunny side of the Rhône valley.

◐ *Continue heading N.*

Leukerbad⚜

Alt. 1 411m/4 628ft. Rathaus.
𝒞(0)27 472 71 71. www.leukerbad.ch.

This high-altitude spa was discovered by the Romans. It nestles in a grandiose **site**★, overlooked by the Gemmi Pass and approached from Leuk via a narrow, often vertiginous road. It was this austere landscape that inspired French author Guy de Maupassant to write his fantastic tale, *L'Auberge*. Bare rocky peaks overlook the valley, which is dotted with attractive chalets and pastureland.

The **Skiing Area** *(50km/31mi of downhill runs and 25km/15mi of cross-country tracks)* extends across the Gemmi and Torrent ranges, at an altitude between 1 400m/4 592ft and 2 800m/9 184ft. Leukerbad is particularly renowned for its **spa**, the largest in Europe, whose sulphurous, calcareous and gypsum-rich waters are recommended for the treatment of rheumatism, circulatory diseases and skin problems. The resort is popular year-round with tourists, who come here to bathe in thermal waters (51°C/124°F at source and between 28°C/82°F and 44°C/111°F in the pools).

🧖 Burgerbad

This spa complex houses an indoor thermal bath and a pool for children, a gym and a bar-restaurant. Outdoor facilities include a swimming pool, two thermal baths, a 70m/230ft water slide, Jacuzzis, a footbath, and a sauna in a grotto.

Lindner Alpentherme

Opened in 1993, this fitness centre has indoor and outdoor thermal baths, a swimming pool, plus a complex where visitors can choose between showers, hot-air baths, massage, steam baths, Jacuzzis, and cold-water baths.

Gemmi Pass
Alt. 2 314m/7 590ft.
Linked to Leukerbad by cable-car, this pass begins in Kandersteg in the Bernese Oberland and ends on the slopes of the Valais in a vertiginous road cut out of the rock, offering superb **views**★ of the Valais and Bernese Alps.

SIERRE TO ZINAL★

67km/42mi. Allow 2hrs. Leave Sierre to the S, heading towards Vissoie.

Val d'Anniviers★
Sierre-Anniviers Tourisme, 3960 Sierre. ✆(0)84 884 80 27. www.sierre-anniviers.ch.

Val d'Anniviers lies between the majestic Weisshorn, Zinalrothorn, Obergabelhorn and Dent Blanche mountains. The valley is known for the extraordinary nomadic habits of the people, continually on the move between the vineyards of the Rhône Valley, the main villages (Vissoie, for instance), mid-mountain pastures known as **mayens** and the Alps.

St Luc✳
Converted into a winter sports resort, the viewing platform at the village entrance offers an impressive **view**★★ of the valley and the mountain range dominated by Mount Marais (2 412m/7 915ft) on the left and Mount Boivin (2 995m/9 825ft) on the right.

Chandolin✳
Alt. 1 936m/6 348ft.
Chandolin is approached by the new village, a ski resort consisting of modern yet traditional chalets. Continue on foot to the old village, which is one of the highest permanently inhabited mountain villages in Europe. From here there is a splendid **panorama**★★ of the Valais Alps (from left to right: Zinalrothorn, Besso, Ober Gabelhorn, the Zinal Peak and the Dent Blanche).

Beyond Chandolin, the road climbs the west face of Roc d'Orzival, which at times becomes a breathtaking *corniche* overlooking the ravine. At the bottom flows the Navisence.

View from Gemmi Pass onto Weisshorn, Matterhorn, and Dent Blanche

Lucia Degonda/Switzerland Tourism

◯ *Return to Vissoie and drive S on the road to Grimentz.*

Grimentz✳
This resort faces the Corne de Sorebois, which separates the Zinal and Moiry valleys. It has preserved several *mazots* or *raccards* (👆 *see p240*), some of which date back to the 15C, and a beautiful **mansion** (1550). In summer, traditional festivals add to the atmosphere and In mid-August, Grimentz is the end of the longest **mountain bike race** in the world, the famous Grand Raid Cristalp. The resort has four waymarked Mountain biking trails, ranging in distance from 12km/7.4mi to 24km/15mi. The start of the **Bendolla** trail can be reached by cable-car, at 400m/1 312ft above the resort.

Grimentz
© Laura Frenkel/Dreamstime.com

Val de Moiry★
13km/8mi from Grimentz.
This valley is an extension of the Val d'Anniviers. After 2km/1.2mi there is a lovely waterfall on the left. At 4km/2.5mi there is a **view**★ of Grimentz and the Anniviers Valley. Less than 1km/.06mi further, the **Moiry Dam** is visible in front of the Dent Blanche; from the middle of the dam (alt. 2 249m/7 379ft) there is a **view**★ of the reservoir, the Pennine Alps and their glaciers. Continue along the road (👆 *poor road surface—drive cau-*

tiously), with its many small waterfalls. Overlooking the reservoir, at the end of the dam, there is a striking **view**★ onto the Moiry and **Zinal** glaciers. The road ends at a small lake facing the **Moiry Glacier**.

Walk to Cabane de Moiry★★★
Alt. 2 825m/9 269ft.
🔌*Allow 2hr45min on foot there and back from the end of the road (*🅿*car park at 2 409m/7 904ft).*
The route first follows the left side of the Moiry Glacier at a reasonable gradient. It runs along a moraine, leading to a refuge after a steep climb. The Cabane de Moiry offers a magnificent **view**★★★ over the Pigne de la Lé (3 396m/11 143ft), Les Bouquetins (3 662m/12 015ft), Grand Cornier (3 962m/13 000ft), Dent des Rosses (3 613m/11 854ft) and the Pointe de Moiry (3 303m/10 837ft). The upper part of the Moiry Glacier sparkles under a thick layer of snow. Experienced hikers can continue (*an added 2hr15min—follow the cairns and yellow signposts*) to the edge of the glacier, for pretty views of the Col de Pigne. In dry, favourable weather (enquire at the refuge beforehand), seasoned climbers may continue to the top. The final section involves walking on *névés* (👆 *remember to bring an ice pick or a stick*). The pass (alt. 3 140m/10 303ft), dominated by the Pigne de la Lé, affords a superb sweeping **panorama**★★★ of the Zinal Valley (Weisshorn, Besso, Zinalrothorn).

◯ *Return to Grimentz and take the road to Zinal.*

Vallée de Zinal★★
The road offers a superb **view**: In the foreground lies the Zinal Valley with the town of Ayer high up on the east side, extended northward by the Val d'Anniviers and in the far distance the Wildstrubel. The valley then narrows and seems to shrink beside the overwhelming Weisshorn Mountain. After crossing the Navisence, the road passes through **Zinal**, and ends 2km/1.2mi farther on at Tsoudounaz, in a small corrie at the foot of the Zinal Glacier.

Zinal ✳
Alt. 1 670m/5 445ft.

Located high up in the mountains, Zinal is a multi-season resort including six villages: Ayer, Mission, Mottec, Curianey, La Combaz, and Les Morands. Zinal is circled by the Imperial Crown, formed by the summits of Weisshorn, Zinalrothorn, Besso, Obergabelhorn, Cervin, and Dent Blanche. Since the 19C it has enjoyed a good reputation as a mountaineering centre. It also offers wonderful opportunities for walking and hiking, with a total of 200km/125mi of signposted paths. The skiing area, virtually unknown outside Switzerland, is powder paradise dominated by the Weisshorn. While there are slopes catering for all levels, Zinal has become a haven for free-riding. It is situated between 1 670m/5 479ft and 2 895m/6 835ft. A skiing pass also accesses the other facilities in the valley (Chandolin, St-Luc, Grimentz, Vercorin), including 46 ski lifts and around 200km/125mi of pistes. Cross-country skiers can enjoy a 12km/7.4mi circuit.

Soreboiss ★★
Alt. 2 441m/8 008ft.

🚠 *Access by cable-car from Zinal: 5min.*
Lovely views of the Mont Durand, the Obergabelhorn, the rocky pyramid of Besso, the imposing Zinalrothorn and, farther to the left, the Weisshorn.

Walk to Petit Mountet ★★★
🚶 *4hrs30min from Soreboiss. Only attempt in dry weather.* ⚠️ *Take care at the start of summer, when damp terrain can be slippery. Turn left on disembarking the Zinal cable-car at Soreboiss.*
The path hugs the side of the moutains and offers a continuous selection of stunning views. After about two hours walking and near the hut, take in a vista of the Col de la Dent Blanche and the peaks of Zinal and Cervin.
At 2 142m/7 000ft is another hut, and from here you pass waterfalls and ever thicker vegetation.

ADDRESSES

🏨 STAY

NEARBY
🛏️ Hôtel Arkanum –
1 Unterdorfstrasse- Salgesch. 📞(0)27 451 21 00. www.hotelarkanum.ch. 28 rooms. 🚗. Seven of the rooms in this hotel are decorated with a wine theme—the beds (very comfortable they are too) are set into a barrel, a wine press and even a vat. The standard rooms are also pleasant. Very good value.

AT SIERRE
🛏️ Hôtel Le Terminus – *1 rue du Bourg. 📞(0)27 455 13 51. www.hotel-terminus.ch. 20 rooms. Closed 2 weeks end of Jun and during Christmas hols. 🚗.* This is really the only decent hotel in the town. The rooms are elegant and decorated with style. The hotel is particularly renowned for its gastronomic restaurant, and its chef Didier de Courten. The hotel's brassserie L'Atelier gourmand is excellent.

🍽️ EAT

🛏️ Château de Villa – *4 rue St Catherine. 📞(0)27 455 18 96. www.chateaudevilla.ch. Daily 10am–1pm, 4.30–8.30pm. Closed 24, 25 and 31 Dec and 1 Jan.* Dishes from the Valais, seasonal menu, raclette. Nicely located in the grounds of a 16C château.

🚴 SPORTS AND LEISURE
👥 HAPPYLAND THEME PARK
This theme park in **Granges** offers 13 rides over an area of 25 000 sq m/27 340 sq yd. Attractions include giant twisting waterslides, Splash River log ride, water jets for older children and a hot air balloon ride. Those who like thrills will want to ride the Low-G helicopter, and aspiring racers take a turn at the wheel of the Auto Moto Formula VS (🕐*open daily 11am–6pm weather permitting;* 🎫*25CHF (22CHF 3–12 years old); 📞(0)27 458 34 25; www.happylandnew.ch).*

Zermatt✶✶

The hooked pyramid of the **Matterhorn** (alt. 4 478m/14 692ft) dominates the centre of Zermatt, situated in the Nikolaital Valley. The mountain has strongly influenced the development of this old mountain village, "discovered" a century ago by the British and launched as a resort in 1855 by the Seilers, a family of hotel-keepers.

A BIT OF HISTORY
Edward Whymper

In the 1860s, Edward Whymper, a young British illustrator thrilled by the mountain shapes had been wandering over the Alps of the Valais, Savoy, and Dauphiné, looking for unconquered peaks. He always came back to Zermatt or the Valtournanche, fascinated by the Matterhorn, which he had already vainly attempted eight times, starting from Breuil with the help of a well-known local guide, Jean-Antoine Carrel.

In 1865, changing his plan of action, Whymper decided to attack the peak along its northeast ridge. On 13 July three British climbers and a guide from Chamonix—Douglas, Hudson, Hadow and Michel Croz—joined Whymper and his two guides from Zermatt and set off for the mountain. Helped by ideal weather, the climbers set foot on the summit of the Matterhorn on 14 July. The climbers began their descent. Suddenly, young Hadow, the least experienced member of the party, slipped, dragging Croz, Hudson and Douglas with him in his fall. The life-line between Douglas and the elder Taugwalder snapped. Whymper and his guides watched the fall of their four companions, 1 200m/4 000ft below. An impressive celestial phenomenon, the appearance of two crosses shining in a great arc of clouds, is said to have appeared before they regained the valley.

RESORT

Zermatt is renowned as an important mountaineering centre, with a dozen peaks over 4 000m/13 120ft within easy access of the resort. It is popular with visitors of all nationalities. The resort is traffic-free, with the exception of small electric vehicles and horse-drawn carriages and sleighs. Zermatt can be reached only by rail either from Brig or Visp (Viège) where most visitors leave their cars, or from Täsch (5km/3.5mi from Zermatt), which has a car park.

SKIING AREA

Zermatt is one of Switzerland's most spectacular ski areas, in part for the view of the Matterhorn from several of the pistes and the opportunity to ski into Italy. It is defined by three high summits with a vertical drop of 2 300m/7 546ft on the Italian side (*a separate lift pass must be purchased for Cervinia, and it should be accessed only in fine weather to prevent being stranded there unable to return to Zermatt*) and 2 200m/7 218ft on the Swiss side. The 260km/161.5mi of gently sloping pistes combine high

▶ **Population:** 5 775.

Michelin Map: Michelin National Map 729: H7.

Info: Bahnhofplatz – 3920. ℰ(0)27 966 81 00. www.zermatt.ch.

Location: The main street runs the length of the village from the train station at one end to the cablecar station at the other. Alt. 1 616m/5 302ft.

Parking: This is a car-free village; you must park down the valley at Täsch and take the electric train the remaining 8km/5mi to the village.

Don't Miss: The view of the iconic Matterhorn from the Stockhorn.

Kids: Children under 9 travel free on all lifts and cable-cars.

Timing: At least two days for skiing (winter) or rambling (other seasons).

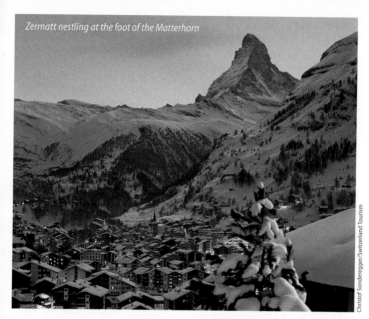

Zermatt nestling at the foot of the Matterhorn

Christof Sonderegger/Switzerland Tourism

and medium altitude slopes. **Telemark** skiing is now one of the resort's specialities. The highest summit is the **Klein Matterhorn** (3 820m/12 533ft), open for both winter and summer skiing along the Theodulgletscher (glacier); the slope here is groomed smooth and ideal for intermediates. Piste *20b* is especially recommended for its splendid views. The **Hörnli** is the starting-point for several excursions.

The **Gornergrat** Massif offers easy slopes near the railway tracks. Experienced skiers will be challenged on the **Rote Nase** (3 247m/10 653ft) and the Stockhorn (3 407m/11 178ft), featuring a difference in height of 1 200m/3 937ft. Finally, the **Rothorn** (3 103m/10 180ft) provides pistes suitable for intermediate skiers, in particular those numbered 22b and 23. There are also 90km/56mi of winter hiking and snowshoeing trails (6 sign-posted trails totalling 26km/16mi) and 9k/5mi of prepared trails for cross-country skiing.

SIGHTS
Bahnhofstrasse

The main street, from the railway station to the parish church and the lower cable-car, is lined with fine hotels, shops, and restaurants. Note the medallion dedicated to Whymper on the façade of the Monte Rosa Hotel, opened in 1855 and a favourite with British high society. Beyond the main street, the quieter district of **Old Zermatt** is dotted with typical Valais chalets and toast-coloured *mazots*. Solar-powered buses and horse-drawn sleighs are the alternative to walking.

Matterhorn Museum

○*Open week after Easter–Jun, 10am–noon, 2pm–6pm; Jul–Sept 11am–6pm; Oct 2pm–6pm; mid-Dec–Easter, Sun–Fri 3pm–7pm.* ○*Closed Nov–mid-Dec.* ✇*10CHF.* ✆*(0)27 967 41 00.*

Recently re-opened in the former casino, entered through the garden of the Grand Hotel Zermatterhof, at the end of the Bahnhofstrasse, the museum incorporates the ongoing archaeological excavations of the old town.

In this experiential environment, the history and nature of the Matterhorn is explored from its geologic origins through the many explorations by climbers. Multi-lingual audio guides and lively video shows brings both the mountain and the town to life for all ages.

VIEWPOINTS ACCESSIBLE BY LIFT

A one-day pass for all lifts below is 119CHF; two-day is 136.50CHF.

Klein Matterhorn★★★

Alt. 3 886m/12 749ft. Access by three successive cable-cars. Allow half a day to discover the panoramas and a whole day if you combine the visit with an excursion. In winter, it can take 2hrs to get to the summit because of the queues. The departure station, accessible by shuttle service or on foot (15min), is at the far end of Zermatt. Departures from Zermatt every 20min, 8am to around 5pm. Fare there and back: 95CHF. (0)27 966 64 64.

The first section has a view straight ahead from the mid-station of **Furi** (alt. 1 865m/6 119ft) to Zermatt. This site has a number of *mazots* and inns, which are open in summer and winter. The second section is within view of the Cervin before ending at **Trockener Steg** (alt. 2 929m/9 610ft), where the **Theodulgletscher★★** can be seen.

The last cable-car climbs over the glacier and stops at the highest altitude station in Europe. The actual summit (3 885m/12 746ft) can be reached by a lift and several flights of steps. The 360° **panorama★★★** is truly breathtaking. To the west: Mont Blanc, Mont Maudit, Les Grandes Jorasses, Grand Combin, Dent d'Hérens, and the iconic Matterhorn; north: Zermatt, Dent Blanche, Obergabelhorn, Zinalrothorn, Dom and the Täschhorn. In the far distance are the Jungfrau, Mönch, and Aletschhorn. The most spectacular sight is the long ice tongue of the Gorner (to the east) and the Breithorn (4 160m/13 648ft), Castor (4 226m/13 865ft) and Pollux (4 091m/13 422ft) summits.

Breithorn★

Alt. 4 164 m. 2hrs30min walk one way. From the Matterhorn Glacier (*see below*) it is possible to reach the summit of the Breithorn, the easiest of the area's 4 000m peaks.

It is not necessary to be an experienced alpinist but hire a guide and be prepared to use crampons. You will need to be fit, to wear appropriate mountain gear and take sun screen.

Schwarzsee★ (Lac Noir)

Alt. 2 582m/8 461ft. Half a day's walk. Cable-car from Schwarzsee. Departures from Zermatt every 20min. Fare there and back: 43.50CHF. (0)27 966 64 64.

From Furi a cable-car goes up (*5min*) to the foot of the Matterhorn, which is mirrored in this small lake. A path goes around it. On its shore stands a chapel. The Black Lake is the starting-point for interesting walks toward Zermatt

Majestic Peaks

Some Swiss mountains over 4 000m/13 123ft:

◆ **Mount Rosa (Valais)**	4 634m/15 203ft
◆ **Dom (Mischabel; Valais)**	4 545m/14 911ft
◆ **Weisshorn (Valais)**	4 505m/14 780ft
◆ **Matterhorn (Valais)**	4 478m/14 692ft
◆ **Dent Blanche (Valais)**	4 357m/14 295ft
◆ **Grand Combin (Valais)**	4 314m/14 153ft
◆ **Finsteraarhorn (Valais)**	4 274m/14 022ft
◆ **Aletschhorn (Valais)**	4 195m/13 763ft
◆ **Breithorn (Valais)**	4 165m/13 665ft
◆ **Jungfrau (Bern-Valais)**	4 158m/13 642ft
◆ **Mönch (Bern-Valais)**	4 099m/13 448ft
◆ **Schreckhorn (Bern)**	4 078m/13 379ft
◆ **Piz Bernina (Graubünden)**	4 049m/13 284ft
◆ **Lauteraarhorn (Bern)**	4 042m/13 261ft

(☞see below). Return to Furi via Stafel and Zmutt.

Gornergrat★★★ ❋

Alt. 3 135/10 272ft. 🚃*1hr40min by rack railway there and back.* 🕐*Open Jun– Oct, 7am–7pm, departures about every 30min.* 🎫*Fare there and back: 76CHF.* ✆*(027) 922 43 11/966 48 11.* ⏱*Allow the whole day if you combine this trip with a walk or the ascent of the Stockhorn.* 🚡*Cable-car from Gornergrat to Stockhorn. Departures every 24min, summer 7.10am–7.55pm (5.55pm mid-Jun to late Oct).* 🎫*Return fare: 67CHF.* ✆*(0)27 921 41 11.*

The steep Gornergrat rack railway is the highest open-air railway in Europe, offering fantastic sweeping **views**★ of Zermatt. After the Riffelberg stop, where there is a very good view of the Matterhorn, you can see **Monte Rosa** (crowning summit: Dufourspitze at 4 634m/15 203ft) and its glaciers. Enjoy the breathtaking **panorama**★★★ of the numerous tongues of ice and the Valais. The excursion can be rounded off by the ascent first to Hohtälli (3 286m/7 499ft), then to **Stockhorn**★★★ (3 405m/11 129ft) in two successive cable-cars (*1hr there and back*). If you do not suffer from vertigo, walk from Gornergrat to Hohtälli, following a narrow **mountain path**★★★ for truly breathtaking views.

Rothorn★★

Alt. 3 103m/10 180ft. 🚡*From Zermatt by funicular (access by a long corridor) to Sunnegga, then by cable-car to Blauherd and then again by cable-car (20min including 5min by funicular).* 🎫*60CHF.*

The funicular climbs through a tunnel (3min) to **Sunnegg**★ (alt. 2 285m/ 7 497ft), on the edge of a plateau of Alpine pastures enhanced by a small lake. Here you get your first glimpse of the Matterhorn (southwest). From **Blauherd** (alt. 2 577m/8 459ft), the second mid-station, in view of a lovely fir forest (on the right), the cable-car arrives on the flat, rocky summit of the Rothorn. From here the spectacular

panorama★★, barred to the east by the Oberrothorn, stretches southwest to the Matterhorn, south to the Findelen Glacier, west to Zermatt, and north to the Nikolaital Valley.

🚶WALKING TOURS

There are around 400km/250mi of footpaths crossing forests and Alpine pastures, dotted with villages, lakes, and glacial cirques.

From Schwarzsee (Lac Noir) to Zermatt★★

🚶*There is a vertical drop of 900m/ 2 952ft down to Zermatt or 700m/ 297ft down to Furi. Remember to wear sturdy mountain shoes. Allow at least half a day. Access to Schwarzsee by cable-car then 5min on foot.*

After walking for a few minutes, you reach a second, smaller lake, a fantastic **setting**★★. Follow the path, which continues to dip steadily: it affords remarkable **views**★★ of the Matterhorn, the Zmutt and Arben glaciers, as well as the Dom and Mont Rose. After 30min walking, keep to the left-hand path then take the track on the right. This steep route brings you to Stafelalp (inn at 2 200m/7 217ft). Then there is a steep descent following the edge of the forest. Ramblers can either walk down to the pretty village of Zmutt or continue toward Furi and then the Gorner Gorges.

From Lac Vert (Grünsee) to Grindjisee and Leisee★★

🚶*Access to Riffelalp (alt. 2 200m/7 218ft) is via the Gornergrat cog train. An easy walk: a half day or full day with variants. Return by the funicular from Sunnegg★.* From Riffelalp, a good path along the edge of the forest takes just 45 minutes to reach Lac Vert, from where there are fantastic views of the Matterhorn, the Dent Blanche, the Obergabelhorn, the Zinalrothorn and the Weisshorn. Another 45 minutes on is the Grindjisee (alt. 2 334m/7 658ft). Experienced walkers can complete the circuit of the lakes by taking a detour by the Stellisee—another 200m of ascent to 2 537m/8 324ft. Complete the day by exploring the traditional hamlet of Eggen, before tackling a short but steep ascent to the beautiful Leisee lake, (2 200m/7 218ft). From this lake climb another 10 minutes to **Sunnegg**★ to catch the funicular railway down. (75 minutes to descend to Zermatt on foot).

Gorges du Gorner (Gornerschlucht)

🏃 *A 2hr walk. From the S side of Zermatt, turn left by the bridge and then follow the signs.*
℘ (0)27 966 81 00. www.zermatt.ch (Zermatt Tourist Office).
This steep path overlooks superb gorges. It passes through forests of arolla pine and larch until it reaches the pretty village of Blatten. After Zumsee take the path which leads you back to Zermatt.

From Riffelberg à Zermatt★★

🏃 *950m of descent which takes 2hr. Take the cog train from Gornergrat.*
The walk to Riffelalp boasts superb alpine scenery. Follow signs to Zermatt through larch and pine forest.

EXCURSION
Stockhorn village

Several **houses**★ of the most majestic Bernese type lend distinction to the entrance to this village on the Spiez side (ℹ*see INTRODUCTION: Rural Architecture*).

Stockhorn★★★   – *5:30 pm*

🚠*Access by cable-car (25min).*
🕐*Operates May–Oct, 8.10am–5.40pm; Dec–mid-Mar, 11.10am–5.10pm (9.10am Sat–Sun); mid-Mar–late Mar, Sat–Sun 9.10am–5.10pm.* 🚠*Fare there and back 3CHF. ℘(033) 681 21 81.*
From the top of Stockhorn (alt. 2 190m/ 7 185ft) is one of the loveliest **panoramas**★★★ in the Oberland. From Erlenbach to the mid-station of Chrindi (alt. 1 637m/5 374ft), the cable-car goes through a valley lined with chalets. From the upper station, walk (*15min return*) to the summit of the Stockhorn. Look

to the north to see Lakes Thun, Amsoldingen and Allmendingen; to the south, Stockensee and Oberstockensee and all around, the legendary white summits of the French and Swiss Alps from the Jungfrau to Mont Blanc.

ADDRESSES

🛏STAY

🛏 **Hotel Jaegerhof** – *Steinmatte 85.* ℘*(0)27 966 38 00. www.hoteljaegerhofzermatt.ch. 45 rooms.* This charming chalet-style hotel is family-owned. Traditional rustic pine décor. Cosy, quiet, and attentive service.

🛏🛏🛏 **Seiler Hotel Schweizerhof** – *Bahnhofstrasse 5.* ℘*(0)27 966 00 00. www.summithotels.com. 95 rooms and suites.* In the heart of the village, owned by the prominent Seiler family, this modern hotel is old-fashioned in style. Also noteworthy for its indoor pool.

🛏🛏🛏 **Christiania** – *Wiestistrasse 7,* ℘*(0)27 966 80 00. www.christiania-zermatt.com. 72 rooms.* Located in the centre, but in a quiet setting, the hotel is good for families, with an indoor pool and play areas. The terrace, dining room, and many of the rooms have picture-perfect views of the Matterhorn.

🍽EAT

🍽 **Walliserstube** – *Gryfelblatte 2.* ℘*(0)27 967 51 11.* Rustic décor, specialises in fondue: cheese, bourgignon (with meat), and chinoise (vegetables). Popular with families.

🍽🍽 **Le Gitan** – *Bahnhofstrasse 64.* ℘*(0)27 968 19 40. www.legitan.ch.* Watch the chef grill racks of lamb, chicken, skewers of meat, and giant prawns in the open kitchen of this casual and centrally located family-run restaurant, which also has a cosy bar.

🍽🍽🍽 **Le Mazot** – *Hofmattstr 23.* ℘*(0)27 966 06 06. www.lemazotzermatt.ch. Closed Mon and late-Apr to mid-June and late Oct.* Traditional grilled specialties and excellent service in a charming old farmhouse. Reservations recommended.

Saas Fee✳✳

Nicknamed the "Pearl of the Alps", Saas Fee enjoys a magnificent setting★★★, where the mountains suddenly and dazzlingly soar to over 4 000m/13 123ft high. The view ranges from the icy dome of the Allalinhorn to the flattened, snow-capped summit of Alphubel and the rocky group of the Mischabel (highest point: Dom—alt. 4 545m/14 941ft, recognisable by its forked peak). Below, the huge Fee Glacier (Feegletscher) divides into two tongues around the rocky promontory of the Längfluh.

▶ **Population:** 1 675.

🜚 **Michelin Map:** Michelin National Map 729: H7.

🛈 **Info:** Postfach 3906 Saas Fee. 𝒫(0)27 958 18 58. www.saas-fee.ch.

◖ **Location:** Southern Valais region. Alt. 1 790m/5 873ft.

🅿 **Parking:** Cars are not permitted in Saas Fee. Park on the outskirts and walk or use electric carts within the town.

⊗ **Don't Miss:** Mittelallalin.

🕔 **Timing:** Allow at least one full day to see the highlights of the area.

A BIT OF HISTORY

Saas Fee is a well-known mountaineering centre. For the sports enthusiast who likes ski touring it has become the terminal of the famous **Haute Route** (Chamonix—Saas Fee, or more often Verbier—Saas Fee). This quiet village became a fashionable resort in the 19C, thanks in part to the abbot Johann Josef Imseng (1806–69), whose statue is in the church square. In his spare time, he acted as a guide, taking tourists into the mountains. He was even heralded as the "best skiier in Switzerland" in 1849, when he skied down the Saas Fee slopes to Saas Grund on wooden skis of his own construction.

SKIING AREA

The Saas Valley covers 145km/92mi of pistes suitable for **downhill skiing**. Beginners will find easy slopes on the edge of the resort and along the Fee Glacier extending down to Längfluh. Do not miss a visit to **Egginerjoch**. In **winter**, the cable-cars of Plattjen and Längfluh serve the area; the Feldskinn cable-car works in **summer** and

Resort of Saas Fee surrounded by soaring mountains

Saas-Fee Tourism/Switzerland Tourism

since 1984 an underground funicular has been operating to **Mittelallalin** (alt. 3 500m/11 483ft). There is an 11km/6.8mi toboggan run, plus air boarding and snow tubing, and ski-joring for experienced skiers (who are pulled by horses). Opportunities for **cross-country skiing** and winter hiking include more than 50km/31mi of prepared trails. The car-free village helps make Saas Fee a favourite for families.

SIGHTS
Saaser Museum
🕐 *Open Mon–Fri 2pm–5pm.*
💶 *5CHF.* ✆ *(0)27 958 18 58.*
This former vicarage (1732) houses a museum devoted to life in the Saas Valley. Local traditions are explored through reconstructed interiors, farming implements, local costume, liturgical objects, minerals, and photographs. Special attention is paid to the development of the spa: The growing expansion of tourism, accommodation, climbing, winter sports and the introduction of new equipment.

EXCURSIONS AND WALKS
Mittelallalin★★★
🕐 *Allow half a day.*
👓 *Remember to dress warmly (trousers, jacket, sturdy mountain boots) and to bring sunglasses.*
Take the Alpin Express cable-car, which affords sweeping views of the Saas Fee resort. Continue the climb up in the funicular (alt. 3 500m/11 482ft). Go to the upper station of the **revolving restaurant** (the highest in the world), where you can enjoy the **panorama**.
🚶 Follow the track marked out in the snow (*in summer only*) behind the restaurant. It dips over 100m/328ft and then climbs up to a rocky crag, dominating the glacier (*20min on foot there and back*). Be sure you use the handrail. To the south and west, the view encompasses the Allalinhorn (4 027m/13 211ft), the Feekopf, the Alphubel, and the Dom. To the north are Saas Fee and Saas Grund lying below at the foot of the Fletschhorn, and the Lagginhorn and the Bernese Oberland (Jungfrau). To the

east, the Hohlaub and the Allalin inch their way toward the Mattmark Dam.

👥 Pavillon des Glaces★
🕐 *At Mittelallalin; 30min tour.*
This 5 000sq m/5 975sq yd cave hollowed out of the Fee Glacier is the highest in Europe. It is a delightful walk in varied icy surroundings with many galleries and rooms embellished with sculptures, ice waterfalls, explanatory texts, and play areas for children.

Egginerjoch and Britanniahütte ★★★
🚶 *Allow 1hr20min.*
From Felskinn (2 998m/9 840ft), the lower station of the cable-car, there are walks through the snow and along the glacier (*it is essential to wear sturdy mountain boots and to bring a walking stick*). After 20min, you will reach **Egginerjoch Pass★★** (2 989m/9 813ft), lying at the foot of the red pyramid of the Egginer. Farther on, the route wends its way against a rocky and glacial backdrop, sometimes difficult to negotiate owing to poor or non-existent snow coverage, especially in late August and September (*enquire beforehand at the Tourist Office*). A 40min stroll will take you to **Britanniahütte** (3 029m/9 935ft), which commands a superb **view★★** of Lake Mattmark, flanked on the right by the lovely tongues of ice of Hohlaub, Allalin and Schwarzberg, and on the left by Stellihorn. The most breathtaking **panorama★★★**, encompassing the whole landscape, can be seen from a promontory on your left.

Plattjen
Alt. 2 570m/8 432ft.
Access by telecabin. Just five minutes walk from the arrival point there are **views★★** across to the Saas glaciers and the man made Mattmark dam.

From Plattjen to Saas Fee★★
🚶 *Allow 1hr45min.*
An easy walk near Berghaus Plattjen, with a beautiful descent through the woods (larch, pine trees, Norway spruce) and rhododendrons.

Längfluh★★★

Alt. 2 870m/9 416ft. ⛰Access by the Gondelbahn Spielboden cable-car, then the Luftseilbahn Längfluh cable-car. Längfluh offers wonderful **views** of the Fee Glacier. Note the lovely panorama of the Täschhorn. There is a restaurant at the site.

Hannig★

Alt. 2 350m/7 709ft.
⛰Access by cable-car.
Lovely **view**★ of Saas Fee, Saas Grund, Saas Almagell and the Fee Glacier to the south, with the Fletschhorn to the northeast. There are many opportunities for interesting walks. In winter, you can return to the resort on foot or by the fine **sledge piste**. In summer, Hannig is the starting-point for fascinating hiking (🚶) toward **Mellig**★ and **Gebiden**★★ (alt. 2 763m/9 064ft, 1hr15min climb). Views of the Hohbalm Glacier dominated by the Nadelhorn (4 327m/14 194ft). Then 3hr30min climb down to Saas Fee via the Bärenfälle waterfalls.

Hohsaas★★★

Alt. 3 098m/10 164ft. Park the car in Saas Grund (alt. 1 560m/5 118ft), a small mountain resort located below Saas Fee. ⛰Access by two cable-cars. 🚶Allow 1hr 45min there and back.
As you walk, enjoy the pretty **views**★★ of the Saas Grund skiing area. The summit affords wonderful **views**★★ of Lagginhorn, the Hohlaub Glacier and Weissmies (4 023m/13 197ft). This peak is frequently used in competitions. Walk up toward Geissrück (15min) for a better view of the stunning séracs. Take in the **panorama**★★★ from Mont Rose to Dürrenhorn, featuring 18 summits above 4 000m/13 122ft.

From Kreuzboden to Saas Fee★★

🚶3hr walk with a 850m/2 788ft drop in altitude as you proceed downwards.
From Kreuzboden (alt. 2 397m/7 863ft), the first cable-car section, take "Höhenweg" in the direction of Almagelleralp. This path, meandering its way across

the slope, is bordered by a small alpine garden (edelweiss, astragalus, gentian, juniper berry). After about 1hr, you will discover broad **views**★★ of the Saas Fee glacial cirque and Lake Mattmark. Note the impressive avalanche barrier. A little farther on, you will come across a path, which you follow, heading downwards toward Saas Grund.
Leave it after 15min and choose a track on the left, marked out as "Alpenblumen-Promenade". This somewhat steep slope, dotted with edelweiss, ends in a forest of larch trees.

Lac de barrage Stausee Mattmark★★

🚗Alt. 2 200m/7 218ft. Take the car or bus to Saas Grund.
A small road runs for some 12km/7.5mi in peaceful country side, through Alpine meadows and woods. There are lovely **views**★★ of the Saas-Fee glaciers. From the parking area at the end of the road, a five minute walk takes you to the left hand side of the dam wall which is 780m/853ft long.
From the lake there is **view**★★ of the four glaciers - Hohlaub, Allalin, Schwarzberg and Seewjinen, plus many waterfalls. Also note the Almagellhorn.
A path takes you around the **lake**— allow 2hr30min.

Monte Moropass★★

🚶Alt. 2 868m/9 409tf. This is a 3hr15min ascent and a 2hr45min descent for good walkers.
Follow the Mattmark lake to its end, which takes about an hour. Then take the narrow path which has is a steady climb, up to the Monte Moro col. After about 45 minutes you will come out onto a flat section of ground from where you can see the mountain. Continue to the right. The access is steep and ends up in a boulder field so ensure you follow the red and white markers.
From the col, where a statue of the Virgin Mary has been erected there is a superb **view**★★ of Mont Rose and its glaciers.
Retrace your steps and upon reaching the lake, take the other bank to return.

ADDRESSES

⌂STAY

⊜♨ **Dom** – ✆(0)27 958 77 00. www.uniquedom.com. 40 rooms. Modern, well situated hotel with ample amenities and a "Popcorn Bar" that hosts live music. Kids will love the the in-room computer consoles ♟♟.

⊜♨ **Rustica** – ✆(0)27 957 21 75. www.hotelgletschergarten.ch. 11 rooms. Family-run B&B-style lodgings in the heart of the resort; private baths for all rooms.

⊜♨🛏 **Imseng** – ✆(0)27 958 12 58. www.hotel-imseng.ch. 22 rooms. Features indoor pool, on-site bar, and lounge with fireplace.

♀/EAT

⊜♨ **Drehrestaurant Allalin** – ✆(0)27 957 17 71. www.drehrestaurant.ch. Accessible via Alpin Express cable-car, the world's highest revolving restaurant serves a variety of Alpine specialties.

⊜♨ **Hohnegg's Fondue-Hütte** – ✆(0)27 957 22 68. www.hohnegg.ch. Closed May–Nov. Reached by 15min hike from town, serving cheese and meat fondue and Valaisian Raclette.

⊜♨🛏🛏 **Waldhotel Fletschhorn** – ✆(0)27 957 21 31. www.fletschhorn.ch. Located a 30min hike from the town centre in a forest clearing. Award-winning food. Ideal for a relaxing meal with amazing views. Cooking courses.

Brig

Brig is located at the confluence of the rivers Rhône and Saltine. This charming town is a lively stopping-place at the junction of the Simplon road and the road to the Rhône Glacier and the Furka Pass. The railway station is important, as it stands on the frontier at the north end of the Simplon Tunnel, the longest rail tunnel in the world (19.8km/12.3mi). Brig is also on the route of the famous Glacier Express linking Zermatt and St Moritz.

A BIT OF HISTORY
The King of the Simplon

Brig owes its great attraction to the ideas and ambitions of **Kaspar Jodok von Stockalper** (1609–1691) who came from a Valais family, traditionally the guardians of the Simplon Defile. Through his enterprise Stockalper amassed great riches from the trade route over the Alps during the Salt Monopoly. He was courted by emperors and kings, but his wealth and success made him enemies and he fled to Italy, leaving his proud fortress unfinished. He returned to Brig to die a respected but ruined man.

▸ **Population:** 12 162.
⬙ **Michelin Map:** Michelin National Map 729: H7.
🛈 **Info:** Bahnhofplatz 1 – 3900. ✆(0)27 921 60 30.
◗ **Location:** Brig is located at the confluence of the River Rhône and River Saltine. Alt. 681m/2 234ft.
🞝 **Don't Miss:** Take an hour or two to visit the open-air thermal baths at Brigerbad, 5km/3mi west of Brig, between Viège and Gamsen (www.brig-belalp.ch).

SIGHT
Stockalperschloss

🗝Guided tours (45min) May–Oct, Tue–Sun, hourly from 9.30am–10.30am, 1.30pm–4.30pm. ◷No visit at 4.30pm in May and Oct. 🎟8CHF. ✆(0)27 921 60 30. www.brig-belalp.ch.

Once the largest private residence in Switzerland, it can be recognised from afar by its three towers with bulbous domes, standing where the road to the Simplon begins. The first building you encounter as you come from the centre of Brig is the Stockalper family dwelling early 16C), flanked by a fine watchtower. The imposing main building (built over the original warehouse by the "Great Stockalper") features eight storeys, including cellars, linked to the smaller house by a picturesque gallery with two tiers of arcades.

The main **courtyard**★ is surrounded by open galleries in two or three storeys. The three towers arranged around it, with their plain stonework, stand in sharp contrast to this elegant building.

EXCURSION

Raron

▶ Drive W from Brig on the E62. 18km/11.25mi. 20min.

The hamlet of Raron or Rarogne (named after an influential feudal family from the Valais) spreads at the foot of a rocky spur. The village centre features a group of pretty 16C and 17C houses made with stone and wood. A steep path leads to the top of the hill.

Near the old tower, which is all that remains of the former castle, stands the 16C **Burgkirche**, clearly dominating the valley. Inside the church, a naïve fresco illustrates the Last Judgement. Note the demons, who have been portrayed in the costumes of Swiss mercenaries. The Austrian poet Rainer Maria Rilke is buried in the cemetery. At the foot of the hill, a small modern church has been carved out of the rock.

🚗 DRIVING TOURS

GOMS★★

54km/33.5mi – allow approx 2hrs. The road that follows the Furka-Oberalp railway at a distance may be blocked by snow between Brig and Oberwald for short periods. Furkastrasse. ℘(0)27 970 10 70. www.goms.ch.

Conches Valley (**Val de Conches** in French or **Goms** in German) begins at Fiesch. The road, as it climbs up the Upper Rhône Valley, enters mountainous terrain; it serves the numerous resorts and ski lifts hanging on the side of the Aletschhorn Massif.

From Brig to the Grengiols fork, the road runs close to the foaming Rhône at the bottom of a narrow, winding cleft. It passes by the large, isolated Baroque **Hohen Flühen Chapel** and serves the lower stations of the Riederalp-Greicheralp cable-car (starting from Mörel) and that of **Bettmeralp**. These lines serve a high Alpine plateau (alt. 2 000m/6 500ft), wonderfully situated within view of the Valais Alps and close to the Aletsch Glacier, the most extensive in the Alps (169sq km/65sq mi with its tributaries).

Riederalp✳, Moosfluh★★

🚠 *Access to Riederalp by cable-car from Mörel; access to Moosfluh by chairlift*

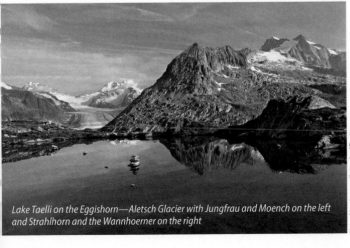

Lake Taelli on the Eggishorn—Aletsch Glacier with Jungfrau and Moench on the left and Strahlhorn and the Wannhoerner on the right

Christof Sonderegger/Switzerland Tourism

283

from Riederalp. ◷*Operates summer, 8am–6pm; winter, 9am–4.30pm.* ⊜*Fare there and back 16CHF.* ℘*(0)27 928 68 11.*

Located in a **site**★ overlooking the Rhône Valley on the valley's north side, the **Riederalp**❋ chalets and hotels are terraced, beginning at 1 930m/6 332ft, and face the mountain range separating Switzerland from Italy. Above its westernmost point stands Villa Cassel, a Victorian-style mansion (1902), now the centre of the **Aletschwald Nature Reserve** with exhibitions on the nature reserve and its larch and arolla pine forests, which are among the highest in Europe. Visitors can also learn about the history of the Aletsch Glacier, which can be visited on excursions organised by the centre.

▶ *From the cable-car's arrival station, walk (a few minutes) to the chairlift's departure station to go to Moosfluh.*

The chairlift passes by the mid-station of Blausee, before arriving at the upper station of **Moosfluh**★★ (alt. 2 335m/7 661ft), set amid a jumble of green rocks and dominating the spectacular curving form of the **Grosser Aletschgletscher**★★★, immediately to the north at the foot of the slopes and tributary glaciers of the Aletschhorn Massif, as well as the Rhône Valley to the south.

The valley's second level stretches from Lax to Fiesch and is marked by the appearance—confirming a gain in height—of arolla pines and small barns on piles (*raccards*). This section marks the start of the Upper Rhône Valley, known as the Conches Valley. Below, in a gorge section, the Rhône is joined by the tributary River Binna. Farther up the valley, when Fiesch comes into view, it is possible to look up the Fieschertal Valley, on the left, and see in the far distance the snowy peak of the Finsteraar-Rothorn.

▶ *Return to the Valley via route 19. After Lax, take the small road on the right which goes to Ernen.*

Ernen★

With its sun bleached chalets, Ernen ❋ one of the most typical villages of th Conches valley, and also one of the mos charming. Several of its houses dat from the 16C and 18C.

L'église St Georges is really worth a visi It was rebuilt in the 16C on the foun dations of a Roman basilica, and ha a variety of works of art, including a important Baroque altar, a pietà fron the 14C, a statue of St Georges, frescoe from the 16C and pews dating from th Renaissance.

▶ *Rejoin after Fiesch where you can take the cable-car to Eggishorn.*

Eggishorn★★★

Alt. 2 927m/9 603ft. ⌁*Access by cable-car from Fiesch.* ◷*Departures every 30min, 9am (7.30am Jun–Sep) to 5pm.* ◷*Closed Nov & May.* ⊜*Fare there and back* ⊜*38CHF summer, 53CHF winter.* ℘*(0)27 971 27 00.*

The first stage takes you up over a spruce forest and a scree of greenish coloured, jagged rocks. From the uppe station (alt. 2 869m/9 413ft) there is a superb **panorama**★★★; below in th immediate foreground the Aletsch Glacier, the Fiesch Glacier, a nearby cascade farther round to the right, and of all the other neighbouring mountair peaks. For an even wider view, climb to the top of one of the three mounds o scree which are quite close to the station. The Eggishorn summit is marked by a cross (⌁*difficult clamber*). After the next change in level beyond Fiesch, the view extends back downstream to the snow-covered slopes of the Weisshorn (alt. 4 505m/14 780ft).

After a few hairpin bends, notice the village of **Mühlebach**, the birthplace of Cardinal Schiner, on the opposite slope.

Bellwald★

⌁*Access by a winding road 8km/5mi or by cable-car from Fürgangen.*

A small summer and winter resort, Bell-wald (alt. 1 600m/5 249ft), with its old larch wood chalets and hotels set on a curved terrace, presents a wide aerial

Getting the Guns Through

As early as the 17C the Great Stockalper (*see p282*), making the most of his monopolies and the position of Brig, adapted the Simplon road, used until then mainly by smugglers and mercenaries, to commercial traffic. He organised a mail service and built two hostels, which still stand at Gondo. But all this was for mule trains, not for wheeled traffic. The modern Simplon is a product of Napoleon. After a detachment sent by Italy via the Simplon had forced the passage only by perilous manoeuvres, the First Consul decided in 1800 that the road from Brig to Domodossola must be made accessible to artillery. The low altitude of the pass and its relatively scanty snowfall determined his choice, and the project received absolute priority. The undertaking was entrusted to Nicolas Céard, chief engineer of public works in the Léman *département*, who drew up plans for a road 7–8m/22–25ft wide with a maximum gradient of 10% (1 in 10). It was officially opened to traffic in 1805, but Napoleon never had occasion to use it.

iew★ of the Conches Valley—from iesch to Brig—over the Eggishorn dentified by its cross), above and to he right of the Wannenhorn Massif nd its glaciers and left onto the Alps of the Italian frontier. The **Richinen and teibenkreuz chairlift** (*operates in vinter, 9.15am–4.15pm; in summer, 9am– oon, 1.15pm–5.30pm; ask for informa- ion on closed periods; 16CHF; (0)27 71 19 26*) offers a close-up view of the Vannenhorn Glaciers and the majestic **Matterhorn** in the distance. The val- ey opens out again beautifully. The hird level is the longest in the Conches /alley. The Alpine combe now offers a bare, open landscape; the total lack of enclosures, the lone trees and scat- ered chalets make for striking views. he villages, with their blackish wooden ouses adorned with geraniums, are rouped around slim white church owers. Upstream, to the right of the Galenstock summit, you will glimpse he Furka Gap, although the pass itself s out of sight.

⬤ *Rejoin route 19 and go as far as Reckingen.*

Reckingen

Reckingen's **Baroque** church is one of he most beautiful in the Conches val- ey. It was built in the 18C, based on he plans of priest **Jean-Georges Ritz**. Ritz represented a group of artisans who

had produced renowned sculpted altar pieces. The family gained worldwide renown thanks to **César Ritz** (born in Niederwald in 1850, died in 1918), who became a hotelier.

The **Seiler** family who made their for- tune in Zermatt and built two hotels next to the Rhône Glacier (in Gletsch and in Belvédère) is also notable in the history of the Conche valley.

Mûnster

The **église** in the fine village has a bell tower adorned with a fine weather vane is worth a visit thanks to its flamboyant **alter shelf**, dedicated to the Virgin Mary, and created by an artist from Lucerne in 1509. Below **Oberwald**, the last village in the Conches valley, the road descends into decreasingly for- ested terrain where the Rhône tumbles downhill. You emerge onto the Gletsch lake from where you can see the Rhône glacier, source of this great river.

⬤ *Drive on to Gletsch.*

Gletsch★★
Alt. 1 759m/5 771ft.

At the junction of roads from the Furka Pass, the Grimsel Pass and the Conches Valley (Upper Valais) lies Gletsch, on the floor of a desolate basin once covered by the tongue of the Rhône Glacier. Higher up, on the road to the Furka Pass (*see FURKAPASS*), the setting in which the Hôtel Belvédère stands draws many sightseers. This well-known stop offers a sweeping **panorama**★★ of the Bernese and Valais Alps plus the **Rhonegletscher**★★ in which an **Ice Grotto**★ (Eisgrotte; ○open Jun–Oct, 8am–7pm (7.30pm Sat–Sun); ○7CHF; ℘(0)27 973 11 29) has been carved out, its walls reflecting a lovely bluish light.

After Gletsch, the Furka Col road climbs and passes in front of the Hôtel Belvédère. The **Rhône Glacier**★★★ (Rhonegletscher) starts at the same level from the other side of the road (parking). It is one of the most easily accessible European glaciers (200m/218yds from the road), but it is necessary to have the services of a professional guide.

Grotte de glace★ (Eisgrotte)

The access to the glacier and the grotto is via the Hotel Belvédère's souvenir shop.
Jun–Oct 8am–7pm (weekend 7.30pm)
○5 CHF. ○Wear warm clothing.
℘(0)27 924 38 24.
For over 120 years the tunnel underneath the ice has been redug every year. It allows the visitor the possibility to walk in a blue tinged world and to examine the different layers of ice.

○ *Rejoin the route.*

The drive up to the col offers far reaching views of the Valais and Bearnais Alps. To get the best the best possible **view** ★★★, stop at a fork 1500m before the col, where there is a military road (marked no entry) and walk a few metres into the meadow. Looking towards the Conches valley the snows of the Weisshorn and the Mischel glisten; closer at hand in the direction of the Grimsel col, are the 4 000m/13 123ft peaks of the Lauteraarhorn, Finsteraarhorn and Schreckhorn.

Furkapass★★

Alt. 2 431 m/7 976ft.
Stop at the Furkablick hotel to admire the majestic Galenstock. The Furka col, the highest access point to the snaking road which crosses the Swiss Alps from Martigny to Chur is a vital tourist link

betwen French Switzerland, the Andermatt crossroads, and Graubünden. Since 1982 a railway tunnel, re-opened linking Realp to Gletsch. The journey takes 1hr35min to travel the 13.3km/8.3mi. The engine built for the line in 1913 was brought back from Vietnam and restored.

SIMPLONSTRASSE ★★

65km/40mi – allow approx 3hrs.
○*The Simplon Pass is sometimes blocked by snow from December to May in spite of the galleries built to keep it clear year-round.*

The Simplon road is not the boldest in the Alps—the Splügen and the St Gotthard have more daring structures—but it is the noblest and most majestic. It is impossible not to succumb to the beauty of such a **site**★★★ as that which unfolds between the Simplon Pass (alt. 2 005m/6 578ft) and Brig, on the Rhône Valley slope. This gentle winding road along the mountain flank, without sharp hairpin bends, is a model of adaptation to topography.

The Alpine section begins at **Crevoladossola**, where you leave the warm inner plain of the Ossola, somewhat Mediterranean in character with its bushy, stony floor exposed to the meanderings of the River Toce.

From Crevoladossola to the border, the narrow Diveria Valley offers little interesting scenery. A few campaniles and the greenery of thickets of hazel, walnut and ash are not enough to make it attractive. A short distance from Crevoladossola, on the left, are the ruins of the little village of San Giovanni, razed by a landslide in 1958. The ruins increase still farther the bleakness of the valley.

○ *Italian and Swiss customs control are at Paglino and Gondo respectively.*

Simplonpass★★

Alt. 2 005m/6 578ft.
The road runs halfway up the side of this long, winding defile, with its uneven floor. It is overlooked from the south by the Böshorn, in the middle distance, by the snowy Fletschhorn and from the

ast by the greenish slabs of the Hüb-chhorn and the Chaltwassergletscher, oming from Mount Leone. Of the three nain features of this scene, none is more emarkable than the **Alter Spittel** (a ormer hostel built by Stockalper), which s high and flanked by a 17C tower and ell turret. The present hostel (Hospiz) vas built at the same time as the road nd is kept by the monks of the Great St 3ernard. A stone eagle commemorates he watch kept on the frontier during he Second World War.

he **belvedere★★** of the pass is at the ighest point, that is, just before the hol-ow on the Valais side. Beside the Hotel implon-Kulm, it is possible to pick out he summits of the **Bernese Alps** which an be seen between the Schinhorn and he Finsteraarhorn (highest point of the ernese Alps, alt. 4 274m/14 022ft). On he Rhône side, the road between the ass and a tunnel clings to the upper recipices of a rocky cirque laced by the cy waters of the **Chaltwassergletscher** vhich can be seen above, protected by series of concrete galleries and roofs. Approaching the Kapfloch Pass through gap you see the Fletschhorn, flanked n its right by the Böshorn. From the apfloch to Rothwald a long stretch of orniche road under larch woods finally eveals, 1 000m/3 281ft below, the town f Brig framed in the opening of the **Sal-ine Gorges**. The mountains separating he Rhône Valley from the Lötschental ow unfold on the horizon: From left o right, the Bietschhorn, Briethorn, Nesthorn and Schinhorn.

3etween Rothwald and Schallberg, the oad detours into the **Gantertal**. On he north slope of this beautiful valley re many crooked arolla pines (*see NTRODUCTION: Alpine Vegetation*). 3etween Schallberg and Brig the road t first overlooks the Saltine Gorges Saltinaschlucht), the floor of which annot be seen. It then leaves the for-st and drops to the well-tilled slopes f the **Brigerberg**. The towers of the tockalper Castle and of the churches f Brig stand out behind the shining rib-on of the Rhône, often shrouded by the actory smoke of Visp.

Gondoschlucht★

The wildest section of this long valley defile, hemmed in by granite walls, is the confluence of the **Alpienbach** and the **Diveria**, whose falls join at the foot of a spur pierced by a road tunnel. Between Gstein (Gabi) and the pass, the road, leaving the Laggintal in the southwest where it penetrates toward the higher levels of the Weissmies (4 023m/13 199ft), and climbs gradually among the Alpine pastures of the lower Simplon combe.

Above the village of **Simplon** the rug-ged appearance of the terrain still shows the devastating effects of the terrible avalanche of 1901 started by the col-lapse of a whole section of the **Ross-boden Glacier**. Dominating this glacier, the **Fletschhorn** is the most attractive feature of the landscape.

ADDRESSES

🛏STAY / ♀/EAT

⊜⊜ **Schlosshotel Art Furrer** – *Schlosspark (near the château).* ℘*(0)27 922 95 95. www.schlosshotel.ch. 27 rooms.* Classic rooms of varying sizes, many with a balcony. Ask for a view of the château.

ON THE ROAD TO THE FURKA COL
⊜⊜ **Hôtel Belvédère** – *A stone's throw from the Rhône glacier.* ℘*(0)27 924 38 24. www.gletscher.ch. Open Jun–mid-Oct.* If you really want to stay at the glacier, enjoy the charms of this old-fashioned but delightful hotel. Built in 1900, it is perched above the road. The cheapest rooms are on the third floor with a communal shower. Splendid view over Gletsch and the mountains.

⊜⊜ **Commerce** – *Sebastianplatz 2* ℘*(0)27 924 52 41. Daily exc Mon.* Well situated on the main square. Pizzas and fish dishes offer a pleasant change from the usual Valais fare.

⊜⊜⊜ **Schlosskeller** – *Alte Simplonstrasse 34* ℘*(0)27 923 33 52. Closed Sun eve and Mon.* Located on the road that leads to the château, this restaurant for gourmets offers, among other treats, Mediterranean specialities. Pleasant interior courtyard.

TICINO

Ticino is located in the southeast of Switzerland and borders the Italian lakes of Maggiore and Lugano. This Italian-speaking canton, called Tessin by German- and French-speaking Swiss, and pronounced "*Tichino*" by the Italian speakers, is evidence of the cultural diversity typical of Switzerland: food, architecture, culture, climate and outlook on life here couldn't be more different from the cheese and chocolate Alpine cliché of the north and west. It covers 2 811 sq km/1 085 sq mi and is surrounded by the cantons of Valais and Uri in the northwest, by Graubünden in the north and east while the southern part of the canton abuts Italy.

Highlights

A Bit of History

Taking its name from the River Ticino which flows along the Levantina Valley from the St Gotthard Massif in the Lepontine Alps in the north to Lake Maggiore in the south, Ticino is for many the ideal blend of Swiss order and Italian flair. Territory to the north of the Monte Ceneri range is known as the Sopraceneri and to the south it is known as Sottoceneri. Lake Lugano (called Lago Ceresio by Italians) to the east of Maggiore and overlooked by Monte San Salvatore and Monte Generoso, has a wilder appearance than its larger neighbour but is no less beautiful. The city of Lugano, "the Queen of Ceresio", located at the end of a splendid bay, is ideally located for touring the area and Bellinzona, the capital of the canton, is also a fascinating town whose splendid castles constitute a UNESCO World Heritage site.

The region came under the control of the Romans during the reign of Augustus and remained part of Rome until the fall of the Western Empire in the 5C. Various invasions followed until eventually, during the Middle Ages the area, which was contested by both Milan and Como, finally came under the control of the powerful Dukes of Milan. During the 15C and 16C Ticino became part of the Swiss Confederation, the forerunner of the modern Swiss state, dominated by the Cantons of Uri, Scwhyz and Unterwalden, who had defeated the Milanese by securing Bellinzona in 1503. This situation lasted nearly 300 years until finally, following intervention by the French, Ticino became independent in 1798 before achieving canton status as a member of Napoleon's new Swiss Confederation in 1803. During the 19C Ticino suffered political unrest between the rival radical and conservative parties and, whilst things have been calmer since, tensions still remain.

Ticino Today

While the region used to be something of a rural backwater, it has now developed a strong tertiary sector which employs nearly 80% of the population and its banking industry is Switzerland's third largest after Zürich and Geneva. The establishment of a university at Lugano in 1996 further bolstered the region, as it meant that Italian-speaking students no longer have to study elsewhere in Switzerland in another language, or move to Italy.

It is economically closely linked to Italy with many *frontalieri*, Italian nationals who work in the region, contributing to the increasingly important tourist industry, a large number of whom are Swiss from the north and west.

TICINO

0   10 km
0   5 miles

GRAUBÜNDEN

N

Disentis/
Mustér

Vorderrhein

19

URI

19

St. Gothard
Pass
2108
Val Trémola
Airolo

Lago
Ritom

Lai da
Sontga Maria
1916 Lukmanier Pass
Acquacalda

Val Piora

Nufenen Pass
2478

L. di
Naret

Lago Sambuco

Rodi-
Fiesso

Alto Ticino

San Carlo
du Negrentino
Lottigna

Fusio
Mogno

Leventina

Giornico
Malvaglia

San Carlo
Peccia
Prato
Ritorto
Foroglio
Val Bavona
Cavergno
Cevio

Sonogno
Pollegio

Biasca

Bosco/Gurin

Brione

Valle Maggia

Maggia

Corippo

Val Verzasca

Tessin

A2

T I C I N O

Intragna
Ponte
Brolla
Contra

Monte
Carasso

Monte Comino
Verdasio
Centovalli
Locarno
Tenero

BELLINZONA

A 13

CHUR

Palagnedra

Monte
Verità
Ascona
Îles de Brissago

Melezza

Rasa

I T A L Y

Monte Tamaro
1961

S 34

Monte Lema
1624

Miglieglia

Monte Brè
925 Gandria

Lugano
Lago di Lugano

Lago Maggiore

S 394

Caslano
912

MONTE SAN SALVATORE

BELLAGIO, ST. MORITZ

R 229
A 36

Carona
Morcote

Swissminiatur

MONTE GENEROSO
1701

Riva San Vitale
Meride
Ligornetto
Mendrisio

S 235
S 340

Lago di
Como

Varèse

Côme

P 342

A 9

A 8

BELLINZONA ★★★ Highly recommended

Lugano ★★ Recommended

Centovalli ★ Interesting

Biasca Other sight described
in this guide

⇔ Driving tour

Lugano★

The Queen of the Ceresio lies at the end of a beautiful bay framed between the wooded Mount Brè and Mount San Salvatore. It faces south and is an ideal tourist and health resort for its temperate climate, particularly appreciated in spring and autumn. You will find beaches, tennis courts, an 18-hole golf course, riding, boating, and a casino. Lugano is a convenient excursion centre for visiting the Ticino's three lakes: Maggiore, Lugano and Como.

⚓WALKING TOUR

THE OLD CITY★

Begin at Piazza della Riforma (behind the Tourist Office). Allow 2hrs.

Piazza della Riforma

A huge, lively square with outdoor cafés and the Municipio (town hall). In early July, during **Estival Jazz**, the square is swarming with jazz lovers enjoying live performances.
Its pedestrian streets, steep alleys and flights of steps make for an interesting walk or shopping expedition.

▷ *Head W out of Piazza della Riforma along the Via dei Pesci and turn right onto Via Pessina. On the left is the Piazza Cioccaro.*

Piazza Cioccaro

This Piazza, (funicular serving the train station), with the **Palazzo Riva**, a fine patrician villa with wrought-iron balconies gives onto to **Via Cattedrale**, a steep alleyway leading up to the cathedral.

San Lorenzo

The cathedral was built in the Roman-esque style and it presents an elegant façade in addition to three doorways embellished with Renaissance motifs. See a splendid example of Baroque decoration in the Chapel of Santa Maria delle Grazie. The esplanade commands a lovely view of Lugano and its lake.

▷ **Population:** 54 437.
▷ **Michelin Map:** National 729: K7-8.
▷ **Info:** Palazzo Civico ✆(0)91 913 32 32. www.lugano-tourism.ch.
▷ **Location:** Lugano lies about 29.6km/18.4mi southwest of Bellinzona, at the edge of Lake Lugano, between Lake Maggiore and Lake Como. Alt. 273ft/896m.
▷ **Parking:** The town centre is car-free.
▷ **Don't Miss:** Villa Favorita, one of the largest private art museums in Europe.
▷ **Kids:** The adventure playground in the Parco Civico. Kids will also like Swissminiatur, small replicas of important sights, in a lakeside park.
▷ **Timing:** Allow two days for museums and lake excursions.

▷ *Return to Piazza Cioccaro and turn right into Via Pessina. At the end of the street turn right into Via Nassa.*

Via Nassa

This street and its arcades of elegant boutiques form the main axis of Lugano. On **Piazzetta San Carlo** note the Sur-realist sculpture by **Salvador Dalí** called *The Dignity of Time*. At number 66, the **Palazzo Vanoni**, was the seat of the Bishop.

Santa Maria degli Angioli

This former convent church, begun in 1499, contains three fine **frescoes★★** by Bernardo Luini (c.1480–1532). The most impressive represents a *Passion*. Below it are pictured St Sebastian and St Roch. In the first chapel on the right, note the fresco *Virgin with Child and St John*, which was taken from the cloisters. The nave bears a representation of the Last Supper.

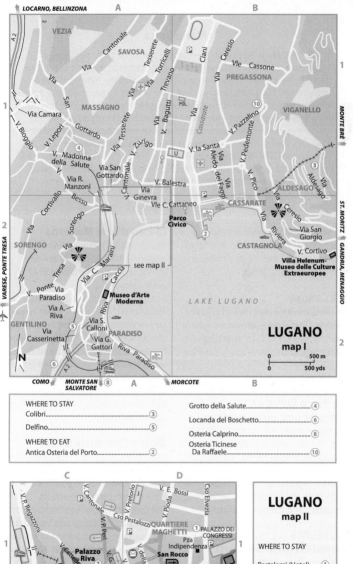

LUGANO
map I

LOCARNO, BELLINZONA

VEZIA
SAVOSA
MASSAGNO
Via Camara
V. Bioggio
V. Lepori
V. Madonna della Salute
Via R. Manzoni
Cortivallo
SORENGO
Via Cantonale
Tesserete
Gottardo
Via San
Via Tesserete
V. Zurigo
Via San Gottardo
Via Ginevra
Via Balestra
Vle C. Cattaneo
Besso
Sorengo
Via
V. C. Maraini
V. Ponte Tresa
Via Paradiso
Via A. Riva
GENTILINO
Via Casserinetta
Caccia
Riva
Via S. Calloni
PARADISO
Via G. Gattori
Riva Paradiso

Torricelli
Trevano
V. Bagutti
Via
Ciani
Cassarate
V. la Santa
Aledo dei Faggi
Parco Civico
see map II

Museo d'Arte Moderna

LAKE LUGANO

Ceresio
Vle Cassone
PREGASSONA
V. Pazzalino
V. Pedemonte
V. Pico
VIGANELLO
ALDESAGO
Via Ceresio
Via Riviera
CASSARATE
CASTAGNOLA
Via San Giorgio
V. Cortivo
Villa Helenum–Museo delle Culture Extraeuropee

MONTE BRÈ
ST. MORITZ, GANDRIA, MENAGGIO
VARESE, PONTE TRESA

N

COMO MONTE SAN SALVATORE MORCOTE

0 — 500 m
0 — 500 yds

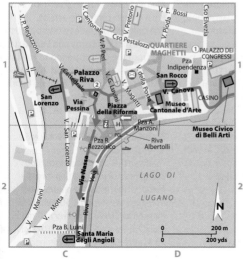

V. P. Regazzoni
San Lorenzo
Via Cattedrale
Palazzo Riva
Via Pessina
V. San Lorenzo
Maraini
V. Motta
Via Nassa
V. G. Luvini
Piazza della Riforma
Pza R. Rezzonico
Riva Albertolli
Pza B. Luini
Santa Maria degli Angioli

Cso Pestalozzi
V. Pretorio
V. Canonica
V. della Posta
QUARTIERE MAGHETTI
San Rocco
V. Canova
Museo Cantonale d'Arte
Pza A. Manzoni

V. E. Bossi
V. Ploda
Cso Elvezia
PALAZZO DEI CONGRESSI
Pza Indipendenza
CASINO
Museo Civico di Belli Arti

LAGO DI LUGANO

N

0 — 200 m
0 — 200 yds

Mario Botta

Born in 1943, Mario Botta is unquestionably one of the most talented and renowned architects of his time. After studying technical design in Lugano, he attended the Institute of Architecture at Venice University. Influenced by Le Corbusier and Louis Kahn, with whom he had worked, he became one of the foremost representatives of the Ticino School. His work aims for a harmonious balance between landscape and architecture, with a curved perspective and compact shapes. His major accomplishments are the school at Morbio Inferiore (1972–77), the Arts Centre in Chambéry (1982–87), the Médiathèque in Villeurbanne (1984–88), the Museum of Modern Art of San Francisco (1990–94), Évry Cathedral (1995), the Tinguely Museum in Basel (1996), the Chiesa Santa Maria degli Angeli at Monte Tamaro (1996) and the Dürrenmatt Centre in Neuchâtel (2000).

Return to the centre along the Riva Bela bordering the Lake. After the Piazza Mazzoni turn left into Via degli Albrizzi then right into Via Canove.

Via Canove

On Via Canove you will pass the **Musée Cantonale d'Arte**, Chiesa San Rocco and the Casino before entering the Piazza Indipendenza.

The Parco Civico is adjacent.

Parco Civico★★

During the summer season and providing the weather is fair, one can attend open-air concerts in the park. Several statues (*Socrates* by the Russian sculptor Antokolsky) and fountains lend charm to the delightful setting. Children will appreciate the adventure playground, the aviary, and the deer enclosure.

MUSEUMS
Museo Civico di Belli Arti

Villa Ciani, Parco Civico ○Tue–Sun 10am–noon, 2pm–6pm. ☜5CHF. ℘(0)58 866 72 14.
Housed in the Villa Ciani in the Parco Civico, the collection includes work by Ticinese artists from the 15–20C as well some work by such renowned painters as Matisse, Rousseau and Monet.

Museo d'Arte Moderna

Riva Caccia 5 ○Open mid-Mar–late Jun and in the fall, Tue–Sun, 10am–6pm, (Fri 9pm). ☜12CHF. ℘(0)58 866 72 01. www.mdam.ch.
Set up in the Villa Malpensata, the Museum of Modern Art hosts temporary exhibitions of an exceptionally high standard. Painters such as Francis Bacon, Nolde, Soutine, Rouault, and Botero were revealed to the public during retrospective shows held here, which brought together works that had been lent by other museums or borrowed from private collections.

Museo Cantonale d'Arte

Via Canova 10. ○Tue 2–5pm; Wed–Sun and Easter Mon 10am–5pm.○Closed Mon and 1 May.☜7CHF. ℘(0)91 910 47 80. www.museo-cantonale-arte.ch.
The collection includes works by artists from Ticino, Lombardy and Venice dating from the Gothic period to the late 18C as well as some 19 and 20C works including one by JMW Turner. There is also some contempoary work.

GREATER LUGANO
Monte San Salvatore★★★

Alt. 912m/2 996ft.
45min there and back, including 20min by funicular, starting from the Paradiso quarter. A five minute walk from the train station. ○Operates 13 Mar–7 Nov. Departures every 30min. ☜28CHF there and back. ℘(0)91 985 28 28. http://montesansalvatore.ch.

An admirable view of Lugano, its lake and the Bernese and Valais Alps. You can return to Lugano from the summit by marked paths.

Monte Brè★★
Alt. 925m/3 051ft.
About 1hr there and back, including 30min by funicular, starting from Cassarate. Access by funicular from Cassarate via Suvigliana, 9.10am–6.45pm. Departures after 9.45am every 30min. 20CHF there and back. (0)91 971 31 71. www.montbre.ch.
You can also go by car, by taking the road to Castagnola and then following the directions. The summit has views of the lake and the Alps (many hiking tours in the area) from the terraces.

LAKE LUGANO★★
The greater part of Lake Lugano lies within Switzerland. The Italians, who call it Ceresio, have only the northeast branch (Porlezza), part of the southwest shore (Porto Ceresio) and a small enclave on the east shore (Campione d'Italia). Lake Lugano looks wilder than Lake Maggiore and Lake Como. It is irregular in shape, with a total length of 33km/21mi and a maximum depth of 288m/947ft or 150 fathoms. From the municipal park up to Paradiso, the promenade following the lake shore is an ideal place for a leisurely stroll.

Paradiso
This district is populated by luxury hotels, restaurants, cafés, nightclubs, and fashionable boutiques.

BY BOAT
The steamer services on Lake Lugano, *(1hr to half-day)*, are among the resort's top attractions. **Società Navigazione Lago di Lugano** *(Viale Castagnola; (0)91 971 52 23; www.lakelugano.ch).* A grand tour of the lake, called Grande Giro del Lago, starts from Lugano.
If you wish to combine the tour of Gandria with that of the Museum of Swiss Customs, allow 3hr.

Gandria★
1hr there and back, if you do not go ashore.
Amid a maze of stepped streets this village, with terraces planted with geraniums, trellises, leafy bowers, arcaded houses and a small Baroque church form a charming picture appreciated by artists and tourists.
Museo Doganale Svizzero – Located on the lake shore in a former Swiss customs post *(at Cantine di Gandria on the south shore of the lake; access by boat 1hr45min there and back, including visit to the museum; accessible by boat only; guided tours Apr–Oct, 1.30pm–5.30pm; no charge; (0)91 910 48 11)*, the museum explains the role, past and present, of the customs

View of Lake Lugano, Monte San Salvatore and the city from Mont Brè

Christof Sonderegger/Switzerland Tourism

officer. Beneath the verandah is a car illustrating the incredible number of tiny hiding places that can be found in an automobile. Other exhibits focus on the perilous role they played during the Second World War, the most common devices (traps, weapons, trick objects) used by smugglers, drug dealers, and forgers (fake passports, fake garments). It also presents the highly sophisticated means used by customs officers to foil smugglers. Perhaps the museum's most unusual exhibit is the Zodiac submarine seized in 1946: its metal tubes were stuffed with salami! Under the eaves are temporary exhibitions on Swiss customs: recruitment and training techniques at the Liestal School near Basel and the role of women in this profession.

EXCURSIONS
Villa Favorita★★
Via Riviera 14. At Castagnola. ○*Take bus 1 leaving from Piazza Manzoni and get off at Villa Favorita.* *It is advisable to take the bus since the car park can only accommodate a few cars.* ○*Open Apr 15–Oct 31, Thu–Sun 10am–5pm.* 12CHF. (0)91 970 11 62.

A garden park overlooking the lake planted with exotic trees and graced with statues leads to this late-17C mansion featuring three staggered storeys and crowned by a birdcage.

Although the greater part of the remarkable collection of paintings gathered since 1920 by Thyssen-Bornemisza, the famous German steel industrialists, has been transferred to the Thyssen-Bornemisza Museum in Madrid, the Villa Favorita regularly holds exhibitions of works taken from this collection, concentrating on a given theme or artistic style (e.g. 19C and 20C American artists Andrew Wyeth, Winslow Homer, and Edward Hopper).

Villa Heleneum – Museo delle Culture Extraeuropee
○*Take bus number 1 leaving from Piazza Manzoni. Get off at San Domenico, then continue on foot for 5min along Via Cortivo 24.* ○*Open Tue–*

Sun, 10am–6pm. 12CHF. (0)58 866 69 60. www.mcl.lugano.ch.

On the edge of the lake, a neo-Classical mansion houses the **Museum of Non-European Cultures**. The collections are laid out on three levels. The ground floor is devoted to Oceania and Southeast Asia. The first floor focuses on New Guinea and the different regional cultures which make up its identity. The second floor is divided into themes, adopting a comparative approach on issues such as death, fertility, and power. Each display is amply illustrated with explanatory panels and objects, including finely carved wooden sculptures.

Caslano
○*5km/3mi SE. Leave Lugano on the airport road heading toward Ponte Tresa.*
Switzerland is invariably associated with chocolate and for those who have a sweet tooth, the visit to a chocolate-making factory is a must. Near the Italian border, the firm **Alprose** welcomes visitors to its **Museo del Cioccolato** (○*open daily 9am–5.30pm (Sat–Sun 4.30pm);* ○*closed 2 Jan, 1 Nov and 24 Dec; film (20min); shop;* 3CHF; (0)91 611 88 56; www.alprose.ch).

The museum unveils the world of chocolate before your eyes, starting with the cocoa plantations in Amazonia and ending with present-day manufacturing and marketing techniques. An upper passageway enables you to observe the methods of fabrication from above. All aspects of the industry are covered: milk, white, or bitter chocolate, small squares to have with coffee, and drinking chocolate, a warm nectar with an enticing aroma. The tour ends with a tasting session.

Swissminiatur★
○*7km/4.5mi S.* ○*Open 13 Mar–23 Oct, 9am–6pm (May–Sept Wed & Fri until 10.30pm), 24 Oct–14 Nov 9am-5pm.* 17CHF. (0)91 640 10 60. www.swissminiatur.ch.

A joy to children and grown-ups alike. Spread over 1ha/2.5 acres of verdant and flowery land on the edge of the lake, the exhibit displays the country's main tourist attractions reproduced in miniature (monuments carved out of stone, mountains, bridges, sites, etc.) and evokes the country's main economic activities. The trains (3km/1.8mi network), boats and cable-cars all function.

🚗 DRIVING TOURS

ROAD TO MORCOTE★

Round trip of 26km/16mi – allow about 3hrs – the route starts on a fairly hilly road. (Alternative access by boat from Lugano; ⏰ operates Apr–Oct; tour lasts for approximately 1hr).

▷ *Leave Lugano through Paradiso, then take the high road to Morcote via Carona.*

This route via Pazzallo and Carona offers magnificent **bird's-eye views**★★ of the lake and the Monte Rosa Massif.

Carona

At the entrance to the village, lined at intervals with picturesque houses, the **Chiesa San Giorgio** (16C) is crowned by an octagonal dome and contains interesting 16C **frescoes**★. Adjoining the church is a portico with Tuscan columns, decorated with heraldic arms and *trompe-l'œil* paintings.

On leaving the locality, follow directions for **Madonna d'Ongero**. You can leave the car at a car park and continue on foot along a forest path. A wide path with Stations of the Cross leads to the church, which has a portico and an octagonal dome. The interior is heavily ornate, with abundant frescoes and stuccowork. Return to the road to Morcote; after a short distance you can stop at a roadside belvedere to enjoy a view of the lake.

Morcote★★

The Lombardic arcaded houses of this village, dubbed the Pearl of the Ceresio, are reflected in Lake Lugano. By a staircase and alleys you will reach the **Church of Santa Maria del Sasso** containing splendid 16C frescoes and a fine organ case. Go through the church to see the Baroque baptistery (Battisteri da Sant Antoni). The whole ensemble forms a remarkable **picture**★★.

▷ *Take the lake shore road back toward Lugano. After approx 4km/3mi turn right onto via Cantonale.*

▷ *Return to Lugano still taking the lake shore road, which is the most attractive.*

Morcote and its church Santa Maria del Sasso

Franziska Pfenniger/Switzerland Tourism

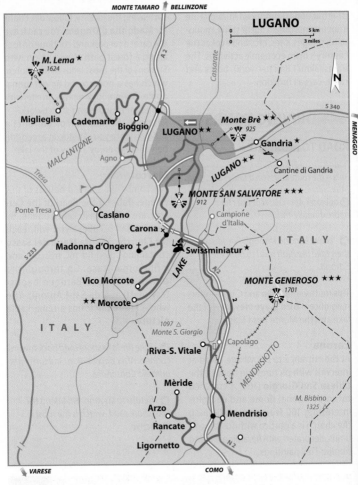

MONTE TAMARO · BELLINZONE

LUGANO

0 ————— 5 km
0 ————— 3 miles

N

MALCANTONE

M. Lema ★
1624

Miglieglia   **Cademario**
   Bioggio

Agno

LUGANO ★★

Monte Brè ★★
925

Gandria ★

Cantine di Gandria

LUGANO ★★

MONTE SAN SALVATORE ★★★
912

Campione
d'Italia

ITALY

Ponte Tresa

Tresa

Caslano

Carona ×

Madonna d'Ongero †

Vico Morcote

★★ **Morcote**

ITALY

1097 △
Monte S. Giorgio

LAKE

Swissminiatur ★

MONTE GENEROSO ★★★
1701

Capolago

MENDRISIOTTO

M. Bisbino
1325

Riva-S. Vitale

Mèride

Arzo

Rancate

Ligornetto

Mendrisio

MENAGGIO

S 340

S 233

VARESE   COMO

MENDRISIOTTO REGION

40km/25mi.

▷ *Leave Lugano S on the lakeside road and drive as far as Capolago. Leave the car and take the rack railway.*

Monte Generoso★★★

Alt. 1 701m/5 581ft. Rack railway from Capolago. ◷*Departure every hour from 19 Mar–1 Nov.* ◷*Open in winter 2 Nov–9 Jan except Mon & Tue.* ≋*49CHF there and back.* ℘*(0)91 648 11 05. www.montegeneroso.ch. Allow 2hrs.* From the summit the splendid **panorama**★★★ extends over the Alps, Lugano, the lakes and the Lombardy

Plain to the distant Apennines on a clear day.

▷ *Return to the main road and turn right to reach Riva San Vitale.*

Riva San Vitale

This village is worth a visit for its 5C baptistery *(battistero)*, in an octagonal room near the parish church. Remains of 11C frescoes adorn part of the walls.

At the opposite end of the village, the **Chiesa Santa Croce** (16C) can be recognised by its octagonal dome; note the sculpted wooden door with grotesque faces. The interior features fine mural paintings.

Mendrisio

This is the town where the famous Ticino architect **Mario Botta** was born. The old city is dominated by the Neoclassical Chiesa Santi Cosma e Damiano (19C) and its characteristic dome. It is reached by a monumental flight of steps; at the foot of these, a square tower is all that remains of the city's medieval ramparts. Note the fine Baroque palace nearby. Take the charming Via San Damiano, continued by Via Stella, which leads to the oratory of Madonna delle Grazie (13C). Behind the oratory, on Piazza dei Serviti, the former convent house contains the Museo d'Arte.

Ligornetto

Ligornetto is the birthplace of the Ticino sculptor **Vincenzo Vela** (1820–1891), a legendary figure in the region. His villa has been converted into a museum.

Rancate

This village is certainly worth a detour, if only to visit the **Pinacoteca Cantonale Giovanni Züst** (◷open Mar–Jun Tue–Sun 9am–noon, 2pm–5pm; Jul–Aug, Tue–Sun 2pm–6pm, Sept–1 Jan Tue–Fri 9am–noon, 2pm–6pm, Sat, Sun and Hols 10am–noon and 2pm–6pm; ◷closed Jan, Feb and Mon; ◉8CHF; ℰ(0)91 646 45 65; www.ti.ch/zuest) which presents a fine selection of works by Ticino artists from the 17C to the 20C. The paintings of Antonio Rinaldi are in Room 3 on the ground floor (The Kitten, Portrait of Angiolino) and in Room 6 on the first floor (Sketch for a Portrait, The Shepherd, The Holy Virgin). Giuseppe Antonio Petrini (1677–1758) is represented with the intensely moving L'Addolorata, in room 7 on the first floor.

Arzo

Renowned for its marble quarry and the clocktower of the Baroque Church is covered with slabs of this material.

Meride

This village in the vines has some 18C houses with galleries and courtyards.

◔ Return to Lugano.

MONTE LEMA★

22km/13mi NW via Bioggio.

◔ *From Bioggio the road winds through woods before entering Cademario.*

Cademario

From this terraced village there is a nice view of the plain below, part of Lake Lugano and the mountains. As you leave the village following directions to Lugano, the old **Chiesa di San Ambrogio** *(for information, call ℰ(091) 605 68 30)* stands alone with its campanile in the Lombardy style and its façade with partly-erased 15C frescoes. Inside are interesting 13C polychrome frescoes.

Miglieglia

At the foot of Monte Lema lies the village and its church, St Stefano (15C). The interior houses 16C–17C frescoes.

Monte Lema★

Alt. 1 624m/5 328ft.
⌁*Access by chairlift from Miglieglia. Departure every 30min 9am–5pm.* ◉*24CHF there and back. ℰ(0)91 609 11 68. www.montelema.ch.*
The climb, above a landscape of fern and rocks, gives a bird's-eye view of Miglieglia and St Stefano church. From the restaurant of the upper station climb to the top *(20min round trip along a steep path)* between a television relay station and a large metal cross for a **panorama★** which extends westwards to Lake Maggiore and the Monte Rosa and eastwards to Lake Lugano and Monte Generoso.

ADDRESSES

⌂STAY

Owing to its ideal location, Lugano offers many opportunities for leisure activities and for boat trips on the lake or into the mountains, where spectacular panoramas can be had. As in many resorts with a prestigious reputation, prices are comparatively high and some visitors may prefer to stay outside the town.

Hôtel Pestalozzi – *Piazza Independencia 9.* *(0)91 92 146 46. www.pestalozzi-lugano.ch. 51 rooms.* Very central and excellent value for money. Limited parking.

Colibri – *In Aldesago, 6km/3.7mi E – Via Bassone 7.* *(0)91 971 42 42. www. hotelcolibri.ch. 30 rooms. Closed Jan and Feb.* A delightful setting atop the Monte Brè, commanding splendid views of the lake, the town, and the Alpine range, especially from the terrace near the swimming pool.

Delfino – *Via Casserinetta 6.* *(0)91 985 99 99. www.delfinolugano.ch. 50 rooms. Open Mar–Dec.* In the Paradiso quarter, away from the lake. Excellent service for a decent price. Terrace with solarium and pool, a definite asset for the summer season.

Ticino – *Piazza Cioccaro 1.* *(0)91 922.77 72. www.ticinohotel.ch. 18 rooms. Closed Jan.* This historic 14C residence nestles at the heart of the old quarter, among pedestrian streets dotted with fashionable boutiques. A touch of romanticism in a modern city.

℣/EAT

Locanda del Boschetto – *Via Boschetto 8 (Cassarina).* *(0)91 994 24 93. Closed Mon and 1–15 Nov.* A rustic setting and lovely terrace. Good fish and seafood dishes are served.

Osteria Ticinese Da Raffaele – *Via Pazzalino 19.* *(0)91 971 66 14. Closed Sat lunchtime, Sun and end Jul–end Aug.* Serves German, Swiss, and Italian local specialties.

Grotto della Salute – *In Massagno, 2km/1mi NW, Via del Sindicatori 4.* *(0)91 966 04 76. Closed Sat, Sun, mid-Dec–mid-Jan and 4–19 Aug.* Reasonably priced menus offering regional specialities which vary by season.

Osteria Calprino – *Via Carona 18 in the Paradiso district.* *(0)91 994 14 80. www.osteriacalprino.ch. Closed Wed.* Three small, cosy rooms, one of which has an open fireplace where polenta is cooked in the winter season. Reservations are recommended.

Antica Osteria del Porto – *Via Foce 9.* *(0)91 971 42 00. www.osteriadelporto.ch. Open daily exc Tue.* Beside the port this relaxed restaurant offers excellent fish and tasty risotto.

⊞ SHOPPING

The town centre, cut by narrow streets, many of which are closed to traffic, is a great shopping area featuring attractive boutiques with eye-catching window displays **(Via Nassa, Via Pelissa, Piazza Cioccaro)**. In the **Quartiere Maghetti** is a modern shopping complex laid out over several levels.

Christmas Market on Via Nassa

⊞ THEATRE AND MUSIC

The high season runs from May to October and many performances are held at the **Palais des Congrès** or on squares throughout the town (Piazza della Riforma, Piazza Maghetti, or Piazza della Chiesa Santa Marta).

⊞ NIGHTLIFE

The Paradiso area offers several fashionable and pleasant choices: the **Golfe** (Riva Paradiso 2), **Charlie's Pub** (Via Guisan 10) and the **Karisma Pub** (Via Geretta 6). In the town centre, sample delightful Ticino wines at the **Bottegone del Vino** (Via Magatti) or the **Trani** (Salira Mario e Antonio Chiattone).

Corso Pestalozzi becomes especially lively after 11pm, when crowds pour out of the **Corso Cinema** and settle down for a drink at the **Etnie** in the Maghetti district or for one of the tempting ice creams at the pavement café Vanini, on Piazza della Riforma. The **New Orleans** (Piazza Indipendenza) has a combination of live music and DJs.

Locarno★

Locarno lies in the hollow of a sunny bay which curves more sharply as the delta formed by the River Maggia juts into the waters of one of Italy's most famous lakes, **Lago Maggiore**★★★. Sheltered by the Alps, Locarno enjoys an exceptional climate in which hydrangeas, magnolias, and camellias blossom as early as March. This is a beautiful town with pleasant walks among the gardens, along the lakeshore, on the vine-covered slopes of Orselina, and in the Cardada Hills.

SIGHTS
Piazza Grande

This paved oblong square is frequented by locals who enjoy coming here for a stroll, as well as by tourists, attracted by the shopping arcades, cafés and restaurants. The old houses with balconies painted in pastel hues add charm to the whole scene. Each August, film buffs meet in Locarno to attend the **International Film Festival**, when Piazza Grande becomes a huge open-air cinema screen. To the east the square is extended by Largo Zorzi: it ends at the landing stage from which boat trips on the lake can be organised.

▶ **Population:** 15 123.
◉ **Michelin Map:** National 729: K7.
ℹ **Info:** Largo Zorzi 1 – 6600. ℘(0)91 791 00 91. www.maggiore.ch.
◐ **Location:** Sits at the Northern tip of Lake Maggiore.
🅿 **Parking:** Use a municipal car park and take public transport.
◈ **Don't Miss:** Boat tours on Lake Maggiore.
◔ **Timing:** Allow at least a full day to fully take in the sights and complete the driving tour.

Visconti Castle
◔*Open mid-Apr–Oct, Tue–Sun 10am–noon, 2pm–5pm; Sat and Sun 10am–5pm ⊘7CHF. ℘(0)91 756 31 70 80.*
The Museo Civico e Archeologico (Municipal and Archaeological Museum) housed within Visconti castle is devoted to the region's Iron and Bronze Age, Roman period, and Middle Ages. One room is devoted to the Pact of Locarno through photographs and press articles.

Piazza Grande during the International Film Festival

Remy Steinegger/Ticino Turismo/Switzerland Tourism

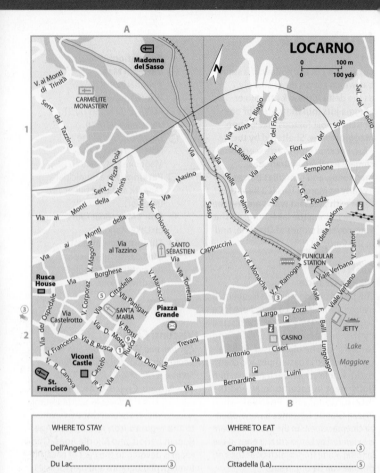

LOCARNO

0   100 m
0   100 yds

WHERE TO STAY		WHERE TO EAT	
Dell'Angello	①	Campagna	③
Du Lac	③	Cittadella (La)	⑤
Piccolo Hotel	⑤	Locanda Locarnese	⑨

Chiesa San Francesco

Consecrated in 1230 by Uberto di Mon-serrato, the Bishop of Como, the church attached to the former Franciscan convent was extensively restored in the 16C. The upper section of the chancel is decorated with a large fresco depicting the Annunciation of the Virgin.

Rusca House

Piazza Sant'Antonio. ⏲*Open Tue–Sun 10am–noon, 2pm–5pm.* ☞*7CHF.* ✆*(0)91 756 31 85.*

Rusca house is a fine example of a 17C patrician residence. The exhibitions, renewed on a regular basis, are devoted to modern and contemporary art, focusing on the work of a specific

artist. Traditionally, featured artists are expected to donate one of their works to the museum, continuously adding to the collections.

GREATER LOCARNO
Madonna del Sasso★★

At Orselina. Recommended access by funicular. Lower station at Via della Stazione.

This church stands on the summit (355m/1 165ft) of a wooded spur which can also be reached by car along the hairpin bends of the Via ai Monti della Trinità. At the upper level, stairs lead down to the basilica (excellent bird's-eye views). In 1480, the Virgin appeared before the brother of Bartolomeo of

The Pact of Locarno, or How to Maintain Peace in Europe

In October 1925, Locarno was at the centre of international politics. World attention was focused on the **Palais de Justice**, where delegations from France, Great Britain, Germany, Italy, Belgium, Poland and Czechoslovakia attended a conference led by their respective foreign ministers Aristide Briand, Austen Chamberlain, Gustav Stresemann, Vittorio Scialoja, Émile Vandervelde, Alexander Skrzynski and Edvard Benes. Seen as a sequel to the 1924 London Conference, which stipulated that the Ruhr area be evacuated within a year and that Germany join the League of Nations, the **Locarno Conference** led to the signing of a treaty on 16 October 1925. Germany recognised its borders with France and Belgium and the demilitarised zone included in the 1919 peace treaty concluded in Versailles. Germany also agreed not to alter her western borders through military action. For his key role in the negotiations and final peace agreement, the head of the British delegation, Austen Chamberlain, was awarded the Nobel Prize for Peace in 1925.

The **Pact of Locarno** was hailed as a resounding success by the international press. It introduced a new era of peaceful cohabitation and Lord d'Abernon, the British ambassador in Berlin, wrote: that it "marks a significant turning-point in the history of post-war Europe. It symbolises the abolition of the dividing line between the conquerors and the conquered." The treaty was ratified in London on **1 December 1925**. Briand, Chamberlain and Stresemann met regularly to supervise its implementation and to pave the way for economic cooperation between countries. Germany was accepted into the **League of Nations** in 1926, signifying reconciliation, it seemed that the future would be free from international tension. But in 1936 **Hitler** violated the treaty by occupying and remilitarising the Rhineland, plunging Europe, and, indeed, the world, into a bloody war three years later.

Ivrea, a monk from the San Francesco convent in Locarno, who had gone into retreat on the Sasso della Rocca. A chapel was erected to commemorate the vision. In the courtyard, follow directions for the "Chiesa". Before reaching the church, you can see several chapels containing groups of wooden sculptures (Chapel of the Pietà, Chapel of the Last Supper, Chapel of the Holy Spirit).

The **Church of the Annunciation** features an arcaded gallery embellished

Madonna del Sasso with a view to the Lake Maggiore

Walter Storto/Switzerland Tourism

with murals. The Baroque interior is particularly interesting for its frescoes and works of art, such as the *Flight into Egypt* painted by Bramantino (1522) and a *Descent from the Cross* (left side aisle) by Antonio Ciseri. The nearby loggia along the church commands a pretty **view**★ of Locarno and Lake Maggiore. Return to the courtyard to visit the **museum** set up in Casa del Padre. It presents 18C sculptures, liturgical objects, ex-votos, and other artefacts. Leaving the church, you can return either by funicular or on foot, following directions for Locarno via Crucis. This will take you along the path traditionally used by pilgrims. The steep climb down, dotted with Stations of the Cross, offers interesting views of the lake.

Cimetta★★

🚡 *Chairlift leaving from Cardada.* 🕐*Operates 15 Mar–Oct, 9.30am–6pm, Mon–Thu, Fri 8am–6pm, Sat and Sun 8am–6pm.* 🚠*33CHF there and back.* 📞*(0)91 735 30 30. www.cardada.ch.*

The funicular going to the Madonna del Sasso is continued by a cable-car which in 10 minutes climbs the **Alpe di Cardada** (alt. 1 350m/4 428ft) from where there is a very extensive **view**★★. From Cardada a chairlift goes to the top of the Cimetta (alt. 1 672m/5 482ft) and a fine **panorama**★★ of the Alps and Lake Maggiore.

Parco delle camelle

2km/1.25mi S, near the swimming pool. 🕐*Open daily 9am–5pm.*

Shaded by poplars and oaks, a unique collection of 520 varieties of camelias flourishes in the beneficial microclimate here.

EXCURSION
Ronco Tour★★

17km/11mi – about 1hr30min – by a corniche road between Ronco and Porto Ronco on which it is difficult to pass. ☀*The trip is very pleasant in the late afternoon.* ▶ *Leave Locarno to the SW by the Ascona road.*

Soon after the bridge over the Maggia, turn right toward Losone. In this village, after the church, turn left (road to Ascona and Veritá Mountain) and right (road to Ronco) at the next crossroads. After running through a small valley, leave the Arcegno road on your right and follow directions for Monte Verita. At the next fork bear right.

The *corniche* byroad, emerging from chestnut woods, opens out above Lake Maggiore and immediately affords a series of beautiful **bird's-eye views**★★. Below, in succession, you will see Ascona,

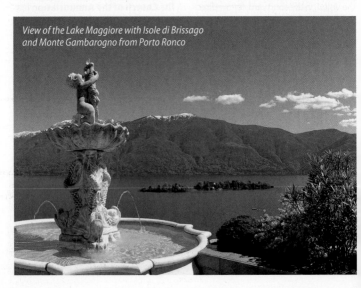

View of the Lake Maggiore with Isole di Brissago and Monte Gambarogno from Porto Ronco

the two wooded **Isole di Brissago** (*see ASCONA*) and finally the lakeside town of Brissago. You come into sight of Ronco.

Ronco

The village clings to a slope in a typically Mediterranean **setting**★★. The church terrace offers a pretty view of Lake Maggiore, the Brissago Islands, and Monte Gambarogno. Take a winding road downward to rejoin the road along the lake at Porto Ronco.

DRIVING TOURS

VALLE MAGGIA★★

28km/17.5mi NW until you reach Bignasco.

▷ *First take the road to Ascona, then follow directions.*

This valley is one of the deepest on the southern slope of the Alps. It is wide at low altitude, with the steep cliff face jutting almost vertically, but narrows farther on, taking on Alpine features with pine and larch forests. Most of the villages have rustic old houses with stone walls, roofs covered in gneiss. As in the Valais canton, you often come across chalets mounted on piles, known as *raccards* or *torbas*, which were used as lofts (*see THE VALAIS*).

▷ *Turn right into a narrow road which branches off the main road.*

Maggia

The village of Maggia has a lovely church, **Santa Maria delle Grazie**, which stands on the edge. Its most notable features are the 16C **frescoes**★ adorning the apse and the walls of the nave and a fine collection of ex-votos painted by Giovanni Antonio Vanoni (1810–1886). This artist born in the small neighbouring hamlet of Aurigeno decorated a great many churches in the Ticino region. The valley becomes narrower and the river bed is littered with huge boulders. Beyond Someo, the **Soladino Waterfall** is on the left.

Cevio

The administrative centre of the Valley Maggia is known for its **Bailiffs' House** (16C), set back behind the main square. The façade is decorated with the coats of arms of the different bailiffs who occupied the premises. On leaving the village, you can visit the **Museo di Vallemaggia** (*open Apr–Oct, Tue–Sat 10am–noon, 2pm–6pm, Sun 2pm–6pm; 6CHF; (0)91 754 13 40/or 23 68 for directions; www.museovalmaggia.ch*).
The museum is divided into two sections. A Folklore Museum in Palazzo Franzoni illustrates the costumes and local crafts of this secluded area. Another display concerns the extraction and use of granite and serpentine, a rare type of rock that is easy to work with and that encouraged the development of local craft. The quarrying of serpentine (deposits at Valle di Peccia, Valle Rovana, Valle Verzasca and Centovalli) ended in the 19C. The second part of the museum lies nearby: the Casa Respini-Moretti is devoted to the Mogheno necropolis discovered in 1994 while a house was being built.

In the hamlet of Rovana (road to Busco/Gurin), near the bridge spanning the river, the church **Beata Vergine del Ponte** is a fine example of Baroque architecture. The interior is lavishly ornamented with stuccowork and frescoes.

▷ *16km/10mi W towards Cerentino.*

Follow the road and its hairpin bends through Alpine landscape to Linescio, then Cerentino. The countryside becomes more rugged and opens onto Bosco/Gurin, a cirque of Alpine pastures. This wild "world's end" is often part of the difficult official circuit of the Swiss Cycling Tour for experienced cyclists.

Bosco/Gurin★

The highest village in the Ticino area (1 503m/4 930ft) is unique: it is the last remaining Walser village where the local population still speaks Gurinerdeutsch or Walser Deutsch, a German dialect which incorporates Italian words.
The Walser probably settled here around the 13C, coming from the Upper Valais to cultivate and defend land belonging to Italian lords. These rugged mountain people, who lived in a state of serfdom, enjoyed certain privileges in return, such as the free hereditary loan of land. The church terrace commands a plunging view of the Lower Valley with wooden houses built on stone bases.
A fine old mansion, the **Walserhaus** (*open mid-April–Oct, Tue–Sun 10am–11.30am, 1.30pm–5pm, Sun 1.30pm–5pm; 3CHF; (091) 754 24 23; www.walserhaus.ch*) contains an Ethnographical Museum explaining the history and traditions of the Walser (household objects, early trades, costumes, religious rites, etc.).

Bignasco

The confluence where the River Maggia (or Lavizzara) meets the River Bavona.

▷ *Choose between two itineraries: Val Lavizzara or Val Bavona.*

VAL LAVIZZARA

17km/10.5mi until Fusio.

Peccia

This village is renowned for its marble. The quarry is located near the small hamlet of Piano di Peccia. The marble is taken to Peccia, where it is worked. The shades go from white, as in the case of Carrara marble, to gray, with blue, brown, or even pink streaks. The road continues to climb, forming hairpin bends.

Mogno

Soon after the bridge, take a small road on the right to the chapel, designed by Ticino architect Mario Botta. The white and gray stone building, shaped as a truncated pyramid, replaces the former church, swept away by an avalanche in 1986.

Fusio

Perched at an altitude of 1 280m/4 199ft, at the foot of a rocky spur, Fusio is the highest village in Val Lavizzara, with many fine old houses. During the high season, you may continue beyond the dam lake (Lago Sambuco). The road becomes steeper and narrower, with more bends (*caution is required here as there is no parapet and only room for one car to pass at a time*). The vegetation is scarce and the landscape appears barren. There are breathtaking views all the way up to the small mountain lakes.

▷ *Return to Bignasco.*

VAL BAVONA

12km/7.4mi until you reach San Carlo, where the road ends.

This wild area is characterised by high cliff faces and huge boulders which accumulated after a series of rockfalls, especially around **Cavergno**. All along the route, you will drive through villages with typical 16C architecture.

Foroglio

The most attractive feature of Foroglio is its waterfall. Leave the car near the bridge, cross the river and follow the green signpost "Punto Panoramico" near the restaurant. The path leads to the foot of the waterfall, whose gushing waters form an imposing sight.

Sonlerto

This little village is worth visiting with its church and its campanile, the fountain, the houses and the torba. The road winds its way upward along a sinuous course. As it crosses the river, it gets closer to the huge mass of rock looming on the horizon.

San Carlo

From the last village in Val Bavona, a cable-car will take you to Mont Robiei (1 894m/6 213ft). Experienced climbers may reach the summit on foot and proceed until they reach the three small mountain lakes: Zött, Robiei, and Bianco.

CENTOVALLI★

19km/11.8mi W.

The region of the Hundred Valleys is extremely popular with both hikers and nature lovers. The train linking Locarno to Domodossola (Italy) makes many stops and allows those who don't have a car to discover a highly attractive area.

▷ *Leave Locarno by the road to Ponte Tresa. At Ponte Brolla, turn left.*

Intragna

The village and its narrow streets are dominated by the campanile. The Baroque church features fine mural paintings in the chancel. To the right of the church, a small alley leads to the **Museo Regionale delle Centovalli e del Pedemonte** (*open Easter–Oct, Tue–Sun 2–6pm; 5CHF; (0)91 796 25 77; www.museo100valli.ch*).
This little museum illustrates the history and life of the region through an exhibition of farming tools, everyday objects, costumes, sacred art, sculptures, and paintings.

Rasa

⚞ Access by cable-car (Funivia Verdasio-Rasa). Allow 10min there and back.
The village perched at an altitude of 900m/2 953ft presents many old stone houses. To the left of the church, a path leads to a fountain and some benches. From there you can enjoy a view of the Lower Valley, lake, and the villages nestling on the slopes. From right to left, you will see Verdasio, Borgnone, Lionza and, farther down, Comedo. Several paths for hikers start from Rasa, such as that of Pizzo Leone *(3hr)*, which affords pretty views of Lake Maggiore.

Monte Comino

⚞ Access by cable-car (Funivia Verdasio-Monte Comino) to the right of the road. Allow 15min there and back.
From the upper station (1 200m/3 936ft), a path winds its way down, toward a fork branching off into two directions. The right-hand path leads to Madonna della Segna, a small church fronted by a porch with three arcades dating back to 1700. The left-hand path will take you to an inn or *grotto* where hikers may stay the night. From the terrace (tables made with local granite), there is a sweeping panorama of the whole valley. The tiny village of Rasa can be glimpsed on the opposite slope.

Verdasio

🅿 Leave the car at the entrance to the village and continue on foot through a charming ensemble of narrow streets and vaulted passageways. The road climbs down toward a small reservoir, then snakes its way up in the direction of Palagnedra.

Palagnedra

The village architecture—one- or two-storey houses scattered over pastureland—provides a striking contrast with the other localities in the area. The road passes the rocky bank of Borgnone.

Camedo

This is the last Swiss village, separated from Italy by a bridge, the Ponte Ribellasca.

VAL VERZASCA★

25km/15.5mi NE.

After **Tenero**, a small village surrounded by vineyards, the road climbs toward the gigantic concrete mass of the Contra Dam.

Contra Dam

Leave the car by the roadside and walk up to the dam, which dominates the valley from a height of over 200m/656ft, built over a lake 5km/3.5mi long. In the centre of the dyke, a contraption has been set up with the inscription "007 Bungy Jumping," used in bungee jumping competitions and films (the famous scene in the James Bond movie *Goldeneye* was shot here). The best record to date is a 220m/722ft jump in 7.5 seconds!
The road skirts the dam, climbs upward and goes through several tunnels.

Vogorno

The houses are built on the mountain side. The church, entirely white with a stone campanile, presents a fine fresco in the Byzantine style. About 2km/1.2mi farther on, take a narrow road on the left which climbs up the opposite side of the valley.

Corippo★

This picturesque village is one of the most popular stopping-places for tourists. The setting is truly magnificent. Note the splendid panorama of the Lower Valley and the lake. Near the church stands the tiny *Sala Communale*.

▷ *Return to the main road, which crosses the river over a bridge with twin arches. The landscape becomes more barren and the river snakes through huge boulders.*

Brione

Situated on a plateau where the Osola stream and the River Verzasca converge, this village is famous for its granite quarries. It is also a starting-point for many hiking excursions. The parish church boasts some beautiful 14C **frescoes★**

attributed to one of Giotto's pupils from the Rimini School, centreing on religious themes *(The Last Supper, Presentation of the Virgin, etc.)*. The small castle with corner turrets (formerly the Trattoria del Castello) was once the private residence of the Marcacci barons of Locarno. Before reaching Frasco, you will see a waterfall on the right.

Sonogno

🅿 *Car park (fee) at the entrance to the village.*

ADDRESSES

🍴 STAY

🛏🍽 **Hotel du Lac** – *Via Ramogna 3.* 📞 *(0)91 751 29 21. www.du-lac-locarno.ch.* *31 rooms.* Located in the pedestrian area near Piazza Grande, barely 5min from the Madonna del Sasso funicular and near the landing for delightful boat trips on the lake. No restaurant.

🛏🍽 **Hotel Garni Muralto** – *Via Sempione.* 📞 *(0)91 743 14 41.* *www.hotelmuralto.ch. 34 rooms. Closed 19 Dec–11 Jan.* A charming and quaint hotel, surrounded by a garden planted with palm trees. Most rooms have a balcony overlooking Lake Maggiore.

🛏🍽 **Piccolo Hotel** – *Via Buetti 11.* 📞 *(0)91 743 02 12. www-piccolo-hotel.ch.* *21 rooms. Closed mid-Nov–mid-Mar.* Good prices and service at this hotel away from the town centre. No restaurant.

🛏🍽 **Dell'Angelo** – *Piazza Grande.* 📞 *(0)91 751 81 75. www.hotel-dell-angelo.ch. 55 rooms.* Centrally located at the heart of the new town, this hotel is a good starting-point for discovering the old quarter. The top floor has a terrace offering nice views of the town and lake.

🍴 EAT

🍽 **Campagna** – *In Minusio, 2km/1mi E – Via Rivapiana 46.* 📞 *(0)91 743 20 54.* *Closed Tue, and Wed evening.* This typical Ticino grotto has been converted into a restaurant with rustic decor. Eating at granite tables outdoors, in the shade of the trees, can be a charming experience.

The last village in Val Verzasca spreads its stone houses at the foot of a rocky barrier. The **Museo di Val Verzasca** (🕐 *open daily May–Oct, 1pm–5pm;* 🎫*4CHF;* 📞*(0)91 746 17 77)* is a small Museum of Ethnography devoted to regional crafts, farming, costumes, and sacred art. Walk up the main street near the church you can see an early bread oven which is still used. The chancel in the church contains frescoes painted by Cherubino Pata, a pupil of Courbet who was born in Sonogno.

🍽🍽 **La Cittadella** – *Via Cittadella 18.* 📞 *(0)91 751 58 85. www.cittadella.ch.* A trattoria on the ground floor and a dining room upstairs - in both the service and cuisine are impeccable.

🍽🍽 **Locanda Locarnese** – *Via Bossi 1/Piazza Grande.* 📞 *(0)91 756 87 56.* *www.locandalocarnese.ch. Closed Sun.* A young talented chef and inventive mediterranean cuisine.

🛒 SHOPPING

The main shopping streets are **Via della Stazione**, **Via della Ramogna**, **Via Sempione**, **Via Cattori**, **Via D. Recinto**, **Via F. Balli** and **Piazza Grande**.

🍸 NIGHTLIFE

Enjoy an apéritif in a typical setting at **Alle Grotto** (in the Grand Albergo Locarno complex, access by Via della Stazione). On weekends, there is live music at **Cantina Canetti** (Piazza Grande 20), a well-known wine bar which has retained its old-fashioned charm. The **Kursaal** casino (Largo Zorzi) attracts the late-night crowd with its discotheque and slot machines.

In the Muralto district, along the lake shores, the **Al Pozz** (Viale Verbano 21) is a bar offering musical entertainment. A little farther on, the **Bussola** is for dedicated jazz enthusiasts.

🏌 SPORTS AND RECREATION

The Navigazione Lago Maggiore company (📞*(0)91 751 61 40; www.navigazionelaghi.it)* books a wide variety of boat tours on Lake Maggiore.

Ascona★★

Ascona's site on Lake Maggiore's shore resembles that of Locarno and its position at the mouth of the River Maggia. Like its larger neighbour, Ascona benefits from the river delta's flat lands, which provide a host of sporting facilities. This colourful fishing village, long a favourite with artists, has become an important venue for cultural events (New Orleans Jazz Festival in July, Classical Music Festival in September).

LAKE

Ente Turistico Lago Maggiore. Viale Papio 5. ℘(0)91 791 00 91. www.maggiore.ch.
The lake front, closed to cars, is a popular promenade area. During the high season, at night, strains of live music add to the festive atmosphere of the town. Regular boat trips leave for Locarno, Porte Ronco, the Brissago islands and destinations in Italy.

SIGHTS
Santa Maria della Misericordia
Via delle Cappelle.
Founded in 1399 and reconstructed in the 15C, the church is known for its 15C–16C polychrome **frescoes** in the nave and on the walls and vaulting of the chancel. The beautiful **altarpiece**, depicting the life of the Virgin, is attributed to Giovanni Antonio della Gaïa (1519).

Santi Pietro e Paolo
Piazza San Pietro.
At the heart of the town's narrow alleys, this parish church, dedicated to St Peter and St Paul, exhibits a fine altarpiece and splendid paintings by **Giovanni Serodine**, a pupil of Caravaggio.

Monte Verità
This wooded hillside which dominates Ascona could also be called "Utopian Hill". This present name was given by the community which established the village at the beginning of the 20C. They

▶ **Population:** 5 533.
⦿ **Michelin Map:** National 729: K7.
🄸 **Info:** The beautiful mansion on the square, whose windows are decorated with sculptures, houses the Tourist Information Centre. Ente Turistico Lago Maggiore Ascona, Via B. Luini 3. ℘(0)91 791 00 91. www.ascona-locarno.com. Alt. 210m/689ft.
🕙 **Timing:** Plan your visit around a boat tour on the Isole di Brissago.
⦿ **Also See:** The Botanical Park at San Pancrazio, created by Baroness Antonietta de Saint-Léger.

were looking for a new way of life, a classless society without money.

Casa Anatta
Monte Verità. ⓞOpen Apr–Oct, Tue–Sun, 2.30pm–6pm. ℘(0)91 791 01 81. ⊜6CHF.
This house of 1904, constructed at the time of the community gives an idea of what life was like.

EXCURSION
Isole di Brissago★
ⓞ*Boat service is available from 28 Mar –19 Sept, daily 9am–6pm.*
🄸 *For information contact the Tourist Office in Ascona or Losone or ask at the offices of Navigazione Lago Maggiore d'Ascona, at Ascona harbour. Exotic park, art exhibition. ⊜8CHF. ℘(0)91 791 00 91.*
The tiny Brissago islands enjoy an exceptional climate and the larger of the two, San Pancrazio, is the most popular holiday destination for tourists staying in Ascona. There is a tour of the Botanical Park which also affords pretty views of the lake. The mild climate permits cultivation of plant and flower species from all five continents. The small shady beach has a distinctly tropical feel.

Isole di Brissago

Christof Sonderegger/Switzerland Tourism

ADDRESSES

STAY

Al Faro – *Piazza G. Motta 27.* ℘ *(0)91 791 85 15. www.hotel-al-faro.ch. Closed Nov–mid-Feb. 18 rooms.* Located in the centre of Ascona's famous Piazza. Newly renovated, now offering Wi-Fi service.

Castello – *Piazza G. Mottta.* ℘ *(0)91 791 01 61. www.castello-s-eeschloss.ch. Closed early Nov–Feb. 46 rooms.* This former medieval castle near the lake and the centre of town is extravagant with its cosy rooms with period furniture. Outdoor pool.

Al Porto – *Piazza G. Motta.* ℘ *(0)91 785 85 85. www.alporto-hotel.ch. 36 rooms.* Simple contemporary rooms in pastel colours and rustic furniture. On-site restaurant.

Tamaro – *Piazza G. Motta 35.* ℘ *(0)91 785 48 48. www.hotel-tamaro.ch. Closed early Jan. 51 rooms.* Situated on the lakeside promenade with a pleasant inner courtyard and garden where meals are served.

LOSONE

Casa Berno – ℘ *(0)91 791 32 32 www.casaberno.ch. Closed Nov–Mar. 65 rooms.* Enchanting location near the panoramic Ronco Tour. Beautiful views of the mountains and lake. Peace and quiet guaranteed.

EAT

Della Carrà – *Carrà dei Nasi.* ℘ *(0)91 791 44 52. www.ristorantedellacarra.ch. Closed Sun and Mon (except Sun evening from Easter–Oct) and 1–20 Dec.* Located in the old town, offering regional cuisine.

LOSONE

Osteria Dell'Enoteca – *Contrada Maggiore 24.* ℘ *(0)91 791 78 17. www. osteriaenoteca.ch. Closed Mon, Tue and 1 Jan–7 Mar.* Friendly osteria with meals served in an enchanting garden.

PONTE BROLLA

Da Enzo – *6652 Tegna.* ℘ *(0)91 796 14 75. www.ristorantedaenzo.ch. Closed Wed all day, Thu at lunchtime and 15 Jan– 1 Mar.* Located at the entrance to the Valle Maggia and surrounded by palm and bamboo this fine restaurant offers Italian specialities in a lovely Ticino house nestling amid the greenery.

BRISSAGO

Mirafiori – *Via Crodolo.* ℘ *(0)91 793 12 34. Closed Nov–Feb.* Enjoy a good meal on the shaded terrace right on the edge of the lake.

Osteria Grotto Borei – *At Piodina 3km/1.8mi SW of Brissago.* ℘ *(0)91 793 01 95. Closed Thu, 15 Dec–18 Mar; weekdays Nov–14 Dec (open Fri, Sat and Sun only).* Family business serving typical Ticino dishes. Splendid location in the mountains with pretty views of the lake.

Bellinzona★★★

Bellinzona is an essential point of passage for traffic using the St Gotthard, Lukmanier or San Bernardino routes. It lies on the Italian side of the Alps and for 1 000 years has been a stronghold guarding the Ticino Valley. In 1803 it became the administrative centre of the canton, which took the name of the river.

HISTORICAL CENTRE
Collegiata dei Santi Pietro e Stefano

On Piazza della Collegiata, this church, dedicated to St Peter and St Stephen, stands out because of its imposing Renaissance façade carved out of Castione stone and adorned with a rose window. The interior is Baroque; fine frescoes decorate the side chapels, the most famous being the *Angel Musicians*, the work of Giuseppe Antonio Felice Orelli (c.1770). This arcaded square of **Piazza Nosetto** is the scene of a lively market held on Saturday mornings. The **Palazzo Civico** (town hall) is heavily influenced by the Italian Renaissance and has an elegant inner courtyard.

Teatro Sociale

Reopened in 1997 following extensive renovation, the Theatre of Bellinzona is the only existing Neoclassical theatre in Switzerland, and recalls Milan's famous La Scala.

CASTLES

The city fortifications rested on three castles, two of which (Castelgrande and Castello di Montebello) were connected by walls, a great part of which can still be seen, even from a distance. These castles are a UNESCO World Heritage Site.

Castelgrande★★

Recommended access by a lift situated on Piazzella Mario della Valle at the foot of the rock. ◐*Open Apr–Oct, daily 10am–6pm; Nov–Mar,10am–5pm. Film (15 min).* ◉*4CHF. (Three Castles ticket* ◉*10CHF).* ℘*(0)91 825 81 45.*

▶ **Population:** 17 286.
◔ **Michelin Map:** National 729: L7.
🖩 **Info:** Palazzo Civico, via Camminata 2 – 6500. ℘(0)91 825 21 31. www.bellinzonaturismo.ch.
◖ **Location:** Bellinzona is positioned at the southern entrance to the St. Gotthard, San Bernardino and Lukmanier passes. Alt. 223m/732ft.
◉ **Don't Miss:** UNESCO World Heritage Sites of Castelgrande, Castellos di Montebello, Sasso Corbaro
◕ **Timing:** Allow at least a half day to visit the three castles.

The oldest of the three castles is built on a rocky spur, its two quadrangular towers (Torre Bianca and Torre Nera) clearly visible from afar and from various vantage points in the town. Castelgrande endowed itself with additional fortifications between 1250 and 1500 following the wars that ravaged the area. The Torre Nera marked the centre of the castle; from there the crenelated ramparts formed three inner baileys. Substantial restoration work was carried out between 1982 and 1992 under the supervision of the Ticino architect Aurelio Galfetti. Buildings in the south courtyard now house a restaurant and a reception area. In the south wing the **Museo Storico Archeologico** (Museum of History and Archaeology) contains rooms explaining the history of castles and a gallery devoted to the gold and silver coins minted in Bellinzona during the 16C. In 1503 the Uri, Schwyz and Nidwalden cantons decided to found a minting factory in Basel, which became famous throughout the Confederation.

Castello di Montebello★★

Access by a ramp which starts from the railway station road (Viale Stazione). 🅿*Car park.* ◐*Museum open Mar–Nov,*

Castello di Montebello

Roland Gerth/Switzerland Tourism

*daily 10am–6pm (Castle 8am–8pm.
5CHF (Three Castles ticket 10CHF).
(0)91 825 13 42.*

This formidable citadel is typical of the Lombard military style in architecture. Built in the 13C by the influential Rusca family, the castle became the property of the Visconti in the late 14C. Under the reign of the Confederates in the 16C, it was renamed Castello di Svitto (Castle of Schwyz) and subsequently San Martino in the 18C. A drawbridge spanning the moat takes you to the defensive core of the stronghold, around which ramparts were erected in the 14C and 15C. The **Museo Civico** (Municipal Museum) presents ancient weapons and artefacts unearthed during digs carried out in the localities of Ticino, Gudo, Gorduno, Ascona, Giubiasco, Madrano, etc.

Castello di Sasso Corbaro

Access by car from the castle described above. Take the steep Via Artore, then Via Bebedetto Ferrini on the right and Via Sasso Corbaro. Car park. Open Apr–Oct, Mon–Sat 10am–6pm. 5CHF (Three Castles ticket 10CHF). (0)91 825 59 06.

This castle is the highest of the three, an isolated fortress standing among chest-nut groves. Built to a square plan, it was commissioned in the 15C by the Duke of Milan to consolidate the defensive network of the city, deemed too vulnerable at that spot.

The terrace in the forecourt affords a beautiful **view**★ of the town and the Lower Ticino Valley as far as Lake Maggiore. Visit the **Museo dell'Arte e delle Tradizioni Popolari** (Museum of Popular Art and Tradition) installed in the keep. Room 3 (Sala Emma-Poglia) features a bedroom with fine wainscoting and a sculpted coffered ceiling taken from the residence belonging to the Poglia d'Olivone family. The following rooms display everyday objects which bring to life the Ticino region and its traditions.

GREATER BELLINZONA
Ravecchia

From Piazza Indipendenza, Via Lugano leads to the peaceful suburb of Ravecchia.

Santa Maria delle Grazie

Formerly attached to a 15C convent run by a minor order of monks, Santa Maria delle Grazie contains some interesting frescoes, including a poignant *Crucifixion*

Scene, surrounded by 15 paintings illustrating the Life of Christ.

San Biagio

This small medieval church with its square belltower and 14C frescoes, both inside and out, was known as the church of Bellinzona even though it was outside the walls.

Museo Villa dei Cedri

Piazza San Biagio 9. Tue–Fri 2pm–6pm, Sat–Sun and Hols 11am–6pm. ⊛8CHF. ℘(0)91 821 85 20. www.villacedri.ch.
Very close to the Chiesa San Biagio this museum is the town's art gallery. Situated in a pleasant park, it houses Suisse and Italian figurative art of the 19 and 20C. These works all donated carry the signatures of Chiesa, Franzoni, Rossi and Guide Tallone amongst many others.

EXCURSIONS
Monte Carasso★

▶ *2km/1.25mi W of Bellinzona.*
This village of 2300 inhabitants on the periphery of Bellinzona is a textbook case of an innovative urban project by the Ticino architect **Luigi Snozzi**. The most visible is the public area around the old convent which has become a community school. Some other buildings such as the Raiffeisen bank, the gymnasium and the new cemetery all contribute to the transformation of the village.

Monte Tamaro★

▶ *15km/9mi NW. Leave Lugano on the Como road and take the freeway towards Bellinzona. Turn off at Rivera.* ◴*Open daily 27 Mar–7 Nov 8.30am–5pm. Reach Alpe Foppa by cable-car (20min). ⊛23CHF. ℘(0)91 946 23 03. www.montemaro.ch.*
Although it looks like a fort, it is the **Chiesa Santa Maria degli Angeli**, designed by the famous Ticino architect Mario Botta. A long upper passageway ends in a belvedere decorated with a metal cross supporting a bell. You can also reach the church via the lower passageway, whose ceilings are embellished with paintings by Enzo Cucchi (the same artist decorated the interior). Notice the two hands symbolically united on a blue background, lit by a luminous source from above. The curved walls present two rows of 11 windows, which make for a light, radiant atmosphere.

Alpe Foppa (alt. 1 530m/4 018ft) is the departure point for many excursions. You can also hire cross-country bicycles or go paragliding from there. The Monte Tamaro summit (alt. 1 960m/6 397ft) commands a sweeping **view★** of Lake Lugano, Lake Maggiore, the Monte Rosa and the Matterhorn.

ADDRESSES

⌂STAY

⊜⊌ **Albergo Internazionale** –
Piazza Stazione 35. ℘(0)91 825 43 33. www.hotel-internazionale.ch. 90 rooms.
Facing the station, the hotel offers modern, comfortable rooms, most with balconies.

⊜⊌⊟ **Unione** – *Via Generale Guisan 1. ℘(0)91 825 55 77. www.hotel-unione.ch. Closed 22 Dec–20 Jan. 40 rooms.*
Conveniently situated near the town centre, this hotel offers good service for highly affordable prices. Meals can be served in the garden.

⊉/EAT

⊜⊌ **Osseria Sasso Corbaro** –
In Castello Sasso Corbaro. ℘(0)91 825 55 32. Closed Dec–mid-Mar. A charming restaurant perched high up in a castle. Regional cuisine. Nice views of the town from the terrace.

⊜⊌⊟ **Castelgrande** – *Salita al Castello (access by lift). ℘(0)91 826 23 53. www.castelgrande.ch. Closed Mon.*
The restaurant lies within the ramparts of the former medieval fortress of Castelgrande. Wines bottled on the estate.

Alto Ticino★★

The Alto or Upper Ticino consists of the valleys and mountains in the north of the Canton. The small town of Biasca, 24km/15m, north of Bellinzona is the gateway to the region and here the Val Levantina, leading northwest to Airolo, and the Val Blenio, leading north to Olivoni, head off to the Alpine passes of St Gotthard and Lukmanier respectively.

🚗 DRIVING TOURS

① LUKMANIER PASS ROAD★
66km/40mi – about 45min.
The Lukmanier Pass is usually blocked by snow from November to May.

To the south, villages consist of groups of stone buildings around slender campaniles; to the north they feature wooden chalets and domed churches. The Lukmanier is the lowest of the Swiss transalpine routes, but due to its roundabout approaches on the north slope of the Alps, international traffic uses the St Gotthard. On the Rhine side, part of the high Alpine hollow is flooded by the waters of the Santa Maria Dam. Between the Santa Maria Dam and Disentis/Mustér, beyond a valley dotted with clumps of dwarf alders and rhododendrons, the road crosses the clear Cristallina Rhine and, as conifers begin to reappear, enters the central basin of the Medel Valley. Sloping pastures cut by zigzag ravines, dark chalets and the domed belfry of Curaglia make this little mountain retreat an attractive **scene★**. Notice the silos in which grain ripens, after being harvested early because of the harsh climate.

Biasca

This small town, at the intersection of the Ticino Valley and the Brenno Valley, is dominated by the 12C **Chiesa dei Santi Pietro e Paolo** (*Contact the Tourist Office for entry*), hollowed out of the rock and accessible by a long stairway. The Romanesque church, made of local granite, has a tall bell tower with arches, its façade, decorated with a fresco partly worn away; the chapel is in the Baroque style with remains of interesting polychrome **frescoes** (14C–15C).

Malvaglia

The Romanesque **campanile★** of the church is in the Lombard fashion, with the number of arches increasing as they approach the summit.

The barrenness of the lower **Val Blenio**, accentuated by the destructive work of the tributaries of the Brenno, decreases beyond Dongio.

A verdant basin opens out with the bold pyramid of the Sosto looming ahead.

Lottigna★

This village stretches along the valley in terraces. The former Bailiffs' House (15C), decorated with the coat of arms of the first Swiss cantons, is now the **Museo della Valle di Blenio** (○*open mid-Apr–31 Oct, Tue–Sun 2pm–5.30pm; ⊙5CHF; ℘(0)91 871 19 77; www.vallediblenio.ch*). The museum houses historic tools, utensils and traditional

⚿ **Michelin Map:**
National 729.

🚊 **Info: Andermatt –**
Verkehrsverein, Gotthardstrasse 2. ℘041 887 14 54. www.andermatt.ch.
Biasca – Ente Turistico, Contrada Cavalier Pellanda 4 – 6710. ℘(0)91 862 33 27. www.biascaturismo.ch.
Faido – Leventina Turismo. ℘091 966 16 16. www.leventinaturismo.ch.

▶ **Location:** Accessible via St Gotthard and Lukmanier Pass roads, and the Nufenenstrasse.

✦ **Don't Miss:** A cable-car ride up Gemsstock.

⏱ **Timing:** Allow a day to make the most of this area and complete the itineraries.

St Gotthard Massif

St Gotthard Road

One of the best-known Alpine passes in Switzerland, the St Gotthard provides a route from Airolo, in the Ticino, to Goschenen, in the canton of Uri, thus connecting the German and Italian-speaking regions. Despite being the shortest route between southern Germany and Milan, Italy, the pass was not heavily trafficked until after the 13C because the trip required fording the Schollen River at a steep gorge near Andermatt. Folktales surround the building of the bridges. Until the late 1700s the bridge carried only foot traffic, and was strengthened to accommodate carriages in 1775. The top of the pass is the continental divide; waters north of it flow into the Rhine and North Sea, and to the south flow to the Po and into the Mediterranean.

The old winding road over the top of the pass was replaced by a tunnel in 1980, but the old road remains and offers a far more scenic, though slower, alternative, especially for those heading south, where magnificent views open up as they descend along raised viaducts. To take the old road, leave the main road at the Goschenen exit, just before the tunnel entrance. At the top of the pass is a tourist centre with a restaurant, gift shop, and a small museum.

The St Gotthard Rail Tunnel

The trip through the pass by train is quite spectacular, not only for the steep cliffs and gorges of the Reuss Valley and the vertigo-inducing bridges of the south side, but for the tunnel itself. It climbs through the mountain in a series of spirals that allows the locomotive to reach the necessary height without making the gradient too steep. The highlight of the tunnel climb is the many sightings of the town of Wassen, with its pretty little church. This tunnel is being replaced by a new one that drills almost straight through the range, from Erstfeld, in Uri, to Bodio, in the Ticino (due to open in 2017).

A popular tourist pass, **The William Tell Express** combines a luncheon trip across the lake from Lucerne to Flüelen by vintage paddle steamer with the train ride through the pass. The programme is offered May to October, and operates in either direction. Reservations are compulsory: *www.raileurope.com/us/rail/specialty/william_tell.htm*.

St Gothard Pass at Val Tremola

egional costumes, religious art and a
arge arms collection (14C to today).

⟩ At Acquarossa bear left onto the
small road that runs along the western
ide of Blenio Valley. Left of the church
in Prugiasco, take the street that
climbs, then narrows, and follow it for
2km/1.2mi. The sanctuary of Negrentino
stands atop a grassy knoll.

Chiesa Negrentino San Carlo★

30min on foot there and back. To visit,
contact the Blenio Tourist Office in
Acquarossa. ℘(0)91 871 14 87.
The interior of this small 11C Romanesque church is painted with a series
of polychrome **frescoes**★★ (11C–16C).
After leaving Castro and Ponto-Valen-
tino, you reach Aquila and the direct
road to Lukmanier. From Olivone to
Acquacalda the road has two series of
hairpin bends separated by the Camp-
erio shelf. Soon the **view**★ opens eastward to the snowy peaks of the Adula
Massif.

Lukmanier Pass
(Passo del Lucomagno)

Alt. 1 916m/6 286ft.

② THE ST GOTTHARD
PASS ROAD★

*See the box opposite for the history
of this road.*
Most of the present siting dates from
1830 but extensive resurfacing and widening has improved it considerably. On
the Ticino side the road is much faster

than along the Reuss. *The St Gotthard
road carries heavy traffic.*

*The St Gotthard Pass is usually blocked
by snow Nov–Jun. 65km/40mi – 2hr.*

Andermatt★
Alt. 1 436m/4 711ft.
Andermatt lies at the junction of the St
Gotthard, Furka and Oberalp roads in
a beautiful curve of the Urseren Valley,
which is the heart of the St Gotthard
Massif. The life of the town flows
along its narrow main street, sections
of which still show the typical Italian **binario** (road with granite paving
stones). In winter, when snow covers
the neighbouring slopes, punctuated
with anti-avalanche barriers, Andermatt is crowded with skiers. The main
ski resorts are in the Nätschen district
(towards the Oberalp Pass), regularly
served by local trains and chairlifts, as
are the Gemsstock slopes, equipped
with a cable-car.
The last climb to the St Gotthard begins
at the foot of the ancient Hospental
watchtower. The road climbs above the
Urseren Valley, to the right of the Furka
Pass, by the snowy Galenstock peaks,
then into the Gams Valley.

Gemsstock★★
*Allow at least 1hr there and back,
including a 40min journey in a cable-
car split up into two trips.*
Many opportunities for hiking.
Proceed to the upper terrace with its
viewing tables. The dramatic **panor**

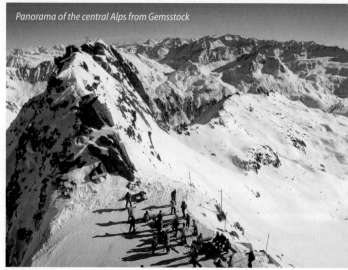

Panorama of the central Alps from Gemsstock

ama★★ sweeps over 600 summits in the distance. The Finsteraarhorn dominates the Bernese Oberland to the east.

In the foreground, the Göschen Valley is overshadowed by Dammastock. To the south lie the Mont Rose and the spectacular range of Italian Alps.

St Gotthard Pass (Passo del San Gottardo)
Alt. 2 108m/6 919ft.

Set in a rugged but breathtaking landscape of rounded rocks and scattered lakes, the pass owes its name to a chapel erected about 1300 in honor of St Gotthard, Bishop of Hildesheim (near Hanover).

Situated at the top of the pass, the **Museo Nazionale del San Gottardo**★ (National St Gotthard Museum; ○open Jun–Oct, daily 9am–6pm; slide show (25min); ⊕8CHF; ℘(0)91 869 15 25) traces the history of this strategic location, used by the Romans and which links together north and south, connecting Switzerland to the rest of Europe. Scale models, photographs, and other artefacts illustrate the road, the tunnel, flora and fauna, postal connections, the St Gotthard Inn (where weary travellers were fed and given a bed) and the relevance of the pass, particularly to the Battle of Tremola on 24 September 1799, during which the French fought against the Russians and the Austrians.

Val Tremola
Access in summer only. 13km/8mi from the St Gotthard Pass.

The road coils loop over loop within this steep corridor, which carries the alarming name of Trembling Valley. Seen from below (*stand on the disused bridge at the bottom of the ravine*), the road, with its interlaced sustaining walls, gives a good idea of the road-builders' audacity.

The modern road, an exceptionally bold piece of work, avoids the difficult crossing of the Tremola Valley by a change of route. It follows the mountainside with only three hairpin bends—one of which is built partly on a curved viaduct, another is a **viewpoint**★—and the third is a tunnel 700m/0.5mi long. The descent is very steep.

The Upper Leventina lies wide open between slopes dotted with villages, nestling at the foot of a campanile. Note the Ticino stone houses and Alpine chalets with wooden upper storeys.

The Ambri-Piotta Basin, between woods of firs and larches, opens out between Airolo and the Piottino Defile. Below the Piottino Defile the valley is gradually shut in by steep spurs with wild ravines, whose torrents end in waterfalls.

Val Piora★

Alt. 1 796m/5 900ft. 🚡 12min by funicular from the Ritom power station.
This is a pleasant walk along clearly laid-out paths, bordered by charming Alpine lakes: The walk affords an opportunity to discover the local vegetation and the many wild animal species inhabiting the region.

Faido

Rich woodlands and gushing waters (La Piumogna Cascades), makes this township a splendid summer resort. The semicircular main square with shady lime trees, a statue dedicated to local glories, houses covered by curious conical stone roofs and dotted with outdoor cafés, compose a lovely Italian scene.

Biasca – 🚗 *See Lukmanier Pass Road*

③ NUFENEN PASS ROAD★★

⚠ *The Nufenen Pass is usually closed November to May.*
Nufenpass is the highest elevation pass to allow motor vehicles in Switzerland, and is also home to many bicycle and hiking trails 🅱. The bicycle tour, suitable for experienced and very fit riders, spans 36.6 km/22.7mi over an altitude variation of 1 340m/4 396ft; this trip takes the average cyclist four to six hours to complete. The road offers many spectacular views.

From **Airolo** (alt. 1 142m/3 747ft) to 8km/5mi from Nufenen, the climb up the Bedretto Valley (and from the River Ticino to its source) begins between slopes covered with fir trees. From Airolo to Fontana there are audacious examples (above and to the right) of the engineers' ingenuity when constructing the road. Then after Ossasco you can see a series of villages halfway up the slope: Bedretto is one of them. Beginning at the hamlet of All'Acqua (*cable-car on the left*) the foliage becomes scarcer, the climb steeper and the hairpin bends offer a succession of views behind onto the valley's slopes. You then ascend the barren right side of the Bedretto Valley. The ascent stops abruptly at the **Nufenen Pass★★** (alt. 2 478m/8 130ft),

Mountain Roads

The highway code states that on difficult mountain roads the ascending vehicle has priority. On "postal" roads, drivers must comply with directions given by the drivers of the yellow postal buses.

where you have climbed more than 1 300m/4 265ft since Airolo. This pass offers an amazing landscape of incredible desolation. Higher up (*to the left of the restaurant*) the **view★★** encompasses the glacier and Gries Reservoir, extending to the Upper Valais Range, the Bernese Oberland (Finsteraarhorn summit) and in the foreground the black, vertically grooved face of the Faulhorn. The downhill road on the Valais side, after a close-up view of the greyish-coloured Gries Glacier and its meltwater lake, plunges dizzily into a mineral landscape, brightened only by patches of very short grass and thistles. The glacier and the Faulhorn can still be seen.

ADDRESSES

🏨 STAY

⊜ **Albergo Ristorante Defanti** – *6746 Lavorgo, Fiado. 2km/1.25m S. ✆(0)91 865 14 34. www.defanti.ch. 26 rooms.* Quiet hotel run by the Defanti family and established for 100 years.

⊜⊜ **Albergo Ristorante Nazionale** – *Via Belinzona 24 CH-6710 Biasca. ✆(0)91 862 13 31. www.albergonazionale.ch. 21 rooms.* Quiet, comfortable modern hotel located in front of the railway station. Excellent restaurant and pizzeria.

⊜⊜ **Zur Sonne** – *Gotthardstrasse 76, Andermatt. ✆(0)41 887 12 26. www.hotelsonneandermatt.ch. 21 rooms. 🍴. Open 20 Dec–21 Apr and 2 Jun–27 Oct only.* Comfortable hotel built in the chalet style. Sauna. A few minutes from the railway station. Two minutes to Gemsstock (alt. 2 961m/9 714ft).

⊜⊜⊜ **Badus** – *Gotthardstrasse 25, Andermatt. ✆(0)41 887 12 86. www. hotelbadus.ch. 23 rooms.* Modern and comfortable.

CENTRAL SWITZERLAND

Central Switzerland is the core of the country, physically and psychologically: It contains the Rütli field where the founding 1291 oath was taken, the three cantons that participated, and is the where the William Tell legend originated. With Lake Lucerne as its epicenter, it is also a visitor's delight offering boat trips on glacial waters, magnificent unimpeded views over a stunning landscape, gilded Baroque churches, unforgettable railway journeys and splendid museums.

Highlights

A Bit of History

Central Switzerland is where the current Swiss confederation started life as a small alliance between the three "early" cantons of Uri, Unterwalden and Schwyz whose oath was sworn in the field of **Rütli**. This is the region that gave Switzerland its **name** (from the canton of Schwyz), its **flag** (from an early version of the Schwyz arms) and its **National Day**. Though the written pact which is preserved in the **Bundesbriefmuseum** in Schwyz only mentions "the month of August" without a specific date, the national day is celebrated on 1 August by convention. Lucerne and Zug quickly joined these three cantons and have become (with Ticino) the Catholic conservative core of Switzerland.

William Tell

This is also the region where the **William Tell** legend takes place. Tell's deed were first described in the **White Book of Sarnen**, a collection of medieval manuscripts found in the capital of Obwalden. He was allegedly born in **Bürglen** in the canton of Uri, a small village southeast of **Altdorf** where the Tell tourist industry now thrives. The newly appointed Austrian governor **Gessler** hung his hat in the middle of a field and demanded that all village folk bow in front of it in reverence and fealty. Tell refused and was punished by having to shoot an apple from the head of his young son with a crossbow. When Gessler asked him why he had two arrows in his quiver, Tell replied that the second was for Gessler in case he missed. Gessler had Tell arrested and carried him on his boat bound for

View from Pilatus—Lake Lucerne with Bürgenstock and Rigi

Mark Twain in Lucerne

Out of all of Mark Twain's celebrated travel memoirs, it is the sections on Switzerland in *A Tramp Abroad* that are among the most frequently quoted. His description of Lucerne in 1878 could still be valid today: *"Lucerne is a charming place. It begins at the water's edge, with a fringe of hotels, and scrambles up and spreads itself over two or three sharp hills in a crowded, disorderly, but picturesque way, offering to the eye a heaped-up confusion of red roofs, quaint gables, dormer windows, toothpick steeples, with here and there a bit of ancient embattled wall bending itself over the ridges, worm-fashion, and here and there an old square tower of heavy masonry."* Though he woke up too late to see the sunset on the Rigi, he does write of the sunset: *"The great cloud-barred disk of the sun stood just above a limitless expanse of tossing white-caps—so to speak—a billowy chaos of massy mountain domes and peaks draped in imperishable snow, and flooded with an opaline glory of changing and dissolving splendors, while through rifts in a black cloud-bank above the sun, radiating lances of diamond dust shot to the zenith. The cloven valleys of the lower world swam in a tinted mist which veiled the ruggedness of their crags and ribs and ragged forests, and turned all the forbidding region into a soft and rich and sensuous paradise."*

Gessler's castle in **Küssnacht** below the **Rigi** mountain, but a storm on **Lake Lucerne** helped Tell escape where the current **Tellkapelle** stands. He then made his way to Gessler's castle and killed him. Tell eventually drowned on the **Schächen** river by Bürglen, trying to save a boy.

All this would have been lost to the world, but **Antoine-Marin Lemierre** revived the legend with a play to inspire Revolutionary France; Napoleon's installed government in the **Helvetic Republic** depicted Tell in the new republic's official seal. **Johann Wolfgang von Goethe** was another admirer of the myth which had since become a symbol of the common man standing against tyranny, and passed it on to his friend **Friedrich von Schiller.** Schiller wrote an epic on William Tell, which **Gioachino Rossini** used in turn as the basis for his eponymous opera—this time as an allegory for the Austrian repression of early 19C Italian nationalist sentiment.

The St Gotthard Pass

There is a reason this was the heart of early Switzerland and even today it is impossible not to see why: the St Gotthard Pass. It has been called the Water Tower of Europe: westwards flows the Rhône through the Valais and Lake Geneva to end in the Mediterranean; southwards the Ticino that joins the Po; eastwards several small Rhines that join at Chur to make up the big Rhine which feeds lake Constance; and northwards the Reuss that flows into the Aare just before the latter joins the Rhine.

This Alpine route is the key trading route between Zürich and Milan, and, more widely, Southern Germany and Northern Italy. Much of the prosperity of the mountain cantons resulted from taxes on the movement of goods through the pass and the provision of guides. Many of the early wars and battles in the area have been fought around its control: the Swiss independence battles of Morgarten (1315) and Sempach (1386); the capture of Ticino to secure the pass during the wars between the Swiss and the Dukes of Milan in the early 15C; and Napoleon's capture of Switzerland in 1798 as a prelude to his campaigns against Italy and Austria. Finally, the threat of dynamiting the Gotthard tunnel was one of several factors that deterred Adolf Hitler from invading Switzerland.

The St Gotthard Pass offers visitors unrivalled access to some of central Switzerland's most dramatic scenery, as well as the opportunity to ride a marvel of engineering, the St Gotthard railway.

CENTRAL SWITZERLAND

0	10 km
0	5 miles

N

SAINT GALLEN

SCHWYZ

GLARIS

GRAUBÜNDEN

Rapperswil

Einsiedeln

Sihlsee

Wägitalersee

Schwyz 1406

Ibergeregg Pass

V⁹ᵉ de la Muota

Stoos

ronalpstock

Grotte de Hölloch

Altdorf

Bürglen

Staübifall

Urner Boden

Klausen Pass 1948

Näfels

Walensee

Klöntal

Glaris

Lake Klöntal

Linthal

Linthkanal

Thur

Limmernsee

Flims

Llanz

Disentis/ Mustér

Vorderrhein

ffensprung

eralppass

Lai da Nalps

Lai da Curnera

msstock

Lai da Sontga Maria

WINTERTHUR

Lake Zürich

2637

CHUR / ST. MORITZ

BAD RAGAZ / CHUR

LUCERNE	★★★	Highly recommended
Zug	★★	Recommended
Schwyz	★	Interesting
Andermatt		Other sight described in this guide
→		Driving tour

321

Lucerne★★★

Lucerne is a picturesque town of squares and churches, with two attractive, covered wooden bridges and an octagonal tower overlooking the River Reuss. It nestles in a remarkable site at the northwest end of Lake Lucerne, dominated by Mount Pilatus and Mount Rigi. Its location on the important north-south transport axis, between the Swiss Plateau and the Alps, helped spur its development, and a recent rail link to Zürich Airport has encouraged investment. Its transformation to a tourism hotspot was established in the 19C after a string of celebrity visitors that included Mark Twain and Queen Victoria.

A BIT OF HISTORY

Early History to Middle Ages – The city's birth was in 1178 when the parish was transferred from the St Leodegar (St Leger) to the city. With the opening of the St Gotthard route around 1220, the town became an important staging-point between Flanders and Italy, and the first city fortifications were built. Lucerne was sold to Rudolf von Habsburg in 1291. The city population protested against the limits on its autonomy and in 1332 pledged a treaty with the Waldstätten (the "forest cantons" around Lake Lucerne), an impor-

▶ **Population:** 59 241.
⚬ **Michelin Map:** Regional Map 551, Suisse Nord/ Schweiz Nord/ Sviizzera Nord.
▯ **Info:** Zentralstrasse 5 (in the railway station). ℘(0)41 227 17 17. www.luzern.org.
◐ **Location:** Lucerne is right by Vierwaldstättersee, 45km/28mi west of Schwyz. Alt. 436m/1 430ft.
▯ **Parking:** The Old Town is pedestrian-only. Attractions beyond walking distance are easily accessible by public transportation.
⊘ **Don't Miss:** Strolling across the covered bridges that are the city's icons.
⚏ **Kids:** The sprawling transport museum, Verkehrshaus, includes the opportunity to experience the weightlessness of space travel.
◕ **Timing:** Allow at least two days to wander the streets and visit the museums.

tant political and commercial alliance that helped ensure the survival of the young Confederation formed in 1291. The Confederation victory at Sempach

Lucerne with Wasserturm and Kapellbruecke

(1386) permanently freed Lucerne from ties to Austria. When the Reformation began, Lucerne led the Catholic resistance. Because the city voted against the Federal Constitution in 1848, it was bypassed as the nation's capital for Bern. In the mid-19C, Lucerne gratefully seized upon opportunities offered by tourism to recapture some of its lost glory.

Development of Tourism – Lucerne remained a small town, with just 4 300 inhabitants at the end of the 18C; that changed with the arrival of tourists beginning in 1830. The Nationalquai and the esplanade by the Jesuit church were laid out during this period, fine hotels were built and the first steamboats began operating on the lake. Today, Lucerne welcomes over five million tourists every year, a quarter of whom are Swiss.

✣.WALKING TOURS

1 ALTSTADT (OLD TOWN)★★

3hrs. Start from Schwanenplatz (Swan Square) and head towards Kapellplatz, fronted by the impressive 18C St Peterskapelle. See map p327.
The old town is built on the side of the mountain and is partially surrounded by vestiges of the old fortifications, of which seven large square towers remain. Note the ornate original covered wooden bridges spanning the river.

Kapellplatz

The centre of the square is adorned with the Fritschibrunnen (Fritschi Fountain), which represents carnival, spring, and joy. **Fritschi** is a legendary character in whose honour a carnival has been held since the 15C. The Kapellgasse, a lively street lined with shops, leads to **Kornmarkt** (Grain Market), a square built in the 16C. A market is held here on Tuesdays and Saturday mornings.

Old City Hall★

This handsome Renaissance Altes Rathaus was built from 1602 to 1606 and overlooks the Kornmarkt, once used as a grain storehouse. The Gasthaus zu Pfistern, to the right, has a fine painted façade. To the left, the Am-Rhyn town house is home to the **Picasso Museum** (see Museums).

▷ *Take Kornmarktgasse, and through an alleyway on the right, to Hirschenplatz.*

Hirschenplatz (Stag Square)

This square is lined with houses with painted façades, which are adorned with wrought-iron signs. The famous Johann Wolfgang von Goethe (1749–1832) stayed at the Hotel Goldener Adler in 1779.

Weinmarkt (Wine Market)★

The old houses in this pretty square, which are covered with paintings and decorated with many signs and flags, were once the seats of the various guilds. Note the Scales' Mansion, and the Wine Market Pharmacy (Weinmarktapotheke) built in 1530. The Gothic fountain represents warriors and St Maurice, patron saint of soldiers. The original is currently displayed in the Regierungsgebaüde.

Follow Kramgasse to **Mühlenplatz** (Mills Square) which dates from the 16C. There is a fine view of the Spreuerbrücke, the old houses on the opposite bank of the Reuss and, in the distance, of Gütsch Hill.

Spreuerbrücke

This covered bridge, part of the fortifications of the old town, spans the River Reuss. It was built in 1408 and restored in the 19C. In German, *Spreu* means "chaff": The bridge was the only point where chaff and dead leaves could be thrown into the river. A small chapel (1568) stands in the middle of the bridge. The decoration of 67 painted panels representing a Dance of Death was executed in the 17C by Caspar Meglinger. From the bridge, there is a view of the quays of the old town and of the façade of the Jesuits' Church.

▷ *Beyond the bridge, follow Pfistergasse.*

LUCERNE
map I

WHERE TO STAY

Pfistergasse

Number 24, formerly the Arsenal, from 1567 to 1983, now houses the **Historisches Museum** (&see Museums).
On the quay, (Reuss-Steg), houses with oriels, painted façades and flower-decked fountains; on the left are the towers from the old town fortifications.

▶ Turn right at Münzgasse to reach Franziskanerplatz.

Franciscan Church★

🕐 *Open Sun–Fri, 10.30am–6.30pm, Sun 12.30–6.30pm.* ✆ *(0)41 210 14 67.*
The Gothic Franzisckankiche, built in the 13C and remodelled many times since, is the oldest in Lucerne. It contains fine stalls, a 17C carved wooden pulpit and flags won by the city over the centuries. A Baroque chapel to the rear of the church is decorated with stucco in the Italian style.

Regierungsgebäude (Government Palace)

This building has ornate stonework in Florentine Renaissance style (1557–64) and since 1804 has housed the cantonal government. In the inner court stands the original Weinmarkt Fountain (*see above*) which dates back to 1481.

Jesuit Church

Built in 1666 by Pater Christoph Vogler, the Jesuitenkirche was the first Baroque church in Switzerland. The plain façade is framed between two tall towers surmounted by domed belfries, and the **interior**★ is nobly proportioned. The high altar is adorned with a huge pink marble stucco altarpiece. The central ceiling painting (1749) depicts the Apotheosis of St Francis Xavier, the patron saint of the church. The three chapels on the right house relics from **St Silvan**, **St Nicholas of Flüe** (*see LAKE LUCERNE*) and **St Karl Borromäus**.

▷ *Exit and continue to your right, past the Rathaus bridge.*

Kapellbrücke★

This covered wooden bridge, rebuilt after a fire in 1993, has been the symbol of Lucerne for more than 600 years. The 200m/656ft-long bridge was built in 1333 to protect the town on the lakeside. In the beginning of the 17C, it was adorned with 110 paintings on the wood triangles formed by the roof beams, depicting the history of Lucerne and Switzerland, as well as of St Leger and St Maurice. Only 47 paintings were salvaged from the fire but 30 have been restored and once again hang inside the

walkway. The bridge has an octagonal tower, called the **Wasserturm**. Dating from around 1300, the tower was once part of the defensive fortifications of the town; in the past it has also been an archives room, a prison and a torture chamber.

▷ *Cross the Reuss on the busy Seebrücke towards the station.*

Culture and Convention Centre

Built in 2000 by the French architect Jean Nouvel, the architecturally controversial Kultur-und Kongresszentrum consisting mainly of a glass structure (12 000sq m/129 120sq ft) and offers splendid views★ of Lucerne and the lake. It houses the Kunstmuseum (*see p328*), and a concert hall (acoustically one of the best in the world) where the Lucerne Festival is held. There is a café on the ground floor.

② TO THE RAMPARTS VIA LÔWENPLATZ★★

👣 *See map opposite. Leave Schwanenplatz and follow the Schweizerhofquai.*

The **Schweizerhofquai** replaced the third covered bridge in Lucerne during the 19C. Both the Schweizerhofquai and the **Nationalquai** afford admirable views★★ of the town and Lake Lucerne, and beyond of the Alpine range stretching from the Rigi to the Pilatus (*viewing tables*). At the end of Carl-Spitteler-quai is the Lido beach.

▷ *Turn left before the Grand Hotel to join the narrow Stiftstraße.*

Collegiate Church★

🕐 *Open 10am–5.30pm.* ✎ *Guided tours available on request.* 🕐 *Closed Nov–Feb, noon–2pm.* ✆ *(0)41 410 52 41.*
The Hofkirche is dedicated to St Leodegar (St Leger), the patron saint of the town, which is said to derive its name from him, founded in 735. In 1633 all except the Gothic towers were destroyed by fire and it was rebuilt in

the Renaissance style. It is a huge building, reached by a monumental stairway, and is surrounded by Italianate cloisters, containing tombs of the old families of Lucerne. The **interior**★ is spacious and well proportioned, in the late Renaissance style. The high altar is black marble and statues of St Maurice and St Leodogar flank it. Two of the altars (*Pietà* in the south aisle; *Death of the Virgin* in the north aisle) are richly adorned and gilded. The organ (1650) is one of the best in Switzerland.

Take Löwenstrasse up to Löwenplatz, where the Bourbaki-Panorama (see Museums) is housed in a domed building. Take Denkmalstrasse up to the Lion's Monument.

Lion's Monument

Known as Löwendenkmal, this statue was carved out of the sandstone cliff face in 1821. It portrays a dying lion with a spear embedded in its left flank and its right paw protecting a fleur de lys. The sculpture (9m/29.5ft long) commemorates the Swiss Guards, whose task it was to protect the royal palace in Paris during the French Revolution: about 850 mercenaries were either killed during the Storming of the Tuileries (Paris) in August 1792 or guillotined soon after. The monument was the brainchild of Karl Pfyffer von Altishofen, a Swiss officer who survived the massacre.

Gletschergarten★ (Glacier Garden)

Denkmalstrasse 4. Open Apr–Oct, 9am–6pm; Nov–Mar, 10am–5pm. Film (12min). 12CHF. (0)41 410 43 40. www.gletschergarten.ch.

In 1872, JW Amrein-Troller, a bank clerk, bought a meadow outside Lucerne with the intention of building a cellar. During construction work, 32 different cavities were discovered, hollowed out from the sandstone by the Reuss Glacier 20 000 years ago, when ice covered the entire plain as far as the Jura. Amrein-Troller built a park around this geological site, which is particularly popular with children.

In the **museum**, **glacier science** is explained in an easy and accessible way. Visitors can touch "cold" ice from Polar glaciers and the more "temperate" ice from Alpine glaciers. Displays document the life of glaciers and animal species, such as the glacial flea (2mm/0.08in long), The region's geological history, which was still subtropical 20 million years ago, is demonstrated by fossils marked with prints of palms and birds. Other exhibits include an old relief model of Central Switzerland made in 1786, a reconstruction of a peasant's bedroom, and lithographs, models and reconstructions of old Lucerne.

After the museum, enjoy a **panoramic walk** with views of Lucerne and Mont Pilatus in the beautiful gardens, planted with Alpine flowers. The gardens also house an unusual **Moorish-style hall of mirrors** built in 1896 for the Geneva National Exhibition. The **Alpineum** is situated opposite the glacier garden.

Return through Löwenplatz to Alpenstrasse, turn right into Hertenstreinstrasse.

Museggmauer (Musegg Ramparts)

Open Easter–All Saints Day, 7.30am–7pm. No charge.

The remains of the fortified city walls (800m/875yds in length) include watch and defensive towers, dating from around 1400. Only one tower has undergone restoration work; three are open to the public: **Schirmerturm**, rebuilt after a fire in 1994; **Zytturm**, which has the oldest clock tower in Lucerne (1535); and **Männliturm**. The towers offer superb **views**★ of the town and the lake.

OLD TOWN MUSEUMS
Rosengart Collection★★

Pilatusstrasse 10. Open Apr–Oct, 10am–6pm; Nov–Mar, 11am–5pm. 15CHF. (0)41 220 16 60. www.rosengart.ch.

The Sammlung Rosengart art gallery was opened in 2002 by Angela Rosengart, daughter of the art dealer Siegfried Rosengart. There are more than

200 modern works of art dating from the 19C and 20C, including paintings by Picasso, Klee and Chagall. More than 100 **works**★★ by **Paul Klee** are displayed in the basement. The collection includes *Belebte Strasse* (1910), *St Germain bei Tunis* (1914), and *Modebild*, 1922.

Among the many graphic works, *Bild mit Hahn* (1919) and *Bergdorf* (1934) are worthy of note.

On the ground floor, the stunning **Picasso collection**★★★ (over 80 works of art painted after 1938) includes many Cubist paintings, such as *Violin at the Café* (1913). Portraits of Nusch Éluard, Dora Maar and Marie-Thérèse Walter, painted in the 1930s and 1940s, are exhibited along with *Woman and Dog Playing*, a painting inspired by Françoise Gilot (1953). *The Studio* (1954) is that of the Villa Californie in Cannes.

Other interesting works include *Jacqueline's Profile* (1957) and *Women in Hats* (1961, 1963). In *Déjeuner sur l'herbe* (1961), inspired by Manet's famous painting, Picasso himself is depicted on the right.

The first floor is devoted to Impressionist works by artists such as Monet, Pissarro, Renoir, Bonnard and Cézanne (*L'Estaque, the village and the sea*, 1882). Léger (*The Staircase*, 1914) and Matisse (*Lemons and Saxifrage*, 1943) are also well represented, as is Braque with his lyrical *Pot and Ivy* (1950). Thirteen works by Chagall are also displayed, ranging from *Evening at the Window* (1950) to *Red Sun* (1983). Other artists exhibited here include Seurat, Vuillard, Utrillo, Dufy, Rouault and Kandinsky.

Picasso Museum

Furrengasse 21. ⏰*Open Apr–Oct, 10am –6pm; Nov–Mar, 11am–5pm.* 🎫*8CHF.* 📞*(0)41 410 35 33. www.rosengart.ch.*

The **Am Rhyn-Haus** contains a small collection of lithographs, engravings and ceramics by Picasso, donated to the city in 1978 by the Rosengart family (⏰*see Rosengart Collection opposite*). Most works date from the last 20 years of the artist's life. The museum also houses photographs taken during the same period (1956–73) by the American David

Douglas Duncan, a close friend of the artist, and include portraits of Picasso and his last muse, Jacqueline Roque.

Art Museum★

Europaplatz 1. ◐*Open Tue–Sun 10am –5pm (8pm Wed).* ◐*Closed 7, 11 and 12 Feb, 24 and 31 Dec.* ◉*10CHF.* ♪*(0)41 226 78 00. www.kunstmuseumluzern.ch.* Since 2000, the **Kunstmuseum** has been housed on the fourth floor of the **Kultur- und Kongresszentrum** designed by Jean Nouvel. The permanent collection of mainly Swiss paintings from the 18C–20C is exhibited in rotation alongside temporary exhibitions of contemporary art. Permanent exhibits include works by the Romantic painter Johann Heinrich Füssli, landscape painters from the School of Geneva such as François Diday and Alexandre Calame, the Symbolist Ferdinand Hodler, and Félix Vallotton (*see INTRODUCTION: Art and Architecture*). Other artists exhibited here include Vlaminck, Soutine, the Expressionist Max Pechstein and the contemporary artists Joseph Beys, Paul Thek, Franz Gertsch, and Jeff Wall.

Historical Museum

Pfistergasse 24. ◐*Open Tue–Sun 10am –5pm.* ◐*Closed 25 Dec.* ◉*10CHF.* ⚒ ♪*(0)41 228 54 24. www.hmluzern.ch.* The **Historisches Museum** displays 16C and 17C armour, traditional dress, and reconstructions of interiors.

Natural History Museum

Kasernenplatz 6 ◐*Open Tue–Sun 10am –5pm.* ◐*Closed 24, 25 Dec.* ◉*6CHF.* ⚒ ♪*(0)41 228 54 11. www.naturmuseum.ch.* Devoted mainly to the natural characteristics of central Switzerland, this museum presents an extensive collection of Alpine minerals and fossils and a remarkable **Gallery of Archeology** exhibiting objects such as weapons and pottery found in the area from the Neolithic lake dwellers, the Bronze Age and Celto-Roman period.

Also in this gallery, models and dioramas depict the life of the lake dweller. On the second floor are zoological and botani-cal collections as well as aquariums, terrariums, etc.

Bourbaki-Panorama★

Löwenplatz 11. ◐*Open Nov–early Apr, Tue–Sun 10am–5pm, Mon 1pm–5pm; mid-Apr–Oct, Tue–Sun 9am–6pm, Mon 1pm–6pm.* ◉*8CHF.* ♪*(0)41 412 30 30. www.bourbakipanorama.ch.* A glass building houses this huge **circular canvas** (1 100sq m/1 315.5sq yds) painted by **Édouard Castres** (1881). The canvas hangs on the second floor, attached by hundreds of magnets, and depicts one of the last episodes of the Franco-Prussian war of 1870–71: the crossing of the Swiss border by French general Bourbaki after his defeat at the **Battle of Lisaine**. The museum on the ground floor provides a thorough portrayal of the war with information given in three languages, and includes an audio-visual presentation.

ADDITIONAL SIGHTS
Verkehrshaus★★★ (Swiss Transport Museum)

Lidostrasse 5 (near the lake) by Haldenstrasse. Buses 6 and 8; Verkehrshaus bus stop. ◐*Open daily Apr–Nov, 10am–6pm; Dec–Mar, 10am–5pm.* ◉*27 CHF.* ⚒ ♪*(08) 48 85 20 20. www.verkehrshaus.ch.* This museum illustrates the **history of transport** in Switzerland. The different sections are housed in a dozen separate buildings dotted around a park, which is interspersed with play areas and snack bars. There is also an Imax cinema (*www. imax.ch*).

Rail transport – An 8 000sq m/ 9 568sq yds exhibition area featuring 1 000m/3 281ft of railway track presents the largest collection in the country. Exhibits include the Vitznau-Rigi loco-motive, dating back to 1873, Switzerland's largest steam engine and the legendary Be 6/8 mountain locomotive, better known as the Crocodile. Exhibits also include tramcars from several Swiss cities and a collection of miniature trains. There is also a lively presentation of the building of the St Gotthard Tun-

© PHOTOPRESS/Verkehrshaus der Schweiz

Rail Transport Hall, Verkehrshaus

nel: visitors are invited to settle in a carriage and be guided through the various stages of this exciting project, accompanied by typical sounds and smells.

Road transport – The dramatic changes during the 19C and 20C are illustrated by the sledge used by the Simplon Post Office and the Grimsel horse-drawn carriage. The impressive Halle du Transport Routier contains more than 30 automobiles used by the Confederation in this thriving industry. The most remarkable exhibit is probably the 1905 racing car designed by Genevan manufacturers Charles and Frédéric Dufaux, presented alongside several Weber, Turicum, Pic-Pic and Martini models. Note the replica of an early Benz tricycle. From the dandy horse to the scooter, two-wheeled vehicles are represented by 50 or so bicycles, including a number of Swiss models.

Media Factory – This section devoted to the history of communication is equipped with radio, television and video-conference facilities as well as interactive systems that enable visitors to experiment with the latest technology.

Aviation and Space Travel Hall – Aviation through the ages: the first biplane—the Dufaux 4—in which Armand Dufaux flew over Lake Geneva in 1910, Swissair's DC 3, the supersonic carrier CV 990 Coronado, hot-air balloons, hang-gliders, microlites, and other aircraft. Exhibits include a Fokker F-VII, a collection of 200 miniature models and 30 engines and turbines. Visitors can try a flight simulator and take over the controls, or they can pose for a photograph on board the Blue Box. In the air traffic control tower, a radar console teaches the complexities of modern safety conditions at airports. On the second upper level, the **Cosmorama** boasts numerous special effects that plunge you into the fascinating world of asteroids and outer space, including experiencing weightlessness.

Planetarium ZEISS Longines – Beneath a huge cupola lies a replica of the firmament, where the life of the planets and their movements is explained.

Navigation, cable-cars, tourism – The ground floor exhibits the machinery of the paddle steamer *Pilatus* (1895), one of the legendary boats to glide on Lake Lucerne. The **Navigation Section** (*first floor*) presents a remarkable collection of reduced models and nautical instruments evoking the progress of navigation through the centuries. Note the shipowner's office, containing a wide range of miniature ships, marine books and seascapes donated to the museum by shipowner Philipp Keller in 1980. The multimedia show **Nautirama** retraces

A National Hero

On 9 July 1386 a decisive battle took place near Sempach between the Swiss Confederates and Austrians commanded by Duke Leopold. **Arnold von Winkelried** spurred forward and grasped as many spears as he could hold in order to make a breach in the Austrian square, bristling with pikes. His heroic sacrifice secured the victory of the Confederates when Duke Leopold lost his life. A monument commemorates the events of that day, which heralded the decline of Habsburg rule in Switzerland.

the history of navigation on Lake Lucerne. The cable-car section displays a cabin of the first public aerial cable-car (1908), which transported passengers to the Wetterhorn, and the ultra-modern cabin of the cable-car, built in 1984, linking Spielboden to Langfluh near Saas Fee. The tourism section displays the country's most typical products and activities and **Swissorama**, a multivision show, illustrates its most famous sites.

Richard Wagner-Museum

Access **by boat** *from the landing-stage near Seebrücke.* **By car**: *leave the town by Hirschmattstrasse; at the Bundersplatz take Tribschenstrasse and follow directions to Tribschen.* **Buses** *6, 7 or 8; bus stop Wartegg.* ◐*Open mid-Mar–Nov, Tue–Sun 10am–noon, 2pm–5pm. Open Easter Mon.* ⊝*8CHF.* ℘*(0)41 360 23 70. www.richard-wagner-museum.ch.*

Rack Railway

The Pilatus railway was opened in 1889 as a steam operated train and switched to electric in 1937. The descent, an average gradient of 38%, takes 10 minutes longer than ascent.

Wagner produced some of his major works here: *Die Meistersinger, Rheingold, Siegfried.* Here, too, he married Cosima, Franz Liszt's daughter, and received Nietzsche. The ground floor houses original scores, Wagner's death mask, a plaster of his right hand, photos, letters and the **Érard piano** that accompanied him on his trips. On the first floor, there is a collection of musical instruments dating from the 17–19C.

EXCURSIONS
Dietschiberg★★
Alt. 629m/2 064ft.
At the station, take **bus** *14, alight at the Konservatorium stop, then walk for 20min, following signposts to Utenberg and Golfplatz.* **By funicular** *from Felsental, on the north bank: follow the lake shore as far as Carl-Spitteler-Quai, then take Gesegnetmattstrasse.*
Splendid **panorama**★★ of Lake Lucerne and Pilatus on the right, the Rigi on the left and the Bernese and Glarus Alps.

Glasi Hergiswil

At Seestrasse 12, Hergiswil, 8km/4.9mi S of Lucerne. Access by boat or train. ◐*Mon–Sat 9am–6pm (4pm Sat).* ⊝*Free.* ℘*(0)41 632 32 32. www.glasi.ch*
The oldest glassworks in the country, operating since 1817, opens its doors to admire the work of its glassblowing artisans. A small collection containing pieces from the 18 and 19C, a direct sales shop, games for children and a cafe on the lake nicely complement the visit.

Pilatus★★★

Pilatus-Bahnen, Schlossweg 1, 6010 Kriens/Lucerne. ℘*(0)41 329 11 13. www.pilatus.ch.*
The proud rock pyramid of Mount Pilatus (highest point: 2 132m/6 995ft at the Tomlishorn) dominates with its sharply defined ridges. The aerial cable-car, along a steep cliff to the top, is a marvel of modern engineering, and the view from the summit is astounding. Pilatus is both a useful landmark for the visitor to central Switzerland and a long time source of superstitious dread, as legend declared that the spirit of Pontius Pilate

Pilatus cog railway

Philipp Giegel/Switzerland Tourism

haunted a small lake near the summit and that anyone who approached that accursed spot would cause fearful storms.

A construction and renovation project of the Pilatus-Kulm and Bellevue Hotels and a panorama gallery aims to make the most of this stunning location.

Pilatus-Kulm railway★★★

The railway climb begins at Alpnachstad. Train time from Lucerne 2hr round trip, including 1hr by rack railway (Apr–Oct). ☞*Return train fare 58CHF. Pilatus-Kulm can also be reached by cable-car from Kriens, in the suburbs of Lucerne. The Golden Tour (90CHF, recommended) combines a boat from Lucerne to Alpnachstadt, ascent by the cogwheel railway and descent by cable-car to Kriens forming a complete circuit. Bus number 1, outside Lucerne station takes 15 mins to Kriens, fare included.* The red cogwheel railway, with a maximum gradient of 48°, is the steepest rack-and-pinion railway in the world, particularly impressive where it crosses the slopes of the Esel.

From the upper station, which has two mountain hotels (*Pilatus-Kulm and Bellevue*), you will climb in a few minutes to the Esel summit (alt. 2 119m/6 952ft). A walk through the gallery hollowed out of the side of the mountain showcasing Alpine plants is recommended.

🚗 DRIVING TOURS

Around Lake Sempach (Sempachsee)

68km/42mi NW of Lucerne. Leave by Highway 2, direction Emmen, then Basel and Sursee, then bear right towards Sempach.

Sempach

Alt. 518m/1 699ft.
Theaterstrasse 9. 📞*(0)41 920 44 44.*
www.sempachersee-tourismus.ch.
Founded by the Habsburgs, Sempach is built near the lake to which it gave its name. For a long time it owed its activity and prosperity to the considerable traffic on the St Gotthard route (Basel-Lucerne-Milan), which now follows the

opposite shore. The main street has an old-fashioned air with its Witches' Tower, its town hall (Rathaus) with a façade made cheerful by a red and white pattern, its flower-decked fountain, and its houses with brown tile roofs.

The **Swiss Ornithological Centre** (Schweizerische Vogelwarte) (⊙ open Tue–Fri 8am–5pm (10am Sat–Sun and public holidays); ⊙ closed Mon and weekends Jan–Mar; ⊚ 5CHF; ♿; ℘ (0)41 462 97 00; www.vogelwarte.ch) is devoted to local birds, as well as the survival of species and bird migration. It consists of several gardens, a number of large aviaries and a small museum presenting stuffed birds.

▷ Take the little lakeside road.

Sursee
Alt. 504m/1 654ft.

The small old town at the northwest corner of Lake Sempach has kept some of its old atmosphere in spite of the fires that ravaged it between the 14C and the 17C.

The **Old Town** boasts a fine town hall (Rathaus) from the Late Gothic period (mid-16C), flanked by two towers. One ends in a slender belfry, whereas the other is hexagonal and crowned by a dome. The façade with a stepped gable is pierced by many mullioned windows. The **Baseltor** or **Untertor**, the town gate, a vestige of the former ramparts, is flanked by a half-timbered house whose white façade is intersected by red beams.

Wallfahrtskirche Mariazell
On the eastern outskirts of town near the road to Beromünster.

Built in the 17C, this pilgrim's chapel is adorned with a ceiling decorated with naïve paintings representing Noah's Ark, the Tower of Babel and other Old Testament scenes. Near the gateway there is a **view**★ of the lake, the Alps and the Jura.

▷ Head E on road 23.

Beromünster
7.5km/4.6mi NE of Sursee.

This little town, near the transmitters of the Swiss National German-language Broadcasting Station, gets its name from the monastery (Münster) founded in 980 by Count Bero of Lenzburg and transformed in the 13C into a priory for lay canons.

Stiftskirche
▸ Guided tours by appointment, Mon–Fri 10am–5pm. ⊚ 5CHF. ℘ (0)41 930 35 85.

The collegiate church was built in the 11C and 12C but almost entirely remodelled in the Baroque style. The porch is adorned with many shields bearing the arms of former canons. The raised chancel is enclosed by a wrought-iron screen and furnished with remarkable **stalls**★ (1609). Their carved panels represent episodes in the Life of Christ. The treasury holds the reliquary of Warnebert (7C).

Schlossmuseum
▸ Guided tours (1hr) May–Oct, Sun and public holidays 3pm–5pm. ⊚ 3CHF. ℘ (041) 930 36 17/14 82.

The museum, housed in the castle's medieval tower, displays a collection of furniture, paintings, local costumes, tools and objects from Beromünster and its environs as well as a reconstruction of the Helyas Heyle print room where, in 1470, the very first book was printed in Switzerland.

Around Entlebuch and Lake Sarnen
105km/65mi W of Lucerne. Leave by Highway 10, direction Wolhusen (19km/12mi), then Schüpfheim and Sörenberg (55km/34mi).

Entlebuch
The region of Entlebuch, southwest of Lucerne, is Switzerland's only **Unesco Biosphere Reserve**: around the valley of the **Kleine Emme**, there is an outstanding protected area of upland moors and bogs, wild gorges and vast karst formations. **Sörenberg**, with its

many hiking paths, is an ideal starting point. From Sörenberg one can continue to the **Glaubenbüelen Pass** to discover the snowy peak of the **Brienzer Rothorn**, and then descend down to **Giswil** by a winding road that provides beautiful views of Lake Sarnen and the surrounding countryside

From Giswil you can continue to **Lungern** and climb to the **Brünig Pass**. Between Giswil and Kaiserstuhl, you will get a good view of the Pilatus ridges rising above the shallow depression, dotted with farms and clumps of trees, partly submerged by Lake Sarnen. Upstream and in the far distance, the three snowy peaks of the Wetterhorn group appear through the Brünig Pass. Between the fir trees and maples, there are wonderful glimpses of **Lake Lungern** (Lungernsee), with its curving shores. Close by to Lungern lies the well known **Schönbühl** ski area in the Brünig Pass with 22km/13.6mi of trails.

▶ *Leave Entlebuch SE on Glaubenbergstrasse, or if coming directly from Lucerne, take the A2 towards Stans, then the A8.*

Sachseln

Sachseln is both the geographic centre of Switzerland and the land of **Nicolas of Flüe**, a saint whose role was crucial in the early formation of the Confederation. Swiss Catholics affirm their attachment to their faith and their patriotic fervor by coming to Sachseln to pray to St Nicholas of Flüe (*see LAKE LUCERNE*). The town, prettily situated on the shore of Lake Sarnen, is as much a moving place of pilgrimage as a trendsetter in environmental achievements. In 2004, Sachseln converted mountain spring-fed drinking water pipelines into hydroelectric power generators, fulfilling two essential requirements; the project was a national pilot, and is considered to be the first of its kind.

The great Baroque **church**, supported by columns of black Melchtal marble, enshrines the relics of **St Nicholas of Flüe** on a special altar at the entrance to the chancel. The remains are enclosed

in a large, embossed recumbent figure (1934). Go around the building to reach the funeral chapel, where the faithful come to meditate before the tombstone, carved in 1518 with the effigy of the saint. Below is the worn step of the original sepulchre.

▶ *Leave Sachseln E on the hill road behind the church.*

Flüeli

Exit Sachseln E towards Flüeli (uphill behind the church). ℙ*Leave the car in the car park on the village's central plaza.* The rustic character of this hamlet, where St Nicholas led the life of a mountain patriarch surrounded by his large family, has been preserved. The chapel (1618) can be seen on its mound from far off; it is reached by stairs and an esplanade. From the terrace there is a pleasant, open view of the Valley of Sarsen, Lake Sarnen, and Pilatus on one side and the deep cleft leading into the Melchtal on the other. Besides this sanctuary, pilgrims still visit the birthplace (the oldest wooden house in Switzerland—14C) and the family home of Nicholas.

Ranft★

Approaches are signposted on leaving Flüeli.

By a steep descent *(ramp or stairs)* toward the floor of the Melchtal Valley you will first reach the hermitage-chapel. The church (17C) is decorated with painted panels recalling the life of the recluse; outstanding is a fine Gothic **Christ**★ taken from the former Sachseln church. The cell nearby where the hermit could not stand upright—was built in 1468 by his fellow-citizens from Obwalden. Below, another chapel was built in the 16C on the spot where the Virgin appeared to St. Nicholas of Flüeli. On returning from Flüeli bound for Lucerne, take the fork to the right toward Kerns; then cross the River Melchaa (or simply Aa) on the **Hohe Brücke**★. This 30m-long bridge was built across the torrent at a height of 100m/329ft in 1943 by Swiss Army Engineers and is the highest covered wooden bridge in Europe.

ADDRESSES

🛏️STAY

Rösli – *Pfistergasse 12 . ℰ(0)41 249 22 77. www.roesli.ch. 6 rooms.* A small pension very well located in a quiet street with great prices for Lucerne. The reception is opposite at the hotel Baslertor in the same street.

Goldener Stern – *Burgerstrasse 35. ℰ(0)41 227 50 60. www.goldener-stern.ch. 16 rooms. Restaurant.* Ten minutes from the railway station, next to the Franciscan church, this simple, family-run hotel has well-maintained rooms at reasonable prices for Lucerne.

Hofgarten - *Stadthofstrasse 14. ℰ(0)41 417 18 19. www.hofgarten.ch. 18 rooms. Restaurant.* Just steps from the Hofkirche, this timber-framed 15C house combining modernity and heritage is surrounded by a secluded garden. The vegetarian restaurant is a haven of peace.

Krone – *Weinmarkt 12. ℰ(0)41 419 44 00. www.krone-luzern.ch. 25 rooms. Restaurant.* Situated in the heart of the old town, this modern hotel has spacious rooms. The restaurant overlooks the Weinmarkt, a pedestrian square with real medieval charm.

Cascada – *Bundesplatz 18. ℰ(0)41 226 80 88. www.cascada.ch. 63 rooms. Restaurant.* Comfortable rooms, private car park 🅿️, Wi-Fi access, close to the station. The Boléro restaurant serves Spanish specialties.

Waldstätterhof – *Zentralstrasse 4. ℰ(0)41 227 12 71. www.hotel-waldstaetterhof.ch. 75 rooms and 2 suites.* Ideally located opposite the station, the hotel has renovated some of the rooms, which are the most expensive. The proximity of bars makes it noisy on weekends. Alcohol-free restaurant.

NEARBY

Seeburg – *Seeburgstrasse 61 at Ost going towards Meggen (north shore of the lake). ℰ(0)41 375 55 55. www.hotelseeburg.ch. 58 rooms. Restaurant.* A handsome,

beautifully preserved residence with old-fashioned charm. The best rooms look over Lake Lucerne and Mount Pilatus. Lakeside garden with a charming creek for mooring boats, two restaurants and a lively lounge.

PILATUS

Bellevue – *Pilatus Kulm. ℰ(0)41 329 12 12. www.pilatus.com. 28 rooms.* Circular structure with views of the sunrise.

Pilatus Kulm – *ℰ(0)41 670 12 55. www.pilatus.com. 20 rooms.* The Bellevue and the Pilatus Kulm both share a reception area located in the Hotel Bellevue and both offer dining.

🍴EAT

Wilhelm Tell – *Schweizerhofquai. ℰ(0)41 410 23 30. www.schiffrestaurant. ch. Closed Mondays.* Huge steamboat, many of which used to be seen gliding on Lake Lucerne. From the bar, you can glimpse the machinery which once operated the paddle wheels. The Art Nouveau dining hall adds a touch of refinement.

Galliker – *Schützenstrasse 1, near Kasernenplatz. ℰ(0)41 240 10 02. Closed Sun and Mon.* Small, cosy and friendly establishment where you immediately feel at ease.

Goldener Löwen – *Eisengasse 1. ℰ(0)41 410 11 33.* Tavern with ambiance to enjoy one of its innumerable Swiss fondues. Even the chocolate fondue is on the menu.

Café Bodu – *Kornmarkt 5. ℰ(0)41 410 01 77.* French cuisine with a Mediterranean accent. Parisian brasserie atmosphere inside and a romantic evening terrace outside. Good service.

NEARBY

Schwendelberg – *Horw. ℰ(0)41 340 35 40. www.schwendelberg. com. Closed May–Sept, Tue; Oct–Apr Tue & Wed.* Traditional guesthouse offering peace and quiet. Sweeping panorama of Lake Lucerne and the Swiss Alps.

Schlössli Utenberg – *Utenbergstrasse 643 (4km/2.5mi NE heading towards Dietschiberg). ℰ(0)41 420 00 22. www.schlössli-utenberg.ch. Closed Mon, Tue.* An 18C mansion built

In the Baroque style houses this ideal lunch-spot. Admire the 18C faience stove (1758) on the first floor. Pretty terrace views of the city and its lake.

NIGHTLIFE

Situated on the seventh floor of the Hôtel Astoria (*Pilatusstrasse 29*), the **Penthouse**, with its soft background music, is a favourite haunt among the young. In the same street, the **Hôtel Schiller** (*Pilatusstrasse 15*) offers two different bars: The **Bar Blue** in an old-fashioned setting and the **Pacifico**, a bar with a Mexican touch.

On the shores of the lake, both the **Hôtel National** and the **Hôtel Palace** feature a piano bar (*Haldenstrasse 4 and 10 respectively*), as does the **Casino**, which also has a large room where weekend shows are held.

In the old town, enjoy a good fondue to the strains of folk music at the **Stadtkeller** (*Sternenplatz 3*). The **Movie Bar** (*Weinmarkt*), whose décor will delight film buffs, attracts a casual crowd and offers a great variety of wines and beers. In the basement, you can order dishes bearing the name of a famous film: Try Al Capone, Jaws, or Love Story.

For dancers and nightclub-goers, the **Mad Wallstreet**, (*Industriestrasse 9, Kriens. www.madwallstreet.ch*) offers live music in Kriens, a few miles away from Lucerne. **Pravda Dance Club** (*Pilatusstrasse 29, www.pravda.ch*) is one of the hippest in the city. **The Loft** (*Haldenstrasse 21, www.theloft.ch*) is the destination for late clubbers and also offers a gay night on Fridays.

The alternative, indie and punk scene is centeed out of town, around the **Musikzentrum Sedel** (*www.sedel.ch*) which used to be a prison. There is a shuttle to the venue from Löwenplatz, Bundesplatz and Kasernenplatz every 30 mins until 2am during the weekends. A taxi from the station costs 15CHF.

For jazz enthusiasts, **Jazzkantine** (*Grabenstrasse 8, www.jsl.ch*) offers most days performances and jam sessions by the pupils of the Lucerne Jazz School.

SHOPPING

The main shopping area is the picturesque, pedestrian streets in the old town.

Department stores: Jelmoli (*Pilatusstrasse 4*), **Manor Warenhäuser** (*Weggisstrasse 5*), **Au Bon Marché** (*Kapellgasse 4*).

The **Emmen Center** (*EmmenBrücke 3, www.emmencenter.ch*) is a large shopping mall with over 80 stores, 13 min from the railway station on bus 53.

A well-stocked fruit and vegetable market is on the right bank of the Reuss River every Tue and Sat. A flea market operates on the Burgerstasse/ Reusssteg every Saturday May–Oct.

THEATRE, MUSIC, CINEMA

Stadttheater – *Theaterstrasse 2. ℘(0)41 228 14 14. www.luzerner-theater.ch.*

Boa cultural centre – *Geissensteinring 41. ℘(0)41 360 45 88. www.boaluzern.ch.*

EVENTS AND FESTIVALS
LUCERNE FESTIVAL

On 25 August 1938, Arturo Toscanini conducted *Siegfried* by Wagner in Tribschen Park. This performance marked the beginning of the **Lucerne Festival**, dedicated to classical and contemporary music, which now attracts over 110 000 people every year. The festival holds events at Easter, during the summer (around 30 concerts in August and September) and in November (piano recitals). For further information, contact *Hirschmattstrasse 13, 6002 Lucerne. ℘(0)41 226 44 00. www. lucernefestival.ch.*

SIGHTSEEING

Lake Lucerne Navigation Company offers trips on the lake, dinner cruises, and links with all the cable-cars and funiculars in the region. *℘(0)41 367 67 67. www.lakelucerne.ch.*

The **Tourist Office** inside the railway station offers a 2hr city walk in English at 9.45am 25CHF. *Daily May–Oct, Wed & Sat Nov–Mar, Wed, Sat & Sun Apr.*

Lake Lucerne ★★★

Lake Lucerne is found on most maps under its German name, Vierwaldstätter See. The Lake Lucerne district offers picturesque old-fashioned villages and cities, and innumerable hills and majestic mountain summits. A total surface area of 114sq km/44sq mi makes Lake Lucerne the second largest lake within the country's boundaries after Lake Neuchâtel. It is comprised of three distinct sections from west to east: namely, the "lakes" of Vitznau, Gersau-Beckenried, and Uri, created by a narrowing of the lake shore. The River Reus joins the lake to the south and leaves it at Lucerne to the north.

- **Michelin Map:** Regional Map 551, Suisse Nord/Schweiz Nord/Svizzera Nord.
- **Info:** Bahnhofplatz 4. (0)41 610 88 33. www.lakeluzern.ch.
- **Location:** The lake is overlooked by the summits of Mount Pilatus and Mount Rigi.
- **Don't Miss:** A boat trip around the lake followed by a climb to one of the surrounding summits. Some of the lakeside sights, namely the historic Field of Rütli, can only be reached by boat.
- **Timing:** The boat trip from Lucerne to Flüelen takes 2h45min non-stop.

A BIT OF HISTORY

The Cradle of Swiss Democracy – Long before the Confederation existed, the **Waldstätten** (forest cantons) on the lake shores had adapted without much difficulty to a symbolic fealty to the Holy Roman Empire. The attachment of the district of Uri to the Empire was formally guaranteed as early as 1231, special treatment due to its strategic location on the vital St Gotthard route. The relative autonomy of these cantons was threatened when the Austrian House of Habsburg, anxious to ensure profitable administration of its possessions, gave officials control over the revenues of estates without consulting with local authorities. These outsiders quickly became unpopular.

The situation became critical when Rudolf I, the first of the Hapsburgs, acceded to the Imperial throne in 1273. His death prompted representatives of Schwyz, Uri, and Unterwalden to form a permanent alliance. This mutual assistance pact is regarded by the Swiss as the founding pact of the Confederation. Its original text is carefully preserved at Schwyz, and the anniversary of its signature (1 August 1291) is celebrated as the national festival (*see Calendar of Events*). The victory of Morgarten (1315) over the troops of Leopold of Austria marked the definite liberation of the three original cantons.

Dawn of liberty – This story gained its fame as a result of one of the treasures of German literature: Schiller's **William Tell** (1804). His story involves a conspiracy long matured by the representatives of the three communities, represented as victims of Bailiff Gessler's despotism, and solemnly sworn on the Field of Rütli, opposite Brunnen, by 33 spokesmen for Schwyz, Uri, and Unterwalden. After having been subjected by Gessler to the famous ordeal of the apple, the archer William Tell became the arm of justice. He killed Gessler in the sunken road (Hohle Gasse) at Küssnacht, paving the way for an era of liberty.

"Protector of the Fatherland" – The district of Unterwalden (more exactly the half-canton of Obwalden) is proud to number among its sons the hermit **Nicholas of Flüe** (canonised in 1947), whose conciliatory intervention left an indelible mark on the Swiss patriotic temperament. Born in 1417 to prosper-

LAKE LUCERNE

0   4 km
0   2 mile

ous peasants, Brother Nicholas (Bruder Klaus), as his fellow citizens called him, led a contemplative life. After decades of family and civic duties, at the age of 50, this father of 10 children separated from his family to live the life of an ascetic in Ranft. Meanwhile the confederates of the cantons (& see INTRODUCTION: History) faced serious internal difficulties. In 1477 the population around Lake Lucerne became agitated when they learned that Lucerne, in agreement with Zürich and Bern, had concluded a separate alliance with Fribourg and Solothurn. When Lucerne maintained the pact, in spite of the entreaties of its neighbours Uri, Schwyz, and Unterwalden, the conflict became acute. In despair the parish priest of Stans went to Ranft to consult Brother Nicholas. He returned with an admirable appeal for peace. A compromise was reached in 1481.

SIGHTS
THE SOUTH SHORE OF THE LAKE

The road round the south shore is far less picturesque than that of the north.

It is advised to travel these shores both by sea and land and take funiculars or lifts that provide access to breathtaking views.

Bürgenstock★★

Ascend the Bürgenstock **by car** *from Stansstad (6km/3.7mi) or* **by funicular** *from the landing stage at Kehrsiten-Bürgenstock in 7min.*

The name Bürgenstock is given to a massive rock ridge and also applies to a group of hotels perched 500m/1 640ft above the central basin (Chrüztrichter) of the lake. A favourite walk here is along the **Felsenweg★★** (about 30min), a cliff road that completes a panoramic circuit around the Hammetschwand lookout. The summit (1 128m/3 701ft) can be reached by a lift up the mountainside which is the highest outdoor elevator in Europe (153m/501 ft).

A high-end hotel, spa and sports resort is set to be developed at Bürgenstock.

Stans

Bahnhofplatz 4. ℘(0)41 610 88 33.
Stans, the capital of canton Nidwalden, is an agreeable town, whose main sell-

Rütli field above the Lake Lucerne

Christof Sonderegger/Switzerland Tourism

Sailing on the Lake

Before becoming solely the domain of tourist ferries, sailing on the lake used to be the only way to transport goods and passengers around the region and to the all-important St Gotthard Pass. From the 13C until the arrival of railways, boats used to roam on this vast expanse of water with the first steamboat brought into service in 1837.

Now, only five renovated vessels, including a paddle steamer and a steamboat, sail regularly. The **Lake Lucerne Navigation Company** (SGV) has the largest fleet of historic boats in the world. The steamship *Schiller* (1906) is considered the most elegant, boasting a Jugendstil (German Art Nouveau) first-class lounge with geometric inlays of mother of pearl and ebony decorated with panels of mermaids. The fleet connects Lucerne's famous resorts on the lake all year and offers cruises with commentary on historical sites (TellKapelle, Schillerstein), cruises at sunset, night cruises offering music and dance in the summer, gastronomic cruises (brunch or lunch) and connections or combinations with all funiculars and cable-cars in the area (Bürgenstock, Klewenalp, Seelisberg, Vitznau, Alpnachstadt). Some coastal sites—primarily the historic field of **Rütli**—are also only practically accessible via the lake. From Lucerne, a complete circumnavigation of all lake branches requires about six hours. In season, boats from Lucerne to Flüelen via Brunnen and from Lucerne to Alpnachstad leave approximately every hour. It is also possible to reach Locarno or Lugano in Ticino by combining a lake crossing on a steamer and a train ride aboard first-class panorama cars on the Gotthard line. This link, called **William Tell Express**, operates daily from May to October, in a north-south direction.

🖪 *www.lakelucerne.ch. www.wilhelmtellexpress.ch.*

Paddle wheel steamer "Schiller" on the Lake Lucerne

D. Brauand/Switzerland Tourism

ing point is its excursions, in particular the funicular/cable-car to the magnificent Stanserhorn belvedere. It is also a convenient place for a stopover when the hotels in the Lucerne district are full.

Pfarrkirche St Peter und Paul

The large Romanesque church **belfry**★, with four tiers of arcades, towers above the main square. The spire was added in the 16C. The spacious interior, in early Baroque style, is impressive: Statues adorning the nave stand out in dazzling white, whereas the chancel and aisles feature altarpieces carved in the local black marble. Below the church note the monument commemorating the sacrifice of Arnold von Winkelried at the Battle of Sempach.

Museum für Geschichte

⊙*Open Apr–Oct, Mon–Sat, 2pm–5pm, Sun, 10am–noon, 2pm–5pm; Nov–Mar, Wed and Sat, 2pm–5pm, Sun, 10am–noon, 2pm–5pm .*⊚*5CHF.* ℘*(0)41 618 73 40.*

This small Museum of Local History situated at the heart of the town features a charming little chapel embellished with a 1604 altarpiece. One of the rooms evokes the Day of Horror—9 September 1798—when the French assault on the local mountain people caused bloodshed (⊙*audio-visual presentation in German only*).

Stanserhorn★★

Alt. 1 898m/6 227ft.

A pleasant ride in a funicular and cable-car (⊙*operates May–Oct; departure every 30min (every 10min at busy periods) 8.30am–5.15pm;* ⊚*fare there and back 48CHF;* ℘*(0)41 618 80 40; www.stanserhorn.ch*) takes you to the upper station (the huge serrated wheels of the winch which hoisted the old funicular can be seen) from where a portion of the view *(viewing table)* seen from the top is offered.

Walk to the summit *(20min there and back)* from where there is a splendid **panorama**★★ of Lake Lucerne to the north, the peaks of the Swiss Alps to the south (Titlis Glacier) and to the south-

---

> ### Switzerland's Largest Lakes
>
> - Lake Geneva: 580sq km/224sq mi
> - Lake Lucerne: 114sq km/44sq mi
> - Lake Constance: 540sq km/208sq mi
> - Lake Zürich: 88sq km/34 sq mi
> - Lake Neuchâtel: 217sq km/84sq mi
> - Lake Lugano: 48sq km/18.5 sq mi
> - Lake Maggiore: 212sq km/ 82sq mi
> - Lake Thun: 48sq km/18.5 sq mi

west, the summits of the Bernese Alps, including the Jungfrau Massif.

Enjoy a hot chocolate or fondue while taking in the views of ten lakes at the new revolving restaurant Rondorama.

Klewenalp

Reached via cable-car starting from Beckenried. Accessible by boat. ⊙*May– Nov.* ⊚ *34CHF.* ℘*(0)41 227 17 17 25. www.klewenalp.ch.*

At 1 593m/5 226ft, Klewenalp offers a useful starting point for hiking and downhill mountain biking. There are also nice beaches lawn Beckenried, especially Freibad *(free)* with cabins, bar and swimming pool for children.

Seelisberg★

Alt. 845m/2 772ft.

Bahnhof, 6377. ℘*(0)41 820 15 63. www.seelisberg.com.*

You can reach Seelisberg by car from Stans (22km/13.5mi; go under the motorway to Buochs on the south bank of the lake, continue along the shore via Niederdorf to the valley of Beckenried, then St Anna and Emmetten) or by funicular, from the Treib landing stage (services connecting with the steamers on Lake Lucerne; duration of the climb: 8min. ⊙*Operates all year round, times vary according to the season.* ⊚*5.80CHF.* ℘*(0)41 820 15 63.*

Seelisberg stands on a wooded spur dipping into Lake Lucerne within view of the Bay of Brunnen and the Schwyz Basin. It is overlooked by the twin peaks of the Mythen. As one of the exclusive summer resorts in central Switzerland, this luxurious retreat is characterised by its isolation, the majesty of its panorama and the quality of its tourist amenities. Visitors may indulge in fondue while on the last funicular ride of the day; the cars slow down and accordion music accompanies the ride.

The trip includes coffee and dessert at the Hotel Treib (summit) before descending at dusk, overlooking the valley lights. From the public belvedere-promenade there is a **view**★★ of the Fronalpstock and Lake Uri.

🚗 DRIVING TOURS

NORTH SHORE★★★

Lucerne to Altdorf. 54km/33.5mi – approx 2hr30min.

Lucerne★★★ – 🕐See LUCERNE.
Between Lucerne, Küssnacht and Weggis, the road skirts Lake Lucerne and Lake Küssnacht as it approaches the slopes of the Rigi. To the south, the foothills of the Nidwalden (Stans-Engelberg district) succeed one another.

Hohle Gasse
From Küssnacht, 3km/1.8mi there and back by the road to Arth (number 2), plus 15min on foot there and back.
Leaving your car at the Hohle Gasse Hotel, take the roughly paved Sunken Road (Hohle Gasse) uphill, where according to tradition William Tell lay in wait for Gessler. The road through the woods ends at the commemorative chapel.

Weggis★★
Weggis is a grand resort situated on the shores of Lake Lucerne within view of the Pilatus and Unterwalden mountains along a promenade quay which leads to the Hertenstein Promontory.

Vitznau★
Passing tourists may leave their cars for a few hours in this elegant resort, enclosed between the Rigi and the lake, to climb the Rigi-Kulm by rack railway. This was the first mountain railway built in Europe (1871).

Rigi-Kulm★★★
Tourist Information Rigi, Casa Margherita, Kaltbad. www.wvrt.ch.
Isolated on all sides by a depression largely covered by the waters of the Lucerne, Zug, and Lauerz lakes, this "island mountain," to quote the term used by German geographers, raises its heavy wooded shoulders, scarred by reddish escarpments, to an altitude of 1 797m/5 896ft. It has been famous for a century for its highest point, the Rigi-Kulm, on the summit of which, traditionally, you should spend the night to see the sun rise over the Alps. Two of the first tourists were Queen Victoria (carried to the summit on a sedan chair) and Mark Twain who made it famous in his book *A Tramp Abroad*. Those who like easy walks through woods and Alpine pastures, or along mountain roads, which always offer interesting views, should stay in one of the hotels scattered high on the mountainside. One of the best-situated resorts is **Rigi-Kaltbad**.
For over 150 years the sunrise seen from the **Rigi-Kulm** has been the climax of a visit to Switzerland. "The splendor of the spectacle drove away memories of the harsh preliminaries, and the shivering, sleepy crowd reached a state of collective exaltation when the first rays of the sun lit up", according to Victor Hugo. However, the sun is often obscured by clouds, as Mark Twain famously found to his annoyance.

Vitznau-Rigi railway
From Arth-Goldau or Vitznau the climb by rack railway to the Rigi-Kulm takes 35min. Another way is to take the cable-car from Weggis to Rigi-Kaltbad and change there to the rack railway for the Rigi-Kulm. From Arth-Goldau, Vitznau or Weggis: 🚡Fare there and back 62CHF. For exact timetables, call 📞 (0)41 399 87 42 (Vitznau Station), 📞 (0)41 859 08 59 (Goldau Station) or 📞 (0)41 390 18 44 (Weggis Station) or contact 📞 (0)41 399 87 87. www.rigi.ch.
A set of cog railways climbs to the top of Mount Rigi. Since the middle of the 19C steam trains have brought visitors to the top of Mount Rigi. Modern equip-

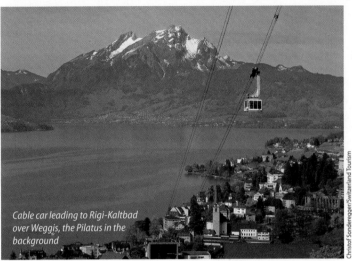

Cable car leading to Rigi-Kaltbad over Weggis, the Pilatus in the background

Christof Sonderegger/Switzerland Tourism

ment has replaced the antique on most runs, but from time to time fully restored antique engines and cars still bring visitors on the same breathtaking trip.

Cog railroads run from Vitznau and from Arth-Goldau up to the Rigi Kulm all year round. The railroad company also runs a modern cable-car from Weggis. The Rigi-Kaltbad lift rises some 274m/900ft and a 91.4m/300ft path at the top connects to the cog train station at Kaltbad. The top is famed for its views and for hiking and other outdoor activities, including winter sports.

Panorama★★★

Alt. 1 797m/5 896ft.

From the terminus station, near to a large hotel, 15min on foot there and back to the signpost and the cross at the summit.

Your eye may wander from end to end of the Alps' tremendous backcloth rising between Säntis and the Bernese Alps (Jungfrau), including the Glarus and Uri Alps and the Titlis Massif. The opposite half of the horizon is less dazzling, but is more attractive.

On this side the rounded hills of the Zürich countryside stretch into the distance, beyond the Lauerzer, Zug, and Lucerne lakes, to merge with the line of the Jura, the Vosges, and the Black Forest.

⚑ Walk from Rigi-Kaltbad to Hinterbergen★★★

A wonderful walk (*2hr–2hr30min*), easy to negotiate and clearly signposted, the perfect complement to a climb up Rigi. Get off the train at Kaltbad station (alt. 1 438m/4 718ft). Follow the path to First, flanked by explanatory panels about the geology of the area. The **view**★★ widens out over Lake Lucerne. The route continues toward Unterstetten, wending its way through spectacularly sheer cliffs. When you catch sight of the hotel, bear left and go up the lawn for 200m/220yds, then turn right in the direction of Gletti (a steep, short climb followed by a descent). From Gletti there is a sweeping **panorama**★★★ of the whole region. To end the tour, go down to Hinterbergen, either by the direct, steep route on the right, or by the gently sloping path on the left. At the heart of the village, look out for the white house with six small windows: It is the terminus of a cable-car that will take you back to Vitznau in 6min.

Horse-Drawn Carriage Rides

Contact the Tourist Office for reservations. 30min, 2hr and 4hr rides are available at Rigi-Kaltbad via three scenic routes.

⊳ *From Vitznau, follow the lakeshore road towards Brunnen.*

Obere Nase★

The very pronounced bend in the road as it passes this cape is arranged as a **belvedere**★. This "Nose", thrown out by a spur of the Rigi, and the Untere Nase, an extreme outcrop of the Bürgenstock facing it, encloses a channel only 825m/2 707ft wide connecting two very different basins. Within a short distance you pass from Lake Vitznau, bounded on the south by the Bürgenstock, to Lake Gersau-Beckenried.

Gersau★

Lying in an open **site**★★ on the Alpine shores of the lake, this small municipality used to be the Independent Republic of Gersau in permanent alliance with the Swiss Confederation, but is now attached to canton Schwyz. You will now begin to skirt the Bay of Brunnen, followed by the Seelisberg.

Brunnen★★

Alt. 439m/1 440ft. Bahnhofstrasse 15.
℘(0)41 825 00 40. www.brunnen
tourismus.ch.

Brunnen is one of the major resorts of Lake Lucerne; **Hans Christian Andersen**, the author of fairy tales, visited often on holiday. Until the opening of Axenstrasse, Brunnen was a key port for traffic between the Schwyz and Uri cantons and a major transit point on the St Gotthard route. It is busy today because tourists on the great transalpine road through Arth and those on the coastal route through Vitznau meet here.

Brunnen deserves a stop for its **site**★★ at the head of the wild Lake Uri (Unnersee), in the heart of picturesque Switzerland. It was here after the victory at Morgarten in 1315, that the three cantons of Uri, Schwyz and Unterwalden renewed their pact of mutual assistance (&see INTRODUCTION: History).

Quays★★

From the shaded quay, the extension of the Axenquai Promenade eastwards below Axenstrasse, there is a sweeping **panorama**★★ of Lake Uri, lying like a fjord between wild mountain spurs. The dominant feature is the Uri-Rotstock, whose bare twin peaks rise above a small glacier.

In the foreground, on the opposite shore, the tender green of the historic field of **Rütli** shows up against the wooded slopes of the Seelisburg spur. At the extreme point of this promontory you can see the natural obelisk known as the **Schillerstein** with an 1859 inscription by the first 3 cantons in memory of Friedrich von Schiller, whose epic "Wilhelm Tell" distilled Swiss nationalist sentiment. (&*A short trip in a motor boat will give a closer view.*)

From Brunnen to Flüelen the Axenstrasse corniche overhangs the romantic **Lake Uri** (Urnersee), with its deep blue waters. Its shores are marked by places of patriotic pilgrimage recalling the birth of the Confederation (Rütli, Tellskapelle).

▷ *This section of road, which is one of the best-known on the St Gotthard route, is also one of the busiest in the country.*

Tellskapelle

From the Hotel Tellsplatte, 30min on foot there and back by a steep path.

On the shore of **Lake Uri**★, this chapel commemorates an episode in the story of William Tell. As Gessler's prisoner after the ordeal of the apple, Tell was thrown into a boat which was assailed by a sudden storm; the bailiff and his minions had to appeal for their captive's help. He took advantage of this to steer the boat toward the shore, leapt out and kicked the boat back into the raging waves.

▷ *Continuing on the Axenstrasse we reach Flüelen and Altdorf (7km/4.3mi).*

FROM ALTDORF TO LINDTHAL

48km/30mi – approx 2hrs.

&*The Klausen road is closed to vehicles with a trailer. The Klausen Pass is usually blocked by snow Nov–May.*

The Escape from Gessler's Boat—*mural by Ernst Stueckelberg, Tellskapelle*

Lucia Degonda/Switzerland Tourism

Altdorf

Alt. 462m/1 516ft.
Tellspielhaus Schützengasse 11. ℘*(0)41*
872 04 50. www.altdorf.ch.

Altdorf stands between Lake Lucerne and the defile of the Upper Reuss Valley. The key to the St Gotthard Pass on the north side of the Alps, Altdorf preserves all the dignity of a small, old-fashioned capital town. Travellers will also notice the southern influences already apparent on restaurant menus, the presence of Ticino characteristics in the people, and traces of the **binario** *(road with granite paving stones)*, which will prepare them for a greater change of scene. It is no exaggeration to say that tourism today revolves rather obsessively about the William Tell myth and that most visitors are, indeed, Swiss.

Telldenkmal

The statue in honour of **William Tell**, the famous archer of Uri, stands in the main square of the town. The work dates from 1895 and is interesting chiefly for the fact that it created Tell's physical type, since made familiar all over the world by a postage stamp bearing his effigy. The statue of this national hero is appropriately erected in this canton, which was the first to throw off foreign control. There is a small **Tell-Museum** (◯*open daily late May–mid Oct, 10am–11.30am, 1.30pm–5pm; 10am–5pm Jul–Aug;*

5CHF; ℘(0)41 870 41 55; www.tellmuseum.ch) at Bürglen on the Klausen Pass road (◖*see KLAUSEN PASS).*

▷ *It is only a short distance from Altdorf to the next stopping-place.*

Bürglen

Bürglen is said to be the birthplace of **William Tell** and the village now has a **Tell Museum**. The exhibits include a host of documents, chronicles, sculptures, paintings, and other items relating to Switzerland's legendary hero over the past 600 years.

Between Bürglen and Unterschächen, the road, lined by chapels, runs at first along the verdant valley through which flows the river Schächen. This widens upstream and is then covered with birch, maple and fruit trees, but the south slope quickly becomes barren and gives a foretaste of harsher sections.

From Unterschächen to the pass, two big hairpin bends facing the mouth of the Brunnital, a tributary valley ending in a cirque at the foot of the Ruchen and the Windgällen precipices, lead to Urigen, the starting-point of a magnificent **corniche section**★★. From then on there is a bird's-eye view of the wild cul-de-sac of the Upper Schächental, enclosed by the gigantic **Chammliberg Cliffs.** The bend marked by a single rock on the side of the escarpment

(600m/656yds above the first tunnel) forms a **viewpoint**★ overlooking the **Stäubi Waterfall** (Stäubifall) and the hamlet of **Aesch**, 400m/1 312ft below. The great snow-laden corniches of the Clariden can be seen behind the Chammliberg Cliffs.

Klausen Pass★
Alt. 1 948m/6 391ft.

The Klausen Pass road combines nearly all the physical and economic features of mountainous Switzerland. Within less than 50km/31mi the traveller passes from a high, wild primitive Alpine combe (Urner Boden) to one of the most industrial valleys in the range (Linth Valley). Motorists usually stop below the summit on the Schächental slope, at the Klausenpasshöhe Hotel.

From a spot near the hotel you can see the snowy crests of the Clariden, the Chammliberg Cliffs, the double Schärhorn peak, the rocky points of the Windgälen, and finally, in line with the Schächen Gap, the Uri-Rotstock Massif on the horizon. After passing the huts of Vorfrütt, where herdsmen shelter in the summer, you will be able to admire the north face of the Clariden and the Chlus, a corrie streaked by two cascades.

Urner Boden★

The run along the bottom of this very regular cleft offers motorists a long, level stretch, unexpected at this altitude (1 300–1 400m /4 250–4 600ft).

The belfry of the church in the main hamlet, standing in the middle of the hollow, behind fir trees, is an attractive feature of the run down from the Klausen Pass. There are hairpin bends as far as Linthal. The Linth Valley opens out below, abutting the walls of the Selbsanft (Tödi Massif) upstream.

SCHÖLLENENSTRASSE (Schöllenen Road)

From Altdorf to Andermatt. 56km/35mi – approx 1hr30min. Between Altdorf and Göschenen, the E 35 motorway runs parallel to road number 2 we recommend.

The itinerary, starting in the Lake Lucerne district and following the Reuss Valley, penetrates into the heart of the **St Gotthard Massif**. Its most unusual site, the Schöllenen Defile, lies at the end of the itinerary.

Altdorf (&see above)

From Altdorf to Amsteg, as the valley narrows, the majestic conical Bristen Peak, rising steeply to 3 072m/10 079ft, catches the eye. The populous centre of **Erstfeld** marks the point where the line begins to climb the ramp to the north entrance of the **St Gotthard Tunnel**, 600m/1 968ft higher up.

Between Amsteg and Wassen, the floor of the **Reuss Valley**, where the mountain section of the road begins, contains pretty shaded nooks. Bends in the road—especially before reaching Wassen, whose church can be seen directly after leaving Gurtnellen—give glimpses of the shapely pyramid of the **Kleine Windgällen** lying below.

Pfaffensprung

From the car park, downstream from the bridge over the Reuss, cross the road to a belvedere overlooking the **Parson's Leap**. The overflow of the dam built nearby forms a spectacular cascade, with beautiful iridescent effects.

Footbridge over the River Reuss at Pfaffensprung

Suvorov's Retreat

During the Napoleonic Wars Switzerland became a battlefield between the French, Austrian and Russian Forces. In March 1799 **General Masséna** prepared an invasion of the Tyrol but he was repulsed and decamped in Zürich. He was further beaten in June by Austrian troops under the **Duke of Teschen** who subsequently left for the Netherlands and entrusted his position to a contingent of Russian troops under **General Korsakov**. He in turn, expected a large expeditionary force under **General Alexander Suvorov** from the south. Masséna sent sentries to harass Suvorov's force, while he attacked Korsakov whom he eventually routed. Suvorov had to make a strategic retreat through the snowy Alps in October and, although he lost many men, he regrouped in Austria undefeated. His crossing of the Alps through Airolo-Andermatt-Altdorf and retreat via the Muothatal, the Pragel pass to Glarus, the Panixer pass to Chur and eventually to Feldkirch and the Vorarlberg has been compared as second only to Hannibal's.

Wassen

Wassen became well-known when the builders of the St Gotthard railway made two successive loops in the track, partly underground, on either side of the village. Uninitiated visitors struggling to keep their sense of direction after seeing three successive views of Wassen church from different angles are a constant source of amusement to regular travellers.

From Wassen to Göschenen the bottom of the corridor is partly obstructed by landslides; among them is an enormous single rock called the **Devil's Stone** (**Teufelsstein**). Impressive road construction has been achieved on this section.

Göschenen

Göschenen is best known for its railway station at the north end of the St Gotthard Tunnel (15km/9.3mi long, opened in 1882). It is a useful halt for tourists, who will find it pleasant to stand near the small central bridge and admire the ice field of the Upper Dammastock, which can be seen through the Göschenertal Gap.

Göscheneralpsee★★

The road that leads to this reservoir-lake offers close-up views of the **Dammastock Glaciers** (on the east side of the Rhône Glacier) which feed it. The road climbs the wild, narrow Göschenen

Valley, with winding sections along the side of superb rock faces.

Leave the car in the car park near the restaurant (alt. 1 783m/5 850ft) and go to the centre of the dam's grassy crest. This gravity dam (capacity 9.3 million cum/204 600 million gal; 700m/2 297ft thick at base; 155m/508ft high; 540m/1 772ft length of crest) dams the reservoir-lake.

Ahead is a magnificent **landscape**★★ that includes the dam, cascades right and left and, separated by a rocky cone, gleaming glaciers below the Winterberg peak.

Schöllenen★★

Andermatt Gotthard Tourismus, Gotthardstrasse 2. ℘(0)41 887 14 54. www.andermatt.ch.

The remarkably smooth and polished granite walls of the Reus Valley form a bottleneck between Göschenen and Andermatt. This is the legendary **Schöllenen gorge**, which was the chief obstacle to the development of traffic on the St Gotthard route until about the 13C, when a road was boldly driven through it. The modern roads may be a bit of an anti-climax, so visitors are advised to walk the old road.

Teufelsbrücke

The bridge is 3km/1.8mi N of Andermatt. In 1830, this bridge replaced one built, according to legend, at the instigation and the co-operation of the Devil. There was one condition: the villagers had to pay for it with the soul of the first one to cross it—but the the wily people of Uri sent across a billy goat. Since motor traffic is no longer permitted, the bridge is an ideal viewing spot to admire the foaming **Reuss Falls** (⌔ best seen in sunlight around noon). Slightly downstream, take note of a cross hewn in the rocky wall of the east bank and an inscription in Cyrillic characters. It commemorates the hazardous venture of Russian **General Suvorov** (⌔ see info box p345).

Skiing in Andermatt

Robert Boesch/Switzerland Tourism

Andermatt – ⌔ See ALTO TICINO.
Andermatt is known worldwide for its grand pistes and challenging downhill ski slopes, but summer in the area has just as many outdoor adventures on offer.

There are several choices of **Mountain Bike** tours with incredible views along the way, from easy ones such as the 20km/12mi circuit Andermatt—Hospental—Zumdorf—Realp—Andermatt (1hr30min, 100m/0.6mi altitude difference) to the very difficult 31km/19mi Andermatt—Oberalp— Maighelspass—Andermatt (4hr, 1 200 m/3 937ft altitude difference). There is a famous **Mountain Climbing** route the **Via Ferrata Diavolo** (450m/1 476ft altitude difference) starting from the Suvorov monument and ending at **Tüfelstalboden**. For more info, ☎(0)41 888 83 21. **Rafting** on the pristine glacial torrents is an experience unlike any other (☎(0)43

888 53 00; www.rafters.ch), or you can find a spot for **fishing** in these green-blue pools with an experienced guide (Fischerpatente Oberalpsee; ☎081 949 12 13, or Fischerpatente übriges, Altdorf, ☎(0)41 875 20 17). Avid **golfers** will not want to miss a round at Golfplatz Realp in Urserntal (☎(0)41 887 01 62; www.golf-gotthard.ch).

Gemsstock★★ –
⌔ See ALTO TICINO.

ADDRESSES

🛏 STAY

RIGI-KULM

⌖⌖⌖ **Bergsonne** – ☎(0)41 399 80 10. www.bergsonne.ch. Closed Apr. Restaurant ⌖⌖⌖. 17 rooms. Its ideal location above the village provides breathtaking views of the Alps and the nearby lake. Rooms are decorated with local furniture.

⌖⌖⌖ **Edelweiss** – ☎(0)41 399 88 00. www.edelweiss-rigi.ch. Closed mid-Mar–mid-Apr. 27 rooms. A blissfully quiet establishment with views of lake and mountains. The older part features rooms appointed with rustic-style furniture.

BRUNNEN

⌖⌖⌖ **Weisses Rössli** –
Bahnhofstrasse 8. ☎(0)41 820 11 22. 17 rooms. Frescoes evoke the memory of Ludwig II of Bavaria, who once stayed at the hotel. The first-floor salon is decorated in blue and white, the official colours of Bavaria, and, naturally, the most prestigious room is the one which was occupied by the sovereign.

⌖⌖⌖ **Schmid und Alfa** –
On the lakeshore. ☎(0)41 820 18 82; www.schmidalfa.ch. 30 rooms. Closed Tue and Wed from 1 Mar to Easter. The best rooms overlook the lake, from where, on a fine day, you can make out the Rütli and the memorial to Schiller on the opposite shore. Excellent service at this modern, comfortable hotel will make your stay even more special.

Engelberg ✳✳

Engelberg stands on a site which, although surrounded by heights, is nonetheless sunny. It is the great mountain resort of central Switzerland famous for both tourist and religious activities. A swimming pool, tea rooms, tennis courts, and a skating rink are found alongside one of the large, imposing Benedictine abbeys which lie concealed in the high valleys of Switzerland. Recently, it has become a resort of much renown in India, because it features regularly in Bollywood films whenever snowy peaks are required in the frame.

The mountaineer can choose between the glacier formation of the Titlis and the jagged crests of the Spannörter and Uri Rotstock, whereas the walker, using the high-tec ski lifts can easily reach attractive sites such as those of Trübsee and the Titlis.

SIGHTS
Benedictine Monastery

Guided tour of monastery (1hr) Tue–Sat, 10am, 4pm; monastery and exhibition hall (1hr30min) Wed and Sat at 4pm. ⊕6CHF (monastery); 8CHF (monastery and exhibition hall). ℘(0)41 639 61 19. www.kloster-engelberg.ch.

▶ **Population:** 3 721.

ℹ **Info:** Klosterstrasse 3 – 6390. ℘(0)41 639 77 77. www.engelberg.ch.

▶ **Location:** Located in the very centre of Switzerland, home to Mt Titlis. Alt. 1 002m/3 287ft.

✦ **Don't Miss:** Excursion to Titlis with the Rotair cable-car, and exploration of its glacial caves or the Engelberg-Titlis ski resort.

The monastery, founded in the 12C, ruled over the whole valley until the French invasion of 1798. Today most of the buildings are used as a religious college. One of the rooms displays an unusual collection of liturgical objects from the 11C to the 20C. The Baroque **parish church** features the arrangement and decoration characteristic of French Regency style (mid 18C) and was fully restored in 2005–2009. The organ is the largest in Switzerland.

EXCURSIONS
Titlis ★★★

Alt. 3 239m/10 627ft. Allow 3hr there and back, preferably during the day, when you can combine the climb with a long walk. Remember to wear warm clothes, sturdy mountain shoes and a

Cable car to Titlis

Christian Perret/Engelberg-Titlis Tourismus/Switzerland Tourism

347

pair of sunglasses. ⏱*Operates Dec–Oct, 8.30am–4.50pm.* 🚠*Fare there and back 76CHF.* 📞*(0)41 639 50 50.*

🚠*A cable-car, the "Rotair", fitted with rotating cabins, operates on the upper section between Strand and Titlis. The journey takes 5min. The rotation of the cabins gives passengers a spectacular panoramic view; there is a restaurant at the top.*

The cable-car service to **Trübsee**, split up into two journeys, commands a full **view**★ of Engelberg and its green pastures. Then take the cable-car to Stand (2 450m/8 038ft).

The splendid **views**★★ of **Trübsee** and the **Titlis Glacier** can be seen from above thanks to the **Rotair** cable-car (**views**★★ of Lake Engtsien). From the terrace (alt. 3 020m/9 909ft) enjoy the breathtaking **panorama**★★★ of Sustenhorn dominating a rough mountain range, the steep rocks of Wendenstöcke and Reissand Nollend and, farther west, the Valais Alps (Dom) and the Bernese Oberland (Jungfrau). A number of curious sights will delight visitors: An ice grotto and a panoramic window hollowed out of the south slope, 45m/145ft beneath the ice.

You are advised to climb up to the viewpoint and its viewing table (*10min*). A ski lift for children leads to a sledge piste. Experienced hikers who want a broader **bird's-eye view**★★★ should proceed to the summit (*40min*), taking care to observe the safety rules. From Stand, there is a panoramic route that takes you back down to Trübsee (*1hr15min*), offering lovely **views**★★ of the valley, interspersed with explanatory panels about the geology of the area.

Trübsee★★

Alt. 1 764m/5 786ft. 🚠*Access in 5min after the second journey in cable-car.*
Lying at the foot of the Titlis Glacier framed by rocky summits, this is one of Europe's most beautiful mountain lakes. Go on a **tour of the lake**★★, proceeding towards the right (allow 1hr10min) and appreciate the pretty path enhanced by clumps of spruce and rhododendron.

Fürenalp★★

Alt. 1 850m/6 069ft. 🚠*Access by cable-car. 3.5km/2.2mi E of Engelberg.*
The route leading to this rocky outcrop perched up high affords spectacular **views**★★ of the whole glacial cirque lining the valley, with its waterfalls, peaks and glaciers.

Walk to Stäfeli★★

1hr45min on foot and 5min by cable-car.
From Fürenalp, bear right onto a gently sloping path bordered by yellow gentian and herds of cows. Continue to walk straight on until you catch sight of Abnet village: Proceed towards it bearing right. For a hair-raising experience, jump into the small cable-car that will take you to Stäfeli, dropping by 300m/985ft amid sheer cliffs. You will eventually get back to your point of departure by a smooth path flanked by steep slopes, in an austere but lush green landscape cut across by a stream.

Brunnihütte★

Alt. 1 860m/6 102ft. www.brunnihuette.ch. 🚠*Access by cable-car, then by chairlift. Allow 1hr there and back.* 📞*(0)41 637 37 32. www.brunnihutte.ch.*
You will enjoy a **view**★ of the whole valley, particularly impressive at sunset. Accommodation and meals available.

Walk to Rugghubelhütte★★

Alt. 2 294m/7 526ft. www.rugghubel.ch.
Make your way down the right-hand path following the mountain slope, bordered with luxuriant alpine flora (*30min*). Proceed straight until the refuge (*1hr15min*). The early part of the climb offers fantastic **views**★★ of the Titlis, Grosser Spannort and the massive Hahnen barrier.

On reaching the top, enjoy views of Gemsispil, Reissend Nollen and the Bernese Alps in the distance. Continue for 100m/100yds beyond the refuge for a **sweeping panorama**★★ including the Griessenfirn Glacier and Wissigstock. Return the same way, then go towards Ristis (*2hr altogether*) by a good path in a charming bucolic **setting**★★. Finish the outing by cable-car.

Zug★★

This charming little town is built at the northeast end of **Zugersee (Lake Zug)★★**, a charming lake nestling among gardens and orchards at the foot of the first wooded foothills of the Zugerberg. Excavations reveal that the site of Zug has been inhabited by man without interruption since the Neolithic Era. In the Middle Ages it belonged successively to the Lenzburg, Kyburg, and Habsburg families before joining the Confederation in 1352. Its 13C castle has now been entirely restored.

▶ **Population:** 25 778.

Info: Bahnhofplatz, ℘(0)41 723 68 00. www.zug-tourismus.ch.

Location: Central Switzerland, just south of Zürich. Alt. 425m/1 394ft.

Don't Miss: Zugersee, or guided tours of the old town.

Timing: Allow a minimum of one day to see the principal sights.

GEOGRAPHY
Zugersee★★

The Zugersee, with a total area of 38sq km/15sq mi and a depth of almost 200m/656ft, is Switzerland's tenth largest lake. It runs in a north-south direction for 14km/9mi and is almost divided in two by a verdant peninsula. The lake, in an attractive hilly setting, is dominated by the Rigi-Kulm in the south and is very popular with visitors for its scenic beauty and many amenities.

SIGHTS
The Quays★

From Seestrasse to Alpenquai, a promenade beside the lake offers **views★** of the summits of central Switzerland (Rigi, Pilatus, Bürgenstock, Stanserhorn) and, in the background, of the Bernese Alps (Finsteraarhorn, Jungfrau, Blümlisalp).

Old Town★

Guided tours of the town (1hr30min) daily by reservation. 140CHF for groups of up to 25. Contact the Tourist Office. ℘(0)41 723 68 00.

Ruined fortifications—Powder Tower (Pulverturm), the Capuchin's Tower (Kapuzinerturm)—still mark the original nucleus of the town. The quarters known as Unter-Altstadt (Lower Old Town) and Ober-Altstadt (Upper Old Town), with their old step-gabled houses, strike a delightfully medieval note.

The **Fischmarkt** (Fish Market) has houses with painted weatherboards and overhanging balconies. The Clock Tower, **Zytturm**, features a tiled roof painted in the Zug colours (blue and white) and is crowned by a slim belfry. Under the clock face are the coats of arms of the first eight cantons of the Confederation, Zug having been the seventh canton to join the alliance.

Kolinplatz is surrounded by old houses, among them the Town House (Stadthaus), a 16C building adorned with a fine flower-decked fountain. This fountain bears the statue of the standard bearer **Wolfgang Kolin**, a local hero who performed brave feats to save his banner at the **Battle of Arbedo** (1422), when the Swiss Confederate forces, who were defending **Bellinzona**, were defeated by the Duke of Milan's army. Kolin's son, to whom the banner had been passed, was also killed.

St Oswald

Open 8am–6pm (5pm in winter). For information on guided tours, call ℘(0)41 711 00 78.

This Late Gothic church (1478–1515) is dedicated to St Oswald of Northumbria. The interior, with ogive vaulting, is darkened by its massive pillars. The nave is separated from the chancel by a partition adorned with frescoes. The interior includes many statues of saints, painted and gilded wooden triptychs in the side chapels, and frescoes on the vaulting.

EXCURSIONS
Zugerberg★
Alt. 988m/3 241ft. ◐ *The easiest way to get to Zugerberg is to take bus number 11 leaving from Zug railway station (Bahnhof Metelli stop), then go to Schöneg and take the funicular.*
Operates all year. Departures every 30min Mon–Fri, every 15min Sat–Sun.
Fare there and back 7CHF.
(0)41 728 58 30.

From the summit there is a almost circular **view**★ to the northwest, of Zug and the lake, to the southwest of the Pilatus, to the south of the Uri-Rotstock and the Uri Alps, and to the east—through a gap in the fir trees—of the village of Unter-Ägeri and its lake. To the north the hills of the Mittelland can be seen rising one behind the other toward Zürich.

Cistercian Abbey Church★
◐ *8km/5mi N by the road to Zürich.*
The imposing silhouette of the former Cistercian abbey church—buttresses, pointed roofs, and slim bell tower—can be seen in the distance with its village huddled against it. It is located not far from where Zwingli was killed. Built in 13C–14C, the abbey illustrates the Early Gothic style with pure lines and elegant lancet windows. The vast nave is highlighted by stalls decorated with human or animal heads (note the bitch with her puppies). Note the remains of 14C frescoes decorating chancel walls (St Martin, Christ and Saints in medallions) and the **stained-glass windows**★.

Schwyz★

This quiet little town gave the Swiss Confederation both its name and its flag. It occupies a majestic **site**★ at the foot of the twin Mythen peaks, between the lakes of Lucerne and Lauerz. The resort of Stoos (alt. 1 295m/4 249ft), at the foot of the Fronalpstock moutain, is built on a sunny plateau with far-reaching views.

A BIT OF HISTORY
For the history of the original cantons, see LAKE LUCERNE: The Cradle of Swiss Democracy.

Soldiers of Fortune
When foreign princes recruited mercenaries for their service from the 16C onwards, the men of Schwyz enlisted in their armies, especially in the French regiments.
Their bravery and military qualities enabled many to return to their country, having made their fortunes, covered with honours and glory. They settled in their homeland and built the sumptuous homes that their descendants still own.

▶ **Population:** 14 183.
▮ **Info:** Oberer Steisteg 14 – 6430. *(0)41 810 19 91. www.info-schwyz.ch.*
◐ **Location:** Central Switzerland, near Lake Lucerne. Alt. 517m/1 696ft.
⊕ **Don't Miss:** Bundesbriefmuseum, housing original Confederation documents.
◷ **Timing:** The town's sights can be seen in under three hours.

SIGHTS
Forum der Schweizer Geschichte
Hofmatt/Zeughausstrasse 5. ◷*Open Tue–Sun, 10am–5pm (Thu until 7pm)* ◷*Closed 1 Jan, Good Fri, Easter Mon, 1 Nov and 25 Dec.* *10CHF.* *(0)41 819 60 11. www.forumschwyz.ch.*
Open to commemorate the 700th anniversary of the Swiss Confederation (1991), this thoroughly modern national museum is dedicated to the history and cultural life of Switzerland from the 14C to the 19C, including a history of the

Swiss knife. A relevant selection of over 800 items helps to understand better the Swiss people and their myths.

Bundesbriefmuseum★

🕐*Open Tue–Fri, 9am–11.30am, 1.30pm–5pm, Sat–Sun 9am–5pm (1.30pm Nov–Apr).* 🕐*Closed Good Fri and 25 Dec.* ✆*4CHF.* ✆*(0)41 819 20 64. www.bundesbriefmuseum.ch.*

A modern building, with a fresco by H Danioth on its façade, it was erected (1934–36) to house the most precious original documents of the Confederation. In the great hall adorned with a fresco, *The Oath* by W Clénin, and banners of the Schwyz canton are displayed. The Original Pact of 1291 (Bundesbrief), the Pact of Brunnen of 1315 (Morgartenbrief), charters of freedom and pacts of alliance concerning the "XIII Cantons" are also on show. Ask at the reception for a free brochure in English.

Hauptplatz

Rebuilt after a fire in the city in 1642 according to plans by a Venetian architect, the buildings define a beautiful Baroque square where five different roads converge. Unfortunately it has been lately turned into a roundabout and the constant traffic tends to dampen some of its charm.

Pfarrkirche St Martin

St Martin's Church (1769–74) has sumptuous 18C Baroque decorations. The nave is adorned with stucco and frescoes; the high altar, the altars in the side chapels, the marble **pulpit**★ and baptistry are all elaborately decorated. In the two transepts lie the reliquaries of St Polycarp (left) and St Lazarus (right).

Rathaus

🕐*Open Mon–Fri, 10am–3pm.* 🕐*Closed public holidays and when there are sittings.* ✆*(0)41 811 45 05.*

Burnt down and rebuilt in 1645, the town hall is ornamented on the two front sides with mural paintings (1891) recalling episodes in Swiss history. Inside are rooms with decorative woodwork and stained-glass windows.

EXCURSIONS
Lauerzer See

▶ *5 km/3mi from Schwyz. Take the exit direction Zürich. In Seewen, take Highway number 2 towards Lucerne.*

The lake shores, lined with reeds on the west side, form small coves for swimming or sunbathing on the eastern side. A tiny island houses a chapel and a restaurant.

Tierpark Goldau

▶ *11km/6.8mi NW of Schwyz.* 🕐*Apr–Oct Mon–Fri 9am–6pm (Sat, Sun & holidays 7pm), Nov–Mar 9am–5pm.* ✆*18CHF (children 10CHF).* ✆*(0)41 859 06 06. www.tierpark.ch.*

Animals from temperate regions live freely in an enclosed forest created in the area where a terrible 1806 landslide buried alive 500 victims. The traces of the catastrophe are clearly visible on the flanks of Rossberg.

Muotathal valley

This valley, southeast of Schwyz, is part of a vast karst area which forks in the village of Muotathal. One branch goes towards Bisisthal and the cable-car to the Glattalp hiking area and a mountain restaurant. The other leads to the canton of Glarus via the Pragel pass and is covered by the largest primeval forest in Europe, 600 acres of spruces barely touched by man.

Höllochgrotte★

▶ *15km/9.3mi by the Muotatal road (SE of the plan) plus 1hr tour.*
Trekking-Team, 6652 Tegna. 🔦*Guided tours by appointment only, half-day, full-day, or two-day.* ✆*14CHF and up.* ✆*0848 808 007. www.trekkingteam.ch.* 🔦*Torches, hard hats and waterproof boots are strongly recommended.*

The Hölloch Cave is known for the size of its galleries, the number of its naturally formed chambers and the beauty of its concretions. It is the largest cave in Europe and, as a geological phenomenon, it enjoys a worldwide reputation. On the way out of Schwyz, take the Muotatal road which is narrow until Hinterthal, then cross the river and turn left into a steep uphill road going to Stalden *(signpost: Stalden-Hölloch)*. The cave must be visited with a guide. When doing this trip you can also go to **Stoos** in a funicular and then to the magnificent viewpoint of the **Fronalpstock**★ (alt. 1 922m/6 306ft).

🚗 DRIVING TOUR

Ibergeregg Road★
11km/7mi.
◐ *Leave Schwyz E via Rickenbachstrasse.*

Beginning at the hill's slope, after crossing Rickenbach, views open out on the left to the Mythen and on the right on part of Lake Lucerne and Lake Lauerz, separated by the Hochfluhe. After a magnificent stretch of corniche through woods above the deep Muotatal Valley and, in a bend in the road, there is a beautiful **view**★ behind this valley and the Lake Lucerne district. During the steep climb that follows, the snowy summits of the Glarus Alps can be seen. At the **Ibergeregg Pass** (alt. 1 406m/4 613ft) admire the remarkable **views**★ of the neighbouring valley. For Einsiedeln, drive down through Unteriberg to Sihlsee and then along the lakeshore road with the water on your right.

Einsiedeln★★
Alt. 881m/2 890ft. Hauptstrasse 85.
℘ (0)55 418 44 88. www.einsiedeln.ch.
The small town of Einsiedeln, in a district of rugged hills and pinewoods, is the most famous and most frequented place of pilgrimage in the whole of Switzerland.

An original church was built on the site of the cell occupied by St Meinradthe hermit, killed by thieves in 861. A monastery was subsequently founded in 934 by Otto I and Duchess Reglinde of Swabia, and subsequently burnt down several times. The town's main street runs into the west side of the huge square on which the abbey church stands. The façade of the Benedictine abbey overlooks a great semicircular courtyard, edged by arcades. in its centre stands a fountain in honour of the Virgin.

Abbey Church (Klosterkirche)★★ *(◐ open 5am–8.30pm)* The church was built (1719–35) in **Vorarlberg Baroque**, popular in regions around Lake Constance, and it is the most remarkable example of this style in Switzerland. Two tall towers flank the façade, which is slightly convex and very graceful. The length of the church, including the upper chancel, is 113m/370ft, the width of the nave 41m/131ft, and the height of the Dome of the Nativity up to the lantern 37m/118ft (Westminster Cathedral 93m/306ft x 47m/156ft x 85m/280ft). Above all, the decoration is extraordinarily ornate: The vaulting, domes and octagonal roof of the nave, the aisles and chancel are embellished with frescoes and stuccoes, largely the work of the Asam brothers from Bavaria. One was known as a painter, the other as an expert in stucco, but many other artists contributed to the construction. The altars were built and painted by the Carlone brothers from Sciara (near Como) and by Milanese artists and the chancel, built between 1674 and 1680, was remodelled later and painted by Kraus of Augsburg. The **Gnadenkapelle**, built in neoclassical style at the entrance to the nave contains the statue of the **Black Madonna**, an object of special veneration for pilgrims.

🐾 Arrive at 4.45pm to see the monks in procession chanting Salve Regina in front off the statue of the Black Madonna.

Grosser Saal
◐ *Open 1.30pm–6pm.* ◐ *Closed during concerts.* 🎟 *3CHF.* ℘ *(0)55 418 62 40.*
The Abbey Great Hall, on the second floor of the monastery buildings, is reached by skirting the church to the right. Enter the first door on the left, in the courtyard. It was built at the beginning of the 18C and is decorated with stuccowork and frescoes by Marsiglio Roncati of Lugano and Johannes Brandenberg of Zug. Exhibitions are held on a regular basis, displaying items from the monastery's different art collections.

Glarus

Glarus lies in a deeply ravined site★ at the foot of the Vorder Glärnisch Cliffs. Since its old quarters were destroyed by fire in 1861 it has had the appearance of a busy city, built on a regular grid plan. The great Zaunplatz holds the canton's open-air assemblies known as Landsgemeinde (see INTRODUCTION) every year on the first Sunday in May.

▶ **Population:** 5 892.
🛈 **Info:** Gemeinde Glarus – Postfach 367. ℘(0)55 610 21 25. www.stadt-glarus.ch.
◉ **Location:** Glarus is in central-eastern Switzerland, and is the capital city of Glarus canton. Alt. 472m/1 549ft.

A BIT OF HISTORY
A Hive of Industry

The row of factories, which gives a peculiar character to the Linth Valley as the main artery of the Glarus canton, recalls the valleys of the Vosges. In the 18C Pastor Andreas Heidegger introduced cotton spinning into the area.

The town enjoyed its golden age about 1860 when printing on cloth was introduced. Indian fabrics made in Glarus then flooded the market, as the town's weavers excelled in this technique. Today Glarus is still the only industrial mountain canton in Switzerland. This municipality is also a tourist area, however; a resort such as **Braunwald** keeps up the traditions of the canton, which was a pioneer of mountaineering (the very first shelter of the Swiss Alpine Club was built in the Tödi Massif in 1863) and skiing (the very first Swiss Ski Championship was held at Glarus in 1905). The Braunwald music weeks are extremely popular events and attract many music lovers every July.

EXCURSIONS
Klöntal★

◉ 13km/8mi – about 45min. Leave Glarus by the road to Zürich, then make for Riedern. In this village follow the road straight on to the Klöntal, running up the Löntsch Valley.

At the top of a steep climb under beech trees is Lake Klöntal (alt. 848m/2 781ft), which was enlarged when the dam was built. The Glärnisch's jagged steep slopes with inaccessible ravines, plunge from a height of 2 000m/6 500ft into the

lake waters. The road climbs to follow the lake shore; after the second hairpin bend, stop at a bench: Facing you is a superb **view**★★ of the Klöntal.

Walensee★★

℘(0)81 720 35 45.
www.walenseeschiff.ch.
Lake Walen forms a deep green-blue mirror beneath the gigantic rock bastions of the Churfisten, a memoravle sight to travellers from Zürich passing through the Wessen-Sargans Gap on their way to Austria, and Graubünden.

NÄFELS TO MURG

Between Näfels and Murg, the lakeside road, parallel with the railway, required large-scale engineering, including the construction of six tunnels and nine stretches of road cut into the mountainside.

It is still possible to go by the old, steep road which, as it climbs to the wooded terrace of the Kerenzerberg, affords many **bird's-eye views**★★ both westwards to the Linth valley and the low alluvial plain into which the torrent flows, and eastwards to the Walensee and the Churfirsten.

Schabzieger

One of the local specialities of the Glarus canton is *Schabzieger*, a green, cone-shaped cheese with no crust, made with skimmed cow's milk and crushed herbs. It owes its spicy flavour, name and colour to one of its ingredients, *ziegerklee* (blue fenugreek).

GRAUBÜNDEN

Graubünden is in the easternmost region of the country, bordering Austria and Italy. Three languages, two religions more or less equally represented, and a political evolution towards democracy similar to that of the original cantons, make Graubünden, the largest Swiss canton, a true model for the Confederation. This is undoubtedly the part of Switzerland where the traveller can enjoy the most complete change of scene: the Engadin, with the charm of its clear blue skies and open countryside, is the tourist lodestar of this little mountain state astride the Alps.

Highlights

1 An unforgettable trip on the **Glacier Express** or the **Bernina Express** (p355)

2 The incomparable view from the **Weisshorn** in Arosa (p365)

3 Snowboarding on the **Jacobshorn** in Davos (p368)

4 Skiing under a full moon in **Diavolezza** (p376)

5 An excursion in the **Swiss National Park** (p383)

A Bit of History

The territory of the canton corresponds with the most mountainous parts of ancient **Rhaetia**, whose "Welsch" tribes originally peopled the area between Lake Constance and Venetia. The Upper Valleys of the Rhine and the Inn, protected from Germanisation, remained Romansh-speaking districts whose language, derived from Latin, was officially recognised as the fourth Swiss national language in 1938.

A Transit Area – Under Roman rule and throughout the Middle Ages, Rhaetia, being crossed by the **High Road** (the Julier and especially the Septimer Pass) and the **Low Road** (the Splügen Pass) monopolised nearly all transalpine traffic through the present territory of the Confederation. The great advantage of the High Road is that there are few passes, so frequent along transalpine roads. The only comparable route was farther west along the Great St Bernard road. The present network of transalpine roads were jointly financed by Switzerland, Austria and Piedmont between 1818 and 1823 and the railways over

and around the Alps were built between 1885 and 1910 (The Bernina line). Already in 1892 posters were appearing in London and other European capitals advertising the Landquart-Klosters-Davos line.

Deeply Independent – The complex network of valleys enclosed by mountains and connected by easily defended alpine passes contributed to the isolation of communities that would speak mutually incomprehensible dialects and yet be only kilometres apart. Rhaetia, like Switzerland, was split into three loose confederations of smaller communities: the 1367 **League of God's House** (Gotteshausbund)—roughly today's Engandin—the **Grey League** in 1395—roughly the area between Dissentis and Flims—named after the colour of the garments worn by those early cantonal forefathers and the **League of Ten Jurisdictions** (Zehngerichtebund)—the area around the bishopric of Chur. All three signed a treaty of mutual assistance in 1471 and it was only in 1803 that the united leagues (Graubünden) joined the Swiss Confederation.

Geography

Graubünden (German), also referred to as Les Grisons (French), Grigioni (Italian) or Grischun (Romansh), contain the sources of the Rhine and Inn rivers. The Vorderrhein has its source in the Oberalp massif and runs from Disentis/Mustér along the Graubünden Oberland; the Hinterrhein comes down from the Adula Glaciers. They meet at the foot of Reichenau Castle near Chur. The Upper Inn Valley (the river joins the Danube at Passau on the borders of Germany and Austria), because of the Engadin, is also part of ancient Rhaetia.

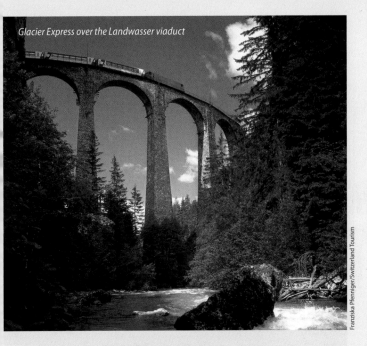
Glacier Express over the Landwasser viaduct

UNESCO Railways

Graubünden has its fair share of Unesco cultural sites but, uniquely, one of them is the 122km/76mi of the railway line from Thusis to St Moritz (the Albula section) and from St Moritz to Tirano (the Bernina section). The first was finished in 1904 and astonished the civil engineering world in that the train climbed from 585m/1 919ft in Chur to 1 775m/5 823ft in St Moritz without using the rack-and-pinion method; it used wheel adhesion via a complex scheme of spiral tunnels over the Albula valley instead. These tunnels are the architectural highlights of the linein addition to the miracle of technology that is the Landwasser viaduct (1902). After St Moritz, the railway engineers went even further and utilised the new available power of the hydroelectric plant at Brusio to design an all-electric railway. The resulting Bernina line goes from the glaciers of the highest pass in Europe at an altitude of 2 253m/7 392ft (an all year operation since 1913) to reach the palms trees at Tirano that stands at only 429m/1 407.5ft above sea level.

Winter Wonderland

Here is where the ski and snowboard connoisseurs descend to: from glitzy St Moritz to youthful, exuberant Davos and elegant Arosa, tourism—and that means winter tourism—is the canton's main source of income. And with 937 mountains, 150 valleys, and 615 lakes reached by 500 cable-cars, chairlifts and mountain railways you can come here every year and never tire of the place. Yet, 100 years ago, the area would be better known by its sanatoriums: in the pre-antibiotic era, a six-month stay in the mountains was what was universally prescribed for lung diseases.

Thomas Mann visited Davos' Waldsanatorium in 1912 which was the inspiration for his famous novel *The Magic Mountain* (1924). It is now the slick Waldhotel, which welcomes visitors seeking a 21C approach to wellness, as well as delegates visiting Davos for the annual meeting of the World Economic Forum.

GRAUBÜNDEN

Chur★

Since the 16C Chur has been the historical, administrative and religious capital of Graubünden. It is built a short distance from the Rhine on a mound of rocky debris formed by a tributary of the Plessur.

GEOGRAPHY

To the east of Chur, the first hairpin bend on the road to Arosa (Arosastrasse) provides an ideal **viewpoint**★ of the whole town and its many belfries, set against a backdrop of steep rocky ridges, covered with the eternal snow of the Calanda.

SIGHTS
Old Town

The old town is grouped around St Martin's church below the cathedral and the bishop's palace, reached by climbing a stairway and passing under an old gateway known as Hoftor. Chur remains a cathedral city with narrow streets with fine houses, occasionally flanked by towers, pretty squares with fountains adorned with flowers and the arms of Graubünden canton, and finally the 15C town hall (Rathaus), all of which make for a picturesque scene.

Chur Cathedral

The **Cathedral of Our Lady** was built in a mixed Romanesque and Gothic style in the 12C and 13C and is unique because the choir lies at an angle to the nave. The exterior was remodelled after a fire in 1811, and restored in 2007. The tower is crowned with a domed belfry, the porch adorned with painted recessed arches. The nave, which is roofed with ribbed vaulting, is very dark, lit only by clerestory windows on the south side. The interior, restored in the 1920s, features massive piers, surmounted by fine, if somewhat unusual, capitals. The chancel contains a 15C **triptych**★ in carved and gilded wood at the high altar; it is dedicated to Our Lady and is the largest Gothic triptych in Switzerland. Four 13C statues depicting the Apostles are arranged on either side of the altar.

▶ **Population:** 32 957.

🛈 **Info:** Grabenstrasse 5 – 7000. ℘(0)81 252 18 18. www.churtourismus.ch.

▶ **Location:** Chur lies in the Rhine Valley at the crossroads of Latin and German influences. Alt. 585m/1 919ft.

◉ **Don't Miss:** The Cathedral and the Bishop's Palace Hof.

◷ **Timing:** It's best to overnight in the town.

Domschatz

☛ Guided tours by appointment only, Mon–Sat 10am–4pm. ◷Closed Good Fri and Corpus Christi and religious holidays ⊕2CHF. ℘(0)81 252 92 50/ 19 70.

The treasury includes reliquaries from the Carolingian period and the Middle Ages and valuable reliquary-busts. The Bishop's Palace **Hof** is an elegant 18C edifice.

Rätisches Museum

Hofstrasse 1 ◷Open Tue–Sun 10am– 5pm. ◷Closed most public holidays. ⊕6CHF. ℘(0)81 254 16 40. www.raetischesmuseum.gr.ch.

This museum is housed in the late 17C Buol Mansion. It contains interesting displays of folklore relating to the canton, a prehistory collection and historical specimens.

Bündner Kunstmuseum

◷Open Tue–Sun 10am–5pm (8pm Thu) ◷Closed most public holidays. ⊕8CHF. ℘(0)81 257 28 68. www.buendner-kunstmuseum.ch.

Most of the works displayed in the **Fine Arts Museum** are by 18C to 20C artists and sculptors from Graubünden by birth or adoption: Barthelemy Menn, Angelica Kauffmann, Giovanni Segantini—and contemporaries, namely Giovanni, Augusto and Alberto Giacometti, and E-L Kirchner.

Chur

Lucia Degonda/Switzerland Tourism

EXCURSIONS

Lenzerheide-Valbella✷✷

www.lenzerheide.com.

The twin resorts of Lenzerheide and Valbella are located in Lenzerheide Valley, their modern buildings are set in a hollow (at an altitude of 1 500m/4 900ft; the hollow forms the top of the first ridge crossed by the road from Chur) enhanced by two lakes. It owes its popularity to the charming **parklike country**★ which the motorist will appreciate between Valbella and Lenzerheide-Centre. In winter the smooth slopes encourage downhill skiing, especially on the Piz Scalottas and the Stätzerhorn. A long chain of chairlifts reaches up the 2 861m/9 382ft of the Parpaner Rothorn.

Parpaner Rothorn★★

⛷*Access by cable-car in 15min from Lenzerheide-Valbella.* ⏱*Departures every 20min, 8.10am–12.10pm, 1.10pm –5.10pm.* ⏱*Closed mid-Apr–late Jun.* ➥*Fare there and back 30CHF.* ✆*(0)81 385 03 85.*

The climb above the fir trees as far as Scharmoin (alt. 1 900m/6 234ft) gives way to barren slopes before reaching the rocky peak of the Parpaner Rothorn (alt. 2 861m/9 382ft). The superb **view**★★, which to the west reveals the Valbella hollow, its resort and clear lake, is blocked to the east by the snowy summits of the Weisshorn, Tschirpen, and Aroser Rothorn. For a more open view, walk (*15min return*) to a nearby

mountain top such as the Ostgipfel (alt. 2 899m/9 511ft). From Lenzerheide to Lenz, approaching the chapel of San-Cassian, the view opens out toward the depression of the Oberhalbstein, its entrance narrowed between the wooded foothills of the Piz Mitgel and the more pasture-like slopes of the Piz Curvèr. The first Romansh houses, giving a foretaste of the Engadin style, (⛨*see INTRODUCTION: Rural Architecture*) can be seen at **Lenz**.

Flims✷✷

▶ *20km/12.5mi W of Chur, on the road towards Disentis. Via Nova 62.* ✆*(0)81 927 77 77. www.flims.com.*

Flims is divided into **Flims-Dorf**, the traditional residential section and **Flims-Waldhaus**, where the hotels are scattered over a forested area of conifers. Thickly wooded slopes all the way to the Vorderrhein Gorge have hardly changed since prehistoric times. This is when an enormous landslide along the axis of the present Flem Valley blocked the Rhine Valley and forced the river to find a new course. The southern facing site of Flims, and its woods that are a joy for walks, make it a much sought-after family resort, with many marked trails for hiking and bike enthusiasts. Swimming is another popular activity because of the proximity of Lake Cresta and Lake Cauma, whose shimmering waters remain beautifully warm all summer. Still, high season here is undoubtedly winter, characterised by a lively, festive atmosphere and a majority of young visitors.

The skiing area

Commonly known as **Alpenarena**, it incorporates three resorts, Flims, Laax and Falera, and is among the largest in Switzerland (220km/137mi of pistes and around 30 ski lifts). Spread out over 4 summits, including the Vorab Glacier, it features altitudes ranging from 1 100m/3 608ft to 3 000m/9 843ft. It is possible to move around by skiing along the many narrow tracks linking together the massifs. These pistes are particularly suitable for intermediate skiers (Crest da Tiarus and Crappa Spessa on Crap Masegn, Curtgani on Crap Sogn Gion and Naraus). Experienced skiers can tackle the few steep slopes such as Fatschas, Sattel, Alp Ruschein and Stretg (**views**★ from the forest). The area is has several snowparks and has become extremely popular with snowboarders; the towns of Flims and Laax host some of the most prestigious snowboard events in November and April.

≗≗ Maienfeld

◐ 17km/11mi. Head NW on Nikolaigasse towardS Grabenstrasse to Route 13/Route 3.

This small town surrounded by vineyards attracts tourists from around the world because of a girl: the famous Heidi. The heroine of Johanna Spyri's (1827–1901) eponymous novel has inspired a "village", Heididorf, with its Heidi house museum, its bucolic hiking trail and gift shop. This appropriation of the myth of a small mountain girl for commercial purposes can cause some gnashing of teeth to those craving old values (Heididorf, Maienfeld (A13, exit 3); ◐open Mar–Nov 10am–5pm; 25min walk from Maienfeld; ⊶5 CHF, children 2 CHF; ℘(0)81 330 19 12. www.heididorf.ch).

Bad Ragaz★

◐ 22km/14mi. As per Maienfeld but follow the signs to Bad Ragaz.

Bad Ragaz is a leading Swiss spa located in one of the Alpine Rhine Valley's finest settings and facing the rugged crests of the Falknis. Since the 11C the resort has been known for its mineral waters, which rise to a temperature of 37ºC/98ºF in the Tamina Gorges below the village of Pfäfers. The waters are particularly recommended for circulatory troubles, rheumatism, paralysis and the after-effects of accidents. Bad Ragaz has been a mid-winter ski resort since a cable-car and ski lifts linked the town with the great snowfields in the Pizol district.

Taminaschlucht★★

2hr there and back on foot by the road branching off the road to Valens on the left, SW of Bad Ragaz. ◐Open May–Oct, 10am–5.30pm (5pm in May and Oct). ⊶4CHF. ℘(0)81 302 71 61.

These gorges are truly breathtaking. To take the waters, before they were piped, patients were lowered down on ropes to the bottom of this tremendous fissure.

🚗 DRIVING TOURS

① VALLEY OF THE VORDERRHEIN

Total distance from Chur to Medel gorge 105 km/65mi – Allow half a day. Exit Chur to the W by Highway 13.

Reichenau

With its three bridges forming a triangle enclosing the confluence of the Vorderrhein and the Hinterrhein, this little settlement owes its existence to a site exceptionally convenient for collecting tolls. It is still an important road junction at the fork of the main roads to the Domleschg (Thusis) and the Graubünden Oberland (Disentis/Mustér). During the French Revolution, buildings here were occupied by an Institute of Education.

Versam Road★

From Bonaduz to Ilanz 21km/13mi.

The road offers vistas of the Rhine Gorges and the Bifertenstock (Tödi Massif) Crests, to the left of the Vorab. The clearing just before the village of Versam is a good place to stop for a **view**★ of the Vorab group, with its great plateau glacier, on the left, and the Ringelspitz on the right. In the foreground stands the Flimserstein promontory, girdled with imposing cliffs.

The narrow road is soon suspended on a ledge along the flank of white precipices formed by the Rhine and its tributary, the Rabiusa, and runs through debris brought down by the Flims landslide.

▷ *Drive W on road number 19.*

Ilanz

Ilanz is the only place in the Graubünden Oberland which bears the official title of "town". It was the former capital of the Grey League, founded here in 1395 (*see p354*), Disentis being considered more of a religious capital.

The most picturesque quarter, reached by crossing the bridge over the Rhine and following the exit route towards Vals or Vrin, has retained its 17C mansions with Baroque ornamentation, especially the Casa Gronda (black and yellow shutters) with its corner turret, window grilles and finely decorated door frames.

▷ *Leave Ilanz S on Valserstrasse.*

Vals★

20km/12.4mi from Ilanz.

A detour along a charming, winding road in the Valsertal Valley leads to this spa resort (alt. 1 248m/4 093ft), which nestles among a grandiose cirque of mountains. **Felsen-Therme**★ was the first spa to be built in natural stone. Opened in 1996, it was designed by the famous Swiss architect Peter Zumthor. The walls of this cube construction are made of quartzite, extracted from within the valley.

The spa's sophisticated facilities include an indoor pool (32°C/89°F), an open-air pool (36°C/96°F), saunas, a cold plunge pool and a "musical" grotto which plays "mineral" music composed by Fritz Hauser.

▷ *Return to Ilanz by the same route and take the direction to Disentis/Mustér.*

Trun

The imposing mass of the **Cuort Ligia Grischa** (black and white shutters) (○*open mid-Apr–Nov, Mon, Wed, Sat and the second and last Sun of the month 2pm–5pm.* ⌖*Guided tours available (1hr) at 2pm, 3pm and 4pm.* ⌖*5CHF.* ✆*(0)81 943 23 09/33 88*), a former residence of the abbots of Disentis built in 1674, once housed the Parliament and Law Court of the League.

Inside, the apartments open to visitors include the Abbot's Bedchamber, with 17C panelling, and the Law Court decorated in the Baroque style. It was in the shade of The maple tree planted from the Maple of Trun that the Pact of the Grey League was solemnly confirmed in 1424.

▷ *After Somvix and its elegant onion dome, beyond the railway bridge and the modern road bridge that crosses the Russeinbach ravine you will arrive at an old covered bridge.*

Disentis/Mustér✳

Via Alpsu 62. ✆*(081) 920 40 30.*
www.disentis-sedrun.ch.

Disentis, the centre of Romansh culture and a health resort, was colonised in the Middle Ages by the monks of St Benedict. From its terrace it overlooks the junction of the Tavetsch Rhine, flowing down from the Oberalp Pass to the west and the Medel Rhine from Lukmanier Pass to the south. In winter, skiers are offered a network of ski lifts which take them up to the runs at an altitude of 3 000m/9 240ft.

Abbey and Abbey Church

This is one of the oldest Benedictine institutions in Switzerland, dating from the 8C. The present buildings date from the 17C, 19C and 20C. The **abbey**, from which the town derives its Romansh name of Mustér, forms a massive quadrilateral ensemble of buildings lying on a long, rugged Alpine slope. The

Abbey Church★ (1695–1712) is flanked by two domed towers. The two tiers of windows are invisible from the nave in accordance with the Baroque rules of indirect lighting.

② SAN BERNADINO PASS ROAD ★★

170km/106mi from Chur to Cama – Allow one day.

The San Bernardino Pass is usually blocked by snow from November to May. The itinerary outlined below follows the old road (blue signposts). Note that Route A 13 goes through the pass via a tunnel.

The San Bernardino Pass is a historic transalpine road linking Bellinzona (near Lake Maggiore) in the sunny Lower Ticino Valley to Chur, the historical capital of Graubünden, located downstream from the confluence of the Vorderrhein and Hinterrhein.

The road goes up the Rhine Valley towards Reichenau, the Rhine and later, Thusis at the entrance of the gorges of the Via Mala.

Via Mala★★

15min, not including the walk through the galleries.

This famous stretch of road, which for centuries has been the main obstacle to the development of traffic along the **Untere Strasse**, is divided into two gorges separated by the small, verdant Rongellen Basin. The **upstream defile**★★ —the Via Mala proper— plunges between formidable schist escarpments connected by four successive bridges. Leave the car by the pavilion at the entrance to the galleries and go to the second bridge (upstream), spanning the gorge under which flows the Rhine, 68m/223ft below.

Visit the **galleries**★ (*open May–Aug, 8am–7pm; Mar, Apr and Nov, 9am–6pm; 5CHF; (0)81 651 11 34; 341 steps—30min there and back*). The road avoids the floor of the ravine downstream and the section called the Verlorenes Loch (Lost Hole).

Zillis★★

Before arriving at Zillis take the road to right marked "zur Kirche" to go to church. Apr–Oct 9am–6pm, Nov–Mar 10am–4pm. 4CHF. Booklet description panels 4CHF. (0)81 661 10 21. Information and Exhibition Centre (slideshow) in the village centre. Apr–Oct 8am–8pm, rest of the year Sat–Sun 10am–4pm. (0)81 661 22 55.

The **ceiling**★★ of the church at Zillis (Kirche St Martin) is a unique example of its kind in Western Europe. Dating from the second half of the 12C, the quality and style of decoration evokes the exquisite work of illuminated manuscripts. 153 square panels are arranged in two cycles. Those in the perimeter symbolise the Primitive Ocean and the Sea of the Apocalypse, its waters inhabited by mythical creatures, and four angels of the Last Judgement in the corners. The inner panel (follow the scenes with your back to the choir, from left to right) relate to the life of Christ and scenes from the life of St Martin.

Upon exiting Zillis, a steep and winding road (7 km) leads to the village of Mathon.

Mathon

Situated in a **site**★ on the slopes of the Piz Beverin, this mountain village (alt. 1 521m/4 990ft) overlooks the Schons Basin in view of the peaks of the basin's east side. Below the church are the ruins of a former church (1528, parts of which date from the 9C).

Make a U-turn on the main road. After Andeer, leave the road for the Val Ferrera, then for the valley of Avers up to Juf (50km/31mi round trip).

Averserrhein Valley★★ (Ferrera Valley, Avers Valley)

The Averserrhein route moves through the Piz Grisch and Piz Platta massifs. Following the torrent, the road climbs through the **Ferrera Valley** within view of Piz Miez, and crosses the village of **Ausserferrera** (waterfalls). After **Innerferrera**, the road deviates southeasterly.

It follows a hilly landscape and opens out onto the Avers Valley and its first village, **Campsut**.

Starting at Cröt, a sudden rise in the road reveals a view of **Avers-Cresta** (charming white church). The road ends at **Juf** (alt. 2 126m/6 975ft). Continuing down the Hinterrhein, the road enters the Schons Basin.

Rofflaschlucht

🕐*May–Oct 9am–7pm.* 🕐*Closed rest of the year.* 🚌*3 CHF.* ✆*(0)81 661 11 97.*
The 300m/985ft-long tunnels, built between 1907 and 1914, allow you to cross the Rhine underground, and lead to a waterfall.

Splügen★

Upon exiting the gorge, past the cliffs and spruces growing along the stream, the road comes to the vast reservoir of Sufers and to the back upper Rhine valley (Rheinwald) around Splügen. The village features fascinating traditional houses and barns as if clothed in green velvet. From edge of Hinterrhein the **view**★ extends upstream, taking in the large Zapportgletscher and the what remains of the cone of Rheinquellhorn.

Houses in Splügen
Lucia Degonda/Switzerland Tourism

San Bernardino Pass

Alt. 2 065/6 775ft.
The **San Bernardino Pass** is littered with rounded rocks left behind by

Quaternary glaciers. Open between the Zapporthorn and the Pizzo Uccello, the pass marks the dividing line between the Moesa, southward, a tributary of the Ticino and thus of the Pô and the Hinterrhein, northward.

On the north side, the **Upper Inner Rhine Valley** (**Hinterrhein**) presents as far as Splügen a landscape which is open and pastoral but still harsh.

From the approach to the Hinterrhein, the **view**★ opens out upstream toward the massif containing the sources of the Rhine. The range is also remarkable for the size of its glaciers: The great Zapportgletscher overlooked by the Rheinquellhorn is particularly impressive.

Between **Splügen** and **Andeer** the road runs through woods of Norway spruce, skirts the vast Sufers Reservoir and crosses the deepest section of the Rheinwald, the Roffla Defile.

The galleries, 300m/984ft long, cut out of the rock (1907–14) in this **gorge** (🕐*open May–Oct, 9am–5pm (otherwise enquire in advance), Thu–Mon 9am–6pm;* 🕐*closed Nov–Easter;* 🚌*3CHF;* ✆*(0)81 661 11 97*) through which the Rhine flows, end under an impressive waterfall, which passes just above the spectator's head. As you leave, notice the **Bärenburg Reservoir**.

▶ *After the pass, along the beautiful lake Moesola in the beginning of Mesolcina, one of the four valleys of the Italian canton of Grabünden. The descent is performed in stages with views of the highway. It passes quickly from a zone of pine forest to one of spruce, followed by beech and fir.*

Castello di Misox★

The feudal ruins of Misox Castle, the most impressive in Graubünden, sits on a high rocky peak. This massive fortified group once belonged to the counts of Sax-Mesocco.

The castle was sold in 1483 to the Trivulce of Milan and dismantled by the Graubünden Leagues in 1526 (⌖*see INTRODUCTION*). It was saved from complete destruction by the intervention of Swiss students in 1924.

Santa Maria del Castello

The key is available at the cancelleria comunale in Mesocco.
℘ (0)91 822 91 40.

This chapel contains an interesting series of 15C **frescoes**★ including images of St George slaying the Dragon, St Bernardino of Siena (patron saint of the valley), and rural life in the Alps.

Castle

Access by the footpath from behind the chapel to the entrance drawbridge.

To enjoy a superb **bird's-eye view**★ of the Mesolcina Valley and the village of Soazza, turn left as soon as you find a gap between the ruined buildings and make for an uncrowned wall on the edge of the escarpment, the top of which can be reached by a staircase without a balustrade.

▷ *From Soazza onwards, note the appearance of chestnut trees and Mediterranean crops: palm trees, plane trees, fig trees and vineyards.*

Cama

The 46 grottos, situated behind the village, is the largest ensemble of its kind in Graubünden and a characteristic example of one style of traditional architecture in Italian Switzerland. A current of cold air coming from below maintains the caves at a constant temperature of 3C to 12C throughout the year. The small stone houses where natives come to spend a cool summer are side by side with restaurants on whose tables iced red wine is served.

THE AROSA CLIMB

29km/18mi – Allow one hour.

The Arosa Express reaches Arosa from Chur in an hour. The train wanders quaintly like a streetcar in the city, along the Plessur river, the Powder Tower and the Obertor before becoming a true mountain railway.

▷ *Leave Chur from the SE in the direction of Arosa.*

The **Arosa road**★, a high, winding, picturesque corniche along the Schanfigg valley, passes through flower-decked villages with quaint churches. During the last part, the road cuts through unusual sharp limestone ridges, which are convex and wooded on the north side and concave and barren on the south side. Note the railway viaduct spanning the chasm on the outskirts of Langwies.

Arosa★★

Alt. 1 742m/5 715ft.
Poststrasse – 7050. ℘ (0)81 378 70 20.

The elegant resort of Arosa spreads its hotels in the Upper Schanfig Basin of the Plessur Valley. It charms the visitor at once with its setting of gently sloping woodlands, reflected in three small lakes. In the summer the section from Arosa to Langwies is free, as are all cable-cars, with every hotel night spent in the resort.

Arosa station was inaugurated in 1880 with the opening of the sanatoriums and hotels as well as the arrival of the first skiers. It remained a minor health resort until the 1950s when it experienced a boom with the construction of many hotels and apartments.

Today, tiny Arosa with only 2 267 permanent inhabitants has become one of the country's major mountain resorts. Its superb setting of gently inclined wooded slopes with shimmering small lakes, which become skating rings in winter, remains undiminished.

Its golf course is one of the main attractions in the summer, as it is the highest in Europe. Other summer attractions include some excellent hikes and mountain biking, while pedalo and boat hire on the lake is free.

The Chur road passes through **Ausser-Arosa**, the chief centre of activity and location of the railway station and the lakes. The road emerges from the forest and ends at **Inner-Arosa**, where the upper depression of the Plessur (Aroser Alp) begins.

The nearby centre of **Maran** is more isolated; visitors to Arosa walk to it along delightful, gently sloping paths through the woods (*Eichhörnliweg*: squirrel path). The settlement spreads over the open Alpine pastures. The Weisshorn cable-car is the ski area's backbone in winter, Arosa's real season. Long, wide runs, some of which drop over 1 000m/3 280ft, make this resort ideal for the beginner or intermediate; the descent from the top of the Weisshorn is only for accomplished skiers and snowboarders. The first week of January every year is **Gay Ski Week** and prices rise accordingly.

Weisshorn★★

Alt. 2 653m/8 704ft. ⚡ *Access in 15min by cable-car.* 🕐 *Departure every 10min, 9am–5pm.* 🕐 *Closed mid-Apr–late Apr.* 🚡 *Free with a hotel stay, otherwise 13CHF.* ℘ *(0)81 378 84 84.*

The climb up to the mid-station, Law Mittel (alt. 2 013m/6 640ft), offers wide vistas of Arosa, its lakes, verdant basin and mountains. From the top (*viewing table*) there is a magnificent **panorama**★★ of the Graubünden Alps' neighbouring heights and snowy ridges, blocked to the south by the Piz Kesch, Piz Ela and Erzhorn; Arosa is visible on one side and Chur can be glimpsed on the other, to the northwest at the foot of Calanda Mountain. The Bernina range is also visible towards the south.

ADDRESSES

🛏 STAY

🛏 **Hotel Drei Könige** – *Reichgasse 18.* ℘ *(0)81 354 90 90. www.dreikoenige.ch.* *38 rooms.* At the heart of Old Town, this is a simple hotel with some cheaper rooms with shared facilities. Restaurant in house with traditional Graubünden cuisine.

🛏🛏 **Hotel Alte Herberge Weiss Kreuz** – *Splügen.* ℘ *(0)81 630 91 30. www.weiss-kreuz.ch. Closed Nov and May. 4 rooms.* A hotel out of place and out of time set in a 18C inn which blends historic and contemporary architecture. Magnificent view of the village.

🛏🛏 **Romantik Hotel Stern** – *Reichsgasse 11, Chur.* ℘ *(0)81 258 57 57. www.stern-chur.ch. 65 rooms.* This quiet house at the entrance of the Old City is home to a hotel for three centuries. Rooms have been renovated in traditional but comfortable style. Tavern with tasty local specialties.

🛏🛏🛏 **Waldhotel National** – *Arosa.* ℘ *(0)81 378 55 55. www.waldhotel.ch.* *83 rooms.* A historic ex-sanatorium, renovated in pine decor. A must if staying in Arosa, since the half board it offers includes a gourmet five-course dinner, itself worth the price of the room.

🍴 EAT

🍴 **Muntsulej** – *Mathon.* ℘ *(0)81 661 20 40. Closed Wed–Thu.* Without doubt one of the most beautiful terraces in Graubünden. Inventive kitchen uses local produce from nearby farms and offers curtgnatsch (local cheese) or Rotel (spicy cherry liqueur).

🍴🍴 **Süsswinkel** – *Süsswinkelgasse 1.* ℘ *(0)81 252 28 56. Closed Sun–Mon.* A bistro with tasty food in an atmosphere of yesteryear.

🍴🍴 **Romantik Hotel Stern** – *Reichsgasse 11.* ℘ *(0)81 258 57 57. www.stern-chur.ch.* Traditional fare served in an historic regional house. Beautiful terrace.

🍴🍴 **Basil** – *Susenbülhstr, 43, on the Malix / Lenzerheide road.* ℘ *(0)81 253 00 22. Closed Mon, Sun noon.* A very creative gourmet restaurant overlooking the city of Chur.

Davos✲✲

Davos is Europe's highest altitude resort, situated in the heart of one of the most famous skiing areas in Switzerland. This is a go-getting, dynamic place that seems more in tune with its twin town Denver, Colorado, than with the genteel, almost Tyrolean old-fashioned village of Klosters just over the Wolfgang Pass. Davos has reinvented itself three times in its history: it first established itself as a sanatorium town during the Belle Époque period when it became very popular with the British. (It was here that Robert Louis Stevenson wrote *Treasure Island* in 1881). From the 1930s onwards it became a sports and holiday resort that at the beginning of the 21C accepts more than 700 000 hotel bookings in the winter. And finally from 1971 onwards, it acquired worldwide fame for staging the World Economic Forum, which put it on the map as a Congress destination.

SIGHTS
The Village

The village of Davos developed in the 13C on the floor of the mountain valley in which the Landwasser flows. To

▸ **Population:** 11 142.
▯ **Info:** Talstrasse 41. ℘(081) 415 21 21. www.davos.ch.
▻ **Location:** The two main stations, Platz and Dorf, are like bookends to the city. Alt. 1 560m/5 120ft.
▯ **Parking:** There is ample parking in garages throughout the city.
◉ **Don't Miss:** The nightlife, with its clubs, casinos and all-night parties in the winter.

the northeast, beyond Lake Davos, the gentle, wooded slope towards Wolfgang offers easy access to the Prättigau (towards Klosters). The site is dominated by the Flüela Schwarzhorn (3 146m/10 318ft) and the Alpihorn (3 006m/9 859ft).

The resort

The resort extends between Davos-Dorf and **Davos-Platz**, the chief administrative centre. Around the central square stand the **Church of St John** (St Johann) and the **town hall**. Davos has the largest **natural skating rink** in Europe and is renowned for its giant **sledge runs**: Rinerhorn and Wiesen (2 505m/8 216ft

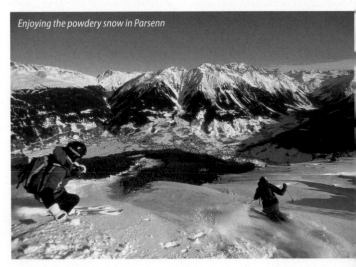

Enjoying the powdery snow in Parsenn

GETTING AROUND

Train – Rhaetian railways – Talstrasse 4, Davos Platz. *(0)81 288 32 50. www.rhb.ch.* Connections to Lanquart and Zürich possible from 8am–9pm and every hour to St Moritz via Filisur by train. Frequent service to Klosters.
Bus – VBD. *www.vbd.ch.* Connection with the Engandin via Susch every two hours by bus via the Flüelapass (summer only). Frequent service between Platz and Dorf as well as in the Sertig and Dischma valleys. Good connections with start and end of hiking paths. All town and cable-car transport is free in the summer when you are staying overnight.

and 3 500m/11 480ft long respectively), and Schatzalp (2 500m/8 200ft in winter and 600m/1 968ft in summer). During the winter, 80km/49.7mi of footpaths remain open to walkers. In summer, visitors can choose from 450km/279.6mi of marked **paths** and superb **mountain bike trails**, including the route (14km/8.7mi) from Weissfluhjoch to Klosters, with an altitude difference of 1 463m/2 340ft.

The skiing area – 44 ski lifts serve 320km/198.8mi of pistes, which run over a difference in altitude of 1 600m/5 249ft as far as Klosters (*see KLOSTERS*). The area extends over seven massifs, most of which are linked by train or bus, rather than by ski lifts. The main section is **Parsenn**✳✳✳ (120km/74.5mi of pistes), accessible by funicular from Davos-Dorf. Skiers leaving from Weissfluhgipfel or Weissfluhjoch will discover splendid, beautifully maintained snowfields of surprising variety suitable for all levels of expertise. From the top (2 844m/9 331ft) you go down to 810m/2 657ft in Küblis (train journey back) or even 190m/623ft in Klosters. Most slopes offer hiking paths with lovely views in the lower sections; the longest run (12km/7.4mi) is from the top of Parsenn to Kublis.

Jacobshorn offers 45km/28mi of pistes characterised by a difference in height of 1 000m/3 281ft, some of which should only be tackled by experienced skiers. This massif is particularly popular with snowboarders.

The remaining massifs are smaller and farther away from Davos: **Pischa** (1 800m/5 905ft to 2 483m/8 146ft) on the Flüelapass road, **Rinerhorn** (1 450m/4 757ft to 2 490m/8 169ft) at Glaris and **Madrisa** (1 120m/3 674ft to 2 600m/8 530ft) at Klosters-Dorf.
Davos is also famous for its 75km/46.6mi of pistes for **cross-country skiing** between Wolfgang and Glaris, which follow the lake shores before reaching the lateral valleys of Flüela.

Kirchnermuseum

Ernst Ludwig Kurchner Platz.
Christmas–Easter and Jul–Sept Tue–Sun 10am–6pm; rest of year 2pm–6pm. 12CHF/children 5CHF. (0)81 410 63 00. www.kirchnermuseum.ch.

Ernst-Ludwig Kirchner (1880–1938), a leading German Expressionist painter, left Berlin in 1917 to settle in Davos. In 1936, his intense artistic style was declared "degenerate" by the Nazis. Kirchner was badly affected by this condemnation of his art and committed suicide in Davos two years later. This museum *(number 67 on the Promenade)* houses the world's largest collection of works by Kirchner, including *Davos in Summer*. It also hosts annual special exhibitions.

Hohe Promenade★

1hr on foot there and back.
The promenade is a perfectly planned road, level and sometimes under trees, kept clear of snow in winter. This walk begins in Davos-Dorf by the road behind the Arabella Sheraton Hotel (near the Parsenn funicular station) or from Davos-Platz by a steep path which continues the lane to the church.
It is high above the town, so it is like a walk on the countryside, while overlooking the city and the Jacobshorn opposite.

The Capital of the World Economy

The **World Economic Forum** is held in January every year in Davos, bringing together heads of state, politicians, economists and business people from around the world. The original idea was launched by Klaus Schwab, a lecturer on corporate strategy, who decided to bring together leading company managers in an informal manner in 1970. The first meeting was held in Davos in January 1971, the year in which Klaus Schwab founded what would eventually become the World Economic Forum. In 2001, the town was the scene of violent clashes between police and pressure groups opposed to globalisation; as a result, and because of 9/11, the Forum was held in New York the following year. Since then, the policing of Davos has been such and restrictions on movement so draconian, that any protest demonstrations have only been held in the capital, Bern.

EXCURSIONS
Walk from Weissfluhjoch to Davos★★

🔲 *Allow 3hr30min without breaks (difference in height 1 000m/3 280ft).*
Walk to the Parsennhütte refuge (*45min*) along a steep, stony path, passing pretty Lake Totalpsee half-way down. Inexperienced hikers may take the cable-car. On reaching the lower station (300m/300yds ahead), bear right and take **Panoramaweg★★**, a smooth path flanked by benches following the mountain slope and offering superb **views★★** of Lake Davos, Dürrboden Valley, Pischa, and Silvretta. After walking for about 1hr15min, turn left and proceed toward the intermediate platform of the funicular. Continue in the direction of Büschalp 1850, with its dreamlike setting, then go back down to Davos-Dorf or Davos-Platz (*allow 1hr30min*).

Jacobshorn★★
Alt. 2 590m/8 497ft. 🥾 *Allow at least 1hr round trip. Access is by two funiculars, then 5min on foot up a steep incline.*
⊙*Daily service leaving every 15min, 8.30am–5pm.* ⊚*Fare 32CHF, free in summer.* ℘*(0)81 415 21 21.*
There is a **panorama★★** over the whole Davos and Klosters area as well as Sertig Valley.

Dischma Valley★★
⊙ *12km/7.4mi SE of Davos.*
Allow 20min. Bus line 13 from Dorf.
This narrow road running along the peaceful waters of the Dischmabach

wends through a heavenly setting. Lovely pastures dotted with woods, cottages, and hillocks, with the Scaletta Glacier in the far distance. To fully enjoy these natural beauties, make good use of the hiking and biking trails that have been marked out for visitors.

Walk to Grialetschhütte★★
Alt. 2 542m/8 340ft.
🅿*Park the car at the end of the road to Dürrboden (2 007m/6 584ft).*
Walk up the gentle slope (*allow 1hr45min*) facing the Scaletta Glacier until you get to **Fuorcia da Grialetsch Pass★★**. From there it is easy to reach the refuge, surrounded by a cluster of lakes. This is a typical bare mountain **setting★★** that contrasts sharply with the luxuriant vegetation thriving down in the valley. The Scaletta and Grialetsch Glaciers are overlooked by Flüela Schwarzhorn and Piz Vadret. To get a **bird's-eye view★★** of the whole area, continue the ascent toward the glacier for 20min and take in the sweeping panorama of the valley and lakes. Go back down along the same route.

Klosters✹✹
⊙ *11km/7mi N. Alte Bahnhofstrasse 6.*
℘*(0)81 410 20 20. www.klosters.ch.*
Klosters (alt. 1 194m/3 917ft) nestles in a valley below Davos, but unlike its neighbour, has remained a traditional Alpine village. In the setting, still quite rural, of the Prättigau, the resort is ideal for both summer and winter holidays. In summer the Silvretta summits, jutting up on the

horizon, are enjoyable expeditions for mountaineers.

In winter, skiers using the cable-cars from Gotschnagrat and Madrisa or the railway shuttle service between Klosters and Davos can reach the famous Parsenn snowfields; skiers in search of more challenging terrain should proceed to the Weisspfluhgipfel (alt. 2 844m/9 328ft). In March and April, spring skiing weeks are organised as excursions led by guides in the Silvretta and Vereina Massifs. Klosters has been fashionable with the rich and famous since the 1950s. Celebrities who have spent time here include Gene Kelly, Vivien Leigh, and Audrey Hepburn. The Prince of Wales is also a regular visitor to the resort.

DRIVING TOUR

③ THE ZÜGEN AND ALBULA PASS ROADS★★
85km/53mi from Davos to St Moritz.

◉ *Leave Davos SE by the Tiefencastel Road. After the village of Glarus, take a left up the hill.*

Monstein★
Its chalets made with heavy timbers are typical of the architecture of this village where Walser settled the highest brewery in Europe. Visits Tues

2.30pm–5.45pm Jul–Oct. ℰ(0)81 420 30 60. www.biervision-monstein.ch.

◉ *Return to the main road.*

Since the opening of the Landwasser tunnel in 1974, the road now avoids the most dramatic area, the "Zügen", so-called due to frequent avalanches (which sound like trains—zügen). Take time to walk towards Bärentritt following the course of the river Landwasser.

Bärentritt★★
2hr on foot there and back by the old road to the Zügen taking the exit E of the tunnel (on the Davos side). 🅿 *Park the car at Schmelzbaden.*

From this point, a projecting parapet forms a belvedere that marks the beginning of the Zügen defile. There is an impressive downward view of the confluence 80m/262ft below, of the Landwasser and of the torrent forming the Sägetobel Cascade on the right. Coming out of the deep Tieftobel Ravine, you will see below you the **Wiesen Viaduct★** (length 210m/689ft, central span 55m/180ft, height 88m/288ft), one of the largest structures of the Rhaetic railways.

◉ *After Schmitten the view plunges to the left onto the Albula and the Landwasser river. After Alvaneu, instead*

Monstein

Raphael Koch/Tourismus Davos Klosters/Switzerland Tourism

of going to Tiefencastel, turn left
towards Alvaneu Bad and Filisur.

Alvaneu Bad

🕐*Baths open daily 9am–10pm.*
🕐*Closed Nov.* 🚃*28CHF (sulphur baths*
and steam, sauna, solarium). 📞*(0)81*
420 44 00. www.bad-alvaneu.ch.
These sulfur springs, perhaps already
exploited in Roman times, enjoyed some
popularity in the second half of the 19C
Closed in 1962, today they have been
resurrected in full spa mode around
a golf course and a pleasant outdoor
pond.

▶ *Follow the road to the Albula Pass*
towards Filisur.

Coming from Chur or Davos the most
impressive way to St Moritz and the
Upper Engadin is via the Julier Pass. Past
Filisur the Albula valley, more and more
wooded and wild, gradually forces the
road to carve a passage through the rock
at the Berguener Steina.

Bergün

This village has several Engadin-style
houses with oriel windows and window
grilles, far more rustic than those of the
Inn Valley.
From Bergün to Preda, while the road
climbs steeply through mossy woods
and fields, you will see the extraordinary contortions (loops and spiral
tunnels) imposed upon the railway to
gain height. Arrival at Preda is marked
by an opening-out of the mountainous
horizon. Between Preda and the pass
are pleasant pastures as far as the little green **Lake Palpuogna**. Higher
up, beyond the Crap Alv, the road
rises among rocky ledges as it skirts a
marshy plateau, where numerous small
cascades indicate one of the sources of
the Albula. You then reach the grassy
coomb marking the pass.

Albulapass

Alt. 2 312m/7 585ft.
😊*The pass is usually blocked by snow*
Nov–Jun. Served by the Tiefencastel–
Samedan rail-car service.

The pass divides the Albula Basin to the
north, a tributary of the Rhine from the
Val d'Alvra, and to the south, a tributary
of the Inn. From La Punt to Samedan follow the flat floor of the Inn Valley until
the peaks of the Bernina Massif appear
through the Pontresina Gap.

ADDRESSES

🛏️STAY

Many hotels in the summer offer half
board included the room price. Check
whether your hotel is part of the Dine
Around scheme whereby you can use
your half-board option to dine in any
of the participating hotels.

🍽️🛏️**Hotel Alpina** – *Richtstattweg 1.*
📞*(0)81 416 47 67. www.alpina-davos.ch.*
Closed Nov and May. 19 rooms. A nice
pension with good service, good value
on the higher slopes of Davos. Ask for a
southern-facing room with balcony.

🍽️🛏️🛏️**Hotel National** – *Obere Strasse*
31. 📞*(0)81 415 10 10. www.national-*
davos.ch. 65 rooms. Very central (near
Platz) and yet quiet, plus parking. Large
rooms, helpful staff. Member of Dine
Around.

🍽️🛏️🛏️**Hotel Bahnhof Terminus** –
Talstrasse 3. 📞*(0)81 414 97 97. www.best*
western.ch/bahnhofterminus. 53 rooms.
This place in front of the railway station
is very convenient. Superb sauna and
three restaurants to choose from.

🍴EAT

🍽️**Flüela Stübli** – *Bahnhofstrasse 5.*
📞*(0)81 410 17 17. www.fluela.ch.*
Closed Apr-Nov. The restaurant of the
eponymous 5-star hotel, this is as
sophisticated a gourmet experience as
you can have in Davos.

🍽️🛏️🛏️ **Morosani Posthotel** –
Promenade 42. 📞*(0)81 415 20 60.*
www.posthotel.morosani.ch. Try to eat
at least once in this restaurant when
in Davos if only to experience the
immaculate service and the superb
wine list. Member of Dine around.

St Moritz ✳✳✳

In St Moritz (San Murezzan in Romansh), the sun shines an average of 322 days a year, more than anywhere else in Switzerland; unsurprisingly, the town's symbol is a sun. Switzerland's most famous ski resort promotes itself as the "Top of the World," its popularity with tourists lasting year-round due to the reliably clear blue sky, stunning scenery, and sport and leisure activities. Local sports include bobsleigh competitions, horse racing, and golf on the frozen lake, while a wide array of elegant boutiques, gourmet dining, and world-class hotels cater for weary bones at the end of the day.

▶ **Population:** 5 175.
◔ **Michelin Map:**
Town plan in the Michelin RED Guide Switzerland.
▤ **Info:** via Maistra 12 – 7500.
℘(0)81 837 33 33.
www.stmoritz.ch.
◑ **Location:** The heart of the village is the Plaza da Scoula (pedestrians only). Alt. 1 865m/6 089ft.
⊛ **Don't Miss:** Take the funicular up to Piz Nair for a memorable view over the Engadin Valley.
◷ **Timing:** Allow at least two days, summer or winter, for exploring, events and excursions.

SKI AREA
Twin Resorts

St Moritz-Dorf has the world's oldest skiing school (1927) and is grouped halfway up a slope at the foot of a campanile. This is where you will find remnants of traditional Engadin architecture, which is also a feature of the typical villages of Silvaplana, Sils, and Pontresina. In contrast, the mostly modern urban sprawl of **St Moritz-Bad** at the lake's southwest corner, is where many of the spa installations are found, offering waters rich in iron. Frequent buses connect the two halves of St Moritz.

The Skiing Area

This resort has hosted the Winter Olympics twice, in 1928 and 1948. The ski area, which extends over the **Piz Nair Massif** (alt. 3 087m/10 128ft), offers slopes for all levels, with more than 80km/50mi of downhill pistes and 23 chairlifts. The Corviglia and Piz Nair peaks offer mostly intermediate terrain on groomed runs. The Ski Engadin pass allows you to enjoy facilities at **Piz Corvatsch** (3 303m/10 837ft, 65km/40mi of pistes), **Diavolezza** (alt. 2 978m/9 755ft, 49km/30mi of pistes

Bar on the Corviglia ski slopes above St Moritz with a view of the Upper Engadine Alps with Piz Corvatsch on the right

Christof Sonderegger/Switzerland Tourism

for more experienced skiers), **Piz Lagalb** (alt. 2 959m/9 708ft, 29km/18mi of pistes), and **Muottas Muragl** (alt. 2 453m/8 048ft, 8km/5mi of pistes), which together form a vast ski area (230km/143mi of pistes). Snowboarders can enjoy numerous "half-pipes" and a "boardercross" at Corviglia (Piz Nair). Cross-country skiers can explore about 150km/93mi of loops throughout the area. Silvaplana and Pontresina are the two most popular resorts for cross-country skiing. St Moritz has been the sight of the Women's Alpine World Cup downhill race and the Engadin Cross-Country Marathon, held annually since 1969, in which thousands of skiers race 42km/26mi from Maloja to Zuos, running through Sils, Silvapana, St Moritz, and Pontresina. Once a month during the full moon, ski lifts remain open until 10pm in Diavolezza for a **moonlight ski experience**★★. Corvatsch offers similar night skiing every Friday, but it is Diavolezza that has become legendary,

In **summer**, St Moritz becomes an ideal setting for hiking excursions through the Engadin Valley. Itineraries go past the nearby villages of Silvaplana-Surlej (&see ENGADIN) and Pontresina (&see MUOTTAS MURAGL).

SIGHTS
Engadiner Museum★

Via del Bagn 39. ⏲Open Mon–Fri, 9.30am–noon, 2pm–5pm; winter, Sun 10am–noon. ⏲Closed Sat, Easter, and Christmas, May and November. ⌖5CHF. ☎(0)81 833 43 33.
This visit is a useful preliminary to an excursion through the villages of the

Engadin. The following rooms are particularly worthy of note: The **Engadin Room no II** (Zuoz house), with its elegant beamed ceiling; the luxurious **State Room no IX** (the Visconti-Venosta house at Grosio); and **State Room no VII** (a nobleman's house at Marca de Mesocco).

Segantini-Museum

Via Somplaz 30. ⏲Open Tue–Sun 10am–noon, 2pm–6pm. ⏲Closed May & Nov. ⌖10CHF. ☎(0)81 833 44 54. www.segantini-museum.ch.
This rotunda contains several works by the painter Giovanni-Segantini (1858–99), who enjoys widespread popularity in Switzerland.
Note especially the symbolic **trilogy**★ To Be—To Pass—To Become, where details of the upper mountain landscape are illustrated.

Berry-Museum

Via Arona 32. ⏲Wed–Mon 10am–1pm, 4pm–7pm. ⌖15 CHF. ☎(0)81 833 30 18. www.berrymuseum.com.
Situated in the spacious Villa Arona, this museum has brought together many works by Peter Robert Berry, a local doctor and painter (1864–1942) who studied in Paris and was influenced by the greatest fin-de-siècle French masters.

HIKING
Piz Nair★★

Alt. 3 057m/10 029ft. About 45min, including 20min by funicular to Corviglia, then by cable-car, and 15min on foot round trip. Cable-car: Departure every 30min Jun–mid-Oct and Dec–Apr,

---

Alpine Palaces

It was at St Moritz in 1896, that the word Hotel and the word Palace were first spoken next to each other after the inauguration of the eponymous Palace by Johannes Bradrutt. The edifice was a neo-Gothic castle which the critics marked as a success. Today called Badrutt's Palace Hotel, it is still the place where glamorous resort celebs like to parade. Above it, the Kulm Hotel, J. Badrutt's first property, is the oldest of the current five-star hotels (1856). Still higher, the Carlton, built for Tsar Nicolas II, is the smallest. In St Moritz Bad, the Kempinski Grand Hotel des Bains looks like a fairytale castle, as does the Suvretta House, in a forest clearance on the road to Champfèr.

8am–5.30pm. Fare there and back
35CHF. (0)81 836 50 50.
From the terrace of the upper cable-
car station look down on the Upper
Engadin and its lakes. Then walk to
the highest point to enjoy the circular **panorama**★★ embracing the
Bernina Summits.

Val Suvretta da
S Murezzan★★

*From the upper station of the gondola to
Piz Nair – 3hr30mins walk. 1 200m/
3 937ft change in altitude during the
decent.*

You start with a descent for about 50
minutes, in a rough rocky peak devoid
of vegetation, to Pass Suvretta. From the
pass (alt. 2 615m/8 580ft), the **view**★★
of Val Suvretta da Samedan dominated
by the Piz Bever and Piz Julier and its
glacier in the south. Turn left and within
10 minutes you reach **lake Suvretta**★★
which provides a superb view south to
the Bernina Massif (Piz Roseg Scerscen
and Bernina).

From there the descent, is more agreeable as it continues along the river,
through alpine meadows with grazing cattle. After 1 hour of walking, the
stream rushes into a cascade. Just after,
turn left onto a path uphill. The steepness is short and the path then continues without a perceptible difference in
altitude on the mountainside, offering
quick **views** ★★ of the village of Surlej,
Piz Corvatsch and Lake Silvaplana. Finish
by following the directions to St Moritz-
Dorf (nice views over the village).

Piz Corvatsch★★★

*Access by cable-car in 16min; leave
from Surlej (to the left of Lake Silvaplana
which is reached by the causeway).
Departure every 20min 8.10am–5pm
Jul–mid-Oct, Dec–Apr 8.20am–5pm.
Return fare 34CHF. (0)81 838 73 73.*

The ride up to the mid-station of Murtel
(alt. 2 702m/8 865ft) offers views onto
Lake Silvaplana and Lake Sils. The upper
station is situated below the superb ski
jump formed by the Piz Corvatsch (alt.
3 451m/11 319ft). Go to the panoramic
terrace, which commands a splendid

overall view★★★ of the surrounding
landscape. To the east you can see the
glaciers of the Piz Tschierva, Morteratsch, Palü, Bernina, Scerscen and Roseg.
To the northwest, one overlooks the
Engadin Valley and its lakes, dominated
by the Piz Lagrev, Julier, Bever and Ot.
And in the background, one can make
out the Säntis and, farther east, the
Jungfraugruppe and the Sustenhorn.

Fuorcia Surlej★★

Alt. 2 755m/9 038ft.

This is an easy, gentle walk, leaving from
the intermediate station of Murtel. From
the pass, where a refuge has been set
up, there is a lovely **view**★★ of the
Bernina Massif. You can return to Surlej
on foot (*2hr30min*) via Hahnensee. This
will take you along a rocky path affording a beautiful **panorama**★★★ of four
lakes: Sils, Silvaplana, Champfer, and St
Moritz.

Chamanna Coaz refuge★★★

Alt. 2 610m/8 562ft.

*Remember to bring sturdy shoes and
a hiking stick. Allow 5hr not including
stops. The walk is challenging, especially
on the way down. Enquire beforehand
about times of buses and carriages to
get back to Surlej in the late afternoon.
This is one of the most popular walks
in the area, after you have climbed Piz
Corvatsch and reached Fuorcia Surlej
early in the morning.*

Starting from the pass, the clearly
signposted path follows the mountain
slope, gradually offering an increasingly stunning **view**★★★ of the glacial
corrie coating the valley, dominated
by Piz Roseg. After following the path
for 2hr, enhanced by burbling streams
and waterfalls, you will see the refuge,
nestled in a secluded **setting**★★ amid
mountain tops. The Roseg and Sella
Glaciers plunge down towards a vast
white lake.

Retrace your steps and after about
15min bear right towards Pontresina
(Puntraschigna). The 40min descent
along a stony path towards Lake Vadret
is very steep and trying. The impressive
glacier (*see INTRODUCTION: Nature*)

View from Muottas Muragl towards Staz forest the lakes of St Moritz, Champfèr, Silvaplana and Sils

ending in the lake, dotted with ice floes, is a truly breathtaking sight. Continue following the stream and notice that the flora gradually becomes more lush: alpine meadows, mountain flowers, larch and pine trees.

After 1hr30min, you reach a hotel (alt. 2 000m/6 561ft) that marks the end of this wonderful outing.

Do not miss the striking **panorama**★★★ of glaciers standing out against bursts of vegetation, basking in the glowing sunset.

At the hotel, treat yourself to a carriage ride to Pontresina, then catch a bus back to Surlej.

Muottas Muragl★★

From the lower station at Punt Muragl, about 1hr there and back, including 30min by funicular.

⌂ ○ *Operates June–mid-Oct and Dec–Mar. Departure every 30min, 8am–11pm.* ⊙ *Summit trail pass 29CHF (more in high season); children up to 12yrs 10CHF; young persons up to 17yrs 20CHF (all tickets more in high season; euros welcome).* ℘ *(0)81 842 83 08. www.muottasmuragl.ch.*

The grassy ridges of Muottas Muragl, easily reached by funicular from the Samedan Basin, form the classic belvedere of the Upper Engadin.

From the upper station (hotel), at an altitude of 2 453m/8 048ft there is a **view**★★ of the Upper Engadin Gap, framed by the small Piz Rosatsch and Piz Julier ranges. The string of lakes between St Moritz and the Maloja are also clearly visible. Farther left are the Roseg corrie and the shining peaks of the Bernina Massif: Piz Morteratsch, Piz Bernina and Piz Palü. Many tourists will enjoy walking on this high ground, famous for its flora and fauna, along broad, gently sloping paths superbly sited on the mountainside, such as the Hochweg.

Walk to Pontresina★★

Allow one day to ascend by funicular to Muottas Muragl, walk to, and then tour Pontresina village. From Muottas Muragl, allow at least 2hr30min on foot. The classic route is through peaceful pastureland to Alp Languard *(3hr on foot)*, offering superb **views**★★ of the Roseg and Morteratsch glaciers and the Pontresina Valley. The climb down from to Pontresina can be done on foot or by chairlift. You may, however, decide to stop at the Unterer Schafberg Restaurant perched at a height of 2 231m/7 319.5ft *(1hr on foot before reaching Alp Languard)* before heading directly for Pontresina through the forest

(*45min*). From Pontresina, a path following the bed of the valley will take you to the foot of the funicular (*45min*), wending its way through many houses whose architecture is typical of the area.

While on this trail, note the 15 informational displays set up by Climate Trail, a project of the SESN (Natural Science Society of the Engadin) and WWF Switzerland. These displays explain the phenomenon of global warming and its effects on the Alpine environment. Also discussed are ways that everyone can help stop and reverse the process on a local and global level.

🚗 DRIVING TOUR

4️⃣ THE BERNINA ROAD★★★

*56km/34mi from St Moritz to Tirano –
Allow 2hr.*

This magnificent mountain road climbs up the Bernina Valley as far as the pass and then descends along the Poschiavo Valley to Tirano.

👁*It is inadvisable to start across the Engadin slope late in the afternoon; it will be difficult to see the Morteratsch. The Bernina Pass is usually blocked by snow from October to May. The pass road is not cleared at night. The railway—the highest in Europe without racks—runs all year round. The Swiss customs control is* at Campocologno and the Italian control at Piattamala.

▷ *Leave St Moritz in the direction of Pontresina.*

Pontresina★★

Alt. 1 777m/5 863ft.
Kongresszentrum Rondo – 7504.
𝒫(0)81) 838 83 00. www.pontresina.ch.
Pontresina, in the heart of the Engadin, is still tied to Romansch traditions. The town is situated in the highest region of the Upper Engadin, at the mouth of the Bernina Valley, within view of the Roseg corrie and the snowy ridges of the Piz Palü. Pushing up the Roseg or the Morteratsch valleys, mountaineers set out from here for magnificent glacier climbs in the Bernina Massif, especially the famous Diavolezza tour. Walkers can continue along the woodland paths of the forest of Tais (Taiswald) or climb the last foothills of the Piz Languard, via a corniche from Muottas Muragl (*7km/4.3mi*).

Old Town

The names of the streets and houses, some dating to the 16C, are in Romansch, which is still spoken here; the façades of many of the buildings are painted with intricate, ancient designs. There are also modern, well-appointed hotels which are more affordable than

Roseg Valley near Pontresina with a view of Piz Bernina, Piz Roseg, Tschierva and Roseg glaciers and the Lake Vadret

Daniel Martinek//Tourismus Engadin St. Moritz/Switzerland Tourism in St Moritz 4km/2.5mi away. The little Romanesque chapel of Santa Maria, near the pentagonal 13C Spaniola Tower, contains a series of mural paintings, created in the 13C and in the 15C. The series devoted to the story of Mary Magdalene will interest tourists familiar with the Golden Legend and the great Provençal traditions.

Skiing Area

The winter season at Pontresina lasts until April. It offers long-distance excursions for skiers and sunny ski runs served by the ski lifts of Alp Languard and the Muottas Muragl funicular. The resort is also popular for **cross-country skiing**. The famous Engadin marathon, which covers a distance of 40km/25mi, is held here every year (🛈 *for further information, contact Engadin Skimarathon, CH 7504 Pontresina*).

Between Pontresina and the Chünetta road fork, the valley quickly becomes wilder. The three glittering peaks of the Piz Palü appear to the right of the Munt Pers, and farther to the right, the snowy summits of the Bellavista.

Chünetta Belvedere★★★

Alt. 2 083m/6 832ft. From the Bernina road 2km/1.2mi there and back – plus 1hr on foot there and back.

After branching off on the road to the Morteratsch Glacier, leave your car before the wooden bridge leading to Morteratsch station. Cross this bridge and the railway track and after passing a bed of stones brought down by the torrent, take a path going uphill to the right, under the larches. After 20min, at the second fork, when the view opens out, turn right to climb to the viewpoint. From there you will see the grand picture formed by the **Morteratsch Corrie**, overlooked from left to right by the Piz Palü, the Piz Bellavista, the cloven summit of the Piz Bernina (highest point: 4 049m/13 284ft), the Piz Morteratsch with its heavy snowcap and the Piz Boval. The lower end of the glacier dies away in the foreground; it is framed by terminal moraines and divided longi-

tudinally by a central moraine. The **view**★★ is splendid after two hairpin bends. To the right of Bellavista the glorious twin peaks of the Bernina Massif—Piz Bernina and Piz Morteratsch—appear. From the latter the Morteratsch Glacier descends—a truly breathtaking sight. After this the road emerges into the Upper Bernina Depression.

Diavolezza★★★

Alt. 2 973m/9 754ft. About 1hr there and back from the Bernina road, including 9min by cable-car. ⛷ Operates in summer only 8.15am–5pm. ⊜Fare there and back: 28CHF. ℘(0)81 842 64 19.

For generations of mountaineers and skiers the Diavolezza refuge (now a restaurant) has been the starting-point of one of the most famous glacier runs in Europe. Thanks to a cable-car, tourists can now reach this high mountain pass and admire its spectacular glacier landscape. Take in the splendid **view** ★★★ encompassing the Piz Palü, Piz Bellavista, Piz Zupó, Crast Agüzza (easily identifiable because of its white peak), Piz Bernina, Piz Morteratsch, and the Boval refuge.

Diavolezza

The Bernina Pass★★

Alt. 2 328m/7 638ft. After leaving the valley, followed throughout its length by the railway and in which the Lago Bianco lies, the road climbs to the Bernina Pass from which there are clear **views**★★★ of the Piz Cambrena and its glacier.

Alp Grüm★★★

Alt. 2 091m/6 860ft. From the "Ospizio Bernina" station (accessible by car along a downhill road starting from the Bernina Pass), about 1hr there and back, including 10min by rail. 4.40CHF for a one-way ticket.

A famous viewpoint overlooking the Palü Glacier and the Poschiavo Valley. From the Bernina Pass to the Rösa Plateau the road dips into the Agone Valley, framed between the warmly coloured slopes of the Piz Campasc and Cima di Cardan. It then follows a winding course, taking advantage of every natural feature to maintain a practicable gradient. Looking back, the Cambrena group offers glimpses of its glaciers. Forest vegetation is once more reduced to a few stunted larch. You will make your entry to La Rösa facing the majestic, rocky Teo cirque.

From La Rösa to Poschiavo the wooded slopes, clothed with spruce, grow darker. 1km/0.6mi after two hairpin bends, in a section where the road winds above a green valley, a widely sweeping stretch of corniche reveals, lying below, the villages of San Carlo and Poschiavo, overshadowed by the icy shoulder of the Pizzo Scalino.

Poschiavo★

Tall, uniform buildings with regularly spaced windows quite unlike those in the Engadin, is typically transalpine in style. The early 16C church of San Vittore on the main square shows the peculiar position of Graubünden as a transitional area for men and goods and for artistic influences. Although the low-pitched roof and slim campanile with five storeys of arches is Lombard style, the intricate star vaulting, most remarkable in the chancel, derives from a typically Germanic style belonging to the last Flamboyant Gothic period (*see INTRODUCTION*). **Lago di Poschiavo** (a hydroelectric reservoir) is the best feature of the Poschiavo-Miralago section. Very high on the steep and wooded

eastern slope stands the steeple of San Romerio.

Miralago

From this hamlet, whose name ("look at the lake") refers to the **view**★, upstream is your last glimpse of a mountain skyline.

ADDRESSES

STAY

Hotel Hauser – *Via Traunter Plazzas 7.* *(0)81 837 50 50. www.hotelhauser.ch. 51 rooms. Restaurant .* Downtown, in a modern building, the Hotel Hauser has very spacious rooms. Brasserie, tearoom and sweet shop on the ground floor.

Igloo Dorf – *Muottas Muragl.* *(0)41 612 27 28. www.iglu-dorf.com. Open from Christmas to April. Offers half board.* A unique experience of sleeping in an igloo in the mountains. Igloos for six or two, with fondue, hiking and breakfast for all, sauna and Jacuzzi for the more expensively priced rooms.

Hotel Soldanella – *Via Somplatz 17.* *(0)81 830 85 00. www.hotel-soldanella.ch. Closed midNov–mid-Dec, late March–late May. 36 rooms.* The hotel offers the allure of a small palace of yesteryear (built 1905). The rooms overlooking the lake are worth the extra cost.

EAT

Grischuna – *Via Maistra 17.* *(0)81 837 04 04. www.monopol.ch. Closed Apr–May, Oct–Nov.* This elegant restaurant offers Italian-influenced cuisine with a contemporary twist, known as *Cucina Casalinga.*

Engiadina – *Plazza da Scoul.* *(0)81 833 32 65. www.restaurantengiadina.ch. Closed Jun and Oct, Sat, Sun and May and Nov.* A friendly family restaurant, far from the luxurious palaces. Graubünden specialties.

Cascade – *Via Somplaz 6.* *(0) 81 833 33 44. www.cascade-stmoritz.ch. Open evenings only. Closed late Apr-Jun, mid Oct–Nov.* International cuisine with Italian influences in an elegant bistro with Belle Epoque atmosphere.

Engadin★★★

Engadin, the valley of the river Inn, traditionally approached by the High Road, presents a different landscape from that of the great, deep valleys of the Alps, where basins and gorges often alternate in a somewhat monotonous manner. Since the altitude averages 1 500m/4 900ft (1 800m/5 900ft in Upper Engadin) motorists travelling from the north through the Julier or Albula Pass will experience only a modest fall. As for motorists coming from Italy through the Maloja Pass, they drive into the cradle of the Upper Inn without any change in altitude.

A BIT OF GEOGRAPHY

The Engadin Mountains reach 4 000m/ 13 000ft (Piz Bernina: 4 049m/13 284ft). They are sought after mainly for the splendour of their glaciers and the continental mountain climate, almost entirely protected against disturbances from the sea.

Romansh in the Engadin

Both Italian and German are spoken in the Engadin Valley, in addition to **Romansh**, which was declared the fourth official language of the Swiss Confederation in 1938. Romansh, a Rheto-Romance language, is distantly related to French and Italian, and is spoken by 40 000 people in Graubünden. Here, the word for bread is *pan*, and child is *uffant*. Romansh developed as a result of the conquest of Rhaetia 2 500 years ago by the Roman legions of Tiberius and Drusus. Latin was mixed with the local languages, evolving into the Romansh dialects spoken today. There are two main dialects: *Putèr* is spoken in the Upper Engadin Valley and *vallader* in the lower valley.

- ℹ **Info:** Via San Gian 30. ℘(0)81 830 08 00. www.engadin.stmoritz.ch.
- ▶ **Location:** Located in the Grabünden region.
- ⊕ **Don't Miss:** Views from Pix Coratsch or the Piz Corvatsch ski area (2 800m/9 185ft).

St Moritz/Muotas Muragl and Pontresina also part of the Upper Engandin but have been considered separately in this guide.

🚗 DRIVING TOURS

5 VAL BREGAGLIA★★

39km/24mi from St-Moritz to Soglio – Allow 1hr30mins.

▶ *Leave St Moritz by the S via route 27, which joins route 3 at Silvaplana.*

On leaving St Moritz, the road goes up the slopes of the upper valley of the Inn along the lakes of **Silvaplana**★★ and Sils, made more vivid by a wooded peninsula.

Sils★

This quiet, elegant resort in the Upper Engadin includes the two townships of Sils-Baselgia and **Sils-Maria**✲, situated at the beginning of the Inn Valley in thickly wooded countryside. The two lakes and the soft lines of the landscape, both in the main valley and in the tributary **Fex Valley**, which is very wide, contribute to the restful atmosphere of the resort. In spite of the large hotels of Sils-Maria, which stand out between the trees, across the way at the foot of the slope, visitors can take in a view to the south of the very wide glacier gap at the beginning of the Fex Valley from between the lakes. The German philosopher **Friedrich Nietzsche** (1844–1900) spent seven summers here (1881–88) and found inspiration for many of his most famous works during his walks along the lake shore. Photos, letters, and other mementoes can be found in the house where he stayed, which has been converted into a museum and which stands near the Church of Sils-Maria.

Passo del Maloja
Alt. 1 815m/5 955ft.
The Maloja Pass, the lowest one between Switzerland and Italy, establishes the actual boundary of the Engadin and is the watershed between the Danube and the Italian sides of Graubünden. Downhill from the pass the **Val Bregaglia**★★ (Bergell) is the continuation of the Inn Valley. A series of hairpin bends leads you to Casaccia, which marks the junction with the old Septimer road from Bivio. Beyond rises the Piz Cacciabella, distinguished by its small rounded snowcap.

Downhill from Löbbia, the **view**★ opens towards Stampa and Vicosoprano framed on the slope facing north by magnificent fir woods interspersed by pale green clumps of larches. The villages between Vicosoprano and Promontogno—including Stampa, Giacometti's native village—show the waning influence of the Engadin style (tall houses with deep, sunken windows, narrow, cobbled streets, and groups of little barns with rows of open gables). Even the Alpine flora gives way to chestnut groves, vineyards, and orchards.

La Porta
This narrow valley, fortified in Roman times, marks naturally the boundary between the Alpine and Southern Val Bregaglia. The Castelmur tower appears on a spur contrasting with the Romanesque Campanile of the church of Nossa Donna, while the remains of the old castle floor and perimeter wall can still be seen. Castelmur was the key position of the High Road on the Italian side.

Soglio★★
Access by a narrow and very steep by road.
The **site**★★ of this village is one of the most picturesque in the Bergell. It stands on a terrace surrounded by chestnut groves facing the rocky cirque that closes off the Bondasca Valley. The smooth slopes of the Pizzo Badile are among the most amazing in the Alps. Standing out against the houses which cluster around the church and its Italian-style campanile, the noble façades of several Salis palaces (one is now the Hotel Palazzo Salis) conjure memories of a Graubünden family best known over-

Village of Soglio

Christof Sonderegger/Switzerland Tourism

seas, since many of its members made their career in the diplomatic service.

6 UPPER ENGADIN

34km/21mi from St Moritz to Zernez – allow 1hr30mins.

▶ *Leave St Moritz N by route number 3, and then take route 27 on the left.*

After the wooded slope separating St Moritz from Celerina, the road goes along the lower plateau of the Upper Engadin.

Celerina

6km/3.7mi NE of St Moritz. Plazza da la Staziun 8. ℘(0)81 830 00 11. www.celerina.ch.

Celerina (Schlarigna in Romansh) lies at the foot of the larch-clad ridge separating the Samedan Basin from the upper levels of the High Engadin lakes. It is rather like an annex of St Moritz in regard to sports opportunities: In the Cresta quarter, where the great hotels of the resort are found, the famous bobsleigh and "skeleton" runs end. Nearer the banks of the Inn, an attractive group of typical **Engadin houses** make up old Celerina.

San Gian

🕓*Open summer, Mon 2pm–4pm, Wed 4pm–5.30pm, Fri 10.30am–noon; winter, Mon and Wed 2pm–4pm, Fri*

Celerina New Orleans Jazz Festival

During one weekend towards the end of August the mountains are alive with the sound of jazz. Big bands parade through the streets, an open air concert is held in the main square and by Lake Staz, an open-ended late-night Jam *really* goes into the early hours and there' a jazz church service on the Sunday. Details at www.celerina-sounds-good.ch.

10.30am–noon. 🔊*Guided tours in summer only: mid-Jul–mid-Sept, Wed 4pm–4.30pm. ℘(0)81 830 00 11.*

Standing alone on a mound to the east of Celerina, the uncrowned tower of **St John's Church** is a familiar landmark of the Inn Valley, dating back to Romanesque times, with a 15C painted ceiling and frescoes.

Samedan

Plazzet 21. ℘(0)81 851 00 60. www.engadin.stmoritz.ch/samedan.

At the entrance to the little triangular plain where the great resorts of the Upper Engadin have found room for a golf course, aerodrome and glider field, Samedan's horizons are bounded by the high summits of the Bernina to the south: Piz Morteratsch and Piz Palü.

This old-fashioned village is dotted with houses in traditional Engadin style. Notice, in the heart of the village, the imposing double Planta House (Chesa Planta, from the name of one of the oldest families in Graubünden), which contains the **Romansch Library**, dedicated to the preservation of local language and traditions. Also don't miss the Old St Peter Parish Church and the 1771 Parish Church (in the square).

Zuoz★★

Alt. 1 716m/5 561ft.

Zuoz is a high-altitude resort, well equipped for a stay in summer.

It has preserved a group of **Engadin houses** ★★, mostly built by members of the Planta family, who played an important part in the history of Graubünden. The town is small and everything can be reached on foot.

Hauptplatz★★

Its fountain is surmounted by the heraldic bear of the Plantas. The square is bounded on the north by the Planta House, designed in the Engadin style but its unusual size and its outdoor staircase with a Rococo balustrade give it a lordly air.

On the main street the Crusch Alva Inn (1570) has a gable decorated with a series of coats of arms.

Hauptplatz, Zuoz

Christof Sonderegger/Switzerland Tourism

Between Punt Ota (the traditional boundary between Upper and Lower Engadin) and Zernez, the valley narrows and near Zernez the Piz Linard looms into sight.

Zernez
Alt. 1 474m/4 836ft.
Chasa Fuschina, ℘ (0)81 856 13 00.
www.zernez.ch.
This large, picturesque village overlooks the confluence of the Rivers Spöl and Inn dividing the valley into Upper and Lower Engandin. It is the gateway of the Swiss National Park (℘ see p383). The park centre and museum is situated here.

7 LOWER ENGADIN
44km/27mi from Zernez to Martina –
Allow 3hrs.

▶ *Leave Zernerz from the N via route numbers 27 and 28.*

From Zernez to Susch, the road, going alongside the Inn river, plunges into the ravine of the Clüs. Piz Linard can be gradually discerned in the axis of this landscape, its rock faces veined with snow. Beyond Susch the valley, guarded from its terraced site by the village of Guarda, grows narrower, which makes the road feel more claustrophobic as it runs next to the blue-green waters of the river Inn.

Leave the main road and drive up from the valley floor to Guarda (2.5 km). To make the most of the sunlight on the slopes, try to drive this route in the direction Guarda–Scuol in the afternoon or Scuol–Guarda in the morning.

Guarda★
With its fountains, houses decorated with sgraffiti and family coats of arms over the doors, and its steep, narrow streets paved with cobblestones, Guarda is regarded as a typical village of the Lower Engadin. Notice the **Steinsberg Tower** standing upstream on a rocky hill, against which the white village of Ardez is built.

Ardez
This village at the foot of the Steinsberg is worth a stop for its painted houses with charming flower-decked oriel windows. The theme of original sin has enabled the decorator of the "Adam and Eve House" to paint a study of luxuriant foliage.
Between Ardez and Schuls the corniche road overlooks a third wooded defile, sinking finally towards its floor. From the start it offers a first glimpse of the proud **Schloss Tarasp** (castle). The many mountain crests of the Lower Engadin Dolomites (Piz Lischana and Piz St Chalambert Mountains) follow one another in the distance as far as the Swiss, Italian and Austrian frontier ridges.

Schloss Tarasp

Scuol/Schuls ✵

Stradun – 7550. ℘ (0)81 861 22 22.
www.scuol.ch.

This spa town and its surrounding area on the eastern tip of the Grabünden region are popular for their dramatic setting of scattered forests and rocky slopes, here in the widest basin of the Lower Engadin. The Lower Engadin Dolomites stand above the town, which enjoys a dry, sheltered climate, and bright sunshine.

The village on the tilled slope of the valley has become a tourist and business centre sustained by traffic using the international Engadin-Austria route (St Moritz-Landeck). At the same time, below the through road, Lower Scuol, the former nucleus of the community still stands around two paved squares built in pure Engadin style.

The most imposing building is the **Chagronda House and Museum** (◷*open mid-May–end Jun and in Oct, Tue–Thu 4pm–6pm; Jul and Sept, Fri–Wed 3pm–6pm;* ◆*guided tours in winter, Tue–Thu at 5pm;* ◉*5CHF;* ℘*(0)81 861 22 22*), which can be recognised thanks to its two superimposed galleries. It houses the Lower Engadin Museum.

Downhill from Scuol, the valley narrows between the crest line marking the Italian side on the right and the slopes streaked with torrents descending from the Silvretta Massif on the left.

Munt la Crusch★

Alt. 1 474m/4 835ft.

From this impressive viewpoint east of Scuol, and beyond Sent, you can admire the pretty **site**★★ of the castle and a **panorama**★ embracing the whole of the Lower Engadin with its Dolomites (Piz Lischana and Piz Pisoc) and its perched villages (Ftan and Sent).

Tarasp

This is the collective name of the communities facing Scuol opposite the Inn. A bus leaves Scuol station every hour.

Vulpera★★

Beautiful scenery and houses as well as some four star hotels. The main attraction is the 9-hole golf course, which is bisected by the road to Tarasp castle. Check out the traffic signs warning the drivers against flying golfballs.

Schloss Tarasp

◆*Guided tours daily (1hr), late May to early Jul, at 2.30 & 3.30pm; Jul to late Aug at 11am, 2.30pm, 3.30pm and 4.30pm; late Aug to late Oct at 2.30pm and 3.30pm; Christmas to Easter, Tue and Thu only at 4.30pm.* ◉*10CHF.* ℘*(0)81 864 93 68.*

This castle remained an Austrian enclave until 1803. The fortress was restored (1907–16) and is now used in certain seasons by the Prince of Hesse-Darmstadt.

Schweizerischer National Park (Swiss National Park)

Hans Lozza/Tourismus Engadin St. Moritz/Switzerland Tourisma

🕐 *Open Jun–Oct, 8.30am–6pm (10pm Tue).*
💶 *No charge.* ✆ *(0)81 856 12 82.*
www.nationalpark.ch.

Switzerland's only national park was also one of the first to be created in Europe. Founded in 1914 by the Nature Protection League, it covers an area of 172sq km/66sq mi between the Müstair Valley, the Inn Valley and the Ofen Pass, ranging in altitude from 1 400m/4 592ft to 3 200m/10 496ft.

The aim of the park is to protect local flora and fauna and to this end visitors are

Larch trees in Swiss National Park

required to leave their car in one of the designated car parks. Walkers must stay on marked trails. Camping, cycling, lighting of fires and picking flowers are forbidden.

🌿**Guided Tours** – The national park and local Tourist Offices provide advice on walks and organise guided tours of the park. Some of the tours follow particular themes, such as deer-watching in the Trupchun Valley, which is especially rich in game. **Special excursions** include a visit to the park during the deer-rutting season in autumn. For further information, contact ℹ️Tourismus Organization Engadin Plaiv/Engadin, 7524 Zuoz, ✆(0)81 20 20, plaiv@spin.ch, www.engadin.ch.

Nationalparkhaus

At Zernez (🕐 see ZERNEZ), along route 28.
🕐 *Open Jun–Oct, 8.30am–6pm (10pm Tue).* 💶 *No charge.* ✆ *(0)81 856 13 78.*
The National Park Centre provides information on the history of the park, as well as hosting temporary exhibitions, illustrated by films, which introduce visitors to the protected species within its boundaries. 📖Topoguides and a 1:45 000 scale map of the park are also available from the centre.

Walks

Access: continue along route 28, which winds its way through the Spöl Valley. Car parks at the entrance to the park. ℹ️*Contact the Tourist Office in Zernez, ✆(0)81 856 13 00 or the Maison du Parc National in Zernez, ✆(0)81 856 13 78.*
The park is dotted with information panels in five languages, some of which are designed specifically for children, and has 80km/50mi of marked paths of varying lengths and difficulty (walking trails are marked with yellow signs; mountain trails that can require crossing steep or slippery sections are marked with a red stripe on a white background; alpine trails that require climbing or glacier traverse are marked by a blue stripe on a white background). One of these starts at Ofen Pass, crosses Stabelchod Valley as far as the Margunet Pass (alt. 2 328m/7 635ft) and then rejoins the Botsch Valley.

The walks cross some magnificent scenery, especially striking from June to August, when the last snow is melting and the woods and meadows are full of flowers, such as edelweiss and gentian. Lucky visitors may even catch a glimpse of a marmot, deer, chamois, ibex or the bearded vulture, reintroduced to the park in 1991.

Gradients in Percentages

Gradients are usually represented as percentages in Switzerland. These figures will give the motorist some idea of slopes ahead.

10% 1:10, 14% 1:7, 18% 1:5.5
20% 1:5, 25% 1:4, 30% 1:3.3

Sent

To reach Sent drive along a little road shaded by maples, traced along the flank of the ridge, within view of the Lower Engadin Dolomites and Tarasp Castle. Sent is a fine village with perfectly kept houses with Baroque gables, known as Sent gables.

⑧ OFENPASS ROAD★★

Müstair Valley: 38km/23.5mi from Zernez to Müstair – Allow 2hrs.

The road links the Engadin with the Val Venosta in Italy and winds its way in the Val dal Spöl before entering the Swiss National Park at the Ova Spin stream. Once in the park you can only park at certain designated areas only.

Pass dal Fuorn (Ofenpass)

Alt. 2 149m/7 051ft.

The pass separates the Val dal Spöl, to the north, from the Val Müstair, to the south, whose torrent, the Rom, is a tributary of the Adige.

From the pass to Tschierv several sections of corniche afford pretty glimpses downstream, especially of the snow-capped Mount Ortler. After Tschierv the road runs pleasantly between stretches of turf and larch woods. It owes some of its character to the Tyrolean note introduced by the domed belfries of Valchava and Fuldera.

Müstaira

7532 Tschierv. ℰ (0)81 858 58 58. www.val-muestair.ch.

Chief town of the **Val Müstair**, Müstair is the only part of Swiss territory in the Adige Basin. **The Abbey of St John the Baptist** is one of the most ancient buildings in Switzerland, founded according to tradition by Charlemagne. The wood used for its construction has been dated to AD 775, so it stems from that period. Originally a Benedictine monastery for men, in 1163 it became a nuns' convent to this day. You can hear the nuns sing at 11am and 5pm during the summer.

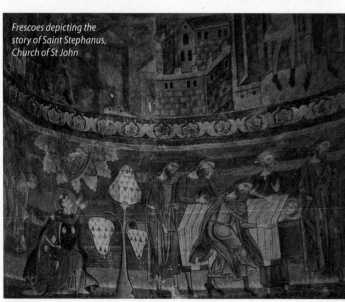

Frescoes depicting the story of Saint Stephanus, Church of St John

Church of St John★★

Guided tours in English available for groups of more than six. Open 7am–8pm. ℘ (0)81 851 62 28. www.muestair.ch.

The nave, originally built in the style of a basilica (8C) was transformed in the 15C by an Abbess of the Planta family (*see ZUOZ*) into a vaulted late Gothic structure with two aisles. The tower stems from c.960 and the bell tower stems from 16C. The Reformation stopped at Müstair and the grateful nuns donated the church to the village which has remained until today. The **frescoes**★★★ on the walls are listed as a **UNESCO World Heritage Site** and are the most imposing cycle of Carolingian frescoes in Europe. The originals (early 9C) are partially overpainted by Romanesque frescoes (1150–70) which are in excellent condition. The series over the north apse show the martyrdom of St Peter and Paul, over central apse the martyrdom of St John the Baptist, and on the right that of St Stephen. Among the other works of art is a 12C statue of Charlemagne.

Convent Museum★ (Planta Tower)

The museum (*open May–Oct Mon–Sat 9am–noon, 1.30pm–5pm, Sun 1.30pm–5pm, Nov–Apr Mon–Sat 10am–noon, 1.30pm–5pm, Sun 1.30pm–4.30pm; 12 CHF*) covers three floors of the 10C Planta tower containing objects of religious art from the baroque era in rooms of the original refectory, dormitory and kitchen; the nuns' 17C cells and the abbess' own (the remarkable 18C Hohenbalken room) can also be visited.

ADDRESSES

STAY

Alpine Astrovillage – *Lü.* ℘(0)76 547 11 33. www.alpineastrovillage.com. *5 rooms.* Relax during the day and look at the stars at night through three high-powered telescopes in this superbly located B&B, in Val Mustair.

Hotel Baer & Post – *Zernez.* ℘ (0)81 851 55 00. www.baer-post.ch. *54 rooms. Hostel accommodation available in an annex with 64 beds (2x4, 7x8). Gourmet restaurant.* In the same family for more than 100 years, this fine hotel has helpful staff who will arrange guides and packed lunches for your National Park hiking. Sauna for guests.

Hotel Il Fuorn – *Between Zernez and the Pass dal Fuorn.* ℘ (0)81 856 12 26. www.ilfuorn.ch. *22 rooms. Restaurant.* The only hotel inside the National Park is easily reached by an hourly bus from Zernez to Mustair.

Hotel Liun – *Müstair.* ℘ (0)81 858 51 54. www.hotel-liun.ch. *20 rooms. Restaurant.* Rooms with valley views and a vast spa centre.

Hotel Piz Buin – *Guarda.* ℘ (0)81 861 30 00. www.pizbuin.ch. *Closed 10–20 Jan, 15 Mar–15 Jun, 30 Oct–end Dec. 22 rooms. Restaurant.* One of those peaceful hotels for writers you read about in novels set in Switzerland. All rooms are comfortable rooms; those that are south facing have magnificent views.

Chasa Belvair – *Scuol.* ℘ (0)81 861 25 00. www.belvair.ch. *33 rooms.* Modern rooms with direct access to the Scuol thermal spa centre.

EAT

Crusch Alba – *Scuol.* ℘ (0)81 864 11 55. www.crusch-alba.ch. Specialities from the Engandin at reasonable prices.

Mürtaröl – *Plaun da Lej, next to Maloja.* ℘ (0)81 826 53 50. *Closed Mon and Tue.* Restaurant specialising in fish freshly caught from the surrounding rivers and lakes.

Stüa Granda – *Soglio.* ℘ (0)81 822 19 88. www.stuagranda.ch. *Closed Jan–Mar, mid Nov–20 Dec, Mon and Tue in Apr and Nov.* Local cuisine with Southern flavours (try the chestnut tagliatelle). Offers a sublime panorama towards Piz Badile.

THE NORTH

People in Austria—in perpetual competition with Switzerland, from the Winter Olympics to the quality of the ski pistes—have a rather unkind saying about their neighbour: "it's a fantastic place to be born and a nice place to die—but what do you do in between?" Maybe this was true in the past, but anyone who has been to Basel and Zürich—the twin pillars of German culture in Switzerland—can only shake their head in disbelief. Basel plays the cultured older brother to Zürich's brash, petulant teenager and their cultural lives complement each other perfectly.

Highlights

Cultural Giants

With German-speaking cities from Cologne to Berlin and Vienna lying in ruins after WWII, Zürich, and to a secondary degree Basel, were catapulted to the centre of German cultural life in the postwar era. With the reputation of their northern neighbour (the great canton up north, as the Swiss refer to Germany) in tatters, it was left to writers and dramatists such as **Friedrich Dürrenmatt** and **Max Frisch** to continue the tradition of Goethe and Schiller. As centres for modern architecture, fine arts and as providers for gallery space for artists, both Basel and Zürich stood up to the challenge and became the hives of activity we see today. Already financially rich—Basel with its pharmaceutical industries and Zürich with its banks—the cities enriched themselves further as cultural centres that now rank them next to Vienna and Berlin in the German-speaking world. One only has to visit the **Kunsthaus** in Zürich or the **Kunstmuseum** in Basel to be immediately impressed with some of the best collections of 20C art in Europe. In addition, generous sponsorship ensures that Zürich's **Opernhaus** offers a varied opera and ballet repertoire every day, something that many cities with more famous opera houses would envy.

Richard Serra's sculpture at Theaterplatz, Basel

LSD and Other Swiss Inventions

Basel's contribution to counter-culture was accidental, but nonetheless as important as they come. One Friday in April 1943, Dr Albert Hoffmann who was working for the company Sandoz Laboratories, was researching the chemistry of a fungal growth on rye when he started having hallucinations. He had accidentally discovered the mind-altering properties of lysergic acid diethylamide, commonly known as **LSD**, which kickstarted the 1960s counter-culture movement a quarter of a century later. This was only one of many Swiss inventions that have changed Western life, including: **the penknife** (or Swiss army knife)—Karl Elsener started the Victorinox company in Ibach, Schwyz in 1884; **Velcro**—Georges de Mestral from canton Vaud patented his invention in 1955; **stockcCubes**—first unveiled to the world by Maggi (now part of the giant Nestlé conglomerate) in 1908; **cellophane**—invented by Jacques E Brandenberger, a textile engineer in 1908 who had the idea of a clear, waterproof film when a waiter spilled wine on his tablecloth at a restaurant. One invention that is frequently and erroneously believed to be Swiss, is the **cuckoo clock**, which actually comes from southern Germany.

Counter-culture and Nightlife

Yet there is also an aspect of life, particularly in Zürich, that is often overlooked. Maybe it was the presence of the banks that spawned a counter culture movement whose traces can be seen today in the **Rote Fabrik** (see p394) and the graffiti that adorns Züri-West. The down side of tolerating the drift to the anti-establishment was the city's descent into heavy drug use in the early 1990s. This is when the triangular park behind the Landesmuseum became known as the **Needle Park**, where the city's heroin addicts injected themselves openly. As the park became more and more crime-ridden, for a time it became the unthinkable: a no-go area in a Swiss city. (Even today, since the area has been cleaned up, there is still saturation policing from the station to the park's end where the Sihl meets the Limmat.) Instead of criminalising addiction and driving the users underground, the city pioneered a programme whereby registered addicts would obtain their drug doses free from designated distribution points. This policy saw the addicts as sick people who need medical treatment rather than criminals who must go to jail. At the same time, a huge rehabilitation and education initiative was established to stop any new addicts and help the existing ones. The success was astonishing. Not only did crime fall as there was no reason to resort to stealing or mugging to fund addiction, but also the number of users actually fell despite the original fears that giving drugs out for free would encourage further use. Fifteen years later, in 2008, the Swiss voted in a national referendum to employ the Zürich experiment countrywide.

The relaxation of the licensing and opening hours in Zürich during the 1990s—a move not followed by Basel—has also resulted in a no-holds-barred nightlife which draws people from miles around, including from Konstanz across the border in Germany. The focus of the nightlife is **Niederdorf**, the area around **Langstrasse** and industrial **Züri-West** with its abandoned warehouses. Indeed, swish **Kaufleuten**, housed in a large building a stone's throw from the Paradeplatz, was voted as one of the top clubs in the world by the New York Times. Away from the cities of northern Switzerland, picture-book pretty green fields surround picturesque Medieval settlements such as Stein am Rhein, castles line the shores of the region's lakes and rivers, and time seems to stand still in the gentle valleys of the Appenzellerland. Take time to visit the tiny Principality of Liechtenstein to take in the museums of Vaduz, its small capital, and walk to breathtaking Tamina Gorge.

THE NORTH

NORTH SWITZERLAND

N

| 0 | | 10 km |
| 0 | 5 miles | |

ZURICH	★★★	Highly recommended
St. Gallen	★★	Recommended
Liestal	★	Interesting
Vaduz		Other sight described in this guide
		Driving tour

Schwenningen

A 81

31

SCHAFFHAUSEN

A 81

34

A 98

31

Überlingen

Ravensburg

WANGEN

1

affhausen

A 4

15

13

Stein am Rhein

33

Constance

Friedrichshafen

467

33

32

BREGENZ

Rheinfall

Arenenberg

Rheinau

Ittingen Charterhouse

Gottlieben

Kreuzlingen

LAKE

Thur

A 7

13

CONSTANCE

Lindau

31

BREGENZ

7

THURGAU

14

2

Winterthur

A 1

Wil

Rorschach

202

Kyburg

ÜRICH

A 53

ZÜRICH

16

ST.
GALLEN

St. Gallen

Trogen

A 1

Altstätten

Gais

A 13

A 14

15

Stein

APPENZELL

Greifensee

A 52

8

Urnäsch

Appenzell

13

BREGENZ

17

Zürichsee

Bubikon Commandery

Thur

Ebenalp
1640

1795

Hoher Kasten

Rapperswil

A 3

Seealp

591

AUSTRIA

G

Sihl

SÄNTIS
2502

16

ST. ANTON

Sihlsee

Lac de Walenstadt

Wildhaus

Werdenberg

Vaduz

Wägitalersee

Linthkanal

Triesenberg

LIECHTENSTEIN

2000

Schwyz

Glaris

Sareiser
Joch

3

SCHWYZ

Linth

17

Bad Ragaz

28

DAVOS

Brunnen

GLARIS

Tamina

Altdorf

17

GRAUBÜNDEN

RHINE

A 13

URI

19

Chur

Zürich★★★

Zürich is built between the wooded slopes of the Uetliberg and the Zürichberg at the point where the river Limmat, emerging from Lake Zürich, merges with the Sihl. It is the most important financial, industrial and commercial centre in Switzerland and its canton has a population of over one million, the largest in Switzerland. It has a reputation for being particularly receptive to contemporary trends and youth culture, and the city is much more lively at night than any other Swiss town, offering a wide choice of restaurants, cinemas, nightclubs and concert halls.

A BIT OF HISTORY

Zwingli and the Reformation – When **Ulrich Zwingli** was made parish priest of Glarus in 1506 at the age of 22, he lost no time denouncing social institutions from his pulpit, attacking the corruption of the magistracy and the practice of mercenary soldiering abroad, which he felt was weakening the nation. After two years at Einsiedeln, he was given the pastorate of the Grossmünster (cathedral) of Zürich and began to institute his most controversial religious reforms, namely that the Bible not the Church is the sole Christian authority. In 1523, after a public debate at the Zürich town

▶ **Population:** 365 132.
⚅ **Michelin Map:** Town plan in The Michelin red Guide Switzerland.
▯ **Info:** Im Bahnhof. ℘(0)44 215 40 40. www.zuerich.com.
◗ **Location:** Bahnhofstrasse, the city's main street, is lined by elegant shops and considered one of the world's most exclusive shopping areas. Alt. 408m/1 339ft.
▣ **Parking:** Leave the car and use the Zürich Card (⚅ see Getting Around), which provides unlimited transportation on trains, buses, trams, boats and cable-cars.
☺ **Don't Miss:** The Swiss National Museum (Landesmuseum) behind the main railway station, or a stroll on the banks of the Limmat in the Old Town.
⚇**Kids:** The Zoo, the lake, the circus when in town.
◷ **Timing:** At least three days for museums, shopping, and lake excursions. Try to fit in a weekend for its famed nightlife.

View of Old Town towards Zürichsee and the Alps

hall between Zwingli supporters and opponents, the Council declared itself in favour of his new ideas. Within three years Zürich had become a stronghold of the Reformation in German-speaking Switzerland. Zwingli closed monasteries, destroyed religious paintings and sculptures, abolished pilgrimages, processions and certain sacraments, and advocated the marriage of priests, setting the example himself in 1524. His authority alarmed the Catholic cantons. Lucerne, Uri, Schwyz, Unterwalden, and Zug allied against Zürich and gradually excluded it from federal affairs. However, another great religious debate took place at Bern in 1528 after which Bern, Basel and St Gallen adopted what we now called Reform Protestantism. War was narrowly avoided in 1529, but broke out in 1531. His death that year at Kappel did not diminish the influence of his religious theories, which spread throughout German Switzerland.

Tremendous growth – Zürich still had only 17 000 inhabitants in 1800. It had to cede the title of federal capital to Bern in 1848, but six years later it became the official seat of the Federal Polytechnic School—the famous Polytechnikum. The democratic constitution it gave itself in 1869 became the model for other cantons and even, in part, for the Federal Constitution of 1874. At the beginning of the 19C the town already extended beyond its fortifications and new buildings were mushrooming in the surrounding country. Industrial suburbs subsequently developed along the lines of communication and today Zürich is the economic capital of the Confederation.

WALKING TOURS

1 WEST BANK OF THE LIMMAT

Bahnhofstrasse★

This avenue (1.4km/0.8mi) is the busiest street in the city. It was built along the former site of the Fröschengraben (Frogs' Moat) and leads from the central station (Hauptbahnhof) to the shore of the lake. With its banks and insurance offices, department stores and luxury boutiques, this is the most important business centre in Switzerland.

▷ *Turn left at Werdmühlestrasse and descend to the Limmat just below Rudolf-Brun-brücke.*

Schipfe

This is the heart of the old town, with narrow, medieval streets running down to the Limmat. Some houses here have roof gardens. Take a detour into Augustinerstrasse, where some of the houses are adorned with oriel windows —a rare sight in Zürich.

Lindenhof

This esplanade, shaded by 90 lime trees and adorned with a fountain, marks the summit of a hill. This strategic location guarded the crossing of the Limmat and

GETTING AROUND
PUBLIC TRANSPORT

It is both difficult and expensive to park in the city centre. However, there is an excellent public transport network of trams, buses, metro (the S-Bahn), boats, and trains, which operates downtown and to the suburbs. Unlimited day passes can be bought from the Tourist Office, railway station, and from automatic ticket machines. Other passes combine public transport with museum entry or excursions.

ZÜRICH CARD

The Zürich Card (*17CHF for 24 hours, 34 CHF for 72 hours*) includes admission to over 40 sights, public transport, and discounts.

BICYCLES

The city is well equipped with cycle lanes. In summer, bicycles can be borrowed free of charge (deposit and passport required) from Bahnhofstrasse near the station, Marktplatz, Oerlikon, and Altstetten.

The Advent of the Dada Movement

The **Cabaret Voltaire** (Spiegelgasse 1—note the commemorative plaque) was inaugurated in 1916 by poet/director Hugo Ball and wife Emmy Jennings, with friends and artists including Tristan Tzara, Marcel Janco, Jean Arp, Richard Huelsenbeck and Sophie Taeuber, to create an avant-garde movement as a reaction to established art. They decided to disrupt conventional rules by staging dance performances, reciting poems, and exhibiting their paintings, an unprecedented approach to cultural life that was a resounding success. The term Dada was coined quite by accident when Ball and Huelsenbeck were trying to find a name for the cabaret singer. The word *Dada* appeared in the first issue of *Cabaret Voltaire,* a magazine published in German, English, and French: it expressed the first quiverings of a moral and intellectual rebellion against the complacency of contemporary society. Although the Cabaret Voltaire had to close down after only six months of existence, the Dadaist magazine managed to survive longer.

was the site of the Celtic and Roman settlements from which Zürich sprang. Note the old Roman stone on the way down with the inscription **Turicum**, the Latin name that became Zürich. From the edge of the terrace you will see the old quarters of the town rising in tiers on the east bank.

◗ *Walk down Pfalzgasse and S on Schlüsselgasse - on your right rises the Peterkirche.*

St Peterkirche

The origins of this church, the oldest in Zürich, date back to the 7C. The largest clock face in Europe (8.70m/28ft in diameter), built in 1534, adorns the 13C bell tower.

Weinplatz

South of the square you will find fine houses with Flemish roofs, the town hall (Rathaus)—a neo-Gothic building dating from 1900—and the Wasserkirche, a recently restored 15C chapel. The cathedral (Grossmünster) dominates the whole with its two tall towers.

Fraumünster

⊙*Open Apr–Oct, Mon–Sat 10am–6pm; Nov–Mar until 4pm daily. ℘(0)44 211 41 00. www.kirche-zh.ch.*
This church replaced a convent founded in 853 by Ludwig the German and his daughters Hildegard and Bertha. Con-

struction began in 1250; the façade was restored in 1911 in neo-Gothic style. The chancel is Romanesque and the nave has pointed vaulting. Note the remarkable **stained-glass windows**★; those in the north transept are by Giacometti (*The Celestial Paradise*, 1947).

The five windows in the chancel (1970) and south transept (1980) are by Marc Chagall and illustrate biblical scenes. On the south side of the church, remains of the Romanesque **cloisters**★ (Kreuzgang) are ornamented with frescoes by Paul Bodmer (1920–41).

◗ *Turn right to Paradeplatz and down the Bleicherweg to reach the old moat.*

Schanzengraben

A detour via the Bleicherweg leads to this old moat, one of the last remains of city's old fortifications, which runs from the railway station to the lake. Panels along the moat provide information on its history.

② EAST BANK OF THE LIMMAT

◗ *Start at the Rathaus, go up the Marktgasse and turn left.*

Niederdorfstrasse

This partially pedestrianised street crossing the Niederdorf district is particularly lively at night, with a good choice of cafés and restaurants. The street is

ZÜRICH

lined with beautiful old houses that bear witness to the past wealth of Zürich's old corporations.

▶ From Hirschenplatz, turn right into the Brunngasse, then the charming old Froschgasse.

Neumarkt

This small street is home to a beautiful baroque facade of the 18C, seat of the ancient guild of shoemakers at number 5. The building now houses a municipal theatre. At number 4 next to the restaurant Kanterei, push the door of the house "Zum Rech", to admire the model representing Zürich in 1800 (note the presence of vines). Free admission.

▷ *Walk down Spiegelgasse.*

Spiegelgasse

A small lane which is full of history! At number 14, Lenin prepared the Russian Revolution of 1916-1917. Political exiles, refugees of war, communists and artists occupied the area in the early 20C. At number 1, the Cabaret Voltaire was the birthplace of Dadaism (&*see info box p392*). It is now a trendy cafe, which perpetuates the movement of Tristan Tzara in programming exhibitions, readings and various artistic events.

▷ *Take the Münstergasse to the cathedral.*

Grossmünster★

🕑*Tower open mid-Mar–Oct, Mon–Sat 9.15am–5pm, Sun 12.30pm–5.30pm; Nov–Mar, Mon–Sat 10am–4.30pm, Sun 12.30pm–4.30pm.* ᴓ*5CHF. Cathedral mid-Mar–Oct, Mon–Sat, 10am–6pm; Nov–mid Mar, Mon–Sat 10am–5pm.* 𝄢*(0)44 252 59 49. www.grossmuenster.ch.*

This impressive cathedral, erected between the 11C and the 13C, replaced a collegiate church said to have been founded by Charlemagne, and is a symbol of the Reformation for German-speaking Swiss. Zwingli preached here from 1519 until he died. Its façade is flanked by three-storey towers surmounted by wooden domes faced with metal plates.

The south tower is crowned by a colossal statue (the original is in the crypt) of Charlemagne seated with a sword across his knees. The bronze doors were sculpted by Otto Münch between 1935

and 1950. The nave has pointed vaulting; the raised chancel ends in a flat chevet, and a gallery runs above the aisles. Traces of frescoes may be seen in the chancel and the crypt with its characteristic triple nave. The modern stained-glass windows are by Augusto Giacometti (1932).

The Romanesque **cloisters** are decorated with groin vaulting. Groups of three arcades, their rounded arches are supported by finely sculpted capitals, open onto a courtyard.

Oberdorf

South of the cathedral unfolds this quaint little neighbourhood. Above Oberdorfstrasse, a handful of steep, cobbled streets contain beautiful old houses and some great art galleries. In this oasis of calm and romance, the bustle of the city seems far away.

RIVERSIDE AND LAKESIDE WALKS★★

This walk starts along the banks of the Limmat, near Quaibrücke which links Bürkliplatz and Bellevueplatz and marks the beginning of Lake Zürich (Zürichsee). Continue the walk along the quays, along which beautifully maintained gardens are dotted with flower beds and several species of trees.

WEST BANK FROM BÜRKLIPLATZ

The landing-stages in Bürkliplatz are always busy with sailing and motor boats, some of which offer boat trips on the lake (&*see Boat trips*).

Heading farther along the **Mythenquai** the **views**★ of the lake and the Alps (with the Oberland Massif in the far distance) become more open. (*About 1hr.*)

Rote Fabrik

Seestrasse 395. Bus 161 or 165 from Bürkliplatz. 𝄢*(0)44 481 91 43. www.rotefabrik.ch.*

This old brick factory is now a popular student haunt, housing artists' studios, the Shedhalle gallery and a large concert hall.

EAST BANK FROM BELLEVUEPLATZ

▶ *Take Utoquai, then Seefeldquai. Trams number 2 or 4, Fröhlisstrasse.*

Zürichhorn Gardens

By Utoquai.

There is an excellent **view**★ of the town from the Zürichhorn Gardens, where a sculpture (*Heureka*, 1964) by the Swiss sculptor Jean Tinguely (↻ *see box p73*) is on permanent display.

Centre Le Corbusier (Heidi Weber museum)

Höschgasse 8.
Free. ♿. ☎*(0)44 383 64 70.*

To the left of the Tinguely sculpture and slightly obscured by trees is Le Corbusier's last building, erected in 1967, which now serves as a permanent exhibition to the architect himself.

Chinese Garden

🕐*Open late Mar to late Oct daily 11am –7pm.* *4CHF (children 1CHF).* ♿.

This park, opened in 1993, was given to Zürich by its twin town, Kunming. Hidden behind the heavy red gates—in central China red is the colour of the emperor—is a perfectly kept garden, where the theme "three friends in winter" is illustrated by pines, bamboo, and winter cherry trees. Canals criss-crossed by small bridges run through the gardens, which are dotted with gingko trees and bamboo.

Mühlerama

Access by Kreuzbühlstrasse, E of the town plan. 🕐*Open Tue–Sat, 1pm–5pm; Sun, 10am–5pm.* *9CHF.* ☎*(0)44 422 76 60. www.muehlerama.ch.*

This Belle Époque-style flour mill, built in 1913, was in operation until 1983 and now houses a museum with functioning milling machines, allowing visitors to learn about the production of flour. The exhibition covers the development of milling techniques; the role of the miller in history; bread in popular culture; and the themes of abundance and famine.

Zoo Zürich★

Access by Gloriastrasse. Tram 6.
🕐*Open 9am–6pm (5pm Nov–Feb).*
22CHF, (6–16 years, 11CHF). ♿.
☎*(0)44 254 25 05/25 31; www.zoo.ch.*

Nicely laid out at Zürichberg, in a very pretty, leafy setting, this zoo houses more than 2 000 animals. Giant tortoises, an otter, and a beaver can be seen playing in the water and on land. Just as fascinating are the monkeys and the elephants' bath (*around 10am*).

Fluntern Cemetery

About 5 minutes in the opposite direction to the Zoo entrance from the final stop of Tram number 6 is the **Fluntern Cemetery** notable for the grave and statue of **James Joyce**★.

Botanical Gardens

Access by Kreuzbühlstrasse, E of the town plan.

The botanical gardens comprise three huge plexiglass domes and are planted with tropical forest vegetation, as well as species from the Alps and the Mediterranean.

MUSEUMS
WEST BANK OF THE LIMMAT
Schweizerisches Landesmuseum★★★

Behind the main railway station.
🕐*Open Tue–Sun 10am–5pm (Thu 7pm)*
10CHF. ☎*(0)44 218 65 11.*
www.landesmuseen.ch.

This French chateau-like building (1898) houses the magnificent collections of the **Swiss National Museum**, with exhibits on all aspects of Switzerland's artistic and cultural heritage. Whole rooms have been dismantled from the regions and painstakingly reassembled in here, such as that of a typical **Schwyz chapel** (1518) with stained-glass windows and ribbed vaulting, the **Mellingen council room** (1467), and **three rooms from the Fraumünster** in Zürich decorated in wood from top to bottom and adorned with friezes and rich metal fittings, as well as a **Gothic corridor** from the same abbey that looks exactly as it would in the Middle Ages.

History of Switzerland exhibition, Schweizerisches Landesmuseum

© The Swiss National Museum

Ground floor – One wing houses exhibits from the Middle Ages and the modern era: Romanesque era religious objets d'art, such as the unusual **Christ with Palms** on a donkey with wheels, and ivory tablets that once adorned Carolingian bindings. The late-Gothic period is represented by stained-glass, paintings on panels (view of Zürich, 1500) and polychrome sculptures, such as the king made from walnut wood (c.1320) with slanting eyes and wavy hair, similar in style to images found in illuminated manuscripts. Note also the ceramic stove decorated with a bearded man dressed in animal skins, representing the forest (1440). Other interesting exhibits include a parchment decorated with 559 coats of arms and 18 banners from (1340).

First floor, west wing – A huge gilded celestial globe with four images of Hermes symbolises the ages of man, made by the Swiss astronomer Jost Bürgi (1594), and the fine reconstructions of **interiors from 1600** are not to be missed. The 16C and 17C stained-glass window cabinets are decorated with coats of arms and biblical scenes. Dating from the same period, a profusion of silverware (cups, goblets with lids, etc.) demonstrates the wealth of the city's corporations. Among the 17C and 18C furniture, note the wardrobe

decorated with Mannerist low reliefs. The Baroque room from the **Zum langen Stadelhof** house, with its gallery of famous men, commemorates Swiss soldiers who fought for foreign armies (c.1660).

First floor, south wing – It is dedicated to the History of Switzerland using multimedia reconstructions and findings from the **Bronze Age** including the remarkable 910g/2lbs golden **Beaker of Altstetten** decorated with animals, the sun and the moon. The **Celtic** and **Roman** eras follow with busts, statues and gold treasure troves as they run into the **Middle Ages** and the invasion of Germanic tribes. A special section on **Huguenot immigration** is followed by rooms on the **Reformation** and **Enlightenment**. The final section 17C–20C shows how the Swiss became a rich nation from the export of watches and clocks to tourism and finance. Don't miss an old set of safe deposit boxes from a bank.

Second and Third Floors – The collection continues with an array of clothes and toys from the late 18C and early 19C. The headdress made of black silk ribbons is typical of the Zürich area around 1770. The **rural costumes** on display are particularly varied: the best known is the shepherd's costume from the Appenzell, which is red and yellow and decorated with cow motifs. Also exhibited here are reconstructions of 19C artisan workshops and the detailed **model of the battle of Murten**, won by the Confederates against Charles the Bold in 1476. Finally on the third floor is the museum's armoury.

Museum für Gestaltung Zürich

Access by Sihlquai. ⊙*Open daily Tue–Thu, 10am–8pm, Fri–Sun 10am–5pm.* ∞*12CHF.* ℘*(0)44 446 67 67. www.museum-gestaltung.ch.*
Exhibits at the **Museum of Design** include applied arts, architecture, graphic art, and industrial design from 1900 onwards. The museum also houses a collection of posters and graphic designs.

Zunfthaus "Zur Meisen"

Opposite the Fraumünster.
This building dates from 1757 and is adorned with a fine wrought-iron balcony from where Winston Churchill gave his famous 1946 speech on a United Europe. It contains the collections of 18C ceramics (faience and porcelain) belonging to the Schweizerisches Landesmuseum. The ceramics are displayed in two Rococo-style rooms on the first floor.

Museum Bärengasse

⊙*Open daily 2pm–6pm, (Tue 8pm)* ⊙*Closed until some time in Autumn 2010.* ∞*8CHF.* ℘*(0)44 211 17 16.*
The museum occupies two adjoining houses of the late 17C, now restored. The permanent exhibition, spread over three floors, offers a glimpse of the daily life and mentality of Zürich between 1750 and 1800. Furniture, ovens and objects of common use or ornaments dating from the mid 17C to the mid 19C are highlighted in the context of their time. On the ground floor, there is a collection of dolls created in the 1920s by a local artist, Sasha Morgenthaler (1893–1975).

Rietbergmuseum★★

Gablerstasse 15. Access by Bleicherweg (off the town plan). Tram 7. ⊙*Open Tue–Sat 10am–5pm (late Feb–Sept until*
8pm Wed & Thu). ⊙*Closed most public holidays.* ∞*12CHF (permanent collections), 16CHF (special exhibitions).* ♿ ℘*(0)44 206 31 31. www.rietberg.ch.*
This museum contains the collections of Baron von der Heydt: statues from India, Cambodia, Java, China, Africa, and the South Sea Islands. The collections of Japanese prints by Willy Boller and Julius Mueller, works of art from the Near East, Tibet and pre-Columbian America, paintings from the Far East, a collection of Swiss masks and some Flemish and Armenian carpets complete the exhibition.

EAST BANK OF THE LIMMAT
Kunsthaus★★★

⊙*Open Sat, Sun & Tue 10am–6pm, Wed–Fri 10am–8pm.* ⊙*Closed some public holidays.* ∞*18CHF (permanent collections).* ℘*(0)44 253 84 84. www.kunsthaus.ch.*

The **Fine Arts Museum** displays paintings, as well as sculpture from the early French, Swiss and German Middle Ages. On the first floor are canvases of Ferdinand Hodler, considered to be the leading Swiss painter of the early 20C, and pictures by Vallotton, Böcklin, Anker, Auberjonois, and Barraud. The French School is represented by works by Delacroix, Toulouse-Lautrec, Cézanne, Renoir, Degas, Matisse, Utrillo, Léger, Braque, and Picasso. One room contains 14 works by Marc Chagall. The museum also houses the largest collection outside Scandinavia of the work of Edvard Munch, as well as Dada works by Man Ray and Hans Arp. Finally the Alberto Giacometti Foundation has on view a considerable collection of the artist's works.

Sammlung Bührle★★

Access by Zeltweg. ⊙*Open Tue, Wed, Fri and Sun 2pm–5pm.* ⊙*Closed most public holidays.* ∞*9CHF.* ℘*(0)44 422 00 86.*
This villa houses one of the most important private art collections in Switzerland: works of art collected by Emil Bührle between 1934 and 1956. A fervent admirer of Claude Monet, Bührle

Kunsthaus

Christoph Schuerpf/Switzerland Tourism

succeeded in barely 20 years in bringing together a superb collection of some 300 paintings, mainly 19C French works. As the result of a major heist in the winter of 2008, the museum was closed to heighten security. To date two of the four paintings stolen have been recovered, but the museum's most famous, Cézanne's, *The Boy in the Red Waistcoat,* is still missing.

Ground floor – Four rooms are devoted to works from the 16C to the 19C: the landing and the Dutch Gallery present Hals *(Portrait of a Man)*, Rembrandt, Van Ruysdael *(View of Rhenen)* and Teniers; works on display in the Louis XVI Salon include paintings by Boucher, Degas *(Portrait of Mme Camus*, with two sketches), Fragonard and Ingres *(Portrait of M. Devillers)*; the Venetian Salon exhibits works by Canaletto, Goya *(Procession in Valencia)*, El Greco and Tiepolo *(Diane Bathing)*.

The Pink Salon and the Music Chamber contain important Impressionist works: *Sunflowers on an Armchair* by Gauguin, *The Road to Versailles at Louveciennes* by Pissarro or Manet's *The Swallows*. The portrait *Little Irène* was painted by Renoir just before he broke loose from the Impressionist movement. *The Poppies near Vétheuil* is a landscape by Monet. *Messalina* by Toulouse-Lautrec was to influence the Fauves by its luminous colour. Finally, the dazzling *Chest-*

nut Tree in Blossom, reflecting the influence of Japanese art, painted by Vincent van Gogh.

Staircase and First Floor – Seven Delacroix paintings *(Self-Portrait)* and canvases by Courbet and Dufy laid out along the first flight of steps are followed by another series by Chagall, Picasso, Rouault, and a *Recumbent Nude* by Modigliani. The landing is devoted to the 20C with Cubist works by Braque *(The Violinist)*, Picasso and Gris, and several Fauvist pictures by Derain, Marquet, Matisse (note the change in technique between *The Pont St-Michel in Paris* and *Still Life*, executed five years later) and Vlaminck *(Barges on the Seine near Le Pecq)*. The Courbet Gallery shows Realist works such as *Free Performance* by Daumier and *Portrait of A Sisley* by Renoir. An adjoining room set aside for Renoir also features the splendid *Garden at Giverny* by Monet and *Sailing Boats* by Boudin. In the Manet Gallery are *La Sultane*, *Pond with Water-Lilies* and *Waterloo Bridge* by Monet, alongside one of the 22 original bronzes of *The Dancer* by Degas. The last three rooms concentrate on Vincent van Gogh *(Self-Portrait* and *The Sower)*, Sisley *(Summer in Bougival)* and Bonnard *(Portrait of Ambroise Vollard*, clearly a tribute to Cézanne). Also of interest are *The Offering* by Gauguin (painted on the Marquise Islands shortly before he died), *The Milliners* by Paul Signac and

Salon Natanson (the meeting-place of the Nabis) signed by E Vuillard. The Gothic Gallery (note two landscapes by Patenier) and the second floor house a set of fine religious sculptures (12C–16C).

Felix-und-Regulakirche★

Access by Talacker, W of the plan.
🕐*Open Mon–Fri, 9am–11.30am, 1.30pm–4.30pm. 𝒫(0)44 405 29 79.*
This modern church is dedicated to St Felix and St Regula, siblings who, according to tradition, were martyred in Zürich, beheaded on the orders of Decius. The tall bell tower is detached from the rest of the building. The interior is unusual: the oblong church is roofed with a barely curving vault supported by sloping pillars. Stained-glass windows near the vault are modern.

Migros Museum für Gegenwartskunst and Kunsthalle★

Limmatstrasse 270. 🕐*Open Tue, Wed and Fri 12pm–6pm, Thu 12pm–8pm, Sat–Sun 11am–5pm.* 🎟*8 CHF (reduced 4CHF); combination ticket: 12CHF (discounted 6CHF). 𝒫(0)44 277 20 50 (Migros Museum). 𝒫 (0)44 272 15 15 (Kunsthalle). www.migrosmuseum.ch. www.kunsthallezurich.ch.*
These two museums of contemporary art that will delight fans of the genre, occupy the former Löwenbräu brewery. They welcome temporary exhibitions throughout the year that are usually dedicated to young promising artists. The cutting-edge facilities and daring works resonate especially in the vast halls of pure white. The brick building also houses several art galleries and a good bookstore on the ground floor.

EXCURSIONS
Uetliberg and Felsenegg ★★

Access by train: 20min on line number 10 from Zürich station, platform 2; departures every 30min. 🎟*14.40CHF.*
🗺*A map is available from the Tourist Office.*
The **Uetliberg** (alt. 871m/2 856ft) is a favourite day trip for locals. The railway journey is mainly through woods. From the arrival station (no cars), there is a fine view of the summits of the Alps. Take the steep path to the nearby terrace of the Gmüetliberg restaurant *(viewing table)*.

You can go to the top of the belvedere tower *(167 steps)* for a sweeping **panorama★★** of the whole Zürich district, the Limmat Valley, Lake Zürich, and the Alpine range—from Säntis in the east to the Jungfrau and Les Diablerets in the southwest. From here, it is possible to follow the ridge to Felsenegg (alt. 804m/2 637ft; a walk of approximately 1hr45min). A "planet path" (Planetenweg) features models of the planets on a scale of 1:1 billion. At Felsenegg, a cable-car climbs to Adliswil (*return to Zürich by train, line number 4*).

Kilchberg

▶ *7km/4mi. Leave Zürich by General Guisan-Quai.*
Highway 3 runs along the west shore of the lake to Kilchberg, a suburb of Zürich. Swiss poet Conrad Ferdinand Meyer (1825–1898) and German writer Thomas Mann (1875–1955) spent their last days in this area and are buried in its small cemetery.

Wildpark Langenberg

This wildlife park extends on either side of the road (mostly on the left side) north of Langnau am Albis on a couple of acres of forest and rocky hillocks: deer, chamois, marmots, ibex and wild boar can sometimes be seen. The road climbs to the Albis Pass (alt. 791m/2 596ft) from where magnificent views extend over the countryside, then descends between Lake Turler and the Albis Mountain before turning left toward Hausen at the foot of the Albishorn.

Some time after Hütten, there is a stretch of corniche *(2km/1mi)* that overlooks the widest part of Lake Zürich. The road then rises as far as Feusisberg in the countryside with glimpses of the lake.

After a winding section of road through woods, there is a plunging **view★**, which reveals both sections of the lake (Obersee on the right) which the Rapperswil causeway divides.

Knie—The Swiss National Circus

In 1803 Friedrich Knie, son of Empress Maria-Theresa's personal physician, was studying medicine at Innsbruck when a chance encounter with a horsewoman from a troupe of travelling artistes changed his life. He joined them, becoming an acrobat. Later, he founded his own troupe and performed throughout Germany, Austria, Switzerland and France, gaining fame as a tightrope walker. His children and grandchildren kept up the tradition. The Knie family became Swiss citizens in 1900; in 1919 Friedrich's cherished dream came true when the Knie Circus was founded. Today the Knies are one of the great circus families; their one-ring circus remains a family affair with the sixth generation now active. It is Switzerland's national circus, although it remains financially independent. The circus and its itinerant zoo tour March to November, giving 375 shows under the big top to capacity audiences of 3 000 in some 60 towns. Their winter quarters are in Rapperswil.

Rapperswil★

Alt. 409m/1 342ft. Hintergasse 16.
℘*(0)848 811 500.*
Sitting on a short peninsula on the north shore of Lake Zürich, the little town of Rapperswil has kept its medieval appearance, emphasised by the imposing mass of its castle. Rapperswil is a pleasant place to stay in summer, with plenty of walks and drives around the lake and in the neighbourhood. Below the town, a wooden crossing, stretching for 841m/0.5mi, bridges the narrowest part of the lake. It has been part of the pilgrims' way to the abbey of Einsiedeln opposite (see p352) for centuries.

Castle

A massive structure flanked by three grim-looking towers, the castle was built by the counts of the district in the 13C. From the outer terrace there is a fine **view** of the town below, Lake Zürich and, beyond it, the Glarus Alps and St Gallen. On the opposite side, above the former ramparts and overlooking the lake, a deer park has been there since the castle was built.

Ritterhaus

○*Open Apr–Oct, Tue–Thu, 1pm–5pm; Fri 1pm–8pm; Sat – Sun and public holidays, 10am–5pm.* ○*Closed Good Fri, Easter Sun and Whitsun.* ∞*8CHF.*
℘*(0)55 243 39 74. www.ritterhaus.ch.*
Founded in 1192 and rebuilt in the 15C and 16C, the Bubikon Commandery of the Order of the Hospital of St John of Jerusalem, is now used as a museum. It recounts the history of the Hospitalliers' Order with the aid of documents, arms, paintings. Also visit the chapel, 16C kitchen, library and large common rooms with their *trompe-l'œil* ceilings and panelling, fireplaces, and Gothic-Renaissance furnishings.

ADDRESSES

🍽 STAY

Affectionately nicknamed the "little big city", Zürich is expensive. During the high season, allow at least 160CHF for a double room, including breakfast. For the younger traveller, there is a **youth hostel** at Mutschellenstrasse 114, ℘01 482 35 44. The **Seebucht campsite** is at Seestrasse 559, on the west bank of the lake; ℘(0)44 482 16 12.

🍴🛏 **City Backpacker** – Niederdorfstrasse 5. ℘(0)44 251 90 15. www.city-backpacker.ch. **65 beds.** An address for backpackers that proves that Zürich is not just for wealthy tourists. The rooms and dorms provide basic comfort, but you will not find anything cheaper or more central (in the middle of Niederdorf). Bathrooms on the landing. Friendly international atmosphere, and a beautiful roof terrace.

🍴🛏 **Splendid** – Rosengasse 5. ℘(0)44 252 58 50. Fax 0(0)44 262 61 40. www.hotelsplendid.ch. **24 rooms.** Splendid might be overdoing it, but this one-star, simple and rather dated hotel is in a decent location (close to the Limmat) for the price. Toilets and showers on the landing.

🍴🛏 **Youth Hostel** - Mutschellenstrasse 114. ℘(0)43 399 78 00. www.youth hostel.ch. **76 rooms.** Globetrotters keen to save money can drop their backpack in this clean, comfortable and well equipped building .The hostel is, alas, away from the centre: the lake is only 10 min walk, but the station is 6.5km/4mi away so downtown is a tram ride away. Reception 24/7, self-service restaurant, bar, washing machines.

🍴🛏🛏 **Altstadt** – Kirchgasse 4. ℘(0)44 250 53 53. Fax 0(0)44 250 53 54. www. hotel-altstadt.ch. **23 rooms.** Pictorial compositions and poems signed by contemporary artists adorn the walls of regularly renovated rooms, at this hotel in the charming district of Oberdorf. Nice bar downstairs.

🍴🛏🛏 **Franziskaner** – Niederdorfstrasse 1. ℘(0)44 250 53 00. Fax 0(0)44 250 53 01. www.hotel-franziskaner.ch. **19 rooms.** A three-star hotel recently refurbished with care and taste. Excellent value for the bustling neighbourhood of Niederdorf. Special rates on weekends (on request). Bar and restaurant.

🍴🛏🛏 **Landhus** – Katzenbachstrasse 10. Zürich-Seebach. ℘(0)44 308 34 00. www.landhus-zuerich.ch. **28 rooms.** This hotel has English-style décor and comfortable rooms.

🍴🛏🛏 **Leoneck** – Leonhardstrasse 1. ℘(0)44 254 22 22. www.leoneck.ch. **78 rooms.** This hotel features an unusual interior which revolves around the world of cows. The whole decoration, including frescoes, depict these large, friendly creatures. Conveniently located on a hill, a few minutes from the old town. No parking facilities.

🍴🛏🛏 **Rex** – Weinbergstrasse 92. ℘(0)44 360 25 25. rex-swiss-quality. www.hotel-rez.com. **37 rooms. Restaurant** 🍴🛏. Modern, recently renovated comfortable hotel near the town centre. On-site parking for guests.

🍴🛏🛏 **Uto Kulm** – Giusep Fry, in Ütliberg. ℘(0)44 457 66 66. www.uto kulm.ch. **55 rooms.** Perched above Zürich, this hotel has a superb view of the city below. Perfect for a restful break in the countryside.

🍴🛏🛏🛏 **Adler** – Rosengasse 10, am Hirschplatz. ℘(0)44 266 96 96. www.hotel-adler.ch. **52 rooms.** Situated in the lively district of Niederdorf (soundproof windows keep out the noise), this old-fashioned hotel, with a charming bohemian touch, displays works of Basel artist Heintz Hum, along with frescoes illustrating the city's main sights. Restaurant serves traditional cuisine (fondues, raclettes).

🍴🛏🛏🛏 **Sorell Hotel Zürichberg** – Orellistrasse 21. ℘(0)44 268 35 35. www.zueerichberg.ch. **66 rooms.** Nestling in the forest not far from the lake, a few minutes from Zürich by tramway, this hotel has a terrace offering lovely city views. The combination of modern and traditional styles creates an unusual atmosphere.

🍴🛏🛏🛏 **Greulich** – Herman Greulich-Strasse 56. ℘(0)43 243 42 43. www.greulich.ch. **18 rooms.** 🍽18 CHF. Fans of contemporary design and architecture will love this stylish hotel which celebrates the marriage of wood, glass and concrete. Arranged around a quiet courtyard, it combines minimalist decor in the rooms with modern comforts. The hotel has a "slow food" restaurant with Mediterranean cuisine and a trendy lounge bar. The hotel is a good 20-minute walk from the Bahnhofstrasse.

⊜⊜🛏🍴 **Rössli** – *Rössligasse 7.* *(0)44 256 70 50. www.hotelroessli.ch. 27 rooms.* This very central hotel, is nestled in an alley in the district of Oberdorf. It occupies a historic building which has been completely refurbished. The decor and the elegant rooms, the impeccable comfort and the professional service is second to none in Zürich. Prices are, of course, high, but you will not find a better example in this category in the city centre. The hotel has no garage (parking close but expensive). Free Internet.

🍴/EAT

⊜🍴 **Zeughauskeller** – *Bahnhofstrasse 28A.* *(0)44 211 26 90. www.zeughauskeller.ch. Closed public holidays.* Generous portions of regional cuisine served in a former 15C arms depot. Art Nouveau décor and shaded terrace in summer.

⊜⊜ **Öpfelchammere** – *Rindermarkt 12.* *(0)44 251 23 36. Closed Sun, Mon 24 Dec –8 Jan and mid-Jul–mid-Aug.* This is Zürich's oldest tavern, dating back to the 13C. The old-fashioned setting, medieval rafters, and traditional furniture make for a delightful dining experience.

⊜🍴 **Zum Kropf** – *In Gassen 16.* *(0)44 221 18 05. www.zumkropf.ch Closed Sun and public holidays.* A stone's throw from the Fraumünster, this large tavern dating from 1888 has three Art Nouveau beer halls, whose ceilings are decorated with frescoes. Generous portions.

⊜⊜🍴 **Zunfthaus zur Schmiden** – *Marktgasse 20.* *(0)44 250 58 48. www.zunfthausschmiden.ch.* This former blacksmiths' guildhall in the old quarter presents a fine 15C Gothic dining hall and an attractive coffered ceiling. Call for opening times.

⊜⊜🍴 **Kronenhalle** – *Rämistrasse 4.* *(0)44 262 99 00. www.kronenhalle.com.* Typical brasserie with an artistic ambience, displaying works by contemporary painters. Charming bar and restaurant serving local fare and wide selection of wines and beers.

⊜⊜🍴 **Haus zum Rüden** – *Limmatquai 42 (1st floor).* *(0)44 261 95 66. www.hauszumrueden.ch. Closed Sat and Sun except for group reservations.* This former guildhall from the 13C features a remarkable dining room with groined vaulting, which adds charm and atmosphere to the restaurant.

⊜⊜🍴 **Zunfthaus zur Zimmerleuten** – *Limmatquai 40 (1st floor).* *(0)44 250 53 63. www.zimmerleuten.ch. Closed public holidays and mid-Jul–mid-Aug.* Charming 18C guild-house. Choose from a rustic, cosy setting with wooden beams, a charming, light room for romantic dinners, and a scenic restaurant overlooking the Limmat.

⊜⊜🍴 **Bodega Española** – *Münstergasse 15.* *(0)44 251 23 10. Closed 25 & 26 Dec.* For over 100 years, this authentic wine cellar has been serving excellent Spanish paella and tapas in an old Zürich café. Iberian atmosphere with hams hanging from the rafters, garlands of garlic and waiters speaking in Spanish. Very busy every night.

⊜⊜🍴 **Hiltl** – *Sihlstrasse 28.* *(0)44 227 70 00. www.hiltl.ch.* Founded in 1898, the oldest vegetarian restaurant in Zürich serves excellent dishes from around the world: curries, paella, tagines, etc. A wide choice which, combined with a cozy and chic environment, has seduced the city. Eat à la carte or, more economically, use the buffet where you pay by weight. Also serves as a takeaway.

⊜⊜🍴 **Alpenrose** – *Fabrikstrasse 12.* *(0)44 271 39 19. Open daily except Mon (Sat, Sun and Tues nights only). Closed mid-Jul–mid-Aug and Christmas/ New Year period.* Draws a clientele of regulars—quite understandably so, as feasting under the high ceiling and panelling define this restaurant as a warm and pretty mountain chalet. The traditional Swiss dishes always manage to surprise. Top recommendations are "Bündner Pizokel", a specialty of the Engadin, and fresh fish from Lake Zürich. Friendly and attentive. A good choice and excellent value for money.

⊜⊜⊜ **Roi International** – *Seestrasse 457.* ℘*(0)44 487 14 14.* Breathtaking view of Lake Zürich and the lights from the windows of this recently revamped (and renamed—it was previously called Blu) restaurant located near the Rote Fabrik. The kitchen uses regional ingredients in Mediterranean-style dishes. Depending on the day, up to the full cost of your meal is given as credit to spend in the adjacent lifestyle (homeware, fashion, gifts) shop.

⊜⊜⊜⊜ **LaSalle** – *Schiffbaustrasse 4 (tram 4 / 13 Escher-Wyss-Platz). ℘(0)44 258 70 71. www.lasalle-restaurant.ch. Open Mon–Fri for lunch and Mon–Sun for dinner until very late.* Located in the renovated Schiffbau factory in Züri-West, this restaurant offers a sophisticated decor and trendy design, which combines raw concrete, metal, and glass (note the Murano chandelier). The menu is varied and daring. Finish the evening in the third floor bar to admire the city lights.

SIGHTSEEING

BOAT TRIPS ON LAKE ZÜRICH

🗓 *Information from the Tourist Office or at the main landing-stage at Bürkliplatz, near Bellevue. Tram numbers 2, 5, 8, 9 and 11 run to the landing stage. Boat trips Mar–Oct. Trips last from 1hr to 5hr; meals are served on board from Apr–Oct. To reserve, call ℘(0)44 487 13 13. www.zsg.ch* Boat trips run along the Limmat *(1hr30min),* from the Schweizerisches Landesmuseum as far as the Zürichhorn. Large boats operate trips on the lake, including a short trip *(1hr30min),* stopping at Erlenbach and Thalwil, and a longer half-day excursion on a steamboat, stopping at Rapperswil *(☉see RAPPERSWIL)* and Schmerikon, at the other end of the lake. If you opt for the longer trip to Rapperswil you can return by rail using the same ticket.

🛒 SHOPPING

Bahnhofstrasse is Zürich's main shopping street. It is lined by smart boutiques with attractive window displays and is home to several **department stores**, such as Globus, Jelmoli and Coop. The street becomes more and more expensive the further you move from the station. Interesting shops selling designer items, wooden toys and confectionery can be found in the **old city**, along the narrow streets surrounding Weinplatz on the left bank and in the district around Niederdorfstrasse on the right bank.

Flea market – *On Bürkliplatz, open Sat from May–Oct, 6am–4pm.*

SOUVENIRS

The long-established confectioner's **Sprüngli** (Bahnhofstrasse 21) sells all kinds of truffles and chocolates, including Luxemburgerli, a local speciality. **Schweizer Heimatwerk** (Rudolf Brun-Brücke) is part of a chain of shops selling typical Swiss souvenirs, including designer items, toys, and children's clothes inspired by traditional costumes. The **Pastorini** toy shop (Weinplatz 3) in the old town specializes in wooden toys.

🎭 THEATRE AND MUSIC

Opernhaus – *Falkenstrasse 1. ℘(0)44 268 66 66. www.opernhaus.ch.* Richard Wagner once conducted in this neo-Baroque opera house (1891).

Tonhalle – *Gotthardstrasse 5 and Claridenstrasse 7. ℘(0)44 206 34 34. www.tonhalle.ch.* Built in 1895, this large hall was inaugurated by Johannes Brahms.

Schauspielhaus – *Rämistrasse 34. ℘(0) 44 258 77 77. www.schauspielhaus.ch.* This theatre (1884) is renowned for excellent music and drama programmes.

Bernhard-Theater – *Theaterplatz. ℘(0) 44 268 66 66. www.bernhardtheater.ch.*

Theater Stok – *Hirschengraben 42. ℘(0)44 251 22 80. www.theater-stok.ch.*

⊙NIGHTLIFE

Niederdorf is buzzing every night—not just on weekends—and a walk down the street is recommended. Before 10–11pm you can sit outside while afterwards you congregate indoors because of noise regulations.

For a more quiet night out try the **Jules Verne bar** at the Brasserie Lipp (*Uraniastrasse 9*) that offers a fine selection of cocktails and affords a lovely view of the city, or enjoy the cosy, intimate atmosphere of the **Hôtel Central Plaza**, not far from Bahnhofbrücke. Sample a *"déci"* (*short for décilitre*) of Swiss wine in the pleasant setting of the **La Barrique** (*Marktgasse 17. www.barrique-wineandbar.ch*) The famous **Café Odéon** (*Limmatquai 2*) with Art Nouveau décor was once frequented by writers and famous personalities such as Thomas Mann and Lenin, but its clientele is now mostly gay. Many of the trendier dance clubs are to be found in industrial Zürich-West. The chic clientele gravitates to **Bling** (*Neufrenkengasse 22, www.bling-zuerich.ch*), electro and hip-hop fans flock to **Besame Mucho** (*Pfingstweidstrasse 6, www.besamemucho.ch*) while **Loop38** attracts an alternative crowd (*Albulastrasse 38, www.loop38.ch*). To watch live bands almost every night check out the **Hive Club** (*Geroldstrasse 5, www.hiveclub.ch*) and if you like eighties music the **Labor Bar** which is gay on Sundays (*Schiffbaustrasse 3, www.laborbar.ch*). Jazz, blues or soul fans should not miss visiting club **Moods** (*Schiffbaustrasse 6. www.moods.ch*) next door. Finally the **Rote Fabrik** (*see Riverside Walks*) houses the **Ziegel oh Lac bistro** (*www.ziegelohlac.ch*) and a huge **concert hall**, popular with Zürich's rock fans. Dance club and concerts are on several times a week.

For a British ambience and a wide selection of beers go to the **Lion Pub** (*Ötenbachgasse, left bank*) or further up to the **Nelson** (*Beatengasse 11*)

BATHS ALONG THE LIMMAT

These traditional, old-fashioned baths are situated along the banks of the Limmat and are open June–August.

Stadthausquai *℘(0)44 211 95 92. www.barfussbar.ch*. These baths, located close to Zürich's city hall, are for women only and include a solarium. Concerts and DJ-hosted events open to all are held here in the evening at the **Barfussbar** (where you enter barefoot).

Schanzengraben (off the town plan) *℘(0)44 211 95 94*. Also in the city centre, near the Stauffacherbrücke and the stock exchange, this swimming pool is for men only.

Flussbad Oberer Letten – *Pier West, Lettensteg 10. ℘(0)44 362 92 00*. Take Limmatstrasse behind the railway station, then turn right toward Sihlquai. These baths, situated in the Letten district, are the oldest in the city. Open to men, women, and children.

⊙EVENTS

The Tourist Office inside the train station offers a weekly guide to what is happening in Zürich.

During the **Sechseläuten** spring festival, usually held on the third Monday in April, the various corporations of Zürich march through the city centre in traditional costume. The city's symbol of winter, the **Böögg**, a snowman made from cotton wool and filled with fireworks, is burned at 6pm on Sechseläutenplatz, at Bellevue.

The **Knabenschiessen**, a shooting competition for children aged between 12 and 16, is one of the oldest festivals in Zürich. It is held on the Albisgütli fields (last stop on tram number 13) on the second weekend in September.

The **Züri-Fäscht**, a large fair held along the banks of the River Limmat in the old town, takes place every three years, over three days in early July and includes firework displays along the lake. The next Züri-Fäscht will take place between 5 and 7 July 2013.

Basel★★★

Situated on the northwest border of Switzerland, facing Alsace and the Baden region, Basel town is washed by the River Rhine at the point when it becomes navigable. The Old Town is part of Grossbasel (Greater Basel) and is separated from Kleinbasel (Lesser Basel) by the wide river which opens up opportunities for maritime trade. The third largest city in the country, Basel is a vibrant cultural centre with over 30 museums: at present, new museums are opening at a rate of one every year. The city's prosperity is derived from banking, insurance, sea traffic and a number of important chemical and pharmaceutical companies based here. Some 30 000 workers commute to Basel each day; approximately a third come from Germany and two-thirds from France, mostly from the Alsace region.

A BIT OF HISTORY

Origins – The city's origins date back to pre-Roman times, as testified by ruins of a fortified Celtic settlement dating from around 100 BC, in the St Johann district. The Roman city of Augusta Raurica (&see AUGST/AUGUSTA RAURICA) was later founded here in 44 BC. In 1032 Basel became part of the Germanic Empire but later came under the rule of a prince-bishop, vassal of the Emperor; these events are recalled in the town's coat of arms, which bears an Episcopal cross.

From the Council of Basel to the Reformation – From 1431–48, the Council of Basel tried to reform the clergy and bring heretics back to the Church. However, its existence was threatened by serious disagreements dividing the Pope and his bishops. The Council offered the papal tiara to Amadeus VIII, Duke of Savoy, who took the title of Pope Felix V. It was only in 1501 that the city joined the Helvetic Confederation.

- ▶ **Population:** 164 937.
- **Info:** Schifflände 5 – 4001. ℰ(0)61 268 68 68. www.baseltourismus.ch.
- **Parking:** Parking may be difficult to find in Old Town. See the map for outlying parking areas. A day-pass for public transport within the city is available from the Tourist Office.
- **Don't Miss:** The Kunstmuseum: The country's largest art museum.
- **Kids:** Basel's large zoo, situated southwest of Old Town and the Museum of Caricature and Comic Strip.
- **Timing:** Allow at least 4 hours for a walking tour of Old Town and the Kunstmuseum. To visit the majority of attractions, reserve 4 days plus an additional day for the excursions.

View of the Rhine with the Middle Rhine Bridge and the cathedral

Philipp Giegel/Switzerland Tourism

The industrial age – Basel welcomed many French Huguenots who had fled following the Revocation of the Edict of Nantes when Protestantism in France was outlawed. They introduced silk weaving into Basel, paving the way for

GETTING AROUND

BY FERRY – Four Fähri routes cross the River Rhine (5min). These passenger-only ferries are propelled solely by the river flow holding on to a cable across the Rhine. *The ferries run daily in summer from 9am–7pm. In winter, the two middle routes run from 11am–5pm.*

BY BICYCLE – A map of cycle routes is available from the Tourist Office. Bikes can be borrowed free of charge in summer from 8am–10pm from the railway station, Theaterplatz, Claraplatz and Schifflände; a deposit is charged. Visitors must show a passport or identity card.

PUBLIC TRANSPORT – Tickets for public transport are available from automatic ticket vendors; a pass valid for one or several days can be bought at the Tourist Office. Anyone spending the night in a hotel in Basel Town is given a Mobility Ticket, which provides unlimited access to all forms of local transport.

---

industrial expansion. The town started to manufacture ribbons, an activity in which it came to specialise. The industry of dyeing was introduced and began to expand; the creation of the Geigy factory in 1785 signaled the beginning of the chemicals industry in Basel. The golden age of the 18C has left its mark in the handsome Classical hotels. During the 19C, the town expanded into the surrounding countryside. After a violent civil conflict, two half-cantons were created in 1883: Basel-Stadt (Basel Town, represented by a black crosier) and Basel-Land (Basel District, represented by a red crosier).

Basler dialect – Compared with other German-speaking areas, this dialect has slightly muffled vowels and is softer on the ear. Situated on the border of three countries, Basel borrows words from French, such as *Baareblyy* (*parapluie*—umbrella), *Boorpmenee* (*portemonnaie*—wallet) and *Exgyysi* (*Excusez-moi*—Excuse me). Unusually, locals say *Aadie* derived from the French *adieu*, meaning goodbye, to say "hello".

◗◖WALKING TOUR

OLD TOWN★★★
Allow approx 3hrs. Leave from Marktplatz (the market place).

Surrounded by corbelled houses the Marktplatz is animated Monday to Saturday by the market stands in front of the arcades of City Hall next to the Coopers' Guildhouse (1578).

Rathaus (H)
◗◖*Guided tours available.* ◌*No charge. Call for info.* ✆*(0)61 268 68 68.* The town hall was erected between 1508 and 1514 in the Late Gothic style and restored between 1898 and 1902. The façade is decorated with frescoes and flanked by a modern belfry adorned with pinnacles. In the inner courtyard, note the fresco on the theme of justice by Hans Bock (1610) and a statue of Munatius Plancus, the founder of Augusta Raurica that developed into Basel.

▷ *Take the Eisengasse to the Rhine and walk right on the Rheinsprung.*

Cathedral★★
◷*Open mid-Apr–mid-Oct, varied hours.* ✆*(0)61 272 91 57. Tower open mid-Apr–mid-Oct, 10am–5pm (1pm Sun, 4pm Sat); mid-Oct–mid-Apr, 11am (2pm Sun) to 4pm.* ◌*3CHF.* ✆*(0)61 272 91 57. www.baslermuenster.ch.*
The great 12C münster was partly rebuilt in the 14C and 15C and restored in the 19C. It is built with red sandstone and surmounted by two Gothic towers (good view of the city). Between the towers is a porch dating from the mid 13C. The recessed arches of the main doorway are decorated with small statues depicting prophets, angels and garlands of foliage and flowers.

The Carnival

The Basel Carnival dates back to the Middle Ages, the only Catholic celebration to have survived the Reformation in a Protestant city. Created to mark the beginning of Lent, the carnival interrupts the daily life of the population with three days of processions and masquerades meticulously governed by coded rituals.

On the first Monday after Ash Wednesday, at 4 o'clock in the morning, all the lights are switched off and the "**Morgestraich**," a custom dating back to the 18C, heralds the start of the festivities. During "**die drei scheenschte Dääg**"— the three most beautiful days—the revellers rule the city.

Participants (whose number can reach 15–18 000) sporting masks and costumes are divided into "groups" (called **cliques,** because you have to be invited to join one) of 20 to 200 people each and line up. Each clique dresses around a subject such as Harlequins, Centurions or American Presidents. They never take their masks off and it is impolite to ask someone to identify himself. The procession marches through the streets to the strains of fifes and drums and under showers of confetti (supposedly invented here) ending up in the local restaurants at 6 o'clock, where they are served onion pie and soup made with flour.

These colourful displays of masks and musical performances—both highly organised and individually celebrated—continue to enliven the town until Wednesday. Tuesday afternoon is reserved for the children's parade; do not miss their procession.

Skirting the building to the left you reach the **portal** of St Gallen (12C) showing *Christ the Judge* on the tympanum, *The Wise and Foolish Virgins* on the lintel and the *Resurrection of the Dead* over the main vault. There is a pretty **view**★ of the Rhine, the town, the Black Forest and the Vosges from the Pfalz terrace. A narrow, dark passage leads into 15C Gothic **cloisters**, extended by other cloisters dating from the same period. The cathedral houses the **tomb of Erasmus**, the writer who made Basel a centre of Humanist learning, and who died here in 1536. Steps lead to the crypt, which houses tombs of the bishops of Basel from the 10C–13C.

◑ *Walk down the Münster hill until Barfüsserplatz.*

Barfüsserplatz

Criss-crossed constantly by the comings and goings of trams, the busiest place in Basel is dominated by the steeple of the church of St Leonard. It houses the Historical Museum (M1. Note at number 10 the beautifully painted façade of the restaurant-brewery Zum Braunnen Mutz.

◑ *Turn left to Steinenberg.*

Fassnachtsbrunnen

The Carnival Fountain designed by **Jean Tinguely** (1925–91) is the center of attraction on the esplanade in front of the municipal theatre. Nine cleverly articulated metallic structures in perpetual motion provide a telling example of Tinguely's wit and ingenuity.

◑ *Rejoin Barfüsserplatz and take Gerbergasse, the main street of the Old City. Walk to the Marktplatz, which extends the Marktgasse (Market Street) to Fischmarktplatz.*

Fischmarktplatz

This lively sector of Basel's shopping district, Fish Market Square, is ornamented with the Fish Market fountain (**Fischmarktbrunnen**), one of the most beautiful Gothic fountains in Switzerland. The fountain (11m/36ft high) is decorated with angels, saints and prophets. The

Cakes and biscuits

The *Leckerli*, a speciality of Basel since the Middle Ages, is a small, rich biscuit made from honey, flour, almonds, walnuts, orange and lemon concentrate, spices and eau-de-vie. It is sold in pastry shops all over town, including the **Läckerlihaus** (Gergerstrasse 57), which specialises in this particular biscuit. Local specialties served at Carnival time include the Fastnachtskiechli, a fried pastry sprinkled with sugar, and the Fastenwähe, a butter brioche flavoured with cumin.

original (1390), sculpted by Jacob Sarbach, is in the Historical Museum.

Old streets★

Take Stadthausgasse on the left and continue along Schneidergasse. This leads to **Spalenberg**, a steep picturesque street lined with art galleries and antique shops. Turn left into **Gemsberg** to a charming square lined with 13C and 14C houses and a flower-decked Chamois fountain. Turn into Untere Heuberg, a side street with attractive houses, then right into **Heuberg** where you see 13C and 14C residences; numbers 24, 20 and 6 have retained the pulley systems once used to lift objects to the attic.

Spalentor

This fine monumental gate was built in 1398 and restored at the end of the 19C. The summit of the west façade is adorned with Basel's coat of arms.

▷ *Go through the Botanical Gardens to the Petersplatz, shaded by trees and bordered by the University.*

St Peter's Church

◷*Open Tue–Sun, 9am–5pm.*
Guided tours available; for further details, contact the Tourist Office on ☏(0)61 268 68 68 or the presbytery on ☏(0)61 261 87 24.
A Late Gothic church, Peterskirche was built in pink sandstone. In the south

aisle and in the chapel to the left of the chancel 14C–15C frescoes can be seen. On the left of the east end of the church, take **Petersgasse**, graced with medieval charm.

▷ *Walk away from the church down the stairs to the Spiegelgasse, which leads to Mittlere Rheinbrücke (Middle Rhine Bridge). This bridge joins the left bank to the Little Basel on the right bank of the Rhine.*

KLEIN BASEL (LITTLE BASEL)

At the end of the bridge on the right, stands the famous Café Spitz. This was where in 1833 the guild of the three main Kleinbasel fraternities (symbolised by the wild, the lion and the griffin) was founded. The terrace of this famous seafood restaurant offers spectacular views over the Rhine.

▷ *Descend a few steps to the right.*

Oberer Rheinweg

This esplanade set along the Rhine affords a panoramic **view★** of the area, especially from the **Wettsteinbrücke**. Narrow alleyways link the esplanade to Rheingasse, which leads to the church of **St Theodore,** where you find some fine late-4C stained-glass windows and a bell tower dating from 1277.

▷ *With the old church on your right, cross the Wettsteinbrücke.*

ST ALBAN TAL

The St Alban district was named after the oldest convent in town, founded by the Bishop of Basel in 1083. Now all that remains is a wing of the Romanesque cloisters, visible from the old graveyard of St Alban's Church (Gothic chancel and tower, 19C nave).
It was in this residence that the painter **Arnold Böcklin** spent his childhood days. The traditional paper industry, dating back to the creation of a canal by monks in the 12C, is evidenced by a number of mills; there is a view over the canal and several mills at the beginning of the street, St Alban-Tal.

Mühlegraben

Next to the Museum of Paper, this wooden walkway, which has been renovated, is one of the remains of walls of Basel, built in the 14C. The medieval fortifications of the city were destroyed, mostly after 1860, a period of population growth due to the industrialisation of the 19C.

◉ *Follow the canal after the Paper Museum.*

St Alban-Berg

Cross the canal, from where you see the foundations of the town's former fortifications; continue along the path up St Alban hill. At the top, St Alban gateway and its portcullis (St Alban-Tor) built in the 13C, are surrounded by a pretty garden.

OUTSIDE THE OLD TOWN
Zoologischer Garten★★★

🕐*Open 8am–5.30pm; extended hours Mar–Oct.* ✎*18CHF (7CHF ages 6–16).* ♿ ℘*(0)61 295 35 35. www.zoobasel.ch.*
This **zoological garden** was founded in 1874 and, with Bern, is one of the largest in Switzerland (13ha/32 acres). It includes more than 6 000 animals from each of the five continents. The zoo specialises in the reproduction and rearing of endangered species such as rhinoceroses, gorillas and spectacled bears. Its park, with ponds where swans, ducks, flamingoes and other exotic birds splash about, is equipped with restaurants, picnic spots, and children's play areas.
The children's zoo has young or newborn animals which children can pet, and ponies or elephants on which they can ride. Several buildings are entirely devoted to one species, such as the Monkey Pavilion, the Aviary, the Elephant House, and the Wild Animal House.
The **vivarium** houses 250 varieties of fish (sea and freshwater), 250 reptile species, and 40 amphibian species, some of which are exceedingly rare. Before leaving, don't miss the zoo's star attractions, the several dozen or so penguins and king penguins.

St Antonius Kirche

Lovers of contemporary architecture will admire the church made out of reinforced concrete, which was erected in 1925–1931, according to the plans of the architect Werner Moser. The nave is set as a system of barrel-vaulted chambers and the aisles are covered with coffered ceilings, while the stained-glass windows of Hans Stocker and Otto Staiger illuminate the immense interior.

Hafen (Port)
Via Klybeckstrasse.
Since the Middle Ages, the town has played a part in trade between the North Sea and the Mediterranean, Swabia and Burgundy. River navigation ceased following the building of the great Alpine roads and railway lines and it was not until 1906 that traffic resumed as far as Antwerp and Rotterdam.
The city's main docks extend downstream as far as Kleinhüningen, where an obelisk in the shape of an unfolding needle—the **Dreiländereck** memorial—and a viewing platform mark the junction of the French, German, and Swiss frontiers.
The ports of Basel Town and Basel District (Basel-Stadt and Basel-Land) are equipped to handle the larger motor vessels and barges. Coal, hydrocarbons, grain, metallurgical products, and industrial raw materials make up most of this traffic, which is mainly concerned with imported goods.

Boat trips
Tours of the harbour passing through the locks, May–Oct. Contact Basler Personenschiffahrts-Gesellschaft AG, Hochbergstrasse 160, Postfach 4019. ℘(0)61 639 95 00/08. www.bpg.ch.
In summer, there are tours of the port along the Rhine and the Kembs Canal. ♿*For details of embarkation points see the town plan.*

GROSSBASEL MUSEUMS
Art Museum★★★
🕐*Open Tue–Sun 10am–5pm .* ✎*12CHF.* ♿ ℘*(0)61 206 62 62. www.kunstmuseumbasel.ch.*

PRACTICAL INFORMATION

MUSEUMS

The **BaselCard**, valid for one, two or three days allows tourists free entry to 25 museums, free ferry rides, city tours, and entry to shows and other cultural events. See *www.basel.com* for prices.

The **Oberrheinischer Museums-Pass** allows free entry to the museums in Basel and the surrounding area for one year and can be purchased at the Tourist Office or participating museums.

In this sprawling Kunstmuseum, which has a large collection of masterpieces, particular emphasis is laid on 15C–17C paintings and drawings from the Upper Rhine and the Netherlands. The museum boasts the world's largest collection of works by the Holbein family. Donated to the city in 1661, they served as a starting-point for the creation of the museum.

Entrance courtyard, gallery, ground floor – Here stand sculptures by Rodin (*The Burghers of Calais*), Alexander Calder (*Die Grosse Spinne*) and Edouardo Chillida, and an extensive collection of works by **Arnold Böcklin**, a Basel native who produced many symbolic and mythological paintings.

The **First floor** covers 15C–17C art in the Upper Rhine, including a series of altarpiece panels, *The Mirror of the Holy Salvation*, by the Basel master **Konrad Witz** (c. 1440–45). The Alsatian painter Martin Schongauer (c.1430–91), drawing on the experience of Witz and his followers, depicts moving family scenes, notably in *Mary and Child in Their Room*. Next is Grünewald (1460–1528) and his *Christ on the Cross*, and his contemporary from Strasbourg, **Hans Baldung Grien** with his *Death and the Maiden* (1517).

Hans Holbein the Younger (1497–1543), one of the greatest painters of all time, marked the peak of the Renaissance. Among some 20 paintings are the admirable *Portrait of the Artist's Wife*

with her Children and *Portrait of Erasmus as an Old Man* with his shrewd gaze. Lucas Cranach the Elder (1472–1553) is present with *Virgin with Child Holding a Piece of Bread* and *Judgement of Paris*. Other rooms contain 17C Dutch paintings, including an outstanding work by the young Rembrandt (1606–69), *David before Saul*.

Portrait of Bonifacius Amerbach (1519) by Hans Holbein the Younger

Kunstmuseum Basel

Another section contains artists such as Rubens, Goltzius, Ruysdael, Brouwer, and Stoskopff, and by masters of Romanticism (Delacroix, Géricault, Daumier) and Realism (Courbet, Manet). These rooms also display a fine collection of Impressionist and Post-Impressionist art, with works by Monet (*Snow Scenes*), Pissarro (*The Harvesters*) and Sisley (*The Banks of the Loing at Moret*); *The Racetrack* by Degas; *Young Girl Lying in the Grass* by Renoir; *Montagne Sainte-Victoire* by Cézanne; landscapes and portraits by Van Gogh; and several works by Gauguin, including *Nafea Faa ipoipo* ("*When Will You Marry?*"), an important painting dating from his Tahitian period, and major works by Caspar Wolf and Johann Heinrich Füssli. The Nazarene movement is represented with pictures by Josef Anton Koch and Johann Friedrich Overbeck.

Second floor – A painting by Georg Baselitz (*Animals*) in the foyer marks the beginning of the remarkable 20C collection. Cubism is particularly well represented with canvases by Braque (*Landscape, Pitcher and Violin*), Picasso (*Bread Loaves and Fruit Bowl on Table*),

Juan Gris (*The Violin*), and Fernand Léger (*The Woman in Blue*). Fauvism can be admired in compositions by Matisse. German Expressionism is present with Franz Marc (*Tierschicksale*), Emil Nolde (*Vorabend: Marschlandschaft*), Oskar Kokoschka (*Die Windsbraut*) and Lovis Corinth (*Ecce Homo*); Surrealism with Giorgio de Chirico, Dalí, Miró, Max Ernst and Yves Tanguy. Some rooms contain Abstract art by Arp, Mondrian (*Composition in Blue, Yellow and White*), Van Doesburg (*Composition in Black and White*), Vantongerloo (*Enigmatic L2 = S*), Kandinsky and Schwitters, and works of Henri Rousseau, Chagall, and Paul Klee. The museum also pays tribute to American art after the year 1945.

Abstract Expressionism, also known as the New York School, is represented with works by Franz Kline *(Andes)* and Clyfford Still *(Painting)*; Colour Field by Barnett Newman *(Day Before One, White Fire II)* and Mark Rothko *(No 1)*; Minimal Art heralded by Frank Stella. Body Art saw a flourishing era with Sam Francis *(Deep Orange and Black)*, Cy Twombly *(Nini's Painting)* and Bruce Nauman. Pop Art is represented with pieces by Jasper Johns, Andy Warhol and Claes Oldenburg.

Museum of Cultures★★

◷Open Tue–Sun, 10am–5pm. ◷Closed 1 Jan, 1 Aug, 24, 25 and 31 Dec. ◉7CHF. ℘(0)61 266 56 00. www.mkb.ch. ⌂Between 27 August 2010 – 15 May 2011 only the special show "Inbetween" is open to the public.

The **Museum der Kulturen** houses the largest collection of its kind in Switzerland, with around 140 000 masks, arms, carvings, along with Oceanian and Pre-Columbian works of art. Of particular note is the Melanesian section (ground floor): a Papuan temple hut, masks, totem poles, etc. Other galleries display objects from Ancient Egypt, such as mummies and sarcophagi. Another section is devoted to European and Swiss customs and traditions, including popular religious art, rural life, and the carnival.

There are also extensive **collections devoted to natural sciences** as well as a prehistory section. Exhibits include information on animals from the region, exotic species and dinosaurs, as well as live animals.

Contemporary Art Museum

◷Open Tue–Sun, 11am–5pm. ◉12CHF. ♿℘(0)61 206 62 62.

A modern, bright building next to a 19C factory provides a pleasant setting for the **Museum für Gegenwartskunst**, part of the Fine Art Museum. It houses temporary exhibitions on prominent contemporary art movements since 1960: Minimal Art, Conceptual Art, Arte Povera and Free Figurative Art, and permanent works by such artists as Frank Stella, Bruce Nauman, Cindy Sherman and Joseph Beuys.

Antikenmuseum Basel und Sammlung Ludwig★★

◷Open Tue–Sun, 10am–5pm. ◷Closed 1 Jan, 1, 9 May, and 24, 25 Dec. ◉5 CHF. ♿℘(0)61 201 12 12. www.antiken museumbasel.ch.

This is the only museum in Switzerland dedicated exclusively to the Ancient art of the Mediterranean. Its exhibits cover five millennia, from 4000 BC to the 7C AD, and include artefacts from Greece, Rome, Egypt and other civilisations in the Middle and Near East.

The Middle East, Cyprus and beginnings of Ancient Greece★★
(Basement)

Some 350 works illustrate the close ties between the island of Cyprus and the civilisations of the Near and Middle East (Iran, Mesopotamia, Syria, Urartu and Anatolia) with the Aegean.

Noteworthy are Syrian cups decorated with lions (8C BC), bronze caldrons from Urartu adorned with a bull's head, and votive statuettes from Cyprus, whose style is influenced by many countries, including Anatolia and Egypt (7C BC). The civilisations of the Near and Middle East also influenced Greek art, as shown by the containers with animal motifs (c.600 BC).

Ancient Egypt★★
(Basement)

This is the most important collection of Egyptian artefacts in Switzerland. The section is arranged in chronological order, with more than 600 exhibits on display. The Predynastic Period is represented by a simple but skillfully sculpted brown ceramic hippopotamus (c.3500 BC). A remarkable head in red jasper and a rare faïence statue of Ramses II with a falcon's head date from the Ramesside Era (c.1250 BC). An almost complete version of a Book of the Dead dating from the Ptolemaic Period (305–30 BC) is on one of the walls. The basement features works from **Roman and Hellenic times**: clay statuettes, small bronzes, funerary stelae from Phrygia, a scene representing Achilles and Penthesilea, and Roman tombs, including a fine marble sarcophagus.

Archaic and Classical eras
(Ground, first and second floors).

Exhibits include marble sculptures and bronze statuettes (600–300 BC). Note the funerary stela (480 BC), locally known as the "relief of the Basel doctor." A superb collection of vases (520–350 BC) includes works by an artist known as the "Berlin painter," as well as a huge amphora complete with lid, bearing the twin figures of Athena and Hercules, plus exhibits of jewellery and coins (from Sicily and southern Italy).

Historisches Museum Basel: Barfüsserkirche★ (M1)

🕐Open Tue–Sun 10am–5pm. 🕐Closed 1 Jan, Good Fri, 1 May, Ascension, 24 and 31 Dec. ⊞7CHF (-13 years, free) no charge one Sun a month. ℘(0)61 205 86 00. www.hmb.ch.

This original Franciscan church belonged to the mendicant monks of the Order (barfüsser means barefoot) who occupied this old triple-aisle church (1231) until the Reformation in 1529. Near the steps leading downstairs stands a 17C painted bronze head of the Lällenkönig (King Lälli) whose significance is still debated and which used to adorn the old Rhine gate.

Downstairs, exhibits retrace the town's history since the days of the Celts, with a strong emphasis on the 13C, when Basel became a truly independent city. Besides this historical exhibition, reconstructed rooms present some fine period furniture. Also in the basement are precious, non-religious objects (such as Erasmus' beaker, 1531, and a provost's crown, 1671) and the cathedral treasury (with a bust-reliquary of St Ursula in partly gilded repoussé silver and copper, 14C; monstrance of the Innocents or the Apostles in gilded silver, 1335–40).

In the chancel, note the large altarpiece with panels from the Church of Santa Maria in Calanca (Graubünden). This polychrome retable made in Ivo Strigel's workshop was carved out of limewood. The rood screen corridor is decorated with fragments of Konrad Witz's Dance of Death (15C), a famous fresco painted in the days of the Council of Basel. The north side aisle is devoted to the Basel Corporations.

During the 18C, they played a major role in the city's political, administrative, religious, social and economic life. The south aisle presents objects from the Upper Rhine region: tapestries woven in Basel workshops, sculpted or painted wooden chests with romantic motifs, bowls, and faience work for the ornamentation of stoves. In the nave, note the magistrates' stalls from Basel Cathedral (solid oak, 16C) and the 16C Holbein Fountain in painted sandstone, known as the Bagpiper's Fountain.

Music Museum

🕐Open Wed–Sat 2pm–6pm, Sun 11am–5pm. 🕐Closed most public holidays. ⊞10CHF. ℘(0)61 205 86 00.

The Musikmuseum, the largest of its kind in Switzerland, is part of the Historisches Museum. Its collection of 650 musical instruments is displayed in the Lohnhof, an old monastery, part of which dates from the 11C. The building, for a long time used as a prison, was restored in 2000. The "Music in Basel" section presents musical instruments in their social context, with rooms dedicated to themes such as public concerts.

Another section, "Concerto, Chorale and Dance," displays instruments played in different musical genres, including chamber music and religious music. "Parade, Celebration and Signals" exhibits instruments played during particular events, such as hunts or at royal courts. Visitors can listen to 200 extracts of music selected via an interactive display, which also provides information in a number of languages.

▲▲ Karikatur & Cartoon Museum

🕐 Open Wed–Sat 2pm–5pm, Sun and public holidays, 10am–5pm. 🕐 Closed during Carnival. 🎫 9CHF (-10 years, free). 📞 (0)61 226 33 60. www.cartoon museum.ch.

Set up in a superbly renovated old house, the Museum of Caricature and Cartoons stands out because of its highly original and refreshing approach. Adults and children will enjoy leafing through original albums, drawn by some of the leading names in this field: Tomi Ungerer, EK Waechter, Claire Bretécher, etc. Children can even try their hand at drawing in a special room set aside for this purpose.

Basel Paper Museum★★

🕐 Open Tue–Sun 2pm–5pm. 🕐 Closed 1 Jan, Carnival, Good Fri, Easter Sun and Whitsun, Ascension, 1 May, 1 Aug, 24 and 25 Dec. 🎫 12CHF. 📞 (0)61 272 96 52. www.papiermuseum.ch.

In 1980, this former flour mill attached to Klingental Convent, later converted into a paper mill (1453), was turned into a museum devoted to the many aspects of the paper industry. It provides a lively presentation of the history of paper and paper-related activities, laid out on four levels. As in former times, the mill is still operated by its paddle wheel. Each floor is devoted to a particular theme.

Visitors can take part in the demonstrations and keep the objects they have made to remind them of their visit. They can choose between papermaking, fonts, typography and binding.

Museum of Pharmacy

Totengässlein 3. 🕐 Tue–Fri 10am–6pm; Sat 5pm. 🕐 Closed Sun, Mon, public holidays. 🎫 5CHF (-12 years, free). 📞 (0)61 264 91 11. www.pharmazie museum.ch.

Endowed with one of the richest collections on the history of pharmacy, the museum houses ancient instruments and drugs used in the past. A chemistry lab and a pharmacy with woodwork from the 18C and 19C has been restored. Note the curious Japanese medicine chest of the 18C, a sort of wooden box fitted with small drawers, and the exhibition on African and its remedies.

Schweizerisches Architekturmuseum

Steinberger 7. 🕐 Mon–Wed 11am–6pm, Thu 11am–8.30pm, Sat/Sun 11am–5pm (hours change during public holidays). 🕐 Closed during Carnival. 🎫 10 CHF (-12 years, free). 📞 (0)61 261 14 13. www.sam-basel.org.

The museum hosts temporary exhibitions of Swiss and international modern architecture. The emphasis is on Swiss architects (Le Corbusier, Baur, Bernoulli, Meyer, Wittwer), whose contribution to modern architecture was fundamental. It also offers guided tours of key monuments of the city (4hrs, in German, English, Italian and French). Individual tours available on request.

Jewish Museum

Kornhausgasse 8. 🕐 Open Mon and Wed 1pm–5pm, Sun 11am–5pm. 🎫 No charge. 📞 (0)61 261 95 14. www.juedisches-museum.ch.

The Jüdisches Museum der Schweiz is the only Jewish Museum in Switzerland. At the encouragement of Theodor Herzl, Jews from throughout Europe and America gathered in Basel to attend the first Zionist Congress, held in the Casino concert hall in August 1897. This momentous event marked a turning point in the long history of the Jewish community of Basel (the earliest Jewish settlements date back to the 12C and Hebrew books were printed here as early as the 16C). Exhibits include

Jewish law, the Jewish year and Jewish life. Artefacts from Jewish communities around the world include tombstones from the Middle Ages, Persian amulets studded with precious stones and sumptuous 19C silver menorahs from Vienna, plus embroidered prayer shawls, inscribed and painted Torah scrolls (*Book of Law*), and passports from World War II with the telltale "J" stamped on them.

Kirschgarten Museum

Open Tue–Sun, 10am–5pm, Sat 1pm –5pm. Closed most public holidays. 7CHF, no charge first Sun in the month. (0)61 205 86 00.
The museum is housed in a beautiful 18C town house owned by the silk ribbon manufacturer JR Burckhardt. There is a fine collection of clocks, balance-cocks and watches from the 16C to the 19C, porcelain stoves and a large collection of porcelain figurines on the ground floor. Upstairs are drawing rooms adorned with Aubusson tapestries, pictures and French furniture; boudoirs and 18C and 19C costumes. The third floor offers a collection of antique toys: dolls' houses, miniature carriages, rocking horses, boats and vintage cars. The basement contains porcelain and ceramics from Switzerland, Germany, France and China; and carved casks, one of which dates from 1723 and holds 10 000l/2 200gal.

Skulpturhalle

Mittlere Strasse 17. Open Mon–Fri 10am–5pm, Sat–Sun 11am–5pm. Closed first Sun of every month 5 CHF (children 3 CHF). (061) 261 52 45 www.skulpturhalle.ch.
Part of the Museum of Ancient Art, it exhibits many Greek and Roman sculptures—including a large collection of sculptures from the Parthenon.

Puppenhausmuseum (M3)

Steinenvorstadt 1. Open daily 10am– 6pm. Closed 25 Dec and Carnival. 7 CHF (-16 years, free). (0)61 225 95 95. www.puppenhausmuseum.ch.
The largest doll museum in Europe on four floors with over 6 000 teddy bears (the largest collection in the world)

and dolls in their original doll houses, assembled by a collector, Ms. Oeri. As for teddy bears, there are yellow, green, blue, mechanical, musical—you name it, there's a bear in that style. The oldest teddy is displayed on the 4th floor and dates from 1904.

Schaulager★★

Ruchfeldstrasse 19 Münchenstein. Open Tue, Wed and Fri midday–6pm, Thu midday–7pm, Sat–Sun 10am–5pm. Closed Oct–May. Tours Thu 11am, Sun 5.30pm. 14 CHF (children, students 8CHF). (0)61 335 32 32. www.schaulager.org.
This huge cube lost in the suburbs of Basel certainly deserves a visit, if only for its futuristic architecture, by Herzog & de Meuron. Neither museum nor warehouse, the Schaulager houses works by the Emmanuel Hoffmann Foundation. It opens its doors only to temporary exhibitions, so it is advisable to inquire before going there. Avant-garde installations are seen at their best in the vast halls of the immaculate ground floor and basement, while the upper floors, lit by neon in a dizzying effect of symmetry, remain closed to the public. End your visit to the library and bar, which seem straight out of Moloko Bar in *A Clockwork Orange*.

Museum Jean Tinguely

Paul Sacher-Anlage 2. At the SBB train station, take tram number 2 to Wettsteinplatz, then bus number 31 in the direction of Habermatten/Hörnli and get off at the Museum Tinguely stop. Open Tue–Sun, 11am–7pm. Closed 1 Jan, Good Fri and 25 Dec. 15CHF. (0)61 681 93 20. www.tinguely.ch.
The renowned Ticino architect Mario Botta designed this museum, located along the banks of the Rhine in Solitude Park, which features a long glassed-in ramp adjoining a construction in pink sandstone. The museum pays tribute to the great metal sculptor **Jean Tinguely**, a dominant post-war artist who conceived the famous "strange machines" (*see FRIBOURG*). Each gal-

lery is devoted to a specific period in the sculptor's life. The 1950s are represented by reliefs driven by engines (*Méta-Mécanique, 1955*). In the 1960s, Tinguely created objects from scrap metal, followed by machine-sculptures painted black. The 1980s are marked by large compositions such as *Lola T 180—Memorial to Joachim B*. The machines can be operated by visitors however they choose. The upper floor displays letters and drawings as well as other sculptures like *Lotus and the Widows of Eva Aeppli*, *Hannibal II*, an impressive work reflecting Tinguely's obsession with death, and an unusual collection of philosophers' busts: *Friedrich Engels, Jean-Jacques Rousseau, Martin Heidegger,* and *Henri Bergson*. The tour finishes where the most striking item in the huge room is unquestionably *Grosse Méta Maxi-Maxi Utopia* (1987), of which the artist himself said: "I would like to make something gay, something for children, who can climb and jump; I would like it to turn into something good, impressive, merry, wild, something suggesting a funfair."

RIEHEN

Although a separate administrative division, Riehen is a suburb of the city.

▷ *Access by car via Wettsteinbrücke and Riehenstrasse. To avoid traffic and parking problems, visitors are advised to take tram number 6 from Marktplatz.*

Fondation Beyeler★★★

Tram no 6, Fondation Beyeler stop. ⊙Open daily, 10am–6pm, Wed until 8pm. ⊙Closed 24, 25 Dec. ⊛23CHF; reduced admission fees every Mon (except holidays). ⌣Guided tours available on request, contact ℘(0)61 645 97 00. www.beyeler.com.

For half a century, Basel art enthusiasts **Hildy and Ernst Beyeler** collected paintings and sculptures from celebrated 20C artists; they commissioned Italian architect **Renzo Piano** and Richard Rogers to design a museum to display this collection. This simple building (2 700sq m/29 052sq ft) was constructed in 1997; three large bays open onto the

lovely Berower Park, where a sculpture by Calder (*The Tree*, 1966) can be admired. A water garden evokes *Pond with Waterlilies* by Monet, a 9m/29ft triptych on display in the museum. A long glass roof supported by red porphyry walls provides excellent lighting.

Around 200 paintings and sculptures trace the development of modern art from Impressionism to Cubism. Famous works include *Seven Bathers* by Cézanne, *Wheatfield with Cornflower* by Vincent van Gogh, *Rouen Cathedral* by Monet, *Woman Reading* by Braque, *Hungry Lion Attacking Antelope* by Douanier Rousseau, *Woman in Green* by Picasso, and *Interior with Black Fern* by Matisse. Abstract Art is represented here by *Fugue* by Kandinsky, and *Painting no 1* by Mondrian.

Tribute is paid to Switzerland in the works of Klee (*Diana, Ein Tor*) and Alberto Giacometti (*Seated Woman, Caroline, The Street*). Post-war Abstract Art is represented by works of Mark Rothko, Robert Rauschenberg (*Windward*) and Roy Lichtenstein (*Girl with Tear III*). One room is devoted to British artist Francis Bacon (1909–92), whose compositions are characterised by distorted perspective and hallucinatory themes (*Portrait of George Dyer Riding a Bicycle*). Paintings by Jean Dubuffet, Georg Baselitz, and Anselm Kiefer are also on display. Tribal art from Alaska, Oceania and Africa are interspersed with the paintings and sculptures.

Spielzeugmuseum★

Access by tram number 6, Riehen Dorf stop. ⊙Open Mon, Wed–Sun 11am–5pm, Sun 10am–5pm. ⊙Closed 1 Jan, Good Fri, 1 May, 1 Aug, 24–26 and 31 Dec. ⊛7CHF. ℘(0)61 641 28 29.

The **Toy Museum** occupies a large section of Wettsteinhaus, a magnificently restored former mansion which belonged to Johan Rudolf Wettstein, mayor of Basel (1645–1666). The collections include an astounding variety of toys and games. Exhibits illustrate the evolution of toy making and reflect the changes in trends and fashions throughout history. The mansion also houses

Events in Basel

The annual **International Art Fair** (*Art Internationale Kunstmesse*), the largest festival of its kind in the world, attracts collectors, brokers and art-gallery owners in June. The **Autumn Fair** has been held in the city since 1471: fairground rides and a big wheel are set up on several squares in the city, including the Barfüsserplatz, Kaserne and Mustermesse.

the **Dorfmuseum**, devoted to daily life in Riehen, and the **Rebbaumuseum**, which explains winemaking techniques and the art of winemaking.

EXCURSIONS
Vitra Design Museum★★
In Weil am Rhein, Germany.
▶ *Take bus number 55 from Claraplatz or Badischer Bahnhof in Basel to Vitra. By car, follow the Riehenstrasse and the Riehenring toward Freiburg.* ◷*Open Mon–Sun 10am–6pm, Wed until 8pm.* ⊜*8CHF.* 🅿 *(free of charge).* ◖◗*2hr guided architectural tours daily 11am. 1pm, 3pm.* ℘*+49 (0)7621 702 32 00. www.design-museum.de.*

This startling white **building**★ at the Vitra Campus is the work of Californian architect Frank Gehry, the first example of his "deconstructivist" style in Europe. The museum has a vast permanent collection of modern furniture design and hosts temporary exhibitions.
The VitraHaus (Herzog & de Meuron) opened in 2010 to showcase a variety of furniture products in different contexts, which you can purchase or order here.

AUGUSTA RAURICA★★
District of Basel. ▶ *11km/6.8mi SE of Basel.* ℘*(0)61 816 22 22. www.augusta-raurica.ch.* ◖◗*Guided tour (30min–1hr depending on the route). The ruins are signposted in French and German. A series of plans explains how buildings were laid out originally.* ◷*Open Mar–Oct, daily 10am–5pm; Nov–Feb,10am–4.30pm.* ⊜*No charge.* ℘*(0)61 816 22 22. www.baselland.ch.*

It is to the Roman general Munatius Plancus, a friend of Julius Caesar, that Switzerland owes the existence of the "Colonia Raurica" ruins, the oldest Roman settlement situated alongside the Rhine, founded in 44–43 BC. It is believed that the actual colonization of the Augst site dates back to the year 10 BC.

An important ancient city – By the year AD 200, Augst had grown to a city of 20 000 people and had become a prosperous centre for both trade and craft. Owing to its privileged location on the northern border of the Roman Empire, artistic activity thrived, as shown by the many imposing public buildings. Towards the end of the 3C, characterised by severe political unrest, most of the city was destroyed when the Alemanni assaulted the defensive system, or *limes*. In order to keep control over this strategic passage of the Rhine, the army built the powerful Kaiseraugst stronghold slightly north of Augst soon after the year AD 300. Most of these fortifications remained standing after the fall of the Roman Empire and served to protect the local population during the early Middle Ages.

Excavation work – During the 16C, influenced by the doctrines of the great Basel humanists, the famous jurist **Amerbach** was the first to carry out scientific research, making use of the excavation work formerly conducted by the tradesman Andreas Ryff. In 1839, the Historical and Archaeological Society of Basel commissioned research on the Roman city. From 1878 onwards, this site has been the subject of in-depth investigations.

Ancient ruins – Restored monuments include the **Theatre**, the largest Roman ruin in Switzerland, with a seating capacity of 8 000. Today it is used as a venue for outdoor concerts and live performances. The administrative, political and religious core of the city was the **forum**, consisting of the basilica, the Temple of Jupiter, and the **curia** (display of mosaics in the cellar). Markets and various local festivities were held at the forum. The **sewers** were designed to evacuate the waters from the central baths to the Violental Valley; visitors may enter this huge cylindrical pipe (*diameter 70cm/28in*), with limestone walls and a sandstone paved floor. The amphitheatre was the scene of many games, races and fights between gladiators and wild beasts.

♣♣ Römermuseum★

🕐*Open daily, 10am–5pm, Mon 1pm–5pm.* 🕐*Closed Nov–Feb, noon–5pm, 1 Jan, 24, 25 and 31 Dec.* 🎫*7CHF (children 5CHF).* ♿ 𝒫*(0)61 816 22 22.*
Adjoining the Roman House, the Roman Museum presents some of the 700 000 objects unearthed during the excavations. The **silver hoard**★★ discovered at the foot of the Kaiseraugst fortifications in 1962 features many precious objects, including 68 items of sumptuous tableware: dishes decorated with mythological scenes, tumblers, spoons, candelabra and platters. This treasure also contained three silver ingots which experts traced back to the year AD 350. It is thought that the treasure might have been buried during the Germanic invasion in AD 352–353. There is also a small **animal park** (*Haustierpark*) ♣♣ of old breeds, some threatened by extinction, including wooly-haired pigs, Alpine sheep and small cattle.

Römisches Wohnhaus★

🕐*Same admission times and charges as the Römermuseum.*
This Roman House was a private residence and is considered to be a faithful reconstruction of the type common in Augst under the Roman Empire. The kitchen, dining room, bedroom, bathroom, workshop and shop contain authentic artefacts and utensils found on the site. The floor of the steamroom carries a diagram of an ingenious heating system devised by the Romans in which hot air circulated under the floor and between double walls. The right wall bears a fragment of the famous **Gladiators' mosaic**, thought to be the largest and finest in the Roman city. It

used to adorn the dining-room floor of a patrician villa nearby.

Rheinfelden★

▶ *15km/8.5mi E of Basel on Highway 3. Marktgasse 16.* 𝒫*(0)61 835 52 00. www.tourismus-rheinfelden.ch.*
Rheinfelden is separated from its German namesake by the Rheinbrücke, an arched stone bridge. Founded in 1130 by the Zähringen, the town is thought to be the oldest in the Aargau. It was given to the Habsburgs in 1330 by Duke Ludwig I of Bavaria and remained in their possession until 1802.

This small town is the last stopping-place for **cruises along the Rhine**, and it has an attractive old centre with narrow streets, as well as a shaded riverside park with thermal baths. For a good **view** of the town, cross the bridge to the German side of the river. The discovery of salt deposits in 1844 allowed the town to develop its renowned spa. The old **no. 6 drilling tower** of Riburg saltworks—now a museum—can be seen in the thermal park (*follow signs to the Kurzentrum*).

The main street is **Marktgasse**, which runs from near the customs post by the bridge. Attractive houses with painted façades and attractive signs line the street; starting from the Tourist Office, numbers 36, 16 and 10 are particularly interesting. Also noteworthy are the painted murals in the courtyard of the **town hall** (Rathaus), recognisable by its medieval tower.

The **Fricktaler Museum** (number 12) (🕐*open May–Dec, Tue and Sat–Sun 2pm–5pm;* 🕐*closed Whitsun and the third Sun in Sept (Bettag);* 🎫*no charge;* 𝒫*(0)61 831 14 50; www.fricktaler-museum.ch*) is dedicated to local history and to the Saint Sebastian Brotherhood. This unique organisation has 12 members, one of whom carries a lantern. The members dress in black and wear long coats and tall hats. On 24 and 31 December, the Brotherhood maintains the tradition of singing canticles (short Biblical songs) in front of the town's fountains in memory of the epidemic of 1541 that killed a large percentage of the population.

The nearby **Albrechtsplatz** is adorned with the Banneret Fountain. Johannmittergasse, a little farther up on the left, leads to the StJohann chapel, which once belonged to the Knights of Malta (note the frescoes). A small road to the left of the chapel leads to a terrace overlooking the Rhine.

Marktgasse leads into Kupfergasse, which runs up to the Storchennestturm and a section of the ramparts. Other streets and squares with attractive façades or fountains include Geissgasse, Obertorplatz, Kapuzinergasse, and Bahnhofstrasse. The Gothic-style church on Kirchplatz, **St Martinskirche**, was heavily restored at the end of the 18C, as shown by its Baroque interior.

Bräuerei Feldschlösschen

Guided tours (1hr30min) Mon–Fri 9.15am–noon, 1.45pm–5pm; first Sat of the month 9.30am–noon. Closed public holidays of the Aargau canton. No charge. (0)61 833 42 58.

Switzerland's largest **brewery** is housed in an imposing red and yellow brick building adorned with towers and ramparts. Founded in 1876, it still delivers beer to its nearest customers by horse-drawn cart. Guided tours provide insight into the production of beer; the huge copper stills and Art Deco interior of the **brewing room** are definitely worth a visit. The tour finishes with a tasting of the brewery's six different beers.

St Chrischona Kapelle★

8km/5mi – allow 15min. Leave Basel by the road to Riehen. At the post office at Riehen turn right toward Bettingen.

The road runs through residential suburbs of Basel and Bettingen before climbing to St Chrischona Chapel. From a terrace nearby there is a **panorama**★ from Säntis in the east to the Jura mountain ranges in the west. Basel can be seen nestling in the Rhine plain.

Wasserturm Bruderholz★

3.5km/2mi. Leave Basel to the S. Bear right in Jacobsbergstrasse to Bruderholz.

A water tower stands on the great Esplanade of the Battery, in memory of the redoubts built by the Confederates in 1815 during the last campaign of the Allies against Napoleon I. A stairway (*164 steps*) leads to the top of the tower, which commands a lovely **panorama**★ of Basel, the Birse Valley, the Jura, and the Black Forest.

Muttenz

5km/3mi SE of Basel.

In the town centre stands **Pfarrkirche**, a strange fortified church surrounded by crenellated circular walls; originally Romanesque, it was remodelled in the 15C and 16C. The small single nave, with its carved wooden ceiling, presents some superb fragments (restored) of early Renaissance religious frescoes.

Liestal★

16km/10mi SE of Basel.

This charming locality, on a promontory between the Ergolz Valley and the Orisbach, is the capital of the canton of Basel-Land. Its main street (**Rathausstrasse**) lined with painted 19C houses, leads from the city's medieval gate to its red sandstone town hall, built in 1586 and extended in 1938. The town hall is decorated with Renaissance frescoes which were restored in 1900.

The **Kantonsmuseum Baselland** (*Zeughausplatz; open Tue–Sun, 10am–noon, 2pm–5pm; Sat–Sun, 10am–5pm; closed 1 May and 1 Aug 5; 18CHF; (0)61 925 59 86*) focuses on the natural environment and especially the ribbon-making industry—an important regional activity for over four centuries. The stages of fabrication, ranging from design to the marketing, are illustrated with display cabinets and equipment. On the heights of Schleifenberg, the Aussichtsturm belvedere affords a lovely **view** of the Rhine and, in fine weather, the landscape stretching to the Alps. The surrounding forests offer many pleasant walks. On summer Sundays, a little

steam train (Waldenburger Dampfzug) links Liestal to Waldenburger, located 14km/8.7mi to the south.

 DRIVING TOUR

PASSWANGSTRASSE★

56km/35mi. The harsh Lüssel Valley, along with the welcoming Birse Valley, make up the major part of this itinerary along the Passwing Road. Leave Basel on road 18 in the direction of Münchenstein, then Reinach and Arlesheim.

Arlesheim

The **collegiate church**★ of Arlesheim is one of the most charming examples of Baroque art in Switzerland. Built in 1680 for the episcopal principality of Basel, it was later transformed in the Rococo style (1769–71). It stands in a quiet, shaded little square bordered by the former canons' houses. The church interior, whose harmony is untarnished by any detail, is adorned with stucco discreetly picked out in pink or pale yellow, while the low vaulting bears large, misty compositions in pale colours by Joseph Appiani (1760).

▷ *Drive to Dornach to the S.*

Goetheanum★★

Rüttiweg 45, Dornach. ○Open daily 8am–9.45pm. ≈15CHF (-14 years, free). ☎(0)61 706 42 49. www.goetheanum.org. The seat of the School of Spiritual Science and centre of the worldwide Anthroposophical Society (founded in 1912 by Rudolf Steiner, proponent of "free schooling") is an immense concrete edifice hugging the slopes above Dornach and Arlesheim, made entirely of concrete and without one right angle. Don't miss the incredible boiler house or other buildings on the campus.

▷ *At Dornach church, head towards Hochwald and Seewen.*

Seewen

On the outskirts of this charming village, huddled in a wooded basin at the foot of its white church, stands the **Musikautomaten-Museum** (☛ *guided tours (1hr) Tue–Sun 11am–6pm;* ○*closed 1 Jan, Good Fri and 25 Dec;* ≈10CHF; ☎(0)61 915 98 80). Its galleries house a total of 800 musical mechanisms dating from the 18C to the early 20C and all in perfect working order: mechanical pianos, barrel organs, street organs, music boxes, orchestrions (imitating orchestra instruments) and especially amusing automata designed to resemble a bird, a painter and a magician.

▷ *Join road 18 and follow the signs to Laufen and Zwingen. Between Büsserach and Erschwll are the ruins of Thierstein tower.*

Passwanggipfel★★

Alt. 1 204m/3 950ft. From the N exit of the Passwang Tunnel, 2km/1.2m along a narrow road with sharp gradients (close the gates behind you), plus 45min on foot there and back.
Leaving the car at the Wirtschaft Ober-Passwang café-restaurant, continue the climb on foot. Upon coming out of a wood, after passing through a gate, leave the road and climb, to the right, to the summit. From this point a varied **panorama**★★ extends, to the north, over the last undulations of the Basel Jura, the Plain of Alsace (note the double ribbon of the Rhine and the Kembs Canal, part of the great Alsace Canal) framed between the Vosges and the Black Forest, and to the south, to the Solothurn Jura and part of the Bernese Alps.
Between the pass and Laufen, the Lüssel Valley shrinks to a narrow wooded cleft. Between Erschwill and Büsserach, the ruins of Thierstein, a massive tower flanked by a turret, stand like a sentinel. You come out in the Laufen Basin where the tilled, undulating floor lies spread before the forest ridges of the Blauen. Between **Laufen**, a little town with fortified gates, and Aesch, the **Birstal** continues green in spite of increasing industrialisation. The keep of the Angenstein Burg, a former residence of the bishops of Basel, seems to block the last defile.

ADDRESSES

🏠STAY

Hostel – *St Alban, Kirchrain 10. ✆(0)61 272 05 72. www.youthhostel.ch/basel. Closed Dec 24–Jan 2. 39 rooms (197 beds).* A whiff of the countryside lingers here.

Easy Hotel – *Riehenring 109. ✆900 327 927 (1.50 CHF/min). www.easyhotel.com. 24 rooms.* Minimalist and clean. The less expensive rooms are no bigger than cupboards.

Hotel Stadthof – *Gerbergasse 84. ✆(0)61 261 87 11. www.stadthof.ch. 9 rooms.* On Barfüsserplatz, one of the cheapest hotels in Basel. Tiled and white rooms are monastic but clean. Shared bathroom facilities.

Rochat – *Petersgraben 23. ✆(0)61 261 81 40. www.hotelrochat.ch. 50 rooms.* Dating from 1899, this listed building with a bright red façade is a stone's throw from the town centre. Light, quiet rooms at reasonable prices.

Hotel Brasserie Au Violon – *Im Lohnhof 4. ✆(0)61 269 87 11. www.au-violon.com. 20 rooms. Brasserie open Tue–Sat.* Hard to believe that in 1995 this elegant hotel perched on the heights of the Old City was a prison. For comfort, opt for rooms with views of the Barfüsserplatz and the cathedral.

Hotel Kraft – *Rheingasse 12. ✆(0)61 690 91 30. www.hotelkraft.ch. 45 rooms.* 🅿. A recommended hotel in Kleinbasel. The rooms are spacious, bright and elegant. The restaurant serves Mediterranean cuisine.

Der Teufelhof Basel – *Leonhardsgraben 47-49. ✆(0)61 261 10 10. www.teufelhof.com. 33 rooms.* 🅿. The term "art hotel" could have been coined for this small group housed in four buildings in the old city: two hotels, a restaurant, café, wine cellar and theatre.

Les Trois Rois – *Blumenrain 8. ✆(0)61 260 50 50. Fax (0)61 260 50 60. www.lestroisrois.com. 101 rooms.* With an 1844 decor, the interior recalls "old Europe". The institution has received royalty and celebrities from Napoleon to Picasso. Three restaurants, a brewery and Belle Epoque ballroom.

St Gotthard – *Central-bahnstrasse 13. ✆(0)61 225 13 13. www.gotthard.ch. 104 rooms.* Well-located just opposite the railway station and close to a tram stop. Easy access to the town centre. Delicious buffet breakfast.

🍴EAT

Rosario's – *Spalenberg 53. ✆(0)61 261 03 76. Open Mon–Sat.* Beautiful Art Nouveau décor in this old wine bistro. The Sicilian boss ensures the quality of Italian wines and Mediterranean dishes.

Lily's – *Rebgasse 1. ✆(0)61 683 11 11. www.lilys.ch.* Fans of wok cooking, curry and spicy noodles will delight in this elegant Asian place in Little Basel. Service is unfussy and smiling.

Bodega zum Strauss – *Barfüsserplatz 16. ✆(0)61 261 22 72. Daily except Sunday lunchtime.* Cosy little downtown pub. Delicious, mostly Italian cuisine.

Harmonie – *Petersgraben 71. ✆(0)61 261 07 18. www.harmonie-basel.ch.* This small, friendly restaurant, situated on Spalenberg Hill, is popular with locals. The restaurant serves generous portions of simple cuisine, featuring dishes such as Zürich-style veal, liver with *Rösti* and a giant-sized *im Schlüsseli* salad.

Noohn – *Henric Petri-Strasse 12. ✆(0)61 281 14 14. www.noohn.ch. Daily except Sat lunchtime and Sun.* The Noohn houses a sushi bar, a self-service restaurant (fusion kitchen) and a bar. Something for every taste and budget.

Torstübli – *Riehentorstrasse 27. ✆(0)61 692 01 10. www.torstuebli.ch. Closed Sat–Sun.* Kleinbasel restaurant with good reputation for the quality of its dishes.

Restaurant Kunsthalle – *Steinenberg 7. ✆(0)61 272 42 33.* Conveniently located near the Tinguely Fountain, it houses both a fancy restaurant and a cheaper bistro with old woodwork and frescoes painted in 1878. Good wine list.

St Alban-Stübli – *St Alban-Vorstadt 74. ✆(0)61 272 54 15. www.st-alban-stuebli.ch. Closed 23 Dec–9 Jan, Sun, Sat lunchtime and public holidays.*

This building is tucked away in a quaint, picturesque street. Affordable meals.

🍽🍷🛏 **Zum Goldenen Sternen** – *St Alban-Rheinweg 70. ☎(0)61 272 16 66. Fax (0)61 272 16 67. Closed Sun evening, Mon and 23 Dec–3 Jan.* On the banks of the Rhine, under the chestnut trees, this is the oldest restaurant in Basel, opened in 1412. Fish specialities and seasonal cuisine are served beneath the dining hall's splendid coffered ceiling.

🍽🍷🛏 **Chez Donati** – *St Johanns-Vorstadt 48. ☎(0)61 322 09 19. www.lestroisrois.com. Closed Sun, Mon, and mid-Jul–mid-Aug.* A fashionable restaurant, decorated with lovely Murano glass lamps, serving fine Italian food and wine.

🍽🍷🛏 **Saffron Zunft** – *Gerbergasse 11. ☎(0)61 269 94 94. www.safran-zunft.ch. Closed Sun.* This old guildhall restaurant offers the amazing "Out of South Africa" menu: crusty antelope, medallions of springbok and kudu steaks.

SIGHTSEEING

BOAT TRIPS

The city offers a number of boat trips, including dinner cruises, excursions through the locks between Basel and Rheinfelden, and night trips. Tickets can be purchased from Basel Personenschiffahrt, Schifflände, next to the Tourist Office, ☎(0)61 639 95 00.

THEATRE AND MUSIC

Theater Basel – *Theaterstrasse 7. ☎(0)61 295 11 33. www.theaterbasel. ch.* This theatre has an excellent reputation for opera, theatre, and dance. **Junges Theater Basel** – *Wettsteinallee 40. ☎(0)61 681 27 80. www.jungestheaterbasel.ch.* **Stadtmusik** – *Steinenberg 14. ☎(0)61 225 93 93. www.casinobasel.ch.* **Musical Theater** – *Feldbergstrasse 151. ☎(0)61 699 88 99.*

SHOPS AND MARKETS

Basel's shopping district is centred around the Marktplatz. The Globus department store and smaller shops selling clothes, designer goods, crystal and souvenirs are on the Freie Strasse and Gebergasse, as far as Barfüsserplatz. The Manor department store is on Greifengasse, in the St Alban district.

SOUVENIRS

The local emblem is the Basilisk, a type of dragon with a cockerel's head, which is often depicted on brooches.

MARKETS

General stalls: Barfüsserplatz, Thu, Jan–mid-Oct, 7am–6.30pm.; **Food, flower and organic market:** Marktplatz, daily every afternoon; Mon, Wed, Fri, until 7pm. NB: prices are often based on pounds and not kilos. **Flea market:** Peterplatz, Sat. **Christmas market:** Dec, on Barfüsserplatz and Claraplatz.

PUBLIC BATHING IN THE RHINE

Rheinbad Breite – *St Alban-Rheinweg 195. ☎(0)61 311 25 75.* View of the cathedral.

Rheinbad St Johann – *St Johanns-Rheinweg. ☎(0)61 322 04 42.*

NIGHTLIFE

The bar of the **Drei Könige** (*Kleinhüningeranlage 39; ☎(0)41 61 631 15 10*) is pleasant, especially in summer with its covered terrace overlooking the Rhine. The **Schiesser** tea-rooms (*Marktplatz 19; ☎(0)41 61 261 60 77*) on the nearby Marktplatz have been serving delicious confectionery since 1870. Beyond the right bank of the river lies **Kleinbasel**, a district where nightlife is particularly active. In Clarastrasse, a lively shopping street, there are several popular places including **le Plaza Club** and its theme evenings (karaoke, concerts, shows) and the **Grischuna Bar** in the Hôtel Alexander (concerts every evening).

Near the railway station, you can have a cocktail in a discreet, refined ambience at the bar of the **Hotel Euler** (*Centralbahnplatz 14*). Those who like soft music and piano bars should visit the **Old City Bar** in the Hotel Hilton (*Aeschengraben 31*).

Le Caveau (*Grünpfahlgasse 4, near the post office*) offers a wide range of Swiss, French, Italian, Californian and other wines. In the heart of the old city, the **Atlantis** (*Klosterberg 9*) is reputed for its excellent jazz concerts.

Aarau

The capital of the Aargau canton, Aarau is one of the richest towns in Switzerland, thanks to the textile and machine industries. Formerly the capital of the short-lived Helvetic Republic, it became a separate canton in 1803. The best view of the old town is from the bridge spanning the River Aare.

OLD TOWN

The narrow streets are lined with fine old houses, some adorned with oriel windows and wrought-iron emblems from the long-standing Bernese domination; other façades are covered with frescoes, and roofs have stepped gables and eaves. The **Stadtkirche** (parish church) is surmounted by an elegant late-17C belfry. The fine **Fountain of Justice** (1643) stands in a small adjacent square. Throughout the city, the painted roofs (*Dachhimmel*) date from the 16C.

EXCURSIONS
Schönenwerd★
▶ *4.5km/2.8mi SW towards Olten.*
Away from the old town, dominated by a collegiate church dating from the 12C, a modern area has developed, which owes its existence to the Bally shoe brand.
The **Bally Schuhmuseum**★★ (Bally Shoe Museum) *(Felsgarten House, Oltnerstrasse 6; ⌕guided tours; ⏰open Jan–mid-Jul and mid-Aug–mid-Dec; ⌕no charge; ℘(0)62 858 61 00)* traces the history of footwear throughout the centuries and across cultures.

Schloss Hallwyl★
▶ *18km/11mi SE towards Suhr.* ⏰*Apr–Oct.* ⌕*10CHF (children 5CHF).* ℘*(0)62 767 60 10. www.schlosshallwyl.ch.*
An enchanting castle, with round towers and sharp, high crenellated walls expanded from the 11C to 16C (and now restored) built on two islets of a tributary of Lake Hallwil. Its entrance is via a drawbridge and a courtyard from where you walk to the second island to visit the main building, a museum of art and popular traditions. In the tower of

- **Population:** 15 753.
- **Info:** Aarau info Verkehrsbüro, Graben 42, 5001 Aarau. ℘(0)62 824 76 24. www.aarauinfo.ch.
- **Location:** Aarau is 46km/28.5mi west of Zürich. Alt. 383m/1 273ft.
- **Don't Miss:** Lenzburg Castle—housing the History Museum of the canton of Aargau as well as offering a spectacular panoramic view.

the main building of the first island you can examine a first floor apartment with 17C furniture and on the second floor a 19C bourgeois apartment.

Olten
▶ *12 km/7.5mi SW of Aarau on Route 5. Klosterplatz 21, 4600.* ℘*(0)62 212 30 88.*
Olten is situated at the boundary of the Jura, on the banks of the River Aare.
A wooden covered bridge (Alte Brücke), reserved for pedestrians, leads to the old town. However, since the beginning of the last century, the appearance of the town, which continues to spread on both sides of the Aare, has been altered by its great industrial activity: Soap and cement works, food processing, and the workshops of the Federal Railways.
The **Kuntsmuseum** (Fine Arts Museum) *(⏰open Tue–Sun 2pm–5pm, Sat–Sun 11am–5pm; ⏰closed most public holidays and during the summer holidays; ⌕7CHF; ℘(0)62 212 86 76; www.kunstmuseumolten.ch)* possesses a fine collection of 19C and 20C paintings and sculpture, including excellent caricatures, studies and drawings by **Martin Disteli** (1802–44). This talented painter and caricaturist interpreted scenes from Swiss military history and political life, as well as fables.

Zofingen
▶ *16km/10mi; Head S on Route 24 then along Highway 1 until Zofingen exit.*

The old part of the town is contained within the quadrilateral formed by the alleys which have taken the place of its ramparts. The Pulvertum, a square 12C tower, is all that remains of the old fortifications. The Niklaus-Thut-Platz (town square) has numerous 17C and 18C houses. The Church of St Maurice, has a 17C Renaissance bell tower. Two large mosaics from the Roman period (*under shelter*) can be seen as you leave the town from the south.

Schloss Habsburg

17km/10.6mi. From Aarau head NE to route 24 and then route 5 to Habsburg village. Open 9am–midnight Closed Mon–Tue Oct–Apr; Mon May–Sept. *(0)56 41 76 73. www.schlosshabsburg.ch.*

A narrow country lane wends its way to the castle, which has been converted into a **restaurant** (). In former days, it was the cradle of the Habsburg dynasty: Several members of this illustrious family were to influence the course of European history for many centuries. Note the family tree and map illustrating the possessions they acquired. Climb the wooden staircase: The **view** at the top encompasses the surrounding countryside, cut across by the pretty meanderings of the River Aare.

Schloss Wildegg★

11km/6.8mi. From Aarau take Route 5 E. Open mid-Mar–end Oct, Tue–Sun 10am–5pm. Closed Good Fri. 7CHF. *(0)62 893 10 33.*

The impressive mass of Wildegg Castle, looming above the Aare Valley, was built in the 12C by a Habsburg Count and enlarged and altered several times since (particularly by the Effinger family who were the owners for four centuries). The castle contains fine **furniture**★ dating from the 17C–19C. The Blue Room, the Armory and the Library deserve special attention for the beauty of their ceilings and furnishings. From the upper storeys there is a wide view of a gently undulating landscape of fields and forests.

Baden★

The spa and the industrial quarters extend below the old town, built on a promontory overlooking the river, dominated by the ruins of Stein Castle (Ruine Stein). This imposing fortress served as an arsenal and a refuge for the Austrians during their unsuccessful campaigns against the Swiss, which ended in the victories for Swiss independence at Morgarten (1315) and Sempach (1386). In 1415 the Confederates seized the city and burnt it. It was rebuilt in the 17C and destroyed again in 1712 by the people of Bern and Zürich.

▶ **Population:** 17 446.

Info: Bahnhofplatz 1 – 5400. *(0)56 210 91 91.*

Location: Baden lies at the foot of the last spurs of the Jura at a picturesque site on the banks of the Limmat. Alt. 385m/1 273ft.

Timing: Allow an hour or two to wander the town and visit the museum. Allow a full day if you plan to do the excursions as well.

A BIT OF HISTORY

Known in Roman times as Aquae Helveticae and famous for its 19 sulphur hot springs (47°C/116°F), Baden became one of Switzerland's most important spas towards the end of the Middle Ages. Famous personalities who have taken the waters here include the writers Goethe, Thomas Mann and Hermann Hesse, and the conductor Karl Böhm. Today, Baden is also a centre of electro-mechanical engineering.

SIGHTS
Old town★

From the modern road bridge (Hochbrücke) there is a fine **view**★ of the old town. Its houses, with their stepped gables and fine brown roofs, pierced by many dormer windows, come down to the Limmat, which is crossed by an old covered wooden bridge (Holzbrücke). The parish church (Stadtkirche) and the city tower (Stadtturm), with a belfry and corner turrets with glazed tiles, dominate the whole scene.

Historiches Museum Baden★

ⓒOpen Tue–Sun, 1pm–5pm, Sat–Sun, 10am–5pm. ⏾7CHF. ℘(0)56 222 75 74. www.museum.baden.ch.

The museum stands near the covered bridge (Holzbrücke) on the right bank of the Limmat. It occupies the central tower of a 15C castle and, since 1992, a modern extension building by Basel architects pair Wilfrid and Katharina Steib as well. The permanent exhibition in the extension is on the industrial history of the city and that of the baths (from 1790–1960), illustrated by an inventive and elegant set design. It also hosts temporary exhibitions. The bay window offers a fine view of the covered bridge and old town with its gables and sawtooth roofs with dormer windows. The tower contains a collection of conventional weapons, antique furniture, paintings and sculptures, pottery, bronzes and coins of Roman origin found in the area and costumes of the Canton of Aargau. A 1930s interior has been restored on the top floor.

Baden in winter

Christof Sonderegger/Switzerland Tourism

Stiftung Langmatt Sidney und Jenny Brown★

Römerstrasse 30. Temporary exhibitions on the first floor. ⓒOpen Apr–Oct, Tue–Sun 2pm–5pm, Sat–Sun 11am–5pm. ⏾10CHF. ℘(0)56 222 58 42. www.langmatt.ch.

The house formerly belonging to the industrialist **Sidney Brown**, whose name is perpetuated by the company ABB (Asea Brown Boveri), contains mostly Impressionist paintings, including two series by Renoir and Cézanne. There are also superb canvases by other famous artists: Study of a Nude by Degas, Return of the Fishing Boats in Trouville by E Boudin, Chestnut Trees in Louveciennes by Pissarro, The Torments of the Seine by Monet, sketches attributed to Henri Matisse, and noteworthy pictures by Corot, Courbet, Fantin-Latour, Gauguin, Sisley, and Vincent van Gogh. A small salon presents 18C French works (Fragonard, Greuze and Watteau) and landscapes by a native of Zürich, S Gessner.

EXCURSIONS
Old Cistercian Abbey at Wettingen★

▶ 3km/1.8mi S of Baden, between the railway and the Limmat. ⓒThe cloisters can be visited Apr–Oct, Mon–Sat 10am–5pm, Sun noon–5pm. Church: guided tours daily Apr–Oct, 2pm–5pm. ⏾5CHF. ℘(0)56 437 24 10.

This former Cistercian abbey, founded by Count Heinrich von Rapperswil in the 13C, presently houses a school. The Gothic **cloisters** have been glazed and now display a collection of stained glass. The **interior**★ is richly decorated in Baroque style with frescoes, paintings, stucco and marble. Note the splendidly carved 17C **choir stalls**★★.

Brugg

▶ 10km/6 mi W of Baden on Route 3. Founded by the Habsburgs in the early 12C, the "city of the bridges", which stands at the confluence of the River Aare and the River Reuss, Brugg has preserved many of its old buildings. An important industrial town that plays a central role in the country's road and railway network. Among the monuments still standing in the **old city** (*leave your car in one of the car parks (fee) located outside this area*) are the Archive Tower, the Storks' Tower (Storchentum) and the imposing 12C and 16C Black Tower, **Schwarzer Turm**, which overlooks the bridge spanning the Aare. This vantage point affords a good view of its wooded banks and old houses. Note the 16C former town hall and the Late Gothic Protestant church with its 18C interior. On the pretty **Hofstatt**, a paved square embellished with a white fountain, you will find the former 17C arsenal and the old storeroom, dating from the 18C.

Vindonissa-Museum

🕐*Open Tue–Sat 1pm–5pm, Sun 10am–5pm.* ⊛*5CHF.* ℘*(0)56 44121 84. www.ag.ch/vindonissa.*

Housed in the newly renovated museum are the finds from the Roman site of Vindonissa: jewellery, arms, coins, statues, pottery, glasswork, plus articles made from wood and leather. Note the 4C skeleton of a Roman woman in a sarcophagus and the model of the Vindonissa military camp. Outside is a lapidary museum (stelae, votive inscriptions).

Kloster Königsfelden (Abbey of Königsfelden)

▶ *9.2km/5.7mi W of Baden.*

The Franciscan abbey of Königsfelden was founded in 1308 by Queen Elizabeth and the Habsburg family on the spot where King Albrecht I was assassinated by Duke Johann of Swabia. The monastic buildings presently house a psychiatric hospital.

Klosterkirche

By the side of the abbey.

🕐*Open Apr–Oct, Tue–Sun 10am–5pm; Nov–Mar, 1pm–4pm.* 🕐*Closed 1 and 2 Jan, Good Fri–Easter Sun, 24, 25 and 26 Dec.* ⊛*5CHF.* ℘*(0)56 441 88 33.*

A pretty park is the setting for this large Gothic church. The nave, lit by clerestory windows, has a flat wooden ceiling, and the aisles are decorated with painted wooden panels representing portraits of knights and coats of arms. A memorial in the nave recalls that Königsfelden became the burial place of the Habsburgs.

The long **chancel**★ is lit by 11 windows of which the **stained glass**★, made between 1325 and 1330, forms an interesting series. You will recognize the Childhood of Christ, the Passion, scenes from Lives of the Saints and Death of the Virgin. The colours, in which a silvery-yellow predominates, are iridescent.

Vindonissa: Roman Amphitheatre

▶ *At Windisch 1km/0.6mi from Brugg via the Zürich road, then to the right of Königsfelden Church take Hauserstrasse.*

This is the most important find of the Vindonissa site, a military camp which, in the 1C AD, was the Roman headquarters for the whole of Switzerland, on the present-day site of Windisch. The huge oval amphitheatre with its double wall of ashlar stone (average height 2m/6.5ft) sat approximately 10 000 people.

Zurzach

▶ *19km/1.5mi N of Baden on Route 17.*

Near the Rhine on the site of the Roman town, Tenedo, Zurzach is now a spa centre (cures for rheumatic disorders). On its main street are some 17C and 18C monuments and houses and beside the river stands a 19C château.

August Deusser Museum

🕐*Open daily 1pm–6pm.* 🕐*Closed 1 Jan, Easter Thu, Fri and Sat, 24 Dec and in Jan and Jul.* ⊛*6CHF, no charge on preview days.* ℘*(0)56 249 20 50.*

The château houses this museum, which contains the personal collection of the German painter **August Deusser** (1870–1942) as well as his own works of art. On the first floor are furnishings, works of art, an 18C Chinese low relief and a carved gilt bed made for Ludwig II of Bavaria. The second floor presents works bequeathed by Deusser. The park contains trees, pond and many modern sculptures by Johann Ulrich Steiger.

Winterthur★

A town named Vitudurum was established here during the Roman era. At the end of the Middle Ages, Winterthur was the manufacturing centre for large porcelain stoves, which can still be admired in some Swiss houses. The industrial development of the town has not interfered with its artistic reputation: the city boasts several museums with fine collections that show a complete record of 19C European painting. Concerts given by the Collegium Musicum, founded in 1629, always draw a large audience. The city is also a lively centre for comedy and cabaret, has a charming old quarter with street cafés and interesting shops, and graceful parks and gardens.

▶ **Population:** 98 238.
◔ **Michelin Map:** Town plan in The Michelin Red Guide to Switzerland.
🛈 **Info:** In the main railway station. ℘(0)52 267 67 00. www.winterthur-tourismus.ch.
◉ **Location:** Zürich region, northern Switzerland. Alt. 439m/1 440ft.
🅿 **Parking:** There are several public car parks; it is easiest to use one and take public transport.
✆ **Don't Miss:** Villa Flora (art museum) or Schloss Kyburg.
👪 **Kids:** Technorama, the interactive science centre.
🕐 **Timing:** Allow at least half a day to see the starred sights; a full day to see everything.

SIGHTS
Oskar Reinhart Collection

Oskar Reinhart (1885–1965) a merchant who made his fortune in textiles, bequeathed his famous private collection, one of the most important of the 20C, to the Swiss Confederation, provided it remains in his hometown. The collection includes nearly 200 works of European art from Late Gothic to the modern avant-garde, dominated by French painting of the 19C. It is divided into two separate museums.

Museum Oskar Reinhart am Stadtgarten★

Stadthausstrasse 6. ◔*Open Tue–Sun 10am–5pm (8pm Tue).* ◉*8CHF.* ℘*(0)52 267 51 72. www.museum oskarreinhart.ch.*

Works by Swiss, German, and Austrian painters from the 18C, 19C, and 20C are displayed. Excellent drawings by Rudolf Wasmann, portraits of children by Anker, works by Böcklin and Koller, paintings by the German Romantics and by artists of the Munich School as well as animal studies by Jacques Laurent Agasse may be seen. The many canvases by Ferdinand Hodler (1853–1918) show the importance attached to this leader of pre-1914 Swiss painting.

Collection Oskar Reinhart "Am Römerholz"★★★

Haldenstrasse 95. ◔*Open Tue–Sun, 10am–5pm, 8pm Wed.* ◉*Closed 1 Jan, Good Fri, Easter Sun, Whitsun, 1 May and 25 Dec.* ◉*10CHF.* ℘*(0)52 269 27 40. www.roemerholz.ch.*

The artwork bequeathed by Reinhart is presented in this house set in large grounds overlooking the town. Works span five centuries including paintings by Brueghel and El Greco and drawings by Rembrandt, French works from the late 17C to the 19C with Poussin, Claude Lorraine, Watteau, Chardin and Fragonard, and sketches by Daumier.

The 19C is represented by artists whose works reflect the main contemporary trends in pictorial art, such as Corot, Delacroix, Courbet, Manet, Renoir, and Cézanne, as well as Van Gogh and, closer to the present, Picasso, with drawings from his Blue period.

Kunstmuseum★★

🕐Open 10am–8pm Tue, Wed–Sun 10am–5pm. 🕐Closed 1 Jan, Good Fri, Easter Sun, Whitsun, Ascension, 1 May, St Alban's Sunday, 1 Aug and 25 Dec. ⊕15CHF. 𝒫(0)52 267 51 62. www.kmw.ch.

The **Fine Arts Museum** contains works from the 16C (Cranach), 17C and 18C regional art (Graff, Mayer, Füssli), and Swiss and German painters from the 19C and 20C (Hodler, Vallotton, Giacometti, Auberjonois, Corinth, and Hofer). The French Schools are represented by artists such as Renoir, Bonnard, Vuillard, and Van Gogh. Part of the building is devoted to sculpture by Rodin, Maillol, Haller, Marini, and Alberto Giacometti. The museum also houses the town's library and a natural history section.

Villa Flora★

Tösstalstrasse 44. 🕐Open Tue–Sat 2pm–5pm, Sun 11am–3pm. 🕐Closed 1 Jan, Good Friday, Easter, 1 May, Whitsun and 25 Dec. ⊕12.50CHF. 𝒫(0)52 212 99 60. www.villaflora.ch.

The post-Impressionist works accumulated between 1907 and 1930 by Arthur and Hedy Hahnloser-Bühler are interesting in that they were acquired not through art dealers, but through their personal friends and relatives of the artists themselves. Visitors will be impressed by the high quality of the works, and the prophetic nature of the paintings, laid out in the house once occupied by these dedicated art lovers. The largest part of the collection is works by the Nabis—artists born between 1860 and 1870, who chose to rebel against academic conventions, including the Swiss Félix Vallotton (The Barrow), E Vuillard (The Game of Draughts, with its incredible plunging perspective)—and to Pierre Bonnard (The Fauns, combining many different viewpoints). Fauvism—the term was first coined by art critic Louis Vauxcelles during the Salon d'Automne in 1905—is represented by H Manguin, a close friend of the Hahnloser-Bühlers, and by Matisse. Besides the Fauves and the Nabis, of particular note is the rare series

of nine paintings (Andromède) by Odilon Redon, dubbed "the artist of the Irrational", of which Hedy Hahnloser-Bühler had already said in 1919: "All the main components characteristic of contemporary artistic inspiration are already present in his work". Finally, note the outstanding Portrait of the Artist by Paul Cézanne, The Sower and Night Café by Vincent van Gogh, and many sculptures (bronzes by Bonnard, C Despiau, A Maillol, Henri Matisse, M Marini, PA Renoir, A Rodin, and F Vallotton). The garden (two sculptures by Aristede Maillol) sadly is open only to groups.

🔬 Technorama★★

Technoramastrasse 1. Leave the motorway at the Oberwinterthur exit and then follow directions. You can also take bus number 12 from the main station. 🕐Open Tue–Sun, 10am–5pm. 🕐Closed 25 Dec. ⊕23CHF. 𝒫(0)52 244 08 44. www.technorama.ch.

This attractive and amusing museum is a perfect tool to introduce young people to the world of science and technology. The permanent exhibitions of the Swiss **Science Centre** include physics, trains and toys, energy, water, nature and chaos, mechanical music, materials, textiles, and automatic technology. The purpose of the visit is to operate the various machines and watch demonstrations, of which the most impressive is no doubt that of high-voltage, one of many interactive opportunities. The "laboratory", supervised by a team of trained instructors, enables visitors to acquire scientific knowledge while having fun. The park can be used to experiment with flying machines (🕐open Sat–Sun only).

Fotomuseum Winterthur★★

Grüzenstrasse 44. 🕐Open Tue–Sun 11am–6pm (8pm Wed.). ⊕8CHF. 𝒫(0)52 234 10 60. www.fotomuseum.ch.

The collections comprise 30 000 works of 19C and 20C master photographers, as well as works of contemporary photographers. Part of its collections document cultural history and sociology with applied photography from industry, architecture, fashion, and other areas of life and work, in line with its mission of representing photography both as an art form and as a means of documenting all facets of life in each era. Each year the exhibits change to display different parts of the vast collection.

EXCURSIONS

Schloss Kyburg

▶ *6km/4mi S. Leave Winterthur by the Seen road. At Sennhof take the small road to the right and follow it along the Töss; after 1km/0.6mi turn left to go to Kyburg village.* ○*Open Tue–Sat 10.30am–5.30pm (4.30pm Nov–Mar).* ○*Closed Mon, some public holidays.* ⊙*8CHF.* ℘*(0)52 232 46 64. www.schlosskyburg.ch.*

This feudal castle was built in the 10C and 11C and passed successively from the line of the Counts of Kyburg to that of the Habsburgs. In 1424 it came within the bailiwick of the town of Zürich and remained so until 1798; since 1917 the castle has belonged to the canton. Inside are remarkable collections of furniture and arms that will interest visitors with a knowledge of history and antiques. There is a good view of the surrounding countryside.

Kartause Ittingen★ (Ittingen Charterhouse)

▶ *The old charterhouse is situated in the small village of Warth, about 20min N of Winterthur (toll).* ○*Open Mon–Fri 2pm–5pm, Sat 11am–5pm; Apr–Sept until 6pm.* ℘*(0)52 748 41 41. www.ittingermuseum.tg.ch.*

The Ittingen Charterhouse stands on a hill overlooking the Thur Valley, surrounded by vineyards, it was founded in 1152 as an Augustinian priory dedicated to St Lawrence and became affiliated to the Carthusian Order in 1461. The monastery was almost entirely rebuilt between the 16C and 18C. A foundation (Stiftung Kartause Ittingen) was established in 1977 to administer the old monastery, which has been carefully restored and now houses two museums run by the canton of Thurgau.

The building is also occupied by a hotel, restaurant, and pottery and furniture workshops. Surrounded by its own agricultural land, including 8ha/20 acres of vines, the monastery enjoys a peaceful location, with magnificent views extending as far as the Alps. The foundation, which also administers a nature reserve (14ha/34.6 acres), has details on walks in the area: Ask for a map at reception.

Ittinger Museum

A small cloistered gallery surrounds the garden where the monks were buried. The history of the charterhouse, from the pillages of the 15C to 18C prosperity, is explained in the old cellar. The museum collections—paintings, models and furniture—provide an insight into the austere life led by the monks, who renounced all worldly pleasures. In the refectory where the monks met for meals on Sundays, without breaking their vow of silence, the decoration is decidedly religious in tone. One of the cells is dedicated to St Bruno, who founded the Carthusian Order in the 11C. Note also the carved **stalls** dating from around 1700 in the chapter house, as well as the religious works of art from Ittingen in the sacristy. A small chapel on the first floor contains a Baroque display cabinet of relics. The guestrooms within the charterhouse have beautiful painted ceilings, 18C four-poster beds and **faience stoves** decorated with emblems and landscape scenes.

Church★

This Baroque church is striking for its exuberant décor: the interior is covered with frescoes recounting the life of St Brun, red-veined green and white stuccowork, statues, and cherubs. Farm workers sat slightly apart from the rest of the church; the gallery was reserved for guests. The superb **choir stalls★** were sculpted in the 18C. The main altar is adorned with Rococo-style ornamentation. There is no organ in the church as the Carthusian monks sang unaccompanied chants.

Kunstmuseum des Kantons Thurgau

This art gallery houses a collection of 20C paintings, most of which are Swiss in origin. Artists exhibited include Adolf Dietrich, with work inspired by the landscapes of Thurgau, Carl Roesch, Ernst Kreidolf and Hans Brühlmann. Of particular interest is the *Self-portrait* by Helen Dahm. Temporary exhibitions of contemporary art are held in the basement.

Kreuzlingen

▶ *48.5km/30mi on Route 1 NE of Wintherthur and then Route 7* Sonnenstrasse 4. &(0)71 672 38 40. www.kreuzlingen.to.
The Swiss town of Kreuzlingen is built on a former moraine of the Rhine Glacier. It forms a single town with the German city of Constance, divided only by the frontier. The town owes its name to a relic of the Holy Cross (Kreuz), which was brought back from the Holy Land in the 10C and deposited in the basilica. It is locally revered as "the first town of Switzerland."

Old Klosterkirche St Ulrich

This basilica was built in the 17C and the Baroque interior decoration completed in the following century. The building was damaged by fire in 1963 and restored in 1967. The Olive Grove Chapel (Ölbergkapelle) contains an extraordinary group of 250 carved wooden figurines set in curious rock work, representing scenes taken from the Passion. The top floor of the sacristy houses a **museum** displaying paintings and documents from the long history of the monastery. (✪*open during services or upon request;* &(0)71 672 22 18).

Gottlieben

▶ *45km/28m NE of Winterthur via A 7 (toll).*
Gottlieben lies at the western end of the arm of the Rhine joining the Untersee, or lower lake, to the main basin of Lake Constance. It has a 13C castle, remodelled in the 19C. In the 15C the building was used as a prison for the deposed Pope John III and for the Czech reformer **Jan Hus**. Prince Louis-Napoleon Bonaparte, the future Napoleon III, lived here from 1837 to 1838.

Schloss Arenenberg

▶ *6km/4mi W of Gottlieben along the Untersee shore road. Thurgau Tourismus, Egelmoosstrasse 1.* &(0)71 414 11 44. www.thurgau-tourismus.ch.
The little Arenenberg Castle, stands on a terrace overlooking the western basin of Lake Constance, Untersee. Built in the 16C, it became, in 1817, the property of Queen Hortense, daughter of Louis Bonaparte, after which the family lived here for generations. In 1906 it became a museum devoted to Napoleon.

Napoleonmuseum★

✪*Open year-round Tue–Sun 10am– 5pm; mid-Apr–mid Oct, Mon 1pm–5pm.* ✪*Closed Good Friday.* ◈10CHF. &(0)71 663 32 60.
Works of art and furniture collected by the Bonapartes have remained in the castle. Note Queen Hortense's drawing room, furnished in the style of the period, and the library, bedrooms and boudoirs, which contain many mementoes of the imperial family. Queen Hortense's bedroom affords a sweeping **view** over Lake Constance and Reichenau Island.

ADDRESSES

🏠 STAY / 🍴 EAT

⊜⊜**Gästehaus** – *Kartause Ittingen.* &(0)52 748 44 11. www.kartause.ch. The hotel run by the foundation has 48 rooms (33 double, 15 single). It is situated in a warm, modern building, attractively decorated.

⊜⊜**Zur Mühle** – *Kartause Ittingen. In the courtyard, on the right.* This restaurant, housed in one of the buildings belonging to the foundation (1870), offers a reasonably priced menu.

Schaffhausen★

The old city of Schaffhausen is home to a host of wonderful Renaissance and classical buildings, making it one of the most attractive towns in Switzerland. The city is also the starting-point for a visit to the Rhine Falls (Rheinfall), traditionally an important attraction of romantic Switzerland.

A BIT OF HISTORY

As the Rhine Falls compelled boatmen to unload their cargoes here, merchants settled in the town and set up a depot. Schaffhausen entered the Swiss Confederation in 1501.

Nowadays, it depends largely on its situation as a communications junction and bridgehead. It has also become an industrial centre, drawing electric power from the river, including, machine and electrical goods factories, spinning mills and steel works.

SIGHTS

Old Town★

Dominated by the remains of the ramparts crowned by the **Munot**, a massive 16C keep (*accessible via stairs and a footbridge across the moat, now a deer park*), the old town forms a **belvedere★** (Ⓞ*open May–Oct, 8am–7pm, Nov–Apr, 9am–5pm;* ∞*5CHF;* ✆*(0)52 632 40 20*) overlooking the town and the Rhine Valley. The lower town has fine houses with painted façades, often embellished with oriel windows. The **Vordergasse★** is one of the most typical streets, its houses adorned with stucco and carvings, its roofs with numerous dormer windows.

The **Haus zum Ritter** (Knight's House) deserves special mention: the paintings adorning the façade were restored in 1938–39 by Care Roesch, signed by the famous Schaffhausen artist, **Tobias Stimmer**. Some of these murals (1570) can be seen in the Museum zu Allerheiligen. You also should see the pretty fountains in Fronwagplatz and the Regierungsgebäude (Government

▶ **Population:** 34 076.

🇮 **Info:** Fronwagplatz 4 – 8200. ✆(0)52 632 40 20. www.schaffhausen-tourismus.ch.

◑ **Location:** Schaffhausen is on the north bank of the Rhine at the foot of the Munot Keep, 51km/32mi north of Zürich. Alt. 403m/1 322ft.

☺ **Don't Miss:** Rheinfall, or the old town's belvedere.

🕑 **Timing:** Allow a minimum of one day to enjoy the sights.

GETTING AROUND

BOAT SERVICES

www.urh.ch, daily July–mid Sep, May–June and Mid Sept–Oct Sat and Sun only. 22CHF to Stein am Rhein one way. ∞*43CHF to Konstanz. Day ticket 37CHF.* Excursion steamers sail between Schaffhausen and Kreuzlingen on the Rhine and the Lower Lake (Untersee), offering glimpses of the river banks, overlooked by ruined castles, and of charming little towns like Diessenhofen and Stein am Rhein.

House), a 17C building with a fine sculptured façade and a stepped gable.

Museum zu Allerheiligen★★

Ⓞ*Open Tue–Sun 11am–5pm.* Ⓞ*Closed 1 Jan, Good Fri and 25 Dec.* ∞*9CHF.* 🎧*Guided tour by appointment.* ♿ ✆*(0)52 633 07 77. www.allerheiligen.ch.* The museum is housed in the former **All Saints Abbey**. It contains prehistoric artefacts from excavations in the region, manuscripts and early printed books, mostly 15C, which belonged to the monastery library, and works of Swiss artists from the 15C–20C.

The most remarkable exhibit is an early-13C onyx, mounted on gold and inlaid with precious stones.

WHERE TO STAY
Sorell Hotel & Zunfthaus Rüden.................... ①

Münster zu Allerheiligen (All Saints Abbey)

🕐 Open 9am–5pm (8am–8pm summer). ☏ (0)52 624 39 71. www.muenster-schaffhausen.ch.
This Romanesque abbey basilica was built in the 11C with yellow ochre-coloured stone. The cloister, abutting the south aisle of the church, has a gallery with Gothic bays and contains numerous tombstones. A bell known as Schiller's Bell, which inspired the poet's famous *Lied von der Glocke*, or *Ballad of the Bell*, is kept in a small courtyard nearby.

Museum of Contemporary Art★

🕐 Open Sat 3pm–5pm, Sun 11am–5pm.
🕐 Closed 25 Dec. 🎟14CHF. ☏ (0)52 625 25 15. www.modern-art.ch.
Situated along the banks of the Rhine, this former textile factory pays tribute to the Conceptual and Minimalist movements of the 1960s–1980s. The Hallen für Neue Kunst is laid out over an area of 5 500sq m/59 200sq ft comprising four different levels; the first is set aside for temporary exhibitions.

The permanent collections feature works by Mario Merz, Dan Flavin, Joseph Beuys (*Das Kapital 1970–77*), Richard Long (*Lightning Fire Wood Circle*), Lawrence Weiner, Bruce Nauman (*Floating Room*), Jannis Kounellis representing Arte Povera, Carl Andre (*Cuts*), Sol Lewitt, and Robert Ryman.

EXCURSIONS

Rheinfall★★

The **Rhine Falls** are the most powerful in Europe. The river plunges from a height of 21m/70ft and its flow sometimes reaches 1 070cu m/37 500cu ft per second (average flow, 700cu m/ 25 000cu ft per second). The spectacle, which Goethe described as "the Source of the Ocean," is best seen in July when the waters are swollen.

The Rhine

Rheinfall by Schloss Laufen

Christof Sonderegger/Switzerland Tourism

The Rhine's source is in the canton of Graubünden, from whence it flows north to Germany, France and the Netherlands. It flows through Switzerland for barely a quarter of its course, reaching Basel after 388km/242mi. Over this relatively short distance it falls from 2 200m to 250m/7 218ft to 820ft, making it a wild and fast-flowing river.

The Rhine Basin is by far the largest river basin in Swiss territory. The Rhine is a typical **Alpine River**, with low levels in winter and flash-flooding in summer. It rises in Graubünden; its two main arms, the Vorderrhein and the Hinterrhein, meet at Reichenau, above Chur, and provide the power for the large-scale hydroelectric works. The courses are followed respectively by the San Bernardino and the Oberalp roads.

The river is swollen at Chur by the Plessur and farther on by the Landquart and the Tamina. It follows the **Rheinthal** cleft, which resembles Alsace by its north-south orientation, its size and its varying vegetation (maize, vines, etc.). It then flows into the immense **Lake Constance** (12km/8mi wide and 64km/40mi long), which acts as a regulator for it, as Lake Geneva does for the Rhône. At Constance, the Rhine leaves the main basin for the Lower Lake (Untersee), from which it escapes at Stein am Rhein.

Between Schaffhausen and Basel the character of the river changes. Hemmed in between the slopes of the Black Forest and the Jura foothills, it forces its way among slabs of hard rock. Below Schaffhausen, where the valley narrows, the flow becomes faster and the river plunges between the rocks, forming impressive falls (⟨ *see Rheinfall*⟩). Farther on, other rocky slabs produce rapids (*Laufen*), whose presence accounts for place names like Laufen and Laufenburg. These breaks in level make navigation impossible, but have enabled hydroelectric power from power stations on the river banks, the most recent of which is the power-dam at Rheinau.

Observing the River

Between Lake Constance and Basel, driving along the Rhine Valley is complicated by the meandering border of the canton of Schaffhausen. Therefore do not try to follow the course of the Rhine very closely in Swiss territory. It is better to choose a few characteristic observation points for excursions:

- The castle, **Burg Hohenklingen**, near Stein am Rhein;
- The **Munot Terrace**, at Schaffhausen;
- The **Laufener Schloss**, at the Rhine Falls (⟨ *see Rheinfall*⟩);
- At **Laufenburg** (Swiss shore), the terrace laid out below an old tower.

Scene from the north bank (Rheinfallquai)

▶ *4km/3mi via Neuhausen, where you will leave the Basel road and follow signs to Rheinfallstrasse.*

Close views from the south bank

▶ *5km/3mi – plus 30min on foot there and back. Leave Schaffhausen on the road to Zürich, which you will then leave to turn right toward Laufen.*

Park the car at the entrance to Laufener Schlosses, which is now a restaurant.

Belvederes

Enter the courtyard of the castle. You will go down a staircase to the level of the falls. View also from a little kiosk the top of the staircase. There are numerous viewpoints along the way. Boats take you to the rock in the middle of the falls and ferry you from one bank to the other.

Rheinau

▶ *Take Route 4 SW from Schaffhausen and then take the Postrasse W at Marthalen Station. Schulstrasse 11.*
℘ *(0)52 305 40 80. www.rheinau.ch.*
Rheinau was the seat of a Benedictine abbey (now converted into a psychiatric hospital) on an island in the river. Its abbey church is an outstanding example of Baroque art. In 1956 a large hydroelectric power station and dam were completed across the Rhine downstream of Rheinau; its reservoir stretches for 6.5km/4mi up to the Rhine Falls.

Klosterkirche

🕐 *Open Apr, May and Oct, Tue–Sat 2pm–4pm, Sun and public holidays 1.30pm–5pm; Jun–Sept, Tue–Sat 10am–noon, 1pm–5pm, Sun and public holidays 10.30am–noon, 1pm–6pm.*
🕐 *Closed Nov–Mar.* 🎫 *3CHF.*
℘ *(0)52 319 31 00.*
The abbey church was rebuilt at the beginning of the 18C. The **interior**★ is striking for its Baroque-style decoration. The nave, whose vaulting is covered with frescoes, is flanked by four chapels adorned with a profusion of marble and gilding. A balustrade runs under the

---

Rhine-Danube Canal

Ever since Roman times, emperors, kings, engineers and visionaries dreamed of linking the Rhine and Danube rivers. Charlemagne began the great enterprise, hence the name Charlemagne's Ditch (Fossa Carolina). Bavaria's Ludwig I made another attempt, building the Ludwig Canal. However, it took until 1992—12 centuries after it was begun—that the waterway linking Europe from the north Sea to the Black Sea became a reality. The 177km/110mi canal with its hundreds of locks takes the barges up and down the 245m/800ft climb. It is truly a marvel of modern engineering. Charlemagne and Ludwig would be proud.

---

clerestory. The chancel, enclosed by an elaborate grille, has beautiful stalls. The organ dates back to 1715.

Stein am Rhein★★

Best reached by boat from Schaffhausen Oberstadt 3. ℘ *(0)52 742 20 90. www.steinamrhein.ch.*
The unbelievably picturesque medieval town of Stein am Rhein is built on the north bank of the Rhine, close by the outflow of the Untersee, the western basin of Lake Constance.

Old Town★★

The old town's character is apparent as you approach the bridge spanning the Rhine; on the right are half-timbered houses, whose foundations dip into the river.

The Town Hall Square (Rathausplatz) and the main street (Hauptstrasse) form an exceptional picture with flower-decked fountains and oriel-windowed houses, whose fully painted façades develop the theme of each house sign: The House of the Pelican, Inn of the Sun, House of the Red Ox and the House of the White Eagle—each has its own motif.

Stein am Rhein

Lucia Degonda / Switzerland Tourism

Historische Sammlung

Housed on the second floor of the town hall (Rathaus). ⚫⚫*Guided tours (45min) 10am–11.30am, 2pm–5pm.* ⏱*Closed Sat–Sun and public holidays.* 🎫*3CHF.* 📞*(0)52 742 20 40.*

A historical collection of weapons, Delft porcelain and historiated stained-glass windows from the 16C and 17C recall the town's past.

Kloster St Georgen

⏱*Open Apr–Oct Tue–Sun, 10am–5pm.* ⏱*Closed Good Fri.* 🎫*3CHF.* 📞*(0)52 741 21 42.*

This former Benedictine monastery, set up at Stein in the 11C by the German Emperor Heinrich II, has kept its medieval character but has been converted into a **museum**★ (history, local art). Rooms are adorned with carved ceilings, panelling and inlaid furniture and are sometimes decorated with 16C monochrome paintings (*grisaille*).

You will notice the monks' cells, with their fine stone paving, the bailiff's room, the cloisters and the chapterhouse. The Romanesque church, a 12C basilica with a flat ceiling and no transept, has been restored.

Burg Hohenklingen★

▶ *2.5km/1.2mi N of Stein am Rhein.*

A steep uphill road running partly among vineyards, partly through woods, leads to Hohenklingen Castle. From the tower you will see a **panorama**★ of Stein am Rhein, the Rhine, the surrounding hills and beyond them the Alps, from which the Säntis emerges.

ADDRESSES

🍽 STAY

SCHAFFHAUSEN

🍴🍽 **Sorell Hotel Rüden & Zunfthaus** - Oberstadt 20. 📞*(0)52 632 36 36.* www.rueden.ch. Closed Dec. 24–Jan 3. 🛏 *30 rooms.* The contemporary decor blends perfectly with the old stones and wooden beams of this historic house, where the guilds of the city once sat. It would be wrong to leave the enjoyment of this very central hotel (in the heart of Old Town) to businessmen, who are the main clients. Hearty breakfast and a reduction of 25CHF per person during weekends.

St Gallen★★

The economic and cultural capital of eastern Switzerland, St Gallen owes its fortune to an abbey, founded on the spot where **Gallus** died in 650. It's Baroque cathedral and magnificent abbey library, both UNESCO World Heritage Sites since 1983, are situated in the old town, surrounded by typical corbelled houses with oriel (Erker) windows.

ABBEY BUILDINGS★★★

The Catholic Abbey was largely destroyed during the Reformation, introduced in 1524 by Joachim von Watt (known as Vadian) a physician and mayor of St Gallen. It was not until the mid 18C that the prince-abbots resumed their secular power with the creation of the church and the library; it soon became the seat of the largest ecclesiastical state in Switzerland. In 1805, the prince-abbots lost their power and the abbey was "secularised". In 1846 it became a separate See.

From the Klosterhof (monastery court-yard) there is a fine view of the former Benedictine abbey. The abbey buildings are attached to the cathedral; they now house the bishop's residence, the famous abbey library, the Cantonal Government and several schools. Along with that of Einsiedeln it is the most important Baroque structure in Switzerland.

Cathedral★★

The cathedral was built from 1755 to 1767 on the site of a 14C Gothic edifice. In the centre of the immense structure, the **dome**★★ is richly decorated. The **chancel**★★★, enclosed by admirable grilles, is adorned with a high altar executed in the Empire style in 1810.

Stiftsbibliothek★★★

🕐 *Open 10am–5pm (4pm Sun); some public holidays, 10am–4pm.* 🕐 *Closed mid-Nov–early Dec & major holidays.* ⌾*7CHF.* 📞*(0)71 227 34 16. www.stiftsbibliothek.ch.*
A UNESCO World Heritage Site, the **Abbey Library** is considered to have

▶ **Population:** 72 040.
🖒 **Michelin Map:** Town plan in the Michelin Red Guide Switzerland.
🚼 **Info:** Bahnhofplatz 1. 📞(0)71 227 37 37. www.st.gallen-bodensee.ch.
◖ **Location:** St Gallen, the highest town in Switzerland, nestles in the narrow Steinach Valley in the east of the country, 10km/6.2mi southeast of Lake Constance (Bodensee). Alt. 668m/2 201ft.
◈ **Don't Miss:** The Abbey Library, the finest secular baroque room in Central Europe.
👫 **Kids:** Peter and Paul Zoo.
🕐 **Timing:** Allow at least two days for museums and excursions. While here, take the 2hr guided city tour from the Tourist Office (🕐*open May–Oct Mon, Wed, Thu, Fri, Sat 2pm; Jul & Aug also Tue & Sun at 2pm; Jan–Apr Sat at 11am;*⌾*15CHF).*

Abbey Library

the finest non-religious Rococo interior in Switzerland, built during the same period as the cathedral (1758–67). Architectural features include a parquet floor, monochrome *(grisaille)* paintings, and ceiling frescoes by the Gigi brothers.

The collections include around 100 000 volumes, including over 2 000 parchments from the 8C–12C, early printed books (prior to 1500), and illuminated manuscripts from the Renaissance period. A mummy from Upper Egypt (700 BC), donated in 1824, can be seen in a double sarcophagus made from sycamore at the back of the library.

OLD TOWN★★

Around the cathedral are many 16C and 18C houses, some with painted façades, often adorned with wrought-iron signs and carved and painted wooden **oriel windows★**, typical of the region. Many houses in this district are noteworthy for their elaborate sculpture and ornamentation; a stroll down the various streets (**Gallusplatz, Gallusstrasse, Marktgasse, etc.**) will afford fine views.

MUSEUMS
Art Museum★

🕐Open Tue–Sun 10am–5pm (8pm Wed). ◉10CHF. ✆(0)71 242 06 71. www.kunstmuseumsg.ch.

The **Kunstmuseum** includes German, Austrian and Swiss art from the 15C-18C, as well as several 19C and 20C paintings. One of the highlights of the museum is its collection of 17C Dutch art. Of particular interest are *Odalisque* by Corot, *Adoration of the Virgin* by Delacroix, *Garden* by Sisley, *Lake Geneva* by Courbet, *Hermitage* by Pissarro and *Palazzo Contarini* by Monet.

The museum also boasts a collection of modern and contemporary art, with works by Sophie Taeuber-Arp, Klee, Picasso, Tapiès, Richard Serra, Donald Judd and Nam June Paik. Temporary exhibitions are also hosted here.

Natural History Museum

🕐Open Tue–Sun 10am–5pm (8pm Wed). ◉10CHF. ✆(0)71 242 06 70. www.naturmuseumsg.ch.

Housed in the same building as the Fine Arts Museum, the **Naturmuseum** has nature exhibits, including displays on birds and mammals of the region. Note the skeletons of a *Plateosaurus*, a *Pterosaurus* and an *Anatosaurus* (around 80 million years old).

Historical Museum

🕐Open Tue–Sun 10am–5pm, Sun 10am–5pm. 🕐Closed major holidays. ◉10CHF. ✆(0)071 242 06 42. www.hmsg.ch.

This **Historisches und Völkerkunde Museum** exhibits the history and traditions of the St Gallen region from the Prehistoric period to the 18C. Also exhibited are artefacts from Africa, the Pacific and Asia, Japan, Inuit articles, and antique Greek and Etruscan sculptures.

Textile Museum

🕐Open daily 10am–5pm. 🕐Closed 1 Jan, Good Fri, 1 Aug, 25 Dec. ◉12CHF. ✆(0)71 222 17 44. www.textilmuseum.ch.

The modern **Textile Museum** pays tribute to a traditional industry that brought prosperity to St Gallen and eastern Switzerland for over seven centuries.

Botanischer Garten

In Neudorf; via Rorschacher Strasse then bear left onto Stephanshornstrasse (off map). 🕐Open 8am–5pm. Greenhouses 9.30am–noon, 2pm–5pm. 🕐Closed 1 Jan and 25 Dec. ◉No charge. ♿ ✆(0)71 288 15 30.

These gardens (1.5ha/3.5 acres) are home to 8 000 species from the five continents. A gazebo stands in front of a pond where rushes and reeds grow, while nearby two tropical greenhouses are teeming with cacti, palm trees, euphorbias, orchids and water lilies .

EXCURSIONS
Dreilinden Hill★
Alt. 738m/2 420ft.

▶ *Take the Mühleggweiher automatic railway (1893). Mühleggbahn station is situated in Moosbruggstrasse. Turn right out of the station.*

The three pools (**Weiher**) on this hill are 200m/220yd long and were created by the monastery to supply the mills, textile workshops and canals of the town; the monks also used to fish in them. At around the turn of the 20C, the pools were made suitable for **swimming**. A Baroque-style house (1677) can be admired near the central pool.

From the pools, a path (**Höhenweg**) winds its way through pine forests and meadows up the Dreilinden Hill,

heading as far as **Freudenberg**★ peak (alt. 884m/2 899ft), from where there is a **view**★ of the old town of St Gallen.

▲▲ Tierpark Peter und Paul

Alt. 793m/2 601ft. 3.5km/2mi N of St Gallen. ◗ *Leave St Gallen by Müller-Friedbergstrasse.*

This zoological park (deer, chamois, mouflons) is situated in an open setting. Ibex from the Gran Paradiso Massif in Italy were brought here in 1911.

Trogen

◐ *10km/6mi SE of St Gallen.*
Speicherstrasse 11. ℰ(0)71 344 13 16.
www.trogen.ch or www.appenzell.ch.
Trogen is in the district of Appenzell
within view of Lake Constance. Built on
a hill, it boasts many bourgeois houses,
some of which are real palaces built
by rich merchants of former days. Its
central square, the Landsgemeindeplatz is where the traditional meeting
(◐ *see INTRODUCTION: Government*) of
the half-canton of Appenzell–Ausserrhoden takes place in even years; in odd
years, the ceremony is held at Hundwil.
Among the fine houses surrounding it
you will notice the Zur Krone, an inn with
its overhanging roof and two superimposed gables. Just outside Trogen, 1km
south on the road to Bühler there is the
Pestalozzi Children's village. Here, the
houses are reserved for war orphans
from different countries. Johann
Heinrich Pestalozzi, a citizen of Zürich
(1746–1827), is honoured throughout
Switzerland and abroad for his educational work and innovative teaching
methods.

🚗 DRIVING TOUR

1 SITTER VALLEY

21km/13mi from St Gallen to Appenzell.

◐ *Leave St Gallen to the S towards*
Altstätten. After 6km/4mi turn right
towards Hundwill.

This recommended route from St
Gallen affords pleasant views all along
the Sitter Valley. This is at first a deep
ravine, but turns into a depression
dotted with traditional farms. Look
especially for a group of buildings
1km/0.6mi southeast of the Hundwil
junction.

Stein

As you cross this village, located on a
plateau (alt. 823m/2 700ft) above its
neighbours, there are sweeping views
of the surrounding countryside. The
Appenzeller Volkskunde Museum

(◐*open Tue–Sun 10am–5pm, Sun 10am–*
5pm; ◐closed 25 Dec; ☞6CHF; ℰ071
368 50 56; www.avm-stein.ch) presents
a reconstruction of a typical Alpine
cheesemaking dairy (*production starts*
at 1.30pm), surrounded by traditional
objects such as bells, saddles, and casks.
In the basement, two craftsmen dem-
onstrate the functioning of a weaving
loom and an embroidery hoop (superb
jacquard fabrics). On the first floor, note
the three 16C wooden panels, illustrated
with naive drawings, which were found
in the nearby district of Gais.

Appenzell – ◐*See APPENZELL.*

ADDRESSES

🛏STAY

◒ ◱ **Vadian Garni** – *Gallustrasse 36.*
ℰ(0)71 228 18 78. www.hotel-vadian.com.
16 rooms. Bright, well-maintained rooms.
Homemade jam for breakfast.

◒ ◱ **DOM** – *Webergasse 22. ℰ(0)71*
227 71 71 www.hoteldom.ch. Closed
Christmas–New Year. 🅿 *31 rooms.*
Conveniently located next to the
cathedral, this hotel offers no-frills,
comfortable and very well kept rooms.

◒ ◱ **City Weissenstein** –
Davidstrasse 22. ℰ(0)71 228 06 28.
www.cityweissenstein.ch. 🅿 *6 rooms*
(suites). Located in a quiet neighbourhood away from the old city, offering all
the comforts of a modern hotel.

◱ **Radisson Blu** – *St Jakob-Strasse 55.*
ℰ(0)71 242 12 12. www.radissonblu.com/
hotel-stgallen.ch. 🛏 *27 CHF. 123 rooms.*
Comfortable, modern and technically
well-equipped rooms. Casino and
restaurant on site.

◒◱◱ **Ekkehard** – *Rorschacher*
Strasse 50. ℰ(0)71 224 04 04.
www.ekkehard.ch. Closed for
refurbishment until late 2011.

◒◱◱◱ **Metropol** – *Bahnhofplatz 3.*
ℰ (0)71 228 32 32. www.hotel-metropol.ch.
🛏 🅿 *32 rooms.* The dull façade of the
building does not do justice to this
hotel, located just opposite the station.
Excellent, very well rated restaurant.

♥/EAT

Marktplatz – *Neugasse 2. ℘(0)71 222 36 41.* This modern brasserie, with its bright walls, brickwork and TV screens offers a variety of dishes at moderate prices: flammeküeche, burgers, salads, fries, Spätzle, grilled meats. Every dish can come in half portions for smaller appetites. It is also open on Sundays, which is quite rare in St Gallen.

Atrium – *Schützengasse 8. ℘(0)71 223 37 17. Closed Sun.* Cream walls, paintings of artists, Art Deco chandeliers: it's enjoyable just to sit in this elegant Italian restaurant. The chef excels in preparing manicotti and risotto. Wide variety of pasta and Mediterranean wines. Impeccable service and reasonable prices.

Zum Goldenen Leuen – *Schmiedgasse 30. ℘(0)71 222 0262. Closed Sun (and Sat after 6pm).* A cosy and popular address rightly so given the warm décor of this perfectly preserved 17C brasserie. At noon you can watch the locals having a soup, salad or a cheese pie, reading the newspapers. The restaurant has been brewing its own beer since 2002.

Zum Goldenen Schäfli – *Metzgergasse 5. ℘(0)71 223 37 37. www.zumgoldenenschaefli.ch. Closed Sun.* This traditional restaurant is in the oldest remaining guildhall dating from the 17C. The sloping ceiling and floor add to the rustic charm.

Maximilian – *Schreinerstrasse 6. ℘(0)71 230 21 21. www.maximilian restaurant.ch. Closed Sun.* This bar-restaurant has a tasteful 70s décor and a small but varied menu.

Seeger – *Oberer Graben 2. ℘(0)71 222 97 90. www.seeger-restaurants.ch.* Businessmen, travellers and regulars like to gather in this pleasant restaurant. Affordable daily specials for lunch just a few steps from the train station and old town.

Schlössli – *Zeughausgasse 17, adjacent to the Spisertor railway station. ℘(0)71 222 12 56. www.schloessli-sg.ch. Closed Sat–Sun and mid-Jul–mid-Aug.* This small 16C château is worth a visit for its frescoes, furniture, salons with vaulted ceilings, and its excellent local food.

David 38 – *Davidstrasse 38. ℘(0)71 230 28 38. www.david38.ch. Closed Sun.* This elegant restaurant attracts the local gourmets of the region by its cuisine, which takes pleasure in mixing styles and flavours. The curry soup and the veal escalope with lemon are worth a taste.

Am Gallusplatz – *Gallustrasse 24. ℘(0)71 223 33 30. www.gallusplatz.ch. Closed Mon, Sat lunch, mid-Jul–early-Aug and 12–18 Oct.* Situated in the medieval district of half-timbered houses around the cathedral. Specialising in hearty roasts, good regional cuisine and a wide choice of wines. Pleasant terrace.

🛒SHOPPING

The main shopping streets are **Multergasse**, **Spisergasse**, **Neugasse**, and **Marktgasse**. Find genuine St Gallen embroidery at **Boutique La Bambola** (*Brühlgasse 35*).

🎭THEATRE AND MUSIC

Stadttheater – *Museumstrasse 24. ℘(0)71 242 06 06. www.theatersg.ch.*

Sinfonieorchester – *Museumstrasse 25. ℘(0)71 242 05 05. www.sinfonie orchestersg.ch.* Classical symphony orchestra concerts in an early-20C building, a reminder of the prosperity brought to the town by the textile industry.

Kellerbühne – *St Georgenstrasse 3. ℘(0)71 223 39 59. www.kellerbuehne.ch.*

Figurentheater (Puppet Theatre) – *Lämmlisbrunnenstrasse 34. ℘(0)71 222 60 60. www.figurentheater-sg.ch.*

🎭NIGHTLIFE

The **Einstein Bar**, the piano bar of the Hôtel Einstein (*Berneggstrasse*) offers a cosy atmosphere, where you can enjoy a cocktail or a local beer.

🎭EVENTS

In-line one-eleven is the longest rollerblade race in Europe (Aug). It starts in St Gallen and runs for 111km/69mi, through 20 villages and two cantons, before finishing back in the town.

Appenzell★

Appenzell is an old-fashioned town which succeeds in reconciling rural and city life, a trait common to many Germanic countries. It is a *flecken*, a word denoting communities that are neither towns nor villages, whose buildings boast highly-decorated façades and undulating gables typical of the region.

A BIT OF HISTORY

The name of Appenzell (*Abbatis cella*, the Abbot's cell) dates from the early settlement of the country by the monks of St Gallen. The **Hauptgasse**★, the main street crossing the village, offers various temptations (embroidery shops; Appenzell cakes decorated with por-traits of cowmen in yellow breeches and scarlet waistcoats). It lies between the church, with its astonishing Baroque embellishments, and the Löwendrog-erie, whose curved gable bears a series of paintings of medicinal plants with this mournful comment: "Many plants against illness, none against death".

SIGHTS
♣♣Museum Appenzell

🕐*Open Apr–1 Nov, daily, 10am–noon, 2pm–5pm; 2 Nov–Mar, Tue–Sun, 2pm–5pm.* ✏*Guided tours on request; free guided tour every Fri.* 🕐*Closed 24, 25 Dec, 1 Jan.* ⌾*5CHF.* ✆*(0)71 788 96 31. www.museum.ai.ch.*

Set up in the town hall and the adjoining house (1560), this museum focuses on regional lore, including a collection of coins which the Inner-Rhoden people were able to mint for only five years (1737–42), a prison cell dating back

- ▶ **Population:** 5 787.
- 🛈 **Info:** Appenzellerland Tourismus, Hauptgasse 4. ✆071 788 96 41. www.appenzell.ch.
- ▶ **Location:** Appenzell lies at the foot of the lush Alpstein hills, 18km/11mi south of St Gallen. Alt. 789m/2 589ft.
- ⌾ **Don't Miss:** The Appenzell Museum with its collections of local crafts and folklore.
- ♣♣ **Kids:** Appenzell Museum.

to 1570, typical Appenzell costumes (featuring the sophisticated black tulle headdress), banners, a 16C triptych attributed to Jacob Girtanner and coffin-shaped hatchments (a bygone practice, they were once used to drive away evil spirits). The museum also boasts an Egyptian sarcophagus (c.1000 BC), found in a temple at Thebes.

Museum Liner

🕐*Open Apr–Nov daily, 10am–noon, 2pm–5pm; Nov–Mar, Mon–Sat 2pm–5pm, Sun 11am–5pm.* ⌾*9CHF.* ✆*(0)71 788 18 00.*

This museum, housed in a postmodern building (1998) by the architects Annette Gigon and Mike Guyer, presents tem-porary exhibitions dedicated to work by local artists, such as the landscape painter Carl-August Liner (1871–1946) and Carl-Walter Liner (1914–1997), an early exponent of Abstract art. A col-lection of modern art by painters such as Arp, Kirchner and Tapiès can also be admired in the museum.

Appenzellerland

The soft, undulating landscape of green hills is dotted with farms and rich townships with their pretty, curvilinear gabled houses which still hold meetings of the traditional Landsgemeinden (⌾*see INTRODUCTION: Government*). Traditions are still very much alive here: special dishes such as Appenzell fat cheese (one of the strongest Swiss cheeses) and small, dry sausages called *Alpenklübler*. Another long-standing custom to have survived is that of fine old-fashioned embroidery, which continues to flourish as a cottage industry in Inner-Rhoden.

EXCURSIONS
Hoher Kasten★★

Alt. 1 795m/5 890ft. ◐ *7km/4.3mi SE on the road to Weissbad and Brülisau.* ⛟ *Cable-car leaves from Brülisau (alt. 924m/3 030ft) every 30min. Fare there and back* ◌◌*26CHF. Information on operating periods* 𝒫*(0)71 799 13 22.*

The ride up in the cable-car (8min) offers a view below of spruce trees, mountain pastures and shepherds' huts and ahead to the massive limestone spur of the Hoher Kasten. The belvedere, with its attractive Alpine garden, is higher than the restaurant but easily accessible. It offers a magnificent **panorama★★**: west and northwest, the town of Appenzell and surrounding hills; eastward, the view plunges down to the Rheinthal and its river, winding from Lake Constance (north) to the Liechtenstein mountains (south), with the Austrian Alps in the background. The Alpstein Massif and its

highest peak, Säntis, are clearly visible to the southeast. There is a marked path to Staubern and on to the lakes of Fälensee and Sämtisersee, as far as Brülisau.

Ebenalp★★

Alt. 1 640m/5 380ft. ◐ *7km/4.3mi – about 1hr30min following the Weissbad-Wasserauen road to its terminus, plus 8min by cable-car.* ⛟ *Cable-car – Departures Jul–Aug, 7.40am–7pm; Jun and Sept, 7.40am–6pm, May and Oct, 8am–5.30pm, Nov–Apr, 8.30am–5pm. Fare there and back* ◌◌*24CHF.* 𝒫*(0)71 799 12 12.*

This Alpine promontory is edged with cliffs jutting out over the Appenzell country. From Ebenalp you can return on foot *(about 1hr30min)* to Wasserauen via the **tunnel-grotto of Wildkirchli** (80m/262ft long), where excavations have exposed traces of the oldest prehistoric settlement in Switzerland. The

THE APPENZELL REGION

path passes the **Seealpsee**★, whose dark waters lie at the foot of the Rossmad.

🚗 DRIVING TOURS

1️⃣ SITTER VALLEY 🦽 see p440.

2️⃣ STOSS ROAD★
16km/10mi – allow 1hr.

▶ *Leave Appenzell to the W.*

Stoss★
In 1405 this plateau was the scene of a battle which secured the liberation of Appenzell from Austrian rule. To enjoy the distant **panorama**★★ of the Rheinthal and the Vorarlberg Alps, proceed towards the commemorative chapel and, 100m/110yd to its right, the obelisk marked out from afar by a clump of trees.

Altstätten
Altstätten lies at the heart of the Rheinthal on a warm inner plain with orchards, vineyards and crops of maize. It has a markedly medieval character: picturesque Marktgasse (Market Street), lined with pointed-gabled houses and pillared arcades. The Engelplatz, with its flower-decked fountain and crooked houses makes another pretty picture.

3️⃣ THE TOGGENBURG★
62km/38.5mi – allow approx 2hr30min.

Urnäsch
The village is known for its **Museum für Appenzeller Brauchtum** (🕐open Apr–Oct, daily 1.30pm–5pm; 🎟5CHF; 📞(0)71 364 23 22; www.museum-urnaesch.ch), a small folklore museum located in a 19C chalet. There is a sumptuous collection of carnival costumes and hats plus daily local costumes, jewels, pipes, paintings and painted figurines, cowbells, as well as a carpenter's workshop. The second floor displays an Appenzell interior with painted furniture, complete with its box bed and the bedroom occupied by the cowherd, a music room, dairy, and a col-

lection of old wooden toys. A short distance past Appenzell, between Urnäsch and Schwägalp, the road emerges from the bottom of a dell dotted with fir and ash trees, at the foot of the cliffs of the north face of Säntis.

Säntis★★★
📞(0)71 365 65 65. www.saentisbahn.ch (Also for Nature Discovery Park.)
Säntis, at an altitude of 2 502m/ 8 207ft is the highest peak in the Alpstein Massif between Toggenburg, the Rhine Valley, Lake Constance and the chief belvedere of eastern Switzerland. The summit calcareous shoulders, sometimes gently folded, sometimes sharply ridged (Wildhuser Schafberg), make this the most easily identified peak in the range.

Summit Climb
From Schwägalp, the terminus of the roads coming from Urnäsch or Neu St Johann: Departure every 30min. 🕐*Open mid-Jun–Oct, 7.30am–6.30pm (9pm Sat–Sun); Jul and Aug, 7.30am–7pm; Nov–mid-Jun, 8.30am–5pm.* 🕐*Does not operate the second fortnight in Jan.* 🎟*33CHF.* 📞*(0)71 365 65 65.*
From the upper station you can easily reach the summit, which is crowned by a telecommunications centre installed in 1956, and whose two restaurants and panoramic terraces have recently been renovated. The **panorama**★★★ of the Vorarlberg Mountains, the Graubünden, Glarus and Bernese Alps and the lakes of Zürich and Constance is incredibly grand. Its immensity is, however, often difficult to appreciate in the height of summer, especially in the middle of the day, when a heat haze obscures distant features. For a better view, go down steps to the Hôtel du Säntis, built above the wild valley of the Seealpsee .

👪 Nature Discovery Park
www.naturerlebnispark.ch.
This interactive park covers topics from plants and wildlife to geology and culture, not to mention guided trails, a working dairy and a technology park. The section from Schwälgalp to Nes-

slau leads along the southwest barrier of the Alpstein (Silberplatten, Lütispitz), where Alpine formations succeed the parklands. The spa of Rietbad is framed in a valley dotted with green knolls. Between Nesslau and Wildhaus, uphill from two wooded clefts, the High Toggenburg Valley spreads harmoniously, with dwellings whose walls are protected by weatherboarding. On the climb from Unterwasser to Wildhaus, admire the deeply folded escarpments of the Wildhuser-Schafberg and the serrated crests of the Churfirsten.

Wildhaus★

This pleasant resort lies on the plateau separating the Toggenburg from the Rheinthal, within sight of the Wildhuser-Schafberg, the Churfirsten and the Drei Schwestern. Wildhaus is the birthplace of the great reformer **Ulrich Zwingli**, whose home may still be seen, but not visited (⊶ *closed to the public*). From Wildhaus to Gams, the road dips towards the Rheinthal. From the hairpin bends immediately before Gams you will appreciate the size of this trough, dominated on its eastern side by the mountains of the Vorarlberg and of Liechtenstein, separated by the Feldkirch Gap, negotiated by the road and railway to the Arlberg region of Austria.

Werdenberg★★

At the north end of the settlement of Buchs, the old village of Werdenberg is a particularly welcome little **scene**★. You enter the tiny hamlet by a narrow alley flanked by a row of well-restored wooden arcaded houses. The atmosphere is typical of small 17C–18C towns from the Rhine Valley. Between numbers 8 and 9, a passageway leads to a path circling the pond. There you face the houses of Werdenberg, closely grouped together at the foot of the Castle of Counts: note the painted façade of the Schlange house.

Schloss

ⓞ*Open Apr–Oct, Tue–Sun 9.30am–5pm;* ⊚*4CHF;* ℘*(0)81 771 29 50; www.schlosswerdenberg.sg.ch).*

The section under the eaves is devoted to the Rhine, and the tower commands a lovely **view** of the Rheinthal.

ADDRESSES

🛌STAY

⊜⊜ **Schwägalp** – *Säntis.* ℘*(0)71 365 66 00. www.saentisbahn.ch. 30 rooms.* Quaint wooden chalet nestling in a peaceful setting with pretty views overlooking the terrace. Within walking distance of the Säntis ski resort.

⊜⊜ **Kaubad** – ℘*(0)71 787 48 44. www.hotel-kaubad.ch.* ⌖ *15 rooms.* This chalet is a haven of peace in a secluded spot surrounded by nature. Heated pool and reasonably priced restaurant.

⊜⊜⊜ **Appenzell** – *Hauptgasse 37.* ℘*(0)71 788 15 15. www.hotel-appenzell.ch.* ⌖ *16 rooms.* A cosy, welcoming establishment at the heart of Appenzell. A good base to rest after an excursion.

⊜⊜⊜ **Säntis** – *Landsgemeindeplatz.* ℘*(0)71 788 11 11. www.saentis-appenzell.ch* ⓟ ⌖ *37 rooms.* Comfortable hotel with a romantic atmosphere and a wooden façade typical of the Appenzell region. Sauna and solarium.

🍴/EAT

⊜ **Rössli** – *Postplatz.* ℘*(0)71 787 12 56. Closed Mon, Tue and mid-Jan–mid-Feb.* Typical old-fashioned café.

⊜ **Bären** – *Schlatt, 5km/3mi from Appenzell.* ℘*(0)71 787 14 13. Closed Tue, Wed, 11 Feb–1 Mar and 15–31 Jul.* Lovely views of the Alps and the valley from the terrace.

⊜⊜ **Bären** – *Hauptstrasse, in Gonten, 6km/3.7mi from Appenzell.* ℘*(0)71 795 40 10. Closed Sun evenings and for 3 weeks from end of Mar.* Delicious regional specialities from the Appenzell area, served in a peaceful, rustic setting.

⊜⊜⊜ **Schäfli** – *In Störgel Nord, 3km/1.8mi from Teufen.* ℘*(0)71 367 11 90. www.schaefli-stein.ch.* This beautiful house, built in the Appenzell tradition, offers regional cuisine.

Liechtenstein

The Principality of Liechtenstein is a fragment of the former Germanic Confederation, whose territory extended from the east bank of the Rhine to the Vorarlberg Mountains. The little state was made a sovereign principality by Emperor Charles VI in 1719 to benefit Prince Jean Adam of Liechtenstein; it owes the preservation of its statute largely to the wise policy followed by Prince Johann II (the Good), whose reign (1858–1929) was the longest of any Western European sovereign except Louis XIV (1638–1715). Today, numerous multinational companies based here benefit from a favourable tax regime.

▶ **Population:** 34 247.
▢ **Info:** Städtle 37, Postfach 139 – 9490. ℘(00423) 239 63 00. www.welcome.li.
◖ **Location:** Liechtenstein is 24km/15mi from north to south. Situated in the Upper Rhein valley of the Alps, its western border is formed by a river.
▣ **Parking:** Ample parking in major areas.
◈ **Don't Miss:** Post Office; philatelists collect stamps issued by this small state.
◷ **Timing:** Allow one day to tour the country by car.

A BIT OF HISTORY

After 1919 Liechtenstein loosened its last bonds with Austria and concluded monetary, postal, customs and diplomatic conventions with the Swiss Confederation; today it is to all intents a part of the Swiss economic sphere. The dividing line between the Germanic and Rhaetic civilisations is, however, clearly marked by the southern boundary; large villages scattered among the orchards at the foot of a castle or around churches with pointed spires make a contrast with the Graubünden cities closely gathered among their vines.

VADUZ

Liechtenstein's small capital lies on the Rhine river valley, with a beautiful view of the Swiss mountains of Faulfirst, Wissifrauen and Alvier opposite.

Lying at the foot of the imposing **castle**, Schloss Vaduz, the residence of the royal family (⦿ *closed to the public*), and seat of the present government, has become a busy international tourist attraction. You can drive (or climb up a very steep hill) to the castle gate (and even ring the bell), but the royal family will not receive you.

Schloss Vaduz

Liechtenstein Fine Arts Museum

◷*Open Tue–Sun, 10am–5pm (8pm Thu).* ◷*Closed 1 Jan, 24, 25 and 31 Dec.* ◉*8CHF.* ♿ *℘(00423) 235 03 00. www.kunstmuseum.li.*

This Fine Arts Museum is devoted primarily to paintings and 20C graphic artwork. It houses some of the works taken from collections belonging to the Prince of Liechtenstein. There is also a fine outdoor sculpture park dotted with modern works.

Liechtensteinisches Landesmuseum

Städle 43, Vaduz. ◷*Open Tue–Sun 10am –5pm (8pm Wed).* ◷*Closed 24, 25, 31 Dec and 1 Jan.* ◉*8CHF.* ℘*(00423) 239 68 20. www.landesmuseum.li.*

In the restored buildings of an old inn, this museum covers the important periods of the principality's history. There is a relief model of the country, a mineralogy collection, and a display of art from the prehistoric age, the Bronze Age, the Roman era (coins, objects), and the Alemanic period (jewellery, arms). Also exhibited are arms (medieval cutting and thrusting weapons, 16C–18C firearms), utensils, local folk art, works of art and cult objects.

Philatelic museum

◷*Open daily 10am–5.30pm (5pm Nov–Mar).* ◷*Closed 1 Jan and 25 Dec.* ◉*No charge.* ℘*(00423) 236 61 05.*

Located in a small gallery of the Fine Arts Museum, this museum highlights the principality's philatelic art and the history of the country's postal system (stamp collections). Temporary exhibitions are regularly organised.

EXCURSIONS
Tamina Gorge★★

2hr there and back on foot by the road branching off the road to Valens on the left, SW of Bad Ragaz.
◷*Open May–Oct, 10am–5.30pm (5pm in May and Oct).* ◉*4CHF.* ℘*(0)81 302 71 61.*

This gorge is breathtaking. To take the waters, before they were pumped up,

National Anthem

The National Anthem of Liechtenstein is **Oben am jungen Rhein** (Up above the young Rhine) which is sung to the tune of **God Save the Queen**. The lyrics were written in the 1850s by a German priest named Jakob Jauch officiating in Balzers. They were changed to the current version by a parliamentary resolution to remove all references to Germany.

patients were lowered down on ropes to the bottom of this tremendous fissure.

Malbuntal (Malbun Valley)

30km/19mi to Malbun. Take the route towards Vaduz castle, follow the signs to Triesen and then enter the valley towards Malbun.

In the heart of the country, this road passes through numerous pretty hamlets of Triesenberg and climbs to the corrie at the foot of the Sareiser Joch (alt. 2 000m/6 562ft), part of the Vorarlberg foothills and which can be reached on foot or by cable-car from Malbun.

INDEX

INDEX

INDEX

INDEX

INDEX

INDEX

INDEX

¶/EAT

INDEX

MAPS AND PLANS

THEMATIC MAPS

MAPS

COMPANION PUBLICATIONS

MICHELIN MAP 729 SUISSE

◆ a practical map on a scale of
1:400 000 which includes an index of
towns and shows the major roads
subject to snow cover.

MICHELIN ATLAS EUROPE

◆ Main road atlas with a full index.
1:1 000 000 scale map of Western
Europe and 1:1 000 000 scale map of
Eastern Europe. 74 town and city plans.
◆ 1136 Small Spiral ◆ 1129 Large Spiral
◆ 1135 Paperback ◆ 1133 Hardback

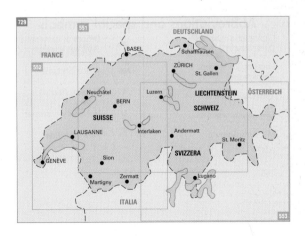

MAP LEGEND

	Sight	Seaside Resort	Winter Sports Resort	Spa
Highly recommended	★★★	立立立	✳✳✳	‡‡‡
Recommended	★★	立立	✳✳	‡‡
Interesting	★	立	✳	‡

Tourism

●━━━➡	Sightseeing route with departure point indicated	AZ B	Map co-ordinates locating sights
♠ ♣ ♠ ♣	Ecclesiastical building	🚩	Tourist information
◫ ◫	Synagogue – Mosque	✕ ∴	Historic house, castle – Ruins
⌐⌐	Building (with main entrance)	∪ ☼	Dam – Factory or power station
■	Statue, small building	☆ ∩	Fort – Cave
†	Wayside cross	⊓	Prehistoric site
◎	Fountain	▼ ♈	Viewing table – View
━●━■━►	Fortified walls – Tower – Gate	▲	Miscellaneous sight

Recreation

🏇	Racecourse	🏃	Waymarked footpath
⛸	Skating rink	◆	Outdoor leisure park/centre
≋ ▨	Outdoor, indoor swimming pool	⛸	Theme/Amusement park
⚓	Marina, moorings	♈	Wildlife/Safari park, zoo
⌂	Mountain refuge hut	❀	Gardens, park, arboretum
□━■━■━□	Overhead cable-car	⊛	Aviary, bird sanctuary
🚂	Tourist or steam railway		

Additional symbols

═ ═	Motorway (unclassified)	⊠ ⊙	Post office – Telephone centre
❶ ❶	Junction: complete, limited	⊠	Covered market
◻━ ■	Pedestrian street	•╳•	Barracks
ɪ═══ɪ	Unsuitable for traffic, street subject to restrictions	△	Swing bridge
⊞⊞⊞ ┄┄	Steps – Footpath	∪ ✕	Quarry – Mine
🚆 🚌	Railway – Coach station	Ⓑ Ⓕ	Ferry (river and lake crossings)
□━━━□	Funicular – Rack-railway	🚢	Ferry services: Passengers and cars
━━ ◉	Tram – Metro, underground	⇌	Foot passengers only
Bert (R.)...	Main shopping street	③	Access route number common to MICHELIN maps and town plans

Abbreviations and special symbols

Ⓒ	Capital of a "Canton" (Kantonshauptort)	P	Offices of cantonal authorities (Kantonale Verwaltung)
G	Local police station (Kantonspolizei)	POL.	Police (Stadtpolizei)
H	Town hall (Rathaus)	T	Theatre (Theater)
J	Law courts (Justizpalast)	U	University (Universität)
M	Museum (Museum)	🅿	Park and Ride

You know
the Green Guide

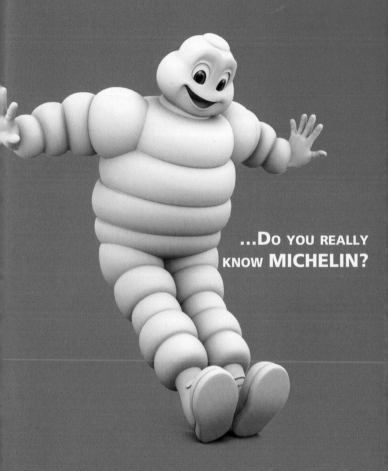

...Do you really
know **MICHELIN**?

● Data 31/12/2009

The world No.1 in tires
with 16.3% of the market

A business presence in over **170 countries**

A manufacturing footprint
at the heart of markets

In 2009 **72** industrial sites in **19** countries produced:

- **150** million tires
- **10** million maps and guides

Highly international **teams**

Over **109 200** employees* from all cultures on all continents

including **6 000** people employed in R&D centers

in Europe, the US and Asia.

*102 692 full-time equivalent staff

The Michelin Group
at a glance

Michelin
competes

At the end of 2009

- **Le Mans 24-hour race**
  12 consecutive years of victories
- **Endurance 2009**
  - 6 victories on 6 stages
  in Le Mans Series
  - 12 victories on 12 stages
  in American Le Mans Series

- **Paris-Dakar**
  Since the beginning of the event,
  the Michelin group has won
  in all categories
- **Moto endurance**
  2009 World Champion
- **Trial**
  Every World Champion title
  since 1981 (except 1992)

Michelin, established close to its customers

○ **72 plants in 19 countries**

- Algeria
- Brazil
- Canada
- China
- Colombia
- France
- Germany
- Hungary
- Italy
- Japan
- Mexico
- Poland
- Romania
- Russia
- Serbia
- Spain
- Thailand
- UK
- USA

● **A Technology Center spread over 3 continents**

- Asia
- Europe
- North America

● **Natural rubber plantations**

- Brazil

Our mission

To make a sustainable contribution to progress in the mobility of goods and people by enhancing freedom of movement, safety, efficiency and the pleasure of travelling.

Michelin committed to environmental-friendliness

Michelin, world leader in low rolling resistance tires, actively reduces fuel consumption and vehicle gas emission.

For its products, Michelin develops state-of-the-art technologies in order to:
- Reduce fuel consumption, while improving overall tire performance.
- Increase life cycle to reduce the number of tires to be processed at the end of their useful lives;
- Use raw materials which have a low impact on the environment.

Furthermore, at the end of 2008, 99.5% of tire production in volume was carried out in ISO 14001* certified plants.

Michelin is committed to implementing recycling channels for end-of-life tires.

*environmental certification

**Passenger Car
Light Truck**

Truck

Michelin
a key mobility enabler

Earthmover

Aircraft

Agricultural

Two-wheel   **Distribution**

Partnered with vehicle manufacturers, in tune with users,
active in competition and in all the distribution channels,
Michelinis continually innovating to promote mobility today
and to invent that of tomorrow.

Maps and   **ViaMichelin,**   **Michelin**
Guides   travel   **Lifestyle,**
                    assistance   for your travel
                    services   accessories

MICHELIN
plays on balanced performance

- ● Long tire life
- ● Fuel savings
- ○ Safety on the road

... MICHELIN tires provide you with the best performance, without making a single sacrifice.

The MICHELIN tire
pure technology

1 **Tread**
A thick layer of rubber
provides contact with the ground.
It has to channel water away
and last as long as possible.

2 **Crown plies**
This double or triple reinforced belt
has both vertical flexibility
and high lateral rigidity.
It provides the steering capacity.

3 **Sidewalls**
These cover and protect the textile casing
whose role is to attach the tire tread
to the wheel rim.

4 **Bead area for attachment to the rim**
Its internal bead wire
clamps the tire firmly
against the wheel rim.

5 **Inner liner**
This makes the tire
almost totally impermeable
and maintains the correct inflation pressure.

Heed
the MICHELIN Man's advice

To improve safety:

- I drive with the correct tire pressure
- I check the tire pressure every month
- I have my car regularly serviced
- I regularly check the appearance
  of my tires (wear, deformation)
- I am responsive behind the wheel
- I change my tires according to the season

www.michelin.com
www.michelin.(your country extension – e.g. .fr for France)

Michelin Apa Publications Ltd

A joint venture between Michelin and Langenscheidt

58 Borough High Street, London SE1 1XF, United Kingdom

No part of this publication may be reproduced in any form
without the prior permission of the publisher.

© 2011 Michelin Apa Publications Ltd
ISBN 978-1-907099-25-0
Printed: November 2010
Printed and bound in Germany